£5

· PENGUIN BOOKS

P.ENGUIN GREAT AUTHORS
THE PENGUIN THOMAS HARDY:
UNDER THE GREENWOOD TREE/FAR FROM THE MADDING CROWD
THE RETURN OF THE NATIVE/THE MAYOR OF CASTERBRIDGE

Thomas Hardy was born at Higher Bockhampton, near Dorchester, on 2 June 1840. He was educated locally at the village school and later in Dorchester, where he learnt Latin. At sixteen he was articled to the Dorchester architect and church restorer, John Hicks, although he continued his studies under the guidance of Horace Moule, a Cambridge graduate, whose later suicide affected Hardy and his writing deeply. In 1862 he went to London to pursue his architectural career and also began writing at this time. He returned to Dorset in 1867 to become assistant to John Hicks, at the same time beginning his first novel, *The Poor Man and the Lady* (of which only fragments remain), and which George Meredith advised him not to publish. In 1870 Hardy was sent to St Juliot in Cornwall and it was here that he met his first wife, Emma Gifford, whom he married in 1874; in the same year *Far from the Madding Crowd* was published and met with considerable success. In the previous three years he had published *Desperate Remedies* (1871), *Under the Greenwood Tree* (1872) and *A Pair of Blue Eyes* (1873). In 1878 Hardy moved back to London and in this year *The Return of the Native* was published. His reputation as a writer grew and he became a well-known figure in London's literary circles. *The Trumpet-Major* was published in 1880; at this time Hardy fell seriously ill and was bedridden for six months, during which time he wrote *A Laodicean*. In 1885 he returned to Dorset to live at Max Gate and over the next three years he published *The Mayor of Casterbridge* (1886), which many regard as his greatest tragic novel, *The Woodlanders* (1887) and his first collection of short stories, *Wessex Tales* (1888). In 1891 he published *Tess of the d'Urbervilles* and in 1896 his last novel, *Jude the Obscure*, which together are thought to form one of the most individual achievements in English literature. These two novels are important for their defiance of social convention but also illustrate Hardy's preoccupation with that malignant fate which dominates the lives of his tragic heroes and heroines. During the latter part of his life Hardy devoted himself to poetry, publishing his first collection of verse, *Wessex Poems*, in 1898. He also worked on his autobiography, *The Early Life of Thomas Hardy* (published posthumously in 1928), at the same time burning his old letters, notebooks and private papers. He died on 11 January 1928. Writing of Hardy in *The English Novel*, Walter Allen says, 'The true index of Hardy's stature is that he is almost the only tragic novelist in our literature and that when we consider him we have ultimately to do so in relation to Shakespeare and Webster and to the Greek dramatists.'

The Penguin

THOMAS HARDY

UNDER THE GREENWOOD TREE (1872)

FAR FROM THE MADDING CROWD (1874)

THE RETURN OF THE NATIVE (1878)

THE MAYOR OF CASTERBRIDGE (1886)

Bloomsbury Books
London

PENGUIN BOOKS
Published by the Penguin Group
Penguin Books Ltd, 27 Wrights Lane, London W8 5TZ, England
Penguin Books USA Inc., 375 Hudson Street, New York, New York 10014, USA
Penguin Books Australia Ltd, Ringwood, Victoria, Australia
Penguin Books Canada Ltd, 10 Alcorn Avenue, Toronto, Ontario, Canada M4V 3B2
Penguin Books (NZ) Ltd, 182–190 Wairau Road, Auckland 10, New Zealand

Penguin Books Ltd, Registered Offices: Harmondsworth, Middlesex, England

This collection published as *The Penguin Thomas Hardy* 1983
This edition published by Bloomsbury Books,
an imprint of Godfrey Cave Associates Limited
42 Bloomsbury Street, London WC1B 3QT,
under licence from Penguin Books Ltd 1994

Printed and bound in Great Britain by
BPC Hazell Books Ltd
A member of
The British Printing Company Ltd

Set in Bembo

CONTENTS

GENERAL PREFACE TO THE
WESSEX EDITION OF 1912

IN accepting a proposal for a definite edition of these productions in prose and verse I have found an opportunity of classifying the novels under heads that show approximately the author's aim, if not his achievement, in each book of the series at the date of its composition. Sometimes the aim was lower than at other times; sometimes, where the intention was primarily high, force of circumstances (among which the chief were the necessities of magazine publication) compelled a modification, great or slight, of the original plan. Of a few, however, of the longer novels, and of many of the shorter tales, it may be assumed that they stand today much as they would have stood if no accidents had obstructed the channel between the writer and the public. That many of them, if any, stand as they would stand if written *now* is not to be supposed.

In the classification of these fictitious chronicles – for which the name of 'The Wessex Novels' was adopted, and is still retained – the first group is called 'Novels of Character and Environment', and contains those which approach most nearly to uninfluenced works; also one or two which, whatever their quality in some few of their episodes, may claim a verisimilitude in general treatment and detail.

The second group is distinguished as 'Romances and Fantasies', a sufficiently descriptive definition. The third class – 'Novels of Ingenuity' – show a not infrequent disregard of the probable in the chain of events, and depend for their interest mainly on the incidents themselves. They might also be characterized as 'Experiments', and were written for the nonce simply; though despite the artificiality of their fable some of their scenes are not without fidelity to life.

It will not be supposed that these differences are distinctly perceptible in every page of every volume. It was inevitable that blendings and alternations should occur in all. Moreover, as it was not thought desirable in every instance to change the arrangement of the shorter stories to which readers have grown accustomed, certain of these may be found under headings to which an acute judgement might deny appropriateness.

It has sometimes been conceived of novels that evolve their action on a circumscribed scene – as do many (though not all) of these – that they cannot be so inclusive in their exhibition of human nature as novels wherein the scenes cover large extents of country, in which events figure amid towns and cities, even wander over the four quarters of the globe.

I am not concerned to argue this point further than to suggest that the conception is an untrue one in respect of the elementary passions. But I would state that the geographical limits of the stage here trodden were not absolutely forced upon the writer by circumstances; he forced them upon himself from judgement. I considered that our magnificent heritage from the Greeks in dramatic literature found sufficient room for a large proportion of its action in an extent of their country not much larger than the half-dozen counties here reunited under the old name of Wessex, that the domestic emotions have throbbed in Wessex nooks with as much intensity as in the palaces of Europe, and that, anyhow, there was quite enough human nature in Wessex for one man's literary purpose. So far was I possessed by this idea that I kept within the frontiers when it would have been easier to overlap them and give more cosmopolitan features to the narrative.

Thus, though the people in most of the novels (and in much of the shorter verse) are dwellers in a province bounded on the north by the Thames, on the south by the English Channel, on the east by a line running from Hayling Island to Windsor Forest, and on the west by the Cornish coast, they were meant to be typically and essentially those of any and every place where

Thought's the slave of life, and life time's fool

– beings in whose hearts and minds that which is apparently local should be really universal.

But whatever the success of this intention, and the value of these novels as delineations of humanity, they have at least a humble supplementary quality of which I may be justified in reminding the reader, though it is one that was quite unintentional and unforeseen. At the dates represented in the various narrations things were like that in Wessex: the inhabitants lived in certain ways, engaged in certain occupations, kept alive certain customs, just as they are shown doing in these pages. And in particularizing such I have often been reminded of Boswell's remarks on the trouble to which he was put and the pilgrimages he was obliged to make to authenticate some detail, though the labour was one which would bring him no praise. Unlike his achievement, however, on which an error would as he says have brought discredit, if these country customs and vocations, obsolete and obsolescent, had been detailed wrongly, nobody would have discovered such errors to the end of Time. Yet I have instituted inquiries to correct tricks of memory, and striven against temptations to exaggerate, in order to preserve for my own satisfaction a fairly true record of a vanishing life.

It is advisable also to state here, in response to inquiries from readers interested in landscape, prehistoric antiquities, and especially old English architecture, that the description of these backgrounds has been done from the real – that is to say, has something real for its basis, however illusively treated. Many features of the first two kinds have been given under their existing names; for instance, the Vale of Blackmoor or

Blakemore, Hambledon Hill, Bulbarrow, Nettlecombe Tout, Dogbury Hill, High-Stoy, Bubb-Down Hill, The Devil's Kitchen, Cross-in-Hand, Long-Ash Lane, Benvill Lane, Giant's Hill, Crimmercrock Lane, and Stonehenge. The rivers Froom, or Frome, and Stour are, of course, well known as such. And the further idea was that large towns and points tending to mark the outline of Wessex – such as Bath, Plymouth, The Start, Portland Bill, Southampton, etc. – should be named clearly. The scheme was not greatly elaborated, but, whatever its value, the names remain still.

In respect of places described under fictitious or ancient names in the novels – for reasons that seemed good at the time of writing them – and kept up in the poems – discerning people have affirmed in print that they clearly recognize the originals: such as Shaftesbury in 'Shaston', Sturminster Newton in 'Stourcastle', Dorchester in 'Casterbridge', Salisbury Plain in 'The Great Plain', Cranborne Chase in 'The Chase', Beaminster in 'Emminster', Bere Regis in 'Kingsbere', Woodbury Hill in 'Greenhill', Wool Bridge in 'Wellbridge', Harfoot or Harput Lane in 'Stagfoot Lane', Hazlebury in 'Nuttlebury', Bridport in 'Port Bredy', Maiden Newton in 'Chalk Newton', a farm near Nettlecombe-Tout in 'Flintcomb Ash', Sherborne in 'Sherton Abbas', Milton Abbey in 'Middleton Abbey', Cerne Abbas in 'Abbot's-Cernel', Evershot in 'Evershed', Taunton in 'Toneborough', Bournemouth in 'Sandbourne', Winchester in 'Wintoncester', Oxford in 'Christminster', Reading in 'Aldbrickham', Newbury in 'Kennetbridge', Wantage in 'Alfredston', Basingstoke in 'Stoke Barehills', and so on. Subject to the qualifications above given, that no detail is guaranteed – that the portraiture of fictitiously named towns and villages was only suggested by certain real places, and wantonly wanders from inventorial descriptions of them – I do not contradict these keen hunters for the real; I am satisfied with their statements as at least an indication of their interest in the scenes.

Thus much for the novels. Turning now to the verse – to myself the more individual part of my literary fruitage – I would say that, unlike some of the fiction, nothing interfered with the writer's freedom in respect of its form or content. Several of the poems – indeed many – were produced before novel-writing had been thought of as a pursuit; but few saw the light till all the novels had been published. The limited stage to which the majority of the latter confine their exhibitions has not been adhered to here in the same proportion, the dramatic part especially having a very broad theatre of action. It may thus relieve the circumscribed areas treated in the prose, if such relief be needed. To be sure, one might argue that by surveying Europe from a celestial point of vision – as in *The Dynasts* – that continent becomes virtually a province – a Wessex, an Attica, even a mere garden – and hence is made to conform to the principle of the novels, however far it outmeasures their region. But that may be as it will.

The few volumes filled by the verse cover a producing period of some eighteen years first and last, while the seventeen or more volumes of novels represent correspondingly about four-and-twenty years. One is reminded by this disproportion in time and result how much more concise and quintessential expression becomes when given in rhythmic form than when shaped in the language of prose.

One word on what has been called the present writer's philosophy of life, as exhibited more particularly in this metrical section of his compositions. Positive views on the Whence and the Wherefore of things have never been advanced by this pen as a consistent philosophy. Nor is it likely, indeed, that imaginative writings extended over more than forty years would exhibit a coherent scientific theory of the universe even if it had been attempted – of that universe concerning which Spencer owns to the 'paralysing thought' that possibly there exists no comprehension of it anywhere. But such objectless consistency never has been attempted, and the sentiments in the following pages have been stated truly to be mere impressions of the moment, and not convictions or arguments.

That these impressions have been condemned as 'pessimistic' – as if that were a very wicked adjective – shows a curious muddle-mindedness. It must be obvious that there is a higher characteristic of philosophy than pessimism, or than meliorism, or even than the optimism of these critics – which is truth. Existence is either ordered in a certain way, or it is not so ordered, and conjectures which harmonize best with experience are removed above all comparison with other conjectures which do not so harmonize. So that to say one view is worse than other views without proving it erroneous implies the possibility of a false view being better or more expedient than a true view; and no pragmatic proppings can make that *idolum specus* stand on its feet, for it postulates a prescience denied to humanity.

And there is another consideration. Differing natures find their tongue in the presence of differing spectacles. Some natures become vocal at tragedy, some are made vocal by comedy, and it seems to me that to whichever of these aspects of life a writer's instinct for expression the more readily responds, to that he should allow it to respond. That before a contrasting side of things he remains undemonstrative need not be assumed to mean that he remains unperceiving.

It was my hope to add to these volumes of verse as many more as would make a fairly comprehensive cycle of the whole. I had wished that those in dramatic, ballad, and narrative form should include most of the cardinal situations which occur in social and public life, and those in lyric form a round of emotional experiences of some completeness. But

The petty done, the undone vast!

The more written the more seems to remain to be written; and the night cometh. I realize that these hopes and plans, except possibly to the extent of a volume or two, must remain unfulfilled.

October 1911

T.H.

HARDY'S WESSEX

HARDY'S Wessex is so familiar that it is hard to realize how odd it is that a novelist should have tied himself by so many strings to a particular tract of territory. Many novelists have set their scenes in real places, or have written with some features of a familiar landscape always before them. But Hardy has done something different. Almost every step taken by his characters is taken along real roads or over real heaths; the towns and villages, the hills, even many of the houses are identifiable. It is as if Hardy's imagination could not work unless with solid ground under its feet, with solid objects to be seen around it. Many of the characters, there is little doubt, contain more or less of one real person, more or less of another, with elements drawn purely from imagination or from the accumulated layers of experience, which comes to much the same thing. But with the topography, Hardy was rarely satisfied with anything less than a one-to-one correspondence between the fictional and the real.

While the detail of Hardy's topographical nomenclature may become tedious, the fact that the landscape is identifiable does give the novels a special quality, as of a day-dream, with half-real figures moving over a real world. One might say –.if it can be said with respect – that it is this which leaves the novels with a touch of the magazine-story still, in which the ingenuous reader may lose himself – or herself – in vicarious adventures. And part of the immense popularity of Hardy certainly derives from the interest of the places written about, and particularly the more picturesque.

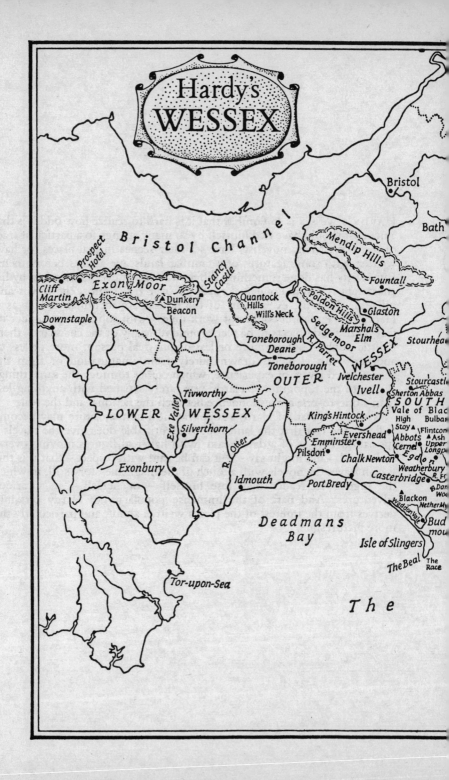

R. Thames
Christminster
Lumsdon
NORTH
The Brown House
Alfredston
Cresscombe
Marygreen
MID
WESSEX
Marlbury Downs
Castle Royal
Gaymead
Kennetbridge
Aldbrickham
Batton Castle
Inkpen Beacon
WESSEX
The Great Plain
Stoke Barehills
Icenway House
Quartershot
Weydon Priors
Stonehenge
UPPER WESSEX
Melchester
Wintoncester
Leddenton
Fernel Hall
Deansleigh Park
aston
Wingreen
The Chase
The Slopes
Trantridge Cross
Chaseborough
Southampton
VESSEX
Fe
Shottsford Forum
Lornton Inn
dleton
Badbury Rings
Yewsholt
The Great Forest
Abbey
Warborne
Bramshurst
Welland
Chene Manor
gsbere
Heath
Havenpool
Solentsea
Talbothays
Portsmouth
bridge
Anglebury
Sandbourne
Corvesgate
The Island
ullwind Cove
Knollsea
tship
channel

N

0   10   20   30 miles

Fictitious names: Exonbury
Real names: Portsmouth

H. A. Shelley

KEY TO PLACE-NAMES

HARDY'S NAME	REAL NAME
Abbot's-Cernel	Cerne Abbas
Abbotsea	Abbotsbury
Aldbrickham	Reading
Alfredston	Wantage
Anglebury	Wareham
Badbury Rings	A hill near Wimborne Minster
Budmouth	Weymouth
Bulbarrow	A hill near Sturminster Newton
Casterbridge	Dorchester
Chalk Newton	Maiden Newton
Chaseborough	Cranborne
Christminster	Oxford
Cresscombe	Letcombe Basset
Damer's Wood	Came Wood near Dorchester
Dogbury	A hill near High Stoy
Durnover	Fordington
Egdon Heath	A composite of the heaths between Bournemouth and Dorchester
Emminster	Beaminster
Evershead	Evershot
Exonbury	Exeter
Fensworth	Letcombe Regis
Flintcombe-Ash	Nettlecombe-Tout
Greenhill	Woodbury Hill near Bere Regis
Hope Cove	Church Hope
Kennetbridge	Newbury
Kingsbere and *King's Bere*	Bere Regis
Leddenton	Gillingham
Longpuddle	Piddlehinton (also called by Hardy *Upper Longpuddle*)
Lulwind Cove	Lulworth Cove
Lumsdon	Cumnor
Marlott	Marnhull
Marygreen	Fawley
Melchester	Salisbury

Mellstock	Stinsford and Lower and Higher Bockhampton
Middleton Abbey	Milton Abbas
Nether-Moynton	Overmoigne
Norcombe Hill	A hill near Toller Down
Nuttlebury	Hazelbury Bryan
Oxwell Hall	Poxwell
Port Bredy	Bridport
Pos'ham	Portisham
Quartershot	Aldershot
Rainbarrow	Rainbarrows, a mound north of the Dorchester–Wareham road
Ridgeway	A road between Dorchester and Weymouth
Roy Town	Troy Town
St Aldhelm's Head	St Alban's Head
Sandbourne	Bournemouth
Shaston	Shaftesbury
Sherton	Sherborne
Shottesford and Shottsford Forum	Blandford
Stoke-Barehills	Basingstoke
Stourcastle	Sturminster Newton
Upper Longpuddle	Piddlehinton
Weatherbury	Puddletown
Wellbridge	Wool
Wintonchester	Winchester
Yalbury Wood	Yellowham Wood

UNDER THE
GREENWOOD TREE

OR

THE
MELLSTOCK QUIRE

**A RURAL PAINTING OF THE
DUTCH SCHOOL**

CONTENTS

CONTENTS

Part The Third · Summer

Part The Fourth · Autumn

Part The Fifth · Conclusion

AUTHOR'S PREFACE

THIS story of the Mellstock Quire and its old established west-gallery musicians, with some supplementary descriptions of similar officials in *Two on a Tower*, *A Few Crusted Characters*, and other places, is intended to be a fairly true picture, at first hand, of the personages, ways, and customs which were common among such orchestral bodies in the villages of fifty or sixty years ago.

One is inclined to regret the displacement of these ecclesiastical bandsmen by an isolated organist (often at first a barrel-organist) or harmonium player; and despite certain advantages in point of control and accomplishment which were, no doubt, secured by installing the single artist, the change has tended to stultify the professed aims of the clergy, its direct result being to curtail and extinguish the interest of parishioners in church doings. Under the old plan, from half a dozen to ten full-grown players, in addition to the numerous more or less grown-up singers, were officially occupied with the Sunday routine, and concerned in trying their best to make it an artistic outcome of the combined musical taste of the congregation. With a musical executive limited, as it mostly is limited now, to the parson's wife or daughter and the school-children, or to the school-teacher and the children, an important union of interests has disappeared.

The zest of these bygone instrumentalists must have been keen and staying, to take them, as it did, on foot every Sunday after a toilsome week through all weathers to the church, which often lay at a distance from their homes. They usually received so little in payment for their performances that their efforts were really a labour of love. In the parish I had in my mind when writing the present tale, the gratuities received yearly by the musicians at Christmas were somewhat as follows: from the manor-house ten shillings and a supper; from the vicar ten shillings; from the farmers five shillings each; from each cottage-household one shilling; amounting altogether to not more than ten shillings a head annually – just enough, as an old executant told me, to pay for their fiddle-strings, repairs, rosin, and music-paper (which they mostly ruled themselves). Their music in those days was all in their own manuscript, copied in the evenings after work, and their music-books were home-bound.

It was customary to inscribe a few jigs, reels, hornpipes, and ballads in the same book, by beginning it at the other end, the insertions being continued from front and back till sacred and secular met together in the middle, often with bizarre effect, the words of some of the songs exhibiting that ancient and broad humour which our grandfathers, and possibly grandmothers, took delight in, and is in these days unquotable.

The aforesaid fiddle-strings, rosin, and music-paper were supplied by a pedlar, who travelled exclusively in such wares from parish to parish, coming to each village about every six months. Tales are told of the consternation once caused among the church fiddlers when, on the occasion of their producing a new Christmas anthem, he did not come to time, owing to being snowed up on the downs, and the straits they were in through having to make shift with whipcord and twine for strings. He was generally a musician himself, and sometimes a composer in a small way, bringing his own new tunes, and tempting each choir to adopt them for a consideration. Some of these compositions which now lie before me, with their repetitions of lines, half-lines, and half-words, their fugues and their intermediate symphonies, are good singing still, though they would hardly be admitted into such hymn-books as are popular in the churches of fashionable society at the present time.

August 1896

Under the Greenwood Tree was first brought out in the summer of 1872 in two volumes. The name of the story was originally intended to be, more appropriately, *The Mellstock Quire*, and this has been appended as a sub-title since the early editions, it having been thought unadvisable to displace for it the title by which the book first became known.

In rereading the narrative after a long interval there occurs the inevitable reflection that the realities out of which it was spun were material for another kind of study of this little group of church musicians than is found in the chapters here penned so lightly, even so farcically and flippantly at times. But circumstances would have rendered any aim at a deeper, more essential, more transcendent handling unadvisable at the date of writing; and the exhibition of the Mellstock Quire in the following pages must remain the only extant one, except for the few glimpses of that perished band which I have given in verse elsewhere.

April 1912   T.H.

PART THE FIRST

WINTER

Mellstock-Lane

To dwellers in a wood almost every species of tree has its voice as well as its feature. At the passing of the breeze the fir-trees sob and moan no less distinctly than they rock; the holly whistles as it battles with itself; the ash hisses amid its quiverings; the beech rustles while its flat boughs rise and fall. And winter, which modifies the note of such trees as shed their leaves, does not destroy its individuality.

On a cold and starry Christmas-eve within living memory a man was passing up a lane towards Mellstock Cross in the darkness of a plantation that whispered thus distinctively to his intelligence. All the evidences of his nature were those afforded by the spirit of his footsteps, which succeeded each other lightly and quickly, and by the liveliness of his voice as he sang in a rural cadence:

> With the rose and the lily
> And the daffodowndilly,
> The lads and the lasses a-sheep-shearing go.

The lonely lane he was following connected one of the hamlets of Mellstock parish with Upper Mellstock and Lewgate, and to his eyes, casually glancing upward, the silver and black-stemmed birches with their characteristic tufts, the pale grey boughs of beech, the dark-creviced elm, all appeared now as black and flat outlines upon the sky, wherein the white stars twinkled so vehemently that their flickering seemed like the flapping of wings. Within the woody pass, at a level anything lower than the horizon, all was dark as the grave. The copse-wood forming the sides of the bower interlaced its branches so densely, even at this season of the year, that the draught from the north-east flew along the channel with scarcely an interruption from lateral breezes.

After passing the plantation and reaching Mellstock Cross the white surface of the lane revealed itself between the dark hedgerows like a ribbon jagged at the edges; the irregularity being caused by temporary accumulations of leaves extending from the ditch on either side.

The song (many times interrupted by flitting thoughts which took the place of several bars, and resumed at a point it would have reached had its continuity been unbroken) now received a more palpable check, in the shape of 'Ho-i-i-i-i-i!' from the crossing lane to Lower Mellstock, on the right of the singer who had just emerged from the trees.

'Ho-i-i-i-i-i!' he answered, stopping and looking round, though with no idea of seeing anything more than imagination pictured.

'Is that thee, young Dick Dewy?' came from the darkness.

'Ay, sure, Michael Mail.'

'Then why not stop for fellow-craters – going to thy own father's house too, as we be, and knowen us so well?'

Dick Dewy faced about and continued his tune in an underwhistle, implying that the business of his mouth could not be checked at a moment's notice by the placid emotion of friendship.

Having come more into the open he could now be seen rising against the sky, his profile appearing on the light background like the portrait of a gentleman in black cardboard. It assumed the form of a low-crowned hat, an ordinary-shaped nose, an ordinary chin, an ordinary neck, and ordinary shoulders. What he consisted of further down was invisible from lack of sky low enough to picture him on.

Shuffling, halting, irregular footsteps of various kinds were now heard coming up the hill, and presently there emerged from the shade severally five men of different ages and gaits, all of them working villagers of the parish of Mellstock. They, too, had lost their rotundity with the daylight, and advanced against the sky in flat outlines, which suggested some processional design on Greek or Etruscan pottery. They represented the chief portion of Mellstock parish choir.

The first was a bowed and bent man, who carried a fiddle under his arm, and walked as if engaged in studying some subject connected with the surface of the road. He was Michael Mail, the man who had hallooed to Dick.

The next was Mr Robert Penny, boot- and shoe-maker; a little man who, though rather round-shouldered, walked as if that fact had not come to his own knowledge, moving on with his back very hollow and his face fixed on the north-east quarter of the heavens before him, so that his lower waistcoat-buttons came first, and then the remainder of his figure. His features were invisible; yet when he occasionally looked round, two faint moons of light gleamed for an instant from the precincts of his eyes, denoting that he wore spectacles of a circular form.

The third was Elias Spinks, who walked perpendicularly and dramatically. The fourth outline was Joseph Bowman's, who had now no distinctive appearance beyond that of a human being. Finally came a weak lath-like form, trotting and stumbling along with one shoulder forward and his head inclined to the left, his arms dangling nervelessly in the wind as if they were empty sleeves. This was Thomas Leaf.

'Where be the boys?' said Dick to this somewhat indifferently-matched assembly.

The eldest of the group, Michael Mail, cleared his throat from a great depth.

'We told them to keep back at home for a time, thinken they wouldn't be wanted yet awhile; and we could choose the tuens, and so on.'

'Father and grandfather William have expected ye a little sooner. I have just been for a run round by Ewelease Stile and Hollow Hill to warm my feet.'

'To be sure father did! To be sure 'a did expect us – to taste the little barrel beyond compare that he's going to tap.'

"Od rabbit it all! Never heard a word of it!' said Mr Penny, gleams of delight appearing upon his spectacle-glasses, Dick meanwhile singing parenthetically –

The lads and the lasses a-sheep-shearing go.

'Neighbours, there's time enough to drink a sight of drink now afore bedtime?' said Mail.

'True, true – time enough to get as drunk as lords!' replied Bowman cheerfully.

This opinion being taken as convincing they all advanced between the varying hedges and the trees dotting them here and there, kicking their toes occasionally among the crumpled leaves. Soon appeared glimmering indications of the few cottages forming the small hamlet of Upper Mellstock for which they were bound, whilst the faint sound of church-bells ringing a Christmas peal could be heard floating over upon the breeze from the direction of Longpuddle and Weatherbury parishes on the other side of the hills. A little wicket admitted them to the garden, and they proceeded up the path to Dick's house.

* II *

The Tranter's

It was a long low cottage with a hipped roof of thatch, having dormer windows breaking up into the eaves, a chimney standing in the middle of the ridge and another at each end. The window-shutters were not yet closed, and the fire- and candle-light within radiated forth upon the thick bushes of box and laurestinus growing in clumps outside, and upon the bare boughs of several codlin-trees hanging about in various distorted shapes, the result of early training as espaliers combined with careless climbing into their boughs in later years. The walls of the dwelling were for the most part covered with creepers, though these were rather beaten back from the doorway – a feature which was worn and scratched by much passing in and out, giving it by day the appearance of an old keyhole. Light streamed through the cracks and joints of outbuildings a little way from the cottage, a sight which nourished a fancy that the purpose of the erection must be rather to veil bright attractions than to shelter unsightly necessaries. The noise of a beetle and wedges and the splintering of wood was periodically heard from this direction; and at some little distance further a steady regular munching and the occasional scurr of a rope betokened a stable, and horses feeding within it.

The choir stamped severally on the door-stone to shake from their boots any fragment of earth or leaf adhering thereto, then entered the house and looked around to survey the condition of things. Through the open doorway of a small inner room on the right hand, of a character between pantry and cellar, was Dick Dewy's father Reuben, by vocation a 'tranter', or irregular carrier. He was a stout florid man about forty years of age, who surveyed people up and down when first making their acquaintance, and generally smiled at the horizon or other distant object during conversations with friends, walking about with a steady sway, and turning out his toes very considerably. Being now occupied in bending over a hogshead that stood in the pantry ready horsed for the process of broaching, he did not take the trouble to turn or raise his eyes at the entry of his visitors, well knowing by their footsteps that they were the expected old comrades.

The main room, on the left, was decked with bunches of holly and other evergreens, and from the middle of the beam bisecting the ceiling hung the mistletoe, of a size out of all proportion to the room, and extending so low that it became necessary for a full-grown person to walk round it in passing, or run the risk of entangling his hair. This apartment contained Mrs Dewy the tranter's wife, and the four remaining children, Susan, Jim, Bessie, and Charley, graduating uniformly though at wide stages from the age of sixteen to that of four years – the eldest of the series being separated from Dick the firstborn by a nearly equal interval.

Some circumstance had apparently caused much grief to Charley just previous to the entry of the choir, and he had absently taken down a small looking-glass, holding it before his face to learn how the human countenance appeared when engaged in crying, which survey led him to pause at the various points in each wail that were more than ordinarily striking, for a thorough appreciation of the general effect. Bessy was leaning against a chair, and glancing under the plaits about the waist of the plaid frock she wore, to notice the original unfaded pattern of the material as there preserved, her face bearing an expression of regret that the brightness had passed away from the visible portions. Mrs Dewy sat in a brown settle by the side of the glowing wood fire – so glowing that with a heedful compression of the lips she would now and then rise and put her hand upon the hams and flitches of bacon lining the chimney, to reassure herself that they were not being broiled instead of smoked – a misfortune that had been known to happen now and then at Christmas-time.

'Hullo my sonnies, here you be, then!' said Reuben Dewy at length, standing up and blowing forth a vehement gust of breath. 'How the blood do puff up in anybody's head, to be sure, a-stooping like that! I was just going out to gate to hark for ye.' He then carefully began to wind a strip of brown paper round a brass tap he held in his hand. 'This in the cask here is a drop o' the right sort' (tapping the cask); ''tis a real drop o' cordial from the best picked apples – Sansoms, Stubbards, Five-corners, and such-like – you d'mind the sort, Michael?' (Michael nodded.) 'And there's a sprinkling of they that grow down by the orchard-rails – streaked ones – rail apples we d'call 'em, as 'tis by the rails they grow, and not knowing the right name. The water-cider from 'em is as good as most people's best cider is.'

'Ay, and of the same make too,' said Bowman. ' "It rained when we wrung it out, and the water got into it," folk will say. But 'tis on'y an excuse. Watered cider is too common among us.'

'Yes, yes; too common it is!' said Spinks with an inward sigh, whilst his eyes seemed to be looking at the case in an abstract form rather than at the scene before him. 'Such poor liquor do make a man's throat feel very melancholy – and is a disgrace to the name of stimmilent.'

'Come in, come in, and draw up to the fire; never mind your shoes,' said Mrs Dewy, seeing that all except Dick had paused to wipe them upon the doormat. 'I am glad that you've stepped up-along at last; and, Susan, you run down to Grammer Kaytes's and see if you can borrow some larger candles than these fourteens. Tommy Leaf, don't ye be afeared! Come and sit here in the settle.'

This was addressed to the young man before mentioned, consisting chiefly of a human skeleton and a smock-frock, who was very awkward in his movements, apparently on account of having grown so very fast that before he had had time to get used to his height he was higher.

'Hee – hee – ay!' replied Leaf, letting his mouth continue to smile for some time after his mind had done smiling, so that his teeth remained in view as the most conspicuous members of his body.

'Here, Mr Penny,' resumed Mrs Dewy, 'you sit in this chair. And how's your daughter, Mrs Brownjohn?'

'Well, I suppose I must say pretty fair.' He adjusted his spectacles a quarter of an inch to the right. 'But she'll be worse before she's better, 'a b'lieve.'

'Indeed – poor soul! And how many will that make in all, four or five?'

'Five; they've buried three. Yes, five; and she not much more than a maid yet. She do know the multiplication table onmistakable well. However, 'twas to be, and none can gainsay it.'

Mrs Dewy resigned Mr Penny. 'Wonder where your grandfather James is?' she inquired of one of the children. 'He said he'd drop in tonight.'

'Out in fuel-house with grandfather William,' said Jimmy.

'Now let's see what we can do,' was heard spoken about this time by the tranter in a private voice to the barrel, beside which he had again established himself, and was stooping to cut away the cork.

'Reuben, don't make such a mess o' tapping that barrel as is mostly made in this house,' Mrs Dewy cried from the fireplace. 'I'd tap a hundred without wasting more than you do in one. Such a squizzling and squirting job as 'tis in your hands! There, he always was such a clumsy man indoors.'

'Ay, ay; I know you'd tap a hundred beautiful, Ann – I know you would; two hundred, perhaps. But I can't promise. This is a' old cask, and the wood's rotted away about the tap-hole. The husbird of a feller Sam Lawson – that ever I should call'n such, now he's dead and gone, poor heart! – took me in completely upon the feat of buying this cask. "Reub," says he – 'a always used to call me plain Reub, poor old heart! – "Reub," he said says he, "that there cask, Reub, is as good as new; yes, good as new. 'Tis a wine-hogshead; the best port-wine in the common-wealth have been in that there cask; and you shall have en for ten shillens, Reub," – 'a said says he – "he's worth twenty, ay, five-and-twenty, if he's worth one; and an iron hoop or two put round en among the wood ones will make en worth thirty shillens of any man's money, if –" '

'I think I should have used the eyes that Providence gave me to use afore I paid any ten shillens for a jimcrack wine-barrel; a saint is sinner enough not to be cheated. But 'tis like all your family was, so easy to be deceived.'

'That's as true as gospel of this member,' said Reuben.

Mrs Dewy began a smile at the answer, then altering her lips and refolding them so that it was not a smile, commenced smoothing little Bessy's hair; the tranter having meanwhile suddenly become oblivious to conversation, occupying himself in a deliberate cutting and arrangement of some more brown paper for the broaching operation.

'Ah, who can believe sellers!' said old Michael Mail in a carefully-cautious voice, by way of tiding-over this critical point of affairs.

'No one at all,' said Joseph Bowman, in the tone of a man fully agreeing with everybody.

'Ay,' said Mail, in the tone of a man who did not agree with everybody as a rule, though he did now; 'I knowed a' auctioneering feller once – a very friendly feller 'a was too. And so one hot day as I was walking down the front street o' Casterbridge, jist below the King's Arms, I passed a' open winder and see him inside, stuck upon his perch, a-selling off. I jist nodded to en in a friendly way as I passed, and went my way, and thought no more about it. Well, next day, as I was oilen my boots by fuel-house door, if a letter didn't come wi' a bill charging me with a feather-bed, bolster, and pillers, that I had bid for at Mr Taylor's sale. The slim-faced martel had knocked 'em down to me because I nodded to en in my friendly way; and I had to pay for 'em too. Now, I hold that that was coming it very close, Reuben?'

''Twas close, there's no denying,' said the general voice.

'Too close, 'twas,' said Reuben, in the rear of the rest. 'And as to Sam Lawson – poor heart! now he's dead and gone too! – I'll warrant, that if so be I've spent one hour in making hoops for that barrel, I've spent fifty, first and last. That's one of my hoops' – touching it with his elbow – 'that's one of mine, and that, and that, and all these.'

'Ah, Sam was a man,' said Mr Penny, contemplatively.

'Sam was!' said Bowman.

'Especially for a drap o' drink,' said the tranter.

'Good, but not religious-good,' suggested Mr Penny.

The tranter nodded. Having at last made the tap and hole quite ready, 'Now then, Suze, bring a mug,' he said. 'Here's luck to us, my sonnies!'

The tap went in, and the cider immediately squirted out in a horizontal shower over Reuben's hands, knees, and leggings, and into the eyes and neck of Charley, who, having temporarily put off his grief under pressure of more interesting proceedings, was squatting down and blinking near his father.

'There 'tis again!' said Mrs Dewy.

'Devil take the hole, the cask, and Sam Lawson too, that good cider should be wasted like this!' exclaimed the tranter. 'Your thumb! Lend me your thumb, Michael! Ram it in here, Michael! I must get a bigger tap, my sonnies.'

'Idd it cold inthide te hole?' inquired Charley of Michael, as he continued in a stooping posture with his thumb in the cork-hole.

'What wonderful odds and ends that chiel has in his head to be sure!' Mrs Dewy admiringly exclaimed from the distance. 'I lay a wager that he thinks more about how 'tis inside that barrel than in all the other parts of the world put together.'

All persons present put on a speaking countenance of admiration for the cleverness alluded to, in the midst of which Reuben returned. The operation was then satisfactorily performed; when Michael arose and stretched his head to the extremest fraction of height that his body would allow of, to restraighten his back and shoulders – thrusting out his arms and twisting his features to a mass of wrinkles to emphasize the relief acquired. A quart or two of the beverage was then brought to table, at which all the new arrivals reseated themselves with wide-spread knees, their eyes meditatively seeking out any speck or knot in the board upon which the gaze might precipitate itself.

'Whatever is father a-biding out in fuel-house so long for?' said the tranter. 'Never such a man as father for two things – cleaving up old dead apple-tree wood and playing the bass-viol. 'A'd pass his life between the two, that 'a would.' He stepped to the door and opened it.

'Father!'

'Ay!' rang thinly from round the corner.

'Here's the barrel tapped, and we all awaiting!'

A series of dull thuds, that had been heard without for some time past, now ceased; and after the light of a lantern had passed the window and made wheeling rays upon the ceiling inside the eldest of the Dewy family appeared.

* III *
The Assembled Quire

WILLIAM DEWY – otherwise grandfather William – was now about seventy; yet an ardent vitality still preserved a warm and roughened bloom upon his face, which reminded gardeners of the sunny side of a ripe ribstone-pippin; though a narrow strip of forehead, that was protected from the weather by lying above the line of his hat-brim, seemed to belong to some town man, so gentlemanly was its whiteness. His was a humorous and kindly nature, not unmixed with a frequent melancholy; and he had a firm religious faith. But to his neighbours he had no character in particular. If they saw him pass by their windows when they had been bottling off old mead, or when they had just been called long-headed men who might do anything in the world if they chose, they thought concerning him, 'Ah, there's that good-hearted man – open as a child!' If they saw him just after losing a shilling or half-a-crown, or accidentally letting fall a piece of crockery, they thought, 'There's that poor weak-minded man Dewy again! Ah, he's never done much in the world either!' If he passed when fortune neither smiled nor frowned on them, they merely thought him old William Dewy.

'Ah, so's – here you be! – Ah, Michael and Joseph and John – and you too, Leaf! a merry Christmas all! We shall have a rare log-wood fire directly, Reub, to reckon by the toughness of the job I had in cleaving 'em.' As he spoke he threw down an armful of logs which fell in the chimney-corner with a rumble, and looked at them with something of the admiring enmity he would have bestowed on living people who had been very obstinate in holding their own. 'Come in, grandfather James.'

Old James (grandfather on the maternal side) had simply called as a visitor. He lived in a cottage by himself, and many people considered him a miser; some, rather slovenly in his habits. He now came forward from behind grandfather William, and his stooping figure formed a well-illuminated picture as he passed towards the fire-place. Being by trade a mason, he wore a long linen apron reaching almost to his toes, corduroy breeches and gaiters, which, together with his boots, graduated in tints of whitish-brown by constant friction against lime and stone. He also wore a very stiff fustian coat, having folds at the elbows and shoulders as unvarying in their arrangement as those in a pair of bellows: the ridges and the projecting parts of the coat collectively exhibiting a shade different from that of the hollows, which were lined with small ditch-like accumulations of stone and mortar-dust. The extremely large side-pockets, sheltered beneath wide flaps, bulged out convexly whether empty or full; and as he was often engaged to work at buildings far away – his breakfasts and dinners being eaten in a strange chimney-corner, by a garden wall, on a heap of stones, or walking along the road – he carried in these pockets a small tin canister of butter, a small canister of sugar, a small canister of tea, a paper of salt, and a paper of pepper; the bread, cheese, and meat, forming the substance of his meals, hanging up behind him in his basket among the hammers and chisels. If a passer-by looked hard at him when he was drawing forth any of these, 'My buttery,' he said, with a pinched smile.

'Better try over number seventy-eight before we start, I suppose?' said William, pointing to a heap of old Christmas-carol books on a side table.

'Wi' all my heart,' said the choir generally.

'Number seventy-eight was always a teaser – always. I can mind him ever since I was growing up a hard boy-chap.'

'But he's a good tune, and worth a mint o' practice,' said Michael.

'He is; though I've been mad enough wi' that tune at times to seize en and tear en all to linnit. Ay, he's a splendid carrel – there's no denying that.'

'The first line is well enough,' said Mr Spinks; 'but when you come to "O, thou man," you make a mess o't.'

'We'll have another go into en, and see what we can make of the martel. Half-an-hour's hammering at en will conquer the toughness of en; I'll warn it.'

'"Od rabbit it all!" said Mr Penny, interrupting with a flash of his spectacles, and at the same time clawing at something in the depths of a large side-pocket. 'If so be I hadn't been as scatter-brained and thirtingill as a chiel I should have called at the schoolhouse wi' a boot as I cam up along. Whatever is coming to me I really can't estimate at all!'

'The brain has its weaknesses,' murmured Mr Spinks, waving his head ominously. Mr Spinks was considered to be a scholar, having once kept a nightschool, and always spoke up to that level.

'Well, I must call with en the first thing tomorrow. And I'll empty my pocket o' this last too, if you don't mind, Mrs Dewy.' He drew forth a last, and placed it on a table at his elbow. The eyes of three or four followed it.

'Well,' said the shoemaker, seeming to perceive that the interest the object had excited was greater than he had anticipated, and warranted the last's being taken up again and exhibited; 'now, whose foot do ye suppose this last was made for? It was made for Geoffrey Day's father, over at Yalbury Wood. Ah, many's the pair o' boots he've had off the last! Well, when 'a died, I used the last for Geoffrey, and have ever since, though a little doctoring was wanted to make it do. Yes, a very queer natured last it is now, 'a b'lieve,' he continued, turning it over caressingly. 'Now, you notice that there' (pointing to a lump of leather bradded to the toe), 'that's a very bad bunion that he've had ever since 'a was a boy. Now, this remarkable large piece' (pointing to a patch nailed to the side), 'shows a' accident he received by the tread of a horse, that squashed his foot a'most to a pomace. The horse-shoe came full-butt on this point, you see. And so I've just been over to Geoffrey's, to know if he wanted his bunion altered or made bigger in the new pair I'm making.'

During the latter part of this speech Mr Penny's left hand wandered towards the cider-cup as if the hand had no connection with the person speaking; and bringing his sentence to an abrupt close all but the extreme margin of the bootmaker's face was eclipsed by the circular brim of the vessel.

'However, I was going to say,' continued Penny, putting down the cup, 'I ought to have called at the school' – here he went groping again in the depths of his pocket – 'to leave this without fail, though I suppose the first thing tomorrow will do.'

He now drew forth and placed upon the table a boot – small, light, and prettily shaped – upon the heel of which he had been operating.

'The new schoolmistress's!'

'Ay, no less, Miss Fancy Day; as neat a little figure of fun as ever I see, and just husband-high.'

'Never Geoffrey's daughter Fancy?' said Bowman, as all glances present converged like wheelspokes upon the boot in the centre of them.

'Yes, sure,' resumed Mr Penny, regarding the boot as if that alone were his auditor; ''tis she that's come here schoolmistress. You knowed his daughter was in training?'

'Strange, isn't it, for her to be here Christmas-night, Master Penny?'

'Yes; but here she is, 'a b'lieve.'

'I know how she comes here – so I do!' chirruped one of the children.

'Why?' Dick inquired with subtle interest.

'Pa'son Maybold was afraid he couldn't manage us all tomorrow at the dinner, and he talked o' getting her just to come over and help him hand about the plates, and see we didn't make pigs of ourselves; and that's what she's come for!'

'And that's the boot, then,' continued its mender imaginatively, 'that she'll walk to church in tomorrow morning. I don't care to mend boots I don't make; but there's no knowing what it may lead to, and her father always comes to me.'

There, between the cider-mug and the candle, stood this interesting receptacle of the little unknown's foot; and a very pretty boot it was. A character, in fact – the flexible bend at the instep, the rounded localities of the small nestling toes, scratches from careless scampers now forgotten – all, as repeated in the tell-tale leather, evidencing a nature and a bias. Dick surveyed it with a delicate feeling that he had no right to do so without having first asked the owner of the foot's permission.

'Now, neighbours, though no common eye can see it,' the shoemaker went on, 'a man in the trade can see the likeness between this boot and that last, although that is so deformed as hardly to recall one of God's creatures, and this is one of as pretty a pair as you'd get for ten-and-sixpence in Casterbridge. To you, nothing; but 'tis father's voot and daughter's voot to me, as plain as houses.'

'I don't doubt there's a likeness, Master Penny – a mild likeness – a fantastical likeness,' said Spinks. 'But I han't got imagination enough to see it, perhaps.'

Mr Penny adjusted his spectacles.

'Now, I'll tell ye what happened to me once on this very point. You used to know Johnson the dairyman, William?'

'Ay, sure; I did.'

'Well, 'twasn't opposite his house, but a little lower down – by his paddock, in front o' Parkmaze Pool. I was a-bearing across towards Bloom's End, and lo and behold, there was a man just brought out o' the Pool, dead; he had un'rayed for a dip, but not being able to pitch it just there had gone in flop over his head. Men looked at en; women looked at en; children looked at en; nobody knowed en. He was covered wi' a sheet; but I catched sight of his voot, just showing out as they carried en along. "I don't care what name that man went by," I said, in my way, "but he's John Woodward's brother; I can swear to the family voot." At that very moment up comes John Woodward, weeping and teaving, "I've lost my brother! I've lost my brother!" '

'Only to think of that!' said Mrs Dewy.

''Tis well enough to know this foot and that foot,' said Mr Spinks. ''Tis long-headed, in fact, as far as feet do go. I know little, 'tis true – I say no more; but show *me* a man's foot, and I'll tell you that man's heart.'

'You must be a cleverer feller, then, than mankind in jineral,' said the tranter.

'Well, that's nothing for me to speak of,' returned Mr Spinks. 'A man lives and learns. Maybe I've read a leaf or two in my time. I don't wish to say anything large, mind you; but nevertheless, maybe I have.'

'Yes, I know,' said Michael soothingly, 'and all the parish knows, that ye've read sommat of everything a'most, and have been a great filler of young folks' brains. Learning's a worthy thing, and ye've got it, Master Spinks.'

'I make no boast, though I may have read and thought a little; and I know – it may be from much perusing, but I make no boast – that by the time a man's head is finished 'tis almost time for him to creep underground. I am over forty-five.'

Mr Spinks emitted a look to signify that if his head was not finished, nobody's head ever could be.

'Talk of knowing people by their feet!' said Reuben. 'Rot me, my sonnies, then, if I can tell what a man is from all his members put together, oftentimes.'

'But still, look is a good deal,' observed grandfather William absently, moving and balancing his head till the tip of grandfather James's nose was exactly in a right line with William's eye and the mouth of a miniature cavern he was discerning in the fire. 'By the way,' he continued in a fresher voice, and looking up, 'that young creature, the schoolmis'ess, must be sung to tonight wi' the rest? If her ear is as fine as her face, we shall have enough to do to be up-sides with her.'

'What about her face?' said young Dewy.

'Well, as to that,' Mr Spinks replied, ''tis a face you can hardly gainsay.

A very good pink face, as far as that do go. Still, only a face, when all is said and done.'

'Come, come, Elias Spinks, say she's a pretty maid and have done wi' her,' said the tranter, again preparing to visit the cider-barrel.

* IV *

Going the Rounds

SHORTLY after ten o'clock the singing-boys arrived at the tranter's house, which was invariably the place of meeting, and preparations were made for the start. The older men and musicians wore thick coats, with stiff perpendicular collars, and coloured handkerchiefs wound round and round the neck till the end came to hand, over all which they just showed their ears and noses, like people looking over a wall. The remainder, stalwart ruddy men and boys, were dressed mainly in snow-white smock-frocks, embroidered upon the shoulders and breasts in ornamental forms of hearts, diamonds, and zigzags. The cider-mug was emptied for the ninth time, the music-books were arranged, and the pieces finally decided upon. The boys in the meantime put the old horn-lanterns in order, cut candles into short lengths to fit the lanterns; and, a thin fleece of snow having fallen since the early part of the evening, those who had no leggings went to the stable and wound wisps of hay round their ankles to keep the insidious flakes from the interior of their boots.

Mellstock was a parish of considerable acreage, the hamlets composing it lying at a much greater distance from each other than is ordinarily the case. Hence several hours were consumed in playing and singing within hearing of every family, even if but a single air were bestowed on each. There was Lower Mellstock, the main village; half a mile from this were the church and vicarage, and a few other houses, the spot being rather lonely now, though in past centuries it had been the most thickly-populated quarter of the parish. A mile north-east lay the hamlet of Upper Mellstock, where the tranter lived; and at other points knots of cottages, besides solitary farmsteads and dairies.

Old William Dewy, with the violoncello, played the bass; his grandson Dick the treble violin; and Reuben and Michael Mail the tenor and second violins respectively. The singers consisted of four men and seven boys, upon whom devolved the task of carrying and attending to the lanterns, and holding the books open for the players. Directly music was the theme old William ever and instinctively came to the front.

'Now mind, neighbours,' he said, as they all went out one by one at the door, he himself holding it ajar and regarding them with a critical face as they passed, like a shepherd counting out his sheep. 'You two counter-boys, keep your ears open to Michael's fingering, and don't ye go straying into the treble part along o' Dick and his set, as ye did last year; and mind this especially when we be in "Arise, and hail." Billy Chimlen, don't you sing quite so raving mad as you fain would; and, all o' ye, whatever ye do, keep from making a great scuffle on the ground when we go in at people's gates; but go quietly, so as to strike up all of a sudden, like spirits.'

'Farmer Ledlow's first?'

'Farmer Ledlow first; the rest as usual.'

'And, Voss,' said the tranter terminatively, 'you keep house here till about half-past two; then heat the metheglin and cider in the warmer you'll find turned up upon the copper; and bring it wi' the victuals to church-hatch, as th'st know.'

Just before the clock struck twelve they lighted the lanterns and started. The moon, in her third quarter, had risen since the snowstorm; but the dense accumulation of snow-cloud weakened her power to a faint twilight which was rather pervasive of the landscape than traceable to the sky. The breeze had gone down, and the rustle of their feet and tones of their speech echoed with an alert rebound from every post, boundary-stone, and ancient wall they passed, even where the distance of the echo's origin was less than a few yards. Beyond their own slight noises nothing was to be heard save the occasional bark of foxes in the direction of Yalbury Wood, or the brush of a rabbit among the grass now and then as it scampered out of their way.

Most of the outlying homesteads and hamlets had been visited by about two o'clock; they then passed across the outskirts of a wooded park toward the main village, nobody being at home at the Manor. Pursuing no recognized track, great care was necessary in walking lest their faces should come in contact with the low-hanging boughs of the old lime-trees, which in many spots formed dense overgrowths of interlaced branches.

'Times have changed from the times they used to be,' said Mail, regarding nobody can tell what interesting old panoramas with an inward eye, and letting his outward glance rest on the ground because it was as convenient a position as any. 'People don't care much about us now! I've been thinking we must be almost the last left in the county of the old string players? Barrel-organs, and the things next door to 'em that you blow wi' your foot, have come in terribly of late years.'

'Ay!' said Bowman shaking his head; and old William on seeing him did the same thing.

'More's the pity,' replied another. 'Time was – long and merry ago now! – when not one of the varmits was to be heard of; but it served some of the quires right. They should have stuck to strings as we did, and kept out clarinets, and done away with serpents. If you'd thrive in musical religion, stick to strings, says I.'

'Strings be safe soul-lifters, as far as that do go,' said Mr Spinks.

'Yet there's worse things than serpents,' said Mr Penny. 'Old things pass away, 'tis true; but a serpent was a good old note: a deep rich note was the serpent.'

'Clar'nets, however, be bad at all times,' said Michael Mail. 'One Christmas – years agone now, years – I went the rounds wi' the Weatherbury quire. 'Twas a hard frosty night, and the keys of all the clar'nets froze – ah, they did freeze! – so that 'twas like drawing a cork every time a key was opened; and the players o' 'em had to go into a hedger-and-ditcher's chimley-corner, and thaw their clar'nets every now and then. An icicle o' spet hung down from the end of every man's clar'net a span long; and as to fingers – well, there, if ye'll believe me, we had no fingers at all, to our knowing.'

'I can well bring back to my mind,' said Mr Penny, 'what I said to poor Joseph Ryme (who took the treble part in Chalk-Newton Church for two-and-forty year) when they thought of having clar'nets there. "Joseph," I said says I, "depend upon't, if so be you have them tooting clar'nets you'll spoil the whole set-out. Clar'nets were not made for the service of the Lard; you can see it by looking at 'em," I said. And what came o't? Why, souls, the parson set up a barrel-organ on his own account within two years o' the time I spoke, and the old quire went to nothing.'

'As far as look is concerned,' said the tranter, 'I don't for my part see that a fiddle is much nearer heaven than a clar'net. 'Tis further off. There's always a rakish, scampish twist about a fiddle's looks that seems to say the Wicked One had a hand in making o'en; while angels be supposed to play clar'nets in heaven, or som'at like 'em if ye may believe picters.'

'Robert Penny, you was in the right,' broke in the eldest Dewy. 'They should ha' stuck to strings. Your brass-man is a rafting dog – well and good; your reed-man is a dab at stirring ye – well and good; your drum-man is a rare bowel-shaker – good again. But I don't care who hears me say it, nothing will spak to your heart wi' the sweetness o' the man of strings!'

'Strings for ever!' said little Jimmy.

'Strings alone would have held their ground against all the new comers in creation.' ('True, true!' said Bowman.) 'But clarinets was death.' ('Death they was!' said Mr Penny.) 'And harmonions,' William continued in a louder voice, and getting excited by these signs of approval, 'harmonions and barrel-organs' ('Ah!' and groans from Spinks) 'be miserable – what shall I call 'em? – miserable –'

'Sinners,' suggested Jimmy, who made large strides like the men and did not lag behind with the other little boys.

'Miserable dumbledores!'

'Right, William, and so they be – miserable dumbledores!' said the choir with unanimity.

By this time they were crossing to a gate in the direction of the school which, standing on a slight eminence at the junction of three ways, now rose in unvarying and dark flatness against the sky. The instruments were retuned, and all the band entered the school enclosure, enjoined by old William to keep upon the grass.

'Number seventy-eight,' he softly gave out as they formed round in a semicircle, the boys opening the lanterns to get a clearer light, and directing their rays on the books.

Then passed forth into the quiet night an ancient and time-worn hymn, embodying a quaint Christianity in words orally transmitted from father to son through several generations down to the present characters, who sang them out right earnestly:

> Remember Adam's fall,
>   O thou Man:
> Remember Adam's fall
>   From Heaven to Hell.
> Remember Adam's fall;
> How he hath condemn'd all
> In Hell perpetual
>   There for to dwell.
>
> Remember God's goodnesse,
>   O thou Man:
> Remember God's goodnesse,
>   His promise made.
> Remember God's goodnesse;
> He sent His Son sinlesse
> Our ails for to redress;
>   Be not afraid!
>
> In Bethlehem He was born,
>   O thou Man:
> In Bethlehem He was born,
>   For mankind's sake.
> In Bethlehem He was born,
> Christmas-day i' the morn:
> Our Saviour thought no scorn
>   Our faults to take.
>
> Give thanks to God alway,
>   O thou Man:
> Give thanks to God alway
>   With heart-most joy.
> Give thanks to God alway
> On this our joyful day:
> Let all men sing and say,
>   Holy, Holy!

Having concluded the last note they listened for a minute or two, but found that no sound issued from the schoolhouse.

'Four breaths, and then, "O, what unbounded goodness!" number fifty-nine,' said William.

This was duly gone through, and no notice whatever seemed to be taken of the performance.

'Good guide us, surely 'tisn't a' empty house, as befell us in the year thirty-nine and forty-three!' said old Dewy.

'Perhaps she's jist come from some musical city, and sneers at our doings?' the tranter whispered.

"Od rabbit her!' said Mr Penny, with an annihilating look at a corner of the school chimney, 'I don't quite stomach her, if this is it. Your plain music well done is as worthy as your other sort done bad, a' b'lieve, souls; so say I.'

'Four breaths, and then the last,' said the leader authoritatively. ' "Rejoice, ye Tenants of the Earth," number sixty-four.'

At the close, waiting yet another minute, he said in a clear loud voice, as he had said in the village at that hour and season for the previous forty years –

'A merry Christmas to ye!'

* V *

The Listeners

WHEN the expectant stillness consequent upon the exclamation had nearly died out of them all, an increasing light made itself visible in one of the windows of the upper floor. It came so close to the blind that the exact position of the flame could be perceived from the outside. Remaining steady for an instant, the blind went upward from before it, revealing to thirty concentrated eyes a young girl framed as a picture by the window architrave, and unconsciously illuminating her countenance to a vivid brightness by a candle she held in her left hand, close to her face, her right hand being extended to the side of the window. She was wrapped in a white robe of some kind, whilst down her shoulders fell a twining profusion of marvellously rich hair, in a wild disorder which proclaimed it to be only during the invisible hours of the night that such a condition was discoverable. Her bright eyes were looking into the grey world outside with an uncertain expression, oscillating between courage and shyness, which, as she recognized the semicircular group of dark forms gathered before her, transformed itself into pleasant resolution.

Opening the window, she said lightly and warmly –

'Thank you, singers, thank you!'

Together went the window quickly and quietly, and the blind started downward on its return to its place. Her fair forehead and eyes vanished; her little mouth; her neck and shoulders; all of her. Then the spot of candlelight shone nebulously as before; then it moved away.

'How pretty!' exclaimed Dick Dewy.

'If she'd been rale wexwork she couldn't ha' been comelier,' said Michael Mail.

'As near a thing to a spiritual vision as ever *I* wish to see!' said tranter Dewy.

'O, sich I never, never see!' said Leaf fervently.

All the rest, after clearing their throats and adjusting their hats, agreed that such a sight was worth singing for.

'Now to Farmer Shiner's, and then replenish our insides, father?' said the tranter.

'Wi' all my heart,' said old William, shouldering his bass-viol.

Farmer Shiner's was a queer lump of a house, standing at the corner of a lane that ran into the principal thoroughfare. The upper windows were much wider than they were high, and this feature, together with a broad bay-window where the door might have been expected, gave it by day the aspect of a human countenance turned askance, and wearing a sly and wicked leer. Tonight nothing was visible but the outline of the roof upon the sky.

The front of this building was reached, and the preliminaries arranged as usual.

'Four breaths, and number thirty-two, "Behold the Morning Star",' said old William.

They had reached the end of the second verse, and the fiddlers were doing the up bow-stroke previously to pouring forth the opening chord of the third verse, when, without a light appearing or any signal being given a roaring voice exclaimed –

'Shut up, woll 'ee! Don't make your blaring row here! A feller wi' a headache enough to split his skull likes a quiet night!'

Slam went the window.

'Hullo, that's a' ugly blow for we!' said the tranter, in a keenly appreciative voice, and turning to his companions.

'Finish the carrel, all who be friends of harmony!' commanded old William; and they continued to the end.

'Four breaths, and number nineteen!' said William firmly. 'Give it him well; the quire can't be insulted in this manner!'

A light now flashed into existence, the window opened, and the farmer stood revealed as one in a terrific passion.

'Drown en! – drown en!' the tranter cried, fiddling frantically. 'Play fortissimy, and drown his spaking!'

'Fortissimy!' said Michael Mail, and the music and singing waxed so loud that it was impossible to know what Mr Shiner had said, was saying, or was about to say; but wildly flinging his arms and body about in the forms of capital Xs and Ys, he appeared to utter enough invectives to consign the whole parish to perdition.

'Very onseemly – very!' said old William, as they retired. 'Never such a dreadful scene in the whole round o' my carrel practice – never! And he a churchwarden!'

'Only a drap o' drink got into his head,' said the tranter. 'Man's well enough when he's in his religious frame. He's in his worldly frame now. Must ask en to our bit of a party tomorrow night, I suppose, and so put en in humour again. We bear no mortal man ill-will.'

They now crossed Mellstock Bridge, and went along an embowered path beside the Froom towards the church and vicarage, meeting Voss with the hot mead and bread-and-cheese as they were approaching the churchyard. This determined them to eat and drink before proceeding further, and they entered the church and ascended to the gallery. The lanterns were opened, and the whole body sat round against the wall on benches and whatever else was available, and made a hearty meal. In the pauses of conversation there could be heard through the floor overhead a little world of undertones and creaks from the halting clockwork, which never spread further than the tower they were born in, and raised in the more meditative minds a fancy that here lay the direct pathway of Time.

Having done eating and drinking they again tuned the instruments, and once more the party emerged into the night air.

'Where's Dick?' said old Dewy.

Every man looked round upon every other man, as if Dick might have been transmuted into one or the other; and then they said they didn't know.

'Well now, that's what I call very nasty of Master Dicky, that I do,' said Michael Mail.

'He've clinked off home-along, depend upon't,' another suggested, though not quite believing that he had.

'Dick!' exclaimed the tranter, and his voice rolled sonorously forth among the yews.

He suspended his muscles rigid as stone whilst listening for an answer, and finding he listened in vain, turned to the assemblage.

'The treble man too! Now if he'd been a tenor or counter chap, we might ha' contrived the rest o't without en, you see. But for a quire to lose the treble, why, my sonnies, you may so well lose your . . .' The tranter paused, unable to mention an image vast enough for the occasion.

'Your head at once,' suggested Mr Penny.

The tranter moved a pace as if it were puerile of people to complete sentences when there were more pressing things to be done.

'Was ever heard such a thing as a young man leaving his work half done and turning tail like this!'

'Never,' replied Bowman, in a tone signifying that he was the last man in the world to wish to withhold the formal finish required of him.

'I hope no fatal tragedy has overtook the lad!' said his grandfather.

'O no,' replied tranter Dewy placidly. 'Wonder where he's put that there fiddle of his. Why that fiddle cost thirty shillings, and good words besides. Somewhere in the damp, without doubt; that instrument will be unglued and spoilt in ten minutes – ten! ay, two.'

'What in the name o' righteousness can have happened?' said old William, more uneasily. 'Perhaps he's drownded!'

Leaving their lanterns and instruments in the belfry they retraced their steps along the waterside track. 'A strapping lad like Dick d'know better than let anything happen onawares,' Reuben remarked. 'There's sure to be some poor little scram reason for't staring us in the face all the while.' He lowered his voice to a mysterious tone: 'Neighbours, have ye noticed any sign of a scornful woman in his head, or suchlike?'

'Not a glimmer of such a body. He's as clear as water yet.'

'And Dicky said he should never marry,' cried Jimmy, 'but live at home always along wi' mother and we!'

'Ay, ay, my sonny; every lad has said that in his time.'

They had now again reached the precincts of Mr Shiner's, but hearing nobody in that direction, one or two went across to the schoolhouse. A light was still burning in the bedroom, and though the blind was down the window had been slightly opened, as if to admit the distant notes of the carollers to the ears of the occupant of the room.

Opposite the window, leaning motionless against a beech tree, was the lost man, his arms folded, his head thrown back, his eyes fixed upon the illuminated lattice.

'Why, Dick, is that thee? What b'st doing here?'

Dick's body instantly flew into a more rational attitude, and his head was seen to turn east and west in the gloom as if endeavouring to discern some proper answer to that question; and at last he said in rather feeble accents –

'Nothing, father.'

'Th'st take long enough time about it then, upon my body,' said the tranter as they all turned anew towards the vicarage.

'I thought you hadn't done having snap in the gallery,' said Dick.

'Why, we've been traypsing and rambling about, looking everywhere, and thinking you'd done fifty deathly things, and here have you been at nothing at all!'

'The stupidness lies in that point of it being nothing at all,' murmured Mr Spinks.

The vicarage front was their next field of operation, and Mr Maybold, the lately-arrived incumbent, duly received his share of the night's harmonies. It was hoped that by reason of his profession he would have been led to open the window, and an extra carol in quick time was added to draw him forth. But Mr Maybold made no stir.

'A bad sign!' said old William, shaking his head.

However, at that same instant a musical voice was heard exclaiming from inner depths of bedclothes –

'Thanks, villagers!'

'What did he say?' asked Bowman, who was rather dull of hearing. Bowman's voice, being therefore loud, had been heard by the vicar within.

'I said, "Thanks, villagers!" ' cried the vicar again.

'Oh, we didn't hear 'ee the first time!' cried Bowman.

'Now don't for heaven's sake spoil the young man's temper by answering like that!' said the tranter.

'You won't do that, my friends!' the vicar shouted.

'Well to be sure, what ears!' said Mr Penny in a whisper. 'Beats any horse or dog in the parish, and depend upon't that's a sign he's a proper clever chap.'

'We shall see that in time,' said the tranter.

Old William, in his gratitude for such thanks from a comparatively new inhabitant, was anxious to play all the tunes over again; but renounced his desire on being reminded by Reuben that it would be best to leave well alone.

'Now putting two and two together,' the tranter continued, as they went their way over the hill, and across to the last remaining houses; 'that is, in the form of that young female vision we zeed just now, and this young tenor-voiced parson, my belief is she'll wind en round her finger, and twist the pore young feller about like the figure of 8 – that she will, my sonnies.'

* VI *

Christmas Morning

THE choir at last reached their beds, and slept like the rest of the parish, Dick's slumbers, through the three or four hours remaining for rest, were disturbed and slight; an exhaustive variation upon the incidents that had passed that night in connection with the school-window going on in his brain every moment of the time.

In the morning, do what he would – go upstairs, downstairs, out of doors, speak of the wind and weather, or what not – he could not refrain from an unceasing renewal, in imagination, of that interesting enactment. Tilted on the edge of one foot he stood beside the fireplace, watching his mother grilling rashers; but there was nothing in grilling, he thought, unless the Vision grilled. The limp rasher hung down between the bars of the gridiron like a cat in a child's arms; but there was nothing in similes unless She uttered them. He looked at the daylight shadows of a yellow hue, dancing with the firelight shadows in blue on the whitewashed chimney corner, but there was nothing in shadows. 'Perhaps the new young wom – sch – Miss Fancy Day will sing in church with us this morning,' he said.

The tranter looked a long time before he replied, 'I fancy she will; and yet I fancy she won't.'

Dick implied that such a remark was rather to be tolerated than admired; though deliberateness in speech was known to have, as a rule, more to do with the machinery of the tranter's throat than with the matter enunciated.

They made preparations for going to church as usual; Dick with extreme alacrity, though he would not definitely consider why he was so religious. His wonderful nicety in brushing and cleaning his best light boots had features which elevated it to the rank of an art. Every particle and speck of last week's mud was scraped and brushed from toe and heel; new blacking from the packet was carefully mixed and made use of, regardless of expense. A coat was laid on and polished; then another coat for increased blackness; and lastly a third, to give the perfect and mirror-like jet which the hoped-for rencounter demanded.

It being Christmas-day, the tranter prepared himself with Sunday particularity. Loud sousing and snorting noises were heard to proceed from a tub in the back quarters of the dwelling, proclaiming that he was there performing his great Sunday wash, lasting half-an-hour, to which his washings on working-day mornings were mere flashes in the pan. Vanishing into the outhouse with a large brown towel, and the above-named bubblings and snortings being carried on for about twenty minutes, the tranter would appear round the edge of the door, smelling like a summer fog, and looking as if he had just narrowly escaped a watery grave with the loss of much of his clothes, having since been weeping bitterly till his eyes were red; a crystal drop of water hanging ornamentally at the bottom of each ear, one at the tip of his nose, and others in the form of spangles about his hair.

After a great deal of crunching upon the sanded stone floor by the feet of father, son, and grandson as they moved to and fro in these preparations, the bass-viol and fiddles were taken from their nook, and the strings examined and screwed a little above concert-pitch that they might keep their tone when the service began, to obviate the awkward contingency of having to retune them at the back of the gallery during a cough, sneeze, or amen – an inconvenience which had been known to arise in damp wintry weather.

The three left the door and paced down Mellstock-lane and across the ewe-lease, bearing under their arms the instruments in faded green-baize bags, and old brown music-books in their hands; Dick continually finding himself in advance of the other two, and the tranter moving on with toes turned outwards to an enormous angle.

At the foot of an incline the church became visible through the north gate, or 'church hatch', as it was called here. Seven agile figures in a clump were observable beyond, which proved to be the choristers waiting; sitting on an altar-tomb to pass the time, and letting their heels dangle against it. The musicians being now in sight the youthful party scampered off and rattled up the old wooden stairs of the gallery like a regiment of cavalry; the other boys of the parish waiting outside and observing birds, cats, and other creatures till the vicar entered, when they suddenly subsided into sober church-goers, and passed down the aisle with echoing heels.

The gallery of Mellstock Church had a status and sentiment of its own. A stranger there was regarded with a feeling altogether differing from that of the congregation below towards him. Banished from the nave as an intruder whom no originality could make interesting, he was received above as a curiosity that no unfitness could render dull. The gallery, too, looked down upon and knew the habits of the nave to its remotest peculiarity, and had an extensive stock of exclusive information about it; while the nave knew nothing of the gallery folk, as gallery folk, beyond their loud-sounding minims and chest notes. Such topics as that the clerk was always chewing tobacco except at the moment of crying amen; that he had a dust-hole in his pew; that during the sermon certain young daughters of the village had left off caring to read anything so mild as the marriage service for some years, and now regularly studied the one which chronologically follows it, that a pair of lovers touched fingers through a knot-hole between their pews in the manner ordained by their great exemplars, Pyramus and Thisbe; that Mrs Ledlow, the farmer's wife, counted her money and reckoned her week's marketing expenses during the first lesson – all news to those below – were stale subjects here.

Old William sat in the centre of the front row, his violoncello between his knees and two singers on each hand. Behind him, on the left, came the treble singers and Dick; and on the right the tranter and the tenors. Further back was old Mail with the altos and supernumeraries.

But before they had taken their places, and whilst they were standing in a circle at the back of the gallery practising a psalm or two, Dick cast his eyes over his grandfather's shoulder, and saw the vision of the past night enter the porch-door as methodically as if she had never been a vision at all. A new atmosphere seemed suddenly to be puffed into the ancient edifice by her movement, which made Dick's body and soul tingle with novel sensations. Directed by Shiner, the churchwarden, she proceeded to the small aisle on the north side of the chancel, a spot now allotted to a throng of Sunday-school girls, and distinctly visible from the gallery-front by looking under the curve of the furthermost arch on that side.

Before this moment the church had seemed comparatively empty – now it was thronged; and as Miss Fancy rose from her knees and looked around her for a permanent place in which to deposit herself – finally choosing the remotest corner – Dick began to breathe more freely the warm new air she had brought with her; to feel rushings of blood, and to have impressions that there was a tie between her and himself visible to all the congregation.

Ever afterwards the young man could recollect individually each part of the service of that bright Christmas morning, and the trifling occurrences which took place as its minutes slowly drew along; the duties of that day dividing themselves by a complete line from the services of other times. The tunes they that morning essayed remained with him for years, apart from all others; also the text; also the appearance of the layer of dust upon the capitals of the piers; that the holly-bough in the chancel archway was hung a little out of the centre – all the ideas, in short, that creep into the mind when reason is only exercising its lowest activity through the eye.

By chance or by fate, another young man who attended Mellstock Church on that Christmas morning had towards the end of the service the same instinctive perception of an interesting presence, in the shape of the same bright maiden, though his emotion reached a far less developed stage. And there was this difference, too, that the person in question was surprised at his condition, and sedulously endeavoured to reduce himself to his normal state of mind. He was the young vicar, Mr Maybold.

The music on Christmas mornings was frequently below the standard of church-performances at other times. The boys were sleepy from the heavy exertions of the night; the men were slightly wearied; and now, in addition to these constant reasons, there was a dampness in the atmosphere that still further aggravated the evil. Their strings, from the recent long exposure to the night air, rose whole semitones, and snapped with a loud twang at the most silent moment; which necessitated more retiring than ever to the back of the gallery, and made the gallery throats quite husky with the quantity of coughing and hemming required for tuning in. The vicar looked cross.

When the singing was in progress there was suddenly discovered to be a strong and shrill reinforcement from some point, ultimately found to be the school-girls' aisle. At every attempt it grew bolder and more distinct. At the third time of singing, these intrusive feminine voices were mighty as those of the regular singers; in fact, the flood of sound from this quarter assumed such an individuality, that it had a time, a key, almost a tune of its own, surging upwards when the gallery plunged downwards, and the reverse.

Now this had never happened before within the memory of man. The girls, like the rest of the congregation, had always been humble and respectful followers of the gallery; singing at sixes and sevens if without gallery leaders; never interfering with the ordinances of these practised artists – having no will, union, power, or proclivity except it was given them from the established choir enthroned above them.

A good deal of desperation became noticeable in the gallery throats and strings, which continued throughout the musical portion of the service. Directly the fiddles were laid down, Mr Penny's spectacles put in their sheath, and the text had been given out, an indignant whispering began.

'Did ye hear that, souls?' Mr Penny said, in a groaning breath.

'Brazen-faced hussies!' said Bowman.

'True; why, they were every note as loud as we, fiddles and all, if not louder!'

'Fiddles and all!' echoed Bowman bitterly.

'Shall anything saucier be found than united 'ooman?' Mr Spinks murmured.

'What I want to know is,' said the tranter (as if he knew already, but that civilization required the form of words), 'what business people have to tell maidens to sing like that when they don't sit in a gallery, and never have entered one in their lives? That's the question, my sonnies.'

''Tis the gallery have got to sing, all the world knows,' said Mr Penny. 'Why, souls, what's the use o' the ancients spending scores of pounds to build galleries if people down in the lowest depths of the church sing like that at a moment's notice?'

'Really, I think we useless ones had better march out of church, fiddles and all!' said Mr Spinks, with a laugh which, to a stranger, would have sounded mild and real. Only the initiated body of men he addressed could understand the horrible bitterness of irony that lurked under the quiet words 'useless ones', and the ghastliness of the laughter apparently so natural.

'Never mind! Let 'em sing too – 'twill make it all the louder – hee, hee!' said Leaf.

'Thomas Leaf, Thomas Leaf! Where have you lived all your life?' said grandfather William sternly.

The quailing Leaf tried to look as if he had lived nowhere at all.

'When all's said and done, my sonnies,' Reuben said, 'there'd have been no real harm in their singing if they had let nobody hear 'em, and only jined in now and then.'

'None at all,' said Mr Penny. 'But though I don't wish to accuse people wrongfully, I'd say before my lord judge that I could hear every note o' that last psalm come from 'em as much as from us – every note as if 'twas their own.'

'Know it! ah, I should think I did know it!' Mr Spinks was heard to observe at this moment without reference to his fellow-players – shaking his head at some idea he seemed to see floating before him, and smiling as if he were attending a funeral at the time. 'Ah, do I or don't I know it!'

No one said, 'Know what?' because all were aware from experience that what he knew would declare itself in process of time.

'I could fancy last night that we should have some trouble wi' that young man,' said the tranter, pending the continuance of Spinks's speech, and looking towards the unconscious Mr Maybold in the pulpit.

'I fancy,' said old William, rather severely, 'I fancy there's too much whispering going on to be of any spiritual use to gentle or simple.' Then folding his lips and concentrating his glance on the vicar, he implied that none but the ignorant would speak again; and accordingly there was silence in the gallery, Mr Spinks's telling speech remaining for ever unspoken.

Dick had said nothing, and the tranter little, on this episode of the morning; for Mrs Dewy at breakfast expressed it as her intention to invite the youthful leader of the culprits to the small party it was customary with them to have on Christmas night – a piece of knowledge which had given a particular brightness to Dick's reflections since he had received it. And in the tranter's slightly cynical nature, party feeling was weaker than in the other members of the choir, though friendliness and faithful partnership still sustained in him a hearty earnestness on their account.

* VII *

The Tranter's Party

DURING the afternoon unusual activity was seen to prevail about the precincts of tranter Dewy's house. The flagstone floor was swept of dust, and a sprinkling of the finest yellow sand from the innermost stratum of the adjoining sand-pit lightly scattered thereupon. Then were produced large knives and forks, which had been shrouded in darkness and grease since the last occasion of the kind, and bearing upon their sides, 'Shear-steel, warranted', in such emphatic letters of assurance, that the warranter's name was not required as further proof, and not given. The key was left in the tap of the cider-barrel instead of being carried in a pocket. And finally the tranter had to stand up in the room and let his wife wheel him round like a turnstile, to see if anything discreditable was visible in his appearance.

'Stand still till I've been for the scissors,' said Mrs Dewy.

The tranter stood as still as a sentinel at the challenge.

The only repairs necessary were a trimming of one or two whiskers that had extended beyond the general contour of the mass; a like trimming of a slightly-frayed edge visible on his shirt-collar; and a final tug at a grey hair – to all of which operations he submitted in resigned silence, except the last, which produced a mild 'Come, come, Ann', by way of expostulation.

'Really, Reuben, 'tis quite a disgrace to see such a man,' said Mrs Dewy, with the severity justifiable in a long-tried companion, giving him another turn round, and picking several of Smiler's hairs from the shoulder of his coat. Reuben's thoughts seemed engaged elsewhere, and he yawned. 'And the collar of your coat is a shame to behold – so plastered with dirt, or dust, or grease, or something. Why, wherever could you have got it?'

' 'Tis my warm nater in summer-time, I suppose. I always did get in such a heat when I bustle about.'

'Ay, the Dewys always were such a coarse-skinned family. There's your brother Bob just as bad – as fat as a porpoise – wi' his low, mean, "How'st do, Ann?" whenever he meets me. I'd "How'st do" him indeed! If the sun only shines out a minute, there be you all streaming in the face – I never see!'

'If I be hot week-days, I must be hot Sundays.'

'If any of the girls should turn after their father 'twill be a bad look-out for 'em, poor things! None of my family was sich vulgar sweaters, not one of 'em. But, Lord-a-mercy, the Dewys! I don't know how ever I cam' into such a family!'

'Your woman's weakness when I asked ye to jine us. That's how it was, I suppose.' But the tranter appeared to have heard some such words from his wife before, and hence his answer had not the energy it might have shown if the inquiry had possessed the charm of novelty.

'You never did look so well in a pair o' trousers as in them,' she continued in the same unimpassioned voice, so that the unfriendly criticism of the Dewy family seemed to have been more normal than spontaneous. 'Such a cheap pair as 'twas too. As big as any man could wish to have, and lined inside, and double-lined in the lower parts, and an extra piece of stiffening at the bottom. And 'tis a nice high cut that comes up right under your armpits, and there's enough turned down inside the seams to make half a pair more, besides a piece of cloth left that will make an honest waistcoat – all by my contriving in buying the stuff at a bargain, and having it made up under my eye. It only shows what may be done by taking a little trouble, and not going straight to the rascally tailors.'

The discourse was cut short by the sudden appearance of Charley on the scene, with a face and hands of hideous blackness, and a nose like a guttering candle. Why, on that particularly cleanly afternoon, he should have discovered that the chimney-crook and chain from which the hams were suspended should have possessed more merits and general interest as playthings than any other articles in the house, is a question for nursing mothers to decide. However, the humour seemed to lie in the result being, as has been seen, that any given player with these articles was in the long-run daubed with soot. The last that was seen of Charley by daylight after this piece of ingenuity was when in the act of vanishing from his father's presence round the corner of the house – looking back over his shoulder with an expression of great sin on his face, like Cain as the Outcast in Bible pictures.

★

The guests had all assembled, and the tranter's party had reached that degree of development which accords with ten o'clock p.m. in rural assemblies. At that hour the sound of a fiddle in process of tuning was heard from the inner pantry.

'That's Dick,' said the tranter. 'That lad's crazy for a jig.'

'Dick! Now I cannot – really, I cannot have any dancing at all till Christmas-day is out,' said old William emphatically. 'When the clock ha' done striking twelve, dance as much as ye like.'

'Well, I must say there's reason in that, William,' said Mrs Penny. 'If you do have a party on Christmas-night, 'tis only fair and honourable to the sky-folk to have it a sit-still party. Jigging parties be all very well on the Devil's holidays; but a jigging party looks suspicious now. O yes; stop till the clock strikes, young folk – so say I.'

It happened that some warm mead accidentally got into Mr Spinks's head about this time.

'Dancing,' he said, 'is a most strengthening, livening, and courting movement, 'specially with a little beverage added! And dancing is good. But why disturb what is ordained, Richard and Reuben, and the company zhinerally? Why, I ask, as far as that do go?'

'Then nothing till after twelve,' said William.

Though Reuben and his wife ruled on social points, religious questions were mostly disposed of by the old man, whose firmness on this head quite counterbalanced a certain weakness in his handling of domestic matters. The hopes of the younger members of the household were therefore relegated to a distance of one hour and three-quarters – a result that took visible shape in them by a remote and listless look about the eyes – the singing of songs being permitted in the interim.

At five minutes to twelve the soft tuning was again heard in the back quarters; and when at length the clock had whizzed forth the last stroke, Dick appeared ready primed, and the instruments were boldly handled; old William very readily taking the bass-viol from its accustomed nail, and touching the strings as irreligiously as could be desired.

The country-dance called the 'Triumph, or Follow my Lover', was the figure with which they opened. The tranter took for his partner Mrs Penny, and Mrs Dewy was chosen by Mr Penny, who made so much of his limited height by a judicious carriage of the head, straightening of the back, and important flashes of his spectacle-glasses, that he seemed almost as tall as the tranter. Mr Shiner, age about thirty-five, farmer and church-warden, a character principally composed of a crimson stare, vigorous breath, and a watch-chain, with a mouth hanging on a dark smile but never smiling, had come quite willingly to the party, and showed a wondrous obliviousness of all his antics on the previous night. But the comely, slender, prettily-dressed prize Fancy Day fell to Dick's lot, in spite of some private machinations of the farmer, for the reason that Mr Shiner, as a richer man, had shown too much assurance in asking the favour, whilst Dick had been duly courteous.

We gain a good view of our heroine as she advances to her place in the ladies' line. She belonged to the taller division of middle height. Flexibility was her first characteristic, by which she appeared to enjoy the most easeful rest when she was in gliding motion. Her dark eyes – arched by brows of so keen, slender, and soft a curve that they resembled nothing so much as two slurs in music – showed primarily a bright sparkle each. This was softened by a frequent thoughtfulness, yet not so frequent as to do away, for more than a few minutes at a time, with a certain coquettishness; which in its turn was never so decided as to banish honesty. Her lips imitated her brows in their clearly-cut outline and softness of bend; and her nose was well shaped – which is saying a great deal, when it is remembered that there are a hundred pretty mouths and eyes for one pretty nose. Add to this, plentiful knots of dark-brown hair, a gauzy dress of white with blue facings; and the slightest idea may be gained of the young maiden who showed, amidst the rest of the dancing-ladies, like a flower among vegetables. And so the dance proceeded. Mr Shiner, according to the interesting rule laid down, deserted his own partner and made off down the middle with this fair one of Dick's – the pair appearing from the top of the room like two persons tripping down a lane to be married. Dick trotted behind with what was intended to be a look of composure, but which was, in fact, a rather silly expression of feature – implying, with too much earnestness, that such an elopement could not be tolerated. Then they turned and came back, when Dick grew more rigid around his mouth, and blushed with ingenuous ardour as he joined hands with the rival and formed the arch over his lady's head, which presumably gave the figure its name; relinquishing her again at setting to partners, when Mr Shiner's new chain quivered in every link, and all the loose flesh upon the tranter – who here came into action again – shook like jelly. Mrs Penny, being always rather concerned for her personal safety when she danced with the tranter, fixed her face to a chronic smile of timidity the whole time it lasted – a peculiarity which filled her features with wrinkles, and reduced her eyes to little straight lines like hyphens, as she jigged up and down opposite him; repeating in her own person not only his proper movements, but also the minor flourishes which the richness of the tranter's imagination led him to introduce from time to time – an imitation which had about it something of slavish obedience, not unmixed with fear.

The ear-rings of the ladies now flung themselves wildly about, turning violent somersaults, banging this way and that, and then swinging quietly against the ears sustaining them. Mrs Crumpler – a heavy woman, who, for some reason which nobody ever thought worth inquiry, danced in a clean apron – moved so smoothly through the figure that her feet were never seen; conveying to imaginative minds the idea that she rolled on castors.

Minute after minute glided by, and the party reached the period when ladies' back-hair begins to look forgotten and dissipated; when a perceptible dampness makes itself apparent upon the faces even of delicate girls – a ghastly dew having for some time rained from the features of their masculine partners; when skirts begin to be torn out of their gathers; when elderly people, who have stood up to please their juniors, begin to feel sundry small tremblings in the region of the knees, and to wish the interminable dance was at Jericho; when (at country parties of the thorough sort) waistcoats begin to be unbuttoned, and when the fiddlers' chairs have been wriggled, by the frantic bowing of their occupiers, to a distance of about two feet from where they originally stood.

Fancy was dancing with Mr Shiner. Dick knew that Fancy, by the law of good manners, was bound to dance as pleasantly with one partner as with another; yet he could not help suggesting to himself that she need not have put *quite* so much spirit into her steps, nor smiled *quite* so frequently whilst in the farmer's hands.

'I'm afraid you didn't cast off,' said Dick mildly to Mr Shiner, before the latter man's watch-chain had done vibrating from a recent whirl.

Fancy made a motion of accepting the correction; but her partner took no notice, and proceeded with the next movement with an affectionate bend towards her.

'That Shiner's too fond of her,' the young man said to himself as he watched them. They came to the top again, Fancy smiling warmly towards her partner, and went to their places.

'Mr Shiner, you didn't cast off,' said Dick, for want of something else to demolish him with; casting off himself, and being put out at the farmer's irregularity.

'Perhaps I shan't cast off for any man,' said Mr Shiner.

'I think you ought to, sir.'

Dick's partner, a young lady of the name of Lizzy – called Lizz for short – tried to mollify.

'I can't say that I myself have much feeling for casting off,' she said.

'Nor I,' said Mrs Penny, following up the argument; 'especially if a friend and neighbour is set against it. Not but that 'tis a terrible tasty thing in good hands and well done; yes, indeed, so say I.'

'All I meant was,' said Dick, rather sorry that he had spoken correctingly to a guest, 'that 'tis in the dance; and a man has hardly any right to hack and mangle what was ordained by the regular dance-maker, who, I daresay, got his living by making 'em, and thought of nothing else all his life.'

'I don't like casting off: then very well; I cast off for no dance-maker that ever lived.'

Dick now appeared to be doing mental arithmetic, the act being really an effort to present to himself, in an abstract form, how far an argument with a formidable rival ought to be carried when that rival was his mother's guest. The dead-lock was put an end to by the stamping arrival up the middle of the tranter, who, despising minutiae on principle, started a theme of his own.

'I assure you, neighbours,' he said, 'the heat of my frame no tongue can tell!' He looked around and endeavoured to give, by a forcible gaze of self-sympathy, some faint idea of the truth.

Mrs Dewy formed one of the next couple.

'Yes,' she said in an auxiliary tone, 'Reuben always was such a hot man.'

Mrs Penny implied the species of sympathy that such a class of affliction required by trying to smile and to look grieved at the same time.

'If he only walk round the garden of a Sunday morning his shirt-collar is as limp as no starch at all,' continued Mrs Dewy, her countenance lapsing parenthetically into a housewifely expression of concern at the reminiscence.

'Come, come, you women-folk; 'tis hands-across – come, come!' said the tranter; and the conversation ceased for the present.

* VIII *

They Dance more Wildly

DICK had at length secured Fancy for that most delightful of country-dances, opening with six-hands-round.

'Before we begin,' said the tranter, 'my proposal is, that 'twould be a right and proper plan for every mortal man in the dance to pull off his jacket, considering the heat.'

'Such low notions as you have, Reuben! Nothing but strip will go down with you when you are a-dancing. Such a hot man as he is!'

'Well, now, look here, my sonnies,' he argued to his wife, whom he often addressed in the plural masculine for economy of epithet merely; 'I don't see that. You dance and get hot as fire; therefore you lighten your clothes. Isn't that nature and reason for gentle and simple? If I strip by myself and not necessary, 'tis rather pot-housey I own; but if we stout chaps strip one and all, why, 'tis the native manners of the country, which no man can gainsay? Hey – what did you say, my sonnies?'

'Strip we will!' said the three other heavy men who were in the dance; and their coats were accordingly taken off and hung in the passage, whence the four sufferers from heat soon reappeared marching in close column, with flapping shirt-sleeves, and having as common to them all a general glance of being now a match for any man or dancer in England or Ireland. Dick, fearing to lose ground in Fancy's good opinion, retained his coat like the rest of the thinner men; and Mr Shiner did the same from superior knowledge.

And now a further phase of revelry had disclosed itself. It was the time of night when a guest may write his name in the dust upon the tables and chairs, and a bluish mist pervades the atmosphere, becoming a distinct halo round the candles; when people's nostrils, wrinkles, and crevices in general seem to be getting gradually plastered up; when the very fiddlers as well as the dancers get red in the face, the dancers having advanced further still towards incandescence, and entered the cadaverous phrase; the fiddlers no longer sit down, but kick back their chairs and saw madly at the strings with legs firmly spread and eyes closed, regardless of the visible world. Again and again did Dick share his Love's hand with another man, and wheel round; then, more delightfully, promenade in a circle with her all to himself, his arm holding her waist more firmly each time, and his elbow getting further and further behind her back, till the distance reached was rather noticeable; and, most blissful, swinging to places shoulder to shoulder, her breath curling round his neck like a summer zephyr that had strayed from its proper date. Threading the couples one by one they reached the bottom, when there arose in Dick's mind a minor misery lest the tune should end before they could work their way to the top again, and have anew the same exciting run down through. Dick's feelings on actually reaching the top in spite of his doubts were supplemented by a mortal fear that the fiddling might even stop at this supreme moment; which prompted him to convey a stealthy whisper to the far-gone musicians to the effect that they were not to leave off till he and his partner had reached the bottom of the dance once more, which remark was replied to by the nearest of those convulsed and quivering men by a private nod to the anxious young man between two semiquavers of the tune, and a simultaneous 'All right, ay, ay', without opening the eyes. Fancy was now held so closely that Dick and she were practically one person. The room became to Dick like a picture in a dream; all that he could remember of it afterwards being the look of the fiddlers going to sleep as humming-tops sleep, by increasing their motion and hum, together with the figures of grandfather James and old Simon Crumpler sitting by the chimney-corner talking and nodding in dumb-show, and beating the air to their emphatic sentences like people near a threshing machine.

The dance ended. 'Piph-h-h-h!' said tranter Dewy, blowing out his breath in the very finest stream of vapour that a man's lips could form. 'A regular tightener, that one, sonnies!' He wiped his forehead, and went to the cider and ale mugs on the table.

'Well!' said Mrs Penny, flopping into a chair, 'my heart haven't been in such a thumping state of uproar since I used to sit up on old Midsummer-eves to see who my husband was going to be.'

'And that's getting on for a good few years ago now, from what I've heard you tell,' said the tranter without lifting his eyes from the cup he was filling. Being now engaged in the business of handing round refreshments he was warranted in keeping his coat off still, though the other heavy men had resumed theirs.

'And a thing I never expected would come to pass, if you'll believe me, came to pass then,' continued Mrs Penny. 'Ah, the first spirit ever I see on a Midsummer-eve was a puzzle to me when he appeared, a hard puzzle, so say I!'

'So I should have fancied,' said Elias Spinks.

'Yes,' said Mrs Penny, throwing her glance into past times and talking on in a running tone of complacent abstraction, as if a listener were not a necessity. 'Yes; never was I in such a taking as on that Midsummer-eve! I sat up, quite determined to see if John Wildway was going to marry me or no. I put the bread-and-cheese and beer quite ready, as the witch's book ordered, and I opened the door, and I waited till the clock struck twelve, my nerves all alive and so strained that I could feel every one of 'em twitching like bell-wires. Yes, sure! and when the clock had struck, lo and behold I could see through the door a *little small* man in the lane wi' a shoemaker's apron on.'

Here Mr Penny stealthily enlarged himself half an inch.

'Now, John Wildway,' Mrs Penny continued, 'who courted me at that time, was a shoemaker, you see, but he was a very fair-sized man, and I couldn't believe that any such a little small man had anything to do wi' me, as anybody might. But on he came, and crossed the threshold – not John, but actually the same little man in the shoemaker's apron –'

'You needn't be so mighty particular about little and small!' said her husband.

'In he walks, and down he sits, and O my goodness me, didn't I flee upstairs, body and soul hardly hanging together! Well, to cut a long story short, by-long and by-late John Wildway and I had a miff and parted; and lo and behold, the coming man came! Penny asked me if I'd go snacks with him, and afore I knew what I was about a'most, the thing was done.'

'I've fancied you never knew better in your life; but I mid be mistaken,' said Mr Penny in a murmur.

After Mrs Penny had spoken, there being no new occupation for her eyes she still let them stay idling on the past scenes just related, which were apparently visible to her in the centre of the room. Mr Penny's remark received no reply.

During this discourse the tranter and his wife might have been observed standing in an unobtrusive corner in mysterious closeness to each other, a just perceptible current of intelligence passing from each to each, which had apparently no relation whatever to the conversation of their guests, but much to their sustenance. A conclusion of some kind having at length been drawn, the palpable confederacy of man and wife was once more obliterated, the tranter marching off into the pantry humming a tune that he couldn't quite recollect, and then breaking into the words of a song of which he could remember about one line and a quarter. Mrs Dewy spoke a few words about preparations for a bit of supper.

That elder portion of the company which loved eating and drinking put on a look to signify that till this moment they had quite forgotten that it was customary to expect suppers on these occasions; going even further than this politeness of feature, and starting irrelevant subjects, the exceeding flatness and forced tone of which rather betrayed their object. The younger members said they were quite hungry, and that supper would be delightful though it was so late.

Good luck attended Dick's love-passes during the meal. He sat next Fancy, and had the thrilling pleasure of using permanently a glass which had been taken by Fancy in mistake; of letting the outer edge of the sole of his boot touch the lower verge of her skirt; and to add to these delights the cat, which had lain unobserved in her lap for several minutes, crept across into his own, touching him with fur that had touched her hand a moment before. There were, besides, some little pleasures in the shape of helping her to vegetable she didn't want, and when it had nearly alighted on her plate taking it across for his own use, on the plea of waste not, want not. He also, from time to time, sipped sweet sly glances at her profile; noticing the set of her head, the curve of her throat, and other artistic properties of the lively goddess, who the while kept up a rather free, not to say too free, conversation with Mr Shiner sitting opposite; which, after some uneasy criticism, and much shifting of argument backwards and forwards in Dick's mind, he decided not to consider of alarming significance.

'A new music greets our ears now,' said Miss Fancy, alluding, with the sharpness that her position as village sharpener demanded, to the contrast between the rattle of knives and forks and the late notes of the fiddlers.

'Ay; and I don't know but what 'tis sweeter in tone when you get above forty,' said the tranter; 'except, in faith, as regards father there. Never such a mortal man as he for tunes. They do move his soul; don't 'em, father?'

The eldest Dewy smiled across from his distant chair an assent to Reuben's remark.

'Spaking of being moved in soul,' said Mr Penny, 'I shall never forget the first time I heard the "Dead March". 'Twas at poor Corp'l Nineman's funeral at Casterbridge. It fairly made my hair creep and fidget about like a vlock of sheep – ah, it did, souls! And when they had done, and the last trump had sounded, and the guns was fired over the dead hero's grave, a' icy-cold drop o' moist sweat hung upon my forehead, and another upon my jawbone. Ah, 'tis a very solemn thing!'

'Well, as to father in the corner there,' the tranter said, pointing to old William, who was in the act of filling his mouth; 'he'd starve to death for music's sake now, as much as when he was a boy-chap of fifteen.'

'Truly, now,' said Michael Mail, clearing the corner of his throat in the manner of a man who meant to be convincing; 'there's a friendly tie of some sort between music and eating.' He lifted the cup to his mouth, and drank himself gradually backwards from a perpendicular position to a slanting one, during which time his looks performed a circuit from the wall opposite him to the ceiling overhead. Then clearing the other corner of his throat: 'Once I was a-setting in the little kitchen of the Dree Mariners at Casterbridge, having a bit of dinner, and a brass band struck

up in the street. Such a beautiful band as that were! I was setting eating
fried liver and lights, I well can mind – ah, I was! and to save my life, I
couldn't help chawing to the tune. Band played six-eight time; six-eight
chaws I, willynilly. Band plays common; common time went my teeth
among the liver and lights as true as a hair. Beautiful 'twere! Ah, I shall
never forget that there band!'

'That's as tuneful a thing as ever I heard of,' said grandfather James,
with the absent gaze which accompanies profound criticism.

'I don't like Michael's tuneful stories then,' said Mrs Dewy. 'They are
quite coarse to a person o' decent taste.'

Old Michael's mouth twitched here and there, as if he wanted to smile
but didn't know where to begin, which gradually settled to an expression
that it was not displeasing for a nice woman like the tranter's wife to
correct him.

'Well, now,' said Reuben, with decisive earnestness, 'that sort o' coarse
touch that's so upsetting to Ann's feelings is to my mind a recommendation; for it do always prove a story to be true. And for the same reason,
I like a story with a bad moral. My sonnies, all true stories have a coarse
touch or a bad moral, depend upon't. If the story-tellers could ha' got
decency and good morals from true stories, who'd have troubled to invent
parables?' Saying this the tranter arose to fetch a new stock of cider, ale,
mead, and home-made wines.

Mrs Dewy sighed and appended a remark (ostensibly behind her
husband's back, though that the words should reach his ears distinctly
was understood by both): 'Such a man as Dewy is! Nobody do know the
trouble I have to keep that man barely respectable. And did you ever hear
too – just now at suppertime – talking about "taties" with Michael in
such a work-folk way. Well, 'tis what I was never brought up to! With
our family 'twas never less than "taters", and very often "pertatoes"
outright; mother was so particular and nice with us girls: there was no
family in the parish that kept themselves up more than we.'

The hour of parting came. Fancy could not remain for the night
because she had engaged a woman to wait up for her. She disappeared
temporarily from the flagging party of dancers, and then came downstairs
wrapped up and looking altogether a different person from whom she
had been hitherto, in fact (to Dick's sadness and disappointment), a
woman somewhat reserved and of a phlegmatic temperament – nothing
left in her of the romping girl that she had seemed but a short quarter-
hour before, who had not minded the weight of Dick's hand upon her
waist, nor shirked the purlieus of the mistletoe.

'What a difference!' thought the young man – hoary cynic *pro tem*.
'What a miserable deceiving difference between the manners of a maid's
life at dancing times and at others! Look at this lovely Fancy! Through
the whole past evening touchable, squeezable – even kissable! For whole
half-hours I held her so close to me that not a sheet of paper could have
been slipped between us; and I could feel her heart only just outside my
own, her life beating on so close to mine, that I was aware of every breath

in it. A flit is made upstairs – a hat and a cloak put on – and I no more dare to touch her than –' Thought failed him, and he returned to realities.

But this was an endurable misery in comparison with what followed. Mr Shiner and his watch-chain, taking the intrusive advantage that ardent bachelors who are going homeward along the same road as a pretty young woman always do take of that circumstance, came forward to assure Fancy – with a total disregard of Dick's emotions, and in tones which were certainly not frigid – that he (Shiner) was not the man to go to bed before seeing his Lady Fair safe within her own door – not he, nobody should say he was that; and that he would not leave her side an inch till the thing was done – drown him if he would. The proposal was assented to by Miss Day, in Dick's foreboding judgement, with one degree – or at any rate, an appreciable fraction of a degree – of warmth beyond that required by a disinterested desire for protection from the dangers of the night.

All was over; and Dick surveyed the chair she had last occupied, looking now like a setting from which the gem has been torn. There stood her glass, and the romantic teaspoonful of elderwine at the bottom that she couldn't drink by trying ever so hard, in obedience to the mighty arguments of the tranter (his hand coming down upon her shoulder the while like a Nasmyth hammer), but the drinker was there no longer. There were the nine or ten pretty little crumbs she had left on her plate; but the eater was no more seen.

There seemed a disagreeable closeness of relationship between himself and the members of his family now that they were left alone again face to face. His father seemed quite offensive for appearing to be in just as high spirits as when the guests were there; and as for grandfather James (who had not yet left), he was quite fiendish in being rather glad they were gone.

'Really,' said the tranter, in a tone of placid satisfaction, 'I've had so little time to attend to myself all the evenen that I mean to enjoy a quiet meal now! A slice of this here ham – neither too fat nor too lean – so; and then a drop of this vinegar and pickles – there, that's it – and I shall be as fresh as a lark again! And to tell the truth, my sonny, my inside has been as dry as a lime-basket all night.'

'I like a party very well once in a while,' said Mrs Dewy, leaving off the adorned tones she had been bound to use throughout the evening and returning to the natural marriage voice; 'but, Lord, 'tis such a sight of heavy work next day! What with the dirty plates, and knives and forks, and dust and smother, and bits kicked off your furniture, and I don't know what all, why a body could a'most wish there were no such things as Christmases . . . Ah'h dear!' she yawned, till the clock in the corner had ticked several beats. She cast her eyes round upon the displaced, dust-laden furniture, and sat down overpowered at the sight.

'Well, I be getting all right by degrees, thank the Lord for't!' said the tranter cheerfully through a mangled mass of ham and bread, without lifting his eyes from his plate, and chopping away with his knife and fork as if he were felling trees. 'Ann, you may as well go on to bed at once, and not bide there making such sleepy faces; you look as long-favoured as a fiddle, upon my life, Ann. There, you must be wearied out, 'tis true. I'll do the doors and draw up the clock; and you go on, or you'll be as white as a sheet tomorrow.'

'Ay; I don't know whether I shan't or no.' The matron passed her hand across her eyes to brush away the film of sleep till she got upstairs.

Dick wondered how it was that when people were married they could be so blind to romance; and was quite certain that if he ever took to wife that dear impossible Fancy, he and she would never be so dreadfully practical and undemonstrative of the Passion as his father and mother were. The most extraordinary thing was that all the fathers and mothers he knew were just as undemonstrative as his own.

* IX *

Dick calls at the School

THE early days of the year drew on, and Fancy, having spent the holiday weeks at home, returned again to Mellstock.

Every spare minute of the week following her return was used by Dick in accidentally passing the schoolhouse in his journeys about the neigh-bourhood; but not once did she make herself visible. A handkerchief belonging to her had been providentially found by his mother in clearing the rooms the day after that of the dance; and by much contrivance Dick got it handed over to him, to leave with her at any time he should be near the school after her return. But he delayed taking the extreme measure of calling with it lest, had she really no sentiment of interest in him, it might be regarded as a slightly absurd errand, the reason guessed, and the sense of the ludicrous, which was rather keen in her, do his dignity considerable injury in her eyes; and what she thought of him, even apart from the question of her loving, was all the world to him now.

But the hour came when the patience of love at twenty-one could endure no longer. One Saturday he approached the school with a mild air of indifference, and had the satisfaction of seeing the object of his quest at the further end of her garden, trying, by the aid of a spade and gloves, to root a bramble that had intruded itself there.

He disguised his feelings from some suspicious-looking cottage-windows opposite by endeavouring to appear like a man in a great hurry of business, who wished to leave the handkerchief and have done with such trifling errands.

This endeavour signally failed; for on approaching the gate he found it locked to keep the children, who were playing 'cross-ladder' in the front, from running into her private grounds.

She did not see him; and he could only think of one thing to be done, which was to shout her name.

'Miss Day!'

The words were uttered with a jerk and a look meant to imply to the cottages opposite that he was now simply one who liked shouting as a pleasant way of passing his time, without any reference to persons in gardens. The name died away, and the unconscious Miss Day continued digging and pulling as before.

He screwed himself up to enduring the cottage-windows yet more stoically, and shouted again. Fancy took no notice whatever.

He shouted the third time, with desperate vehemence, turning suddenly about and retiring a little distance as if it were by no means for his own pleasure that he had come.

This time she heard him, came down the garden, and entered the school at the back. Footsteps echoed across the interior, the door opened, and three-quarters of the blooming young schoolmistress's face and figure stood revealed before him; a slice on her left-hand side being cut off by the edge of the door. Having surveyed and recognized him she came to the gate.

At sight of him had the pink of her cheeks increased, lessened, or did it continue to cover its normal area of ground? It was a question meditated several hundreds of times by her visitor in after-hours – the meditation, after wearying involutions, always ending in one way, that it was impossible to say.

'Your handkerchief: Miss Day: I called with.' He held it out spasmodically and awkwardly. 'Mother found it: under a chair.'

'O, thank you very much for bringing it, Mr Dewy. I couldn't think where I had dropped it.'

Now Dick, not being an experienced lover – indeed, never before having been engaged in the practice of love-making at all, except in a small schoolboy way – could not take advantage of the situation; and out came the blunder which afterwards cost him so many bitter moments and a sleepless night:

'Good morning, Miss Day.'

'Good morning, Mr Dewy.'

The gate was closed; she was gone; and Dick was standing outside, unchanged in his condition from what he had been before he called. Of course the Angel was not to blame – a young woman living alone in a house could not ask him indoors unless she had known him better – he should have kept her outside before floundering into that fatal farewell. He wished that before he called he had realized more fully than he did the pleasure of being about to call; and turned away.

PART THE SECOND

SPRING

* I *

Passing by the School

It followed that as the spring advanced Dick walked abroad much more frequently than had hitherto been usual with him, and was continually finding that his nearest way to or from home lay by the road which skirted the garden of the school. The first-fruits of his perseverance were that, on turning the angle on the nineteenth journey by that track, he saw Miss Fancy's figure, clothed in a dark-grey dress, looking from a high open window upon the crown of his hat. The friendly greeting resulting from this rencounter was considered so valuable an elixir that Dick passed still oftener; and by the time he had almost trodden a little path under the fence where never a path was before, he was rewarded with an actual meeting face to face on the open road before her gate. This brought another meeting, and another, Fancy faintly showing by her bearing that it was a pleasure to her of some kind to see him there; but the sort of pleasure she derived, whether exultation at the hope her exceeding fairness inspired, or the true feeling which was alone Dick's concern, he could not anyhow decide, although he meditated on her every little movement for hours after it was made.

* II *

A Meeting of the Quire

It was the evening of a fine spring day. The descending sun appeared as a nebulous blaze of amber light, its outline being lost in cloudy masses hanging round it like wild locks of hair.

The chief members of Mellstock parish choir were standing in a group in front of Mr Penny's workshop in the lower village. They were all brightly illuminated, and each was backed up by a shadow as long as a steeple; the lowness of the source of light rendering the brims of their hats of no use at all as a protection to the eyes.

Mr Penny's was the last house in that part of the parish, and stood in a hollow by the roadside; so that cart-wheels and horses' legs were about level with the sill of his shop-window. This was low and wide, and was open from morning till evening, Mr Penny himself being invariably seen working inside like a framed portrait of a shoemaker by some modern Moroni. He sat facing the road, with a boot on his knees and the awl in his hand, only looking up for a moment as he stretched out his arms and bent forward at the pull, when his spectacles flashed in the passer's face with a shine of flat whiteness, and then returned again to the boot as usual. Rows of lasts, small and large, stout and slender, covered the wall which formed the background, in the extreme shadow of which a kind of dummy was seen sitting, in the shape of an apprentice with a string tied round his hair (probably to keep it out of his eyes). He smiled at remarks that floated in from without, but was never known to answer them in Mr Penny's presence. Outside the window the upper-leather of a Wellington-boot was usually hung, pegged to a board as if to dry. No sign was over his door; in fact – as with old banks and mercantile houses – advertising in any shape was scorned, and it would have been felt as beneath his dignity to paint up, for the benefit of strangers, the name of an establishment whose trade came solely by connection based on personal respect.

His visitors now came and stood on the outside of his window, sometimes leaning against the sill, sometimes moving a pace or two backwards and forwards in front of it. They talked with deliberate gesticulations to Mr Penny, enthroned in the shadow of the interior.

'I do like a man to stick to men who be in the same line o' life – o' Sundays, anyway – that I do so.'

' 'Tis like all the doings of folk who don't know what a day's work is, that's what I say.'

'My belief is the man's not to blame; 'tis *she* – she's the bitter weed!'

'No, not altogether. He's a poor gawk-hammer. Look at his sermon yesterday.'

'His sermon was well enough, a very good guessable sermon, only he couldn't put it into words and speak it. That's all was the matter wi' the sermon. He hadn't been able to get it past his pen.'

'Well – ay, the sermon might have been good; for, 'tis true, the sermon of Old Eccl'iastes himself lay in Eccl'iastes's ink-bottle afore he got it out.'

Mr Penny, being in the act of drawing the last stitch tight, could afford time to look up and throw in a word at this point.

'He's no spouter – that must be said, 'a b'lieve.'

' 'Tis a terrible muddle sometimes with the man, as far as spout do go,' said Spinks.

'Well, we'll say nothing about that,' the tranter answered; 'for I don't believe 'twill make a penneth o' difference to we poor martels here or hereafter whether his sermons be good or bad, my sonnies.'

Mr Penny made another hole with his awl, pushed in the thread, and looked up and spoke again at the extension of arms.

' 'Tis his goings-on, souls, that's what it is.' He clenched his features for an Herculean addition to the ordinary pull, and continued, 'The first thing he done when he came here was to be hot and strong about church business.'

'True,' said Spinks; 'that was the very first thing he done.'

Mr Penny, having now been offered the ear of the assembly, accepted it, ceased stitching, swallowed an unimportant quantity of air as if it were a pill, and continued:

'The next thing he do do is to think about altering the church, until he found 'twould be a matter o' cost and what not, and then not to think no more about it.'

'True: that was the next thing he done.'

'And the next thing was to tell the young chaps that they were not on no account to put their hats in the christening font during service.'

'True.'

'And then 'twas this, and then 'twas that, and now 'tis –'

Words were not forcible enough to conclude the sentence, and Mr Penny gave a huge pull to signify the concluding word.

'Now 'tis to turn us out of the quire neck and crop,' said the tranter after an interval of half a minute, not by way of explaining the pause and pull, which had been quite understood, but as a means of keeping the subject well before the meeting.

Mrs Penny came to the door at this point in the discussion. Like all good wives, however much she was inclined to play the Tory to her husband's Whiggism, and *vice versa*, in times of peace, she coalesced with him heartily enough in time of war.

'It must be owned he's not all there,' she replied in a general way to the fragments of talk she had heard from indoors. 'Far below poor Mr Grinham' (the late vicar).

'Ay, there was this to be said for he, that you were quite sure he'd never come mumbudgeting to see ye, just as you were in the middle of your work, and put you out with his fuss and trouble about ye.'

'Never. But as for this new Mr Maybold, though he mid be a very well-intending party in that respect, he's unbearable; for as to sifting your cinders, scrubbing your floors, or emptying your slops, why, you can't do it. I assure you I've not been able to empt them for several days, unless I throw 'em up the chimley or out of winder; for as sure as the sun you meet him at the door, coming to ask how you are, and 'tis such a confusing thing to meet a gentleman at the door when ye are in the mess o' washing.'

' 'Tis only for want of knowing better, poor gentleman,' said the tranter. 'His meaning's good enough. Ay, your pa'son comes by fate: 'tis heads or tails, like pitch-halfpenny, and no choosing; so we must take en as he is, my sonnies, and thank God he's no worse, I suppose.'

'I fancy I've seen him look across at Miss Day in a warmer way than Christianity asked for,' said Mrs Penny musingly; 'but I don't quite like to say it.'

'O no; there's nothing in that,' said grandfather William.

'If there's nothing, we shall see nothing,' Mrs Penny replied in the tone of a woman who might possibly have private opinions still.

'Ah, Mr Grinham was the man!' said Bowman. 'Why, he never troubled us wi' a visit from year's end to year's end. You might go anywhere, do anything: you'd be sure never to see him.'

'Yes; he was a right sensible pa'son,' said Michael. 'He never entered our door but once in his life, and that was to tell my poor wife – ay, poor soul, dead and gone now, as we all shall! – that as she was such a' old aged person, and lived so far from the church, he didn't at all expect her to come any more to the service.'

'And 'a was a very jinerous gentleman about choosing the psalms and hymns o' Sundays. "Confound ye," says he, "blare and scrape what ye will, but don't bother me!"'

'And he was a very honourable man in not wanting any of us to come and hear him if we were all on-end for a jaunt or spree, or to bring the babies to be christened if they were inclined to squalling. There's good in a man's not putting a parish to unnecessary trouble.'

'And there's this here man never letting us have a bit o' peace; but keeping on about being good and upright till 'tis carried to such a pitch as I never see the like afore nor since!'

'No sooner had he got here than he found the font wouldn't hold water, as it hadn't for years off and on; and when I told him that Mr Grinham never minded it, but used to spet upon his vinger and christen 'em just as well, 'a said, "Good Heavens! Send for a workman immediate. What place have I come to!" Which was no compliment to us, come to that.'

'Still, for my part,' said old William, 'though he's arrayed against us, I like the hearty borus-snorus ways of the new pa'son.'

'You, ready to die for the quire,' said Bowman reproachfully, 'to stick up for the quire's enemy, William!'

'Nobody will feel the loss of our church-work so much as I,' said the old man firmly: 'that you d'all know. I've a-been in the quire man and boy ever since I was a chiel of seven. But for all that 'tisn't in me to call the man a bad man, because I truly and sincerely believe en to be a good young feller.'

Some of the youthful sparkle that used to reside there animated William's eye as he uttered the words, and a certain nobility of aspect was also imparted to him by the setting sun, which gave him a Titanic shadow at least thirty feet in length, stretching away to the east in outlines of imposing magnitude, his head finally terminating upon the trunk of a grand old oak-tree.

'Mayble's a hearty feller enough,' the tranter replied, 'and will spak to you be you dirty or be you clane. The first time I met en was in a drong, and though 'a didn't know me no more than the dead 'a passed the time of day. "D'ye do!" he said says he, nodding his head. "A fine day." Then the second time I met en was full-buff in town street, when my breeches were tore into a long strent by getting through a copse of thorns and brimbles for a short cut home-along; and not wanting to disgrace the man by spaking in that state, I fixed my eye on the weathercock to let en pass me as a stranger. But no: "How d'ye do, Reuben?" says he, right hearty, and shook my hand. If I'd been dressed in silver spangles from top to toe the man couldn't have been civiller.'

At this moment Dick was seen coming up the village-street, and they turned and watched him.

* III *

A Turn in the Discussion

'I'M afraid Dick's a lost man,' said the tranter.

'What? – no!' said Mail, implying by his manner that it was a far commoner thing for his ears to report what was not said than that his judgement should be at fault.

'Ay,' said the tranter, still gazing at Dick's unconscious advance. 'I don't at all like what I see! There's too many o' them looks out of the winder without noticing anything: too much shining of boots; too much peeping round corners; too much looking at the clock; telling about clever things *she* did till you be sick of it, and then upon a hint to that effect a horrible silence about her. I've walked the path once in my life and know the country, neighbours; and Dick's a lost man!' The tranter turned a quarter round and smiled a smile of miserable satire at the setting new moon, which happened to catch his eye.

The others became far too serious at this announcement to allow them to speak; and they still regarded Dick in the distance.

' 'Twas his mother's fault,' the tranter continued, 'in asking the young woman to our party last Christmas. When I eyed the blue frock and light heels o' the maid, I had my thoughts directly. "God bless thee, Dicky my sonny," I said to myself, "there's a delusion for thee!" '

'They seemed to be rather distant in manner last Sunday, I thought?' Mail tentatively observed, as became one who was not a member of the family.

'Ay, that's a part of the zickness. Distance belongs to it, slyness belongs to it, queerest things on earth belongs to it! There, 'tmay as well come early as late s'far as I know. The sooner begun, the sooner over; for come it will.'

'The question I ask is,' said Mr Spinks, connecting into one thread the two subjects of discourse, as became a man learned in rhetoric, and beating with his hand in a way which signified that the manner rather than the matter of his speech was to be observed, 'how did Mr Maybold know she could play the organ? You know we had it from her own lips, as far as lips go, that she has never, first or last, breathed such a thing to him; much less that she ever would play.'

In the midst of this puzzle Dick joined the party, and the news which had caused such a convulsion among the ancient musicians was unfolded to him. 'Well,' he said, blushing at the allusion to Miss Day, 'I know by some words of hers that she has a particular wish not to play, because she is a friend of ours; and how the alteration comes I don't know.'

'Now, this is my plan,' said the tranter, reviving the spirit of the discussion by the infusion of new ideas, as was his custom – 'this is my plan; if you don't like it, no harm's done. We all know one another very well, don't we, neighbours?'

That they knew one another very well was received as a statement which, though familiar, should not be omitted in introductory speeches.

'Then I say this' – and the tranter in his emphasis slapped down his hand on Mr Spinks's shoulder with a momentum of several pounds, upon which Mr Spinks tried to look not in the least startled – 'I say that we all move down-along straight as a line to Pa'son Mayble's when the clock has gone six tomorrow night. There we one and all stand in the passage; then one or two of us go in and spak to en, man and man, and say, "Pa'son Mayble, every tradesman d'like to have his own way in his workshop, and Mellstock Church is yours. Instead of turning us out neck and crop, let us stay on till Christmas, and we'll gie way to the young woman, Mr Mayble, and make no more ado about it. And we shall always be quite willing to touch our hats when we meet ye, Mr Mayble, just as before." That sounds very well? Hey?'

'Proper well, in faith, Reuben Dewy.'

'And we won't sit down in his house; 'twould be looking too familiar when only just reconciled?'

'No need at all to sit down. Just do our duty man and man, turn round, and march out – he'll think all the more of us for it.'

'I hardly think Leaf had better go wi' us?' said Michael, turning to Leaf and taking his measure from top to bottom by the eye. 'He's so terrible silly that he might ruin the concern.'

'He don't want to go much; do ye, Thomas Leaf?' said William.

'Hee-hee! no; I don't want to. Only a teeny bit!'

'I be mortal afeard, Leaf, that you'll never be able to tell how many cuts d'take to sharpen a spar,' said Mail.

'I never had no head, never! that's how it happened to happen, hee-hee!'

They all assented to this, not with any sense of humiliating Leaf by disparaging him after an open confession, but because it was an accepted thing that Leaf didn't in the least mind having no head, that deficiency of his being an unimpassioned matter of parish history.

'But I can sing my treble!' continued Thomas Leaf, quite delighted at being called a fool in such a friendly way; 'I can sing my treble well as any maid, or married woman either, and better! And if Jim had lived, I should have had a clever brother! Tomorrow is poor Jim's birthday. He'd ha' been twenty-six if he'd lived till tomorrow.'

'You always seem very sorry for Jim,' said old William musingly.

'Ah! I do. Such a stay to mother as he'd always have been! She'd never have had to work in her old age if he had continued strong, poor Jim!'

'What was his age when 'a died?'

'Four hours and twenty minutes, poor Jim. 'A was born as might be at night; and 'a didn't last as might be till the morning. No, 'a didn't last. Mother called en Jim on the day that would ha' been his christening-day if he had lived; and she's always thinking about en. You see he died so very young.'

'Well, 'twas rather youthful,' said Michael.

'Now to my mind that woman is very romantical on the matter o' children?' said the tranter, his eye sweeping his audience.

'Ah, well she mid be,' said Leaf. 'She had twelve regular one after another, and they all, except myself, died very young; either before they was born or just afterwards.'

'Pore feller, too. I suppose th'st want to come wi' us?' the tranter murmured.

'Well, Leaf, you shall come wi' us as yours is such a melancholy family,' said old William rather sadly.

'I never see such a melancholy family as that afore in my life,' said Reuben. 'There's Leaf's mother, poor woman! Every morning I see her eyes mooning out through the panes of glass like a pot-sick winder-flower; and as Leaf sings a very high treble, and we don't know what we should do without en for upper G, we'll let en come as a trate, poor feller.'

'Ay, we'll let en come, 'a b'lieve,' said Mr Penny, looking up, as the pull happened to be at that moment.

'Now,' continued the tranter, dispersing by a new tone of voice these digressions about Leaf; 'as to going to see the pa'son, one of us might call and ask en his meaning, and 'twould be just as well done; but it will add a bit of a flourish to the cause if the quire waits on him as a body. Then the great thing to mind is, not for any of our fellers to be nervous; so before starting we'll one and all come to my house and have a rasher of bacon; then every man-jack het a pint a cider into his inside; then we'll warm up an extra drop wi' some mead and a bit of ginger; every one take a thimbleful – just a glimmer of a drop, mind ye, no more, to finish off his inner man – and march off to Pa'son Mayble. Why, sonnies, a man's not himself till he is fortified wi' a bit and a drop? We shall be able to look any gentleman in the face without shrink or shame.'

Mail recovered from a deep meditation and downward glance into the earth in time to give a cordial approval to this line of action, and the meeting adjourned.

* IV *

The Interview with the Vicar

AT six o'clock next day the whole body of men in the choir emerged from the tranter's door, and advanced with a firm step down the lane. This dignity of march gradually became obliterated as they went on, and by the time they reached the hill behind the vicarage a faint resemblance to a flock of sheep might have been discerned in the venerable party. A word from the tranter, however, set them right again; and as they descended the hill, the regular tramp, tramp, tramp of the united feet was clearly audible from the vicarage garden. At the opening of the gate there was another short interval of irregular shuffling, caused by a rather peculiar habit the gate had, when swung open quickly, of striking against the bank and slamming back into the opener's face.

'Now keep step again, will ye?' said the tranter. 'It looks better, and more becomes the high class of arrant which has brought us here.' Thus they advanced to the door.

At Reuben's ring the more modest of the group turned aside, adjusted their hats, and looked critically at any shrub that happened to lie in the line of vision; endeavouring thus to give a person who chanced to look out of the windows the impression that their request, whatever it was going to be, was rather a casual thought occurring whilst they were inspecting the vicar's shrubbery and grass-plot than a predetermined thing. The tranter who, coming frequently to the vicarage with luggage, coals, firewood, etc., had none of the awe for its precincts that filled the breasts of most of the others, fixed his eyes firmly on the knocker during this interval of waiting. The knocker having no characteristic worthy of notice he relinquished it for a knot in one of the door-panels, and studied the winding lines of the grain.

'O, sir, please, here's Tranter Dewy, and old William Dewy, and young Richard Dewy, O, and all the quire too, sir, except the boys, a-come to see you!' said Mr Maybold's maid-servant to Mr Maybold, the pupils of her eyes dilating like circles in a pond.

'All the choir?' said the astonished vicar (who may be shortly described as a good-looking young man with courageous eyes, timid mouth, and neutral nose), abandoning his writing and looking at his parlourmaid after speaking, like a man who fancied he had seen her face before but couldn't recollect where.

'And they looks very firm, and Tranter Dewy do turn neither to the right hand nor to the left, but stares quite straight and solemn with his mind made up!'

'O, all the choir,' repeated the vicar to himself, trying by that simple device to trot out his thoughts on what the choir could come for.

'Yes; every man-jack of 'em, as I be alive!' (The parlour-maid was rather local in manner, having in fact been raised in the same village.) 'Really, sir, 'tis thoughted by many in town and country that –'

'Town and country! – Heavens, I had no idea that I was public property in this way!' said the vicar, his face acquiring a hue somewhere between that of the rose and the peony. 'Well, "It is thought in town and country that –" '

'It is thought that you be going to get it hot and strong! – excusen my incivility, sir.'

The vicar suddenly recalled to his recollection that he had long ago settled it to be decidedly a mistake to encourage his servant Jane in giving personal opinions. The servant Jane saw by the vicar's face that he recalled this fact to his mind; and removing her forehead from the edge of the door, and rubbing away the indent that edge had made, vanished into the passage as Mr Maybold remarked, 'Show them in, Jane.'

A few minutes later a shuffling and jostling (reduced to as refined a form as was compatible with the nature of shuffles and jostles) was heard in the passage; then an earnest and prolonged wiping of shoes, conveying the notion that volumes of mud had to be removed; but the roads being so clean that not a particle of dirt appeared on the choir's boots (those of all the elder members being newly oiled, and Dick's brightly polished), this wiping might have been set down simply as a desire to show that respectable men had no wish to take a mean advantage of clean roads for curtailing proper ceremonies. Next there came a powerful whisper from the same quarter:

'Now stand stock-still there, my sonnies, one and all! And don't make no noise; and keep your backs close to the wall, that company may pass in and out easy if they want to without squeezing through ye; and we two are enough to go in.' . . . The voice was the tranter's.

'I wish I could go in too and see the sight!' said a reedy voice – that of Leaf.

' 'Tis a pity Leaf is so terrible silly, or else he might,' another said.

'I never in my life seed a quire go into a study to have it out about the playing and singing,' pleaded Leaf; 'and I should like to see it just once!'

'Very well; we'll let en come in,' said the tranter. 'You'll be like chips in porridge,* Leaf – neither good nor hurt. All right, my sonny, come along;' and immediately himself, old William, and Leaf appeared in the room.

'We took the liberty to come and see 'ee, sir,' said Reuben, letting his hat hang in his left hand, and touching with his right the brim of an imaginary one on his head. 'We've come to see 'ee, sir, man and man, and no offence, I hope?'

'None at all,' said Mr Maybold.

'This old aged man standing by my side is father; William Dewy by name, sir.'

'Yes; I see it is,' said the vicar, nodding aside to old William, who smiled.

'I thought ye mightn't know en without his bass-viol,' the tranter apologized. 'You see, he always wears his best clothes and his bass-viol a-Sundays, and it do make such a difference in a' old man's look.'

'And who's that young man?' the vicar said.

'Tell the pa'son yer name,' said the tranter, turning to Leaf, who stood with his elbows nailed back to a bookcase.

'Please, Thomas Leaf, your holiness!' said Leaf, trembling.

'I hope you'll excuse his looks being so very thin,' continued the tranter deprecatingly, turning to the vicar again. 'But 'tisn't his fault, poor feller. He's rather silly by nature, and could never get fat; though he's a' excellent treble, and so we keep him on.'

'I never had no head, sir,' said Leaf, eagerly grasping at this opportunity for being forgiven his existence.

'Ah, poor young man!' said Mr Maybold.

'Bless you, he don't mind it a bit, if you don't, sir,' said the tranter assuringly. 'Do ye, Leaf?'

'Not I – not a morsel – hee, hee! I was afeard it mightn't please your holiness, sir, that's all.'

The tranter, finding Leaf get on so very well through his negative qualities, was tempted in a fit of generosity to advance him still higher, by giving him credit for positive ones. 'He's very clever for a silly chap, good-now, sir. You never knowed a young feller keep his smock-frocks so clane; very honest too. His ghastly looks is all there is against en, poor feller; but we can't help our looks, you know, sir.'

'True: we cannot. You live with your mother, I think, Leaf?'

The tranter looked at Leaf to express that the most friendly assistant to his tongue could do no more for him now, and that he must be left to his own resources.

'Yes, sir: a widder, sir. Ah, if brother Jim had lived she'd have had a clever son to keep her without work!'

'Indeed! poor woman. Give her this half-crown. I'll call and see your mother.'

'Say, "Thank you, sir," ' the tranter whispered imperatively towards Leaf.

* This, a local expression, must be a corruption of something less questionable.

'Thank you, sir!' said Leaf.

'That's it, then; sit down, Leaf,' said Mr Maybold.

'Y-yes, sir!'

The tranter cleared his throat after this accidental parenthesis about Leaf, rectified his bodily position, and began his speech.

'Mr Mayble,' he said, 'I hope you'll excuse my common way, but I always like to look things in the face.'

Reuben made a point of fixing his sentence in the vicar's mind by gazing hard at him at the conclusion of it, and then out of the window.

Mr Maybold and old William looked in the same direction, apparently under the impression that the things' faces alluded to were there visible.

'What I have been thinking' – the tranter implied by this use of the past tense that he was hardly so discourteous as to be positively thinking it then – 'is that the quire ought to be gie'd a little time, and not done away wi' till Christmas, as a fair thing between man and man. And, Mr Mayble, I hope you'll excuse my common way?'

'I will, I will. Till Christmas,' the vicar murmured, stretching the two words to a great length, as if the distance to Christmas might be measured in that way. 'Well, I want you all to understand that I have no personal fault to find, and that I don't wish to change the church music by forcible means, or in a way which should hurt the feelings of any parishioners. Why I have at last spoken definitely on the subject is that a player has been brought under – I may say pressed upon – my notice several times by one of the churchwardens. And as the organ I brought with me is here waiting' (pointing to a cabinet-organ standing in the study), 'there is no reason for longer delay.'

'We made a mistake I suppose then, sir? But we understood the young woman didn't want to play particularly?' The tranter arranged his countenance to signify that he did not want to be inquisitive in the least.

'No, nor did she. Nor did I definitely wish her to just yet; for your playing is very good. But, as I said, one of the churchwardens has been so anxious for a change that, as matters stand, I couldn't consistently refuse my consent.'

Now for some reason or other the vicar at this point seemed to have an idea that he had prevaricated; and as an honest vicar it was a thing he determined not to do. He corrected himself, blushing as he did so, though why he should blush was not known to Reuben.

'Understand me rightly,' he said: 'the churchwarden proposed it to me, but I had thought myself of getting – Miss Day to play.'

'Which churchwarden might that be who proposed her, sir? – excusing my common way.' The tranter intimated by his tone that so far from being inquisitive he did not even wish to ask a single question.

'Mr Shiner, I believe.'

'Clk, my sonny! – beg your pardon, sir, that's only a form of words of mine, and slipped out accidental – he nourishes enmity against us for some reason or another; perhaps because we played rather hard upon en Christmas night. Anyhow 'tis certain sure that Mr Shiner's real love for music of a particular kind isn't his reason. He've no more ear than that chair. But let that be.'

'I don't think you should conclude that, because Mr Shiner wants a different music, he has any ill-feeling for you. I myself, I must own, prefer organ-music to any other. I consider it most proper, and feel justified in endeavouring to introduce it; but then, although other music is better, I don't say yours is not good.'

'Well then, Mr Mayble, since death's to be, we'll die like men any day you name (excusing my common way).'

Mr Maybold bowed his head.

'All we thought was, that for us old ancient singers to be choked off quiet at no time in particular, as now, in the Sundays after Easter, would seem rather mean in the eyes of other parishes, sir. But if we fell glorious with a bit of a flourish at Christmas, we should have a respectable end, and not dwindle away at some nameless paltry second-Sunday-after or Sunday-next-before something, that's got no name of his own.'

'Yes, yes, that's reasonable; I own it's reasonable.'

'You see, Mr Mayble, we've got – do I keep you inconvenient long, sir?'

'No, no.'

'We've got our feelings – father there especially.'

The tranter, in his earnestness, had advanced his person to within six inches of the vicar's.

'Certainly, certainly!' said Mr Maybold, retreating a little for convenience of seeing. 'You are all enthusiastic on the subject, and I am all the more gratified to find you so. A Laodicean luke-warmness is worse than wrongheadedness itself.'

'Exactly, sir. In fact now, Mr Mayble,' Reuben continued more impressively, and advancing a little closer still to the vicar, 'father there is a perfect figure o' wonder, in the way of being fond of music!'

The vicar drew back a little further, the tranter suddenly also standing back a foot or two to throw open the view of his father, and pointing to him at the same time.

Old William moved uneasily in the large chair, and with a minute smile on the mere edge of his lips for good-manners, said he was indeed very fond of tunes.

'Now, you see exactly how it is,' Reuben continued, appealing to Mr Maybold's sense of justice by looking sideways into his eyes. The vicar seemed to see how it was so well that the gratified tranter walked up to him again with even vehement eagerness, so that his waistcoat-buttons almost rubbed against the vicar's as he continued: 'As to father, if you or I, or any man or woman of the present generation, at the time music is a-playing, was to shake your fist in father's face, as may be this way, and say, "Don't you be delighted with that music!" ' – the tranter went back to where Leaf was sitting, and held his fist so close to Leaf's face that the latter pressed his head back against the wall: 'All right, Leaf, my sonny, I won't hurt you; 'tis just to show my meaning to Mr Mayble. – As I was saying, if you or I, or any man, was to shake your fist in father's face this

way, and say, "William, your life or your music!" he'd say, "My life!"
Now that's father's nature all over; and you see, sir, it must hurt the
feelings of a man of that kind for him and his bass-viol to be done away
wi' neck and crop.'

The tranter went back to the vicar's front and again looked earnestly at
his face.

'True, true, Dewy,' Mr Maybold answered, trying to withdraw his
head and shoulders without moving his feet; but finding this impracticable
edging back another inch. These frequent retreats had at last jammed Mr
Maybold between his easy-chair and the edge of the table.

And at the moment of the announcement of the choir Mr Maybold had
just re-dipped the pen he was using; at their entry, instead of wiping it,
he had laid it on the table with the nib overhanging. At the last retreat his
coat-tails came in contact with the pen, and down it rolled, first against
the back of the chair, thence turning a somersault into the seat, thence
falling to the floor with a rattle.

The vicar stooped for his pen, and the tranter, wishing to show that,
however great their ecclesiastical differences, his mind was not so small
as to let this affect his social feelings, stooped also.

'And have you anything else you want to explain to me, Dewy?' said
Mr Maybold from under the table.

'Nothing, sir. And, Mr Mayble, you be not offended? I hope you see
our desire is reason?' said the tranter from under the chair.

'Quite, quite; and I shouldn't think of refusing to listen to such a
reasonable request,' the vicar replied. Seeing that Reuben had secured the
pen he resumed his vertical position, and added, 'You know, Dewy, it is
often said how difficult a matter it is to act up to our convictions and
please all parties. It may be said with equal truth, that it is difficult for a
man of any appreciativeness to have convictions at all. Now in my case,
I see right in you, and right in Shiner. I see that violins are good, and that
an organ is good; and when we introduce the organ it will not be that
fiddles were bad, but that an organ was better. That you'll clearly
understand, Dewy?'

'I will; and thank you very much for such feelings, sir. Piph-h-h-h!
How the blood do get into my head, to be sure, whenever I quat down
like that!' said Reuben, who having also risen to his feet stuck the pen
vertically in the inkstand and almost through the bottom, that it might
not roll down again under any circumstances whatever.

Now the ancient body of minstrels in the passage felt their curiosity
surging higher and higher as the minutes passed. Dick, not having much
affection for this errand, soon grew tired, and went away in the direction
of the school. Yet their sense of propriety would probably have restrained
them from any attempt to discover what was going on in the study had
not the vicar's pen fallen to the floor. The conviction that the movement
of chairs, &c., necessitated by the search, could only have been caused by
the catastrophe of a bloody fight beginning, overpowered all other
considerations; and they advanced to the door, which had only just fallen

to. Thus, when Mr Maybold raised his eyes after the stooping he beheld glaring through the door Mr Penny in full-length portraiture, Mail's face and shoulders above Mr Penny's head, Spinks's forehead and eyes over Mail's crown, and a fractional part of Bowman's countenance under Spinks's arm – crescent-shaped portions of other heads and faces being visible behind these – the whole dozen and odd eyes bristling with eager inquiry.

Mr Penny, as is the case with excitable bootmakers and men, seeing the vicar look at him and hearing no word spoken, thought it incumbent upon himself to say something of any kind. Nothing suggested itself till he had looked for about half a minute at the vicar.

'You'll excuse my naming of it, sir,' he said, regarding with much commiseration the mere surface of the vicar's face; 'but perhaps you don't know that your chin have bust out a-bleeding where you cut yourself a-shaving this morning, sir.'

'Now, that was the stooping, depend upon't,' the tranter suggested, also looking with much interest at the vicar's chin. 'Blood always will bust out again if you hang down the member that's been bleeding.'

Old William raised his eyes and watched the vicar's bleeding chin likewise; and Leaf advanced two or three paces from the bookcase, absorbed in the contemplation of the same phenomenon with parted lips and delighted eyes.

'Dear me, dear me!' said Mr Maybold hastily, looking very red and brushing his chin with his hand, then taking out his handkerchief and wiping the place.

'That's it, sir; all right again now, 'a b'lieve – a mere nothing,' said Mr Penny. 'A little bit of fur off your hat will stop it in a minute if it should bust out again.'

'I'll let 'ee have a bit off mine,' said Reuben, to show his good feeling; 'my hat isn't so new as yours, sir, and 'twon't hurt mine a bit.'

'No, no; thank you, thank you,' Mr Maybold again nervously replied.

' 'Twas rather a deep cut seemingly?' said Reuben, feeling these to be the kindest and best remarks he could make.

'O, no; not particularly.'

'Well, sir, your hand will shake sometimes a-shaving, and just when it comes into your head that you may cut yourself, there's the blood.'

'I have been revolving in my mind that question of the time at which we make the change,' said Mr Maybold, 'and I know you'll meet me half-way. I think Christmas-day as much too late for me as the present time is too early for you. I suggest Michaelmas or thereabout as a convenient time for both parties; for I think your objection to a Sunday which has no name is not one of any real weight.'

'Very good, sir. I suppose mortal men mustn't expect their own way entirely; and I express in all our names that we'll make shift and be satisfied with what you say.' The tranter touched the brim of his imaginary hat again, and all the choir did the same. 'About Michaelmas, then, as far as you concerned, sir, and then we make room for the next generation.'

'About Michaelmas,' said the vicar.

* V *

Returning Homeward

' 'A took it very well, then?' said Mail, as they all walked up the hill.

'He behaved like a man; 'a did so,' said the tranter. 'And I'm glad we've let en know our minds. And though, beyond that, we ha'n't got much by going, 'twas worth while. He won't forget it. Yes, he took it very well. Supposing this tree here was Pa'son Mayble, and I standing here, and thik gr't stone is father sitting in the easy-chair. "Dewy," says he, "I don't wish to change the church music in a forcible way." '

'That was very nice o' the man, even though words be wind.'

'Proper nice – out and out nice. The fact is,' said Reuben confidentially, ' 'tis how you take a man. Everybody must be managed. Queens must be managed: kings must be managed; for men want managing almost as much as women, and that's saying a good deal.'

' 'Tis truly!' murmured the husbands.

'Pa'son Mayble and I were as good friends all through it as if we'd been sworn brothers. Ay, the man's well enough; 'tis what's put in his head that spoils him, and that's why we've got to go.'

'There's really no believing half you hear about people nowadays.'

'Bless ye, my sonnies, 'tisn't the pa'son's move at all. That gentleman over there' (the tranter nodded in the direction of Shiner's farm) 'is at the root of the mischty.'

'What! Shiner?'

'Ay; and I see what the pa'son don't see. Why, Shiner is for putting forward that young woman that only last night I was saying was our Dick's sweetheart, but I suppose can't be, and making much of her in the sight of the congregation, and thinking he'll win her by showing her off. Well, perhaps 'a woll.'

'Then the music is second to the woman, the other churchwarden is second to Shiner, the pa'son is second to the churchwardens, and God A'mighty is nowhere at all.'

'That's true; and you see,' continued Reuben, 'at the very beginning it put me in a stud as to how to quarrel wi' en. In short, to save my soul, I couldn't quarrel wi' such a civil man without belying my conscience. Says he to father there, in a voice as quiet as a lamb's, "William, you are a' old aged man, as all shall be, so sit down in my easy-chair, and rest yourself." And down father zot. I could fain ha' laughed at thee, father; for thou'st take it so unconcerned at first, and then looked so frightened when the chair-bottom sunk in.'

'You see,' said old William, hastening to explain, 'I was scared to find the bottom gie way – what should I know o' spring bottoms? – and thought I had broke it down: and of course as to breaking down a man's chair, I didn't wish any such thing.'

'And, neighbours, when a feller, ever so much up for a miff, d'see his own father sitting in his enemy's easy-chair, and a poor chap like Leaf made the best of, as if he almost had brains – why, it knocks all the wind out of his sail at once; it did out of mine.'

'If that young figure of fun – Fance Day, I mean,' said Bowman, 'hadn't been so mighty forward wi' showing herself off to Shiner and Dick and the rest, 'tis my belief we should never ha' left the gallery.'

' 'Tis my belief that though Shiner fired the bullets, the parson made 'em,' said Mr Penny. 'My wife sticks to it that he's in love wi' her.'

'That's a thing we shall never know. I can't onriddle her, nohow.'

'Thou'st ought to be able to onriddle such a little chiel as she,' the tranter observed.

'The littler the maid, the bigger the riddle, to my mind. And coming of such a stock, too, she may well be a twister.'

'Yes; Geoffrey Day is a clever man if ever there was one. Never says anything: not he.'

'Never.'

'You might live wi' that man, my sonnies, a hundred years, and never know there was anything in him.'

'Ay; one o' these up-country London ink-bottle chaps would call Geoffrey a fool.'

'Ye never find out what's in that man: never,' said Spinks. 'Close? ah, he is close! He can hold his tongue well. That man's dumbness is wonderful to listen to.'

'There's so much sense in it. Every moment of it is brimmen over wi' sound understanding.'

' 'A can hold his tongue very clever – very clever truly,' echoed Leaf. ' 'A do look at me if 'a could see my thoughts running round like the works of a clock.'

'Well, all will agree that the man can halt well in his talk, be it a long time or be it a short time. And though we can't expect his daughter to inherit his closeness, she may have a few dribblets from his sense.'

'And his pocket, perhaps.'

'Yes; the nine hundred pound that everybody says he's worth; but I call it four hundred and fifty; for I never believe more than half I hear.'

'Well, he've made a pound or two, and I suppose the maid will have it, since there's nobody else. But 'tis rather sharp upon her, if she's born to fortune, to bring her up as if not born for it, and letting her work so hard.'

' 'Tis all upon his principle. A long-headed feller!'

'Ah,' murmured Spinks, ' 'twould be sharper upon her if she were born for fortune, and not to it! I suffer from that affliction.'

* VI *

Yalbury Wood and the Keeper's House

A MOOD of blitheness rarely experienced even by young men was Dick's on the following Monday morning. It was the week after the Easter holidays, and he was journeying along with Smart the mare and the light spring-cart, watching the damp slopes of the hill-sides as they streamed in the warmth of the sun, which at this unsettled season shone on the grass with the freshness of an occasional inspector rather than as an accustomed proprietor. His errand was to fetch Fancy, and some additional household goods, from her father's house in the neighbouring parish to her dwelling at Mellstock. The distant view was darkly shaded with clouds; but the nearer parts of the landscape were whitely illumined by the visible rays of the sun streaming down across the heavy grey shade behind.

The tranter had not yet told his son of the state of Shiner's heart that had been suggested to him by Shiner's movements. He preferred to let such delicate affairs right themselves; experience having taught him that the uncertain phenomenon of love, as it existed in other people, was not a groundwork upon which a single action of his own life could be founded.

Geoffrey Day lived in the depths of Yalbury Wood, which formed portion of one of the outlying estates of the Earl of Wessex, to whom Day was head gamekeeper, timber-steward, and general overlooker for this district. The wood was intersected by the highway from Casterbridge to London at a place not far from the house, and some trees had of late years been felled between its windows and the ascent of Yalbury Hill, to give the solitary cottager a glimpse of the passers-by.

It was a satisfaction to walk into the keeper's house, even as a stranger, on a fine spring morning like the present. A curl of wood-smoke came from the chimney and drooped over the roof like a blue feather in a lady's hat; and the sun shone obliquely upon the patch of grass in front, which reflected its brightness through the open doorway and up the staircase opposite, lighting up each riser with a shiny green radiance and leaving the top of each step in shade.

The window-sill of the front room was between four and five feet from the floor, dropping inwardly to a broad low bench, over which, as well as over the whole surface of the wall beneath, there always hung a deep shade, which was considered objectionable on every ground save one, namely, that the perpetual sprinkling of seeds and water by the caged canary above was not noticed as an eyesore by visitors. The window was set with thickly-leaded diamond glazing, formed, especially in the lower panes, of knotty glass of various shades of green. Nothing was better known to Fancy than the extravagant manner in which these circular knots or eyes distorted everything seen through them from the outside – lifting hats from heads, shoulders from bodies; scattering the spokes of cart-wheels, and bending the straight fir-trunks into semicircles. The ceiling was carried by a beam traversing its midst, from the side of which projected a large nail, used solely and constantly as a peg for Geoffrey's hat; the nail was arched by a rainbow-shaped stain, imprinted by the brim of the said hat when it was hung there dripping wet.

The most striking point about the room was the furniture. This was a repetition upon inanimate objects of the old principle introduced by Noah, consisting for the most part of two articles of every sort. The duplicate system of furnishing owed its existence to the forethought of Fancy's mother, exercised from the date of Fancy's birthday onwards. The arrangement spoke for itself: nobody who knew the tone of the household could look at the goods without being aware that the second set was a provision for Fancy when she should marry and have a house of her own. The most noticeable instance was a pair of green-faced eight-day clocks ticking alternately, which were severally two-and-a-half minutes and three minutes striking the hour of twelve, one proclaiming, in Italian flourishes, Thomas Wood as the name of its maker, and the other – arched at the top, and altogether of more cynical appearance – that of Ezekiel Saunders. They were two departed clockmakers of Casterbridge, whose desperate rivalry throughout their lives was nowhere more emphatically perpetuated than here at Geoffrey's. These chief specimens of the marriage provision were supported on the right by a couple of kitchen dressers, each fitted complete with their cups, dishes, and plates, in their turn followed by two dumb-waiters, two family Bibles, two warming-pans, and two intermixed sets of chairs.

But the position last reached – the chimney-corner – was, after all, the most attractive side of the parallelogram. It was large enough to admit, in addition to Geoffrey himself, Geoffrey's wife, her chair, and her work-table, entirely within the line of the mantel, without danger or even inconvenience from the heat of the fire; and was spacious enough overhead to allow of the insertion of wood poles for the hanging of bacon, which were cloaked with long shreds of soot floating on the draught like the tattered banners on the walls of ancient aisles.

These points were common to most chimney-corners of the neigh-bourhood; but one feature there was which made Geoffrey's fireside not only an object of interest to casual aristocratic visitors – to whom every cottage fireside was more or less a curiosity – but the admiration of friends who were accustomed to fireplaces of the ordinary hamlet model. This peculiarity was a little window in the chimney-back, almost over the fire, around which the smoke crept caressingly when it left the perpendicular course. The window-board was curiously stamped with black circles, burnt thereon by the heated bottoms of drinking-cups which had rested there after previously standing on the hot ashes of the hearth for the purpose of warming their contents, the result giving to the ledge the look of an envelope which has passed through innumerable post-offices.

Fancy was gliding about the room preparing dinner, her head inclining now to the right, now to the left, and singing the tips and ends of tunes that sprang up in her mind like mushrooms. The footsteps of Mrs Day could be heard in the room overhead. Fancy went finally to the door.

'Father! Dinner.'

A tall spare figure was seen advancing by the window with periodical steps, and the keeper entered from the garden. He appeared to be a man who was always looking down as if trying to recollect something he said yesterday. The surface of his face was fissured rather than wrinkled, and over and under his eyes were folds which seemed as a kind of exterior eyelids. His nose had been thrown backwards by a blow in a poaching fray, so that when the sun was low and shining in his face people could see far into his head. There was in him a quiet grimness which would in his moments of displeasure have become surliness, had it not been tempered by honesty of soul, and which was often wrongheadedness because not allied with subtlety.

Although not an extraordinarily taciturn man among friends slightly richer than himself, he never wasted words upon outsiders, and to his trapper Enoch his ideas were seldom conveyed by any other means than nods and shakes of the head. Their long acquaintance with each other's ways, and the nature of their labours, rendered words between them almost superfluous as vehicles of thought, whilst the coincidences of their horizons, and the astonishing equality of their social views, by startling the keeper from time to time as very damaging to the theory of master and man, strictly forbade any indulgence in words of courtesies.

Behind the keeper came Enoch (who had been assisting in the garden) at the well-considered chronological distance of three minutes – an interval of non-appearance on the trapper's part not arrived at without some reflection. Four minutes had been found to express indifference to indoor arrangements, and simultaneousness had implied too great an anxiety about meals.

'A little earlier than usual, Fancy,' the keeper said, as he sat down and looked at the clocks. 'That Ezekiel Saunders o' thine is tearing on afore Thomas Wood again.'

'I kept in the middle between them,' said Fancy, also looking at the two clocks.

'Better stick to Thomas,' said her father. 'There's a healthy beat in Thomas that would lead a man to swear by en offhand. He is as true as the town time. How is it your stap-mother isn't here?'

As Fancy was about to reply the rattle of wheels was heard, and 'Weh-hey, Smart!' in Mr Richard Dewy's voice rolled into the cottage from round the corner of the house.

'Hullo! there's Dewy's cart come for thee, Fancy – Dick driving – afore time, too. Well, ask the lad to have pot-luck with us.'

Dick on entering made a point of implying by his general bearing that he took an interest in Fancy simply as in one of the same race and country as himself; and they all sat down. Dick could have wished her manner had not been so entirely free from all apparent consciousness of those accidental meetings of theirs; but he let the thought pass. Enoch sat diagonally at a table afar off under the corner cupboard, and drank his cider from a long perpendicular pint cup having tall fir-trees done in brown on its sides. He threw occasional remarks into the general tide of conversation, and with this advantage to himself, that he participated in the pleasures of a talk (slight as it was) at meal-times, without saddling himself with the responsibility of sustaining it.

'Why don't your stap-mother come down, Fancy?' said Geoffrey. 'You'll excuse her, Mister Dick, she's a little queer sometimes.'

'O yes – quite,' said Richard, as if he were in the habit of excusing people every day.

'She d'belong to that class of womankind that become second wives: a rum class rather.'

'Indeed,' said Dick, with sympathy for an indefinite something.

'Yes; and 'tis trying to a female, especially if you've been a first wife, as she have.'

'Very trying it must be.'

'Yes; you see her first husband was a young man who let her go too far; in fact, she used to kick up Bob's-a-dying at the least thing in the world. And when I'd married her and found it out, I thought, thinks I, " 'Tis too late now to being to cure 'ee;" and so I let her bide. But she's queer, – very queer, at times!'

'I'm sorry to hear that.'

'Yes; there; wives be such a provoking class of society because, though they be never right, they be never more than half wrong.'

Fancy seemed uneasy under the infliction of this household moralizing, which might tend to damage the airy-fairy nature that Dick, as maiden shrewdness told her, had accredited her with. Her dead silence impressed Geoffrey with the notion that something in his words did not agree with her educated ideas, and he changed the conversation.

'Did Fred Shiner send the cask 'o drink, Fancy?'

'I think he did: O yes, he did.'

'Nice solid feller, Fred Shiner!' said Geoffrey to Dick as he helped himself to gravy, bringing the spoon round to his plate by way of the potato-dish, to obviate a stain on the cloth in the event of a spill.

Now Geoffrey's eyes had been fixed upon his plate for the previous four or five minutes, and in removing them he had only carried them to the spoon, which, from its fulness and the distance of its transit, necessitated a steady watching through the whole of the route. Just as intently as the keeper's eyes had been fixed on the spoon Fancy's had been fixed on her father's, without premeditation or the slightest phase of furtiveness; but there they were fastened. This was the reason why:

Dick was sitting next to her on the right side, and on the side of the table opposite her father. Fancy had laid her right hand lightly down upon the tablecloth for an instant, and to her alarm Dick, after dropping his fork and brushing his forehead as a reason, flung down his own left hand, overlapping a third of Fancy's with it, and keeping it there. So the innocent Fancy, instead of pulling her hand from the trap, settled her eyes on her father's, to guard against his discovery of this perilous game of Dick's. Dick finished his mouthful; Fancy finished her crumb, and nothing was done beyond watching Geoffrey's eyes. Then the hands slid apart; Fancy's going over six inches of cloth, Dick's over one. Geoffrey's eye had risen.

'I said Fred Shiner is a nice solid feller,' he repeated more emphatically.

'He is; yes, he is,' stammered Dick; 'but to me he is little more than a stranger.'

'O, sure. Now I know en as well as any man can be known. And you know en very well too, don't ye, Fancy?'

Geoffrey put on a tone expressing that these words signified at present about one hundred times the amount of meaning they conveyed literally.

Dick looked anxious.

'Will you pass me some bread?' said Fancy in a flurry, the red of her face becoming slightly disordered, and looking as solicitous as a human being could look about a piece of bread.

'Ay, that I will,' replied the unconscious Geoffrey. 'Ay,' he continued, returning to the displaced idea, 'we are likely to remain friendly wi' Mr Shiner if the wheels d'run smooth.'

'An excellent thing – a very capital thing, as I should say,' the youth answered with exceeding relevance, considering that his thoughts, instead of following Geoffrey's remark, were nestling at a distance of about two feet on his left the whole time.

'A young woman's face will turn the north wind, Master Richard: my heart if 'twon't.' Dick looked more anxious and was attentive in earnest at these words. 'Yes; turn the north wind,' added Geoffrey after an impressive pause. 'And though she's one of my own flesh and blood . . .'

'Will you fetch down a bit of raw-mil' cheese from pantry-shelf?' Fancy interrupted as if she were famishing.

'Ay, that I will, chiel; chiel, says I, and Mr Shiner only asking last Saturday night . . . cheese you said, Fancy?'

Dick controlled his emotion at these mysterious allusions to Mr Shiner

– the better enabled to do so by perceiving that Fancy's heart went not with her father's – and spoke like a stranger to the affairs of the neighbourhood. 'Yes, there's a great deal to be said upon the power of maiden faces in settling your courses,' he ventured, as the keeper retreated for the cheese.

'The conversation is taking a very strange turn: nothing that *I* have ever done warrants such things as being said!' murmured Fancy with emphasis just loud enough to reach Dick's ears.

'You think to yourself, 'twas to be,' cried Enoch from his distant corner, by way of filling up the vacancy caused by Geoffrey's momentary absence. 'And so you marry her, Master Dewy, and there's an end o't.'

'Pray don't say such things, Enoch,' came from Fancy severely, upon which Enoch relapsed into servitude.

'If we be doomed to marry, we marry; if we be doomed to remain single, we do,' replied Dick.

Geoffrey had by this time sat down again, and he now made his lips thin by severely straining them across his gums, and looked out of the window along the vista to the distant highway up Yalbury Hill. 'That's not the case with some folk,' he said at length, as if he read the words on a board at the further end of the vista.

Fancy looked interested, and Dick said, 'No?'

'There's that wife o' mine. It was her doom to be nobody's wife at all in the wide universe. But she made up her mind that she would, and did it twice over. Doom? Doom is nothing beside a elderly woman – quite a chiel in her hands!'

A movement was now heard along the upstairs passage, and footsteps descending. The door at the foot of the stairs opened and the second Mrs Day appeared in view, looking fixedly at the table as she advanced towards it, with apparent obliviousness of the presence of any other human being than herself. In short, if the table had been the personage, and the persons the table, her glance would have been the most natural imaginable.

She showed herself to possess an ordinary woman's face, iron-grey hair, hardly any hips, and a great deal of cleanliness in a broad white apron-string as it appeared upon the waist of her dark stuff dress.

'People will run away with a story now, I suppose,' she began saying, 'that Jane Day's tablecloths are as poor and ragged as any union beggar's!'

Dick now perceived that the tablecloth was a little the worse for wear, and reflecting for a moment concluded that 'people' in step-mother language probably meant himself. On lifting his eyes he found that Mrs Day had vanished again upstairs, and presently returned with an armful of new damask-linen table-cloths folded square and hard as boards by long compression. These she flounced down into a chair; then took one, shook it out from its folds, and spread it on the table by instalments, transferring the plates and dishes one by one from the old to the new cloth.

'And I suppose they'll say, too, that she ha'n't a decent knife and fork in her house!'

'I shouldn't say any such ill-natured thing, I am sure —' began Dick. But Mrs Day had vanished into the next room. Fancy appeared distressed.

'Very strange woman, isn't she?' said Geoffrey, quietly going on with his dinner. 'But 'tis too late to attempt curing. My heart! 'tis so growed into her that 'twould kill her to take it out. Ay, she's very queer: you'd be amazed to see what valuable goods we've got stowed away upstairs.'

Back again came Mrs Day with a box of bright steel horn-handled knives, silver-plated forks, carver, and all complete. These were wiped of the preservative oil which coated them, and then a knife and fork were laid down to each individual with a bang, the carving knife and fork thrust into the meat dish, and the old ones they had hitherto used tossed away.

Geoffrey placidly cut a slice with the new knife and fork, and asked Dick if he wanted any more.

The table had been spread for the mixed midday meal of dinner and tea which was common among frugal countryfolk. 'The parishioners about here,' continued Mrs Day, not looking at any living being, but snatching up the brown delf tea-things, 'are the laziest, gossipest, poachest, jailest set of any ever I came among. And they'll talk about my teapot and tea-things next, I suppose!' She vanished with the teapot, cups, and saucers, and reappeared with a tea-service in white china, and a packet wrapped in brown paper. This was removed, together with folds of tissue-paper underneath; and a brilliant silver teapot appeared.

'I'll help to put the things right,' said Fancy soothingly, and rising from her seat. 'I ought to have laid out better things, I suppose. But' (here she enlarged her looks so as to include Dick) 'I have been away from home a good deal, and I make shocking blunders in my housekeeping.' Smiles and suavity were then dispensed all around by this bright little bird.

After a little more preparation and modification Mrs Day took her seat at the head of the table, and during the latter or tea division of the meal presided with much composure. It may cause some surprise to learn that, now her vagary was over, she showed herself to be an excellent person with much common sense, and even a religious seriousness of tone on matters pertaining to her afflictions.

* VII *

Dick makes himself Useful

THE effect of Geoffrey's incidental allusions to Mr Shiner was to restrain a considerable flow of spontaneous chat that would otherwise have burst from young Dewy along the drive homeward. And a certain remark he had hazarded to her, in rather too blunt and eager a manner, kept the young lady herself even more silent than Dick. On both sides there was an unwillingness to talk on any but the most trivial subjects, and their sentences rarely took a larger form than could be expressed in two or three words.

Owing to Fancy being later in the day than she had promised the charwoman had given up expecting her; whereupon Dick could do no less than stay and see her comfortably tided over the disagreeable time of entering and establishing herself in an empty house after an absence of a week. The additional furniture and utensils that had been brought (a canary and cage among the rest) were taken out of the vehicle, and the horse was unharnessed and put in the plot opposite, where there was some tender grass. Dick lighted the fire already laid; and activity began to loosen their tongues a little.

'There!' said Fancy, 'we forgot to bring the fire-irons!'

She had originally found in her sitting-room, to bear out the expression 'nearly furnished' which the school-manager had used in his letter to her, a table, three chairs, a fender, and a piece of carpet. This 'nearly' had been supplemented hitherto by a kind friend, who had lent her fire-irons and crockery until she should fetch some from home.

Dick attended to the young lady's fire, using his whip-handle for a poker till it was spoilt, and then flourishing a hurdle stick for the remainder of the time.

'The kettle boils; now you shall have a cup of tea,' said Fancy, diving into the hamper she had brought.

'Thank you,' said Dick, whose drive had made him ready for some, especially in her company.

'Well, here's only one cup-and-saucer, as I breathe! Whatever could mother be thinking about? Do you mind making shift, Mr Dewy?'

'Not at all, Miss Day,' said that civil person.

'– And only having a cup by itself? or a saucer by itself?'

'Don't mind in the least.'

'Which do you mean by that?'

'I mean the cup if you like the saucer.'

'And the saucer if I like the cup?'

'Exactly, Miss Day.'

'Thank you, Mr Dewy, for I like the cup decidedly. Stop a minute; there are no spoons now!' She dived into the hamper again, and at the end of two or three minutes looked up and said, 'I suppose you don't mind if I can't find a spoon?'

'Not at all,' said the agreeable Richard.

'The fact is the spoons have slipped down somewhere; right under the other things. O yes, here's one, and only one. You would rather have one than not I suppose, Mr Dewy?'

'Rather not. I never did care much about spoons.'

'Then I'll have it. I do care about them. You must stir up your tea with a knife. Would you mind lifting the kettle off, that it may not boil dry?'

Dick leapt to the fireplace, and earnestly removed the kettle.

'There! you did it so wildly that you have made your hand black. We always use kettle-holders; didn't you learn housewifery as far as that, Mr Dewy? Well, never mind the soot on your hand. Come here. I am going to rinse mine, too.'

They went to a basin she had placed in the back room. 'This is the only basin I have,' she said. 'Turn up your sleeves, and by that time my hands will be washed, and you can come.'

Her hands were in the water now. 'O, how vexing!' she exclaimed. 'There's not a drop of water left for you unless you draw it, and the well is I don't know how many furlongs deep; all that was in the pitcher I used for the kettle and this basin. Do you mind dipping the tips of your fingers in the same?'

'Not at all. And to save time I won't wait till you have done, if you have no objection?'

Thereupon he plunged in his hands, and they paddled together. It being the first time in his life that he had touched female fingers under water, Dick duly registered the sensation as rather a nice one.

'Really, I hardly know which are my own hands and which are yours, they have got so mixed up together,' she said, withdrawing her own very suddenly.

'It doesn't matter at all,' said Dick, 'at least as far as I am concerned.'

'There! no towel! Whoever thinks of a towel till the hands are wet?'

'Nobody.'

' "Nobody." How very dull it is when people are so friendly! Come here, Mr Dewy. Now do you think you could lift the lid of that box with your elbow, and then, with something or other, take out a towel you will find under the clean clothes? Be *sure* don't touch any of them with your wet hands, for the things at the top are all Starched and Ironed.'

Dick managed by the aid of a knife and fork to extract a towel from under a muslin dress without wetting the latter; and for a moment he ventured to assume a tone of criticism.

'I fear for that dress,' he said, as they wiped their hands together.

'What?' said Miss Day, looking into the box at the dress alluded to. 'O, I know what you mean – that the vicar will never let me wear muslin?'

'Yes.'

'Well, I know it is condemned by all orders in the church as flaunting, and unfit for common wear for girls who've their living to get; but we'll see.'

'In the interest of the church I hope you don't speak seriously.'

'Yes, I do; but we'll see.' There was a comely determination on her lip, very pleasant to a beholder who was neither bishop, priest, nor deacon. 'I think I can manage any vicar's views about me if he's under forty.'

Dick rather wished she had never thought of managing vicars.

'I certainly shall be glad to get some of your delicious tea,' he said in a rather free way, yet modestly, as became one in a position between that of visitor and inmate, and looking wistfully at his lonely saucer.

'So shall I. Now is there anything else we want, Mr Dewy?'

'I really think there's nothing else, Miss Day.'

She prepared to sit down, looking musingly out of the window at Smart's enjoyment of the rich grass. 'Nobody seems to care about me,' she murmured, with large lost eyes fixed upon the sky beyond Smart.

'Perhaps Mr Shiner does,' said Dick, in the tone of a slightly injured man.

'Yes, I forgot – he does, I know.' Dick precipitately regretted that he had suggested Shiner since it had produced such a miserable result as this.

'I'll warrant you'll care for somebody very much indeed another day, won't you, Mr Dewy?' she continued, looking very feelingly into the mathematical centre of his eyes.

'Ah, I'll warrant I shall,' said Dick, feelingly too, and looking back into her dark pupils, whereupon they were turned aside.

'I meant,' she went on, preventing him from speaking just as he was going to narrate a forcible story about his feelings; 'I meant that nobody comes to see if I have returned – not even the vicar.'

'If you want to see him, I'll call at the vicarage directly we have had some tea.'

'No, no! Don't let him come down here, whatever you do, whilst I am in such a state of disarrangement. Parsons look so miserable and awkward when one's house is in a muddle; walking about and making impossible suggestions in quaint academic phrases till your flesh creeps and you wish them dead. Do you take sugar?'

Mr Maybold was at this instant seen coming up the path.

'There! That's he coming! How I wish you were not here! – that is, how awkward – dear, dear!' she exclaimed, with a quick ascent of blood to her face, and irritated with Dick rather than the vicar, as it seemed.

'Pray don't be alarmed on my account, Miss Day – good-afternoon!' said Dick in a huff, putting on his hat and leaving the room hastily by the back-door.

The horse was caught and put in, and on mounting the shafts to start he saw through the window the vicar, standing upon some books piled in a chair, and driving a nail into the wall; Fancy, with a demure glance, holding the canary-cage up to him as if she had never in her life thought of anything but vicars and canaries.

* VIII *

Dick meets his Father

FOR several minutes Dick drove along homeward, with the inner eye of reflection so anxiously set on his passages at arms with Fancy that the road and scenery were as a thin mist over the real pictures of his mind. Was she a coquette? The balance between the evidence that she did love him and that she did not was so nicely struck that his opinion had no stability. She had let him put his hand upon hers; she had allowed her gaze to drop plumb into the depths of his – his into hers – three or four times; her manner had been very free with regard to the basin and towel; she had appeared vexed at the mention of Shiner. On the other hand, she had driven him about the house like a quiet dog or cat, said Shiner cared for her, and seemed anxious that Mr Maybold should do the same.

Thinking thus as he neared the handpost at Mellstock Cross, sitting on the front board of the spring cart – his legs on the outside, and his whole frame jigging up and down like a candle-flame to the time of Smart's trotting – who should he see coming down the hill but his father in the light wagon, quivering up and down on a smaller scale of shakes, those merely caused by the stones in the road. They were soon crossing each other's front.

'Weh-hey!' said the tranter to Smiler.

'Weh-hey!' said Dick to Smart, in an echo of the same voice.

'Th'st hauled her back, I suppose?' Reuben inquired peaceably.

'Yes,' said Dick, with such a clinching period at the end that it seemed he was never going to add another word. Smiler, thinking this the close of the conversation, prepared to move on.

'Weh-hey!' said the tranter. 'I tell thee what it is, Dick. That there maid is taking up thy thoughts more than's good for thee, my sonny. Thou'rt never happy now unless th'rt making thyself miserable about her in one way or another.'

'I don't know about that, father,' said Dick rather stupidly.

'But I do – Wey, Smiler! – 'Od rot the women, 'tis nothing else wi' 'em nowadays but getting young men and leading 'em astray.'

'Pooh, father! you just repeat what all the common world says; that's all you do.'

'The world's a very sensible feller on things in jineral, Dick; very sensible indeed.'

Dick looked into the distance at a vast expanse of mortgaged estate. 'I wish I was as rich as a squire when he's as poor as a crow,' he murmured; 'I'd soon ask Fancy something.'

'I wish so too, wi' all my heart, sonny; that I do. Well, mind what beest about, that's all.'

Smart moved on a step or two. 'Supposing now, father – Weh-hey,

Smart! – I did think a little about her, and I had a chance, which I ha'n't; don't you think she's a very good sort of – of – one?'

'Ay, good; she's good enough. When you've made up your mind to marry, take the first respectable body that comes to hand – she's as good as any other; they be all alike in the groundwork; 'tis only in the flourishes there's a difference. She's good enough; but I can't see what the nation a young feller like you – wi' a comfortable house and home, and father and mother to take care o' thee, and who sent 'ee to a school so good that 'twas hardly fair to the other children – should want to go hollering after a young woman for, when she's quietly making a husband in her pocket, and not troubled by chick nor chiel, to make a poverty-stric' wife and family of her, and neither hat, cap, wig, nor waistcoat to set 'em up with: be drowned if I can see it, and that's the long and short o't, my sonny!'

Dick looked at Smart's ears, then up the hill; but no reason was suggested by any object that met his gaze.

'For about the same reason that you did, father, I suppose.'

'Dang it, my sonny, thou'st got me there!' And the tranter gave vent to a grim admiration, with the mien of a man who was too magnanimous not to appreciate artistically a slight rap on the knuckles, even if they were his own.

'Whether or no,' said Dick, 'I asked her a thing going along the road.'

'Come to that, is it? Turk! won't thy mother be in a taking! Well, she's ready, I don't doubt?'

'I didn't ask her anything about having me; and if you'll let me speak, I'll tell 'ee what I want to know. I just said, Did she care about me?'

'Piph-ph-ph!'

'And then she said nothing for a quarter of a mile, and then she said she didn't know. Now, what I want to know is, what was the meaning of that speech?' The latter words were spoken resolutely, as if he didn't care for the ridicule of all the fathers in creation.

'The meaning of that speech is,' the tranter replied deliberately, 'that the meaning is meant to be rather hid at present. Well, Dick, as an honest father to thee, I don't pretend to deny what you d'know well enough; that is, that her father being rather better in the pocket than we, I should welcome her ready enough if it must be somebody.'

'But what d'ye think she really did mean?' said the unsatisfied Dick.

'I'm afeard I am not o' much account in guessing, especially as I was not there when she said it, and seeing that your mother was the only 'ooman I ever cam' into such close quarters as that with.'

'And what did mother say to you when you asked her?' said Dick musingly.

'I don't see that that will help 'ee.'

'The principle is the same.'

'Well – ay: what did she say? Let's see. I was oiling my working-day boots without taking 'em off, and wi' my head hanging down, when she just brushed on by the garden hatch like a flittering leaf. "Ann," I said says I, and then, – but, Dick, I'm afeard 'twill be no help to thee; for we were such a rum couple, your mother and I, leastways one half was, that is myself – and your mother's charms was more in the manner than the material.'

'Never mind! "Ann," said you.'

' "Ann," said I, as I was saying . . . "Ann," I said to her when I was oiling my working-day boots wi' my head hanging down, "Woot hae me?" . . . What came next I can't quite call up at this distance o' time. Perhaps your mother would know, – she's got a better memory for her little triumphs than I. However, the long and the short o' the story is that we were married somehow, as I found afterwards. 'Twas on White Tuesday, – Mellstock Club walked the same day, every man two and two, and a fine day 'twas, – hot as fire; how the sun did strike down upon my back going to church! I well can mind what a bath o' sweating I was in, body and soul! But Fance will ha' thee, Dick – she won't walk with another chap – no such good luck.'

'I don't know about that,' said Dick, whipping at Smart's flank in a fanciful way which, as Smart knew, meant nothing in connection with going on. 'There's Pa'son Maybold, too – that's all against me.'

'What about he? She's never been stuffing into thy innocent heart that he's in love with her? Lord, the vanity o' maidens!'

'No, no. But he called, and she looked at him in such a way, and at me in such a way – quite different the ways were, – and as I was coming off there was he hanging up her birdcage.'

'Well, why shouldn't the man hang up her birdcage? Turk seize it all, what's that got to do wi' it? Dick, that thou beest a white-lyvered chap I don't say, but if thou beestn't as mad as a cappel-faced bull let me smile no more.'

'O, ay.'

'And what's think now, Dick?'

'I don't know.'

'Here's another pretty kettle o' fish for thee. Who d'ye think's the bitter weed in our being turned out? Did our party tell 'ee?'

'No. Why, Pa'son Maybold, I suppose.'

'Shiner, – because he's in love with thy young woman, and d'want to see her young figure sitting up at that queer instrument, and her young fingers rum-strumming upon the keys.'

A sharp ado of sweet and bitter was going on in Dick during this communication from his father. 'Shiner's a fool! – no, that's not it; I don't believe any such thing, father. Why, Shiner would never take a bold step like that unless she'd been a little made up to, and had taken it kindly. Pooh!'

'Who's to say she didn't?'

'I do.'

'The more fool you.'

'Why, father of me?'

'Has she ever done more to thee?'

'No.'

'Then she has done as much to he – rot 'em! Now, Dick, this is how a maid is. She'll swear she's dying for thee; and she is dying for thee, and she will die for thee; but she'll fling a look over t'other shoulder at another young feller, though never leaving off dying for thee just the same.'

'She's not dying for me, and so she didn't fling a look at him.'

'But she may be dying for him, for she looked at thee.'

'I don't know what to make of it all,' said Dick gloomily.

'All I can make of it is,' the tranter said, raising his whip, arranging his different joints and muscles, and motioning to the horse to move on, 'that if you can't read a maid's mind by her motions, nature d'seem to say thou'st ought to be a bachelor. Clk, clk! Smiler!' And the tranter moved on.

Dick held Smart's rein firmly, and the whole concern of horse, cart, and man remained rooted in the lane. How long this condition would have lasted is unknown, had not Dick's thoughts, after adding up numerous items of misery, gradually wandered round to the fact that as something must be done it could not be done by staying there all night.

Reaching home he went up to his bedroom, shut the door as if he were going to be seen no more in this life, and taking a sheet of paper and uncorking the ink-bottle he began a letter. The dignity of the writer's mind was so powerfully apparent in every line of this effusion that it obscured the logical sequence of facts and intentions to an appreciable degree; and it was not at all clear to a reader whether he there and then left off loving Miss Fancy Day; whether he had never loved her seriously and never meant to; whether he had been dying up to the present moment and now intended to get well again; or whether he had hitherto been in good health and intended to die for her forthwith.

He put this letter in an envelope, sealed it up, directed it in a stern handwriting of straight dashes – easy flourishes being rigorously excluded. He walked with it in his pocket down the lane in strides not an inch less than three feet long. Reaching her gate he put on a resolute expression – then put it off again, turned back homeward, tore up his letter, and sat down.

That letter was altogether in a wrong tone – that he must own. A heartless man-of-the-world tone was what the juncture required. That he rather wanted her, and rather did not want her – the latter for choice; but that as a member of society he didn't mind making a query in jaunty terms, which could only be answered in the same way: did she mean anything by her bearing towards him, or did she not?

This letter was considered so satisfactory in every way that, being put into the hands of a little boy and the order given that he was to run with it to the school, he was told in addition not to look behind him if Dick called after him to bring it back, but to run along with it just the same. Having taken this precaution against vacillation Dick watched his messenger down the road, and turned into the house whistling an air in such ghastly jerks and starts that whistling seemed to be the act the very furthest removed from that which was instinctive in such a youth.

The letter was left as ordered: the next morning came and passed – and no answer. The next. The next. Friday night came. Dick resolved that if no answer or sign were given by her the next day, on Sunday he would meet her face to face, and have it all out by word of mouth.

'Dick,' said his father, coming in from the garden at that moment – in each hand a hive of bees tied in a cloth to prevent their egress – 'I think you'd better take these two swarms of bees to Mrs Maybold's tomorrow, instead o' me, and I'll go wi' Smiler and the wagon.'

It was a relief; for Mrs Maybold, the vicar's mother, who had just taken into her head a fancy for keeping bees (pleasantly disguised under the pretence of its being an economical wish to produce her own honey), lived near the watering-place of Budmouth Regis, ten miles off, and the business of transporting the hives thither would occupy the whole day, and to some extent annihilate the vacant time between this evening and the coming Sunday. The best spring-cart was washed throughout, the axles oiled, and the bees placed therein for the journey.

PART THE THIRD

SUMMER

Driving out of Budmouth

AN easy bend of neck and graceful set of head; full and wavy bundles of dark-brown hair; light fall of little feet; pretty devices on the skirt of the dress; clear deep eyes; in short, a bunch of sweets: it was Fancy! Dick's heart went round to her with a rush.

The scene was the corner of Mary Street in Budmouth Regis, near the King's statue, at which point the white angle of the last house in the row cut perpendicularly an embayed and nearly motionless expanse of salt water projected from the outer ocean – today lit in bright tones of green and opal. Dick and Smart had just emerged from the street, and there on the right, against the brilliant sheet of liquid colour, stood Fancy Day; and she turned and recognized him.

Dick suspended his thoughts of the letter and wonder at how she came there by driving close to the chains of the Esplanade – incontinently displacing two chairmen, who had just come to life for the summer in new clean shirts and revivified clothes, and being almost displaced in turn by a rigid boy rattling along with a baker's cart and looking neither to the right nor the left. He asked if she were going to Mellstock that night.

'Yes, I'm waiting for the carrier,' she replied, seeming, too, to suspend thoughts of the letter.

'Now I can drive you home nicely, and you save half an hour. Will ye come with me?'

As Fancy's power to will anything seemed to have departed in some mysterious manner at that moment, Dick settled the matter by getting out and assisting her into the vehicle without another word.

The temporary flush upon her cheek changed to a lesser hue which was permanent, and at length their eyes met; there was present between them a certain feeling of embarrassment, which arises at such moments when all the instinctive acts dictated by the position have been performed. Dick, being engaged with the reins, thought less of this awkwardness than did Fancy, who had nothing to do but to feel his presence, and to be more and more conscious of the fact that by accepting a seat beside him in this way she succumbed to the tone of his note. Smart jogged along, and Dick jogged, and the helpless Fancy necessarily jogged too; and she felt that she was in a measure captured and made a prisoner.

'I am so much obliged to you for your company, Miss Day,' he observed, as they drove past the two semicircular bays of the Old Royal

Hotel, where His Majesty King George the Third had many a time attended the balls of the burgesses.

To Miss Day, crediting him with the same consciousness of mastery – a consciousness of which he was perfectly innocent – this remark sounded like a magnanimous intention to soothe her, the captive.

'I didn't come for the pleasure of obliging you with my company,' she said.

The answer had an unexpected manner of incivility in it that must have been rather surprising to young Dewy. At the same time it may be observed that when a young woman returns a rude answer to a young man's civil remark her heart is in a state which argues rather hopefully for his case than otherwise.

There was silence between them till they had left the seafront and passed about twenty of the trees that ornamented the road leading up out of the town towards Casterbridge and Mellstock.

'Though I didn't come for that purpose either, I would have done it,' said Dick at the twenty-first tree.

'Now, Mr Dewy, no flirtation, because it's wrong, and I don't wish it.'

Dick seated himself afresh just as he had been sitting before, arranged his looks very emphatically, and cleared his throat.

'Really, anybody would think you had met me on business and were just going to commence,' said the lady intractably.

'Yes, they would.'

'Why, you never have, to be sure!'

This was a shaky beginning. He chopped round and said cheerily, as a man who had resolved never to spoil his jollity by loving one of womankind –

'Well, how are you getting on, Miss Day, at the present time? Gaily, I don't doubt for a moment.'

'I am not gay, Dick; you know that.'

'Gaily doesn't mean decked in gay dresses.'

'I didn't suppose gaily was gaily dressed. Mighty me, what a scholar you've grown!'

'Lots of things have happened to you this spring, I see.'

'What have you seen?'

'O, nothing; I've heard, I mean!'

'What have you heard?'

'The name of a pretty man with brass studs, and a copper ring, and a tin watch-chain, a little mixed up with your own. That's all.'

'That's a very unkind picture of Mr Shiner, for that's who you mean! The studs are gold as you know, and it's a real silver chain; the ring I can't conscientiously defend, and he only wore it once.'

'He might have worn it a hundred times without showing it half so much.'

'Well, he's nothing to me,' she serenely observed.

'Not any more than I am?'

'Now, Mr Dewy,' said Fancy severely, 'certainly he isn't any more to me than you are!'

'Not so much?'

She looked aside to consider the precise compass of that question. 'That I can't exactly answer,' she replied with soft archness.

As they were going rather slowly another spring-cart, containing a farmer, farmer's wife, and farmer's man, jogged past them; and the farmer's wife and farmer's man eyed the couple very curiously. The farmer never looked up from the horse's tail.

'Why can't you exactly answer?' said Dick, quickening Smart a little, and jogging on just behind the farmer and farmer's wife and man.

As no answer came, and as their eyes had nothing else to do, they both contemplated the picture presented in front, and noticed how the farmer's wife sat flattened between the two men, who bulged over each end of the seat to give her room till they almost sat upon their respective wheels; and they looked too at the farmer's wife's silk mantle inflating itself between her shoulders like a balloon and sinking flat again at each jog of the horse. The farmer's wife, feeling their eyes sticking into her back, looked over her shoulder. Dick dropped ten yards further behind.

'Fancy, why can't you answer?' he repeated.

'Because how much you are to me depends upon how much I am to you,' said she in low tones.

'Everything,' said Dick, putting his hand towards hers, and casting emphatic eyes upon the upper curve of her cheek.

'Now, Richard Dewy, no touching me! I didn't say in what way your thinking of me affected the question – perhaps inversely, don't you see? No touching, sir! Look; goodness me, don't, Dick!'

The cause of her sudden start was the unpleasant appearance over Dick's right shoulder of an empty timber-wagon and four journeymen-carpenters reclining in lazy postures inside it, their eyes directed upwards at various oblique angles into the surrounding world, the chief object of their existence being apparently to criticize to the very backbone and marrow every animate object that came within the compass of their vision. This difficulty of Dick's was overcome by trotting on till the wagon and carpenters were beginning to look rather misty by reason of a film of dust that accompanied their wagon-wheels and rose around their heads like a fog.

'Say you love me, Fancy.'

'No, Dick, certainly not; 'tisn't time to do that yet.'

'Why, Fancy?'

' "Miss Day" is better at present – don't mind my saying so; and I ought not to have called you Dick.'

'Nonsense! when you know that I would do anything on earth for your love. Why, you make any one think that loving is a thing that can be done and undone, and put on and put off at a mere whim.'

'No, no, I don't,' she said gently; 'but there are things which tell me I ought not to give way to much thinking about you, even if –'

'But you want to, don't you? Yes, say you do; it is best to be truthful. Whatever they may say about a woman's right to conceal where her love lies, and pretend it doesn't exist, and things like that, it is not best; I do know it, Fancy. And an honest woman in that, as well as in all her daily concerns, shines most brightly, and is thought most of in the long run.'

'Well then, perhaps, Dick, I do love you a little,' she whispered tenderly; 'but I wish you wouldn't say any more now.'

'I won't say any more now, then, if you don't like it, dear. But you do love me a little, don't you?'

'Now you ought not to want me to keep saying things twice; I can't say any more now, and you must content with what you have.'

'I may at any rate call you Fancy? There's no harm in that.'

'Yes, you may.'

'And you'll not call me Mr Dewy any more?'

'Very well.'

* II *

Further along the Road

DICK'S spirits having risen in the course of these admissions of his sweetheart he now touched Smart with the whip; and on Smart's neck, not far behind his ears. Smart, who had been lost in thought for some time, never dreaming that Dick could reach so far with a whip which, on this particular journey, had never been extended further than his flank, tossed his head and scampered along with exceeding briskness, which was very pleasant to the young couple behind him till, turning a bend in the road, they came instantly upon the farmer, farmer's man, and farmer's wife with the flapping mantle, all jogging on just the same as ever.

'Bother those people! Here we are upon them again.'

'Well, of course. They have as much right to the road as we.'

'Yes, but it is provoking to be overlooked so. I like a road all to myself. Look what a lumbering affair theirs is!' The wheels of the farmer's cart just at that moment jogged into a depression running across the road, giving the cart a twist, whereupon all three nodded to the left, and on coming out of it all three nodded to the right, and went on jerking their backs in and out as usual. 'We'll pass them when the road gets wider.'

When an opportunity seemed to offer itself for carrying this intention into effect they heard light flying wheels behind, and on their quartering there whizzed along past them a brand-new gig, so brightly polished that the spokes of the wheels sent forth a continual quivering of light at one point in their circle, and all the panels glared like mirrors in Dick and Fancy's eyes. The driver, and owner as it appeared, was really a handsome man; his companion was Shiner. Both turned round as they passed Dick and Fancy and stared with bold admiration in her face till they were obliged to attend to the operation of passing the farmer. Dick glanced for an instant at Fancy while she was undergoing their scrutiny; then returned to his driving with rather a sad countenance.

'Why are you so silent?' she said after a while, with real concern.

'Nothing.'

'Yes, it is, Dick. I couldn't help those people passing.'

'I know that.'

'You look offended with me. What have I done?'

'I can't tell without offending you.'

'Better out.'

'Well,' said Dick, who seemed longing to tell even at the risk of offending her, 'I was thinking how different you in love are from me in love. Whilst those men were staring you dismissed me from your thoughts altogether and –'

'You can't offend me further now; tell all!'

'And showed upon your face a pleased sense of being attractive to 'em.'

'Don't be silly, Dick! You know very well I didn't.'

Dick shook his head sceptically and smiled.

'Dick, I always believe flattery *if possible* – and it was possible then. Now there's an open confession of weakness. But I showed no consciousness of it.'

Dick, perceiving by her look that she would adhere to her statement, charitably forbore saying anything that could make her prevaricate. The sight of Shiner, too, had recalled another branch of the subject to his mind; that which had been his greatest trouble till her company and words had obscured its probability.

'By the way, Fancy, do you know why our quire is to be dismissed?'

'No: except that it is Mr Maybold's wish for me to play the organ.'

'Do you know how it came to be his wish?'

'That I don't.'

'Mr Shiner, being churchwarden, has persuaded the vicar; who, however, was willing enough before. Shiner, I know, is crazy to see you playing every Sunday; I suppose he'll turn over your music, for the organ will be close to his pew. But – I know you have never encouraged him?'

'Never once!' said Fancy emphatically, and with eyes full of earnest truth. 'I don't like him indeed, and I never heard of his doing this before! I have always felt that I should like to play in a church, but I never wished to turn you and your choir out; and I never even said that I could play till I was asked. You don't think for a moment that I did, surely, do you?'

'I know you didn't, dear.'

'Or that I care the least morsel of a bit for him?'

'I know you don't.'

The distance between Budmouth and Mellstock was ten or eleven miles, and there being a good inn, 'The Ship', four miles out of Budmouth, with a mast and cross-trees in front, Dick's custom in driving thither was to divide his journey into three stages by resting at this inn going and coming, and not troubling the Budmouth stables, at all, whenever his visit to the town was a mere call and deposit, as today.

Fancy was ushered into a little tea-room and Dick went to the stables to see to the feeding of Smart. In face of the significant twitches of feature that were visible in the ostler and labouring men idling around, Dick endeavoured to look unconscious of the fact that there was any sentiment between him and Fancy beyond a tranter's desire to carry a passenger home. He presently entered the inn and opened the door of Fancy's room.

'Dick, do you know, it has struck me that it is rather awkward my being here alone with you like this. I don't think you had better come in with me.'

'That's rather unpleasant, dear.'

'Yes, it is, and I wanted you to have some tea as well as myself too, because you must be tired.'

'Well, let me have some with you, then. I was denied once before, if you recollect, Fancy.'

'Yes, yes, never mind! And it seems unfriendly of me now, but I don't know what to do.'

'It shall be as you say, then.' Dick began to retreat with a dissatisfied wrinkling of face, and a farewell glance at the cosy tea-tray.

'But you don't see how it is, Dick, when you speak like that,' she said with more earnestness than she had ever shown before. 'You do know that even if I care very much for you I must remember that I have a difficult position to maintain. The vicar would not like me, as his schoolmistress, to indulge in a *tête-à-tête* anywhere with anybody.'

'But I am not *any* body!' exclaimed Dick.

'No, no, I mean with a young man,' and she added softly, 'unless I were really engaged to be married to him.'

'Is that all? Then, dearest, dearest, why we'll be engaged at once, to be sure we will, and down I sit! There it is, as easy as a glove!'

'Ah! but suppose I won't! And, goodness me, what have I done!' she faltered, getting very red. 'Positively, it seems as if I meant you to say that!'

'Let's do it! I mean get engaged,' said Dick. 'Now, Fancy, will you be my wife?'

'Do you know, Dick, it was rather unkind of you to say what you did coming along the road,' she remarked as if she had not heard the latter part of his speech; though an acute observer might have noticed about her breast as the word 'wife' fell from Dick's lips a soft silent escape of breaths, with very short rests between each.

'What did I say?'

'About my trying to look attractive to those men in the gig.'

'You couldn't help looking so, whether you tried or no. And, Fancy, you do care for me?'

'Yes.'

'Very much?'

'Yes.'

'And you'll be my own wife?'

Her heart quickened, adding to and withdrawing from her cheek varying tones of red to match each varying thought. Dick looked expectantly at the ripe tint of her delicate mouth, waiting for what was coming forth.

'Yes – if father will let me.'

Dick drew himself close to her, compressing his lips and pouting them out as if he were about to whistle the softest melody known.

'O no!' said Fancy solemnly.

The modest Dick drew back a little.

'Dick, Dick, kiss me and let me go instantly! – here's somebody coming!' she whisperingly exclaimed.

Half an hour afterwards Dick emerged from the inn, and if Fancy's lips had been real cherries probably Dick's would have appeared deeply stained. The landlord was standing in the yard.

'Heu-heu! hay-hay, Master Dewy? Ho-ho!' he laughed, letting the laugh slip out gently and by degrees that it might make little noise in its exit, and smiting Dick under the fifth rib at the same time. 'This will never do, upon my life, Master Dewy! calling for tay for a feymel passenger, and then going in and sitting down and having some too, and biding such a fine long time!'

'But surely you know?' said Dick, with great apparent surprise. 'Yes, yes! Ha-ha!' smiting the landlord under the ribs in return.

'Why, what? Yes, yes; ha-ha!'

'You know, of course!'

'Yes, of course! But – that is – I don't.'

'Why about – between that young lady and me?' nodding to the window of the room that Fancy occupied.

'No; not I!' said the innkeeper, bringing his eyes into circles.

'And you don't!'

'Not a word, I'll take my oath!'

'But you laughed when I laughed.'

'Ay, that was me sympathy; so did you when I laughed!'

'Really, you don't know? Goodness – not knowing that!'

'I'll take my oath I don't!'

'O yes,' said Dick, with frigid rhetoric of pitying astonishment, 'we're engaged to be married, you see, and I naturally look after her.'

'Of course, of course! I didn't know that, and I hope ye'll excuse any little freedom of mine, Mr Dewy. But it is a very odd thing; I was talking to your father very intimate about family matters only last Friday in the world, and who should come in but Keeper Day and we all then fell a-talking o' family matters; but neither one o' them said a mortal word about it; knowen me too so many years, and I at your father's own wedding. 'Tisn't what I should have expected from an old neighbour!'

'Well, to say the truth, we hadn't told father of the engagement at that time; in fact, 'twasn't settled.'

'Ah! the business was done Sunday. Yes, yes, Sunday's the courting day. Heu-heu!'

'No, 'twasn't done Sunday in particular.'

'After school-hours this week? Well, a very good time, a very proper good time.'

'O no, 'twasn't done then.'

'Coming along the road today then, I suppose?'

'Not at all; I wouldn't think of getting engaged in a dog-cart.'

'Dammy – might as well have said at once the *when* be blowed! Anyhow, 'tis a fine day, and I hope next time you'll come as one.'

Fancy was duly brought out and assisted into the vehicle, and the newly affianced youth and maiden passed up the steep hill to the Ridgeway, and vanished in the direction of Mellstock.

* III *

A Confession

IT was a morning of the latter summer-time; a morning of lingering dews, when the grass is never dry in the shade. Fuchsias and dahlias were laden till eleven o'clock with small drops and dashes of water, changing the colour of their sparkle at every movement of the air; and elsewhere hanging on twigs like small silver fruit. The threads of garden-spiders appeared thick and polished. In the dry and sunny places dozens of long-legged crane-flies whizzed off the grass at every step the passer took.

Fancy Day and her friend Susan Dewy the tranter's daughter were in such a spot as this, pulling down a bough laden with early apples. Three months had elapsed since Dick and Fancy had journeyed together from Budmouth, and the course of their love had run on vigorously during the whole time. There had been just enough difficulty attending its development, and just enough finesse required in keeping it private, to lend the passion an ever-increasing freshness on Fancy's part, whilst, whether from these accessories or not, Dick's heart had been at all times as fond as could be desired. But there was a cloud on Fancy's horizon now.

'She is so well off – better than any of us,' Susan Dewy was saying. 'Her father farms five hundred acres, and she might marry a doctor or curate or anything of that kind if she contrived a little.'

'I don't think Dick ought to have gone to that gipsy-party at all when he knew I couldn't go,' replied Fancy uneasily.

'He didn't know that you would not be there till it was too late to refuse the invitation,' said Susan.

'And what was she like? Tell me.'

'Well, she was rather pretty, I must own.'

'Tell straight on about her, can't you! Come, do, Susan. How many times did you say he danced with her?'

'Once.'

'Twice, I think you said?'

'Indeed I'm sure I didn't.'

'Well, and he wanted to again, I expect.'

'No; I don't think he did. She wanted to dance with him again bad enough, I know. Everybody does with Dick, because he's so handsome and such a clever courter.'

'O, I wish! – How did you say she wore her hair?'

'In long curls, – and her hair is light, and it curls without being put in paper: that's how it is she's so attractive.'

'She's trying to get him away! yes, yes, she is! And through keeping this miserable school I mustn't wear my hair in curls! But I will; I don't care if I leave the school and go home, I will wear my curls! Look, Susan, do! is her hair as soft and long as this?' Fancy pulled from its coil under her hat a twine of her own hair and stretched it down her shoulder to show its length, looking at Susan to catch her opinion from her eyes.

'It is about the same length as that, I think,' said Miss Dewy.

Fancy paused hopelessly. 'I wish mine was lighter, like hers!' she continued mournfully. 'But hers isn't so soft, is it? Tell me, now.'

'I don't know.'

Fancy abstractedly extended her vision to survey a yellow butterfly and a red-and-black butterfly that were flitting along in company, and then became aware that Dick was advancing up the garden.

'Susan, here's Dick coming; I suppose that's because we've been talking about him.'

'Well, then, I shall go indoors now – you won't want me,' and Susan turned practically and walked off.

Enter the single-minded Dick, whose only fault at the gipsying, or picnic, had been that of loving Fancy too exclusively and depriving himself of the innocent pleasure the gathering might have afforded him, by sighing regretfully at her absence, – who had danced with the rival in sheer despair of ever being able to get through that stale, flat, and unprofitable afternoon in any other way; but this she would not believe.

Fancy had settled her plan of emotion. To reproach Dick? O no, no. 'I am in great trouble,' said she, taking what was intended to be a hopelessly melancholy survey of a few small apples lying under the tree;

yet a critical ear might have noticed in her small voice a tentative tone as to the effect of the words upon Dick when she uttered them.

'What are you in trouble about? Tell me of it,' said Dick earnestly. 'Darling, I will share it with 'ee and help 'ee.'

'No, no: you can't! Nobody can!'

'Why not? You don't deserve it, whatever it is. Tell me, dear.'

'O, it isn't what you think! It is dreadful: my own sin!'

'Sin, Fancy! as if you could sin! I know it can't be.'

' 'Tis, 'tis!' said the young lady, in a pretty little frenzy of sorrow. 'I have done wrong, and I don't like to tell it! Nobody will forgive me, nobody! and you above all will not! . . . I have allowed myself to – to – fl –'

'What, – not flirt!' he said, controlling his emotion as it were by a sudden pressure inward from his surface. 'And you said only the day before yesterday that you hadn't flirted in your life!'

'Yes, I did; and that was a wicked story! I have let another love me, and –'

'Good G –! Well, I'll forgive you, – yes, if you couldn't help it, – yes, I will!' said the now dismal Dick. 'Did you encourage him?'

'O, – I don't know, – yes – no. O, I think so!'

'Who was it?'

A pause.

'Tell me!'

'Mr Shiner.'

After a silence that was only disturbed by the fall of an apple, a long-checked sigh from Dick, and a sob from Fancy, he said with real austerity –

'Tell it all; – every word!'

'He looked at me, and I looked at him, and he said, "Will you let me show you how to catch bullfinches down here by the stream?" And I – wanted to know very much – I did so long to have a bullfinch! I couldn't help that! – and I said, "Yes!" and then he said, "Come here." And I went with him down to the lovely river, and then he said to me, "Look and see how I do it, and then you'll know: I put this birdlime round this twig, and then I go here," he said, "and hide away under a bush; and presently clever Mister Bird comes and perches upon the twig, and flaps his wings, and you've got him before you can say Jack" – something; O, O, O, I forget what!'

'Jack Sprat,' mournfully suggested Dick through the cloud of his misery.

'No, not Jack Sprat,' she sobbed.

'Then 'twas Jack Robinson!' he said with the emphasis of a man who had resolved to discover every iota of the truth or die.

'Yes, that was it! And then I put my hand upon the rail of the bridge to get across, and – That's all.'

'Well, that isn't much, either,' said Dick critically and more cheerfully. 'Not that I see what business Shiner has to take upon himself to teach you anything. But it seems – it do seem there must have been more than that to set you up in such a dreadful taking?'

He looked into Fancy's eyes. Misery of miseries! – guilt was written there still.

'Now, Fancy, you've not told me all!' said Dick, rather sternly for a quiet young man.

'O, don't speak so cruelly! I am afraid to tell now! If you hadn't been harsh I was going on to tell all; now I can't!'

'Come, dear Fancy, tell: come. I'll forgive; I must, – by heaven and earth, I must, whether I will or no; I love you so!'

'Well, when I put my hand on the bridge, he touched it –'

'A scamp!' said Dick, grinding an imaginary human frame to powder.

'And then he looked at me, and at last he said, "Are you in love with Dick Dewy?" And I said, "Perhaps I am!" and then he said, "I wish you weren't then, for I want to marry you, with all my soul." '

'There's a villain now! Want to marry you!' And Dick quivered with the bitterness of satirical laughter. Then suddenly remembering that he might be reckoning without his host: 'Unless, to be sure, you are willing to have him, – perhaps you are,' he said, with the wretched indifference of a castaway.

'No, indeed I am not!' she said, her sobs just beginning to take a favourable turn towards cure.

'Well, then,' said Dick, coming a little to his senses, 'you've been stretching it very much in giving such a dreadful beginning to such a mere nothing. And I know what you've done it for, – just because of that gipsy-party!' He turned away from her and took five paces decisively, as if he were tired of an ungrateful country, including herself. 'You did it to make me jealous, and I won't stand for it!' He flung the words to her over his shoulder and then stalked on, apparently very anxious to walk to the remotest of the Colonies that very minute.

'O, O, O, Dick – Dick!' she cried, trotting after him like a pet lamb and really seriously alarmed at last, 'you'll kill me! My impulses are bad – miserably wicked, – and I can't help it; forgive me, Dick! And I love you always; and those times when you look silly and don't seem quite good enough for me – just the same, I do, Dick! And there is something more serious, though not concerning that walk with him.'

'Well, what is it?' said Dick, altering his mind about walking to the Colonies; in fact, passing to the other extreme, and standing so rooted to the road that he was apparently not even going home.

'Why this,' she said, drying the beginning of a new flood of tears she had been going to shed, 'this is the serious part. Father has told Mr Shiner that he would like him for a son-in-law if he could get me – that he has his right hearty consent to come courting me!'

* IV *

An Arrangement

'THAT *is* serious,' said Dick, more intellectually than he had spoken for a long time.

The truth was that Geoffrey knew nothing about his daughter's continued walks and meetings with Dick. When a hint that there were symptoms of an attachment between them had first reached Geoffrey's ears he stated so emphatically that he must think the matter over before any such thing could be allowed that, rather unwisely on Dick's part, whatever it might have been on the lady's, the lovers were careful to be seen together no more in public; and Geoffrey, forgetting the report, did not think over the matter at all. So Mr Shiner resumed his old position in Geoffrey's brain by mere flux of time. Even Shiner began to believe that Dick existed for Fancy no more, – though that remarkably easy-going man had taken no active steps on his own account as yet.

'And father has not only told Mr Shiner that,' continued Fancy, 'but he has written me a letter to say he should wish me to encourage Mr Shiner if 'twas convenient!'

'I must start off and see your father at once!' said Dick, taking two or three vehement steps to the south, recollecting that Mr Day lived to the north, and coming back again.

'I think we had better see him together. Not tell him what you come for, or anything of the kind, until he likes you, and so win his brain through his heart, which is always the way to manage people. I mean in this way: I am going home on Saturday week to help them in the honey-taking. You might come there to me, have something to eat and drink, and let him guess what your coming signifies, without saying it in so many words.'

'We'll do it, dearest. But I shall ask him for you, flat and plain; not wait for his guessing.' And the lover then stepped close to her, and attempted to give her one little kiss on the cheek, his lips alighting, however, on an outlying tract of her back hair by reason of an impulse that had caused her to turn her head with a jerk. 'Yes, and I'll put on my second-best suit and a clean shirt and collar, and black my boots as if 'twas a Sunday. 'Twill have a good appearance, you see, and that's a great deal to start with.'

'You won't wear that old waistcoat, will you, Dick?'

'Bless you, no! Why I –'

'I didn't mean to be personal, dear Dick,' she said, fearing she had hurt his feelings. ' 'Tis a very nice waistcoat, but what I meant was, that though it is an excellent waistcoat for a settled-down man, it is not quite one for' (she waited, and a blush expanded over her face, and then she went on again) – 'for going courting in.'

'No, I'll wear my best winter one, with the leather lining, that mother made. It is a beautiful, handsome waistcoat inside, yes, as ever anybody saw. In fact, only the other day, I unbuttoned it to show a chap that very lining, and he said it was the strongest handsomest lining you could wish to see on the king's waistcoat himself.'

'*I* don't quite know what to wear,' she said, as if her habitual indifference alone to dress had kept back so important a subject till now.

'Why, that blue frock you wore last week.'

'Doesn't set well round the neck. I couldn't wear that.'

'But I shan't care.'

'No, you won't mind.'

'Well, then it's all right. Because you only care how you look to me, do you, dear? I only dress for you, that's certain.'

'Yes, but you see I couldn't appear in it again very well.'

'Any strange gentleman you mid meet in your journey might notice the set of it, I suppose. Fancy, men in love don't think so much about how they look to other women.' It is difficult to say whether a tone of playful banter or of gentle reproach prevailed in the speech.

'Well then, Dick,' she said, with good-humoured frankness, 'I'll own it. I shouldn't like a stranger to see me dressed badly even though I am in love. 'Tis our nature, I suppose.'

'You perfect woman!'

'Yes; if you lay the stress on "woman",' she murmured, looking at a group of hollyhocks in flower, round which a crowd of butterflies had gathered like female idlers round a bonnet-shop.

'But about the dress. Why not wear the one you wore at our party?'

'That sets well, but a girl of the name of Bet Tallor, who lives near our house, has had one made almost like it (only in pattern, though of miserably cheap stuff), and I couldn't wear it on that account. Dear me, I am afraid I can't go now.'

'O yes, you must; I know you will!' said Dick, with dismay. 'Why not wear what you've got on?'

'What! this old one! After all, I think that by wearing my grey one Saturday, I can make the blue one do for Sunday. Yes, I will. A hat or a bonnet, which shall it be? Which do I look best in?'

'Well, I think the bonnet is nicest, more quiet and matronly.'

'What's the objection to the hat? Does it make me look old?'

'O no; the hat is well enough; but it makes you look rather too – you won't mind me saying it, dear?'

'Not at all, for I shall wear the bonnet.'

'– Rather too coquettish and flirty for an engaged young woman.'

She reflected a minute. 'Yes; yes. Still, after all, the hat would do best; hats *are* best, you see. Yes, I must wear the hat, dear Dicky, because I ought to wear a hat, you know.'

PART THE FOURTH

AUTUMN

* I *

Going Nutting

DICK, dressed in his second-best suit, burst into Fancy's sitting-room with a glow of pleasure on his face.

It was two o'clock on Friday, the day before her contemplated visit to her father, and for some reason connected with cleaning the school the children had been given this Friday afternoon for pastime, in addition to the usual Saturday.

'Fancy! it happens just right that it is a leisure half day with you. Smart is lame in his near-foot-afore, and so, as I can't do anything, I've made a holiday afternoon of it, and am come for you to go nutting with me!'

She was sitting by the parlour window with a blue frock lying across her lap and scissors in her hand.

'Go nutting! Yes. But I'm afraid I can't go for an hour or so.'

'Why not? 'Tis the only spare afternoon we may both have together for weeks.'

'This dress of mine, that I am going to wear on Sunday at Yalbury; – I find it fits so badly that I must alter it a little, after all. I told the dressmaker to make it by a pattern I gave her at the time; instead of that, she did it her own way, and made me look a perfect fright.'

'How long will you be?' he inquired, looking rather disappointed.

'Not long. Do wait and talk to me; come, do, dear.'

Dick sat down. The talking progressed very favourably amid the snipping and sewing till about half-past two, at which time his conversation began to be varied by a slight tapping upon his toe with a walking-stick he had cut from the hedge as he came along. Fancy talked and answered him, but sometimes the answers were so negligently given that it was evident her thoughts lay for the greater part in her lap with the blue dress.

The clock struck three. Dick arose from his seat, walked round the room with his hands behind him, examined all the furniture, then sounded a few notes on the harmonium, then looked inside all the books he could find, then smoothed Fancy's head with his hand. Still the snipping and sewing went on.

The clock struck four. Dick fidgeted about, yawned privately; counted the knots in the table, yawned publicly; counted the flies on the ceiling, yawned horribly; went into the kitchen and scullery and so thoroughly studied the principle upon which the pump was constructed that he could have delivered a lecture on the subject. Stepping back to Fancy, and finding still that she had not done, he went into her garden and looked at her cabbages and potatoes, and reminded himself that they seemed to him to wear a decidedly feminine aspect; then pulled up several weeds and came in again. The clock struck five, and still the snipping and sewing went on.

Dick attempted to kill a fly, peeled all the rind off his walking-stick, then threw the stick into the scullery because it was spoilt, produced hideous discords from the harmonium, and accidentally overturned a vase of flowers, the water from which ran in a rill across the table and dribbled to the floor, where it formed a lake, the shape of which, after the lapse of a few minutes, he began to modify considerably with his foot till it was like a map of England and Wales.

'Well, Dick, you needn't have made quite such a mess.'

'Well, I needn't, I suppose.' He walked up to the blue dress, and looked at it with a rigid gaze. Then an idea seemed to cross his brain.

'Fancy.'

'Yes.'

'I thought you said you were going to wear your grey gown all day tomorrow on your trip to Yalbury, and in the evening too, when I shall be with you, and ask your father for you?'

'So I am.'

'And the blue one only on Sunday?'

'And the blue one Sunday.'

'Well, dear, I shan't be at Yalbury Sunday to see it.'

'No, but I shall walk to Longpuddle church in the afternoon with father, and such lots of people will be looking at me there, you know; and it did set so badly round the neck.'

'I never noticed it, and 'tis like nobody else would.'

'They might.'

'Then why not wear the grey one on Sunday as well? 'Tis as pretty as the blue one.'

'I might make the grey one do, certainly. But it isn't so good; it didn't cost half so much as this one, and besides, it would be the same I wore Saturday.'

'Then wear the striped one, dear.'

'I might.'

'Or the dark one.'

'Yes, I might; but I want to wear a fresh one they haven't seen.'

'I see, I see,' said Dick, in a voice in which the tones of love were decidedly inconvenienced by a considerable emphasis, his thoughts meanwhile running as follows: 'I, the man she loves best in the world, as she says, am to understand that my poor half-holiday is to be lost, because she wants to wear on Sunday a gown there is not the slightest necessity for wearing, simply, in fact, to appear more striking than usual in the eyes of the Longpuddle young men; and I not there, either.'

'Then there are three dresses good enough for my eyes, but neither is good enough for the youths of Longpuddle,' he said.

'No, not that exactly, Dick. Still, you see, I do want – to look pretty to them – there, that's honest! But I shan't be much longer.'

'How much?'

'A quarter of an hour.'

'Very well; I'll come in in a quarter of an hour.'

'Why go away?'

'I mid as well.'

He went out, walked down the road, and sat upon a gate. Here he meditated and meditated, and the more he meditated the more decidedly did he begin to fume, and the more positive was he that his time had been scandalously trifled with by Miss Fancy Day – that, so far from being the simple girl who had never had a sweetheart before, as she had solemnly assured him time after time, she was, if not a flirt, a woman who had had no end of admirers; a girl most certainly too anxious about her frocks; a girl, whose feelings, though warm, were not deep; a girl who cared a great deal too much how she appeared in the eyes of other men. 'What she loves best in the world,' he thought, with an incipient spice of his father's grimness, 'is her hair and complexion. What she loves next best, her gowns and hats; what she loves next best, myself, perhaps!'

Suffering great anguish at this disloyalty in himself and harshness to his darling, yet disposed to persevere in it, a horribly cruel thought crossed his mind. He would not call for her, as he had promised, at the end of a quarter of an hour! Yes, it would be a punishment she well deserved. Although the best part of the afternoon had been wasted he would go nutting as he had intended, and go by himself.

He leaped over the gate, and pushed up the lane for nearly two miles, till a winding path called Snail-Creep sloped up a hill and entered a hazel copse by a hole like a rabbit's burrow. In he plunged, vanished among the bushes, and in a short time there was no sign of his existence upon earth save an occasional rustling of boughs and snapping of twigs in divers points of Grey's Wood.

Never man nutted as Dick nutted that afternoon. He worked like a galley slave. Half-hour after half-hour passed away, and still he gathered without ceasing. At last, when the sun had set, and bunches of nuts could not be distinguished from the leaves which nourished them, he shouldered his bag, containing quite two pecks of the finest produce of the wood, about as much use to him as two pecks of stones from the road, strolled down the woodland track, crossed the highway and entered the homeward lane, whistling as he went.

Probably, Miss Fancy Day never before or after stood so low in Mr Dewy's opinion as on that afternoon. In fact, it is just possible that a few more blue dresses on the Longpuddle young men's account would have clarified Dick's brain entirely, and made him once more a free man.

But Venus had planned other developments, at any rate for the present. Cuckoo-Lane, the way he pursued, passed over a ridge which rose keenly against the sky about fifty yards in his van. Here, upon the bright after-glow about the horizon, was now visible an irregular shape, which at first he conceived to be a bough standing a little beyond the line of its neighbours. Then it seemed to move, and, as he advanced still further, there was no doubt that it was a living being sitting in the bank, head bowed on hand. The grassy margin entirely prevented his footsteps from being heard, and it was not till he was close that the figure recognized him. Up it sprang, and he was face to face with Fancy.

'Dick, Dick! O, is it you, Dick!'

'Yes, Fancy,' said Dick, in a rather repentant tone, and lowering his nuts.

She ran up to him, flung her parasol on the grass, put her little head against his breast, and then there began a narrative disjointed by such a hysterical weeping as was never surpassed for intensity in the whole history of love.

'O Dick,' she sobbed out, 'where have you been away from me? O, I have suffered agony, and thought you would never come any more! 'Tis cruel, Dick; no 'tisn't, it is justice! I've been walking miles and miles up and down Grey's Wood, trying to find you, till I was wearied and worn out, and I could walk no further, and had come back this far! O Dick, directly you were gone I thought I had offended you and I put down the dress; 'tisn't finished now, and I never will finish it, and I'll wear an old one Sunday! Yes, Dick, I will, because I don't care what I wear when you are not by my side – ha, you think I do, but I don't! – and I ran after you, and I saw you go up Snail-Creep and not look back once, and then you plunged in, and I after you; but I was too far behind. O, I did wish the horrid bushes had been cut down so that I could see your dear shape again! And then I called out to you and nobody answered, and I was afraid to call very loud lest anybody else should hear me. Then I kept wandering and wandering about, and it was dreadful misery, Dick. And then I shut my eyes and fell to picturing you looking at some other woman, very pretty and nice, but with no affection or truth in her at all, and then imagined you saying to yourself. "Ah, she's as good as Fancy, for Fancy told me a story, and was a flirt, and cared for herself more than me, so now I'll have this one for my sweetheart." O, you won't, will you, Dick, for I do love you so!'

It is scarcely necessary to add that Dick renounced his freedom there and then, and kissed her ten times over, and promised that no pretty woman of the kind alluded to should ever engross his thoughts; in short, that though he had been vexed with her all such vexation was past, and that henceforth and for ever it was simply Fancy or death for him. And then they set about proceeding homewards, very slowly on account of Fancy's weariness, she leaning upon his shoulder and in addition receiving support from his arm round her waist; though she had sufficiently recovered from her desperate condition to sing to him, 'Why are you wandering here, I pray?' during the latter part of their walk. Nor is it necessary to describe in detail how the bag of nuts was quite forgotten until three days later, when it was found among the brambles and restored empty to Mrs Dewy, her initials being marked thereon in red cotton; and how she puzzled herself till her head ached upon the question of how on earth her meal-bag could have got into Cuckoo-Lane.

* II *

Honey-taking, and Afterwards

SATURDAY evening saw Dick Dewy journeying on foot to Yalbury Wood, according to the arrangement with Fancy.

The landscape being concave, at the going down of the sun everything suddenly assumed a uniform robe of shade. The evening advanced from sunset to dusk long before Dick's arrival, and his progress during the latter portion of his walk through the trees was indicated by the flutter of terrified birds that had been roosting over the path. And in crossing the glades, masses of hot dry air that had been formed on the hills during the day greeted his cheeks alternately with clouds of damp night air from the valleys. He reached the keeper-steward's house, where the grass-plot and the garden in front appeared light and pale against the unbroken darkness of the grove from which he had emerged, and paused at the garden gate.

He had scarcely been there a minute when he beheld a sort of procession advancing from the door in his front. It consisted first of Enoch the trapper, carrying a spade on his shoulder and a lantern dangling in his hand; then came Mrs Day, the light of the lantern revealing that she bore in her arms curious objects about a foot long in the form of Latin crosses (made of lath and brown paper dipped in brimstone – called matches by bee-masters); next came Miss Day with a shawl thrown over her head; and behind all, in the gloom, Mr Frederic Shiner.

Dick in his consternation at finding Shiner present was at a loss how to proceed, and retired under a tree to collect his thoughts.

'Here I be, Enoch,' said a voice; and the procession advancing further, the lantern's rays illuminated the figure of Geoffrey awaiting their arrival beside a row of bee-hives in front of the path. Taking the spade from Enoch he proceeded to dig two holes in the earth beside the hives, the others standing round in a circle except Mrs Day, who deposited her matches in the fork of an apple-tree and returned to the house. The party remaining were now lit up in front by the lantern in their midst, their shadows radiating each way upon the garden-plot like the spoke of a wheel. An apparent embarrassment of Fancy at the presence of Shiner caused a silence in the assembly, during which the preliminaries of execution were arranged, the matches fixed, the stake kindled, the two hives placed over the two holes, and the earth stopped round the edges. Geoffrey then stood erect, and rather more, to straighten his backbone after the digging.

'They were a peculiar family,' said Mr Shiner, regarding the hives reflectively.

Geoffrey nodded.

'Those holes will be the grave of thousands!' said Fancy. 'I think 'tis rather a cruel thing to do.'

Her father shook his head. 'No,' he said, tapping the hives to shake the dead bees from their cells, 'if you suffocate 'em this way, they only die once; if you fumigate 'em in the new way, they come to life again, and die o' starvation; so the pangs o' death be twice upon 'em.'

'I incline to Fancy's notion,' said Mr Shiner, laughing lightly.

'The proper way to take honey, so that the bees be neither starved nor murdered, is a puzzling matter,' said the keeper steadily.

'I should like never to take it from them,' said Fancy.

'But 'tis the money,' said Enoch musingly. 'For without money man is a shadder!'

The lantern-light had disturbed many bees that had escaped from hives destroyed some days earlier, and, demoralized by affliction, were now getting a living as marauders about the doors of other hives. Several flew round the head and neck of Geoffrey; then darted upon him with an irritated bizz.

Enoch threw down the lantern and ran off and pushed his head into a currant bush; Fancy scudded up the path; and Mr Shiner floundered away helter-skelter among the cabbages. Geoffrey stood his ground, unmoved and firm as a rock. Fancy was the first to return, followed by Enoch picking up the lantern. Mr Shiner still remained invisible.

'Have the craters stung ye?' said Enoch to Geoffrey.

'No, not much – on'y a little here and there,' he said with leisurely solemnity, shaking one bee out of his shirt sleeve, pulling another from among his hair, and two or three more from his neck. The rest looked on during this proceeding with a complacent sense of being out of it, – much as a European nation in a state of internal commotion is watched by its neighbours.

'Are those all of them, father?' said Fancy, when Geoffrey had pulled away five.

'Almost all, – though I feel one or two more sticking into my shoulder and side. Ah! there's another just begun again upon my backbone. You lively young mortals, how did you get inside there? However, they can't sting me many times more, poor things, for they must be getting weak. They mid as well stay in me till bedtime now, I suppose.'

As he himself was the only person affected by this arrangement it seemed satisfactory enough; and after a noise of feet kicking against cabbages in a blundering progress among them the voice of Mr Shiner was heard from the darkness in that direction.

'Is all quite safe again?'

No answer being returned to this query he apparently assumed that he might venture forth, and gradually drew near the lantern again. The hives were now removed from their position over the holes, one being handed to Enoch to carry indoors, and one being taken by Geoffrey himself.

'Bring hither the lantern, Fancy: the spade can bide.'

Geoffrey and Enoch then went towards the house, leaving Shiner and Fancy standing side by side on the garden-plot.

'Allow me,' said Shiner, stooping for the lantern and seizing it at the same time with Fancy.

'I can carry it,' said Fancy, religiously repressing all inclination to trifle. She had thoroughly considered that subject after the tearful explanation of the bird-catching adventure to Dick, and had decided that it would be dishonest in her as an engaged young woman to trifle with men's eyes and hands any more. Finding that Shiner still retained his hold of the lantern she relinquished it, and he, having found her retaining it, also let go. The lantern fell and was extinguished. Fancy moved on.

'Where is the path?' said Mr Shiner.

'Here,' said Fancy. 'Your eyes will get used to the dark in a minute or two.'

'Till that time will ye lend me your hand?'

Fancy gave him the extreme tips of her fingers and they stepped from the plot into the path.

'You don't accept attentions very freely.'

'It depends upon who offers them.'

'A fellow like me, for instance.'

A dead silence.

'Well, what do you say, Missie?'

'It then depends upon how they are offered.'

'Not wildly, and yet not careless-like; not purposely, and yet not by chance; not too quick nor yet too slow.'

'How then?' said Fancy.

'Coolly and practically,' he said. 'How would that kind of love be taken?'

'Not anxiously, and yet not indifferently; neither blushing nor pale; nor religiously not yet quite wickedly.'

'Well, how?'

'Not at all.'

Geoffrey Day's storehouse at the back of his dwelling was hung with bunches of dried horehound, mint, and sage; brown-paper bags of thyme and lavender; and long ropes of clean onions. On shelves were spread large red and yellow apples, and choice selections of early potatoes for seed next year; — vulgar crowds of commoner kind lying beneath in heaps. A few empty beehives were clustered around a nail in one corner, under which stood two or three barrels of new cider of the first crop, each bubbling and squirting forth from the yet open bunghole.

Fancy was now kneeling beside the two inverted hives, one of which rested against her lap for convenience in operating upon the contents. She thrust her sleeves above her elbows, and inserted her small pink hand edgewise between each white lobe of honeycomb, performing the act so adroitly and gently as not to unseal a single cell. Then cracking the piece off at the crown of the hive by a slight backward and forward movement she lifted each portion as it was loosened into a large blue platter placed on a bench at her side.

'Bother these little mortals!' said Geoffrey, who was holding the light to her and giving his back an uneasy twist. 'I really think I may as well go indoors and take 'em out, poor things! for they won't let me alone. There's two a stinging wi' all their might now. I'm sure I wonder their strength can last so long.'

'All right, friend; I'll hold the candle whilst you are gone,' said Mr Shiner, leisurely taking the light and allowing Geoffrey to depart, which he did with his usual long paces.

He could hardly have gone round to the housedoor when other footsteps were heard approaching the outbuilding; the tip of a finger appeared in the hole through which the wood latch was lifted, and Dick Dewy came in, having been all this time walking up and down the wood vainly waiting for Shiner's departure.

Fancy looked up and welcomed him rather confusedly. Shiner grasped the candlestick more firmly, and, lest doing this in silence should not imply to Dick with sufficient force that he was quite at home and cool, he sang invincibly –

'King Arthur he had three sons.'

'Father here?' said Dick.

'Indoors, I think,' said Fancy, looking pleasantly at him.

Dick surveyed the scene and did not seem inclined to hurry off just at that moment. Shiner went on singing –

'The miller was drown'd in his pond,
    The weaver was hung in his yarn,
And the d— ran away with the little tail-or,
    With the broadcloth under his arm.'

'That's a terrible crippled rhyme, if that's your rhyme!' said Dick, with a grain of superciliousness in his tone.

'It's no use your complaining to me about the rhyme!' said Mr Shiner. 'You must go to the man that made it.'

Fancy by this time had acquired confidence.

'Taste a bit, Mr Dewy,' she said, holding up to him a small circular piece of honeycomb that had been the last in the row of layers, remaining still on her knees and flinging back her head to look at his face; 'and then I'll taste a bit too.'

'And I, if you please,' said Mr Shiner. Nevertheless the farmer looked superior, as if he could even now hardly join the trifling from very importance of station; and after receiving the honeycomb from Fancy he turned it over in his hand till the cells began to be crushed, and the liquid honey ran down from his fingers in a thin string.

Suddenly a faint cry from Fancy caused them to gaze at her.

'What's the matter, dear?' said Dick.

'It is nothing, but – O-o! – a bee has stung the inside of my lip! He was in one of the cells I was eating!'

'We must keep down the swelling or it may be serious!' said Shiner, stepping up and kneeling beside her. 'Let me see it.'

'No, no!'

'Just let *me* see it,' said Dick kneeling on the other side; and after some hesitation she pressed down her lip with one finger to show the place. 'O, I hope 'twill soon be better! I don't mind a sting in ordinary places, but it is so bad upon your lip,' she added with tears in her eyes, and writhing a little from the pain.

Shiner held the light above his head and pushed his face close to Fancy's, as if the lip had been shown exclusively to himself, upon which Dick pushed closer, as if Shiner were not there at all.

'It is swelling,' said Dick to her right aspect.

'It isn't swelling,' said Shiner to her left aspect.

'Is it dangerous on the lip?' cried Fancy. 'I know it is dangerous on the tongue.'

'O no, not dangerous,' answered Dick.

'Rather dangerous,' had answered Shiner simultaneously.

'I must try to bear it!' said Fancy, turning again to the hives.

'Hartshorn-and-oil is a good thing to put to it, Miss Day,' said Shiner with great concern.

'Sweet-oil-and-hartshorn I've found to be a good thing to cure stings, Miss Day,' said Dick with greater concern.

'We have some mixed indoors; would you kindly run and get it for me?' she said.

Now whether by inadvertence or whether by mischievous intention, the individuality of the *you* was so carelessly denoted that both Dick and Shiner sprang to their feet like twin acrobats, and marched abreast to the door; both seized the latch and lifted it, and continued marching on shoulder to shoulder in the same manner to the dwelling-house. Not only so but, entering the room, they marched as before straight up to Mrs Day's chair, letting the door in the oak partition slam so forcibly that the rows of pewter on the dresser rang like a bell.

'Mrs Day, Fancy has stung her lip and wants you to give me the hartshorn, please,' said Mr Shiner, very close to Mrs Day's face.

'O, Mrs Day, Fancy has asked me to bring out the hartshorn, please, because she has stung her lip!' said Dick, a little closer to Mrs Day's face.

'Well, men alive! that's no reason why you should eat me, I suppose!' said Mrs Day, drawing back.

She searched in the corner-cupboard, produced the bottle, and began to dust the cork, the rim, and every other part very carefully, Dick's hand and Shiner's hand waiting side by side.

'Which is head man?' said Mrs Day. 'Now, don't come mumbudgeting so close again. Which is head man?'

Neither spoke; and the bottle was inclined towards Shiner. Shiner, as a high-class man, would not look in the least triumphant, and turned to go off with it as Geoffrey came downstairs after the search in his linen for concealed bees.

'O – that you, Master Dewy?'

Dick assured the keeper that it was; and the young man then determined upon a bold stroke for the attainment of his end, forgetting that the worst of bold strokes is the disastrous consequences they involve if they fail.

'I've come on purpose to speak to you very particular, Mr Day,' he said, with a crushing emphasis intended for the ears of Mr Shiner, who was vanishing round the door-post at that moment.

'Well, I've been forced to go upstairs and unrind myself, and shake some bees out o' me,' said Geoffrey, walking slowly towards the open door and standing on the threshold. 'The young rascals got into my shirt and wouldn't be quiet nohow.'

Dick followed him to the door.

'I've come to speak a word to you,' he repeated, looking out at the pale mist creeping up from the gloom of the valley. 'You may perhaps guess what it is about.'

The keeper lowered his hands into the depths of his pockets, twirled his eyes, balanced himself on his toes, looked as perpendicularly downward as if his glance were a plumb-line, then horizontally, collecting together the cracks that lay about his face till they were all in the neighbourhood of his eyes.

'Maybe I don't know,' he replied.

Dick said nothing; and the stillness was disturbed only by some small bird that was being killed by an owl in the adjoining wood, whose cry passed into the silence without mingling with it.

'I've left my hat up in chammer,' said Geoffrey; 'wait while I step up and get en.'

'I'll be in the garden,' said Dick.

He went round by a side wicket into the garden, and Geoffrey went upstairs. It was the custom in Mellstock and its vicinity to discuss matters of pleasure and ordinary business inside the house, and to reserve the garden for very important affairs, a custom which, as is supposed, originated in the desirability of getting away at such times from the other members of the family when there was only one room for living in, though it was now quite as frequently practised by those who suffered from no such limitation to the size of their domiciles.

The head-keeper's form appeared in the dusky garden, and Dick walked towards him. The elder paused and leant over the rail of a piggery that stood on the left of the path, upon which Dick did the same; and they both contemplated a whitish shadowy shape that was moving about and grunting among the straw of the interior.

'I've come to ask for Fancy,' said Dick.

'I'd as lief you hadn't.'

'Why should that be, Mr Day?'

'Because it makes me say that you've come to ask what ye be'n't likely to have. Have ye come for anything else?'

'Nothing.'

'Then I'll just tell 'ee you've come on a very foolish errand. D'ye know what her mother was?'

'No.'

'A teacher in a landed family's nursery, who was foolish enough to marry the keeper of the same establishment; for I was only a keeper then, though now I've a dozen other irons in the fire as steward here for my lord, what with the timber sales and the yearly fellings, and the gravel and sand sales, and one thing and t'other. However, d'ye think Fancy picked up her good manners, the smooth turn of her tongue, her musical notes, and her knowledge of books, in a homely hole like this?'

'No.'

'D'ye know where?'

'No.'

'Well, when I went a-wandering after her mother's death she lived with her aunt, who kept a boarding-school, till her aunt married Lawyer Green – a man as sharp as a needle – and the school was broke up. Did ye know that then she went to the training-school, and that her name stood first among the Queen's scholars of her year?'

'I've heard so.'

'And that when she sat for her certificate as Government teacher, she had the highest of the first class?'

'Yes.'

'Well, and do ye know what I live in such a miserly way for when I've got enough to do without it, and why I make her work as a schoolmistress instead of living here?'

'No.'

'That if any gentleman, who sees her to be his equal in polish, should want to marry her, and she want to marry him, he shan't be superior to her in pocket. Now do ye think after this that you be good enough for her?'

'No.'

'Then good-night t'ee, Master Dewy.'

'Good-night, Mr Day.'

Modest Dick's reply had faltered upon his tongue, and he turned away wondering at his presumption in asking for a woman whom he had seen from the beginning to be so superior to him.

Fancy in the Rain

THE next scene is a tempestuous afternoon in the following month, and Fancy Day is discovered walking from her father's home towards Mellstock.

A single vast grey cloud covered the country, from which the small rain and mist had just begun to blow in wavy sheets, alternately thick and thin. The trees of the fields and plantations writhed like miserable men as the air wound its way swiftly among them: the lowest portions of their trunks, that had hardly ever been known to move, were visibly rocked by the fiercer gusts, distressing the mind by its painful unwontedness, as when a strong man is seen to shed tears. Low-hanging boughs went up and down; high and erect boughs went to and fro; the blasts being so irregular, and divided into so many cross-currents, that neighbouring branches of the same tree swept the skies in independent motions, crossed each other, or became entangled. Across the open spaces flew flocks of green and yellowish leaves which, after travelling a long distance from their parent trees, reached the ground and lay there with their under-sides upward.

As the rain and wind increased, and Fancy's bonnet-ribbons leapt more and more snappishly against her chin, she paused on entering Mellstock Lane to consider her latitude, and the distance to a place of shelter. The nearest house was Elizabeth Endorfield's in Higher Mellstock, whose cottage and garden stood not far from the junction of that hamlet with the road she followed. Fancy hastened onward, and in five minutes entered a gate which shed upon her toes a flood of water-drops as she opened it.

'Come in, chiel!' a voice exclaimed before Fancy had knocked: a promptness that would have surprised her had she not known that Mrs Endorfield was an exceedingly and exceptionally sharp woman in the use of her eyes and ears.

Fancy went in and sat down. Elizabeth was paring potatoes for her husband's supper.

Scrape, scrape, scrape; then a toss, and splash went a potato into a bucket of water.

Now as Fancy listlessly noted these proceedings of the dame she began to reconsider an old subject that lay uppermost in her heart. Since the interview between her father and Dick the days had been melancholy days for her. Geoffrey's firm opposition to the notion of Dick as a son-in-law was more than she had expected. She had frequently seen her lover since that time, it is true, and had loved him more for the opposition than she would have otherwise dreamt of doing – which was a happiness of a certain kind. Yet, though love is thus an end in itself it must be believed to be the means to another end if it is to assume the rosy hues of an unalloyed pleasure. And such a belief Fancy and Dick were emphatically denied just now.

Elizabeth Endorfield had a repute among women which was in its nature something between distinction and notoriety. It was founded on the following items of character. She was shrewd and penetrating; her house stood in a lonely place; she never went to church; she wore a red cloak; she always retained her bonnet indoors; and she had a pointed chin. Thus far her attributes were distinctly Satanic; and those who looked no further called her, in plain terms, a witch. But she was not gaunt, nor ugly in the upper part of her face, nor particularly strange in manner; so that, when her more intimate acquaintances spoke of her the term was softened, and she became simply a Deep Body, who was as long-headed as she was high. It may be stated that Elizabeth belonged to a class of suspects who were gradually losing their mysterious character-istics under the administration of the young vicar; though during the long reign of Mr Grinham the parish of Mellstock had proved extremely favourable to the growth of witches.

While Fancy was revolving all this in her mind, and putting it to herself whether it was worth while to tell her troubles to Elizabeth, and ask her advice in getting out of them, the witch spoke.

'You be down – proper down,' she said suddenly, dropping another potato into the bucket.

Fancy took no notice.

'About your young man.'

Fancy reddened. Elizabeth seemed to be watching her thoughts. Really one would almost think she must have the powers people ascribed to her.

'Father not in the humour for't, hey?' Another potato was finished and flung in. 'Ah, I know about it. Little birds tell me things that people don't dream of my knowing.'

Fancy was desperate about Dick, and here was a chance – O, such a wicked chance! – of getting help; and what was goodness beside love!

'I wish you'd tell me how to put him in the humour for it?' she said.

'That I could soon do,' said the witch quietly.

'Really? O, do; anyhow – I don't care – so that it is done! How could I do it, Mrs Endorfield?'

'Nothing so mighty wonderful in it.'

'Well, but how?'

'By witchery, of course!' said Elizabeth.

'No!' said Fancy.

' 'Tis, I assure ye. Didn't you ever hear I was a witch?'

'Well,' hesitated Fancy, 'I have heard you called so.'

'And you believed it?'

'I can't say that I did exactly believe it, for 'tis very horrible and wicked; but, O, how I do wish it was possible for you to be one!'

'So I am. And I'll tell you how to bewitch your father to let you marry Dick Dewy.'

'Will it hurt him, poor thing?'

'Hurt who?'

'Father.'

'No; the charm is worked by common sense, and the spell can only be broke by your acting stupidly.'

Fancy looked rather perplexed, and Elizabeth went on:

> 'This fear of Lizz – whatever 'tis –
> By great and small,
> She makes pretence to common sense,
> And that's all.

You must do it like this.' The witch laid down her knife and potato, and then poured into Fancy's ear a long and detailed list of directions, glancing up from the corner of her eye into Fancy's face with an expression of sinister humour. Fancy's face brightened, clouded, rose and sank, as the narrative proceeded. 'There,' said Elizabeth at length, stooping for the knife and another potato, 'do that, and you'll have him by-long and by-late, my dear.'

'And do it I will,' said Fancy.

She then turned her attention to the external world once more. The rain continued as usual, but the wind had abated considerably during the discourse. Judging that it was now possible to keep an umbrella erect she pulled her hood again over her bonnet, bade the witch good-bye, and went her way.

* IV *

The Spell

MRS ENDORFIELD'S advice was duly followed.

'I be proper sorry that your daughter isn't so well as she might be,' said a Mellstock man to Geoffrey one morning.

'But is there anything in it?' said Geoffrey uneasily, as he shifted his hat to the right. 'I can't understand the report. She didn't complain to me a bit when I saw her.'

'No appetite at all, they say.'

Geoffrey crossed to Mellstock and called at the school that afternoon. Fancy welcomed him as usual, and asked him to stay and take tea with her.

'I be'n't much for tea this time o' day,' he said, but stayed.

During the meal he watched her narrowly. And to his great conster-nation discovered the following unprecedented change in the healthy girl – that she cut herself only a diaphanous slice of bread-and-butter, and, laying it on her plate, passed the meal-time in breaking it into pieces, but eating no more than about one-tenth of the slice. Geoffrey hoped she would say something about Dick and finish up by weeping, as she had done after the decision against him a few days subsequent to the interview in the garden. But nothing was said, and in due time Geoffrey departed again for Yalbury Wood.

' 'Tis to be hoped poor Miss Fancy will be able to keep on her school,' said Geoffrey's man Enoch to Geoffrey the following week, as they were shovelling up ant-hills in the wood.

Geoffrey stuck in the shovel, swept seven or eight ants from his sleeve, and killed another that was prowling round his ear, then looked perpendicularly into the earth, as usual, waiting for Enoch to say more. 'Well, why shouldn't she?' said the keeper at last.

'The baker told me yesterday,' continued Enoch, shaking out another emmet that had run merrily up his thigh, 'that the bread he've left at that there school-house this last month would starve any mouse in the three creations; that 'twould so! And afterwards I had a pint o' small down at Morris's, and there I heard more.'

'What might that ha' been?'

'That she used to have a pound o' the best rolled butter a week, regular as clockwork, from Dairyman Viney's for herself, as well as just so much salted for the helping girl, and the 'ooman she calls in; but now the same quantity d'last her three weeks, and then 'tis thoughted she throws it away sour.'

'Finish doing the emmets, and carry the bag home-along.' The keeper resumed his gun, tucked it under his arm, and went on without whistling to the dogs, who however followed with a bearing meant to imply that they did not expect any such attentions when their master was reflecting.

On Saturday morning a note came from Fancy. He was not to trouble about sending her the couple of rabbits as was intended, because she feared she should not want them. Later in the day Geoffrey went to Casterbridge and called upon the butcher who served Fancy with fresh meat, which was put down to her father's account.

'I've called to pay up our little bill, Neighbour Haylock, and you can gie me the chiel's account at the same time.'

Mr Haylock turned round three-quarters of a circle in the midst of a heap of joints, altered the expression of his face from meat to money, went into a little office consisting only of a door and a window, looked very vigorously into a book which possessed length but no breadth; and then, seizing a piece of paper and scribbling thereupon, handed the bill.

Probably it was the first time in the history of commercial transactions that the quality of shortness in a butcher's bill was a cause of tribulation to the debtor. 'Why, this isn't all she've had in a whole month!' said Geoffrey.

'Every mossel,' said the butcher – '(now, Dan, take that leg and shoulder to Mrs White's, and this eleven pound here to Mr Martin's) – you've been treating her to smaller joints lately, to my thinking, Mr Day?'

'Only two or three little scram rabbits this week, as I am alive – I wish I had!'

'Well, my wife said to me – (Dan! not too much, not too much on that tray at a time; better go twice) – my wife said to me as she posted up the books: "Haylock," she says, "Miss Day must have been affronted this summer during that hot muggy weather that spoilt so much for us; for depend upon't," she says, "she've been trying John Grimmett unknown to us: see her account else." 'Tis little, of course, at the best of times, being only for one, but now 'tis next kin to nothing.'

'I'll inquire,' said Geoffrey despondingly.

He returned by way of Mellstock, and called upon Fancy in fulfilment of a promise. It being Saturday the children were enjoying a holiday, and on entering the residence Fancy was nowhere to be seen. Nan the charwoman was sweeping the kitchen.

'Where's my da'ter?' said the keeper.

'Well, you see she was tired with the week's teaching, and this morning she said, "Nan, I shan't get up till the evening." You see, Mr Day, if people don't eat they can't work; and as she've gie'd up eating she must gie up working.'

'Have ye carried up any dinner to her?'

'No; she don't want any. There, we all know that such things don't come without good reason – not that I wish to say anything about a broken heart, or anything of the kind.'

Geoffrey's own heart felt inconveniently large just then. He went to the staircase and ascended to his daughter's door.

'Fancy!'

'Come in, father.'

To see a person in bed from any cause whatever on a fine afternoon is depressing enough; and here was his only child Fancy not only in bed, but looking very pale. Geoffrey was visibly disturbed.

'Fancy, I didn't expect to see thee here, chiel,' he said. 'What's the matter?'

'I'm not well, father.'

'How's that?'

'Because I think of things.'

'What things can you have to think o' so mortal much?'

'You know, father.'

'You think I've been cruel to thee in saying that that penniless Dick o' thine shan't marry thee, I suppose?'

No answer.

'Well, you know, Fancy, I do it for the best, and he isn't good enough for thee. You know that well enough.' Here he again looked at her as she lay. 'Well, Fancy, I can't let my only chiel die; and if you can't live without en, you must ha' en, I suppose.'

'O, I don't want him like that; all against your will, and everything so disobedient!' sighed the invalid.

'No, no, 'tisn't against my will. My wish is, now I d'see how 'tis hurten thee to live without en, that he shall marry thee as soon as we've considered a little. That's my wish flat and plain, Fancy. There, never cry, my little maid! You ought to have cried afore; no need o' crying now 'tis all over. Well, howsoever, try to step over and see me and mother-law tomorrow, and ha' a bit of dinner wi' us.'

'And – Dick too?'

'Ay, Dick too, 'far's I know.'

'And *when* do you think you'll have considered, father, and he may marry me?' she coaxed.

'Well, there, say next Midsummer; that's not a day too long to wait.'

On leaving the school Geoffrey went to the tranter's. Old William opened the door.

'Is your grandson Dick in 'ithin, William?'

'No, not just now, Mr Day. Though he've been at home a good deal lately.'

'O, how's that?'

'What wi' one thing, and what wi' t'other, he's all in a mope, as might be said. Don't seem the feller he used to be. Ay, 'a will sit studding and thinking as if 'a were going to turn chapel-member, and then do nothing but traypse and wamble about. Used to be such a chatty boy, too, Dick did; and now 'a don't speak at all. But won't ye step inside? Reuben will be home soon, 'a b'lieve.'

'No, thank you, I can't stay now. Will ye just ask Dick if he'll do me the kindness to step over to Yalbury tomorrow with my da'ter Fancy, if she's well enough? I don't like her to come by herself, now she's not so terrible topping in health.'

'So I've heard. Ay, sure, I'll tell him without fail.'

V

After gaining her Point

THE visit to Geoffrey passed off as delightfully as a visit might have been expected to pass off when it was the first day of smooth experience in a hitherto obstructed love-course. And then came a series of several happy days of the same undisturbed serenity. Dick could court her when he chose; stay away when he chose, – which was never; walk with her by winding streams and waterfalls and autumn scenery till dews and twilight sent them home. And thus they drew near the day of the Harvest Thanksgiving, which was also the time chosen for opening the organ in Mellstock Church.

It chanced that Dick on that very day was called away from Mellstock. A young acquaintance had died of consumption at Charmley, a neighbouring village, on the previous Monday, and Dick in fulfilment of a long-standing promise was to assist in carrying him to the grave. When on Tuesday Dick went towards the school to acquaint Fancy with the fact it is difficult to say whether his own disappointment at being denied the sight of her triumphant *début* as organist, was greater than his vexation that his pet should be on this great occasion be deprived of the pleasure of his presence. However, the intelligence was communicated. She bore it as she best could, not without many expressions of regret and convictions that her performance would be nothing to her now.

Just before eleven o'clock on Sunday he set out upon his sad errand. The funeral was to be immediately after the morning service, and as there were four good miles to walk, driving being inconvenient, it became necessary to start comparatively early. Half an hour later would certainly have answered his purpose quite as well, yet at the last moment nothing would content his ardent mind but that he must go a mile out of his way in the direction of the school, in the hope of getting a glimpse of his Love as she started for church.

Striking therefore into the lane towards the school, instead of across the ewelease direct to Charmley, he arrived opposite her door as his goddess emerged.

If ever a woman look a divinity Fancy Day appeared one that morning as she floated down those school steps, in the form of a nebulous collection of colours inclining to blue. With an audacity unparalleled in the whole history of village-schoolmistresses at this date – partly owing, no doubt, to papa's respectable accumulation of cash, which rendered her profession not altogether one of necessity – she had actually donned a hat and feather and lowered her hitherto plainly looped-up hair, which now fell about her shoulders in a profusion of curls. Poor Dick was astonished: he had never seen her look so distractingly beautiful before save on Christmas-eve, when her hair was in the same luxuriant condition of freedom. But his first burst of delighted surprise was followed by less comfortable feelings as soon as his brain recovered its power to think.

Fancy had blushed; – was it with confusion? She had also involuntarily pressed back her curls. She had not expected him.

'Fancy, you didn't know me for a moment in my funeral clothes, did you?'

'Good-morning, Dick – no, really, I didn't know you for an instant in such a sad suit.'

He looked again at the gay tresses and hat. 'You've never dressed so charming before, dearest.'

'I like to hear you praise me in that way, Dick,' she said, smiling archly. 'It is meat and drink to a woman. Do I look nice really?'

'Fie! you know it. Did you remember, – I mean didn't you remember about my going away today?'

'Well, yes, I did, Dick; but, you know, I wanted to look well; – forgive me.'

'Yes, darling; yes, of course, – there's nothing to forgive. No, I was only thinking that when we talked on Tuesday and Wednesday and Thursday and Friday about my absence today, and I was so sorry for it, you said, Fancy, so were you sorry, and almost cried, and said it would be no pleasure to you to be the attraction of the church today since I could not be there.'

'My dear one, neither will it be so much pleasure to me . . . But I do take a little delight in my life, I suppose,' she pouted.

'Apart from mine?'

She looked at him with perplexed eyes. 'I know you are vexed with me, Dick, and it is because the first Sunday I have curls and a hat and feather since I have been here happens to be the very day you are away and won't be with me. Yes, say it is, for that is it! And you think that all this week I ought to have remembered you wouldn't be here today, and not have cared to be better dressed than usual. Yes, you do, Dick, and it is rather unkind!'

'No, no,' said Dick earnestly and simply, 'I didn't think so badly of you as that. I only thought that – if *you* had been going away, I shouldn't have tried new attractions for the eyes of other people. But then of course you and I are different, naturally.'

'Well, perhaps we are.'

'Whatever will the vicar say, Fancy?'

'I don't fear what he says in the least!' she answered proudly. 'But he won't say anything of the sort you think. No, no.'

'He can hardly have conscience to, indeed.'

'Now come, you say, Dick, that you quite forgive me, for I must go,' she said with sudden gaiety, and skipped backwards into the porch. 'Come here, sir; – say you forgive me, and then you shall kiss me; – you never have yet when I have worn curls, you know. Yes, just where you want to so much, – yes, you may!'

Dick followed her into the inner corner, where he was probably not slow in availing himself of the privilege offered.

'Now that's a treat for you, isn't it?' she continued. 'Good-bye, or I shall be late. Come and see me tomorrow: you'll be tired tonight.'

Thus they parted, and Fancy proceeded to the church. The organ stood on one side of the chancel, close to and under the immediate eye of the vicar when he was in the pulpit and also in full view of the congregation. Here she sat down, for the first time in such a conspicuous position, her seat having previously been in a remote spot in the aisle.

'Good heavens – disgraceful! Curls and a hat and feather!' said the daughters of the small gentry, who had either only curly hair without a hat and feather, or a hat and feather without curly hair. 'A bonnet for church always!' said sober matrons.

That Mr Maybold was conscious of her presence close beside him during his sermon; that he was not at all angry at her development of costume; that he admired her, she perceived. But she did not see that he loved her during that sermon-time as he had never loved a woman before; that her proximity was a strange delight to him; and that he gloried in her musical success that morning in a spirit quite beyond a mere cleric's glory at the inauguration of a new order of things.

The old choir, with humbled hearts, no longer took their seats in the gallery as heretofore (which was now given up to the school-children who were not singers, and a pupil-teacher), but were scattered about with their wives in different parts of the church. Having nothing to do with conducting the service for almost the first time in their lives they all felt awkward, out of place, abashed, and inconvenienced by their hands. The tranter had proposed that they should stay away today and go nutting, but grandfather William would not hear of such a thing for a moment. 'No,' he replied reproachfully, and quoted a verse: ' "Though this has come upon us let not our hearts be turned back, or our steps go out of the way." '

So they stood and watched the curls of hair trailing down the back of the successful rival, and the waving of her feather as she swayed her head. After a few timid notes and uncertain touches her playing became markedly correct, and towards the end full and free. But, whether from prejudice or unbiased judgement, the venerable body of musicians could not help thinking that the simpler notes they had been wont to bring forth were more in keeping with the simplicity of their old church than the crowded chords and interludes it was her pleasure to produce.

* VI *

Into Temptation

THE day was done, and Fancy was again in the school-house. About five o'clock it began to rain, and in rather a dull frame of mind she wandered into the schoolroom for want of something better to do. She was thinking – of her lover Dick Dewy? Not precisely. Of how weary she was of living alone; how unbearable it would be to return to Yalbury under the rule of her strange-tempered step-mother; that it was far better to be married to anybody than do that; that eight or nine long months had yet to be lived through ere the wedding could take place.

At the side of the room were high windows of Ham-hill stone, upon either sill of which she could sit by first mounting a desk and using it as a footstool. As the evening advanced here she perched herself, as was her custom on such wet and gloomy occasions, put on a light shawl and bonnet, opened the window, and looked out at the rain.

The window overlooked a field called the Grove, and it was the position from which she used to survey the crown of Dick's passing hat in the early days of their acquaintance and meetings. Not a living soul was now visible anywhere; the rain kept all people indoors who were not forced abroad by necessity, and necessity was less importunate on Sundays than during the week.

Sitting here and thinking again – of her lover, or of the sensation she had created at church that day? – well, it is unknown – thinking and thinking she saw a dark masculine figure arising into distinctness at the further end of the Grove – a man without an umbrella. Nearer and nearer he came, and she perceived that he was in deep mourning, and then that it was Dick. Yes, in the fondness and foolishness of his young heart, after walking four miles in a drizzling rain without overcoat or umbrella and in face of a remark from his love that he was not to come because he would be tired, he had made it his business to wander this mile out of his way again from sheer wish of spending ten minutes in her presence.

'O Dick, how wet you are!' she said, as he drew up under the window. 'Why, your coat shines as if it had been varnished, and your hat – my goodness, there's a streaming hat!'

'O, I don't mind, darling!' said Dick cheerfully. 'Wet never hurts me, though I am rather sorry for my best clothes. However, it couldn't be helped; we lent all the umbrellas to the women. I don't know when I shall get mine back.'

'And look, there's a nasty patch of something just on your shoulder.'

'Ah, that's japanning; it rubbed off the clamps of poor Jack's coffin when we lowered him from our shoulders upon the bier! I don't care about that, for 'twas the last deed I could do for him; and 'tis hard if you can't afford a coat for an old friend.'

Fancy put her hand to her mouth for half a minute. Underneath the palm of that little hand there existed for that half-minute a little yawn.

'Dick, I don't like you to stand there in the wet. And you mustn't sit down. Go home and change your things. Don't stay another minute.'

'One kiss after coming so far,' he pleaded.

'If I can reach, then.'

He looked rather disappointed at not being invited round to the door. She twisted from her seated position and bent herself downwards, but not even by standing on the plinth was it possible for Dick to get his lips into contact with hers as she held them. By great exertion she might have reached a little lower; but then she would have exposed her head to the rain.

'Never mind, Dick; kiss my hand,' she said, flinging it down to him. 'Now, good-bye.'

'Good-bye.'

He walked slowly away, turning and turning again to look at her till he was out of sight. During the retreat she said to herself, almost involuntarily, and still conscious of that morning's triumph –

'I like Dick, and I love him; but how plain and sorry a man looks in the rain, with no umbrella, and wet through!'

As he vanished she made as if to descend from her seat; but glancing in the other direction she saw another form coming along the same track. It was also that of a man. He, too, was in black from top to toe; but he carried an umbrella.

He drew nearer, and the direction of the rain caused him so to slant his umbrella that from her height above the ground his head was invisible, as she was also to him. He passed in due time directly beneath her, and in looking down upon the exterior of his umbrella her feminine eyes perceived it to be of superior silk – less common at that date than since – and of elegant make. He reached the entrance to the building, and Fancy suddenly lost sight of him. Instead of pursuing the roadway as Dick had done he had turned sharply round into her own porch.

She jumped to the floor, hastily flung off her shawl and bonnet, smoothed and patted her hair till the curls hung in passable condition, and listened. No knock. Nearly a minute passed, and still there was no knock. Then there arose a soft series of raps no louder than the tapping of a distant woodpecker, and barely distinct enough to reach her ears. She composed herself and flung open the door.

In the porch stood Mr Maybold.

There was a warm flush upon his face and a bright flash in his eyes which made him look handsomer than she had ever seen him before.

'Good-evening, Miss Day.'

'Good-evening, Mr Maybold,' she said, in a strange state of mind. She had noticed, beyond the ardent hue of his face, that his voice had a singular tremor in it, and that his hand shook like an aspen leaf when he laid his umbrella in the corner of the porch. Without another word being spoken by either he came into the schoolroom, shut the door, and moved close to her. Once inside the expression of his face was no more discernible by reason of the increasing dusk of evening.

'I want to speak to you,' he then said; 'seriously – on a perhaps unexpected subject, but one which is all the world to me – I don't know what it may be to you, Miss Day.'

No reply.

'Fancy, I have come to ask you if you will be my wife?'

As a person who has been idly amusing himself with rolling a snowball might start at finding he had set in motion an avalanche, so did Fancy start at these words from the young vicar. And in the dead silence which followed them the breathings of the man and of the woman could be distinctly and separately heard; and there was this difference between them – his respirations gradually grew quieter and less rapid after the enunciation; hers, from having been low and regular, increased in quickness and force till she almost panted.

'I cannot, I cannot, Mr Maybold – I cannot! Don't ask me!' she said.

'Don't answer in a hurry!' he entreated. 'And do listen to me. This is no sudden feeling on my part. I have loved you for more than six months! Perhaps my late interest in teaching the children here has not been so single-minded as it seemed. You will understand my motive – like me better, perhaps, for honestly telling you that I have struggled against my emotion continually, because I have thought that it was not well for me to love you! But I resolved to struggle no longer; I have examined the feeling; and the love I bear you is as genuine as that I could bear any woman! I see your great charm; I respect your natural talents, and the refinement they have brought into your nature – they are quite enough, and more than enough for me! They are equal to anything ever required of the mistress of a quiet parsonage-house – the place in which I shall pass my days, wherever it may be situated. O Fancy, I have watched you, criticized you even severely, brought my feelings to the light of judgement, and still have found them rational, and such as any man might have expected to be inspired with by a woman like you! So there is nothing hurried, secret, or untoward in my desire to do this. Fancy, will you marry me?'

No answer was returned.

'Don't refuse; don't,' he implored. 'It would be foolish of you – I mean cruel! Of course we would not live here, Fancy. I have had for a long time the offer of an exchange of livings with a friend in Yorkshire, but I have hitherto refused on account of my mother. There we would go. Your musical powers shall be still further developed; you shall have whatever pianoforte you like; you shall have anything, Fancy, anything to make you happy – pony-carriage, flowers, birds, pleasant society; yes, you have enough in you for any society, after a few months of travel with me! Will you, Fancy, marry me?'

Another pause ensued, varied only by the surging of the rain against the window-panes, and then Fancy spoke, in a faint and broken voice.

'Yes, I will,' she said.

'God bless you, my own!' He advanced quickly, and put his arm out to embrace her. She drew back hastily. 'No, no, not now!' she said in an agitated whisper. 'There are things; – but the temptation is, O, too strong, and I can't resist it; I can't tell you now, but I must tell you! Don't, please, don't come near me now! I want to think. I can scarcely get myself used to the idea of what I have promised yet.' The next minute she turned to a desk, buried her face in her hands, and burst into a hysterical fit of weeping. 'O, leave me to myself!' she sobbed; 'leave me! O, leave me!'

'Don't be distressed; don't, dearest!' It was with visible difficulty that he restrained himself from approaching her. 'You shall tell me at your leisure what it is that grieves you so; I am happy – beyond all measure happy! – at having your simple promise.'

'And do go and leave me now!'

'But I must not, in justice to you, leave for a minute, until you are yourself again.'

'There then,' she said, controlling her emotion, and standing up; 'I am not disturbed now.'

He reluctantly moved towards the door. 'Good-bye!' he murmured tenderly. 'I'll come tomorrow about this time.'

* VII *

Second Thoughts

THE next morning the vicar rose early. The first thing he did was to write a long and careful letter to his friend in Yorkshire. Then, eating a little breakfast, he crossed the meadows in the direction of Casterbridge, bearing his letter in his pocket, that he might post it at the town office, and obviate the loss of one day in its transmission that would have resulted had he left it for the foot-post through the village.

It was a foggy morning, and the trees shed in noisy water-drops the moisture they had collected from the thick air, an acorn occasionally falling from its cup to the ground in company with the drippings. In the meads sheets of spiders'-web, almost opaque with wet, hung in folds over the fences, and the falling leaves appeared in every variety of brown, green, and yellow hue.

A low and merry whistling was heard on the highway he was approaching, then the light footsteps of a man going in the same direction as himself. On reaching the junction of his path with the road the vicar beheld Dick Dewy's open and cheerful face. Dick lifted his hat, and the vicar came out into the highway that Dick was pursuing.

'Good-morning, Dewy. How well you are looking!' said Mr Maybold.

'Yes, sir, I am well – quite well! I am going to Casterbridge now, to get Smart's collar; we left it there Saturday to be repaired.'

'I am going to Casterbridge, so we'll walk together,' the vicar said. Dick gave a hop with one foot to put himself in step with Mr Maybold, who proceeded: 'I fancy I didn't see you at church yesterday, Dewy. Or were you behind the pier?'

'No; I went to Charmley. Poor John Dunford chose me to be one of his bearers a long time before he died, and yesterday was the funeral. Of course I couldn't refuse, though I should have liked particularly to have been at home as 'twas the day of the new music.'

'Yes, you should have been. The musical portion of the service was successful – very successful indeed; and what is more to the purpose no ill-feeling whatever was evinced by any of the members of the old choir. They joined in the singing with the greatest good-will.'

' 'Twas natural enough that I should want to be there, I suppose,' said Dick, smiling a private smile; 'considering who the organ-player was.'

At this the vicar reddened a little, and said, 'Yes, yes,' though not at all comprehending Dick's true meaning, who, as he received no further reply, continued hesitatingly, and with another smile denoting his pride as a lover –

'I suppose you know what I mean, sir? You've heard about me and – Miss Day?'

The red in Maybold's countenance went away: he turned and looked Dick in the face.

'No,' he said constrainedly, 'I've heard nothing whatever about you and Miss Day.'

'Why, she's my sweetheart, and we are going to be married next Midsummer. We are keeping it rather close just at present, because 'tis a good many months to wait; but it is her father's wish that we don't marry before, and of course we must submit. But the time 'ill soon slip along.'

'Yes, the time will soon slip along – Time glides away every day – yes.'

Maybold said these words, but he had no idea of what they were. He was conscious of a cold and sickly thrill throughout him; and all he reasoned was this that the young creature whose graces had intoxicated him into making the most imprudent resolution of his life was less an angel than a woman.

'You see, sir,' continued the ingenuous Dick, ' 'twill be better in one sense. I shall by that time be the regular manager of a branch o' father's business which we think of starting elsewhere. It has very much increased lately, and we expect next year to keep a' extra couple of horses. We've already our eye on one – brown as a berry, neck like a rainbow, fifteen hands, and not a grey hair in her – offered us at twenty-five want a crown. And to kip pace with the times I have had some cards prented, and I beg leave to hand you one, sir.'

'Certainly,' said the vicar, mechanically taking the card that Dick offered him.

'I turn in here by Grey's Bridge,' said Dick. 'I suppose you go straight on and up town?'

'Yes.'

'Good-morning, sir.'

'Good-morning, Dewy.'

Maybold stood still upon the bridge, holding the card as it had been put into his hand, and Dick's footsteps died away towards Durnover Mill. The vicar's first voluntary action was to read the card:

DEWY AND SON,

TRANTERS AND HAULIERS

MELLSTOCK.

N.B. – *Furniture, Coals, Potatoes, Live and Dead Stock,*
removed to any distance on the shortest notice.

Mr Maybold leant over the parapet of the bridge and looked into the river. He saw – without heeding – how the water came rapidly from beneath the arches, glided down a little steep, then spread itself over a pool in which dace, trout, and minnows sported at ease among the long green locks of weed that lay heaving and sinking with their roots towards the current. At the end of ten minutes spent leaning thus he drew from his pocket the letter to his friend, tore it deliberately into such minute fragments that scarcely two syllables remained in juxtaposition, and sent the whole handful of shreds fluttering into the water. Here he watched them eddy, dart, and turn, as they were carried downwards towards the ocean and gradually disappeared from his view. Finally he moved off, and pursued his way at a rapid pace back again to Mellstock Vicarage.

Nerving himself by a long and intense effort he sat down in his study and wrote as follows:

DEAR MISS DAY, – The meaning of your words, 'the temptation is too strong', of your sadness and your tears, has been brought home to me by an accident. I know today what I did not know yesterday – that you are not a free woman.

Why did you not tell me – why didn't you? Did you suppose I knew? No. Had I known, my conduct in coming to you as I did would have been reprehensible.

But I don't chide you! Perhaps no blame attaches to you – I can't tell. Fancy, though my opinion of you is assailed and disturbed in a way which cannot be expressed, I love you still, and my word to you holds good yet. But will you, in justice to an honest man who relies upon your word to him, consider whether, under the circumstances, you can honourably forsake him? – yours ever sincerely.

ARTHUR MAYBOLD.

He rang the bell. 'Tell Charles to take these copybooks and this note to the school at once.'

The maid took the parcel and the letter, and in a few minutes a boy was seen to leave the vicarage gate with the one under his arm and the other in his hand. The vicar sat with his hand to his brow, watching the lad as he descended Church Lane and entered the waterside path which intervened between that spot and the school.

Here he was met by another boy, and after a free salutation and pugilistic frisk had passed between the two the second boy came on his way to the vicarage, and the other vanished out of sight.

The boy came to the door, and a note for Mr Maybold was brought in.

He knew the writing. Opening the envelope with an unsteady hand he read the subjoined words:

DEAR MR MAYBOLD, – I have been thinking seriously and sadly through the whole of the night of the question you put to me last evening; and of my answer. That answer, as an honest woman, I had no right to give.

It is my nature – perhaps all women's – to love refinement of mind and manners; but even more than this, to be ever fascinated with the idea of surroundings more elegant and pleasing than those which have been customary. And you praised me, and praise is life to me. It was alone my sensations at these things which prompted my reply. Ambition and vanity they would be called; perhaps they are so.

After this explanation I hope you will generously allow me to withdraw the answer I too hastily gave.

And one more request. To keep the meeting of last night, and all that passed between us there, for ever a secret. Were it to become known it would utterly blight the happiness of a trusting and generous man, whom I love still, and shall love always. – yours sincerely,

FANCY DAY

The last written communication that ever passed from the vicar to Fancy was a note containing these words only:

Tell him everything; it is best. He will forgive you.

PART THE FIFTH

CONCLUSION

'The Knot there's no Untying'

THE last day of the story is dated just subsequent to that point in the development of the seasons when country people go to bed among nearly naked trees, are lulled to sleep by a fall of rain, and awake next morning among green ones; when the landscape appears embarrassed with the sudden weight and brilliancy of its leaves; when the night-jar comes and strikes up for the summer his tune of one note; when the apple-trees have bloomed, and the roads and orchard-grass become spotted with fallen petals; when the faces of the delicate flowers are darkened and their heads weighed down by the throng of honey-bees, which increase their humming till humming is too mild a term for the all-pervading sound; and when cuckoos, blackbirds, and sparrows, that have hitherto been merry and respectful neighbours, become noisy and persistent intimates.

The exterior of Geoffrey Day's house in Yalbury Wood appeared exactly as was usual at that season, but a frantic barking of the dogs at the back told of unwonted movements somewhere within. Inside the door the eyes beheld a gathering which was a rarity indeed for the dwelling of the solitary wood-steward and keeper.

About the room were sitting and standing, in various gnarled attitudes, our old acquaintance grandfathers James and William, the tranter, Mr Penny, two or three children, including Jimmy and Charley, besides three or four country ladies and gentlemen from a greater distance who do not require any distinction by name. Geoffrey was seen and heard stamping about the outhouse and among the bushes of the garden, attending to details of daily routine before the proper time arrived for their performance, in order that they might be off his hands for the day. He appeared with his shirt-sleeves rolled up; his best new nether garments, in which he had arrayed himself that morning, being temporarily disguised under a week-day apron whilst these proceedings were in operation. He occasionally glanced at the hives in passing to see if his wife's bees were swarming, ultimately rolling down his shirt-sleeves and going indoors, talking to tranter Dewy whilst buttoning the wristbands, to save time; next going upstairs for his best waistcoat, and coming down again to make another remark whilst buttoning that, during the time looking fixedly in the tranter's face as if he were a looking-glass.

The furniture had undergone attenuation to an alarming extent, every duplicate piece having been removed, including the clock by Thomas Wood; Ezekiel Saunders being at last left sole referee in matters of time.

Fancy was stationary upstairs, receiving her layers of clothes and adornments and answering by short fragments of laughter which had more fidgetiness than mirth in them, remarks that were made from time to time by Mrs Dewy and Mrs Penny, who were assisting her at the toilet, Mrs Day having pleaded a queerness in her head as a reason for shutting herself up in an inner bedroom for the whole morning. Mrs Penny appeared with nine corkscrew curls on each side of her temples, and a back comb stuck upon her crown like a castle on a steep.

The conversation just now going on was concerning the banns, the last publication of which had been on the Sunday previous.

'And how did they sound?' Fancy subtly inquired.

'Very beautiful indeed,' said Mrs Penny. 'I never heard any sound better.'

'But *how?*'

'O, *so* natural and elegant, didn't they, Reuben!' she cried through the chinks of the unceiled floor to the tranter downstairs.

'What's that?' said the tranter, looking up inquiringly at the floor above him for an answer.

'Didn't Dick and Fancy sound well when they were called home in church last Sunday?' came downwards again in Mrs Penny's voice.

'Ay, that they did, my sonnies! – especially the first time. There was a terrible whispering piece of work in the congregation, wasn't there, neighbour Penny?' said the tranter, taking up the thread of conversation on his own account and, in order to be heard in the room above, speaking very loud to Mr Penny, who sat at the distance of three feet from him, or rather less.

'I never can mind seeing such a whispering as there was,' said Mr Penny, also loudly, to the room above. 'And such sorrowful envy on the maidens' faces; really, I never did see such envy as there was!'

Fancy's lineaments varied in innumerable little flushes and her heart palpitated innumerable little tremors of pleasure. 'But perhaps,' she said, with assumed indifference, 'it was only because no religion was going on just then?'

'O, no; nothing to do with that. 'Twas because of your high standing in the parish. It was just as if they had one and all caught Dick kissing and coling ye to death, wasn't,it, Mrs Dewy?'

'Ay; that 'twas.'

'How people will talk about one's doings!' Fancy exclaimed.

'Well, if you make songs about yourself, my dear, you can't blame other people for singing 'em.'

'Mercy me! how shall I go through it?' said the young lady again, but merely to those in the bedroom, with a breathing of a kind between a sigh and a pant, round shining eyes, and warm face.

'O, you'll get through it well enough, child,' said Mrs Dewy placidly. 'The edge of the performance is took off at the calling home; and when once you get up to the chancel end o' the church you feel as saucy as you please. I'm sure I felt as brave as a sodger all through the deed – though of course I dropped my face and looked modest, as was becoming to a maid. Mind you do that, Fancy.'

'And I walked into the church as quiet as a lamb, I'm sure,' subjoined Mrs Penny. 'There, you see Penny is such a little small man. But certainly I was flurried in the inside o' me. Well, thinks I, 'tis to be, and here goes! And do you do the same: say, " 'Tis to be, and here goes!" '

'Is there such wonderful virtue in " 'Tis to be, and here goes!"?' inquired Fancy.

'Wonderful! 'Twill carry a body through it all from wedding to churching, if you only let it out with spirit enough.'

'Very well, then,' said Fancy, blushing. ' 'Tis to be, and here goes!'

'That's a girl for a husband!' said Mrs Dewy.

'I do hope he'll come in time!' continued the bride-elect, inventing a new cause of affright now that the other was demolished.

' 'Twould be a thousand pities if he didn't come, now you be so brave,' said Mrs Penny.

Grandfather James, having overheard some of these remarks, said downstairs with mischievous loudness –

'I've known some would-be weddings when the men didn't come.'

'They've happened not to come, before now, certainly,' said Mr Penny, cleaning one of the glasses of his spectacles.

'O, do hear what they are saying downstairs,' whispered Fancy, 'Hush, hush!'

She listened.

'They have, haven't they, Geoffrey?' continued grim grandfather James, as Geoffrey entered.

'Have what?' said Geoffrey.

'The men have been known not to come.'

'That they have,' said the keeper.

'Ay; I've knowed times when the wedding had to be put off through his not appearing, being tired of the woman. And another case I knowed was when the man was catched in a man-trap crossing Oaker's Wood, and the three months had run out before he got well, and the banns had to be published over again.'

'How horrible!' said Fancy.

'They only say it on purpose to tease 'ee, my dear,' said Mrs Dewy.

' 'Tis quite sad to think what wretched shifts poor maids have been put to,' came again from downstairs. 'Ye should hear Clerk Wilkins, my brother-in-law, tell his experiences in marrying couples these last thirty year: sometimes one thing, sometimes another – 'tis quite heart-rending – enough to make your hair stand on end.'

'Those things don't happen very often, I know,' said Fancy with smouldering uneasiness.

'Well, really 'tis time Dick was here,' said the tranter.

'Don't keep on at me so, grandfather James and Mr Dewy, and all you down there!' Fancy broke out, unable to endure any longer. 'I am sure I shall die, or do something, if you do!'

'Never you hearken to these old chaps, Miss Day!' cried Nat Callcome the best man, who had just entered, and threw his voice upward through the chinks of the floor as the others had done. ' 'Tis all right; Dick's coming on like a wild feller; he'll be here in a minute. The hive o' bees his mother gie'd en for his new garden swarmed jist as he was starting, and he said, "I can't afford to lose a stock o' bees; no, that I can't, though I fain would; and Fancy wouldn't wish it on any account." So he jist stopped to ting to 'em and shake 'em.'

'A genuine wise man,' said Geoffrey.

'To be sure what a day's work we had yesterday!' Mr Callcome continued, lowering his voice as if it were not necessary any longer to include those in the room above among his audience, and selecting a remote corner of his best clean handkerchief for wiping his face. 'To be sure!'

'Things so heavy, I suppose,' said Geoffrey, as if reading through the chimney-window from the far end of the vista.

'Ay,' said Nat, looking round the room at points from which furniture had been removed. 'And so awkward to carry, too. 'Twas ath'art and across Dick's garden; in and out Dick's door; up and down Dick's stairs; round and round Dick's chammers till legs were worn to stumps: and Dick is so particular, too. And the stores of victuals and drink that lad has laid in: why, 'tis enough for Noah's ark! I'm sure I never wish to see a choicer half-dozen of hams than he's got there in his chimley; and the cider I tasted was a very pretty drop, indeed; – none could desire a prettier cider.'

'They be for the love and the stalled ox both. Ah, the greedy martels!' said grandfather James.

'Well, may-be they be. "Surely," says I, "that couple between 'em have heaped up so much furniture and victuals that anybody would think they were going to take hold the big end of married life first, and begin wi' a grown-up family." Ah, what a bath of heat we two chaps were in, to be sure, a-getting that furniture in order!'

'I do wish the room below was ceiled,' said Fancy, as the dressing went on; 'we can hear all they say and do down there.'

'Hark! Who's that?' exclaimed a small pupil-teacher, who also assisted this morning to her great delight. She ran half-way down the stairs and peeped round the banister. 'O, you should, you should, you should!' she exclaimed, scrambling up to the room again.

'What?' said Fancy.

'See the bridesmaids! They've just a-come! 'Tis wonderful, really! 'tis wonderful how muslin can be brought to it. There, they don't look a bit like themselves, but like some very rich sisters o' theirs that nobody knew they had!'

'Make them come up to me, make them come up!' cried Fancy ecstatically; and the four damsels appointed, namely, Miss Susan Dewy,

Miss Bessie Dewy, Miss Vashti Sniff, and Miss Mercy Onmey surged upstairs and floated along the passage.

'I wish Dick would come!' was again the burden of Fancy.

The same instant a small twig and flower from the creeper outside the door flew in at the open window, and a masculine voice said, 'Ready, Fancy dearest?'

'There he is, he is!' cried Fancy, tittering spasmodically and breathing as it were for the first time that morning.

The bridesmaids crowded to the window and turned their heads in the direction pointed out, at which motion eight ear-rings all swung as one: – not looking at Dick because they particularly wanted to see him, but with an important sense of their duty as obedient minister of the will of that apotheosised being – the Bride.

'He looks very taking!' said Miss Vashti Sniff, a young lady who blushed cream-colour and wore yellow bonnet-ribbons.

Dick was advancing to the door in a painfully new coat of shining cloth, primrose-coloured waistcoat, hat of the same painful style of newness, and with an extra quantity of whiskers shaved off his face and hair cut to an unwonted shortness in honour of the occasion.

'Now I'll run down,' said Fancy, looking at herself over her shoulder in the glass, and flitting off.

'O Dick!' she exclaimed, 'I am so glad you are come! I knew you would, of course, but I thought, O, if you shouldn't!'

'Not come, Fancy! Het or wet, blow or snow, here come I today! Why, what's possessing your little soul? You never used to mind such things a bit.'

'Ah, Mr Dick, I hadn't hoisted my colours and committed myself then!' said Fancy.

' 'Tis a pity I can't marry the whole five of ye!' said Dick, surveying them all round.

'Heh-heh-heh!' laughed the four bridesmaids, and Fancy privately touched Dick and smoothed him down behind his shoulder as if to assure herself that he was there in flesh and blood as her own property.

'Well, whoever would have thought such a thing?' said Dick, taking off his hat, sinking into a chair, and turning to the elder members of the company.

The latter arranged their eyes and lips to signify that in their opinion nobody could have thought such a thing, whatever it was.

'That my bees should ha' swarmed just then, of all times and seasons!' continued Dick, throwing a comprehensive glance like a net over the whole auditory. 'And 'tis a fine swarm, too: I haven't seen such a fine swarm for these ten years.'

'A' excellent sign,' said Mrs Penny, from the depths of experience. 'A' excellent sign.'

'I am glad everything seems so right,' said Fancy with a breath of relief.

'And so am I,' said the four bridesmaids with much sympathy.

'Well, bees can't be put off,' observed the inharmonious grandfather James. 'Marrying a woman is a thing you can do at any moment; but a swarm o'bees won't come for the asking.'

Dick fanned himself with his hat. 'I can't think,' he said thoughtfully, 'whatever 'twas I did to offend Mr Maybold – a man I like so much, too. He rather took to me when he came first, and used to say he should like to see me married, and that he'd marry me, whether the young woman I chose lived in his parish or no. I just hinted to him of it when I put in the banns, but he didn't seem to take kindly to the notion now, and so I said no more. I wonder how it was.'

'I wonder!' said Fancy, looking into vacancy with those beautiful eyes of hers – too refined and too beautiful for a tranter's wife; but, perhaps, not too good.

'Altered his mind, as folks will, I suppose,' said the tranter. 'Well, my sonnies, there'll be a good strong party looking at us today as we go along.'

'And the body of the church,' said Geoffrey, 'will be lined with females, and a row of young fellers' heads, as far down as the eyes, will be noticed just above the sills of the chancel-winders.'

'Ay, you've been through it twice,' said Reuben, 'and well mid know.'

'I can put up with it for once,' said Dick, 'or twice either, or a dozen times.'

'O Dick!' said Fancy reproachfully.

'Why, dear, that's nothing – only just a bit of a flourish. You be as nervous as a cat today.'

'And then, of course, when 'tis all over,' continued the tranter, 'we shall march two and two round the parish.'

'Yes, sure,' said Mr Penny: 'two and two: every man hitched up to his woman, 'a b'lieve.'

'I never can make a show of myself in that way!' said Fancy, looking at Dick to ascertain if he could.

'I'm agreed to anything you and the company like, my dear!' said Mr Richard Dewy heartily.

'Why, we did when we were married, didn't we, Ann?' said the tranter; 'and so do everybody, my sonnies.'

'And so did we,' said Fancy's father.

'And so did Penny and I,' said Mrs Penny: 'I wore my best Bath clogs, I remember, and Penny was cross because it made me look so tall.'

'And so did father and mother,' said Miss Mercy Onmey.

'And I mean to, come next Christmas!' said Nat the groomsman vigorously, and looking towards the person of Miss Vashti Sniff.

'Respectable people don't nowadays,' said Fancy. 'Still, since poor mother did, I will.'

'Ay,' resumed the tranter, ' 'twas on a White Tuesday when I committed it. Mellstock Club walked the same day, and we new-married folk went a-gaying round the parish behind 'em. Everybody used to wear something white at Whitsuntide in them days. My sonnies, I've got the very white trousers that I wore, at home in box now. Ha'n't I, Ann?'

'You had till I cut 'em up for Jimmy,' said Mrs Dewy.

'And we ought, by rights, after doing this parish, to go round Higher and Lower Mellstock, and call at Viney's, and so work our way hither again across He'th,' said Mr Penny, recovering scent of the matter in hand. 'Dairyman Viney is a very respectable man, and so is Farmer Kex, and we ought to show ourselves to them.'

'True,' said the tranter, 'we ought to go round Mellstock to do the thing well. We shall form a very striking object walking along in rotation, good-now, neighbours?'

'That we shall: a proper pretty sight for the nation,' said Mrs Penny.

'Hullo!' said the tranter, suddenly catching sight of a singular human figure standing in the doorway, and wearing a long smock-frock of pillow-case cut and of snowy whiteness. 'Why, Leaf! whatever dost thou do here?'

'I've come to know if so be I can come to the wedding – hee-hee!' said Leaf in a voice of timidity.

'Now, Leaf,' said the tranter reproachfully, 'you know we don't want 'ee here today: we've got no room for 'ee, Leaf.'

'Thomas Leaf, Thomas Leaf, fie upon 'ee for prying!' said old William.

'I know I've got no head, but I thought, if I washed and put on a clane shirt and smock-frock, I might just call,' said Leaf, turning away disappointed and trembling.

'Poor feller!' said the tranter, turning to Geoffrey. 'Suppose we must let en come? His looks are rather against en, and he is terrible silly; but 'a have never been in jail, and 'a won't do no harm.'

Leaf looked with gratitude at the tranter for these praises, and then anxiously at Geoffrey, to see what effect they would have in helping his cause.

'Ay, let en come,' said Geoffrey decisively. 'Leaf, th'rt welcome, 'st know'; and Leaf accordingly remained.

They were now all ready for leaving the house, and began to form a procession in the following order: Fancy and her father, Dick and Susan Dewy, Nat Callcome and Vashti Sniff, Ted Waywood and Mercy Onmey, and Jimmy and Bessie Dewy. These formed the executive and all appeared in strict wedding attire. Then came the tranter and Mrs Dewy, and last of all Mr and Mrs Penny; – the tranter conspicuous by his enormous gloves, size eleven and threequarter, which appeared at a distance like boxing gloves bleached and sat rather awkwardly upon his brown hands; this hall-mark of respectability having been set upon himself today (by Fancy's special request) for the first time in his life.

'The proper way is for the bridemaids to walk together,' suggested Fancy.

'What? 'Twas always young man and young woman, arm in crook, in my time!' said Geoffrey, astounded.

'And in mine!' said the tranter.

'And in ours!' said Mr and Mrs Penny.

'Never heard o' such a thing as woman and woman!' said old William; who, with grandfather James and Mrs Day, was to stay at home.

'Whichever way you and the company like, my dear!' said Dick, who, being on the point of securing his right to Fancy, seemed willing to renounce all other rights in the world with the greatest pleasure. The decision was left to Fancy.

'Well, I think I'd rather have it the way mother had it,' she said, and the couples moved along under the trees, every man to his maid.

'Ah!' said grandfather James to grandfather William as they retired, 'I wonder which she thinks most about, Dick or her wedding raiment!'

'Well, 'tis their nature,' said grandfather William. 'Remember the words of the prophet Jeremiah: "Can a maid forget her ornaments, or a bride her attire?" '

Now among dark perpendicular firs, like the shafted columns of a cathedral; now through a hazel copse, matted with primroses and wild hyacinths; now under broad beeches in bright young leaves they threaded their way into the high road over Yalbury Hill, which dipped at that point directly into the village of Geoffrey Day's parish; and in the space of a quarter of an hour Fancy found herself to be Mrs Richard Dewy, though, much to her surprise, feeling no other than Fancy Day still.

On the circuitous return walk through the lanes and fields, amid much chattering and laughter, especially when they came to stiles, Dick discerned a brown spot far up a turnip field.

'Why, 'tis Enoch!' he said to Fancy. 'I thought I missed him at the house this morning. How is it he's left you?'

'He drank too much cider, and it got into his head, and they put him in Weatherbury stocks for it. Father was obliged to get somebody else for a day or two, and Enoch hasn't had anything to do with the woods since.'

'We might ask him to call down tonight. Stocks are nothing for once, considering 'tis our wedding day.' The bridal party was ordered to halt.

'Eno-o-o-o-ch!' cried Dick at the top of his voice.

'Y-a-a-a-a-as!' said Enoch from the distance.

'D'ye know who I be-e-e-e-e-e?'

'No-o-o-o-o-o-o!'

'Dick Dew-w-w-w-wy!'

'O-h-h-h-h-h!'

'Just a-ma-a-a-a-a-arried!'

'O-h-h-h-h-h!'

'This is my wife, Fa-a-a-a-a-a-ancy!' (holding her up to Enoch's view as if she had been a nosegay).

'O-h-h-h-h-h!'

'Will ye come across to the party to-ni-i-i-i-i-ight!'

'Ca-a-a-a-a-an't!'

'Why n-o-o-o-o-ot?'

'Don't work for the family no-o-o-o-ow!'

'Not nice of Master Enoch,' said Dick as they resumed their walk.

'You mustn't blame en,' said Geoffrey; 'the man's not hisself now; he's in his morning frame of mind. When he's had a gallon o' cider or ale, or a pint or two of mead, the man's well enough, and his manners be as good as anybody's in the kingdom.'

* II *

Under the Greenwood Tree

THE point in Yalbury Wood which abutted on the end of Geoffrey Day's premises was closed with an ancient tree, horizontally of enormous extent, though having no great pretensions to height. Many hundreds of birds had been born amidst the boughs of this single tree; tribes of rabbits and hares had nibbled at its bark from year to year; quaint tufts of fungi had sprung from the cavities of its forks; and countless families of moles and earthworms had crept about its roots. Beneath and beyond its shade spread a carefully-tended grass-plot, its purpose being to supply a healthy exercise-ground for young chickens and pheasants; the hens, their mothers, being enclosed in coops placed upon the same green flooring.

All these encumbrances were now removed, and as the afternoon advanced the guests gathered on the spot, where music, dancing, and the singing of songs went forward with great spirit throughout the evening. The propriety of every one was intense, by reason of the influence of Fancy, who, as an additional precaution in this direction had strictly charged her father and the tranter to carefully avoid saying 'thee' and 'thou' in their conversation, on the plea that those ancient words sounded very humiliating to persons of newer taste; also that they were never to be seen drawing the back of the hand across the mouth after drinking – a local English custom of extraordinary antiquity, but stated by Fancy to be decidedly dying out among the better classes of society.

In addition to the local musicians present a man who had a thorough knowledge of the tambourine was invited from the village of Tantrum Clangley, – a place long celebrated for the skill of its inhabitants as performers on instruments of percussion. These important members of the assembly were relegated to a height of two or three feet from the ground, upon a temporary erection of planks supported by barrels. Whilst the dancing progressed the older persons sat in a group under the trunk of the tree, – the space being allotted to them somewhat grudgingly by the young ones, who were greedy of pirouetting room, – and fortified by a table against the heels of the dancers. Here the gaffers and gammers whose dancing days were over told stories of great impressiveness, and at intervals surveyed the advancing and retiring couples from the same retreat, as people on shore might be supposed to survey a naval engagement in the bay beyond; returning again to their tales when the pause was over. Those of the whirling throng who, during the rests between each figure, turned their eyes in the direction of these seated ones, were only to discover, on account of the music and bustle, that a very striking circumstance was in course of narration – denoted by an emphatic sweep of the hand, snapping of the fingers, close of the lips, and a fixed look into the centre of the listener's eye for the space of a quarter of a minute, which raised in that listener such a reciprocating working of face as to sometimes make the distant dancers half wish to know what such an interesting tale could refer to.

Fancy caused her looks to wear as much matronly expression as was obtainable out of six hours' experience as a wife, in order that the contrast between her own state of life and that of the unmarried young women present might be duly impressed upon the company: occasionally stealing glances of admiration at her left hand, but this quite privately; for her ostensible bearing concerning the matter was intended to show that, though she undoubtedly occupied the most wondrous position in the eyes of the world that had ever been attained, she was almost unconscious of the circumstances, and that the somewhat prominent position in which that wonderfully-emblazoned left hand was continually found to be placed when handing cups and saucers, knives, forks, and glasses, was quite the result of accident. As to wishing to excite envy in the bosoms of her maiden companions by the exhibition of the shining ring, every one was to know it was quite foreign to the dignity of such an experienced married woman. Dick's imagination in the meantime was far less capable of drawing so much wontedness from his new condition. He had been for two or three hours trying to feel himself merely a newly-married man, but had been able to get no further in the attempt than to realize that he was Dick Dewy, the tranter's son, at a party given by Lord Wessex's head man-in-charge, on the outlying Yalbury estate, dancing and chatting with Fancy Day.

Five country dances, including 'Haste to the Wedding', two reels, and three fragments of hornpipes, brought them to the time for supper which, on account of the dampness of the grass from the immaturity of the summer season, was spread indoors. At the conclusion of the meal Dick went out to put the horse in; and Fancy, with the elder half of the four bridesmaids, retired upstairs to dress for the journey to Dick's new cottage near Mellstock.

'How long will you be putting on your bonnet, Fancy?' Dick inquired at the foot of the staircase. Being now a man of business and married he was strong on the importance of time, and doubled the emphasis of his words in conversing, and added vigour to his nods.

'Only a minute.'

'How long is that?'

'Well, dear, five.'

'Ah, sonnies!' said the tranter, as Dick retired, ' 'tis a talent of the female race that low numbers should stand for high, more especially in matters of waiting, matters of age, and matters of money.'

'True, true, upon my body,' said Geoffrey.

'Ye spak with feeling, Geoffrey, seemingly.'

'Anybody that d'know my experience might guess that.'

'What's she doing now, Geoffrey?'

'Claning out all the upstairs drawers and cupboards, and dusting the second-best chainey – a thing that's only done once a year. "If there's work to be done I must do it," says she, "wedding or no." '

' 'Tis my belief she's a very good woman at bottom.'

'She's terrible deep, then.'

Mrs Penny turned round. 'Well, 'tis humps and hollers with the best of us; but still and for all that, Dick and Fancy stand as fair a chance of having a bit of sunsheen as any married pair in the land.'

'Ay, there's no gainsaying it.'

Mrs Dewy came up, talking to one person and looking at another. 'Happy, yes,' she said. ' 'Tis always so when a couple is so exactly in tune with one another as Dick and she.'

'When they be'n't too poor to have time to sing,' said grandfather James.

'I tell ye, neighbours, when the pinch comes,' said the tranter: 'when the oldest daughter's boots be only a size less than her mother's, and the rest o' the flock close behind her. A sharp time for a man that, my sonnies; a very sharp time! Chanticleer's comb is a-cut then, 'a believe.'

'That's about the form o't,' said Mr Penny. 'That'll put the stuns upon a man, when you must measure mother and daughters' lasts to tell 'em apart.'

'You've no cause to complain, Reuben, of such a close-coming flock,' said Mrs Dewy; 'for ours was a straggling lot enough, God knows!'

'I d'know it, I d'know it,' said the tranter. 'You be a well-enough woman, Ann.'

Mrs Dewy put her mouth in the form of a smile and put it back again without smiling.

'And if they come together, they go together,' said Mrs Penny, whose family had been the reverse of the tranter's; 'and a little money will make either fate tolerable. And money can be made by our young couple, I know.'

'Yes, that it can!' said the impulsive voice of Leaf, who had hitherto humbly admired the proceedings from a corner. 'It can be done – all that's wanted is a few pounds to begin with. That's all! I know a story about it!'

'Let's hear thy story, Leaf,' said the tranter. 'I never knew you were clever enough to tell a story. Silence, all of ye! Mr Leaf will tell a story.'

'Tell your story, Thomas Leaf,' said grandfather William in the tone of a schoolmaster.

'Once,' said the delighted Leaf, in an uncertain voice, 'there was a man who lived in a house! Well, this man went thinking and thinking night and day. At last, he said to himself, as I might, "If I had only ten pound, I'd make a fortune." At last by hook or by crook, behold he got the ten pounds!'

'Only think of that!' said Nat Callcome satirically.

'Silence!' said the tranter.

'Well, now comes the interesting part of the story! In a little time he had made that ten pounds twenty. Then a little time after that he doubled it, and made it forty. Well, he went on, and a good while after that he made it eighty, and on to a hundred. Well, by-and-by he made it two hundred! Well, you'd never believe it, but – he went on and made it four hundred! He went on, and what did he do? Why, he made it eight hundred! Yes, he did,' continued Leaf in the highest pitch of excitement, bringing down his fist upon his knee with such force that he quivered with pain; 'yes, and he went on and made it A THOUSAND!'

'Hear, hear!' said the tranter. 'Better than the history of England, my sonnies!'

'Thank you for your story, Thomas Leaf,' said grandfather William; and then Leaf gradually sank into nothingness again.

Amid a medley of laughter, old shoes, and elderwine, Dick and his bride took their departure side by side in the excellent new spring-cart which the young tranter now possessed. The moon was just over the full, rendering any light from the lamps or their own beauties quite unnecessary to the pair. They drove slowly along Yalbury Bottom, where the road passed between two copses. Dick was talking to his companion.

'Fancy,' he said, 'why we are so happy is because there is such full confidence between us. Ever since that time you confessed to that little flirtation with Shiner by the river (which was really no flirtation at all), I have thought how artless and good you must be to tell me o' such a trifling thing, and to be so frightened about it as you were. It has won me to tell you my every deed and word since then. We'll have no secrets from each other, darling, will we ever? – no secret at all.'

'None from today,' said Fancy. 'Hark! what's that?'

From a neighbouring thicket was suddenly heard to issue in a loud, musical, and liquid voice –

'Tippiwit! swe-e-et! ki-ki-ki! Come hither, come hither, come hither!'

'O, 'tis the nightingale,' murmured she, and thought of a secret she would never tell.

FAR FROM
THE
MADDING CROWD

CONTENTS

AUTHOR'S PREFACE

IN reprinting this story for a new edition I am reminded that it was in the chapters of 'Far from the Madding Crowd', as they appeared month by month in a popular magazine, that I first ventured to adopt the word 'Wessex' from the pages of early English history, and give it a fictitious significance as the existing name of the district once included in that extinct kingdom. The series of novels I projected being mainly of the kind called local, they seemed to require a territorial definition of some sort to lend unity to their scene. Finding that the area of a single county did not afford a canvas large enough for this purpose, and that there were objections to an invented name, I disinterred the old one. The region designated was known but vaguely, and I was often asked even by educated people where it lay. However, the press and the public were kind enough to welcome the fanciful plan, and willingly joined me in the anachronism of imagining a Wessex population living under Queen Victoria; – a modern Wessex of railways, the penny post, mowing and reaping machines, union workhouses, lucifer matches, labourers who could read and write, and National school children. But I believe I am correct in stating that, until the existence of this contemporaneous Wessex in place of the usual counties was announced in the present story, in 1874, it had never been heard of in fiction and current speech, if at all, and that the expression, 'a Wessex peasant', or 'a Wessex custom', would theretofore have been taken to refer to nothing later in date than the Norman Conquest.

I did not anticipate that this application of the word to modern story would extend outside the chapters of these particular chronicles. But it was soon taken up elsewhere, the first to adopt it being the now defunct *Examiner*, which, in the impression bearing date July 15, 1876, entitled one of its articles 'The Wessex Labourer', the article turning out to be no dissertation on farming during the Heptarchy, but on the modern peasant of the south-west counties.

Since then the appellation which I had thought to reserve to the horizons and landscapes of a partly real, partly dream country, has become more and more popular as a practical provincial definition; and the dream-country has, by degrees, solidified into a utilitarian region which people can go to, take a house in, and write to the papers from. But I ask all good and idealistic readers to forget this, and to refuse steadfastly to believe that there are any inhabitants of a Victorian Wessex outside these volumes in which their lives and conversations are detailed.

Moreover, the village called Weatherbury, wherein the scenes of the present story of the series are for the most part laid, would perhaps be hardly discernible by the explorer, without help, in any existing place nowadays; though at the time, comparatively recent, at which the tale was written, a sufficient reality to meet the descriptions, both of backgrounds and personages, might have been traced easily enough. The church remains, by great good fortune, unrestored and intact* and a few of the old houses; but the ancient malt-house, which was formerly so character-istic of the parish, has been pulled down these twenty years; also most of the thatched and dormered cottages that were once lifeholds. The heroine's fine old Jacobean house would be found in the story to have taken a witch's ride of a mile or more from its actual position; though with that difference its features are described as they still show themselves to the sun and moonlight. The game of prisoner's-base, which not so long ago seemed to enjoy a perennial vitality in front of the worn-out stocks, may, so far as I can say, be entirely unknown to the rising generation of schoolboys there. The practice of divination by Bible and key, the regarding of valentines as things of serious import, the shearing-supper, the long smock-frocks, and the harvest-home, have, too, nearly disappeared in the wake of the old houses; and with them has gone, it is said, much of that love of fuddling to which the village at one time was notoriously prone. The change at the root of this has been the recent supplanting of the class of stationary cottagers, who carried on the local traditions and humours, by a population of more or less migratory labourers, which has led to a break of continuity in local history, more fatal than any other thing to the preservation of legend, folklore, close inter-social relations, and eccentric individualities. For these the indis-pensable conditions of existence are attachment to the soil of one particular spot by generation after generation.

1895–1902   T.H.

---

* This is no longer the case (1912).

* I *

Description of Farmer Oak – An Incident

WHEN Farmer Oak smiled, the corners of his mouth spread till they were within an unimportant distance of his ears, his eyes were reduced to chinks, and diverging wrinkles appeared round them, extending upon his countenance like the rays in a rudimentary sketch of the rising sun.

His Christian name was Gabriel, and on working days he was a young man of sound judgement, easy motions, proper dress, and general good character. On Sundays he was a man of misty views, rather given to postponing, and hampered by his best clothes and umbrella: upon the whole, one who felt himself to occupy morally that vast middle space of Laodicean neutrality which lay between the Communion people of the parish and the drunken section – that is, he went to church, but yawned privately by the time the congregation reached the Nicene creed, and thought of what there would be for dinner when he meant to be listening to the sermon. Or, to state his character as it stood in the scale of public opinion, when his friends and critics were in tantrums, he was considered rather a bad man; when they were pleased, he was rather a good man; when they were neither, he was a man whose moral colour was a kind of pepper-and-salt mixture.

Since he lived six times as many working days as Sundays, Oak's appearance in his old clothes was most peculiarly his own – the mental picture formed by his neighbours in imagining him being always dressed in that way. He wore a low-crowned felt hat, spread out at the base by tight jamming upon the head for security in high winds, and a coat like Dr Johnson's; his lower extremities being encased in ordinary leather leggings and boots emphatically large, affording to each foot a roomy apartment so constructed that any wearer might stand in a river all day long and know nothing of damp – their maker being a conscientious man who endeavoured to compensate for any weakness in his cut by unstinted dimension and solidity.

Mr Oak carried about him, by way of watch, what may be called a small silver clock; in other words, it was a watch as to shape and intention, and a small clock as to size. This instrument being several years older than Oak's grandfather, had the peculiarity of going either too fast or not at all. The smaller of its hands, too, occasionally slipped round on the pivot, and thus, though the minutes were told with precision, nobody could be quite certain of the hour they belonged to. The stopping peculiarity of his watch Oak remedied by thumps and shakes, and he escaped any evil consequences from the other two defects by constant comparisons with and observations of the sun and stars, and by pressing his face close to the glass of his neighbours' windows, till he could discern the hour marked by the green-faced time-keepers within. It may be mentioned that Oak's fob being difficult of access, by reason of its somewhat high situation in the waistband of his trousers (which also lay at a remote height under his waistcoat), the watch was as a necessity pulled out by throwing the body to one side, compressing the mouth and face to a mere mass of ruddy flesh on account of the exertion, and drawing up the watch by its chain, like a bucket from a well.

But some thoughtful persons, who had seen him walking across one of his fields on a certain December morning – sunny and exceedingly mild – might have regarded Gabriel Oak in other aspects than these. In his face one might notice that many of the hues and curves of youth had tarried on to manhood: there even remained in his remoter crannies some relics of the boy. His height and breadth would have been sufficient to make his presence imposing, had they been exhibited with due consideration. But there is a way some men have, rural and urban alike, for which the mind is more responsible than flesh and sinew: it is a way of curtailing their dimensions by their manner of showing them. And from a quiet modesty that would have become a vestal, which seemed continually to impress upon him that he had no great claim on the world's room, Oak walked unassumingly, and with a faintly perceptible bend, yet distinct from a bowing of the shoulders. This may be said to be a defect in an individual if he depends for his valuation more upon his appearance than upon his capacity to wear well, which Oak did not.

He had just reached the time of life at which 'young' is ceasing to be the prefix of 'man' in speaking of one. He was at the brightest period of masculine growth, for his intellect and his emotions were clearly separated: he had passed the time during which the influence of youth indiscriminately mingles them in the character of impulse, and he had not yet arrived at the stage wherein they become united again, in the character of prejudice, by the influence of a wife and family. In short, he was twenty-eight, and a bachelor.

The field he was in this morning sloped to a ridge called Norcombe Hill. Through a spur of this hill ran the highway between Emminster and Chalk-Newton. Casually glancing over the hedge, Oak saw coming down the incline before him an ornamental spring waggon, painted yellow and gaily marked, drawn by two horses, a waggoner walking alongside bearing a whip perpendicularly. The waggon was laden with household goods and window plants, and on the apex of the whole sat a woman, young and attractive. Gabriel had not beheld the sight for more than half a minute, when the vehicle was brought to a standstill just beneath his eyes.

'The tailboard of the waggon is gone, Miss,' said the waggoner.

'Then I heard it fall,' said the girl, in a soft, though not particularly low voice. 'I heard a noise I could not account for when we were coming up the hill.'

'I'll run back.'

'Do,' she answered.

The sensible horses stood perfectly still, and the waggoner's steps sank fainter and fainter in the distance.

The girl on the summit of the load sat motionless, surrounded by tables and chairs with their legs upwards, backed by an oak settle, and ornamented in front by pots of geraniums, myrtles and cactuses, together with a caged canary – all probably from the windows of the house just vacated. There was also a cat in a willow basket, from the partly-opened lid of which she gazed with half-closed eyes, and affectionately surveyed the small birds around.

The handsome girl waited for some time idly in her place, and the only sound heard in the stillness was the hopping of the canary up and down the perches of its prison. Then she looked attentively downwards. It was not at the bird, nor at the cat; it was at an oblong package tied in paper, and lying between them. She turned her head to learn if the waggoner were coming. He was not yet in sight; and her eyes crept back to the package, her thoughts seeming to run upon what was inside it. At length she drew the article into her lap, and untied the paper covering; a small swing looking-glass was disclosed, in which she proceeded to survey herself attentively. She parted her lips and smiled.

It was a fine morning, and the sun lighted up to a scarlet glow the crimson jacket she wore, and painted a soft lustre upon her bright face and dark hair. The myrtles, geraniums, and cactuses packed around her were fresh and green, and at such a leafless season they invested the whole concern of horses, waggon, furniture, and girl with a peculiar vernal charm. What possessed her to indulge in such a performance in the sight of the sparrows, blackbirds, and unperceived farmer who were alone its spectators – whether the smile began as a factitious one, to test her capacity in that art – nobody knows; it ended certainly in a real smile. She blushed at herself, and seeing her reflection blush, blushed the more.

The change from the customary spot and necessary occasion of such an act – from the dressing hour in a bedroom to a time of travelling out of doors – lent to the idle deed a novelty it did not intrinsically possess. The picture was a delicate one. Woman's prescriptive infirmity had stalked into the sunlight, which had clothed it in the freshness of an originality. A cynical inference was irresistible by Gabriel Oak as he regarded the scene, generous though he fain would have been. There was no necessity whatever for her looking in the glass. She did not adjust her hat, or pat her hair, or press a dimple into shape, or do one thing to signify that any such intention had been her motive in taking up the glass. She simply observed herself as a fair product of Nature in the feminine kind, her thoughts seeming to glide into far-off though likely dramas in which men would play a part – vistas of probable triumphs – the smiles being of a phase suggesting that hearts were imagined as lost and won. Still, this was but conjecture, and the whole series of actions was so idly put forth as to make it rash to assert that intention had any part in them at all.

The waggoner's steps were heard returning. She put the glass in the paper, and the whole again into its place.

When the waggon had passed on, Gabriel withdrew from his point of espial, and descending into the road, followed the vehicle to the turnpike-gate some way beyond the bottom of the hill, where the object of his contemplation now halted for the payment of toll. About twenty steps still remained between him and the gate, when he heard a dispute. It was a difference concerning twopence between the persons with the waggon and the man at the toll-bar.

'Mis'ess's niece is upon the top of the things, and she says that's enough that I've offered ye, you great miser, and she won't pay any more.' These were the waggoner's words.

'Very well; then mis'ess's niece can't pass,' said the turnpike-keeper, closing the gate.

Oak looked from one to the other of the disputants, and fell into a reverie. There was something in the tone of twopence remarkably insignificant. Threepence had a definite value as money – it was an appreciable infringement on a day's wages, and, as such, a higgling matter: but twopence – 'Here,' he said, stepping forward and handing twopence to the gatekeeper; 'let the young woman pass.' He looked up at her then; she heard his words, and looked down.

Gabriel's features adhered throughout their form so exactly to the middle line between the beauty of St John and the ugliness of Judas Iscariot, as represented in a window of the church he attended, that not a single lineament could be selected and called worthy either of distinction or notoriety. The red-jacketed and dark-haired maiden seemed to think so too, for she carelessly glanced over him, and told her man to drive on. She might have looked her thanks to Gabriel on a minute scale, but she did not speak them; more probably she felt none, for in gaining her a passage he had lost her her point, and we know how women take a favour of that kind.

The gatekeeper surveyed the retreating vehicle. 'That's a handsome maid,' he said to Oak.

'But she has her faults,' said Gabriel.

'True, farmer.'

'And the greatest of them is – well, what it is always.'

'Beating people down? ay, 'tis so.'

'O no.'

'What, then?'

Gabriel, perhaps a little piqued by the comely traveller's indifference, glanced to where he had witnessed her performance over the hedge, and said, 'Vanity.'

Night – The Flock – An Interior – Another Interior

IT was nearly midnight on the eve of St Thomas's, the shortest day in the year. A desolating wind wandered from the north over the hill whereon Oak had watched the yellow waggon and its occupant in the sunshine of a few days earlier.

Norcombe Hill – not far from lonely Toller-Down – was one of the spots which suggest to a passer-by that he is in the presence of a shape approaching the indestructible as nearly as any to be found on earth. It was a featureless convexity of chalk and soil – an ordinary specimen of those smoothly-outlined protuberances of the globe which may remain undisturbed on some great day of confusion, when far grander heights and dizzy granite precipices topple down.

The hill was covered on its northern side by an ancient and decaying plantation of beeches, whose upper verge formed a line over the crest, fringing its arched curve against the sky, like a mane. To-night these trees sheltered the southern slope from the keenest blasts, which smote the wood and floundered through it with a sound as of grumbling, or gushed over its crowning boughs in a weakened moan. The dry leaves in the ditch simmered and boiled in the same breezes, a tongue of air occasionally ferreting out a few, and sending them spinning across the grass. A group or two of the latest in date amongst the dead multitude had remained till this very mid-winter time on the twigs which bore them, and in falling rattled against the trunks with smart taps.

Between this half-wooded half-naked hill, and the vague still horizon that its summit indistinctly commanded, was a mysterious sheet of fathomless shade – the sounds from which suggested that what it concealed bore some reduced resemblance to features here. The thin grasses, more or less coating the hill, were touched by the wind in breezes of differing powers, and almost of differing natures – one rubbing the blades heavily, another raking them piercingly, another brushing them like a soft broom. The instinctive act of humankind was to stand and listen, and learn how the trees on the right and the trees on the left wailed or chaunted to each other in the regular antiphonies of a cathedral choir; how hedges and other shapes to leeward then caught the note, lowering it to the tenderest sob; and how the hurrying gust then plunged into the south, to be heard no more.

The sky was clear – remarkably clear – and the twinkling of all the stars seemed to be but throbs of one body, timed by a common pulse. The North Star was directly in the wind's eye, and since evening the Bear had swung round it outwardly to the east, till he was now at a right angle with the meridian. A difference of colour in the stars – oftener read of than seen in England – was really perceptible here. The sovereign brilliancy of Sirius pierced the eye with a steely glitter, the star called Capella was yellow, Aldebaran and Betelgueux shone with a fiery red.

To persons standing alone on a hill during a clear midnight such as this, the roll of the world eastward is almost a palpable movement. The sensation may be caused by the panoramic glide of the stars past earthly objects, which is perceptible in a few minutes of stillness, or by the better outlook upon space that a hill affords, or by the wind, or by the solitude; but whatever be its origin the impression of riding along is vivid and abiding. The poetry of motion is a phrase much in use, and to enjoy the epic form of that gratification it is necessary to stand on a hill at a small hour of the night, and, having first expanded with a sense of difference from the mass of civilized mankind, who are dreamwrapt and disregardful of all such proceedings at this time, long and quietly watch your stately progress through the stars. After such a nocturnal reconnoitre it is hard to get back to earth, and to believe that the consciousness of such majestic speeding is derived from a tiny human frame.

Suddenly an unexpected series of sounds began to be heard in this place up against the sky. They had a clearness which was to be found nowhere in the wind, and a sequence which was to be found nowhere in nature. They were the notes of Farmer Oak's flute.

The tune was not floating unhindered into the open air: it seemed muffled in some way, and was altogether too curtailed in power to spread high or wide. It came from the direction of a small dark object under the plantation hedge – a shepherd's hut – now presenting an outline to which an uninitiated person might have been puzzled to attach either meaning or use.

The image as a whole was that of a small Noah's Ark on a small Ararat, allowing the traditionary outlines and general form of the Ark which are followed by toy-makers – and by these means are established in men's imaginations among their firmest, because earliest impressions – to pass as an approximate pattern. The hut stood on little wheels, which raised its floor about a foot from the ground. Such shepherds' huts are dragged into the field when the lambing season comes on, to shelter the shepherd in his enforced nightly attendance.

It was only latterly that people had begun to call Gabriel 'Farmer' Oak. During the twelvemonth preceding this time he had been enabled by sustained efforts of industry and chronic good spirits to lease the small sheep-farm of which Norcombe Hill was a portion, and stock it with two hundred sheep. Previously he had been a bailiff for a short time, and earlier still a shepherd only, having from his childhood assisted his father in tending the flocks of large proprietors, till old Gabriel sank to rest.

This venture, unaided and alone, into the paths of farming as master and not as man, with an advance of sheep not yet paid for, was a critical juncture with Gabriel Oak, and he recognized his position clearly. The first movement in his new progress was the lambing of his ewes, and sheep having been his speciality from his youth, he wisely refrained from deputing the task of tending them at this season to a hireling or a novice.

The wind continued to beat about the corners of the hut, but the flute-playing ceased. A rectangular space of light appeared in the side of the hut, and in the opening the outline of Farmer Oak's figure. He carried a lantern in his hand, and closing the door behind him came forward and busied himself about this nook of the field for nearly twenty minutes, the lantern light appearing and disappearing here and there, and brightening him or darkening him as he stood before or behind it.

Oak's motions, though they had a quiet energy, were slow, and their deliberateness accorded well with his occupation. Fitness being the basis of beauty, nobody could have denied that his steady swings and turns in and about the flock had elements of grace. Yet, although if occasion demanded he could do or think a thing with as mercurial a dash as can the men of towns who are more to the manner born, his special power, morally, physically, and mentally, was static, owing little or nothing to momentum as a rule.

A close examination of the ground hereabout, even by the wan starlight only, revealed how a portion of what would have been casually called a wild slope had been appropriated by Farmer Oak for his great purpose this winter. Detached hurdles thatched with straw were struck into the ground at various scattered points, amid and under which the whitish forms of his meek ewes moved and rustled. The ring of the sheep-bell, which had been silent during his absence, recommenced, in tones that had more mellowness than clearness, owing to an increasing growth of surrounding wool. This continued till Oak withdrew again from the flock. He returned to the hut, bringing in his arms a new-born lamb, consisting of four legs large enough for a full-grown sheep, united by a seemingly inconsiderable membrane about half the substance of the legs collectively, which constituted the animal's entire body just at present.

The little speck of life he placed on a wisp of hay before the small stove, where a can of milk was simmering. Oak extinguished the lantern by blowing into it and then pinching the snuff, the cot being lighted by a candle suspended by a twisted wire. A rather hard couch, formed of a few corn sacks thrown carelessly down, covered half the floor of this little habitation, and here the young man stretched himself along, loosened his woollen cravat, and closed his eyes. In about the time a person unaccustomed to bodily labour would have decided upon which side to lie, Farmer Oak was asleep.

The inside of the hut, as it now presented itself, was cosy and alluring, and the scarlet handful of fire in addition to the candle, reflecting its own genial colour upon whatever it could reach, flung associations of enjoyment even over utensils and tools. In the corner stood the sheep-crook, and along a shelf at one side were ranged bottles and canisters of the simple preparations pertaining to ovine surgery and physic; spirits of wine, turpentine, tar, magnesia, ginger, and castor-oil being the chief. On a triangular shelf across the corner stood bread, bacon, cheese, and a cup for ale or cider, which was supplied from a flagon beneath.

Beside the provisions lay the flute, whose notes had lately been called
forth by the lonely watcher to beguile a tedious hour. The house was
ventilated by two round holes, like the lights of a ship's cabin, with
wood slides.

The lamb, revived by the warmth, began to bleat, and the sound
entered Gabriel's ears and brain with an instant meaning, as expected
sounds will. Passing from the profoundest sleep to the most alert
wakefulness with the same ease that had accompanied the reverse
operation, he looked at his watch, found that the hour-hand had shifted
again, put on his hat, took the lamb in his arms, and carried it into the
darkness. After placing the little creature with its mother he stood and
carefully examined the sky, to ascertain the time of night from the
altitude of the stars.

The Dog-star and Aldebaran, pointing to the restless Pleiades, were
half-way up the Southern sky, and between them hung Orion, which
gorgeous constellation never burnt more vividly than now, as it soared
forth above the rim of the landscape. Castor and Pollux with their quiet
shine were almost on the meridian: the barren and gloomy Square of
Pegasus was creeping round to the north-west; far away through the
plantation Vega sparkled like a lamp suspended amid the leafless trees,
and Cassiopeia's chair stood daintily poised on the uppermost boughs.

'One o'clock,' said Gabriel.

Being a man not without a frequent consciousness that there was some
charm in this life he led, he stood still after looking at the sky as a useful
instrument, and regarded it in an appreciative spirit, as a work of art
superlatively beautiful. For a moment he seemed impressed with the
speaking loneliness of the scene, or rather with the complete abstraction
from all its compass of the sights and sounds of man. Human shapes,
interferences, troubles, and joys were all as if they were not, and there
seemed to be on the shaded hemisphere of the globe no sentient being
save himself; he could fancy them all gone round to the sunny side.

Occupied thus, with eyes stretched afar, Oak gradually perceived that
what he had previously taken to be a star low down behind the outskirts
of the plantation was in reality no such thing. It was an artificial light,
almost close at hand.

To find themselves utterly alone at night where company is desirable
and expected makes some people fearful; but a case more trying by far to
the nerves is to discover some mysterious companionship when intuition,
sensation, memory, analogy, testimony, probability, induction – every
kind of evidence in the logician's list – have united to persuade consciousness that it is quite in isolation.

Farmer Oak went towards the plantation and pushed through its lower
boughs to the windy side. A dim mass under the slope reminded him that
a shed occupied a place here, the site being a cutting into the slope of the
hill, so that at its back part the roof was almost level with the ground. In
front it was formed of board nailed to posts and covered with tar as a
preservative. Through crevices in the roof and side spread streaks and

dots of light, a combination of which made the radiance that had attracted him. Oak stepped up behind, where, leaning down upon the roof and putting his eye close to a hole, he could see into the interior clearly.

The place contained two women and two cows. By the side of the latter a steaming bran-mash stood in a bucket. One of the women was past middle age. Her companion was apparently young and graceful; he could form no decided opinion upon her looks, her position being almost beneath his eye, so that he saw her in a bird's-eye view, as Milton's Satan first saw Paradise. She wore no bonnet or hat, but had enveloped herself in a large cloak, which was carelessly flung over her head as a covering.

'There, now we'll go home,' said the elder of the two, resting her knuckles upon her hips, and looking at their goings-on as a whole. 'I do hope Daisy will fetch round again now. I have never been more frightened in my life, but I don't mind breaking my rest if she recovers.'

The young woman, whose eyelids were apparently inclined to fall together on the smallest provocation of silence, yawned without parting her lips to any inconvenient extent, whereupon Gabriel caught the infection and slightly yawned in sympathy.

'I wish we were rich enough to pay a man to do these things,' she said.

'As we are not, we must do them ourselves,' said the other; 'for you must help me if you stay.'

'Well, my hat is gone, however,' continued the younger. 'It went over the hedge, I think. The idea of such a slight wind catching it.'

The cow standing erect was of the Devon breed, and was encased in a tight warm hide of rich Indian red, as absolutely uniform from eyes to tail as if the animal had been dipped in a dye of that colour, her long back being mathematically level. The other was spotted, grey and white. Beside her Oak now noticed a little calf about a day old, looking idiotically at the two women, which showed that it had not long been accustomed to the phenomenon of eyesight, and often turning to the lantern, which it apparently mistook for the moon, inherited instinct having as yet had little time for correction by experience. Between the sheep and the cows Lucina had been busy on Norcombe Hill lately.

'I think we had better send for some oatmeal,' said the elder woman; 'there's no more bran.'

'Yes, aunt; and I'll ride over for it as soon as it is light.'

'But there's no side-saddle.'

'I can ride on the other: trust me.'

Oak, upon hearing these remarks, became more curious to observe her features, but this prospect being denied him by the hooding effect of the cloak, and by his aërial position, he felt himself drawing upon his fancy for their details. In making even horizontal and clear inspections we colour and mould according to the wants within us whatever our eyes bring in. Had Gabriel been able from the first to get a distinct view of her countenance, his estimate of it as very handsome or slightly so would have been as his soul required a divinity at the moment or was ready supplied with one. Having for some time known the want of satisfactory form to fill an increasing void within him, his position moreover affording the widest scope for his fancy, he painted her a beauty.

By one of those whimsical coincidences in which Nature, like a busy mother, seems to spare a moment from her unremitting labours to turn and make her children smile, the girl now dropped the cloak, and forth tumbled ropes of black hair over a red jacket. Oak knew her instantly as the heroine of the yellow waggon, myrtles, and looking-glass: prosily, as the woman who owed him twopence.

They placed the calf beside its mother again, took up the lantern, and went out, the light sinking down the hill till it was no more than a nebula. Gabriel Oak returned to his flock.

* III *

A Girl on Horseback – Conversation

THE sluggish day began to break. Even its position terrestrially is one of the elements of a new interest, and for no particular reason save that the incident of the night had occurred there Oak went again into the plantation. Lingering and musing here he heard the steps of a horse at the foot of the hill, and soon there appeared in view an auburn pony with a girl on its back, ascending by the path leading past the cattle-shed. She was the young woman of the night before. Gabriel instantly thought of the hat she had mentioned as having lost in the wind; possibly she had come to look for it. He hastily scanned the ditch, and after walking about ten yards along it found the hat among the leaves. Gabriel took it in his hand and returned to his hut. Here he ensconced himself, and peeped through the loophole in the direction of the rider's approach.

She came up and looked around – then on the other side of the hedge. Gabriel was about to advance and restore the missing article, when an unexpected performance induced him to suspend the action for the present. The path, after passing the cowshed, bisected the plantation. It was not a bridle-path – merely a pedestrian's track, and the boughs spread horizontally at a height not greater than several feet above the ground, which made it impossible to ride erect beneath them. The girl, who wore no riding-habit, looked around for a moment, as if to assure herself that all humanity was out of view, then dexterously dropped backwards flat upon the pony's back, her head over its tail, her feet against its shoulders, and her eyes to the sky. The rapidity of her glide into this position was that of a kingfisher – its noiselessness that of a hawk. Gabriel's eyes had scarcely been able to follow her. The tall lank pony seemed used to such doings, and ambled along unconcerned. Thus she passed under the level boughs.

The performer seemed quite at home anywhere between a horse's head and its tail, and the necessity for this abnormal attitude having ceased with the passage of the plantation, she began to adopt another, even more obviously convenient than the first. She had no side-saddle, and it was very apparent that a firm seat upon the smooth leather beneath her was unattainable sideways. Springing to her accustomed perpendicular like a bowed sapling, and satisfying herself that nobody was in sight, she seated herself in the manner demanded by the saddle, though hardly expected of the woman, and trotted off in the direction of Tewnell Mill.

Oak was amused, perhaps a little astonished, and hanging up the hat in his hut went again among his ewes. An hour passed, the girl returned, properly seated now, with a bag of bran in front of her. On nearing the cattle-shed she was met by a boy bringing a milking-pail, who held the reins of the pony whilst she slid off. The boy led away the horse leaving the pail with the young woman.

Soon soft spirts alternating with loud spirts came in regular succession from within the shed, the obvious sounds of a person milking a cow. Gabriel took the lost hat in his hand, and waited beside the path she would follow in leaving the hill.

She came, the pail in one hand, hanging against her knee. The left arm was extended as a balance, enough of it being shown bare to make Oak wish that the event had happened in the summer, when the whole would have been revealed. There was a bright air and manner about her now, by which she seemed to imply that the desirability of her existence could not be questioned; and this rather saucy assumption failed in being offensive because a beholder felt it to be, upon the whole, true. Like exceptional emphasis in the tone of a genius, that which would have made mediocrity ridiculous was an addition to recognized power. It was with some surprise that she saw Gabriel's face rising like the moon behind the hedge.

The adjustment of the farmer's hazy conceptions of her charms to the portrait of herself she now presented him with was less a diminution than a difference. The starting-point selected by the judgement was her height. She seemed tall, but the pail was a small one, and the hedge diminutive; hence, making allowance for error by comparison with these, she could have been not above the height to be chosen by women as best. All features of consequence were severe and regular. It may have been observed by persons who go about the shires with eyes for beauty that in Englishwomen a classically-formed face is seldom found to be united with a figure of the same pattern, the highly-finished features being generally too large for the remainder of the frame; that a graceful and proportionate figure of eight heads usually goes off into random facial curves. Without throwing a Nymphean tissue over a milkmaid, let it be said that here criticism checked itself as out of place, and looked at her proportions with a long consciousness of pleasure. From the contours of her figure in its upper part she must have had a beautiful neck and shoulders; but since her infancy nobody had ever seen them. Had she been put into a low dress she would have run and thrust her head into a bush. Yet she was not a shy girl by any means; it was merely her instinct to draw the line dividing the seen from the unseen higher than they do it in towns.

That the girl's thoughts hovered about her face and form as soon as she caught Oak's eyes conning the same page was natural, and almost certain. The self-consciousness shown would have been vanity if a little more pronounced, dignity if a little less. Rays of male vision seem to have a tickling effect upon virgin faces in rural districts; she brushed hers with her hand, as if Gabriel had been irritating its pink surface by actual touch, and the free air of her previous movements was reduced at the same time to a chastened phase of itself. Yet it was the man who blushed, the maid not at all.

'I found a hat,' said Oak.

'It is mine,' said she, and, from a sense of proportion, kept down to a small smile an inclination to laugh distinctly: 'it flew away last night.'

'One o'clock this morning?'

'Well – it was.' She was surprised. 'How did you know?' she said.

'I was here.'

'You are Farmer Oak, are you not?'

'That or thereabouts. I'm lately come to this place.'

'A large farm?' she inquired, casting her eyes round, and swinging back her hair, which was black in the shaded hollows of its mass; but it being now an hour past sunrise the rays touched its prominent curve with a colour of their own.

'No; not large. About a hundred.' (In speaking of farms the word 'acres' is omitted by the natives, by analogy to such old expressions as 'a stag of ten'.)

'I wanted my hat this morning,' she went on. 'I had to ride to Tewnell Mill.'

'Yes, you had.'

'How do you know?'

'I saw you.'

'Where?' she inquired, a misgiving bringing every muscle of her lineaments and frame to a standstill.

'Here – going through the plantation, and all down the hill,' said Farmer Oak, with an aspect excessively knowing with regard to some matter in his mind, as he gazed at a remote point in the direction named, and then turned back to meet his colloquist's eyes.

A perception caused him to withdraw his own eyes from hers as suddenly as if he had been caught in a theft. Recollection of the strange antics she had indulged in when passing through the trees was succeeded in the girl by a nettled palpitation, and that by a hot face. It was a time to see a woman redden who was not given to reddening as a rule; not a point in the milkmaid but was of the deepest rose-colour. From the Maiden's Blush, through all varieties of the Provence down to the Crimson Tuscany the countenance of Oak's acquaintance quickly graduated; whereupon he, in considerateness, turned away his head.

The sympathetic man still looked the other way, and wondered when she would recover sufficient to justify him in facing her again. He heard what seemed to be the flitting of a dead leaf upon the breeze, and looked. She had gone away.

With an air between that of Tragedy and Comedy Gabriel returned to his work.

Five mornings and evenings passed. The young woman came regularly to milk the healthy cow or to attend to the sick one, but never allowed her vision to stray in the direction of Oak's person. His want of tact had deeply offended her – not by seeing what he could not help, but by letting her know that he had seen it. For, as without law there is no sin, without eyes there is no indecorum; and she appeared to feel that Gabriel's espial had made her an indecorous woman without her own connivance. It was food for great regret with him; it was also a *contretemps* which touched into life a latent heat he had experienced in that direction.

The acquaintanceship might, however, have ended in a slow forgetting but for an incident which occurred at the end of the same week. One afternoon it began to freeze, and the frost increased with evening, which drew on like a stealthy tightening of bonds. It was a time when in cottages the breath of the sleepers freezes to the sheets; when round the drawing-room fire of a thick-walled mansion the sitters' backs are cold, even whilst their faces are all aglow. Many a small bird went to bed supperless that night among the bare boughs.

As the milking-hour drew near Oak kept his usual watch upon the cowshed. At last he felt cold, and shaking an extra quantity of bedding round the yeaning ewes he entered the hut and heaped more fuel upon the stove. The wind came in at the bottom of the door, and to prevent it Oak laid a sack there and wheeled the cot round a little more to the south. Then the wind spouted in at a ventilating hole – of which there was one on each side of the hut.

Gabriel had always known that when the fire was lighted and the door closed one of these must be kept open – that chosen being always on the side away from the wind. Closing the slide to windward he turned to open the other; on second thoughts the farmer considered that he would first sit down, leaving both closed for a minute or two, till the temperature of the hut was a little raised. He sat down.

His head began to ache in an unwonted manner and, fancying himself weary by reason of the broken rests of the preceding nights, Oak decided to get up, open the slide, and then allow himself to fall asleep. He fell asleep, however, without having performed the necessary preliminary.

How long he remained unconscious Gabriel never knew. During the first stages of his return to perception peculiar deeds seemed to be in course of enactment. His dog was howling, his head was aching fearfully – somebody was pulling him about, hands were loosening his neckerchief.

On opening his eyes he found that evening had sunk to dusk in a strange manner of unexpectedness. The young girl with the remarkably pleasant lips and white teeth was beside him. More than this – astonishingly more – his head was upon her lap, his face and neck were disagreeably wet, and her fingers were unbuttoning his collar.

'Whatever is the matter?' said Oak vacantly.

She seemed to experience mirth, but of too insignificant a kind to start enjoyment.

'Nothing now,' she answered, 'since you are not dead. It is a wonder you were not suffocated in this hut of yours.'

'Ah, the hut!' murmured Gabriel. 'I gave ten pounds for that hut. But I'll sell it, and sit under thatched hurdles as they did in old times, and curl up to sleep in a lock of straw! It played me nearly the same trick the other day!' Gabriel, by way of emphasis, brought down his fist upon the floor.

'It was not exactly the fault of the hut,' she observed in a tone which showed her to be that novelty among women – one who finished a thought before beginning the sentence which was to convey it. 'You should, I think, have considered, and not have been so foolish as to leave the slides closed.'

'Yes, I suppose I should,' said Oak absently. He was endeavouring to catch and appreciate the sensation of being thus with her, his head upon her dress, before the event passed on into the heap of bygone things. He wished she knew his impressions; but he would as soon have thought of carrying an odour in a net as of attempting to convey the intangibilities of his feeling in the coarse meshes of language. So he remained silent.

She made him sit up, and then Oak began wiping his face and shaking himself like a Samson. 'How can I thank 'ee?' he said at last gratefully, some of the natural, rusty red having returned to his face.

'Oh, never mind that,' said the girl, smiling, and allowing her smile to hold good for Gabriel's next remark, whatever that might prove to be.

'How did you find me?'

'I heard your dog howling and scratching at the door of the hut when I came to the milking (it was so lucky. Daisy's milking is almost over for the season, and I shall not come here after this week or the next). The dog saw me, and jumped over to me, and laid hold of my skirt. I came across and looked round the hut the very first thing to see if the slides were closed. My uncle has a hut like this one, and I have heard him tell his shepherd not to go to sleep without leaving a slide open. I opened the door, and there you were like dead. I threw the milk over you, as there was no water, forgetting it was warm, and no use.'

'I wonder if I should have died?' Gabriel said in a low voice, which was rather meant to travel back to himself than to her.

'O no!' the girl replied. She seemed to prefer a less tragic probability; to have saved a man from death involved talk that should harmonize with the dignity of such a deed – and she shunned it.

'I believe you saved my life, Miss – I don't know your name. I know your aunt's, but not yours.'

'I would just as soon not tell it – rather not. There is no reason either why I should, as you probably will never have much to do with me.'

'Still I should like to know.'

'You can inquire at my aunt's – she will tell you.'

'My name is Gabriel Oak.'

'And mine isn't. You seem fond of yours in speaking it so decisively, Gabriel Oak.'

'You see, it is the only one I shall ever have, and I must make the most of it.'

'I always think mine sounds odd and disagreeable.'

'I should think you might soon get a new one.'

'Mercy! – how many opinions you keep about you concerning other people, Gabriel Oak.'

'Well, Miss – excuse the words – I thought you would like them. But I can't match you, I know, in mapping out my mind upon my tongue. I never was very clever in my inside. But I thank you. Come, give me your hand!'

She hesitated, somewhat disconcerted at Oak's old-fashioned earnest conclusion to a dialogue lightly carried on. 'Very well,' she said, and gave him her hand, compressing her lips to a demure impassivity. He held it but an instant, and in his fear of being too demonstrative, swerved to the opposite extreme, touching her fingers with the lightness of a small-hearted person.

'I am sorry,' he said the instant after.

'What for?'

'Letting your hand go so quick.'

'You may have it again if you like; there it is.' She gave him her hand again.

Oak held it longer this time – indeed, curiously long. 'How soft it is – being winter time, too – not chapped or rough, or anything!' he said.

'There – that's long enough,' said she, though without pulling it away. 'But I suppose you are thinking you would like to kiss it? You may if you want to.'

'I wasn't thinking of any such thing,' said Gabriel simply; 'but I will –'

'That you won't!' She snatched back her hand.

Gabriel felt himself guilty of another want of tact.

'Now find out my name,' she said teasingly; and withdrew.

* IV *

Gabriel's Resolve – The Visit – The Mistake

THE only superiority in women that is tolerable to the rival sex is, as a rule, that of the unconscious kind; but a superiority which recognizes itself may sometimes please by suggesting possibilities of capture to the subordinated man.

This well-favoured and comely girl soon made appreciable inroads upon the emotional constitution of young Farmer Oak.

Love being an extremely exacting usurer (a sense of exorbitant profit, spiritually, by an exchange of hearts, being at the bottom of pure passions, as that of exorbitant profit, bodily or materially, is at the bottom of those of lower atmosphere), every morning Oak's feelings were as sensitive as the money-market in calculations upon his chances. His dog waited for his meals in a way so like that in which Oak waited for the girl's presence that the farmer was quite struck with the resemblance, felt it lowering, and would not look at the dog. However, he continued to watch through the hedge for her regular coming, and thus his sentiments towards her were deepened without any corresponding effect being produced upon herself. Oak had nothing finished and ready to say as yet, and not being able to frame love phrases which end where they begin; passionate tales –

– Full of sound and fury
– Signifying nothing –

he said no word at all.

By making inquiries he found that the girl's name was Bathsheba Everdene, and that the cow would go dry in about seven days. He dreaded the eighth day.

At last the eighth day came. The cow had ceased to give milk for that year, and Bathsheba Everdene came up the hill no more. Gabriel had reached a pitch of existence he never could have anticipated a short time before. He liked saying 'Bathsheba' as a private enjoyment instead of whistling; turned over his taste to black hair, though he had sworn by brown ever since he was a boy, isolated himself till the space he filled in the public eye was contemptibly small. Love is a possible strength in an actual weakness. Marriage transforms a distraction into a support, the power of which should be, and happily often is, in direct proportion to the degree of imbecility it supplants. Oak began now to see light in this direction, and said to himself, 'I'll make her my wife, or upon my soul I shall be good for nothing!'

All this while he was perplexing himself about an errand on which he might consistently visit the cottage of Bathsheba's aunt.

He found his opportunity in the death of a ewe, mother of a living lamb. On a day which had a summer face and a winter constitution – a fine January morning, when there was just enough blue sky visible to make cheerfully-disposed people wish for more, and an occasional gleam of silvery sunshine, Oak put the lamb into a respectable Sunday basket, and stalked across the fields to the house of Mrs Hurst, the aunt – George, the dog, walking behind, with a countenance of great concern at the serious turn pastoral affairs seemed to be taking.

Gabriel had watched the blue wood-smoke curling from the chimney with strange meditation. At evening he had fancifully traced it down the chimney to the spot of its origin – seen the hearth and Bathsheba beside it – beside it in her outdoor dress; for the clothes she had worn on the hill were by association equally with her person included in the compass of his affection; they seemed at this early time of his love a necessary ingredient of the sweet mixture called Bathsheba Everdene.

He had made a toilet of a nicely-adjusted kind – of a nature between the carefully neat and the carelessly ornate – of a degree between fine-market-day and wet-Sunday selection. He thoroughly cleaned his silver watch-chain with whiting, put new lacing straps to his boots, looked to the brass eyelet-holes, went to the inmost heart of the plantation for a new walking-stick, and trimmed it vigorously on his way back; took a new handkerchief from the bottom of his clothes-box, put on the light waistcoat patterned all over with sprigs of an elegant flower uniting the beauties of both rose and lily without the defects of either, and used all the hair-oil he possessed upon his usually dry, sandy, and inextricably curly hair, till he had deepened it to a splendidly novel colour, between that of guano and Roman cement, making it stick to his head like mace round a nutmeg, or wet seaweed round a boulder after the ebb.

Nothing disturbed the stillness of the cottage save the chatter of a knot of sparrows on the eaves; one might fancy scandal and rumour to be no less the staple topic of these little coteries on roofs than of those under them. It seemed that the omen was an unpropitious one, for, as the rather untoward commencement of Oak's overtures, just as he arrived by the garden gate he saw a cat inside, going into various arched shapes and fiendish convulsions at the sight of his dog George. The dog took no notice, for he had arrived at an age at which all superfluous barking was cynically avoided as a waste of breath – in fact, he never barked even at the sheep except to order, when it was done with an absolutely neutral countenance, as a sort of Commination-service which, though offensive, had to be gone through once now and then to frighten the flock for their own good.

A voice came from behind some laurel-bushes into which the cat had run:

'Poor dear! Did a nasty brute of a dog want to kill it; – did he, poor dear!'

'I beg yer pardon,' said Oak to the voice, 'but George was walking on behind me with a temper as mild as milk.'

Almost before he had ceased speaking Oak was seized with a misgiving as to whose ear was the recipient of his answer. Nobody appeared, and he heard the person retreat among the bushes.

Gabriel meditated, and so deeply that he brought small furrows into his forehead by sheer force of reverie. Where the issue of an interview is as likely to be a vast change for the worse as for the better, any initial difference from expectation causes nipping sensations of failure. Oak went up to the door a little abashed: his mental rehearsal and the reality had had no common grounds of opening.

Bathsheba's aunt was indoors. 'Will you tell Miss Everdene that somebody would be glad to speak to her?' said Mr Oak. (Calling one's self merely Somebody, without giving a name, is not to be taken as an example of the ill-breeding of the rural world: it springs from a refined modesty of which townspeople, with their cards and announcements, have no notion whatever.)

Bathsheba was out. The voice had evidently been hers.

'Will you come in, Mr Oak?'

'Oh, thank 'ee,' said Gabriel, following her to the fireplace. 'I've brought a lamb for Miss Everdene. I thought she might like one to rear; girls do.'

'She might,' said Mrs Hurst musingly; 'though she's only a visitor here. If you will wait a minute Bathsheba will be in.'

'Yes, I will wait,' said Gabriel, sitting down. 'The lamb isn't really the business I came about, Mrs Hurst. In short, I was going to ask her if she'd like to be married.'

'And were you indeed?'

'Yes. Because if she would I should be very glad to marry her. D'ye know if she's got any other young man hanging about her at all?'

'Let me think,' said Mrs Hurst, poking the fire superfluously . . . 'Yes – bless you, ever so many young men. You see, Farmer Oak, she's so good-looking, and an excellent scholar besides – she was going to be a governess once, you know, only she was too wild. Not that her young men ever come here – but Lord, in the nature of women, she must have a dozen!'

'That's unfortunate,' said Farmer Oak, contemplating a crack in the stone floor with sorrow. 'I'm only an every-day sort of man, and my only chance was in being the first comer . . . Well, there's no use in my waiting, for that was all I came about: so I'll take myself off home-along, Mrs Hurst.'

When Gabriel had gone about two hundred yards along the down, he heard a 'hoi-hoi!' uttered behind him, in a piping note of more treble quality than that in which the exclamation usually embodies itself when shouted across a field. He looked round, and saw a girl racing after him, waving a white handkerchief.

Oak stood still – and the runner drew nearer. It was Bathsheba Everdene. Gabriel's colour deepened: hers was already deep, not, as it appeared, from emotion, but from running.

'Farmer Oak – I –' she said, pausing for want of breath, pulling up in front of him with a slanted face, and putting her hand to her side.

'I have just called to see you,' said Gabriel pending her further speech.

'Yes – I know that,' she said, panting like a robin, her face red and moist from her exertions, like a peony petal before the sun dries off the dew. 'I didn't know you had come to ask to have me, or I should have come in from the garden instantly. I ran after you to say – that my aunt made a mistake in sending you away from courting me.'

Gabriel expanded. 'I'm sorry to have made you run so fast, my dear,' he said, with a grateful sense of favours to come. 'Wait a bit till you've found your breath.'

'– It was quite a mistake – aunt's telling you I had a young man already,' Bathsheba went on. 'I haven't a sweetheart at all – and I never had one, and I thought that, as times go with women, it was *such* a pity to send you away thinking that I had several.'

'Really and truly I am glad to hear that!' said Farmer Oak, smiling one of his long special smiles, and blushing with gladness. He held out his hand to take hers, which, when she had eased her side by pressing it there, was prettily extended upon her bosom to still her loud-beating heart. Directly he seized it she put it behind her, so that it slipped through his fingers like an eel.

'I have a nice snug little farm,' said Gabriel, with half a degree less assurance than when he had seized her hand.

'Yes; you have.'

'A man has advanced me money to begin with, but still, it will soon be paid off, and though I am only an every-day sort of man I have got on a little since I was a boy.' Gabriel uttered 'a little' in a tone to show her that it was the complacent form of 'a great deal'. He continued: 'When we be married, I am quite sure I can work twice as hard as I do now.'

He went forward and stretched out his arm again. Bathsheba had overtaken him at a point beside which stood a low stunted holly bush, now laden with red berries. Seeing his advance take the form of an attitude threatening a possible enclosure, if not compression, of her person, she edged off round the bush.

'Why, Farmer Oak,' she said over the top, looking at him with rounded eyes, 'I never said I was going to marry you.'

'Well – that *is* a tale!' said Oak with dismay. 'To run after anybody like this, and then say you don't want him!'

'What I meant to tell you was only this,' she said eagerly, and yet half conscious of the absurdity of the position she had made for herself – 'that nobody has got me yet as a sweetheart, instead of my having a dozen, as my aunt said; I *hate* to be thought men's property in that way, though possibly I shall be had some day. Why, if I'd wanted you I shouldn't have run after you like this; 'twould have been the *forwardest* thing! But there was no harm in hurrying to correct a piece of false news that had been told you.'

'Oh, no – no harm at all.' But there is such a thing as being too generous in expressing a judgement impulsively, and Oak added with a more appreciative sense of all the circumstances – 'Well, I am not quite certain it was no harm.'

'Indeed, I hadn't time to think before starting whether I wanted to marry or not, for you'd have been gone over the hill.'

'Come,' said Gabriel, freshening again; 'think a minute or two. I'll wait a while, Miss Everdene. Will you marry me? Do, Bathsheba. I love you far more than common!'

'I'll try to think,' she observed rather more timorously; 'if I can think out of doors; my mind spreads away so.'

'But you can give a guess.'

'Then give me time.' Bathsheba looked thoughtfully into the distance, away from the direction in which Gabriel stood.

'I can make you happy,' said he to the back of her head, across the bush. 'You shall have a piano in a year or two – farmers' wives are getting to have pianos now – and I'll practise up the flute right well to play with you in the evenings.'

'Yes; I should like that.'

'And have one of those little ten-pound gigs for market – and nice flowers, and birds – cocks and hens I mean, because they be useful,' continued Gabriel, feeling balanced between poetry and practicality.

'I should like it very much.'

'And a frame for cucumbers – like a gentleman and lady.'

'Yes.'

'And when the wedding was over, we'd have it put in the newspaper list of marriages.'

'Dearly I should like that!'

'And the babies in the births – every man jack of 'em! And at home by the fire, whenever you look up, there I shall be – and whenever I look up, there will be you.'

'Wait, wait, and don't be improper!'

Her countenance fell, and she was silent awhile. He regarded the red berries between them over and over again, to such an extent that holly seemed in his after life to be a cypher signifying a proposal of marriage. Bathsheba decisively turned to him.

'No; 'tis no use,' she said. 'I don't want to marry you.'

'Try.'

'I've tried hard all the time I've been thinking; for a marriage would be very nice in one sense. People would talk about me and think I had won my battle, and I should feel triumphant, and all that. But a husband –'

'Well!'

'Why, he'd always be there, as you say; whenever I looked up, there he'd be.'

'Of course he would – I, that is.'

'Well, what I mean is that I shouldn't mind being a bride at a wedding, if I could be one without having a husband. But since a woman can't show off in that way by herself, I shan't marry – at least yet.'

'That's a terrible wooden story!'

At this criticism of her statement Bathsheba made an addition to her dignity by a slight sweep away from him.

'Upon my heart and soul I don't know what a maid can say stupider than that,' said Oak. 'But dearest,' he continued in a palliative voice, 'don't be like it!' Oak sighed a deep honest sigh – none the less so in that, being like the sigh of a pine plantation, it was rather noticeable as a disturbance of the atmosphere. 'Why won't you have me?' he appealed, creeping round the holly to reach her side.

'I cannot,' she said, retreating.

'But why?' he persisted, standing still at last in despair of ever reaching her, and facing over the bush.

'Because I don't love you.'

'Yes, but –'

She contracted a yawn to an inoffensive smallness, so that it was hardly ill-mannered at all. 'I don't love you,' she said.

'But I love you – and, as for myself, I am content to be liked.'

'O Mr Oak – that's very fine! You'd get to despise me.'

'Never,' said Mr Oak, so earnestly that he seemed to be coming, by the force of his words, straight through the bush and into her arms. 'I shall do one thing in this life – one thing certain – that is, love you, and long for you, and *keep wanting you* till I die.' His voice had a genuine pathos now, and his large brown hands perceptibly trembled.

'It seems dreadfully wrong not to have you when you feel so much!' she said with a little distress, and looking hopelessly around for some means of escape from her moral dilemma. 'How I wish I hadn't run after you!' However, she seemed to have a short cut for getting back to cheerfulness and set her face to signify archness. 'It wouldn't do, Mr Oak. I want somebody to tame me; I am too independent; and you would never be able to, I know.'

Oak cast his eyes down the field in a way implying that it was useless to attempt argument.

'Mr Oak,' she said, with luminous distinctness and common sense, 'you are better off than I. I have hardly a penny in the world – I am staying with my aunt for my bare sustenance. I am better educated than you – and I don't love you a bit: that's my side of the case. Now yours: you are a farmer just beginning, and you ought in common prudence, if you marry at all (which you should certainly not think of doing at present, to marry a woman with money, who would stock a larger farm for you than you have now.'

Gabriel looked at her with a little surprise and much admiration.

'That's the very thing I had been thinking myself!' he naïvely said.

Farmer Oak had one-and-a-half Christian characteristics too many to succeed with Bathsheba: his humility, and a superfluous moiety of honesty. Bathsheba was decidedly disconcerted.

'Well, then, why did you come and disturb me?' she said, almost angrily, if not quite, an enlarging red spot rising in each cheek.

'I can't do what I think would be – would be –'

'Right?'

'No: wise.'

'You have made an admission *now*, Mr Oak,' she exclaimed with even more hauteur, and rocking her head disdainfully. 'After that, do you think I could marry you? Not if I know it.'

He broke in passionately: 'But don't mistake me like that! Because I am open enough to own what every man in my shoes would have thought of, you make your colours come up your face and get crabbed with me. That about you not being good enough for me is nonsense. You speak like a lady – all the parish notice it, and your uncle at Weatherbury is, I've heerd, a large farmer – much larger than ever I shall be. May I call in the evening, or will you walk along with me o' Sundays? I don't want you to make up your mind at once, if you'd rather not.'

'No – no – I cannot. Don't press me any more – don't. I don't love you – so 'twould be ridiculous,' she said, with a laugh.

No man likes to see his emotions the sport of a merry-go-round of skittishness. 'Very well,' said Oak firmly, with the bearing of one who was going to give his days and nights to Ecclesiastes for ever. 'Then I'll ask you no more.'

* V *

Departure of Bathsheba – A Pastoral Tragedy

THE news which one day reached Gabriel that Bathsheba Everdene had left the neighbourhood, had an influence upon him which might have surprised any who never suspected that the more emphatic the renunciation the less absolute its character.

It may have been observed that there is no regular path for getting out of love as there is for getting in. Some people look upon marriage as a short cut that way, but it has been known to fail. Separation, which was the means that chance offered to Gabriel Oak by Bathsheba's disappearance, though effectual with people of certain humours, is apt to idealize the removed object with others – notably those whose affection, placid and regular as it may be, flows deep and long. Oak belonged to the even-tempered order of humanity, and felt the secret fusion of himself in Bathsheba to be burning with a finer flame now that she was gone – that was all.

His incipient friendship with her aunt had been nipped by the failure of his suit, and all that Oak learnt of Bathsheba's movements was done indirectly. It appeared that she had gone to a place called Weatherbury, more than twenty miles off, but in what capacity – whether as a visitor or permanently, he could not discover.

Gabriel had two dogs. George, the elder, exhibited an ebony-tipped nose, surrounded by a narrow margin of pink flesh, and a coat marked in random splotches approximating in colour to white and slaty grey; but the grey, after years of sun and rain, had been scorched and washed out of the more prominent locks, leaving them a reddish-brown, as if the blue component of the grey had faded, like the indigo from the same colour in Turner's pictures. In substance it had originally been hair, but long contact with sheep seemed to be turning it by degrees into wool of a poor quality and staple.

This dog had originally belonged to a shepherd of inferior morals and dreadful temper, and the result was that George knew the exact degrees of condemnation signified by cursing and swearing of all descriptions better than the wickedest old man in the neighbourhood. Long experience had so precisely taught the animal the difference between such exclamations as 'Come in!' and 'D— ye, come in!' that he knew to a hair's breadth the rate of trotting back from the ewes' tails that each call involved, if a staggerer with the sheep-crook was to be escaped. Though old, he was clever and trustworthy still.

The young dog, George's son, might possibly have been the image of his mother, for there was not much resemblance between him and George. He was learning the sheep-keeping business, so as to follow on at the flock when the other should die, but had got no further than the rudiments as yet – still finding an insuperable difficulty in distinguishing between doing a thing well enough and doing it too well. So earnest and yet so wrong-headed was this young dog (he had no name in particular, and answered with perfect readiness to any pleasant interjection) that if sent behind the flock to help them on he did it so thoroughly that he would have chased them across the whole county with the greatest pleasure if not called off, or reminded when to stop by the example of old George.

Thus much for the dogs. On the further side of Norcombe Hill was a chalk-pit, from which chalk had been drawn for generations, and spread over adjacent farms. Two hedges converged upon it in the form of a V, but without quite meeting. The narrow opening left, which was immediately over the brow of the pit, was protected by a rough railing.

One night, when Farmer Oak had returned to his house, believing there would be no further necessity for his attendance on the down, he called as usual to the dogs, previously to shutting them up in the outhouse till next morning. Only one responded – old George; the other could not be found, either in the house, lane, or garden. Gabriel then remembered that he had left the two dogs on the hill eating a dead lamb (a kind of meat he usually kept from them, except when other food ran short), and concluding that the young one had not finished his meal he went indoors to the luxury of a bed, which latterly he had only enjoyed on Sundays.

It was a still, moist night. Just before dawn he was assisted in waking by the abnormal reverberation of familiar music. To the shepherd, the note of the sheep-bell, like the ticking of the clock to other people, is a chronic sound that only makes itself noticed by ceasing or altering in some unusual manner from the well-known idle tinkle which signifies to the accustomed ear, however distant, that all is well in the fold. In the solemn calm of the awakening morn that note was heard by Gabriel, beating with unusual violence and rapidity. This exceptional ringing may be caused in two ways – by the rapid feeding of the sheep bearing the bell, as when the flock breaks into new pasture, which gives it an intermittent rapidity, or by the sheep starting off in a run, when the sound has a regular palpitation. The experienced ear of Oak knew the sound he now heard to be caused by the running of the flock with great velocity.

He jumped out of bed, dressed, tore down the lane through a foggy dawn, and ascended the hill. The forward ewes were kept apart from those among which the fall of lambs would be later, there being two hundred of the latter class in Gabriel's flock. These two hundred seemed to have absolutely vanished from the hill. There were the fifty with their lambs, enclosed at the other end as he had left them, but the rest, forming the bulk of the flock, were nowhere. Gabriel called at the top of his voice the shepherd's call:

'Ovey, ovey, ovey!'

Not a single bleat. He went to the hedge; a gap had been broken through it, and in the gap were the footprints of the sheep. Rather surprised to find them break fence at this season, yet putting it down instantly to their great fondness for ivy in winter-time, of which a great deal grew in the plantation, he followed through the hedge. They were not in the plantation. He called again: the valleys and furthest hills resounded as when the sailors invoked the lost Hylas on the Mysian shore; but no sheep. He passed through the trees and along the ridge of the hill. On the extreme summit, where the ends of the two converging hedges of which we have spoken were stopped short by meeting the brow of the chalk-pit, he saw the younger dog standing against the sky – dark and motionless as Napoleon at St Helena.

A horrible conviction darted through Oak. With a sensation of bodily faintness he advanced: at one point the rails were broken through, and there he saw the footprints of his ewes. The dog came up, licked his hand, and made signs implying that he expected some great reward for signal services rendered. Oak looked over the precipice. The ewes lay dead and dying at its foot – a heap of two hundred mangled carcases, representing in their condition just now at least two hundred more.

Oak was an intensely humane man: indeed, his humanity often tore in pieces any politic intentions of his which bordered on strategy, carried him on as by gravitation. A shadow in his life had always been that his flock ended in mutton – that a day came and found every shepherd an arrant traitor to his defenceless sheep. His first feeling now was one of pity for the untimely fate of these gentle ewes and their unborn lambs.

It was a second to remember another phase of the matter. The sheep were not insured. All the savings of a frugal life had been dispersed at a blow; his hopes of being an independent farmer were laid low – possibly for ever. Gabriel's energies, patience, and industry had been so severely taxed during the years of his life between eighteen and eight-and-twenty, to reach his present stage of progress, that no more seemed to be left in him. He leant down upon a rail, and covered his face with his hands.

Stupors, however, do not last for ever, and Farmer Oak recovered from his. It was as remarkable as it was characteristic that the one sentence he uttered was in thankfulness:

'Thank God I am not married: what would *she* have done in the poverty now coming upon me!'

Oak raised his head, and wondering what he could do, listlessly surveyed the scene. By the outer margin of the pit was an oval pond, and over it hung the attenuated skeleton of a chrome-yellow moon, which had only a few days to last – the morning star dogging her on the left hand. The pool glittered like a dead man's eye, and as the world awoke a breeze blew, shaking and elongating the reflection of the moon without breaking it, and turning the image of the star to a phosphoric streak upon the water. All this Oak saw and remembered.

As far as could be learnt it appeared that the poor young dog, still under the impression that since he was kept for running after sheep, the more he ran after them the better, had at the end of his meal off the dead lamb, which may have given him additional energy and spirits, collected all the ewes into a corner, driven the timid creatures through the hedge, across the upper field, and by main force of worrying had given them momentum enough to break down a portion of the rotten railing, and so hurled them over the edge.

George's son had done his work so thoroughly that he was considered too good a workman to live, and was, in fact, taken and tragically shot at twelve o'clock that same day – another instance of the untoward fate which so often attends dogs and other philosophers who follow out a train of reasoning to its logical conclusion, and attempt perfectly consistent conduct in a world made up so largely of compromise.

Gabriel's farm had been stocked by a dealer – on the strength of Oak's promising look and character – who was receiving a percentage from the farmer till such time as the advance should be cleared off. Oak found that the value of stock, plant, and implements which were really his own would be about sufficient to pay his debts, leaving himself a free man with the clothes he stood up in, and nothing more.

VI

The Fair – The Journey – The Fire

TWO months passed away. We are brought on to a day in February, on which was held the yearly statute or hiring fair in the county-town of Casterbridge.

At one end of the streets stood from two to three hundred blithe and hearty labourers waiting upon Chance – all men of the stamp to whom labour suggests nothing worse than a wrestle with gravitation, and pleasure nothing better than a renunciation of the same. Among these, carters and waggoners were distinguished by having a piece of whip-cord twisted round their hats; thatchers wore a fragment of woven straw; shepherds held their sheep-crooks in their hands; and thus the situation required was known to the hirers at a glance.

In the crowd was an athletic young fellow of somewhat superior appearance to the rest – in fact, his superiority was marked enough to lead several ruddy peasants standing by to speak to him inquiringly, as to a farmer, and to use 'Sir' as a finishing word. His answer always was, –

'I am looking for a place myself – a bailiff's. Do ye know of anybody who wants one?'

Gabriel was paler now. His eyes were more meditative, and his expression was more sad. He had passed through an ordeal of wretchedness which had given him more than it had taken away. He had sunk from his modest elevation as pastoral king into the very slime-pits of Siddim; but there was left to him a dignified calm he had never before known, and that indifference to fate which, though it often makes a villain of a man, is the basis of his sublimity when it does not. And thus the abasement had been exaltation, and the loss gain.

In the morning a regiment of cavalry had left the town, and a sergeant and his party had been beating up for recruits through the four streets. As the end of the day drew on, and he found himself not hired, Gabriel almost wished that he had joined them, and gone off to serve his country. Weary of standing in the market-place, and not much minding the kind of work he turned his hand to, he decided to offer himself in some other capacity than that of bailiff.

All the farmers seemed to be wanting shepherds. Sheep-tending was Gabriel's speciality. Turning down an obscure street and entering an obscurer lane, he went up to a smith's shop.

'How long would it take you to make a shepherd's crook?'

'Twenty minutes.'

'How much?'

'Two shillings.'

He sat on a bench and the crook was made, a stem being given him into the bargain.

He then went to a ready-made clothes shop, the owner of which had a large rural connection. As the crook had absorbed most of Gabriel's money, he attempted, and carried out, an exchange of his overcoat for a shepherd's regulation smock-frock.

This transaction having been completed he again hurried off to the centre of the town, and stood on the kerb of the pavement, as a shepherd, crook in hand.

Now that Oak had turned himself into a shepherd it seemed that bailiffs were most in demand. However, two or three farmers noticed him and drew near. Dialogues followed, more or less in the subjoined form:

'Where do you come from?'

'Norcombe.'

'That's a long way.'

'Fifteen miles.'

'Whose farm were you on last?'

'My own.'

This reply invariably operated like a rumour of cholera. The inquiring farmer would edge away and shake his head dubiously. Gabriel, like his dog, was too good to be trustworthy, and he never made advance beyond this point.

It is safer to accept any chance that offers itself, and extemporize a procedure to fit it, than to get a good plan matured, and wait for a chance of using it. Gabriel wished he had not nailed up his colours as a shepherd, but had laid himself out for anything in the whole cycle of labour that was required in the fair. It grew dusk. Some merry men were whistling and singing by the corn-exchange. Gabriel's hand, which had lain for some time idle in his smock-frock pocket, touched his flute, which he carried there. Here was an opportunity for putting his dearly bought wisdom into practice.

He drew out his flute and began to play 'Jockey to the Fair' in the style of a man who had never known a moment's sorrow. Oak could pipe with Arcadian sweetness, and the sound of the well-known notes cheered his own heart as well as those of the loungers. He played on with spirit, and in half an hour had earned in pence what was a small fortune to a destitute man.

By making inquiries he learnt that there was another fair at Shottsford the next day.

'How far is Shottsford?'

'Ten miles t'other side of Weatherbury.'

Weatherbury! It was where Bathsheba had gone two months before. This information was like coming from night into noon.

'How far is it to Weatherbury?'

'Five or six miles.'

Bathsheba had probably left Weatherbury long before this time, but the place had enough interest attaching to it to lead Oak to choose Shottsford fair as his next field of inquiry, because it lay in the Weatherbury quarter. Moreover, the Weatherbury folk were by no means uninteresting intrinsically. If report spoke truly they were as hardy, merry, thriving, wicked a set as any in the whole county. Oak resolved to sleep at Weatherbury that night on his way to Shottsford, and struck out at once into the high road which had been recommended as the direct route to the village in question.

The road stretched through water-meadows traversed by little brooks, whose quivering surfaces were braided along their centres, and folded into creases at the sides; or, where the flow was more rapid, the stream was pied with spots of white froth, which rode on in undisturbed serenity. On the higher levels the dead and dry carcases of leaves tapped the ground as they bowled along helter-skelter upon the shoulders of the wind, and little birds in the hedges were rustling their feathers and tucking themselves in comfortably for the night, retaining their places if Oak kept moving, but flying away if he stopped to look at them. He passed by Yalbury Wood where the game-birds were rising to their roosts, and heard the crack-voiced cock-pheasants' 'cu-uck, cuck', and the wheezy whistle of the hens.

By the time he had walked three or four miles every shape in the landscape had assumed a uniform hue of blackness. He descended Yalbury Hill and could just discern ahead of him a waggon, drawn up under a great over-hanging tree by the roadside.

On coming close, he found there were no horses attached to it, the spot being apparently quite deserted. The waggon, from its position, seemed to have been left there for the night, for beyond about half a truss of hay which was heaped in the bottom, it was quite empty. Gabriel sat down on the shafts of the vehicle and considered his position. He calculated that he had walked a very fair proportion of the journey; and having been on foot since daybreak, he felt tempted to lie down upon the hay in the waggon instead of pushing on to the village of Weatherbury, and having to pay for a lodging.

Eating his last slices of bread and ham, and drinking from the bottle of cider he had taken the precaution to bring with him, he got into the lonely waggon. Here he spread half of the hay as a bed, and, as well as he could in the darkness, pulled the other half over him by way of bed-clothes, covering himself entirely, and feeling, physically, as comfortable as ever he had been in his life. Inward melancholy it was impossible for a man like Oak, introspective far beyond his neighbours, to banish quite, whilst conning the present untoward page of his history. So, thinking of his misfortunes, amorous and pastoral, he fell asleep, shepherds enjoying, in common with sailors, the privilege of being able to summon the god instead of having to wait for him.

On somewhat suddenly awaking, after a sleep of whose length he had no idea, Oak found that the waggon was in motion. He was being carried along the road at a rate rather considerable for a vehicle without springs, and under circumstances of physical uneasiness, his head being dandled up and down on the bed of the waggon like a kettledrum-stick. He then distinguished voices in conversation, coming from the forepart of the waggon. His concern at this dilemma (which would have been alarm, had he been a thriving man; but misfortune is a fine opiate to personal terror) led him to peer cautiously from the hay, and the first sight he beheld was the stars above him. Charles's Wain was getting towards a right angle with the Pole star, and Gabriel concluded that it must be about nine o'clock – in other words, that he had slept two hours. This small astronomical calculation was made without any positive effort, and whilst he was stealthily turning to discover, if possible, into whose hands he had fallen.

Two figures were dimly visible in front, sitting with their legs outside the waggon, one of whom was driving. Gabriel soon found that this was the waggoner, and it appeared they had come from Casterbridge fair, like himself.

A conversation was in progress, which continued thus:

'Be as 'twill, she's a fine handsome body as far's looks be concerned. But that's only the skin of the woman, and these dandy cattle be as proud as a lucifer in their insides.'

'Ay – so 'a do seem, Billy Smallbury – so 'a do seem.' This utterance was very shaky by nature, and more so by circumstance, the jolting of the waggon not being without its effect upon the speaker's larynx. It came from the man who held the reins.

'She's a very vain feymell – so 'tis said here and there.'

'Ah, now. If so be 'tis like that, I can't look her in the face. Lord, no: not I – heh-heh-heh! Such a shy man as I be!'

'Yes – she's very vain. 'Tis said that every night at going to bed she looks in the glass to put on her nightcap properly.'

'And not a married woman. Oh, the world!'

'And 'a can play the peanner, so 'tis said. Can play so clever that 'a can make a psalm tune sound as well as the merriest loose song a man can wish for.'

'D'ye tell o't! A happy time for us, and I feel quite a new man! And how do she play?'

'That I don't know, Master Poorgrass.'

On hearing these and other similar remarks, a wild thought flashed into Gabriel's mind that they might be speaking of Bathsheba. There were, however, no grounds for retaining such a supposition, for the waggon, though going in the direction of Weatherbury, might be going beyond it, and the woman alluded to seemed to be the mistress of some estate. They were now apparently close upon Weatherbury, and not to alarm the speakers unnecessarily Gabriel slipped out of the waggon unseen.

He turned to an opening in the hedge, which he found to be a gate, and mounting thereon he sat meditating whether to seek a cheap lodging in the village, or to ensure a cheaper one by lying under some hay or corn stack. The crunching jangle of the waggon died upon his ear. He was about to walk on, when he noticed on his left hand an unusual light – appearing about half a mile distant. Oak watched it, and the glow increased. Something was on fire.

Gabriel again mounted the gate, and, leaping down on the other side upon what he found to be ploughed soil, made across the field in the exact direction of the fire. The blaze, enlarging in a double ratio by his approach and its own increase, showed him as he drew nearer the outlines of ricks beside it, lighted up to great distinctness. A rick-yard was the source of the fire. His weary face now began to be painted over with a rich orange glow, and the whole front of his smock-front and gaiters was covered with a dancing shadow pattern of thorn-twigs – the light reaching him through a leafless intervening hedge – and the metallic curve of his sheep-crook shone silver-bright in the same abounding rays. He came up to the boundary fence, and stood to regain breath. It seemed as if the spot was unoccupied by a living soul.

The fire was issuing from a long straw-stack, which was so far gone as to preclude a possibility of saving it. A rick burns differently from a house. As the wind blows the fire inwards, the portion in flames completely disappears like melting sugar, and the outline is lost to the eye. However, a hay or a wheat rick, well put together, will resist combustion for a length of time if it begins on the outside.

This before Gabriel's eyes was a rick of straw, loosely put together, and the flames darted into it with lightning swiftness. It glowed on the windward side, rising and falling in intensity like the coal of a cigar. Then a superincumbent bundle rolled down with a whisking noise; flames elongated, and bent themselves about with a quiet roar, but no crackle. Banks of smoke went off horizontally at the back like passing clouds, and behind these burned hidden pyres, illuminating the semi-transparent sheet of smoke to a lustrous yellow uniformity. Individual straws in the foreground were consumed in a creeping movement of ruddy heat, as if they were knots of red worms, and above shone imaginary fiery faces, tongues hanging from lips, glaring eyes, and other impish forms, from which at intervals sparks flew in clusters like birds from a nest.

Oak suddenly ceased from being a mere spectator by discovering the case to be more serious than he had at first imagined. A scroll of smoke blew aside and revealed to him a wheat-rick in startling juxtaposition with the decaying one, and behind this a series of others, composing the main corn produce of the farm; so that instead of the straw-stack standing, as he had imagined, comparatively isolated, there was a regular connection between it and the remaining stacks of the group.

Gabriel leapt over the hedge, and saw that he was not alone. The first man he came to was running about in a great hurry, as if his thoughts were several yards in advance of his body, which they could never drag on fast enough.

'O, man – fire, fire! A good master and a bad servant is fire, fire! – I mane a bad servant and a good master. O Mark Clark – come! And you, Billy Smallbury – and you, Maryann Money – and you, Jan Coggan, and Matthew there!' Other figures now appeared behind this shouting man and among the smoke, and Gabriel found that, far from being alone, he was in a great company – whose shadows danced merrily up and down, timed by the jigging of the flames, and not at all by their owners' movements. The assemblage – belonging to that class of society which casts its thoughts into the form of feeling, and its feelings into the form of commotion – set to work with a remarkable confusion of purpose.

'Stop that draught under the wheat-rick!' cried Gabriel to those nearest to him. The corn stood on stone staddles, and between these, tongues of yellow hue from the burning straw licked and darted playfully. If the fire once got *under* this stack, all would be lost.

'Get a tarpaulin – quick!' said Gabriel.

A rick-cloth was brought, and they hung it like a curtain across the channel. The flames immediately ceased to go under the bottom of the corn-stack, and stood up vertical.

'Stand here with a bucket of water and keep the cloth wet,' said Gabriel again.

The flames, now driven upwards, began to attack the angles of the huge roof covering the wheat-stack.

'A ladder,' cried Gabriel.

'The ladder was against the straw-rick and is burnt to a cinder,' said a spectre-like form in the smoke.

Oak seized the cut ends of the sheaves, as if he were going to engage in the operation of 'reed-drawing', and digging in his feet, and occasionally sticking in the stem of his sheep-crook, he clambered up the beetling face. He at once sat astride the very apex, and began with his crook to beat off the fiery fragments which had lodged thereon, shouting to the others to get him a bough and a ladder, and some water.

Billy Smallbury – one of the men who had been on the waggon – by this time had found a ladder, which Mark Clark ascended, holding on beside Oak upon the thatch. The smoke at this corner was stifling, and Clark, a nimble fellow, having been handed a bucket of water, bathed Oak's face and sprinkled him generally, whilst Gabriel, now with a long beech-bough in one hand, in addition to his crook in the other, kept sweeping the stack and dislodging all fiery particles.

On the ground the groups of villagers were still occupied in doing all they could to keep down the conflagration, which was not much. They were all tinged orange, and backed up by shadows of varying pattern. Round the corner of the largest stack, out of the direct rays of the fire, stood a pony, bearing a young woman on its back. By her side was another woman, on foot. These two seemed to keep at a distance from the fire, that the horse might not become restive.

'He's a shepherd,' said the woman on foot. 'Yes – he is. See how his crook shines as he beats the rick with it. And his smock-frock is burnt in two holes, I declare! A fine young shepherd he is too, ma'am.'

'Whose shepherd is he?' said the equestrian in a clear voice.

'Don't know, ma'am.'

'Don't any of the others know?'

'Nobody at all – I've asked 'em. Quite a stranger, they say.'

The young woman on the pony rode out from the shade and looked anxiously around.

'Do you think the barn is safe?' she said.

'D'ye think the barn is safe, Jan Coggan?' said the second woman, passing on the question to the nearest man in that direction.

'Safe now – leastwise I think so. If this rick had gone the barn would have followed. 'Tis that bold shepherd up there that have done the most good – he sitting on the top o' rick, whizzing his great long arms about like a windmill.'

'He does work hard,' said the young woman on horseback, looking up at Gabriel through her thick woollen veil. 'I wish he was shepherd here. Don't any of you know his name?'

'Never heard the man's name in my life, or seed his form afore.'

The fire began to get worsted, and Gabriel's elevated position being no longer required of him, he made as if to descend.

'Maryann,' said the girl on horseback, 'go to him as he comes down, and say that the farmer wishes to thank him for the great service he has done.'

Maryann stalked off towards the rick and met Oak at the foot of the ladder. She delivered her message.

'Where is your master the farmer?' asked Gabriel, kindling with the idea of getting employment that seemed to strike him now.

' 'Tisn't a master; 'tis a mistress, shepherd.'

'A woman farmer?'

'Ay, 'a believe, and a rich one too!' said a bystander. 'Lately 'a came here from a distance. Took on her uncle's farm, who died suddenly. Used to measure his money in half-pint cups. They say now that she've business in every bank in Casterbridge, and thinks no more of playing pitch-and-toss sovereign than you and I do pitch-halfpenny – not a bit in the world, shepherd.'

'That's she, back there upon the pony,' said Maryann; 'wi' her face a-covered up in that black cloth with holes in it.'

Oak, his features smudged, grimy, and undiscoverable from the smoke and heat, his smock-frock burnt into holes and dripping with water, the ash stem of his sheep-crook charred six inches shorter, advanced with the humility stern adversity had thrust upon him up to the slight female form in the saddle. He lifted his hat with respect, and not without gallantry: stepping close to her hanging feet he said in a hesitating voice, –

'Do you happen to want a shepherd, ma'am?'

She lifted the wool veil tied round her face, and looked all astonishment. Gabriel and his cold-hearted darling, Bathsheba Everdene, were face to face.

Bathsheba did not speak, and he mechanically repeated in an abashed and sad voice, –

'Do you want a shepherd, ma'am?'

* VII *

Recognition – A Timid Girl

BATHSHEBA withdrew into the shade. She scarcely knew whether most to be amused at the singularity of the meeting, or to be concerned at its awkwardness. There was room for a little pity, also for a very little exultation: the former at his position, the latter at her own. Embarrassed she was not, and she remembered Gabriel's declaration of love to her at Norcombe only to think she had nearly forgotten it.

'Yes,' she murmured, putting on an air of dignity, and turning again to him with a little warmth of cheek; 'I do want a shepherd. But –'

'He's the very man, ma'am,' said one of the villagers, quietly.

Conviction breeds conviction. 'Ay, that 'a is,' said a second, decisively.

'The man, truly!' said a third, with heartiness.

'He's all there!' said number four, fervidly.

'Then will you tell him to speak to the bailiff?' said Bathsheba.

All was practical again now. A summer eve and loneliness would have been necessary to give the meeting its proper fulness of romance.

The bailiff was pointed out to Gabriel, who, checking the palpitation within his breast at discovering that this Ashtoreth of strange report was only a modification of Venus the well-known and admired, retired with him to talk over the necessary preliminaries of hiring.

The fire before them wasted away. 'Men,' said Bathsheba, 'you shall take a little refreshment after this extra work. Will you come to the house?'

'We could knock in a bit and a drop a good deal freer, Miss, if so be ye'd send it to Warren's Malthouse,' replied the spokesman.

Bathsheba then rode off into the darkness, and the men straggled on to the village in twos and threes – Oak and the bailiff being left by the rick alone.

'And now,' said the bailiff, finally, 'all is settled, I think, about your coming, and I am going home-along. Good-night to ye, shepherd.'

'Can you get me a lodging?' inquired Gabriel.

'That I can't, indeed,' he said, moving past Oak as a Christian edges past an offertory-plate when he does not mean to contribute. 'If you follow on the road till you come to Warren's Malthouse, where they are all gone to have their snap of victuals, I daresay some of 'em will tell you of a place. Good-night to ye, shepherd.'

The bailiff who showed this nervous dread of loving his neighbour as himself, went up the hill, and Oak walked on to the village, still astonished at the rencounter with Bathsheba, glad of his nearness to her, and perplexed at the rapidity with which the unpractised girl of Norcombe had developed into the supervising and cool woman here. But some women only require an emergency to make them fit for one.

Obliged to some extent to forgo dreaming in order to find the way, he reached the churchyard, and passed round it under the wall where several ancient trees grew. There was a wide margin of grass along here, and Gabriel's footsteps were deadened by its softness, even at this indurating period of the year. When abreast of a trunk which appeared to be the oldest of the old, he became aware that a figure was standing behind it. Gabriel did not pause in his walk, and in another moment he accidentally kicked a loose stone. The noise was enough to disturb the motionless stranger, who started and assumed a careless position.

It was a slim girl, rather thinly clad.

'Good-night to you,' said Gabriel heartily.

'Good-night,' said the girl to Gabriel.

The voice was unexpectedly attractive; it was the low and dulcet note suggestive of romance; common in descriptions, rare in experience.

'I'll thank you to tell me if I'm in the way for Warren's Malthouse?' Gabriel resumed, primarily to gain the information, indirectly to get more of the music.

'Quite right. It's at the bottom of the hill. And do you know –' The girl hesitated and then went on again. 'Do you know how late they keep open the Buck's Head Inn?' She seemed to be won by Gabriel's heartiness, as Gabriel had been won by her modulations.

'I don't know where the Buck's Head is, or anything about it. Do you think of going there to-night?'

'Yes –' The woman again paused. There was no necessity for any continuance of speech, and the fact that she did add more seemed to proceed from an unconscious desire to show unconcern by making a remark, which is noticeable in the ingenuous when they are acting by stealth. 'You are not a Weatherbury man?' she said timorously.

'I am not. I am the new shepherd – just arrived.'

'Only a shepherd – and you seem almost a farmer by your ways.'

'Only a shepherd,' Gabriel repeated, in a dull cadence of finality. His thoughts were directed to the past, his eyes to the feet of the girl; and for the first time he saw lying there a bundle of some sort. She may have perceived the direction of his face, for she said coaxingly, –

'You won't say anything in the parish about having seen me here, will you – at least, not for a day or two?'

'I won't if you wish me not to,' said Oak.

'Thank you, indeed,' the other replied. 'I am rather poor, and I don't want people to know anything about me.' Then she was silent and shivered.

'You ought to have a cloak on such a cold night,' Gabriel observed. 'I would advise 'ee to get indoors.'

'O no! Would you mind going on and leaving me? I thank you much for what you have told me.'

'I will go on,' he said; adding hesitatingly, – 'Since you are not very well off, perhaps you would accept this trifle from me. It is only a shilling, but it is all I have to spare.'

'Yes, I will take it,' said the stranger gratefully.

She extended her hand; Gabriel his. In feeling for each other's palm in the gloom before the money could be passed, a minute incident occurred which told much. Gabriel's fingers alighted on the young woman's wrist. It was beating with a throb of tragic intensity. He had frequently felt the same quick, hard beat in the femoral artery of his lambs when overdriven. It suggested a consumption too great of a vitality which, to judge from her figure and stature, was already too little.

'What is the matter?'

'Nothing.'

'But there is.'

'No, no, no! Let your having seen me be a secret!'

'Very well; I will. Good-night, again.'

'Good-night.'

The young girl remained motionless by the tree, and Gabriel descended into the village of Weatherbury, or Lower Longpuddle as it was sometimes called. He fancied that he had felt himself in the penumbra of a very deep sadness when touching that slight and fragile creature. But wisdom lies in moderating mere impressions, and Gabriel endeavoured to think little of this.

* VIII *

The Malthouse – The Chat – News

WARREN'S Malthouse was enclosed by an old wall inwrapped with ivy, and though not much of the exterior was visible at this hour, the character and purposes of the building were clearly enough shown by its outline upon the sky. From the walls an overhanging thatched roof sloped up to a point in the centre, upon which rose a small wooden lantern, fitted with louvre-boards on all the four sides, and from these openings a mist was dim perceived to be escaping into the night air. There was no window in front; but a square hole in the door was glazed with a single pane, through which red, comfortable rays now stretched out upon the ivied wall in front. Voices were to be heard inside.

Oak's hand skimmed the surface of the door with fingers extended to an Elymas-the-Sorcerer pattern, till he found a leathern strap, which he pulled. This lifted a wooden latch, and the door swung open.

The room inside was lighted only by the ruddy glow from the kiln mouth, which shone over the floor with the streaming horizontality of the setting sun, and threw upwards the shadows of all facial irregularities in those assembled around. The stone-flag floor was worn into a path from the doorway to the kiln, and into undulations everywhere. A curved settle of unplaned oak stretched along one side, and in a remote corner was a small bed and bedstead, the owner and frequent occupier of which was the maltster.

This aged man was now sitting opposite the fire, his frosty white hair and beard overgrowing his gnarled figure like the grey moss and lichen upon the leafless apple-tree. He wore breeches and the laced-up shoes called ankle-jacks; he kept his eyes fixed upon the fire.

Gabriel's nose was greeted by an atmosphere laden with the sweet smell of new malt. The conversation (which seemed to have been concerning the origin of the fire) immediately ceased, and every one ocularly criticized him to the degree expressed by contracting the flesh of their foreheads and looking at him with narrowed eyelids, as if he had been a light too strong for their sight. Several exclaimed meditatively, after this operation had been completed: –

'Oh, 'tis the new shepherd, 'a b'lieve.'

'We thought we heard a hand pawing about the door for the bobbin. but weren't sure 'twere not a dead leaf blowed across,' said another. 'Come in, shepherd; sure ye be welcome, though we don't know yer name.'

'Gabriel Oak, that's my name, neighbours.'

The ancient maltster sitting in the midst turned at this – his turning being as the turning of a rusty crane.

'That's never Gable Oak's grandson over at Norcombe – never!' he said, as a formula expressive of surprise, which nobody was supposed to take literally.

'My father and my grandfather were old men of the name of Gabriel,' said the shepherd placidly.

'Thought I knowed the man's face as I seed him on the rick! – thought I did! And where be ye trading o't to now, shepherd?'

'I'm thinking of biding here,' said Mr Oak.

'Knowed yer grandfather for years and years!' continued the maltster, the words coming forth of their own accord as if the momentum previously imparted had been sufficient.

'Ah – and did you!'

'Knowed yer grandmother.'

'And her too!'

'Likewise knowed yer father when he was a child. Why, my boy Jacob there and your father were sworn brothers – that they were sure – weren't ye Jacob?'

'Ay, sure,' said his son, a young man about sixty-five, with a semi-bald head and one tooth in the left centre of his upper jaw, which made much of itself by standing prominent, like a milestone in a bank. 'But 'twas Joe had most to do with him. However, my son William must have knowed the very man afore us – didn't ye, Billy, afore ye left Norcombe?'

'No, 'twas Andrew,' said Jacob's son Billy, a child of forty, or thereabouts, who manifested the peculiarity of possessing a cheerful soul in a gloomy body, and whose whiskers were assuming a chinchilla shade here and there.

'I can mind Andrew,' said Oak, 'as being a man in the place when I was quite a child.'

'Ay – the other day I and my youngest daughter, Liddy, were over at my grandson's christening,' continued Billy. 'We were talking about this very family, and 'twas only last Purification Day in this very world, when the use-money is gied away to the second-best poor folk, you know, shepherd, and I can mind the day because they all had to traypse up to the vestry – yes, this very man's family.'

'Come, shepherd, and drink. 'Tis gape and swaller with us – a drap of sommit, but not of much account,' said the maltster, removing from the fire his eyes, which were vermilion-red and bleared by gazing into it for so many years. 'Take up the God-forgive-me, Jacob. See if 'tis warm, Jacob.'

Jacob stooped to the God-forgive-me, which was a two-handled tall mug standing in the ashes, cracked and charred with heat: it was rather furred with extraneous matter about the outside, especially in the crevices of the handles, the innermost curves of which may not have seen daylight for several years by reason of this encrustation thereon – formed of ashes accidentally wetted with cider and baked hard; but to the mind of any sensible drinker the cup was no worse for that, being incontestably clean on the inside and about the rim. It may be observed that such a class of mug is called a God-forgive-me in Weatherbury and its vicinity for uncertain reasons; probably because its size makes any given toper feel ashamed of himself when he sees its bottom in drinking it empty.

Jacob, on receiving the order to see if the liquor was warm enough, placidly dipped his forefinger into it by way of thermometer, and having pronounced it nearly of the proper degree, raised the cup and very civilly attempted to dust some of the ashes from the bottom with the skirt of his smock-frock, because Shepherd Oak was a stranger.

'A clane cup for the shepherd,' said the maltster commandingly.

'No – not at all,' said Gabriel, in a reproving tone of considerateness. 'I never fuss about dirt in its pure state, and when I know what sort it is.' Taking the mug he drank an inch or more from the depth of its contents, and duly passed it to the next man. 'I wouldn't think of giving such trouble to neighbours in washing up when there's so much work to be done in the world already,' continued Oak in a moister tone, after recovering from the stoppage of breath which is occasioned by pulls at large mugs.

'A right sensible man,' said Jacob.

'True, true; it can't be gainsaid!' observed a brisk young man – Mark

Clark by name, a genial and pleasant gentleman, whom to meet anywhere in your travels was to know, to know was to drink with, and to drink with was, unfortunately, to pay for.

'And here's a mouthful of bread and bacon that mis'ess have sent, shepherd. The cider will go down better with a bit of victuals. Don't ye chaw quite close, shepherd, for I let the bacon fall in the road outside as I was bringing it along, and may be 'tis rather gritty. There, 'tis clane dirt; and we all know what that is, as you say, and you bain't a particular man we see, shepherd.'

'True, true – not at all,' said the friendly Oak.

'Don't let your teeth quite meet, and you won't feel the sandiness at all. Ah! 'tis wonderful what can be done by contrivance!'

'My own mind exactly, neighbour.'

'Ah, he's his granfer's own grandson! – his granfer were just such a nice unparticular man!' said the maltster.

'Drink, Henry Fray – drink,' magnanimously said Jan Coggan, a person who held Saint-Simonian notions of share and share alike where liquor was concerned, as the vessel showed signs of approaching him in its gradual revolution among them.

Having at this moment reached the end of a wistful gaze into mid-air, Henry did not refuse. He was a man of more than middle age, with eyebrows high up in his forehead, who laid it down that the law of the world was bad, with a long-suffering look through his listeners at the world alluded to, as it presented itself to his imagination. He always signed his name 'Henery' – strenuously insisting upon that spelling, and if any passing schoolmaster ventured to remark that the second 'e' was superfluous and old-fashioned, he received the reply that 'H-e-n-e-r-y' was the name he was christened and the name he would stick to – in the tone of one to whom orthographical differences were matters which had a great deal to do with personal character.

Mr Jan Coggan, who had passed the cup to Henery, was a crimson man with a spacious countenance and private glimmer in his eye, whose name had appeared on the marriage register of Weatherbury and neighbouring parishes as best man and chief witness in countless unions of the previous twenty years; he also very frequently filled the post of head godfather in baptisms of the subtly-jovial kind.

'Come, Mark Clark – come. Ther's plenty more in the barrel,' said Jan.

'Ay – that I will; 'tis my only doctor,' replied Mr Clark, who, twenty years younger than Jan Coggan, revolved in the same orbit. He secreted mirth on all occasions for special discharge at popular parties.

'Why, Joseph Poorgrass, ye han't had a drop!' said Mr Coggan to a self-conscious man in the background, thrusting the cup towards him.

'Such a modest man as he is!' said Jacob Smallbury. 'Why, ye've hardly had strength of eye enough to look in our young mis'ess's face, so I hear, Joseph?'

All looked at Joseph Poorgrass with pitying reproach.

'No – I've hardly looked at her at all,' simpered Joseph, reducing his body smaller whilst talking, apparently from a meek sense of undue prominence. 'And when I seed her, 'twas nothing but blushes with me!'

'Poor feller,' said Mr Clark.

' 'Tis a curious nature for a man,' said Jan Coggan.

'Yes,' continued Joseph Poorgrass – his shyness, which was so painful as a defect, filling him with a mild complacency now that it was regarded as an interesting study. ' 'Twere blush, blush, blush with me every minute of the time, when she was speaking to me.'

'I believe ye, Joseph Poorgrass, for we all know ye to be a very bashful man.'

' 'Tis a' awkward gift for a man, poor soul,' said the maltster. 'And ye have suffered from it a long time, we know.'

'Ay, ever since I was a boy. Yes – mother was concerned to her heart about it – yes. But 'twas all nought.'

'Did ye ever go into the world to try and stop it, Joseph Poorgrass?'

'Oh ay, tried all sorts o' company. They took me to Greenhill Fair, and into a great gay jerry-go-nimble show, where there were women-folk riding round – standing upon horses, with hardly anything on but their smocks; but it didn't cure me a morsel. And then I was put errand-man at the Women's Skittle Alley at the back of the Tailor's Arms in Casterbridge. 'Twas a horrible sinful situation, and a very curious place for a good man. I had to stand and look ba'dy people in the face from morning till night; but 'twas no use – I was just as bad as ever after all. Blushes hev been in the family for generations. There, 'tis a happy providence that I be no worse.'

'True,' said Jacob Smallbury, deepening his thoughts to a profounder view of the subject. ' 'Tis a thought to look at, that ye might have been worse; but even as you be, 'tis a very bad affliction for 'ee, Joseph. For ye see, shepherd, though 'tis very well for a woman, dang it all, 'tis awkward for a man like him, poor feller?'

' 'Tis – 'tis,' said Gabriel, recovering from a meditation. 'Yes, very awkward for the man.'

'Ay, and he's very timid, too,' observed Jan Coggan. 'Once he had been working late at Yalbury Bottom, and had had a drap of drink, and lost his way as he was coming home-along through Yalbury Wood, didn't ye, Master Poorgrass?'

'No, no, no; not that story!' expostulated the modest man, forcing a laugh to bury his concern.

'– And so 'a lost himself quite,' continued Mr Coggan, with an impassive face, implying that a true narrative, like time and tide, must run its course and would respect no man. 'And as he was coming along in the middle of the night, much afeared, and not able to find his way out of the trees nohow, 'a cried out, "Man-a-lost! man-a-lost!" A owl in a tree happened to be crying "Whoo-whoo-whoo!" as owls do, you know, shepherd' (Gabriel nodded), 'and Joseph, all in a tremble, said, "Joseph Poorgrass, of Weatherbury, sir!" '

'No, no, now – that's too much!' said the timid man, becoming a man of brazen courage all of a sudden. 'I didn't say *sir*. I'll take my oath I didn't say "Joseph Poorgrass o' Weatherbury, sir". No, no; what's right is right, and I never said sir to the bird, knowing very well that no man of a gentleman's rank would be hollering there at that time o' night. "Joseph Poorgrass of Weatherbury", – that's every word I said, and I shouldn't ha' said that if 't hadn't been for Keeper Day's metheglin . . . There, 'twas a merciful thing it ended where it did.'

The question of which was right being tacitly waived by the company, Jan went on meditatively: –

'And he's the fearfullest man, bain't ye, Joseph? Ay, another time ye were lost by Lambing-Down Gate, weren't ye, Joseph?'

'I was,' replied Poorgrass, as if there were some conditions too serious even for modesty to remember itself under, this being one.

'Yes; that were the middle of the night, too. The gate would not open, try how he would, and knowing there was the Devil's hand in it, he kneeled down.'

'Ay,' said Joseph, acquiring confidence from the warmth of the fire, the cider, and a perception of the narrative capabilities of the experience alluded to. 'My heart died within me, that time; but I kneeled down and said the Lord's Prayer, and then the Belief right through, and then the Ten Commandments, in earnest prayer. But no, the gate wouldn't open; and then I went on with Dearly Beloved Brethren, and, thinks I, this makes four, and 'tis all I know out of book, and if this don't do it nothing will, and I'm a lost man. Well, when I got to Saying After Me, I rose from my knees and found the gate would open – yes, neighbours, the gate opened the same as ever.'

A meditation on the obvious inference was indulged in by all, and during its continuance each directed his vision into the ashpit, which glowed like a desert in the tropics under a vertical sun, shaping their eyes long and liny, partly because of the light, partly from the depth of the subject discussed.

Gabriel broke the silence. 'What sort of a place is this to live at, and what sort of a miss'ess is she to work under?' Gabriel's bosom thrilled gently as he thus slipped under the notice of the assembly the innermost subject of his heart.

'We d'know little of her – nothing. She only showed herself a few days ago. Her uncle was took bad, and the doctor was called with his world-wide skill; but he couldn't save the man. As I take it, she's going to keep on the farm.'

'That's about the shape o't, 'a b'lieve,' said Jan Coggan. 'Ay, 'tis a very good family. I'd as soon be under 'em as under one here and there. Her uncle was a very fair sort of man. Did ye know en, shepherd – a bachelor-man?'

'Not at all.'

'I used to go to his house a-courting my first wife, Charlotte, who was his dairymaid. Well, a very good-hearted man were Farmer Everdene, and I being a respectable young fellow was allowed to call and see her and drink as much ale as I liked, but not to carry away any – outside my skin I mane, of course.'

'Ay, ay, Jan Coggan; we know yer maning.'

'And so you see 'twas beautiful ale, and I wished to value his kindness as much as I could, and not to be so ill-mannered as to drink only a thimbleful, which would have been insulting the man's generosity –'

'True, Master Coggan, 'twould so,' corroborated Mark Clark.

'– And so I used to eat a lot of salt fish afore going, and then by the time I got there I were as dry as a lime-basket – so thorough dry that that ale would slip down – ah, 'twould slip down sweet! Happy times! heavenly times! Such lovely drunks as I used to have at that house! You can mind, Jacob? You used to go wi' me sometimes.'

'I can – I can,' said Jacob. 'That one, too, that we had at Buck's Head on a White Monday was a pretty tipple.'

' 'Twas. But for a wet of the better class, that brought you no nearer to the horned man than you were afore you begun, there was none like those in Farmer Everdene's kitchen. Not a single damn allowed; no, not a bare poor one, even at the most cheerful moment when all were blindest, though the good old word of sin thrown in here and there at such times is a great relief to a merry soul.'

'True,' said the maltster. 'Nater requires her swearing at the regular times, or she's not herself; and unholy exclamations is a necessity of life.'

'But Charlotte,' continued Coggan – 'not a word of the sort would Charlotte allow, nor the smallest item of taking in vain . . . Ay, poor Charlotte, I wonder if she had the good fortune to get into Heaven when 'a died! But 'a was never much in luck's way and perhaps 'a went downstairs after all, poor soul.'

'And did any of you know Miss Everdene's father and mother?' inquired the shepherd, who found some difficulty in keeping the conversation in the desired channel.

'I knew them a little,' said Jacob Smallbury; 'but they were townsfolk, and didn't live here. They've been dead for years. Father, what sort of people were mis'ess' father and mother?'

'Well,' said the maltster, 'he wasn't much to look at; but she was a lovely woman. He was fond enough of her as his sweetheart.'

'Used to kiss her scores and long-hundreds o' times, so 'twas said,' observed Coggan.

'He was very proud of her, too, when they were married, as I've been told,' said the maltster.

'Ay,' said Coggan. 'He admired her so much that he used to light the candle three times a night to look at her.'

'Boundless love; I shouldn't have supposed it in the universe!' murmured Joseph Poorgrass, who habitually spoke on a large scale in his moral reflections.

'Well, to be sure,' said Gabriel.

'Oh, 'tis true enough. I knowed the man and woman both well. Levi

Everdene – that was the man's name, sure. "Man", saith I in my hurry, but he were of a higher circle of life than that – 'a was a gentleman-tailor really, worth scores of pounds. And he became a very celebrated bankrupt two or three times.'

'Oh, I thought he was quite a common man!' said Joseph.

'O no, no! That man failed for heaps of money; hundreds in gold and silver.'

The maltster being rather short of breath, Mr Coggan, after absently scrutinizing a coal which had fallen among the ashes, took up the narrative, with a private twirl of his eye: –

'Well, now, you'd hardly believe it, but that man – our Miss Everdene's father – was one of the ficklest husbands alive, after a while. Understand, 'a didn't want to be fickle, but he couldn't help it. The poor feller were faithful and true enough to her in his wish, but his heart would rove, do what he would. He spoke to me in real tribulation about it once. "Coggan," he said, "I could never wish for a handsomer woman than I've got, but feeling she's ticketed as my lawful wife, I can't help my wicked heart wandering, do what I will." But at last I believe he cured it by making her take off her wedding-ring and calling her by her maiden name as they sat together after the shop was shut, and so 'a would get to fancy she was only his sweetheart, and not married to him at all. And as soon as he could thoroughly fancy he was doing wrong and committing the seventh, 'a got to like her as well as ever, and they lived on a perfect picture of mutel love.'

'Well, 'twas a most ungodly remedy,' murmured Joseph Poorgrass; 'but we ought to feel deep cheerfulness that a happy Providence kept it from being any worse. You see, he might have gone the bad road and given his eyes to unlawfulness entirely – yes, gross unlawfulness, so to say it.'

'You see,' said Billy Smallbury, 'the man's will was to do right, sure enough, but his heart didn't chime in.'

'He got so much better that he was quite godly in his later years, wasn't he, Jan?' said Joseph Poorgrass. 'He got himself confirmed over again in a more serious way, and took to saying "Amen" almost as loud as the clerk, and he liked to copy comforting verses from the tombstones. He used, too, to hold the money–plate at Let Your Light so Shine, and stand godfather to poor little come-by-chance children; and he kept a missionary box upon his table to nab folks unawares when they called; yes, and he would box the charity-boys' ears, if they laughed in church, till they could hardly stand upright, and do other deeds of piety natural to the saintly inclined.'

'Ay, at that time he thought of nothing but high things,' added Billy Smallbury. 'One day Parson Thirdly met him and said, "Good-morning, Mister Everdene; 'tis a fine day!" "Amen", said Everdene, quite absent-like, thinking only of religion when he seed a parson. Yes, he was a very Christian man.'

'Their daughter was not at all a pretty chiel at that time,' said Henery

Fray. 'Never should have thought she'd have growed up such a handsome body as she is.'

' 'Tis to be hoped her temper is as good as her face.'

'Well, yes; but the baily will have most to do with the business and ourselves. Ah!' Henery gazed into the ashpit, and smiled volumes of ironical knowledge.

'A queer Christian, like the Devil's head in a cowl,* as the saying is,' volunteered Mark Clark.

'He is,' said Henery, implying that irony must cease at a certain point. 'Between we two, man and man, I believe that man would as soon tell a lie Sundays as working-days – that I do so.'

'Good faith, you do talk!' said Gabriel.

'True enough,' said the man of bitter moods, looking round upon the company with the antithetic laughter that comes from a keener appreciation of the miseries of life than ordinary men are capable of. 'Ah, there's people of one sort, and people of another, but that man – bless your souls!'

Gabriel thought fit to change the subject. 'You must be a very aged man, malter, to have sons growed up so old and ancient,' he remarked.

'Father's so old that 'a can't mind his age, can ye, father?' interposed Jacob. 'And he's growed terrible crooked, too, lately,' Jacob continued, surveying his father's figure, which was rather more bowed than his own. 'Really, one may say that father there is three-double.'

'Crooked folk will last a long while,' said the maltster, grimly, and not in the best humour.

'Shepherd would like to hear the pedigree of yer life, father – wouldn't ye, shepherd?'

'Ay, that I should,' said Gabriel, with the heartiness of a man who had longed to hear it for several months. 'What may your age be, malter?'

The maltster cleared his throat in an exaggerated form for emphasis, and elongating his gaze to the remotest point of the ashpit, said, in the slow speech justifiable when the importance of a subject is so generally felt that any mannerism must be tolerated in getting at it, 'Well, I don't mind the year I were born in, but perhaps I can reckon up the places I've lived at, and so get it that way. I bode at Upper Longpuddle across there' (nodding to the north) 'till I were eleven. I bode seven at Kingsbere' (nodding to the east) 'where I took to malting. I went therefrom to Norcombe, and malted there two-and-twenty years, and two-and-twenty years I was there turnip-hoeing and harvesting. Ah, I knowed that old place, Norcombe, years afore you were thought of, Master Oak' (Oak smiled sincere belief in the fact). 'Then I malted at Durnover four year, and four year turnip-hoeing; and I was fourteen times eleven months at Millpond St Jude's' (nodding north-west-by-north). 'Old Twills wouldn't hire me for more than eleven months at a time, to keep me from being chargeable to the parish if so be I was disabled. Then I was three year at

* This phrase is a conjectural emendation of the unintelligible expression, 'as the Devil said to the owl', used by the natives.

Mellstock, and I've been here one-and-thirty year come Candlemas. How much is that?'

'Hundred and seventeen,' chuckled another old gentleman, given to mental arithmetic and little conversation, who had hitherto sat unobserved in a corner.

'Well, then, that's my age,' said the maltster emphatically.

'O no, father!' said Jacob. 'Your turnip-hoeing were in the summer and your malting in the winter of the same years, and ye don't ought to count both halves, father.'

'Chok' it all! I lived through the summers, didn't I? That's my question. I suppose ye'll say next I be no age at all to speak of?'

'Sure we shan't,' said Gabriel soothingly.

'Ye be a very old aged person, malter,' attested Jan Coggan, also soothingly. 'We all know that, and ye must have a wonderful talented constitution to be able to live so long, mustn't he, neighbours?'

'True, true; ye must, malter, wonderful;' said the meeting unanimously.

The maltster, being now pacified, was even generous enough to voluntarily disparage in a slight degree the virtue of having lived a great many years, by mentioning that the cup they were drinking out of was three years older than he.

While the cup was being examined, the end of Gabriel Oak's flute became visible over his smock-frock pocket, and Henery Fray exclaimed, 'Surely, shepherd, I seed you blowing into a great flute by now at Casterbridge?'

'You did,' said Gabriel, blushing faintly. 'I've been in great trouble, neighbours, and was driven to it. I used not to be so poor as I be now.'

'Never mind, heart!' said Mark Clark. 'You should take it careless-like, shepherd, and your time will come. But we could thank ye for a tune if ye bain't too tired?'

'Neither drum nor trumpet have I heard since Christmas,' said Jan Coggan. 'Come, raise a tune, Master Oak!'

'That I will,' said Gabriel, pulling out his flute and putting it together. 'A poor tool, neighbours; but such as I can do ye shall have and welcome.'

Oak then struck up 'Jockey to the Fair', and played that sparkling melody three times through, accenting the notes in the third round in a most artistic and lively manner by bending his body in small jerks and tapping with his foot to beat time.

'He can blow the flute very well – that 'a can,' said a young married man, who having no individuality worth mentioning was known as 'Susan Tall's husband'. He continued, 'I'd as lief as not be able to blow into a flute as well as that.'

'He's a clever man, and 'tis a true comfort for us to have such a shepherd,' murmured Joseph Poorgrass, in a soft cadence. 'We ought to feel full o' thanksgiving that he's not a player of ba'dy songs instead of these merry tunes; for 'twould have been just as easy for God to have made the shepherd a loose low man – a man of iniquity, so to speak it – as what he is. Yes, for our wives' and daughters' sakes we should feel real thanksgiving.'

'True, true – real thanksgiving!' dashed in Mark Clark conclusively, not feeling it to be of any consequence to his opinion that he had only heard about a word and three-quarters of what Joseph had said.

'Yes,' added Joseph, beginning to feel like a man in the Bible; 'for evil do thrive so in these times that ye may be as much deceived in the clanest shaved and whitest shirted man as in the raggedest tramp upon the turnpike, if I may term it so.'

'Ay, I can mind yer face now, shepherd,' said Henery Fray, criticizing Gabriel with misty eyes as he entered upon his second tune. 'Yes – now I see 'ee blowing into the flute I know 'ee to be the same man I see play at Casterbridge, for yer mouth were scrimped up and yer eyes a-staring out like a strangled man's – just as they be now.'

' 'Tis a pity that playing the flute should make a man look such a scarecrow,' observed Mr Mark Clark, with additional criticism of Gabriel's countenance, the latter person jerking out, with the ghastly grimace required by the instrument, the chorus of 'Dame Durden':

> 'Twas Moll' and Bet', and Doll' and Kate',
> And Dor'-othy Drag'-gle Tail'.

'I hope you don't mind that young man's bad manners in naming your features?' whispered Joseph to Gabriel.

'Not at all,' said Mr Oak.

'For by nature ye be a very handsome man, shepherd,' continued Joseph Poorgrass with winning suavity.

'Ay, that ye be, shepherd,' said the company.

'Thank you very much,' said Oak, in the modest tone good manners demanded, thinking, however, that he would never let Bathsheba see him playing the flute; in this resolve showing a discretion equal to that related of its sagacious inventress, the divine Minerva herself.

'Ah, when I and my wife were married at Norcombe Church,' said the old maltster, not pleased at finding himself left out of the subject, 'we were called the handsomest couple in the neighbourhood – everybody said so.'

'Danged if ye bain't altered now, malter,' said a voice with the vigour natural to the enunciation of a remarkable evident truism. It came from the old man in the background, whose offensiveness and spiteful ways were barely atoned for by the occasional chuckle he contributed to general laughs.

'O no, no,' said Gabriel.

'Don't ye play no more, shepherd,' said Susan Tall's husband, the young married man who had spoken once before. 'I must be moving, and when there's tunes going on I seem as if hung in wires. If I thought after I'd left that music was still playing, and I not there, I should be quite melancholy-like.'

'What's yer hurry then, Laban?' inquired Coggan. 'You used to bide as late as the latest.'

'Well, ye see, neighbours, I was lately married to a woman, and she's my vocation now, and so ye see –' The young man halted lamely.

'New lords new laws, as the saying is, I suppose,' remarked Coggan.

'Ay, 'a b'lieve – ha, ha!' said Susan Tall's husband, in a tone intended to imply his habitual reception of jokes without minding them at all. The young man then wished them good-night and withdrew.

Henery Fray was the first to follow. Then Gabriel arose and went off with Jan Coggan, who had offered him a lodging. A few minutes later, when the remaining ones were on their legs and about to depart, Fray came back again in a hurry. Flourishing his finger ominously he threw a gaze teeming with tidings just where his eye alighted by accident, which happened to be in Joseph Poorgrass's face.

'O – what's the matter, what's the matter, Henery?' said Joseph, starting back.

'What's a-brewing, Henery?' asked Jacob and Mark Clark.

'Baily Pennyways – Baily Pennyways – I said so; yes, I said so!'

'What, found out stealing anything?'

'Stealing it is. The news is, that after Miss Everdene got home she went out again to see all was safe, as she usually do, and coming in found Baily Pennyways creeping down the granary steps with half a bushel of barley. She fleed at him like a cat – never such a tomboy as she is – of course I speak with closed doors?'

'You do – you do, Henery.'

'She fleed at him, and, to cut a long story short, he owned to having carried off five sack altogether, upon her promising not to persecute him. Well, he's turned out neck and crop, and my question is, who's going to be baily now?'

The question was such a profound one that Henery was obliged to drink there and then from the large cup till the bottom was distinctly visible inside. Before he had replaced it on the table, in came the young man, Susan Tall's husband, in a still greater hurry.

'Have ye heard the news that's all over parish?'

'About Baily Pennyways?'

'But besides that?'

'No – not a morsel of it!' they replied, looking into the very midst of Laban Tall as if to meet his words half-way down his throat.

'What a night of horrors!' murmured Joseph Poorgrass, waving his hands spasmodically. 'I've had the news-bell ringing in my left ear quite bad enough for a murder, and I've seen a magpie all alone!'

'Fanny Robin – Miss Everdene's youngest servant – can't be found. They've been wanting to lock up the door these two hours, but she isn't come in. And they don't know what to do about going to bed for fear of locking her out. They wouldn't be so concerned if she hadn't been noticed in such low spirits these last few days, and Maryann d' think the beginning of a crowner's inquest has happened to the poor girl.'

'O – 'tis burned – 'tis burned!' came from Joseph Poorgrass's dry lips.

'No – 'tis drowned!' said Tall.

'Or 'tis her father's razor!' suggested Billy Smallbury with a vivid sense of detail.

'Well – Miss Everdene wants to speak to one or two of us before we go to bed. What with this trouble about the baily, and now about the girl, mis'ess is almost wild.'

They all hastened up the lane to the farmhouse, excepting the old maltster, whom neither news, fire, rain, nor thunder could draw from his hole. There, as the others' footsteps died away, he sat down again, and continued gazing as usual into the furnace with his red, bleared eyes.

From the bedroom window above their heads Bathsheba's head and shoulders, robed in mystic white, were dimly seen extended into the air.

'Are any of my men among you?' she said anxiously.

'Yes, ma'am, several,' said Susan Tall's husband.

'To-morrow morning I wish two or three of you to make inquiries in the villages round if they have seen such a person as Fanny Robin. Do it quietly; there is no reason for alarm as yet. She must have left whilst we were all at the fire.'

'I beg yer pardon, but had she any young man courting her in the parish, ma'am?' asked Jacob Smallbury.

'I don't know,' said Bathsheba.

'I've never heard of any such thing, ma'am,' said two or three.

'It is hardly likely, either,' continued Bathsheba. 'For any lover of hers might have come to the house if he had been a respectable lad. The most mysterious matter connected with her absence – indeed, the only thing which gives me serious alarm – is that she was seen to go out of the house by Maryann with only her indoor working gown on – not even a bonnet.'

'And you mean, ma'am, excusing my words, that a young woman would hardly go to see her young man without dressing up,' said Jacob, turning his mental vision upon past experiences. 'That's true – she would not, ma'am.'

'She had, I think, a bundle, though I couldn't see very well,' said a female voice from another window, which seemed that of Maryann. 'But she had no young man about here. Hers lives in Casterbridge, and I believe he's a soldier.'

'Do you know his name?' Bathsheba said.

'No, mistress; she was very close about it.'

'Perhaps I might be able to find out if I went to Casterbridge barracks,' said William Smallbury.

'Very well; if she doesn't return to-morrow, mind you go there and try to discover which man it is, and see him. I feel more responsible than I should if she had had any friends or relations alive. I do hope she has come to no harm through a man of that kind . . . And then there's this disgraceful affair of the bailiff – but I can't speak of him now.'

Bathsheba had so many reasons for uneasiness that it seemed she did not think it worth while to dwell upon any particular one. 'Do as I told you, then,' she said in conclusion, closing the casement.

'Ay, ay, mistress; we will,' they replied, and moved away.

That night at Coggan's Gabriel Oak, beneath the screen of closed eyelids, was busy with fancies, and full of movement, like a river flowing rapidly under its ice. Night had always been the time at which he saw Bathsheba most vividly, and through the slow hours of shadow he tenderly regarded her image now. It is rarely that the pleasures of the imagination will compensate for the pain of sleeplessness, but they possibly did with Oak to-night, for the delight of merely seeing her effaced for the time his perception of the great difference between seeing and possessing.

He also thought of plans for fetching his few utensils and books from Norcombe. *The Young Man's Best Companion*, *The Farrier's Sure Guide*, *The Veterinary Surgeon*, *Paradise Lost*, *The Pilgrim's Progress*, *Robinson Crusoe*, Ash's *Dictionary*, and Walkingame's *Arithmetic*, constituted his library; and though a limited series, it was one from which he had acquired more sound information by diligent perusal than many a man of opportunities has done from a furlong of laden shelves.

* IX *

The Homestead – A Visitor – Half-Confidences

By daylight, the bower of Oak's new-found mistress, Bathsheba Everdene, presented itself as a hoary building, of the early stage of Classic Renaissance as regards its architecture, and of a proportion which told at a glance that, as is so frequently the case, it had once been the manorial hall upon a small estate around it, now altogether effaced as a distinct property, and merged in the vast tract of a non-resident landlord, which comprised several such modest demesnes.

Fluted pilasters, worked from the solid stone, decorated its front, and above the roof the chimneys were panelled or columnar, some coped gables with finials and like features still retaining traces of their Gothic extraction. Soft brown mosses, like faded velveteen, formed cushions upon the stone tiling, and tufts of the houseleek or sengreen sprouted from the eaves of the low surrounding buildings. A gravel walk leading from the door to the road in front was encrusted at the sides with more moss – here it was a silver-green variety, the nut-brown of the gravel being visible to the width of only a foot or two in the centre. This circumstance, and the generally sleepy air of the whole prospect here, together with the animated and contrasting state of the reverse façade, suggested to the imagination that on the adaptation of the building for farming purposes the vital principles of the house had turned round inside its body to face the other way. Reversals of this kind, strange deformities, tremendous paralyses, are often seen to be inflicted by trade upon edifices – either individual or in the aggregate as streets and towns – which were originally planned for pleasure alone.

Lively voices were heard this morning in the upper rooms, the main staircase to which was of hard oak, the balusters, heavy as bed-posts, being turned and moulded in the quaint fashion of their century, the handrail as stout as a parapet-top, and the stairs themselves continually twisting round like a person trying to look over his shoulder. Going up, the floors above were found to have a very irregular surface, rising to ridges, sinking into valleys; and being just then uncarpeted, the face of the boards was seen to be eaten into innumerable vermiculations. Every window replied by a clang to the opening and shutting of every door, a tremble followed every bustling movement, and a creak accompanied a walker about the house, like a spirit, wherever he went.

In the room from which the conversation proceeded Bathsheba and her servant-companion, Liddy Smallbury, were to be discovered sitting upon the floor, and sorting a complication of papers, books, bottles, and rubbish spread out thereon – remnants from the household stores of the late occupier. Liddy, the maltster's great-granddaughter, was about Bathsheba's equal in age, and her face was a prominent advertisement of the light-hearted English country girl. The beauty her features might have lacked in form was amply made up for by perfection of hue, which at this winter-time was the softened ruddiness on a surface of high rotundity that we meet with in a Terburg or a Gerard Douw; and, like the presentations of those great colourists, it was a face which kept well back from the boundary between comeliness and the ideal. Though elastic in nature she was less daring then Bathsheba, and occasionally showed some earnestness, which consisted half of genuine feeling, and half of manner-liness superadded by way of duty.

Through a partly-opened door the noise of a scrubbing-brush led up to the charwoman, Maryann Money, a person who for a face had a circular disc, furrowed less by age than by long gazes of perplexity at distant objects. To think of her was to get good-humoured; to speak of her was to raise the image of a dried Normandy pippin.

'Stop your scrubbing a moment,' said Bathsheba through the door to her. 'I hear something.'

Maryann suspended the brush.

The tramp of a horse was apparent, approaching the front of the building. The paces slackened, turned in at the wicket, and, what was most unusual, came up the mossy path close to the door. The door was tapped with the end of a crop or stick.

'What impertinence!' said Liddy, in a low voice. 'To ride up to the footpath like that! Why didn't he stop at the gate? Lord! 'tis a gentleman! I see the top of his hat.'

'Be quiet!' said Bathsheba.

The further expression of Liddy's concern was continued by aspect instead of narrative.

'Why doesn't Mrs Coggan go to the door?' Bathsheba continued.

Rat-tat-tat-tat resounded more decisively from Bathsheba's oak.

'Maryann, you go!' said she, fluttering under the onset of a crowd of romantic possibilities.

'O ma'am – see, here's a mess!'

The argument was unanswerable after a glance at Maryann.

'Liddy – you must,' said Bathsheba.

Liddy held up her hands and arms, coated with dust from the rubbish they were sorting, and looked imploringly at her mistress.

'There – Mrs Coggan is going!' said Bathsheba, exhaling her relief in the form of a long breath which had lain in her bosom a minute or more.

The door opened, and a deep voice said –

'Is Miss Everdene at home?'

'I'll see, sir,' said Mrs Coggan, and in a minute appeared in the room.

'Dear, what a thirtover place this world is!' continued Mrs Coggan (a wholesome-looking lady who had a voice for each class of remark according to the emotion involved; who could toss a pancake or twirl a mop with the accuracy of pure mathematics, and who at this moment showed hands shaggy with fragments of dough and arms encrusted with flour). 'I am never up to my elbows, miss, in making a pudding but one of two things do happen – either my nose must needs begin tickling, and I can't live without scratching it, or somebody knocks at the door. Here's Mr Boldwood wanting to see you, Miss Everdene.'

A woman's dress being a part of her countenance, and any disorder in the one being of the same nature with a malformation or wound in the other, Bathsheba said at once –

'I can't see him in this state. Whatever shall I do?'

Not-at-homes were hardly naturalized in Weatherbury farmhouses, so Liddy suggested – 'Say you're a fright with dust, and can't come down.'

'Yes – that sounds very well,' said Mrs Coggan critically.

'Say I can't see him – that will do.'

Mrs Coggan went downstairs, and returned the answer as requested, adding, however, on her own responsibility, 'Miss is dusting bottles, sir, and is quite a object – that's why 'tis.'

'Oh, very well,' said the deep voice indifferently. 'All I wanted to ask was, if anything had been heard of Fanny Robin?'

'Nothing, sir – but we may know to-night. William Smallbury is gone to Casterbridge, where her young man lives, as is supposed, and the other men be inquiring about everywhere.'

The horse's tramp then recommenced and retreated, and the door closed.

'Who is Mr Boldwood?' said Bathsheba.

'A gentleman-farmer at Little Weatherbury.'

'Married?'

'No, miss.'

'How old is he?'

'Forty, I should say – very handsome – rather stern-looking – and rich.'

'What a bother this dusting is! I am always in some unfortunate plight or other,' Bathsheba said complainingly. 'Why should he inquire about Fanny?'

'Oh, because, as she had no friends in her childhood, he took her and put her to school, and got her her place here under your uncle. He's a very kind man that way, but Lord – there!'

'What?'

'Never was such a hopeless man for a woman! He's been courted by sixes and sevens – all the girls, gentle and simple, for miles round, have tried him. Jane Perkins worked at him for two months like a slave, and the two Miss Taylors spent a year upon him, and he cost Farmer Ives's daughter nights of tears and twenty pounds' worth of new clothes; but Lord – the money might as well have been thrown out of the window.'

A little boy came up at this moment and looked in upon them. This child was one of the Coggans, who, with the Smallburys, were as common among the families of this district as the Avons and Derwents among our rivers. He always had a loosened tooth or a cut finger to show to particular friends, which he did with an air of being thereby elevated above the common herd of afflictionless humanity – to which exhibition people were expected to say 'Poor child!' with a dash of congratulation as well as pity.

'I've got a pen-nee!' said Master Coggan in a scanning measure.

'Well – who gave it you, Teddy?' said Liddy.

'Mis-terr Bold-wood! He gave it to me for opening the gate.'

'What did he say?'

'He said, "Where are you going, my little man?" and I said, "To Miss Everdene's, please"; and he said, "She is a staid woman, isn't she, my little man?" and I said, "Yes." '

'You naughty child! What did you say that for?'

"Cause he gave me the penny!'

'What a pucker everything is in!' said Bathsheba discontentedly, when the child had gone. 'Get away, Maryann, or go on with your scrubbing, or do something! You ought to be married by this time, and not here troubling me!'

'Ay, mistress – so I did. But what between the poor men I won't have, and the rich men who won't have me, I stand as a pelican in the wilderness!'

'Did anybody ever want to marry you, miss?' Liddy ventured to ask when they were again alone. 'Lots of 'em, I daresay?'

Bathsheba paused, as if about to refuse a reply, but the temptation to say yes, since it really was in her power, was irresistible by aspiring virginity, in spite of her spleen at having been published as old.

'A man wanted to once,' she said, in a highly experienced tone, and the image of Gabriel Oak, as the farmer, rose before her.

'How nice it must seem!' said Liddy, with the fixed features of mental realization. 'And you wouldn't have him?'

'He wasn't quite good enough for me.'

'How sweet to be able to disdain, when most of us are glad to say, "Thank you!" I seem I hear it. "No, sir – I'm your better," or "Kiss my foot, sir; my face is for mouths of consequence." And did you love him, miss?'

'Oh, no. But I rather liked him.'

'Do you now?'

'Of course not – what footsteps are those I hear?'

Liddy looked from a back window into the courtyard behind, which was now getting low-toned and dim with the earliest films of night. A crooked file of men was approaching the back door. The whole string of trailing individuals advanced in the completest balance of intention, like the remarkable creatures known as Chain Salpae, which, distinctly organized in other respects, have one will common to a whole family. Some were, as usual, in snow-white smock-frocks of Russia duck, and some in whitey-brown ones of drabbet – marked on the wrists, breasts, backs, and sleeves with honeycomb-work. Two or three women in pattens brought up the rear.

'The Philistines be upon us,' said Liddy, making her nose white against the glass.

'Oh, very well. Maryann, go down and keep them in the kitchen till I am dressed, and then show them in to me in the hall.'

* X *

Mistress and Men

HALF-AN-HOUR later Bathsheba, in finished dress, and followed by Liddy, entered the upper end of the old hall to find that her men had all deposited themselves on a long form and a settle at the lower extremity. She sat down at a table and opened the time-book, pen in her hand, with a canvas money-bag beside her. From this she poured a small heap of coin. Liddy chose a position at her elbow and began to sew, sometimes pausing and looking round, or, with the air of a privileged person, taking up one of the half-sovereigns lying before her, and surveying it merely as a work of art, while strictly preventing her countenance from expressing any wish to possess it as money.

'Now, before I begin, men,' said Bathsheba, 'I have two matters to speak of. The first is that the bailiff is dismissed for thieving, and that I have formed a resolution to have no bailiff, at all, but to manage everything with my own head and hands.'

The men breathed an audible breath of amazement.

'The next matter is, have you heard anything of Fanny?'

'Nothing, ma'am.'

'Have you done anything?'

'I met Farmer Boldwood,' said Jacob Smallbury, 'and I went with him and two of his men, and dragged Newmill Pond, but we found nothing.'

'And the new shepherd have been to Buck's Head, by Yalbury, thinking she had gone there, but nobody had seed her,' said Laban Tall.

'Hasn't William Smallbury been to Casterbridge?'

'Yes, ma'am, but he's not yet come home. He promised to be back by six.'

'It wants a quarter to six at present,' siad Bathsheba, looking at her watch. 'I daresay he'll be in directly. Well, now then' – she looked into the book – 'Joseph Poorgrass, are you there?'

'Yes, sir – ma'am I mane,' said the person addressed. 'I be the person name of Poorgrass.'

'And what are you?'

'Nothing in my own eye. In the eye of other people – well, I don't say it; though public thought will out.'

'What do you do on the farm?'

'I do do carting things all the year, and in seed time I shoots the rooks and sparrows, and helps at pig-killing, sir.'

'How much to you?'

'Please nine and ninepence and a good halfpenny where 'twas a bad one, sir – ma'am I mane.'

'Quite correct. Now here are ten shillings in addition as a small present, as I am a new comer.'

Bathsheba blushed slightly at the sense of being generous in public, and Henery Fray, who had drawn up towards her chair, lifted his eyebrows and fingers to express amazement on a small-scale.

'How much do I owe you – that man in the corner – what's your name?' continued Bathsheba.

'Matthew Moon, ma'am,' said a singular framework of clothes with nothing of any consequence inside them, which advanced with the toes in no definite direction forwards, but turned in or out as they chanced to swing.

'Matthew Mark, did you say? – speak out – I shall not hurt you,' inquired the young farmer kindly.

'Matthew Moon, mem,' said Henery Fray, correctingly, from behind her chair, to which point he had edged himself.

'Matthew Moon,' murmured Bathsheba, turning her bright eyes to the book. 'Ten and twopence halfpenny is the sum put down to you, I see?'

'Yes, mis'ess,' said Matthew, as the rustle of wind among dead leaves.

'Here it is, and ten shillings. Now the next – Andrew Randle, you are a new man, I hear. How came you to leave your last farm?'

'P-p-p-p-p-pl-pl-pl-pl-l-l-l-l-ease, ma'am, p-p-p-p-pl-pl-pl-pl-please, ma'am-please'm-please'm –'

"A's a stammering man, mem,' said Henery Fray in an undertone, 'and they turned him away because the only time he ever did speak plain he said his soul was his own, and other iniquities, to the squire. 'A can cuss, mem, as well as you or I, but 'a can't speak a common speech to save his life.'

'Andrew Randle, here's yours – finish thanking me in a day or two. Temperance Miller – oh, here's another, Soberness – both women, I suppose?'

'Yes'm. Here we be, 'a b'lieve,' was echoed in shrill unison.

'What have you been doing?'

'Tending thrashing-machine, and wimbling haybonds, and saying "Hoosh!" to the cocks and hens when they go upon your seeds, and planting Early Flourballs and Thompson's Wonderfuls with a dibble.'

'Yes – I see. Are they satisfactory women?' she inquired softly of Henery Fray.

'O mem – don't ask me! Yielding women – as scarlet a pair as ever was!' groaned Henery under his breath.

'Sit down.'

'Who, mem?'

'Sit down.'

Joseph Poorgrass, in the background, twitched, and his lips became dry with fear of some terrible consequences, as he saw Bathsheba summarily speaking, and Henery slinking off to a corner.

'Now the next. Laban Tall, you'll stay on working for me?'

'For you or anybody that pays me well, ma'am,' replied the young married man.

'True – the man must live!' said a woman in the back quarter, who had just entered with clicking pattens.

'What woman is that?' Bathsheba asked.

'I be his lawful wife!' continued the voice with greater prominence of manner and tone. This lady called herself five-and-twenty, looked thirty, passed as thirty-five, and was forty. She was a woman who never, like some newly married, showed conjugal tenderness in public, perhaps because she had none to show.

'Oh, you are,' said Bathsheba. 'Well, Laban, will you stay on?'

'Yes, he'll stay, ma'am!' said again the shrill tongue of Laban's lawful wife.

'Well, he can speak for himself, I suppose.'

'O Lord, not he, ma'am! A simple tool. Well enough, but a poor gawkhammer mortal,' the wife replied.

'Heh-heh-heh!' laughed the married man, with a hideous effort of appreciation, for he was as irrepressibly good-humoured under ghastly snubs as a parliamentary candidate on the hustings.

The names remaining were called in the same manner.

'Now I think I have done with you,' said Bathsheba, closing the book and shaking back a stray twine of hair. 'Has William Smallbury returned?'

'No, ma'am.'

'The new shepherd will want a man under him,' suggested Henery Fray, trying to make himself official again by a sideway approach towards her chair.

'Oh – he will. Who can he have?'

'Young Cain Ball is a very good lad,' Henery said, 'and Shepherd Oak don't mind his mouth?' he added, turning with an apologetic smile to the shepherd, who had just appeared on the scene, and was now leaning against the doorpost with his arms folded.

'No, I don't mind that,' said Gabriel.

'How did Cain come by such a name?' asked Bathsheba.

'Oh you see, mem, his pore mother, not being a Scripture-read woman, made a mistake at his christening, thinking 'twas Abel killed Cain, and called en Cain, meaning Abel all the time. The parson put it right, but 'twas too late, for the name could never be got rid of in the parish. 'Tis very unfortunate for the boy.'

'It is rather unfortunate.'

'Yes. However, we soften it down as much as we can, and call him Cainy. Ah, pore widow-woman! she cried her heart out about it almost. She was brought up by a very heathen father and mother, who never sent her to church or school, and it shows how the sins of the parents are visited upon the children, mem.'

Mr Fray here drew up his features to the mild degree of melancholy required when the persons involved in the given misfortune do not belong to your own family.

'Very well then, Cainy Ball to be under-shepherd. And you quite understand your duties? – you I mean, Gabriel Oak?'

'Quite well, I thank you, Miss Everdene,' said Shepherd Oak from the doorpost. 'If I don't, I'll inquire.' Gabriel was rather staggered by the remarkable coolness of her manner. Certainly nobody without previous information would have dreamt that Oak and the handsome woman before whom he stood had ever been other than strangers. But perhaps her air was the inevitable result of the social rise which had advanced her from a cottage to a large house and fields. The case is not unexampled in high places. When, in the writings of the later poets, Jove and his family are found to have moved from their cramped quarters on the peak of Olympus into the wide sky above it, their words show a proportionate increase of arrogance and reserve.

Footsteps were heard in the passage, combining in their character the qualities both of weight and measure, rather at the expense of velocity.

(All.) 'Here's Billy Smallbury come from Casterbridge.'

'And what's the news?' said Bathsheba, as William, after marching to the middle of the hall, took a handkerchief from his hat and wiped his forehead from its centre to its remoter boundaries.

'I should have been sooner, miss,' he said, 'if it hadn't been for the weather.' He then stamped with each foot severely, and on looking down his boots were perceived to be clogged with snow.

'Come at last, is it?' said Henery.

'Well, what about Fanny?' said Bathsheba.

'Well, ma'am, in round numbers, she's run away with the soldiers,' said William.

'No; not a steady girl like Fanny!'

'I'll tell ye all particulars. When I got to Casterbridge Barracks, they said, "The Eleventh Dragoon Guards be gone away, and new troops have come." The Eleventh left last week for Melchester and onwards. The Route came from Government like a thief in the night, as is his nature to, and afore the Eleventh knew it almost, they were on the march. They passed near here.'

Gabriel had listened with interest. 'I saw them go,' he said.

'Yes,' continued William, 'they pranced down the street playing "The Girl I Left Behind Me", so 'tis said, in glorious notes of triumph. Every looker-on's inside shook with the blows of the great drum to his deepest vitals, and there was not a dry eye throughout the town among the public-house people and the nameless women!'

'But they're not gone to any war?'

'No, ma'am; but they be gone to take the places of them who may, which is very close connected. And so I said to myself, Fanny's young man was one of the regiment, and she's gone after him. There, ma'am, that's it in black and white.'

'Did you find out his name?'

'No; nobody knew it. I believe he was higher in rank than a private.'

Gabriel remained musing and said nothing, for he was in doubt.

'Well, we are not likely to know more to-night, at any rate,' said Bathsheba. 'But one of you had better run across to Farmer Boldwood's and tell him that much.'

She then rose; but before retiring, addressed a few words to them with a pretty dignity, to which her mourning dress added a soberness that was hardly to be found in the words themselves:

'Now mind, you have a mistress instead of a master. I don't yet know my powers or my talents in farming; but I shall do my best, and if you serve me well, so shall I serve you. Don't any unfair ones among you (if there are any such, but I hope not) suppose that because I'm a woman I don't understand the difference between bad goings-on and good.'

(All.) 'No'm!'

(Liddy.) 'Excellent well said.'

'I shall be up before you are awake; I shall be afield before you are up; and I shall have breakfasted before you are afield. In short, I shall astonish you all.'

(All.) 'Yes'm!'

'And so good-night.'

(All.) 'Good-night, ma'am.'

Then this small thesmothete stepped from the table, and surged out of the hall, her black silk dress licking up a few straws and dragging them along with a scratching noise upon the floor. Liddy, elevating her feelings to the occasion from a sense of grandeur, floated off behind Bathsheba with a milder dignity not entirely free from travesty, and the door was closed.

* XI *

Outside the Barracks – Snow – A Meeting

FOR dreariness nothing could surpass a prospect in the outskirts of a certain town and military station, many miles north of Weatherbury, at a later hour on this same snowy evening – if that may be called a prospect of which the chief constituent was darkness.

It was a night when sorrow may come to the brightest without causing any great sense of incongruity: when, with impressible persons, love becomes solicitousness, hope sinks to misgivings, and faith to hope: when the exercise of memory does not stir feelings of regret at opportunities for ambition that have been passed by, and anticipation does not prompt to enterprise.

The scene was a public path, bordered on the left hand by a river, behind which rose a high wall. On the right was a tract of land, partly meadow and partly moor, reaching, at its remote verge, to a wide undulating upland.

The changes of the seasons are less obtrusive on spots of this kind than amid woodland scenery. Still, to a close observer, they are just as perceptible; the difference is that their media of manifestation are less trite and familiar than such well-known ones as the bursting of the buds or the fall of the leaf. Many are not so stealthy and gradual as we may be apt to imagine in considering the general torpidity of a moor or waste. Winter, in coming to the country hereabout, advanced in well-marked stages, wherein might have been successively observed the retreat of the snakes, the transformation of the ferns, the filling of the pools, a rising of fogs, the embrowning by frost, the collapse of the fungi, and an obliteration by snow.

This climax of the series had been reached to-night on the aforesaid moor, and for the first time in the season its irregularities were forms without features; suggestive of anything, proclaiming nothing, and without more character than that of being the limit of something else – the lowest layer of a firmament of snow. From this chaotic skyful of crowding flakes the mead and moor momentarily received additional clothing, only to appear momentarily more naked thereby. The vast arch of cloud above was strangely low, and formed as it were the roof of a large dark cavern, gradually sinking in upon its floor; for the instinctive thought was that the snow lining the heavens and that encrusting the earth would soon unite into one mass without any intervening stratum of air at all.

We turn our attention to the left-hand characteristics; which were flatness in respect of the river, verticality in respect of the wall behind it, and darkness as to both. These features made up the mass. If anything could be darker than the sky, it was the wall, and if anything could be gloomier than the wall it was the river beneath. The indistinct summit of the façade was notched and prolonged by chimneys here and there, and upon its face were faintly signified the oblong shapes of windows, though only in the upper part. Below, down to the water's edge, the flat was unbroken by hole or projection.

An indescribable succession of dull blows, perplexing in their regularity, sent their sound with difficulty through the fluffy atmosphere. It was a neighbouring clock striking ten. The bell was in the open air, and being overlaid with several inches of muffling snow, had lost its voice for the time.

About this hour the snow abated: ten flakes fell where twenty had fallen, then one had the room of ten. Not long after a form moved by the brink of the river.

By its outline upon the colourless background a close observer might have seen that it was small. This was all that was positively discoverable, though it seemed human.

The shape went slowly along, but without much exertion, for the snow, though sudden, was not as yet more than two inches deep. At this time some words were spoken aloud:

'One. Two. Three. Four. Five.'

Between each utterance the little shape advanced about half-a-dozen yards. It was evident now that the windows high in the wall were being counted. The word 'Five' represented the fifth window from the end of the wall.

Here the spot stopped, and dwindled smaller. The figure was stooping. Then a morsel of snow flew across the river towards the fifth window. It smacked against the wall at a point several yards from its mark. The throw was the idea of a man conjoined with the execution of a woman.

No man who had ever seen bird, rabbit, or squirrel in his childhood, could possibly have thrown with such utter imbecility as was shown here.

Another attempt, and another; till by degrees the wall must have become pimpled with the adhering lumps of snow. At last one fragment struck the fifth window.

The river would have been seen by day to be of that deep smooth sort which races middle and sides with the same gliding precision, any irregularities of speed being immediately corrected by a small whirlpool. Nothing was heard in reply to the signal but the gurgle and cluck of one of these invisible wheels – together with a few small sounds which a sad man would have called moans, and a happy man laughter – caused by the flapping of the waters against trifling objects in other parts of the stream.

The window was struck again in the same manner.

Then a noise was heard, apparently produced by the opening of the window. This was followed by a voice from the same quarter:

'Who's there?'

The tones were masculine, and not those of surprise. The high wall being that of a barrack, and marriage being looked upon with disfavour in the army, assignations and communications had probably been made across the river before to-night.

'Is it Sergeant Troy?' said the blurred spot in the snow, tremulously.

This person was so much like a mere shade upon the earth, and the other speaker so much a part of the building, that one would have said the wall was holding a conversation with the snow.

'Yes,' came suspiciously from the shadow. 'What girl are you?'

'O, Frank – don't you know me?' said the spot. 'Your wife, Fanny Robin.'

'Fanny!' said the wall, in utter astonishment.

'Yes,' said the girl, with a half-suppressed gasp of emotion.

There was something in the woman's tone which is not that of the wife, and there was a manner in the man which is rarely a husband's. The dialogue went on:

'How did you come here?'

'I asked which was your window. Forgive me!'

'I did not expect you to-night. Indeed, I did not think you would come at all. It was a wonder you found me here. I am orderly to-morrow.'

'You said I was to come.'

'Well – I said that you might.'

'Yes, I mean that I might. You are glad to see me, Frank?'

'O yes – of course.'

'Can you – come to me?'

'My dear Fan, no! The bugle has sounded, the barrack gates are closed, and I have no leave. We are all of us as good as in the county gaol till to-morrow morning.'

'Then I shan't see you till then!' The words were in a faltering tone of disappointment.

'How did you get here from Weatherbury?'

'I walked – some part of the way – the rest by the carriers.'

'I am surprised.'

'Yes – so am I. And Frank, when will it be?'

'What?'

'That you promised.'

'I don't quite recollect.'

'O you do! Don't speak like that. It weighs me to the earth. It makes me say what ought to be said first by you.'

'Never mind – say it.'

'O, must I? – it is, when shall we be married, Frank?'

'Oh, I see. Well – you have to get proper clothes.'

'I have money. Will it be by banns or license?'

'Banns, I should think.'

'And we live in two parishes.'

'Do we? What then?'

'My lodgings are in St Mary's, and this is not. So they will have to be published in both.'

'Is that the law?'

'Yes. O Frank – you think me forward, I am afraid! Don't, dear Frank – will you – for I love you so. And you said lots of times you would marry me, and – and I – I – I –'

'Don't cry, now! It is foolish. If I said so, of course I will.'

'And shall I put up the banns in my parish, and will you in yours?'

'Yes.'

'Tomorrow?'

'Not tomorrow. We'll settle in a few days.'

'You have the permission of the officers?'

'No – not yet.'

'O – how is it? You said you almost had before you left Casterbridge.'

'The fact is, I forgot to ask. Your coming like this is so sudden and unexpected.'

'Yes – yes – it is. It was wrong of me to worry you. I'll go away now. Will you come and see me to-morrow, at Mrs Twills's, in North Street? I don't like to come to the Barracks. There are bad women about, and they think me one.'

'Quite so. I'll come to you, my dear. Good-night.'

'Good-night, Frank – good-night!'

And the noise was again heard of a window closing. The little spot moved away. When she passed the corner a subdued exclamation was heard inside the wall.

'Ho – ho – Sergeant – ho – ho!' An expostulation followed, but it was indistinct; and it became lost amid a low peal of laughter, which was hardly distinguishable from the gurgle of the tiny whirlpools outside.

XII

Farmers – A Rule – An Exception

THE first public evidence of Bathsheba's decision to be a farmer in her own person and by proxy no more was her appearance the following market-day in the cornmarket at Casterbridge.

The low though extensive hall, supported by beams and pillars, and latterly dignified by the name of Corn Exchange, was thronged with hot men who talked among each other in twos and threes, the speaker of the minute looking sideways into his auditor's face and concentrating his argument by a contraction of one eyelid during delivery. The greater number carried in their hands ground-ash saplings, using them partly as walking-sticks and partly for poking up pigs, sheep, neighbours with their backs turned, and restful things in general, which seemed to require such treatment in the course of their peregrinations. During conversations each subjected his sapling to great varieties of usage – bending it round his back, forming an arch of it between his two hands, overweighting it on the ground till it reached nearly a semicircle; or perhaps it was hastily tucked under the arm whilst the sample-bag was pulled forth and a handful of corn poured into the palm, which, after criticism, was flung upon the floor, an issue of events perfectly well known to half-a-dozen acute town-bred fowls which had as usual crept into the building unobserved, and waited the fulfilment of their anticipations with a high-stretched neck and oblique eye.

Among these heavy yeomen a feminine figure glided, the single one of her sex that the room contained. She was prettily and even daintily dressed. She moved between them as a chaise between carts, was heard after them as a romance after sermons, was felt among them like a breeze among furnaces. It had required a little determination – far more than she had at first imagined – to take up a position here, for at her first entry the lumbering dialogues had ceased, nearly every face had been turned towards her, and those that were already turned rigidly fixed there.

Two or three only of the farmers were personally known to Bathsheba, and to these she had made her way. But if she was to be the practical woman she had intended to show herself, business must be carried on, introductions or none, and she ultimately acquired confidence enough to speak and reply boldly to men merely known to her by hearsay. Bathsheba too had her sample-bags, and by degrees adopted the professional pour into the hand – holding up the grains in her narrow palm for inspection, in perfect Casterbridge manner.

Something in the exact arch of her upper unbroken row of teeth, and in the keenly pointed corners of her red mouth when, with parted lips, she somewhat defiantly turned up her face to argue a point with a tall man, suggested that there was potentiality enough in that lithe slip of humanity for alarming exploits of sex, and daring enough to carry them out. But her eyes had a softness – invariably a softness – which, had they not been dark, would have seemed mistiness; as they were, it lowered an expression that might have been piercing to simple clearness.

Strange to say of a woman in full bloom and vigour, she always allowed her interlocutors to finish their statements before rejoining with hers. In arguing on prices she held to her own firmly, as was natural in a dealer, and reduced theirs persistently, as was inevitable in a woman. But there was an elasticity in her firmness which removed it from obstinacy, as there was a *naïveté* in her cheapening which saved it from meanness.

Those of the farmers with whom she had no dealings (by far the greater part) were continually asking each other, 'Who is she?' The reply would be –

'Farmer Everdene's niece; took on Weatherbury Upper Farm; turned away the baily, and swears she'll do everything herself.'

The other man would then shake his head.

'Yes, 'tis a pity she's so headstrong,' the first would say. 'But we ought to be proud of her here – she lightens up the old place. 'Tis such a shapely maid, however, that she'll soon get picked up.'

It would be ungallant to suggest that the novelty of her engagement in such an occupation had almost as much to do with the magnetism as had the beauty of her face and movements. However, the interest was general, and this Saturday's *début* in the forum, whatever it may have been to Bathsheba as the buying and selling farmer, was unquestionably a triumph to her as the maiden. Indeed, the sensation was so pronounced that her instinct on two or three occasions was merely to walk as a queen among these gods of the fallow, like a little sister of a little Jove, and to neglect closing prices altogether.

The numerous evidences of her power to attract were only thrown into greater relief by a marked exception. Women seem to have eyes in their ribbons for such matters as these. Bathsheba, without looking within a right angle of him, was conscious of a black sheep among the flock.

It perplexed her first. If there had been a respectable minority on either side, the case would have been most natural. If nobody had regarded her, she would have taken the matter indifferently – such cases had occurred. If everybody, this man included, she would have taken it as a matter of course – people had done so before. But the smallness of the exception made the mystery.

She soon knew thus much of the recusant's appearance. He was a gentlemanly man, with full and distinctly outlined Roman features, the prominences of which glowed in the sun with a bronze-like richness of tone. He was erect in attitude, and quiet in demeanour. One characteristic pre-eminently marked him – dignity.

Apparently he had some time ago reached that entrance to middle age at which a man's aspect naturally ceases to alter for the term of a dozen years or so; and, artificially, a woman's does likewise. Thirty-five and fifty were his limits of variation – he might have been either, or anywhere between the two.

It may be said that married men of forty are usually ready and generous enough to fling passing glances at any specimen of moderate beauty they may discern by the way. Probably, as with persons playing whist for love, the consciousness of a certain immunity under any circumstances from that worst possible ultimate, the having to pay, makes them unduly speculative. Bathsheba was convinced that this unmoved person was not a married man.

When marketing was over, she rushed off to Liddy, who was waiting for her beside the yellow gig in which they had driven to town. The horse was put in, and on they trotted – Bathsheba's sugar, tea, and drapery parcels being packed behind, and expressing in some indescribable manner, by their colour, shape, and general lineaments, that they were that young lady-farmer's property, and the grocer's and draper's no more.

'I've been through it, Liddy, and it is over. I shan't mind it again, for they will all have grown accustomed to seeing me there; but this morning it was as bad as being married – eyes everywhere!'

'I knowed it would be,' Liddy said. 'Men be such a terrible class of society to look at a body.'

'But there was one man who had more sense than to waste his time upon me.' The information was put in this form that Liddy might not for a moment suppose her mistress was at all piqued. 'A very good-looking man,' she continued, 'upright; about forty, I should think. Do you know at all who he could be?'

Liddy couldn't think.

'Can't you guess at all?' said Bathsheba with some disappointment.

'I haven't a notion; besides, 'tis no difference, since he took less notice of you than any of the rest. Now, if he'd taken more, it would have mattered a great deal.'

Bathsheba was suffering from the reverse feeling just then, and they bowled along in silence. A low carriage, bowling along still more rapidly behind a horse of unimpeachable breed, overtook and passed them.

'Why, there he is!' she said.

Liddy looked. 'That! That's Farmer Boldwood – of course 'tis – the man you couldn't see the other day when he called.'

'Oh, Farmer Boldwood,' murmured Bathsheba, and looked at him as he outstripped them. The farmer had never turned his head once, but with eyes fixed on the most advanced point along the road, passed as unconsciously and abstractedly as if Bathsheba and her charms were thin air.

'He's an interesting man – don't you think so?' she remarked.

'O yes, very. Everybody owns it,' replied Liddy.

'I wonder why he is so wrapt up and indifferent, and seemingly so far away from all he sees around him.'

'It is said – but not known for certain – that he met with some bitter disappointment when he was a young man and merry. A woman jilted him, they say.'

'People always say that – and we know very well women scarcely ever jilt men; 'tis the men who jilt us. I expect it is simply his nature to be so reserved.'

'Simply his nature – I expect so, miss – nothing else in the world.'

'Still, 'tis more romantic to think he has been served cruelly, poor thing! Perhaps, after all, he has.'

'Depend upon it he has. O yes, miss, he has! I feel he must have.'

'However, we are very apt to think extremes of people. I shouldn't wonder after all if it wasn't a little of both – just between the two – rather cruelly used and rather reserved.'

'O dear no, miss – I can't think it between the two!'

'That's most likely.'

'Well, yes, so it is. I am convinced it is most likely. You may take my word, miss, that that's what's the matter with him.'

* XIII *

Sortes Sanctorum – The Valentine

IT was Sunday afternoon in the farmhouse, on the thirteenth of February. Dinner being over, Bathsheba, for want of a better companion, had asked Liddy to come and sit with her. The mouldy pile was dreary in winter-time before the candles were lighted and the shutters closed; the atmosphere of the place seemed as old as the walls; every nook behind the furniture had a temperature of its own, for the fire was not kindled in this part of the house early in the day; and Bathsheba's new piano, which was an old one in other annals, looked particularly sloping and out of level on the warped floor before night threw a shade over its less prominent angles and hid the unpleasantness. Liddy, like a little brook, though shallow, was always rippling; her presence had not so much weight as to task thought, and yet enough to exercise it.

On the table lay an old quarto Bible, bound in leather. Liddy looking at it said, –

'Did you ever find out, miss, who you are going to marry by means of the Bible and key?'

'Don't be so foolish, Liddy. As if such things could be.'

'Well, there's a good deal in it, all the same.'

'Nonsense, child.'

'And it makes your heart beat fearful. Some believe in it; some don't; I do.'

'Very well, let's try it,' said Bathsheba, bounding from her seat with that total disregard of consistency which can be indulged in towards a dependant, and entering into the spirit of divination at once. 'Go and get the front door key.'

Liddy fetched it. 'I wish it wasn't Sunday,' she said, on returning. 'Perhaps 'tis wrong.'

'What's right week days is right Sundays,' replied her mistress in a tone which was a proof in itself.

The book was opened – the leaves, drab with age, being quite worn away at much-read verses by the forefingers of unpractised readers in former days, where they were moved along under the line as an aid to the vision. The special verse in the Book of Ruth was sought out by Bathsheba, and the sublime words met her eye. They slightly thrilled and abashed her. It was Wisdom in the abstract facing Folly in the concrete. Folly in the concrete blushed, persisted in her intention, and placed the key on the book. A rusty patch immediately upon the verse, caused by previous pressure of an iron substance thereon, told that this was not the first time the old volume had been used for the purpose.

'Now keep steady, and be silent,' said Bathsheba.

The verse was repeated; the book turned round; Bathsheba blushed guiltily.

'Who did you try?' said Liddy curiously.

'I shall not tell you.'

'Did you notice Mr Boldwood's doings in church this morning, miss?' Liddy continued, adumbrating by the remark the track her thoughts had taken.

'No, indeed,' said Bathsheba, with serene indifference.

'His pew is exactly opposite yours, miss.'

'I know it.'

'And you did not see his goings on!'

'Certainly I did not, I tell you.'

Liddy assumed a smaller physiognomy, and shut her lips decisively.

This move was unexpected, and proportionately disconcerting. 'What did he do?' Bathsheba said perforce.

'Didn't turn his head to look at you once all the service.'

'Why should he?' again demanded her mistress, wearing a nettled look. 'I didn't ask him to.'

'Oh, no. But everybody else was noticing you; and it was odd he didn't. There, 'tis like him. Rich and gentlemanly, what does he care?'

Bathsheba dropped into a silence intended to express that she had opinions on the matter too abstruse for Liddy's comprehension, rather than that she had nothing to say.

'Dear me – I had nearly forgotten the valentine I bought yesterday,' she exclaimed at length.

'Valentine! who for, miss?' said Liddy. 'Farmer Boldwood?'

It was the single name among all possible wrong ones that just at this moment seemed to Bathsheba more pertinent than the right.

'Well, no. It is only for little Teddy Coggan. I have promised him something, and this will be a pretty surprise for him. Liddy, you may as well bring me my desk and I'll direct it at once.'

Bathsheba took from her desk a gorgeously illuminated and embossed design in post-octavo, which had been bought on the previous market-day at the chief stationer's in Casterbridge. In the centre was a small oval enclosure; this was left blank, that the sender might insert tender words more appropriate to the special occasion than any generalities by a printer could possibly be.

'Here's a place for writing,' said Bathsheba. 'What shall I put?'

'Something of this sort, I should think,' returned Liddy promptly:

> 'The rose is red,
> The violet blue,
> Carnation's sweet,
> And so are you.'

'Yes, that shall be it. It just suits itself to a chubby-faced child like him,' said Bathsheba. She inserted the words in a small though legible handwriting; enclosed the sheet in an envelope, and dipped her pen for the direction.

'What fun it would be to send it to the stupid old Boldwood, and how he would wonder!' said the irrepressible Liddy, lifting her eyebrows, and indulging in an awful mirth on the verge of fear as she thought of the moral and social magnitude of the man contemplated.

Bathsheba paused to regard the idea at full length. Boldwood's had begun to be a troublesome image – a species of Daniel in her kingdom who persisted in kneeling eastward when reason and common sense said that he might just as well follow suit with the rest, and afford her the official glance of admiration which cost nothing at all. She was far from being seriously concerned about his nonconformity. Still, it was faintly depressing that the most dignified and valuable man in the parish should withhold his eyes, and that a girl like Liddy should talk about it. So Liddy's idea was at first rather harassing than piquant.

'No, I won't do that. He wouldn't see any humour in it.'

'He'd worry to death,' said the persistent Liddy.

'Really, I don't care particularly to send it to Teddy,' remarked her mistress. 'He's rather a naughty child sometimes.'

'Yes – that he is.'

'Let's toss, as men do,' said Bathsheba idly. 'Now then, head, Boldwood; tail, Teddy. No, we won't toss money on a Sunday, that would be tempting the devil indeed.'

'Toss this hymn-book; there can't be no sinfulness in that, miss.'

'Very well. Open, Boldwood – shut, Teddy. No; it's more likely to fall open. Open, Teddy – shut, Boldwood.'

The book went fluttering in the air and came down shut.

Bathsheba, a small yawn upon her mouth, took the pen, and with off-hand serenity directed the missive to Boldwood.

'Now light a candle, Liddy. Which seal shall we use? Here's a unicorn's head – there's nothing in that. What's this? – two doves – no. It ought to be something extraordinary, ought it not, Lidd? Here's one with a motto – I remember it is some funny one, but I can't read it. We'll try this, and if it doesn't do we'll have another.'

A large red seal was duly affixed. Bathsheba looked closely at the hot wax to discover the words.

'Capital!' she exclaimed, throwing down the letter frolicsomely. ''Twould upset the solemnity of a parson and clerk too.'

Liddy looked at the words of the seal, and read –

'MARRY ME.'

The same evening the letter was sent, and was duly sorted in Casterbridge post-office that night, to be returned to Weatherbury again in the morning.

So very idly and unreflectingly was this deed done. Of love as a spectacle Bathsheba had a fair knowledge; but of love subjectively she knew nothing.

* XIV *

Effect of the Letter – Sunrise

AT dusk on the evening of St Valentine's Day Boldwood sat down to supper as usual, by a beaming fire of aged logs. Upon the mantel-shelf before him was a time-piece, surmounted by a spread eagle, and upon the eagle's wings was the letter Bathsheba had sent. Here the bachelor's gaze was continually fastening itself, till the large red seal became as a blot of blood on the retina of his eye; and as he ate and drank he still read in fancy the words thereon, although they were too remote for his sight –

'MARRY ME.'

The pert injunction was like those crystal substances, which, colourless themselves, assume the tone of objects about them. Here, in the quiet of Boldwood's parlour, where everything that was not grave was extraneous, and where the atmosphere was that of a Puritan Sunday lasting all the week, the letter and its dictum changed their tenor from the thoughtless-ness of their origin to a deep solemnity, imbibed from their accessories now.

Since the receipt of the missive in the morning, Boldwood had felt the symmetry of his existence to be slowly getting distorted in the direction of an ideal passion. The disturbance was as the first floating weed to Columbus – the contemptibly little suggesting possibilities of the infi-nitely great.

The letter must have had an origin and a motive. That the latter was of the smallest magnitude compatible with its existence at all, Boldwood, of course, did not know. And such an explanation did not strike him as a possibility even. It is foreign to a mystified condition of mind to realize of the mystifier that the processes of approving a course suggested by circumstance, and of striking out a course from inner impulse, would look the same in the result. The vast difference between starting a train of events, and directing into a particular groove a series already started, is rarely apparent to the person confounded by the issue.

When Boldwood went to bed he placed the valentine in the corner of the looking-glass. He was conscious of its presence, even when his back was turned upon it. It was the first time in Boldwood's life that such an event had occurred. The same fascination that caused him to think it an act which had a deliberate motive prevented him from regarding it as an impertinence. He looked again at the direction. The mysterious influences of night invested the writing with the presence of the unknown writer. Somebody's – some *woman's* – hand had travelled softly over the paper bearing his name; her unrevealed eyes had watched every curve as she formed it; her brain had seen him in imagination the while. Why should she have imagined him? Her mouth – were the lips red or pale, plump or creased? – had curved itself to a certain expression as the pen went on – the corners had moved with all their natural tremulousness: what had been the expression?

The vision of the woman writing, as a supplement to the words written, had no individuality. She was a misty shape, and well she might be, considering that her original was at that moment sound asleep and oblivious of all love and letter-writing under the sky. Whenever Bold-wood dozed she took a form, and comparatively ceased to be a vision; when he awoke there was the letter justifying the dream.

The moon shone to-night, and its light was not of a customary kind. His window admitted only a reflection of its rays, and the pale sheen had that reverse direction which snow gives, coming upward and lighting up his ceiling in an unnatural way, casting shadows in strange places, and putting lights where shadows had used to be.

The substance of the epistle had occupied him but little in comparison with the fact of its arrival. He suddenly wondered if anything more might be found in the envelope than what he had withdrawn. He jumped out of bed in the weird light, took the letter, pulled out the flimsy sheet, shook the envelope – searched it. Nothing more was there. Boldwood looked,

as he had a hundred times the preceding day, at the insistent red seal:
'Marry me,' he said aloud.

The solemn and reserved yeoman again closed the letter, and stuck it
in the frame of the glass. In doing so he caught sight of his reflected
features, wan in expression, and insubstantial in form. He saw how
closely compressed was his mouth, and that his eyes were wide-spread
and vacant. Feeling uneasy and dissatisfied with himself for his nervous
excitability, he returned to bed.

Then the dawn drew on. The full power of the clear heaven was not
equal to that of a cloudy sky at noon, when Boldwood arose and dressed
himself. He descended the stairs and went out towards the gate of a field
to the east, leaning over which he paused and looked around.

It was one of the usual slow sunrises of this time of the year, and the sky,
violet in the zenith, was leaden to the northward and murky to the east,
where, over the snowy down or ewe-lease on Weatherbury Upper Farm,
and apparently resting upon the ridge, the only half of the sun yet visible
burnt rayless, like a red and flameless fire shining over a white hearthstone.
The whole effect resembled a sunset as childhood resembles age.

In other directions the fields and sky were so much of one colour by the
snow that it was difficult in a hasty glance to tell whereabouts the horizon
occurred; and in general there was here, too, that before-mentioned
preternatural inversion of light and shade which attends the prospect
when the garish brightness commonly in the sky is found on the earth,
and the shades of earth are in the sky. Over the west hung the wasting
moon, now dull and greenish-yellow, like tarnished brass.

Boldwood was listlessly noting how the frost had hardened and glazed
the surface of the snow, till it shone in the red eastern light with the
polish of marble; how, in some portions of the slope, withered grass-
bents, encased in icicles, bristled through the smooth wan coverlet in the
twisted and curved shapes of old Venetian glass; and how the footprints
of a few birds, which had hopped over the snow whilst it lay in the state
of a soft fleece, were now frozen to a short permanency. A half-muffled
noise of light wheels interrupted him. Boldwood turned back into the
road. It was the mail-cart – a crazy two-wheeled vehicle, hardly heavy
enough to resist a puff of wind. The driver held out a letter. Boldwood
seized it and opened it, expecting another anonymous one – so greatly are
people's ideas of probability a mere sense that precedent will repeat itself.

'I don't think it is for you, sir,' said the man, when he saw Boldwood's
action. 'Though there is no name, I think it is for your shepherd.'

Boldwood looked then at the address –

> To the New Shepherd,
> Weatherbury Farm,
> Near Casterbridge.

'Oh – what a mistake! – it is not mine. Nor is it for my shepherd. It is
for Miss Everdene's. You had better take it on to him – Gabriel Oak – and
say I opened it in mistake.'

At this moment on the ridge, up against the blazing sky, a figure was visible, like the black snuff in the midst of a candle-flame. Then it moved and began to bustle about vigorously from place to place, carrying square skeleton masses, which were riddled by the same rays. A small figure on all fours followed behind. The tall form was that of Gabriel Oak; the small one that of George; the articles in course of transit were hurdles.

'Wait,' said Boldwood. 'That's the man on the hill. I'll take the letter to him myself.'

To Boldwood it was now no longer merely a letter to another man. It was an opportunity. Exhibiting a face pregnant with intention, he entered the snowy field.

Gabriel, at that minute, descended the hill towards the right. The glow stretched down in this direction now, and touched the distant roof of Warren's Malthouse – whither the shepherd was apparently bent. Boldwood followed at a distance.

* XV *

A Morning Meeting – The Letter again

THE scarlet and orange light outside the malthouse did not penetrate to its interior, which was, as usual, lighted by a rival glow of similar hue, radiating from the hearth.

The maltster, after having lain down in his clothes for a few hours, was now sitting beside a three-legged table, breakfasting off bread and bacon. This was eaten on the plateless system, which is performed by placing a slice of bread upon the table, the meat flat upon the bread, a mustard plaster upon the meat, and a pinch of salt upon the whole, then cutting them vertically downwards with a large pocket-knife till wood is reached, when the severed lump is impaled on the knife, elevated, and sent the proper way of food.

The maltster's lack of teeth appeared not to sensibly diminish his powers as a mill. He had been without them for so many years that toothlessness was felt less to be a defect than hard gums an acquisition. Indeed, he seemed to approach the grave as a hyperbolic curve approaches a straight line – less directly as he got nearer, till it was doubtful if he would ever reach it at all.

In the ashpit was a heap of potatoes roasting, and a boiling pipkin of charred bread, called 'coffee', for the benefit of whomsoever should call, for Warren's was a sort of clubhouse, used as an alternative to the inn.

'I say, says I, we get a fine day, and then down comes a snapper at night,' was a remark now suddenly heard spreading into the malthouse from the door, which had been opened the previous moment. The form of Henery Fray advanced to the fire, stamping the snow from his boots when about half-way there. The speech and entry had not seemed to be at all an abrupt beginning to the maltster, introductory matter being often omitted in this neighbourhood, both from word and deed, and the maltster having the same latitude allowed him, did not hurry to reply. He picked up a fragment of cheese by pecking upon it with his knife, as a butcher picks up skewers.

Henery appeared in a drab kerseymere great-coat, buttoned over his smock-frock, the white skirts of the latter being visible to the distance of about a foot below the coat-tails, which, when you got used to the style of dress, looked natural enough, and even ornamental – it certainly was comfortable.

Matthew Moon, Joseph Poorgrass, and other carters and waggoners followed at his heels, with great lanterns dangling from their hands, which showed that they had just come from the cart-horse stables, where they had been busily engaged since four o'clock that morning.

'And how is she getting on without a baily?' the maltster inquired.

Henery shook his head, and smiled one of the bitter smiles, dragging all the flesh of his forehead into a corrugated heap in the centre.

'She'll rue it – surely, surely!' he said. 'Benjy Pennyways were not a true man or an honest baily – as big a betrayer as Joey Iscariot himself. But to think she can carr' on alone!' He allowed his head to swing laterally three or four times in silence. 'Never in all my creeping up – never!'

This was recognized by all as the conclusion of some gloomy speech which had been expressed in thought alone during the shake of the head; Henery meanwhile retained several marks of despair upon his face, to imply that they would be required for use again directly he should go on speaking.

'All will be ruined, and ourselves too, or there's no meat in gentlemen's houses!' said Mark Clark.

'A headstrong maid, that's what she is – and won't listen to no advice at all. Pride and vanity have ruined many a cobbler's dog. Dear, dear, when I think o' it, I sorrows like a man in travel!'

'True, Henery, you do, I've heard ye,' said Joseph Poorgrass, in a voice of thorough attestation, and with a wire-drawn smile of misery.

''Twould do a martel man no harm to have what's under her bonnet,' said Billy Smallbury, who had just entered, bearing his one tooth before him. 'She can spaik real language, and must have some sense somewhere. Do ye foller me?'

'I do; but no baily – I deserved that place,' wailed Henery, signifying wasted genius by gazing blankly at visions of a high destiny apparently visible to him on Billy Smallbury's smock-frock. 'There, 'twas to be, I suppose. Your lot is your lot, and Scripture is nothing; for if you do good you don't get rewarded according to your works, but be cheated in some mean way out of your recompense.'

'No, no; I don't agree with'ee there,' said Mark Clark. 'God's a perfect gentleman in that respect.'

'Good works good pay, so to speak it,' attested Joseph Poorgrass.

A short pause ensued, and as a sort of *entr'acte* Henery turned and blew out the lanterns, which the increase of daylight rendered no longer necessary even in the malthouse, with its one pane of glass.

'I wonder what a farmer-woman can want with a harpsichord, dulcimer, pianner, or whatever 'tis they d'call it?' said the maltster. 'Liddy saith she've a new one.'

'Got a pianner?'

'Ay. Seems her old uncle's things were not good enough for her. She've bought all but everything new. There's heavy chairs for the stout, weak and wiry ones for the slender; great watches, getting on to the size of clocks, to stand upon the chimbley-piece.'

'Pictures, for the most part wonderful frames.'

'And long horse-hair settles for the drunk, with horse-hair pillows at each end,' said Mr Clark. 'Likewise looking-glasses for the pretty, and lying books for the wicked.'

A firm loud tread was now heard stamping outside; the door was opened about six inches, and somebody on the other side exclaimed –

'Neighbours, have ye got room for a few new-born lambs?'

'Ay, sure, shepherd,' said the conclave.

The door was flung back till it kicked the wall and trembled from top to bottom with the blow. Mr Oak appeared in the entry with a steaming face, haybands wound about his ankles to keep out the snow, a leather strap round his waist outside the smock-frock, and looking altogether an epitome of the world's health and vigour. Four lambs hung in various embarrassing attitudes over his shoulders, and the dog George, whom Gabriel had contrived to fetch from Norcombe, stalked solemnly behind.

'Well, Shepherd Oak, and how's lambing this year, if I mid say it?' inquired Joseph Poorgrass.

'Terrible trying,' said Oak. 'I've been wet through twice a-day, either snow or rain, this last fortnight. Cainy and I haven't tined our eyes tonight.'

'A good few twins, too, I hear?'

'Too many by half. Yes; 'tis a very queer lambing this year. We shan't have done by Lady Day.'

'And last year 'twer all over by Sexajessamine Sunday,' Joseph remarked.

'Bring on the rest, Cain,' said Gabriel, 'and then run back to the ewes. I'll follow you soon.'

Cainy Ball – a cheery-faced young lad, with a small circular orifice by way of mouth, advanced and deposited two others, and retired as he was bidden. Oak lowered the lambs from their unnatural elevation, wrapped them in hay, and placed them round the fire.

'We've no lambing-hut here, as I used to have at Norcombe,' said Gabriel, 'and 'tis such a plague to bring the weakly ones to a house. If 'twasn't for your place here, malter, I don't know what I should do, this keen weather. And how is it with you today, malter?'

'Oh, neither sick nor sorry, shepherd; but no younger.'

'Ay – I understand.'

'Sit down, Shepherd Oak,' continued the ancient man of malt. 'And how was the old place at Norcombe, when ye went for your dog? I should like to see the old familiar spot; but faith, I shouldn't know a soul there now.'

'I suppose you wouldn't. 'Tis altered very much.'

'Is it true that Dicky Hill's wooden cider-house is pulled down?'

'O yes – years ago, and Dicky's cottage just above it.'

'Well, to be sure!'

'Yes; and Tompkins's old apple-tree is rooted that used to bear two hogsheads of cider, and no help from other trees.'

'Rooted? – you don't say it! Ah! stirring times we live in – stirring times.'

'And you can mind the old well that used to be in the middle of the place? That's turned into a solid iron pump with a large stone trough, and all complete.'

'Dear, dear – how the face of nations alter, and what we live to see nowadays! Yes – and 'tis the same here. They've been talking but now of the mis'ess's strange doings.'

'What have you been saying about her?' inquired Oak, sharply turning to the rest, and getting very warm.

'These middle-aged men have been pulling her over the coals for pride and vanity,' said Mark Clark; 'but I say, let her have rope enough. Bless her pretty face – shouldn't I like to do so – upon her cherry lips!' The gallant Mark Clark here made a peculiar and well-known sound with his own.

'Mark,' said Gabriel sternly, 'now you mind this: none of that dalliance-talk – that smack-and-coddle style of yours – about Miss Everdene. I don't allow it. Do you hear?'

'With all my heart, as I've got no chance,' replied Mr Clark cordially.

'I suppose you've been speaking against her?' said Oak, turning to Joseph Poorgrass with a very grim look.

'No, no – not a word I – 'tis a real joyful thing that she's no worse, that's what I say,' said Joseph, trembling and blushing with terror. 'Matthew just said –'

'Matthew Moon, what have you been saying?' asked Oak.

'I? Why ye know I wouldn't harm a worm – no, not one underground worm?' said Matthew Moon, looking very uneasy.

'Well, somebody has – and look here, neighbours.' Gabriel, though one of the quietest and most gentle men on earth, rose to the occasion, with martial promptness and vigour. 'That's my fist.' Here he placed his fist, rather smaller in size than a common loaf, in the mathematical centre of the maltster's little table, and with it gave a bump or two thereon, as if to ensure that their eyes all thoroughly took in the idea of fistiness before he went further. 'Now – the first man in the parish that I hear prophesying bad of our mistress, why' (here the fist was raised and let fall, as Thor might have done with his hammer in assaying it) – 'he'll smell and taste that – or I'm a Dutchman.'

All earnestly expressed by their features that their minds did not wander to Holland for a moment on account of this statement, but were deploring the difference which gave rise to the figure; and Mark Clark cried 'Hear, hear; just what I should ha' said.' The dog George looked up at the same time after the shepherd's menace, and, though he understood English but imperfectly, began to growl.

'Now, don't ye take on so, shepherd, and sit down!' said Henery with a deprecating peacefulness equal to anything of the kind in Christianity.

'We hear that ye be a extraordinary good and clever man, shepherd,' said Joseph Poorgrass with considerable anxiety from behind the malts-ter's bedstead, whither he had retired for safety. ' 'Tis a great thing to be clever, I'm sure,' he added, making movements associated with states of mind rather than body; 'we wish we were, don't we, neighbours?'

'Ay, that we do, sure,' said Matthew Moon, with a small anxious laugh towards Oak, to show how very friendly disposed he was likewise.

'Who's been telling you I'm clever?' said Oak.

' 'Tis blowed about from pillar to post quite common,' said Matthew. 'We hear that ye can tell the time as well by the stars as we can by the sun and moon, shepherd.'

'Yes, I can do a little that way,' said Gabriel, as a man of medium sentiments on the subject.

'And that ye can make sun-dials, and prent folks' names upon their waggons almost like copper-plate, with beautiful flourishes, and great long tails. A excellent fine thing for ye to be such a clever man, shepherd. Joseph Poorgrass used to prent to Farmer James Everdene's waggon before you came, and 'a could never mind which way to turn the J's and E's – could ye, Joseph?' Joseph shook his head to express how absolute was the fact that he couldn't. 'And so you used to do 'em the wrong way, like this, didn't ye, Joseph?' Matthew marked on the dusty floor with his whip-handle

ſAMƎƨ

'And how Farmer James would cuss, and call thee a fool, wouldn't he, Joseph, when 'a seed his name looking so inside-out-like?' continued Matthew Moon, with feeling.

'Ay – 'a would,' said James meekly. 'But you see, I wasn't so much to blame, for them J's and E's be such trying sons o' witches for the memory to mind whether they face backward or forward; and I always had such a forgetful memory, too.'

' 'Tis a bad affliction for ye, being such a man of calamities in other ways.'

'Well, 'tis; but a happy Providence ordered that it should be no worse, and I feel my thanks. As to shepherd, there, I'm sure mis'ess ought to have made ye her baily – such a fitting man for't as you be.'

'I don't mind owning that I expected it,' said Oak frankly. 'Indeed, I hoped for the place. At the same time, Miss Everdene has a right to be her own baily if she choose – and to keep me down to be a common shepherd only.' Oak drew a slow breath, looked sadly into the bright ashpit, and seemed lost in thoughts not of the most hopeful hue.

The genial warmth of the fire now began to stimulate the nearly lifeless lambs to bleat and move their limbs briskly upon the hay, and to recognize for the first time the fact that they were born. Their noise increased to a chorus of baas, upon which Oak pulled the milk-can from before the fire, and taking a small tea-pot from the pocket of his smock-frock, filled it with milk, and taught those of the helpless creatures which were not to be restored to their dams how to drink from the spout – a trick they acquired with astonishing aptitude.

'And she don't even let ye have the skins of the dead lambs, I hear?' resumed Joseph Poorgrass, his eyes lingering on the operations of Oak with the necessary melancholy.

'I don't have them,' said Gabriel.

'Ye be very badly used, shepherd,' hazarded Joseph again, in the hope of getting Oak as an ally in lamentation after all. 'I think she's took against ye – that I do.'

'O no – not at all,' replied Gabriel hastily, and a sigh escaped him, which the deprivation of lamb skins could hardly have caused.

Before any further remark had been added a shade darkened the door, and Boldwood entered the malthouse, bestowing upon each a nod of a quality between friendliness and condescension.

'Ah! Oak, I thought you were here,' he said. 'I met the mail-cart ten minutes ago, and a letter was put into my hand, which I opened without reading the address. I believe it is yours. You must excuse the accident, please.'

'O yes – not a bit of difference, Mr Boldwood – not a bit,' said Gabriel readily. He had not a correspondent on earth, nor was there a possible letter coming to him whose contents the whole parish would not have have been welcome to peruse.

Oak stepped aside, and read the following in an unknown hand:

DEAR FRIEND – I do not know your name, but I think these few lines will reach you, which I write to thank you for your kindness to me the night I left Weatherbury in a reckless way. I also return the money I owe you, which you will excuse my not keeping as a gift. All has ended well, and I am happy to say I am going to be married to the young man who has courted me for some time – Sergeant Troy, of the 11th Dragoon Guards, now quartered in this town. He would, I know, object to my having received anything except as a loan, being a man of great respectability and high honour – indeed, a nobleman by blood.

I should be much obliged to you if you would keep the contents of this letter a secret for the present, dear friend. We mean to surprise Weatherbury by coming there soon as husband and wife, though I blush to state it to one nearly a stranger. The sergeant grew up in Weatherbury. Thanking you again for your kindness,

I am, your sincere well-wisher,

FANNY ROBIN

'Have you read it, Mr Boldwood?' said Gabriel; 'if not, you had better do so. I know you are interested in Fanny Robin.'

Boldwood read the letter and looked grieved.

'Fanny – poor Fanny! the end she is so confident of has not yet come, she should remember – and may never come. I see she gives no address.'

'What sort of a man is this Sergeant Troy?' said Gabriel.

'H'm – I'm afraid not one to build much hope upon in such a case as this,' the farmer murmured, 'though he's a clever fellow, and up to everything. A slight romance attaches to him, too. His mother was a French governess, and it seems that a secret attachment existed between her and the late Lord Severn. She was married to a poor medical man, and soon after an infant was born; and while money was forthcoming all went on well. Unfortunately for her boy, his best friends died; and he got then a situation as second clerk at a lawyer's in Casterbridge. He stayed there for some time, and might have worked himself into a dignified position of some sort had he not indulged in the wild freak of enlisting. I have much doubt if ever little Fanny will surprise us in the way she mentions – very much doubt. A silly girl – silly girl!'

The door was hurriedly burst open again, and in came running Cainy Ball out of breath, his mouth red and open, like the bell of a penny trumpet, from which he coughed with noisy vigour and great distension of face.

'Now, Cain Ball,' said Oak sternly, 'why will you run so fast and lose your breath so? I'm always telling you of it.'

'O – I – a puff of mee breath – went – the wrong way, please, Mister Oak, and made me cough – hok – hok!'

'Well – what have you come for?'

'I've run to tell ye,' said the junior shepherd, supporting his exhausted youthful frame against the doorpost, 'that you must come directly. Two more ewes have twinned – that's what's the matter, Shepherd Oak.'

'Oh, that's it,' said Oak, jumping up, and dismissing for the present his thoughts on poor Fanny. 'You are a good boy to run and tell me, Cain, and you shall smell a large plum pudding some day as a treat. But, before we go, Cainy, bring the tarpot, and we'll mark this lot and have done with 'em.'

Oak took from his illimitable pockets a marking iron, dipped it into the pot, and imprinted on the buttocks of the infant sheep the initials of her he delighted to muse on – 'B.E.', which signified to all the region round that henceforth the lambs belonged to Farmer Bathsheba Everdene, and to no one else.

'Now, Cainy, shoulder your two, and off. Good morning, Mr

Boldwood.' The shepherd lifted the sixteen large legs and four small bodies he had himself brought, and vanished with them in the direction of the lambing field hard by – their frames being now in a sleek and hopeful state, pleasantly contrasting with their death's-door plight of half an hour before.

Boldwood followed him a little way up the field, hesitated, and turned back. He followed him again with a last resolve, annihilating return. On approaching the nook in which the fold was constructed, the farmer drew out his pocket-book, unfastened it, and allowed it to lie open on his hand. A letter was revealed – Bathsheba's.

'I was going to ask you, Oak,' he said, with unreal carelessness, 'if you know whose writing this is?'

Oak glanced into the book, and replied instantly, with a flushed face, 'Miss Everdene's.'

Oak had coloured simply at the consciousness of sounding her name. He now felt a strangely distressing qualm from a new thought. The letter could of course be no other than anonymous, or the inquiry would not have been necessary.

Boldwood mistook his confusion: sensitive persons are always ready with their 'Is it I?' in preference to objective reasoning.

'The question was perfectly fair,' he returned – and there was something incongruous in the serious earnestness with which he applied himself to an argument on a valentine. 'You know it is always expected that privy inquiries will be made: that's where the – fun lies.' If the word 'fun' had been 'torture', it could not have been uttered with a more constrained and restless countenance than was Boldwood's then.

Soon parting from Gabriel, the lonely and reserved man returned to his house to breakfast – feeling twinges of shame and regret at having so far exposed his mood by those fevered questions to a stranger. He again placed the letter on the mantelpiece, and sat down to think of the circumstances attending it by the light of Gabriel's information.

* XVI *

All Saints' and All Souls'

ON a week-day morning a small congregation, consisting mainly of women and girls, rose from its knees in the mouldy nave of a church called All Saints', in the distant barrack-town before-mentioned, at the end of a service without a sermon. They were about to disperse when a smart footstep, entering the porch and coming up the central passage, arrested their attention. The step echoed with a ring unusual in a church; it was the clink of spurs. Everybody looked. A young cavalry soldier in a red uniform, with the three chevrons of a sergeant upon his sleeve, strode up the aisle, with an embarrassment which was only the more marked by the intense vigour of his step, and by the determination upon his face to show none. A slight flush had mounted his cheek by the time he had run the gauntlet between these women; but, passing on through the chancel arch, he never paused till he came close to the altar railing. Here for a moment he stood alone.

The officiating curate, who had not yet doffed his surplice, perceived the new-comer, and followed him to the communion-space. He whispered to the soldier, and then beckoned to the clerk, who in his turn whispered to an elderly woman, apparently his wife, and they also went up the chancel steps.

' 'Tis a wedding!' murmured some of the women, brightening. 'Let's wait!'

The majority again sat down.

There was a creaking of machinery behind, and some of the young ones turned their heads. From the interior face of the west wall of the tower projected a little canopy with a quarter-jack and small bell beneath it, the automaton being driven by the same clock machinery that struck the large bell in the tower. Between the tower and the church was a close screen, the door of which was kept shut during services, hiding this grotesque clockwork from sight. At present, however, the door was open, and the egress of the jack, the blows on the bell, and the mannikin's retreat into the nook again, were visible to many, and audible throughout the church.

The jack had struck half-past eleven.

'Where's the woman?' whispered some of the spectators.

The young sergeant stood still with the abnormal rigidity of the old pillars around. He faced the south-east, and was as silent as he was still.

The silence grew to be a noticeable thing as the minutes went on, and nobody else appeared, and not a soul moved. The rattle of the quarter-jack again from its niche, its blows for three-quarters, its fussy retreat, were almost painfully abrupt, and caused many of the congregation to start palpably.

'I wonder where the woman is!' a voice whispered again.

There began now that slight shifting of feet, that artificial coughing among several, which betrays a nervous suspense. At length there was a titter. But the soldier never moved. There he stood, his face to the south-east, upright as a column, his cap in his hand.

The clock ticked on. The women threw off their nervousness, and titters and giggling became more frequent. Then came a dead silence. Every one was waiting for the end. Some persons may have noticed how extraordinarily the striking of quarters seems to quicken the flight of time. It was hardly credible that the jack had not got wrong with the minutes when the rattle began again, the puppet emerged, and the four quarters were struck fitfully as before. One could almost be positive that there was a malicious leer upon the hideous creature's face, and a mischievous delight in its twitchings. Then followed the dull and remote resonance of the twelve heavy strokes in the tower above. The women were impressed, and there was no giggle this time.

The clergyman glided into the vestry, and the clerk vanished. The sergeant had not yet turned; every woman in the church was waiting to see his face, and he appeared to know it. At last he did turn, and stalked resolutely down the nave, braving them all, with a compressed lip. Two bowed and toothless old almsmen then looked at each other and chuckled, innocently enough; but the sound had a strange weird effect in that place.

Opposite to the church was a paved square, around which several overhanging wood buildings of old time cast a picturesque shade. The young man on leaving the door went to cross the square, when, in the middle, he met a little woman. The expression of her face, which had been one of intense anxiety, sank at the sight of his nearly to terror.

'Well?' he said, in a suppressed passion, fixedly looking at her.

'O Frank – I made a mistake! – I thought that church with the spire was All Saints', and I was at the door at half past eleven to a minute as you said. I waited till quarter to twelve, and found then that I was in All Souls'. But I wasn't much frightened, for I thought it could be to-morrow as well.'

'You fool, for so fooling me! But say no more.'

'Shall it be to-morrow, Frank?' she asked blankly.

'To-morrow!' and he gave vent to a hoarse laugh. 'I don't go through that experience again for some time, I warrant you!'

'But after all,' she expostulated in a trembling voice, 'the mistake was not such a terrible thing! Now, dear Frank, when shall it be?'

'Ah, when? God knows!' he said, with a light irony, and turning from her walked rapidly away.

* XVII *

In the Market-place

ON Saturday Boldwood was in Casterbridge market-house as usual when the disturber of his dreams entered, and became visible to him. Adam had awakened from his deep sleep, and behold! there was Eve. The farmer took courage, and for the first time really looked at her.

Material causes and emotional effects are not to be arranged in regular equation. The result from capital employed in the production of any movement of a mental nature is sometimes as tremendous as the cause itself is absurdly minute. When women are in a freakish mood their usual intuition, either from carelessness or inherent defect, seemingly fails to teach them this, and hence it was that Bathsheba was fated to be astonished to-day.

Boldwood looked at her – not slily, critically, or understandingly, but blankly at gaze, in the way a reaper looks up at a passing train – as something foreign to his element, and but dimly understood. To Boldwood women had been remote phenomena rather than necessary complements – comets of such uncertain aspect, movement, and permanence, that whether their orbits were as geometrical, unchangeable, and as subject to laws as his own, or as absolutely erratic as they superficially appeared, he had not deemed it his duty to consider.

He saw her black hair, her correct facial curves and profile, and the roundness of her chin and throat. He saw then the side of her eyelids, eyes, and lashes, and the shape of her ear. Next he noticed her figure, her skirt, and the very soles of her shoes.

Boldwood thought her beautiful, but wondered whether he was right in his thought, for it seemed impossible that this romance in the flesh, if so sweet as he imagined, could have been going on long without creating a commotion of delight among men, and provoking more inquiry than Bathsheba had done, even though that was not a little. To the best of his judgement neither nature nor art could improve this perfect one of an imperfect many. His heart began to move within him. Boldwood, it must be remembered, though forty years of age, had never before inspected a woman with the very centre and force of his glance; they had struck upon all his senses at wide angles.

Was she really beautiful? He could not assure himself that his opinion was true even now. He furtively said to a neighbour, 'Is Miss Everdene considered handsome?'

'O yes; she was a good deal noticed the first time she came, if you remember. A very handsome girl indeed.'

A man is never more credulous than in receiving favourable opinions on the beauty of a woman he is half, or quite, in love with; a mere child's word on the point has the weight of an R.A.'s. Boldwood was satisfied now.

And this charming woman had in effect said to him, 'Marry me.' Why should she have done that strange thing? Boldwood's blindness to the difference between approving of what circumstances suggest, and originating what they do not suggest, was well matched by Bathsheba's insensibility to the possibly great issues of little beginnings.

She was at this moment coolly dealing with a dashing young farmer, adding up accounts with him as indifferently as if his face had been the pages of a ledger. It was evident that such a nature as his had no attraction for a woman of Bathsheba's taste. But Boldwood grew hot down to his hands with an incipient jealousy; he trod for the first time the threshold of 'the injured lover's hell'. His first impulse was to go and thrust himself between them. This could be done, but only in one way – by asking to see a sample of her corn. Boldwood renounced the idea. He could not make the request; it was debasing loveliness to ask it to buy and sell, and jarred with his conceptions of her.

All this time Bathsheba was conscious of having broken into that dignified stronghold at last. His eyes, she knew, were following her everywhere. This was a triumph;. and had it come naturally, such a triumph would have been the sweeter to her for this piquing delay. But it had been brought about by misdirected ingenuity, and she valued it only as she valued an artificial flower or a wax fruit.

Being a woman with some good sense of reasoning on subjects wherein her heart was not involved, Bathsheba genuinely repented that a freak which had owed its existence as much to Liddy as to herself, should ever have been undertaken, to disturb the placidity of a man she respected too highly to deliberately tease.

She that day nearly formed the intention of begging his pardon on the very next occasion of their meeting. The worst features of this arrangement were that, if he thought she ridiculed him, an apology would increase the offence by being disbelieved; and if he thought she wanted him to woo her, it would read like additional evidence of her forwardness.

XVIII

Boldwood in Meditation – Regret

BOLDWOOD was tenant of what was called Little Weatherbury Farm, and his person was the nearest approach to aristocracy that this remoter quarter of the parish could boast of. Genteel strangers, whose god was their town, who might happen to be compelled to linger about this nook for a day, heard the sound of light wheels, and prayed to see good society, to the degree of a solitary lord, or squire at the very least, but it was only Mr Boldwood going out for the day. They heard the sound of wheels yet once more, and were re-animated to expectancy: it was only Mr Boldwood coming home again.

His house stood recessed from the road, and the stables, which are to a farm what a fireplace is to a room, were behind, their lower portions being lost amid bushes of laurel. Inside the blue door, open half-way down, were to be seen at this time the backs and tails of half-a-dozen warm and contented horses standing in their stalls; and as thus viewed, they presented alternations of roan and bay, in shapes like a Moorish arch, the tail being a streak down the midst of each. Over these, and lost to the eye gazing in from the outer light, the mouths of the same animals could be heard busily sustaining the above-named warmth and plumpness by quantities of oats and hay. The restless and shadowy figure of a colt wandered about a loose-box at the end, whilst the steady grind of all the eaters was occasionally diversified by the rattle of a rope or the stamp of a foot.

Pacing up and down at the heels of the animals was Farmer Boldwood himself. This place was his almonry and cloister in one: here, after looking to the feeding of his four-footed dependants, the celibate would walk and meditate of an evening till the moon's rays streamed in through the cobwebbed windows, or total darkness enveloped the scene.

His square-framed perpendicularity showed more fully now than in the crowd and bustle of the market-house. In this meditative walk his foot met the floor with heel and toe simultaneously, and his fine reddish-fleshed face was bent downwards just enough to render obscure the still mouth and the well-rounded though rather prominent and broad chin. A few clear and thread-like horizontal lines were the only interruption to the otherwise smooth surface of his large forehead.

The phases of Boldwood's life were ordinary enough, but his was not an ordinary nature. That stillness, which struck casual observers more than anything else in his character and habit, and seemed so precisely like the rest of inanition, may have been the perfect balance of enormous antagonistic forces – positives and negatives in fine adjustment. His equilibrium disturbed, he was in extremity at once. If an emotion possessed him at all, it ruled him; a feeling not mastering him was entirely latent. Stagnant or rapid, it was never slow. He was always hit mortally, or he was missed.

He had no light and careless touches in his constitution, either for good or for evil. Stern in the outlines of action, mild in the details, he was serious throughout all. He saw no absurd sides to the follies of life, and thus, though not quite companionable in the eyes of merry men and scoffers, and those to whom all things show life as a jest, he was not intolerable to the earnest and those acquainted with grief. Being a man who read all the dramas of life seriously, if he failed to please when they were comedies, there was no frivolous treatment to reproach him for when they chanced to end tragically.

Bathsheba was far from dreaming that the dark and silent shape upon which she had so carelessly thrown a seed was a hotbed of tropic intensity. Had she known Boldwood's moods her blame would have been fearful, and the stain upon her heart ineradicable. Moreover, had she known her present power for good or evil over this man, she would have trembled at her responsibility. Luckily for her present, unluckily for her future tranquillity, her understanding had not yet told her what Boldwood was. Nobody knew entirely; for though it was possible to form guesses concerning his wild capabilities from old flood-marks faintly visible, he had never been seen at the high tides which caused them.

Farmer Boldwood came to the stable-door and looked forth across the level fields. Beyond the first enclosure was a hedge, and on the other side of this a meadow belonging to Bathsheba's farm.

It was now early spring – the time of going to grass with the sheep, when they have the first feed of the meadows, before these are laid up for mowing. The winds, which had been blowing east for several weeks, had veered to the southward, and the middle of spring had come abruptly – almost without a beginning. It was that period in the vernal quarter when we may suppose the Dryads to be waking for the season. The vegetable world begins to move and swell and the saps to rise, till in the completest silence of lone gardens and trackless plantations, where everything seems helpless and still after the bond and slavery of frost, there are bustlings, strainings, united thrusts, and pulls-all-together, in comparison with which the powerful tugs of cranes and pulleys in a noisy city are but pigmy efforts.

Boldwood, looking into the distant meadows, saw there three figures. They were those of Miss Everdene, Shepherd Oak, and Cainy Ball.

When Bathsheba's figure shone upon the farmer's eyes it lighted him up as the moon lights up a great tower. A man's body is as the shell, or the tablet, of his soul, as he is reserved or ingenuous, overflowing or self-contained. There was a change in Boldwood's exterior from its former impassibleness; and his face showed that he was now living outside his defences for the first time, and with a fearful sense of exposure. It is the usual experience of strong natures when they love.

At last he arrived at a conclusion. It was to go across and inquire boldly of her.

The insulation of his heart by reserve during these many years, without a channel of any kind for disposable emotion, had worked its effect. It has been observed more than once that the causes of love are chiefly subjective, and Boldwood was a living testimony to the truth of the proposition. No mother existed to absorb his devotion, no sister for his tenderness, no idle ties for sense. He became surcharged with the compound, which was genuine lover's love.

He approached the gate of the meadow. Beyond it the ground was melodious with ripples, and the sky with larks; the low bleating of the flock mingling with both. Mistress and man were engaged in the operation of making a lamb 'take', which is performed whenever an ewe had lost her own offspring, one of the twins of another ewe being given her as a substitute. Gabriel had skinned the dead lamb, and was tying the skin over the body of the live lamb in the customary manner, whilst Bathsheba was holding open a little pen of four hurdles, into which the mother and foisted lamb were driven, where they would remain till the old sheep conceived an affection for the young one.

Bathsheba looked up at the completion of the manoeuvre and saw the farmer by the gate, where he was overhung by a willow tree in full bloom. Gabriel, to whom her face was as the uncertain glory of an April day, was very regardful of its faintest changes, and instantly discerned thereon the mark of some influence from without, in the form of a keenly self-conscious reddening. He also turned and beheld Boldwood.

At once connecting these signs with the letter Boldwood had shown him, Gabriel suspected her of some coquettish procedure begun by that means, and carried on since, he knew not how.

Farmer Boldwood had read the pantomime denoting that they were aware of his presence, and the perception was as too much light turned upon his new sensibility. He was still in the road, and by moving on he hoped that neither would recognize that he had originally intended to enter the field. He passed by with an utter and overwhelming sensation of ignorance, shyness, and doubt. Perhaps in her manner there were signs that she wished to see him – perhaps not – he could not read a woman. The cabala of this erotic philosophy seemed to consist of the subtlest meanings expressed in misleading ways. Every turn, look, word, and accent contained a mystery quite distinct from its obvious import, and not one had ever been pondered by him until now.

As for Bathsheba, she was not deceived into the belief that Farmer Boldwood had walked by on business or in idleness. She collected the probabilities of the case, and concluded that she was herself responsible for Boldwood's appearance there. It troubled her much to see what a great flame a little wildfire was likely to kindle. Bathsheba was no schemer for marriage, nor was she deliberately a trifler with the affections of men, and a censor's experience on seeing an actual flirt after observing her would have been a feeling of surprise that Bathsheba could be so different from such a one, and yet so like what a flirt is supposed to be.

She resolved never again, by look or by sign, to interrupt the steady flow of this man's life. But a resolution to avoid an evil is seldom framed till the evil is so far advanced as to make avoidance impossible.

* XIX *

The Sheep-washing – The Offer

BOLDWOOD did eventually call upon her. She was not at home. 'Of course not,' he murmured. In contemplating Bathsheba as a woman, he had forgotten the accidents of her position as an agriculturist – that being as much of a farmer, and as extensive a farmer, as himself, her probable whereabouts was out-of-doors at this time of the year. This, and the other oversights Boldwood was guilty of, were natural to the mood, and still more natural to the circumstances. The great aids to idealization in love were present here: occasional observation of her from a distance, and the absence of social intercourse with her – visual familiarity, oral strangeness. The smaller human elements were kept out of sight; the pettinesses that enter so largely into all earthly living and doing were disguised by the accident of lover and loved-one not being on visiting terms; and there was hardly awakened a thought in Boldwood that sorry household realities appertained to her, or that she, like all others, had moments of commonplace, when to be least plainly seen was to be most prettily remembered. Thus a mild sort of apotheosis took place in his fancy, whilst she still lived and breathed within his own horizon, a troubled creature like himself.

It was the end of May when the farmer determined to be no longer repulsed by trivialities or distracted by suspense. He had by this time grown used to being in love; the passion now startled him less even when it tortured him more, and he felt himself adequate to the situation. On inquiring for her at her house they had told him she was at the sheep-washing, and he went off to seek her there.

The sheep-washing pool was a perfectly circular basin of brickwork in the meadows, full of the clearest water. To birds on the wing its glassy surface, reflecting the light sky, must have been visible for miles around as a glistening Cyclops' eye in a green face. The grass about the margin at this season was a sight to remember long – in a minor sort of way. Its activity in sucking the moisture from the rich damp sod was almost a process observable by the eye. The outskirts of this level water-meadow were diversified by rounded and hollow pastures, where just now every flower that was not a buttercup was a daisy. The river slid along noiselessly as a shade, the swelling reeds and sedge forming a flexible palisade upon its moist brink. To the north of the meadow were trees, the leaves of which were new, soft, and moist, not yet having stiffened and darkened under summer sun and drought, their colour being yellow beside a green – green beside a yellow. From the recesses of this knot of foliage the loud notes of three cuckoos were resounding through the still air.

Boldwood went meditating down the slopes with his eyes on his boots, which the yellow pollen from the buttercups had bronzed in artistic gradations. A tributary of the main stream flowed through the basin of the pool by an inlet and outlet at opposite points of its diameter. Shepherd Oak, Jan Coggan, Moon, Poorgrass, Cain Ball, and several others were assembled here, all dripping wet to the very roots of their hair, and Bathsheba was standing by in a new riding-habit – the most elegant she had ever worn – the reins of her horse being looped over her arm. Flagons of cider were rolling about upon the green. The meek sheep were pushed into the pool by Coggan and Matthew Moon, who stood by the lower hatch, immersed to their waists; then Gabriel, who stood on the brink thrust them under as they swam along, with an instrument like a crutch, formed for the purpose, and also for assisting the exhausted animals when the wool became saturated and they began to sink. They were let out against the stream, and through the upper opening, all impurities flowing away below. Cainy Ball and Joseph, who performed this latter operation, were if possible wetter than the rest; they resembled dolphins under a fountain, every protuberance and angle of their clothes dribbling forth a small rill.

Boldwood came close and bade her good morning with such constraint that she could not but think he had stepped across to the washing for its own sake, hoping not to find her there; more, she fancied his brow severe and his eye slighting. Bathsheba immediately contrived to withdraw, and glided along by the river till she was a stone's throw off. She heard footsteps brushing the grass, and had a consciousness that love was encircling her like a perfume. Instead of turning or waiting, Bathsheba went further among the high sedges, but Boldwood seemed determined, and pressed on till they were completely past the bend of the river. Here, without being seen, they could hear the splashing and shouts of the washers above.

'Miss Everdene!' said the farmer.

She trembled, turned, and said 'Good morning'. His tone was so utterly removed from all she had expected as a beginning. It was lowness and quiet accentuated: an emphasis of deep meanings, their form, at the same time, being scarcely expressed. Silence has sometimes a remarkable power of showing itself as the disembodied soul of feeling wandering without its carcase, and it is then more impressive than speech. In the same way, to say a little is often to tell more than to say a great deal. Boldwood told everything in that word.

As the consciousness expands on learning that what was fancied to be the rumble of wheels is the reverberation of thunder, so did Bathsheba's at her intuitive conviction.

'I feel – almost too much – to think,' he said, with a solemn simplicity. 'I have come to speak to you without preface. My life is not my own since I have beheld you clearly, Miss Everdene – I come to make you an offer of marriage.'

Bathsheba tried to preserve an absolutely neutral countenance, and all the motion she made was that of closing lips which had previously been a little parted.

'I am now forty-one years old,' he went on. 'I may have been called a confirmed bachelor, and I was a confirmed bachelor. I had never any views of myself as a husband in my earlier days, nor have I made any calculation on the subject since I have been older. But we all change, and my change, in this matter, came with seeing you. I have felt lately, more and more, that my present way of living is bad in every respect. Beyond all things, I want you as my wife.'

'I feel, Mr Boldwood, that though I respect you much, I do not feel – what would justify me to – in accepting your offer,' she stammered.

This giving back of dignity for dignity seemed to open the sluices of feeling that Boldwood had as yet kept closed.

'My life is a burden without you,' he exclaimed, in a low voice. 'I want you – I want you to let me say I love you again and again!'

Bathsheba answered nothing, and the mare upon her arm seemed so impressed that instead of cropping the herbage she looked up.

'I think and hope you care enough for me to listen to what I have to tell!'

Bathsheba's momentary impulse at hearing this was to ask why he thought that, till she remembered that, far from being a conceited assumption on Boldwood's part, it was but the natural conclusion of serious reflection based on deceptive premises of her own offering.

'I wish I could say courteous flatteries to you,' the farmer continued in an easier tone, 'and put my rugged feeling into a graceful shape: but I have neither power nor patience to learn such things. I want you for my wife – so wildly that no other feeling can abide in me; but I should not have spoken out had I not been led to hope.'

'The valentine again! O that valentine!' she said to herself, but not a word to him.

'If you can love me say so, Miss Everdene. If not – don't say no!'

'Mr Boldwood, it is painful to have to say I am surprised, so that I don't know how to answer you with propriety and respect – but am only just able to speak out my feeling – I mean my meaning; that I am afraid I can't marry you, much as I respect you. You are too dignified for me to suit you, sir.'

'But, Miss Everdene!'

'I – I didn't – I know I ought never to have dreamt of sending that valentine – forgive me, sir – it was a wanton thing which no woman with any self-respect should have done. If you will only pardon my thought-lessness, I promise never to –'

'No, no, no. Don't say thoughtlessness! Make me think it was something more – that it was a sort of prophetic instinct – the beginning of a feeling that you would like me. You torture me to say it was done in thoughtlessness – I never thought of it in that light, and I can't endure it. Ah! I wish I knew how to win you! but that I can't do – I can only ask if I have already got you. If I have not, and it is not true that you have come unwittingly to me as I have to you, I can say no more.'

'I have not fallen in love with you, Mr Boldwood – certainly I must say that.' She allowed a very small smile to creep for the first time over her serious face in saying this, and the white row of upper teeth, and keenly-cut lips already noticed, suggested an idea of heartlessness, which was immediately contradicted by the pleasant eyes.

'But you will just think – in kindness and condescension think – if you cannot bear with me as a husband! I fear I am too old for you, but believe me I will take more care of you than would many a man of your own age. I will protect and cherish you with all my strength – I will indeed! You shall have no cares – be worried by no household affairs, and live quite at ease, Miss Everdene. The dairy superintendence shall be done by a man – I can afford it well – you shall never have so much as to look out of doors at haymaking time, or to think of weather in the harvest. I rather cling to the chaise, because it is the same my poor father and mother drove, but if you don't like it I will sell it, and you shall have a pony-carriage of your own. I cannot say how far above every other idea and object on earth you seem to me – nobody knows – God only knows – how much you are to me!'

Bathsheba's heart was young, and it swelled with sympathy for the deep-natured man who spoke so simply.

'Don't say it: don't! I cannot bear you to feel so much, and me to feel nothing. And I am afraid they will notice us, Mr Boldwood. Will you let the matter rest now? I cannot think collectedly. I did not know you were going to say this to me. O, I am wicked to have made you suffer so!' She was frightened as well as agitated at his vehemence.

'Say then, that you don't absolutely refuse. Do not quite refuse?'

'I can do nothing. I cannot answer.'

'I may speak to you again on the subject?'

'Yes.'

'I may think of you?'

'Yes, I suppose you may think of me.'

'And hope to obtain you?'

'No – do not hope! Let us go on.'

'I will call upon you again tomorrow.'

'No – please not. Give me time.'

'Yes – I will give you any time,' he said earnestly and gratefully. 'I am happier now.'

'No – I beg you! Don't be happier if happiness only comes from my agreeing. Be neutral, Mr Boldwood! I must think.'

'I will wait,' he said.

And then she turned away. Boldwood dropped his gaze to the ground, and stood long like a man who did not know where he was. Realities then returned upon him like the pain of a wound received in an excitement which eclipses it, and he, too, then went on.

* XX *

Perplexity – Grinding the Shears – A Quarrel

'HE is so disinterested and kind to offer me all that I can desire,' Bathsheba mused.

Yet Farmer Boldwood whether by nature kind or the reverse to kind, did not exercise kindness here. The rarest offerings of the purest loves are but a self-indulgence, and no generosity at all.

Bathsheba, not being the least in love with him, was eventually able to look calmly at his offer. It was one which many women of her own station in the neighbourhood, and not a few of higher rank, would have been wild to accept and proud to publish. In every point of view, ranging from politic to passionate, it was desirable that she, a lonely girl, should marry, and marry this earnest, well-to-do, and respected man. He was close to her doors: his standing was sufficient: his qualities were even supererogatory. Had she felt, which she did not, any wish whatever for the married state in the abstract, she could not reasonably have rejected him, being a woman who frequently appealed to her understanding for deliverance from her whims. Boldwood as a means to marriage was unexceptionable: she esteemed and liked him, yet she did not want him. It appears that ordinary men take wives because possession is not possible without marriage, and that ordinary women accept husbands because marriage is not possible without possession; with totally differing aims the method is the same on both sides. But the understood incentive on the woman's part was wanting here. Besides, Bathsheba's position as absolute mistress of a farm and house was a novel one, and the novelty had not yet begun to wear off.

But a disquiet filled her which was somewhat to her credit, for it would have affected few. Beyond the mentioned reasons with which she combated her objections, she had a strong feeling that, having been the one who began the game, she ought in honesty to accept the consequences. Still the reluctance remained. She said in the same breath that it would be ungenerous not to marry Boldwood, and that she couldn't do it to save her life.

Bathsheba's was an impulsive nature under a deliberative aspect. An Elizabeth in brain and a Mary Stuart in spirit, she often performed actions of the greatest temerity with a manner of extreme discretion. Many of her thoughts were perfect syllogisms; unluckily they always remained thoughts. Only a few were irrational assumptions; but, unfortunately, they were the ones which most frequently grew into deeds.

The next day to that of the declaration she found Gabriel Oak at the bottom of her garden, grinding his shears for the sheep-shearing. All the surrounding cottages were more or less scenes of the same operation; the scurr of whetting spread into the sky from all parts of the village as from an armoury previous to a campaign. Peace and war kiss each other at their hours of preparation – sickles, scythes, shears, and pruning-hooks ranking with swords, bayonets, and lances, in their common necessity for point and edge.

Cainy Ball turned the handle of Gabriel's grindstone, his head performing a melancholy see-saw up and down with each turn of the wheel. Oak stood somewhat as Eros is represented when in the act of sharpening his arrows: his figure slightly bent, the weight of his body thrown over on the shears, and his head balanced sideways, with a critical compression of the lips and contraction of the eyelids to crown the attitude.

His mistress came up and looked upon them in silence for a minute or two; then she said –

'Cain, go to the lower mead and catch the bay mare. I'll turn the winch of the grindstone. I want to speak to you, Gabriel.'

Cain departed, and Bathsheba took the handle. Gabriel had glanced up in intense surprise, quelled its expression, and looked down again. Bathsheba turned the winch, and Gabriel applied the shears.

The peculiar motion involved in turning a wheel has a wonderful tendency to benumb the mind. It is a sort of attenuated variety of Ixion's punishment, and contributes a dismal chapter to the history of gaols. The brain gets muddled, the head grows heavy, and the body's centre of gravity seems to settle by degrees in a leaden lump somewhere between the eyebrows and the crown. Bathsheba felt the unpleasant symptoms after two or three dozen turns.

'Will you turn, Gabriel, and let me hold the shears?' she said. 'My head is in a whirl, and I can't talk.'

Gabriel turned. Bathsheba then began, with some awkwardness, allowing her thoughts to stray occasionally from her story to attend to the shears, which required a little nicety in sharpening.

'I wanted to ask you if the men made any observations on my going behind the sedge with Mr Boldwood yesterday?'

'Yes, they did,' said Gabriel. 'You don't hold the shears right, miss – I knew you wouldn't know the way – hold like this.'

He relinquished the winch, and enclosing her two hands completely in his own (taking each as we sometimes clasp a child's hand in teaching him to write), grasped the shears with her. 'Incline the edge so,' he said.

Hands and shears were inclined to suit the words, and held thus for a peculiarly long time by the instructor as he spoke.

'That will do,' exclaimed Bathsheba. 'Loose my hands. I won't have them held! Turn the winch.'

Gabriel freed her hands quietly, retired to his handle, and the grinding went on.

'Did the men think it odd?' she said again.

'Odd was not the idea, miss.'

'What did they say?'

'That Farmer Boldwood's name and your own were likely to be flung over pulpit together before the year was out.'

'I thought so by the look of them! Why, there's nothing in it. A more foolish remark was never made, and I want you to contradict it: that's what I came for.'

Gabriel looked incredulous and sad, but between his moment of incredulity, relieved.

'They must have heard our conversation,' she continued.

'Well, then, Bathsheba!' said Oak, stopping the handle, and gazing into her face with astonishment.

'Miss Everdene, you mean,' she said with dignity.

'I mean this, that if Mr Boldwood really spoke of marriage, I bain't going to tell a story and say he didn't to please you. I have already tried to please you too much for my own good!'

Bathsheba regarded him with round-eyed perplexity. She did not know whether to pity him for disappointed love of her, or to be angry with him for having got over it – his tone being ambiguous.

'I said I wanted you just to mention that it was not true I was going to be married to him,' she murmured, with a slight decline in her assurance.

'I can say that to them if you wish, Miss Everdene. And I could likewise give an opinion to 'ee on what you have done.'

'I daresay. But I don't want your opinion.'

'I suppose not,' said Gabriel bitterly, and going on with his turning; his words rising and falling in a regular swell and cadence as he stood or rose with the winch, which directed them, according to his position, perpendicularly into the earth, or horizontally along the garden, his eyes being fixed on a leaf upon the ground.

With Bathsheba a hastened act was a rash act; but, as does not always happen, time gained was prudence ensured. It must be added, however, that time was very seldom gained. At this period the single opinion in the parish on herself and her doings that she valued as sounder than her own was Gabriel Oak's. And the outspoken honesty of his character was such that on any subject, even that of her love for, or marriage with, another man, the same disinterestedness of opinion might be calculated on, and be had for the asking. Thoroughly convinced of the impossibility of his own suit, a high resolve constrained him not to injure that of another. This is a lover's most stoical virtue, as the lack of it is a lover's most venial sin. Knowing he would reply truly she asked the question, painful as she must have known the subject would be. Such is the selfishness of some charming women. Perhaps it was some excuse for her thus torturing honesty to her own advantage, that she had absolutely no other sound judgement within easy reach.

'Well, what is your opinion of my conduct?' she said quietly.

'That it is unworthy of any thoughtful, and meek, and comely woman.'

In an instant Bathsheba's face coloured with the angry crimson of a Danby sunset. But she forbore to utter this feeling, and the reticence of her tongue only made the loquacity of her face the more noticeable.

The next thing Gabriel did was to make a mistake.

'Perhaps you don't like the rudeness of my reprimanding you, for I know it is rudeness; but I thought it would do good.'

She instantly replied sarcastically –

'On the contrary, my opinion of you is so low, that I see in your abuse the praise of discerning people!'

'I am glad you don't mind it, for I said it honestly and with every serious meaning.'

'I see. But, unfortunately, when you try not to speak in jest you are amusing – just as when you wish to avoid seriousness you sometimes say a sensible word.'

It was a hard hit, but Bathsheba had unmistakably lost her temper, and on that account Gabriel had never in his life kept his own better. He said nothing. She then broke out –

'I may ask, I suppose, where in particular my unworthiness lies? In my not marrying you, perhaps!'

'Not by any means,' said Gabriel quietly. 'I have long given up thinking of that matter.'

'Or wishing it, I suppose,' she said; and it was apparent that she expected an unhesitating denial of this supposition.

Whatever Gabriel felt, he coolly echoed her words –

'Or wishing it either.'

A woman may be treated with bitterness which is sweet to her, and with a rudeness which is not offensive. Bathsheba would have submitted to an indignant chastisement for her levity had Gabriel protested that he was loving her at the same time; the impetuosity of passion unrequited is bearable, even if it stings and anathematizes – there is a triumph in the humiliation, and a tenderness in the strife. This was what she had been expecting, and what she had not got. To be lectured because the lecturer saw her in the cold morning light of open-shuttered disillusion was exasperating. He had not finished, either. He continued in a more agitated voice:

'My opinion is (since you ask it) that you are greatly to blame for playing pranks upon a man like Mr Boldwood, merely as a pastime. Leading on a man you don't care for is not a praiseworthy action. And even, Miss Everdene, if you seriously inclined towards him, you might have let him find it out in some way of true loving-kindness, and not by sending him a valentine's letter.'

Bathsheba laid down the shears.

'I cannot allow any man to – to criticize my private conduct!' she exclaimed. 'Nor will I for a minute. So you'll please leave the farm at the end of the week!'

It may have been a peculiarity – at any rate it was a fact – that when Bathsheba was swayed by an emotion of an earthly sort her lower lip trembled: when by a refined emotion, her upper or heavenward one. Her nether lip quivered now.

'Very well, so I will,' said Gabriel calmly. He had been held to her by a beautiful thread which it pained him to spoil by breaking, rather than by a chain he could not break. 'I should be even better pleased to go at once,' he added.

'Go at once then, in Heaven's name!' said she, her eyes flashing at his, though never meeting them. 'Don't let me see your face any more.'

'Very well, Miss Everdene – so it shall be.'

And he took his shears and went away from her in placid dignity, as Moses left the presence of Pharaoh.

* XXI *

Troubles in the Fold – A Message

GABRIEL OAK had ceased to feed the Weatherbury flock for about four-and-twenty hours, when on Sunday afternoon the elderly gentlemen Joseph Poorgrass, Matthew Moon, Fray, and half-a-dozen others, came running up to the house of the mistress of the Upper Farm.

'Whatever *is* the matter, men?' she said, meeting them at the door just as she was coming out on her way to church, and ceasing in a moment from the close compression of her two red lips, with which she had accompanied the exertion of pulling on a tight glove.

'Sixty!' said Joseph Poorgrass.

'Seventy!' said Moon.

'Fifty-nine!' said Susan Tall's husband.

'Sheep have broken fence,' said Fray.

'– And got into a field of young clover,' said Tall.

'– Young clover!' said Moon.

'– Clover!' said Joseph Poorgrass.

'And they be getting blasted,' said Henery Fray.

'That they be,' said Joseph.

'And will all die as dead as nits, if they bain't got out and cured!' said Tall.

Joseph's countenance was drawn into lines and puckers by his concern. Fray's forehead was wrinkled both perpendicularly and crosswise, after the pattern of a portcullis, expressive of a double despair. Laban Tall's lips were thin, and his face was rigid. Matthew's jaws sank, and his eyes turned whichever way the strongest muscle happened to pull them.

'Yes,' said Joseph, 'and I was sitting at home looking for Ephesians, and says I to myself, " 'Tis nothing but Corinthians and Thessalonians in this danged Testament," when who should come in but Henery there: "Joseph," he said, "the sheep have blasted theirselves –" '

With Bathsheba it was a moment when thought was speech and speech exclamation. Moreover, she had hardly recovered her equanimity since the disturbance which she had suffered from Oak's remarks.

'That's enough – that's enough! – O you fools!' she cried, throwing the parasol and Prayer-book into the passage, and running out of doors in the direction signified. 'To come to me, and not go and get them out directly! O, the stupid numskulls!'

Her eyes were at their darkest and brightest now. Bathsheba's beauty belonging rather to the demonian than to the angelic school, she never looked so well as when she was angry – particularly when the effect was heightened by a rather dashing velvet dress, carefully put on before a glass.

All the ancient men ran in a jumbled throng after her to the clover-field, Joseph sinking down in the midst when about half-way, like an individual withering in a world which was more and more insupportable. Having once received the stimulus that her presence always gave them they went round among the sheep with a will. The majority of the afflicted animals were lying down, and could not be stirred. These were bodily lifted out, and the others driven into the adjoining field. Here, after the lapse of a few minutes, several more fell down, and lay helpless and livid as the rest.

Bathsheba, with a sad, bursting heart, looked at these primest specimens of her prime flock as they rolled there –

> Swoln with wind and the rank mist they drew.

Many of them foamed at the mouth, their breathing being quick and short, whilst the bodies of all were fearfully distended.

'O, what can I do, what can I do!' said Bathsheba, helplessly. 'Sheep are such unfortunate animals! – there's always something happening to them! I never knew a flock pass a year without getting into some scrape or other.'

'There's only one way of saving them,' said Tall.

'What way? Tell me quick!'

'They must be pierced in the side with a thing made on purpose.'

'Can you do it? Can I?'

'No, ma'am. We can't, nor you neither. It must be done in a particular spot. If ye go to the right or left but an inch you stab the ewe and kill her. Not even a shepherd can do it, as a rule.'

'Then they must die,' she said, in a resigned tone.

'Only one man in the neighbourhood knows the way,' said Joseph, now just come up. 'He could cure 'em all if he were here.'

'Who is he? Let's get him!'

'Shepherd Oak,' said Matthew. 'Ah, he's a clever man in talents!'

'Ah, that he is so!' said Joseph Poorgrass.

'True – he's the man,' said Laban Tall.

'How dare you name that man in my presence!' she said excitedly. 'I told you never to allude to him, nor shall you if you stay with me. Ah!' she added, brightening, 'Farmer Boldwood knows!'

'O no, ma'am,' said Matthew. 'Two of his store ewes got into some vetches t'other day, and were just like these. He sent a man on horseback here post-haste for Gable, and Gable went and saved 'em. Farmer Boldwood hev got the thing they do it with. 'Tis a holler pipe, with a sharp pricker inside. Isn't it, Joseph?'

'Ay – a holler pipe,' echoed Joseph. 'That's what 'tis.'

'Ay, sure – that's the machine,' chimed in Henery Fray reflectively, with an Oriental indifference to the flight of time.

'Well,' burst out Bathsheba, 'don't stand there with your "ayes" and your "sures", talking at me! Get somebody to cure the sheep instantly!'

All then stalked off in consternation, to get somebody as directed, without any idea of who it was to be. In a minute they had vanished through the gate, and she stood alone with the dying flock.

'Never will I send for him – never!' she said firmly.

One of the ewes here contracted its muscles horribly, extended itself, and jumped high into the air. The leap was an astonishing one. The ewe fell heavily, and lay still.

Bathsheba went up to it. The sheep was dead.

'O, what shall I do – what shall I do!' she again exclaimed, wringing her hands. 'I won't send for him. No, I won't!'

The most vigorous expression of a resolution does not always coincide with the greatest vigour of the resolution itself. It is often flung out as a sort of prop to support a decaying conviction which, whilst strong, required no enunciation to prove it so. The 'No, I won't' of Bathsheba meant virtually, 'I think I must.'

She followed her assistants through the gate, and lifted her hand to one of them. Laban answered to her signal.

'Where is Oak staying?'

'Across the valley at Nest Cottage.'

'Jump on the bay mare, and ride across, and say he must return instantly – that I say so.'

Tall scrambled off to the field, and in two minutes was on Poll, the bay, bare-backed, and with only a halter by way of rein. He diminished down the hill.

Bathsheba watched. So did all the rest. Tall cantered along the bridle-path through Sixteen Acres, Sheeplands, Middle Field, The Flats, Cappel's Piece, shrank almost to a point, crossed the bridge, and ascended from the valley through Springmead and Whitepits on the other side. The cottage to which Gabriel had retired before taking his final departure from the locality was visible as a white spot on the opposite hill, backed by blue firs. Bathsheba walked up and down. The men entered the field and endeavoured to ease the anguish of the dumb creatures by rubbing them. Nothing availed.

Bathsheba continued walking. The horse was seen descending the hill, and the wearisome series had to be repeated in reverse order: Whitepits, Springmead, Cappel's Piece, The Flats, Middle Field, Sheeplands, Sixteen Acres. She hoped Tall had had presence of mind enough to give the mare up to Gabriel, and return himself on foot. The rider neared them. It was Tall.

'O what folly!' said Bathsheba.

Gabriel was not visible anywhere.

'Perhaps he is already gone!' she said.

Tall came into the inclosure, and leapt off, his face tragic as Morton's after the battle of Shrewsbury.

'Well?' said Bathsheba, unwilling to believe that her verbal *lettre-de-cachet* could possibly have miscarried.

'He says *beggars mustn't be choosers*,' replied Laban.

'What!' said the young farmer, opening her eyes and drawing in her breath for an outburst. Joseph Poorgrass retired a few steps behind a hurdle.

'He says he shall not come onless you request en to come civilly and in a proper manner, as becomes any 'ooman begging a favour.'

'Oh, oh, that's his answer! Where does he get his airs? Who am I, then, to be treated like that? Shall I beg to a man who has begged to me?'

Another of the flock sprang into the air, and fell dead.

The men looked grave, as if they suppressed opinion.

Bathsheba turned aside, her eyes full of tears. The strait she was in through pride and shrewishness could not be disguised longer: she burst out crying bitterly; they all saw it; and she attempted no further concealment.

'I wouldn't cry about it, miss,' said William Smallbury compassionately. 'Why not ask him softer like? I'm sure he'd come then. Gable is a true man in that way.'

Bathsheba checked her grief and wiped her eyes. 'O, it is a wicked cruelty to me – it is – it is!' she murmured. 'And he drives me to do what I wouldn't; yes, he does! – Tall, come indoors.'

After this collapse, not very dignified for the head of an establishment, she went into the house, Tall at her heels. Here she sat down and hastily scribbled a note between the small convulsive sobs of convalescence which follow a fit of crying as a ground-swell follows a storm. The note was none the less polite for being written in a hurry. She held it at a distance, was about to fold it, then added these words at the bottom:

Do not desert me, Gabriel!

She looked a little redder in refolding it, and closed her lips, as if thereby to suspend till too late the action of conscience in examining whether such strategy were justifiable. The note was despatched as the message had been, and Bathsheba waited indoors for the result.

It was an anxious quarter of an hour that intervened between the messenger's departure and the sound of the horse's tramp again outside. She could not watch this time, but, leaning over the old bureau at which she had written the letter, closed her eyes, as if to keep out both hope and fear.

The case, however, was a promising one. Gabriel was not angry: he was simply neutral, although her first command had been so haughty. Such imperiousness would have damned a little less beauty; and on the other hand, such beauty would have redeemed a little less imperiousness.

She went out when the horse was heard, and looked up. A mounted figure passed between her and the sky, and drew on towards the field of sheep, the rider turning his face in receding. Gabriel looked at her. It was a moment when a woman's eyes and tongue tell distinctly opposite tales. Bathsheba looked full of gratitude, and she said:

'O, Gabriel, how could you serve me so unkindly!'

Such a tenderly-shaped reproach for his previous delay was the one speech in the language that he could pardon for not being commendation of his readiness now.

Gabriel murmured a confused reply, and hastened on. She knew from the look which sentence in her note had brought him. Bathsheba followed to the field.

Gabriel was already among the turgid, prostrate forms. He had flung off his coat, rolled up his shirt-sleeves, and taken from his pocket the instrument of salvation. It was a small tube or trochar, with a lance passing down the inside; and Gabriel began to use it with a dexterity that would have graced a hospital-surgeon. Passing his hand over the sheep's left flank, and selecting the proper point, he punctured the skin and rumen with the lance as it stood in the tube; then he suddenly withdrew the lance, retaining the tube in its place. A current of air rushed up the tube, forcible enough to have extinguished a candle held at the orifice.

It has been said that mere ease after torment is delight for a time; and the countenances of these poor creatures expressed it now. Forty-nine operations were successfully performed. Owing to the great hurry necessitated by the far-gone state of some of the flock, Gabriel missed his aim in one case, and in one only – striking wide of the mark, and inflicting a mortal blow at once upon the suffering ewe. Four had died; three recovered without an operation. The total number of sheep which had thus strayed and injured themselves so dangerously was fifty-seven.

When the love-led man had ceased from his labours Bathsheba came and looked him in the face.

'Gabriel, will you stay on with me?' she said, smiling winningly, and not troubling to bring her lips quite together again at the end, because there was going to be another smile soon.

'I will,' said Gabriel.

And she smiled on him again.

* XXII *

The Great Barn and the Sheep-shearers

MEN thin away to insignificance and oblivion quite as often by not making the most of good spirits when they have them as by lacking good spirits when they are indispensable. Gabriel lately, for the first time since his prostration by misfortune, had been independent in thought and vigorous in action to a marked extent – conditions which, powerless without an opportunity as an opportunity without them is barren, would have given him a sure lift upwards when the favourable conjunction should have occurred. But this incurable loitering beside Bathsheba Everdene stole his time ruinously. The spring tides were going by without floating him off, and the neap might soon come which could not.

It was the first day of June, and the sheep-shearing season culminated, the landscape, even to the leanest pasture, being all health and colour. Every green was young, every pore was open, and every stalk was swollen with racing currents of juice. God was palpably present in the country, and the devil had gone with the world to town. Flossy catkins of the later kinds, fern-sprouts like bishops' croziers, the square-headed moschatel, the odd cuckoo-pint, – like an apoplectic saint in a niche of malachite, – snow-white ladies'-smocks, the toothwort, approximating to human flesh, the enchanter's night-shade, and the black-petalled doleful-bells, were among the quainter objects of the vegetable world in and about Weatherbury at this teeming time; and of the animal, the metamorphosed figures of Mr Jan Coggan, the master-shearer; the second and third shearers, who travelled in the exercise of their calling, and do not require definition by name; Henery Fray the fourth shearer, Susan Tall's husband the fifth, Joseph Poorgrass the sixth, young Cain Ball as assistant-shearer, and Gabriel Oak as general supervisor. None of these were clothed to any extent worth mentioning, each appearing to have hit in the matter of raiment the decent mean between a high and low caste Hindoo. An angularity of lineament, and a fixity of facial machinery in general, proclaimed that serious work was the order of the day.

They sheared in the great barn, called for the nonce the Shearing-barn, which on ground-plan resembled a church with transepts. It not only emulated the form of the neighbouring church of the parish, but vied with it in antiquity. Whether the barn had ever formed one of a group of conventual buildings nobody seemed to be aware; no trace of such surroundings remained. The vast porches at the sides, lofty enough to admit a waggon laden to its highest with corn in the sheaf, were spanned by heavy-pointed arches of stone, broadly and boldly cut, whose very simplicity was the origin of a grandeur not apparent in erections where more ornament has been attempted. The dusky, filmed, chestnut roof, braced and tied in by huge collars, curves, and diagonals, was far nobler in design, because more wealthy in material, than nine-tenths of those in our modern churches. Along each side wall was a range of striding buttresses, throwing deep shadows on the spaces between them, which were perforated by lancet openings, combining in their proportions the precise requirements both of beauty and ventilation.

One could say about this barn, what could hardly be said of either the church or the castle, akin to it in age and style, that the purpose which had dictated its original erection was the same with that to which it was still applied. Unlike and superior to either of those two typical remnants of mediaevalism, the old barn embodied practices which had suffered no mutilation at the hands of time. Here at least the spirit of the ancient builders was at one with the spirit of the modern beholder. Standing before this abraded pile, the eye regarded its present usage, the mind dwelt upon its past history, with a satisfied sense of functional continuity throughout – a feeling almost of gratitude, and quite of pride, at the permanence of the idea which had heaped it up. The fact that four centuries had neither proved it to be founded on a mistake, inspired any hatred of its purpose, nor given rise to any reaction that had battered it down, invested this simple grey effort of old minds with a repose, if not a grandeur, which a too curious reflection was apt to disturb in its ecclesiastical and military compeers. For once mediaevalism and modernism had a common standpoint. The lanceolate windows, the time-eaten arch-stones and chamfers, the orientation of the axis, the misty chestnut work of the rafters, referred to no exploded fortifying art or worn-out religious creed. The defence and salvation of the body by daily bread is still a study, a religion, and a desire.

To-day the large side doors were thrown open towards the sun to admit a bountiful light to the immediate spot of the shearers' operations, which was the wood threshing-floor in the centre, formed of thick oak, black with age and polished by the beating of flails for many generations, till it had grown as slippery and as rich in hue as the state-room floors of an Elizabethan mansion. Here the shearers knelt, the sun slanting in upon their bleached shirts, tanned arms, and the polished shears they flourished, causing these to bristle with a thousand rays strong enough to blind a weak-eyed man. Beneath them a captive sheep lay panting, quickening its pants as misgiving merged in terror, till it quivered like the hot landscape outside.

This picture of to-day in its frame of four hundred years ago did not produce that marked contrast between ancient and modern which is implied by the contrast of date. In comparison with cities, Weatherbury was immutable. The citizen's *Then* is the rustic's *Now*. In London, twenty or thirty years ago are old times; in Paris ten years, or five; in Weatherbury three or four score years were included in the mere present, and nothing less than a century set a mark on its face or tone. Five decades hardly modified the cut of a gaiter, the embroidery of a smock-frock, by the breadth of a hair. Ten generations failed to alter the turn of a single phrase. In these Wessex nooks the busy outsider's ancient times are only old; his old times are still new; his present is futurity.

So the barn was natural to the shearers, and the shearers were in harmony with the barn.

The spacious ends of the building, answering ecclesiastically to nave and chancel extremities, were fenced off with hurdles, the sheep being all collected in a crowd within these two enclosures; and in one angle a catching-pen was formed, in which three or four sheep were continuously kept ready for the shearers to seize without loss of time. In the background, mellowed by tawny shade, were the three women, Maryann Money, and Temperance and Soberness Miller, gathering up the fleeces and twisting ropes of wool with a wimble for tying them round. They were indifferently well assisted by the old maltster, who, when the malting season from October to April had passed, made himself useful upon any of the bordering farmsteads.

Behind all was Bathsheba, carefully watching the men to see that there was no cutting or wounding through carelessness, and that the animals were shorn close. Gabriel, who flitted and hovered under her bright eyes like a moth, did not shear continuously, half his time being spent in attending to the others and selecting the sheep for them. At the present moment he was engaged in handing round a mug of mild liquor, supplied from a barrel in the corner, and cut pieces of bread and cheese.

Bathsheba, after throwing a glance here, a caution there, and lecturing one of the younger operators who had allowed his last finished sheep to go off among the flock without restamping it with her initials, came again to Gabriel, as he put down the luncheon to drag a frightened ewe to his shear-station, flinging it over upon its back with a dexterous twist of the arm. He lopped off the tresses about its head, and opened up the neck and collar, his mistress quietly looking on.

'She blushes at the insult,' murmured Bathsheba, watching the pink flush which arose and overspread the neck and shoulders of the ewe where they were left bare by the clicking shears – a flush which was enviable, for its delicacy, by many queens of coteries, and would have been creditable, for its promptness, to any woman in the world.

Poor Gabriel's soul was fed with a luxury of content by having her over him, her eyes critically regarding his skilful shears, which apparently were going to gather up a piece of the flesh at every close, and yet never did so. Like Guildenstern, Oak was happy in that he was not over happy. He had no wish to converse with her: that his bright lady and himself formed one group, exclusively their own, and containing no others in the world, was enough.

So the chatter was all on her side. There is a loquacity that tells nothing, which was Bathsheba's; and there is a silence which says much: that was Gabriel's. Full of this dim and temperate bliss he went on to fling the ewe over upon her other side, covering her head with his knee, gradually running the shears line after line round her dewlap, thence about her flank and back, and finishing over the tail.

'Well done, and done quickly!' said Bathsheba, looking at her watch as the last snip resounded.

'How long, miss?' said Gabriel, wiping his brow.

'Three-and-twenty minutes and a half since you took the first lock from its forehead. It is the first time I have ever seen one done in less than half an hour.'

The clean, sleek creature arose from its fleece – how perfectly like Aphrodite rising from the foam should have been seen to be realized – looking startled and shy at the loss of its garment, which lay on the floor in one soft cloud, united throughout, the portion visible being the inner surface only, which, never before exposed, was white as snow, and without flaw or blemish of the minutest kind.

'Cain Ball!'

'Yes, Mister Oak; here I be!'

Cainy now runs forward with the tar-pot. 'B.E.' is newly stamped upon the shorn skin, and away the simple dam leaps, panting, over the board into the shirtless flock outside. Then up comes Maryann; throws the loose locks into the middle of the fleece, rolls it up, and carries it into the battleground as three-and-a-half pounds of unadulterated warmth for the winter enjoyment of persons unknown and far away, who will, however, never experience the superlative comfort derivable from the wool as it here exists, new and pure – before the unctuousness of its nature whilst in a living state has dried, stiffened, and been washed out – rendering it just now as superior to anything *woollen* as cream is superior to milk-and-water.

But heartless circumstances could not leave entire Gabriel's happiness of this morning. The rams, old ewes, and two-shear ewes had duly undergone their stripping, and the men were proceeding with the shearlings and hogs, when Oak's belief that she was going to stand pleasantly by and time him through another performance was painfully interrupted by Farmer Boldwood's appearance in the extremest corner of the barn. Nobody seemed to have perceived his entry, but there he certainly was. Boldwood always carried with him a social atmosphere of his own, which everybody felt who came near him; and the talk, which

Bathsheba's presence had somewhat suppressed, was now totally suspended.

He crossed over towards Bathsheba, who turned to greet him with a carriage of perfect ease. He spoke to her in low tones, and she instinctively modulated her own to the same pitch, and her voice ultimately even caught the inflection of his. She was far from having a wish to appear mysteriously connected with him; but woman at the impressionable age gravitates to the larger body not only in her choice of words, which is apparent every day, but even in her shades of tone and humour when the influence is great.

What they conversed about was not audible to Gabriel, who was too independent to get near, though too concerned to disregard. The issue of their dialogue was the taking of her hand by the courteous farmer to help her over the spreading-board into the bright June sunlight outside. Standing beside the sheep already shorn, they went on talking again. Concerning the flock? Apparently not. Gabriel theorized, not without truth, that in quiet discussion of any matter within reach of the speakers' eyes, these are usually fixed upon it. Bathsheba demurely regarded a contemptible straw lying upon the ground, in a way which suggested less ovine criticism than womanly embarrassment. She became more or less red in the cheek, the blood wavering in uncertain flux and reflux over the sensitive space between ebb and flood. Gabriel sheared on, constrained and sad.

She left Boldwood's side, and he walked up and down alone for nearly a quarter of an hour. Then she reappeared in her new riding-habit of myrtle-green, which fitted her to the waist as a rind fits its fruit; and young Bob Coggan led on her mare, Boldwood fetching his own horse from the tree under which it had been tied.

Oak's eyes could not forsake them; and in endeavouring to continue shearing at the same time that he watched Boldwood's manner, he snipped the sheep in the groin. The animal plunged; Bathsheba instantly gazed towards it, and saw the blood.

'O Gabriel!' she exclaimed, with severe remonstrance, 'you who are so strict with the other men – see what you are doing yourself!'

To an outsider there was not much to complain of in this remark; but to Oak, who knew Bathsheba to be well aware that she herself was the cause of the poor ewe's wound, because she had wounded the ewe's shearer in a still more vital part, it had a sting which the abiding sense of his inferiority to both herself and Boldwood was not calculated to heal. But a manly resolve to recognize boldly that he had no longer a lover's interest in her, helped him occasionally to conceal a feeling.

'Bottle!' he shouted, in an unmoved voice of routine. Cainy Ball ran up, the wounded was anointed, and the shearing continued.

Boldwood gently tossed Bathsheba into the saddle, and before they turned away she again spoke out to Oak with the same dominative and tantalizing graciousness.

'I am going now to see Mr Boldwood's Leicesters. Take my place in the barn, Gabriel, and keep the men carefully to their work.'

The horses' heads were put about, and they trotted away.

Boldwood's deep attachment was a matter of great interest among all around him; but, after having been pointed out for so many years as the perfect exemplar of thriving bachelorship, his lapse was an anticlimax somewhat resembling that of St John Long's death by consumption in the midst of his proofs that it was not a fatal disease.

'That means matrimony,' said Temperance Miller, following them out of sight with her eyes.

'I reckon that's the size o't,' said Coggan, working along without looking up.

'Well, better wed over the mixen than over the moor,' said Laban Tall, turning his sheep.

Henery Fray spoke, exhibiting miserable eyes at the same time: 'I don't see why a maid should take a husband when she's bold enough to fight her own battles, and don't want a home; for 'tis keeping another woman out. But let it be, for 'tis a pity he and she should trouble two houses.'

As usual with decided characters, Bathsheba invariably provoked the criticism of individuals like Henery Fray. Her emblazoned fault was to be too pronounced in her objections, and not sufficiently overt in her likings. We learn that it is not the rays which bodies absorb, but those which they reject, that give them the colours they are known by; and in the same way people are specialized by their dislikes and antagonisms, whilst their goodwill is looked upon as no attribute at all.

Henery continued in a more complaisant mood: 'I once hinted my mind to her on a few things, as nearly as a battered frame dared to do so to such a froward piece. You all know, neighbours, what a man I be, and how I come down with my powerful words when my pride is boiling wi' scarn?'

'We do, we do, Henery.'

'So I said, "Miss Everdene, there's places empty, and there's gifted men willing; but the spite" – no, not the spite – I didn't say spite – "but the villainy of the contrarikind," I said (meaning womankind), "keeps 'em out." That wasn't too strong for her, say?'

'Passably well put.'

'Yes; and I would have said it, had death and salvation overtook me for it. Such is my spirit when I have a mind.'

'A true man, and proud as a lucifer.'

'You see the artfulness? Why, 'twas about being baily really; but I didn't put it so plain that she could understand my meaning, so I could lay it on all the stronger. That was my depth! . . . However, let her marry as she will. Perhaps 'tis high time. I believe Farmer Boldwood kissed her behind the spear-bed at the sheep-washing t'other day – that I do.'

'What a lie!' said Gabriel.

'Ah, neighbour Oak – how'st know?' said Henery mildly.

'Because she told me all that passed,' said Oak, with a pharisaical sense that he was not as other shearers in this matter.

'Ye have a right to believe it,' said Henery, with dudgeon; 'a very true right. But I mid see a little distance into things! To be long-headed enough for a baily's place is a poor mere trifle – yet a trifle more than nothing. However, I look round upon life quite cool. Do you heed me, neighbours? My words, though made as simple as I can, mid be rather deep for some heads.'

'O yes, Henery, we quite heed ye.'

'A strange old piece, goodmen – whirled about from here to yonder, as if I were nothing! A little warped, too. But I have my depths; ha, and even my great depth! I might gird at a certain shepherd, brain to brain. But no – O no!'

'A strange old piece, ye say!' interposed the maltster, in a querulous voice. 'At the same time ye be no old man worth naming – no old man at all. Yer teeth bain't half gone yet; and what's a old man's standing if so be his teeth bain't gone? Weren't I stale in wedlock afore ye were out of arms? 'Tis a poor thing to be sixty, when there's people far past four-score – a boast weak as water.'

It was the unvarying custom in Weatherbury to sink minor differences when the maltster had to be pacified.

'Weak as water! yes,' said Jan Coggan. 'Malter, we feel ye to be a wonderful veteran man, and nobody can gainsay it.'

'Nobody,' said Joseph Poorgrass. 'Ye be a very rare old spectacle, malter, and we all admire ye for that gift.'

'Ay, and as a young man, when my senses were in prosperity, I was likewise liked by a good-few who knowed me,' said the maltster.

' 'Ithout doubt you was – 'ithout doubt.'

The bent and hoary man was satisfied, and so apparently was Henery Fray. That matters should continue pleasant Maryann spoke, who, what with her brown complexion, and the working wrapper of rusty linsey, had at present the mellow hue of an old sketch in oils – notably some of Nicholas Poussin's:

'Do anybody know of a crooked man, or a lame, or any second-hand fellow at all that would do for poor me?' said Maryann. 'A perfect one I don't expect to get at my time of life. If I could hear of such a thing 'twould do me more good than toast and ale.'

Coggan furnished a suitable reply. Oak went on with his shearing, and said not another word. Pestilent moods had come, and teased away his quiet. Bathsheba had shown indications of anointing him above his fellows by installing him as the bailiff that the farm imperatively required. He did not covet the post relatively to the farm: in relation to herself, as beloved by him and unmarried to another, he had coveted it. His readings of her seemed now to be vapoury and indistinct. His lecture to her was, he thought, one of the absurdest mistakes. Far from coquetting with Boldwood, she had trifled with himself in thus feigning that she had trifled with another. He was inwardly convinced that, in accordance with the anticipations of his easy-going and worse-educated comrades, that day would see Boldwood the accepted husband of Miss Everdene. Gabriel at this time of his life had outgrown the instinctive dislike which every Christian boy has for reading the Bible, perusing it now quite frequently, and he inwardly said, ' "I find more bitter than death the woman whose heart is snares and nets!" ' This was mere exclamation – the froth of the storm. He adored Bathsheba just the same.

'We workfolk shall have some lordly junketing to-night,' said Cainy Ball, casting forth his thoughts in a new direction. 'This morning I see 'em making the great puddens in the milking-pail – lumps of fat as big as yer thumb, Mister Oak! I've never seed such splendid large knobs of fat before in the days of my life – they never used to be bigger than a horse-bean. And there was a great black crock upon the brandise with his legs a-sticking out, but I don't know what was in within.'

'And there's two bushels of biffins for apple-pies,' said Maryann.

'Well, I hope to do my duty by it all,' said Joseph Poorgrass, in a pleasant, masticating manner of anticipation. 'Yes; victuals and drink is a cheerful thing, and gives nerves to the nerveless, if the form of words may be used. 'Tis the gospel of the body, without which we perish, so to speak it.'

* XXIII *

Eventide – A Second Declaration

FOR the shearing-supper a long table was placed on the grass-plot beside the house, the end of the table being thrust over the sill of the wide parlour window and a foot or two into the room. Miss Everdene sat inside the window, facing down the table. She was thus at the head without mingling with the men.

This evening Bathsheba was unusually excited, her red cheeks and lips contrasting lustrously with the mazy skeins of her shadowy hair. She seemed to expect assistance, and the seat at the bottom of the table was at her request left vacant until after they had begun the meal. She then asked Gabriel to take the place and the duties appertaining to that end, which he did with great readiness.

At this moment Mr Boldwood came in at the gate, and crossed the green to Bathsheba at the window. He apologized for his lateness: his arrival was evidently by arrangement.

'Gabriel,' said she, 'will you move again, please, and let Mr Boldwood come there?'

Oak moved in silence back to his original seat.

The gentleman-farmer was dressed in cheerful style, in a new coat and white waistcoat, quite contrasting with his usual sober suits of grey. Inwardly, too, he was blithe, and consequently chatty to an exceptional degree. So also was Bathsheba now that he had come, though the uninvited presence of Pennyways, the bailiff who had been dismissed for theft, disturbed her equanimity for a while.

Supper being ended, Coggan began on his own private account, without reference to listeners:

> I've lost my love, and I care not,
> I've lost my love, and I care not;
>   I shall soon have another
>   That's better than t'other;
> I've lost my love, and I care not.

This lyric, when concluded, was received with a silently appreciative gaze at the table, implying that the performance, like a work by those established authors who are independent of notices in the papers, was a well-known delight which required no applause.

'Now, Master Poorgrass, your song!' said Coggan.

'I be all but in liquor, and the gift is wanting in me,' said Joseph, diminishing himself.

'Nonsense; wou'st never be so ungrateful, Joseph – never!' said Coggan, expressing hurt feelings by an inflection of voice. 'And mistress is looking hard at ye, as much as to say, "Sing at once, Joseph Poorgrass." '

'Faith, so she is; well, I must suffer it! . . . Just eye my features, and see if the tell-tale blood overheats me much, neighbours?'

'No, yer blushes be quite reasonable,' said Coggan.

'I always tries to keep my colours from rising when a beauty's eyes get fixed on me,' said Joseph differently; 'but if so be 'tis willed they do, they must.'

'Now, Joseph, your song, please,' said Bathsheba from the window.

'Well, really, ma'am,' he replied in a yielding tone, 'I don't know what to say. It would be a poor plain ballet of my own composure.'

'Hear, hear!' said the supper-party.

Poorgrass, thus assured, trilled forth a flickering yet commendable piece of sentiment, the tune of which consisted of the key-note and another, the latter being the sound chiefly dwelt upon. This was so successful that he rashly plunged into a second in the same breath, after a few false starts:

> I sow'-ed th'-e . . .
> I sow'-ed . . .
> I sow'-ed the'-e seeds' of' love',
>   I-it was' all' i'-in the'-e spring',
> I-in A'-pril', Ma'-ay, a'-nd sun'-ny' June',
>   When sma'-all bi'-irds they' do' sing.

'Well put out of hand,' said Coggan, at the end of the verse. ' "They do sing" was a very taking paragraph.'

'Ay; and there was a pretty place at "seeds of love", and 'twas well heaved out. Though "love" is a nasty high corner when a man's voice is getting crazed. Next verse, Master Poorgrass.'

But during this rendering young Bob Coggan exhibited one of those anomalies which will afflict little people when other persons are particularly serious: in trying to check his laughter, he pushed down his throat as much of the table-cloth as he could get hold of, when, after continuing hermetically sealed for a short time, his mirth burst out through his nose. Joseph perceived it, and with hectic cheeks of indignation instantly ceased singing. Coggan boxed Bob's ears immediately.

'Go on, Joseph – go on, and never mind the young scamp,' said Coggan. ' 'Tis a very catching ballet. Now then again – the next bar; I'll help ye to flourish up the shrill notes where yer wind is rather wheezy:

> O the wi'-il-lo'-ow tree' will' twist',
> And the wil'-low' tre'-ee wi'-ill twine'.'

But the singer could not be set going again. Bob Coggan was sent home for his ill manners, and tranquillity was restored by Jacob Smallbury, who volunteered a ballad as inclusive and interminable as that with which the worthy toper old Silenus amused on a similar occasion the swains Chromis and Mnasylus, and other jolly dogs of his day.

It was still the beaming time of evening, though night was stealthily making itself low down upon the ground, the western lines of light raking the earth without alighting upon it to any extent, or illuminating the dead levels at all. The sun had crept round the tree as a last effort before death, and then began to sink, the shearers' lower parts becoming steeped in embrowning twilight, whilst their heads and shoulders were still enjoying day, touched with a yellow of self-sustained brilliancy that seemed inherent rather than acquired.

The sun went down in an ochreous mist; but they sat, and talked on, and grew as merry as the gods in Homer's heaven. Bathsheba still remained enthroned inside the window, and occupied herself in knitting, from which she sometimes looked up to view the fading scene outside. The slow twilight expanded and enveloped them completely before the signs of moving were shown.

Gabriel suddenly missed Farmer Boldwood from his place at the bottom of the table. How long he had been gone Oak did not know; but he had apparently withdrawn into the encircling dusk. Whilst he was thinking of this Liddy brought candles into the back part of the room overlooking the shearers, and their lively new flames shone down the table and over the men, and dispersed among the green shadows behind. Bathsheba's form, still in its original position, was now again distinct between their eyes and the light, which revealed that Boldwood had gone inside the room, and was sitting near her.

Next came the question of the evening. Would Miss Everdene sing to them the song she always sang so charmingly – 'The Banks of Allan Water' – before they went home?

After a moment's consideration Bathsheba assented, beckoning to Gabriel, who hastened up into the coveted atmosphere.

'Have you brought your flute?' she whispered.

'Yes, miss.'

'Play to my singing, then.'

She stood up in the window-opening, facing the men, the candles behind her, Gabriel on her right hand, immediately outside the sashframe. Boldwood had drawn up on her left, within the room. Her singing was soft and rather tremulous at first, but it soon swelled to a steady clearness. Subsequent events caused one of the verses to be remembered for many months, and even years, by more than one of those who were gathered there:

> For his bride a soldier sought her,
>   And a winning tongue had he:
> On the banks of Allan Water
>   None was gay as she!

In addition to the dulcet piping of Gabriel's flute Boldwood supplied a bass in his customary profound voice, uttering his notes so softly, however, as to abstain entirely from making anything like an ordinary duet of the song; they rather formed a rich unexplored shadow, which threw her tones into relief. The shearers reclined against each other as at suppers in the early ages of the world, and so silent and absorbed were they that her breathing could almost be heard between the bars; and at the end of the ballad, when the last tone loitered on to an inexpressible close, there arose that buzz of pleasure which is the attar of applause.

It is scarcely necessary to state that Gabriel could not avoid noting the farmer's bearing to-night towards their entertainer. Yet there was nothing exceptional in his actions beyond what appertained to his time of performing them. It was when the rest were all looking away that Boldwood observed her; when they regarded her he turned aside; when they thanked or praised he was silent; when they were inattentive he murmured his thanks. The meaning lay in the difference between actions none of which had any meaning of itself; and the necessity of being jealous, which lovers are troubled with, did not lead Oak to underestimate these signs.

Bathsheba then wished them good-night, withdrew from the window, and retired to the back part of the room, Boldwood thereupon closing the sash and the shutters, and remaining inside with her. Oak wandered away under the quiet and scented trees. Recovering from the softer impressions produced by Bathsheba's voice, the shearers rose to leave, Coggan turning to Pennyways as he pushed back the bench to pass out:

'I like to give praise where praise is due, and the man deserves it – that 'a do so,' he remarked, looking at the worthy thief as if he were the masterpiece of some world-renowned artist.

'I'm sure I should never have believed it if we hadn't proved it, so to allude,' hiccupped Joseph Poorgrass, 'that every cup, every one of the best knives and forks, and every empty bottle be in their place as perfect now as at the beginning, and not one stole at all.'

'I'm sure I don't deserve half the praise you give me,' said the virtuous thief grimly.

'Well, I'll say this for Pennyways,' added Coggan, 'that whenever he do really make up his mind to do a noble thing in the shape of a good action, as I could see by his face he did to-night afore sitting down, he's generally able to carry it out. Yes, I'm proud to say, neighbours, that he's stole nothing at all.'

'Well, 'tis an honest deed, and we thank ye for it, Pennyways,' said Joseph; to which opinion the remainder of the company subscribed unanimously.

At this time of departure, when nothing more was visible of the inside of the parlour than a thin and still chink of light between the shutters, a passionate scene was in course of enactment there.

Miss Everdene and Boldwood were alone. Her cheeks had lost a great deal of their healthful fire from the very seriousness of her position; but her eye was bright with the excitement of a triumph – though it was a triumph which had rather been contemplated than desired.

She was standing behind a low arm-chair, from which she had just risen, and he was kneeling in it – inclining himself over its back towards her, and holding her hand in both his own. His body moved restlessly, and it was with what Keats daintily calls a too happy happiness. This unwonted abstraction by love of all dignity from a man of whom it had ever seemed the chief component, was, in its distressing incongruity, a pain to her which quenched much of the pleasure she derived from the proof that she was idolized.

'I will try to love you,' she was saying, in a trembling voice quite unlike her usual self-confidence. 'And if I can believe in any way that I shall make you a good wife I shall indeed be willing to marry you. But, Mr Boldwood, hesitation on so high a matter is honourable in any woman, and I don't want to give a solemn promise to-night. I would rather ask you to wait a few weeks till I can see my situation better.'

'But you have every reason to believe that then –'

'I have every reason to hope that at the end of the five or six weeks, between this time and harvest, that you say you are going to be away from home, I shall be able to promise to be your wife,' she said firmly. 'But remember this distinctly, I don't promise yet.'

'It is enough; I don't ask more. I can wait on those dear words. And now, Miss Everdene, good-night!'

'Good-night,' she said graciously – almost tenderly; and Boldwood withdrew with a serene smile.

Bathsheba knew more of him now; he had entirely bared his heart before her, even until he had almost worn in her eyes the sorry look of a grand bird without the feathers that make it grand. She had been awestruck at her past temerity, and was struggling to make amends without thinking whether the sin quite deserved the penalty she was schooling herself to pay. To have brought all this about her ears was terrible; but after a while the situation was not without a fearful joy. The facility with which even the most timid women sometimes acquire a relish for the dreadful when that is amalgamated with a little triumph, is marvellous.

* XXIV *

The same Night – The Fir Plantation

AMONG the multifarious duties which Bathsheba had voluntarily imposed upon herself by dispensing with the services of a bailiff, was the particular one of looking around the homestead before going to bed, to see that all was right and safe for the night. Gabriel had almost constantly preceded her in this tour every evening, watching her affairs as carefully as any specially appointed officer of surveillance could have done; but this tender devotion was to a great extent unknown to his mistress, and as much as was known was somewhat thanklessly received. Women are never tired of bewailing man's fickleness in love, but they only seem to snub his constancy.

As watching is best done invisibly, she usually carried a dark lantern in her hand, and every now and then turned on the light to examine nooks and corners with the coolness of a metropolitan policeman. This coolness may have owed its existence not so much to her fearlessness of expected danger as to her freedom from the suspicion of any; her worst anticipated discovery being that a horse might not be well bedded, the fowls not all in, or a door not closed.

This night the buildings were inspected as usual, and she went round to the farm paddock. Here the only sounds disturbing the stillness were steady munchings of many mouths, and stentorian breathings from all but invisible noses, ending in snores and puffs like the blowing of bellows slowly. Then the munching would recommence, when the lively imagination might assist the eye to discern a group of pink-white nostrils shaped as caverns, and very clammy and humid on their surfaces, not exactly pleasant to the touch until one got used to them; the mouths beneath having a great partiality for closing upon any loose end of Bathsheba's apparel which came within reach of their tongues. Above each of these a still keener vision suggested a brown forehead and two staring though not unfriendly eyes, and above all a pair of whitish crescent-shaped horns like two particularly new moons, an occasional stolid 'moo!' proclaiming beyond the shade of a doubt that these phenomena were the features and persons of Daisy, Whitefoot, Bonny-lass, Jolly-O, Spot, Twinkle-eye, etc., etc., etc. – the respectable dairy of Devon cows belonging to Bathsheba aforesaid.

Her way back to the house was by a path through a young plantation of tapering firs, which had been planted some years earlier to shelter the premises from the north wind. By reason of the density of the interwoven foliage overhead it was gloomy there at cloudless noontide, twilight in the evening, dark as midnight at dusk, and black as the ninth plague of Egypt at midnight. To describe the spot is to call it a vast, low, naturally formed hall, the plumy ceiling of which was supported by slender pillars of living wood, the floor being covered with a soft dun carpet of dead spikelets and mildewed cones, with a tuft of grass-blades here and there.

This bit of the path was always the crux of the night's ramble, though, before starting, her apprehensions of danger were not vivid enough to lead her to take a companion. Slipping along here covertly as Time, Bathsheba fancied she could hear footsteps entering the track at the opposite end. It was certainly a rustle of footsteps. Her own instantly fell as gently as snowflakes. She reassured herself by a remembrance that the path was public, and that the traveller was probably some villager returning home; regretting, at the same time, that the meeting should be about to occur in the darkest point of her route, even though only just outside her own door.

The noise approached, came close, and a figure was apparently on the point of gliding past her when something tugged at her skirt and pinned it forcibly to the ground. The instantaneous check nearly threw Bathsheba off her balance. In recovering she struck against warm clothes and buttons.

'A rum start, upon my soul!' said a masculine voice, a foot or so above her head. 'Have I hurt you, mate?'

'No,' said Bathsheba, attempting to shrink away.

'We have got hitched together somehow, I think.'

'Yes.'

'Are you a woman?'

'Yes.'

'A lady, I should have said.'

'It doesn't matter.'

'I am a man.'

'Oh!'

Bathsheba softly tugged again, but to no purpose.

'Is that a dark lantern you have? I fancy so,' said the man.

'Yes.'

'If you'll allow me I'll open it, and set you free.'

A hand seized the lantern, the door was opened, the rays burst out from their prison, and Bathsheba beheld her position with astonishment.

The man to whom she was hooked was brilliant in brass and scarlet. He was a soldier. His sudden appearance was to darkness what the sound of a trumpet is to silence. Gloom, the *genius loci* at all times hitherto, was now totally overthrown, less by the lantern-light than by what the lantern lighted. The contrast of this revelation with her anticipations of some sinister figure in sombre garb was so great that it had upon her the effect of a fairy transformation.

It was immediately apparent that the military man's spur had become entangled in the gimp which decorated the skirt of her dress. He caught a view of her face.

'I'll unfasten you in one moment, miss,' he said, with newborn gallantry.

'O no – I can do it, thank you,' she hastily replied, and stooped for the performance.

The unfastening was not such a trifling affair. The rowel of the spur had so wound itself among the gimp cords in those few moments, that separation was likely to be a matter of time.

He too stooped, and the lantern standing on the ground betwixt them threw the gleam from its open side among the fir-tree needles and the blades of long damp grass with the effect of a large glow-worm. It radiated upwards into their faces, and sent over half the plantation gigantic shadows of both man and woman, each dusky shape becoming distorted and mangled upon the tree-trunks till it wasted to nothing.

He looked hard into her eyes when she raised them for a moment; Bathsheba looked down again, for his gaze was too strong to be received point-blank with her own. But she had obliquely noticed that he was young and slim, and that he wore three chevrons upon his sleeve.

Bathsheba pulled again.

'You are a prisoner, miss; it is no use blinking the matter,' said the soldier drily. 'I must cut your dress if you are in such a hurry.'

'Yes – please do!' she exclaimed helplessly.

'It wouldn't be necessary if you could wait a moment'; and he unwound a cord from the little wheel. She withdrew her own hand, but, whether by accident or design, he touched it. Bathsheba was vexed; she hardly knew why.

His unravelling went on, but it nevertheless seemed coming to no end. She looked at him again.

'Thank you for the sight of such a beautiful face!' said the young sergeant, without ceremony.

She coloured with embarrassment. ' 'Twas unwillingly shown,' she replied stiffly, and with as much dignity – which was very little – as she could infuse into a position of captivity.

'I like you the better for that incivility, miss,' he said.

'I should have liked – I wish – you had never shown yourself to me by intruding here!' She pulled again, and the gathers of her dress began to give way like lilliputian musketry.

'I deserve the chastisement your words give me. But why should such a fair and dutiful girl have such an aversion to her father's sex?'

'Go on your way, please.'

'What, Beauty, and drag you after me? Do but look; I never saw such a tangle!'

'O, 'tis shameful of you; you have been making it worse on purpose to keep me here – you have!'

'Indeed, I don't think so,' said the sergeant, with a merry twinkle.

'I tell you you have!' she exclaimed, in high temper. 'I insist upon undoing it. Now, allow me!'

'Certainly, miss; I am not of steel.' He added a sigh which had as much archness in it as a sigh could possess without losing its nature altogether. 'I am thankful for beauty, even when 'tis thrown to me like a bone to a dog. These moments will be over soon!'

She closed her lips in a determined silence.

Bathsheba was revolving in her mind whether by a bold and desperate rush she could free herself at the risk of leaving her skirt bodily behind her. The thought was too dreadful. The dress – which she had put on to appear stately at the supper – was the head and front of her wardrobe; not another in her stock became her so well. What woman in Bathsheba's position, not naturally timid, and within call of her retainers, would have bought escape from a dashing soldier at so dear a price?

'All in good time; it will soon be done, I perceive,' said her cool friend.

'This trifling provokes, and – and –'

'Not too cruel!'

'– Insults me!'

'It is done in order that I may have the pleasure of apologizing to so charming a woman, which I straightway do most humbly, madam,' he said, bowing low.

Bathsheba really knew not what to say.

'I've seen a good many women in my time,' continued the young man in a murmur, and more thoughtfully than hitherto, critically regarding her bent head at the same time; 'but I've never seen a woman so beautiful as you. Take it or leave it – be offended or like it – I don't care.'

'Who are you, then, who can so well afford to despise opinion?'

'No stranger. Sergeant Troy. I am staying in this place. – There! it is undone at last, you see. Your light fingers were more eager than mine. I wish it had been the knot of knots, which there's no untying!'

This was worse and worse. She started up, and so did he. How to decently get away from him – that was her difficulty now. She sidled off inch by inch, the lantern in her hand, till she could see the redness of his coat no longer.

'Ah, Beauty; good-bye!' he said.

She made no reply, and, reaching a distance of twenty or thirty yards, turned about, and ran indoors.

Liddy had just retired to rest. In ascending to her own chamber, Bathsheba opened the girl's door an inch or two, and, panting, said –

'Liddy, is any soldier staying in the village – sergeant somebody – rather gentlemanly for a sergeant, and good looking – a red coat with blue facings?'

'No, miss . . . No, I say; but really it might be Sergeant Troy home on furlough, though I have not seen him. He was here once in that way when the regiment was at Casterbridge.'

'Yes; that's the name. Had he a moustache – no whiskers or beard?'

'He had.'

'What kind of person is he?'

'O! miss – I blush to name it – a gay man! But I know him to be very quick and trim, who might have made his thousands, like a squire. Such a clever young dand as he is! He's a doctor's son by name, which is a great deal; and he's an earl's son by nature!'

'Which is a great deal more. Fancy! Is it true?'

'Yes. And he was brought up so well, and sent to Casterbridge Grammar School for years and years. Learnt all languages while he was there; and it was said he got on so far that he could take down Chinese in shorthand; but that I don't answer for, as it was only reported. However, he wasted his gifted lot, and listed a soldier; but even then he rose to be a sergeant without trying at all. Ah! such a blessing it is to be high-born; nobility of blood will shine out even in the ranks and files. And is he really come home, miss?'

'I believe so. Good-night, Liddy.'

After all, how could a cheerful wearer of skirts be permanently offended with the man? There are occasions when girls like Bathsheba will put up with a great deal of unconventional behaviour. When they want to be praised, which is often; when they want to be mastered, which is sometimes; and when they want no nonsense, which is seldom. Just now the first feeling was in the ascendant with Bathsheba, with a dash of the second. Moreover, by chance or by devilry, the ministrant was antecedently made interesting by being a handsome stranger who had evidently seen better days.

So she could not clearly decide whether it was her opinion that he had insulted her or not.

'Was ever anything so odd!' she at last exclaimed to herself, in her own room. 'And was ever anything so meanly done as what I did – to skulk away like that from a man who was only civil and kind!' Clearly she did not think his barefaced praise of her person an insult now.

It was a fatal omission of Boldwood's that he had never once told her she was beautiful.

XXV

The New Acquaintance described

IDIOSYNCRASY and vicissitude had combined to stamp Sergeant Troy as an exceptional being.

He was a man to whom memories were an incumbrance, and anticipations a superfluity. Simply feeling, considering, and caring for what was before his eyes, he was vulnerable only in the present. His outlook upon time was as a transient flash of the eye now and then: that projection of consciousness into days gone by and to come, which makes the past a synonym for the pathetic and the future a word for circum-spection, was foreign to Troy. With him the past was yesterday; the future, to-morrow; never, the day after.

On this account he might, in certain lights, have been regarded as one of the most fortunate of his order. For it may be argued with great plausibility that reminiscence is less an endowment than a disease, and that expectation in its only comfortable form – that of absolute faith – is practically an impossibility; whilst in the form of hope and the secondary compounds, patience, impatience, resolve, curiosity, it is a constant fluctuation between pleasure and pain.

Sergeant Troy, being entirely innocent of the practice of expectation, was never disappointed. To set against this negative gain there may have been some positive losses from a certain narrowing of the higher tastes and sensations which it entailed. But limitation of the capacity is never recognized as a loss by the loser therefrom: in this attribute moral or aesthetic poverty contrasts plausibly with material, since those who suffer do not mind it, whilst those who mind it soon cease to suffer. It is not a denial of anything to have been always without it, and what Troy had never enjoyed he did not miss; but, being fully conscious that what sober people missed he enjoyed, his capacity, though really less, seemed greater than theirs.

He was moderately truthful towards men, but to women lied like a Cretan – a system of ethics above all others calculated to win popularity at the first flush of admission into lively society; and the possibility of the favour gained being transitory had reference only to the future.

He never passed the line which divides the spruce vices from the ugly; and hence, though his morals had hardly been applauded, disapproval of them had frequently been tempered with a smile. This treatment had led to his becoming a sort of regrater of other men's gallantries, to his own aggrandizement as a Corinthian, rather than to the moral profit of his hearers.

His reason and his propensities had seldom any reciprocating influence, having separated by mutual consent long ago: thence it sometimes happened that, while his intentions were as honourable as could be wished, any particular deed formed a dark background which threw them into fine relief. The sergeant's vicious phases being the offspring of impulse, and his virtuous phases of cool meditation, the latter had a modest tendency to be oftener heard of than seen.

Troy was full of activity, but his activities were less of a locomotive than a vegetable nature; and, never being based upon any original choice of foundation or direction, they were exercised on whatever object chance might place in their way. Hence, whilst he sometimes reached the brilliant in speech because that was spontaneous, he fell below the commonplace in action, from inability to guide incipient effort. He had a quick comprehension and considerable force of character; but, being without the power to combine them, the comprehension became engaged with trivialities whilst waiting for the will to direct it, and the force wasted itself in useless grooves through unheeding the comprehension.

He was a fairly well-educated man for one of middle class – exceptionally well educated for a common soldier. He spoke fluently and unceasingly. He could in this way be one thing and seem another; for instance, he could speak of love and think of dinner; call on the husband to look at the wife; be eager to pay and intend to owe.

The wondrous power of flattery in *passados* at women is a perception so universal as to be remarked upon by many people almost as automatically as they repeat a proverb, or say that they are Christians and the like, without thinking much of the enormous corollaries which spring from the proposition. Still less is it acted upon for the good of the complemental being alluded to. With the majority such an opinion is shelved with all those trite aphorisms which require some catastrophe to bring their tremendous meanings thoroughly home. When expressed with some amount of reflectiveness it seems co-ordinate with a belief that this flattery must be reasonable to be effective. It is to the credit of men that few attempt to settle the question by experiment, and it is for their happiness, perhaps, that accident has never settled it for them. Nevertheless, that a male dissembler who by deluging her with untenable fictions charms the female wisely, may acquire powers reaching to the extremity of perdition, is a truth taught to many by unsought and wringing occurrences. And some profess to have attained to the same knowledge by experiment as aforesaid, and jauntily continue their indulgence in such experiments with terrible effect. Sergeant Troy was one.

He had been known to observe casually that in dealing with womankind the only alternative to flattery was cursing and swearing. There was no third method. 'Treat them fairly, and you are a lost man,' he would say.

This philosopher's public appearance in Weatherbury promptly followed his arrival there. A week or two after the shearing Bathsheba, feeling a nameless relief of spirits on account of Boldwood's absence, approached her hayfields and looked over the hedge towards the haymakers. They consisted in about equal proportions of gnarled and flexuous forms, the former being the men, the latter the women, who wore tilt bonnets covered with nankeen, which hung in a curtain upon their shoulders. Coggan and Mark Clark were mowing in a less forward meadow, Clark humming a tune to the strokes of his scythe, to which Jan made no attempt to keep time with his. In the first mead they were already loading hay, the women raking it into cocks and windrows, and the men tossing it upon the waggon.

From behind the waggon a bright scarlet spot emerged, and went on loading unconcernedly with the rest. It was the gallant sergeant, who had come haymaking for pleasure; and nobody could deny that he was doing the mistress of the farm real knight-service by this voluntary contribution of his labour at a busy time.

As soon as she had entered the field Troy saw her, and sticking his pitchfork into the ground and picking up his crop or cane, he came forward. Bathsheba blushed with half-angry embarrassment, and adjusted her eyes as well as her feet to the direct line of her path.

* XXVI *

Scene on the Verge of the Hay-mead

'Ah, Miss Everdene!' said the sergeant, touching his diminutive cap. 'Little did I think it was you I was speaking to the other night. And yet, if I had reflected, the "Queen of the Corn-market" (truth is truth at any hour of the day or night, and I heard you so named in Casterbridge yesterday), the "Queen of the Corn-market", I say, could be no other woman. I step across now to beg your forgiveness a thousand times for having been led by my feelings to express myself too strongly for a stranger. To be sure I am no stranger to the place – I am Sergeant Troy, as I told you, and I have assisted your uncle in these fields no end of times when I was a lad. I have been doing the same for you to-day.'

'I suppose I must thank you for that, Sergeant Troy,' said the Queen of the Corn-market in an indifferently grateful tone.

The sergeant looked hurt and sad. 'Indeed you must not, Miss Everdene,' he said. 'Why could you think such a thing necessary?'

'I am glad it is not.'

'Why? if I may ask without offence.'

'Because I don't want to thank you for anything.'

'I am afraid I have made a hole in my tongue that my heart will never mend. O these intolerable times: that ill-luck should follow a man for honestly telling a woman she is beautiful! 'Twas the most I said – you must own that; and the least I could say – that I own myself.'

'There is some talk I could do without more easily than money.'

'Indeed. That remark is a sort of digression.'

'No. It means that I would rather have your room than your company.'

'And I would rather have curses from you than kisses from any other woman; so I'll stay here.'

Bathsheba was absolutely speechless. And yet she could not help feeling that the assistance he was rendering forbade a harsh repulse.

'Well,' continued Troy. 'I suppose there is a praise which is rudeness, and that may be mine. At the same time there is a treatment which is injustice, and that may be yours. Because a plain blunt man, who has never been taught concealment, speaks out his mind without exactly intending it, he's to be snapped off like the son of a sinner.'

'Indeed there's no such case between us,' she said, turning away. 'I don't allow strangers to be bold and impudent – even in praise of me.'

'Ah – it is not the fact but the method which offends you,' he said carelessly. 'But I have the sad satisfaction of knowing that my words, whether pleasing or offensive, are unmistakably true. Would you have had me look at you, and tell my acquaintance that you are quite a common-place woman, to save you the embarrassment of being stared at if they come near you? Not I. I couldn't tell any such ridiculous lie about a beauty to encourage a single woman in England in too excessive a modesty.'

'It is all pretence – what you are saying!' exclaimed Bathsheba, laughing in spite of herself at the sergeant's sly method. 'You have a rare invention, Sergeant Troy. Why couldn't you have passed by me that night, and said nothing? – that was all I meant to reproach you for.'

'Because I wasn't going to. Half the pleasure of a feeling lies in being able to express it on the spur of the moment, and I let out mine. It would have been just the same if you had been the reverse person – ugly and old – I should have exclaimed about it in the same way.'

'How long is it since you have been so afflicted with strong feeling, then?'

'Oh, ever since I was big enough to know loveliness from deformity.'

' 'Tis to be hoped your sense of the difference you speak of doesn't stop at faces, but extends to morals as well.'

'I won't speak of morals or religion – my own or anybody else's. Though perhaps I should have been a very good Christian if you pretty women hadn't made me an idolater.'

Bathsheba moved on to hide the irrepressible dimplings of merriment. Troy followed, whirling his crop.

'But – Miss Everdene – you do forgive me?'

'Hardly.'

'Why?'

'You say such things.'

'I said you were beautiful and I'll say so still, by— so you are! The most beautiful ever I saw, or may I fall dead this instant! Why, upon my –'

'Don't – don't! I won't listen to you – you are so profane!' she said, in a restless state between distress at hearing him and a *penchant* to hear more.

'I again say you are a most fascinating woman. There's nothing remarkable in my saying so, is there? I'm sure the fact is evident enough. Miss Everdene, my opinion may be too forcibly let out to please you, and, for the matter of that, too insignificant to convince you, but surely it is honest, and why can't it be excused?'

'Because it – it isn't a correct one,' she femininely murmured.

'O, fie – fie! Am I any worse for breaking the third of that Terrible Ten than you for breaking the ninth?'

'Well, it doesn't seem *quite* true to me that I am fascinating,' she replied evasively.

'Not so to you: then I say with all respect that, if so, it is owing to your modesty, Miss Everdene. But surely you must have been told by everybody of what everybody notices? And you should take their words for it.'

'They don't say so exactly.'

'O yes, they must!'

'Well, I mean to my face, as you do,' she went on, allowing herself to be further lured into a conversation that intention had rigorously forbidden.

'But you know they think so?'

'No – that is – I certainly have heard Liddy say they do, but –' She paused.

Capitulation – that was the purport of the simple reply, guarded as it was – capitulation, unknown to herself. Never did a fragile tailless sentence convey a more perfect meaning. The careless sergeant smiled within himself, and probably too the devil smiled from a loop-hole in Tophet, for the moment was the turning-point of a career. Her tone and mien signified beyond mistake that the seed which was to lift the foundation had taken root in the chink: the remainder was a mere question of time and natural changes.

'There the truth comes out!' said the soldier, in reply. 'Never tell me that a young lady can live in a buzz of admiration without knowing something about it. Ah, well, Miss Everdene, you are – pardon my blunt way – you are rather an injury to our race than otherwise.'

'How – indeed?' she said, opening her eyes.

'O, it is true enough. I may as well be hung for a sheep as a lamb (an old country saying, not of much account, but it will do for a rough soldier), and so I will speak my mind, regardless of your pleasure, and without hoping or intending to get your pardon. Why, Miss Everdene, it is in this manner that your good looks may do more harm than good in the world.' The sergeant looked down the mead in critical abstraction. 'Probably some one man on an average falls in love with each ordinary woman. She can marry him: he is content, and leads a useful life. Such women as you a hundred men always covet – your eyes will bewitch scores on scores into an unavailing fancy for you – you can only marry one of that many. Out of these say twenty will endeavour to drown the bitterness of despised love in drink; twenty more will mope away their lives without a wish or attempt to make a mark in the world, because they have no ambition apart from their attachment to you; twenty more – the susceptible person myself possibly among them – will be always draggling after you, getting where they may just see you, doing desperate things. Men are such constant fools! The rest may try to get over their passion with more or less success. But all these men will be saddened. And not only those ninety-nine men, but the ninety-nine women they might have married are saddened with them. There's my tale. That's why I say that a woman so charming as yourself, Miss Everdene, is hardly a blessing to her race.'

The handsome sergeant's features were during this speech as rigid and stern as John Knox's in addressing his gay young queen.

Seeing she made no reply, he said, 'Do you read French?'

'No; I began, but when I got to the verbs, father died,' she said simply.

'I do – when I have an opportunity, which latterly has not been often (my mother was a Parisienne) – and there's a proverb they have, *Qui aime bien châtie bien* – "He chastens who loves well." Do you understand me?'

'Ah!' she replied, and there was even a little tremulousness in the usually cool girl's voice; 'if you can only fight half as winningly as you can talk, you are able to make a pleasure of a bayonet wound!' And then poor Bathsheba instantly perceived her slip in making this admission: in hastily trying to retrieve it, she went from bad to worse. 'Don't, however, suppose that *I* derive any pleasure from what you tell me.'

'I know you do not – I know it perfectly,' said Troy, with much hearty conviction on the exterior of his face: and altering the expression to moodiness; 'when a dozen men are ready to speak tenderly to you, and give the admiration you deserve without adding the warning you need, it stands to reason that my poor rough-and-ready mixture of praise and blame cannot convey much pleasure. Fool as I may be, I am not so conceited as to suppose that!'

'I think you – are conceited, nevertheless,' said Bathsheba, looking askance at a reed she was fitfully pulling with one hand, having lately grown feverish under the soldier's system of procedure – not because the nature of his cajolery was entirely unperceived, but because its vigour was overwhelming.

'I would not own it to anybody else – nor do I exactly to you. Still, there might have been some self-conceit in my foolish supposition the other night. I knew that what I said in admiration might be an opinion too often forced upon you to give any pleasure, but I certainly did think that the kindness of your nature might prevent you judging an uncontrolled tongue harshly – which you have done – and thinking badly of me and wounding me this morning, when I am working hard to save your hay.'

'Well, you need not think more of that: perhaps you did not mean to be rude to me by speaking out of your mind: indeed, I believe you did not,' said the shrewd woman, in painfully innocent earnest. 'And I thank you for giving help here. But – but mind you don't speak to me again in that way, or in any other, unless I speak to you.'

'O Miss Bathsheba! That is too hard!'

'No, it isn't. Why is it?'

'You will never speak to me; for I shall not be here long. I am soon going back to the miserable monotony of drill – and perhaps our regiment will be ordered out soon. And yet you take away the one little ewe-lamb of pleasure that I have in this dull life of mine. Well, perhaps generosity is not a woman's most marked characteristic.'

'When are you going from here?' she asked with some interest.

'In a month.'

'But how can it give you pleasure to speak to me?'

'Can you ask, Miss Everdene – knowing as you do – what my offence is based on?'

'If you do care so much for a silly trifle of that kind, then, I don't mind doing it,' she uncertainly and doubtingly answered. 'But you can't really care for a word from me? you only say so – I think you only say so.'

'That's unjust – but I won't repeat the remark. I am too gratified to get such a mark of your friendship at any price to cavil at the tone. I *do*, Miss Everdene, care for it. You may think a man foolish to want a mere word – just a good morning. Perhaps he is – I don't know. But you have never been a man looking upon a woman, and the woman yourself.'

'Well.'

'Then you know nothing of what such an experience is like – and heaven forbid that you ever should!'

'Nonsense, flatterer! What is it like? I am interested in knowing.'

'Put shortly, it is not being able to think, hear, or look in any direction except one without wretchedness, nor there without torture.'

'Ah, sergeant, it won't do – you are pretending!' she said, shaking her head. 'Your words are too dashing to be true.'

'I am not, upon the honour of a soldier.'

'But *why* is it so? – Of course I ask for mere pastime.'

'Because you are so distracting – and I am so distracted.'

'You look like it.'

'I am indeed.'

'Why, you only saw me the other night!'

'That makes no difference. The lightning works instantaneously. I loved you then, at once – as I do now.'

Bathsheba surveyed him curiously, from the feet upward, as high as she liked to venture her glance, which was not quite so high as his eyes.

'You cannot and you don't,' she said demurely. 'There is no such sudden feeling in people. I won't listen to you any longer. Dear me, I wish I knew what o'clock it is – I am going – I have wasted too much time here already!'

The sergeant looked at his watch and told her. 'What, haven't you a watch, miss?' he inquired.

'I have not just at present – I am about to get a new one.'

'No. You shall be given one. Yes – you shall. A gift, Miss Everdene – a gift.'

And before she knew what the young man was intending, a heavy gold watch was in her hand.

'It is an unusually good one for a man like me to possess,' he quietly said. 'That watch has a history. Press the spring and open the back.'

She did so.

'What do you see?'

'A crest and a motto.'

'A coronet with five points, and beneath, *Cedit amor rebus* – "Love yields to circumstance." It's the motto of the Earls of Severn. That watch belonged to the last lord, and was given to my mother's husband, a medical man, for his use till I came of age, when it was to be given to me. It was all the fortune that ever I inherited. That watch has regulated imperial interests in its time – the stately ceremonial, the courtly assignation, pompous travels, and lordly sleeps. Now it is yours.'

'But Sergeant Troy, I cannot take this – I cannot!' she exclaimed with round-eyed wonder. 'A gold watch! What are you doing? Don't be such a dissembler!'

The sergeant retreated to avoid receiving back his gift, which she held out persistently towards him. Bathsheba followed as he retired.

'Keep it – do, Miss Everdene – keep it!' said the erratic child of impulse. 'The fact of your possessing it makes it worth ten times as much to me. A more plebeian one will answer my purpose just as well, and the pleasure of knowing whose heart my old one beats against – well, I won't speak of that. It is in far worthier hands than ever it has been in before.'

'But indeed I can't have it!' she said, in a perfect simmer of distress. 'O, how can you do such a thing; that is, if you really mean it! Give me your dead father's watch, and such a valuable one! You should not be so reckless, indeed, Sergeant Troy!'

'I loved my father: good; but better, I love you more. That's how I can do it,' said the sergeant with an intonation of such exquisite fidelity to nature that it was evidently not all acted now. Her beauty, which, whilst it had been quiescent, he had praised in jest, had in its animated phases moved him to earnest; and though his seriousness was less than she imagined, it was probably more than he imagined himself.

Bathsheba was brimming with agitated bewilderment, and she said, in half-suspicious accents of feeling, 'Can it be! O, how can it be, that you care for me, and so suddenly! You have seen so little of me: I may not be really so – so nice-looking as I seem to you. Please, do take it; O, do! I cannot and will not have it. Believe me, your generosity is too great. I have never done you a single kindness, and why should you be so kind to me?'

A factitious reply had been again upon his lips, but it was again suspended, and he looked at her with an arrested eye. The truth was, that as she now stood – excited, wild, and honest as the day – her alluring beauty bore out so fully the epithets he had bestowed upon it that he was quite startled at his temerity in advancing them as false. He said mechanically, 'Ah, why?' and continued to look at her.

'And my workfolk see me following you about the field, and are wondering. O, this is dreadful!' she went on, unconscious of the transmutation she was effecting.

'I did not quite mean you to accept it at first, for it was my one poor patent of nobility,' he broke out bluntly; 'but, upon my soul, I wish you would now. Without any shamming, come! Don't deny me the happiness of wearing it for my sake! But you are too lovely even to care to be kind as others are.'

'No, no; don't say so! I have reasons for reserve which I cannot explain.'

'Let it be, then, let it be,' he said, receiving back the watch at last; 'I must be leaving you now. And will you speak to me for these few weeks of my stay?'

'Indeed I will. Yet, I don't know if I will! O, why did you come and disturb me so!'

'Perhaps in setting a gin, I have caught myself. Such things have happened. Well, will you let me work in your fields?' he coaxed.

'Yes, I suppose so; if it is any pleasure to you.'

'Miss Everdene, I thank you.'

'No, no.'

'Good-bye!'

The sergeant brought his hand to the cap on the slope of his head, saluted, and returned to the distant group of haymakers.

Bathsheba could not face the haymakers now. Her heart erratically flitting hither and thither from perplexed excitement, hot, and almost tearful, she retreated homeward, murmuring, 'O, what have I done! What does it mean! I wish I knew how much of it was true!'

* XXVII *

Hiving the Bees

THE Weatherbury bees were late in their swarming this year. It was in the latter part of June, and the day after the interview with Troy in the hayfield, that Bathsheba was standing in her garden, watching a swarm in the air and guessing their probable settling place. Not only were they late this year, but unruly. Sometimes throughout a whole season all the swarms would alight on the lowest attainable bough – such as part of a currant-bush or espalier apple-tree; next year they would, with just the same unanimity, make straight off to the uppermost member of some tall, gaunt costard, or quarrenden, and there defy all invaders who did not come armed with ladders and staves to take them.

This was the case at present. Bathsheba's eyes, shaded by one hand, were following the ascending multitude against the unexplorable stretch of blue till they ultimately halted by one of the unwieldy trees spoken of. A process somewhat analogous to that of alleged formations of the universe, time and times ago, was observable. The bustling swarm had swept the sky in a scattered and uniform haze, which now thickened to a nebulous centre: this glided on to a bough and grew still denser till it formed a solid black spot upon the light.

The men and women being all busily engaged in saving the hay – even Liddy had left the house for the purpose of lending a hand – Bathsheba resolved to hive the bees herself, if possible. She had dressed the hive with herbs and honey, fetched a ladder, brush, and crook, made herself impregnable with armour of leather gloves, straw hat, and large gauze veil – once green but now faded to snuff colour – and ascended a dozen rungs of the ladder. At once she heard, not ten yards off, a voice that was beginning to have a strange power in agitating her.

'Miss Everdene, let me assist you; you should not attempt such a thing alone.'

Troy was just opening the garden gate.

Bathsheba flung down the brush, crook, and empty hive, pulled the skirt of her dress tightly round her ankles in a tremendous flurry, and as well as she could slid down the ladder. By the time she reached the bottom Troy was there also, and he stooped to pick up the hive.

'How fortunate I am to have dropped in at this moment!' exclaimed the sergeant.

She found her voice in a minute. 'What! and will you shake them in for me?' she asked, in what, for a defiant girl, was a faltering way; though, for a timid girl, it would have seemed a brave way enough.

'Will I!' said Troy. 'Why of course I will. How blooming you are to-day!' Troy flung down his cane and put his foot on the ladder to ascend.

'But you must have on the veil and gloves, or you'll be stung fearfully!'

'Ah, yes. I must put on the veil and gloves. Will you kindly show me how to fix them properly?'

'And you must have the broad-brimmed hat, too; for your cap has no brim to keep the veil off, and they'd reach your face.'

'The broad-brimmed hat, too, by all means.'

So a whimsical fate ordered that her hat should be taken off – veil and all attached – and placed upon his head, Troy tossing his own into a gooseberry bush. Then the veil had to be tied at its lower edge round his collar and the gloves put on him.

He looked such an extraordinary object in this guise that, flurried as she was, she could not avoid laughing outright. It was the removal of yet another stake from the palisade of cold manners which had kept him off.

Bathsheba looked on from the ground whilst he was busy sweeping and shaking the bees from the tree, holding up the hive with the other hand for them to fall into. She made use of an unobserved minute whilst his attention was absorbed in the operation to arrange her plumes a little. He came down holding the hive at arm's length, behind which trailed a cloud of bees.

'Upon my life,' said Troy, through the veil, 'holding up this hive makes one's arm ache worse than a week of sword-exercise.' When the manoeuvre was completed he approached her. 'Would you be good enough to untie me and let me out? I am nearly stifled inside this silk cage.'

To hide her embarrassment during the unwonted process of untying the string about his neck, she said:–

'I have never seen that you spoke of.'

'What?'

'The sword-exercise.'

'Ah! would you like to?' said Troy.

Bathsheba hesitated. She had heard wondrous reports from time to time by dwellers in Weatherbury, who had by chance sojourned awhile in Casterbridge, near the barracks, of this strange and glorious perform-ance, the sword-exercise. Men and boys who had peeped through chinks or over walls into the barrack-yard returned with accounts of its being the most flashing affair conceivable; accoutrements and weapons glistening like stars – here, there, around – yet all by rule and compass. So she said mildly what she felt strongly:

'Yes; I should like to see it very much.'

'And so you shall; you shall see me go through it.'

'No! How?'

'Let me consider.'

'Not with a walking-stick – I don't care to see that. It must be a real sword.'

'Yes, I know; and I have no sword here; but I think I could get one by the evening. Now, will you do this?'

Troy bent over her and murmured some suggestion in a low voice.

'Oh no, indeed!' said Bathsheba, blushing. 'Thank you very much, but I couldn't on any account.'

'Surely you might? Nobody would know.'

She shook her head, but with a weakened negation. 'If I were to,' she said, 'I must bring Liddy too. Might I not?'

Troy looked far away. 'I don't see why you want to bring her,' he said coldly.

An unconscious look of assent in Bathsheba's eyes betrayed that something more than his coldness had made her also feel that Liddy would be superfluous in the suggested scene. She had felt it, even whilst making the proposal.

'Well, I won't bring Liddy – and I'll come. But only for a very short time,' she added; 'a very short time.'

'It will not take five minutes,' said Troy.

* XXVIII *

The Hollow amid the Ferns

THE hill opposite Bathsheba's dwelling extended, a mile off, into an uncultivated tract of land, dotted at this season with tall thickets of brake fern, plump and diaphanous from recent rapid growth, and radiant in hues of clear and untainted green.

At eight o'clock this midsummer evening, whilst the bristling ball of gold in the west still swept the tips of the ferns with its long, luxuriant rays, a soft brushing-by of garments might have been heard among them, and Bathsheba appeared in their midst, their soft, feathery arms caressing her up to her shoulders. She paused, turned, went back over the hill and half-way to her own door, whence she cast a farewell glance upon the spot she had just left, having resolved not to remain near the place after all.

She saw a dim spot of artificial red moving round the shoulder of the rise. It disappeared on the other side.

She waited one minute – two minutes – thought of Troy's disappointment at her non-fulfilment of a promised engagement, till she again ran along the field, clambered over the bank, and followed the original direction. She was now literally trembling and panting at this her temerity in such an errant undertaking; her breath came and went quickly, and her eyes shone with an infrequent light. Yet go she must. She reached the verge of a pit in the middle of the ferns. Troy stood in the bottom, looking up towards her.

'I heard you rustling through the fern before I saw you,' he said, coming up and giving her his hand to help her down the slope.

The pit was a saucer-shaped concave, naturally formed, with a top diameter of about thirty feet, and shallow enough to allow the sunshine to reach their heads. Standing in the centre, the sky overhead was met by a circular horizon of fern: this grew nearly to the bottom of the slope and then abruptly ceased. The middle within the belt of verdure was floored with a thick flossy carpet of moss and grass intermingled, so yielding that the foot was half-buried within it.

'Now,' said Troy, producing the sword, which, as he raised it into the sunlight, gleamed a sort of greeting, like a living thing; 'first, we have four right and four left cuts; four right and four left thrusts. Infantry cuts and guards are more interesting than ours, to my mind; but they are not so swashing. They have seven cuts and three thrusts. So much as a preliminary. Well, next, our cut one is as if you were sowing your corn – so.' Bathsheba saw a sort of rainbow, upside down in the air, and Troy's arm was still again. 'Cut two, as if you were hedging – so. Three, as if you were reaping – so. Four, as if you were threshing – in that way. Then the same on the left. The thrusts are these: one, two, three, four, right; one, two, three, four, left.' He repeated them. 'Have 'em again?' he said. 'One, two –'

She hurriedly interrupted: 'I'd rather not; though I don't mind your twos and fours; but your ones and threes are terrible!'

'Very well, I'll let you off the ones and threes. Next, cuts, points and guards altogether.' Troy duly exhibited them. 'Then there's pursuing practice, in this way.' He gave the movements as before. 'There, those are the stereotyped forms. The infantry have two most diabolical upward cuts, which we are too humane to use. Like this – three, four.'

'How murderous and bloodthirsty!'

'They are rather deathy. Now I'll be more interesting, and let you see some loose play – giving all the cuts and points, infantry and cavalry, quicker than lightning, and as promiscuously – with just enough rule to regulate instinct and yet not to fetter it. You are my antagonist, with this difference from real warfare, that I shall miss you every time by one hair's breadth, or perhaps two. Mind you don't flinch, whatever you do.'

'I'll be sure not to!' she said invincibly.

He pointed to about a yard in front of him.

Bathsheba's adventurous spirit was beginning to find some grains of relish in these highly novel proceedings. She took up her position as directed, facing Troy.

'Now just to learn whether you have pluck enough to let me do what I wish, I'll give you a preliminary test.'

He flourished the sword by way of introduction number two, and the next thing of which she was conscious was that the point and blade of the sword were darting with a gleam towards her left side, just above her hip;

then of their reappearance on her right side, emerging as it were from between her ribs, having apparently passed through her body. The third item of consciousness was that of seeing the same sword, perfectly clean and free from blood held vertically in Troy's hand (in the position technically called 'recover swords'). All was as quick as electricity.

'Oh!' she cried out in affright, pressing her hand to her side. 'Have you run me through? – no, you have not! Whatever have you done!'

'I have not touched you,' said Troy quietly. 'It was mere sleight of hand. The sword passed behind you. Now you are not afraid, are you? Because if you are I can't perform. I give my word that I will not only not hurt you, but not once touch you.'

'I don't think I am afraid. You are quite sure you will not hurt me?'

'Quite sure.'

'Is the sword very sharp?'

'O no – only stand as still as a statue. Now!'

In an instant the atmosphere was transformed to Bathsheba's eyes. Beams of light caught from the low sun's rays, above, around, in front of her, well-nigh shut out earth and heaven – all emitted in the marvellous evolutions of Troy's reflecting blade, which seemed everywhere at once, and yet nowhere specially. These circling gleams were accompanied by a keen rush that was almost a whistling – also springing from all sides of her at once. In short, she was enclosed in a firmament of light, and of sharp hisses, resembling a sky-full of meteors close at hand.

Never since the broadsword became the national weapon had there been more dexterity shown in its management than by the hands of Sergeant Troy, and never had he been in such splendid temper for the performance as now in the evening sunshine among the ferns with Bathsheba. It may safely be asserted with respect to the closeness of his cuts, that had it been possible for the edge of the sword to leave in the air a permanent substance wherever it flew past, the space left untouched would have been almost a mould of Bathsheba's figure.

Behind the luminous streams of this *aurora militaris*, she could see the hue of Troy's sword arm, spread in a scarlet haze over the space covered by its motions, like a twanged harpstring, and behind all Troy himself, mostly facing her; sometimes, to show the rear cuts, half turned away, his eye nevertheless always keenly measuring her breadth and outline, and his lips tightly closed in sustained effort. Next, his movements lapsed slower, and she could see them individually. The hissing of the sword ceased, and he stopped entirely.

'That outer loose lock of hair wants tidying,' he said, before she had moved or spoken. 'Wait: I'll do it for you.'

An arc of silver shone on her right side: the sword had descended. The lock dropped to the ground.

'Bravely borne!' said Troy. 'You didn't flinch a shade's thickness. Wonderful in a woman!'

'It was because I didn't expect it. O, you have spoilt my hair!'

'Only once more.'

'No – no! I am afraid of you – indeed I am!' she cried.

'I won't touch you at all – not even your hair. I am only going to kill that caterpillar settling on you. Now: still!'

It appeared that a caterpillar had come from the fern and chosen the front of her bodice as his resting place. She saw the point glisten towards her bosom, and seemingly enter it. Bathsheba closed her eyes in the full persuasion that she was killed at last. However, feeling just as usual, she opened them again.

'There it is, look,' said the sergeant, holding his sword before her eyes. The caterpillar was spitted upon its point.

'Why, it is magic!' said Bathsheba, amazed.

'O no – dexterity. I merely gave point to your bosom where the caterpillar was, and instead of running you through checked the extension a thousandth of an inch short of your surface.'

'But how could you chop off a curl of my hair with a sword that has no edge?'

'No edge! This sword will shave like a razor. Look here.'

He touched the palm of his hand with the blade, and then, lifting it, showed her a thin shaving of scarf-skin dangling therefrom.

'But you said before beginning that it was blunt and couldn't cut me!'

'That was to get you to stand still, and so make sure of your safety. The risk of injuring you through your moving was too great not to force me to tell you a fib to escape it.'

She shuddered. 'I have been within an inch of my life, and didn't know it!'

'More precisely speaking, you have been within half an inch of being pared alive two hundred and ninety-five times.'

'Cruel, cruel, 'tis of you!'

'You have been perfectly safe, nevertheless. My sword never errs.' And Troy returned the weapon to the scabbard.

Bathsheba, overcome by a hundred tumultuous feelings resulting from the scene, abstractedly sat down on a tuft of heather.

'I must leave you now,' said Troy softly. 'And I'll venture to take and keep this in remembrance of you.'

She saw him stoop to the grass, pick up the winding lock which he had severed from her manifold tresses, twist it round his fingers, unfasten a button in the breast of his coat, and carefully put it inside. She felt powerless to withstand or deny him. He was altogether too much for her, and Bathsheba seemed as one who, facing a reviving wind, finds it blow so strongly that it stops the breath.

He drew near and said, 'I must be leaving you.' He drew nearer still. A minute later and she saw his scarlet form disappear amid the ferny thicket, almost in a flash, like a brand swiftly waved.

That minute's interval had brought the blood beating into her face, set her stinging as if aflame to the very hollows of her feet, and enlarged emotion to a compass which quite swamped thought. It had brought upon her a stroke resulting, as did that of Moses in Horeb, in a liquid stream – here a stream of tears. She felt like one who has sinned a great sin.

The circumstance had been the gentle dip of Troy's mouth downwards upon her own. He had kissed her.

* XXIX *

Particulars of a Twilight Walk

WE now see the element of folly distinctly mingling with the many varying particulars which made up the character of Bathsheba Everdene. It was almost foreign to her intrinsic nature. Introduced as lymph on the dart of Eros it eventually permeated and coloured her whole constitution. Bathsheba, though she had too much understanding to be entirely governed by her womanliness, had too much womanliness to use her understanding to the best advantage. Perhaps in no minor point does woman astonish her helpmate more than in the strange power she possesses of believing cajoleries that she knows to be false – except, indeed, in that of being utterly sceptical on strictures that she knows to be true.

Bathsheba loved Troy in the way that only self-reliant women love when they abandon their self-reliance. When a strong woman recklessly throws away her strength she is worse than a weak woman who has never had any strength to throw away. One source of her inadequacy is the novelty of the occasion. She has never had practice in making the best of such a condition. Weakness is doubly weak by being new.

Bathsheba was not conscious of guile in this matter. Though in one sense a woman of the world, it was, after all, that world of daylight coteries and green carpets wherein cattle form the passing crowd and winds the busy hum; where a quiet family of rabbits or hares lives on the other side of your party-wall, where your neighbour is everybody in the tything, and where calculation is confined to market-days. Of the fabricated tastes of good fashionable society she knew but little, and of the formulated self-indulgence of bad, nothing at all. Had her utmost thoughts in this direction been distinctly worded (and by herself they never were), they would only have amounted to such a matter as that she felt her impulses to be pleasanter guides than her discretion. Her love was entire as a child's, and though warm as summer it was fresh as spring. Her culpability lay in her making no attempt to control feeling by subtle and careful inquiry into consequences. She could show others the steep and thorny way, but 'reck'd not her own rede'.

And Troy's deformities lay deep down from a woman's vision, whilst his embellishments were upon the very surface; thus contrasting with homely Oak, whose defects were patent to the blindest, and whose virtues were as metals in a mine.

The difference between love and respect was markedly shown in her conduct. Bathsheba had spoken of her interest in Boldwood with the greatest freedom to Liddy, but she had only communed with her own heart concerning Troy.

All this infatuation Gabriel saw, and was troubled thereby from the time of his daily journey a-field to the time of his return, and on to the small hours of many a night. That he was not beloved had hitherto been his great sorrow; that Bathsheba was getting into the toils was now a sorrow greater than the first, and one which nearly obscured it. It was a result which paralleled the oft-quoted observation of Hippocrates concerning physical pains.

That is a noble though perhaps an unpromising love which not even the fear of breeding aversion in the bosom of the one beloved can deter from combating his or her errors. Oak determined to speak to his mistress. He would base his appeal on what he considered her unfair treatment of Farmer Boldwood, now absent from home.

An opportunity occurred one evening when she had gone for a short walk by a path through the neighbouring cornfields. It was dusk when Oak, who had not been far a-field that day, took the same path and met her returning, quite pensively, as he thought.

The wheat was not tall, and the path was narrow; thus the way was quite a sunken groove between the embowing thicket on either side. Two persons could not walk abreast without damaging the crop, and Oak stood aside to let her pass.

'Oh, is it Gabriel?' she said. 'You are taking a walk too. Good-night.'

'I thought I would come to meet you, as it is rather late,' said Oak, turning and following at her heels when she had brushed somewhat quickly by him.

'Thank you, indeed, but I am not very fearful.'

'O no; but there are bad characters about.'

'I never meet them.'

Now Oak, with marvellous ingenuity, had been going to introduce the gallant sergeant through the channel of 'bad characters'. But all at once the scheme broke down, it suddenly occurring to him that this was rather a clumsy way, and too barefaced to begin with. He tried another preamble.

'And as the man who would naturally come to meet you is away from home, too – I mean Farmer Boldwood – why, thinks I, I'll go,' he said.

'Ah, yes.' She walked on without turning her head, and for many steps nothing further was heard from her quarter than the rustle of her dress against the heavy corn-ears. Then she resumed rather tartly –

'I don't quite understand what you meant by saying that Mr Boldwood would naturally come to meet me.'

'I meant on account of the wedding which they say is likely to take place between you and him, miss. Forgive my speaking plainly.'

'They say what is not true,' she returned quickly. 'No marriage is likely to take place between us.'

Gabriel now put forth his unobscured opinion, for the moment had come. 'Well, Miss Everdene,' he said, 'putting aside what people say, I never in my life saw any courting if his is not a courting of you.'

Bathsheba would probably have terminated the conversation there and then by flatly forbidding the subject, had not her conscious weakness of position allured her to palter and argue in endeavours to better it.

'Since this subject has been mentioned,' she said very emphatically, 'I am glad of the opportunity of clearing up a mistake which is very common and very provoking. I didn't definitely promise Mr Boldwood anything. I have never cared for him. I respect him, and he has urged me to marry him. But I have given him no distinct answer. As soon as he returns I shall do so; and the answer will be that I cannot think of marrying him.'

'People are full of mistakes, seemingly.'

'They are.'

'The other day they said you were trifling with him, and you almost proved that you were not; lately they have said that you be not, and you straightway begin to show –'

'That I am, I suppose you mean.'

'Well, I hope they speak the truth.'

'They do, but wrongly applied. I don't trifle with him; but then, I have nothing to do with him.'

Oak was unfortunately led on to speak of Boldwood's rival in a wrong tone to her after all. 'I wish you had never met that young Sergeant Troy, miss,' he sighed.

Bathsheba's steps became faintly spasmodic. 'Why?' she asked.

'He is not good enough for 'ee.'

'Did any one tell you to speak to me like this?'

'Nobody at all.'

'Then it appears to me that Sergeant Troy does not concern us here,' she said intractably. 'Yet I must say that Sergeant Troy is an educated man, and quite worthy of any woman. He is well born.'

'His being higher in learning and birth than the ruck o' soldiers is anything but a proof of his worth. It shows his course to be down'ard.'

'I cannot see what this has to do with our conversation. Mr Troy's course is not by any means downward; and his superiority *is* a proof of his worth!'

'I believe him to have no conscience at all. And I cannot help begging you, miss, to have nothing to do with him. Listen to me this once – only this once! I don't say he's such a bad man as I have fancied – I pray to God he is not. But since we don't exactly know what he is, why not behave as if he *might* be bad, simply for your own safety? Don't trust him, mistress; I ask you not to trust him so.'

'Why, pray?'

'I like soldiers, but this one I do not like,' he said sturdily. 'His cleverness in his calling may have tempted him astray, and what is mirth to the neighbours is ruin to the woman. When he tries to talk to 'ee again, why not turn away with a short "Good Day"; and when you see him coming one way, turn the other. When he says anything laughable, fail to see the point and don't smile, and speak of him before those who will report your talk as "that fantastical man", or "that Sergent What's-his-name". "That man of a family that has come to the dogs." Don't be unmannerly towards en, but harmless–uncivil, and so get rid of the man.'

No Christmas robin detained by a window-pane ever pulsed as did Bathsheba now.

'I say – I say again – that it doesn't become you to talk about him. Why he should be mentioned passes me quite!' she exclaimed desperately. 'I know this, th-th-that he is a thoroughly conscientious man – blunt sometimes even to rudeness – but always speaking his mind about you plain to your face!'

'Oh.'

'He is as good as anybody in this parish! He is very particular, too, about going to church – yes, he is!'

'I am afeard nobody ever saw him there. I never did, certainly.'

'The reason of that is,' she said eagerly, 'that he goes in privately by the old tower door, just when the service commences, and sits at the back of the gallery. He told me so.'

This supreme instance of Troy's goodness fell upon Gabriel's ears like the thirteenth stroke of a crazy clock. It was not only received with utter incredulity as regarded itself, but threw a doubt on all the assurances that had preceded it.

Oak was grieved to find how entirely she trusted him. He brimmed with deep feeling as he replied in a steady voice, the steadiness of which was spoilt by the palpableness of his great effort to keep it so:

'You know, mistress, that I love you, and shall love you always. I only mention this to bring to your mind that at any rate I would wish to do you no harm; beyond that I put it aside. I have lost in the race for money and good things, and I am not such a fool as to pretend to 'ee now I am poor, and you have got altogether above me. But Bathsheba, dear mistress, this I beg you to consider – that, both to keep yourself well honoured among the workfolk, and in common generosity to an honourable man who loves you as well as I, you should be more discreet in your bearing towards this soldier.'

'Don't, don't, don't!' she exclaimed, in a choking voice.

'Are ye not more to me than my own affairs, and even life!' he went on. 'Come, listen to me! I am six years older than you, and Mr Boldwood is ten years older than I, and consider – I do beg of 'ee to consider before it is too late – how safe you would be in his hands!'

Oak's allusion to his own love for her lessened, to some extent, her anger at his interference; but she could not really forgive him for letting his wish to marry her be eclipsed by his wish to do her good, any more than for his slighting treatment of Troy.

'I wish you to go elsewhere,' she commanded, a paleness of face invisible to the eye being suggested by the trembling words. 'Do not remain on this farm any longer. I don't want you – I beg you to go!'

'That's nonsense,' said Oak calmly. 'This is the second time you have pretended to dismiss me; and what's the use o' it?'

'Pretended! You shall go, sir – your lecturing I will not hear! I am mistress here.'

'Go, indeed – what folly will you say next? Treating me like Dick, Tom and Harry when you know that a short time ago my position was as good as yours! Upon my life, Bathsheba, it is too barefaced. You know, too, that I can't go without putting things in such a strait as you wouldn't get out of I can't tell when. Unless, indeed, you'll promise to have an understanding man as bailiff, or manager, or something. I'll go at once if you'll promise that.'

'I shall have no bailiff; I shall continue to be my own manager,' she said decisively.

'Very well, then; you should be thankful to me for biding. How would the farm go on with nobody to mind it but a woman? But mind this. I don't wish 'ee to feel you owe me anything. Not I. What I do, I do. Sometimes I say I should be as glad as a bird to leave the place – for don't suppose I'm content to be a nobody. I was made for better things. However, I don't like to see your concerns going to ruin, as they must if you keep in this mind . . . I hate taking my own measure so plain, but, upon my life, your provoking ways make a man say what he wouldn't dream of at other times! I own to being rather interfering. But you know well enough how it is, and who she is that I like too well, and feel too much like a fool about to be civil to her!'

It is more than probable that she privately and unconsciously respected him a little for this grim fidelity, which had been shown in his tone even more than in his words. At any rate she murmured something to the effect that he might stay if he wished. She said more distinctly, 'Will you leave me alone now? I don't order it as a mistress – I ask it as a woman, and I expect you not to be so uncourteous as to refuse.'

'Certainly I will, Miss Everdene,' said Gabriel gently. He wondered that the request should have come at this moment, for the strife was over, and they were on a most desolate hill, far from every human habitation, and the hour was getting late. He stood still and allowed her to get far ahead of him till he could only see her form upon the sky.

A distressing explanation of this anxiety to be rid of him at that point now ensued. A figure apparently rose from the earth beside her. The shape beyond all doubt was Troy's. Oak would not be even a possible listener, and at once turned back till a good two hundred yards were between the lovers and himself.

Gabriel went home by way of the churchyard. In passing the tower he thought of what she had said about the sergeant's virtuous habit of entering the church unperceived at the beginning of service. Believing that the little gallery door alluded to was quite disused, he ascended the external flight of steps at the top of which it stood, and examined it. The pale lustre yet hanging in the north-western heaven was sufficient to show that a sprig of ivy had grown from the wall across the door to a length of more than a foot, delicately tying the panel to the stone jamb. It was a decisive proof that the door had not been opened at least since Troy came · back to Weatherbury.

* XXX *

Hot Cheeks and Tearful Eyes

HALF an hour later Bathsheba entered her own house. There burnt upon her face when she met the light of the candles the flush and excitement which were little less than chronic with her now. The farewell words of Troy, who had accompanied her to the very door, still lingered in her ears. He had bidden her adieu for two days, which were, so he stated, to be spent at Bath in visiting some friends. He had also kissed her a second time.

It is only fair to Bathsheba to explain here a little fact which did not come to light till a long time afterwards: that Troy's presentation of himself so aptly at the roadside this evening was not by any distinctly preconcerted arrangement. He had hinted – she had forbidden; and it was only on the chance of his still coming that she had dismissed Oak, fearing a meeting between them just then.

She now sank down into a chair, wild and perturbed by all these new and fevering sequences. Then she jumped up with a manner of decision, and fetched her desk from a side table.

In three minutes, without pause or modification, she had written a letter to Boldwood, at his address beyond Casterbridge, saying mildly but firmly that she had well considered the whole subject he had brought before her and kindly given her time to decide upon; that her final decision was that she could not marry him. She had expressed to Oak an intention to wait till Boldwood came home before communicating to him her conclusive reply. But Bathsheba found that she could not wait.

It was impossible to send this letter till the next day; yet to quell her uneasiness by getting it out of her hands, and so, as it were, setting the act in motion at once, she arose to take it to any one of the women who might be in the kitchen.

She paused in the passage. A dialogue was going on in the kitchen, and Bathsheba and Troy were the subject of it.

'If he marry her, she'll gie up farming.'

' 'Twill be a gallant life, but may bring some trouble between the mirth – so say I.'

'Well, I wish I had half such a husband.'

Bathsheba had too much sense to mind seriously what her servitors said about her; but too much womanly redundance of speech to leave alone what was said till it died the natural death of unminded things. She burst in upon them.

'Who are you speaking of?' she asked.

There was a pause before anybody replied. At last Liddy said frankly, 'What was passing was a bit of a word about yourself, miss.'

'I thought so! Maryann and Liddy and Temperance – now I forbid you to suppose such things. You know I don't care the least for Mr Troy – not I. Everybody knows how much I hate him. – Yes,' repeated the froward young person, '*hate* him!'

'We know you do, miss,' said Liddy; 'and so do we all.'

'I hate him too,' said Maryann.

'Maryann – O you perjured woman! How can you speak that wicked story!' said Bathsheba excitedly. 'You admired him from your heart only this morning in the very world, you did. Yes. Maryann, you know it!'

'Yes, miss, but so did you. He is a wild scamp now, and you are right to hate him.'

'He's *not* a wild scamp! How dare you to my face! I have no right to hate him, nor you, nor anybody. But I am a silly woman! What is it to me what he is? You know it is nothing. I don't care for him; I don't mean to defend his good name, not I. Mind this, if any of you say a word against him you'll be dismissed instantly!'

She flung down the letter and surged back into the parlour, with a big heart and tearful eyes, Liddy following her.

'O miss!' said mild Liddy, looking pitifully into Bathsheba's face. 'I am sorry we mistook you so! I did think you cared for him; but I see you don't now.'

'Shut the door, Liddy.'

Liddy closed the door, and went on: 'People always say such foolery, miss. I'll make answer hencefor'ard, "Of course a lady like Miss Everdene can't love him", I'll say it out in plain black and white.'

Bathsheba burst out: 'O Liddy, are you such a simpleton? Can't you read riddles? Can't you see? Are you a woman yourself?'

Liddy's clear eyes rounded with wonderment.

'Yes; you must be a blind thing, Liddy!' she said in reckless abandonment and grief. 'Oh, I love him to very distraction and misery and agony! Don't be frightened at me, though perhaps I am enough to frighten any innocent woman. Come closer – closer.' She put her arms round Liddy's neck. 'I must let it out to somebody; it is wearing me away! Don't you yet know enough of me to see through that miserable denial of mine? O God, what a lie it was! Heaven and my Love forgive me. And don't you know that a woman who loves at all thinks nothing of perjury when it is balanced against her love? There, go out of the room; I want to be quite alone.'

Liddy went towards the door.

'Liddy, come here. Solemnly swear to me that he's not a fast man; that it is all lies they say about him!'

'But, miss, how can I say he is not if –'

'You graceless girl! How can you have the cruel heart to repeat what they say? Unfeeling thing that you are . . . But *I'll* see if you or anybody else in the village, or town either, dare do such a thing!' She started off, pacing from fireplace to door, and back again.

'No, miss. I don't – I know it is not true!' said Liddy, frightened at Bathsheba's unwonted vehemence.

'I suppose you only agree with me like that to please me. But Liddy, he *cannot be* bad, as is said. Do you hear?'

'Yes, miss, yes.'

'And you don't believe he is?'

'I don't know what to say, miss,' said Liddy, beginning to cry. 'If I say No, you don't believe me; and if I say Yes, you rage at me!'

'Say you don't believe it – say you don't!'

'I don't believe him to be so bad as they make out.'

'He is not bad at all . . . My poor life and heart, how weak I am!' she moaned, in a relaxed, desultory way, heedless of Liddy's presence. 'O, how I wish I had never seen him! Loving is misery for women always. I shall never forgive God for making me a woman, and dearly am I beginning to pay for the honour of owning a pretty face.' She freshened and turned to Liddy suddenly. 'Mind this, Lydia Smallbury, if you repeat anywhere a single word of what I have said to you inside this closed door, I'll never trust you, or love you, or have you with me a moment longer – not a moment!'

'I don't want to repeat anything,' said Liddy, with womanly dignity of a diminutive order; 'but I don't wish to stay with you. And, if you please, I'll go at the end of the harvest, or this week, or today . . . I don't see that I deserve to be put upon and stormed at for nothing!' concluded the small woman, bigly.

'No, no, Liddy; you must stay!' said Bathsheba, dropping from haughtiness to entreaty with capricious inconsequence. 'You must not notice my being in a taking just now. You are not as a servant – you are a companion to me. Dear, dear – I don't know what I am doing since this miserable ache o' my heart has weighted and worn upon me so! What shall I come to! I suppose I shall get further and further into troubles. I wonder sometimes if I am doomed to die in the Union. I am friendless enough, God knows!'

'I won't notice anything, nor will I leave you!' sobbed Liddy, impulsively putting up her lips to Bathsheba's, and kissing her.

Then Bathsheba kissed Liddy, and all was smooth again.

'I don't often cry, do I, Lidd? but you have made tears come into my eyes,' she said, a smile shining through the moisture. 'Try to think him a good man, won't you, dear Liddy?'

'I will, miss, indeed.'

'He is a sort of steady man in a wild way, you know. That's better than to be as some are, wild in a steady way. I am afraid that's how I am. And promise me to keep my secret – do, Liddy! And do not let them know that I have been crying about him, because it will be dreadful for me, and no good to him, poor thing!'

'Death's head himself shan't wring it from me, mistress, if I've a mind to keep anything; and I'll always be your friend,' replied Liddy emphatically, at the same time bringing a few more tears into her own eyes, not from any particular necessity, but from an artistic sense of making herself in keeping with the remainder of the picture, which seems to influence women at such times. 'I think God likes us to be good friends, don't you?'

'Indeed I do.'

'And, dear miss, you won't harry me and storm at me, will you? because you seem to swell so tall as a lion then, and it frightens me! Do you know, I fancy you would be a match for any man when you are in one o' your takings.'

'Never! do you?' said Bathsheba, slightly laughing, though somewhat seriously alarmed by this Amazonian picture of herself. 'I hope I am not a bold sort of maid – mannish?' she continued with some anxiety.

'O no, not mannish; but so almighty womanish that 'tis getting on that way sometimes. Ah! miss,' she said, after having drawn her breath very sadly in and sent it very sadly out, 'I wish I had half your failing that way. 'Tis a great protection to a poor maid in these illegit'mate days!'

* XXXI *

Blame – Fury

THE next evening Bathsheba, with the idea of getting out of the way of Mr Boldwood in the event of his returning to answer her note in person, proceeded to fulfil an engagement made with Liddy some few hours earlier. Bathsheba's companion, as a gage of their reconciliation, had been granted a week's holiday to visit her sister, who was married to a thriving hurdler and cattle-crib-maker living in a delightful labyrinth of hazel copse not far beyond Yalbury. The arrangement was that Miss Everdene should honour them by coming there for a day or two to inspect some ingenious contrivances which this man of the woods had introduced into his wares.

Leaving her instructions with Gabriel and Maryann, that they were to see everything carefully locked up for the night, she went out of the house just at the close of a timely thunder-shower, which had refined the air, and daintily bathed the coat of the land, though all beneath was dry as ever. Freshness was exhaled in an essence from the varied contours of bank and hollow, as if the earth breathed maiden breath; and the pleased birds were hymning to the scene. Before her, among the clouds, there was a contrast in the shape of lairs of fierce light which showed themselves in the neighbourhood of a hidden sun, lingering on to the farthest north-west corner of the heavens that his midsummer season allowed.

She had walked nearly two miles of her journey, watching how the day was retreating, and thinking how the time of deeds was quietly melting into the time of thought, to give place in its turn to the time of prayer and sleep, when she beheld advancing over Yalbury hill the very man she sought so anxiously to elude. Boldwood was stepping on, not with that quiet tread of reserved strength which was his customary gait, in which he always seemed to be balancing two thoughts. His manner was stunned and sluggish now.

Boldwood had for the first time been awakened to woman's privileges in tergiversation even when it involves another person's possible blight. That Bathsheba was a firm and positive girl, far less inconsequent than her fellows, had been the very lung of his hope; for he had held that these qualities would lead her to adhere to a straight course for consistency's sake, and accept him, though her fancy might not flood him with the iridescent hues of uncritical love. But the argument now came back as sorry gleams from a broken mirror. The discovery was no less a scourge than a surprise.

He came on looking upon the ground, and did not see Bathsheba till they were less than a stone's throw apart. He looked up at the sound of her pit-pat, and his changed appearance sufficiently denoted to her the depth and strength of the feelings paralysed by her letter.

'Oh; is it you, Mr Boldwood?' she faltered, a guilty warmth pulsing in her face.

Those who have the power of reproaching in silence may find it a means more effective than words. There are accents in the eye which are not on the tongue, and more tales come from pale lips than can enter an ear. It is both the grandeur and the pain of the remoter moods that they avoid the pathway of sound. Boldwood's look was unanswerable.

Seeing she turned a little aside, he said, 'What, are you afraid of me?'

'Why should you say that?' said Bathsheba.

'I fancied you looked so,' said he. 'And it is most strange, because of its contrast with my feeling for you.'

She regained self-possession, fixed her eyes calmly, and waited.

'You know what that feeling is,' continued Boldwood deliberately. 'A thing strong as death. No dismissal by a hasty letter affects that.'

'I wish you did not feel so strongly about me,' she murmured. 'It is generous of you, and more than I deserve, but I must not hear it now.'

'Hear it? What do you think I have to say, then? I am not to marry you, and that's enough. Your letter was excellently plain. I want you to hear nothing – not I.'

Bathsheba was unable to direct her will into any definite groove for freeing herself from this fearfully awkward position. She confusedly said, 'Good evening', and was moving on. Boldwood walked up to her heavily and dully.

'Bathsheba – darling – is it final indeed?'

'Indeed it is.'

'O Bathsheba – have pity upon me!' Boldwood burst out. 'God's sake, yes – I am come to that low, lowest stage – to ask a woman for pity! Still, she is you – she is you.'

Bathsheba commanded herself well. But she could hardly get a clear voice for what came instinctively to her lips: 'There is little honour to the woman in that speech.' It was only whispered, for something unutterably mournful no less than distressing in this spectacle of a man showing himself to be so entirely the vane of a passion enervated the feminine instinct for punctilios.

'I am beyond myself about this, and am mad,' he said. 'I am no stoic at all to be supplicating here; but I do supplicate to you. I wish you knew what is in me of devotion to you; but it is impossible, that. In bare human mercy to a lonely man, don't throw me off now!'

'I don't throw you off – indeed, how can I? I never had you.' In her noon-clear sense that she had never loved him she forgot for a moment her thoughtless angle on that day in February.

'But there was a time when you turned to me, before I thought of you! I don't reproach you, for even now I feel that the ignorant and cold darkness that I should have lived in if you had not attracted me by that letter – valentine you call it – would have been worse than my knowledge of you, though it has brought this misery. But, I say, there was a time when I knew nothing of you, and cared nothing for you, and yet you drew me on. And if you say you gave me no encouragement, I cannot but contradict you.'

'What you call encouragement was the childish game of an idle minute. I have bitterly repented of it – ay, bitterly, and in tears. Can you still go on reminding me?'

'I don't accuse you of it – I deplore it. I took for earnest what you insist was jest, and now this that I pray to be jest you say is awful, wretched earnest. Our moods meet at wrong places. I wish your feeling was more like mine, or my feeling more like yours! O, could I but have foreseen the torture that trifling trick was going to lead me into, how I should have cursed you; but only having been able to see it since, I cannot do that for I love you too well! But it is weak, idle drivelling to go on like this . . . Bathsheba, you are the first woman of any shade or nature that I have ever looked at to love, and it is the having been so near claiming you for my own that makes this denial so hard to bear. How nearly you promised me! But I don't speak now to move your heart, and make you grieve because of my pain; it is no use, that. I must bear it; my pain would get no less by paining you.'

'But I do pity you – deeply – O, so deeply!' she earnestly said.

'Do no such thing – do no such thing. Your dear love, Bathsheba, is such a vast thing beside your pity, that the loss of your pity as well as your love is no great addition to my sorrow, nor does the gain of your pity make it sensibly less. O sweet – how dearly you spoke to me behind the spear-bed at the washing-pool, and in the barn at the shearing, and that dearest last time in the evening at your home! Where are your pleasant words all gone – your earnest hope to be able to love me? Where is your firm conviction that you would get to care for me very much? Really forgotten? – really?'

She checked emotion, looked him quietly and clearly in the face, and said in her low, firm voice, 'Mr Boldwood, I promised you nothing. Would you have had me a woman of clay when you paid me that furthest, highest compliment a man can pay a woman – telling her he loves her? I was bound to show some feeling, if I would not be a graceless shrew. Yet each of those pleasures were just for the day – the day just for the pleasure. How was I to know that what is a pastime to all other men was death to you? Have reason, do, and think more kindly of me!'

'Well, never mind arguing – never mind. One thing is sure: you were all but mine, and now you are not nearly mine. Everything is changed, and that by you alone, remember. You were nothing to me once, and I was contented; you are now nothing to me again, and how different the second nothing is from the first! Would to God you had never taken me up, since it was only to throw me down!'

Bathsheba, in spite of her mettle, began to feel unmistakable signs that she was inherently the weaker vessel. She strove miserably against this femininity which would insist upon supplying unbidden emotions in stronger and stronger current. She had tried to elude agitation by fixing her mind on the trees, sky, any trivial object before her eyes, whilst his reproaches fell, but ingenuity could not save her now.

'I did not take you up – surely I did not!' she answered as heroically as she could. 'But don't be in this mood with me. I can endure being told I am in the wrong, if you will only tell it me gently! O sir, will you not kindly forgive me, and look at it cheerfully?'

'Cheerfully! Can a man fooled to utter heart-burning find a reason for being merry? If I have lost, how can I be as if I had won? Heavens, you must be heartless quite! Had I known what a fearfully bitter sweet this was to be, how I would have avoided you, and never seen you, and been deaf to you. I tell you all this, but what do you care! You don't care.'

She returned silent and weak denials to his charges, and swayed her head desperately, as if to thrust away the words as they came showering about her ears from the lips of the trembling man in the climax of life, with his bronzed Roman face and fine frame.

'Dearest, dearest, I am wavering even now between the two opposites of recklessly renouncing you, and labouring humbly for you again. Forget that you have said No, and let it be as it was! Say, Bathsheba, that you only wrote that refusal to me in fun – come, say it to me!'

'It would be untrue, and painful to both of us. You overrate my capacity for love. I don't possess half the warmth of nature you believe me to have. An unprotected childhood in a cold world has beaten gentleness out of me.'

He immediately said with more resentment: 'That may be true, somewhat; but ah, Miss Everdene, it won't do as a reason! You are not the cold woman you would have me believe. No, no! It isn't because you have no feeling in you that you don't love me. You naturally would have me think so – you would hide from me that you have a burning heart like mine. You have love enough, but it is turned into a new channel. I know where.'

The swift music of her heart became hubbub now, and she throbbed to extremity. He was coming to Troy. He did then know what had occurred! And the name fell from his lips the next moment.

'Why did Troy not leave my treasure alone?' he asked fiercely. 'When I had no thought of injuring him, why did he force himself upon your notice! Before he worried you your inclination was to have me; when next I should have come to you your answer would have been Yes. Can you deny it – I ask, can you deny it?'

She delayed the reply, but was too honest to withhold it. 'I cannot,' she whispered.

'I know you cannot. But he stole in in my absence and robbed me. Why didn't he win you away before, when nobody would have been grieved? – when nobody would have been set tale-bearing. Now the people sneer at me – the very hills and sky seem to laugh at me till I blush shamefully for my folly. I have lost my respect, my good name, my standing – lost it, never to get it again. Go and marry your man – go on!'

'O sir – Mr Boldwood!'

'You may as well. I have no further claim upon you. As for me, I had better go somewhere alone, and hide – and pray. I loved a woman once. I am now ashamed. When I am dead they'll say, Miserable love-sick man that he was. Heaven – heaven – if I had got jilted secretly, and the dishonour not known, and my position kept! But no matter, it is gone, and the woman not gained. Shame upon him – shame!'

His unreasonable anger terrified her, and she glided from him, without obviously moving, as she said, 'I am only a girl – do not speak to me so!'

'All the time you knew – how very well you knew – that your new freak was my misery. Dazzled by brass and scarlet – O, Bathsheba – this is woman's folly indeed!'

She fired up at once. 'You are taking too much upon yourself!' she said vehemently. 'Everybody is upon me – everybody. It is unmanly to attack a woman so! I have nobody in the world to fight my battles for me; but no mercy is shown. Yet if a thousand of you sneer and say things against me, I *will not* be put down.'

'You'll chatter with him doubtless about me. Say to him, "Boldwood would have died for me." Yes, and you have given way to him, knowing him to be not the man for you. He has kissed you – claimed you as his. Do you hear – he has kissed you. Deny it!'

The most tragic woman is cowed by a tragic man, and although Boldwood was, in vehemence and glow, nearly her own self rendered into another sex, Bathsheba's cheek quivered. She gasped, 'Leave me, sir – leave me! I am nothing to you. Let me go on!'

'Deny that he has kissed you.'

'I shall not.'

'Ha – then he has!' came hoarsely from the farmer.

'He has,' she said slowly, and, in spite of her fear, defiantly. 'I am not ashamed to speak the truth.'

'Then curse him; and curse him!' said Boldwood, breaking into a whispered fury. 'Whilst I would have given worlds to touch your hand, you have let a rake come in without right or ceremony and – kiss you! Heaven's mercy – kiss you! . . . Ah, a time of his life shall come when he will have to repent, and think wretchedly of the pain he has caused another man; and then may he ache, and wish, and curse, and yearn – as I do now!'

'Don't, don't, O, don't pray down evil upon him!' she implored in a miserable cry. 'Anything but that – anything. O, be kind to him, sir, for I love him true!'

Boldwood's ideas had reached that point of fusion at which outline and consistency entirely disappear. The impending night appeared to concentrate in his eye. He did not hear her at all now.

'I'll punish him – by my soul, that will I! I'll meet him, soldier or no, and I'll horsewhip the untimely stripling for this reckless theft of my one delight. If he were a hundred men I'd horsewhip him –' He dropped his voice suddenly and unnaturally. 'Bathsheba, sweet, lost coquette, pardon me! I've been blaming you, threatening you, behaving like a churl to you, when he's the greatest sinner. He stole your dear heart away with his unfathomable lies! . . . It is a fortunate thing for him that he's gone back to his regiment – that he's away up the country, and not here! I hope he may not return here just yet. I pray God he may not come into my sight, for I may be tempted beyond myself. O, Bathsheba, keep him away – yes, keep him away from me!'

For a moment Boldwood stood so inertly after this that his soul seemed to have been entirely exhaled with the breath of his passionate words. He turned his face away, and withdrew, and his form was soon covered over by the twilight as his footsteps mixed in with the low hiss of the leafy trees.

Bathsheba, who had been standing motionless as a model all this latter time, flung her hands to her face, and wildly attempted to ponder on the exhibition which had just passed away. Such astounding wells of fevered feeling in a still man like Mr Boldwood were incomprehensible, dreadful. Instead of being a man trained to repression he was – what she had seen him.

The force of the farmer's threats lay in their relation to a circumstance known at present only to herself: her lover was coming back to Weatherbury in the course of the very next day or two. Troy had not returned to his distant barracks as Boldwood and others supposed, but had merely gone to visit some acquaintance in Bath, and had yet a week or more remaining to his furlough.

She felt wretchedly certain that if he revisited her just at this nick of time, and came into contact with Boldwood, a fierce quarrel would be the consequence. She panted with solicitude when she thought of possible injury to Troy. The least spark would kindle the farmer's swift feelings of rage and jealousy; he would lose his self-mastery as he had this evening; Troy's blitheness might become aggressive; it might take the direction of derision, and Boldwood's anger might then take the direction of revenge.

With almost a morbid dread of being thought a gushing girl, this guideless woman too well concealed from the world under a manner of carelessness the warm depths of her strong emotions. But now there was no reserve. In her distraction, instead of advancing further she walked up and down, beating the air with her fingers, pressing her brow, and sobbing brokenly to herself. Then she sat down on a heap of stones by the wayside to think. There she remained long. Above the dark margin of the earth appeared foreshores and promontories of coppery cloud, bounding a green and pellucid expanse in the western sky. Amaranthine glosses came over them then, and the unresting world wheeled her round to a contrasting prospect eastward, in the shape of indecisive and palpitating stars. She gazed upon their silent throes amid the shades of space, but realized none at all. Her troubled spirit was far away with Troy.

* XXXII *

Night – Horses tramping

THE village of Weatherbury was quiet as the graveyard in its midst, and
the living were lying well-nigh as still as the dead. The church clock
struck eleven. The air was so empty of other sounds that the whirr of the
clock-work immediately before the strokes was distinct, and so was also
the click of the same at their close. The notes flew forth with the usual
blind obtuseness of inanimate things – flapping and rebounding among
walls, undulating against the scattered clouds, spreading through their
interstices into unexplored miles of space.

Bathsheba's crannied and mouldy halls were tonight occupied only by
Maryann, Liddy being, as was stated, with her sister, whom Bathsheba
had set out to visit. A few minutes after eleven had struck, Maryann
turned in her bed with a sense of being disturbed. She was totally
unconscious of the nature of the interruption to her sleep. It led to a
dream, and the dream to an awakening, with an uneasy sensation that
something had happened. She left her bed and looked out of the window.
The paddock abutted on this end of the building, and in the paddock she
could just discern by the uncertain grey a moving figure approaching the
horse that was feeding there. The figure seized the horse by the forelock,
and led it to the corner of the field. Here she could see some object which
circumstances proved to be a vehicle, for after a few minutes spent
apparently in harnessing, she heard the trot of the horse down the road,
mingled with the sound of light wheels.

Two varieties only of humanity could have entered the paddock with
the ghost-like glide of that mysterious figure. They were a woman and
a gipsy man. A woman was out of the question in such an occupation at
this hour, and the comer could be no less than a thief, who might
probably have known the weakness of the household on this particular
night, and have chosen it on that account for his daring attempt.
Moreover, to raise suspicion to conviction itself, there were gipsies in
Weatherbury Bottom.

Maryann, who had been afraid to shout in the robber's presence,
having seen him depart had no fear. She hastily slipped on her clothes,
stumped down the disjointed staircase with its hundred creaks, ran to
Coggan's, the nearest house, and raised an alarm. Coggan called Gabriel,
who now again lodged in his house as at first, and together they went to
the paddock. Beyond all doubt the horse was gone.

'Hark!' said Gabriel.

They listened. Distinct upon the stagnant air came the sounds of a
trotting horse passing up Longpuddle Lane – just beyond the gipsies'
encampment in Weatherbury Bottom.

'That's our Dainty – I'll swear to her step,' said Jan.

'Mighty me! Won't mis'ess storm and call us stupids when she comes back!' moaned Maryann. 'How I wish it had happened when she was at home, and none of us had been answerable!'

'We must ride after,' said Gabriel decisively. 'I'll be responsible to Miss Everdene for what we do. Yes, we'll follow.'

'Faith, I don't see how,' said Coggan. 'All our horses are too heavy for that trick except little Poppet, and what's she between two of us? – if we only had that pair over the hedge we might do something.'

'Which pair?'

'Mr Boldwood's Tidy and Moll.'

'Then wait here till I come hither again,' said Gabriel. He ran down the hill towards Farmer Boldwood's.

'Farmer Boldwood is not at home,' said Maryann.

'All the better,' said Coggan. 'I know what he's gone for.'

Less than five minutes brought up Oak again, running at the same pace, with two halters dangling from his hand.

'Where did you find 'em?' said Coggan, turning round and leaping upon the hedge without waiting for an answer.

'Under the eaves. I knew where they were kept,' said Gabriel, following him. 'Coggan, you can ride bare-backed? there's no time to look for saddles.'

'Like a hero!' said Jan.

'Maryann, you go to bed,' Gabriel shouted to her from the top of the hedge.

Springing down into Boldwood's pastures, each pocketed his halter to hide it from the horses, who, seeing the men empty-handed, docilely allowed themselves to be seized by the mane, when the halters were dexterously slipped on. Having neither bit nor bridle, Oak and Coggan extemporized the former by passing the rope in each case through the animal's mouth and looping it on the other side. Oak vaulted astride, and Coggan clambered up by aid of the bank, when they ascended to the gate and galloped off in the direction taken by Bathsheba's horse and the robber. Whose vehicle the horse had been harnessed to was a matter of some uncertainty.

Weatherbury Bottom was reached in three or four minutes. They scanned the shady green patch by the roadside. The gipsies were gone.

'The villains!' said Gabriel. 'Which way have they gone, I wonder?'

'Straight on, as sure as God made little apples,' said Jan.

'Very well; we are better mounted, and must overtake 'em,' said Oak. 'Now, on at full speed!'

No sound of the rider in their van could now be discovered. The road-metal grew softer and more clayey as Weatherbury was left behind, and the late rain had wetted its surface to a somewhat plastic, but not muddy state. They came to cross-roads. Coggan suddenly pulled up Moll and slipped off.

'What's the matter?' said Gabriel.

'We must try to track 'em, since we can't hear 'em,' said Jan, fumbling in his pockets. He struck a light, and held the match to the ground. The rain had been heavier here, and all foot and horse tracks made previous to the storm had been abraded and blurred by the drops, and they were now so many little scoops of water, which reflected the flame of the match like eyes. One set of tracks was fresh and had no water in them; one pair of ruts was also empty, and not small canals, like the others. The footprints forming this recent impression were full of information as to pace; they were in equidistant pairs, three or four feet apart, the right and left foot of each pair being exactly opposite one another.

'Straight on!' Jan exclaimed. 'Tracks like that mean a stiff gallop. No wonder we don't hear him. And the horse is harnessed – look at the ruts. Ay, that's our mare, sure enough!'

'How do you know?'

'Old Jimmy Harris only shoed her last week, and I'd swear to his make among ten thousand.'

'The rest of the gipsies must ha' gone on earlier, or some other way,' said Oak. 'You saw there were no other tracks?'

'True.' They rode along silently for a long weary time. Coggan carried an old pinchbeck repeater which he had inherited from some genius in his family; and it now struck one. He lighted another match, and examined the ground again.

"Tis a canter now,' he said, throwing away the light. 'A twisty, rickety pace for a gig. The fact is, they overdrove her at starting; we shall catch 'em yet.'

Again they hastened on, and entered Blackmore Vale. Coggan's watch struck two. When they looked again the hoof-marks were so spaced as to form a sort of zigzag if united, like the lamps along a street.

'That's a trot, I know,' said Gabriel.

'Only a trot now,' said Coggan cheerfully. 'We shall overtake him in time.'

They pushed rapidly on for yet two or three miles. 'Ah! a moment,' said Jan. 'Let's see how she was driven up this hill. 'Twill help us.' A light was promptly struck upon his gaiters as before, and the examination made.

'Hurrah!' said Coggan. 'She walked up here – and well she might. We shall get them in two miles, for a crown.'

They rode three, and listened. No sound was to be heard save a mill-pond trickling hoarsely through a hatch, and suggesting gloomy possibilities of drowning by jumping in. Gabriel dismounted when they came to a turning. The tracks were absolutely the only guide as to the direction that they now had, and great caution was necessary to avoid confusing them with some others which had made their appearance lately.

'What does this mean? – though I guess,' said Gabriel, looking up at Coggan as he moved the match over the ground about the turning. Coggan, who, no less than the panting horses, had latterly shown signs of weariness, again scrutinized the mystic characters. This time only three were of the regular horseshoe shape. Every fourth was a dot.

He screwed up his face, and emitted a long 'whew-w-w!'

'Lame,' said Oak.

'Yes. Dainty is lamed; the near-foot-afore,' said Coggan slowly, staring still at the footprints.

'We'll push on,' said Gabriel, remounting his humid steed.

Although the road along its greater part had been as good as any turnpike-road in the country, it was nominally only a byway. The last turning had brought them into the high road leading to Bath. Coggan recollected himself.

'We shall have him now!' he exclaimed.

'Where?'

'Sherton Turnpike. The keeper of that gate is the sleepiest man between here and London – Dan Randall, that's his name – knowed en for years, when he was at Casterbridge gate. Between the lameness and the gate 'tis a done job.'

They now advanced with extreme caution. Nothing was said until, against a shady background of foliage, five white bars were visible, crossing their route a little way ahead.

'Hush – we are almost close!' said Gabriel.

'Amble on upon the grass,' said Coggan.

The white bars were blotted out in the midst by a dark shape in front of them. The silence of this lonely time was pierced by an exclamation from that quarter.

'Hoy-a-hoy! Gate!'

It appeared that there had been a previous call which they had not noticed, for on their close approach the door of the turnpike-house opened, and the keeper came out half-dressed, with a candle in his hand. The rays illumined the whole group.

'Keep the gate close!' shouted Gabriel. 'He has stolen the horse!'

'Who?' said the turnpike-man.

Gabriel looked at the driver of the gig, and saw a woman – Bathsheba, his mistress.

On hearing his voice she had turned her face away from the light. Coggan had, however, caught sight of her in the meanwhile.

'Why, 'tis mistress – I'll take my oath!' he said, amazed.

Bathsheba it certainly was, and she had by this time done the trick she could do so well in crises not of love, namely, mask a surprise by coolness of manner.

'Well, Gabriel,' she inquired quietly, 'where are you going?'

'We thought –' began Gabriel.

'I am driving to Bath,' she said, taking for her own use the assurance that Gabriel lacked. 'An important matter made it necessary for me to give up my visit to Liddy, and go off at once. What, then, were you following me?'

'We thought the horse was stole.'

'Well – what a thing! How very foolish of you not to know that I had taken the trap and horse. I could neither wake Maryann nor get into the house, though I hammered for ten minutes against her window-sill. Fortunately, I could get the key of the coach-house, so I troubled no one further. Didn't you think it might be me?'

'Why should we, miss?'

'Perhaps not. Why, those are never Farmer Boldwood's horses! Goodness mercy! what have you been doing – bringing trouble upon me in this way? What! mustn't a lady move an inch from her door without being dogged like a thief?'

'But how was we to know, if you left no account of your doings?' expostulated Coggan, 'and ladies don't drive at these hours, miss, as a jineral rule of society.'

'I did leave an account – and you would have seen it in the morning. I wrote in chalk on the coach-house doors that I had come back for the horse and gig, and driven off; that I could arouse nobody, and should return soon.'

'But you'll consider, ma'am, that we couldn't see that till it got daylight.'

'True,' she said, and though vexed at first she had too much sense to blame them long or seriously for a devotion to her that was as valuable as it was rare. She added with a very pretty grace, 'Well, I really thank you heartily for taking all this trouble; but I wish you had borrowed anybody's horses but Mr Boldwood's.'

'Dainty is lame, miss,' said Coggan. 'Can ye go on?'

'It was only a stone in her shoe. I got down and pulled it out a hundred yards back. I can manage very well, thank you. I shall be in Bath by daylight. Will you now return, please?'

She turned her head – the gateman's candle shimmering upon her quick, clear eyes as she did so – passed through the gate, and was soon wrapped in the embowering shades of mysterious summer boughs. Coggan and Gabriel put about their horses, and, fanned by the velvety air of this July night, retraced the road by which they had come.

'A strange vagary, this of hers, isn't it, Oak?' said Coggan curiously.

'Yes,' said Gabriel shortly.

'She won't be in Bath by no daylight!'

'Coggan, suppose we keep this night's work as quiet as we can?'

'I am of one and the same mind.'

'Very well. We shall be home by three o'clock or so, and can creep into the parish like lambs.'

Bathsheba's perturbed meditations by the roadside had ultimately evolved a conclusion that there were only two remedies for the present desperate state of affairs. The first was merely to keep Troy away from Weatherbury till Boldwood's indignation had cooled; the second to listen to Oak's entreaties, and Boldwood's denunciations, and give up Troy altogether.

Alas! Could she give up this new love – induce him to renounce her by saying she did not like him – could no more speak to him, and beg him, for her good, to end his furlough in Bath, and see her and Weatherbury no more?

It was a picture full of misery, but for a while she contemplated it firmly, allowing herself, nevertheless, as girls will, to dwell upon the happy life she would have enjoyed had Troy been Boldwood, and the path of love the path of duty – inflicting upon herself gratuitous tortures by imagining him the lover of another woman after forgetting her; for she had penetrated Troy's nature so far as to estimate his tendencies pretty accurately, but unfortunately loved him no less in thinking that he might soon cease to love her – indeed, considerably more.

She jumped to her feet. She would see him at once. Yes, she would implore him by word of mouth to assist her in this dilemma. A letter to keep him away could not reach him in time, even if he should be disposed to listen to it.

Was Bathsheba altogether blind to the obvious fact that the support of a lover's arms is not of a kind best calculated to assist a resolve to renounce him? Or was she sophistically sensible, with a thrill of pleasure, that by adopting this course for getting rid of him she was ensuring a meeting with him, at any rate, once more?

It was now dark, and the hour must have been nearly ten. The only way to accomplish her purpose was to give up her idea of visiting Liddy at Yalbury, return to Weatherbury Farm, put the horse into the gig, and drive at once to Bath. The scheme seemed at first impossible: the journey was a fearfully heavy one, even for a strong horse, at her own estimate; and she much underrated the distance. It was most venturesome for a woman, at night, and alone.

But could she go on to Liddy's and leave things to take their course? No, no; anything but that. Bathsheba was full of a stimulating turbulence, beside which caution vainly prayed for a hearing. She turned back towards the village.

Her walk was slow, for she wished not to enter Weatherbury till the cottagers were in bed, and, particularly, till Boldwood was secure. Her plan was now to drive to Bath during the night, see Sergeant Troy in the morning before he set out to come to her, bid him farewell, and dismiss him: then to rest the horse thoroughly (herself to weep the while, she thought), starting early the next morning on her return journey. By this arrangement she could trot Dainty gently all the day, reach Liddy at Yalbury in the evening, and come home to Weatherbury with her whenever they chose – so nobody would know she had been to Bath at all.

Such was Bathsheba's scheme. But in her topographical ignorance as a late comer to the place, she misreckoned the distance of her journey as not much more than half what it really was. Her idea, however, she proceeded to carry out, with what initial success we have already seen.

* XXXIII *

In the Sun – A Harbinger

A WEEK passed, and there were no tidings of Bathsheba; nor was there any explanation of her Gilpin's rig.

Then a note came for Maryann, stating that the business which had called her mistress to Bath still detained her there; but that she hoped to return in the course of another week.

Another week passed. The oat-harvest began, and all the men were a-field under a monochromatic Lammas sky, amid the trembling air and short shadows of noon. Indoors nothing was to be heard save the droning of blue-bottle flies; out-of-doors the whetting of scythes and the hiss of tressy oat-ears rubbing together as their perpendicular stalks of amber-yellow fell heavily to each swath. Every drop of moisture not in the men's bottles and flagons in the form of cider was raining as perspiration from their foreheads and cheeks. Drought was everywhere else.

They were about to withdraw for a while into the charitable shade of a tree in the fence, when Coggan saw a figure in a blue coat and brass buttons running to them across the field.

'I wonder who that is?' he said.

'I hope nothing is wrong about mistress,' said Maryann, who with some other women was tying the bundles (oats being always sheafed on this farm), 'but an unlucky token came to me indoors this morning. I went to unlock the door and dropped the key, and it fell upon the stone floor and broke into two pieces. Breaking a key is a dreadful bodement. I wish mis'ess was home.'

''Tis Cain Ball,' said Gabriel, pausing from whetting his reap-hook.

Oak was not bound by his agreement to assist in the cornfield; but the harvest month is an anxious time for a farmer, and the corn was Bathsheba's, so he lent a hand.

'He's dressed up in his best clothes,' said Matthew Moon. 'He hev been away from home for a few days, since he's had that felon upon his finger; for 'a said, since I can't work I'll have a hollerday.'

'A good time for one – a' excellent time,' said Joseph Poorgrass, straightening his back; for he, like some of the others, had a way of resting a while from his labour on such hot days for reasons preternaturally small; of which Cain Ball's advent on a week-day in his Sunday-clothes was one of the first magnitude. ''Twas a bad leg allowed me to read the *Pilgrim's Progress*, and Mark Clark learnt All-Fours in a whitlow.'

'Ay, and my father put his arm out of joint to have time to go courting,' said Jan Coggan, in an eclipsing tone, wiping his face with his shirt-sleeve and thrusting back his hat upon the nape of his neck.

By this time Cainy was nearing the group of harvesters, and was perceived to be carrying a large slice of bread and ham in one hand, from which he took mouthfuls as he ran, the other being wrapped in a bandage. When he came close, his mouth assumed the bell shape, and he began to cough violently.

'Now, Cainy!' said Gabriel sternly. 'How many more times must I tell you to keep from running so fast when you be eating? You'll choke yourself some day, that's what you'll do, Cain Ball.'

'Hok-hok-hok!' replied Cain. 'A crumb of my victuals went the wrong way – hok-hok! That's what 'tis, Mister Oak! And I've been visiting to Bath because I had a felon on my thumb; yes, and I've seen – ahok-hok!'

Directly Cain mentioned Bath, they all threw down their hooks and forks and drew round him. Unfortunately the erratic crumb did not improve his narrative powers, and a supplementary hindrance was that of a sneeze, jerking from his pocket his rather large watch, which dangled in front of the young man pendulum-wise.

'Yes,' he continued, directing his thoughts to Bath and letting his eyes follow, 'I've seed the world at last – yes – and I've seed our mis'ess – ahok-hok-hok!'

'Bother the boy!' said Gabriel. 'Something is always going the wrong way down your throat, so that you can't tell what's necessary to be told.'

'Ahok! there! Please, Mister Oak, a gnat have just fleed into my stomach and brought the cough on again!'

'Yes, that's just it. Your mouth is always open, you young rascal!'

''Tis terrible bad to have a gnat fly down yer throat, pore boy!' said Matthew Moon.

'Well, at Bath you saw –' prompted Gabriel.

'I saw our mistress,' continued the junior shepherd, 'and a sojer, walking along. And bymeby they got closer and closer, and then they went arm-in-crook, like courting complete – hok-hok! like courting complete – hok! – courting complete –' Losing the thread of his narrative at this point simultaneously with his loss of breath, their informant looked up and down the field apparently for some clue to it. 'Well, I see our mis'ess and a soldier – a-ha-a-wk!'

'Damn the boy!' said Gabriel.

''Tis only my manner, Mister Oak, if ye'll excuse it,' said Cain Ball, looking reproachfully at Oak, with eyes drenched in their own dew.

'Here's some cider for him – that'll cure his throat,' said Jan Coggan, lifting a flagon of cider, pulling out the cork, and applying the hole to Cainy's mouth; Joseph Poorgrass in the meantime beginning to think apprehensively of the serious consequences that would follow Cainy Ball's strangulation in his cough, and the history of his Bath adventures dying with him.

'For my poor self, I always say "please God" afore I do anything,' said Joseph, in an unboastful voice; 'and so should you, Cain Ball. 'Tis a great safeguard, and might perhaps save you from being choked to death some day.'

Mr Coggan poured the liquor with unstinted liberality at the suffering Cain's circular mouth; half of it running down the side of the flagon, and half of what reached his mouth running down outside his throat, and half of what ran in going the wrong way, and being coughed and sneezed around the persons of the gathered reapers in the form of a cider fog, which for a moment hung in the sunny air like a small exhalation.

'There's a great clumsy sneeze! Why can't ye have better manners, you young dog!' said Coggan, withdrawing the flagon.

'The cider went up my nose!' cried Cainy, as soon as he could speak; 'and now 'tis gone down my neck, and into my poor dumb felon, and over my shiny buttons and all my best cloze!'

'The poor lad's cough is terrible onfortunate,' said Matthew Moon. 'And a great history on hand, too. Bump his back, shepherd.'

''Tis my nater,' mourned Cain. 'Mother says I always was so excitable when my feelings were worked up to a point!'

'True, true,' said Joseph Poorgrass. 'The Balls were always a very excitable family. I knowed the boy's grandfather – a truly nervous and modest man, even to genteel refinery. 'Twas blush, blush with him, almost as much as 'tis with me – not but that 'tis a fault in me!'

'Not at all, Master Poorgrass,' said Coggan. ''Tis a very noble quality in ye.'

'Heh-heh! well, I wish to noise nothing abroad – nothing at all,' murmured Poorgrass diffidently. 'But we be born to things – that's true. Yet I would rather my trifle were hid; though, perhaps, a high nater is a little high, and at my birth all things were possible to my Maker, and he may have begrudged no gifts . . . But under your bushel, Joseph! under your bushel with 'ee! A strange desire, neighbours, this desire to hide, and no praise due. Yet there is a Sermon on the Mount with a calendar of the blessed at the head, and certain meek men may be named therein.'

'Cainy's grandfather was a very clever man,' said Matthew Moon. 'Invented a' apple-tree out of his own head, which is called by his name to this day – the Early Ball. You know 'em, Jan? A Quarrenden grafted on a Tom Putt, and a Rathe-ripe upon top o' that again. 'Tis trew 'a used to bide about in a public-house wi' a 'ooman in a way he had no business to by rights, but there – 'a were a clever man in the sense of the term.'

'Now then,' said Gabriel impatiently, 'what did you see, Cain?'

'I seed our mis'ess go into a sort of a park place, where there's seats, and shrubs and flowers, arm-in-crook with a sojer,' continued Cainy firmly, and with a dim sense that his words were very effective as regarded Gabriel's emotions. 'And I think the sojer was Sergeant Troy. And they sat there together for more than half-an-hour, talking moving things, and she once was crying a'most to death. And when they came out her eyes were shining and she was as white as a lily; and they looked into one another's faces, as far gone friendly as a man and woman can be.'

Gabriel's features seemed to get thinner. 'Well, what did you see besides?'

'Oh, all sorts.'

'White as a lily? You are sure 'twas she?'

'Yes.'

'Well, what besides?'

'Great glass windows to the shops, and great clouds in the sky, full of rain, and old wooden trees in the country round.'

'You stun-poll! What will ye say next?' said Coggan.

'Let en alone,' interposed Joseph Poorgrass. 'The boy's maning is that the sky and the earth in the kingdom of Bath is not altogether different from ours here. 'Tis for our good to gain knowledge of strange cities, and as such the boy's words should be suffered, so to speak it.'

'And the people of Bath,' continued Cain, 'never need to light their fires except as a luxury, for the water springs up out of the earth ready boiled for use.'

''Tis true as the light,' testified Matthew Moon. 'I've hear other navigators say the same thing.'

'They drink nothing else there,' said Cain, 'and seem to enjoy it, to see how they swaller it down.'

'Well, it seems a barbarian practice enough to us, but I daresay the natives think nothing o' it,' said Matthew.

'And don't victuals spring up as well as drink?' asked Coggan, twirling his eye.

'No – I own to a blot there in Bath – a true blot. God didn't provide 'em with victuals as well as drink, and 'twas a drawback I couldn't get over at all.'

'Well, 'tis a curious place, to say the least,' observed Moon; 'and it must be a curious people that live therein.'

'Miss Everdene and the soldier were walking about together, you say?' said Gabriel, returning to the group.

'Ay, and she wore a beautiful gold-colour silk gown, trimmed with black lace, that would have stood alone 'ithout legs inside if required. 'Twas a very winsome sight; and her hair was brushed splendid. And when the sun shone upon the bright gown and his red coat – my! how handsome they looked. You could see 'em all the length of the street.'

'And what then?' murmured Gabriel.

'And then I went into Griffin's to hae my boots hobbed, and then I went to Riggs's batty-cake shop, and asked 'em for a penneth of the cheapest and nicest stales, that were all but blue-mouldy, but not quite. And whilst I was chawing 'em down I walked on and seed a clock with a face as big as a baking trendle –'

'But that's nothing to do with mistress!'

'I'm coming to that, if you'll leave me alone, Mister Oak!' remonstrated Cainy. 'If you excites me, perhaps you'll bring on my cough, and then I shan't be able to tell ye nothing.'

'Yes – let him tell it his own way,' said Coggan.

Gabriel settled into a despairing attitude of patience, and Cainy went on:

'And there were great large houses, and more people all the week long than at Weatherbury club-walking on White Tuesdays. And I went to grand churches and chapels. And how the parson would pray! Yes; he would kneel down and put up his hands together, and make the holy gold rings on his fingers gleam and twinkle in yer eyes, that he'd earned by praying so excellent well! – Ah yes, I wish I lived there.'

'Our poor Parson Thirdly can't get no money to buy such rings,' said Matthew Moon thoughtfully. 'And as good a man as ever walked. I don't believe poor Thirdly have a single one, even of humblest tin or copper. Such a great ornament as they'd be to him on a dull a'ternoon, when he's up in the pulpit lighted by the wax candles! But 'tis impossible, poor man. Ah, to think how unequal things be.'

'Perhaps he's made of different stuff than to wear 'em,' said Gabriel grimly. 'Well, that's enough of this. Go on, Cainy – quick.'

'Oh – and the new style of pa'sons wear moustaches and long beards,' continued the illustrious traveller, 'and look like Moses and Aaron complete, and make we fokes in the congregation feel all over like the children of Israel.'

'A very right feeling – very,' said Joseph Poorgrass.

'And there's two religions going on in the nation now – High Church and High Chapel. And, thinks I, I'll play fair; so I went to High Church in the morning, and High Chapel in the afternoon.'

'A right and proper boy,' said Joseph Poorgrass.

'Well, at High Church they pray singing, and worship all the colours of the rainbow; and at High Chapel they pray preaching, and worship drab and whitewash only. And then – I didn't see no more of Miss Everdene at all.'

'Why didn't you say so afore, then?' exclaimed Oak, with much disappointment.

'Ah,' said Matthew Moon, 'she'll wish her cake dough if so be she's ever intimate with that man.'

'She's not over intimate with him,' said Gabriel indignantly.

'She would know better,' said Coggan. 'Our mis'ess has too much sense under the knots of black hair to do such a mad thing.'

'You see, he's not a coarse, ignorant man, for he was well brought up,' said Matthew dubiously. ''Twas only wildness that made him a soldier, and maids rather like your man of sin.'

'Now, Cain Ball,' said Gabriel restlessly, 'can you swear in the most awful form that the woman you saw was Miss Everdene?'

'Cain Ball, you be no longer a babe and suckling,' said Joseph in the sepulchral tone the circumstances demanded, 'and you know what taking an oath is. 'Tis a horrible testament mind ye, which you say and seal with your blood-stone, and the prophet Matthew tells us that on whomsoever it shall fall it will grind him to powder. Now, before all the workfolk here assembled, can you swear to your words as the shepherd asks ye?'

'Please no, Mister Oak!' said Cainy, looking from one to the other with great uneasiness at the spiritual magnitude of the position. 'I don't mind saying 'tis true, but I don't like to say 'tis damn true, if that's what you mane.'

'Cain, Cain, how can you?' asked Joseph sternly. 'You be asked to swear in a holy manner, and you swear like wicked Shimei, the son of Gera, who cursed as he came. Young man, fie!'

'No, I don't! 'Tis you want to squander a pore boy's soul, Joseph Poorgrass – that's what 'tis!' said Cain, beginning to cry. 'All I mane is that in common truth 'twas Miss Everdene and Sergeant Troy, but in the horrible so-help-me truth that ye want to make of it perhaps 'twas somebody else!'

'There's no getting at the rights of it,' said Gabriel, turning to his work.

'Cain Ball, you'll come to a bit of bread!' groaned Joseph Poorgrass.

Then the reapers' hooks were flourished again, and the old sounds went on. Gabriel, without making any pretence of being lively, did nothing to show that he was particularly dull. However, Coggan knew pretty nearly how the land lay, and when they were in a nook together he said –

'Don't take on about her, Gabriel. What difference does it make whose sweetheart she is, since she can't be yours?'

'That's the very thing I say to myself,' said Gabriel.

* XXXIV *

Home again – A Trickster

THAT same evening at dusk Gabriel was leaning over Coggan's garden-gate, taking an up-and-down survey before retiring to rest.

A vehicle of some kind was softly creeping along the grassy margin of the lane. From it spread the tones of two women talking. The tones were natural and not at all suppressed. Oak instantly knew the voices to be those of Bathsheba and Liddy.

The carriage came opposite and passed by. It was Miss Everdene's gig, and Liddy and her mistress were the only occupants of the seat. Liddy was asking questions about the city of Bath, and her companion was answering them listlessly and unconcernedly. Both Bathsheba and the horse seemed weary.

The exquisite relief of finding that she was here again, safe and sound, overpowered all reflection, and Oak could only luxuriate in the sense of it. All grave reports were forgotten.

He lingered and lingered on, till there was no difference between the eastern and western expanses of sky, and the timid hares began to limp courageously round the dim hillocks. Gabriel might have been there an additional half-hour when a dark form walked slowly by. 'Good-night, Gabriel,' the passer said.

It was Boldwood. 'Good-night, sir,' said Gabriel.

Boldwood likewise vanished up the road, and Oak shortly afterwards turned indoors to bed.

Farmer Boldwood went on towards Miss Everdene's house. He reached the front, and approaching the entrance, saw a light in the parlour. The blind was not drawn down, and inside the room was Bathsheba, looking over some papers or letters. Her back was towards Boldwood. He went to the door, knocked, and waited with tense muscles and an aching brow.

Boldwood had not been outside his garden since his meeting with Bathsheba in the road to Yalbury. Silent and alone, he had remained in moody meditation on woman's ways, deeming as essentials of the whole sex the accidents of the single one of their number he had ever closely beheld. By degrees a more charitable temper had pervaded him, and this was the reason of his sally tonight. He had come to apologize and beg forgiveness of Bathsheba with something like a sense of shame at his violence, having but just now learnt that she had returned – only from a visit to Liddy, as he supposed, the Bath escapade being quite unknown to him.

He inquired for Miss Everdene. Liddy's manner was odd, but he did not notice it. She went in, leaving him standing there, and in her absence the blind of the room containing Bathsheba was pulled down. Boldwood augured ill from that sign. Liddy came out.

'My mistress cannot see you, sir,' she said.

The farmer instantly went out by the gate. He was unforgiven – that was the issue of it all. He had seen her who was to him simultaneously a delight and a torture, sitting in the room he had shared with her as a peculiarly privileged guest only a little earlier in the summer, and she had denied him an entrance there now.

Boldwood did not hurry homeward. It was ten o'clock at least, when, walking deliberately through the lower part of Weatherbury, he heard the carrier's spring van entering the village. The van ran to and from a town in a northern direction, and it was owned and driven by a Weatherbury man, at the door of whose house it now pulled up. The lamp fixed to the head of the hood illuminated a scarlet and gilded form, who was the first to alight.

'Ah!' said Boldwood to himself, 'come to see her again.'

Troy entered the carrier's house, which had been the place of his lodging on his last visit to his native place. Boldwood was moved by a sudden determination. He hastened home. In ten minutes he was back again, and made as if he were going to call upon Troy at the carrier's. But as he approached, some one opened the door and came out. He heard this person say 'Good-night' to the inmates, and the voice was Troy's. This was strange, coming so immediately after his arrival. Boldwood, however, hastened up to him. Troy had what appeared to be a carpet-bag in his hand – the same that he had brought with him. It seemed as if he were going to leave again this very night.

Troy turned up the hill and quickened his pace. Boldwood stepped forward.

'Sergeant Troy?'

'Yes – I'm Sergeant Troy.'

'Just arrived from up the country, I think?'

'Just arrived from Bath.'

'I am William Boldwood.'

'Indeed.'

The tone in which this word was uttered was all that had been wanted to bring Boldwood to the point.

'I wish to speak a word with you,' he said.

'What about?'

'About her who lives just ahead there – and about a woman you have wronged.'

'I wonder at your impertinence,' said Troy, moving on.

'Now look here,' said Boldwood, standing in front of him, 'wonder or not, you are going to hold a conversation with me.'

Troy heard the dull determination in Boldwood's voice, looked at his stalwart frame, then at the thick cudgel he carried in his hand. He remembered it was past ten o'clock. It seemed worth while to be civil to Boldwood.

'Very well, I'll listen with pleasure,' said Troy, placing his bag on the ground, 'only speak low, for somebody or other may overhear us in the farmhouse there.'

'Well then – I know a good deal concerning your – Fanny Robin's attachment to you. I may say, too, that I believe I am the only person in the village, excepting Gabriel Oak, who does know it. You ought to marry her.'

'I suppose I ought. Indeed, I wish to, but I cannot.'

'Why?'

Troy was about to utter something hastily; he then checked himself and said, 'I am too poor.' His voice was changed. Previously it had had a devil-may-care tone. It was the voice of a trickster now.

Boldwood's present mood was not critical enough to notice tones. He continued, 'I may as well speak plainly; and understand, I don't wish to enter into the questions of right or wrong, woman's honour and shame, or to express any opinion on your conduct. I intend a business transaction with you.'

'I see,' said Troy. 'Suppose we sit down here.'

An old tree trunk lay under the hedge immediately opposite, and they sat down.

'I was engaged to be married to Miss Everdene,' said Boldwood, 'but you came and –'

'Not engaged,' said Troy.

'As good as engaged.'

'If I had not turned up she might have become engaged to you.'

'Hang might!'

'Would, then.'

'If you had not come I should certainly – yes, *certainly* – have been accepted by this time. If you had not seen her you might have been married to Fanny. Well, there's too much difference between Miss Everdene's station and your own for this flirtation with her ever to benefit you by ending in marriage. So all I ask is, don't molest her any more. Marry Fanny. I'll make it worth your while.'

'How will you?'

'I'll pay you well now, I'll settle a sum of money upon her, and I'll see that you don't suffer from poverty in the future. I'll put it clearly. Bathsheba is only playing with you: you are too poor for her as I said; so give up wasting your time about a great match you'll never make for a moderate and rightful match you may make tomorrow; take up your carpet-bag, turn about, leave Weatherbury now, this night, and you shall take fifty pounds with you. Fanny shall have fifty to enable her to prepare for the wedding, when you have told me where she is living, and she shall have five hundred paid down on her wedding-day.'

In making this statement Boldwood's voice revealed only too clearly a consciousness of the weakness of his position, his aims, and his method. His manner had lapsed quite from that of the firm and dignified Boldwood of former times; and such a scheme as he had now engaged in he would have condemned as childishly imbecile only a few months ago. We discern a grand force in the lover which he lacks whilst a free man; but there is a breadth of vision in the free man which in the lover we vainly seek. Where there is much bias there must be some narrowness, and love, though added emotion, is subtracted capacity. Boldwood exemplified this to an abnormal degree: he knew nothing of Fanny Robin's circumstances or whereabouts, he knew nothing of Troy's possibilities, yet that was what he said.

'I like Fanny best,' said Troy; 'and if, as you say, Miss Everdene is out of my reach, why I have all to gain by accepting your money, and marrying Fan. But she's only a servant.'

'Never mind – do you agree to my arrangement?'

'I do.'

'Ah!' said Boldwood, in a more elastic voice. 'O, Troy, if you like her best, why then did you step in here and injure my happiness?'

'I love Fanny best now,' said Troy. 'But Bathsh – Miss Everdene inflamed me, and displaced Fanny for a time. It is over now.'

'Why should it be over so soon? And why then did you come here again?'

'There are weighty reasons. Fifty pounds at once, you said!'

'I did,' said Boldwood, 'and here they are – fifty sovereigns.' He handed Troy a small packet.

'You have everything ready – it seems that you calculated on my accepting them,' said the sergeant, taking the packet.

'I thought you might accept them,' said Boldwood.

'You've only my word that the programme shall be adhered to, whilst I at any rate have fifty pounds.'

'I had thought of that, and I have considered that if I can't appeal to your honour I can trust to your – well, shrewdness we'll call it – not to lose five hundred pounds in prospect, and also make a bitter enemy of a man who is willing to be an extremely useful friend.'

'Stop, listen!' said Troy in a whisper.

A light pit-pat was audible upon the road just above them.

'By George – 'tis she,' he continued. 'I must go on and meet her.'

'She – who?'

'Bathsheba.'

'Bathsheba – out alone at this time o' night!' said Boldwood in amazement, and starting up. 'Why must you meet her?'

'She was expecting me to-night – and I must now speak to her, and wish her good-bye, according to your wish.'

'I don't see the necessity of speaking.'

'It can do no harm – and she'll be wandering about looking for me if I don't. You shall hear all I say to her. It will help you in your love-making when I am gone.'

'Your tone is mocking.'

'O no. And remember this, if she does not know what has become of me, she will think more about me than if I tell her flatly I have come to give her up.'

'Will you confine your words to that one point? – Shall I hear every word you say?'

'Every word. Now sit still there, and hold my carpet bag for me, and mark what you hear.'

The light footstep came closer, halting occasionally, as if the walker listened for a sound. Troy whistled a double note in a soft, fluty tone.

'Come to that, is it!' murmured Boldwood uneasily.

'You promised silence,' said Troy.

'I promise again.'

Troy stepped forward.

'Frank, dearest, is that you?' The tones were Bathsheba's.

'O God!' said Boldwood.

'Yes,' said Troy to her.

'How late you are,' she continued tenderly. 'Did you come by the carrier? I listened and heard his wheels entering the village, but it was some time ago, and I had almost given you up, Frank.'

'I was sure to come,' said Frank. 'You knew I should, did you not?'

'Well, I thought you would,' she said playfully; 'and, Frank, it is so lucky! There's not a soul in my house but me to-night. I've packed them all off, so nobody on earth will know of your visit to your lady's bower. Liddy wanted to go to her grandfather's to tell him about her holiday, and I said she might stay with them till to-morrow – when you'll be gone again.'

'Capital,' said Troy. 'But, dear me, I had better go back for my bag, because my slippers and brush and comb are in it; you run home whilst I fetch it, and I'll promise to be in your parlour in ten minutes.'

'Yes.' She turned and tripped up the hill again.

During the progress of this dialogue there was a nervous twitching of Boldwood's tightly closed lips, and his face became bathed in a clammy dew. He now started forward towards Troy. Troy turned to him and took up the bag.

'Shall I tell her I have come to give her up and cannot marry her?' said the soldier mockingly.

'No, no; wait a minute. I want to say more to you – more to you!' said Boldwood, in a hoarse whisper.

'Now,' said Troy, 'you see my dilemma. Perhaps I am a bad man – the victim of my impulses – led away to do what I ought to leave undone. I can't, however, marry them both. And I have two reasons for choosing Fanny. First, I like her best upon the whole, and second, you make it worth my while.'

At the same instant Boldwood sprang upon him, and held him by the neck. Troy felt Boldwood's grasp slowly tightening. The move was absolutely unexpected.

'A moment,' he gasped. 'You are injuring her you love!'

'Well, what do you mean?' said the farmer.

'Give me breath,' said Troy.

Boldwood loosened his hand, saying, 'By Heaven, I've a mind to kill you!'

'And ruin her.'

'Save her.'

'Oh, how can she be saved now, unless I marry her?'

Boldwood groaned. He reluctantly released the soldier, and flung him back against the hedge. 'Devil, you torture me!' said he.

Troy rebounded like a ball, and was about to make a dash at the farmer; but he checked himself, saying lightly –

'It is not worth while to measure my strength with you. Indeed it is a barbarous way of settling a quarrel. I shall shortly leave the army because of the same conviction. Now after that revelation of how the land lies with Bathsheba, 'twould be a mistake to kill me, would it not?'

''Twould be a mistake to kill you,' repeated Boldwood, mechanically, with a bowed head.

'Better kill yourself.'

'Far better.'

'I'm glad you see it.'

'Troy, make her your wife, and don't act upon what I arranged just now. The alternative is dreadful, but take Bathsheba; I give her up! She must love you indeed to sell soul and body to you so utterly as she has done. Wretched woman – deluded woman – you are, Bathsheba!'

'But about Fanny?'

'Bathsheba is a woman well to do,' continued Boldwood, in nervous anxiety, 'and, Troy, she will make a good wife; and, indeed, she is worth your hastening on your marriage with her!'

'But she has a will – not to say a temper, and I shall be a mere slave to her. I could do anything with poor Fanny Robin.'

'Troy,' said Boldwood imploringly, 'I'll do anything for you, only don't desert her; pray don't desert her, Troy.'

'Which, poor Fanny?'

'No; Bathsheba Everdene. Love her best! Love her tenderly! How shall I get you to see how advantageous it will be to you to secure her at once?'

'I don't wish to secure her in any new way.'

Boldwood's arm moved spasmodically towards Troy's person again. He repressed the instinct, and his form drooped as with pain.

Troy went on –

'I shall soon purchase my discharge, and then –'

'But I wish you to hasten on this marriage! It will be better for you both. You love each other, and you must let me help you to do it.'

'How?'

'Why, by settling the five hundred on Bathsheba instead of Fanny, to enable you to marry at once. No; she wouldn't have it of me. I'll pay it down to you on the wedding-day.'

Troy paused in secret amazement at Boldwood's wild infatuation. He carelessly said, 'And am I to have anything now?'

'Yes, if you wish to. But I have not much additional money with me. I did not expect this; but all I have is yours.'

Boldwood, more like a somnambulist than a wakeful man, pulled out the large canvas bag he carried by way of a purse, and searched it.

'I have twenty-one pounds more with me,' he said. 'Two notes and a sovereign. But before I leave you I must have a paper signed –'

'Pay me the money, and we'll go straight to her parlour, and make any arrangement you please to secure my compliance with your wishes. But she must know nothing of this cash business.'

'Nothing, nothing,' said Boldwood hastily. 'Here is the sum, and if you'll come to my house we'll write out the agreement for the remainder, and the terms also.'

'First we'll call upon her.'

'But why? Come with me to-night, and go with me to-morrow to the surrogate's.'

'But she must be consulted; at any rate informed.'

'Very well; go on.'

They went up the hill to Bathsheba's house. When they stood at the entrance, Troy said, 'Wait here a moment.' Opening the door, he glided inside, leaving the door ajar.

Boldwood waited. In two minutes a light appeared in the passage. Boldwood then saw the chain had been fastened across the door. Troy appeared inside carrying a bedroom candlestick.

'What, did you think I should break in?' said Boldwood contemptuously.

'Oh, no; it is merely my humour to secure things. Will you read this a moment? I'll hold the light.'

Troy handed a folded newspaper through the slit between door and door-post, and put the candle close. 'That's the paragraph,' he said, placing his finger on a line.

Boldwood looked and read –

'MARRIAGES

'On the 17th inst., at St Ambrose's Church, Bath, by the Rev. G. Mincing, B.A., Francis Troy, only son of the late Edward Troy, Esq., M.D., of Weatherbury, and sergeant 11th Dragoon Guards, to Bathsheba, only surviving daughter of the late Mr John Everdene, of Casterbridge.'

'This may be called Fort meeting Feeble, hey, Boldwood?' said Troy. A low gurgle of derisive laughter followed the words.

The paper fell from Boldwood's hands. Troy continued –

'Fifty pounds to marry Fanny. Good. Twenty-one pounds not to marry Fanny, but Bathsheba. Good. Finale: already Bathsheba's husband. Now, Boldwood, yours is the ridiculous fate which always attends interference between a man and his wife. And another word. Bad as I am, I am not such a villain as to make the marriage or misery of any woman a matter of huckster and sale. Fanny has long ago left me. I don't know where she is. I have searched everywhere. Another word yet. You say you love Bathsheba; yet on the merest apparent evidence you instantly believe in her dishonour. A fig for such love! Now that I've taught you a lesson, take your money back again.'

'I will not; I will not!' said Boldwood, in a hiss.

'Anyhow I won't have it,' said Troy contemptuously. He wrapped the packet of gold in the notes, and threw the whole into the the road.

Boldwood shook his clenched fist at him. 'You juggler of Satan! You black hound! But I'll punish you yet; mark me, I'll punish you yet!'

Another peal of laughter. Troy then closed the door, and locked himself in.

Throughout the whole of that night Boldwood's dark form might have been seen walking about the hills and downs of Weatherbury like an unhappy Shade in the Mournful Fields by Acheron.

* XXXV *

At an Upper Window

IT was very early the next morning – a time of sun and dew. The confused beginnings of many birds' songs spread into the healthy air, and the wan blue of the heaven was here and there coated with thin webs of incorporeal cloud which were of no effect in obscuring day. All the lights in the scene were yellow as to colour, and all the shadows were attenuated as to form. The creeping plants about the old manor-house were bowed with rows of heavy water drops, which had upon objects behind them the effect of minute lenses of high magnifying power.

Just before the clock struck five Gabriel Oak and Coggan passed the village cross, and went on together to the fields. They were yet barely in view of their mistress's house, when Oak fancied he saw the opening of a casement in one of the upper windows. The two men were at this moment partially screened by an elder bush, now beginning to be enriched with black bunches of fruit, and they paused before emerging from its shade.

A handsome man leaned idly from the lattice. He looked east and then west, in the manner of one who makes a first morning survey. The man was Sergeant Troy. His red jacket was loosely thrown on, but not buttoned, and he had altogether the relaxed bearing of a soldier taking his ease.

Coggan spoke first, looking quietly at the window.

'She has married him!' he said.

Gabriel had previously beheld the sight, and he now stood with his back turned, making no reply.

'I fancied we should know something to-day,' continued Coggan. 'I heard wheels pass my door just after dark – you were out somewhere.' He glanced round upon Gabriel. 'Good heavens above us, Oak, how white your face is; you look like a corpse!'

'Do I?' said Oak, with a faint smile.

'Lean on the gate: I'll wait a bit.'

'All right, all right.'

They stood by the gate awhile, Gabriel listlessly staring at the ground. His mind sped into the future, and saw there enacted in years of leisure the scenes of repentance that would ensue from this work of haste. That they were married he had instantly decided. Why had it been so mysteriously managed? It had become known that she had had a fearful journey to Bath, owing to her miscalculating the distance: that the horse had broken down, and that she had been more than two days getting there. It was not Bathsheba's way to do things furtively. With all her faults she was candour itself. Could she have been entrapped? The union was not only an unutterable grief to him: it amazed him, notwithstanding that he had passed the preceding week in a suspicion that such might be the issue of Troy's meeting her away from home. Her quiet return with Liddy had to some extent dispersed the dread. Just as that imperceptible motion which appears like stillness is infinitely divided in its properties from stillness itself, so had his hope undistinguishable from despair differed from despair indeed.

In a few minutes they moved on again towards the house. The sergeant still looked from the window.

'Morning, comrades!' he shouted, in a cheery voice, when they came up.

Coggan replied to the greeting. 'Bain't ye going to answer the man?' he then said to Gabriel. 'I'd say good morning – you needn't spend a hapeth of meaning upon it, and yet keep the man civil.'

Gabriel soon decided too that, since the deed was done, to put the best face upon the matter would be the greatest kindness to her he loved.

'Good morning, Sergeant Troy,' he returned, in a ghastly voice.

'A rambling, gloomy house this,' said Troy, smiling.

'Why – they *may* not be married!' suggested Coggan. 'Perhaps she's not there.'

Gabriel shook his head. The soldier turned a little towards the east, and the sun kindled his scarlet coat to an orange glow.

'But it is a nice old house,' responded Gabriel.

'Yes – I suppose so; but I feel like new wine in an old bottle here. My notion is that sash-windows should be put throughout, and these old wainscoted walls brightened up a bit; or the oak cleared quite away, and the walls papered.'

'It would be a pity, I think.'

'Well, no. A philosopher once said in my hearing that the old builders, who worked when art was a living thing, had no respect for the work of builders who went before them, but pulled down and altered as they thought fit; and why shouldn't we? "Creation and preservation don't do well together," says he, "and a million of antiquarians can't invent a style." My mind exactly. I am for making this place more modern, that we may be cheerful whilst we can.'

The military man turned and surveyed the interior of the room, to assist his ideas of improvement in this direction. Gabriel and Coggan began to move on.

'Oh, Coggan,' said Troy, as if inspired by a recollection, 'do you know if insanity has ever appeared in Mr Boldwood's family?'

Jan reflected for a moment.

'I once heard that an uncle of his was queer in his head, but I don't know the rights o't,' he said.

'It is of no importance,' said Troy lightly. 'Well, I shall be down in the fields with you some time this week; but I have a few matters to attend to first. So good-day to you. We shall, of course, keep on just as friendly terms as usual. I'm not a proud man: nobody is ever able to say that of

Sergeant Troy. However, what is must be, and here's half-a-crown to drink my health, men.'

Troy threw the coin dexterously across the front plot and over the fence towards Gabriel, who shunned it in its fall, his face turning to an angry red. Coggan twirled his eye, edged forward, and caught the money in its ricochet upon the road.

'Very well – you keep it, Coggan,' said Gabriel with disdain, and almost fiercely. 'As for me, I'll do without gifts from him!'

'Don't show it too much,' said Coggan musingly. 'For if he's married to her, mark my words, he'll buy his discharge and be our master here. Therefore 'tis well to say "Friend" outwardly, though you say "Troublesome" within.'

'Well – perhaps it is best to be silent; but I can't go further than that. I can't flatter, and if my place here is only to be kept by smoothing him down, my place must be lost.'

A horseman, whom they had for some time seen in the distance, now appeared close beside them.

'There's Mr Boldwood,' said Oak. 'I wonder what Troy meant by his question.'

Coggan and Oak nodded respectfully to the farmer, just checked their paces to discover if they were wanted, and finding they were not, stood back to let him pass on.

The only signs of the terrible sorrow Boldwood had been combating through the night, and was combating now, were the want of colour in his well-defined face, the enlarged appearance of the veins in his forehead and temples, and the sharper lines about his mouth. The horse bore him away, and the very step of the animal seemed significant of dogged despair. Gabriel, for a minute, rose above his own grief in noticing Boldwood's. He saw the square figure sitting erect upon the horse, the head turned to neither side, the elbows steady by the hips, the brim of the hat level and undisturbed in its onward glide, until the keen edges of Boldwood's shape sank by degrees over the hill. To one who knew the man and his story there was something more striking in this immobility than in a collapse. The clash of discord between mood and matter here was forced painfully home to the heart; and, as in laughter there are more dreadful phases than in tears, so was there in the steadiness of this agonized man an expression deeper than a cry.

* XXXVI *

Wealth in Jeopardy – The Revel

ONE night, at the end of August, when Bathsheba's experiences as a married woman were still new, and when the weather was yet dry and sultry, a man stood motionless in the stackyard of Weatherbury Upper Farm, looking at the moon and sky.

The night had a sinister aspect. A heated breeze from the south slowly fanned the summits of lofty objects, and in the sky dashes of buoyant cloud were sailing in a course at right angles to that of another stratum, neither of them in the direction of the breeze below. The moon, as seen through these films, had a lurid metallic look. The fields were sallow with the impure light, and all were tinged in monochrome, as if beheld through stained glass. The same evening the sheep had trailed homeward head to tail, the behaviour of the rooks had been confused, and the horses had moved with timidity and caution.

Thunder was imminent, and, taking some secondary appearances into consideration, it was likely to be followed by one of the lengthened rains which mark the close of dry weather for the season. Before twelve hours had passed a harvest atmosphere would be a bygone thing.

Oak gazed with misgiving at eight naked and unprotected ricks, massive and heavy with the rich produce of one-half the farm for that year. He went on to the barn.

This was the night which had been selected by Sergeant Troy – ruling now in the room of his wife – for giving the harvest supper and dance. As Oak approached the building the sound of violins and a tambourine, and the regular jigging of many feet, grew more distinct. He came close to the large doors, one of which stood slightly ajar, and looked in.

The central space, together with the recess at one end, was emptied of all incumbrances, and this area, covering about two-thirds of the whole, was appropriated for the gathering, the remaining end, which was piled to the ceiling with oats, being screened off with sail-cloth. Tufts and garlands of green foliage decorated the walls, beams, and extemporized chandeliers, and immediately opposite to Oak a rostrum had been erected, bearing a table and chairs. Here sat three fiddlers, and beside them stood a frantic man with his hair on end, perspiration streaming down his cheeks, and a tambourine quivering in his hand.

The dance ended, and on the black oak floor in the midst a new row of couples formed for another.

'Now, ma'am and no offence I hope, I ask what dance you would like next?' said the first violin.

'Really, it makes no difference,' said the clear voice of Bathsheba, who stood at the inner end of the building, observing the scene from behind a table covered with cups and viands. Troy was lolling beside her.

'Then,' said the fiddler, 'I'll venture to name that the right and proper thing is "The Soldier's Joy" there being a gallant soldier married into the farm – hey, my sonnies, and gentlemen all?'

'It shall be "The Soldier's Joy",' exclaimed a chorus.

'Thanks for the compliment,' said the sergeant gaily, taking Bathsheba by the hand and leading her to the top of the dance. 'For though I have purchased my discharge from Her Most Gracious Majesty's regiment of cavalry the 11th Dragoon Guards, to attend to the new duties awaiting me here, I shall continue a soldier in spirit and feeling as long as I live.'

So the dance began. As to the merits of 'The Soldier's Joy', there cannot be, and never were, two opinions. It has been observed in the musical circles of Weatherbury and its vicinity that this melody, at the end of three-quarters of an hour of thunderous footing, still possesses more stimulative properties for the heel and toe than the majority of other dances at their first opening. 'The Soldier's Joy' has, too, an additional charm, in being so admirably adapted to the tambourine aforesaid – no mean instrument in the hands of a performer who understands the proper convulsions, spasms, St Vitus's dances, and fearful frenzies necessary when exhibiting its tones in their highest perfection.

The immortal tune ended, a fine DD rolling forth from the bass-viol with the sonorousness of a cannonade, and Gabriel delayed his entry no longer. He avoided Bathsheba, and got as near as possible to the platform, where Sergeant Troy was now seated, drinking brandy-and-water, though the others drank without exception cider and ale. Gabriel could not easily thrust himself within speaking distance of the sergeant, and he sent a message, asking him to come down for a moment. The sergeant said he could not attend.

'Will you tell him, then,' said Gabriel, 'that I only stepped ath'art to say that a heavy rain is sure to fall soon, and that something should be done to protect the ricks?'

'Mr Troy says it will not rain,' returned the messenger, 'and he cannot stop to talk to you about such fidgets.'

In juxtaposition with Troy, Oak had a melancholy tendency to look like a candle beside gas, and ill at ease he went out again, thinking he would go home; for, under the circumstances, he had no heart for the scene in the barn. At the door he paused for a moment: Troy was speaking.

'Friends, it is not only the harvest home that we are celebrating tonight; but this is also a Wedding Feast. A short time ago I had the happiness to lead to the altar this lady, your mistress, and not until now have we been able to give any public flourish to the event in Weatherbury. That it may be thoroughly well done, and that every man may go happy to bed, I have ordered to be brought here some bottles of brandy and kettles of hot water. A treble-strong goblet will be handed round to each guest.'

Bathsheba put her hand upon his arm, and, with upturned pale face, said imploringly, 'No – don't give it to them – pray don't, Frank! It will only do them harm: they have had enough of everything.'

'True – we don't wish for no more, thank ye,' said one or two.

'Pooh!' said the sergeant contemptuously, and raised his voice as if lighted up by a new idea. 'Friends,' he said, 'we'll send the women-folk home! 'Tis time they were in bed. Then we cockbirds will have a jolly carouse to ourselves! If any of the men show the white feather, let them look elsewhere for a winter's work.'

Bathsheba indignantly left the barn, followed by all the women and children. The musicians, not looking upon themselves as 'company', slipped quietly away to their spring-waggon and put in the horse. Thus Troy and the men on the farm were left sole occupants of the place. Oak, not to appear unnecessarily disagreeable, stayed a little while; then he, too, arose and quietly took his departure, followed by a friendly oath from the sergeant for not staying to a second round of grog.

Gabriel proceeded towards his home. In approaching the door, his toe kicked something which felt and sounded soft, leathery, and distended, like a boxing-glove. It was a large toad humbly travelling across the path. Oak took it up, thinking it might be better to kill the creature to save it from pain; but finding it uninjured, he placed it again among the grass. He knew what this direct message from the Great Mother meant. And soon came another.

When he struck a light indoors there appeared upon the table a thin glistening streak, as if a brush of varnish had been lightly dragged across it. Oak's eyes followed the serpentine sheen to the other side, where it led up to a huge brown garden-slug, which had come indoors to-night for reasons of its own. It was Nature's second way of hinting to him that he was to prepare for foul weather.

Oak sat down meditating for nearly an hour. During this time two black spiders, of the kind common in thatched houses, promenaded the ceiling, ultimately dropping to the floor. This reminded him that if there was one class of manifestation on this matter that he thoroughly understood, it was the instincts of sheep. He left the room, ran across two or three fields towards the flock, got upon a hedge, and looked over among them.

They were crowded close together on the other side around some furze bushes, and the first peculiarity observable was that, on the sudden appearance of Oak's head over the fence, they did not stir or run away. They had now a terror of something greater than their terror of man. But this was not the most noteworthy feature: they were all grouped in such a way that their tails, without a single exception, were towards that half of the horizon from which the storm threatened. There was an inner circle closely huddled, and outside these they radiated wider apart, the pattern formed by the flock as a whole not being unlike a vandyked lace collar, to which the clump of furze-bushes stood in the position of a wearer's neck.

This was enough to re-establish him in his original opinion. He knew now that he was right, and that Troy was wrong. Every voice in nature was unanimous in bespeaking change. But two distinct translations attached to these dumb expressions. Apparently there was to be a thunder-storm, and afterwards a cold continuous rain. The creeping things seemed to know all about the later rain, but little of the interpolated thunder-storm; whilst the sheep knew all about the thunderstorm and nothing of the later rain.

This complication of weathers being uncommon, was all the more to be feared. Oak returned to the stackyard. All was silent here, and the conical tips of the ricks jutted darkly into the sky. There were five wheat-ricks in this yard, and three stacks of barley. The wheat when threshed would average about thirty quarters to each stack; the barley, at least forty. Their value to Bathsheba, and indeed to anybody, Oak mentally estimated by the following simple calculation:

$$5 \times 30 = 150 \text{ quarters} = 500l.$$
$$3 \times 40 = 120 \text{ quarters} = 250l.$$

$$\text{Total } 750l.$$

Seven hundred and fifty pounds in the divinest form that money can wear – that of necessary food for man and beast: should the risk be run of deteriorating this bulk of corn to less than half its value, because of the instability of a woman? 'Never, if I can prevent it!' said Gabriel.

Such was the argument that Oak set outwardly before him. But man, even to himself, is a palimpsest, having an ostensible writing, and another beneath the lines. It is possible that there was this golden legend under the utilitarian one: 'I will help to my last effort the woman I have loved so dearly.'

He went back to the barn to endeavour to obtain assistance for covering the ricks that very night. All was silent within, and he would have passed on in the belief that the party had broken up, had not a dim light, yellow as saffron by contrast with the greenish whiteness outside, streamed through a knot-hole in the folding doors.

Gabriel looked in. An unusual picture met his eye.

The candles suspended among the evergreens had burnt down to their sockets, and in some cases the leaves tied about them were scorched. Many of the lights had quite gone out, others smoked and stank, grease dropping from them upon the floor. Here, under the table, and leaning against forms and chairs in every conceivable attitude except the perpen-dicular, were the wretched persons of all the work-folk, the hair of their heads at such low levels being suggestive of mops and brooms. In the midst of these shone red and distinct the figure of Sergeant Troy, leaning back in a chair. Coggan was on his back, with his mouth open, buzzing forth snores, as were several others; the united breathings of the horizontal assemblage forming a subdued roar like London from a distance. Joseph Poorgrass was curled round in the fashion of a hedgehog, apparently in attempts to present the least possible portion of his surface to the air; and behind him was dimly visible an unimportant remnant of William Smallbury. The glasses and cups still stood upon the table, a water-jug being overturned, from which a small rill, after tracing its course with marvellous precision down the centre of the long table, fell into the neck of the unconscious Mark Clark, in a steady, monotonous drip, like the dripping of a stalactite in a cave.

Gabriel glanced hopelessly at the group, which, with one or two exceptions, composed all the able-bodied men upon the farm. He saw at once that if the ricks were to be saved that night, or even the next morning, he must save them with his own hands.

A faint 'ting-ting' resounded from under Coggan's waist-coat. It was Coggan's watch striking the hour of two.

Oak went to the recumbent form of Matthew Moon, who usually undertook the rough thatching of the homestead, and shook him. The shaking was without effect.

Gabriel shouted in his ear, 'Where's your thatching-beetle and rick-stick and spars?'

'Under the staddles,' said Moon mechanically, with the unconscious promptness of a medium.

Gabriel let go his head, and it dropped upon the floor like a bowl. He then went to Susan Tall's husband.

'Where's the key of the granary?'

No answer. The question was repeated, with the same result. To be shouted to at night was evidently less of a novelty to Susan Tall's husband than to Matthew Moon. Oak flung down Tall's head into the corner again and turned away.

To be just, the men were not greatly to blame for this painful and demoralizing termination to the evening's entertainment. Sergeant Troy had so strenuously insisted, glass in hand, that drinking should be the bond of their union, that those who wished to refuse hardly liked to be so unmannerly under the circumstances. Having from their youth up been entirely unaccustomed to any liquor stronger than cider or mild ale, it was no wonder that they had succumbed, one and all, with extraordinary uniformity, after the lapse of about an hour.

Gabriel was greatly depressed. This debauch boded ill for that wilful and fascinating mistress whom the faithful man even now felt within him as the embodiment of all that was sweet and bright and hopeless.

He put out the expiring lights, that the barn might not be endangered, closed the door upon the men in their deep oblivious sleep, and went again into the lone night. A hot breeze, as if breathed from the parted lips of some dragon about to swallow the globe, fanned him from the south, while directly opposite in the north rose a grim misshapen body of cloud, in the very teeth of the wind. So unnaturally did it rise that one could fancy it to be lifted by machinery from below. Meanwhile the faint cloudlets had flown back into the southeast corner of the sky, as if in terror of the large cloud, like a young brood gazed in upon by some monster.

Going on to the village, Oak flung a small stone against the window of Laban Tall's bedroom, expecting Susan to open it; but nobody stirred.

He went round to the back door, which had been left unfastened for Laban's entry, and passed in to the foot of the staircase.

'Mrs Tall, I've come for the key of the granary, to get at the rick-cloths,' said Oak, in a stentorian voice.

'Is that you?' said Mrs Susan Tall, half awake.

'Yes,' said Gabriel.

'Come along to bed, do, you draw-latching rogue – keeping a body awake like this!'

'It isn't Laban – 'tis Gabriel Oak. I want the key of the granary.'

'Gabriel! What in the name of fortune did you pretend to be Laban for?'

'I didn't. I thought you meant –'

'Yes you did! What do you want here?'

'The key of the granary.'

'Take it then. 'Tis on the nail. People coming disturbing women at this time of night ought –'

Gabriel took the key, without waiting to hear the conclusion of the tirade. Ten minutes later his lonely figure might have been seen dragging four large waterproof coverings across the yard, and soon two of these heaps of treasure in grain were covered snug – two cloths to each. Two hundred pounds were secured. Three wheat-stacks remained open, and there were no more cloths. Oak looked under the staddles and found a fork. He mounted the third pile of wealth and began operating, adopting the plan of sloping the upper sheaves one over the other; and, in addition, filling the interstices with the material of some untied sheaves.

So far all was well. By this hurried contrivance Bathsheba's property in wheat was safe for at any rate a week or two, provided always that there was not much wind.

Next came the barley. This it was only possible to protect by systematic thatching. Time went on, and the moon vanished not to reappear. It was the farewell of the ambassador previous to war. The night had a haggard look, like a sick thing; and there came finally an utter expiration of air from the whole heaven in the form of a slow breeze, which might have been likened to a death. And now nothing was heard in the yard but the dull thuds of the beetle which drove in the spars, and the rustle of thatch in the intervals.

* XXXVII *

The Storm – The Two together

A LIGHT flapped over the scene, as if reflected from phosphorescent wings crossing the sky, and a rumble filled the air. It was the first move of the approaching storm.

The second peal was noisy, with comparatively little visible lightning. Gabriel saw a candle shining in Bathsheba's bedroom, and soon a shadow swept to and fro upon the blind.

Then there came a third flash. Manoeuvres of a most extraordinary kind were going on in the vast firmamental hollows overhead. The lightning now was the colour of silver, and gleamed in the heavens like a mailed army. Rumbles became rattles. Gabriel from his elevated position could see over the landscape at least half-a-dozen miles in front. Every hedge, bush, and tree was distinct as in a line engraving. In a paddock in the same direction was a herd of heifers, and the forms of these were visible at this moment in the act of galloping about in the wildest and maddest confusion, flinging their heels and tails high into the air, their heads to earth. A poplar in the immediate foreground was like an ink stroke on burnished tin. Then the picture vanished, leaving the darkness so intense that Gabriel worked entirely by feeling with his hands.

He had stuck his ricking-rod, or poniard, as it was indifferently called – a long iron lance, polished by handling – into the stack, used to support the sheaves instead of the support called a groom used on houses. A blue light appeared in the zenith, and in some indescribable manner flickered down near the top of the rod. It was the fourth of the larger flashes. A moment later and there was a smack – smart, clear, and short. Gabriel felt his position to be anything but a safe one, and he resolved to descend.

Not a drop of rain had fallen as yet. He wiped his weary brow, and looked again at the black forms of the unprotected stacks. Was his life so valuable to him after all? What were his prospects that he should be so chary of running risk, when important and urgent labour could not be carried on without such risk? He resolved to stick to the stack. However, he took a precaution. Under the staddles was a long tethering chain, used to prevent the escape of errant horses. This he carried up the ladder, and sticking his rod through the clog at one end, allowed the other end of the chain to trail upon the ground. The spike attached to it he drove in. Under the shadow of this extemporized lightning-conductor he felt himself comparatively safe.

Before Oak had laid his hands upon his tools again out leapt the fifth flash, with the spring of a serpent and the shout of a fiend. It was green as an emerald, and the reverberation was stunning. What was this the light revealed to him? In the open ground before him, as he looked over the ridge of the rick, was a dark and apparently female form. Could it be that of the only venturesome woman in the parish – Bathsheba? The form moved on a step: then he could see no more.

'Is that you, ma'am?' said Gabriel to the darkness.

'Who is there?' said the voice of Bathsheba.

'Gabriel. I am on the rick, thatching.'

'O, Gabriel! – and are you? I have come about them. The weather awoke me, and I thought of the corn. I am so distressed about it – can we save it anyhow? I cannot find my husband. Is he with you?'

'He is not here.'

'Do you know where he is?'

'Asleep in the barn.'

'He promised that the stacks should be seen to, and now they are all neglected! Can I do anything to help? Liddy is afraid to come out. Fancy finding you here at such an hour! Surely I can do something?'

'You can bring up some reed-sheaves to me, one by one, ma'am; if you are not afraid to come up the ladder in the dark,' said Gabriel. 'Every moment is precious now, and that would save a good deal of time. It is not very dark when the lightning has been gone a bit.'

'I'll do anything!' she said resolutely. She instantly took a sheaf upon her shoulder, clambered up close to his heels, placed it behind the rod, and descended for another. At her third ascent the rick suddenly brightened with the brazen glare of shining majolica – every knot in every straw was visible. On the slope in front of him appeared two human shapes, black as jet. The rick lost its sheen – the shapes vanished. Gabriel turned his head. It had been the sixth flash which had come from the east behind him, and the two dark forms on the slope had been the shadows of himself and Bathsheba.

Then came the peal. It hardly was credible that such a heavenly light could be the parent of such a diabolical sound.

'How terrible!' she exclaimed, and clutched him by the sleeve. Gabriel turned, and steadied her on her aerial perch by holding her arm. At the same moment, while he was still reversed in his attitude, there was more light, and he saw, as it were, a copy of the tall poplar tree on the hill drawn in black on the wall of the barn. It was the shadow of that tree, thrown across by a secondary flash in the west.

The next flare came. Bathsheba was on the ground now, shouldering another sheaf, and she bore its dazzle without flinching – thunder and all – and again ascended with the load. There was then a silence everywhere for four or five minutes, and the crunch of the spars, as Gabriel hastily drove them in, could again be distinctly heard. He thought the crisis of the storm had passed. But there came a burst of light.

'Hold on!' said Gabriel, taking the sheaf from her shoulder, and grasping her arm again.

Heaven opened then, indeed. The flash was almost too novel for its inexpressibly dangerous nature to be at once realized, and they could only comprehend the magnificence of its beauty. It sprang from east, west, north, south, and was a perfect dance of death. The forms of skeletons appeared in the air, shaped with blue fire for bones – dancing, leaping, striding, racing around, and mingling altogether in unparalleled confusion. With these were intertwined undulating snakes of green, and behind these was a broad mass of lesser light. Simultaneously came from every part of the tumbling sky what may be called a shout; since, though no shout ever came near it, it was more of the nature of a shout than of anything else earthly. In the meantime one of the grisly forms had alighted upon the point of Gabriel's rod, to run invisibly down it, down the chain, and into the earth. Gabriel was almost blinded, and he could feel Bathsheba's warm arm tremble in his hand – a sensation novel and thrilling enough; but love, life, everything human, seemed small and trifling in such close juxtaposition with an infuriated universe.

Oak had hardly time to gather up these impressions into a thought, and to see how strangely the red feathers of her hat shone in this light, when the tall tree on the hill before mentioned seemed on fire to a white heat, and a new one among these terrible voices mingled with the last crash of those preceding. It was a stupefying blast, harsh and pitiless, and it fell upon their ears in a dead, flat blow, without that reverberation which lends the tones of a drum to more distant thunder. By the lustre reflected from every part of the earth and from the wide domical scoop above it, he saw that the tree was sliced down the whole length of its tall, straight stem, a huge riband of bark being apparently flung off. The other portion remained erect, and revealed the bared surface as a strip of white down the front. The lightning had struck the tree. A sulphurous smell filled the air; then all was silent, and black as a cave in Hinnom.

'We had a narrow escape!' said Gabriel hurriedly. 'You had better go down.'

Bathsheba said nothing; but he could distinctly hear her rhythmical pants, and the recurrent rustle of the sheaf beside her in response to her frightened pulsations. She descended the ladder, and, on second thoughts, he followed her. The darkness was now impenetrable by the sharpest vision. They both stood still at the bottom, side by side. Bathsheba appeared to think only of the weather – Oak thought only of her just then. At last he said –

'The storm seems to have passed now, at any rate.'

'I think so too,' said Bathsheba. 'Though there are multitudes of gleams, look!'

The sky was now filled with an incessant light, frequent repetition melting into complete continuity, as an unbroken sound results from the successive strokes on a gong.

'Nothing serious,' said he. 'I cannot understand no rain falling. But Heaven be praised, it is all the better for us. I am going up again.'

'Gabriel, you are kinder than I deserve! I will stay and help you yet. O, why are not some of the others here!'

'They would have been here if they could,' said Oak, in a hesitating way.

'O, I know it all – all,' she said, adding slowly: 'They are all asleep in the barn, in a drunken sleep, and my husband among them. That's it, is it not? Don't think I am a timid woman and can't endure things.'

'I am not certain,' said Gabriel. 'I will go and see.'

He crossed to the barn, leaving her there alone. He looked through the chinks of the door. All was in total darkness, as he had left it, and there still arose, as at the former time, the steady buzz of many snores.

He felt a zephyr curling about his cheek, and turned. It was Bathsheba's breath – she had followed him, and was looking into the same chink.

He endeavoured to put off the immediate and painful subject of their thoughts by remarking gently, 'If you'll come back again, miss – ma'am, and hand up a few more, it would save much time.'

Then Oak went back again, ascended to the top, stepped off the ladder for greater expedition, and went on thatching. She followed, but without a sheaf.

'Gabriel,' she said, in a strange and impressive voice.

Oak looked up at her. She had not spoken since he left the barn. The soft and continual shimmer of the dying lightning showed a marble face high against the black sky of the opposite quarter. Bathsheba was sitting almost on the apex of the stack, her feet gathered up beneath her, and resting on the top round of the ladder.

'Yes, mistress,' he said.

'I suppose you thought that when I galloped away to Bath that night it was on purpose to be married?'

'I did at last – not at first,' he answered, somewhat surprised at the abruptness with which this new subject was broached.

'And others thought so, too!'

'Yes.'

'And you blamed me for it?'

'Well – a little.'

'I thought so. Now, I care a little for your good opinion, and I want to explain something – I have longed to do it ever since I returned, and you looked so gravely at me. For if I were to die – and I may die soon – it would be dreadful that you should always think mistakenly of me. Now, listen.'

Gabriel ceased his rustling.

'I went to Bath that night in the full intention of breaking off my engagement to Troy. It was owing to circumstances which occurred after I got there that – that we were married. Now, do you see the matter in a new light?'

'I do – somewhat.'

'I must, I suppose, say more, now that I have begun. And perhaps it's no harm, for you are certainly under no delusion that I ever loved you, or that I can have any object in speaking, more than that object I have mentioned. Well, I was alone in a strange city, and the horse was lame. And at last I didn't know what to do. I saw, when it was too late, that scandal might seize hold of me for meeting him alone in that way. But I was coming away, when he suddenly said he had that day seen a woman more beautiful than I, and that his constancy could not be counted on unless I at once became his . . . And I was grieved and troubled –' She cleared her voice, and waited a moment, as if to gather breath. 'And then, between jealousy and distraction, I married him!' she whispered with desperate impetuosity.

Gabriel made no reply.

'He was not to blame, for it was perfectly true about – about his seeing somebody else,' she quickly added. 'And now I don't wish for a single remark from you upon the subject – indeed, I forbid it. I only wanted you to know that misunderstood bit of my history before a time comes when you could never know it. – You want some more sheaves?'

She went down the ladder, and the work proceeded. Gabriel soon perceived a languor in the movements of his mistress up and down, and he said to her, gently as a mother –

'I think you had better go indoors now, you are tired. I can finish the rest alone. If the wind does not change the rain is likely to keep off.'

'If I am useless I will go,' said Bathsheba, in a flagging cadence. 'But O, if your life should be lost!'

'You are not useless; but I would rather not tire you longer. You have done well.'

'And you better!' she said gratefully. 'Thank you for your devotion, a thousand times, Gabriel! Good-night – I know you are doing your very best for me.'

She diminished in the gloom, and vanished, and he heard the latch of the gate fall as she passed through. He worked in a reverie now, musing upon her story, and upon the contradictoriness of that feminine heart which had caused her to speak more warmly to him to-night than she ever had done whilst unmarried and free to speak as warmly as she chose.

He was disturbed in his meditation by a grating noise from the coach-house. It was the vane on the roof turning round, and this change in the wind was the signal for a disastrous rain.

* XXXVIII *

Rain – One Solitary meets another

IT was now five o'clock, and the dawn was promising to break in hues of drab and ash.

The air changed its temperature and stirred itself more vigorously.

Cool breezes coursed in transparent eddies round Oak's face. The wind shifted yet a point or two and blew stronger. In ten minutes every wind of heaven seemed to be roaming at large. Some of the thatching on the wheat-stacks was now whirled fantastically aloft, and had to be replaced and weighted with some rails that lay near at hand. This done, Oak slaved away again at the barley. A huge drop of rain smote his face, the wind snarled round every corner, the trees rocked to the bases of their trunks, and the twigs clashed in strife. Driving in spars at any point and on any system, inch by inch he covered more and more safely from ruin this distracting impersonation of seven hundred pounds. The rain came on in earnest, and Oak soon felt the water to be tracking cold and clammy routes down his back. Ultimately he was reduced well-nigh to a homogeneous sop, and the dyes of his clothes trickled down and stood in a pool at the foot of the ladder. The rain stretched obliquely through the dull atmosphere in liquid spines, unbroken in continuity between their beginnings in the clouds and their points in him.

Oak suddenly remembered that eight months before this time he had been fighting against fire in the same spot as desperately as he was fighting against water now – and for a futile love of the same woman. As for her – But Oak was generous and true, and dismissed his reflections.

It was about seven o'clock in the dark leaden morning when Gabriel came down from the last stack, and thankfully exclaimed, 'It is done!' He was drenched, weary, and sad, and yet not so sad as drenched and weary, for he was cheered by a sense of success in a good cause.

Faint sounds came from the barn, and he looked that way. Figures stepped singly and in pairs through the doors – all walking awkwardly, and abashed, save the foremost, who wore a red jacket, and advanced with his hands in his pockets, whistling. The others shambled after with a conscience-stricken air: the whole procession was not unlike Flaxman's group of suitors tottering on towards the infernal regions under the conduct of Mercury. The gnarled shapes passed into the village, Troy, their leader, entering the farmhouse. Not a single one of them had turned his face to the ricks, or apparently bestowed one thought upon their condition.

Soon Oak too went homeward, by a different route from theirs. In front of him against the wet glazed surface of the lane he saw a person walking yet more slowly than himself under an umbrella. The man turned and plainly started; he was Boldwood.

'How are you this morning, sir?' said Oak.

'Yes, it is a wet day. – Oh, I am well, very well, I thank you; quite well.'

'I am glad to hear it, sir.'

Boldwood seemed to awake to the present by degrees. 'You look tired and ill, Oak,' he said then, desultorily regarding his companion.

'I am tired. You look strangely altered, sir.'

'I? Not a bit of it; I am well enough. What put that into your head?'

'I thought you didn't look quite so topping as you used to, that was all.'

'Indeed, then you are mistaken,' said Boldwood shortly. 'Nothing hurts me. My constitution is an iron one.'

'I've been working hard to get our ricks covered, and was barely in time. Never had such a struggle in my life . . . Yours of course are safe, sir.'

'O yes.' Boldwood added, after an interval of silence: 'What did you ask, Oak?'

'Your ricks are all covered before this time?'

'No.'

'At any rate, the large ones upon the stone staddles?'

'They are not.'

'Them under the hedge?'

'No. I forgot to tell the thatcher to set about it.'

'Nor the little one by the stile?'

'Nor the little one by the stile. I overlooked the ricks this year.'

'Then not a tenth of your corn will come to measure, sir.'

'Possibly not.'

'Overlooked them,' repeated Gabriel slowly to himself. It is difficult to describe the intensely dramatic effect that announcement had upon Oak at such a moment. All the night he had been feeling that the neglect he was labouring to repair was abnormal and isolated – the only instance of the kind within the circuit of the county. Yet at this very time, within the same parish, a greater waste had been going on, uncomplained of and disregarded. A few months earlier Boldwood's forgetting his husbandry would have been as preposterous an idea as a sailor forgetting he was in a ship. Oak was just thinking that whatever he himself might have suffered from Bathsheba's marriage, here was a man who had suffered more, when Boldwood spoke in a changed voice – that of one who yearned to make a confidence and relieve his heart by an outpouring.

'Oak, you know as well as I that things have gone wrong with me lately. I may as well own it. I was going to get a little settled in life; but in some way my plan has come to nothing.'

'I thought my mistress would have married you,' said Gabriel, not knowing enough of the full depths of Boldwood's love to keep silence on the farmer's account, and determined not to evade discipline by doing so on his own. 'However, it is so sometimes, and nothing happens that we expect,' he added, with the repose of a man whom misfortune had inured rather than subdued.

'I daresay I am a joke about the parish,' said Boldwood, as if the subject came irresistibly to his tongue, and with a miserable lightness meant to express his indifference.

'O no – I don't think that.'

'– But the real truth of the matter is that there was not, as some fancy, any jilting on – her part. No engagement ever existed between me and Miss Everdene. People say so, but it is untrue: she never promised me!' Boldwood stood still now and turned his wild face to Oak. 'O, Gabriel,' he continued, 'I am weak and foolish, and I don't know what, and I can't fend off my miserable grief! . . . I had some faint belief in the mercy of God till I lost that woman. Yes, He prepared a gourd to shade me, and like the prophet I thanked Him and was glad. But the next day He prepared a worm to smite the gourd and wither it; and I feel it is better to die than to live!'

A silence followed. Boldwood aroused himself from the momentary mood of confidence into which he had drifted, and walked on again, resuming his usual reserve.

'No, Gabriel,' he resumed, with a carelessness which was like the smile on the countenance of a skull: 'it was made more of by other people than ever it was by us. I do feel a little regret occasionally, but no woman ever had power over me for any length of time. Well, good morning; I can trust you not to mention to others what has passed between us two here.'

* XXXIX *

Coming Home – A Cry

ON the turnpike road, between Casterbridge and Weatherbury, and about three miles from the former place, is Yalbury Hill, one of those steep long ascents which pervade the highways of this undulating part of South Wessex. In returning from market it is usual for the farmers and other gig-gentry to alight at the bottom and walk up.

One Saturday evening in the month of October Bathsheba's vehicle was duly creeping up this incline. She was sitting listlessly in the second seat of the gig, whilst walking beside her in a farmer's marketing suit of unusually fashionable cut was an erect, well-made young man. Though on foot, he held the reins and whip, and occasionally aimed light cuts at the horse's ear with the end of the lash, as a recreation. This man was her husband, formerly Sergeant Troy, who, having bought his discharge with Bathsheba's money, was gradually transforming himself into a farmer of a spirited and very modern school. People of unalterable ideas still insisted upon calling him 'Sergeant' when they met him, which was in some degree owing to his having still retained the well-shaped moustache of his military days, and the soldierly bearing inseparable from his form and training.

'Yes, if it hadn't been for that wretched rain I should have cleared two hundred as easy as looking, my love,' he was saying. 'Don't you see, it altered all the chances? To speak like a book I once read, wet weather is the narrative, and fine days are the episodes, of our country's history; now, isn't that true?'

'But the time of year is come for changeable weather.'

'Well, yes. The fact is, these autumn races are the ruin of everybody. Never did I see such a day as 'twas! 'Tis a wild open place, just out of Budmouth, and a drab sea rolled in towards us like liquid misery. Wind and rain – good Lord! Dark? Why. 'Twas as black as my hat before the last race was run. 'Twas five o'clock, and you couldn't see the horses till they were almost in, leave alone colours. The ground was as heavy as lead, and all judgement from a fellow's experience went for nothing. Horses, riders, people, were all blown about like ships at sea. Three booths were blown over, and the wretched folk inside crawled out upon their hands and knees; and in the next field were as many as a dozen hats at one time. Ay, Pimpernel regularly stuck fast, when about sixty yards off, and when I saw Policy stepping on, it did knock my heart against the lining of my ribs, I assure you, my love!'

'And you mean, Frank,' said Bathsheba sadly – her voice was painfully lowered from the fulness and vivacity of the previous summer – 'that you have lost more than a hundred pounds in a month by this dreadful horse-racing? O, Frank, it is cruel; it is foolish of you to take away my money so. We shall have to leave the farm; that will be the end of it!'

'Humbug about cruel. Now, there 'tis again – turn on the water-works; that's just like you.'

'But you'll promise me not to go to Budmouth second meeting, won't you?' she implored. Bathsheba was at the full depth for tears, but she maintained a dry eye.

'I don't see why I should; in fact, if it turns out to be a fine day, I was thinking of taking you.'

'Never, never! I'll go a hundred miles the other way first. I hate the sound of the very word!'

'But the question of going to see the race or staying at home has very little to do with the matter. Bets are all booked safely enough before the race begins, you may depend. Whether it is a bad race for me or a good one, will have very little to do with our going there next Monday.'

'But you don't mean to say that you have risked anything on this one too!' she exclaimed, with an agonized look.

'There now, don't you be a little fool. Wait till you are told. Why, Bathsheba, you have lost all the pluck and sauciness you formerly had, and upon my life if I had known what a chicken-hearted creature you were under all your boldness, I'd never have – I know what.'

A flash of indignation might have been seen in Bathsheba's dark eyes as she looked resolutely ahead after this reply. They moved on without further speech, some early-withered leaves from the trees which hooded the road at this spot occasionally spinning downward across their path to the earth.

A woman appeared on the brow of the hill. The ridge was in a cutting, so that she was very near the husband and wife before she became visible.

Troy had turned towards the gig to remount, and whilst putting his foot on the step the woman passed behind him.

Though the overshadowing trees and the approach of eventide enveloped them in gloom, Bathsheba could see plainly enough to discern the extreme poverty of the woman's garb, and the sadness of her face.

'Please, sir, do you know at what time Casterbridge Union-house closes at night?'

The woman said these words to Troy over his shoulder.

Troy started visibly at the sound of the voice; yet he seemed to recover presence of mind sufficient to prevent himself from giving way to his impulse to suddenly turn and face her. He said, slowly –

'I don't know.'

The woman, on hearing him speak, quickly looked up, examined the side of his face, and recognized the soldier under the yeoman's garb. Her face was drawn into an expression which had gladness and agony both among its elements. She uttered an hysterical cry, and fell down.

'O, poor thing!' exclaimed Bathsheba, instantly preparing to alight.

'Stay where you are, and attend to the horse!' said Troy peremptorily, throwing her the reins and the whip. 'Walk the horse to the top: I'll see to the woman.'

'But I –'

'Do you hear? Clk – Poppet!'

The horse, gig, and Bathsheba moved on.

'How on earth did you come here? I thought you were miles away, or dead! Why didn't you write to me?' said Troy to the woman, in a strangely gentle, yet hurried voice, as he lifted her up.

'I feared to.'

'Have you any money?'

'None.'

'Good Heaven – I wish I had more to give you! Here's – wretched – the merest trifle. It is every farthing I have left. I have none but what my wife gives me, you know, and I can't ask her now.'

The woman made no answer.

'I have only another moment,' continued Troy; 'and now listen. Where are you going to-night? Casterbridge Union?'

'Yes; I thought to go there.'

'You shan't go there; yet, wait. Yes, perhaps for to-night; I can do nothing better – worse luck! Sleep there to-night, and stay there to-morrow. Monday is the first free day I have, and on Monday morning, at ten exactly, meet me on Grey's Bridge, just out of the town. I'll bring all the money I can muster. You shan't want – I'll see that, Fanny; then I'll get you a lodging somewhere. Good-bye till then. I am a brute – but good-bye!'

After advancing the distance which completed the ascent of the hill, Bathsheba turned her head. The woman was upon her feet, and Bathsheba saw her withdrawing from Troy, and going feebly down the hill by the third milestone from Casterbridge. Troy then came on towards his wife, stepped into the gig, took the reins from her hand, and without making any observation whipped the horse into a trot. He was rather agitated.

'Do you know who that woman was?' said Bathsheba, looking searchingly into his face.

'I do,' he said, looking boldly back into hers.

'I thought you did,' said she, with angry hauteur, and still regarding him. 'Who is she?'

He suddenly seemed to think that frankness would benefit neither of the women.

'Nothing to either of us,' he said. 'I know her by sight.'

'What is her name?'

'How should I know her name?'

'I think you do.'

'Think if you will, and be –' The sentence was completed by a smart cut of the whip round Poppet's flank, which caused the animal to start forward at a wild pace. No more was said.

* XL *

On Casterbridge Highway

FOR a considerable time the woman walked on. Her steps became feebler, and she strained her eyes to look afar upon the naked road, now indistinct amid the penumbrae of night. At length her onward walk dwindled to the merest totter, and she opened a gate within which was a haystack. Underneath this she sat down and presently slept.

When the woman awoke it was to find herself in the depths of a moonless and starless night. A heavy unbroken crust of cloud stretched across the sky, shutting out every speck of heaven; and a distant halo which hung over the town of Casterbridge was visible against the black concave, the luminosity appearing the brighter by its great contrast with the circumscribing darkness. Towards this weak, soft glow the woman turned her eyes.

'If I could only get there!' she said. 'Meet him the day after to-morrow: God help me! Perhaps I shall be in my grave before then.'

A manor-house clock from the far depths of shadow struck the hour, one, in a small, attenuated tone. After midnight the voice of a clock seems to lose in breadth as much as in length, and to diminish its sonorousness to a thin falsetto.

Afterwards a light – two lights – arose from the remote shade, and grew larger. A carriage rolled along the road, and passed the gate. It probably contained some late diners-out. The beams from one lamp shone for a moment upon the crouching woman, and threw her face into vivid relief. The face was young in the ground-work, old in the finish; the general contours were flexuous and childlike, but the finer lineaments had begun to be sharp and thin.

The pedestrian stood up, apparently with a revived determination, and looked around. The road appeared to be familiar to her, and she carefully scanned the fence as she slowly walked along. Presently there became visible a dim white shape; it was another milestone. She drew her fingers across its face to feel the marks.

'Two more!' she said.

She leant against the stone as a means of rest for a short interval, then bestirred herself, and again pursued her way. For a slight distance she bore up bravely, afterwards flagging as before. This was beside a lone copsewood, wherein heaps of white chips strewn upon the leafy ground showed that woodmen had been faggoting and making hurdles during the day. Now there was not a rustle, not a breeze, not the faintest clash of twigs to keep her company. The woman looked over the gate, opened it, and went in. Close to the entrance stood a row of faggots, bound and unbound, together with stakes of all sizes.

For a few seconds the wayfarer stood with that tense stillness which signifies itself to be not the end, but merely the suspension, of a previous motion. Her attitude was that of a person who listens, either to the external world of sound, or to the imagined discourse of thought. A close criticism might have detected signs proving that she was intent on the latter alternative. Moreover, as was shown by what followed, she was oddly exercising the faculty of invention upon the speciality of the clever Jacquet Droz, the designer of automatic substitutes for human limbs.

By the aid of the Casterbridge aurora, and by feeling with her hands, the woman selected two sticks from the heaps. These sticks were nearly straight to the height of three or four feet, where each branched into a fork like the letter Y. She sat down, snapped off the small upper twigs, and carried the remainder with her into the road. She placed one of these forks under each arm as a crutch, tested them, timidly threw her whole weight upon them – so little that it was – and swung herself forward. The girl had made for herself a material aid.

The crutches answered well. The pat of her feet, and the tap of her sticks upon the highway, were all the sounds that came from the traveller now. She had passed the last milestone by a good long distance, and began to look wistfully towards the bank as if calculating upon another milestone soon. The crutches, though so very useful, had their limits of power. Mechanism only transfers labour, being powerless to supersede it, and the original amount of exertion was not cleared away; it was thrown into the body and arms. She was exhausted, and each swing forward became fainter. At last she swayed sideways, and fell.

Here she lay, a shapeless heap, for ten minutes and more. The morning wind began to boom dully over the flats, and to move afresh dead leaves which had lain still since yesterday. The woman desperately turned round upon her knees, and next rose to her feet. Steadying herself by the help of one crutch, she essayed a step, then another, then a third, using the crutches now as walking-sticks only. Thus she progressed till descending Mellstock Hill another milestone appeared, and soon the beginning of an iron-railed fence came into view. She staggered across to the first post, clung to it, and looked around.

The Casterbridge lights were now individually visible. It was getting towards morning, and vehicles might be hoped for, if not expected soon. She listened. There was not a sound of life save that acme and sublimation of all dismal sounds, the bark of a fox, its three hollow notes being rendered at intervals of a minute with the precision of a funeral bell.

'Less than a mile!' the woman murmured. 'No; more,' she added, after a pause. 'The mile is to the county-hall, and my resting-place is on the other side Casterbridge. A little over a mile, and there I am!' After an interval she again spoke. 'Five or six steps to a yard – six perhaps. I have to go seventeen hundred yards. A hundred times six, six hundred. Seventeen times that. O pity me, Lord!'

Holding to the rails, she advanced, thrusting one hand forward upon the rail, then the other, then leaning over it whilst she dragged her feet on beneath.

This woman was not given to soliloquy; but extremity of feeling lessens the individuality of the weak, as it increases that of the strong. She said again in the same tone, 'I'll believe that the end lies five posts forward, and no further, and so get strength to pass them.'

This was a practical application of the principle that a half-feigned and fictitious faith is better than no faith at all.

She passed five posts and held on to the fifth.

'I'll pass five more by believing my longed-for spot is at the next fifth. I can do it.'

She passed five more.

'It lies only five further.'

She passed five more.

'But it is five further.'

She passed them.

'That stone bridge is the end of my journey,' she said, when the bridge over the Froom was in view.

She crawled to the bridge. During the effort each breath of the woman went into the air as if never to return again.

'Now for the truth of the matter,' she said, sitting down. 'The truth is, that I have less than half a mile.' Self-beguilement with what she had known all the time to be false had given her strength to come over half a mile that she would have been powerless to face in the lump. The artifice showed that the woman, by some mysterious intuition, had grasped the paradoxical truth that blindness may operate more vigorously than prescience, and the short-sighted effect more than the far-seeing; that limitation, and not comprehensiveness, is needed for striking a blow.

The half-mile stood now before the sick and weary woman like a stolid Juggernaut. It was an impassive King of her world. The road here ran across Durnover Moor, open to the road on either side. She surveyed the wide space, the lights, herself, sighed, and lay down against a guard-stone of the bridge.

Never was ingenuity exercised so sorely as the traveller here exercised hers. Every conceivable aid, method, stratagem, mechanism, by which these last desperate eight hundred yards could be overpassed by a human being unperceived, was revolved in her busy brain, and dismissed as impracticable. She thought of sticks, wheels, crawling – she even thought of rolling. But the exertion demanded by either of these latter two was greater than to walk erect. The faculty of contrivance was worn out. Hopelessness had come at last.

'No further!' she whispered, and closed her eyes.

From the stripe of shadow on the opposite side of the bridge a portion of shade seemed to detach itself and move into isolation upon the pale white of the road. It glided noiselessly towards the recumbent woman.

She became conscious of something touching her hand; it was softness and it was warmth. She opened her eyes, and the substance touched her face. A dog was licking her cheek.

He was a huge, heavy, and quiet creature, standing darkly against the low horizon, and at least two feet higher than the present position of her eyes. Whether Newfoundland, mastiff, bloodhound, or what not, it was impossible to say. He seemed to be of too strange and mysterious a nature to belong to any variety among those of popular nomenclature. Being thus assignable to no breed, he was the ideal embodiment of canine greatness – a generalization from what was common to all. Night, in its sad, solemn, and benevolent aspect, apart from its stealthy and cruel side, was personified in this form. Darkness endows the small and ordinary ones among mankind with poetical power, and even the suffering woman threw her idea into figure.

In her reclining position she looked up to him just as in earlier times she had, when standing, looked up to a man. The animal, who was as homeless as she, respectfully withdrew a step or two when the woman moved, and, seeing that she did not repulse him, he licked her hand again.

A thought moved within her like lightning. 'Perhaps I can make use of him – I might do it then!'

She pointed in the direction of Casterbridge, and the dog seemed to misunderstand: he trotted on. Then, finding she could not follow, he came back and whined.

The ultimate and saddest singularity of woman's effort and invention was reached when, with a quickened breathing, she rose to a stooping posture, and, resting her two little arms upon the shoulders of the dog, leant firmly thereon, and murmured stimulating words. Whilst she sorrowed in her heart she cheered with her voice, and what was stranger than that the strong should need encouragement from the weak was that cheerfulness should be so well stimulated by such utter dejection. Her friend moved forward slowly, and she with small mincing steps moved forward beside him, half her weight being thrown upon the animal. Sometimes she sank as she had sunk from walking erect, from the crutches, from the rails. The dog, who now thoroughly understood her desire and her incapacity, was frantic in his distress on these occasions; he would tug at her dress and run forward. She always called him back, and it was now to be observed that the woman listened for human sounds only to avoid them. It was evident that she had an object in keeping her presence on the road and her forlorn state unknown.

Their progress was necessarily very slow. They reached the bottom of the town and the Casterbridge lamps lay before them like fallen Pleiads as they turned to the left into the dense shade of a deserted avenue of chestnuts, and so skirted the borough. Thus the town was passed, and the goal was reached.

On this much-desired spot outside the town rose a picturesque building. Originally it had been a mere case to hold people. The shell had been so thin, so devoid of excrescence, and so closely drawn over the accommodation granted, that the grim character of what was beneath showed through it, as the shape of a body is visible under a winding-sheet.

Then Nature, as if offended, lent a hand. Masses of ivy grew up, completely covering the walls, till the place looked like an abbey; and it was discovered that the view from the front, over the Casterbridge chimneys, was one of the most magnificent in the county. A neighbouring earl once said that he would give up a year's rental to have at his own door the view enjoyed by the inmates from theirs – and very probably the inmates would have given up the view for his year's rental.

This stone edifice consisted of a central mass and two wings, whereon stood as sentinels a few slim chimneys, now gurgling sorrowfully to the slow wind. In the wall was a gate, and by the gate a bell-pull formed of a hanging wire. The woman raised herself as high as possible upon her knees, and could just reach the handle. She moved it and fell forwards in a bowed attitude, her face upon her bosom.

It was getting on towards six o'clock, and sounds of movement were to be heard inside the building which was the haven of rest to this wearied soul. A little door by the large one was opened, and a man appeared inside. He discerned the panting heap of clothes, went back for a light, and came again. He entered a second time, and returned with two women.

These lifted the prostrate figure and assisted her in through the doorway. The man then closed the door.

'How did she get here?' said one of the women.

'The Lord knows,' said the other.

'There is a dog outside,' murmured the overcome traveller. 'Where is he gone? He helped me.'

'I stoned him away,' said the man.

The little procession then moved forward – the man in front bearing the light, the two bony women next, supporting between them the small and supple one. Thus they entered the house and disappeared.

* XLI *

Suspicion – Fanny is sent for

BATHSHEBA said very little to her husband all that evening of their return from market, and he was not disposed to say much to her. He exhibited the unpleasant combination of a restless condition with a silent tongue. The next day, which was Sunday, passed nearly in the same manner as regarded their taciturnity, Bathsheba going to church both morning and afternoon. This was the day before the Budmouth races. In the evening Troy said, suddenly –

'Bathsheba, could you let me have twenty pounds?'

Her countenance instantly sank. 'Twenty pounds?' she said.

'The fact is, I want it badly.' The anxiety upon Troy's face was unusual and very marked. It was a culmination of the mood he had been in all the day.

'Ah! for those races to-morrow.'

Troy for the moment made no reply. Her mistake had its advantages to a man who shrank from having his mind inspected as he did now. 'Well, suppose I do want it for races?' he said, at last.

'Oh, Frank!' Bathsheba replied, and there was such a volume of entreaty in the words. 'Only such a few weeks ago you said that I was far sweeter than all your other pleasures put together, and that you would give them all up for me; and now, won't you give up this one, which is more a worry than a pleasure? Do, Frank. Come, let me fascinate you by all I can do – by pretty words and pretty looks, and everything I can think of – to stay at home. Say yes to your wife – say yes!'

The tenderest and softest phases of Bathsheba's nature were prominent now – advanced impulsively for his acceptance, without any of the disguises and defences which the wariness of her character when she was cool too frequently threw over them. Few men could have resisted the arch yet dignified entreaty of the beautiful face, thrown a little back and sideways in the well-known attitude that expresses more than the words it accompanies, and which seems to have been designed for these special occasions. Had the woman not been his wife, Troy would have succumbed instantly; as it was, he thought he would not deceive her longer.

'The money is not wanted for racing debts at all,' he said.

'What is it for?' she asked. 'You worry me a great deal by these mysterious responsibilities, Frank.'

Troy hesitated. He did not now love her enough to allow himself to be carried too far by her ways. Yet it was necessary to be civil. 'You wrong me by such a suspicious manner,' he said. 'Such strait-waistcoating as you treat me to is not becoming in you at so early a date.'

'I think that I have a right to grumble a little if I pay,' she said, with features between a smile and a pout.

'Exactly; and, the former being done, suppose we proceed to the latter. Bathsheba, fun is all very well, but don't go too far, or you may have cause to regret something.'

She reddened. 'I do that already,' she said quickly.

'What do you regret?'

'That my romance has come to an end.'

'All romances end at marriage.'

'I wish you wouldn't talk like that. You grieve me to my soul by being smart at my expense.'

'You are dull enough at mine. I believe you hate me.'

'Not you – only your faults. I do hate them.'

' 'Twould be much more becoming if you set yourself to cure them. Come, let's strike a balance with the twenty pounds, and be friends.'

She gave a sigh of resignation. 'I have about that sum here for household expenses. If you must have it, take it.'

'Very good. Thank you. I expect I shall have gone away before you are in to breakfast to-morrow.'

'And must you go? Ah! there was a time, Frank, when it would have taken a good many promises to other people to drag you away from me. You used to called me darling, then. But it doesn't matter to you how my days are passed now.'

'I must go, in spite of sentiment.' Troy, as he spoke, looked at his watch, and, apparently actuated by *non lucendo* principles, opened the case at the back, revealing, snugly stowed within it, a small coil of hair.

Bathsheba's eyes had been accidentally lifted at that moment, and she saw the action and saw the hair. She flushed in pain and surprise, and some words escaped her before she had thought whether or not it was wise to utter them. 'A woman's curl of hair!' she said. 'O, Frank, whose is that?'

Troy had instantly closed his watch. He carelessly replied, as one who cloaked some feelings that the sight had stirred: 'Why, yours, of course. Whose should it be? I had quite forgotten that I had it.'

'What a dreadful fib, Frank!'

'I tell you I had forgotten it!' he said loudly.

'I don't mean that – it was yellow hair.'

'Nonsense.'

'That's insulting me. I know it was yellow. Now whose was it? I want to know.'

'Very well – I'll tell you, so make no more ado. It is the hair of a young woman I was going to marry before I knew you.'

'You ought to tell me her name, then.'

'I cannot do that.'

'Is she married yet?'

'No.'

'Is she alive?'

'Yes.'

'Is she pretty?'

'Yes.'

'It is wonderful how she can be, poor thing, under such an awful affliction!'

'Affliction – what affliction?' he inquired quickly.

'Having hair of that dreadful colour.'

'Oh – ho – I like that!' said Troy, recovering himself. 'Why her hair has been admired by everybody who has seen her since she has worn it loose, which has not been long. It is beautiful hair. People used to turn their heads to look at it, poor girl!'

'Pooh! that's nothing – that's nothing!' she exclaimed, in incipient accents of pique. 'If I cared for your love as much as I used to I could say people had turned to look at mine.'

'Bathsheba, don't be so fitful and jealous. You knew what married life would be like, and shouldn't have entered it if you feared these contingencies.'

Troy had by this time driven her to bitterness: her heart was big in her throat, and the ducts to her eyes were painfully full. Ashamed as she was to show emotion, at last she burst out:

'This is all I get for loving you so well! Ah! when I married you your life was dearer to me than my own. I would have died for you – how truly I can say that I would have died for you! And now you sneer at my foolishness in marrying you. O! is it kind to me to throw my mistake in my face? Whatever opinion you may have of my wisdom, you should not tell me of it so mercilessly, now that I am in your power.'

'I can't help how things fall out,' said Troy; 'upon my heart, women will be the death of me!'

'Well, you shouldn't keep people's hair. You'll burn it, won't you, Frank?'

Frank went on as if he had not heard her. 'There are considerations even before my consideration for you; reparations to be made – ties you know nothing of. If you repent of marrying, so do I.'

Trembling now, she put her hand upon his arm, saying, in mingled tones of wretchedness and coaxing, 'I only repent it if you don't love me better than any woman in the world! I don't otherwise, Frank. You don't repent because you already love somebody better than you love me, do you?'

'I don't know. Why do you say that?'

'You won't burn that curl. You like the woman who owns that pretty hair – yes; it is pretty – more beautiful than my miserable black mane! Well, it is no use; I can't help being ugly. You must like her best, if you will!'

'Until to-day, when I took it from a drawer, I have never looked upon that bit of hair for several months – that I am ready to swear.'

'But just now you said "ties"; and then – that woman we met?'

'   'Twas the meeting with her that reminded me of the hair.'

'Is it hers, then?'

'Yes. There, now that you have wormed it out of me, I hope you are content.'

'And what are the ties?'

'Oh! that meant nothing – a mere jest.'

'A mere jest!' she said, in mournful astonishment. 'Can you jest when I am so wretchedly in earnest? Tell me the truth, Frank. I am not a fool, you know, although I am a woman, and have my woman's moments. Come! treat me fairly,' she said, looking honestly and fearlessly into his face. 'I don't want much; bare justice – that's all! Ah! once I felt I could be content with nothing less than the highest homage from the husband I should choose. Now, anything short of cruelty will content me. Yes! the independent and spirited Bathsheba is come to this!'

'For Heaven's sake don't be so desperate!' Troy said snappishly, rising as he did so, and leaving the room.

Directly he had gone, Bathsheba burst into great sobs – dry-eyed sobs, which cut as they came, without any softening by tears. But she determined to repress all evidences of feeling. She was conquered; but she would never own it as long as she lived. Her pride was indeed brought low by despairing discoveries of her spoliation by marriage with a less pure nature than her own. She chafed to and fro in rebelliousness, like a caged leopard; her whole soul was in arms, and the blood fired her face. Until she had met Troy, Bathsheba had been proud of her position as a woman; it had been a glory to her to know that her lips had been touched by no man's on earth – that her waist had never been encircled by a lover's arm. She hated herself now. In those earlier days she had always nourished a secret contempt for girls who were slaves of the first good-looking young fellow who should choose to salute them. She had never taken kindly to the idea of marriage in the abstract as did the majority of women she saw about her. In the turmoil of her anxiety for her lover she had agreed to marry him; but the perception that had accompanied her happiest hours on this account was rather that of self-sacrifice than of promotion and honour. Although she scarcely knew the divinity's name, Diana was the goddess whom Bathsheba instinctively adored. That she had never, by look, word, or sign, encouraged a man to approach her – that she had felt herself sufficient to herself, and had in the independence of her girlish heart fancied there was a certain degradation in renouncing the simplicity of a maiden existence to become the humbler half of an indifferent matrimonial whole – were facts now bitterly remembered. O, if she had never stooped to folly of this kind, respectable as it was, and could only stand again, as she had stood on the hill at Norcombe, and dare Troy or any other man to pollute a hair of her head by this interference!

The next morning she rose earlier than usual, and had the horse saddled for her ride round the farm in the customary way. When she came in at half-past eight – their usual hour for breakfasting – she was informed that her husband had risen, taken his breakfast, and driven off to Casterbridge with the gig and Poppet.

After breakfast she was cool and collected – quite herself in fact – and she rambled to the gate, intending to walk to another quarter of the farm, which she still personally superintended as well as her duties in the house would permit, continually, however, finding herself preceded in fore-thought by Gabriel Oak, for whom she began to entertain the genuine friendship of a sister. Of course, she sometimes thought of him in the light of an old lover, and had momentary imaginings of what life with him as a husband would have been like; also of life with Boldwood under the same conditions. But Bathsheba, though she could feel, was not much given to futile dreaming, and her musings under this head were short and entirely confined to the times when Troy's neglect was more than ordinarily evident.

She saw coming up the road a man like Mr Boldwood. It was Mr Boldwood. Bathsheba blushed painfully, and watched. The farmer stopped when still a long way off, and held up his hand to Gabriel Oak, who was in a footpath across the field. The two men then approached each other and seemed to engage in earnest conversation.

Thus they continued for a long time. Joseph Poorgrass now passed near them, wheeling a barrow of apples up the hill to Bathsheba's residence. Boldwood and Gabriel called to him, spoke to him for a few minutes, and then all three parted, Joseph immediately coming up the hill with his barrow.

Bathsheba, who had seen this pantomime with some surprise, experienced great relief when Boldwood turned back again. 'Well, what's the message, Joseph?' she said.

He set down his barrow, and, putting upon himself the refined aspect that a conversation with a lady required, spoke to Bathsheba over the gate.

'You'll never see Fanny Robin no more – use nor principle – ma'am.'

'Why?'

'Because she's dead in the Union.'

'Fanny dead – never!'

'Yes, ma'am.'

'What did she die from?'

'I don't know for certain; but I should be inclined to think it was from general neshness of constitution. She was such a limber maid that 'a could stand no hardship, even when I knowed her, and 'a went like a candlesnoff, so 'tis said. She was took bad in the morning, and being quite feeble and worn out, she died in the evening. She belongs by law to our parish; and Mr Boldwood is going to send a waggon at three this afternoon to fetch her home here and bury her.'

'Indeed I shall not let Mr Boldwood do any such thing – I shall do it! Fanny was my uncle's servant, and, although I only knew her for a couple of days, she belongs to me. How very, very sad this is! – the idea of Fanny being in a workhouse.' Bathsheba had begun to know what suffering was, and she spoke with real feeling . . . 'Send across to Mr Boldwood's, and say that Mrs Troy will take upon herself the duty of fetching an old servant of the family . . . We ought not to put her in a waggon; we'll get a hearse.'

'There will hardly be time, ma'am, will there?'

'Perhaps not,' she said, musingly. 'When did you say we must be at the door – three o'clock?'

'Three o'clock this afternoon, ma'am, so to speak it.'

'Very well – you go with it. A pretty waggon is better than an ugly hearse, after all. Joseph, have the new spring waggon with the blue body and red wheels, and wash it very clean. And, Joseph –'

'Yes, ma'am.'

'Carry with you some evergreens and flowers to put upon her coffin – indeed, gather a great many, and completely bury her in them. Get some boughs of laurustinus, and variegated box, and yew, and boy's-love; ay, and some bunches of chrysanthemum. And let old Pleasant draw her, because she knew him so well.'

'I will, ma'am. I ought to have said that the Union, in the form of four labouring men, will meet me when I gets to our churchyard gate, and take her and bury her according to the rites of the Boards of Guardians, as by law ordained.'

'Dear me – Casterbridge Union – and is Fanny come to this?' said Bathsheba, musing. 'I wish I had known of it sooner. I thought she was far away. How long has she lived there?'

'On'y been there a day or two.'

'Oh! – then she has not been staying there as a regular inmate?'

'No. She first went to live in a garrison-town t'other side o' Wessex, and since then she'd been picking up a living at seampstering in Melchester for several months, at the house of a very respectable widow-woman who takes in work of that sort. She only got handy the Union-house on Sunday morning 'a b'lieve, and 'tis supposed here and there that she had traipsed every step of the way from Melchester. Why she left her place I can't say, for I don't know; and as to a lie, why, I wouldn't tell it. That's the short of the story, ma'am.'

'Ah-h!'

No gem ever flashed from a rosy ray to a white one more rapidly than changed the young wife's countenance whilst this word came from her in a long-drawn breath. 'Did she walk along our turnpike-road?' she said, in a suddenly restless and eager voice.

'I believe she did . . . Ma'am, shall I call Liddy? You bain't well, ma'am, surely? You look like a lily – so pale and fainty!'

'No; don't call her, it is nothing. When did she pass Weatherbury?'

'Last Saturday night.'

'That will do, Joseph; now you may go.'

'Certainly, ma'am.'

'Joseph, come hither a moment. What was the colour of Fanny Robin's hair?'

'Really, mistress, now that 'tis put to me so judge-and-jury like, I can't call to mind, if ye'll believe me!'

'Never mind; go on and do what I told you. Stop – well, no, go on.'

She turned herself away from him, that he might no longer notice the mood which had set its sign so visibly upon her, and went indoors with a distressing sense of faintness and a beating brow. About an hour after, she heard the noise of the waggon and went out, still with a painful consciousness of her bewildered and troubled look. Joseph, dressed in his best suit of clothes, was putting in the horse to start. The shrubs and flowers were all piled in the waggon, as she had directed. Bathsheba hardly saw them now.

'Whose sweetheart did you say, Joseph?'

'I don't know, ma'am.'

'Are you quite sure?'

'Yes, ma'am, quite sure.'

'Sure of what?'

'I'm sure that all I know is that she arrived in the morning and died in the evening without further parley. What Oak and Mr Boldwood told me was only these few words. "Little Fanny Robin is dead, Joseph," Gabriel said, looking in my face in his steady old way. I was very sorry, and I said, "Ah! – and how did she come to die?" "Well, she's dead in Casterbridge Union," he said; "and perhaps 'tisn't much matter about how she came to die. She reached the Union early Sunday morning, and died in the afternoon – that's clear enough." Then I asked what she'd been doing lately, and Mr Boldwood turned round to me then, and left off spitting a thistle with the end of his stick. He told me about her having lived by seampstering in Melchester, as I mentioned to you, and that she walked therefrom at the end of last week, passing near here Saturday night in the dusk. They then said I had better just name a hent of her death to you, and away they went. Her death might have been brought on by biding in the night wind, you know, ma'am; for people used to say she'd go off in a decline; she used to cough a good deal in winter time. However, 'tisn't much odds to us about that now, for 'tis all over.'

'Have you heard a different story at all?' She looked at him so intently that Joseph's eyes quailed.

'Not a word, mistress, I assure 'ee!' he said. 'Hardly anybody in the parish knows the news yet.'

'I wonder why Gabriel didn't bring the message to me himself. He mostly makes a point of seeing me upon the most trifling errand.' These words were merely murmured, and she was looking upon the ground.

'Perhaps he was busy, ma'am,' Joseph suggested. 'And sometimes he seems to suffer from things upon his mind, connected with the time when he was better off than 'a is now. 'A's rather a curious item, but a very understanding shepherd, and learned in books.'

'Did anything seem upon his mind whilst he was speaking to you about this?'

'I cannot but say that there did, ma'am. He was terrible down, and so was Farmer Boldwood.'

'Thank you, Joseph. That will do. Go on now, or you'll be late.'

Bathsheba, still unhappy, went indoors again. In the course of the afternoon she said to Liddy, who had been informed of the occurrence, 'What was the colour of poor Fanny Robin's hair? Do you know? I cannot recollect – I only saw her for a day or two.'

'It was light, ma'am; but she wore it rather short, and packed away under her cap, so that you would hardly notice it. But I have seen her let it down when she was going to bed, and it looked beautiful then. Real golden hair.'

'Her young man was a soldier, was he not?'

'Yes. In the same regiment as Mr Troy. He says he knew him very well.'

'What, Mr Troy says so? How came he to say that?'

'One day I just named it to him, and asked him if he knew Fanny's young man. He said, "O yes, he knew the young man as well as he knew himself, and that there wasn't a man in the regiment he liked better." '

'Ah! Said that, did he?'

'Yes; and he said there was a strong likeness between himself and the other young man, so that sometimes people mistook them –'

'Liddy, for Heaven's sake stop your talking!' said Bathsheba, with the nervous petulance that comes from worrying perceptions.

* XLII *

Joseph and his Burden – Buck's Head

A WALL bounded the site of Casterbridge Union-house, except along a portion of the end. Here a high gable stood prominent, and it was covered like the front with a mat of ivy. In this gable was no window, chimney, ornament, or protuberance of any kind. The single feature appertaining to it, beyond the expanse of dark green leaves, was a small door.

The situation of the door was peculiar. The sill was three or four feet above the ground, and for a moment one was at a loss for an explanation of this exceptional altitude, till ruts immediately beneath suggested that the door was used solely for the passage of articles and persons to and from the level of a vehicle standing on the outside. Upon the whole, the door seemed to advertise itself as a species of Traitor's Gate translated to another sphere. That entry and exit hereby was only at rare intervals became apparent on noting that tufts of grass were allowed to flourish undisturbed in the chinks of the sill.

As the clock over the South-street Alms-house pointed to five minutes to three, a blue spring waggon, picked out with red, and containing boughs and flowers, passed the end of the street, and up towards this side of the building. Whilst the chimes were yet stammering out a shattered form of 'Malbrook', Joseph Poorgrass rang the bell, and received directions to back his waggon against the high door under the gable. The door then opened, and a plain elm coffin was slowly thrust forth, and laid by two men in fustian along the middle of the vehicle.

One of the men then stepped up beside it, took from his pocket a lump of chalk, and wrote upon the cover the name and a few other words in a large scrawling hand. (We believe that they do these things more tenderly now, and provide a plate.) He covered the whole with a black cloth, threadbare, but decent, the tail-board of the waggon was returned to its place, one of the men handed a certificate of registry to Poorgrass, and both entered the door, closing it behind them. Their connection with her, short as it had been, was over for ever.

Joseph then placed the flowers as enjoined, and the evergreens around the flowers till it was difficult to divine what the waggon contained; he smacked his whip, and the rather pleasing funeral car crept down the hill, and along the road to Weatherbury.

The afternoon drew on apace, and, looking to the right towards the sea as he walked beside the horse, Poorgrass saw strange clouds and scrolls of mist rolling over the long ridges which girt the landscape in that quarter. They came in yet greater volumes, and indolently crept across the intervening valleys, and around the withered papery flags of the moor and river brinks. Then their dank spongy forms closed in upon the sky. It was a sudden overgrowth of atmospheric fungi which had their roots in the neighbouring sea, and by the time that horse, man, and corpse entered Yalbury Great Wood, these silent workings of an invisible hand had reached them, and they were completely enveloped, this being the first arrival of the autumn fogs, and the first fog of the series.

The air was as an eye suddenly struck blind. The waggon and its load rolled no longer on the horizontal division between clearness and opacity, but were imbedded in an elastic body of a monotonous pallor throughout. There was no perceptible motion in the air, not a visible drop of water fell upon a leaf of the beeches, birches, and firs composing the wood on either side. The trees stood in an attitude of intentness, as if they waited longingly for a wind to come and rock them. A startling quiet overhung all surrounding things – so completely, that the crunching of the waggon-wheels was as a great noise, and small rustles, which had never obtained a hearing except by night, were distinctly individualized.

Joseph Poorgrass looked round upon his sad burden as it loomed faintly through the flowering laurustinus, then at the unfathomable gloom amid the high trees on each hand, indistinct, shadowless, and spectre-like in their monochrome of grey. He felt anything but cheerful, and wished he had the company even of a child or dog. Stopping the horse he listened. Not a footstep or wheel was audible anywhere around, and the dead silence was broken only by a heavy particle falling from a tree through the evergreens and alighting with a smart rap upon the coffin of poor Fanny. The fog had by this time saturated the trees, and this was the first dropping of water from the overbrimming leaves. The hollow echo of its fall reminded the waggoner painfully of the grim Leveller. Then hard by came down another drop, then two or three. Presently there was a continual tapping of these heavy drops upon the dead leaves, the road, and the travellers. The nearer boughs were beaded with the mist to the greyness of aged men, and the rusty-red leaves of the beeches were hung with similar drops, like diamonds on auburn hair.

At the roadside hamlet called Roy-Town, just beyond this wood, was the old inn Buck's Head. It was about a mile and a half from Weatherbury, and in the meridian times of stage-coach travelling had been the place where many coaches changed and kept their relays of horses. All the old stabling was now pulled down, and little remained besides the habitable inn itself, which, standing a little way back from the road, signified its existence to people far up and down the highway by a sign hanging from the horizontal bough of an elm on the opposite side of the way.

Travellers – for the variety *tourist* had hardly developed into a distinct species at this date – sometimes said in passing, when they cast their eyes up to the sign-bearing tree, that artists were fond of representing the signboard hanging thus, but that they themselves had never before noticed so perfect an instance in actual working order. It was near this tree that the waggon was standing into which Gabriel Oak crept on his first journey to Wetherbury; but, owing to the darkness, the sign and the inn had been unobserved.

The manners of the inn were of the old-established type. Indeed, in the minds of its frequenters they existed as unalterable formulae: e.g. –

> Rap with the bottom of your pint for more liquor.
> For tobacco, shout.
> In calling for the girl in waiting, say, 'Maid!'
> Ditto for the landlady, 'Old Soul!', etc., etc.

It was a relief to Joseph's heart when the friendly signboard came in view, and, stopping his horse immediately beneath it, he proceeded to fulfil an intention made a long time before. His spirits were oozing out of him quite. He turned the horse's head to the green bank, and entered the hostel for a mug of ale.

Going down into the kitchen of the inn, the floor of which was a step below the passage, which in its turn was a step below the road outside, what should Joseph see to gladden his eyes but two copper-coloured discs, in the form of the countenances of Mr Jan Coggan and Mr Mark Clark. These owners of the two most appreciative throats in the neighbourhood, within the pale of respectability, were now sitting face to face over a three-legged circular table, having an iron rim to keep cups and pots from being accidentally elbowed off; they might have been said to resemble the setting sun and the full moon shining vis-à-vis across the globe.

'Why, 'tis neighbour Poorgrass!' said Mark Clark. 'I'm sure your face don't praise your mistress's table, Joseph.'

'I've had a very pale companion for the last four miles,' said Joseph, indulging in a shudder toned down by resignation. 'And to speak the truth, 'twas beginning to tell upon me. I assure ye, I ha'n't seed the colour of victuals or drink since breakfast time this morning, and that was no more than a dew-bit afield.'

'Then drink, Joseph, and don't restrain yourself!' said Coggan, handing him a hooped mug three-quarters full.

Joseph drank for a moderately long time, then for a longer time, saying, as he lowered the jug, ' 'Tis pretty drinking – very pretty drinking, and is more than cheerful on my melancholy errand, so to speak it.'

'True, drink is a pleasant delight,' said Jan, as one who repeated a truism so familiar to his brain that he hardly noticed its passage over his tongue; and, lifting the cup, Coggan tilted his head gradually backwards, with closed eyes, that his expectant soul might not be diverted for one instant from its bliss by irrelevant surroundings.

'Well, I must be on again,' said Poorgrass. 'Not but that I should like another nip with ye; but the parish might lose confidence in me if I was seed here.'

'Where be ye trading o't to to-day, then, Joseph?'

'Back to Weatherbury. I've got poor little Fanny Robin in my waggon outside, and I must be at the churchyard gates at a quarter to five with her.'

'Ay – I've heard of it. And so she's nailed up in parish boards after all, and nobody to pay the bell shilling and the grave half-crown.'

'The parish pays the grave half-crown, but not the bell shilling, because the bell's a luxery: but 'a can hardly do without the grave, poor body. However, I expect our mistress will pay all.'

'A pretty maid as ever I see! But what's yer hurry, Joseph? The poor woman's dead, and you can't bring her to life, and you may as well sit down comfortable, and finish another with us.'

'I don't mind taking just the least thimbleful ye can dream of more with ye, sonnies. But only a few minutes, because 'tis as 'tis.'

'Of course, you'll have another drop. A man's twice the man afterwards.

You feel so warm and glorious, and you whop and slap at your work without any trouble, and everything goes on like sticks a-breaking. Too much liquor is bad, and leads us to that horned man in the smoky house; but after all, many people haven't the gift of enjoying a wet, and since we be highly favoured with a power that way, we should make the most o't.'

'True,' said Mark Clark. ' 'Tis a talent the Lord has mercifly bestowed upon us, and we ought not to neglect it. But, what with the parsons and clerks and school-people and serious tea-parties, the merry old ways of good life have gone to the dogs – upon my carcase, they have!'

'Well, really, I must be onward again now,' said Joseph.

'Not, now, Joseph; nonsense! The poor woman is dead, isn't she, and what's your hurry?'

'Well, I hope Providence won't be in a way with me for my doings,' said Joseph, again sitting down. 'I've been troubled with weak moments lately, 'tis true. I've been drinky once this month already, and I did not go to church a-Sunday, and I dropped a curse or two yesterday; so I don't want to go too far for my safety. Your next world is your next world, and not to be squandered offhand.'

'I believe ye to be a chapel-member, Joseph. That I do.'

'Oh, no, no! I don't go so far as that.'

'For my part,' said Coggan, 'I'm staunch Church of England.'

'Ay, and faith, so be I,' said Mark Clark.

'I won't say much for myself; I don't wish to,' Coggan continued, with that tendency to talk on principles which is characteristic of the barley-corn. 'But I've never changed a single doctrine: I've stuck like a plaster to the old faith I was born in. Yes; there's this to be said for the Church, a man can belong to the Church and bide in his cheerful old inn, and never trouble or worry his mind about doctrines at all. But to be a meetinger, you must go to chapel in all winds and weathers, and make yourself as frantic as a skit. Not but that chapel-members be clever chaps enough in their way. They can lift up beautiful prayers out of their own heads, all about their families and shipwracks in the newspaper.'

'They can – they can,' said Mark Clark, with corroborative feeling: 'but we Churchmen, you see, must have it all printed aforehand, or, dang it all, we should no more know what to say to a great gaffer like the Lord than babes unborn.'

'Chapel-folk be more hand-in-glove with them above than we,' said Joseph thoughtfully.

'Yes,' said Coggan. 'We know very well that if anybody do go to heaven, they will. They've worked hard for it, and they deserve to have it, such as 'tis. I bain't such a fool as to pretend that we who stick to the Church have the same chance as they, because we know we have not. But I hate a feller who'll change his old ancient doctrines for the sake of getting to heaven. I'd as soon turn king's-evidence for the few pounds you get. Why, neighbours, when every one of my taties were frosted, our Pa'son Thirdly were the man who gave me a sack for seed, though he hardly had one for his own use, and no money to buy 'em. If it hadn't been for him, I shouldn't hae had a tatie to put in my garden. D'ye think I'd turn after that? No, I'll stick to my side; and if we be in the wrong, so be it; I'll fall with the fallen!'

'Well said – very well said,' observed Joseph. – 'However, folks, I must be moving now: upon my life I must. Pa'son Thirdly will be waiting at the church gates, and there's the woman a-biding outside in the waggon.'

'Joseph Poorgrass, don't be so miserable! Pa'son Thirdly won't mind. He's a generous man; he's found me in tracts for years, and I've consumed a good many in the course of a long and shady life; but he's never been the man to cry out at the expense. Sit down.'

The longer Joseph Poorgrass remained, the less his spirit was troubled by the duties which devolved upon him this afternoon. The minutes glided by uncounted, until the evening shades began perceptibly to deepen, and the eyes of the three were but sparkling points on the surface of darkness. Coggan's repeater struck six from his pocket in the usual still small tones.

At that moment hasty steps were heard in the entry, and the door opened to admit the figure of Gabriel Oak, followed by the maid of the inn bearing a candle. He stared sternly at the one lengthy and two round faces of the sitters, which confronted him with the expressions of a fiddle and a couple of warming-pans. Joseph Poorgrass blinked, and shrank several inches into the background.

'Upon my soul, I'm ashamed of you; 'tis disgraceful, Joseph, disgraceful!' said Gabriel indignantly. 'Coggan, you call yourself a man, and don't know better than this.'

Coggan looked up indefinitely at Oak, one or other of his eyes occasionally opening and closing of its own accord, as if it were not a member, but a dozy individual with a distinct personality.

'Don't take on so, shepherd!' said Mark Clark, looking reproachfully at the candle, which appeared to possess special features of interest for his eyes.

'Nobody can hurt a dead woman,' at length said Coggan, with the precision of a machine. 'All that could be done for her is done – she's beyond us: and why should a man put himself in a tearing hurry for lifeless clay that can neither feel nor see, and don't know what you do with her at all? If she'd been alive, I would have been the first to help her. If she now wanted victuals and drink, I'd pay for it, money down. But she's dead, and no speed of ours will bring her to life. The woman's past us – time spent upon her is throwed away: why should we hurry to do what's not required? Drink, shepherd, and be friends, for to-morrow we may be like her.'

'We may,' added Mark Clark emphatically, at once drinking himself, to run no further risk of losing his chance by the event alluded to, Jan meanwhile merging his additional thoughts of to-morrow in a song:

'To-mor-row, to-mor-row!
And while peace and plenty I find at my board,

With a heart free from sick-ness and sor-row,
With my friends will I share what to-day may af-ford,
And let them spread the ta-ble to-mor-row.
To-mor-row, to-mor –'

'Do hold thy horning, Jan!' said Oak; and turning upon Poorgrass, 'as for you, Joseph, who do your wicked deeds in such confoundedly holy ways, you are as drunk as you can stand.'

'No, Shepherd Oak, no! Listen to reason, shepherd. All that's the matter with me is the affliction called a multiplying eye, and that's how it is I look double to you – I mean, you look double to me.'

'A multiplying eye is a very bad thing,' said Mark Clark.

'It always comes on when I have been in a public-house a little time,' said Joseph Poorgrass meekly. 'Yes; I see two of every sort, as if I were some holy man living in the times of King Noah and entering into the ark . . . Y-y-y-yes,' he added, becoming much affected by the picture of himself as a person thrown away, and shedding tears; 'I feel too good for England: I ought to have lived in Genesis by rights, like the other men of sacrifice, and then I shouldn't have b-b-been called a d-d-drunkard in such a way!'

'I wish you'd show yourself a man of spirit, and not sit whining there!'

'Show myself a man of spirit? . . . Ah well! let me take the name of drunkard humbly – let me be a man of contrite knees – let it be! I know that I always do say "Please God" afore I do anything, from my getting up to my doing down of the same, and I be willing to take as much disgrace as there is in that holy act. Hah, yes! . . . But not a man of spirit? Have I ever allowed the toe of pride to be lifted against my hinder parts without groaning manfully that I question the right to do so? I inquire that query boldly?'

'We can't say that you have, Hero Poorgrass,' admitted Jan.

'Never have I allowed such treatment to pass unquestioned! Yet the shepherd says in the face of that rich testimony that I be not a man of spirit! Well, let it pass by, and death is a kind friend!'

Gabriel, seeing that neither of the three was in a fit state to take charge of the waggon for the remainder of the journey, made no reply, but, closing the door again upon them, went across to where the vehicle stood, now getting indistinct in the fog and gloom of this mildewy time. He pulled the horse's head from the large patch of turf it had eaten bare, readjusted the boughs over the coffin, and drove along through the unwholesome night.

It had gradually become rumoured in the village that the body to be brought and buried that day was all that was left of the unfortunate Fanny Robin who had followed the Eleventh from Casterbridge through Melchester and onwards. But, thanks to Boldwood's reticence and Oak's generosity, the lover she had followed had never been individualized as Troy. Gabriel hoped that the whole truth of the matter might not be published till at any rate the girl had been in her grave for a few days, when the interposing barriers of earth and time, and a sense that the events had been somewhat shut into oblivion, would deaden the sting that revelation and invidious remark would have for Bathsheba just now.

By the time that Gabriel reached the old manor-house, her residence, which lay in his way to the church, it was quite dark. A man came from the gate and said through the fog, which hung between them like blown flour –

'Is that Poorgrass with the corpse?'

Gabriel recognized the voice as that of the parson.

'The corpse is here, sir,' said Gabriel.

'I have just been to inquire of Mrs Troy if she could tell me the reason of the delay. I am afraid it is too late now for the funeral to be performed with proper decency. Have you the registrar's certificate?'

'No,' said Gabriel. 'I expect Poorgrass has that; and he's at the Buck's Head. I forgot to ask him for it.'

'Then that settles the matter. We'll put off the funeral till to-morrow morning. The body may be brought on to the church, or it may be left here at the farm and fetched by the bearers in the morning. They waited more than an hour, and have now gone home.'

Gabriel had his reasons for thinking the latter a most objectionable plan, notwithstanding that Fanny had been an inmate of the farm-house for several years in the lifetime of Bathsheba's uncle. Visions of several unhappy contingencies which might arise from this delay flitted before him. But his will was not law, and he went indoors to inquire of his mistress what were her wishes on the subject. He found her in an unusual mood: her eyes as she looked up to him were suspicious and perplexed as with some antecedent thought. Troy had not yet returned. At first Bathsheba assented with a mien of indifference to his proposition that they should go on to the church at once with their burden; but immediately afterwards, following Gabriel to the gate, she swerved to the extreme of solicitousness on Fanny's account, and desired that the girl might be brought into the house. Oak argued upon the convenience of leaving her in the waggon, just as she lay now, with her flowers and green leaves about her, merely wheeling the vehicle into the coach-house till the morning, but to no purpose. 'It is unkind and unchristian,' she said, 'to leave the poor thing in a coach-house all night.'

'Very well, then,' said the parson. 'And I will arrange that the funeral shall take place early to-morrow. Perhaps Mrs Troy is right in feeling that we cannot treat a dead fellow-creature too thoughtfully. We must remember that though she may have erred grievously in leaving her home, she is still our sister; and it is to be believed that God's uncovenanted mercies are extended towards her, and that she is a member of the flock of Christ.'

The parson's words spread into the heavy air with a sad yet unperturbed cadence, and Gabriel shed an honest tear. Bathsheba seemed unmoved. Mr Thirdly then left them, and Gabriel lighted a lantern. Fetching three other men to assist him, they bore the unconscious truant indoors, placing the coffin on two benches in the middle of a little sitting-room next the hall, as Bathsheba directed.

Every one except Gabriel Oak then left the room. He still indecisively lingered beside the body. He was deeply troubled at the wretchedly ironical aspect that circumstances were putting on with regard to Troy's wife, and at his own powerlessness to counteract them. In spite of his careful manoeuvring all this day, the very worst event that could in any way have happened in connection with the burial had happened now. Oak imagined a terrible discovery resulting from this afternoon's work that might cast over Bathsheba's life a shade which the interposition of many lapsing years might but indifferently lighten, and which nothing at all might altogether remove.

Suddenly, as in a last attempt to save Bathsheba from, at any rate, immediate anguish, he looked again, as he had looked before, at the chalk writing upon the coffin-lid. The scrawl was this simple one, 'Fanny Robin and child'. Gabriel took his handkerchief and carefully rubbed out the two latter words, leaving visible one inscription 'Fanny Robin' only. He then left the room, and went out quietly by the front door.

* XLIII *

Fanny's Revenge

'Do you want me any longer, ma'am?' inquired Liddy, at a later hour the same evening, standing by the door with a chamber candle-stick in her hand, and addressing Bathsheba, who sat cheerless and alone in the large parlour beside the first fire of the season.

'No more tonight, Liddy.'

'I'll sit up for master if you like, ma'am. I am not at all afraid of Fanny, if I may sit in my own room and have a candle. She was such a childlike, nesh young thing that her spirit couldn't appear to anybody if it tried, I'm quite sure.'

'O no, no! You go to bed. I'll sit up for him myself till twelve o'clock, and if he has not arrived by that time, I shall give him up and go to bed too.'

'It is half past ten now.'

'Oh: is it?'

'Why don't you sit upstairs, ma'am?'

'Why don't I?' said Bathsheba desultorily. 'It isn't worth while – there's a fire here, Liddy.' She suddenly exclaimed in an impulsive and excited whisper, 'Have you heard anything strange said of Fanny?' The words had no sooner escaped her than an expression of unutterable regret crossed her face, and she burst into tears.

'No – not a word!' said Liddy, looking at the weeping woman with astonishment. 'What is it makes you cry so, ma'am; has anything hurt you?' She came to Bathsheba's side with a face full of sympathy.

'No, Liddy – I don't want you any more. I can hardly say why I have taken so to crying lately; I never used to cry. Good-night.'

Liddy then left the parlour and closed the door.

Bathsheba was lonely and miserable now; not lonelier actually than she had been before her marriage; but her loneliness then was to that of the present time as the solitude of a mountain is to the solitude of a cave. And within the last day or two had come these disquieting thoughts about her husband's past. Her wayward sentiment that evening concerning Fanny's temporary resting-place had been the result of a strange complication of impulses in Bathsheba's bosom. Perhaps it would be more accurately described as a determined rebellion against her prejudices, a revulsion from a lower instinct of uncharitableness, which would have withheld all sympathy from the dead woman, because in life she had preceded Bathsheba in the attentions of a man whom Bathsheba had by no means ceased from loving, though her love was sick to death just now with the gravity of a further misgiving.

In five or ten minutes there was another tap at the door. Liddy reappeared, and coming in a little way stood hesitating, until at length she said, 'Maryann has just heard something very strange, but I know it isn't true. And we shall be sure to know the rights of it in a day or two.'

'What is it?'

'Oh, nothing connected with you or us, ma'am. It is about Fanny. That same thing you have heard.'

'I have heard nothing.'

'I mean that a wicked story is got to Weatherbury within this last hour – that – ' Liddy came close to her mistress and whispered the remainder of the sentence slowly into her ear, inclining her head as she spoke in the direction of the room where Fanny lay.

Bathsheba trembled from head to foot.

'I don't believe it!' she said excitedly. 'And there's only one name written on the coffin-cover.'

'Nor I, ma'am. And a good many others don't; for we should surely have been told more about it if it had been true – don't you think so, ma'am?'

'We might or we might not.'

Bathsheba turned and looked into the fire, that Liddy might not see her face. Finding that her mistress was going to say no more, Liddy glided out, closed the door softly, and went to bed.

Bathsheba's face, as she continued looking into the fire that evening, might have excited solicitousness on her account even among those who loved her least. The sadness of Fanny Robin's fate did not make Bathsheba's glorious, although she was the Esther to this poor Vashti, and their fates might be supposed to stand in some respects as contrasts to each other. When Liddy came into the room a second time the beautiful eyes which met hers had worn a listless, weary look. When she went out after telling the story they had expressed wretchedness in full activity. Her simple country nature, fed on old-fashioned principles, was troubled by that which would have troubled a woman of the world very little, both Fanny and her child, if she had one, being dead.

Bathsheba had grounds for conjecturing a connection between her own history and the dimly suspected tragedy of Fanny's end which Oak and Boldwood never for a moment credited her with possessing. The meeting with the lonely woman on the previous Saturday night had been unwitnessed and unspoken of. Oak may have had the best of intentions in withholding for as many days as possible the details of what had happened to Fanny; but had he known that Bathsheba's perceptions had already been exercised in the matter, he would have done nothing to lengthen the minutes of suspense she was now undergoing, when the certainty which must terminate it would be the worst fact suspected after all.

She suddenly felt a longing desire to speak to some one stronger than herself, and so get strength to sustain her surmised position with dignity and her carking doubts with stoicism. Where could she find such a friend? nowhere in the house. She was by far the coolest of the women under her roof. Patience and suspension of judgement for a few hours were what she wanted to learn, and there was nobody to teach her. Might she but go to Gabriel Oak! – but that could not be. What a way Oak had, she thought, of enduring things. Boldwood, who seemed so much deeper and higher and stronger in feeling than Gabriel, had not yet learnt, any more than she herself, the simple lesson which Oak showed a mastery of by every turn and look he gave – that among the multitude of interests by which he was surrounded, those which affected his personal well-being were not the most absorbing and important in his eyes. Oak meditatively looked upon the horizon of circumstances without any special regard to his own standpoint in the midst. That was how she would wish to be. But then Oak was not racked by incertitude upon the inmost matter of his bosom, as she was at this moment. Oak knew all about Fanny that she wished to know – she felt convinced of that. If she were to go to him now at once and say no more than these few words, 'What is the truth of the story?' he would feel bound in honour to tell her. It would be an inexpressible relief. No further speech would need to be uttered. He knew her so well that no eccentricity of behaviour in her would alarm him.

She flung a cloak round her, went to the door and opened it. Every blade, every twig was still. The air was yet thick with moisture, though somewhat less dense than during the afternoon, and a steady smack of drops upon the fallen leaves under the boughs was almost musical in its soothing regularity. It seemed better to be out of the house than within it, and Bathsheba closed the door, and walked slowly down the lane till she came opposite to Gabriel's cottage, where he now lived alone, having left Coggan's house through being pinched for room. There was a light in one window only, and that was downstairs. The shutters were not closed, nor was any blind or curtain drawn over the window, neither robbery nor observation being a contingency which could do much injury to the occupant of the domicile. Yes, it was Gabriel himself who was sitting up: he was reading. From her standing-place in the road she could see him plainly, sitting quite still, his light curly head upon his hand, and only occasionally looking up to snuff the candle which stood beside him. At length he looked at the clock, seemed surprised at the lateness of the hour, closed his book, and arose. He was going to bed, she knew, and if she tapped it must be done at once.

Alas for her resolve! She felt she could not do it. Not for worlds now could she give a hint about her misery to him, much less ask him plainly for information on the cause of Fanny's death. She must suspect, and guess, and chafe, and bear it all alone.

Like a homeless wanderer she lingered by the bank, as if lulled and fascinated by the atmosphere of content which seemed to spread from that little dwelling, and was so sadly lacking in her own. Gabriel appeared in an upper room, placed his light in the window-bench, and then – knelt down to pray. The contrast of the picture with her rebellious and agitated existence at this same time was too much for her to bear to look upon longer. It was not for her to make a truce with trouble by any such means. She must tread her giddy distracting measure to its last note, as she had begun it. With a swollen heart she went again up the lane, and entered her own door.

More fevered now by a reaction from the first feelings which Oak's example had raised in her, she paused in the hall, looking at the door of the room wherein Fanny lay. She locked her fingers, threw back her head, and strained her hot hands rigidly across her forehead, saying, with a hysterical sob, 'Would to God you would speak and tell me your secret, Fanny! . . . O, I hope, hope it is not true that there are two of you! . . . If I could only look in upon you for one little minute, I should know all!'

A few moments passed, and she added, slowly, '*And I will.*'

Bathsheba in after times could never gauge the mood which carried her through the actions following this murmured resolution on this memorable evening of her life. She went to the lumber-closet for a screw-driver. At the end of a short though undefined time she found herself in the small room, quivering with emotion, a mist before her eyes, and an excruciating pulsation in her brain, standing beside the uncovered coffin of the girl whose conjectured end had so entirely engrossed her, and saying to herself in a husky voice as she gazed within –

'It was best to know the worst, and I know it now!'

She was conscious of having brought about this situation by a series of actions done as by one in an extravagant dream; of following that idea as to method, which had burst upon her in the hall with glaring obviousness, by gliding to the top of the stairs, assuring herself by listening to the heavy breathing of her maids that they were asleep, gliding down again, turning the handle of the door within which the young girl lay, and deliberately setting herself to do what, if she had anticipated any such undertaking at night and alone, would have horrified her, but which, when done, was not so dreadful as was the conclusive proof of her husband's conduct which came with knowing beyond doubt the last chapter of Fanny's story.

Bathsheba's head sank upon her bosom, and the breath which had been bated in suspense, curiosity, and interest, was exhaled now in the form of a whispered wail: 'Oh-h-h!' she said, and the silent room added length to her moan.

Her tears fell fast beside the unconscious pair in the coffin: tears of a complicated origin, of a nature indescribable, almost indefinable except as other than those of simple sorrow. Assuredly their wonted fires must have lived in Fanny's ashes when events were so shaped as to chariot her hither in this natural, unobtrusive, yet effectual manner. The one feat alone – that of dying – by which a mean condition could be resolved into a grand one, Fanny had achieved. And to that had destiny subjoined this rencounter tonight, which had, in Bathsheba's wild imagining, turned her companion's failure to success, her humiliation to triumph, her lucklessness to ascendency; it had thrown over herself a garish light of mockery, and set upon all things about her an ironical smile.

Fanny's face was framed in by that yellow hair of hers; and there was no longer much room for doubt as to the origin of the curl owned by Troy. In Bathsheba's heated fancy the innocent white countenance expressed a dim triumphant consciousness of the pain she was retaliating for her pain with all the merciless rigour of the Mosaic law: 'Burning for burning; wound for wound; strife for strife.'

Bathsheba indulged in contemplations of escape from her position by immediate death, which, thought she, though it was an inconvenient and awful way, had limits to its inconvenience and awfulness that could not be overpassed; whilst the shames of life were measureless. Yet even this scheme of extinction by death was but tamely copying her rival's method without the reasons which had glorified it in her rival's case. She glided rapidly up and down the room, as was mostly her habit when excited, her hands hanging clasped in front of her, as she thought and in part expressed in broken words: 'O, I hate her, yet I don't mean that I hate her, for it is grievous and wicked; and yet I hate her a little! Yes, my flesh insists upon hating her, whether my spirit is willing or no! . . . If she had only lived, I could have been angry and cruel towards her with some justification; but to be vindictive towards a poor dead woman recoils upon myself. O God, have mercy! I am miserable at all this!'

Bathsheba became at this moment so terrified at her own state of mind that she looked around for some sort of refuge from herself. The vision of Oak kneeling down that night recurred to her, and with the imitative instinct which animates women she seized upon the idea, resolved to kneel, and, if possible, pray. Gabriel had prayed; so would she.

She knelt beside the coffin, covered her face with her hands, and for a time the room was silent as a tomb. Whether from a purely mechanical, or from any other cause, when Bathsheba arose it was with a quieted spirit, and a regret for the antagonistic instincts which had seized upon her just before.

In her desire to make atonement she took flowers from a vase by the window, and began laying them around the dead girl's head. Bathsheba knew no other way of showing kindness to persons departed than by giving them flowers. She knew not how long she remained engaged thus. She forgot time, life, where she was, what she was doing. A slamming together of the coach house doors in the yard brought her to herself again. An instant after, the front door opened and closed, steps crossed the hall, and her husband appeared at the entrance to the room, looking in upon her.

He beheld it all by degrees, stared in stupefaction at the scene, as if he thought it an illusion raised by some fiendish incantation. Bathsheba, pallid as a corpse on end, gazed back at him in the same wild way.

So little are instinctive guesses the fruit of a legitimate induction that, at this moment, as he stood with the door in his hand, Troy never once thought of Fanny in connection with what he saw. His first confused idea was that somebody in the house had died.

'Well – what?' said Troy blankly.

'I must go! I must go!' said Bathsheba, to herself more than to him. She came with a dilated eye towards the door, to push past him.

'What's the matter, in God's name? who's dead?' said Troy.

'I cannot say; let me go out, I want air!' she continued.

'But no; stay, I insist!' He seized her hand, and then volition seemed to leave her, and she went off into a state of passivity. He, still holding her, came up the room, and thus, hand in hand, Troy and Bathsheba approached the coffin's side.

The candle was standing on a bureau close by them, and the light slanted down, distinctly enkindling the cold features of both mother and babe. Troy looked in, dropped his wife's hand, knowledge of it all come over him in a lurid sheen, and he stood still.

So still he remained that he could be imagined to have left in him no motive power whatever. The clashes of feeling in all directions confounded one another, produced a neutrality, and there was motion in none.

'Do you know her?' said Bathsheba, in a small enclosed echo, as from the interior of a cell.

'I do,' said Troy.

'Is it she?'

'It is.'

He had originally stood perfectly erect. And now, in the well-nigh congealed immobility of his frame could be discerned an incipient movement, as in the darkest night may be discerned light after a while. He was gradually sinking forwards. The lines of his features softened, and dismay modulated to illimitable sadness. Bathsheba was regarding him from the other side, still with parted lips and distracted eyes. Capacity for intense feeling is proportionate to the general intensity of the nature, and perhaps in all Fanny's sufferings, much greater relatively to her strength, there never was a time when she suffered in an absolute sense what Bathsheba suffered now.

What Troy did was to sink upon his knees with an indefinable union of remorse and reverence upon his face, and, bending over Fanny Robin, gently kissed her, as one would kiss an infant asleep to avoid awakening it.

At the sight and sound of that, to her, unendurable act, Bathsheba sprang towards him. All the strong feelings which had been scattered over her existence since she knew what feeling was, seemed gathered together into one pulsation now. The revulsion from her indignant mood a little earlier, when she had meditated upon compromised honour, forestalment, eclipse in maternity by another, was violent and entire. All that was forgotten in the simple and still strong attachment of wife to husband. She had sighed for her self-completeness then, and now she cried aloud against the severance of the union she had deplored. She flung her arms round Troy's neck, exclaiming wildly from the deepest deep of her heart –

'Don't – don't kiss them! O, Frank, I can't bear it – I can't! I love you better than she did: kiss me too, Frank – kiss me! *You will, Frank, kiss me too!*'

There was something so abnormal and startling in the childlike pain and simplicity of this appeal from a woman of Bathsheba's calibre and independence, that Troy, loosening her tightly clasped arms from his neck, looked at her in bewilderment. It was such an unexpected revelation of all women being alike at heart, even those so different in their accessories as Fanny and this one beside him, that Troy could hardly seem to believe her to be his proud wife Bathsheba. Fanny's own spirit seemed to be animating her frame. But this was the mood of a few instants only. When the momentary surprise had passed, his expression changed to a silencing imperious gaze.

'I will not kiss you!' he said, pushing her away.

Had the wife now but gone no further. Yet, perhaps, under the harrowing circumstances, to speak out was the one wrong act which can be better understood, if not forgiven in her, than the right and politic one, her rival being now but a corpse. All the feeling she had been betrayed into showing she drew back to herself again by a strenuous effort of self-command.

'What have you to say as your reason?' she asked, her bitter voice being strangely low – quite that of another woman now.

'I have to say that I have been a bad, black-hearted man,' he answered.

'And that this woman is your victim; and I not less than she.'

'Ah! don't taunt me, madam. This woman is more to me, dead as she is, than ever you were, or are, or can be. If Satan had not tempted me with that face of yours, and those cursed coquetries, I should have married her. I never had another thought till you came in my way. Would to God that I had; but it is all too late! I deserve to live in torment for this!' He turned to Fanny then. 'But never mind, darling,' he said; 'in the sight of Heaven you are my very, very wife!'

At these words arose from Bathsheba's lips a long, low cry of measureless despair and indignation, such a wail of anguish as had never been heard within those old-inhabited walls. It was the Τετέλεσται of her union with Troy.

'If she's – that, – what – am I?' she added, as a continuation of the same cry, and sobbing pitifully: and the rarity with her of such abandonment only made the condition more dire.

'You are nothing to me – nothing,' said Troy heartlessly. 'A ceremony before a priest doesn't make a marriage. I am not morally yours.'

A vehement impulse to flee from him, to run from this place, hide, and escape his words at any price, not stopping short of death itself, mastered Bathsheba now. She waited not an instant, but turned to the door and ran out.

* XLIV *

Under a Tree – Reaction

BATHSHEBA went along the dark road, neither knowing nor caring about the direction or issue of her flight. The first time that she definitely noticed her position was when she reached a gate leading into a thicket overhung by some large oak and beech trees. On looking into the place, it occurred to her that she had seen it by daylight on some previous occasion, and that what appeared like an impassable thicket was in reality a brake of fern now withering fast. She could think of nothing better to do with her palpitating self than to go in here and hide; and entering, she lighted on a spot sheltered from the damp fog by a reclining trunk, where she sank down upon a tangled couch of fronds and stems. She mechanically pulled some armfuls round her to keep off the breezes, and closed her eyes.

Whether she slept or not that night Bathsheba was not clearly aware. But it was with a freshened existence and a cooler brain that, a long time afterwards, she became conscious of some interested proceedings which were going on in the trees above her head and around.

A coarse-throated chatter was the first sound.

It was a sparrow just waking.

Next: 'Chee-weeze-weeze-weeze!' from another retreat.

It was a finch.

Third: 'Tink-tink-tink-tink-a-chink!' from the hedge.

It was a robin.

'Chuck-chuck-chuck!' overhead.

A squirrel.

Then, from the road, 'With my ra-ta-ta, and my rum-tum-tum!'

It was a ploughboy. Presently he came opposite, and she believed from his voice that he was one of the boys on her own farm. He was followed by a shambling tramp of heavy feet, and looking through the ferns Bathsheba could just discern in the wan light of daybreak a team of her own horses. They stopped to drink at a pond on the other side of the way. She watched them flouncing into the pool, drinking, tossing up their heads, drinking again, the water dribbling from their lips in silver threads. There was another flounce, and they came out of the pond, and turned back again towards the farm.

She looked further around. Day was just dawning, and beside its cool air and colours her heated actions and resolves of the night stood out in lurid contrast. She perceived that in her lap, and clinging to her hair, were red and yellow leaves which had come down from the tree and settled silently upon her during her partial sleep. Bathsheba shook her dress to get rid of them, when multitudes of the same family lying round about her rose and fluttered away in the breeze thus created, 'like ghosts from an enchanter fleeing'.

There was an opening towards the east, and the glow from the as yet unrisen sun attracted her eyes thither. From her feet, and between the beautiful yellowing ferns with their feathery arms, the ground sloped downwards to a hollow, in which was a species of swamp, dotted with fungi. A morning mist hung over it now – a fulsome yet magnificent silvery veil, full of light from the sun, yet semi-opaque – the hedge behind it being in some measure hidden by its hazy luminousness. Up the sides of this depression grew sheaves of the common rush, and here and there a peculiar species of flag, the blades of which glistened in the emerging sun, like scythes. But the general aspect of the swamp was malignant. From its moist and poisonous coat seemed to be exhaled the essences of evil things in the earth, and in the waters under the earth. The fungi grew in all manner of positions from rotting leaves and tree stumps, some exhibiting to her listless gaze their clammy tops, others their oozing gills. Some were marked with great splotches, red as arterial blood, others were saffron yellow, and others tall and attenuated, with stems like macaroni. Some were leathery and of richest browns. The hollow seemed a nursery of pestilences small and great, in the immediate neighbourhood of comfort and health, and Bathsheba arose with a tremor at the thought of having passed the night on the brink of so dismal a place.

There were now other footsteps to be heard along the road. Bathsheba's nerves were still unstrung: she crouched down out of sight again, and the pedestrian came into view. He was a schoolboy, with a bag slung over his shoulder containing his dinner, and a book in his hand. He paused by the gate, and, without looking up, continued murmuring words in tones quite loud enough to reach her ears.

' "O Lord, O Lord, O Lord, O Lord, O Lord" – that I know out o' book. "Give us, give us, give us, give us, give us" – that I know. "Grace that, grace that, grace that, grace that" – that I know.' Other words followed to the same effect. The boy was of the dunce class apparently; the book was a psalter, and this was his way of learning the collect. In the worst attacks of trouble there appears to be always a superficial film of consciousness which is left disengaged and open to the notice of trifles, and Bathsheba was faintly amused at the boy's method, till he too passed on.

By this time stupor had given place to anxiety, and anxiety began to make room for hunger and thirst. A form now appeared upon the rise on the other side of the swamp, half-hidden by the mist, and came towards Bathsheba. The woman – for it was a woman – approached with her face askance, as if looking earnestly on all sides of her. When she got a little further round to the left, and drew nearer, Bathsheba could see the newcomer's profile against the sunny sky, and knew the wavy sweep from forehead to chin, with neither angle nor decisive line anywhere about it, to be the familiar contour of Liddy Smallbury.

Bathsheba's heart bounded with gratitude in the thought that she was not altogether deserted, and she jumped up. 'O, Liddy!' she said, or attempted to say; but the words had only been framed by her lips; there came no sound. She had lost her voice by exposure to the clogged atmosphere all these hours of night.

'O, ma'am! I am so glad I have found you,' said the girl, as soon as she saw Bathsheba.

'You can't come across,' Bathsheba said in a whisper, which she vainly endeavoured to make loud enough to reach Liddy's ears. Liddy, not knowing this, stepped down upon the swamp, saying, as she did so, 'It will bear me up, I think.'

Bathsheba never forgot that transient little picture of Liddy crossing the swamp to her there in the morning light. Iridescent bubbles of dank subterranean breath rose from the sweating sod beside the waiting-maid's feet as she trod, hissing as they burst and expanded away to join the vapoury firmament above. Liddy did not sink, as Bathsheba had anticipated.

She landed safely on the other side, and looked up at the beautiful though pale and weary face of her young mistress.

'Poor thing!' said Liddy, with tears in her eyes. 'Do hearten yourself up a little, ma'am. However did –'

'I can't speak above a whisper – my voice is gone for the present,' said Bathsheba hurriedly. 'I suppose the damp air from that hollow has taken it away. Liddy, don't question me, mind. Who sent you – anybody?'

'Nobody. I thought, when I found you were not at home, that something cruel had happened. I fancy I heard his voice late last night; and so, knowing something was wrong –'

'Is he at home?'

'No; he left just before I came out.'

'Is Fanny taken away?'

'Not yet. She will soon be – at nine o'clock.'

'We won't go home at present, then. Suppose we walk about in this wood?'

Liddy, without exactly understanding everything, or anything, in this episode, assented, and they walked together further among the trees.

'But you had better come in, ma'am, and have something to eat. You will die of a chill!'

'I shall not come indoors yet – perhaps never.'

'Shall I get you something to eat, and something else to put over your head besides that little shawl?'

'If you will, Liddy.'

Liddy vanished, and at the end of twenty minutes returned with a cloak, hat, some slices of bread and butter, a tea-cup, and some hot tea in a little china jug.

'Is Fanny gone?' said Bathsheba.

'No,' said her companion, pouring out the tea.

Bathsheba wrapped herself up and ate and drank sparingly. Her voice was then a little clearer, and a trifling colour returned to her face. 'Now we'll walk about again,' she said.

They wandered about the woods for nearly two hours, Bathsheba replying in monosyllables to Liddy's prattle, for her mind ran on one subject, and one only. She interrupted with –

'I wonder if Fanny is gone by this time?'

'I will go and see.'

She came back with the information that the men were just taking away the corpse; that Bathsheba had been inquired for; that she had replied to the effect that her mistress was unwell and could not be seen.

'Then they think I am in my bedroom?'

'Yes.' Liddy then ventured to add: 'You said when I first found you that you might never go home again – you didn't mean it, ma'am?'

'No; I've altered my mind. It is only women with no pride in them who run away from their husbands. There is one position worse than that of being found dead in your husband's house from his ill-usage, and that is, to be found alive through having gone away to the house of somebody else. I've thought of it all this morning, and I've chosen my course. A runaway wife is an encumbrance to everybody, a burden to herself and a byword – all of which make up a heap of misery greater than any that comes by staying at home – though this may include the trifling items of insult, beating, and starvation. Liddy, if ever you marry – God forbid that you ever should! – you'll find yourself in a fearful situation; but mind this, don't you flinch. Stand your ground, and be cut to pieces. That's what I'm going to do.'

'O, mistress, don't talk so!' said Liddy, taking her hand, 'but I knew you had too much sense to bide away. May I ask what dreadful thing it is that has happened between you and him?'

'You may ask; but I may not tell.'

In about ten minutes they returned to the house by a circuitous route, entering at the rear. Bathsheba glided up the back stairs to a disused attic, and her companion followed.

'Liddy,' she said, with a lighter heart, for youth and hope had begun to reassert themselves; 'you are to be my confidante for the present – somebody must be – and I choose you. Well, I shall take up my abode here for a while. Will you get a fire lighted, put down a piece of carpet, and help me to make the place comfortable? Afterwards, I want you and Maryann to bring up that little stump bedstead in the small room, and the bed belonging to it, and a table, and some other things . . . What shall I do to pass the heavy time away?'

'Hemming handkerchiefs is a very good thing,' said Liddy.

'O no, no! I hate needlework – I always did.'

'Knitting?'

'And that, too.'

'You might finish your sampler. Only the carnations and peacocks want filling in; and then it could be framed and glazed, and hung beside your aunt's, ma'am.'

'Samplers are out of date – horribly countrified. No, Liddy, I'll read. Bring up some books – not new ones. I haven't heart to read anything new.'

'Some of your uncle's old ones, ma'am?'

'Yes. Some of those we stowed away in boxes.' A faint gleam of humour passed over her face as she said: 'Bring Beaumont and Fletcher's *Maid's Tragedy*; and the *Mourning Bride*; and – let me see – *Night Thoughts*, and the *Vanity of Human Wishes*.'

'And that story of the black man, who murdered his wife Desdemona? It is a nice dismal one that would suit you excellent just now.'

'Now, Lidd, you've been looking into my books, without telling me; and I said you were not to! How do you know it would suit me? It wouldn't suit me at all.'

'But if the others do –'

'No, they don't; and I won't read dismal books. Why should I read dismal books, indeed? Bring me *Love in a Village*, and the *Maid of the Mill*, and *Doctor Syntax*, and some volumes of the *Spectator*.'

All that day Bathsheba and Liddy lived in the attic in a state of barricade; a precaution which proved to be needless as against Troy, for he did not appear in the neighbourhood or trouble them at all. Bathsheba sat at the window till sunset, sometimes attempting to read, at other times watching every movement outside without much purpose, and listening without much interest to every sound.

The sun went down almost blood-red that night, and a livid cloud received its rays in the east. Up against this dark background the west front of the church tower – the only part of the edifice visible from the farm-house windows – rose distinct and lustrous, the vane upon the summit bristling with rays. Hereabouts, at six o'clock, the young men of the village gathered, as was their custom, for a game of Prisoners' base. The spot had been consecrated to this ancient diversion from time immemorial, the old stocks conveniently forming a base facing the boundary of the churchyard, in front of which the ground was trodden hard and bare as a pavement by the players. She could see the brown and black heads of the young lads darting about right and left, their white shirt-sleeves gleaming in the sun; whilst occasionally a shout and a peal of hearty laughter varied the stillness of the evening air. They continued playing for a quarter of an hour or so, when the game concluded abruptly, and the players leapt over the wall and vanished round to the other side behind a yew-tree, which was also half behind a beech, now spreading in one mass of golden foliage, on which the branches traced black lines.

'Why did the base-players finish their game so suddenly?' Bathsheba inquired, the next time that Liddy entered the room.

'I think 'twas because two men came just then from Casterbridge and began putting up a grand carved tombstone,' said Liddy. 'The lads went to see whose it was.'

'Do you know?' Bathsheba asked.

'I don't,' said Liddy.

* XLV *

Troy's Romanticism

WHEN Troy's wife had left the house at the previous midnight his first act was to cover the dead from sight. This done he ascended the stairs, and throwing himself down upon the bed dressed as he was, he waited miserably for the morning.

Fate had dealt grimly with him through the last four-and-twenty hours. His day had been spent in a way which varied very materially from his intentions regarding it. There is always an inertia to be overcome in striking out a new line of conduct – not more in ourselves, it seems, than in circumscribing events, which appear as if leagued together to allow no novelties in the way of amelioration.

Twenty pounds having been secured from Bathsheba, he had managed to add to the sum every farthing he could muster on his own account, which had been seven pounds ten. With this money, twenty-seven pounds ten in all, he had hastily driven from the gate that morning to keep his appointment with Fanny Robin.

On reaching Casterbridge he left the horse and trap at an inn, and at five minutes before ten came back to the bridge at the lower end of the town, and sat himself upon the parapet. The clocks struck the hour, and no Fanny appeared. In fact, at that moment she was being robed in her grave-clothes by two attendants at the Union poor-house – the first and last tiring-women the gentle creature had ever been honoured with. The quarter went, the half hour. A rush of recollection came upon Troy as he waited: this was the second time she had broken a serious engagement with him. In anger he vowed it should be the last, and at eleven o'clock, when he had lingered and watched the stones of the bridge till he knew every lichen upon their faces, and heard the chink of the ripples underneath till they oppressed him, he jumped from his seat, went to the inn for his gig, and in a bitter mood of indifference concerning the past, and recklessness about the future, drove on to Budmouth races.

He reached the race-course at two o'clock, and remained either there or in the town till nine. But Fanny's image, as it had appeared to him in the sombre shadows of that Saturday evening, returned to his mind, backed up by Bathsheba's reproaches. He vowed he would not bet, and he kept his vow, for on leaving the town at nine o'clock in the evening he had diminished his cash only to the extent of a few shillings.

He trotted slowly homeward, and it was now that he was struck for the first time with a thought that Fanny had been really prevented by illness from keeping her promise. This time she could have made no mistake. He regretted that he had not remained in Casterbridge and made inquiries. Reaching home he quietly unharnessed the horse and came indoors, as we have seen, to the fearful shock that awaited him.

As soon as it grew light enough to distinguish objects, Troy arose from the coverlet of the bed, and in a mood of absolute indifference to Bathsheba's whereabouts, and almost oblivious of her existence, he stalked downstairs and left the house by the back door. His walk was towards the churchyard, entering which he searched around till he found a newly dug unoccupied grave – the grave dug the day before for Fanny. The position of this having been marked, he hastened on to Casterbridge, only pausing and musing for a while at the hill whereon he had last seen Fanny alive.

Reaching the town, Troy descended into a side street and entered a pair of gates surmounted by a board bearing the words, 'Lester, stone and marble mason'. Within were lying about stones of all sizes and designs, inscribed as being sacred to the memory of unnamed persons who had not yet died.

Troy was so unlike himself now in look, word and deed, that the want of likeness was perceptible even to his own consciousness. His method of engaging himself in this business of purchasing a tomb was that of an absolutely unpractised man. He could not bring himself to consider, calculate, or economize. He waywardly wished for something, and set about obtaining it like a child in a nursery. 'I want a good tomb,' he said to the man who stood in a little office within the yard. 'I want as good a one as you can give me for twenty-seven pounds.'

It was all the money he possessed.

'That sum to include everything?'

'Everything. Cutting the name, carriage to Weatherbury, and erection. And I want it now, at once.'

'We could not get anything special worked this week.'

'I must have it now.'

'If you would like one of these in stock it could be got ready immediately.'

'Very well,' said Troy, impatiently. 'Let's see what you have.'

'The best I have in stock is this one,' said the stone-cutter, going into a shed. 'Here's a marble headstone beautifully crocketed, with medallions beneath of typical subjects; here's the footstone after the same pattern, and here's the coping to enclose the grave. The polishing alone of the set cost me eleven pounds – the slabs are the best of their kind, and I can warrant them to resist rain and frost for a hundred years without flying.'

'And how much?'

'Well, I could add the name, and put it up at Weatherbury for the sum you mention.'

'Get it done to-day, and I'll pay the money now.'

The man agreed, and wondered at such a mood in a visitor who wore not a shred of mourning. Troy then wrote the words which were to form the inscription, settled the account and went away. In the afternoon he came back again, and found that the lettering was almost done. He waited in the yard till the tomb was packed, and saw it placed in the cart and starting on its way to Weatherbury, giving directions to the two men who were to accompany it to inquire of the sexton for the grave of the person named in the inscription.

It was quite dark when Troy came out of Casterbridge. He carried rather a heavy basket upon his arm, with which he strode moodily along the road, resting occasionally at bridges and gates, whereon he deposited his burden for a time. Midway on his journey he met, returning in the darkness, the men and the waggon which had conveyed the tomb. He merely inquired if the work was done, and, on being assured that it was, passed on again.

Troy entered Weatherbury churchyard about ten o'clock, and went immediately to the corner where he had marked the vacant grave early in the morning. It was on the obscure side of the tower, screened to a great extent from the view of passers along the road – a spot which until lately had been abandoned to heaps of stones and bushes of alder, but now it was cleared and made orderly for interments, by reason of the rapid filling of the ground elsewhere.

Here now stood the tomb as the men had stated, snow-white and shapely in the gloom, consisting of head and foot stone, an enclosing border of marble-work uniting them. In the midst was mould, suitable for plants.

Troy deposited his basket beside the tomb, and vanished for a few minutes. When he returned he carried a spade and a lantern, the light of which he directed for a few moments upon the marble, whilst he read the inscription. He hung his lantern on the lowest bough of the yew-tree, and took from his basket flower-roots of several varieties. There were bundles of snowdrop, hyacinth and crocus bulbs, violets and double daisies, which were to bloom in early spring, and of carnations, pinks, picotees, lilies of the valley, forget-me-not, summer's farewell, meadow-saffron and others, for the later seasons of the year.

Troy laid these out upon the grass, and with an impassive face set to work to plant them. The snowdrops were arranged in a line on the outside of the coping, the remainder within the enclosure of the grave. The crocuses and hyacinths were to grow in rows; some of the summer flowers he placed over her head and feet, the lilies and forget-me-nots over her heart. The remainder were dispersed in the spaces between these.

Troy, in his prostration at this time, had no perception that in the futility of these romantic doings, dictated by a remorseful reaction from previous indifference, there was any element of absurdity. Deriving his idiosyncrasies from both sides of the Channel, he showed at such junctures as the present the inelasticity of the Englishman, together with that blindness to the line where sentiment verges on mawkishness, character-istic of the French.

It was a cloudy, muggy, and very dark night, and the rays from Troy's lantern spread into the two old yews with a strange illuminating power, flickering, as it seemed, up to the black ceiling of cloud above. He felt a large drop of rain upon the back of his hand, and presently one came and entered one of the holes of the lantern, whereupon the candle sputtered and went out. Troy was weary, and it being now not far from midnight, and the rain threatening to increase, he resolved to leave the finishing touches of his labour until the day should break. He groped along the wall and over the graves in the dark till he found himself round at the north side. Here he entered the porch, and, reclining upon the bench within, fell asleep.

* XLVI *

The Gurgoyle: its Doings

THE tower of Weatherbury Church was a square erection of fourteenth-century date, having two stone gurgoyles on each of the four faces of its parapet. Of these eight carved protuberances only two at this time continued to serve the purpose of their erection – that of spouting the water from the lead roof within. One mouth in each front had been closed by bygone churchwardens as superfluous, and two others were broken away and choked – a matter not of much consequence to the well-being of the tower, for the two mouths which still remained open and active were gaping enough to do all the work.

It has been sometimes argued that there is no truer criterion of the vitality of any given art-period than the power of the master-spirits of that time in grotesque; and certainly in the instance of Gothic art there is no disputing the proposition. Weatherbury tower was a somewhat early instance of the use of an ornamental parapet in parish as distinct from cathedral churches, and the gurgoyles, which are the necessary correlatives of a parapet, were exceptionally prominent – of the boldest cut that the hand could shape, and of the most original design that a human brain could conceive. There was, so to speak, that symmetry in their distortion which is less the characteristic of British than of Continental grotesques of the period. All the eight were different from each other. A beholder was convinced that nothing on earth could be more hideous than those he saw on the north side until he went round to the south. Of the two on this latter face, only that at the south-eastern corner concerns the story. It was too human to be called like a dragon, too impish to be like a man, too animal to be like a fiend, and not enough like a bird to be called a griffin. This horrible stone entity was fashioned as if covered with a wrinkled hide; it had short, erect ears, eyes starting from their sockets, and its fingers and hands were seizing the corners of its mouth, which they thus seemed to pull open to give free passage to the water it vomited. The lower row of teeth was quite washed away, though the upper still remained. Here and thus, jutting a couple of feet from the wall against which its feet rested as a support, the creature had for four hundred years laughed at the surrounding landscape, voicelessly in dry weather, and in wet with a gurgling and snorting sound.

Troy slept on in the porch, and the rain increased outside. Presently the gurgoyle spat. In due time a small stream began to trickle through the seventy feet of aerial space between its mouth and the ground, which the water-drops smote like duckshot in their accelerated velocity. The stream thickened in substance, and increased in power, gradually spouting further and yet further from the side of the tower. When the rain fell in a steady and ceaseless torrent the stream dashed downward in volumes.

We follow its course to the ground at this point of time. The end of the liquid parabola has come forward from the wall, has advanced over the plinth mouldings, over a heap of stones, over the marble border, into the midst of Fanny Robin's grave.

The force of the stream had, until very lately, been received upon some loose stones spread thereabout, which had acted as a shield to the soil under the onset. These during the summer had been cleared from the ground, and there was now nothing to resist the downfall but the bare earth. For several years the stream had not spouted so far from the tower as it was doing on this night, and such a contingency had been overlooked. Sometimes this obscure corner received no inhabitant for the space of two or three years, and then it was usually but a pauper, a poacher, or other sinner of undignified sins.

The persistent torrent from the gurgoyle's jaws directed all its vengeance into the grave. The rich tawny mould was stirred into motion, and boiled like chocolate. The water accumulated and washed deeper down, and the roar of the pool thus formed spread into the night as the head and chief among other noises of the kind created by the deluging rain. The flowers so carefully planted by Fanny's repentant lover began to move and writhe in their bed. The winter-violets turned slowly upside down, and became a mere mat of mud. Soon the snowdrop and other bulbs danced in the boiling mass like ingredients in a cauldron. Plants of the tufted species were loosened, rose to the surface, and floated off.

Troy did not awake from his comfortless sleep till it was broad day. Not having been in bed for two nights his shoulders felt stiff, his feet tender, and his head heavy. He remembered his position, arose, shivered, took the spade, and again went out.

The rain had quite ceased, and the sun was shining through the green, brown, and yellow leaves, now sparkling and varnished by the raindrops to the brightness of similar effects in the landscapes of Ruysdael and Hobbema, and full of all those infinite beauties that arise from the union of water and colour with high lights. The air was rendered so transparent by the heavy fall of rain that the autumn hues of the middle distance were as rich as those near at hand, and the remote fields intercepted by the angle of the tower appeared in the same plane as the tower itself.

He entered the gravel path which would take him behind the tower. The path, instead of being stony as it had been the night before, was browned over with a thin coating of mud. At one place in the path he saw a tuft of stringy roots washed white and clean as a bundle of tendons. He picked it up – surely it could not be one of the primroses he had planted? He saw a bulb, another, and another as he advanced. Beyond doubt they were the crocuses. With a face of perplexed dismay Troy turned the corner and then beheld the wreck the stream had made.

The pool upon the grave had soaked away into the ground, and in its place was a hollow. The disturbed earth was washed over the grass and pathway in the guise of the brown mud he had already seen, and it spotted the marble tombstone with the same stains. Nearly all the flowers were washed clean out of the ground, and they lay roots upwards, on the spots whither they had been splashed by the stream.

Troy's brow became heavily contracted. He set his teeth closely, and his compressed lips moved as those of one in great pain. This singular accident, by a strange confluence of emotions in him, was felt as the sharpest sting of all. Troy's face was very expressive, and any observer who had seen him now would hardly have believed him to be a man who had laughed, and sung, and poured love-trifles into a woman's ear. To curse his miserable lot was at first his impulse, but even that lowest stage of rebellion needed an activity whose absence was necessarily antecedent to the existence of the morbid misery which wrung him. The sight, coming as it did, superimposed upon the other dark scenery of the previous days, formed a sort of climax to the whole panorama, and it was more than he could endure. Sanguine by nature, Troy had a power of eluding grief by simply adjourning it. He could put off the consideration of any particular spectre till the matter had become old and softened by time. The planting of flowers on Fanny's grave had been perhaps but a species of elusion of the primary grief, and now it was as if his intention had been known and circumvented.

Almost for the first time in his life Troy, as he stood by this dismantled grave, wished himself another man. It is seldom that a person with much animal spirit does not feel that the fact of his life being his own is the one qualification which singles it out as a more hopeful life than that of others who may actually resemble him in every particular. Troy had felt, in his transient way, hundreds of times, that he could not envy other people their condition, because the possession of that condition would have necessitated a different personality, when he desired no other than his own. He had not minded the peculiarities of his birth, the vicissitudes of his life, the meteorlike uncertainty of all that related to him, because these appertained to the hero of his story, without whom there would have been no story at all for him; and it seemed to be only in the nature of things that matters would right themselves at some proper date and wind up well. This very morning the illusion completed its disappearance, and, as it were, all of a sudden, Troy hated himself. The suddenness was probably more apparent than real. A coral reef which just comes short of the ocean surface is no more to the horizon than if it had never been begun, and the mere finishing stroke is what often appears to create an event which has long been potentially an accomplished thing.

He stood and meditated – a miserable man. Whither should he go? 'He that is accursed, let him be accursed still,' was the pitiless anathema written in this spoliated effort of his new-born solicitousness. A man who has spent his primal strength in journeying in one direction has not much spirit left for reversing his course. Troy had, since yesterday, faintly reversed his; but the merest opposition had disheartened him. To turn about would have been hard enough under the greatest providential encouragement; but to find that Providence, far from helping him into a new course, or showing any wish that he might adopt one, actually jeered his first trembling and critical attempt in that kind, was more than nature could bear.

He slowly withdrew from the grave. He did not attempt to fill up the hole, replace the flowers, or do anything at all. He simply threw up his cards and forswore his game for that time and always. Going out of the churchyard silently and unobserved – none of the villagers having yet risen – he passed down some fields at the back, and emerged just as secretly upon the high road. Shortly afterwards he had gone from the village.

Meanwhile, Bathsheba remained a voluntary prisoner in the attic. The door was kept locked, except during the entries and exits of Liddy, for whom a bed had been arranged in a small adjoining room. The light of Troy's lantern in the churchyard was noticed about ten o'clock by the maid-servant, who casually glanced from the window in that direction whilst taking her supper, and she called Bathsheba's attention to it. They looked curiously at the phenomenon for a time, until Liddy was sent to bed.

Bathsheba did not sleep very heavily that night. When her attendant was unconscious and softly breathing in the next room, the mistress of the house was still looking out of the window at the faint gleam spreading from among the trees – not in a steady shine, but blinking like a revolving coast-light, though this appearance failed to suggest to her that a person was passing and repassing in front of it. Bathsheba sat here till it began to rain, and the light vanished, when she withdrew to lie restlessly in her bed and re-enact in a worn mind the lurid scene of yesternight.

Almost before the first faint sign of dawn appeared she arose again, and opened the window to obtain a full breathing of the new morning air, the panes being now wet with trembling tears left by the night rain, each one rounded with a pale lustre caught from primrose-hued slashes through a cloud low down in the awakening sky. From the trees came the sound of steady dripping upon the drifted leaves under them, and from the direction of the church she could hear another noise – peculiar, and not intermittent like the rest, the purl of water falling into a pool.

Liddy knocked at eight o'clock, and Bathsheba unlocked the door.

'What a heavy rain we've had in the night, ma'am!' said Liddy, when her inquiries about breakfast had been made.

'Yes; very heavy.'

'Did you hear the strange noise from the churchyard?'

'I heard one strange noise. I've been thinking it must have been the water from the tower spouts.'

'Well, that's what the shepherd was saying, ma'am. He's now gone on to see.'

'Oh! Gabriel has been here this morning?'

'Only just looked in in passing – quite in his old way, which I thought he had left off lately. But the tower spouts used to spatter on the stones, and we are puzzled, for this was like the boiling of a pot.'

Not being able to read, think, or work, Bathsheba asked Liddy to stay and breakfast with her. The tongue of the more childish woman still ran upon recent events. 'Are you going across to the church, ma'am?' she asked.

'Not that I know of,' said Bathsheba.

'I thought you might like to go and see where they have put Fanny. The trees hide the place from your window.'

Bathsheba had all sorts of dreads about meeting her husband. 'Has Mr Troy been in tonight?' she said.

'No, ma'am; I think he's gone to Budmouth.'

Budmouth! The sound of the word carried with it a much diminished perspective of him and his deeds; there were thirteen miles interval betwixt them now. She hated questioning Liddy about her husband's movements, and indeed had hitherto sedulously avoided doing so; but now all the house knew that there had been some dreadful disagreement between them, and it was futile to attempt disguise. Bathsheba had reached a stage at which people cease to have any appreciative regard for public opinion.

'What makes you think he has gone there?' she said.

'Laban Tall saw him on the Budmouth road this morning before breakfast.'

Bathsheba was momentarily relieved of that wayward heaviness of the past twenty-four hours which had quenched the vitality of youth in her without substituting the philosophy of maturer years, and she resolved to go out and walk a little way. So when breakfast was over she put on her bonnet, and took a direction towards the church. It was nine o'clock, and the men having returned to work again from their first meal, she was not likely to meet many of them in the road. Knowing that Fanny had been laid in the reprobates' quarter of the graveyard, called in the parish 'behind church', which was invisible from the road, it was impossible to resist the impulse to enter and look upon a spot which, from nameless feelings, she at the same time dreaded to see. She had been unable to overcome an impression that some connection existed between her rival and the light through the trees.

Bathsheba skirted the buttress, and beheld the hole and the tomb, its delicately veined surface splashed and stained just as Troy had seen it and left it two hours earlier. On the other side of the scene stood Gabriel. His eyes, too, were fixed on the tomb, and her arrival having been noiseless, she had not as yet attracted his attention. Bathsheba did not at once perceive that the grand tomb and the disturbed grave were Fanny's, and she looked on both sides and around for some humbler mound, earthed up and clodded in the usual way. Then her eye followed Oak's, and she read the words with which the inscription opened:

ERECTED BY FRANCIS TROY IN BELOVED MEMORY OF FANNY ROBIN

Oak saw her, and his first act was to gaze inquiringly and learn how she received this knowledge of the authorship of the work, which to himself had caused considerable astonishment. But such discoveries did not much affect her now. Emotional convulsions seemed to have become the commonplaces of her history, and she bade him good morning, and asked him to fill in the hole with the spade which was standing by. Whilst Oak was doing as she desired, Bathsheba collected the flowers, and began planting them with that sympathetic manipulation of roots and leaves which is so conspicuous in a woman's gardening, and which flowers seem to understand and thrive upon. She requested Oak to get the church-wardens to turn the lead-work at the mouth of the gurgoyle that hung gaping down upon them, that by this means the stream might be directed sideways, and a repetition of the accident prevented. Finally, with the superfluous magnanimity of a woman whose narrower instincts have brought down bitterness upon her instead of love, she wiped the mud spots from the tomb as if she rather liked its words than otherwise, and went home again.*

* XLVII *

Adventures by the Shore

TROY wandered along towards the south. A composite feeling, made up of disgust with the, to him, humdrum tediousness of a farmer's life, gloomy images of her who lay in the churchyard, remorse, and a general averseness to his wife's society, impelled him to seek a home in any place on earth save Weatherbury. The sad accessories of Fanny's end confronted him as vivid pictures which threatened to be indelible, and made life in Bathsheba's house intolerable. At three in the afternoon he found himself at the foot of a slope more than a mile in length, which ran to the ridge of a range of hills lying parallel with the shore, and formed a monotonous barrier between the basin of cultivated country inland and the wilder scenery of the coast. Up the hill stretched a road nearly straight and perfectly white, the two sides approaching each other in a gradual taper till they met the sky at the top about two miles off. Throughout the length of this narrow and irksome inclined plane not a sign of life was visible on this garish afternoon. Troy toiled up the road with a languor and depression greater than any he had experienced for many a day and year before. The air was warm and muggy, and the top seemed to recede as he approached.

At last he reached the summit, and a wide and novel prospect burst

* The local tower and churchyard do not answer precisely to the foregoing description.

upon him with an effect almost like that of the Pacific upon Balboa's gaze. The broad steely sea, marked only by faint lines, which had a semblance of being etched thereon to a degree not deep enough to disturb its general evenness, stretched the whole width of his front and round to the right, where, near the town and port of Budmouth, the sun bristled down upon it, and banished all colour, to substitute in its place a clear oily polish. Nothing moved in sky, land, or sea, except a frill of milkwhite foam along the nearer angles of the shores, shreds of which licked the contiguous stones like tongues.

He descended and came to a small basin of sea enclosed by the cliffs. Troy's nature freshened within him; he thought he would rest and bathe here before going further. He undressed and plunged in. Inside the cove the water was uninteresting to a swimmer, being smooth as a pond, and to get a little of the ocean swell Troy presently swam between the two projecting spurs of rock which formed the pillars of Hercules to this miniature Mediterranean. Unfortunately for Troy a current unknown to him existed outside, which, unimportant to craft of any burden, was awkward for a swimmer who might be taken in it unawares. Troy found himself carried to the left and then round in a swoop out to sea.

He now recollected the place and its sinister character. Many bathers had there prayed for a dry death from time to time, and, like Gonzalo also, had been unanswered; and Troy began to deem it possible that he might be added to their number. Not a boat of any kind was at present within sight, but far in the distance Budmouth lay upon the sea, as it were quietly regarding his efforts, and beside the town the harbour showed its position by a dim meshwork of ropes and spars. After well-nigh exhausting himself in attempts to get back to the mouth of the cove, in his weakness swimming several inches deeper than was his wont, keeping up his breathing entirely by his nostrils turning upon his back a dozen times over, swimming *en papillon*, and so on, Troy resolved as a last resource to tread water at a slight incline, and so endeavour to reach the shore at any point, merely giving himself a gentle impetus inwards whilst carried on in the general direction of the tide. This, necessarily a slow process, he found to be not altogether so difficult, and though there was no choice of a landing-place – the objects on shore passing by him in a sad and slow procession – he perceptibly approached the extremity of a spit of land yet further to the right, now well defined against the sunny portion of the horizon. While the swimmer's eyes were fixed upon the spit as his only means of salvation on this side of the Unknown, a moving object broke the outline of the extremity, and immediately a ship's boat appeared, manned with several sailor lads, her bows towards the sea.

All Troy's vigour spasmodically revived to prolong the struggle yet a little further. Swimming with his right arm, he held up his left to hail them, splashing upon the waves, and shouting with all his might. From the position of the setting sun his white form was distinctly visible upon the now deep-hued bosom of the sea to the east of the boat, and the men saw him at once. Backing their oars and putting the boat about, they pulled towards him with a will, and in five or six minutes from the time of his first halloo, two of the sailors hauled him in over the stern.

They formed part of a brig's crew, and had come ashore for sand. Lending him what little clothing they could spare among them as a slight protection against the rapidly cooling air, they agreed to land him in the morning; and without further delay, for it was growing late, they made again towards the roadstead where their vessel lay.

And now night drooped slowly upon the wide watery levels in front; and at no great distance from them, where the shore-line curved round, and formed a long riband of shape upon the horizon, a series of points of yellow light began to start into existence, denoting the spot to be the site of Budmouth, where the lamps were being lighted along the parade. The cluck of their oars was the only sound of any distinctness upon the sea, and as they laboured amid the thickening shades the lamp-lights grew larger, each appearing to send a flaming sword deep down into the waves before it, until there arose, among other dim shapes of the kind, the form of the vessel for which they were bound.

* XLVIII *

Doubts arise – Doubts linger

BATHSHEBA underwent the enlargement of her husband's absence from hours to days with a slight feeling of surprise, and a slight feeling of relief; yet neither sensation rose at any time far above the level commonly designated as indifference. She belonged to him: the certainties of that position were so well defined, and the reasonable probabilities of its issue so bounded, that she could not speculate on contingencies. Taking no further interest in herself as a splendid woman, she acquired the indifferent feelings of an outsider in contemplating her probable fate as a singular wretch; for Bathsheba drew herself and her future in colours that no reality could exceed for darkness. Her original vigorous pride of youth had sickened, and with it had declined all her anxieties about coming years, since anxiety recognizes a better and a worse alternative, and Bathsheba had made up her mind that alternatives on any noteworthy scale had ceased for her. Soon, or later – and that not very late – her husband would be home again. And then the days of their tenancy of the Upper Farm would be numbered. There had originally been shown by the agent to the estate some distrust of Bathsheba's tenure as James

Everdene's successor, on the score of her sex, and her youth, and her beauty; but the peculiar nature of her uncle's will, his own frequent testimony before his death to her cleverness in such a pursuit, and her vigorous marshalling of the numerous flocks and herds which came suddenly into her hands before negotiations were concluded, had won confidence in her powers, and no further objections had been raised. She had latterly been in great doubt as to what the legal effects of her marriage would be upon her position; but no notice had been taken as yet of her change of name, and only one point was clear – that, in the event of her own or her husband's inability to meet the agent at the forthcoming January rent-day, very little consideration would be shown, and, for that matter, very little would be deserved. Once out of the farm the approach of poverty would be sure.

Hence Bathsheba lived in a perception that her purposes were broken off. She was not a woman who could hope on without good materials for the process, differing thus from the less far-sighted and energetic, though more petted ones of the sex, with whom hope goes on as a sort of clockwork which the merest food and shelter are sufficient to wind up; and perceiving clearly that her mistake had been a fatal one, she accepted her position, and waited coldly for the end.

The first Saturday after Troy's departure she went to Casterbridge alone, a journey she had not before taken since her marriage. On this Saturday Bathsheba was passing slowly on foot through the crowd of rural business-men gathered as usual in front of the market-house, who were as usual gazed upon by the burghers with feelings that those healthy lives were dearly paid for by exclusion from possible aldermanship, when a man, who had apparently been following her, said some words to another on her left hand. Bathsheba's ears were keen as those of any wild animal, and she distinctly heard what the speaker said, though her back was towards him.

'I am looking for Mrs Troy. Is that she there?'

'Yes; that's the young lady, I believe,' said the person addressed.

'I have some awkward news to break to her. Her husband is drowned.'

As if endowed with the spirit of prophecy, Bathsheba gasped out, 'No, it is not true; it cannot be true!' Then she said and heard no more. The ice of self-command which had latterly gathered over her was broken, and the currents burst forth again, and overwhelmed her. A darkness came into her eyes, and she fell.

But not to the ground. A gloomy man, who had been observing her from under the portico of the old corn-exchange when she passed through the group without, stepped quickly to her side at the moment of her exclamation, and caught her in his arms as she sank down.

'What is it?' said Boldwood, looking up at the bringer of the big news, as he supported her.

'Her husband was drowned this week while bathing in Lulwind Cove. A coastguard found his clothes, and brought them into Budmouth yesterday.'

Thereupon a strange fire lighted up Boldwood's eye, and his face flushed with the suppressed excitement of an unutterable thought. Everybody's glance was now centred upon him and the unconscious Bathsheba. He lifted her bodily off the ground, and smoothed down the folds of her dress as a child might have taken a storm-beaten bird and arranged its ruffled plumes, and bore her along the pavement to the King's Arms inn. Here he passed with her under the archway into a private room; and by the time he had deposited – so lothly – the precious burden upon a sofa, Bathsheba had opened her eyes. Remembering all that had occurred, she murmured, 'I want to go home!'

Boldwood left the room. He stood for a moment in the passage to recover his senses. The experience had been too much for his consciousness to keep up with, and now that he had grasped it it had gone again. For those few heavenly, golden moments she had been in his arms. What did it matter about her not knowing it? She had been close to his breast; he had been close to hers.

He started onward again, and sending a woman to her, went out to ascertain all the facts of the case. These appeared to be limited to what he had already heard. He then ordered her horse to be put into the gig, and when all was ready returned to inform her. He found that, though still pale and unwell, she had in the meantime sent for the Budmouth man who brought the tidings, and learnt from him all there was to know.

Being hardly in a condition to drive home as she had driven to town, Boldwood, with every delicacy of manner and feeling, offered to get her a driver, or to give her a seat in his phaeton, which was more comfortable than her own conveyance. These proposals Bathsheba gently declined, and the farmer at once departed.

About half-an-hour later she invigorated herself by an effort, and took her seat and the reins as usual – in external appearance much as if nothing had happened. She went out of the town by a tortuous back street, and drove slowly along, unconscious of the road and the scene. The first shades of evening were showing themselves when Bathsheba reached home, where, silently alighting and leaving the horse in the hands of the boy, she proceeded at once upstairs. Liddy met her on the landing. The news had preceded Bathsheba to Weatherbury by half-an-hour, and Liddy looked inquiringly into her mistress's face. Bathsheba had nothing to say.

She entered her bedroom and sat by the window, and thought and thought till night enveloped her, and the extreme lines only of her shape were visible. Somebody came to the door, knocked, and opened it.

'Well, what is it, Liddy?' she said.

'I was thinking there must be something got for you to wear,' said Liddy, with hesitation.

'What do you mean?'

'Mourning.'

'No, no, no,' said Bathsheba hurriedly.

'But I suppose there must be something done for poor –'

'Not at present, I think. It is not necessary.'

'Why not, ma'am?'

'Because he's still alive.'

'How do you know that?' said Liddy, amazed.

'I don't know it. But wouldn't it have been different, or shouldn't I have heard more, or wouldn't they have found him, Liddy? – or – I don't know how it is, but death would have been different from how this is. I am perfectly convinced that he is still alive!'

Bathsheba remained firm in this opinion till Monday, when two circumstances conjoined to shake it. The first was a short paragraph in the local newspaper, which, beyond making by a methodizing pen formidable presumptive evidence of Troy's death by drowning, contained the important testimony of a young Mr Barker, M.D., of Budmouth, who spoke to being an eyewitness of the accident, in a letter to the editor. In this he stated that he was passing over the cliff on the remoter side of the cove just as the sun was setting. At that time he saw a bather carried along in the current outside the mouth of the cove, and guessed in an instant that there was but a poor chance for him unless he should be possessed of unusual muscular powers. He drifted behind a projection of the coast, and Mr Barker followed along the shore in the same direction. But by the time that he could reach an elevation sufficiently great to command a view of the sea beyond, dusk had set in, and nothing further was to be seen.

The other circumstance was the arrival of his clothes, when it became necessary for her to examine and identify them – though this had virtually been done long before by those who inspected the letters in his pockets. It was so evident to her in the midst of her agitation that Troy had undressed in the full conviction of dressing again almost immediately, that the notion that anything but death could have prevented him was a perverse one to entertain.

Then Bathsheba said to herself that others were assured in their opinion; strange that she should not be. A strange reflection occurred to her, causing her face to flush. Suppose that Troy had followed Fanny into another world. Had he done this intentionally, yet contrived to make his death appear like an accident? Nevertheless, this thought of how the apparent might differ from the real – made vivid by her bygone jealousy of Fanny, and the remorse he had shown that night – did not blind her to the perception of a likelier difference, less tragic, but to herself far more disastrous.

When alone late that evening beside a small fire, and much calmed down, Bathsheba took Troy's watch into her hand, which had been restored to her with the rest of the articles belonging to him. She opened the case as he had opened it before her a week ago. There was the little coil of pale hair which had been as the fuse to this great explosion.

'He was hers and she was his; they should be gone together,' she said.

'I am nothing to either of them, and why should I keep her hair?' She took it in her hand, and held it over the fire. 'No – I'll not burn it – I'll keep it in memory of her, poor thing!' she added, snatching back her hand.

* XLIX *

Oak's Advancement – A Great Hope

THE late autumn and the winter drew on apace, and the leaves lay thick upon the turf of the glades and the mosses of the woods. Bathsheba, having previously been living in a state of suspended feeling which was not suspense, now lived in a mood of quietude which was not precisely peacefulness. While she had known him to be alive she could have thought of his death with equanimity; but now that it might be she had lost him, she regretted that he was not hers still. She kept the farm going, raked in her profits without caring keenly about them, and expended money on ventures because she had done so in bygone days, which, though not long gone by, seemed infinitely removed from her present. She looked back upon the past over a great gulf, as if she were now a dead person, having the faculty of meditation still left in her, by means of which, like the mouldering gentlefolk of the poet's story, she could sit and ponder what a gift life used to be.

However, one excellent result of her general apathy was the long-delayed installation of Oak as bailiff; but he having virtually exercised that function for a long time already, the change, beyond the substantial increase of wages it brought, was little more than a nominal one addressed to the outside world.

Boldwood lived secluded and inactive. Much of his wheat and all his barley of that season had been spoilt by the rain. It sprouted, grew into intricate mats, and was ultimately thrown to the pigs in armfuls. The strange neglect which had produced this ruin and waste became the subject of whispered talk among all the people round; and it was elicited from one of Boldwood's men that forgetfulness had nothing to do with it, for he had been reminded of the danger to his corn as many times and as persistently as inferiors dared to do. The sight of the pigs turning in disgust from the rotten ears seemed to arouse Boldwood, and he one evening sent for Oak. Whether it was suggested by Bathsheba's recent act of promotion or not, the farmer proposed at the interview that Gabriel should undertake the superintendence of the Lower Farm as well as of Bathsheba's, because of the necessity Boldwood felt for such aid, and the impossibility of discovering a more trustworthy man. Gabriel's malignant star was assuredly setting fast.

Bathsheba, when she learnt of this proposal – for Oak was obliged to consult her – at first languidly objected. She considered that the two farms together were too extensive for the observation of one man. Boldwood, who was apparently determined by personal rather than commercial reasons, suggested that Oak should be furnished with a horse for his sole use, when the plan would present no difficulty, the two farms lying side by side. Boldwood did not directly communicate with her during these negotiations, only speaking to Oak, who was the go-between throughout. All was harmoniously arranged at last, and we now see Oak mounted on a strong cob, and daily trotting the length and breadth of about two thousand acres in a cheerful spirit of surveillance, as if the crops all belonged to him – the actual mistress of the one-half, and the master of the other, sitting in their respective homes in gloomy and sad seclusion.

Out of this there arose, during the spring succeeding, a talk in the parish that Gabriel Oak was feathering his nest fast.

'Whatever d'ye think?' said Susan Tall. 'Gabriel Oak is coming it quite the dand. He now wears shining boots with hardly a hob in 'em, two or three times a-week, and a tall hat a-Sundays, and 'a hardly knows the name of smock-frock. When I see people strut enough to be cut up into bantam cocks, I stand dormant with wonder, and says no more!'

It was eventually known that Gabriel, though paid a fixed wage by Bathsheba independent of the fluctuation of agricultural profits, had made an engagement with Boldwood by which Oak was to receive a share of the receipts – a small share certainly, yet it was money of a higher quality than mere wages, and capable of expansion in a way that wages were not. Some were beginning to consider Oak a 'near' man, for though his condition had thus far improved, he lived in no better style than before, occupying the same cottage, paring his own potatoes, mending his stockings, and sometimes even making his bed with his own hands. But as Oak was not only provokingly indifferent to public opinion, but a man who clung persistently to old habits and usages, simply because they were old, there was room for doubt as to his motives.

A great hope had latterly germinated in Boldwood, whose unreasoning devotion to Bathsheba could only be characterized as a fond madness which neither time nor circumstance, evil nor good report, could weaken or destroy. This fevered hope had grown up again like a grain of mustard-seed during the quiet which followed the hasty conjecture that Troy was drowned. He nourished it fearfully, and almost shunned the contemplation of it in earnest, lest facts should reveal the wildness of the dream. Bathsheba having at last been persuaded to wear mourning, her appearance as she entered the church in that guise was in itself a weekly addition to his faith that a time was coming – very far off perhaps, yet surely nearing – when his waiting on events should have its reward. How long he might have to wait he had not yet closely considered. What he would try to recognize was that the severe schooling she had been subjected to had made Bathsheba much more considerate than she had formerly been of the feelings of others, and he trusted that, should she be willing at any time in the future to marry any man at all, that man would be himself. There was a substratum of good feeling in her: her self-reproach for the injury she had thoughtlessly done him might be depended upon now to a much greater extent than before her infatuation and disappointment. It would be possible to approach her by the channel of her good nature, and to suggest a friendly business-like compact between them for fulfilment at some future day, keeping the passionate side of his desire entirely out of her sight. Such was Boldwood's hope.

To the eyes of the middle-aged, Bathsheba was perhaps additionally charming just now. Her exuberance of spirit was pruned down; the original phantom of delight had shown herself to be not too bright for human nature's daily food, and she had been able to enter this second poetical phase without losing much of the first in the process.

Bathsheba's return from a two months' visit to her old aunt at Norcombe afforded the impassioned and yearning farmer a pretext for inquiring directly after her – now possibly in the ninth month of her widowhood – and endeavouring to get a notion of her state of mind regarding him. This occurred in the middle of the haymaking, and Boldwood contrived to be near Liddy, who was assisting in the fields.

'I am glad to see you out of doors, Lydia,' he said pleasantly.

She simpered, and wondered in her heart why he should speak so frankly to her.

'I hope Mrs Troy is quite well after her long absence,' he continued, in a manner expressing that the coldest-hearted neighbour could scarcely say less about her.

'She is quite well, sir.'

'And cheerful, I suppose.'

'Yes, cheerful.'

'Fearful, did you say?'

'O no. I merely said she was cheerful.'

'Tells you all her affairs?'

'No, sir.'

'Some of them?'

'Yes, sir.'

'Mrs Troy puts much confidence in you, Lydia; and very wisely, perhaps.'

'She do, sir. I've been with her all through her troubles, and was with her at the time of Mr Troy's going and all. And if she were to marry again I expect I should bide with her.'

'She promises that you shall – quite natural,' said the strategic lover, throbbing throughout him at the presumption which Liddy's words appeared to warrant – that his darling had thought of re-marriage.

'No – she doesn't promise it exactly. I merely judge on my own account.'

'Yes, yes, I understand. When she alludes to the possibility of marrying again, you conclude –'

'She never do allude to it, sir,' said Liddy, thinking how very stupid Mr Boldwood was getting.

'Of course not,' he returned hastily, his hope falling again. 'You needn't take quite such long reaches with your rake, Lydia – short and quick ones are best. Well, perhaps, as she is absolute mistress again now, it is wise of her to resolve never to give up her freedom.'

'My mistress did certainly once say, though not seriously, that she supposed she might marry again at the end of seven years from last year, if she cared to risk Mr Troy's coming back and claiming her.'

'Ah, six years from the present time. Said that she might. She might marry at once in every reasonable person's opinion, whatever the lawyers may say to the contrary.'

'Have you been to ask them?' said Liddy innocently.

'Not I,' said Boldwood, growing red. 'Liddy, you needn't stay here a minute later than you wish, so Mr Oak says. I am now going on a little further. Good-afternoon.'

He went away vexed with himself, and ashamed of having for this one time in his life done anything which could be called underhand. Poor Boldwood had no more skill in finesse than a battering-ram, and he was uneasy with a sense of having made himself to appear stupid and, what was worse, mean. But he had, after all, lighted upon one fact by way of repayment. It was a singularly fresh and fascinating fact, and though not without its sadness it was pertinent and real. In little more than six years from this time Bathsheba might certainly marry him. There was something definite in that hope, for admitting that there might have been no deep thought in her words to Liddy about marriage, they showed at least her creed on the matter.

This pleasant notion was now continually in his mind. Six years were a long time, but how much shorter than never, the idea he had for so long been obliged to endure! Jacob had served twice seven years for Rachel; what were six for such a woman as this? He tried to like the notion of waiting for her better than that of winning her at once. Boldwood felt his love to be so deep and strong and eternal, that it was possible she had never yet known its full volume, and this patience in delay would afford him an opportunity of giving sweet proof on the point. He would annihilate the six years of his life as if they were minutes – so little did he value his time on earth beside her love. He would let her see, all those six years of intangible ethereal courtship, how little care he had for anything but as it bore upon the consummation.

Meanwhile the early and the late summer brought round the week in which Greenhill Fair was held. This fair was frequently attended by the folk of Weatherbury.

L

The Sheep Fair – Troy touches his Wife's Hand

GREENHILL was the Nijni Novgorod of South Wessex; and the busiest, merriest, noisiest day of the whole statute number was the day of the sheep fair. This yearly gathering was upon the summit of a hill which retained in good preservation the remains of an ancient earthwork, consisting of a huge rampart and entrenchment of an oval form encircling the top of the hill, though somewhat broken down here and there. To each of the two chief openings on opposite sides a winding road ascended, and the level green space of ten or fifteen acres enclosed by the bank was the site of the fair. A few permanent erections dotted the spot, but the majority of visitors patronized canvas alone for resting and feeding under during the time of their sojourn here.

Shepherds who attended with their flocks from long distances started from home two or three days, or even a week, before the fair, driving their charges a few miles each day – not more than ten or twelve – and resting them at night in hired fields by the wayside at previously chosen points, where they fed, having fasted since morning. The shepherd of each flock marched behind, a bundle containing his kit for the week strapped upon his shoulders, and in his hand his crook, which he used as the staff of his pilgrimage. Several of the sheep would get worn and lame, and occasionally a lambing occurred on the road. To meet these contingencies, there was frequently provided, to accompany the flocks from the remoter points, a pony and waggon into which the weakly ones were taken for the remainder of the journey.

The Weatherbury Farms, however, were no such long distance from the hill, and those arrangements were not necessary in their case. But the large united flocks of Bathsheba and Farmer Boldwood formed a valuable and imposing multitude which demanded much attention, and on this account Gabriel, in addition to Boldwood's shepherd and Cain Ball, accompanied them along the way, through the decayed old town of Kingsbere, and upward to the plateau, – old George the dog of course behind them.

When the autumn sun slanted over Greenhill this morning and lighted the dewy flat upon its crest, nebulous clouds of dust were to be seen floating between the pairs of hedges which streaked the wide prospect around in all directions. These gradually converged upon the base of the hill, and the flocks became individually visible, climbing the serpentine ways which led to the top. Thus, in a slow procession, they entered the opening to which the roads tended, multitude after multitude, horned and hornless – blue flocks and red flocks, buff flocks and brown flocks, even green and salmon-tinted flocks, according to the fancy of the colourist and custom of the farm. Men were shouting, dogs were barking, with greatest animation, but the thronging travellers in so long a journey had grown nearly indifferent to such terrors, though they still bleated piteously at the unwontedness of their experiences, a tall shepherd rising here and there in the midst of them, like a gigantic idol amid a crowd of prostrate devotees.

The great mass of sheep in the fair consisted of South Downs and the old Wessex horned breeds; to the latter class Bathsheba's and Farmer Boldwood's mainly belonged. These filed in about nine o'clock, their vermiculated horns lopping gracefully on each side of their cheeks in geometrically perfect spirals, a small pink and white ear nestling under each horn. Before and behind came other varieties, perfect leopards as to the full rich substance of their coats, and only lacking the spots. There were also a few of the Oxfordshire breed, whose wool was beginning to curl like a child's flaxen hair, though surpassed in this respect by the effeminate Leicesters, which were in turn less curly than the Cotswolds. But the most picturesque by far was a small flock of Exmoors, which chanced to be there this year. Their pied faces and legs, dark and heavy horns, tresses of wool hanging round their swarthy foreheads, quite relieved the monotony of the flocks in that quarter.

All these bleating, panting, and weary thousands had entered and were penned before the morning had far advanced, the dog belonging to each flock being tied to the corner of the pen containing it. Alleys for pedestrians intersected the pens, which soon became crowded with buyers and sellers from far and near.

In another part of the hill an altogether different scene began to force itself upon the eye towards midday. A circular tent, of exceptional newness and size, was in course of erection here. As the day drew on, the flocks began to change hands, lightening the shepherds' responsibilities; and they turned their attention to this tent and inquired of a man at work there, whose soul seemed concentrated on tying a bothering knot in no time, what was going on.

'The Royal Hippodrome Performance of Turpin's Ride to York and the Death of Black Bess,' replied the man promptly, without turning his eyes or leaving off tying.

As soon as the tent was completed the band struck up highly stimulating harmonies, and the announcement was publicly made, Black Bess standing in a conspicuous position on the outside, as a living proof, if proof were wanted, of the truth of the oracular utterances from the stage over which the people were to enter. These were so convinced by such genuine appeals to heart and understanding both that they soon began to crowd in abundantly, among the foremost being visible Jan Coggan and Joseph Poorgrass, who were holiday keeping here to-day.

'That's the great ruffen pushing me!' screamed a woman in front of Jan over her shoulder at him when the rush was at its fiercest.

'How can I help pushing ye when the folk behind push me?' said Coggan, in a deprecating tone, turning his head towards the aforesaid folk as far as he could without turning his body, which was jammed as in a vice.

There was silence; then the drums and trumpets again sent forth their echoing notes. The crowd was again ecstasied, and gave another lurch in which Coggan and Poorgrass were again thrust by those behind upon the women in front.

'O that helpless feymels should be at the mercy of such ruffens!' exclaimed one of these ladies again, as she swayed like a reed shaken by the wind.

'Now,' said Coggan, appealing in an earnest voice to the public at large as it stood clustered about his shoulder-blades, 'did ye ever hear such a onreasonable woman as that? Upon my carcase, neighbours, if I could get out of this cheese-wring the damn women might eat the show for me!'

'Don't ye lose yer temper, Jan!' implored Joseph Poorgrass, in a whisper. 'They might get their men to murder us, for I think by the shine of their eyes that they be a sinful form of womankind.'

Jan held his tongue, as if he had no objection to be pacified to please a friend, and they gradually reached the foot of the ladder, Poorgrass being flattened like a jumping-jack, and the sixpence, for admission, which he had got ready half-an-hour earlier, having become so reeking hot in the tight squeeze of his excited hand that the woman in spangles, brazen rings set with glass diamonds, and with chalked face and shoulders, who took the money of him, hastily dropped it again from a fear that some trick had been played to burn her fingers. So they all entered, and the cloth of the tent, to the eyes of an observer on the outside, became bulged into innumerable pimples such as we observe on a sack of potatoes, caused by the various human heads, backs, and elbows at high pressure within.

At the rear of the large tent there were two small dressing-tents. One of these, allotted to the male performers, was partitioned into halves by a cloth; and in one of the divisions there was sitting on the grass, pulling on a pair of jack-boots, a young man whom we instantly recognize as Sergeant Troy.

Troy's appearance in this position may be briefly accounted for. The brig aboard which he was taken in Budmouth Roads was about to start on a voyage, though somewhat short of hands. Troy read the articles and joined, but before they sailed a boat was despatched across the bay to Lulwind Cove; as he had half expected, his clothes were gone. He ultimately worked his passage to the United States, where he made a precarious living in various towns as Professor of Gymnastics, Sword Exercise, Fencing, and Pugilism. A few months were sufficient to give him a distaste for this kind of life. There was a certain animal form of refinement in his nature; and however pleasant a strange condition might be whilst privations were easily warded off, it was disadvantageously coarse when money was short. There was ever present, too, the idea that he could claim a home and its comforts did he but choose to return to

England and Weatherbury Farm. Whether Bathsheba thought him dead was a frequent subject of curious conjecture. To England he did return at last; but the fact of drawing nearer to Weatherbury abstracted its fascination, and his intention to enter his old groove at that place became modified. It was with gloom he considered on landing at Liverpool that if he were to go home his reception would be of a kind very unpleasant to contemplate; for what Troy had in the way of emotion was an occasional fitful sentiment which sometimes caused him as much inconvenience as emotion of a strong and healthy kind. Bathsheba was not a woman to be made a fool of, or a woman to suffer in silence; and how could he endure existence with a spirited wife to whom at first entering he would be beholden for food and lodging? Moreover, it was not at all unlikely that his wife would fail at her farming, if she had not already done so; and he would then become liable for her maintenance: and what a life such a future of poverty with her would be, the spectre of Fanny constantly between them, harrowing his temper and embittering her words! Thus, for reasons touching on distaste, regret, and shame commingled, he put off his return from day to day, and would have decided to put it off altogether if he could have found anywhere else the ready-made establishment which existed for him there.

At this time – the July preceding the September in which we find him at Greenhill Fair – he fell in with a travelling circus which was performing in the outskirts of a northern town. Troy introduced himself to the manager by taming a restive horse of the troupe, hitting a suspended apple with a pistol-bullet fired from the animal's back when in full gallop, and other feats. For his merits in these – all more or less based upon his experience as a dragoon-guardsman – Troy was taken into the company, and the play of Turpin was prepared with a view to his personation of the chief character. Troy was not greatly elated by the appreciative spirit in which he was undoubtedly treated, but he thought the engagement might afford him a few weeks for consideration. It was thus carelessly, and without having formed any definite plan for the future, that Troy found himself at Greenhill Fair with the rest of the company on this day.

And now the mild autumn sun got lower, and in front of the pavilion the following incident had taken place. Bathsheba – who was driven to the fair that day by her odd man Poorgrass – had, like every one else, read or heard the announcement that Mr Francis, the Great Cosmopolitan Equestrian and Roughrider, would enact the part of Turpin, and she was not yet too old and careworn to be without a little curiosity to see him. This particular show was by far the largest and grandest in the fair, a horde of little shows grouping themselves under its shade like chickens around a hen. The crowd had passed in, and Boldwood, who had been watching all the day for an opportunity of speaking to her, seeing her comparatively isolated, came up to her side.

'I hope the sheep have done well to-day, Mrs Troy?' he said nervously.

'O yes, thank you,' said Bathsheba, colour springing up in the centre of her cheeks. 'I was fortunate enough to sell them all just as we got upon the hill, so we hadn't to pen at all.'

'And now you are entirely at leisure?'

'Yes, except that I have to see one more dealer in two hours' time: otherwise I should be going home. I was looking at this large tent and the announcement. Have you ever seen the play of "Turpin's Ride to York"? Turpin was a real man, was he not?'

'O yes, perfectly true – all of it. Indeed, I think I've heard Jan Coggan say that a relation of his knew Tom King, Turpin's friend, quite well.'

'Coggan is rather given to strange stories connected with his relations, we must remember. I hope they can all be believed.'

'Yes, yes; we know Coggan. But Turpin is true enough. You have never seen it played, I suppose?'

'Never. I was not allowed to go into these places when I was young. Hark! What's that prancing? How they shout!'

'Black Bess just started off, I suppose. Am I right in supposing you would like to see the performance, Mrs Troy? Please excuse my mistake, if it is one; but if you would like to, I'll get a seat for you with pleasure.' Perceiving that she hesitated, he added, 'I myself shall not stay to see it: I've seen it before.'

Now Bathsheba did care a little to see the show, and had only withheld her feet from the ladder because she feared to go in alone. She had been hoping that Oak might appear, whose assistance in such cases was always accepted as an inalienable right, but Oak was nowhere to be seen; and hence it was that she said, 'Then if you will just look in first, to see if there's room, I think I will go in for a minute or two.'

And so a short time after this Bathsheba appeared in the tent with Boldwood at her elbow, who, taking her to a 'reserved' seat, again withdrew.

This feature consisted of one raised bench in a very conspicuous part of the circle, covered with red cloth, and floored with a piece of carpet, and Bathsheba immediately found, to her confusion, that she was the single reserved individual in the tent, the rest of the crowded spectators, one and all, standing on their legs on the borders of the arena, where they got twice as good a view of the performance for half the money. Hence as many eyes were turned upon her, enthroned alone in this place of honour, against a scarlet background, as upon the ponies and clown who were engaged in preliminary exploits in the centre, Turpin not having yet appeared. Once there, Bathsheba was forced to make the best of it and remain: she sat down, spreading her skirts with some dignity over the unoccupied space on each side of her, and giving a new and feminine aspect to the pavilion. In a few minutes she noticed the fat red nape of Coggan's neck among those standing just below her, and Joseph Poorgrass's saintly profile a little further on.

The interior was shadowy with a peculiar shade. The strange luminous semi-opacities of fine autumn afternoons and eves intensified into Rembrandt effects the few yellow sunbeams which came through holes and divisions in the canvas, and spirted like jets of gold-dust across the dusky blue atmosphere of haze pervading the tent, until they alighted on inner surfaces of cloth opposite, and shone like little lamps suspended there.

Troy, on peeping from his dressing-tent through a slit for a reconnoitre before entering, saw his unconscious wife on high before him as described, sitting as queen of the tournament. He started back in utter confusion, for although his disguise effectually concealed his personality, he instantly felt that she would be sure to recognize his voice. He had several times during the day thought of the possibility of some Weatherbury person or other appearing and recognizing him; but he had taken the risk carelessly. If they see me, let them, he had said. But here was Bathsheba in her own person; and the reality of the scene was so much intenser than any of his prefigurings that he felt he had not half enough considered the point.

She looked so charming and fair that his cool mood about Weatherbury people was changed. He had not expected her to exercise this power over him in the twinkling of an eye. Should he go on, and care nothing? He could not bring himself to do that. Beyond a politic wish to remain unknown, there suddenly arose in him now a sense of shame at the possibility that his attractive young wife, who already despised him, should despise him more by discovering him in so mean a condition after so long a time. He actually blushed at the thought, and was vexed beyond measure that his sentiments of dislike towards Weatherbury should have led him to dally about the country in this way.

But Troy was never more clever than when absolutely at his wits' end. He hastily thrust aside the curtain dividing his own little dressing space from that of the manager and proprietor, who now appeared as the individual called Tom King as far down as his waist, and as the aforesaid respectable manager thence to his toes.

'Here's the devil to pay!' said Troy.

'How's that?'

'Why, there's a blackguard creditor in the tent I don't want to see, who'll discover me and nab me as sure as Satan if I open my mouth. What's to be done?'

'You must appear now, I think.'

'I can't.'

'But the play must proceed.'

'Do you give out that Turpin has got a bad cold, and can't speak his part, but that he'll perform it just the same without speaking.'

The proprietor shook his head.

'Anyhow, play or no play, I won't open my mouth,' said Troy firmly.

'Very well, then let me see. I tell you how we'll manage,' said the other, who perhaps felt it would be extremely awkward to offend his leading man just at this time. 'I won't tell 'em anything about your keeping silence; go on with the piece and say nothing, doing what you can by a judicious wink now and then, and a few indomitable nods in the heroic places, you know. They'll never find out that the speeches are omitted.'

This seemed feasible enough, for Turpin's speeches were not many or long, the fascination of the piece lying entirely in the action; and accordingly the play began, and at the appointed time Black Bess leapt into the grassy circle amid the plaudits of the spectators. At the turnpike scene, where Bess and Turpin are hotly pursued at midnight by the officers, and the half-awake gatekeeper in his tasselled nightcap denies that any horseman has passed, Coggan uttered a broad-chested 'Well done!' which could be heard all over the fair above the bleating, and Poorgrass smiled delightedly with a nice sense of dramatic contrast between our hero, who coolly leaps the gate, and halting justice in the form of his enemies, who must needs pull up cumbersomely and wait to be let through. At the death of Tom King, he could not refrain from seizing Coggan by the hand, and whispering, with tears in his eyes, 'Of course he's not really shot, Jan – only seemingly!' And when the last sad scene came on, and the body of the gallant and faithful Bess had to be carried out on a shutter by twelve volunteers from among the spectators, nothing could restrain Poorgrass from lending a hand, exclaiming, as he asked Jan to join him, ' 'Twill be something to tell of at Warren's in future years, Jan, and hand down to our children.' For many a year in Weatherbury, Joseph told, with the air of a man who had had experiences in his time, that he touched with his own hand the hoof of Bess as she lay upon the board upon his shoulder. If, as some thinkers hold, immortality consists in being enshrined in others' memories, then did Black Bess become immortal that day if she never had done so before.

Meanwhile Troy had added a few touches to his ordinary make-up for the character, the more effectually to disguise himself, and though he had felt faint qualms on first entering, the metamorphosis effected by judiciously 'lining' his face with a wire rendered him safe from the eyes of Bathsheba and her men. Nevertheless, he was relieved when it was got through.

There was a second performance in the evening, and the tent was lighted up. Troy had taken his part very quietly this time, venturing to introduce a few speeches on occasion; and was just concluding it when, whilst standing at the edge of the circle contiguous to the first row of spectators, he observed within a yard of him the eye of a man darted keenly into his side features. Troy hastily shifted his position, after having recognized in the scrutineer the knavish bailiff Pennyways, his wife's sworn enemy, who still hung about the outskirts of Weatherbury.

At first Troy resolved to take no notice and abide by circumstances. That he had been recognized by this man was highly probable; yet there was room for doubt. Then the great objection he had felt to allowing news of his proximity to precede him to Weatherbury in the event of his return, based on a feeling that knowledge of his present occupation would discredit him still further in his wife's eyes, returned in full force. Moreover, should he resolve not to return at all, a tale of his being alive and being in the neighbourhood would be awkward; and he was anxious to acquire a knowledge of his wife's temporal affairs before deciding which to do.

In this dilemma Troy at once went out to reconnoitre. It occurred to him that to find Pennyways, and make a friend of him if possible, would be a very wise act. He had put on a thick beard borrowed from the establishment, and in this he wandered about the fair-field. It was now almost dark, and respectable people were getting their carts and gigs ready to go home.

The largest refreshment booth in the fair was provided by an innkeeper from a neighbouring town. This was considered an unexceptionable place for obtaining the necessary food and rest: Host Trencher (as he was jauntily called by the local newspaper) being a substantial man of high repute for catering through all the country round. The tent was divided into first and second-class compartments, and at the end of the first-class division was a yet further enclosure for the most exclusive, fenced off from the body of the tent by a luncheon-bar, behind which the host himself stood, bustling about in white apron and shirt-sleeves, and looking as if he had never lived anywhere but under canvas all his life. In these penetralia were chairs and a table, which, on candles being lighted, made quite a cosy and luxurious show, with an urn, plated tea and coffee pots, china teacups, and plum cakes.

Troy stood at the entrance to the booth, where a gipsy-woman was frying pancakes over a little fire of sticks and selling them at a penny a-piece, and looked over the heads of the people within. He could see nothing of Pennyways, but he soon discerned Bathsheba through an opening into the reserved space at the further end. Troy thereupon retreated, went round the tent into the darkness, and listened. He could hear Bathsheba's voice immediately inside the canvas; she was conversing with a man. A warmth overspread his face: surely she was not so unprincipled as to flirt in a fair! He wondered if, then, she reckoned upon his death as an absolute certainty. To get at the root of the matter, Troy took a penknife from his pocket and softly made two little cuts crosswise in the cloth, which, by folding back the corners, left a hole the size of a wafer. Close to this he placed his face, withdrawing it again in a movement of surprise; for his eye had been within twelve inches of the top of Bathsheba's head. It was too near to be convenient. He made another hole a little to one side and lower down, in a shaded place beside her chair, from which it was easy and safe to survey her by looking horizontally.

Troy took in the scene completely now. She was leaning back, sipping a cup of tea that she held in her hand, and the owner of the male voice was Boldwood, who had apparently just brought the cup to her. Bathsheba, being in a negligent mood, leant so idly against the canvas that it was pressed to the shape of her shoulder, and she was, in fact, as good as in Troy's arms; and he was obliged to keep his breast carefully backward that she might not feel its warmth through the cloth as he gazed in.

Troy found unexpected chords of feeling to be stirred again within him as they had been stirred earlier in the day. She was handsome as ever, and she was his. It was some minutes before he could counteract his sudden wish to go in, and claim her. Then he thought how the proud girl who had always looked down upon him even whilst it was to love him, would hate him on discovering him to be a strolling player. Were he to make himself known, that chapter of his life must at all risks be kept for ever from her and from the Weatherbury people or his name would be a byword throughout the parish. He would be nicknamed 'Turpin' as long as he lived. Assuredly before he could claim her these few past months of his existence must be entirely blotted out.

'Shall I get you another cup before you start, ma'am?' said Farmer Boldwood.

'Thank you,' said Bathsheba. 'But I must be going at once. It was great neglect in that man to keep me waiting here till so late. I should have gone two hours ago, if it had not been for him. I had no idea of coming in here; but there's nothing so refreshing as a cup of tea, though I should never have got one if you hadn't helped me.'

Troy scrutinized her cheek as lit by the candles, and watched each varying shade thereon, and the white shell-like sinuosities of her little ear. She took out her purse and was insisting to Boldwood on paying for her tea for herself, when at this moment Pennyways entered the tent. Troy trembled: here was his scheme for respectability endangered at once. He was about to leave his hole of espial, attempt to follow Pennyways, and find out if the ex-bailiff had recognized him, when he was arrested by the conversation, and found he was too late.

'Excuse me, ma'am,' said Pennyways; 'I've some private information for your ear alone.'

'I cannot hear it now,' she said coldly. That Bathsheba could not endure this man was evident; in fact, he was continually coming to her with some tale or other, by which he might creep into favour at the expense of persons maligned.

'I'll write it down,' said Pennyways confidently. He stooped over the table, pulled a leaf from a warped pocket-book, and wrote upon the paper, in a round hand –

'*Your husband is here. I've seen him. Who's the fool now?*'

This he folded small, and handed towards her. Bathsheba would not read it; she would not even put out her hand to take it. Pennyways, then, with a laugh of derision, tossed it into her lap, and, turning away, left her.

From the words and action of Pennyways, Troy, though he had not been able to see what the ex-bailiff wrote, had not a moment's doubt that the note referred to him. Nothing that he could think of could be done to check the exposure. 'Curse my luck!' he whispered, and added imprecations which rustled in the gloom like a pestilent wind. Meanwhile Boldwood said, taking up the note from her lap –

'Don't you wish to read it, Mrs Troy? If not, I'll destroy it.'

'Oh, well,' said Bathsheba carelessly, 'perhaps it is unjust not to read it; but I can guess what it is about. He wants me to recommend him, or it is to tell me of some little scandal or another connected with my work-people. He's always doing that.'

Bathsheba held the note in her right hand. Boldwood handed towards her a plate of cut bread-and-butter; when, in order to take a slice, she put the note into her left hand, where she was still holding the purse, and then allowed her hand to drop beside her close to the canvas. The moment had come for saving his game, and Troy impulsively felt that he would play the card. For yet another time he looked at the fair hand, and saw the pink finger-tips, and the blue veins of the wrist, encircled by a bracelet of coral chippings which she wore: how familiar it all was to him! Then, with the lightning action in which he was such an adept, he noiselessly slipped his hand under the bottom of the tent-cloth, which was far from being pinned tightly down, lifted it a little way, keeping his eye to the hole, snatched the note from her fingers, dropped the canvas, and ran away in the gloom towards the bank and ditch, smiling at the scream of astonishment which burst from her. Troy then slid down on the outside of the rampart, hastened round in the bottom of the entrenchment to a distance of a hundred yards, ascended again, and crossed boldly in a slow walk towards the front entrance of the tent. His object was now to get to Pennyways, and prevent a repetition of the announcement until such times as he should choose.

Troy reached the tent door, and standing among the groups there gathered, looked anxiously for Pennyways, evidently not wishing to make himself prominent by inquiring for him. One or two men were speaking of a daring attempt that had just been made to rob a young lady by lifting the canvas of the tent beside her. It was supposed that the rogue had imagined a slip of paper which she held in her hand to be a bank note, for he had seized it, and made off with it, leaving her purse behind. His chagrin and disappointment at discovering its worthlessness would be a good joke, it was said. However, the occurrence seemed to have become known to few, for it had not interrupted a fiddler, who had lately begun playing by the door of the tent, nor the four bowed old men with grim countenances and walking-sticks in hand, who were dancing 'Major Malley's Reel' to the tune. Behind these stood Pennyways. Troy glided up to him, beckoned, and whispered a few words; and with a mutual glance of concurrence the two men went into the night together.

* LI *

Bathsheba talks with her Outrider

THE arrangement for getting back again to Weatherbury had been that Oak should take the place of Poorgrass in Bathsheba's conveyance and drive her home, it being discovered late in the afternoon that Joseph was suffering from his old complaint, a multiplying eye, and was, therefore, hardly trustworthy as coachman and protector to a woman. But Oak had found himself so occupied, and was full of so many cares relative to those portions of Boldwood's flocks that were not disposed of, that Bathsheba, without telling Oak or anybody, resolved to drive home herself, as she had many times done from Casterbridge Market, and trust to her good angel for performing the journey unmolested. But having fallen in with Farmer Boldwood accidentally (on her part at least) at the refreshment-tent, she found it impossible to refuse his offer to ride on horseback beside her as escort. It had grown twilight before she was aware, but Boldwood assured her that there was no cause for uneasiness, as the moon would be up in half-an-hour.

Immediately after the incident in the tent she had risen to go – now absolutely alarmed and really grateful for her old lover's protection – though regretting Gabriel's absence, whose company she would have much preferred, as being more proper as well as more pleasant, since he was her own managing-man and servant. This, however, could not be helped; she would not, on any consideration, treat Boldwood harshly, having once already ill-used him, and the moon having risen, and the gig being ready, she drove across the hill-top in the wending ways which led downwards – to oblivious obscurity, as it seemed, for the moon and the hill it flooded with light were in appearance on a level, the rest of the world lying as a vast shady concave between them. Boldwood mounted his horse, and followed in close attendance behind. Thus they descended into the lowlands, and the sounds of those left on the hill came like voices from the sky, and the lights were as those of a camp in heaven. They soon passed the merry stragglers in the immediate vicinity of the hill, traversed Kingsbere, and got upon the high road.

The keen instincts of Bathsheba had perceived that the farmer's staunch devotion to herself was still undiminished, and she sympathized deeply. The sight had quite depressed her this evening; had reminded her of her folly; she wished anew, as she had wished many months ago, for some means of making reparation for her fault. Hence her pity for the man who so persistently loved on to his own injury and permanent gloom had betrayed Bathsheba into an injudicious considerateness of manner, which appeared almost like tenderness, and gave new vigour to the exquisite dream of a Jacob's seven years' service in poor Boldwood's mind.

He soon found an excuse for advancing from his position in the rear, and rode close by her side. They had gone two or three miles in the moonlight, speaking desultorily across the wheel of her gig concerning the fair, farming, Oak's usefulness to them both, and other indifferent subjects, when Boldwood said suddenly and simply –

'Mrs Troy, you will marry again some day?'

This point-blank query unmistakably confused her, and it was not till a minute or more had elapsed that she said, 'I have not seriously thought of any such subject.'

'I quite understand that. Yet your late husband has been dead nearly one year, and –'

'You forget that his death was never absolutely proved, and may not have taken place; so that I may not be really a widow,' she said, catching at the straw of escape that the fact afforded.

'Not absolutely proved, perhaps, but it was proved circumstantially. A man saw him drowning, too. No reasonable person has any doubt of his death; nor have you, ma'am, I should imagine.'

'O yes I have, or I should have acted differently,' she said gently. 'From the first I have had a strange unaccountable feeling that he could not have perished. But I have been able to explain that in several ways since. Even were I half persuaded that I shall see him no more, I am far from thinking of marriage with another. I should be very contemptible to indulge in such a thought.'

They were silent now awhile, and having struck into an unfrequented track across a common, the creaks of Boldwood's saddle and her gig springs were all the sounds to be heard. Boldwood ended the pause.

'Do you remember when I carried you fainting in my arms into the King's Arms, in Casterbridge? Every dog has his day: that was mine.'

'I know – I know it all,' she said, hurriedly.

'I, for one, shall never cease regretting that events so fell out as to deny you to me.'

'I, too, am very sorry,' she said, and then checked herself. 'I mean, you know, I am sorry you thought I –'

'I have always this dreary pleasure in thinking over those past times with you – that I was something to you before *he* was anything, and that you belonged *almost* to me. But of course, that's nothing. You never liked me.'

'I did; and respected you, too.'

'Do you now?'

'Yes.'

'Which?'

'How do you mean which?'

'Do you like me, or do you respect me?'

'I don't know – at least, I cannot tell you. It is difficult for a woman to define her feelings in language which is chiefly made by men to express theirs. My treatment of you was thoughtless, inexcusable, wicked! I shall eternally regret it. If there had been anything I could have done to make amends I would most gladly have done it – there was nothing on earth I so longed to do as to repair the error. But that was not possible.'

'Don't blame yourself – you were not so far in the wrong as you suppose. Bathsheba, suppose you had real complete proof that you are what, in fact, you are – a widow – would you repair the old wrong to me by marrying me?'

'I cannot say. I shouldn't yet, at any rate.'

'But you might at some future time of your life?'

'O yes, I might at some time.'

'Well, then, do you know that without further proof of any kind you may marry again in about six years from the present – subject to nobody's objection or blame?'

'O yes,' she said, quickly. 'I know all that. But don't talk of it – seven or six years – where may we all be by that time?'

'They will soon glide by, and it will seem an astonishingly short time to look back upon when they are past – much less than to look forward to now.'

'Yes, yes; I have found that in my own experience.'

'Now, listen once more,' Boldwood pleaded. 'If I wait that time, will you marry me? You own that you owe me amends – let that be your way of making them.'

'But, Mr Boldwood – six years –'

'Do you want to be the wife of any other man?'

'No indeed! I mean, that I don't like to talk about this matter now. Perhaps it is not proper, and I ought not to allow it. Let us drop it. My husband may be living, as I said.'

'Of course, I'll drop the subject if you wish. But propriety has nothing to do with reasons. I am a middle-aged man, willing to protect you for the remainder of our lives. On your side, at least, there is no passion or blamable haste – on mine, perhaps, there is. But I can't help seeing that if you choose from a feeling of pity, and, as you say, a wish to make amends, to make a bargain with me for a far-ahead time – an agreement which will set all things right and make me happy, late though it may be – there is no fault to be found with you as a woman. Hadn't I the first place beside you? Haven't you been almost mine once already? Surely you can say to me as much as this, you will have me back again should circumstances permit? Now, pray speak! O Bathsheba, promise – it is only a little promise – that if you marry again, you will marry me!'

His tone was so excited that she almost feared him at this moment, even whilst she sympathized. It was a simple physical fear – the weak of the strong; there was no emotional aversion or inner repugnance. She said, with some distress in her voice, for she remembered vividly his outburst on the Yalbury Road, and shrank from a repetition of his anger:

'I will never marry another man whilst you wish me to be your wife, whatever comes – but to say more – you have taken me so by surprise –'

'But let it stand in these simple words – that in six years' time you will be my wife? Unexpected accidents we'll not mention, because those, of course, must be given way to. Now, this time I know you will keep your word.'

'That's why I hesitate to give it.'

'But do give it! Remember the past, and be kind.'

She breathed; and then said mournfully: 'O what shall I do? I don't love you, and I much fear that I never shall love you as much as a woman ought to love a husband. If you, sir, know that, and I can yet give you happiness by a mere promise to marry at the end of six years, if my husband should not come back, it is a great honour to me. And if you value such an act of friendship from a woman who doesn't esteem herself as she did, and has little love left, why I – I will –'

'Promise!'

' – Consider, if I cannot promise soon.'

'But soon is perhaps never?'

'O no, it is not! I mean soon. Christmas, we'll say.'

'Christmas!' He said nothing further till he added: 'Well, I'll say no more about it till that time.'

Bathsheba was in a very peculiar state of mind, which showed how entirely the soul is the slave of the body, the ethereal spirit dependent for its quality upon the tangible flesh and blood. It is hardly too much to say that she felt coerced by a force stronger than her own will, not only into the act of promising upon this singularly remote and vague matter, but into the emotion of fancying that she ought to promise. When the weeks intervening between the night of this conversation and Christmas day began perceptibly to diminish, her anxiety and perplexity increased.

One day she was led by an accident into an oddly confidential dialogue with Gabriel about her difficulty. It afforded her a little relief – of a dull and cheerless kind. They were auditing accounts, and something occurred in the course of their labours which led Oak to say, speaking of Boldwood, 'He'll never forget you, ma'am, never.'

Then out came her trouble before she was aware; and she told him how she had again got into the toils; what Boldwood had asked her, and how he was expecting her assent. 'The most mournful reason of all for my agreeing to it,' she said sadly, 'and the true reason why I think to do so for good or for evil, is this – it is a thing I have not breathed to a living soul as yet – I believe that if I don't give my word, he'll go out of his mind.'

'Really, do ye?' said Gabriel gravely.

'I believe this,' she continued, with reckless frankness; 'and Heaven knows I say it in a spirit the very reverse of vain, for I am grieved and troubled to my soul about it – I believe I hold that man's future in my hand. His career depends entirely upon my treatment of him. O Gabriel, I tremble at my responsibility, for it is terrible!'

'Well, I think this much, ma'am, as I told you years ago,' said Oak, 'that his life is a total blank whenever he isn't hoping for 'ee; but I can't suppose – I hope that nothing so dreadful hangs on to it as you fancy. His natural manner has always been dark and strange, you know. But since the case is so sad and odd-like, why don't yer give the conditional promise? I think I would.'

'But is it right? Some rash acts of my past life have taught me that a watched woman must have very much circumspection to retain only a very little credit, and I do want and long to be discreet in this! And six years – why we may all be in our graves by that time, even if Mr Troy does not come back again, which he may not impossibly do! Such thoughts give a sort of absurdity to the scheme. Now, isn't it preposterous, Gabriel? However he came to dream of it, I cannot think. But is it wrong? You know – you are older than I.'

'Eight years older, ma'am.'

'Yes, eight years – and is it wrong?'

'Perhaps it would be an uncommon agreement for a man and woman to make: I don't see anything really wrong about it,' said Oak, slowly. 'In fact the very thing that makes it doubtful if you ought to marry en under any condition, that is, your not caring about him – for I may suppose –'

'Yes, you may suppose that love is wanting,' she said shortly. 'Love is an utterly bygone, sorry, worn-out, miserable thing with me – for him or any one else.'

'Well, your want of love seems to me the one thing that takes away harm from such an agreement with him. If wild heat had to do wi' it, making ye long to overcome the awkwardness about your husband's vanishing, it mid be wrong; but a cold-hearted agreement to oblige a man seems different, somehow. The real sin, ma'am, in my mind, lies in thinking of ever wedding wi' a man you don't love honest and true.'

'That I'm willing to pay the penalty of,' said Bathsheba, firmly. 'You know, Gabriel, this is what I cannot get off my conscience – that I once seriously injured him in sheer idleness. If I had never played a trick upon him, he would never have wanted to marry me. O if I could only pay some heavy damages in money to him for the harm I did, and so get the sin off my soul that way! . . . Well, there's the debt, which can only be discharged in one way, and I believe I am bound to do it if it honestly lies in my power, without any consideration of my own future at all. When a rake gambles away his expectations, the fact that it is an inconvenient debt doesn't make him the less liable. I've been a rake, and the single point I ask you is, considering that my own scruples, and the fact that in the eye of the law my husband is only missing, will keep any man from marrying me until seven years have passed – am I free to entertain such an idea, even though 'tis a sort of penance – for it will be that! I *hate* the act of marriage under such circumstances, and the class of women I should seem to belong to by doing it!'

'It seems to me that all depends upon whe'r you think, as everybody else do, that your husband is dead.'

'I shall get to, I suppose, because I cannot help feeling what would have brought him back long before this time if he had lived.'

'Well, then, in a religious sense you will be as free to *think* o' marrying again as any real widow of one year's standing. But why don't ye ask Mr Thirdly's advice on how to treat Mr Boldwood?'

'No. When I want a broad-minded opinion for general enlightenment, distinct from special advice, I never go to a man who deals in the subject professionally. So I like the parson's opinion on law, the lawyer's on doctoring, the doctor's on business, and my businessman's – that is, yours – on morals.'

'And on love –'

'My own.'

'I'm afraid there's a hitch in that argument,' said Oak, with a grave smile.

She did not reply at once, and then saying, 'Good evening, Mr Oak,' went away.

She had spoken frankly, and neither asked nor expected any reply from Gabriel more satisfactory than that she had obtained. Yet in the centremost parts of her complicated heart there existed at this minute a little pang of disappointment, for a reason she would not allow herself to recognize. Oak had not once wished her free that he might marry her himself – had not once said, 'I could wait for you as well as he.' That was the insect sting. Not that she would have listened to any such hypothesis. O no – for wasn't she saying all the time that such thoughts of the future were improper, and wasn't Gabriel far too poor a man to speak sentiment to her? Yet he might have just hinted about that old love of his, and asked, in a playful off-hand way, if he might speak of it. It would have seemed pretty and sweet, if no more; and then she would have shown how kind and inoffensive a woman's 'No' can sometimes be. But to give such cool advice – the very advice she had asked for – it ruffled our heroine all the afternoon.

* LII *

Converging Courses

CHRISTMAS-EVE came, and a party that Boldwood was to give in the evening was the great subject of talk in Weatherbury. It was not that the rarity of Christmas parties in the parish made this one a wonder, but that Boldwood should be the giver. The announcement had had an abnormal and incongruous sound, as if one should hear of croquet-playing in a cathedral aisle, or that some much-respected judge was going upon the stage. That the party was intended to be a truly jovial one there was no room for doubt. A large bough of mistletoe had been brought from the woods that day, and suspended in the hall of the bachelor's home. Holly and ivy had followed in armfuls. From six that morning till past noon the huge wood fire in the kitchen roared and sparkled at its highest, the kettle, the saucepan, and the three-legged pot appearing in the midst of the flames like Shadrach, Meshach, and Abednego; moreover, roasting and basting operations were continually carried on in front of the genial blaze.

As it grew later the fire was made up in the large long hall into which the staircase descended, and all encumbrances were cleared out for dancing. The log which was to form the back-brand of the evening fire was the uncleft trunk of a tree, so unwieldy that it could be neither brought nor rolled to its place; and accordingly two men were to be observed dragging and heaving it in by chains and levers as the hour of assembly drew near.

In spite of all this, the spirit of revelry was wanting in the atmosphere of the house. Such a thing had never been attempted before by its owner, and it was now done as by a wrench. Intended gaieties would insist upon appearing like solemn grandeurs, the organization of the whole effort was carried out coldly by hirelings, and a shadow seemed to move about the rooms, saying that the proceedings were unnatural to the place and the lone man who lived therein, and hence not good.

II

Bathsheba was at this time in her room, dressing for the event. She had called for candles, and Liddy entered and placed one on each side of her mistress's glass.

'Don't go away, Liddy,' said Bathsheba, almost timidly. 'I am foolishly agitated – I cannot tell why. I wish I had not been obliged to go to this dance; but there's no escaping now. I have not spoken to Mr Boldwood since the autumn, when I promised to see him at Christmas on business, but I had no idea there was to be anything of this kind.'

'But I would go now,' said Liddy, who was going with her; for Boldwood had been indiscriminate in his invitations.

'Yes, I shall make my appearance, of course,' said Bathsheba. 'But I am *the cause* of the party, and that upsets me! – Don't tell, Liddy.'

'O no, ma'am. You the cause of it, ma'am?'

'Yes. I am the reason of the party – I. If it had not been for me, there would never have been one. I can't explain any more – there's no more to be explained. I wish I had never seen Weatherbury.'

'That's wicked of you – to wish to be worse off than you are.'

'No, Liddy. I have never been free from trouble since I have lived here, and this party is likely to bring me more. Now, fetch my black silk dress, and see how it sits upon me.'

'But you will leave off that, surely, ma'am? You have been a widow-lady fourteen months, and ought to brighten up a little on such a night as this.'

'Is it necessary? No; I will appear as usual, for if I were to wear any light dress people would say things about me, and I should seem to be rejoicing when I am solemn all the time. The party doesn't suit me a bit; but never mind, stay and help to finish me off.'

III

Boldwood was dressing also at this hour. A tailor from Casterbridge was with him, assisting him in the operation of trying on a new coat that had just been brought home.

Never had Boldwood been so fastidious, unreasonable about the fit, and generally difficult to please. The tailor walked round and round him, tugged at the waist, pulled the sleeve, pressed out the collar, and for the first time in his experience Boldwood was not bored. Times had been when the farmer had exclaimed against all such niceties as childish, but now no philosophic or hasty rebuke whatever was provided by this man for attaching as much importance to a crease in the coat as to an earthquake in South America. Boldwood at last expressed himself nearly satisfied, and paid the bill, the tailor passing out of the door just as Oak came in to report progress for the day.

'Oh, Oak,' said Boldwood. 'I shall of course see you here to-night. Make yourself merry. I am determined that neither expense nor trouble shall be spared.'

'I'll try to be here, sir, though perhaps it may not be very early,' said Gabriel, quietly. 'I am glad to see such a change in 'ee from what it used to be.'

'Yes – I must own it – I am bright to-night: cheerful and more than cheerful – so much so that I am almost sad again with the sense that all of it is passing away. And sometimes, when I am excessively hopeful and blithe, a trouble is looming in the distance: so that I often get to look upon gloom in me with content, and to fear a happy mood. Still this may be absurd – I feel that it is absurd. Perhaps my day is dawning at last.'

'I hope it'll be a long and a fair one.'

'Thank you – thank you. Yet perhaps my cheerfulness rests on a slender hope. And yet I trust my hope. It is faith, not hope. I think this time I reckon with my host. – Oak, my hands are a little shaky, or something: I can't tie this neckerchief properly. Perhaps you will tie it for me. The fact is, I have not been well lately, you know.'

'I am sorry to hear that, sir.'

'Oh, it's nothing. I want it done as well as you can, please. Is there any late knot in fashion, Oak?'

'I don't know, sir,' said Oak. His tone had sunk to sadness.

Boldwood approached Gabriel, and as Oak tied the neckerchief the farmer went on feverishly –

'Does a woman keep her promise, Gabriel?'

'If it is not inconvenient to her she may.'

'– Or rather an implied promise.'

'I won't answer for her implying,' said Oak, with faint bitterness. 'That's a word as full o' holes as a sieve with them.'

'Oak, don't talk like that. You have got quite cynical lately – how is it? We seem to have shifted our positions: I have become the young and hopeful man, and you the old and unbelieving one. However, does a woman keep a promise, not to marry, but to enter on an engagement to marry at some time? Now you know women better than I – tell me.'

'I am afeard you honour my understanding too much. However, she may keep such a promise, if it is made with an honest meaning to repair a wrong.'

'It has not gone far yet, but I think it will soon – yes, I know it will,' he said, in an impulsive whisper. 'I have pressed her upon the subject, and she inclines to be kind to me, and to think of me as a husband at a long future time, and that's enough for me. How can I expect more? She has a notion that a woman should not marry within seven years of her husband's disappearance – that her own self shouldn't, I mean – because his body was not found. It may be merely this legal reason which influences her, or it may be a religious one, but she is reluctant to talk on the point. Yet she has promised – implied – that she will ratify an engagement to-night.'

'Seven years,' murmured Oak.

'No, no – it's no such thing!' he said, with impatience. 'Five years, nine months, and a few days. Fifteen months nearly have passed since he vanished, and is there anything so wonderful in an engagement of little more than five years?'

'It seems long in a forward view. Don't build too much upon such promises, sir. Remember, you have once be'n deceived. Her meaning may be good; but there – she's young yet.'

'Deceived? Never!' said Boldwood, vehemently. 'She never promised me at that first time, and hence she did not break her promise! If she promises me, she'll marry me. Bathsheba is a woman to her word.'

IV

Troy was sitting in a corner of The White Hart tavern at Casterbridge, smoking and drinking a steaming mixture from a glass. A knock was given at the door, and Pennyways entered.

'Well, have you seen him?' Troy inquired, pointing to a chair.

'Boldwood?'

'No – Lawyer Long.'

'He wadn' at home. I went there first, too.'

'That's a nuisance.'

''Tis rather, I suppose.'

'Yet I don't see that, because a man appears to be drowned and was not, he should be liable for anything. I shan't ask any lawyer – not I.'

'But that's not it, exactly. If a man changes his name and so forth, and takes steps to deceive the world and his own wife, he's a cheat, and that in the eye of the law is ayless a rogue, and that is ayless a lammocken vagabond; and that's a punishable situation.'

'Ha-ha! Well done, Pennyways.' Troy had laughed, but it was with some anxiety that he said, 'Now, what I want to know is this, do you think there's really anything going on between her and Boldwood? Upon my soul, I should never have believed it! How she must detest me! Have you found out whether she has encouraged him?'

'I haen't been able to learn. There's a deal of feeling on his side seemingly, but I don't answer for her. I didn't know a word about any such thing till yesterday, and all I heard then was that she was gwine to the party at his house to-night. This is the first time she has ever gone there, they say. And they say that she've not so much as spoke to him since they were at Greenhill Fair: but what can folk believe o't? However, she's not fond of him – quite offish and quite careless, I know.'

'I'm not too sure of that . . . She's a handsome woman, Pennyways, is she not? Own that you never saw a finer or more splendid creature in your life. Upon my honour, when I set eyes upon her that day I wondered what I could have been made of to be able to leave her by herself so long. And then I was hampered with that bothering show, which I'm free of at last, thank the stars.' He smoked on awhile, and then added, 'How did she look when you passed by yesterday?'

'Oh, she took no great heed of me, ye may well fancy; but she looked well enough, far's I know. Just flashed her haughty eyes upon my poor scram body, and then let them go past me to what was yond, much as if I'd been no more than a leafless tree. She had just got off her mare to look at the last wring-down of cider for the year; she had been riding, and so her colours were up and her breath rather quick, so that her bosom plimmed and fell – plimmed and fell – every time plain to my eye. Ay, and there were the fellers round her wringing down the cheese and bustling about and saying, "Ware o' the pommy, ma'am: 'twill spoil yer gown." "Never mind me," says she. Then Gabe brought her some of the new cider, and she must needs go drinking it through a strawmote, and not in a nateral way at all. "Liddy," says she, "bring indoors a few gallons, and I'll make some cider-wine." Sergeant, I was no more to her than a morsel of scroff in the fuel-house!'

'I must go and find her out at once – O yes, I see that – I must go. Oak is head man still, isn't he?'

'Yes, 'a b'lieve. And at Little Weatherbury Farm too. He manages everything.'

'"Twill puzzle him to manage her, or any other man of his compass!'

'I don't know about that. She can't do without him, and knowing it well he's pretty independent. And she've a few soft corners to her mind, though I've never been able to get into one, the devil's in't!'

'Ah, baily, she's a notch above you, and you must own it: a higher class of animal – a finer tissue. However, stick to me, and neither this haughty goddess, dashing piece of womanhood, Juno-wife of mine (Juno was a goddess, you know), nor anybody else shall hurt you. But all this wants looking into, I perceive. What with one thing and another, I see that my work is well cut out for me.'

V

'How do I look to-night, Liddy?' said Bathsheba, giving a final adjustment to her dress before leaving the glass.

'I never saw you look so well before. Yes – I'll tell you when you looked like it – that night, a year and a half ago, when you came in so wild-like, and scolded us for making remarks about you and Mr Troy.'

'Everybody will think that I am setting myself to captivate Mr Boldwood, I suppose,' she murmured. 'At least they'll say so. Can't my hair be brushed down a little flatter? I dread going – yet I dread the risk of wounding him by staying away.'

'Anyhow, ma'am, you can't well be dressed plainer than you are, unless you go in sackcloth at once. 'Tis your excitement is what makes you look so noticeable tonight.'

'I don't know what's the matter, I feel wretched at one time, and buoyant at another. I wish I could have continued quite alone as I have been for the last year or so, with no hopes and no fears, and no pleasure and no grief.'

'Now just suppose Mr Boldwood should ask you – only just suppose it – to run away with him, what would you do ma'am?'

'Liddy – none of that,' said Bathsheba, gravely. 'Mind, I won't hear joking on any such matter. Do you hear?'

'I beg pardon, ma'am. But knowing what rum things we women be, I just said – however, I won't speak of it again.'

'No marrying for me yet for many a year; if ever 'twill be for reasons very, very different from those you think, or others will believe! Now get my cloak for it is time to go.'

VI

'Oak,' said Boldwood, 'before you go I want to mention what has been passing in my mind lately – that little arrangement we made about your share in the farm I mean. That share is small, too small, considering how little I attend to business now, and how much time and thought you give to it. Well, since the world is brightening for me, I want to show my sense of it by increasing your proportion in the partnership. I'll make a memorandum of the arrangement which struck me as likely to be convenient, for I haven't time to talk about it now; and then we'll discuss it at our leisure. My intention is ultimately to retire from the management altogether, and until you can take all the expenditure upon your shoulders,

I'll be a sleeping partner in the stock. Then, if I marry her – and I hope – I feel I shall, why –'

'Pray don't speak of it, sir,' said Oak, hastily. 'We don't know what may happen. So many upsets may befall 'ee. There's many a slip, as they say – and I would advise you – I know you'll pardon me this once – not to be *too sure.*'

'I know, I know. But the feeling I have about increasing your share is on account of what I know of you. Oak, I have learnt a little about your secret: your interest in her is more than that of bailiff for an employer. But you have behaved like a man, and I, as a sort of successful rival – successful partly through your goodness of heart – should like definitely to show my sense of friendship under what must have been a great pain to you.'

'O that's not necessary, thank 'ee,' said Oak, hurriedly. 'I must get used to such as that; other men have, and so shall I.'

Oak then left him. He was uneasy on Boldwood's account, for he saw anew that this constant passion of the farmer made him not the man he once had been.

As Boldwood continued awhile in his room alone – ready and dressed to receive his company – the mood of anxiety about his appearance seemed to pass away, and to be succeeded by a deep solemnity. He looked out of the window, and regarded the dim outline of the trees upon the sky, and the twilight deepening to darkness.

Then he went to a locked closet, and took from a locked drawer therein a small circular case the size of a pill-box, and was about to put it into his pocket. But he lingered to open the cover and take a momentary glance inside. It contained a woman's finger-ring, set all the way round with small diamonds, and from its appearance had evidently been recently purchased. Boldwood's eyes dwelt upon its many sparkles a long time, though that its material aspect concerned him little was plain from his manner and mien, which were those of a mind following out the presumed thread of that jewel's future history.

The noise of wheels at the front of the house became audible. Boldwood closed the box, stowed it away carefully in his pocket, and went out upon the landing. The old man who was his indoor factotum came at the same moment to the foot of the stairs.

'They be coming, sir – lots of 'em – a-foot and a-driving!'

'I was coming down this moment. Those wheels I heard – is it Mrs Troy?'

'No, sir – 'tis not she yet.'

A reserved and sombre expression had returned to Boldwood's face again, but it poorly cloaked his feelings when he pronounced Bathsheba's name; and his feverish anxiety continued to show its existence by a galloping motion of his fingers upon the side of his thigh as he went down the stairs.

VII

'How does this cover me?' said Troy to Pennyways. 'Nobody would recognize me now, I'm sure.'

He was buttoning on a heavy grey overcoat of Noachian cut, with cape and high collar, the latter being erect and rigid, like a girdling wall, and nearly reaching to the verge of a travelling cap which was pulled down over his ears.

Pennyways snuffed the candle, and then looked up and deliberately inspected Troy.

'You've made up your mind to go then?' he said.

'Made up my mind? Yes; of course I have.'

'Why not write to her? 'Tis a very queer corner that you have got into, sergeant. You see, all these things will come to light if you go back, and they won't sound well at all. Faith, if I was you I'd even bide as you be – a single man of the name of Francis. A good wife is good, but the best wife is not so good as no wife at all. Now that's my outspoke mind, and I've been called a long-headed feller here and there.'

'All nonsense!' said Troy, angrily. 'There she is with plenty of money, and a house and farm, and horses, and comfort, and here am I living from hand to mouth – a needy adventurer. Besides, it is no use talking now; it is too late, and I am glad of it; I've been seen and recognized here this very afternoon. I should have gone back to her the day after the fair, if it hadn't been for you talking about the law, the rubbish about getting a separation; and I don't put it off any longer. What the deuce put it into my head to run away at all, I can't think! Humbugging sentiment – that's what it was. But what man on earth was to know that his wife would be in such a hurry to get rid of his name!'

'I should have known it. She's bad enough for anything.'

'Pennyways, mind who you are talking to.'

'Well, sergeant, all I say is this, that if I were you I'd go abroad again where I came from – 'tisn't too late to do it now. I wouldn't stir up the business and get a bad name for the sake of living with her – for all that about your play-acting is sure to come out, you know, although you think otherwise. My eyes and limbs, there'll be a racket if you go back just now – in the middle of Boldwood's Christmasing!'

'H'm, yes. I expect I shall not be a very welcome guest if he has her there,' said the sergeant, with a slight laugh. 'A sort of Alonzo the Brave; and when I go in the guests will sit in silence and fear, and all laughter and pleasure will be hushed, and the lights in the chamber burn blue, and the worms – Ugh, horrible! – Ring for some more brandy, Pennyways, I felt an awful shudder just then! Well, what is there besides? A stick – I must have a walking-stick.'

Pennyways now felt himself to be in something of a difficulty, for should Bathsheba and Troy become reconciled it would be necessary to regain her good opinion if he would secure the patronage of her husband. 'I sometimes think she likes you yet, and is a good woman at bottom,' he said, as a saving sentence. 'But there's no telling to a certainty from a body's outside. Well, you'll do as you like about going, of course, sergeant, and as for me, I'll do as you tell me.'

'Now, let me see what the time is,' said Troy, after emptying his glass in one draught as he stood. 'Half past six o'clock. I shall not hurry along the road, and shall be there then before nine.'

* LIII *

Concurritur – Horae Momento

OUTSIDE the front of Boldwood's house a group of men stood in the dark, with their faces towards the door, which occasionally opened and closed for the passage of some guest or servant, when a golden rod of light would stripe the ground for the moment and vanish again, leaving nothing outside but the glowworm shine of the pale lamp amid the evergreens over the door.

'He was seen in Casterbridge this afternoon – so the boy said,' one of them remarked in a whisper. 'And I for one believe it. His body was never found, you know.'

''Tis a strange story,' said the next. 'You may depend upon't that she knows nothing about it.'

'Not a word.'

'Perhaps he don't mean that she shall,' said another man.

'If he's alive and here in the neighbourhood, he means mischief,' said the first. 'Poor young thing: I do pity her, if 'tis true. He'll drag her to the dogs.'

'O no; he'll settle down quiet enough,' said one disposed to take a more hopeful view of the case.

'What a fool she must have been ever to have had anything to do with the man! She is so self-willed and independent too, that one is more minded to say it serves her right than pity her.'

'No, no! I don't hold with 'ee there. She was no otherwise than a girl, mind, and how could she tell what the man was made of? If 'tis really true, 'tis too hard a punishment, and more than she ought to hae. – Hullo, who's that?' This was to some footsteps that were heard approaching.

'William Smallbury,' said a dim figure in the shades, coming up and joining them. 'Dark as a hedge, to-night, isn't it? I all but missed the plank over the river ath'art there in the bottom – never did such a thing before in my life. Be ye any of Boldwood's workfolk?' He peered into their faces.

'Yes – all o' us. We met here a few minutes ago.'

'Oh, I hear now – that's Sam Samway: thought I knowed the voice, too. Going in?'

'Presently. But I say, William,' Samway whispered, 'have ye heard this strange tale?'

'What – that about Sergeant Troy being seen, d'ye mean, souls?' said Smallbury, also lowering his voice.

'Ay: in Casterbridge.'

'Yes, I have. Laban Tall named a hint of it to me but now – but I don't think it. Hark, here Laban comes himself, 'a b'lieve.' A footstep drew near.

'Laban?'

'Yes, 'tis I,' said Tall.

'Have ye heard any more about that?'

'No,' said Tall, joining the group. 'And I'm inclined to think we'd better keep quiet. If so be 'tis not true, 'twill flurry her, and do her much harm to repeat it; and if so be 'tis true, 'twill do no good to forestall her time o' trouble. God send that it mid be a lie, for though Henery Fray and some of 'em do speak against her, she's never been anything but fair to me. She's hot and hasty, but she's a brave girl who'll never tell a lie however much the truth may harm her, and I've no cause to wish her evil.'

'She never do tell women's little lies, that's true; and 'tis a thing that can be said of very few. Ay, all the harm she thinks she says to yer face: there's nothing underhand wi' her.'

They stood silent then, every man busied with his own thoughts, during which interval sounds of merriment could be heard within. Then the front door again opened, the rays streamed out, the well-known form of Boldwood was seen in the rectangular area of light, the door closed, and Boldwood walked slowly down the path.

''Tis master,' one of the men whispered, as he neared them. 'We'd better stand quiet – he'll go in again directly. He would think it unseemly o' us to be loitering here.'

Boldwood came on, and passed by the men without seeing them, they being under the bushes on the grass. He paused, leant over the gate, and breathed a long breath. They heard low words come from him.

'I hope to God she'll come, or this night will be nothing but misery to me! O my darling, my darling, why do you keep me in suspense like this?'

He said this to himself, and they all distinctly heard it. Boldwood remained silent after that, and the noise from indoors was again just audible, until, a few minutes later, light wheels could be distinguished coming down the hill. They drew nearer, and ceased at the gate. Boldwood hastened back to the door, and opened it; and the light shone upon Bathsheba coming up the path.

Boldwood compressed his emotion to mere welcome: the men marked her light laugh and apology as she met him: he took her into the house; and the door closed again.

'Gracious heaven, I didn't know it was like that with him!' said one of the men. 'I thought that fancy of his was over long ago.'

'You don't know much of master, if you thought that,' said Samway.

'I wouldn't he should know we heard what 'a said for the world,' remarked a third.

'I wish we had told of the report at once,' the first uneasily continued. 'More harm may come of this than we know of. Poor Mr Boldwood, it will be hard upon en. I wish Troy was in – Well, God forgive me for such a wish! A scoundrel to play a poor wife such tricks. Nothing has prospered in Weatherbury since he came here. And now I've no heart to go in. Let's look into Warren's for a few minutes first, shall us, neighbours?'

Samway, Tall, and Smallbury agreed to go to Warren's, and went out at the gate, the remaining ones entering the house. The three soon drew near the malt-house, approaching it from the adjoining orchard, and not by way of the street. The pane of glass was illuminated as usual. Smallbury was a little in advance of the rest, when, pausing, he turned suddenly to his companions and said, 'Hist! See there.'

The light from the pane was now perceived to be shining not upon the ivied wall as usual, but upon some object close to the glass. It was a human face.

'Let's come closer,' whispered Samway; and they approached on tiptoe. There was no disbelieving the report any longer. Troy's face was almost close to the pane, and he was looking in. Not only was he looking in, but he appeared to have been arrested by a conversation which was in progress in the malt-house, the voices of the interlocutors being those of Oak and the maltster.

'The spree is all in her honour, isn't it – hey?' said the old man. 'Although he made believe 'tis only keeping up o' Christmas?'

'I cannot say,' replied Oak.

'O 'tis true enough, faith. I cannot understand Farmer Boldwood being such a fool at his time of life as to ho and hanker after thik woman in the way 'a do, and she not care a bit about en.'

The men, after recognizing Troy's features, withdrew across the orchard as quietly as they had come. The air was big with Bathsheba's fortunes to-night: every word everywhere concerned her. When they were quite out of earshot all by one instinct paused.

'It gave me quite a turn – his face,' said Tall, breathing.

'And so it did me,' said Samway. 'What's to be done?'

'I don't see that 'tis any business of ours,' Smallbury murmured dubiously.

'But it is! 'Tis a thing which is everybody's business,' said Samway. 'We know very well that master's on a wrong tack, and that she's quite in the dark, and we should let 'em know at once. Laban, you know her best – you'd better go and ask to speak to her.'

'I bain't fit for any such thing,' said Laban nervously. 'I should think William ought to do it if anybody. He's oldest.'

'I shall have nothing to do with it,' said Smallbury. ''Tis a ticklish business altogether. Why, he'll go on to her himself in a few minutes, ye'll see.'

'We don't know that he will. Come, Laban.'

'Very well, if I must I must, I suppose,' Tall reluctantly answered. 'What must I say?'

'Just ask to see master.'

'O no; I shan't speak to Mr Boldwood. If I tell anybody, 'twill be mistress.'

'Very well,' said Samway.

Laban then went to the door. When he opened it the hum of bustle rolled out as a wave upon a still strand – the assemblage being immediately inside the hall – and was deadened to a murmur as he closed it again. Each man waited intently, and looked around at the dark tree tops gently rocking against the sky and occasionally shivering in a slight wind, as if he took interest in the scene, which neither did. One of them began walking up and down, and then came to where he started from and stopped again, with a sense that walking was a thing not worth doing now.

'I should think Laban must have seen mistress by this time,' said Smallbury, breaking the silence. 'Perhaps she won't come and speak to him.'

The door opened. Tall appeared, and joined them.

'Well?' said both.

'I didn't like to ask for her after all,' Laban faltered out. 'They were all in such a stir, trying to put a little spirit into the party. Somehow the fun seems to hang fire, though everything's there that a heart can desire, and I couldn't for my soul interfere and throw damp upon it – if 'twas to save my life, I couldn't!'

'I suppose we had better all go in together,' said Samway, gloomily. 'Perhaps I may have a chance of saying a word to master.'

So the men entered the hall, which was the room selected and arranged for the gathering because of its size. The younger men and maids were at last just beginning a dance. Bathsheba had been perplexed how to act, for she was not much more than a slim young maid herself, and the weight of stateliness sat heavy upon her. Sometimes she thought she ought not to have come under any circumstances; then she considered what cold unkindness that would have been, and finally resolved upon the middle course of staying for about an hour only, and gliding off unobserved, having from the first made up her mind that she could on no account dance, sing, or take any active part in the proceedings.

Her allotted hour having been passed in chatting and looking on, Bathsheba told Liddy not to hurry herself, and went to the small parlour to prepare for departure, which, like the hall, was decorated with holly and ivy, and well lighted up.

Nobody was in the room, but she had hardly been there a moment when the master of the house entered.

'Mrs Troy – you are not going?' he said. 'We've hardly begun!'

'If you'll excuse me, I should like to go now.' Her manner was restive, for she remembered her promise, and imagined what he was about to say. 'But as it is not late,' she added, 'I can walk home, and leave my man and Liddy to come when they choose.'

'I've been trying to get an opportunity of speaking to you,' said Boldwood. 'You know perhaps what I long to say?'

Bathsheba silently looked on the floor.

'You do give it?' he said, eagerly.

'What?' she whispered.

'Now, that's evasion! Why, the promise. I don't want to intrude upon you at all, or to let it become known to anybody. But do give your word! A mere business compact, you know, between two people who are beyond the influence of passion.' Boldwood knew how false this picture was as regarded himself; but he had proved that it was the only tone in which she would allow him to approach her. 'A promise to marry me at the end of five years and three-quarters. You owe it to me!'

'I feel that I do,' said Bathsheba; 'that is, if you demand it. But I am a changed woman – an unhappy woman – and not – not –'

'You are still a very beautiful woman,' said Boldwood. Honesty and pure conviction suggested the remark, unaccompanied by any perception that it might have been adopted by blunt flattery to soothe and win her.

However, it had not much effect now, for she said, in a passionless murmur which was in itself a proof of her words: 'I have no feeling in the matter at all. And I don't at all know what is right to do in my difficult position, and I have nobody to advise me. But I give my promise, if I must. I give it as the rendering of a debt, conditionally, of course, on my being a widow.'

'You'll marry me between five and six years hence?'

'Don't press me too hard. I'll marry nobody else.'

'But surely you will name the time, or there's nothing in the promise at all?'

'O, I don't know, pray let me go!' she said, her bosom beginning to rise. 'I am afraid what to do! I want to be just to you, and to be that seems to be wronging myself, and perhaps it is breaking the commandments. There is considerable doubt of his death, and then it is dreadful; let me ask a solicitor, Mr Boldwood, if I ought or no!'

'Say the words, dear one, and the subject shall be dismissed; a blissful loving intimacy of six years, and then marriage – O Bathsheba, say them!' he begged in a husky voice, unable to sustain the forms of mere friendship any longer. 'Promise yourself to me; I deserve it, indeed I do, for I have loved you more than anybody in the world! And if I said hasty words and showed uncalled-for heat of manner towards you, believe me, dear, I did not mean to distress you; I was in agony, Bathsheba, and I did not know what I said. You wouldn't let a dog suffer what I have suffered, could you but know it! Sometimes I shrink from your knowing what I have felt for you, and sometimes I am distressed that all of it you never will know. Be gracious, and give up a little to me, when I would give up my life for you!'

The trimmings of her dress, as they quivered against the light, showed how agitated she was, and at last she burst out crying. 'And you'll not – press me – about anything more – if I say in five or six years?' she sobbed, when she had power to frame the words.

'Yes, then I'll leave it to time.'

'Very well. If he does not return, I'll marry you in six years from this day, if we both live,' she said solemnly.

'And you'll take this as a token from me.'

Boldwood had come close to her side, and now he clasped one of her hands in both his own, and lifted it to his breast.

'What is it? Oh I cannot wear a ring!' she exclaimed, on seeing what he held; 'besides, I wouldn't have a soul know that it's an engagement! Perhaps it is improper? Besides, we are not engaged in the usual sense, are we? Don't insist, Mr Boldwood – don't!' In her trouble at not being able to get her hand away from him at once, she stamped passionately on the floor with one foot, and tears crowded to her eyes again.

'It means simply a pledge – no sentiment – the seal of a practical compact,' he said more quietly, but still retaining her hand in his firm grasp. 'Come, now!' And Boldwood slipped the ring on her finger.

'I cannot wear it,' she said, weeping as if her heart would break. 'You frighten me, almost. So wild a scheme! Please let me go home!'

'Only to-night: wear it just to-night, to please me!'

Bathsheba sat down in a chair, and buried her face in her handkerchief, though Boldwood kept her hand yet. At length she said, in a sort of hopeless whisper –

'Very well, then, I will to-night, if you wish it so earnestly. Now loosen my hand; I will, indeed I will wear it to-night.'

'And it shall be the beginning of a pleasant secret courtship of six years, with a wedding at the end?'

'It must be, I suppose, since you will have it so!' she said, fairly beaten into non-resistance.

Boldwood pressed her hand, and allowed it to drop in her lap. 'I am happy now,' he said. 'God bless you!'

He left the room, and when he thought she might be sufficiently composed sent one of the maids to her. Bathsheba cloaked the effects of the late scene as she best could, followed the girl, and in a few moments came downstairs with her hat and cloak on, ready to go. To get to the door it was necessary to pass through the hall, and before doing so she paused on the bottom of the staircase which descended into one corner, to take a last look at the gathering.

There was no music or dancing in progress just now. At the lower end, which had been arranged for the work-folk specially, a group conversed in whispers, and with clouded looks. Boldwood was standing by the fireplace, and he, too, though so absorbed in visions arising from her promise that he scarcely saw anything, seemed at that moment to have observed their peculiar manner, and their looks askance.

'What is it you are in doubt about, men?' he said.

One of them turned and replied uneasily: 'It was something Laban heard of, that's all, sir.'

'News? Anybody married or engaged, born or dead?' inquired the farmer, gaily. 'Tell it to us, Tall. One would think from your looks and mysterious ways that it was something very dreadful indeed.'

'O no, sir, nobody is dead,' said Tall.

'I wish somebody was,' said Samway, in a whisper.

'What do you say, Samway?' asked Boldwood, somewhat sharply. 'If you have anything to say, speak out; if not, get up another dance.'

'Mrs Troy has come downstairs,' said Samway to Tall. 'If you want to tell her, you had better do it now.'

'Do you know what they mean?' the farmer asked Bathsheba, across the room.

'I don't in the least,' said Bathsheba.

There was a smart rapping at the door. One of the men opened it instantly, and went outside.

'Mrs Troy is wanted,' he said, on returning.

'Quite ready,' said Bathsheba. 'Though I didn't tell them to send.'

'It is a stranger, ma'am,' said the man by the door.

'A stranger?' she said.

'Ask him to come in,' said Boldwood.

The message was given, and Troy, wrapped up to his eyes as we have seen him, stood in the doorway.

There was an unearthly silence, all looking towards the newcomer. Those who had just learnt that he was in the neighbourhood recognized him instantly; those who did not were perplexed. Nobody noted Bathsheba. She was leaning on the stairs. Her brow had heavily contracted; her whole face was pallid, her lips apart, her eyes rigidly staring at their visitor.

Boldwood was among those who did not notice that he was Troy. 'Come in, come in!' he repeated, cheerfully, 'and drain a Christmas beaker with us, stranger!'

Troy next advanced into the middle of the room, took off his cap, turned down his coat-collar, and looked Boldwood in the face. Even then Boldwood did not recognize that the impersonator of Heaven's persistent irony towards him, who had once before broken in upon his bliss, scourged him, and snatched his delight away, had come to do these things a second time. Troy began to laugh a mechanical laugh: Boldwood recognized him now.

Troy turned to Bathsheba. The poor girl's wretchedness at this time was beyond all fancy or narration. She had sunk down on the lowest stair; and there she sat, her mouth blue and dry, and her dark eyes fixed vacantly upon him, as if she wondered whether it were not all a terrible illusion.

Then Troy spoke. 'Bathsheba, I come here for you!'

She made no reply.

'Come home with me; come!'

Bathsheba moved her feet a little, but did not rise.

Troy went across to her.

'Come, madam, do you hear what I say?' he said, peremptorily.

A strange voice came from the fireplace – a voice sounding far off and confined, as if from a dungeon. Hardly a soul in the assembly recognized the thin tones to be those of Boldwood. Sudden despair had transformed him.

'Bathsheba, go with your husband!'

Nevertheless, she did not move. The truth was that Bathsheba was beyond the pale of activity – and yet not in a swoon. She was in a state of mental *gutta serena*; her mind was for the minute totally deprived of light at the same time that no obscuration was apparent from without.

Troy stretched out his hand to pull her towards him, when she quickly shrank back. This visible dread of him seemed to irritate Troy, and he seized her arm and pulled it sharply. Whether his grasp pinched her, or whether his mere touch was the cause, was never known, but at the moment of his seizure she writhed, and gave a quick, low scream.

The scream had been heard but a few seconds when it was followed by a sudden deafening report that echoed through the room and stupefied them all. The oak partition shook with the concussion, and the place was filled with grey smoke.

In bewilderment they turned their eyes to Boldwood. At his back, as he stood before the fireplace, was a gun-rack, as is usual in farmhouses, constructed to hold two guns. When Bathsheba had cried out in her husband's grasp, Boldwood's face of gnashing despair had changed. The veins had swollen, and a frenzied look had gleamed in his eye. He had turned quickly, taken one of the guns, cocked it, and at once discharged it at Troy.

Troy fell. The distance apart of the two men was so small that the charge of shot did not spread in the least, but passed like a bullet into his body. He uttered a long guttural sigh – there was a contraction – an extension – then his muscles relaxed, and he lay still.

Boldwood was seen through the smoke to be now again engaged with the gun. It was double-barrelled, and he had, meanwhile, in some way fastened his handkerchief to the trigger, and with his foot on the other end was in the act of turning the second barrel upon himself. Samway his man was the first to see this, and in the midst of the general horror darted up to him. Boldwood had already twitched the handkerchief, and the gun exploded a second time, sending its contents, by a timely blow from Samway, into the beam which crossed the ceiling.

'Well, it makes no difference!' Boldwood gasped. 'There is another way for me to die.'

Then he broke from Samway, crossed the room to Bathsheba, and kissed her hand. He put on his hat, opened the door, and went into the darkness, nobody thinking of preventing him.

* LIV *

After the Shock

BOLDWOOD passed into the high road, and turned in the direction of Casterbridge. Here he walked at an even, steady pace over Yalbury Hill, along the dead level beyond, mounted Mellstock Hill, and between eleven and twelve o'clock crossed the Moor into the town. The streets were nearly deserted now, and the waving lamp-flames only lighted up rows of grey shop-shutters, and strips of white paving upon which his step echoed as he passed along. He turned to the right, and halted before an archway of heavy stonework, which was closed by an iron-studded pair of doors. This was the entrance to the gaol, and over it a lamp was fixed, the light enabling the wretched traveller to find a bell-pull.

The small wicket at last opened, and a porter appeared. Boldwood stepped forward, and said something in a low tone, when, after a delay, another man came. Boldwood entered, and the door was closed behind him, and he walked the world no more.

Long before this time Weatherbury had been thoroughly aroused, and the wild deed which had terminated Boldwood's merrymaking became known to all. Of those out of the house Oak was one of the first to hear of the catastrophe, and when he entered the room, which was about five minutes after Boldwood's exit, the scene was terrible. All the female guests were huddled aghast against the walls like sheep in a storm, and the men were bewildered as to what to do. As for Bathsheba, she had changed. She was sitting on the floor beside the body of Troy, his head pillowed in her lap, where she had herself lifted it. With one hand she held her handkerchief to his breast and covered the wound, though scarcely a single drop of blood had flowed, and with the other she tightly clasped one of his. The household convulsion had made her herself again. The temporary coma had ceased, and activity had come with the necessity for it. Deeds of endurance which seem ordinary in philosophy are rare in conduct, and Bathsheba was astonishing all around her now, for her philosophy was her conduct, and she seldom thought practicable what she did not practise. She was of the stuff of which great men's mothers are made. She was indispensable to high generation, hated at tea parties, feared in shops, and loved at crises. Troy recumbent in his wife's lap formed now the sole spectacle in the middle of the spacious room.

'Gabriel,' she said, automatically, when he entered, turning up a face of which only the well-known lines remained to tell him it was hers, all else in the picture having faded quite. 'Ride to Casterbridge instantly for a surgeon. It is, I believe, useless, but go. Mr Boldwood has shot my husband.'

Her statement of the fact in such quiet and simple words came with more force than a tragic declamation, and had somewhat the effect of setting the distorted images in each mind present into proper focus. Oak, almost before he had comprehended anything beyond the briefest abstract of the event, hurried out of the room, saddled a horse and rode away. Not till he had ridden more than a mile did it occur to him that he would have done better by sending some other man on this errand, remaining himself in the house. What had become of Boldwood? He should have been looked after. Was he mad – had there been a quarrel? Then how had Troy got there? Where had he come from? How did this remarkable reappearance effect itself when he was supposed by many to be at the bottom of the sea? Oak had in some measure been prepared for the presence of Troy by hearing a rumour of his return just before entering Boldwood's house; but before he had weighed that information, this fatal event had been superimposed. However, it was too late now to think of sending another messenger, and he rode on, in the excitement of these self-inquiries not discerning, when about three miles from Casterbridge, a square-figured pedestrian passing along under the dark hedge in the same direction as his own.

The miles necessary to be traversed, and other hindrances incidental to the lateness of the hour and the darkness of the night, delayed the arrival of Mr Aldritch, the surgeon; and more than three hours passed between the time at which the shot was fired and that of his entering the house. Oak was additionally detained in Casterbridge through having to give notice to the authorities of what had happened; and he then found that Boldwood had also entered the town, and delivered himself up.

In the meantime the surgeon, having hastened into the hall at Boldwood's, found it in darkness and quite deserted. He went on to the back of the house, where he discovered in the kitchen an old man, of whom he made inquiries.

'She's had him took away to her own house, sir,' said his informant.

'Who has?' said the doctor.

'Mrs Troy. 'A was quite dead, sir.'

This was astonishing information. 'She had no right to do that,' said the doctor. 'There will have to be an inquest, and she should have waited to know what to do.'

'Yes sir; it was hinted to her that she had better wait till the law was known. But she said law was nothing to her, and she wouldn't let her dear husband's corpse bide neglected for folks to stare at for all the crowners in England.'

Mr Aldritch drove at once back again up the hill to Bathsheba's. The first person he met was poor Liddy, who seemed literally to have dwindled smaller in these few latter hours. 'What has been done?' he said.

'I don't know, sir,' said Liddy, with suspended breath. 'My mistress has done it all.'

'Where is she?'

'Upstairs with him, sir. When he was brought home and taken upstairs, she said she wanted no further help from the men. And then she called me, and made me fill the bath, and after that told me I had better go and lie down because I looked so ill. Then she locked herself into the room alone with him, and would not let a nurse come in, or anybody at all. But I thought I'd wait in the next room in case she should want me. I heard her moving about inside for more than an hour, but she only came out once, and that was for more candles, because hers had burnt down into the socket. She said we were to let her know when you or Mr Thirdly came, sir.'

Oak entered with the parson at this moment, and they all went upstairs together, preceded by Liddy Smallbury. Everything was silent as the grave when they paused on the landing. Liddy knocked, and Bathsheba's dress was heard rustling across the room: the key turned in the lock, and she opened the door. Her looks were calm and nearly rigid, like a slightly animated bust of Melpomene.

'Oh, Mr Aldritch, you have come at last,' she murmured from her lips merely, and threw back the door. 'Ah, and Mr Thirdly. Well, all is done, and anybody in the world may see him now.' She then passed by him, crossed the landing, and entered another room.

Looking into the chamber of death she had vacated they saw by the light of the candles which were on the drawers a tall straight shape lying at the further end of the bedroom, wrapped in white. Everything around was quite orderly. The doctor went in, and after a few minutes returned to the landing again, where Oak and the parson still waited.

'It is all done, indeed, as she says,' remarked Mr Aldritch, in a subdued voice. 'The body has been undressed and properly laid out in grave-clothes. Gracious Heaven – this mere girl! She must have the nerve of a stoic!'

'The heart of a wife merely,' floated in a whisper about the ears of the three, and turning they saw Bathsheba in the midst of them. Then, as if at that instant to prove that her fortitude had been more of will than of spontaneity, she silently sank down between them and was a shapeless heap of drapery on the floor. The simple consciousness that superhuman strain was no longer required had at once put a period to her power to continue it.

They took her away into a further room, and the medical attendance which had been useless in Troy's case was invaluable in Bathsheba's, who fell into a series of fainting-fits that had a serious aspect for a time. The sufferer was got to bed and Oak, finding from the bulletins that nothing really dreadful was to be apprehended on her score, left the house. Liddy kept watch in Bathsheba's chamber, where she heard her mistress moaning in whispers through the dull slow hours of that wretched night: 'O it is my fault – how can I live! O Heaven, how can I live!'

* LV *

The Following March – 'Bathsheba Boldwood'

WE pass rapidly on into the month of March, to a breezy day without sunshine, frost, or dew. On Yalbury Hill, about midway between Weatherbury and Casterbridge, where the turnpike road passes over the crest, a numerous concourse of people had gathered, the eyes of the greater number being frequently stretched afar in a northerly direction. The groups consisted of a throng of idlers, a party of javelin-men, and two trumpeters, and in the midst were carriages, one of which contained the high sheriff. With the idlers, many of whom had mounted to the top of a cutting formed for the road, were several Weatherbury men and boys – among others Poorgrass, Coggan, and Cain Ball.

At the end of half-an-hour a faint dust was seen in the expected quarter, and shortly after a travelling-carriage, bringing one of the two judges on the Western Circuit, came up the hill and halted on the top. The judge changed carriages whilst a flourish was blown by the big-cheeked trumpeters, and a procession being formed of the vehicles and javelin-men, they all proceeded towards the town, excepting the Weatherbury men, who as soon as they had seen the judge move off returned home again to their work.

'Joseph, I zeed you squeezing close to the carriage,' said Coggan, as they walked. 'Did ye notice my lord judge's face?'

'I did,' said Poorgrass, 'I looked hard at en, as if I would read his very soul; and there was mercy in his eyes – or to speak with the exact truth required of us at this solemn time, in the eye that was towards me.'

'Well, I hope for the best,' said Coggan, 'though bad that must be. However, I shan't go to the trial, and I'd advise the rest of ye that bain't wanted to bide away. 'Twill disturb his mind more than anything to see us there staring at him as if he were a show.'

'The very thing I said this morning,' observed Joseph. ' "Justice is come to weigh him in the balances," I said in my reflectious way, "and if he's found wanting, so be it unto him," and a bystander said "Hear, hear! A man who can talk like that ought to be heard." But I don't like dwelling upon it, for my few words are my few words, and not much; though the speech of some men is rumoured abroad as though by nature formed for such.'

'So 'tis, Joseph. And now, neighbours, as I said, every man bide at home.'

The resolution was adhered to; and all waited anxiously for the news next day. Their suspense was diverted, however, by a discovery which was made in the afternoon, throwing more light on Boldwood's conduct and condition than any details which had preceded it.

That he had been from the time of Greenhill Fair until the fatal Christmas Eve in excited and unusual moods was known to those who had been intimate with him; but nobody imagined that there had shown in him unequivocal symptoms of the mental derangement which Bath-sheba and Oak, alone of all others and at different times, had momentarily suspected. In a locked closet was now discovered an extraordinary collection of articles. There were several sets of ladies' dresses in the piece, of sundry expensive materials; silks and satins, poplins and velvets, all of colours which from Bathsheba's style of dress might have been judged to be her favourites. There were two muffs, sable and ermine. Above all there was a case of jewellery, containing four heavy gold bracelets and several lockets and rings, all of fine quality and manufacture. These things had been bought in Bath and other towns from time to time, and brought home by stealth. They were all carefully packed in paper, and each package was labelled 'Bathsheba Boldwood', a date being subjoined six years in advance in every instance.

These somewhat pathetic evidences of a mind crazed with care and love were the subject of discourse in Warren's malt-house when Oak entered from Casterbridge with tidings of the sentence. He came in the afternoon, and his face, as the kiln glow shone upon it, told the tale sufficiently well. Boldwood, as every one supposed he would do, had pleaded guilty, and had been sentenced to death.

The conviction that Boldwood had not been morally responsible for his later acts now became general. Facts elicited previous to the trial had pointed strongly in the same direction, but they had not been of sufficient weight to lead to an order for an examination into the state of Boldwood's mind. It was astonishing, now that a presumption of insanity was raised, how many collateral circumstances were remembered to which a condition of mental disease seemed to afford the only explanation – among others, the unprecedented neglect of his corn stacks in the previous summer.

A petition was addressed to the Home Secretary, advancing the circumstances which appeared to justify a request for a reconsideration of the sentence. It was not 'numerously signed' by the inhabitants of Casterbridge, as is usual in such cases, for Boldwood had never made many friends over the counter. The shops thought it very natural that a man who, by importing direct from the producer, had daringly set aside the first great principle of provincial existence, namely, that God made country villages to supply customers to country towns, should have confused ideas about the Decalogue. The prompters were a few merciful men who had perhaps too feelingly considered the facts latterly unearthed, and the result was that evidence was taken which it was hoped might remove the crime, in a moral point of view, out of the category of wilful murder, and lead it to be regarded as a sheer outcome of madness.

The upshot of the petition was waited for in Weatherbury with solicitous interest. The execution had been fixed for eight o'clock on a Saturday morning about a fortnight after the sentence was passed, and up to Friday afternoon no answer had been received. At that time Gabriel came from Casterbridge Gaol, whither he had been to wish Boldwood good-bye, and turned down a by-street to avoid the town. When past the last house he heard a hammering, and lifting his bowed head he looked back for a moment. Over the chimneys he could see the upper part of the gaol entrance, rich and glowing in the afternoon sun, and some figures were there. They were carpenters lifting a post into a vertical position within the parapet. He withdrew his eyes quickly and hastened on.

It was dark when he reached home, and half the village was out to meet him.

'No tidings,' Gabriel said, wearily. 'And I'm afraid there's no hope. I've been with him more than two hours.'

'Do ye think he *really* was out of his mind when he did it?' said Smallbury.

'I can't honestly say that I do,' Oak replied. 'However, that we can talk of another time. Has there been any change in mistress this afternoon?'

'None at all.'

'Is she downstairs?'

'No. And getting on so nicely as she was too. She's but very little better now again than she was at Christmas. She keeps on asking if you be come, and if there's news, till one's wearied out wi' answering her. Shall I go and say you've come?'

'No,' said Oak. 'There's a chance yet; but I couldn't stay in town any longer – after seeing him too. So Laban – Laban is here, isn't he?'

'Yes,' said Tall.

'What I've arranged is, that you shall ride to town the last thing to-night; leave here about nine, and wait a while there, getting home about twelve. If nothing has been received by eleven to-night, they say there's no chance at all.'

'I do so hope his life will be spared,' said Liddy. 'If it is not, she'll go out of her mind too. Poor thing; her sufferings have been dreadful; she deserves anybody's pity.'

'Is she altered much?' said Coggan.

'If you haven't seen poor mistress since Christmas, you wouldn't know her,' said Liddy. 'Her eyes are so miserable that she's not the same woman. Only two years ago she was a romping girl, and now she's this!'

Laban departed as directed, and at eleven o'clock that night several of the villagers strolled along the road to Casterbridge and awaited his arrival – among them Oak, and nearly all the rest of Bathsheba's men. Gabriel's anxiety was great that Boldwood might be saved, even though in his conscience he felt that he ought to die; for there had been qualities in the farmer which Oak loved. At last, when they all were weary the tramp of a horse was heard in the distance –

> First dead, as if on turf it trode,
> Then, clattering, on the village road
> In other pace than forth he yode.

'We shall soon know now, one way or other,' said Coggan, and they all stepped down from the bank on which they had been standing into the road, and the rider pranced into the midst of them.

'Is that you, Laban?' said Gabriel.

'Yes – 'tis come. He's not to die. 'Tis confinement during Her Majesty's pleasure.'

'Hurrah!' said Coggan, with a swelling heart. 'God's above the devil yet!'

* LVI *

Beauty in Loneliness – After All

BATHSHEBA revived with the spring. The utter prostration that had followed the low fever from which she had suffered diminished perceptibly when all uncertainty upon every subject had come to an end.

But she remained alone now for the greater part of her time, and stayed in the house, or at furthest went into the garden. She shunned every one, even Liddy, and could be brought to make no confidences and to ask for no sympathy.

As the summer drew on she passed more of her time in the open air, and began to examine into farming matters from sheer necessity, though she never rode out or personally superintended as at former times. One Friday evening in August she walked a little way along the road and entered the village for the first time since the sombre event of the preceding Christmas. None of the old colour had as yet come to her cheek, and its absolute paleness was heightened by the jet black of her gown, till it appeared preternatural. When she reached a little shop at the other end of the place, which stood nearly opposite to the churchyard, Bathsheba heard singing inside the church, and she knew that the singers were practising. She crossed the road, opened the gate, and entered the graveyard, the high sills of the church windows effectually screening her from the eyes of those gathered within. Her stealthy walk was to the nook wherein Troy had worked at planting flowers upon Fanny Robin's grave, and she came to the marble tombstone.

A motion of satisfaction enlivened her face as she read the complete inscription. First came the words of Troy himself:

> ERECTED BY FRANCIS TROY
> IN BELOVED MEMORY OF
> FANNY ROBIN,
> WHO DIED OCTOBER 9, 18—,
> AGED 20 YEARS.

Underneath this was now inscribed in new letters:

> IN THE SAME GRAVE LIE
> THE REMAINS OF THE AFORESAID
> FRANCIS TROY,
> WHO DIED DECEMBER 24TH, 18—,
> AGED 26 YEARS.

Whilst she stood and read and meditated the tones of the organ began again in the church, and she went with the same light step round to the porch and listened. The door was closed, and the choir was learning a new hymn. Bathsheba was stirred by emotions which latterly she had assumed to be altogether dead within her. The little attenuated voices of the children brought to her ear in distinct utterance the words they sang without thought or comprehension –

> Lead, kindly Light, amid the encircling gloom,
> Lead Thou me on.

Bathsheba's feeling was always to some extent dependent upon her whim, as is the case with many other women. Something big came into her throat and an uprising to her eyes – and she thought that she would allow the imminent tears to flow if they wished. They did flow and plenteously, and one fell upon the stone bench beside her. Once that she had begun to cry for she hardly knew what, she could not leave off for crowding thoughts she knew too well. She would have given anything in the world to be, as those children were, unconcerned at the meaning of their words, because too innocent to feel the necessity for any such expression. All the impassioned scenes of her brief experience seemed to revive with added emotion at that moment, and those scenes which had been without emotion during enactment had emotion then. Yet grief came to her rather as a luxury than as the scourge of former times.

Owing to Bathsheba's face being buried in her hands she did not notice a form which came quietly into the porch, and on seeing her, first moved as if to retreat, then paused and regarded her. Bathsheba did not raise her head for some time, and when she looked round her face was wet, and her eyes drowned and dim. 'Mr Oak,' exclaimed she, disconcerted, 'how long have you been here?'

'A few minutes, ma'am,' said Oak, respectfully.

'Are you going in?' said Bathsheba; and there came from within the church as from a prompter –

> I loved the garish day, and, spite of fears,
> Pride ruled my will: remember not past years.

'I was,' said Gabriel. 'I am one of the bass singers, you know. I have sung bass for several months.'

'Indeed: I wasn't aware of that. I'll leave you, then.'

> Which I have loved long since, and lost awhile,

sang the children.

'Don't let me drive you away, mistress. I think I won't go in to-night.'

'O no – you don't drive me away.'

Then they stood in a state of some embarrassment, Bathsheba trying to wipe her dreadfully drenched and inflamed face without his noticing her. At length Oak said, 'I've not seen you – I mean spoken to you – since ever so long, have I?' But he feared to bring distressing memories back, and interrupted himself with: 'Were you going into church?'

'No,' she said. 'I came to see the tombstone privately – to see if they had cut the inscription as I wished. Mr Oak, you needn't mind speaking to me, if you wish to, on the matter which is in both our minds at this moment.'

'And have they done it as you wished?' said Oak.

'Yes. Come and see it, if you have not already.'

So together they went and read the tomb. 'Eight months ago!' Gabriel murmured when he saw the date. 'It seems like yesterday to me.'

'And to me as if it were years ago – long years, and I had been dead between. And now I am going home, Mr Oak.'

Oak walked after her. 'I wanted to name a small matter to you as soon as I could,' he said with hesitation. 'Merely about business, and I think I may just mention it now, if you'll allow me.'

'O yes, certainly.'

'It is that I may soon have to give up the management of your farm, Mrs Troy. The fact is, I am thinking of leaving England – not yet, you know – next spring.'

'Leaving England!' she said, in surprise and genuine disappointment. 'Why, Gabriel, what are you going to do that for?'

'Well, I've thought it best,' Oak stammered out. 'California is the spot I've had in my mind to try.'

'But it is understood everywhere that you are going to take poor Mr Boldwood's farm on your own account?'

'I've had the refusal o' it 'tis true; but nothing is settled yet, and I have reasons for gieing up. I shall finish out my year there as manager for the trustees, but no more.'

'And what shall I do without you? Oh, Gabriel, I don't think you ought to go away. You've been with me so long – through bright times and dark times – such old friends as we are – that it seems unkind almost. I had fancied that if you leased the other farm as master, you might still give a helping look across at mine. And now going away!'

'I would have willingly.'

'Yet now that I am more helpless than ever you go away!'

'Yes, that's the ill fortune o' it,' said Gabriel, in a distressed tone. 'And it is because of that very helplessness that I feel bound to go. Good afternoon, ma'am,' he concluded, in evident anxiety to get away, and at once went out of the churchyard by a path she could follow on no pretence whatever.

Bathsheba went home, her mind occupied with a new trouble, which being rather harassing than deadly was calculated to do good by diverting her from the chronic gloom of her life. She was set thinking a great deal about Oak and of his wish to shun her; and there occurred to Bathsheba several incidents of her latter intercourse with him, which, trivial when singly viewed, amounted together to a perceptible disinclination for her society. It broke upon her at length as a great pain that her last old disciple was about to foresake her and flee. He who had believed in her and argued on her side when all the rest of the world was against her, had at last like the others become weary and neglectful of the old cause, and was leaving her to fight her battles alone.

Three weeks went on, and more evidence of his want of interest in her was forthcoming. She noticed that instead of entering the small parlour or office where the farm accounts were kept, and waiting, or leaving a memorandum as he had hitherto done during her seclusion, Oak never came at all when she was likely to be there, only entering at unseasonable hours when her presence in that part of the house was least to be expected. Whenever he wanted directions he sent a message, or note with neither heading nor signature, to which she was obliged to reply in the same off-hand style. Poor Bathsheba began to suffer now from the most torturing sting of all – a sensation that she was despised.

The autumn wore away gloomily enough amid these melancholy conjectures, and Christmas-day came, completing a year of her legal widowhood, and two years and a quarter of her life alone. On examining her heart it appeared beyond measure strange that the subject of which the season might have been supposed suggestive – the event in the hall at Boldwood's – was not agitating her at all; but instead, an agonizing conviction that everybody abjured her – for what she could not tell – and that Oak was the ringleader of the recusants. Coming out of church that day she looked round in hope that Oak, whose bass voice she had heard rolling out from the gallery overhead in a most unconcerned manner, might chance to linger in her path in the old way. There he was, as usual, coming down the path behind her. But on seeing Bathsheba turn, he looked aside, and as soon as he got beyond the gate, and there was the barest excuse for a divergence, he made one, and vanished.

The next morning brought the culminating stroke; she had been expecting it long. It was a formal notice by letter from him that he should not renew his engagement with her for the following Lady-day.

Bathsheba actually sat and cried over this letter most bitterly. She was aggrieved and wounded that the possession of hopeless love from Gabriel, which she had grown to regard as her inalienable right for life, should have been withdrawn just at his own pleasure in this way. She was bewildered too by the prospect of having to rely on her own resources again: it seemed to herself that she never could again acquire energy sufficient to go to market, barter, and sell. Since Troy's death Oak had attended all sales and fairs for her, transacting her business at the same time with his own. What should she do now? Her life was becoming a desolation.

So desolate was Bathsheba this evening, that in an absolute hunger for pity and sympathy, and miserable in that she appeared to have outlived the only true friendship she had ever owned, she put on her bonnet and cloak and went down to Oak's house just after sunset, guided on her way by the pale primrose rays of a crescent moon a few days old.

A lively firelight shone from the window, but nobody was visible in the room. She tapped nervously, and then thought it doubtful if it were right for a single woman to call upon a bachelor who lived alone, although he was her manager, and she might be supposed to call on business without any real impropriety. Gabriel opened the door, and the moon shone upon his forehead.

'Mr Oak,' said Bathsheba faintly.

'Yes; I am Mr Oak,' said Gabriel. 'Who have I the honour – O how stupid of me, not to know you, mistress!'

'I shall not be your mistress much longer, shall I, Gabriel?' she said in pathetic tones.

'Well, no. I suppose – But come in, ma'am. Oh – and I'll get a light,' Oak replied, with some awkwardness.

'No; not on my account.'

'It is so seldom that I have a lady visitor that I'm afraid I haven't proper accommodation. Will you sit down, please? Here's a chair, and there's one, too. I am sorry that my chairs all have wood seats, and are rather hard, but I – was thinking of getting some new ones.' Oak placed two or three for her.

'They are quite easy enough for me.'

So down she sat, and down he sat, the fire dancing in their faces, and upon the old furniture,

all a-sheenen
Wi' long years o' handlen,*

that formed Oak's array of household possessions, which sent back a dancing reflection in reply. It was very odd to these two persons, who

* W. Barnes.

knew each other passing well, that the mere circumstance of their meeting in a new place and in a new way should make them so awkward and constrained. In the fields, or at her house, there had never been any embarrassment; but now that Oak had become the entertainer their lives seemed to be moved back again to the days when they were strangers.

'You'll think it strange that I have come, but –'

'O no; not at all.'

'But I thought – Gabriel, I have been uneasy in the belief that I have offended you, and that you are going away on that account. It grieved me very much, and I couldn't help coming.'

'Offended me! As if you could do that, Bathsheba!'

'Haven't I?' she asked, gladly. 'But, what are you going away for else?'

'I am not going to emigrate, you know; I wasn't aware that you would wish me not to when I told 'ee, or I shouldn't have thought of doing it,' he said, simply. 'I have arranged for Little Weatherbury Farm, and shall have it in my own hands at Lady-day. You know I've had a share in it for some time. Still, that wouldn't prevent my attending to your business as before, hadn't it been that things have been said about us.'

'What?' said Bathsheba in surprise. 'Things said about you and me! What are they?'

'I cannot tell you.'

'It would be wiser if you were to, I think. You have played the part of mentor to me many times, and I don't see why you should fear to do it now.'

'It is nothing that you have done, this time. The top and tail o't is this – that I'm sniffing about here, and waiting for poor Boldwood's farm, with a thought of getting you some day.'

'Getting me! What does that mean?'

'Marrying of 'ee, in plain British. You asked me to tell, so you mustn't blame me.'

Bathsheba did not look quite so alarmed as if a cannon had been discharged by her ear, which was what Oak had expected. 'Marrying me! I didn't know it was that you meant,' she said, quietly. 'Such a thing as that is too absurd – too soon – to think of, by far!'

'Yes; of course, it is too absurd. I don't desire any such thing; I should think that was plain enough by this time. Surely, surely you be the last person in the world I think of marrying. It is too absurd, as you say.'

' "Too – s-s-soon" were the words I used.'

'I must beg your pardon for correcting you, but you said, "Too absurd", and so do I.'

'I beg your pardon too!' she returned, with tears in her eyes. ' "Too soon" was what I said. But it doesn't matter a bit – not at all – but I only meant, "too soon". Indeed, I don't, Mr Oak, and you must believe me!'

Gabriel looked her long in the face, but the firelight being faint there was not much to be seen. 'Bathsheba,' he said, tenderly and in surprise, and coming closer: 'If I only knew one thing – whether you would allow me to love you and win you, and marry you after all – If I only knew that!'

'But you never will know,' she murmured.

'Why?'

'Because you never ask.'

'Oh – Oh!' said Gabriel, with a low laugh of joyousness. 'My own dear –'

'You ought not to have sent me that harsh letter this morning,' she interrupted. 'It shows you didn't care a bit about me, and were ready to desert me like all the rest of them! It was very cruel of you, considering I was the first sweetheart that you ever had, and you were the first I ever had; and I shall not forget it!'

'Now, Bathsheba, was ever anybody so provoking?' he said, laughing. 'You know it was purely that I, as an unmarried man, carrying on a business for you as a very taking young woman, had a proper hard part to play – more particular that people knew I had a sort of feeling for 'ee; and I fancied, from the way we were mentioned together, that it might injure your good name. Nobody knows the heat and fret I have been caused by it.'

'And was that all?'

'All.'

'Oh, how glad I am I came!' she exclaimed, thankfully, as she rose from her seat. 'I have thought so much more of you since I fancied you did not want even to see me again. But I must be going now, or I shall be missed. Why, Gabriel,' she said, with a slight laugh, as they went to the door, 'it seems exactly as if I had come courting you – how dreadful!'

'And quite right, too,' said Oak. 'I've danced at your skittish heels, my beautiful Bathsheba, for many a long mile, and many a long day; and it is hard to begrudge me this one visit.'

He accompanied her up the hill, explaining to her the details of his forthcoming tenure of the other farm. They spoke very little of their mutual feelings; pretty phrases and warm expressions being probably unnecessary between such tried friends. Theirs was that substantial affection which arises (if any arises at all) when the two who are thrown together begin first by knowing the rougher sides of each other's character, and not the best till further on, the romance growing up in the interstices of a mass of hard prosaic reality. This good-fellowship – *camaraderie* – usually occurring through similarity of pursuits, is unfortunately seldom superadded to love between the sexes, because men and women associate, not in their labours, but in their pleasures merely. Where, however, happy circumstance permits its development, the compounded feeling proves itself to be the only love which is strong as death – that love which many waters cannot quench, nor the floods drown, beside which the passion usually called by the name is evanescent as steam.

LVII

A Foggy Night and Morning – Conclusion

'THE most private, secret, plainest wedding that it is possible to have.'

Those had been Bathsheba's words to Oak one evening, some time after the event of the preceding chapter, and he meditated a full hour by the clock upon how to carry out her wishes to the letter.

'A license – O yes, it must be a license,' he said to himself at last. 'Very well, then; first, a license.'

On a dark night, a few days later, Oak came with mysterious steps from the surrogate's door in Casterbridge. On the way home he heard a heavy tread in front of him, and, overtaking the man, found him to be Coggan. They walked together into the village until they came to a little lane behind the church, leading down to the cottage of Laban Tall, who had lately been installed as clerk of the parish, and was yet in mortal terror at church on Sundays when he heard his lone voice among certain hard words of the Psalms, whither no man ventured to follow him.

'Well, good-night, Coggan,' said Oak, 'I'm going down this way.'

'Oh!' said Coggan, surprised; 'what's going on to-night, then, make so bold, Mr Oak?'

It seemed rather ungenerous not to tell Coggan, under the circumstances, for Coggan had been true as steel all through the time of Gabriel's unhappiness about Bathsheba, and Gabriel said, 'You can keep a secret, Coggan?'

'You've proved me, and you know.'

'Yes, I have, and I do know. Well, then mistress and I mean to get married to-morrow morning.'

'Heaven's high tower! And yet I've thought of such a thing from time to time; true, I have. But keeping it so close! Well, there 'tis no consarn of mine, and I wish 'ee joy o' her.'

'Thank you, Coggan. But I assure 'ee that this great hush is not what I wished for at all, or what either of us would have wished if it hadn't been for certain things that would make a gay wedding seem hardly the thing. Bathsheba has a great wish that all the parish shall not be in church, looking at her – she's shy-like and nervous about it, in fact – so I be doing this to humour her.'

'Ay, I see: quite right, too, I suppose I must say. And you be now going down to the clerk.'

'Yes; you may as well come with me.'

'I am afeard your labour in keeping it close will be throwed away,' said Coggan, as they walked along. 'Labe Tall's old woman will horn it all over parish in half-an-hour.'

'So she will, upon my life; I never thought of that,' said Oak, pausing.

'Yet I must tell him to-night, I suppose, for he's working so far off, and leaves early.'

'I'll tell 'ee how we could tackle her,' said Coggan. 'I'll knock and ask to speak to Laban outside the door, you standing in the background. Then he'll come out, and you can tell yer tale. She'll never guess what I want en for; and I'll make up a few words about the farm-work, as a blind.'

This scheme was considered feasible; and Coggan advanced boldly, and rapped at Mrs Tall's door. Mrs Tall herself opened it.

'I want to have a word with Laban.'

'He's not at home, and won't be this side of eleven o'clock. He've been forced to go over to Yalbury since shutting out work. I shall do quite as well.'

'I hardly think you will. Stop a moment,' and Coggan stepped round the corner of the porch to consult Oak.

'Who's t'other man, then?' said Mrs Tall.

'Only a friend,' said Coggan.

'Say he's wanted to meet mistress near church-hatch to-morrow morning at ten,' said Oak, in a whisper. 'That he must come without fail, and wear his best clothes.'

'The clothes will floor us as safe as houses!' said Coggan.

'It can't be helped,' said Oak. 'Tell her.'

So Coggan delivered the message. 'Mind, het or wet, blow or snow, he must come,' added Jan. ' 'Tis very particular, indeed. The fact is, 'tis to witness her sign some law-work about taking shares wi' another farmer for a long span o' years. There, that's what 'tis, and now I've told 'ee, Mother Tall, in a way I shouldn't ha' done if I hadn't loved 'ee so hopeless well.'

Coggan retired before she could ask any further; and next they called at the vicar's in a manner which excited no curiosity at all. Then Gabriel went home, and prepared for the morrow.

'Liddy,' said Bathsheba, on going to bed that night, 'I want you to call me at seven o'clock to-morrow, in case I shouldn't wake.'

'But you always do wake afore then, ma'am.'

'Yes, but I have something important to do, which I'll tell you of when the time comes, and it's best to make sure.'

Bathsheba, however, awoke voluntarily at four, nor could she by any contrivance get to sleep again. About six, being quite positive that her watch had stopped during the night, she could wait no longer. She went and tapped at Liddy's door, and after some labour awoke her.

'But I thought it was I who had to call you?' said the bewildered Liddy. 'And it isn't six yet.'

'Indeed it is; how can you tell such a story, Liddy! I know it must be ever so much past seven. Come to my room as soon as you can; I want you to give my hair a good brushing.'

When Liddy came to Bathsheba's room her mistress was already waiting. Liddy could not understand this extraordinary promptness. 'Whatever *is* going on, ma'am?' she said.

'Well, I'll tell you,' said Bathsheba, with a mischievous smile in her bright eyes. 'Farmer Oak is coming here to dine with me to-day!'

'Farmer Oak – and nobody else? – you two alone?'

'Yes.'

'But is it safe, ma'am, after what's been said?' asked her companion, dubiously. 'A woman's good name is such a perishable article that –'

Bathsheba laughed with a flushed cheek, and whispered in Liddy's ear, although there was nobody present. Then Liddy stared and exclaimed, 'Souls alive, what news! It makes my heart go quite bumpity-bump!'

'It makes mine rather furious, too,' said Bathsheba. 'However, there's no getting out of it now!'

It was a damp disagreeable morning. Nevertheless, at twenty minutes to ten o'clock, Oak came out of his house, and

> Went up the hill side
> With that sort of stride
> A man puts out when walking in search of a bride,

and knocked at Bathsheba's door. Ten minutes later a large and smaller umbrella might have been seen moving from the same door, and through the mist along the road to the church. The distance was not more than a quarter of a mile, and these two sensible persons deemed it unnecessary to drive. An observer must have been very close indeed to discover that the forms under the umbrellas were those of Oak and Bathsheba, arm-in-arm for the first time in their lives, Oak in a greatcoat extending to his knees, and Bathsheba in a cloak that reached her clogs. Yet, though so plainly dressed, there was a certain rejuvenated appearance about her:

> As though a rose should shut and be a bud again.

Repose had again incarnadined her cheeks; and having, at Gabriel's request, arranged her hair this morning as she had worn it years ago on Norcombe Hill, she seemed in his eyes remarkably like the girl of that fascinating dream, which, considering that she was now only three or four-and-twenty, was perhaps not very wonderful. In the church were Tall, Liddy, and the parson, and in a remarkably short space of time the deed was done.

The two sat down very quietly to tea in Bathsheba's parlour in the evening of the same day, for it had been arranged that Farmer Oak should go there to live, since he had as yet neither money, house, nor furniture worthy of the name, though he was on a sure way towards them, whilst Bathsheba was, comparatively, in a plethora of all three.

Just as Bathsheba was pouring out a cup of tea, their ears were greeted by the firing of a cannon, followed by what seemed like a tremendous blowing of trumpets, in the front of the house.

'There!' said Oak, laughing, 'I knew those fellows were up to something, by the look on their faces.'

Oak took up the light and went into the porch, followed by Bathsheba with a shawl over her head. The rays fell upon a group of male figures gathered upon the gravel in front, who, when they saw the newly-married couple in the porch, set up a loud 'Hurrah!' and at the same moment bang again went the cannon in the background, followed by a hideous clang of music from a drum, tambourine, clarionet, serpent, hautboy, tenor-viol, and double-bass – the only remaining relics of the true and original Weatherbury band – venerable worm-eaten instruments, which had celebrated in their own persons the victories of Marlborough, under the finger of the forefathers of those who played them now. The performers came forward, and marched up to the front.

'Those bright boys, Mark Clark and Jan, are at the bottom of all this,' said Oak. 'Come in, souls, and have something to eat and drink wi' me and my wife.'

'Not to-night,' said Mr Clark, with evident self-denial. 'Thank ye all the same; but we'll call at a more seemly time. However, we couldn't think of letting the day pass without a note of admiration of some sort. If ye could send a drop of som'at down to Warren's, why so it is. Here's long life and happiness to neighbour Oak and his comely bride!'

'Thank ye; thank ye all,' said Gabriel. 'A bit and a drop shall be sent to Warren's for ye at once. I had a thought that we might very likely get a salute of some sort from our old friends, and I was saying so to my wife but now.'

'Faith,' said Coggan, in a critical tone, turning to his companions, 'the man hev learnt to say "my wife" in a wonderful naterel way, considering how very youthful he is in wedlock as yet – hey, neighbours all?'

'I never heerd a skilful old married feller of twenty years' standing pipe "my wife" in a more used note than 'a did,' said Jacob Smallbury. 'It might have been a little more true to nater if't had been spoke a little chillier, but that wasn't to be expected just now.'

'That improvement will come wi' time,' said Jan, twirling his eye.

Then Oak laughed, and Bathsheba smiled (for she never laughed readily now), and their friends turned to go.

'Yes; I suppose that's the size o't,' said Joseph Poorgrass with a cheerful sigh as they moved away; 'and I wish him joy o' her; though I were once or twice upon saying to-day with holy Hosea, in my scripture manner, which is my second nature, "Ephraim is joined to idols: let him alone." But since 'tis as 'tis, why, it might have been worse, and I feel my thanks accordingly.'

THE RETURN
OF THE NATIVE

CONTENTS

Book Third: The Fascination

Book Fourth: The Closed Door

Book Fifth: The Discovery

Book Sixth: Aftercourses

'To sorrow
            I bade good morrow,
And thought to leave her far away behind;
            But cheerly, cheerly,
            She loves me dearly;
She is so constant to me, and so kind.
            I would deceive her,
            And so leave her,
But ah! she is so constant and so kind.'

AUTHOR'S PREFACE

THE date at which the following events are assumed to have occurred may be set down as between 1840 and 1850, when the old watering-place herein called 'Budmouth' still retained sufficient afterglow from its Georgian gaiety and prestige to lend it an absorbing attractiveness to the romantic and imaginative soul of a lovely dweller inland.

Under the general name of 'Egdon Heath', which has been given to the sombre scene of the story, are united or typified heaths of various real names, to the number of at least a dozen; these being virtually one in character and aspect, though their original unity, or partial unity, is now somewhat disguised by intrusive strips and slices brought under the plough with varying degrees of success, or planted to woodland.

It is pleasant to dream that some spot in the extensive tract whose south-western quarter is here described, may be the heath of that traditional King of Wessex – Lear.

July 1895

POSTSCRIPT

TO prevent disappointment to searchers for scenery it should be added that though the action of the narrative is supposed to proceed in the central and most secluded part of the heaths united into one whole, as above described, certain topographical features resembling those delineated really lie on the margin of the waste, several miles to the westward of the centre. In some other respects also there has been a bringing together of scattered characteristics.

The first edition of this novel was published in three volumes in 1878.

April 1912   T.H.

BOOK FIRST

THE THREE WOMEN

* I *

A Face on Which Time Makes But Little Impression

A SATURDAY afternoon in November was approaching the time of twilight, and the vast tract of unenclosed wild known as Egdon Heath embrowned itself moment by moment. Overhead the hollow stretch of whitish cloud shutting out the sky was as a tent which had the whole heath for its floor.

The heaven being spread with this pallid screen and the earth with the darkest vegetation, their meeting-line at the horizon was clearly marked. In such contrast the heath wore the appearance of an instalment of night which had taken up its place before its astronomical hour was come: darkness had to a great extent arrived hereon, while day stood distinct in the sky. Looking upwards, a furze-cutter would have been inclined to continue work; looking down, he would have decided to finish his faggot and go home. The distant rims of the world and of the firmament seemed to be a division in time no less than a division in matter. The face of the heath by its mere complexion added half an hour to evening; it could in like manner retard the dawn, sadden noon, anticipate the frowning of storms scarcely generated, and intensify the opacity of a moonless midnight to a cause of shaking dread.

In fact, precisely at this transitional point of its nightly roll into darkness the great and particular glory of the Egdon waste began, and nobody could be said to understand the heath who had not been there at such a time. It could best be felt when it could not clearly be seen, its complete effect and explanation lying in this and the succeeding hours before the next dawn: then, and only then, did it tell its true tale. The spot was, indeed, a near relation of night, and when night showed itself an apparent tendency to gravitate together could be perceived in its shades and the scene. The sombre stretch of rounds and hollows seemed to rise and meet the evening gloom in pure sympathy, the heath exhaling darkness as rapidly as the heavens precipitated it. And so the obscurity in the air and the obscurity in the land closed together in a black fraternization towards which each advanced half-way.

The place became full of a watchful intentness now; for when other things sank brooding to sleep the heath appeared slowly to awake and listen. Every night its Titanic form seemed to await something; but it had waited thus, unmoved, during so many centuries, through the crises of so many things, that it could only be imagined to await one last crisis – the final overthrow.

It was a spot which returned upon the memory of those who loved it with an aspect of peculiar and kindly congruity. Smiling champaigns of flowers and fruit hardly do this, for they are permanently harmonious only with an existence of better reputation as to its issues than the present. Twilight combined with the scenery of Egdon Heath to evolve a thing majestic without severity, impressive without showiness, emphatic in its admonitions, grand in its simplicity. The qualifications which frequently invest the façade of a prison with far more dignity than is found in the façade of a palace double its size lent to this heath a sublimity in which spots renowned for beauty of the accepted kind are utterly wanting. Fair prospects wed happily with fair times; but alas, if times be not fair! Men have oftener suffered from the mockery of a place too smiling for their reason than from the oppression of surroundings oversadly tinged. Haggard Egdon appealed to a subtler and scarcer instinct, to a more recently learnt emotion, than that which responds to the sort of beauty called charming and fair.

Indeed, it is a question if the exclusive reign of this orthodox beauty is not approaching its last quarter. The new Vale of Tempe may be a gaunt waste in Thule: human souls may find themselves in closer and closer harmony with external things wearing a sombreness distasteful to our race when it was young. The time seems near, if it has not actually arrived, when the chastened sublimity of a moor, a sea, or a mountain will be all of nature that is absolutely in keeping with the moods of the more thinking among mankind. And ultimately, to the commonest tourist, spots like Iceland may become what the vineyards and myrtle-gardens of South Europe are to him now; and Heidelberg and Baden be passed unheeded as he hastens from the Alps to the sand-dunes of Scheveningen.

The most thorough-going ascetic could feel that he had a natural right to wander on Egdon: he was keeping within the line of legitimate indulgence when he laid himself open to influences such as these. Colours and beauties so far subdued were, at least, the birthright of all. Only in summer days of highest feather did its mood touch the level of gaiety. Intensity was more usually reached by way of the solemn than by way of the brilliant, and such a sort of intensity was often arrived at during winter darkness, tempests, and mists. Then Egdon was aroused to reciprocity; for the storm was its lover, and the wind its friend. Then it became the home of strange phantoms; and it was found to be the hitherto unrecognized original of those wild regions of obscurity which are vaguely felt to be compassing us about in midnight dreams of flight and disaster, and are never thought of after the dream till revived by scenes like this.

It was at present a place perfectly accordant with man's nature – neither ghastly, hateful, nor ugly: neither common-place, unmeaning, nor tame; but, like man, slighted and enduring; and withal singularly colossal and mysterious in its swarthy monotony. As with some persons who have long lived apart, solitude seemed to look out of its countenance. It had a lonely face, suggesting tragical possibilities.

This obscure, obsolete, superseded country figures in Domesday. Its condition is recorded therein as that of heathy, furzy, briary wilderness – 'Bruaria'. Then follows the length and breadth in leagues; and, though some uncertainty exists as to the exact extent of this ancient lineal measure, it appears from the figures that the area of Egdon down to the present day has but little diminished. 'Turbaria Bruaria' – the right of cutting heath-turf – occurs in charters relating to the district. 'Overgrown with heth and mosse', says Leland of the same dark sweep of the country.

Here at least were intelligible facts regarding landscape – far-reaching proofs productive of genuine satisfaction. The untameable, Ishmaelitish thing that Egdon now was it always had been. Civilization was its enemy; and ever since the beginning of vegetation its soil had worn the same antique brown dress, the natural and invariable garment of the particular formation. In its venerable one coat lay a certain vein of satire on human vanity in clothes. A person on a heath in raiment of modern cut and colours has more or less an anomalous look. We seem to want the oldest and simplest human clothing where the clothing of the earth is so primitive.

To recline on a stump of thorn in the central valley of Egdon, between afternoon and night, as now, where the eye could reach nothing of the world outside the summits and shoulders of heathland which filled the whole circumference of its glance, and to know that everything around and underneath had been from prehistoric times as unaltered as the stars overhead, gave ballast to the mind adrift on change, and harassed by the irrepressible New. The great inviolate place had an ancient permanence which the sea cannot claim. Who can say of a particular sea that it is old? Distilled by the sun, kneaded by the moon, it is renewed in a year, in a day, or in an hour. The sea changed, the fields changed, the rivers, the villages, and the people changed, yet Egdon remained. Those surfaces were neither so steep as to be destructible by weather, nor so flat as to be the victims of floods and deposits. With the exception of an aged highway, and a still more aged barrow presently to be referred to – themselves almost crystallized to natural products by long continuance – even the trifling irregularities were not caused by pickaxe, plough, or spade, but remained as the very finger-touches of the last geological change.

The above-mentioned highway traversed the lower levels of the heath, from one horizon to another. In many portions of its course it overlaid an old vicinal way, which branched from the great Western road of the Romans, the Via Iceniana, or Ikenild Street, hard by. On the evening under consideration it would have been noticed that, though the gloom had increased sufficiently to confuse the minor features of the heath, the white surface of the road remained almost as clear as ever.

II

Humanity Appears upon the Scene, Hand in Hand with Trouble

ALONG the road walked an old man. He was white-headed as a mountain, bowed in the shoulders, and faded in general aspect. He wore a glazed hat, an ancient boat-cloak, and shoes; his brass buttons bearing an anchor upon their face. In his hand was a silver-headed walking-stick, which he used as a veritable third leg, perseveringly dotting the ground with its point at every few inches' interval. One would have said that he had been, in his day, a naval officer of some sort or other.

Before him stretched the long, laborious road, dry, empty, and white. It was quite open to the heath on each side, and bisected that vast dark surface like the parting-line on a head of black hair, diminishing and bending away on the furthest horizon.

The old man frequently stretched his eyes ahead to gaze over the tract that he had yet to traverse. At length he discerned, a long distance in front of him, a moving spot, which appeared to be a vehicle, and it proved to be going the same way as that in which he himself was journeying. It was the single atom of life that the scene contained, and it only served to render the general loneliness more evident. Its rate of advance was slow, and the old man gained upon it sensibly.

When he drew nearer he perceived it to be a spring van, ordinary in shape, but singular in colour, this being a lurid red. The driver walked beside it; and, like his van, he was completely red. One dye of that tincture covered his clothes, the cap upon his head, his boots, his face, and his hands. He was not temporarily overlaid with the colour: it permeated him.

The old man knew the meaning of this. The traveller with the cart was a reddleman – a person whose vocation it was to supply farmers with redding for their sheep. He was one of a class rapidly becoming extinct in Wessex, filling at present in the rural world the place which, during the last century, the dodo occupied in the world of animals. He is a curious, interesting, and nearly perished link between obsolete forms of life and those which generally prevail.

The decayed officer, by degrees, came up alongside his fellow-wayfarer, and wished him good evening. The reddleman turned his head, and replied in sad and occupied tones. He was young, and his face, if not exactly handsome, approached so near to handsome that nobody would have contradicted an assertion that it really was so in its natural colour. His eye, which glared so strangely through his stain, was in itself attractive – keen as that of a bird of prey, and blue as autumn mist. He had neither whisker nor moustache, which allowed the soft curves of the lower part of his face to be apparent. His lips were thin, and though, as it seemed, compressed by thought, there was a pleasant twitch at their corners now and then. He was clothed throughout in a tight-fitting suit of corduroy, excellent in quality, not much worn, and well-chosen for its purpose; but deprived of its original colour by his trade. It showed to advantage the good shape of his figure. A certain well-to-do air about the man suggested that he was not poor for his degree. The natural query of an observer would have been, Why should such a promising being as this have hidden his prepossessing exterior by adopting that singular occupation?

After replying to the old man's greeting he showed no inclination to continue in talk, although they still walked side by side, for the elder traveller seemed to desire company. There were no sounds but that of the booming wind upon the stretch of tawny herbage around them, the crackling wheels, the tread of men, and the footsteps of the two shaggy ponies which drew the van. They were small, hardy animals, of a breed between Galloway and Exmoor, and were known as 'heath-croppers' here.

Now, as they thus pursued their way, the reddleman occasionally left his companion's side, and, stepping behind the van, looked into its interior through a small window. The look was always anxious. He would then return to the old man, who made another remark about the state of the country and so on, to which the reddleman again abstractedly replied, and then again they would lapse into silence. The silence conveyed to neither any sense of awkwardness; in these lonely places wayfarers, after a first greeting, frequently plod on for miles without speech; contiguity amounts to a tacit conversation where, otherwise than in cities, such contiguity can be put an end to on the merest inclination, and where not to put an end to it is intercourse in itself.

Possibly these two might not have spoken again till their parting, had it not been for the reddleman's visit to his van. When he returned from his fifth time of looking in the old man said, 'You have something inside there besides your load?'

'Yes.'

'Somebody who wants looking after?'

'Yes.'

Not long after this a faint cry sounded from the interior. The reddleman hastened to the back, looked in, and came away again.

'You have a child there, my man?'

'No, sir, I have a woman.'

'The deuce you have! Why did she cry out?'

'Oh, she has fallen asleep, and not being used to travelling, she's uneasy, and keeps dreaming.'

'A young woman?'

'Yes, a young woman.'

'That would have interested me forty years ago. Perhaps she's your wife?'

'My wife!' said the other bitterly. 'She's above mating with such as I. But there's no reason why I should tell you about that.'

'That's true. And there's no reason why you should not. What harm can I do to you or to her?'

The reddleman looked in the old man's face. 'Well, sir,' he said at last, 'I knew her before today, though perhaps it would have been better if I had not. But she's nothing to me, and I am nothing to her; and she wouldn't have been in my van if any better carriage had been there to take her.'

'Where, may I ask?'

'At Anglebury.'

'I know the town well. What was she doing there?'

'Oh, not much – to gossip about. However, she's tired to death now, and not at all well, and that's what makes her so restless. She dropped off into a nap about an hour ago, and 'twill do her good.'

'A nice-looking girl, no doubt?'

'You would say so.'

The other traveller turned his eyes with interest towards the van window, and, without withdrawing them said, 'I presume I might look in upon her?'

'No,' said the reddleman abruptly. 'It is getting too dark for you to see much of her; and, more than that, I have no right to allow you. Thank God she sleeps so well: I hope she won't wake till she's home.'

'Who is she? One of the neighbourhood?'

' 'Tis no matter who, excuse me.'

'It is not that girl of Blooms-End, who has been talked about more or less lately? If so, I know her; and I can guess what has happened.'

' 'Tis no matter . . . Now, sir, I am sorry to say that we shall soon have to part company. My ponies are tired, and I have further to go, and I am going to rest them under this bank for an hour.'

The elder traveller nodded his head indifferently, and the reddleman turned his horses and van in upon the turf, saying, 'Good night.' The old man replied, and proceeded on his way as before.

The reddleman watched his form as it diminished to a speck on the road and became absorbed in the thickening films of night. He then took some hay from a truss which was slung up under the van, and, throwing a portion of it in front of the horses, made a pad of the rest, which he laid on the ground beside his vehicle. Upon this he sat down, leaning his back against the wheel. From the interior a low soft breathing came to his ear. It appeared to satisfy him, and he musingly surveyed the scene, as if considering the next step that he should take.

To do things musingly, and by small degrees, seemed, indeed, to be a duty in the Egdon valleys at this transitional hour, for there was that in the condition of the heath itself which resembled protracted and halting dubiousness. It was the quality of the repose appertaining to the scene. This was not the repose of actual stagnation, but the apparent repose of incredible slowness. A condition of healthy life so nearly resembling the torpor of death is a noticeable thing of its sort; to exhibit the inertness of the desert, and at the same time to be exercising powers akin to those of the meadow, and even of the forest, awakened in those who thought of it the attentiveness usually engendered by understatement and reserve.

The scene before the reddleman's eyes was a gradual series of ascents from the level of the road backward into the heart of the heath. It embraced hillocks, pits, ridges, acclivities, one behind the other, till all was finished by a high hill cutting against the still light sky. The traveller's eye hovered about these things for a time, and finally settled upon one noteworthy object up there. It was a barrow. This bossy projection of earth above its natural level occupied the loftiest ground of the loneliest height that the heath contained. Although from the vale it appeared but as a wart on an Atlantean brow, its actual bulk was great. It formed the pole and axis of this heathery world.

As the resting man looked at the barrow he became aware that its summit, hitherto the highest object in the whole prospect round, was surmounted by something higher. It rose from the semi-globular mound like a spike from a helmet. The first instinct of an imaginative stranger might have been to suppose it the person of one of the Celts who built the barrow, so far had all of modern date withdrawn from the scene. It seemed a sort of last man among them, musing for a moment before dropping into eternal night with the rest of his race.

There the form stood, motionless as the hill beneath. Above the plain rose the hill, above the hill rose the barrow, and above the barrow rose the figure. Above the figure was nothing that could be mapped elsewhere than on a celestial globe.

Such a perfect, delicate, and necessary finish did the figure give to the dark pile of hills that it seemed to be the only obvious justification of their outline. Without it, there was the dome without the lantern; with it the architectural demands of the mass were satisfied. The scene was strangely homogeneous, in that the vale, the upland, the barrow, and the figure above it amounted only to unity. Looking at this or that member of the group was not observing a complete thing, but a fraction of a thing.

The form was so much like an organic part of the entire motionless structure that to see it move would have impressed the mind of a strange phenomenon. Immobility being the chief characteristic of that whole which the person formed portion of, the discontinuance of immobility in any quarter suggested confusion.

Yet that is what happened. The figure perceptibly gave up its fixity, shifted a step or two, and turned round. As if alarmed, it descended on the right side of the barrow, with the glide of a water-drop down a bud, and then vanished. The movement had been sufficient to show more clearly the characteristics of the figure, and that it was a woman's.

The reason of her sudden displacement now appeared. With her dropping out of sight on the right side, a new-comer, bearing a burden, protruded into the sky on the left side, ascended the tumulus, and deposited the burden on the top. A second followed, then a third, a fourth, a fifth, and ultimately the whole barrow was peopled with burdened figures.

The only intelligible meaning in this sky-backed pantomime of silhouettes was that the woman had no relation to the forms who had taken her place, was sedulously avoiding these, and had come thither for another object than theirs. The imagination of the observer clung by preference to that vanished, solitary figure, as to something more interesting, more important, more likely to have a history worth knowing than these new-comers, and unconsciously regarded them as intruders. But they remained, and established themselves; and the lonely person who hitherto had been queen of the solitude did not at present seem likely to return.

* III *

The Custom of the Country

HAD a looker-on been posted in the immediate vicinity of the barrow, he would have learned that these persons were boys and men of the neighbouring hamlets. Each, as he ascended the barrow, had been heavily laden with furze-faggots, carried upon the shoulder by means of a long stake sharpened at each end for impaling them easily – two in front and two behind. They came from a part of the heath a quarter of a mile to the rear, where furze almost exclusively prevailed as a product.

Every individual was so involved in furze by his method of carrying the faggots that he appeared like a bush on legs till he had thrown them down. The party had marched in trail, like a travelling flock of sheep; that is to say, the strongest first, the weak and young behind.

The loads were all laid together, and a pyramid of furze thirty feet in circumference now occupied the crown of the tumulus, which was known as Rainbarrow for many miles round. Some made themselves busy with matches, and in selecting the driest tufts of furze, others in loosening the bramble bonds which held the faggots together. Others, again, while this was in progress, lifted their eyes and swept the vast expanse of country commanded by their position, now lying nearly obliterated by shade. In the valleys of the heath nothing save its own wild face was visible at any time of day; but this spot commanded a horizon enclosing a tract of far extent, and in many cases lying beyond the heath country. None of its features could be seen now, but the whole made itself felt as a vague stretch of remoteness.

While the men and lads were building the pile, a change took place in the mass of shade which denoted the distant landscape. Red suns and tufts of fire one by one began to arise, flecking the whole country round. They were the bonfires of other parishes and hamlets that were engaged in the same sort of commemoration. Some were distant, and stood in a dense atmosphere, so that bundles of pale strawlike beams radiated around them in the shape of a fan. Some were large and near, glowing scarlet-red from the shade, like wounds in a black hide. Some were Maenades, with winy faces and blown hair. These tinctured the silent bosom of the clouds above them and lit up their ephemeral caves, which seemed thenceforth to become scalding caldrons. Perhaps as many as thirty bonfires could be counted within the whole bounds of the district; and as the hour may be told on a clock-face when the figures themselves are invisible, so did the men recognize the locality of each fire by its angle and direction, though nothing of the scenery could be viewed.

The first tall flame from Rainbarrow sprang into the sky, attracting all eyes that had been fixed on the distant conflagrations back to their own attempt in the same kind. The cheerful blaze streaked the inner surface of the human circle – now increased by other stragglers, male and female – with its own gold livery, and even overlaid the dark turf around with a lively luminousness, which softened off into obscurity where the barrow rounded downwards out of sight. It showed the barrow to be the segment of a globe, as perfect as on the day when it was thrown up, even the little ditch remaining from which the earth was dug. Not a plough had ever disturbed a grain of that stubborn soil. In the heath's barrenness to the farmer lay its fertility to the historian. There had been no obliteration, because there had been no tending.

It seemed as if the bonfire-makers were standing in some radiant upper storey of the world, detached from and independent of the dark stretches below. The heath down there was now a vast abyss, and no longer a continuation of what they stood on; for their eyes, adapted to the blaze, could see nothing of the deep beyond its influence. Occasionally, it is true, a more vigorous flare than usual from their faggots sent darting lights like aides-de-camp down the inclines to some distant bush, pool, or patch of white sand, kindling these to replies of the same colour, till all was lost in darkness again. Then the whole black phenomenon beneath represented Limbo as viewed from the brink by the sublime Florentine in his vision, and the muttered articulations of the wind in the hollows were as complaints and petitions from the 'souls of mighty worth' suspended therein.

It was as if these men and boys had suddenly dived into past ages, and fetched therefrom an hour and deed which had before been familiar with this spot. The ashes of the original British pyre which blazed from that summit lay fresh and undisturbed in the barrow beneath their tread. The flames from funeral piles long ago kindled there had shone down upon the lowlands as these were shining now. Festival fires to Thor and Woden had followed on the same gound and duly had their day. Indeed, it is pretty well known that such blazes as this the heathmen were now enjoying are rather the lineal descendants from jumbled Druidical rites and Saxon ceremonies than the invention of popular feeling about Gunpowder Plot.

Moreover to light a fire is the instinctive and resistant act of man when, at the winter ingress, the curfew is sounded throughout Nature. It indicates a spontaneous, Promethean rebelliousness against the fiat that this recurrent season shall bring foul times, cold darkness, misery and death. Black chaos comes, and the fettered gods of the earth say, Let there be light.

The brilliant lights and sooty shades which struggled upon the skin and clothes of the persons standing round caused their lineaments and general contours to be drawn with Dureresque vigour and dash. Yet the permanent moral expression of each face it was impossible to discover, for as the nimble flames towered, nodded, and swooped through the surrounding air, the blots of shade and flakes of light upon the countenances of the group changed shape and position endlessly. All was unstable; quivering as leaves, evanescent as lightning. Shadowy eye-sockets, deep as those of a death's head, suddenly turned into pits of lustre: a lantern-jaw cavernous, then it was shining; wrinkles were emphasized to ravines, or obliterated entirely by a changed ray. Nostrils were dark wells; sinews in old necks were gilt mouldings; things with no particular polish on them were glazed; bright objects, such as the tip of a furze-hook one of the men carried, were as glass; eyeballs glowed like little lanterns. Those whom Nature had depicted as merely quaint became grotesque, the grotesque became preternatural; for all was in extremity.

Hence it may be that the face of an old man, who had like others been called to the heights by the rising flames, was not really the mere nose and chin that it appeared to be, but an appreciable quantity of human countenance. He stood complacently sunning himself in the heat. With a speäker, or stake, he tossed the outlying scraps of fuel into the conflagration, looking at the midst of the pile, occasionally lifting his eyes to measure the height of the flame, or to follow the great sparks which rose with and sailed away into darkness. The beaming sight, and the penetrating warmth, seemed to breed in him a cumulative cheerfulness, which soon amounted to delight. With his stick in his hand he began to jig a private minuet, a bunch of copper seals shining and swinging like a pendulum from under his waistcoat: he also began to sing, in the voice of a bee up a flue –

> ' The King' call'd down' his no-bles all',
>   By one', by two', by three';
> Earl Mar'-shal, I'll' go shrive' the queen',
>   And thou' shalt wend' with me'.
>
> 'A boon', a boon', quoth Earl' Mar-shal',
>   And fell' on his bend'-ded knee',
> That what'-so-e'er' the queen' shall say',
>   No harm' there-of' may be'.'

Want of breath prevented a continuance of the songs; and the breakdown attracted the attention of a firm-standing man of middle age, who kept each corner of his crescent-shaped mouth rigorously drawn back into his cheek, as if to do away with any suspicion of mirthfulness which might erroneously have attached to him.

'A fair stave, Grandfer Cantle; but I am afeard 'tis too much for the mouldy weasand of such a old man as you,' he said to the wrinkled reveller. 'Dostn't wish th' wast three sixes again, Grandfer, as you was when you first learnt to sing it?'

'Hey?' said Grandfer Cantle, stopping in his dance.

'Dostn't wish wast young again, I say? There's a hole in thy poor bellows nowadays seemingly.'

'But there's a good art in me? If I couldn't make a little wind go a long ways I should seem no younger than the most aged man, should I, Timothy?'

'And how about the new-married folks down there at the Quiet Woman Inn?' the other inquired, pointing towards a dim light in the direction of the distant highway, but considerably apart from where the reddleman was at that moment resting. 'What's the rights of the matter about 'em? You ought to know, being an understanding man.'

'But a little rakish, hey? I own to it. Master Cantle is that, or he's nothing. Yet 'tis a gay fault, neighbour Fairway, that age will cure.'

'I heard they were coming home to-night. By this time they must have come. What besides?'

'The next thing is for us to go and wish 'em joy, I suppose?'

'Well, no.'

'No? Now, I thought we must. *I* must, or 'twould be very unlike me – the first in every spree that's going!'

> 'Do thou' put on' a fri'-ar's coat',
> And I'll' put on' a-no'-ther,
> And we' will to' Queen Ele'anor go',
> Like Fri'ar and' his bro'ther.'

I met Mis'ess Yeobright, the young bride's aunt, last night, and she told me that her son Clym was coming home a' Christmas. Wonderful clever, 'a believe – ah, I should like to have all that's under that young man's hair. Well, then, I spoke to her in my well-known merry way, and she said, "O that what's shaped so venerable should talk like a fool!" – that's what she said to me. I don't care for her, be jowned if I do, and so I told her. "Be jowned if I care for 'ee," I said. I had her there – hey?'

'I rather think she had you,' said Fairway.

'No,' said Granfer Cantle, his countenance slightly flagging. ''Tisn't so bad as that with me?'

'Seemingly 'tis; however, is it because of the wedding that Clym is coming home a' Christmas – to make a new arrangement because his mother is now left in the house alone?'

'Yes, yes – that's it. But Timothy, hearken to me,' said the Grandfer earnestly. 'Though known as such a joker, I be an understanding man if you catch me serious, and I am serious now. I can tell 'ee lots about the married couple. Yes, this morning at six o'clock they went up the country to do the job, and neither vell nor mark have been seen of 'em since, though I reckon that this afternoon has brought 'em home again, man and woman – wife, that is. Isn't it spoke like a man, Timothy, and wasn't Mis'ess Yeobright wrong about me?'

'Yes, it will do. I didn't know the two had walked together since last fall, when her aunt forbad the banns. How long has this new set-to been mangling them? Do you know, Humphrey?'

'Yes, how long?' said Grandfer Cantle smartly, likewise turning to Humphrey. 'I ask that question.'

'Ever since her aunt altered her mind, and said she might hae the man after all,' replied Humphrey, without removing his eyes from the fire. He was a somewhat solemn young fellow, and carried the hook and leather gloves of a furze-cutter, his legs, by reason of that occupation, being sheathed in bulging leggings as stiff as the Philistine's greaves of brass. 'That's why they went away to be married, I count. You see, after kicking up such a nunny-watch and forbidding the banns 'twould have made Mis'ess Yeobright seem foolish-like to have a banging wedding in the same parish all as if she'd never gainsaid it.'

'Exactly – seem foolish-like; and that's very bad for the poor things that be so, though I only guess as much, to be sure,' said Grandfer Cantle, still strenuously preserving a sensible bearing and mien.

'Ah, well, I was at church that day,' said Fairway, 'which was a very curious thing to happen.'

'If 'twasn't my name's Simple,' said the Grandfer emphatically. 'I ha'n't been there to-year; and now the winter is a-coming on I won't say I shall.'

'I ha'n't been these three years,' said Humphrey; 'for I'm so dead sleepy of a Sunday; and 'tis so terrible far to get there; and when you do get there 'tis such a mortal poor chance that you'll be chose for up above, when so many bain't, that I bide at home and don't go at all.'

'I not only happened to be there,' said Fairway, with a fresh collection of emphasis, 'but I was sitting in the same pew as Mis'ess Yeobright. And though you may not see it as such, it fairly made my blood run cold to hear her. Yes, it is a curious thing; but it made my blood run cold, for I was close to her elbow.' The speaker looked round upon the bystanders, now drawing closer to hear him, with his lips gathered tighter than ever in the rigorousness of his descriptive moderation.

' 'Tis a serious job to have things happen to 'ee there,' said a woman behind.

' "Ye are to declare it," was the parson's words,' Fairway continued. 'And then up stood a woman at my side – a-touching of me. "Well, be damned if there isn't Mis'ess Yeobright a-standing up," I said to myself. Yes, neighbours, though I was in the temple of prayer that's what I said. 'Tis against my conscience to curse and swear in company, and I hope any woman here will overlook it. Still what I did say I did say, and 'twould be a lie if I didn't own it.'

'So 'twould, neighbour Fairway.'

' "Be damned if there isn't Mis'ess Yeobright a-standing up," I said,' the narrator repeated, giving out the bad word with the same passionless severity of face as before, which proved how entirely necessity and not gusto had to do with the iteration. 'And the next thing I heard was, "I forbid the banns," from her. "I'll speak to you after the service," said the parson, in quite a homely way – yes, turning all at once into a common man no holier than you or I. Ah, her face was pale! Maybe you can call to mind that monument in Weatherbury church – the cross-legged soldier that have had his arm knocked away by the school-children? Well, he would about have matched that woman's face, when she said, "I forbid the banns." '

The audience cleared their throats and tossed a few stalks into the fire, not because these deeds were urgent, but to give themselves time to weigh the moral of the story.

'I'm sure when I heard they'd been forbid I felt as glad as if anybody had gied me sixpence,' said an earnest voice – that of Olly Dowden, a woman who lived by making heath brooms, or besoms. Her nature was to be civil to enemies as well as to friends, and grateful to all the world for letting her remain alive.

'And now the maid have married him just the same,' said Humphrey.

'After that Mis'ess Yeobright came round and was quite agreeable,' Fairway resumed, with an unheeding air, to show that his words were no appendage to Humphrey's, but the result of independent reflection.

'Supposing they were ashamed, I don't see why they shouldn't have done it here-right,' said a wide-spread woman whose stays creaked like shoes whenever she stopped or turned. ' 'Tis well to call the neighbours together and to hae a good racket once now and then; and it may as well be when there's a wedding as at tide-times. I don't care for close ways.'

'Ah, now, you'd hardly believe it, but I don't care for gay weddings,' said Timothy Fairway, his eyes again travelling round. 'I hardly blame Thomasin Yeobright and neighbour Wildeve for doing it quiet, if I own it. A wedding at home means five and six-handed reels by the hour; and they do a man's legs no good when he's over forty.'

'True. Once at the woman's house you can hardly say nay to being one in a jig, knowing all the time that you be expected to make yourself worth your victuals.'

'You be bound to dance at Christmas because 'tis the time o' year; you must dance at weddings because 'tis the time o' life. At christenings folk will even smuggle in a reel or two, if 'tis no further on than the first or second chiel. And this is not naming the songs you've got to sing . . . For my part I like a good hearty funeral as well as anything. You've as splendid victuals and drinks as at other parties, and even better. And it don't wear your legs to stumps in talking over a poor fellow's ways as it do to stand up in hornpipes.'

'Nine folks out of ten would own 'twas going too far to dance then, I suppose?' suggested Grandfer Cantle.

' 'Tis the only sort of party a staid man can feel safe at after the mug have been round a few times.'

'Well, I can't understand a quiet lady-like little body like Tamsin Yeobright caring to be married in such a mean way,' said Susan Nunsuch, the wide woman, who preferred the original subject. ' 'Tis worse than the poorest do. And I shouldn't have cared about the man, though some may say he's good-looking.'

'To give him his due he's a clever, learned fellow in his way – a'most as clever as Clym Yeobright used to be. He was brought up to better things than keeping the Quiet Woman. An engineer – that's what the man was, as we know; but he threw away his chance, and so 'a took a public-house to live. His learning was no use to him at all.'

'Very often the case,' said Olly, the besom-maker. 'And yet how people do strive after it and get it! The class of folk that couldn't use to make a round O to save their bones from the pit can write their names now without a sputter of the pen, oftentimes without a single blot: what do I say? – why, almost without a desk to lean their stomachs and elbows upon.'

'True: 'tis amazing what a polish the world have been brought to,' said Humphrey.

'Why, afore I went a soldier in the Bang-up Locals (as we was called), in the year four,' chimed in Grandfer Cantle brightly, 'I didn't know no more what the world was like than the commonest man among ye. And now, jown it all, I won't say what I bain't fit for, hey?'

'Couldst sign the book, no doubt,' said Fairway, 'if wast young enough to join hands with a woman again, like Wildeve and Mis'ess Tamsin, which is more than Humph there could do, for he follows his father in learning. Ah, Humph, well I can mind when I was married how I zid thy father's mark staring me in the face as I went to put down my name. He and your mother were the couple married just afore we were, and there stood thy father's cross with arms stretched out like a great banging scarecrow. What a terrible black cross that was – thy father's very likeness in en! To save my soul I couldn't help laughing when I zid en, though all the time I was as hot as dog-days, what with the marrying, and what with the woman a-hanging to me, and what with Jack Changley and a lot more chaps grinning at me through church window. But the next moment a strawmote would have knocked me down, for I called to mind that if thy father and mother had had high words once, they'd been at it twenty times since they'd been man and wife, and I zid myself as the next poor stunpoll to get into the same mess . . . Ah – well, what a day 'twas!'

'Wildeve is older than Tamsin Yeobright by a goodfew summers. A pretty maid too she is. A young woman with a home must be a fool to tear her smock for a man like that.'

The speaker, a peat or turf-cutter, who had newly joined the group, carried across his shoulder the singular heart-shaped spade of large dimensions used in that species of labour; and its well-whetted edge gleamed like a silver bow in the beams of the fire.

'A hundred maidens would have had him if he'd asked 'em,' said the wide woman.

'Didst ever know a man, neighbour, that no woman at all would marry?' inquired Humphrey.

'I never did,' said the turf-cutter.

'Nor I,' said another.

'Nor I,' said Grandfer Cantle.

'Well, now, I did once,' said Timothy Fairway, adding more firmness to one of his legs. 'I did know of such a man. But only once, mind.' He gave his throat a thorough rake round, as if it were the duty of every person not to be mistaken through thickness of voice. 'Yes, I knew of such a man,' he said.

'And what ghastly gallicrow might the poor fellow have been like, Master Fairway?' asked the turf-cutter.

'Well, 'a was neither a deaf man, nor a dumb man, nor a blind man. What 'a was I don't say.'

'Is he known in these parts?' said Olly Dowden.

'Hardly,' said Timothy; 'but I name no name. . . . Come, keep the fire up there, youngsters.'

'Whatever is Christian Cantle's teeth a-chattering for?' said a boy from amid the smoke and shades on the other side of the blaze. 'Be ye a-cold, Christian?'

A thin jibbering voice was heard to reply, 'No, not at all.'

'Come forward, Christian, and show yourself. I didn't know you were here,' said Fairway, with a humane look across towards the quarter.

Thus requested, a faltering man, with reedy hair, no shoulders and a great quantity of wrist and ankle beyond his clothes, advanced a step or two by his own will, and was pushed by the will of others half a dozen steps more. He was Grandfer Cantle's youngest son.

'What be ye quaking for, Christian?' said the turf-cutter kindly.

'I'm the man.'

'What man?'

'The man no woman will marry.'

'The deuce you be!' said Timothy Fairway, enlarging his gaze to cover Christian's whole surface and a great deal more; Grandfer Cantle meanwhile staring as a hen stares at the duck she has hatched.

'Yes, I be he; and it makes me afeared,' said Christian. 'D'ye think 'twill hurt me? I shall always say I don't care, and swear to it, though I do care all the while.'

'Well, be damned if this isn't the queerest start ever I know'd,' said Mr Fairway. 'I didn't mean you at all. There's another in the country, then! Why did ye reveal yer misfortune, Christian?'

' 'Twas to be if 'twas, I suppose. I can't help it, can I?' He turned upon them his painfully circular eyes, surrounded by concentric lines like targets.

'No, that's true. But 'tis a melancholy thing, and my blood ran cold when you spoke, for I felt there were two poor fellows where I had thought only one. 'Tis a sad thing for ye, Christian. How'st know the women won't hae thee?'

'I've asked 'em.'

'Sure I should never have thought you had the face. Well, and what did the last one say to ye? Nothing that can't be got over, perhaps, after all?'

' "Get out of my sight, you slack-twisted, slim-looking maphrotight fool," was the woman's words to me.'

'Not encouraging, I own,' said Fairway. ' "Get out of my sight, you slack-twisted, slim-looking maphrotight fool," is rather a hard way of saying, No. But even that might be overcome by time and patience, so as to let a few grey hairs show themselves in the hussy's head. How old be you, Christian?'

'Thirty-one last tatie-digging, Mister Fairway.'

'Not a boy – not a boy. Still there's hope yet.'

'That's my age by baptism, because that's put down in the great book of the Judgment that they keep in church vestry; but mother told me I was born some time afore I was christened.'

'Ah!'

'But she couldn't tell when, to save her life, except that there was no moon.'

'No moon: that's bad. Hey, neighbours, that's bad for him!'

'Yes, 'tis bad,' said Grandfer Cantle, shaking his head.

'Mother know'd 'twas no moon, for she asked another woman that had an almanac, as she did whenever a boy was born to her, because of the saying, "No moon, no man," which made her afeard every man-child she had. Do ye really think it serious, Mister Fairway, that there was no moon?'

'Yes; "No moon, no man." 'Tis one of the truest sayings ever spit out. The boy never comes to anything that's born at new moon. A bad job for thee, Christian, that you should have showed your nose then of all days in the month.'

'I suppose the moon was terrible full when you were born?' said Christian, with a look of hopeless admiration at Fairway.

'Well, 'a was not new,' Mr Fairway replied, with a disinterested gaze.

'I'd sooner go without drink at Lammas-tide than be a man of no moon,' continued Christian, in the same shattered recitative. ' 'Tis said I be only the rames of a man, and no good for my race at all; and I suppose that's the cause o't.'

'Ay,' said Grandfer Cantle, somewhat subdued in spirit; 'and yet his mother cried for scores of hours when 'a was a boy, for fear he should outgrow hisself and go for a soldier.'

'Well, there's many just as bad as he,' said Fairway. 'Wethers must live their time as well as other sheep, poor soul.'

'So perhaps I shall rub on? Ought to be afeard o' nights, Master Fairway?'

'You'll have to lie alone all your life; and 'tis not to married couples but to single sleepers that a ghost shows himself when a' do come. One has been seen lately, too. A very strange one.'

'No – don't talk about it if 'tis agreeable of ye not to! 'Twill make my skin crawl when I think of it in bed alone. But you will – ah, you will, I know, Timothy; and I shall dream all night o't! A very strange one? What sort of a spirit did ye mean when ye said, a very strange one, Timothy? – no, no – don't tell me.'

'I don't half believe in spirits myself. But I think it ghostly enough – what I was told. 'Twas a little boy that zid it.'

'What was it like? – no, don't –'

'A red one. Yes, most ghosts be white; but this is as if it had been dipped in blood.'

Christian drew a deep breath without letting it expand his body, and Humphrey said, 'Where has it been seen?'

'Not exactly here; but in this same heth. But 'tisn't a thing to talk about. What do ye say,' continued Fairway in brisker tones, and turning upon them as if the idea had not been Grandfer Cantle's – 'what do you say to giving the new man and wife a bit of a song to-night afore we go to bed – being their wedding-day? When folks are just married 'tis as well to look glad o't, since looking sorry won't unjoin 'em. I am no drinker, as we know, but when the womenfolk and youngsters have gone home we can drop down across to the Quiet Woman, and strike up a ballet in front of the married folks' door. 'Twill please the young wife, and that's what I should like to do, for many's the skinful I've had at her hands when she lived with her aunt at Blooms-End.'

'Hey? And so we will!' said Grandfer Cantle, turning so briskly that his copper seals swung extravagantly. 'I'm as dry as a kex with biding up here in the wind, and I haven't seen the colour of drink since nammet-time today. 'Tis said that the last brew at the Woman is very pretty drinking. And, neighbours, if we should be a little late in the finishing, why, tomorrow's Sunday, and we can sleep it off?'

'Grandfer Cantle! you take things very careless for an old man,' said the wide woman.

'I take things careless; I do – too careless to please the women! Klk! I'll sing the "Jovial Crew," or any other song, when a weak old man would cry his eyes out. Jown it; I am up for anything.

> 'The King' look'd o'ver his left' shoul-der',
>   And a grim' look look'-ed hee',
>   Earl Mar'-shal, he said', but for' my oath'
>   Or hang'-ed thou' shouldst bee'.'

'Well, that's what we'll do,' said Fairway. 'We'll give 'em a song, an' it please the Lord. What's the good of Thomasin's cousin Clym a-coming home after the deed's done? He should have come afore, if so be he wanted to stop it, and marry her himself.'

'Perhaps he's coming to bide with his mother a little time, as she must feel lonely now the maid's gone.'

'Now, 'tis very odd, but I never feel lonely – no, not at all,' said Grandfer Cantle. 'I am as brave in the night-time as a' admiral!'

The bonfire was by this time beginning to sink low, for the fuel had not been of that substantial sort which can support a blaze long. Most of the other fires within the wide horizon were also dwindling weak. Attentive observation of their brightness, colour, and length of existence would have revealed the quality of the material burnt; and through that, to some extent the natural produce of the district in which each bonfire was situate. The clear, kingly effulgence that had characterized the majority expressed a heath and furze country like their own, which in one direction extended an unlimited number of miles: the rapid flares and extinctions at other points of the compass showed the lightest of fuel – straw, beanstalks, and the usual waste from arable land. The most enduring of all – steady unaltering eyes like planets – signified wood, such as hazel-branches, thorn-faggots, and stout billets. Fires of the last-mentioned materials were rare, and, though comparatively small in magnitude beside the transient blazes, now began to get the best of them by mere long-continuance. The great ones had perished, but these remained. They occupied the remotest visible positions – sky-backed summits rising out of rich coppice and plantation districts to the north, where the soil was different, and heath foreign and strange.

Save one; and this was the nearest of any, the moon of the whole shining throng. It lay in a direction precisely opposite to that of the little window in the vale below. Its nearness was such that, notwithstanding its actual smallness, its glow infinitely transcended theirs.

This quiet eye had attracted attention from time to time; and when their own fire had become sunken and dim it attracted more; some even of the wood fires more recently lighted had reached their decline, but no change was perceptible here.

'To be sure, how near that fire is!' said Fairway. 'Seemingly, I can see a fellow of some sort walking round it. Little and good must be said of that fire, surely.'

'I can throw a stone there,' said the boy.

'And so can I!' said Grandfer Cantle.

'No, no, you can't, my sonnies. That fire is not much less than a mile off, for all that 'a seems so near.'

' 'Tis in the heath, but not furze,' said the turf-cutter.

' 'Tis cleft-wood, that's what 'tis,' said Timothy Fairway. 'Nothing would burn like that except clean timber. And 'tis on the knap afore the old captain's house at Mistover. Such a queer mortal as that man is! To have a little fire inside your own bank and ditch, that nobody else may enjoy it or come anigh it! And what a zany an old chap must be, to light a bonfire when there's no youngsters to please.'

'Cap'n Vye has been for a long walk to-day, and is quite tired out,' said Grandfer Cantle, 'so 'tisn't likely to be he.'

'And he would hardly afford a good fuel like that,' said the wide woman.

'Then it must be his granddaughter,' said Fairway. 'Not that a body of her age can want a fire much.'

'She is very strange in her ways, living up there by herself, and such things please her,' said Susan.

'She's a well-favoured maid enough,' said Humphrey the furze-cutter; 'especially when she's got one of her dandy gowns on.'

'That's true,' said Fairway. 'Well, let her bonfire burn an't will. Ours is well-nigh out by the look o't.'

'How dark 'tis now the fire's gone down!' said Christian Cantle, looking behind him with his hare eyes. 'Don't ye think we'd better get home-along, neighbours? The heth isn't haunted, I know; but we'd better get home . . . Ah, what was that?'

'Only the wind,' said the turf-cutter.

'I don't think Fifth-of-Novembers ought to be kept up by night except in towns. It should be by day in outstep, ill-accounted places like this!'

'Nonsense, Christian. Lift up your spirits like a man! Susy, dear, you and I will have a jig – hey, my honey? – before 'tis quite too dark to see how well-favoured you be still, though so many summers have passed since your husband, a son of a witch, snapped you up from me.'

This was addressed to Susan Nunsuch; and the next circumstance of which the beholders were conscious was a vision of the matron's broad form whisking off towards the space whereon the fire had been kindled. She was lifted bodily by Mr Fairway's arm, which had been flung round her waist before she had become aware of his intention. The site of the fire was now merely a circle of ashes flecked with red embers and sparks, the furze having burnt completely away. Once within the circle he whirled her round and round in a dance. She was a woman noisily constructed; in addition to her enclosing framework of whalebone and lath, she wore pattens summer and winter, in wet weather and in dry, to preserve her boots from wear; and when Fairway began to jump about with her, the clicking of the pattens, the creaking of the stays, and her screams of surprise, formed a very audible concert.

'I'll crack thy numskull for thee, you mandy chap!' said Mrs Nunsuch, as she helplessly danced round with him, her feet playing like drumsticks among the sparks. 'My ankles were all in a fever before, from walking through that prickly furze, and now you must make 'em worse with these vlankers!'

The vagary of Timothy Fairway was infectious. The turf-cutter seized old Olly Dowden, and, somewhat more gently, poussetted with her likewise. The young men were not slow to imitate the example of their elders, and seized the maids; Grandfer Cantle and his stick jigged in the form of a three-legged object among the rest; and in half a minute all that could be seen on Rainbarrow was a whirling of dark shapes amid a boiling confusion of sparks, which leapt around the dancers as high as their waists. The chief noises were women's shrill cries, men's laughter, Susan's stays and pattens, Olly Dowden's 'heu-heu-heu!' and the strumming of the wind upon the furze-bushes, which formed a kind of tune of the demoniac measure they trod. Christian alone stood aloof, uneasily rocking himself as he murmured, 'They ought not to do it – how the vlankers do fly! 'tis tempting the Wicked one, 'tis.'

'What was that?' said one of the lads, stopping.

'Ah – where?' said Christian, hastily closing up to the rest.

The dancers all lessened their speed.

' 'Twas behind you, Christian, that I heard it – down there.'

'Yes – 'tis behind me!' Christian said. 'Matthew, Mark, Luke, and John, bless the bed that I lie on; four angels guard –'

'Hold your tongue. What is it?' said Fairway.

'Hoi-i-i-i!' cried a voice from the darkness.

'Halloo-o-o-o!' said Fairway.

'Is there any cart-track up across here to Mis'ess Yeobright's, of Blooms-End?' came to them in the same voice, as a long, slim, indistinct figure approached the barrow.

'Ought we not to run home as hard as we can, neighbours, as 'tis getting late?' said Christian. 'Not run away from one another, you know; run close together, I mean.'

'Scrape up a few stray locks of furze, and make a blaze, so that we can see who the man is,' said Fairway.

When the flame arose it revealed a young man in tight raiment, and red from top to toe. 'Is there a track across here to Mis'ess Yeobright's house?' he repeated.

'Ay – keep along the path down there.'

'I mean a way two horses and a van can travel over?'

'Well, yes; you can get up the vale below here with time. The track is rough, but if you've got a light your horses may pick along wi' care. Have ye brought your cart far up, neighbour reddleman?'

'I've left it in the bottom, about half a mile back. I stepped on in front to make sure of the way, as 'tis night-time, and I hadn't been here for so long.'

'Oh, well, you can get up,' said Fairway. 'What a turn it did give me when I saw him!' he added to the whole group, the reddleman included. 'Lord's sake, I thought, whatever fiery mommet is this come to trouble us? No slight to your looks, reddleman, for ye bain't bad-looking in the groundwork, though the finish is queer. My meaning is just to say how curious I felt. I half thought it 'twas the devil or the red ghost the boy told of.'

'It gied me a turn likewise,' said Susan Nunsuch, 'for I had a dream last night of a death's head.'

'Don't ye talk o't no more,' said Christian. 'If he had handkerchief over his head he'd look for all the world like the Devil in the picture of the Temptation.'

'Well, thank you for telling me,' said the young reddleman, smiling faintly. 'And good night t'ye all.'

He withdrew from their sight down the barrow.

'I fancy I've seen that young man's face before,' said Humphrey. 'But where, or how, or what his name is, I don't know.'

The reddleman had not been gone more than a few minutes when another person approached the partially revived bonfire. It proved to be a well-known and respected widow of the neighbourhood, of a standing which can only be expressed by the word genteel. Her face, encompassed by the blackness of the receding heath, showed whitely, and without half-lights, like a cameo.

She was a woman of middle-age, with well-formed features of the type usually found where perspicacity is the chief quality enthroned within. At moments she seemed to be regarding issues from a Nebo denied to others around. She had something of an estranged mien: the solitude exhaled from the heath was concentrated in this face that had risen from it. The air with which she looked at the heathmen betokened a certain unconcern at their presence, or at what might be their opinions of her for walking in that lonely spot at such an hour, this indirectly implying that in some respect or other they were not up to her level. The explanation lay in the fact that though her husband had been a small farmer she herself was a curate's daughter, who had once dreamt of doing better things.

Persons with any weight of character carry, like planets, their atmospheres along with them in their orbits; and the matron who entered now upon the scene could, and usually did, bring her own tone into a company. Her normal manner among the heathfolk had that reticence which results from the consciousness of superior communicative power. But the effect of coming into society and light after lonely wandering in darkness is a sociability in the comer above its usual pitch, expressed in the features even more than in the words.

'Why, 'tis Mis'ess Yeobright,' said Fairway. 'Mis'ess Yeobright, not ten minutes ago a man was here asking for you – reddleman.'

'What did he want?' said she.

'He didn't tell us.'

'Something to sell, I suppose; what it can be I am at a loss to understand.'

'I am glad to hear that your son Mr Clym is coming home at Christmas, ma'am,' said Sam, the turf-cutter. 'What a dog he used to be for bonfires!'

'Yes. I believe he is coming,' she said.

'He must be a fine fellow by this time,' said Fairway.

'He is a man now,' she replied quietly.

' 'Tis very lonesome for 'ee in the heth tonight, mis'ess,' said Christian, coming from the seclusion he had hitherto maintained. 'Mind you don't get lost. Egdon Heth is a bad place to get lost in, and the winds do huffle queerer tonight than ever I heard 'em afore. Them that know Egdon best have been pixy-led here at times.'

'Is that you, Christian?' said Mrs Yeobright. 'What made you hide away from me?'

' 'Twas that I didn't know you in this light, mis'ess; and being a man of the mournfullest make, I was scared a little, that's all. Oftentimes if you could see how terrible down I get in my mind, 'twould make 'ee quite nervous for fear I should die by my hand.'

'You don't take after your father,' said Mrs Yeobright, looking towards the fire, where Grandfer Cantle, with some want of originality, was dancing by himself among the sparks, as the others had done before.

'Now, Grandfer,' said Timothy Fairway, 'we are shamed of ye. A reverent old patriarch man as you be – seventy if a day – to go hornpiping like that by yourself!'

'A harrowing old man, Mis'ess Yeobright,' said Christian despondingly. 'I wouldn't live with him a week, so playward as he is, if I could get away.'

' 'Twould be more seemly in ye to stand still and welcome Mis'ess Yeobright, and you the venerablest here, Grandfer Cantle,' said the besom-woman.

'Faith, and so it would,' said the reveller, checking himself repentantly. 'I've such a bad memory, Mis'ess Yeobright, that I forget how I'm looked up to by the rest of 'em. My spirits must be wonderful good, you'll say? But not always. 'Tis a weight upon a man to be looked up to as commander, and I often feel it.'

'I am sorry to stop the talk,' said Mrs Yeobright. 'But I must be leaving you now. I was passing down the Anglebury Road, towards my niece's new home, who is returning tonight with her husband; and seeing the bonfire and hearing Olly's voice among the rest I came up here to learn what was going on. I should like her to walk with me, as her way is mine.'

'Ay, sure, ma'am, I'm just thinking of moving,' said Olly.

'Why, you'll be safe to meet the reddleman that I told ye of,' said Fairway. 'He's only gone back to get his van. We heard that your niece and her husband were coming straight home as soon as they were married, and we are going down there shortly, to give 'em a song o' welcome.'

'Thank you indeed,' said Mrs Yeobright.

'But we shall take a shorter cut through the furze than you can go with long clothes; so we won't trouble you to wait.'

'Very well – are you ready, Olly?'

'Yes, ma'am. And there's a light shining from your niece's window, see. It will help to keep us in the path.'

She indicated the faint light at the bottom of the valley which Fairway had pointed out; and the two women descended the tumulus.

* IV *

The Halt on the Turnpike Road

DOWN, downward they went, and yet further down – their descent at each step seeming to outmeasure their advance. Their skirts were scratched noisily by the furze, their shoulders brushed by the ferns, which, though dead and dry, stood erect as when alive, no sufficient winter weather having as yet arrived to beat them down. Their Tartarean situation might by some have been called an imprudent one for two unattended women. But these shaggy recesses were at all seasons a familiar surrounding to Olly and Mrs Yeobright; and the addition of darkness lends no frightfulness to the face of a friend.

'And so Tamsin has married him at last,' said Olly, when the incline had become so much less steep that their footsteps no longer required undivided attention.

Mrs Yeobright answered slowly, 'Yes: at last.'

'How you will miss her – living with 'ee as a daughter, as she always have.'

'I do miss her.'

Olly, though without the tact to perceive when remarks were untimely, was saved by her very simplicity from rendering them offensive. Questions that would have been resented in others she could ask with impunity. This accounted for Mrs Yeobright's acquiescence in the revival of an evidently sore subject.

'I was quite strook to hear you'd agreed to it, ma'am, that I was,' continued the besom-maker.

'You were not more struck by it than I should have been last year this time, Olly. There are a good many sides to that wedding. I could not tell you all of them, even if I tried.'

'I felt myself that he was hardly solid-going enough to mate with your family. Keeping an inn – what is it? But 'a's clever, that's true, and they say he was an engineering gentleman once, but has come down by being too outwardly given.'

'I saw that, upon the whole, it would be better she should marry where she wished.'

'Poor little thing, her feelings got the better of her, no doubt, 'Tis nature. Well, they may call him what they will – he've several acres of heth-ground broke up here, besides the public-house, and the heth-croppers, and his manners be quite like a gentleman's. And what's done cannot be undone.'

'It cannot,' said Mrs Yeobright. 'See, here's the waggon-track at last. Now we shall get along better.'

The wedding subject was no further dwelt upon; and soon a faint diverging path was reached, where they parted company, Olly first begging her companion to remind Mr Wildeve that he had not sent her sick husband the bottle of wine promised on the occasion of his marriage. The besom-maker turned to the left towards her own house, behind a spur of the hill, and Mrs Yeobright followed the straight track, which further on joined the highway by the Quiet Woman Inn, whither she supposed her niece to have returned with Wildeve from their wedding at Anglebury that day.

She first reached Wildeve's Patch, as it was called, a plot of land redeemed from the heath, and after long and laborious years brought into cultivation. The man who had discovered that it could be tilled died of the labour: the man who succeeded him in possession ruined himself in fertilizing it. Wildeve came like Amerigo Vespucci, and received the honours due to those who had gone before.

When Mrs Yeobright had drawn near to the inn, and was about to enter, she saw a horse and vehicle some two hundred yards beyond it, coming towards her, a man walking alongside with a lantern in his hand. It was soon evident that this was the reddleman who had inquired for her. Instead of entering the inn at once, she walked by it and towards the van.

The conveyance came close, and the man was about to pass her with little notice, when she turned to him and said, 'I think you have been inquiring for me? I am Mrs Yeobright of Blooms-End.'

The reddleman started, and held up his finger. He stopped the horses, and beckoned to her to withdraw with him a few yards aside, which she did, wondering.

'You don't know me, ma'am, I suppose?' he said.

'I do not,' said she. 'Why, yes, I do! You are young Venn – your father was a dairyman somewhere here?'

'Yes; and I knew your niece, Miss Tamsin, a little. I have something bad to tell you.'

'About her – no? She has just come home, I believe, with her husband. They arranged to return this afternoon – to the inn beyond here?'

'She's not there.'

'How do you know?'

'Because she's here. She's in my van,' he added slowly.

'What new trouble has come?' murmured Mrs Yeobright, putting her hand over her eyes.

'I can't explain much, ma'am. All I know is that, as I was going along the road this morning, about a mile out of Anglebury, I heard something trotting after me like a doe, and looking round there she was, white as death itself. "Oh, Diggory Venn!" she said, "I thought 'twas you: will you help me? I am in trouble."'

'How did she know your Christian name?' said Mrs Yeobright doubtingly.

'I had met her as a lad before I went away in this trade. She asked then if she might ride, and then down she fell in a faint. I picked her up and put her in, and there she has been ever since. She has cried a good deal, but she has hardly spoke; all she has told me being that she was to have been married this morning. I tried to get her to eat something, but she couldn't; and at last she fell asleep.'

'Let me see her at once,' said Mrs Yeobright, hastening towards the van.

The reddleman followed with the lantern, and, stepping up first, assisted Mrs Yeobright to mount beside him. On the door being opened she perceived at the end of the van an extemporized couch, around which was hung apparently all the drapery that the reddleman possessed, to keep the occupant of the little couch from contact with the red materials of his trade. A young girl lay thereon, covered with a cloak. She was asleep, and the light of the lantern fell upon her features.

A fair, sweet, and honest country face was revealed, reposing in a nest of wavy chestnut hair. It was between pretty and beautiful. Though her eyes were closed, one could easily imagine the light necessarily shining in them as the culmination of the luminous workmanship around. The groundwork of the face was hopefulness; but over it now lay like a foreign substance a film of anxiety and grief. The grief had been there so shortly as to have abstracted nothing of the bloom, and had as yet but given a dignity to what it might eventually undermine. The scarlet of her lips had not had time to abate, and just now it appeared still more intense by the absence of the neighbouring and more transient colour of her cheek. The lips frequently parted, with a murmur of words. She seemed to belong rightly to a madrigal – to require viewing through rhyme and harmony.

One thing at least was obvious: she was not made to be looked at thus. The reddleman had appeared conscious of as much, and, while Mrs Yeobright looked in upon her, he cast his eyes aside with a delicacy which well became him. The sleeper apparently thought so too, for the next moment she opened her own.

The lips then parted with something of anticipation, something more of doubt; and her several thoughts and fractions of thoughts, as signalled by the changes on her face, were exhibited by the light to the utmost nicety. An ingenuous, transparent life was disclosed; as if the flow of her existence could be seen passing within her. She understood the scene in a moment.

'Oh yes, it is I, aunt,' she cried. 'I know how frightened you are, and how you cannot believe it; but all the same, it is I who have come home like this!'

'Tamsin, Tamsin!' said Mrs Yeobright, stooping over the young woman and kissing her. 'O my dear girl!'

Thomasin was now on the verge of a sob; but by an unexpected self-command she uttered no sound. With a gentle panting breath she sat upright.

'I did not expect to see you in this state, any more than you me,' she went on quickly. 'Where am I, aunt?'

'Nearly home, my dear. In Egdon Bottom. What dreadful thing is it?'

'I'll tell you in a moment. So near, are we? Then I will get out and walk. I want to go home by the path.'

'But this kind man who has done so much will, I am sure, take you right on to my house?' said the aunt, turning to the reddleman, who had withdrawn from the front of the van on the awakening of the girl, and stood in the road.

'Why should you think it necessary to ask me? I will, of course,' said he.

'He is indeed kind,' murmured Thomasin. 'I was once acquainted with him, aunt, and when I saw him today I thought I should prefer his van to any conveyance of a stranger. But I'll walk now. Reddleman, stop the horses, please.'

The man regarded her with tender reluctance, but stopped them.

Aunt and niece then descended from the van, Mrs Yeobright saying to its owner, 'I quite recognize you now. What made you change from the nice business your father left you?'

'Well, I did,' he said, and looked at Thomasin, who blushed a little. 'Then you'll not be wanting me any more to-night, ma'am?'

Mrs Yeobright glanced around at the dark sky, at the hills, at the perishing bonfires, and at the lighted window of the inn they had neared. 'I think not,' she said, 'since Thomasin wishes to walk. We can soon run up the path and reach home: we know it well.'

And after a few further words they parted, the reddleman moving onwards with his van, and the two women remaining standing in the road. As soon as the vehicle and its driver had withdrawn so far as to be beyond all possible reach of her voice, Mrs Yeobright turned to her niece.

'Now, Thomasin,' she said sternly, 'what's the meaning of this disgraceful performance?'

* V *

Perplexity among Honest People

THOMASIN looked as if quite overcome by her aunt's change of manner. 'It means just what it seems to mean: I am – not married,' she replied faintly. 'Excuse me – for humiliating you, aunt, by this mishap: I am sorry for it. But I cannot help it.'

'Me? Think of yourself first.'

'It was nobody's fault. When we got there the parson wouldn't marry us because of some trifling irregularity in the licence.'

'What irregularity?'

'I don't know. Mr Wildeve can explain. I did not think when I went away this morning that I should come back like this.' It being dark, Thomasin allowed her emotion to escape her by the silent way of tears, which could roll down her cheek unseen.

'I could almost say that it serves you right – if I did not feel that you don't deserve it,' continued Mrs Yeobright, who, possessing two distinct moods in close contiguity, a gentle mood and an angry, flew from one to the other without the least warning. 'Remember, Thomasin, this business was none of my seeking; from the very first, when you began to feel foolish about that man, I warned you he would not make you happy. I felt it so strongly that I did what I would never have believed myself capable of doing – stood up in the church, and made myself the public talk for weeks. But having once consented, I don't submit to these fancies without good reason. Marry him you must after this.'

'Do you think I wish to do otherwise for one moment?' said Thomasin, with a heavy sigh. 'I know how wrong it was of me to love him, but don't pain me by talking like that, aunt! You would not have had me stay there with him, would you? – and your house is the only home I have to return to. He says we can be married in a day or two.'

'I wish he had never seen you.'

'Very well; then I will be the miserablest woman in the world, and not let him see me again. No, I won't have him!'

'It is too late to speak so. Come with me. I am going to the inn to see if he has returned. Of course I shall get to the bottom of this story at once. Mr Wildeve must not suppose he can play tricks upon me, or any belonging to me.'

'It was not that. The licence was wrong, and he couldn't get another the same day. He will tell you in a moment how it was, if he comes.'

'Why didn't he bring you back?'

'That was me!' again sobbed Thomasin. 'When I found we could not be married I didn't like to come back with him, and I was very ill. Then I saw Diggory Venn, and was glad to get him to take me home. I cannot explain it any better, and you must be angry with me if you will.'

'I shall see about that,' said Mrs Yeobright; and they turned towards the inn, known in the neighbourhood as the Quiet Woman, the sign of which represented the figure of a matron carrying her head under her arm, beneath which gruesome design was written the couplet so well known to frequenters of the inn:

> SINCE THE WOMAN'S QUIET
> LET NO MAN BREED A RIOT.

The front of the house was towards the heath and Rainbarrow, whose dark shape seemed to threaten it from the sky. Upon the door was a neglected brass plate, bearing the unexpected inscription, 'Mr Wildeve, Engineer' – useless yet cherished relic from the time when he had been started in that profession in an office at Budmouth by those who had hoped much from him, and had been disappointed. The garden was at the back, and behind this ran a still deep stream, forming the margin of the heath in that direction, meadow-land appearing beyond the stream.

But the thick obscurity permitted only sky-lines to be visible of any scene at present. The water at the back of the house could be heard, idly spinning whirlpools in its creep between the rows of dry feather-headed reeds which formed a stockade along each bank. Their presence was denoted by sounds as of a congregation praying humbly, produced by their rubbing against each other in the slow wind.

The window, whence the candlelight had shone up the vale to the eyes of the bonfire group, was uncurtained, but the sill lay too high for a pedestrian on the outside to look over it into the room. A vast shadow, in which could be dimly traced portions of a masculine contour, blotted half the ceiling.

'He seems to be at home,' said Mrs Yeobright.

'Must I come in, too, aunt?' asked Thomasin faintly. 'I suppose not; it would be wrong.'

'You must come, certainly – to confront him, so that he may make no false representations to me. We shall not be five minutes in the house, and then we'll walk home.'

Entering the open passage she tapped at the door of the private parlour, unfastened it, and looked in.

The back and shoulders of a man came between Mrs Yeobright's eyes and the fire. Wildeve, whose form it was, immediately turned, arose, and advanced to meet his visitors.

He was quite a young man, and of the two properties, form and motion, the latter first attracted the eye in him. The grace of his movement was singular: it was the pantomimic expression of a lady-killing career. Next came into notice the more material qualities, among which was a profuse crop of hair impending over the top of his face, lending to his forehead the high-cornered outline of an early Gothic shield; and a neck which was smooth and round as a cylinder. The lower half of his figure was of light build. Altogether he was one in whom no man would have seen anything to admire, and in whom no woman would have seen anything to dislike.

He discerned the young girl's form in the passage, and said, 'Thomasin, then, has reached home. How could you leave me in that way, darling?' And turning to Mrs Yeobright: 'It was useless to argue with her. She would go, and go alone.'

'But what's the meaning of it all?' demanded Mrs Yeobright haughtily.

'Take a seat,' said Wildeve, placing chairs for the two women. 'Well, it was a very stupid mistake, but such mistakes will happen. The licence was useless at Anglebury. It was made out for Budmouth, but as I didn't read it I wasn't aware of that.'

'But you had been staying at Anglebury?'

'No. I had been at Budmouth – till two days ago – and that was where I had intended to take her; but when I came to fetch her we decided upon Anglebury, forgetting that a new licence would be necessary. There was not time to get to Budmouth afterwards.'

'I think you are very much to blame,' said Mrs Yeobright.

'It was quite my fault we chose Anglebury,' Thomasin pleaded. 'I proposed it because I was not known there.'

'I know so well that I am to blame that you need not remind me of it,' replied Wildeve shortly.

'Such things don't happen for nothing,' said the aunt. 'It's a great slight to me and my family; and when it gets known there will be a very unpleasant time for us. How can she look her friends in the face tomorrow? It is a very great injury, and one I cannot easily forgive. It may even reflect on her character.'

'Nonsense,' said Wildeve.

Thomasin's large eyes had flown from the face of one to the face of the other during this discussion, and she now said anxiously, 'Will you allow me, aunt, to talk it over alone with Damon for five minutes? Will you, Damon?'

'Certainly, dear,' said Wildeve, 'if your aunt will excuse us.' He led her into an adjoining room, leaving Mrs Yeobright by the fire.

As soon as they were alone, and the door closed, Thomasin said, turning up her pale, tearful face to him, 'It is killing me, this, Damon! I did not mean to part from you in anger at Anglebury this morning; but I was frightened, and hardly knew what I said. I've not let aunt know how much I have suffered to-day; and it is so hard to command my face and voice, and to smile as if it were a slight thing to me; but I try to do so, that she may not be still more indignant with you. I know you would not help it, dear, whatever aunt may think.'

'She is very unpleasant.'

'Yes,' Thomasin murmured, 'and I suppose I seem so now . . . Damon, what do you mean to do about me?'

'Do about you?'

'Yes. Those who don't like you whisper things which at moments make me doubt you. We mean to marry, I suppose, don't we?'

'Of course we do. We have only to go to Budmouth on Monday, and we may marry at once.'

'Then do let us go! – O Damon, what you make me say!' She hid her face in her handkerchief. 'Here am I asking you to marry me; when by rights you ought to be on your knees imploring me, your cruel mistress, not to refuse you, and saying it would break your heart if I did. I used to think it would be pretty and sweet like that; but how different!'

'Yes, real life is never at all like that.'

'But I don't care personally if it never takes place,' she added with a little dignity; 'no, I can live without you. It is aunt I think of. She is so proud, and thinks so much of her family respectability, that she will be cut down with mortification if this story should get abroad before – it is done. My cousin Clym, too, will be much wounded.'

'Then he will be very unreasonable. In fact, you are all rather unreasonable.'

Thomasin coloured a little, and not with love. But whatever the momentary feeling which caused that flush in her, it went as it came, and she humbly said, 'I never mean to be, if I can help it. I merely feel that you have my aunt to some extent in your power at last.'

'As a matter of justice, it is almost due to me,' said Wildeve. 'Think what I have gone through to win her consent; the insult that it is to any man to have the banns forbidden: the double insult to a man unlucky enough to be cursed with sensitiveness, and blue demons, and Heaven knows what, as I am. I can never forget those banns. A harsher man would rejoice now in the power I have of turning upon your aunt by going no further in the business.'

She looked wistfully at him with her sorrowful eyes as he said those words, and her aspect showed that more than one person in the room could deplore the possession of sensitiveness. Seeing that she was really suffering he seemed disturbed and added, 'This is merely a reflection, you know. I have not the least intention to refuse to complete the marriage, Tamsie mine – I could not bear it.'

'You could not, I know!' said the fair girl, brightening. 'You, who cannot bear the sight of pain in even an insect, or any disagreeable sound, or unpleasant smell even, will not long cause pain to me and mine.'

'I will not, if I can help it.'

'Your hand upon it, Damon.'

He carelessly gave her his hand.

'Ah, by my crown, what's that?' he said suddenly.

There fell upon their ears the sound of numerous voices singing in front of the house. Among these, two made themselves prominent by their peculiarity: one was a very strong bass, the other a wheezy thin piping. Thomasin recognized them as belonging to Timothy Fairway and Grandfer Cantle respectively.

'What does it mean – it is not skimmity-riding, I hope?' she said, with a frightened gaze at Wildeve.

'Of course not; no, it is that the heath-folk have come to sing to us a welcome. This is intolerable!' He began pacing about, the men outside singing cheerily –

> 'He told' her that she' was the joy' of his life',
> And if' she'd con-sent' he would make her his wife';
> She could' not refuse' him; to church' so they went',
> Young Will was forgot', and young Sue' was content';
> And then' was she kiss'd' and set down' on his knee',
> No man' in the world' was so lov'-ing as he'!

Mrs Yeobright burst in from the outer room. 'Thomasin, Thomasin!'

she said, looking indignantly at Wildeve; 'here's a pretty exposure! Let us escape at once. Come!'

It was, however, too late to get away by the passage. A rugged knocking had begun upon the door of the front room. Wildeve, who had gone to the window, came back.

'Stop!' he said imperiously, putting his hand upon Mrs Yeobright's arm. 'We are regularly besieged. There are fifty of them out there if there's one. You stay in this room with Thomasin; I'll go out and face them. You must stay now, for my sake, till they are gone, so that it may seem as if all was right. Come, Tamsie dear, don't go making a scene – we must marry after this; that you can see as well as I. Sit still, that's all – and don't speak much. I'll manage them. Blundering fools!'

He pressed the agitated girl into a seat, returned to the outer room and opened the door. Immediately outside, in the passage, appeared Grandfer Cantle singing in concert with those still standing in front of the house. He came into the room and nodded abstractedly to Wildeve, his lips still parted, and his features excruciatingly strained in the emission of the chorus. This being ended, he said heartily, 'Here's welcome to the new-made couple, and God bless 'em!'

'Thank you,' said Wildeve, with dry resentment, his face as gloomy as a thunderstorm.

At the Grandfer's heels now came the rest of the group, which included Fairway, Christian, Sam the turf-cutter, Humphrey, and a dozen others. All smiled upon Wildeve, and upon his tables and chairs likewise, from a general sense of friendliness towards the articles as well as towards their owner.

'We be not here afore Mrs Yeobright after all,' said Fairway, recognizing the matron's bonnet through the glass partition which divided the public apartment they had entered from the room where the women sat. 'We struck down across, d'ye see, Mr Wildeve, and she went round by the path.'

'And I see the young bride's little head!' said Grandfer, peeping in the same direction, and discerning Thomasin, who was waiting beside her aunt in a miserable and awkward way. 'Not quite settled in yet – well, well, there's plenty of time.'

Wildeve made no reply; and probably feeling that the sooner he treated them the sooner they would go, he produced a stone jar, which threw a warm halo over matters at once.

'That's a drop of the right sort, I can see,' said Grandfer Cantle, with the air of a man too well-mannered to show any hurry to taste it.

'Yes,' said Wildeve, ' 'tis some old mead. I hope you will like it.'

'O ay!' replied the guests, in the hearty tones natural when the words demanded by politeness coincide with those of deepest feeling. 'There isn't a prettier drink under the sun.'

'I'll take my oath there isn't,' added Grandfer Cantle. 'All that can be said against mead is that 'tis rather heady, and apt to lie about a man a good while. But tomorrow's Sunday, thank God.'

'I feel'd for all the world like some bold soldier after I had had some once,' said Christian.

'You shall feel so again,' said Wildeve, with condescension. 'Cups or glasses, gentlemen?'

'Well, if you don't mind, we'll have the beaker, and pass 'em round: 'tis better than heling it out in dribbles.'

'Jown the slippery glasses,' said Grandfer Cantle. 'What's the good of a thing that you can't put down in the ashes to warm, hey, neighbours; that's what I ask?'

'Right, Grandfer,' said Sam; and the mead then circulated.

'Well,' said Timothy Fairway, feeling demands upon his praise in some form or other, ' 'tis a worthy thing to be married, Mr Wildeve; and the woman you've got is a dimant, so says I. Yes,' he continued, to Grandfer Cantle, raising his voice so as to be heard through the partition; 'her father (inclining his head towards the inner room) was as good a feller as ever lived. He always had his great indignation ready against anything underhand.'

'Is that very dangerous?' said Christian.

'And there were few in these parts that were upsides with him,' said Sam. 'Whenever a club walked he'd play the clarinet in the band that marched before 'em as if he'd never touched anything but a clarinet all his life. And then, when they got to church-door he'd throw down the clarinet, mount the gallery, snatch up the bass-viol, and rozum away as if he'd never played anything but a bass-viol. Folk would say – folk that knowed what a true stave was – "Surely, surely that's never the same man that I saw handling the clarinet so masterly by now!" '

'I can mind it,' said the furze-cutter. ' 'Twas a wonderful thing that one body could hold it all and never mix the fingering.'

'There was Kingsbere church likewise,' Fairway recommenced, as one opening a new vein of the same mine of interest.

Wildeve breathed the breath of one intolerably bored, and glanced through the partition at the prisoners.

'He used to walk over there of a Sunday afternoon to visit his old acquaintance Andrew Brown, the first clarinet there; a good man enough, but rather screechy in his music, if you can mind?'

' 'A was.'

'And neighbour Yeobright would take Andrey's place for some part of the service, to let Andrey have a bit of a nap, as any friend would naturally do.'

'As any friend would,' said Grandfer Cantle, the other listeners expressing the same accord by the shorter way of nodding their heads.

'No sooner was Andrey asleep and the first whiff of neighbour Yeobright's wind had got inside Andrey's clarinet than every one in church felt in a moment there was a great soul among 'em. All heads would turn, and they'd say, "Ah, I thought 'twas he!" One Sunday I can well mind – a bass-viol day that time, and Yeobright had brought his own. 'Twas the Hundred-and-thirty-third to "Lydia"; and when they'd come to "Ran down his beard and o'er his robes its costly moisture shed", neighbour Yeobright, who had just warmed to his work, drove his bow into them strings that glorious grand that he e'en a'most sawed the bass-viol into two pieces. Every winder in church rattled as if 'twere a thunderstorm. Old Pa'son Williams lifted his hands in his great holy surplice as natural as if he'd been in common clothes, and seemed to say to hisself, "O for such a man in our parish!" But not a soul in Kingsbere could hold a candle to Yeobright.'

'Was it quite safe when the winder shook?' Christian inquired.

He received no answer; all for the moment sitting rapt in admiration of the performance described. As with Farinelli's singing before the prin-cesses, Sheridan's renowned Begum Speech, and other such examples, the fortunate condition of its being for ever lost to the world invested the deceased Mr Yeobright's *tour de force* on that memorable afternoon with a cumulative glory which comparative criticism, had that been possible, might considerably have shorn down.

'He was the last you'd have expected to drop off in the prime of life,' said Humphrey.

'Ah, well: he was looking for the earth some months afore he went. At that time women used to run for smocks and gown-pieces at Greenhill Fair, and my wife that is now, being a long-legged slittering maid, hardly husband-high, went with the rest of the maidens, for 'a was a good runner afore she got so heavy. When she came home I said – we were then just beginning to walk together – "What have ye got, my honey?" "I've won – well, I've won – a gown-piece," says she, her colours coming up in a moment. 'Tis a smock for a crown, I thought; and so it turned out. Ay, when I think what she'll say to me now without a mossel of red in her face, it do seem strange that 'a wouldn't say such a little thing then . . . However, then she went on, and that's what made me bring up the story, "Well, whatever clothes I've won, white or figured, for eyes to see or for eyes not to see" ('a could do a pretty stroke of modesty in those days), "I'd sooner have lost it than have seen what I have. Poor Mr Yeobright was took bad directly he reached the fair ground, and was forced to go home again." That was the last time he ever went out of the parish.'

' 'A faltered on from one day to another, and then we heard he was gone.'

'D'ye think he had great pain when 'a died?' said Christian.

'Oh no: quite different. Nor any pain of mind. He was lucky enough to be God A'mighty's own man.'

'And other folk – d'ye think 'twill be much pain to 'em, Mister Fairway?'

'That depends on whether they be afeard.'

'I bain't afeard at all, I thank God!' said Christian strenuously. 'I'm glad I bain't, for then 'twon't pain me . . . I don't think I be afeard – or if I be I can't help it, and I don't deserve to suffer. I wish I was not afeard at all!'

There was a solemn silence, and looking from the window, which was unshuttered and unblinded, Timothy said, 'Well, what a fess little bonfire that one is, out by Cap'n Vye's! 'Tis burning just the same now as ever, upon my life.'

All glances went through the window, and nobody noticed that Wildeve disguised a brief, tell-tale look. Far away up the sombre valley of heath, and to the right of Rainbarrow, could indeed be seen the light, small, but steady and persistent as before.

'It was lighted before ours was,' Fairway continued; 'and yet every one in the country round is out afore 'n.'

'Perhaps there's meaning in it!' murmured Christian.

'How meaning?' said Wildeve sharply.

Christian was too scattered to reply, and Timothy helped him.

'He means, sir, that the lonesome dark-eyed creature up there that some say is a witch – ever I should call a fine young woman such a name – is always up to some odd conceit or other; and so perhaps 'tis she.'

'I'd be very glad to ask her in wedlock, if she'd hae me, and take the risk of her wild dark eyes ill-wishing me,' said Grandfer Cantle staunchly.

'Don't ye say it, father!' implored Christian.

'Well, be dazed if he who do marry the maid won't hae an uncommon picture for his best parlour,' said Fairway in a liquid tone, placing down the cup of mead at the end of a good pull.

'And a partner as deep as the North Star,' said Sam, taking up the cup and finishing the little that remained.

'Well, really, now I think we must be moving,' said Humphrey, observing the emptiness of the vessel.

'But we'll gie 'em another song?' said Grandfer Cantle. 'I'm as full of notes as a bird!'

'Thank you, Grandfer,' said Wildeve. 'But we will not trouble you now. Some other day must do for that – when I have a party.'

'Be jown'd if I don't learn ten new songs for't, or I won't learn a line!' said Grandfer Cantle. 'And you may be sure I won't disappoint ye by biding away, Mr Wildeve.'

'I quite believe you,' said that gentleman.

All then took their leave, wishing their entertainer long life and happiness as a married man, with recapitulations which occupied some time. Wildeve attended them to the door, beyond which the deep-dyed upward stretch of heath stood awaiting them, an amplitude of darkness reigning from their feet almost to the zenith, where a definite form first became visible in the lowering forehead of Rainbarrow. Diving into the dense obscurity in a line headed by Sam the turf-cutter, they pursued their trackless way home.

When the scratching of the furze against their leggings had fainted upon the ear, Wildeve returned to the room where he had left Thomasin and her aunt. The women were gone.

They could only have left the house in one way, by the back window; and this was open.

Wildeve laughed to himself, remained a moment thinking, and idly returned to the front room. Here his glance fell upon a bottle of wine which stood on the mantelpiece. 'Ah – old Dowden!' he murmured; and going to the kitchen door shouted, 'Is anybody here who can take something to old Dowden?'

There was no reply. The room was empty, the lad who acted as his factotum having gone to bed. Wildeve came back, put on his hat, took the bottle, and left the house, turning the key in the door, for there was no guest at the inn tonight. As soon as he was on the road the little bonfire on Mistover Knap again met his eye.

'Still waiting, are you, my lady?' he murmured.

However, he did not proceed that way just then; but leaving the hill to the left of him, he stumbled over a rutted road that brought him to a cottage which, like all other habitations on the heath at this hour, was only saved from being invisible by a faint shine from its bedroom window. This house was the home of Olly Dowden, the besom-maker, and he entered.

The lower room was in darkness; but by feeling his way he found a table, whereon he placed the bottle, and a minute later emerged again upon the heath. He stood up and looked north-east at the undying little fire – high up above him, though not so high as Rainbarrow.

We have been told what happens when a woman deliberates; and the epigram is not always terminable with woman, provided that one be in the case, and that a fair one. Wildeve stood, and stood longer, and breathed perplexedly, and then said to himself with resignation, 'Yes – by Heaven, I must go to her, I suppose!'

Instead of turning in the direction of home he pressed on rapidly by a path under Rainbarrow towards what was evidently a signal light.

* VI *

The Figure against the Sky

WHEN the whole Egdon concourse had left the site of the bonfire to its accustomed loneliness, a closely wrapped female figure approached the barrow from that quarter of the heath in which the little fire lay. Had the reddleman been watching he might have recognized her as the woman who had first stood there so singularly, and vanished at the approach of strangers. She ascended to her old position at the top, where the red coals of the perishing fire greeted her like living eyes in the corpse of day. There she stood still, around her stretching the vast night atmosphere, whose incomplete darkness in comparison with the total darkness of the heath below it might have represented a venial beside a mortal sin.

That she was tall and straight in build, that she was ladylike in her movements, was all that could be learnt of her just now, her form being wrapped in a shawl folded in the old cornerwise fashion, and her head in a large kerchief, a protection not superfluous at this hour and place. Her back was towards the wind, which blew from the north-west; but whether she had avoided that aspect because of the chilly gusts which played about her exceptional position, or because her interest lay in the south-east, did not at first appear.

Her reason for standing so dead still as the pivot of this circle of heath-country was just as obscure. Her extraordinary fixity, her conspicuous loneliness, her heedlessness of night, betokened among other things an utter absence of fear. A tract of country unaltered from that sinister condition which made Caesar anxious every year to get clear of its glooms before the autumnal equinox, a kind of landscape and weather which leads travellers from the South to describe our island as Homer's Cimmerian land, was not, on the face of it, friendly to women.

It might reasonably have been supposed that she was listening to the wind, which rose somewhat as the night advanced, and laid hold of the attention. The wind, indeed, seemed made for the scene, as the scene seemed made for the hour. Part of its tone was quite special; what was heard there could be heard nowhere else. Gusts in innumerable series followed each other from the north-west, and when each one of them raced past the sound of its progress resolved into three. Treble, tenor, and bass notes were to be found therein. The general ricochet of the whole over pits and prominences had the gravest pitch of the chime. Next there could be heard the baritone buzz of a holly tree. Below these in force, above them in pitch, a dwindled voice strove hard at a husky tune, which was the peculiar local sound alluded to. Thinner and less immediately traceable than the other two, it was far more impressive than either. In it lay what may be called the linguistic peculiarity of the heath; and being audible nowhere on earth off a heath, it afforded a shadow of reason for the woman's tenseness, which continued as unbroken as ever.

Throughout the blowing of these plaintive November winds that note bore a great resemblance to the ruins of human song which remain to the throat of fourscore and ten. It was a worn whisper, dry and papery, and it brushed so distinctly across the ear that, by the accustomed, the material minutiae in which it originated could be realized as by touch. It was the united products of infinitesimal vegetable causes, and these were neither stems, leaves, fruit, blades, prickles, lichen, nor moss.

They were the mummied heath-bells of the past summer, originally tender and purple, now washed colourless by Michaelmas rains, and dried to dead skins by October suns. So low was an individual sound from these that a combination of hundreds only just emerged from silence, and the myriads of the whole declivity reached the woman's ear but as a shrivelled and intermittent recitative. Yet scarcely a single accent among the many afloat tonight could have such power to impress a listener with thoughts of its origin. One inwardly saw the infinity of those combined multitudes; and perceived that each of the tiny trumpets was seized on, entered, scoured and emerged from by the wind as thoroughly as if it were as vast as a crater.

'The spirit moved them.' A meaning of the phrase forced itself upon the attention; and an emotional listener's fetichistic mood might have ended in one of more advanced quality. It was not, after all, that the left-hand expanse of old blooms spoke, or the right-hand, or those of the slope in front; but it was the single person of something else speaking through each at once.

Suddenly, on the barrow, there mingled with all this wild rhetoric of night a sound which modulated so naturally into the rest that its beginning and ending were hardly to be distinguished. The bluffs, and the bushes, and the heather-bells had broken silence; at last, so did the woman; and her articulation was but as another phrase of the same discourse as theirs. Thrown out on the winds it became twined in with them, and with them it flew away.

What she uttered was a lengthened sighing, apparently at something in her mind which had led to her presence here. There was a spasmodic abandonment about it as if, in allowing herself to utter the sound, the woman's brain had authorized what it could not regulate. One point was evident in this; that she had been existing in a suppressed state, and not in one of languor, or stagnation.

Far away down the valley the faint shine from the window of the inn still lasted on; and a few additional moments proved that the window, or what was within it, had more to do with the woman's sigh than had either her own actions or the scene immediately around. She lifted her left hand, which held a closed telescope. This she rapidly extended, as if she were well accustomed to the operation, and raising it to her eye directed it towards the light beaming from the inn.

The handkerchief which had hooded her head was now a little thrown back, her face being somewhat elevated. A profile was visible against the dull monochrome of cloud around her; and it was as though side shadows from the features of Sappho and Mrs Siddons had converged upwards from the tomb to form an image like neither but suggesting both. This, however, was mere superficiality. In respect of character a face may make certain admissions by its outline; but it fully confesses only in its changes. So much is this the case that what is called the play of the features often helps more in understanding a man or woman than the earnest labours of all the other members together. Thus the night revealed little of her whose form it was embracing, for the mobile parts of her countenance could not be seen.

At last she gave up her spying attitude, closed the telescope, and turned to the decaying embers. From these no appreciable beams now radiated, except when a more than usually smart gust brushed over their faces and raised a fitful glow which came and went like the blush of a girl. She stooped over the silent circle, and selecting from the brands a piece of stick which bore the largest live coal at its end, brought it to where she had been standing before.

She held the brand to the ground, blowing the red coal with her mouth at the same time; till it faintly illuminated the sod, and revealed a small object, which turned out to be an hour-glass, though she wore a watch. She blew long enough to show that the sand had all slipped through.

'Ah!' she said, as if surprised.

The light raised by her breath had been very fitful, and a momentary irradiation of flesh was all that it had disclosed of her face. That consisted of two matchless lips and a cheek only, her head being still enveloped. She threw away the stick, took the glass in her hand, the telescope under her arm, and moved on.

Along the ridge ran a faint foot-track, which the lady followed. Those who knew it well called it a path; and, while a mere visitor would have passed it unnoticed even by day, the regular haunters of the heath were at no loss for it at midnight. The whole secret of following these incipient paths, when there was not light enough in the atmosphere to show a turnpike-road, lay in the development of the sense of touch in the feet, which comes with years of night-rambling in little-trodden spots. To a walker practised in such places a difference between impact on maiden herbage, and on the crippled stalks of a slight footway, is perceptible through the thickest boot or shoe.

The solitary figure who walked this beat took no notice of the windy tune still played on the dead heath-bells. She did not turn her head to look at a group of dark creatures further on, who fled from her presence as she skirted a ravine where they fed. They were about a score of the small wild ponies known as heath-croppers. They roamed at large on the undulations of Egdon, but in numbers too few to detract much from the solitude.

The pedestrian noticed nothing just now, and a clue to her abstraction was afforded by a trivial incident. A bramble caught hold of her skirt, and checked her progress. Instead of putting it off and hastening along, she yielded herself up to the pull, and stood passively still. When she began to extricate herself it was by turning round and round, and so unwinding the prickly switch. She was in a desponding reverie.

Her course was in the direction of the small undying fire which had drawn the attention of the men on Rainbarrow and of Wildeve in the valley below. A faint illumination from its rays began to glow upon her face, and the fire soon revealed itself to be lit, not on the level ground, but on a salient corner or redan of earth, at the junction of two converging bank fences. Outside was a ditch, dry except immediately under the fire, where there was a large pool, bearded all round by heather and rushes. In the smooth water of the pool the fire appeared upside down.

The banks meeting behind were bare of a hedge, save such as was formed by disconnected tufts of furze, standing upon stems along the top, liked impaled heads above a city wall. A white mast, fitted up with spars and other nautical tackle, could be seen rising against the dark clouds whenever the flames played brightly enough to reach it. Altogether the scene had much the appearance of a fortification upon which had been kindled a beacon fire.

Nobody was visible; but ever and anon a whitish something moved above the bank from behind, and vanished again. This was a small human hand, in the act of lifting pieces of fuel into the fire; but for all that could be seen the hand, like that which troubled Belshazzar, was there alone. Occasionally an ember rolled off the bank, and dropped with a hiss into the pool.

At one side of the pool rough steps built of clods enabled any one who wished to do so to mount the bank; which the woman did. Within was a paddock in an uncultivated state, though bearing evidence of having once been tilled; but the heath and fern had insidiously crept in, and were reasserting their old supremacy. Further ahead were dimly visible an irregular dwelling-house, garden, and outbuildings, backed by a clump of firs.

The young lady – for youth had revealed its presence in her buoyant bound up the bank – walked along the top instead of descending inside, and came to the corner where the fire was burning. One reason for the permanence of the blaze was now manifest: the fuel consisted of hard pieces of wood, cleft and sawn – the knotty boles of old thorn trees which grew in twos and threes about the hillsides. A yet unconsumed pile of these lay in the inner angle of the bank; and from this corner the upturned face of a little boy greeted her eyes. He was dilatorily throwing up a piece of wood into the fire every now and then, a business which seemed to have engaged him a considerable part of the evening, for his face was somewhat weary.

'I am glad you have come, Miss Eustacia,' he said, with a sigh of relief. 'I don't like biding by myself.'

'Nonsense. I have only been a little way for a walk. I have been gone only twenty minutes.'

'It seemed long,' murmured the sad boy. 'And you have been so many times.'

'Why, I thought you would be pleased to have a bonfire. Are you not much obliged to me for making you one?'

'Yes; but there's nobody here to play wi' me.'

'I suppose nobody has come while I've been away?'

'Nobody except your grandfather: he looked out of doors once for 'ee. I told him you were walking round upon the hill to look at the other bonfires.'

'A good boy.'

'I think I hear him coming again, miss.'

An old man came into the remoter light of the fire from the direction of the homestead. He was the same who had overtaken the reddleman on the road that afternoon. He looked wistfully to the top of the bank at the woman who stood there, and his teeth, which were quite unimpaired, showed like parian from his parted lips.

'When are you coming indoors, Eustacia?' he asked. ' 'Tis almost bedtime. I've been home these two hours, and am tired out. Surely 'tis somewhat childish of you to stay out playing at bonfires so long, and wasting such fuel. My precious thorn roots, the rarest of all firing, that I laid by on purpose for Christmas – you have burnt 'em nearly all!'

'I promised Johnny a bonfire, and it pleases him not to let it go out just yet,' said Eustacia, in a way which told at once that she was absolute queen here. 'Grandfather, you go in to bed. I shall follow you soon. You like the fire, don't you, Johnny?'

The boy looked up doubtfully at her and murmured, 'I don't think I want it any longer.'

Her grandfather had turned back again, and did not hear the boy's reply. As soon as the white-haired man had vanished she said in a tone of pique to the child, 'Ungrateful little boy, how can you contradict me? Never shall you have a bonfire again unless you keep it up now. Come, tell me you like to do things for me, and don't deny it.'

The repressed child said, 'Yes, I do, miss,' and continued to stir the fire perfunctorily.

'Stay a little longer and I will give you a crooked sixpence,' said Eustacia, more gently. 'Put in one piece of wood every two or three minutes, but not too much at once. I am going to walk along the ridge a little longer, but I shall keep on coming to you. And if you hear a frog jump into the pond with a flounce like a stone thrown in, be sure you run and tell me, because it is a sign of rain.'

'Yes, Eustacia.'

'Miss Vye, sir.'

'Miss Vy – stacia.'

'That will do. Now put in one stick more.'

The little slave went on feeding the fire as before. He seemed a mere automaton, galvanized into moving and speaking by the wayward Eustacia's will. He might have been the brass statue which Albertus Magnus is said to have animated just so far as to make it chatter, and move, and be his servant.

Before going on her walk again the young girl stood still on the bank for a few instants and listened. It was to the full as lonely a place as Rainbarrow, though at rather a lower level; and it was more sheltered from wind and weather on account of the few firs to the north. The bank which enclosed the homestead, and protected it from the lawless state of the world without, was formed of thick square clods, dug from the ditch on the outside, and built up with a slight batter or incline, which forms no slight defence where hedges will not grow because of the wind and the wilderness, and where wall materials are unattainable. Otherwise the situation was quite open, commanding the whole length of the valley which reached to the river behind Wildeve's house. High above this to the right, and much nearer thitherward than the Quiet Woman Inn, the blurred contour of Rainbarrow obstructed the sky.

After her attentive survey of the wild slopes and hollow ravines a gesture of impatience escaped Eustacia. She vented petulant words every now and then; but there were sighs between her words, and sudden listenings between her sighs. Descending from her perch she again sauntered off towards Rainbarrow, though this time she did not go the whole way.

Twice she reappeared at intervals of a few minutes and each time she said –

'Not any flounce into the pond yet, little man?'

'No, Miss Eustacia,' the child replied.

'Well,' she said at last, 'I shall be going in, and then I will give you the crooked sixpence, and let you go home.'

'Thank'ee, Miss Eustacia,' said the tired stoker, breathing more easily. And Eustacia again strolled away from the fire, but this time not towards Rainbarrow. She skirted the bank and went round to the wicket before the house, where she stood motionless, looking at the scene.

Fifty yards off rose the corner of the two converging banks, with the fire upon it: within the bank, lifting up to the fire one stick at a time, just as before, the figure of the little child. She idly watched him as he occasionally climbed up in the nook of the bank and stood beside the brands. The wind blew the smoke, and the child's hair, and the corner of his pinafore, all in the same direction; the breeze died, and the pinafore and hair lay still, and the smoke went up straight.

While Eustacia looked on from this distance the boy's form visibly started: he slid down the bank and ran across towards the white gate.

'Well?' said Eustacia.

'A hop-frog have jumped into the pond. Yes, I heard 'en!'

'Then it is going to rain, and you had better go home. You will not be afraid?' She spoke hurriedly, as if her heart had leapt into her throat at the boy's words.

'No, because I shall hae the crooked sixpence.'

'Yes, here it is. Now run as fast as you can – not that way – through the garden here. No other boy in the heath has had such a bonfire as yours.'

The boy, who clearly had had too much of a good thing, marched away into the shadows with alacrity. When he was gone Eustacia, leaving her telescope and hour-glass by the gate, brushed forward from the wicket towards the angle of the bank, under the fire.

Here, screened by the outwork, she waited. In a few moments a splash was audible from the pond outside. Had the child been there he would have said that a second frog had jumped in; but by most people the sound would have been likened to the fall of a stone into the water. Eustacia stepped upon the bank.

'Yes?' she said, and held her breath.

Thereupon the contour of a man became dimly visible against the low-reaching sky over the valley, beyond the outer margin of the pool. He came round it and leapt upon the bank beside her. A low laugh escaped her – the third utterance which the girl had indulged in tonight. The first, when she stood upon Rainbarrow, had expressed anxiety; the second, on the ridge, had expressed impatience; the present was one of triumphant pleasure. She let her joyous eyes rest upon him without speaking, as upon some wondrous thing she had created out of chaos.

'I have come,' said the man, who was Wildeve. 'You give me no peace. Why do you not leave me alone? I have seen your bonfire all the evening.' The words were not without emotion, and retained their level tone as if by a careful equipoise between imminent extremes.

At this unexpectedly repressing manner in her lover the girl seemed to repress herself also. 'Of course you have seen my fire,' she answered with languid calmness, artificially maintained. 'Why shouldn't I have a bonfire on the Fifth of November, like other denizens of the heath?'

'I knew it was meant for me.'

'How did you know it? I have had no word with you since you – you chose her, and walked about with her, and deserted me entirely, as if I had never been yours life and soul so irretrievably!'

'Eustacia! could I forget that last autumn at this same day of the month and at this same place you lighted exactly such a fire as a signal for me to come and see you? Why should there have been a bonfire again by Captain Vye's house if not for the same purpose?'

'Yes, yes – I own it,' she cried under her breath, with a drowsy fervour of manner and tone which was quite peculiar to her. 'Don't begin speaking to me as you did, Damon; you will drive me to say words I would not wish to say to you. I had given you up, and resolved not to think of you any more; and then I heard the news, and I came out and got the fire ready because I thought that you had been faithful to me.'

'What have you heard to make you think that?' said Wildeve, astonished.

'That you did not marry her!' she murmured exultingly. 'And I knew it was because you loved me best, and couldn't do it . . . Damon, you have been cruel to me to go away, and I have said I would never forgive you. I do not think I can forgive you entirely, even now – it is too much for a woman of any spirit to quite overlook.'

'If I had known you wished to call me up here only to reproach me, I wouldn't have come.'

'But I don't mind it, and I do forgive you now that you have not married her, and have come back to me!'

'Who told you that I had not married her?'

'My grandfather. He took a long walk today, and as he was coming home he overtook some person who told him of a broken-off wedding; he thought it might be yours; and I knew it was.'

'Does anybody else know?'

'I suppose not. Now Damon, do you see why I lit my signal fire? You did not think I would have lit it if I had imagined you to have become the husband of this woman. It is insulting my pride to suppose that.'

Wildeve was silent: it was evident that he had supposed as much.

'Did you indeed think I believed you were married?' she again demanded earnestly. 'Then you wronged me; and upon my life and heart I can hardly bear to recognize that you have such ill thoughts of me! Damon, you are not worthy of me: I see it, and yet I love you. Never mind: let it go – I must bear your mean opinion as best I may . . . It is true, is it not,' she added with ill-concealed anxiety, on his making no demonstration, 'that you could not bring yourself to give me up, and are still going to love me best of all?'

'Yes; or why should I have come?' he said touchily. 'Not that fidelity will be any great merit in me after your kind speech about my unworthiness, which should have been said by myself if by anybody, and comes with an ill grace from you. However, the curse of inflammability is upon me, and I must live under it, and take any snub from a woman. It has brought me down from engineering to innkeeping: what lower stage it has in store for me I have yet to learn.' He continued to look upon her gloomily.

She seized the moment, and throwing back the shawl so that the firelight shone full upon her face and throat, said with a smile, 'Have you seen anything better than that in your travels?'

Eustacia was not one to commit herself to such a position without good ground. He said quietly, 'No.'

'Not even on the shoulders of Thomasin?'

'Thomasin is a pleasing and innocent woman.'

'That's nothing to do with it,' she cried with quick passionateness. 'We will leave her out; there are only you and me now to think of.' After a long look at him she resumed with the old quiescent warmth: 'Must I go on weakly confessing to you things a woman ought to conceal; and own that no words can express how gloomy I have been because of that dreadful belief I held till two hours ago – that you had quite deserted me?'

'I am sorry I caused you that pain.'

'But perhaps it is not wholly because of you that I get gloomy,' she archly added. 'It is in my nature to feel like that. It was born in my blood, I suppose.'

'Hypochondriasis.'

'Or else it was coming into this wild heath. I was happy enough at Budmouth. O the times, O the days at Budmouth! But Egdon will be brighter again now.'

'I hope it will,' said Wildeve moodily. 'Do you know the consequence of this recall to me, my old darling? I shall come to see you again as before, at Rainbarrow.'

'Of course you will.'

'And yet I declare that until I got here tonight I intended, after this one good-bye, never to meet you again.'

'I don't thank you for that,' she said, turning away, while indignation spread through her like subterranean heat. 'You may come again to Rainbarrow if you like, but you won't see me; and you may call, but I shall not listen; and you may tempt me, but I won't give myself to you any more.'

'You have said as much before, sweet; but such natures as yours don't so easily adhere to their words. Neither, for the matter of that, do such natures as mine.'

'This is the pleasure I have won by my trouble,' she whispered bitterly. 'Why did I try to recall you? Damon, a strange warring takes place in my mind occasionally. I think when I become calm after your woundings, "Do I embrace a cloud of common fog after all?" You are a chameleon, and now you are at your worst colour. Go home, or I shall hate you!'

He looked absently towards Rainbarrow while one might have counted twenty, and said, as if he did not much mind all this, 'Yes, I will go home. Do you mean to see me again?'

'If you own to me that the wedding is broken off because you love me best.'

'I don't think it would be good policy,' said Wildeve, smiling. 'You would get to know the extent of your power too clearly.'

'But tell me!'

'You know.'

'Where is she now?'

'I don't know. I prefer not to speak of her to you. I have not yet married her: I have come in obedience to your call. That is enough.'

'I merely lit the fire because I was dull, and thought I would get a little excitement by calling you up and triumphing over you as the Witch of Endor called up Samuel. I determined you should come; and you have come! I have shown my power. A mile and half hither, and a mile and half back again to your home – three miles in the dark for me. Have I not shown my power?'

He shook his head at her. 'I know you too well, my Eustacia; I know you too well. There isn't a note in you which I don't know; and that hot little bosom couldn't play such a cold-blooded trick to save its life. I saw a woman on Rainbarrow at dusk looking down towards my house. I think I drew out you before you drew out me.'

The revived embers of an old passion glowed clearly in Wildeve now; and he leant forward as if about to put his face towards her cheek.

'O no,' she said, intractably moving to the other side of the decayed fire. 'What did you mean by that?'

'Perhaps I may kiss your hand?'

'No, you may not.'

'Then I may shake your hand?'

'No.'

'Then I wish you good-night without caring for either. Good-bye, good-bye.'

She returned no answer, and with the bow of a dancing-master he vanished on the other side of the pool as he had come.

Eustacia sighed: it was no fragile maiden sigh, but a sigh which shook her like a shiver. Whenever a flash of reason darted like an electric light upon her lover – as it sometimes would – and showed his imperfections, she shivered thus. But it was over in a second, and she loved on. She knew that he trifled with her; but she loved on. She scattered the half-burnt brands, went indoors immediately, and up to her bedroom without a light. Amid the rustles which denoted her to be undressing in the darkness other heavy breaths frequently came; and the same kind of shudder occasionally moved through her when, ten minutes later, she lay on her bed asleep.

* VII *

Queen of Night

EUSTACIA VYE was the raw material of a divinity. On Olympus she would have done well with a little preparation. She had the passions and instincts which make a model goddess, that is, those which make not quite a model woman. Had it been possible for the earth and mankind to be entirely in her grasp for a while, had she handled the distaff, the spindle, and the shears at her own free will, few in the world would have noticed the change of government. There would have been the same inequality of lot, the same heaping up of favours here, of contumely there, the same generosity before justice, the same perpetual dilemmas, the same captious alternation of caresses and blows that we endure now.

She was in person full-limbed and somewhat heavy; without ruddiness, as without pallor; and soft to the touch as a cloud. To see her hair was to fancy that a whole winter did not contain darkness enough to form its shadow: it closed over her forehead like nightfall extinguishing the western glow.

Her nerves extended into those tresses, and her temper could always be softened by stroking them down. When her hair was brushed she would instantly sink into stillness and look like the Sphinx. If, in passing under one of the Egdon banks, any of its thick skeins were caught, as they sometimes were, by a prickly tuft of the large *Ulex Europaeus* – which will act as a sort of hairbrush – she would go back a few steps, and pass against it a second time.

She had Pagan eyes, full of nocturnal mysteries, and their light, as it came and went, and came again, was partially hampered by their oppressive lids and lashes; and of these the under lid was much fuller than it usually is with English women. This enabled her to indulge in reverie

without seeming to do so: she might have been believed capable of
sleeping without closing them up. Assuming that the souls of men and
women were visible essences, you could fancy the colour of Eustacia's
soul to be flame-like. The sparks from it that rose into her dark pupils
gave the same impression.

The mouth seemed formed less to speak than to quiver, less to quiver
than to kiss. Some might have added, less to kiss than to curl. Viewed
sideways, the closing-line of her lips formed, with almost geometric
precision, the curve so well known in the arts of design as the cima-recta,
or ogee. The sight of such a flexible bend as that on grim Egdon was
quite an apparition. It was felt at once that that mouth did not come over
from Sleswig with a band of Saxon pirates whose lips met like the two
halves of a muffin. One had fancied that such lip-curves were mostly
lurking underground in the South as fragments of forgotten marbles. So
fine were the lines of her lips that, though full, each corner of her mouth
was as clearly cut as the point of a spear. This keenness of corner was only
blunted when she was given over to sudden fits of gloom, one of the
phases of the night-side of sentiment which she knew too well for her
years.

Her presence brought memories of such things as Bourbon roses,
rubies, and tropical midnights; her moods recalled lotus-eaters and the
march in 'Athalie'; her motions, the ebb and flow of the sea; her voice,
the viola. In a dim light, and with a slight rearrangement of her hair, her
general figure might have stood for that of either of the higher female
deities. The new moon behind her head, an old helmet upon it, a diadem
of accidental dewdrops round her brow, would have been adjuncts
sufficient to strike the note of Artemis, Athena, or Hera respectively,
with as close an approximation to the antique as that which passes muster
on many respected canvases.

But celestial imperiousness, love, wrath, and fervour had proved to be
somewhat thrown away on netherward Egdon. Her power was limited,
and the consciousness of this limitation had biassed her development.
Egdon was her Hades, and since coming there she had imbibed much of
what was dark in its tone, though inwardly and eternally unreconciled
thereto. Her appearance accorded well with this smouldering rebelliousness, and the shady splendour of her beauty was the real surface of the sad
and stifled warmth within her. A true Tartarean dignity sat upon her
brow, and not factitiously or with marks of constraint, for it had grown
in her with years.

Across the upper part of her head she wore a thin fillet of black velvet,
restraining the luxuriance of her shady hair, in a way which added much
to this class of majesty by irregularly clouding her forehead. 'Nothing
can embellish a beautiful face more than a narrow band drawn over the
brow,' says Richter. Some of the neighbouring girls wore coloured ribbon
for the same purpose, and sported metallic ornaments elsewhere; but if
any one suggested coloured ribbons and metallic ornaments to Eustacia
Vye she laughed and went on.

Why did a woman of this sort live on Egdon Heath? Budmouth was her native place, a fashionable seaside resort at that date. She was the daughter of the bandmaster of a regiment which had been quartered there – a Corfiote by birth, and a fine musician – who met his future wife during her trip thither with her father the captain, a man of good family. The marriage was scarcely in accord with the old man's wishes, for the bandmaster's pockets were as light as his occupation. But the musician did his best; adopted his wife's name, made England permanently his home, took great trouble with his child's education, the expenses of which were defrayed by the grandfather, and throve as the chief local musician till her mother's death, when he left off thriving, drank, and died also. The girl was left to the care of her grandfather, who, since three of his ribs became broken in a shipwreck, had lived in this airy perch on Egdon, a spot which had taken his fancy because the house was to be had for next to nothing, and because a remote blue tinge on the horizon between the hills, visible from the cottage door, was traditionally believed to be the English Channel. She hated the change; she felt like one banished; but here she was forced to abide.

Thus it happened that in Eustacia's brain were juxtaposed the strangest assortment of ideas, from old time and from new. There was no middle distance in her perspective; romantic recollections of sunny afternoons on an esplanade, with military bands, officers, and gallants around, stood like gilded letters upon the dark tablet of surrounding Egdon. Every bizarre effect that could result from the random intertwining of watering-place glitter with the grand solemnity of a heath, was to be found in her. Seeing nothing of human life now, she imagined all the more of what she had seen.

Where did her dignity come from? By a latent vein from Alcinous' line, her father hailing from Phaeacia's isle? – or from Fitzalan and De Vere, her maternal grandfather having had a cousin in the peerage? Perhaps it was the gift of Heaven – a happy convergence of natural laws. Among other things opportunity had of late years been denied her of learning to be undignified, for she lived lonely. Isolation on a heath renders vulgarity well-nigh impossible. It would have been as easy for the heath-ponies, bats, and snakes to be vulgar as for her. A narrow life in Budmouth might have completely demeaned her.

The only way to look queenly without realms or hearts to queen it over is to look as if you had lost them; and Eustacia did that to a triumph. In the captain's cottage she could suggest mansions she had never seen. Perhaps that was because she frequented a vaster mansion than any of them, the open hills. Like the summer condition of the place around her, she was an embodiment of the phrase 'a populous solitude' – apparently so listless, void, and quiet, she was really busy and full.

To be loved to madness – such was her great desire. Love was to her the one cordial which could drive away the eating loneliness of her days. And she seemed to long for the abstraction called passionate love more than for any particular lover.

She could show a most reproachful look at times, but it was directed less against human beings than against certain creatures of her mind, the chief of these being Destiny, through whose interference she dimly fancied it arose that love alighted only on gliding youth – that any love she might win would sink simultaneously with the sand in the glass. She thought of it with an ever-growing consciousness of cruelty, which tended to breed actions of reckless unconventionality, framed to snatch a year's, a week's, even an hour's passion from anywhere while it could be won. Through want of it she had sung without being merry, possessed without enjoying, outshone without triumphing. Her loneliness deepened her desire. On Egdon, coldest and meanest kisses were at famine prices; and where was a mouth matching hers to be found?

Fidelity in love for fidelity's sake had less attraction for her than for most women: fidelity because of love's grip had much. A blaze of love, and extinction, was better than a lantern glimmer of the same which should last long years. On this head she knew by prevision what most women learn only by experience: she had mentally walked round love, told the towers thereof, considered its palaces; and concluded that love was but a doleful joy. Yet she desired it, as one in a desert would be thankful for brackish water.

She often repeated her prayers; not at particular times, but, like the unaffectedly devout, when she desired to pray. Her prayer was always spontaneous, and often ran thus, 'O deliver my heart from this fearful gloom and loneliness: send me great love from somewhere, else I shall die.'

Her high gods were William the Conqueror, Strafford, and Napoleon Buonaparte, as they had appeared in the Lady's History used at the establishment in which she was educated. Had she been a mother she would have christened her boys such names as Saul or Sisera in preference to Jacob or David, neither of whom she admired. At school she had used to side with the Philistines in several battles, and had wondered if Pontius Pilate were as handsome as he was frank and fair.

Thus she was a girl of some forwardness of mind, indeed, weighed in relation to her situation among the very rearward of thinkers, very original. Her instincts towards social nonconformity were at the root of this. In the matter of holidays, her mood was that of horses who, when turned out to grass, enjoy looking upon their kind at work on the highway. She only valued rest to herself when it came in the midst of other people's labour. Hence she hated Sundays when all was at rest, and often said they would be the death of her. To see the heathmen in their Sunday condition, that is, with their hands in their pockets, their boots newly oiled, and not laced up (a particularly Sunday sign), walking leisurely among the turves and furze-faggots they had cut during the week, and kicking them critically as if their use were unknown, was a fearful heaviness to her. To relieve the tedium of this untimely day she would overhaul the cupboards containing her grandfather's old charts and other rubbish, humming Saturday-night ballads of the country people the while. But on Saturday nights she would frequently sing a psalm, and it was always on a week-day that she read the Bible, that she might be unoppressed with a sense of doing her duty.

Such views of life were to some extent the natural begettings of her situation upon her nature. To dwell on a heath without studying its meanings was like wedding a foreigner without learning his tongue. The subtle beauties of the heath were lost to Eustacia; she only caught its vapours. An environment which would have made a contented woman a poet, a suffering woman a devotee, a pious woman a psalmist, even a giddy woman thoughtful, made a rebellious woman saturnine.

Eustacia had got beyond the vision of some marriage of inexpressible glory; yet, though her emotions were in full vigour, she cared for no meaner union. Thus we see her in a strange state of isolation. To have lost the godlike conceit that we may do what we will, and not to have acquired a homely zest for doing what we can, shows a grandeur of temper which cannot be objected to in the abstract, for it denotes a mind that, though disappointed, forswears compromise. But, if congenial to philosophy, it is apt to be dangerous to the commonwealth. In a world where doing means marrying, and the commonwealth is one of hearts and hands, the same peril attends the condition.

And so we see our Eustacia – for at times she was not altogether unlovable – arriving at that stage of enlightenment which feels that nothing is worth while, and filling up the spare hours of her existence by idealizing Wildeve for want of a better object. This was the sole reason of his ascendency: she knew it herself. At moments her pride rebelled against her passion for him, and she even had longed to be free. But there was only one circumstance which could dislodge him, and that was the advent of a greater man.

For the rest, she suffered much from depression of spirits, and took slow walks to recover them, in which she carried her grandfather's telescope and her grandmother's hour-glass – the latter because of a peculiar pleasure she derived from watching a material representation of time's gradual glide away. She seldom schemed, but when she did scheme, her plans showed rather the comprehensive strategy of a general than the small arts called womanish, though she could utter oracles of Delphian ambiguity when she did not choose to be direct. In heaven she will probably sit between the Héloïses and the Cleopatras.

VIII

Those Who Are Found Where There Is Said to Be Nobody

As soon as the sad little boy had withdrawn from the fire he clasped the money tight in the palm of his hand, as if thereby to fortify his courage, and began to run. There was really little danger in allowing a child to go home alone on this part of Egdon Heath. The distance to the boy's house was not more than three-eighths of a mile, his father's cottage, and one other a few yards further on, forming part of the small hamlet of Mistover Knap: the third and only remaining house was that of Captain Vye and Eustacia, which stood quite away from the small cottages, and was the loneliest of lonely houses on these thinly populated slopes.

He ran until he was out of breath, and then, becoming more courageous, walked leisurely along, singing in an old voice a little song about a sailor-boy and a fair one, and bright gold in store. In the middle of this the child stopped: from a pit under the hill ahead of him shone a light, whence proceeded a cloud of floating dust and a smacking noise.

Only unusual sights and sounds frightened the boy. The shrivelled voice of the heath did not alarm him, for that was familiar. The thorn-bushes which arose in his path from time to time were less satisfactory, for they whistled gloomily, and had a ghastly habit after dark of putting on the shapes of jumping madmen, sprawling giants, and hideous cripples. Lights were not uncommon this evening, but the nature of all of them was different from this. Discretion rather than terror prompted the boy to turn back instead of passing the light, with a view of asking Miss Eustacia Vye to let her servant accompany him home.

When the boy had reascended to the top of the valley he found the fire to be still burning on the bank, though lower than before. Beside it, instead of Eustacia's solitary form, he saw two persons, the second being a man. The boy crept along under the bank to ascertain from the nature of the proceedings if it would be prudent to interrupt so splendid a creature as Miss Eustacia on his poor trivial account.

After listening under the bank for some minutes to the talk he turned in a perplexed and doubting manner and began to withdraw as silently as he had come. That he did not, upon the whole, think it advisable to interrupt her conversation with Wildeve, without being prepared to bear the whole weight of her displeasure, was obvious.

Here was a Scyllaeo-Charybdean position for a poor boy. Pausing when again safe from discovery he finally decided to face the pit phenomenon as the lesser evil. With a heavy sigh he retraced the slope, and followed the path he had followed before.

The light had gone, the rising dust had disappeared – he hoped for ever. He marched resolutely along, and found nothing to alarm him till, coming within a few yards of the sandpit he heard a slight noise in front, which led him to halt. The halt was but momentary, for the noise resolved itself into the steady bites of two animals grazing.

'Two he'th-croppers down here,' he said aloud. 'I have never known 'em come down so far afore.'

The animals were in the direct line of his path, but that the child thought little of; he had played round the fetlocks of horses from his infancy. On coming nearer, however, the boy was somewhat surprised to find that the little creatures did not run off, and that each wore a clog, to prevent his going astray; this signified that they had been broken in. He could now see the interior of the pit, which, being in the side of the hill, had a level entrance. In the innermost corner the square outline of a van appeared, with its back towards him. A light came from the interior, and threw a moving shadow upon the vertical face of gravel at the further side of the pit into which the vehicle faced.

The child assumed that this was the cart of a gipsy, and his dread of those wanderers reached but to that mild pitch which titillates rather than pains. Only a few inches of mud wall kept him and his family from being gipsies themselves. He skirted the gravel-pit at a respectful distance, ascended the slope, and came forward upon the brow, in order to look into the open door of the van and see the original of the shadow.

The picture alarmed the boy. By a little stove inside the van sat a figure red from head to heels – the man who had been Thomasin's friend. He was darning a stocking, which was red like the rest of him. Moreover, as he darned he smoked a pipe, the stem and bowl of which were red also.

At this moment one of the heath-croppers feeding in the outer shadows was audibly shaking off the clog attached to its foot. Aroused by the sound the reddleman laid down his stocking, lit a lantern which hung beside him, and came out from the van. In sticking up the candle he lifted the lantern to his face, and the light shone into the whites of his eyes and upon his ivory teeth, which, in contrast with the red surrounding, lent him a startling aspect enough to the gaze of a juvenile. The boy knew too well for his peace of mind upon whose lair he had lighted. Uglier persons than gipsies were known to cross Egdon at times, and a reddleman was one of them.

'How I wish 'twas only a gipsy!' he murmured.

The man was by this time coming back from the horses. In his fear of being seen the boy rendered detection certain by nervous motion. The heather and peat stratum overhung the brow of the pit in mats, hiding the actual verge. The boy had stepped beyond the solid ground; the heather now gave way, and down he rolled over the scarp of grey sand to the very foot of the man.

The red man opened the lantern and turned it upon the figure of the prostrate boy.

'Who be ye?' he said.

'Johnny Nunsuch, master!'

'What were you doing up there?'

'I don't know.'

'Watching me, I suppose?'

'Yes, master.'

'What did you watch me for?'

'Because I was coming home from Miss Vye's bonfire.'

'Beest hurt?'

'No.'

'Why yes, you be: your hand is bleeding. Come under my tilt and let me tie it up.'

'Please let me look for my sixpence.'

'How did you come by that?'

'Miss Vye gied it to me for keeping up her bonfire.'

The sixpence was found, and the man went to the van, the boy behind, almost holding his breath.

The man took a piece of rag from a satchel containing sewing materials, tore off a strip, which, like everything else, was tinged red, and proceeded to bind up the wound.

'My eyes have got foggy-like – please may I sit down, master?' said the boy.

'To be sure, poor chap. 'Tis enough to make you feel fainty. Sit on that bundle.'

The man finished tying up the gash, and the boy said, 'I think I'll go home now, master.'

'You are rather afraid of me. Do you know what I be?'

The child surveyed his vermilion figure up and down with much misgiving, and finally said, 'Yes.'

'Well, what?'

'The reddleman!' he faltered.

'Yes, that's what I be. Though there's more than one. You little children think there's only one cuckoo, one fox, one giant, one devil, and one reddleman, when there's lots of us all.'

'Is there? You won't carry me off in your bags, will ye, master? 'Tis said that the reddleman will sometimes.'

'Nonsense. All that reddlemen do is sell reddle. You see all these bags at the back of my cart? They are not full of little boys – only full of red stuff.'

'Was you born a reddleman?'

'No, I took to it. I should be as white as you if I were to give up the trade – that is, I should be white in time – perhaps six months: not at first, because 'tis grow'd into my skin and won't wash out. Now, you'll never be afraid of a reddleman again, will ye?'

'No, never. Willy Orchard said he seed a red ghost here t'other day – perhaps that was you?'

'I was here t'other day.'

'Were you making that dusty light I saw by now?'

'O yes: I was beating out some bags. And have you had a good bonfire up there? I saw the light. Why did Miss Vye want a bonfire so bad that she should give you sixpence to keep it up?'

'I don't know. I was tired, but she made me bide and keep up the fire just the same, while she kept going up across Rainbarrow way.'

'And how long did that last?'

'Until a hopfrog jumped into the pond.'

The reddleman suddenly ceased to talk idly. 'A hopfrog?' he inquired. 'Hopfrogs don't jump into ponds this time of year.'

'They do, for I heard one.'

'Certain-sure?'

'Yes. She told me afore that I should hear'n; and so I did. They say she's clever and deep, and perhaps she charmed 'en to come.'

'And what then?'

'Then I came down here, and I was afeard, and I went back; but I didn't like to speak to her, because of the gentleman, and I came on here again.'

'A gentleman – ah! What did she say to him, my man?'

'Told him she supposed he had not married the other woman because he liked his old sweetheart best; and things like that.'

'What did the gentleman say to her, my sonny?'

'He only said he liked her best, and how he was coming to see her again under Rainbarrow o' nights.'

'Ha!' cried the reddleman, slapping his hand against the side of his van so that the whole fabric shook under the blow. 'That's the secret o't!'

The little boy jumped clean from the stool.

'My man, don't you be afraid,' said the dealer in red, suddenly becoming gentle. 'I forgot you were here. That's only a curious way reddlemen have of going mad for a moment; but they don't hurt anybody. And what did the lady say then?'

'I can't mind. Please, Master Reddleman, may I go home-along now?'

'Ay, to be sure you may. I'll go a bit of ways with you.'

He conducted the boy out of the gravel-pit and into the path leading to his mother's cottage. When the little figure had vanished in the darkness the reddleman returned, resumed his seat by the fire, and proceeded to darn again.

* IX *

Love Leads a Shrewd Man into Strategy

REDDLEMEN of the old school are now but seldom seen. Since the introduction of railways Wessex farmers have managed to do without these Mephistophelian visitants, and the bright pigment so largely used by shepherds in preparing sheep for the fair is obtained by other routes. Even those who yet survive are losing the poetry of existence which characterized them when the pursuit of the trade meant periodical journeys to the pit whence the material was dug, a regular camping out from month to month, except in the depth of winter, a peregrination among farms which could be counted by the hundred, and in spite of this Arab existence the preservation of that respectability which is insured by the never-failing production of a well-lined purse.

Reddle spreads its lively hues over everything it lights on, and stamps unmistakably, as with the mark of Cain, any person who has handled it half an hour.

A child's first sight of a reddleman was an epoch in his life. That blood-coloured figure was a sublimation of all the horrid dreams which had afflicted the juvenile spirit since imagination began. 'The reddleman is coming for you!' had been the formulated threat of Wessex mothers for many generations. He was successfully supplanted for a while, at the beginning of the present century, by Buonaparte; but as process of time rendered the latter personage stale and ineffective the older phrase resumed its early prominence. And now the reddleman has in his turn followed Buonaparte to the land of worn-out bogeys, and his place is filled by modern inventions.

The reddleman lived like a gipsy; but gipsies he scorned. He was about as thriving as travelling basket and mat makers; but he had nothing to do with them. He was more decently born and brought up than the cattle-drovers who passed and repassed him in his wanderings; but they merely nodded to him. His stock was more valuable than that of pedlars; but they did not think so, and passed his cart with eyes straight ahead. He was such an unnatural colour to look at that the men of round-abouts and wax-work shows seemed gentlemen beside him; but he considered them low company, and remained aloof. Among all these squatters and folks of the road the reddleman continually found himself; yet he was not of them. His occupation tended to isolate him, and isolated he was mostly seen to be.

It was sometimes suggested that reddlemen were criminals for whose misdeeds other men had wrongfully suffered: that in escaping the law they had not escaped their own consciences, and had taken to the trade as a lifelong penance. Else why should they have chosen it? In the present case such a question would have been particularly apposite. The reddleman who had entered Egdon that afternoon was an instance of the pleasing being wasted to form the ground-work of the singular, when an ugly foundation would have done just as well for that purpose. The one point that was forbidding about this reddleman was his colour. Freed from that he would have been as agreeable a specimen of rustic manhood as one would often see. A keen observer might have been inclined to think – which was, indeed, partly the truth – that he had relinquished his proper station in life for want of interest in it. Moreover, after looking at him one would have hazarded the guess that good-nature, and an acuteness as extreme as it could be without verging on craft, formed the frame-work of his character.

While he darned the stocking his face became rigid with thought. Softer expressions followed this, and then again recurred the tender sadness which had sat upon him during his drive along the highway that afternoon. Presently his needle stopped. He laid down the stocking, arose from his seat, and took a leather pouch from a hook in the corner of the van. This contained among other articles a brown-paper packet, which, to judge from the hinge-like character of its worn folds, seemed to have been carefully opened and closed a good many times. He sat down on a three-legged milking-stool that formed the only seat in the van, and, examining his packet by the light of a candle, took thence an old letter and spread it open. The writing had originally been traced on white paper, but the letter had now assumed a pale red tinge from the accident of its situation; and the black strokes of writing thereon looked like the twigs of a winter hedge against a vermilion sunset. The letter bore a date some two years previous to that time, and was signed 'Thomasin Yeobright'. It rans as follows:

DEAR DIGGORY VENN – The question you put when you overtook me coming home from Pond-close gave me such a surprise that I am afraid I did not make you exactly understand what I meant. Of course, if my aunt had not met me I could have explained all then at once, but as it was there was no chance. I have been quite uneasy since, as you know I do not wish to pain you, yet I fear I shall be doing so now in contradicting what I seemed to say then. I cannot, Diggory, marry you, or think of letting you call me your sweetheart. I could not, indeed, Diggory. I hope you will not much mind my saying this, and feel in a great pain. It makes me very sad when I think it may, for I like you very much, and I always put you next to my cousin Clym in my mind. There are so many reasons why we cannot be married that I can hardly name them all in a letter. I did not in the least expect that you were going to speak on such a thing when you followed me, because I had never thought of you in the sense of a lover at all. You must not becall me for laughing when you spoke; you mistook when you thought I laughed at you as a foolish man. I laughed because the idea was so odd, and not at you at all. The great reason with my own personal self for not letting you court me is, that I do not feel the things a woman ought to feel who consents to walk with you with the meaning of being your wife. It is not as you think, that I have another in my mind, for I do not encourage anybody, and never have in my life. Another reason is my aunt. She would not, I know, agree to it, even if I wished to have you. She likes you very well, but she will want me to look a little higher than a small dairy-farmer, and marry a professional man. I hope you will not set your heart against me for writing plainly, but I felt you might try to see me again, and it is better that we should not meet. I shall always think of you as a good man, and be anxious for your well-doing. I send this by Jane Orchard's little maid, – And remain Diggory, your faithful friend,

                                                    THOMASIN YEOBRIGHT

TO MR VENN, Dairy-farmer

Since the arrival of that letter, on a certain autumn morning long ago, the reddleman and Thomasin had not met till today. During the interval he had shifted his position even further from hers than it had originally been, by adopting the reddle trade; though he was really in very good circumstances still. Indeed, seeing that his expenditure was only one-fourth of his income, he might have been called a prosperous man.

Rejected suitors take to roaming as naturally as unhived bees; and the business to which he had cynically devoted himself was in many ways congenial to Venn. But his wanderings, by mere stress of old emotions, had frequently taken an Egdon direction, though he never intruded upon her who attracted him thither. To be in Thomasin's heath, and near her, yet unseen, was the one ewe-lamb of pleasure left to him.

Then came the incident of that day, and the reddleman, still loving her well, was excited by this accidental service to her at a critical juncture to vow an active devotion to her cause, instead of, as hitherto, sighing and holding aloof. After what had happened, it was impossible that he should not doubt the honesty of Wildeve's intentions. But her hope was apparently centred upon him; and dismissing his regrets Venn determined to aid her to be happy in his own chosen way. That this way was, of all others, the most distressing to himself, was awkward enough; but the reddleman's love was generous.

His first active step in watching over Thomasin's interests was taken about seven o'clock the next morning, and was dictated by the news which he had learnt from the sad boy. That Eustacia was somehow the cause of Wildeve's carelessness in relation to the marriage had at once been Venn's conclusion on hearing of the secret meeting between them. It did not occur to his mind that Eustacia's love-signal to Wildeve was the tender effect upon the deserted beauty of the intelligence which her grandfather had brought home. His instinct was to regard her as a conspirator against rather than as an antecedent obstacle to Thomasin's happiness.

During the day he had been exceedingly anxious to learn the condition of Thomasin; but he did not venture to intrude upon a threshold to which he was a stranger, particularly at such an unpleasant moment as this. He had occupied his time in moving with his ponies and load to a new point in the heath, eastward to his previous station; and here he selected a nook with a careful eye to shelter from wind and rain, which seemed to mean that his stay there was to be a comparatively extended one. After this he returned on foot some part of the way that he had come; and, it being now dark, he diverged to the left till he stood behind a holly-bush on the edge of a pit not twenty yards from Rainbarrow.

He watched for a meeting there, but he watched in vain. Nobody except himself came near the spot that night.

But the loss of his labour produced little effect upon the reddleman. He had stood in the shoes of Tantalus, and seemed to look upon a certain mass of disappointment as the natural preface to all realizations, without which preface they would give cause for alarm.

The same hour the next evening found him again at the same place; but Eustacia and Wildeve, the expected trysters, did not appear.

He pursued precisely the same course yet four nights longer, and without success. But on the next, being the day-week of their previous meeting, he saw a female shape floating along the ridge and the outline of a young man ascending from the valley. They met in the little ditch encircling the tumulus – the original excavation from which it had been thrown up by the ancient British people.

The reddleman, stung with suspicion of wrong to Thomasin, was aroused to strategy in a moment. He instantly left the bush and crept forward on his hands and knees. When he had got as close as he might safely venture without discovery he found that, owing to a cross-wind, the conversation of the trysting pair could not be overheard.

Near him, as in divers places about the heath, were areas strewn with large turves, which lay edgeways and upside-down awaiting removal by Timothy Fairway, previous to the winter weather. He took two of these as he lay, and dragged them over him till one covered his head and shoulders, the other his back and legs. The reddleman would now have been quite invisible, even by daylight; the turves, standing upon him with the heather upwards, looked precisely as if they were growing. He crept along again, and the turves upon his back crept with him. Had he approached without any covering the chances are that he would not have been perceived in the dusk; approaching thus, it was as though he burrowed underground. In this manner he came quite close to where the two were standing.

'Wish to consult me on the matter?' reached his ears in the rich, impetuous accents of Eustacia Vye. 'Consult me? It is an indignity to me to talk so: I won't bear it any longer!' She began weeping. 'I have loved you, and have shown you that I loved you, much to my regret; and yet you can come and say in that frigid way that you wish to consult with me whether it would not be better to marry Thomasin. Better – of course it would be. Marry her: she is nearer to your own position in life than I am!'

'Yes, yes; that's very well,' said Wildeve peremptorily. 'But we must look at things as they are. Whatever blame may attach to me for having brought it about, Thomasin's position is at present much worse than yours. I simply tell you that I am in a strait.'

'But you shall not tell me! You must see that it is only harassing me. Damon, you have not acted well; you have sunk in my opinion. You have

not valued my courtesy – the courtesy of a lady in loving you – who used
to think of far more ambitious things. But it was Thomasin's fault. She
won you away from me, and she deserves to suffer for it. Where is she
staying now? Not that I care, nor where I am myself. Ah, if I were dead
and gone how glad she would be! Where is she, I ask?'

'Thomasin is now staying at her aunt's shut up in a bedroom, and
keeping out of everybody's sight,' he said indifferently.

'I don't think you care much about her even now,' said Eustacia with
sudden joyousness: 'for if you did you wouldn't talk so coolly about her.
Do you talk so coolly to her about me? Ah, I expect you do! Why did you
originally go away from me? I don't think I can ever forgive you, except
on one condition, that whenever you desert me, you come back again,
sorry that you served me so.'

'I never wish to desert you.'

'I do not thank you for that. I should hate it to be all smooth. Indeed,
I think I like you to desert me a little once now and then. Love is the
dismallest thing where the lover is quite honest. O, it is a shame to say so;
but it is true!' She indulged in a little laugh. 'My low spirits begin at the
very idea. Don't you offer me tame love, or away you go!'

'I wish Tamsie were not such a confoundedly good little woman,' said
Wildeve, 'so that I could be faithful to you without injuring a worthy
person. It is I who am the sinner after all; I am not worth the little finger
of either of you.'

'But you must not sacrifice yourself to her from any sense of justice,'
replied Eustacia quickly. 'If you do not love her it is the most merciful
thing in the long run to leave her as she is. That's always the best way.
There, now I have been unwomanly, I suppose. When you have left me
I am always angry with myself for things that I have said to you.'

Wildeve walked a pace of two among the heather without replying.
The pause was filled up by the intonation of a pollard thorn a little way
to windward, the breezes filtering through its unyielding twigs as through
a strainer. It was as if the night sang dirges with clenched teeth.

She continued, half sorrowfully, 'Since meeting you last, it has occurred
to me once or twice that perhaps it was not for love of me you did not
marry her. Tell me, Damon: I'll try to bear it. Had I nothing whatever to
do with the matter?'

'Do you press me to tell?'

'Yes, I must know. I see I have been too ready to believe in my own
power.'

'Well, the immediate reason was that the licence would not do for the
place, and before I could get another she ran away. Up to that point you
had nothing to do with it. Since then her aunt has spoken to me in a tone
which I don't at all like.'

'Yes, yes! I am nothing in it – I am nothing in it. You only trifle with
me. Heaven, what can I, Eustacia Vye, be made of to think so much of
you!'

'None; do not be so passionate . . . Eustacia, how we roved among these bushes last year, when the hot days had got cool, and the shades of the hills kept us almost invisible in the hollows!'

She remained in moody silence till she said, 'Yes, and how I used to laugh at you for daring to look up to me! But you have well made me suffer for that since.'

'Yes, you served me cruelly enough until I thought I had found some one fairer than you. A blessed find for me, Eustacia.'

'Do you still think you found somebody fairer?'

'Sometimes I do, sometimes I don't. The scales are balanced so nicely that a feather would turn them.'

'But don't you really care whether I meet you or whether I don't?' she said slowly.

'I care a little, but not enough to break my rest,' replied the young man languidly. 'No, all that's past. I find there are two flowers where I thought there was only one. Perhaps there are three, or four, or any number as good as the first . . . Mine is a curious fate. Who would have thought that all this could happen to me?'

She interrupted with a suppressed fire of which either love or anger seemed an equally possible issue, 'Do you love me now?'

'Who can say?'

'Tell me; I will know it!'

'I do, and I do not,' said he mischievously. 'That is, I have my times and my seasons. One moment you are too tall, another moment you are too do-nothing, another too melancholy, another too dark, another I don't know what, except – that you are not the whole world to me that you used to be, my dear. But you are a pleasant lady to know, and nice to meet, and I dare say as sweet as ever – almost.'

Eustacia was silent, and she turned from him, till she said, in a voice of suspended mightiness, 'I am for a walk, and this is my way.'

'Well, I can do worse than follow you.'

'You know you can't do otherwise, for all your moods and changes!' she answered defiantly. 'Say what you will; try as you may; keep away from me all that you can – you will never forget me. You will love me all your life long. You would jump to marry me!'

'So I would!' said Wildeve. 'Such strange thoughts as I've had from time to time, Eustacia; and they come to me this moment. You hate the heath as much as ever; that I know.'

'I do,' she murmured deeply. ' 'Tis my cross, my shame, and will be my death!'

'I abhor it too,' said he. 'How mournfully the wind blows round us now!'

She did not answer. Its tone was indeed solemn and pervasive. Compound utterances addressed themselves to their senses, and it was possible to view by ear the features of the neighbourhood. Acoustic pictures were returned from the darkened scenery; they could hear where the tracts of heather began and ended; where the furze was growing stalky and tall; where it had been recently cut; in what direction the fir-clump lay, and how near was the pit in which the hollies grew; for these differing features had their voices no less than their shapes and colours.

'God, how lonely it is!' resumed Wildeve. 'What are picturesque ravines and mists to us who see nothing else? Why should we stay here? Will you go with me to America? I have kindred in Wisconsin.'

'That wants consideration.'

'It seems impossible to do well here, unless one were a wild bird or a landscape-painter. Well?'

'Give me time,' she softly said, taking his hand. 'America is so far away. Are you going to walk with me a little way?'

As Eustacia uttered the latter words she retired from the base of the barrow, and Wildeve followed her, so that the reddleman could hear no more.

He lifted the turves and arose. Their black figures sank and disappeared from against the sky. They were as two horns which the sluggish heath had put forth from its crown, like a mollusc, and had now again drawn in.

The reddleman's walk across the vale, and over into the next where his cart lay, was not sprightly for a slim young fellow of twenty-four. His spirit was perturbed to aching. The breezes that blew around his mouth in that walk carried off upon them the accents of a commination.

He entered the van, where there was a fire in a stove. Without lighting his candle he sat down at once on the three-legged stool, and pondered on what he had seen and heard touching that still loved-one of his. He uttered a sound which was neither sigh nor sob, but was even more indicative than either of a troubled mind.

'My Tamsie,' he whispered heavily. 'What can be done? Yes, I will see that Eustacia Vye.'

* X *

A Desperate Attempt at Persuasion

THE next morning, at the time when the height of the sun appeared very insignificant from any part of the heath as compared with the altitude of Rainbarrow, and when all the little hills in the lower levels were like an archipelago in a fog-formed Aegean, the reddleman came from the brambled nook which he had adopted as his quarters and ascended the slopes of Mistover Knap.

Though these shaggy hills were apparently so solitary, several keen round eyes were always ready on such a wintry morning as this to converge upon a passer-by. Feathered species sojourned here in hiding which would have created wonder if found elsewhere. A bustard haunted the spot and not many years before this five and twenty might have been seen in Egdon at one time. Marsh-harriers looked up from the valley by Wildeve's. A cream-coloured courser had used to visit this hill, a bird so rare that not more than a dozen have ever been seen in England; but a barbarian rested neither night nor day till he had shot the African truant, and after that event cream-coloured coursers thought fit to enter Egdon no more.

A traveller who should walk and observe any of these visitants as Venn observed them now could feel himself to be in direct communication with regions unknown to man. Here in front of him was a wild mallard – just arrived from the home of the north wind. The creatures brought within him an amplitude of Northern knowledge. Glacial catastrophes, snowstorm episodes, glittering auroral effects, Polaris in the zenith, Franklin underfoot – the category of his commonplaces was wonderful. But the bird, like many other philosophers, seemed as he looked at the reddleman to think that a present moment of comfortable reality was worth a decade of memories.

Venn passed on through these towards the house of the isolated beauty who lived up among and despised them. The day was Sunday; but as going to church, except to be married or buried, was exceptional at Egdon, this made little difference. He had determined upon the bold stroke of asking for an interview with Miss Vye – to attack her position as Thomasin's rival either by art or by storm, showing therein, somewhat too conspicuously, the want of gallantry characteristic of a certain astute sort of men, from clowns to kings. The great Frederick making war on the beautiful Archduchess, Napoleon refusing terms to the beautiful Queen of Prussia, were not more dead to difference of sex than the reddleman was, in his peculiar way, in planning the displacement of Eustacia.

To call at the captain's cottage was always more or less an undertaking for the inferior inhabitants. Though occasionally chatty, his moods were erratic, and nobody could be certain how he would behave at any particular moment. Eustacia was reserved, and lived very much to herself. Except the daughter of one of the cotters, who was their servant, and a lad who worked in the garden and stable, scarcely any one but themselves ever entered the house. They were the only genteel people of the district except the Yeobrights, and though far from rich, they did not feel that necessity for preserving a friendly face towards every man, bird, and beast which influenced their poorer neighbours.

When the reddleman entered the garden the old man was looking through his glass at the stain of blue sea in the distant landscape, the little anchors on his buttons twinkling in the sun. He recognized Venn as his companion on the highway, but made no remark on that circumstance, merely saying, 'Ah, reddleman – you here? Have a glass of grog?'

Venn declined, on the plea of it being too early, and stated that his business was with Miss Vye. The captain surveyed him from cap to waistcoat and from waistcoat to leggings for a few moments, and finally asked him to go indoors.

Miss Vye was not to be seen by anybody just then; and the reddleman waited in the window-bench of the kitchen, his hands hanging across his divergent knees, and his cap hanging from his hands.

'I suppose the young lady is not up yet?' he presently said to the servant.

'Not quite yet. Folks never call upon ladies at this time of day.'

'Then I'll step outside,' said Venn. 'If she is willing to see me, will she please send out word, and I'll come in.'

The reddleman left the house and loitered on the hill adjoining. A considerable time elapsed, and no request for his presence was brought. He was beginning to think that his scheme had failed, when he beheld the form of Eustacia herself coming leisurely towards him. A sense of novelty in giving audience to that singular figure had been sufficient to draw her forth.

She seemed to feel, after a bare look at Diggory Venn, that the man had come on a strange errand, and that he was not so mean as she had thought him; for her close approach did not cause him to writhe uneasily, or shift his feet, or show any of those little signs which escape an ingenuous rustic at the advent of the uncommon in womankind. On his inquiring if he might have a conversation with her she replied, 'Yes, walk beside me'; and continued to move on.

Before they had gone far it occurred to the perspicacious reddleman that he would have acted more wisely by appearing less unimpressionable, and he resolved to correct the error as soon as he could find opportunity.

'I have made so bold, miss, as to step across and tell you some strange news which has come to my ears about that man.'

'Ah! what man?'

He jerked his elbow to south-east – the direction of the Quiet Woman.

Eustacia turned quickly to him. 'Do you mean Mr Wildeve?'

'Yes, there is trouble in a household on account of him, and I have come to let you know of it, because I believe you might have power to drive it away.'

'I? What is the trouble?'

'It is quite a secret. It is that he may refuse to marry Thomasin Yeobright after all.'

Eustacia, though set inwardly pulsing by his words, was equal to her part in such a drama as this. She replied coldly, 'I do not wish to listen to this, and you must not expect me to interfere.'

'But, miss, you will hear one word?'

'I cannot. I am not interested in the marriage, and even if I were I could not compel Mr Wildeve to do my bidding.'

'As the only lady on the heath I think you might,' said Venn with subtle indirectness. 'This is how the case stands. Mr Wildeve would marry Thomasin at once, and make all matters smooth, if so be there were not another woman in the case. This other woman is some person he has picked up with, and meets on the heath occasionally, I believe. He will never marry her, and yet through her he may never marry the woman who loves him dearly. Now, if you, miss, who have so much sway over us men-folk, were to insist that he should treat your young neighbour Tamsin with honourable kindness and give up the other woman, he would perhaps do it, and save her a good deal of misery.'

'Ah, my life!' said Eustacia, with a laugh which unclosed her lips so that the sun shone into her mouth as into a tulip, and lent it a similar scarlet fire. 'You think too much of my influence over men-folk indeed, reddleman. If I had such a power as you imagine I would go straight and use it for the good of anybody who has been kind to me – which Thomasin Yeobright has not particularly, to my knowledge.'

'Can it be that you really don't know of it – how much she has always thought of you?'

'I have never heard a word of it. Although we live only two miles apart I have never been inside her aunt's house in my life.'

The superciliousness that lurked in her manner told Venn that thus far he had utterly failed. He inwardly sighed and felt it necessary to unmask his second argument.

'Well, leaving that out of the question, 'tis in your power, I assure you, Miss Vye, to do a great deal of good to another woman.'

She shook her head.

'Your comeliness is law with Mr Wildeve. It is law with all men who see 'ee. They say, "This well-favoured lady coming – what's her name? How handsome!" Handsomer than Thomasin Yeobright,' the reddleman persisted, saying to himself, 'God forgive a rascal for lying!' And she was handsomer, but the reddleman was far from thinking so. There was a certain obscurity in Eustacia's beauty, and Venn's eye was not trained. In her winter dress, as now, she was like the tiger-beetle, which, when observed in dull situations, seems to be of the quietest neutral colour, but under a full illumination blazes with dazzling splendour.

Eustacia could not help replying, though conscious that she endangered her dignity thereby. 'Many women are lovelier than Thomasin,' she said; 'so not much attaches to that.'

The reddleman suffered the wound and went on: 'He is a man who notices the looks of women, and you could twist him to your will like withywind, if you only had the mind.'

'Surely what she cannot do who has been so much with him I cannot do living up here away from him.'

The reddleman wheeled and looked her in the face. 'Miss Vye!' he said.

'Why do you say that – as if you doubted me?' She spoke faintly, and her breathing was quick. 'The idea of your speaking in that tone to me!' she added, with a forced smile of hauteur. 'What could have been in your mind to lead you to speak like that?'

'Miss Vye, why should you make-believe that you don't know this man? – I know why, certainly. He is beneath you, and you are ashamed.'

'You are mistaken. What do you mean?'

The reddleman had decided to play the card of truth. 'I was at the meeting by Rainbarrow last night and heard every word,' he said. 'The woman that stands between Wildeve and Thomasin is yourself.'

It was a disconcerting lift of the curtain, and the mortification of Canduales' wife glowed in her. The moment had arrived when her lip would tremble in spite of herself, and when the gasp could no longer be kept down.

'I am unwell,' she said hurriedly. 'No – it is not that – I am not in a humour to hear you further. Leave me, please.'

'I must speak, Miss Vye, in spite of paining you. What I would put before you is this. However it may come about – whether she is to blame, or you – her case is without doubt worse than yours. Your giving up Mr Wildeve will be a real advantage to you, for how could you marry him? Now she cannot get off so easily – everybody will blame her if she loses him. Then I ask you – not because her right is best, but because her situation is worst – to give him up to her.'

'No – I won't, I won't!' she said impetuously, quite forgetful of her previous manner towards the reddleman as an underling. 'Nobody has ever been served so! It was going on well – I will not be beaten down – by an inferior woman like her. It is very well for you to come and plead for her, but is she not herself the cause of all her own trouble? Am I not to show favour to any person I may choose without asking permission of a parcel of cottagers? She has come between me and my inclination, and now that she finds herself rightly punished she gets you to plead for her!'

'Indeed,' said Venn earnestly, 'she knows nothing whatever about it. It is only I who ask you to give him up. It will be better for her and you both. People will say bad things if they find out that a lady secretly meets a man who has ill-used another woman.'

'I have *not* injured her: he was mine before he was hers! He came back – because – because he liked me best!' she said wildly. 'But I lose all self-respect in talking to you. What am I giving way to?'

'I can keep secrets,' said Venn gently. 'You need not fear. I am the only man who knows of your meeting with him. There is but one thing more to speak of, and then I will be gone. I heard you say to him that you hated living here – that Egdon heath was a jail to you.'

'I did say so. There is a sort of beauty in the scenery, I know; but it is a jail to me. The man you mention does not save me from that feeling, though he lives here. I should have cared nothing for him had there been a better person near.'

The reddleman looked hopeful: after these words from her his third attempt seemed promising. 'As we have now opened our minds a bit, miss,' he said, 'I'll tell you what I have got to propose. Since I have taken to the reddle trade I travel a good deal, as you know.'

She inclined her head, and swept round so that her eyes rested in the misty vale beneath them.

'And in my travels I go near Budmouth. Now Budmouth is a wonderful place – wonderful – a great salt sheening sea bending into the land like a bow – thousands of gentlepeople walking up and down – bands of music playing – officers by sea and officers by land walking among the rest – out of every ten folk you meet nine of 'em in love.'

'I know it,' she said disdainfully. 'I know Budmouth better than you. I was born there. My father came to be a military musician there from abroad. Ah, my soul, Budmouth! I wish I was there now.'

The reddleman was surprised to see how a slow fire could blaze on occasion. 'If you were, miss,' he replied, 'in a week's time you would think no more of Wildeve than of one of those he'th-croppers that we see yond. Now, I could get you there.'

'How?' said Eustacia, with intense curiosity in her heavy eyes.

'My uncle has been for five and twenty years the trusty man of a rich widow-lady who has a beautiful house facing the sea. This lady has become old and lame, and she wants a young company-keeper to read and sing to her, but can't get one to her mind to save her life, though she've advertised in the papers, and tried half a dozen. She would jump to get you, and uncle would make it all easy.'

'I should have to work, perhaps?'

'No, not real work: you'd have a little to do, such as reading and that. You would not be wanted till New Year's Day.'

'I knew it meant work,' she said, drooping to languor again.

'I confess there would be a trifle to do in the way of amusing her; but though idle people might call it work, working people would call it play. Think of the company and the life you'd lead, miss; the gaiety you'd see, and the gentleman you'd marry. My uncle is to inquire for a trustworthy young lady from the country, as she don't like town girls.'

'It is to wear myself out to please her! and I won't go. O, if I could live in a gay town as a lady should, and go my own ways, and do my own doings, I'd give the wrinkled half of my life! Yes, reddleman, that would I.'

'Help me to get Thomasin happy, miss, and the chance shall be yours,' urged her companion.

'Chance! – 'tis no chance,' she said proudly. 'What can a poor man like you offer me, indeed? – I am going indoors. I have nothing more to say. Don't your horses want feeding, or your reddlebags want mending, or don't you want to find buyers for your goods, that you stay idling here like this?'

Venn spoke not another word. With his hands behind him he turned away, that she might not see the hopeless disappointment in his face. The mental clearness and power he had found in this lonely girl had indeed filled his manner with misgiving even from the first few minutes of close quarters with her. Her youth and situation had led him to expect a simplicity quite at the beck of his method. But a system of inducement which might have carried weaker country lasses along with it had merely repelled Eustacia. As a rule, the word Budmouth meant fascination on Egdon. That Royal port and watering-place, if truly mirrored in the minds of the heath-folk, must have combined, in a charming and indescribable manner, a Carthaginian bustle of building with Tarentine luxuriousness and Baian health and beauty. Eustacia felt little less extravagantly about the place; but she would not sink her independence to get there.

When Diggory Venn had gone quite away, Eustacia walked to the bank and looked down the wild and picturesque vale towards the sun, which was also in the direction of Wildeve's. The mist had now so far collapsed that the tips of the trees and bushes around his house could just be discerned, as if boring upwards through a vast white cobweb which cloaked them from the day. There was no doubt that her mind was inclined thitherward; indefinitely, fancifully – twining and untwining about him as the single object within her horizon on which dreams might crystallize. The man who had begun by being merely her amusement, and would never have been more than her hobby but for his skill in deserting her at the right moments, was now again her desire. Cessation in his love-making had revivified her love. Such feeling as Eustacia had idly given to Wildeve was dammed into a flood by Thomasin. She had used to tease Wildeve, but that was before another had favoured him. Often a drop of irony into an indifferent situation renders the whole piquant.

'I will never give him up – never!' she said impetuously.

The reddleman's hint that rumour might show her to disadvantage had no permanent terror for Eustacia. She was as unconcerned at that contingency as a goddess at a lack of linen. This did not originate in inherent shamelessness, but in her living too far from the world to feel the impact of public opinion. Zenobia in the desert could hardly have cared what was said about her in Rome. As far as social ethics were concerned Eustacia approached the savage state, though in emotion she was all the while an epicure. She had advanced to the secret recesses of sensuousness, yet had hardly crossed the threshold of conventionality.

* XI *

The Dishonesty of an Honest Woman

THE reddleman had left Eustacia's presence with desponding views on
Thomasin's future happiness; but he was awakened to the fact that one
other channel remained untried by seeing, as he followed the way to his
van, the form of Mrs Yeobright slowly walking towards the Quiet
Woman. He went across to her; and could almost perceive in her anxious
face that this journey of hers to Wildeve was undertaken with the same
objects as his own to Eustacia.

She did not conceal the fact. 'Then,' said the reddleman, 'you may as
well leave it alone, Mrs Yeobright.'

'I half think so myself,' she said. 'But nothing else remains to be done
besides pressing the question upon him.'

'I should like to say a word first,' said Venn firmly. 'Mr Wildeve is not
the only man who has asked Thomasin to marry him; and why should
not another have a chance? Mrs Yeobright, I should be glad to marry
your niece, and would have done it any time these last two years. There,
now it is out, and I have never told anybody before but herself.'

Mrs Yeobright was not demonstrative, but her eyes involuntarily
glanced towards his singular though shapely figure.

'Looks are not everything,' said the reddleman, noticing the glance.
'There's many a calling that don't bring in so much as mine, if it comes
to money; and perhaps I am not so much worse off than Wildeve. There
is nobody so poor as these professional fellows who have failed; and if
you shouldn't like my redness – well, I am not red by birth, you know;
I only took to this business for a freak; and I might turn my hand to
something else in good time.'

'I am much obliged to you for your interest in my niece; but I fear
there would be objections. More than that, she is devoted to this
man.'

'True; or I shouldn't have done what I have this morning.'

'Otherwise there would be no pain in the case, and you would not see
me going to his house now. What was Thomasin's answer when you told
her of your feelings?'

'She wrote that you would object to me; and other things.'

'She was in a measure right. You must not take this unkindly: I merely
state it as a truth. You have been good to her, and we do not forget it. But
as she was unwilling on her own account to be your wife, that settles the
point without my wishes being concerned.'

'Yes. But there is a difference between then and now, ma'am. She is
distressed now, and I have thought that if you were to talk to her about
me, and think favourably of me yourself, there might be a chance of
winning her round, and getting her quite independent of this Wildeve's

backward and forward play, and his not knowing whether he'll have her or no.'

Mrs Yeobright shook her head. 'Thomasin thinks, and I think with her, that she ought to be Wildeve's wife, if she means to appear before the world without a slur upon her name. If they marry soon, everybody will believe that an accident did really prevent the wedding. If not, it may cast a shade upon her character – at any rate make her ridiculous. In short, if it is anyhow possible they must marry now.'

'I thought that till half an hour ago. But, after all, why should her going off with him to Anglebury for a few hours do her any harm? Anybody who knows how pure she is will feel any such thought to be quite unjust. I have been trying this morning to help on this marriage with Wildeve – yes, I, ma'am – in the belief that I ought to do it, because she was so wrapped up in him. But I much question if I was right, after all. However, nothing came of it. And now I offer myself.'

Mrs Yeobright appeared disinclined to enter further into the question. 'I fear I must go on,' she said. 'I do not see that anything else can be done.'

And she went on. But though this conversation did not divert Thomasin's aunt from her purposed interview with Wildeve, it made a considerable difference in her mode of conducting that interview. She thanked God for the weapon which the reddleman had put into her hands.

Wildeve was at home when she reached the inn. He showed her silently into the parlour, and closed the door. Mrs Yeobright began –

'I have thought it my duty to call today. A new proposal has been made to me, which has rather astonished me. It will affect Thomasin greatly; and I have decided that it should at least be mentioned to you.'

'Yes? What is it?' he said civilly.

'It is, of course, in reference to her future. You may not be aware that another man has shown himself anxious to marry Thomasin. Now, though I have not encouraged him yet, I cannot conscientiously refuse him a chance any longer. I don't wish to be short with you; but I must be fair to him and to her.'

'Who is the man?' said Wildeve with surprise.

'One who has been in love with her longer than she has with you. He proposed to her two years ago. At that time she refused him.'

'Well?'

'He has seen her lately, and has asked me for permission to pay his addresses to her. She may not refuse him twice.'

'What is his name?'

Mrs Yeobright declined to say. 'He is a man Thomasin likes,' she added, 'and one whose constancy she respects at least. It seems to me that what she refused then he would be glad to get now. She is much annoyed at her awkward position.'

'She never once told me of this old lover.'

'The gentlest women are not such fools as to show *every* card.'

'Well, if she wants him I suppose she must have him.'

'It is easy enough to say that; but you don't see the difficulty. He wants her much more than she wants him; and before I can encourage anything of the sort I must have a clear understanding from you that you will not interfere to injure an arrangement which I promote in the belief that it is for the best. Suppose, when they are engaged, and everything is smoothly arranged for their marriage, that you should step between them and renew your suit? You might not win her back, but you might cause much unhappiness.'

'Of course I should do no such thing,' said Wildeve. 'But they are not engaged yet. How do you know that Thomasin would accept him?'

'That's a question I have carefully put to myself; and upon the whole the probabilities are in favour of her accepting him in time. I flatter myself that I have some influence over her. She is pliable, and I can be strong in my recommendations of him.'

'And in your disparagement of me at the same time.'

'Well, you may depend upon my not praising you,' she said drily. 'And if this seems like manoeuvring, you must remember that her position is peculiar, and that she has been hardly used. I shall also be helped in making the match by her own desire to escape from the humiliation of her present state; and a woman's pride in these cases will lead her a very great way. A little managing may be required to bring her round; but I am equal to that, provided that you agree to the one thing indispensable; that is, to make a distinct declaration that she is to think no more of you as a possible husband. That will pique her into accepting him.'

'I can hardly say that just now, Mrs Yeobright. It is so sudden.'

'And so my whole plan is interfered with! It is very inconvenient that you refuse to help my family even to the small extent of saying distinctly you will have nothing to do with us.'

Wildeve reflected uncomfortably. 'I confess I was not prepared for this,' he said. 'Of course I'll give her up if you wish, if it is necessary. But I thought I might be her husband.'

'We have heard that before.'

'Now, Mrs Yeobright, don't let us disagree. Give me a fair time. I don't want to stand in the way of any better chance she may have; only I wish you had let me know earlier. I will write to you or call in a day or two. Will that suffice?'

'Yes,' she replied, 'provided you promise not to communicate with Thomasin without my knowledge.'

'I promise that,' he said. And the interview then terminated, Mrs Yeobright returning homeward as she had come.

By far the greatest effect of her simple strategy on that day was, as often happens, in a quarter quite outside her view when arranging it. In the first place, her visit sent Wildeve the same evening after dark to Eustacia's house at Mistover.

At this hour the lonely dwelling was closely blinded and shuttered from the chill and darkness without. Wildeve's clandestine plan with her was to take a little gravel in his hand and hold it to the crevice at the top of the window-shutter, which was on the outside, so that it should fall with a gentle rustle, resembling that of a mouse, between shutter and glass. This precaution in attracting her attention was to avoid arousing the suspicions of her grandfather.

The soft words, 'I hear; wait for me,' in Eustacia's voice from within told him that she was alone.

He waited in his customary manner by walking round the enclosure and idling by the pool, for Wildeve was never asked into the house by his proud though condescending mistress. She showed no sign of coming out in a hurry. The time wore on, and he began to grow impatient. In the course of twenty minutes she appeared from round the corner, and advanced as if merely taking an airing.

'You would not have kept me so long had you known what I come about,' he said with bitterness. 'Still, you are worth waiting for.'

'What has happened?' said Eustacia. 'I did not know you were in trouble. I too am gloomy enough.'

'I am not in trouble,' said he. 'It is merely that affairs have come to a head, and I must take a clear course.'

'What course is that?' she asked with attentive interest.

'And can you forget so soon what I proposed to you the other night? Why, take you from this place, and carry you away with me abroad.'

'I have not forgotten. But why have you come so unexpectedly to repeat the question, when you only promised to come next Saturday? I thought I was to have plenty of time to consider.'

'Yes, but the situation is different now.'

'Explain to me.'

'I don't want to explain, for I may pain you.'

'But I must know the reason of this hurry.'

'It is simply my ardour, dear Eustacia. Everything is smooth now.'

'Then why are you so ruffled?'

'I am not aware of it. All is as it should be. Mrs Yeobright – but she is nothing to us.'

'Ah, I knew she had something to do with it! Come, I don't like reserve.'

'No – she has nothing. She only says she wishes me to give up Thomasin because another man is anxious to marry her. The woman, now she no longer needs me, actually shows off!' Wildeve's vexation had escaped him in spite of himself.

Eustacia was silent a long while. 'You are in the awkward position of an official who is no longer wanted,' she said in a changed tone.

'It seems so. But I have not yet seen Thomasin.'

'And that irritates you. Don't deny it, Damon. You are actually nettled by this slight from an unexpected quarter.'

'Well?'

'And you come to get me because you cannot get her. This is certainly a new position altogether. I am to be a stop-gap.'

'Please remember that I proposed the same thing the other day.'

Eustacia again remained in a sort of stupefied silence. What curious feeling was this coming over her? Was it really possible that her interest in Wildeve had been so entirely the result of antagonism that the glory and the dream departed from the man with the first sound that he was no longer coveted by her rival? She was, then, secure of him at last. Thomasin no longer required him. What a humiliating victory! He loved her best, she thought; and yet – dared she to murmur such treacherous criticism ever so softly? – what was the man worth whom a woman inferior to herself did not value? The sentiment which lurks more or less in all animate nature – that of not desiring the undesired of others – was lively as a passion in the super-subtle, epicurean heart of Eustacia. Her social superiority over him, which hitherto had scarcely ever impressed her, became unpleasantly insistent, and for the first time she felt that she had stooped in loving him.

'Well, darling, you agree?' said Wildeve.

'If it could be London, or even Budmouth, instead of America,' she murmured languidly. 'Well, I will think. It is too great a thing for me to decide offhand. I wish I hated the heath less – or loved it more.'

'You can be painfully frank. You loved me a month ago warmly enough to go anywhere with me.'

'And you loved Thomasin.'

'Yes, perhaps that was where the reason lay,' he returned, with almost a sneer. 'I don't hate her now.'

'Exactly. The only thing is that you can no longer get her.'

'Come – no taunts, Eustacia, or we shall quarrel. If you don't agree to go with me, and agree shortly, I shall go by myself.'

'Or try Thomasin again. Damon, how strange it seems that you could have married her or me indifferently, and only have come to me because I am – cheapest! Yes, yes – it is true. There was a time when I should have exclaimed against a man of that sort, and been quite wild; but it is all past now.'

'Will you go, dearest? Come secretly with me to Bristol, marry me, and turn our backs upon this dog-hole of England for ever? Say Yes.'

'I want to get away from here at almost any cost,' she said with weariness, 'but I don't like to go with you. Give me more time to decide.'

'I have already,' said Wildeve. 'Well, I give you one more week.'

'A little longer, so that I may tell you decisively. I have to consider so many things. Fancy Thomasin being anxious to get rid of you! I cannot forget it.'

'Never mind that. Say Monday week. I will be here precisely at this time.'

'Let it be at Rainbarrow,' said she. 'This is too near home; my grandfather may be walking out.'

'Thank you, dear. On Monday week at this time I will be at the Barrow. Till then good-bye.'

'Good-bye. No, no, you must not touch me now. Shaking hands is enough till I have made up my mind.'

Eustacia watched his shadowy form till it had disappeared. She placed her hand to her forehead and breathed heavily; and then her rich, romantic lips parted under that homely impulse – a yawn. She was immediately angry at having betrayed even to herself the possible evanescence of her passion for him. She could not admit at once that she might have over-estimated Wildeve, for to perceive his mediocrity now was to admit her own great folly heretofore. And the discovery that she was the owner of a disposition so purely that of the dog in the manger had something in it which at first made her ashamed.

The fruit of Mrs Yeobright's diplomacy was indeed remarkable, though not as yet of the kind she had anticipated. It had appreciably influenced Wildeve, but it was influencing Eustacia far more. Her lover was no longer to her an exciting man whom many women strove for, and herself could only retain by striving with them. He was a superfluity.

She went indoors in that peculiar state of misery which is not exactly grief, and which especially attends the dawnings of reason in the latter days of an ill-judged, transient love. To be conscious that the end of the dream is approaching, and yet has not absolutely come, is one of the most wearisome as well as the most curious stages along the course between the beginning of a passion and its end.

Her grandfather had returned, and was busily engaged in pouring some gallons of newly arrived rum into the square bottles of his square cellaret. Whenever these home supplies were exhausted he would go to the Quiet Woman, and, standing with his back to the fire, grog in hand, tell remarkable stories of how he had lived seven years under the water-line of his ship, and other naval wonders, to the natives, who hoped too earnestly for a treat of ale from the teller to exhibit any doubts of his truth.

He had been there this evening. 'I suppose you have heard the Egdon news, Eustacia?' he said, without looking up from the bottles. 'The men have been talking about it at the Woman as if it were of national importance.'

'I have heard none,' she said.

'Young Clym Yeobright, as they call him, is coming home next week to spend Christmas with his mother. He is a fine fellow by this time, it seems. I suppose you remember him?'

'I never saw him in my life.'

'Ah, true; he left before you came here. I well remember him as a promising boy.'

'Where has he been living all these years?'

'In that rookery of pomp and vanity, Paris, I believe.'

BOOK SECOND

THE ARRIVAL

* I *

Tidings of the Comer

On fine days at this time of the year, and earlier, certain ephemeral operations were apt to disturb, in their trifling way, the majestic calm of Egdon Heath. They were activities which, beside those of a town, a village, or even a farm, would have appeared as the ferment of stagnation merely, a creeping of the flesh of somnolence. But here, away from comparisons, shut in by the stable hills, among which mere walking had the novelty of pageantry, and where any man could imagine himself to be Adam without the least difficulty, they attracted the attention of every bird within eyeshot, every reptile not yet asleep, and set the surrounding rabbits curiously watching from hillocks at a safe distance.

The performance was that of bringing together and building into a stack the furze-faggots which Humphrey had been cutting for the captain's use during the foregoing fine days. The stack was at the end of the dwelling, and the man engaged in building it were Humphrey and Sam, the old man looking on.

It was a fine and quiet afternoon, about three o'clock; but the winter solstice having stealthily come on, the lowness of the sun caused the hour to seem later than it actually was, there being little here to remind an inhabitant that he must unlearn his summer experience of the sky as a dial. In the course of many days and weeks sunrise had advanced its quarters from north-east to south-east, sunset had receded from north-west to south-west; but Egdon had hardly heeded the change.

Eustacia was indoors in the dining-room, which was really more like a kitchen, having a stone floor and a gaping chimney-corner. The air was still, and while she lingered a moment here alone sounds of voices in conversation came to her ears directly down the chimney. She entered the recess, and, listening, looked up the old irregular shaft, with its cavernous hollows, where the smoke blundered about on its way to the square bit of sky at the top, from which the daylight struck down with a pallid glare upon the pattern of soot draping the flue as seaweed drapes a rocky fissure.

She remembered: the furze-stack not far from the chimney, and the voices were those of the workers.

Her grandfather joined in the conversation. 'That lad ought never to have left home. His father's occupation would have suited him best, and the boy should have followed on. I don't believe in these new moves in families. My father was a sailor, so was I, and so should my son have been if I had had one.'

'The place he's been living at is Paris,' said Humphrey, 'and they tell me 'tis where the king's head was cut off years ago. My poor mother used to tell me about that business. "Hummy," she used to say, "I was a young maid then, and as I was at home ironing mother's caps one afternoon, the parson came in and said, 'They've cut the king's head off, Jane; and what 'twill be next God knows.' " '

'A good many of us knew as well as He before long,' said the captain, chuckling. 'I lived seven years under water on account of it in my boyhood – in that damned surgery of the *Triumph*, seeing men brought down to the cockpit with their legs and arms blown to Jericho . . . And so the young man has settled in Paris. Manager to a diamond merchant, or some such thing, is he not?'

'Yes, sir, that's it. 'Tis a blazing great business that he belongs to, so I've heard his mother say – like a king's palace, as far as diments go.'

'I can well mind when he left home,' said Sam.

' 'Tis a good thing for the feller,' said Humphrey. 'A sight of times better to be selling diments than nobbling about here.'

'It must cost a good few shillings to deal at such a place.'

'A good few indeed, my man,' replied the captain. 'Yes, you may make away with a deal of money and be neither drunkard nor glutton.'

'They say, too, that Clym Yeobright is become a real perusing man, with the strangest notions about things. There, that's because he went to school early, such as the school was.'

'Strange notions, has he?' said the old man. 'Ah, there's too much of that sending to school in these days! It only does harm. Every gatepost and barn's door you come to is sure to have some bad word or other chalked upon it by the young rascals: a woman can hardly pass for shame some times. If they'd never been taught how to write they wouldn't have been able to scribble such villainy. Their fathers couldn't do it, and the country was all the better for it.'

'Now, I should think, cap'n, that Miss Eustacia had about as much in her head that comes from books as anybody about here?'

'Perhaps if Miss Eustacia, too, had less romantic nonsense in her head it would be better for her,' said the captain shortly; after which he walked away.

'I say, Sam,' observed Humphrey when the old man was gone, 'she and Clym Yeobright would make a very pretty pigeon-pair – hey? If they wouldn't I'll be dazed! Both of one mind about niceties for certain, and learned in print, and always thinking about high doctrine – there couldn't be a better couple if they were made o' purpose. Clym's family is as good as hers. His father was a farmer, that's true; but his mother was a sort of lady, as we know. Nothing would please me better than to see them two man and wife.'

'They'd look very natty, arm-in-crook together, and their best clothes on, whether or no, if he's at all the well-favoured fellow he used to be.'

'They would,' said Humphrey. 'Well, I should like to see the chap terrible much after so many years. If I knew for certain when he was coming I'd stroll out three or four miles to meet him and help carry anything for'n; though I suppose he's altered from the boy he was. They say he can talk French as fast as a maid can eat blackberries; and if so, depend upon it we who have stayed at home shall seem no more than scroff in his eyes.'

'Coming across the water to Budmouth by steamer, isn't he?'

'Yes; but how he's coming from Budmouth I don't know.'

'That's a bad trouble about his cousin Thomasin. I wonder such a nice-notioned fellow as Clym likes to come home into it. What a nunnywatch we were in, to be sure, when we heard they weren't married at all, after singing to 'em as man and wife that night! Be dazed if I should like a relation of mine to have been made such a fool of by a man. It makes the family look small.'

'Yes. Poor maid, her heart has ached enough about it. Her health is suffering from it, I hear, for she will bide entirely indoors. We never see her out now, scampering over the furze with a face as red as a rose, as she used to do.'

'I've heard she wouldn't have Wildeve now if he asked her.'

'You have? 'Tis news to me.'

While the furze-gatherers had desultorily conversed thus Eustacia's face gradually bent to the hearth in a profound reverie, her toe unconsciously tapping the dry turf which lay burning at her feet.

The subject of their discourse had been keenly interesting to her. A young and clever man was coming into that lonely heath from, of all contrasting places in the world, Paris. It was like a man coming from heaven. More singular still, the heathmen had instinctively coupled her and this man together in their minds as a pair born for each other.

That five minutes of overhearing furnished Eustacia with visions enough to fill the whole blank afternoon. Such sudden alternations from mental vacuity do sometimes occur thus quietly. She could never have believed in the morning that her colourless inner world would before night become as animated as water under a microscope, and that without the arrival of a single visitor. The words of Sam and Humphrey on the harmony between the unknown and herself had on her mind the effect of the invading Bard's prelude in the 'Castle of Indolence', at which myriads of imprisoned shapes arose where had previously appeared the stillness of a void.

Involved in these imaginings she knew nothing of time. When she became conscious of externals it was dusk. The furze-rick was finished; the men had gone home. Eustacia went upstairs, thinking that she would take a walk at this her usual time; and she determined that her walk should be in the direction of Blooms-End, the birthplace of young Yeobright and the present home of his mother. She had no reason for walking elsewhere, and why should she not go that way? The scene of a day-dream is sufficient for a pilgrimage at nineteen. To look at the palings before the Yeobrights' house had the dignity of a necessary performance. Strange that such a piece of idling should have seemed an important errand.

She put on her bonnet, and, leaving the house, descended the hill on the side towards Blooms-End, where she walked slowly along the valley for a distance of a mile and a half. This brought her to a spot in which the green bottom of the dale began to widen, the furze bushes to recede yet further from the path on each side, till they were diminished to an isolated one here and there by the increasing fertility of the soil. Beyond the irregular carpet of grass was a row of white palings, which marked the verge of the heath in this latitude. They showed upon the dusky scene that they bordered as distinctly as white lace on velvet. Behind the white palings was a little garden; behind the garden an old, irregular, thatched house, facing the heath, and commanding a full view of the valley. This was the obscure, removed spot to which was about to return a man whose latter life had been passed in the French capital – the centre and vortex of the fashionable world.

* II *

The People at Blooms-End Make Ready

ALL that afternoon the expected arrival of the subject of Eustacia's ruminations created a bustle of preparation at Blooms-End. Thomasin had been persuaded by her aunt, and by an instinctive impulse of loyalty towards her cousin Clym, to bestir herself on his account with an alacrity unusual in her during these most sorrowful days of her life. At the time that Eustacia was listening to the rickmakers' conversation on Clym's return, Thomasin was climbing into a loft over her aunt's fuel house, where the store-apples were kept, to search out the best and largest of them for the coming holiday-time.

The loft was lighted by a semicircular hole, through which the pigeons crept to their lodgings in the same high quarters of the premises; and from this hole the sun shone in a bright yellow patch upon the figure of the maiden as she knelt and plunged her naked arms into the soft brown fern, which, from its abundance, was used on Egdon in packing away stores of all kinds. The pigeons were flying about her head with the greatest unconcern, and the face of her aunt was just visible above the floor of the loft, lit by a few stray motes of light, as she stood half-way up the ladder, looking at a spot into which she was not climber enough to venture.

'Now a few russets, Tamsin. He used to like them almost as much as ribstones.'

Thomasin turned and rolled aside the fern from another nook, where more mellow fruit greeted her with its ripe smell. Before picking them out she stopped a moment.

'Dear Clym, I wonder how your face looks now?' she said, gazing abstractedly at the pigeon-hole, which admitted the sunlight so directly upon her brown hair and transparent tissues that it almost seemed to shine through her.

'If he could have been dear to you in another way,' said Mrs Yeobright from the ladder, 'this might have been a happy meeting.'

'Is there any use in saying what can do no good, aunt?'

'Yes,' said her aunt, with some warmth. 'To thoroughly fill the air with the past misfortune, so that other girls may take warning and keep clear of it.'

Thomasin lowered her face to the apples again. 'I am a warning to others, just as thieves and drunkards and gamblers are,' she said in a low voice. 'What a class to belong to! Do I really belong to them? 'Tis absurd! Yet why, aunt, does everybody keep on making me think that I do, by the way they behave towards me? Why don't people judge me by my acts? Now, look at me as I kneel here, picking up these apples – do I look like a lost woman? . . . I wish all good women were as good as I!' she added vehemently.

'Strangers don't see you as I do,' said Mrs Yeobright; 'they judge from false report. Well, it is a silly job, and I am partly to blame.'

'How quickly a rash thing can be done!' replied the girl. Her lips were quivering, and tears so crowded themselves into her eyes that she could hardly distinguish apples from fern as she continued industriously searching to hide her weakness.

'As soon as you have finished getting the apples,' her aunt said, descending the ladder, 'come down, and we'll go for the holly. There is nobody on the heath this afternoon, and you need not fear being stared at. We must get some berries, or Clym will never believe in our preparations.'

Thomasin came down when the apples were collected, and together they went through the white palings to the heath beyond. The open hills were airy and clear, and the remote atmosphere appeared, as it often appears on a fine winter day, in distinct planes of illumination independently toned, the rays which lit the nearer tracts of landscape streaming visibly across those further off; a stratum of ensaffroned light was imposed on a stratum of deep blue, and behind these lay still remoter scenes wrapped in frigid grey.

They reached the place where the hollies grew, which was in a conical pit, so that the tops of the trees were not much above the general level of the ground. Thomasin stepped up into a fork of one of the bushes, as she had done under happier circumstances on many similar occasions, and with a small chopper that they had brought she began to lop off the heavily-berried boughs.

'Don't scratch your face,' said her aunt, who stood at the edge of the pit, regarding the girl as she held on amid the glistening green and scarlet masses of the tree. 'Will you walk with me to meet him this evening?'

'I should like to. Else it would seem as if I had forgotten him,' said Thomasin, tossing out a bough. 'Not that that would matter much; I belong to one man; nothing can alter that. And that man I must marry, for my pride's sake.'

'I am afraid –' began Mrs Yeobright.

'Ah, you think, "That weak girl – how is she going to get a man to marry her when she chooses?" But let me tell you one thing, aunt: Mr Wildeve is not a profligate man, any more than I am an improper woman. He has an unfortunate manner, and doesn't try to make people like him if they don't wish to do it of their own accord.'

'Thomasin,' said Mrs Yeobright quietly, fixing her eye upon her niece, 'do you think you deceive me in your defence of Mr Wildeve?'

'How do you mean?'

'I have long had a suspicion that your love for him has changed its colour since you have found him not to be the saint you thought him, and that you act a part to me.'

'He wished to marry me, and I wish to marry him.'

'Now, I put it to you: would you at this present moment agree to be his wife if that had not happened to entangle you with him?'

Thomasin looked into the tree and appeared much disturbed. 'Aunt,' she said presently, 'I have, I think, a right to refuse to answer that question.'

'Yes, you have.'

'You may think what you choose. I have never implied to you by word or deed that I have grown to think otherwise of him, and I never will. And I shall marry him.'

'Well, wait till he repeats his offer. I think he may do it, now that he knows – something I told him. I don't for a moment dispute that it is the most proper thing for you to marry him. Much as I have objected to him in bygone days, I agree with you now, you may be sure. It is the only way out of a false position, and a very galling one.'

'What did you tell him?'

'That he was standing in the way of another lover of yours.'

'Aunt,' said Thomasin, with round eyes, 'what *do* you mean?'

'Don't be alarmed; it was my duty. I can say no more about it now, but when it is over I will tell you exactly what I said, and why I said it.'

Thomasin was perforce content.

'And you will keep the secret of my would-be marriage from Clym for the present?' she next asked.

'I have given my word to. But what is the use of it? He must soon know what has happened. A mere look at your face will show him that something is wrong.'

Thomasin turned and regarded her aunt from the tree. 'Now, hearken to me,' she said, her delicate voice expanding into firmness by a force which was other than physical. 'Tell him nothing. If he finds out that I am not worthy to be his cousin, let him. But, since he loved me once, we will not pain him by telling him my trouble too soon. The air is full of the story, I know; but gossips will not dare to speak of it to him for the first few days. His closeness to me is the very thing that will hinder the tale from reaching him early. If I am not made safe from sneers in a week or two I will tell him myself.'

The earnestness with which Thomasin spoke prevented further objections. Her aunt simply said, 'Very well. He should by rights have been told at the time that the wedding was going to be. He will never forgive you for your secrecy.'

'Yes, he will, when he knows it was because I wished to spare him, and that I did not expect him home so soon. And you must not let me stand in the way of your Christmas party. Putting it off would only make matters worse.'

'Of course I shall not. I do not wish to show myself beaten before all Egdon, and the sport of a man like Wildeve. We have enough berries now, I think, and we had better take them home. By the time we have decked the house with this and hung up the mistletoe, we must think of starting to meet him.'

Thomasin came out of the tree, shook from her hair and dress the loose berries which had fallen thereon, and went down the hill with her aunt, each woman bearing half the gathered boughs. It was now nearly four o'clock, and the sunlight was leaving the vales. When the west grew red the two relatives came again from the house and plunged into the heath in a different direction from the first, towards a point in the distant highway along which the expected man was to return.

* III *

How a Little Sound Produced a Great Dream

EUSTACIA stood just within the heath, straining her eyes in the direction of Mrs Yeobright's house and premises. No light, sound, or movement was perceptible there. The evening was chilly; the spot was dark and lonely. She inferred that the guest had not yet come; and after lingering ten or fifteen minutes she turned again towards home.

She had not far retraced her steps when sounds in front of her betokened the approach of persons in conversation along the same path. Soon their heads became visible against the sky. They were walking slowly; and though it was too dark for much discovery of character from aspect, the gait of them showed that they were not workers on the heath. Eustacia stepped a little out of the foot-track to let them pass. They were two women and a man; and the voices of the women were those of Mrs Yeobright and Thomasin.

They went by her, and at the moment of passing appeared to discern her dusky form. There came to her ears in a masculine voice, 'Good night!'

She murmured a reply, glided by them, and turned round. She could not, for a moment, believe that chance, unrequested, had brought into her presence the soul of the house she had gone to inspect, the man without whom her inspection would not have been thought of.

She strained her eyes to see them, but was unable. Such was her intentness, however, that it seemed as if her ears were performing the functions of seeing as well as hearing. This extension of power can almost be believed in at such moments. The deaf Dr Kitto was probably under the influence of a parallel fancy when he described his body as having become, by long endeavour, so sensitive to vibrations that he had gained the power of perceiving by it as by ears.

She could follow every word that the ramblers uttered. They were talking no secrets. They were merely indulging in the ordinary vivacious chat of relatives who have long been parted in person though not in soul. But it was not to the words that Eustacia listened; she could not even have recalled, a few minutes later, what the words were. It was to the alternating voice that gave out about one-tenth of them – the voice that had wished her good night. Sometimes this throat uttered Yes, sometimes it uttered No; sometimes it made inquiries about a timeworn denizen of the place. Once it surprised her notions by remarking upon the friendliness and geniality written in the faces of the hills around.

The three voices passed on, and decayed and died out upon her ear. This much had been granted her; and all besides withheld. No event could have been more exciting. During the greater part of the afternoon she had been entrancing herself by imagining the fascination which must attend a man come direct from beautiful Paris – laden with its atmosphere, familiar with its charms. And this man had greeted her.

With the departure of the figures the profuse articulations of the women wasted away from her memory; but the accents of the other stayed on. Was there anything in the voice of Mrs Yeobright's son – for Clym it was – startling as a sound? No: it was simply comprehensive. All emotional things were possible to the speaker of that 'good night'. Eustacia's imagination supplied the rest – except the solution to one riddle. What *could* the tastes of that man be who saw friendliness and geniality in these shaggy hills?

On such occasions as this a thousand ideas pass through a highly charged woman's head; and they indicate themselves on her face; but the changes, though actual, are minute. Eustacia's features went through a rhythmical succession of them. She glowed; remembering the mendacity of the imagination, she flagged; then she freshened; then she fired; then she cooled again. It was a cycle of aspects, produced by a cycle of visions.

Eustacia entered her own house; she was excited. Her grandfather was enjoying himself over the fire, raking about the ashes and exposing the red-hot surface of the turves, so that their lurid glare irradiated the chimney-corner with the hues of a furnace.

'Why is it that we are never friendly with the Yeobrights?' she said, coming forward and stretching her soft hands over the warmth. 'I wish we were. They seem to be very nice people.'

'Be hanged if I know why,' said the captain. 'I liked the old man well enough, though he was as rough as a hedge. But you would never have cared to go there, even if you might have, I am well sure.'

'Why shouldn't I?'

'Your town tastes would find them far too countrified. They sit in the kitchen, drink mead and elderwine, and sand the floor to keep it clean. A sensible way of life; but how would you like it?'

'I thought Mrs Yeobright was a ladylike woman? A curate's daughter, was she not?'

'Yes; but she was obliged to live as her husband did; and I suppose she has taken kindly to it by this time. Ah, I recollect that I once accidentally offended her, and I have never seen her since.'

That night was an eventful one to Eustacia's brain, and one which she hardly ever forgot. She dreamt a dream; and few human beings, from Nebuchadnezzar to the Swaffham tinker, ever dreamt a more remarkable one. Such an elaborately developed, perplexing, exciting dream was certainly never dreamed by a girl in Eustacia's situation before. It had as many ramifications as the Cretan labyrinth, as many fluctuations as the Northern Lights, as much colour as a parterre in June, and was as crowded with figures as a coronation. To Queen Scheherazade the dream might have seemed not far removed from commonplace; and to a girl just returned from all the courts of Europe it might have seemed not more than interesting. But amid the circumstances of Eustacia's life it was as wonderful as a dream could be.

There was, however, gradually evolved from its transformation scenes a less extravagant episode, in which the heath dimly appeared behind the general brilliancy of the action. She was dancing to wondrous music, and her partner was the man in silver armour who had accompanied her through the previous fantastic changes, the visor of his helmet being closed. The mazes of the dance were ecstatic. Soft whispering came into her ear from under the radiant helmet, and she felt like a woman in Paradise. Suddenly these two wheeled out from the mass of dancers, dived into one of the pools of the heath, and came out somewhere beneath into an iridescent hollow, arched with rainbows. 'It must be here,' said the voice by her side, and blushingly looking up she saw him removing his casque to kiss her. At that moment there was a cracking noise, and his figure fell into fragments like a pack of cards.

She cried aloud, 'O that I had seen his face!'

Eustacia awoke. The cracking had been that of the window-shutter downstairs, which the maid-servant was opening to let in the day, now slowly increasing to Nature's meagre allowance at this sickly time of the year. 'O that I had seen his face!' she said again. ' 'Twas meant for Mr Yeobright!'

When she became cooler she perceived that many of the phases of the dream had naturally arisen out of the images and fancies of the day before. But this detracted little from its interest, which lay in the excellent fuel it provided for newly kindled fervour. She was at the modulating point between indifference and love, at the stage called 'having a fancy for'. It occurs once in the history of the most gigantic passions, and it is a period when they are in the hands of the weakest will.

The perfervid woman was by this time half in love with a vision. The fantastic nature of her passion, which lowered her as an intellect, raised her as a soul. If she had had a little more self-control she would have attenuated the emotion to nothing by sheer reasoning, and so have killed it off. If she had had a little less pride she might have gone and circumambulated the Yeobrights' premises at Blooms-End at any maidenly sacrifice until she had seen him. But Eustacia did neither of these things. She acted as the most exemplary might have acted, being so influenced; she took an airing twice or thrice a day upon the Egdon hills, and kept her eyes employed.

The first occasion passed, and he did not come that way.

She promenaded a second time, and was again the sole wanderer there.

The third time there was a dense fog: she looked around, but without much hope. Even if he had been walking within twenty yards of her she could not have seen him.

At the fourth attempt to encounter him it began to rain in torrents, and she turned back.

The fifth sally was in the afternoon: it was fine, and she remained out long, walking to the very top of the valley in which Blooms-End lay. She saw the white paling about half a mile off; but he did not appear. It was almost with heart-sickness that she came home, and with a sense of shame at her weakness. She resolved to look for the man from Paris no more.

But Providence is nothing if not coquettish; and no sooner had Eustacia formed this resolve than the opportunity came which, while sought, had been entirely withholden.

* IV *

Eustacia Is Led On to an Adventure

IN the evening of this last day of expectation, which was the twenty-third of December, Eustacia was at home alone. She had passed the recent hour in lamenting over a rumour newly come to her ears – that Yeobright's visit to his mother was to be of short duration, and would end some time the next week. 'Naturally,' she said to herself. A man in the full swing of his activities in a gay city could not afford to linger long on Egdon Heath. That she would behold face to face the owner of the awakening voice within the limits of such a holiday was most unlikely, unless she were to haunt the environs of his mother's house like a robin, to do which was difficult and unseemly.

The customary expedient of provincial girls and men in such circumstances is churchgoing. In an ordinary village or country town one can safely calculate that, either on Christmas-day or the Sunday contiguous, any native home for the holidays, who has not through age or *ennui* lost the appetite for seeing and being seen, will turn up in some pew or other, shining with hope, self-consciousness, and new clothes. Thus the congregation on Christmas morning is mostly a Tussaud collection of celebrities who have been born in the neighbourhood. Hither the mistress, left neglected at home all the year, can steal and observe the development of the returned lover who has forgotten her, and think as she watches him over her prayer-book that he may throb with a renewed fidelity when novelties have lost their charm. And hither a comparatively recent settler like Eustacia may betake herself to scrutinize the person of a native son who left home before her advent upon the scene, and consider if the friendship of his parents be worth cultivating during his next absence in order to secure a knowledge of him on his next return.

But these tender schemes were not feasible among the scattered inhabitants of Egdon Heath. In name they were parishioners, but virtually they belonged to no parish at all. People who came to these few isolated houses to keep Christmas with their friends remained in their friends' chimney-corners drinking mead and other comforting liquors till they left again for good and all. Rain, snow, ice, mud everywhere around, they did not care to trudge two or three miles to sit wet-footed and splashed to the nape of their necks among those who, though in some measure neighbours, lived close to the church, and entered it clean and dry. Eustacia knew it was ten to one that Clym Yeobright would go to no church at all during his few days of leave, and that it would be a waste of labour for her to go driving the pony and gig over a bad road in hope to see him there.

It was dusk, and she was sitting by the fire in the dining-room or hall, which they occupied at this time of the year in preference to the parlour, because of its large hearth, constructed for turf-fires, a fuel the captain was partial to in the winter season. The only visible articles in the room were those on the window-sill, which showed their shapes against the low sky: the middle article being the old hour-glass, and the other two a pair of ancient British urns which had been dug from a barrow near, and were used as flower-pots for two razor-leaved cactuses. Somebody knocked at the door. The servant was out; so was her grandfather. The person, after waiting a minute, came in and tapped at the door of the room.

'Who's there?' said Eustacia.

'Please, Cap'n Vye, will you let us –'

Eustacia arose and went to the door. 'I cannot allow you to come in so boldly. You should have waited.'

'The cap'n said I might come in without any fuss,' was answered in a lad's pleasant voice.

'Oh, did he?' said Eustacia more gently. 'What do you want, Charley?'

'Please will your grandfather lend us his fuel-house to try over our parts in, tonight at seven o'clock?'

'What, are you one of the Egdon mummers for this year?'

'Yes, miss. The cap'n used to let the old mummers practise here.'

'I know it. Yes, you may use the fuel-house if you like,' said Eustacia languidly.

The choice of Captain Vye's fuel-house as the scene of rehearsal was dictated by the fact that his dwelling was nearly in the centre of the heath. The fuel-house was as roomy as a barn, and was a most desirable place for such a purpose. The lads who formed the company of players lived at different scattered points around, and by meeting in this spot the distances to be traversed by all the comers would be about equally proportioned.

For mummers and mumming Eustacia had the greatest contempt. The mummers themselves were not afflicted with any such feeling for their art, though at the same time they were not enthusiastic. A traditional pastime is to be distinguished from a mere revival in no more striking feature than in this, that while in the revival all is excitement and fervour, the survival is carried on with a stolidity and absence of stir which sets one wondering why a thing that is done so perfunctorily should be kept up at all. Like Balaam and other unwilling prophets, the agents seem moved by an inner compulsion to say and do their allotted parts whether they will or no. This unweeting manner of performance is the true ring by which, in this refurbishing age, a fossilized survival may be known from a spurious reproduction.

The piece was the well-known play of 'Saint George', and all who were behind the scenes assisted in the preparations, including the women of each household. Without the co-operation of sisters and sweethearts the dresses were likely to be a failure; but on the other hand, this class of assistance was not without its drawbacks. The girls could never be brought to respect tradition in designing and decorating the armour; they insisted on attaching loops and bows of silk and velvet in any situation pleasing to their taste. Gorget, gusset, basinet, cuirass, gauntlet, sleeve, all alike in the view of these feminine eyes were practicable spaces whereon to sew scraps of fluttering colour.

It might be that Joe, who fought on the side of Christendom, had a sweetheart, and that Jim, who fought on the side of the Moslem, had one likewise. During the making of the costumes it would come to the knowledge of Joe's sweetheart that Jim's was putting brilliant silk scallops at the bottom of her lover's surcoat, in addition to the ribbons of the visor, the bars of which, being invariably formed of coloured strips about half an inch wide hanging before the face, were mostly of that material. Joe's sweetheart straightway placed brilliant silk on the scallops of the hem in question, and, going a little further, added ribbon tufts to the shoulder pieces. Jim's, not to be outdone, would affix bows and rosettes everywhere.

The result was that in the end the Valiant Soldier, of the Christian army, was distinguished by no peculiarity of accoutrement from the Turkish Knight; and what was worse, on a casual view Saint George himself might be mistaken for his deadly enemy, the Saracen. The guisers themselves, though inwardly regretting this confusion of persons, could not afford to offend those by whose assistance they so largely profited, and the innovations were allowed to stand.

There was, it is true, a limit to this tendency to uniformity. The Leech or Doctor preserved his character intact: his darker habiliments, peculiar hat, and the bottle of physic slung under his arm, could never be mistaken. And the same might be said of the conventional figure of Father Christmas, with his gigantic club, an older man, who accompanied the band as general protector in long night journeys from parish to parish, and was bearer of the purse.

Seven o'clock, the hour of the rehearsal, came round, and in a short time Eustacia could hear voices in the fuel-house. To dissipate in some trifling measure her abiding sense of the murkiness of human life she went to the 'linhay' or lean-to shed, which formed the root-store of their dwelling and abutted on the fuel-house. Here was a small rough hole in the mud wall, originally made for pigeons, through which the interior of the next shed could be viewed. A light came from it now; and Eustacia stepped upon a stool to look in upon the scene.

On a ledge in the fuel-house stood three tall rush-lights, and by the light of them seven or eight lads were marching about, haranguing, and confusing each other, in endeavours to perfect themselves in the play. Humphrey and Sam, the furze and turf cutters, were there looking on, so also was Timothy Fairway, who leant against the wall and prompted the boys from memory, interspersing among the set words remarks and anecdotes of the superior days when he and others were the Egdon mummers-elect that these lads were now.

'Well, ye be as well up to it as ever ye will be,' he said. 'Not that such mumming would have passed in our time. Harry as the Saracen should strut a bit more, and John needn't holler his inside out. Beyond that perhaps you'll do. Have you got all your clothes ready?'

'We shall by Monday.'

'Your first outing will be Monday night, I suppose?'

'Yes. At Mrs Yeobright's.'

'Oh, Mrs Yeobright's. What makes her want to see ye? I should think a middle-aged woman was tired of mumming.'

'She's got up a bit of a party, because 'tis the first Christmas that her son Clym has been home for a long time.'

'To be sure, to be sure – her party! I am going myself. I almost forgot it, upon my life.'

Eustacia's face flagged. There was to be a party at the Yeobrights'; she, naturally, had nothing to do with it. She was a stranger to all such local gatherings, and had always held them as scarcely appertaining to her sphere. But had she been going, what an opportunity would have been afforded her of seeing the man whose influence was penetrating her like summer sun! To increase that influence was coveted excitement; to cast it off might be to regain serenity: to leave it as it stood was tantalizing.

The lads and men prepared to leave the premises, and Eustacia returned to her fireside. She was immersed in thought, but not for long. In a few minutes the lad Charley, who had come to ask permission to use the place, returned with the key to the kitchen. Eustacia heard him, and opening the door into the passage said, 'Charley, come here.'

The lad was surprised. He entered the front room not without blushing; for he, like many, had felt the power of this girl's face and form.

She pointed to a seat by the fire, and entered the other side of the chimney-corner herself. It could be seen in her face that whatever motive she might have had in asking the youth indoors would soon appear.

'Which part do you play, Charley – the Turkish Knight, do you not?' inquired the beauty, looking across the smoke of the fire to him on the other side.

'Yes, miss, the Turkish Knight,' he replied diffidently.

'Is yours a long part?'

'Nine speeches, about.'

'Can you repeat them to me? If so I should like to hear them.'

The lad smiled into the glowing turf and began –

> 'Here come I, a Turkish Knight,
> Who learnt in Turkish land to fight,'

continuing the discourse throughout the scenes to the concluding catastrophe of his fall by the hand of Saint George.

Eustacia had occasionally heard the part recited before. When the lad ended she began, precisely in the same words, and ranted on without hitch or divergence till she too reached the end. It was the same thing, yet how different. Like in form, it had the added softness and finish of a Raffaelle after Perugino, which, while faithfully reproducing the original subject, entirely distances the original art.

Charley's eyes rounded with surprise. 'Well, you be a clever lady!' he said, in admiration. 'I've been three weeks learning mine.'

'I have heard it before,' she quietly observed. 'Now, would you do anything to please me, Charley?'

'I'd do a good deal, miss.'

'Would you let me play your part for one night?'

'O, miss! But your woman's gown – you couldn't.'

'I can get boy's clothes – at least all that would be wanted besides the mumming dress. What should I have to give you to lend me your things, to let me take your place for an hour or two on Monday night, and on no account to say a word about who or what I am? You would, of course, have to excuse yourself from playing that night, and to say that somebody – a cousin of Miss Vye's – would act for you. The other mummers have never spoken to me in their lives, so that it would be safe enough; and if it were not, I should not mind. Now, what must I give you to agree to this? Half a crown?'

The youth shook his head.

'Five shillings?'

He shook his head again. 'Money won't do it,' he said, brushing the iron head of the fire-dog with the hollow of his hand.

'What will, then, Charley?' said Eustacia in a disappointed tone.

'You know what you forbad me at the maypoling, miss,' murmured the lad, without looking at her, and still stroking the fire-dog's head.

'Yes,' said Eustacia, with a little more hauteur. 'You wanted to join hands with me in the ring, if I recollect?'

'Half an hour of that, and I'll agree, miss.'

Eustacia regarded the youth steadfastly. He was three years younger than herself, but apparently not backward for his age. 'Half an hour of what?' she said, though she guessed what.

'Holding your hand in mine.'

She was silent. 'Make it a quarter of an hour,' she said.

'Yes, Miss Eustacia – I will, if I may kiss it too. A quarter of an hour. And I'll swear to do the best I can to let you take my place without anybody knowing. Don't you think somebody might know your tongue, miss?'

'It is possible. But I will put a pebble in my mouth to make it less likely. Very well; you shall be allowed to have my hand as soon as you bring the dress and your sword and staff. I don't want you any longer now.'

Charley departed, and Eustacia felt more and more interest in life. Here was something to do: here was some one to see, and a charmingly adventurous way to see him. 'Ah,' she said to herself, 'want of an object to live for – that's all is the matter with me!'

Eustacia's manner was as a rule of a slumberous sort, her passions being of the massive rather than the vivacious kind. But when aroused she would make a dash which, just for the time, was not unlike the move of a naturally lively person.

On the question of recognition she was somewhat indifferent. By the acting lads themselves she was not likely to be known. With the guests who might be assembled she was hardly so secure. Yet detection, after all, would be no such dreadful thing. The fact only could be detected, her true motive never. It would be instantly set down as the passing freak of a girl whose ways were already considered singular. That she was doing for an earnest reason what would most naturally be done in jest was at any rate a safe secret.

The next evening Eustacia stood punctually at the fuel-house door, waiting for the dusk which was to bring Charley with the trappings. Her grandfather was at home tonight, and she would be unable to ask her confederate indoors.

He appeared on the dark ridge of heathland, like a fly on a negro, bearing the articles with him, and came up breathless with his walk.

'Here are the things,' he whispered, placing them upon the threshold. 'And now, Miss Eustacia –'

'The payment. It is quite ready. I am as good as my word.'

She leant against the door-post, and gave him her hand. Charley took it in both his own with a tenderness beyond description, unless it was like that of a child holding a captured sparrow.

'Why, there's a glove on it!' he said in a deprecating way.

'I have been walking,' she observed.

'But, miss!'

'Well – it is hardly fair.' She pulled off the glove, and gave him her bare hand.

They stood together minute after minute, without further speech, each looking at the blackening scene, and each thinking his and her own thoughts.

'I think I won't use it all up tonight,' said Charley devotedly, when six or eight minutes had been passed by him caressing her hand. 'May I have the other few minutes another time?'

'As you like,' said she without the least emotion. 'But it must be over in a week. Now, there is only one thing I want you to do: to wait while I put on the dress, and then to see if I do my part properly. But let me look first indoors.'

She vanished for a minute or two, and went in. Her grandfather was safely asleep in his chair. 'Now, then,' she said, on returning, 'walk down the garden a little way, and when I am ready I'll call you.'

Charley walked and waited, and presently heard a soft whistle. He returned to the fuel-house door.

'Did you whistle, Miss Vye?'

'Yes; come in,' reached him in Eustacia's voice from a back quarter. 'I must not strike a light till the door is shut, or it may be seen shining. Push your hat into the hole through to the wash-house, if you can feel your way across.'

Charley did as commanded, and she struck the light, revealing herself to be changed in sex, brilliant in colours, and armed from top to toe. Perhaps she quailed a little under Charley's vigorous gaze, but whether any shyness at her male attire appeared upon her countenance could not be seen by reason of the strips of ribbon which used to cover the face in mumming costumes, representing the barred visor of the medieval helmet.

'It fits pretty well,' she said, looking down at the white overalls, 'except that the tunic, or whatever you call it, is long in the sleeve. The bottom of the overalls I can turn up inside. Now pay attention.'

Eustacia then proceeded in her delivery, striking the sword against the staff or lance at the minatory phrases, in the orthodox mumming manner, and strutting up and down. Charley seasoned his admiration with criticism of the gentlest kind, for the touch of Eustacia's hand yet remained with him.

'And now for your excuse to the others,' she said. 'Where do you meet before you go to Mrs Yeobright's?'

'We thought of meeting here, miss, if you have nothing to say against it. At eight o'clock, so as to get there by nine.'

'Yes. Well, you of course must not appear. I will march in about five minutes late, ready-dressed, and tell them that you can't come. I have decided that the best plan will be for you to be sent somewhere by me, to make a real thing of the excuse. Our two heath-croppers are in the habit of straying into the meads, and tomorrow evening you can go and see if they are gone there. I'll manage the rest. Now you may leave me.'

'Yes, miss. But I think I'll have one minute more of what I am owed, if you don't mind.'

Eustacia gave him her hand as before.

'One minute,' she said, and counted on till she reached seven or eight minutes. Hand and person she then withdrew to a distance of several feet, and recovered some of her old dignity. The contract completed, she raised between them a barrier impenetrable as a wall.

'There, 'tis all gone; and I didn't mean quite all,' he said, with a sigh.

'You had good measure,' said she, turning away.

'Yes, miss. Well, 'tis over, and now I'll get home-along.'

V

Through the Moonlight

THE next evening the mummers were assembled in the same spot, awaiting the entrance of the Turkish Knight.

'Twenty minutes after eight by the Quiet Woman, and Charley not come.'

'Ten minutes past by Blooms-End.'

'It wants ten minutes to, by Grandfer Cantle's watch.'

'And 'tis five minutes past by the captain's clock.'

On Egdon there was no absolute hour of the day. The time at any moment was a number of varying doctrines professed by the different hamlets, some of them having originally grown up from a common root, and then become divided by secession, some having been alien from the beginning. West Egdon believed in Blooms-End time, East Egdon in the time of the Quiet Woman Inn. Grandfer Cantle's watch had numbered many followers in years gone by, but since he had grown older faiths were shaken. Thus, the mummers having gathered hither from scattered points, each came with his own tenets on early and late; and they waited a little longer as a compromise.

Eustacia had watched the assemblage through the hole; and seeing that now was the proper moment to enter, she went from the 'linhay' and boldly pulled the bobbin of the fuel-house door. Her grandfather was safe at the Quiet Woman.

'Here's Charley at last! How late you be, Charley.'

' 'Tis not Charley,' said the Turkish Knight from within his visor. ' 'Tis a cousin of Miss Vye's, come to take Charley's place from curiosity. He was obliged to go and look for the heath-croppers that have got into the meads, and I agreed to take his place, as he knew he couldn't come back here again tonight. I know the part as well as he.'

Her graceful gait, elegant figure, and dignified manner in general won the mummers to the opinion that they had gained by the exchange, if the newcomer were perfect in his part.

'It don't matter – if you be not too young,' said Saint George. Eustacia's voice had sounded somewhat more juvenile and fluty than Charley's.

'I know every word of it, I tell you,' said Eustacia decisively. Dash being all that was required to carry her triumphantly through, she adopted as much as was necessary. 'Go ahead, lads, take the try-over. I'll challenge any of you to find a mistake in me.'

The play was hastily rehearsed, whereupon the other mummers were delighted with the new knight. They extinguished the candles at half-past eight, and set out upon the heath in the direction of Mrs Yeobright's house at Blooms-End.

There was a slight hoar-frost that night, and the moon, though not more than half full, threw a spirited and enticing brightness upon the fantastic figures of the mumming band, whose plumes and ribbons rustled in their walk like autumn leaves. Their path was not over Rainbarrow now, but down a valley which left that ancient elevation a little to the east. The bottom of the vale was green to a width of ten yards or thereabouts, and the shining facets of frost upon the blades of grass seemed to move on with the shadows of those they surrounded. The masses of furze and heath to the right and left were dark as ever; a mere half-moon was powerless to silver such sable features as theirs.

Half-an-hour of walking and talking brought them to the spot in the valley where the grass riband widened and led down to the front of the house. At sight of the place Eustacia, who had felt a few passing doubts during her walk with the youths, again was glad that the adventure had been undertaken. She had come out to see a man who might possibly have the power to deliver her soul from a most deadly oppression. What was Wildeve? Interesting, but inadequate. Perhaps she would see a sufficient hero tonight.

As they drew nearer to the front of the house the mummers became aware that music and dancing were briskly flourishing within. Every now and then a long low note from the serpent, which was the chief wind instrument played at these times, advanced further into the heath than the thin treble part, and reached their ears alone; and next a more than usually loud tread from a dancer would come the same way. With nearer approach these fragmentary sounds became pieced together, and were found to be the salient points of the tune called 'Nancy's Fancy'.

He was there, of course. Who was she that he danced with? Perhaps some unknown woman, far beneath herself in culture, was by that most subtle of lures sealing his fate this very instant. To dance with a man is to concentrate a twelve-month's regulation fire upon him in the fragment of an hour. To pass to courtship without acquaintance, to pass to marriage without courtship, is a skipping of terms reserved for those alone who tread this royal road. She would see how his heart lay by keen observation of them all.

The enterprising lady followed the mumming company through the gate in the white paling, and stood before the open porch. The house was encrusted with heavy thatchings, which dropped between the upper windows: the front, upon which the moonbeams directly played, had originally been white; but a huge pyracanth now darkened the greater portion.

It became at once evident that the dance was proceeding immediately within the surface of the door, no apartment intervening. The brushing of skirts and elbows, sometimes the bumping of shoulders, could be heard against the very panels. Eustacia, though living within two miles of the place, had never seen the interior of this quaint old habitation. Between Captain Vye and the Yeobrights there had never existed much acquaintance, the former having come as a stranger and purchased the long-empty house at Mistover Knap not long before the death of Mrs

Yeobright's husband; and with that event and the departure of her son such friendship as had grown up became quite broken off.

'Is there no passage inside the door, then?' asked Eustacia as they stood within the porch.

'No,' said the lad who played the Saracen. 'The door opens right upon the front sitting-room, where the spree's going on.'

'So that we cannot open the door without stopping the dance.'

'That's it. Here we must bide till they have done, for they always bolt the back door after dark.'

'They won't be much longer,' said Father Christmas.

This assertion, however, was hardly borne out by the event. Again the instruments ended the tune; again they recommenced with as much fire and pathos as if it were the first strain. The air was now that one without any particular beginning, middle, or end, which perhaps, among all the dances which throng an inspired fiddler's fancy, best conveys the idea of the interminable – the celebrated 'Devil's Dream'. The fury of personal movement that was kindled by the fury of the notes could be approximately imagined by these outsiders under the moon, from the occasional kicks of toes and heels against the door, whenever the whirl round had been of more than customary velocity.

The first five minutes of listening was interesting enough to the mummers. The five minutes extended to ten minutes, and these to a quarter of an hour; but no signs of ceasing were audible in the lively Dream. The bumping against the door, the laughter, the stamping, were all as vigorous as ever, and the pleasure in being outside lessened considerably.

'Why does Mrs Yeobright give parties of this sort?' Eustacia asked, a little surprised to hear merriment so pronounced.

'It is not one of her bettermost parlour-parties. She's asked the plain neighbours and workpeople without drawing any lines, just to give 'em a good supper and such like. Her son and she wait upon the folks.'

'I see,' said Eustacia.

' 'Tis the last strain, I think,' said Saint George, with his ear to the panel. 'A young man and woman have just swung into this corner, and he's saying to her, "Ah, the pity; 'tis over for us this time, my own." '

'Thank God!' said the Turkish Knight, stamping, and taking from the wall the conventional lance that each of the mummers carried. Her boots being thinner than those of the young men, the hoar had damped her feet and made them cold.

'Upon my song 'tis another ten minutes for us,' said the Valiant Soldier, looking through the keyhole as the tune modulated into another without stopping. 'Grandfer Cantle is standing in this corner, waiting his turn.'

' 'Twon't be long; 'tis a six-handed reel,' said the Doctor.

'Why not go in, dancing or no? They sent for us,' said the Saracen.

'Certainly not,' said Eustacia authoritatively as she paced smartly up and down from door to gate to warm herself. 'We should burst into the middle of them and stop the dance, and that would be unmannerly.'

'He thinks himself somebody because he has had a bit more schooling than we,' said the Doctor.

'You may go to the deuce!' said Eustacia.

There was a whispered conversation between three or four of them, and one turned to her.

'Will you tell us one thing?' he said, not without gentleness. 'Be you Miss Vye? We think you must be.'

'You may think what you like,' said Eustacia slowly. 'But honourable lads will not tell tales upon a lady.'

'We'll say nothing, miss. That's upon our honour.'

'Thank you,' she replied.

At this moment the fiddles finished off with a screech, and the serpent emitted a last note that nearly lifted the roof. When, from the comparative quiet within, the mummers judged that the dancers had taken their seats, Father Christmas advanced, lifted the latch, and put his head inside the door.

'Ah, the mummers, the mummers!' cried several guests at once. 'Clear a space for the mummers.'

Hump-backed Father Christmas then made a complete entry, swinging his huge club, and in a general way clearing the stage for the actors proper, while he informed the company in smart verse that he was come, welcome or welcome not; concluding his speech with

> 'Make room, make room, my gallant boys,
>   And give us space to rhyme;
> We've come to show Saint George's play,
>   Upon this Christmas time.'

The guests were now arranging themselves at one end of the room, the fiddler was mending a string, the serpent-player was emptying his mouthpiece, and the play began. First of those outside the Valiant Soldier entered, in the interest of Saint George –

> 'Here come I, the Valiant Soldier;
>   Slasher is my name;'

and so on. This speech concluded with a challenge to the infidel, at the end of which it was Eustacia's duty to enter as the Turkish Knight. She, with the rest who were not yet on, had hitherto remained in the moonlight which streamed down under the porch. With no apparent effort or backwardness she came in, beginning –

> 'Here come I, a Turkish Knight,
>   Who learnt in Turkish land to fight;
> I'll fight this man with courage bold;
>   If his blood's hot I'll make it cold!'

During her declamation Eustacia held her head erect, and spoke as roughly as she could, feeling pretty secure from observation. But the concentration upon her part necessary to prevent discovery, the newness of the scene, the shine of the candles, and the confusing effect upon her vision of the ribboned visor which hid her features, left her absolutely unable to perceive who were present as spectators. On the further side of table bearing candles she could faintly discern faces, and that was all.

Meanwhile Jim Starks as the Valiant Soldier had come forward, and, with a glare upon the Turk, replied –

> 'If, then, thou art that Turkish Knight,
> Draw out thy sword, and let us fight!'

And fight they did; the issue of the combat being that the Valiant Soldier was slain by a preternaturally inadequate thrust from Eustacia, Jim, in his ardour for genuine histrionic art, coming down like a log upon the stone floor with force enough to dislocate his shoulder. Then, after more words from the Turkish Knight, rather too faintly delivered, and statements that he'd fight Saint George and all his crew, Saint George himself magnificently entered with the well-known flourish –

> 'Here come I, Saint George, the valiant man,
> With naked sword and spear in hand,
> Who fought the dragon and brought him to the slaughter,
> And by this won fair Sabra, the King of Egypt's daughter;
> What mortal man would dare to stand
> Before me with my sword in hand?'

This was the lad who had first recognized Eustacia; and when she now, as the Turk, replied with suitable defiance, and at once began to combat, the young fellow took especial care to use his sword as gently as possible. Being wounded, the Knight fell upon one knee, according to the direction. The Doctor now entered, restored the Knight by giving him a draught from the bottle which he carried, and the fight was again resumed, the Turk sinking by degrees until quite overcome – dying as hard in his venerable drama as he is said to do at the present day.

This gradual sinking to the earth was, in fact, one reason why Eustacia had thought that the part of the Turkish Knight, though not the shortest, would suit her best. A direct fall from upright to horizontal, which was the end of the other fighting characters, was not an elegant or decorous part for a girl. But it was easy to die like a Turk, by a dogged decline.

Eustacia was now among the number of the slain, though not on the floor, for she had managed to sink into a sloping position against the clock-case, so that her head was well elevated. The play proceeded between Saint George, the Saracen, the Doctor, and Father Christmas; and Eustacia, having no more to do, for the first time found leisure to observe the scene around, and to search for the form that had drawn her hither.

* VI *

The Two Stand Face to Face

THE room had been arranged with a view to the dancing, the large oak table having been moved back till it stood as a breastwork to the fireplace. At each end, behind, and in the chimney-corner were grouped the guests, many of them being warm-faced and panting, among whom Eustacia cursorily recognized some well-to-do persons from beyond the heath. Thomasin, as she had expected, was not visible, and Eustacia recollected that a light had shone from an upper window when they were outside – the window, probably, of Thomasin's room. A nose, chin, hands, knees, and toes projected from the seat within the chimney opening; which members she found to unite in the person of Grandfer Cantle, Mrs Yeobright's occasional assistant in the garden, and therefore one of the invited. The smoke went up from an Etna of peat in front of him, played round the notches of the chimney-crook, struck against the saltbox, and got lost among the flitches.

Another part of the room soon riveted her gaze. At the other side of the chimney stood the settle, which is the necessary supplement to a fire so open that nothing less than a strong breeze will carry up the smoke. It is, to the hearths of old-fashioned cavernous fireplaces, what the east belt of trees is to the exposed country estate, or the north wall to the garden. Outside the settle candles gutter, locks of hair wave, young women shiver, and old men sneeze. Inside is Paradise. Not a symptom of a draught disturbs the air; the sitters' backs are as warm as their faces, and songs and old tales are drawn from the occupant by the comfortable heat, like fruit from melon-plants in a frame.

It was, however, now with those who sat in the settle that Eustacia was concerned. A face showed itself with marked distinctness against the dark-tanned wood of the upper part. The owner, who was leaning against the settle's outer end, was Clement Yeobright, or Clym, as he was called here; she knew it could be nobody else. The spectacle constituted an area of two feet in Rembrandt's intensest manner. A strange power in the lounger's appearance lay in the fact that, though his whole figure was visible, the observer's eye was only aware of his face.

To one of middle age the countenance was that of a young man, though a youth might hardly have seen any necessity for the term of immaturity. But it was really one of those faces which convey less the idea of so many years as its age than of so much experience as its store. The number of their years may have adequately summed up Jared, Mahalaleel, and the rest of the antediluvians, but the age of a modern man is to be measured by the intensity of his history.

The face was well shaped, even excellently. But the mind within was be-ginning to use it as a mere waste tablet whereon to trace its idiosyncrasies as they developed themselves. The beauty here visible would in no long time be ruthlessly overrun by its parasite, thought, which might just as well have fed upon a plainer exterior where there was nothing it could harm. Had Heaven preserved Yeobright from a wearing habit of meditation, people would have said, 'A handsome man.' Had his brain unfolded under sharper contours they would have said, 'A thoughtful man.' But an inner strenuousness was preying upon an outer symmetry, and they rated his look as singular.

Hence people who began by beholding him ended by perusing him. His countenance was overlaid with legible meanings. Without being thought-worn he yet had certain marks derived from a perception of his surroundings, such as are not unfrequently found on men at the end of the four or five years of endeavour which follow the close of placid pupilage. He already showed that thought is a disease of flesh, and indirectly bore evidence that ideal physical beauty is incompatible with emotional development and a full recognition of the coil of things. Mental luminousness must be fed with the oil of life, even though there is already a physical need for it; and the pitiful sight of two demands on one supply was just showing itself here.

When standing before certain men the philosopher regrets that thinkers are but perishable tissue, the artist that perishable tissue has to think. Thus to deplore, each from his point of view, the mutually destructive interdependence of spirit and flesh would have been instinctive with these in critically observing Yeobright.

As for his look, it was a natural cheerfulness striving against depression from without, and not quite succeeding. The look suggested isolation, but it revealed something more. As is usual with bright natures, the deity that lies ignominiously chained within an ephemeral human carcase shone out of him like a ray.

The effect upon Eustacia was palpable. The extraordinary pitch of excitement that she had reached beforehand would, indeed, have caused her to be influenced by the most commonplace man. She was troubled at Yeobright's presence.

The remainder of the play ended: the Saracen's head was cut off, and Saint George stood as victor. Nobody commented, any more than they would have commented on the fact of mushrooms coming in autumn or snowdrops in spring. They took the piece as phlegmatically as did the actors themselves. It was a phase of cheerfulness which was, as a matter of course, to be passed through every Christmas; and there was no more to be said.

They sang the plaintive chant which follows the play, during which all the dead men rise to their feet in a silent and awful manner, like the ghosts of Napoleon's soldiers in the Midnight Review. Afterwards the door opened, and Fairway appeared on the threshold, accompanied by Christian and another. They had been waiting outside for the conclusion of the play, as the players had waited for the conclusion of the dance.

'Come in, come in,' said Mrs Yeobright; and Clym went forward to welcome them. 'How is it you are so late? Grandfer Cantle has been here ever so long, and we thought you'd have come with him, as you live so near one another.'

'Well, I should have come earlier,' Mr Fairway said, and paused to look along the beam of the ceiling for a nail to hang his hat on; but, finding his accustomed one to be occupied by the mistletoe, and all the nails in the walls to be burdened with bunches of holly, he at last relieved himself of the hat by ticklishly balancing it between the candlebox and the head of the clock-case. 'I should have come earlier, ma'am,' he resumed, with a more composed air, 'but I know what parties be, and how there's none too much room in folks' houses at such times, so I thought I wouldn't come till you'd got settled a bit.'

'And I thought so too, Mrs Yeobright,' said Christian earnestly; 'but father there was so eager that he had no manners at all, and left home almost afore 'twas dark. I told him 'twas barely decent in a' old man to come so oversoon; but words be wind.'

'Klk! I wasn't going to bide waiting about till half the game was over! I'm as light as a kite when anything's going on!' crowed Grandfer Cantle from the chimney-seat.

Fairway had meanwhile concluded a critical gaze at Yeobright. 'Now, you may not believe it,' he said to the rest of the room, 'but I should never have knowed this gentleman if I had met him anywhere off his own he'th: he's altered so much.'

'You too have altered, and for the better, I think, Timothy,' said Yeobright, surveying the firm figure of Fairway.

'Master Yeobright, look me over too. I have altered for the better, haven't I, hey?' said Grandfer Cantle, rising, and placing himself something above half a foot from Clym's eye, to induce the most searching criticism.

'To be sure we will,' said Fairway, taking the candle and moving it over the surface of the Grandfer's countenance, the subject of his scrutiny irradiating himself with light and pleasant smiles, and giving himself jerks of juvenility.

'You haven't changed much,' said Yeobright.

'If there's any difference, Grandfer is younger,' appended Fairway decisively.

'And yet not my own doing, and I feel no pride in it,' said the pleased ancient. 'But I can't be cured of my vagaries; them I plead guilty to. Yes, Master Cantle always was that, as we know. But I am nothing by the side of you, Mister Clym.'

'Nor any o' us,' said Humphrey, in a low rich tone of admiration, not intended to reach anybody's ears.

'Really, there would have been nobody here who could have stood as decent second to him, or even third, if I hadn't been a soldier in the Bang-up Locals (as we was called for our smartness),' said Grandfer Cantle. 'And even as 'tis we all look a little scammish beside him. But in the year four 'twas said there wasn't a finer figure in the whole South Wessex than

I, as I looked when dashing past the shop-winders with the rest of our company on the day we ran out o' Budmouth because it was thoughted that Boney had landed round the point. There was I, straight as a young poplar, wi' my firelock, and my bagnet, and my spatter-dashes, and my stock sawing my jaws off, and my accoutrements sheening like the seven stars! Yes, neighbours, I was a pretty sight in my soldiering days. You ought to have seen me in four!'

' 'Tis his mother's side where Master Clym's figure comes from, bless ye,' said Timothy. 'I know'd her brothers well. Longer coffins were never made in the whole county of South Wessex, and 'tis said that poor George's knees were crumpled up a little e'en as 'twas.'

'Coffins, where?' inquired Christian, drawing nearer. 'Have the ghost of one appeared to anybody, Master Fairway?'

'No, no. Don't let your mind so mislead your ears, Christian; and be a man,' said Timothy reproachfully.

'I will,' said Christian. 'But now I think o't my shadder last night seemed just the shape of a coffin. What is it a sign of when your shade's like a coffin, neighbours? It can't be nothing to be afeard of, I suppose?'

'Afeard, no!' said the Grandfer. 'Faith, I was never afeard of nothing except Boney, or I shouldn't ha' been the soldier I was. Yes, 'tis a thousand pities you didn't see me in four!'

By this time the mummers were preparing to leave; but Mrs Yeobright stopped them by asking them to sit down and have a little supper. To this invitation Father Christmas, in the name of them all, readily agreed.

Eustacia was happy in the opportunity of staying a little longer. The cold and frosty night without was doubly frigid to her. But the lingering was not without its difficulties. Mrs Yeobright, for want of room in the larger apartment, placed a bench for the mummers half-way through the pantry-door, which opened from the sitting-room. Here they seated themselves in a row, the door being left open; thus they were still virtually in the same apartment. Mrs Yeobright now murmured a few words to her son, who crossed the room to the pantry-door, striking his head against the mistletoe as he passed, and brought the mummers beef and bread, cake, pastry, mead, and elder-wine, the waiting being done by him and his mother, that the little maid-servant might sit as guest. The mummers doffed their helmets, and began to eat and drink.

'But you will surely have some?' said Clym to the Turkish Knight, as he stood before that warrior, tray in hand. She had refused, and still sat covered, only the sparkle of her eyes being visible between the ribbons which covered her face.

'None, thank you,' replied Eustacia.

'He's quite a youngster,' said the Saracen apologetically, 'and you must excuse him. He's not one of the old set, but have jined us because t'other couldn't come.'

'But he will take something?' persisted Yeobright. 'Try a glass of mead or elderwine.'

'Yes, you had better try that,' said the Saracen. 'It will keep the cold out going home-along.'

Though Eustacia could not eat without uncovering her face she could drink easily enough beneath her disguise. The elderwine was accordingly accepted, and the glass vanished inside the ribbons.

At moments during this performance Eustacia was half in doubt about the security of her position; yet it had a fearful joy. A series of attentions paid to her, and yet not to her but to some imaginary person, by the first man she had ever been inclined to adore, complicated her emotions indescribably. She had loved him partly because he was exceptional in this scene, partly because she had determined to love him, chiefly because she was in desperate need of loving somebody after wearying of Wildeve. Believing that she must love him in spite of herself, she had been influenced after the fashion of the second Lord Lyttleton and other persons, who have dreamed that they were to die on a certain day, and by stress of a morbid imagination have actually brought about that event. Once let a maiden admit the possibility of her being stricken with love for some one at a certain hour and place, and the thing is as good as done.

Did anything at this moment suggest to Yeobright the sex of the creature whom that fantastic guise inclosed, how extended was her scope both in feeling and in making others feel, and how far her compass transcended that of her companions in the band? When the disguised Queen of Love appeared before Aeneas a preternatural perfume accompanied her presence and betrayed her quality. If such a mysterious emanation ever was projected by the emotions of an earthly woman upon their object, it must have signified Eustacia's presence to Yeobright now. He looked at her wistfully, then seemed to fall into a reverie, as if he were forgetting what he observed. The momentary situation ended, he passed on, and Eustacia sipped her wine without knowing what she drank. The man for whom she had predetermined to nourish a passion went into the small room, and across it to the further extremity.

The mummers, as had been stated, were seated on a bench, one end of which extended into the small apartment, or pantry, for want of space in the outer room. Eustacia, partly from shyness, had chosen the midmost seat, which thus commanded a view of the interior of the pantry as well as the room containing the guests. When Clym passed down the pantry her eyes followed him in the gloom which prevailed there. At the remote end was a door which, just as he was about to open it for himself, was opened by somebody within; and light streamed forth.

The person was Thomasin, with a candle, looking anxious, pale, and interesting. Yeobright appeared glad to see her, and pressed her hand. That's right, Tamsie,' he said heartily, as though recalled to himself by the sight of her: 'you have decided to come down. I am glad of it.'

'Hush – no, no,' she said quickly. 'I only came to speak to you.'

'But why not join us?'

'I cannot. At least I would rather not. I am not well enough, and we shall have plenty of time together now you are going to be home a good long holiday.'

'It isn't nearly so pleasant without you. Are you really ill?'

'Just a little, my old cousin – here,' she said, playfully sweeping her hand across her heart.

'Ah, mother should have asked somebody else to be present tonight, perhaps?'

'O no, indeed. I merely stepped down, Clym, to ask you –' Here he followed her through the doorway into the private room beyond, and, the door closing, Eustacia and the mummer who sat next to her, the only other witness of the performance, saw and heard no more.

The heat flew to Eustacia's head and cheeks. She instantly guessed that Clym, having been home only these two or three days, had not as yet been made acquainted with Thomasin's painful situation with regard to Wildeve; and seeing her living there just as she had been living before he left home, he naturally suspected nothing. Eustacia felt a wild jealousy of Thomasin on the instant. Though Thomasin might possibly have tender sentiments towards another man as yet, how long could they be expected to last when she was shut up here with this interesting and travelled cousin of hers? There was no knowing what affection might not soon break out between the two, so constantly in each other's society, and not a distracting object near. Clym's boyish love for her might have languished, but it might easily be revived again.

Eustacia was nettled by her own contrivances. What a sheer waste of herself to be dressed thus while another was shining to advantage! Had she known the full effect of the encounter she would have moved heaven and earth to get here in a natural manner. The power of her face all lost, the charm of her emotions all disguised, the fascinations of her coquetry denied existence, nothing but a voice left to her: she had a sense of the doom of Echo. 'Nobody here respects me,' she said. She had overlooked the fact that, in coming as a boy among other boys, she would be treated as a boy. The slight, though of her own causing, and self-explanatory, she was unable to dismiss as unwittingly shown, so sensitive had the situation made her.

Women have done much for themselves in histrionic dress. To look far below those who, like a certain fair personator of Polly Peachum early in the last century, and another of Lydia Languish early in this, have won not only love but ducal coronets into the bargain, whole shoals of them have reached to the initial satisfaction of getting love almost whence they would. But the Turkish Knight was denied even the chance of achieving this by the fluttering ribbons which she dared not brush aside.

Yeobright returned to the room without his cousin. When within two or three feet of Eustacia he stopped, as if again arrested by a thought. He was gazing at her. She looked another way, disconcerted, and wondered how long this purgatory was to last. After lingering a few seconds he passed on again.

To court their own discomfiture by love is a common instinct with certain perfervid women. Conflicting sensations of love, fear, and shame reduced Eustacia to a state of the utmost uneasiness. To escape was her great and immediate desire. The other mummers appeared to be in no hurry to leave; and murmuring to the lad who sat next to her that she preferred waiting for them outside the house, she moved to the door as imperceptibly as possible, opened it, and slipped out.

The calm, lone scene reassured her. She went forward to the palings and leant over them, looking at the moon. She had stood thus but a little time when the door again opened. Expecting to see the remainder of the band Eustacia turned; but no – Clym Yeobright came out as softly as she had done, and closed the door behind him.

He advanced and stood beside her. 'I have an odd opinion,' he said, 'and should like to ask you a question. Are you a woman – or am I wrong?'

'I am a woman.'

His eyes lingered on her with great interest. 'Do girls often play as mummers now? They never used to.'

'They don't now.'

'Why did you?'

'To get excitement and shake off depression,' she said in low tones.

'What depressed you?'

'Life.'

'That's a cause of depression a good many have to put up with.'

'Yes.'

A long silence. 'And do you find excitement?' asked Clym at last.

'At this moment, perhaps.'

'Then you are vexed at being discovered?'

'Yes; though I thought I might be.'

'I would gladly have asked you to our party had I known you wished to come. Have I ever been acquainted with you in my youth?'

'Never.'

'Won't you come in again, and stay as long as you like?'

'No. I wish not to be further recognized.'

'Well, you are safe with me.' After remaining in thought a minute he added gently, 'I will not intrude upon you longer. It is a strange way of meeting, and I will not ask why I find a cultivated woman playing such a part as this.'

She did not volunteer the reason which he seemed to hope for, and he wished her good night, going thence round to the back of the house, where he walked up and down by himself for some time before re-entering.

Eustacia, warmed with an inner fire, could not wait for her companions after this. She flung back the ribbons from her face, opened the gate, and at once struck into the heath. She did not hasten along. Her grandfather was in bed at this hour, for she so frequently walked upon the hills on moonlight nights that he took no notice of her comings and goings, and, enjoying himself in his own way, left her to do likewise. A more important subject than that of getting indoors now engrossed her. Yeobright, if he had the least curiosity, would infallibly discover her name. What then? She first felt a sort of exultation at the way in which the adventure had terminated, even though at moments between her exultations she was abashed and blushful. Then this consideration recurred to chill her: What was the use of her exploit? She was at present a total stranger to the Yeobright family. The unreasonable nimbus of romance with which she had encircled that man might be her misery. How could she allow herself to become so infatuated with a stranger? And to fill the cup of her sorrow there would be Thomasin, living day after day in inflammable proximity to him; for she had just learnt that, contrary to her first belief, he was going to stay at home some considerable time.

She reached the wicket at Mistover Knap, but before opening it she turned and faced the heath once more. The form of Rainbarrow stood above the hills, and the moon stood above Rainbarrow. The air was charged with silence and frost. The scene reminded Eustacia of a circumstance which till that moment she had totally forgotten. She had promised to meet Wildeve by the Barrow this very night at eight, to give a final answer to his pleading for an elopement.

She herself had fixed the evening and the hour. He had probably come to the spot, waited there in the cold, and been greatly disappointed.

'Well, so much the better: it did not hurt him,' she said serenely. Wildeve had at present the rayless outline of the sun through smoked glass, and she could say such things as that with the greatest facility.

She remained deeply pondering; and Thomasin's winning manner towards her cousin arose again upon Eustacia's mind.

'O that she had been married to Damon before this!' she said. 'And she would if it hadn't been for me! If I had only known – if I had only known!'

Eustacia once more filled her deep stormy eyes to the moonlight, and, sighing that tragic sigh of hers which was so much like a shudder, entered the shadow of the roof. She threw off her trappings in the out-house, rolled them up, and went indoors to her chamber.

* VII *

A Coalition between Beauty and Oddness

THE old captain's prevailing indifference to his granddaughter's movements left her free as a bird to follow her own courses; but it so happened that he did take upon himself the next morning to ask her why she had walked out so late.

'Only in search of events, grandfather,' she said, looking out of the window with that drowsy latency of manner which discovered so much force behind it whenever the trigger was pressed.

'Search of events – one would think you were one of the bucks I knew at one-and-twenty.'

'It is so lonely here.'

'So much the better. If I were living in a town my whole time would be taken up in looking after you. I fully expected you would have been home when I returned from the Woman.'

'I won't conceal what I did. I wanted an adventure, and I went with the mummers. I played the part of the Turkish Knight.'

'No, never? Ha, ha! Good gad! I didn't expect it of you, Eustacia.'

'It was my first performance, and it certainly will be my last. Now I have told you – and remember it is a secret.'

'Of course. But, Eustacia, you never did – ha! ha! Dammy, how 'twould have pleased me forty years ago! But remember, no more of it, my girl. You may walk on the heath night or day, as you choose, so that you don't bother me; but no figuring in breeches again.'

'You need have no fear for me, grandpapa.'

Here the conversation ceased, Eustacia's moral training never exceeding in severity to a dialogue of this sort, which, if it ever became profitable to good works, would be a result not dear at the price. But her thoughts soon strayed far from her own personality; and, full of a passionate and indescribable solicitude for one to whom she was not even a name, she went forth into the amplitude of tanned wild around her, restless as Ahasuerus the Jew. She was about half a mile from her residence when she beheld a sinister redness arising from a ravine a little way in advance – dull and lurid like a flame in sunlight, and she guessed it to signify Diggory Venn.

When the farmers who had wished to buy in a new stock of reddle during the last month had inquired where Venn was to be found, people replied, 'On Egdon Heath.' Day after day the answer was the same. Now, since Egdon was populated with heath-croppers and furze-cutters rather than with sheep and shepherds, and the downs where most of the latter were to be found lay some to the north, some to the west of Egdon, his reason for camping about there like Israel in Zin was not apparent. The position was central and occasionally desirable. But the sale of reddle was not Diggory's primary object in remaining on the heath, particularly at so late a period of the year, when most travellers of his class had gone into winter quarters.

Eustacia looked at the lonely man. Wildeve had told her at their last meeting that Venn had been thrust forward by Mrs Yeobright as one ready and anxious to take his place as Thomasin's betrothed. His figure was perfect, his face young and well outlined, his eye bright, his intelligence keen, and his position one which he could readily better if he chose. But in spite of possibilities it was not likely that Thomasin would accept this Ishmaelitish creature while she had a cousin like Yeobright at her elbow, and Wildeve at the same time not absolutely indifferent. Eustacia was not long in guessing that poor Mrs Yeobright, in her anxiety for her niece's future, had mentioned this lover to stimulate the zeal of the other. Eustacia was on the side of the Yeobrights now, and entered into the spirit of the aunt's desire.

'Good morning, miss,' said the reddleman, taking off his cap of hareskin, and apparently bearing her no ill-will from recollection of their last meeting.

'Good morning, reddleman,' she said, hardly troubling to lift her heavily shaded eyes to his. 'I did not know you were so near. Is your van here too?'

Venn moved his elbow towards a hollow in which a dense brake of purple-stemmed brambles had grown to such vast dimensions as almost to form a dell. Brambles, though churlish when handled, are kindly shelter in early winter, being the latest of the deciduous bushes to lose their leaves. The roof and chimney of Venn's caravan showed behind the tracery and tangles of the brake.

'You remain near this part?' she asked with more interest.

'Yes, I have business here.'

'Not altogether the selling of reddle?'

'It has nothing to do with that.'

'It has to do with Miss Yeobright?'

Her face seemed to ask for an armed peace, and he therefore said frankly, 'Yes, miss; it is on account of her.'

'On account of your approaching marriage with her?'

Venn flushed through his stain. 'Don't make sport of me, Miss Vye,' he said.

'It isn't true?'

'Certainly not.'

She was thus convinced that the reddleman was a mere *pis aller* in Mrs Yeobright's mind; one, moreover, who had not even been informed of his promotion to that lowly standing. 'It was a mere notion of mine,' she said quietly; and was about to pass by without further speech when, looking round to the right, she saw a painfully well-known figure serpentining upwards by one of the little paths which led to the top where she stood. Owing to the necessary windings of his course his back was at present towards them. She glanced quickly round; to escape that man there was only one way. Turning to Venn, she said, 'Would you allow me to rest a few minutes in your van? The banks are damp for sitting on.'

'Certainly, miss; I'll make a place for you.'

She followed him behind the dell of brambles to his wheeled dwelling, into which Venn mounted, placing the three-legged stool just within the door.

'That is the best I can do for you,' he said, stepping down and retiring to the path, where he resumed the smoking of his pipe as he walked up and down.

Eustacia bounded into the vehicle and sat on the stool, ensconced from view on the side towards the trackway. Soon she heard the brushing of other feet than the reddleman's, a not very friendly 'Good day' uttered by two men in passing each other, and then the dwindling of the footfall of one of them in a direction onwards. Eustacia stretched her neck forward till she caught a glimpse of a receding back and shoulders; and she felt a wretched twinge of misery, she knew not why. It was the sickening feeling which, if the changed heart has any generosity at all in its composition, accompanies the sudden sight of a once-loved one who is beloved no more.

When Eustacia descended to proceed on her way the reddleman came near. 'That was Mr Wildeve who passed, miss,' he said slowly, and expressed by his face that he expected her to feel vexed at having been sitting unseen.

'Yes, I saw him coming up the hill,' replied Eustacia. 'Why should you tell me that?' It was a bold question, considering the reddleman's knowledge of her past love; but her undemonstrative manner had power to repress the opinions of those she treated as remote from her.

'I am glad to hear that you can ask it,' said the reddleman bluntly. 'And, now I think of it, it agrees with what I saw last night.'

'Ah – what was that?' Eustacia wished to leave him, but wished to know.

'Mr Wildeve stayed at Rainbarrow a long time waiting for a lady who didn't come.'

'You waited too, it seems?'

'Yes, I always do. I was glad to see him disappointed. He will be there again tonight.'

'To be again disappointed. The truth is, reddleman, that that lady, so far from wishing to stand in the way of Thomasin's marriage with Mr Wildeve, would be very glad to promote it.'

Venn felt much astonishment at this avowal, though he did not show it clearly; that exhibition may greet remarks which are one remove from expectation, but it is usually withheld in complicated cases of two removes and upwards. 'Indeed, miss,' he replied.

'How do you know that Mr Wildeve will come to Rainbarrow again tonight?' she asked.

'I heard him say to himself that he would. He's in a regular temper.'

Eustacia looked for a moment what she felt, and she murmured, lifting

her deep dark eyes anxiously to his, 'I wish I knew what to do. I don't
want to be uncivil to him; but I don't wish to see him again; and I have
some few little things to return to him.'

'If you choose to send 'em by me, miss, and a note to tell him that you
wish to say no more to him, I'll take it for you quite privately. That
would be the most straightforward way of letting him know your mind.'

'Very well,' said Eustacia. 'Come towards my house, and I will bring
it out to you.'

She went on, and as the path was an infinitely small parting in the
shaggy locks of the heath, the reddleman followed exactly in her trail. She
saw from a distance that the captain was on the bank sweeping the
horizon with his telescope; and bidding Venn to wait where he stood she
entered the house alone.

In ten minutes she returned with a parcel and a note, and said, in
placing them in his hand, 'Why are you so ready to take these for me?'

'Can you ask that?'

'I suppose you think to serve Thomasin in some way by it. Are you
as anxious as ever to help on her marriage?'

Venn was a little moved. 'I would sooner have married her myself,' he
said in a low voice. 'But what I feel is that if she cannot be happy without
him I will do my duty in helping her to get him, as a man ought.'

Eustacia looked curiously at the singular man who spoke thus. What
a strange sort of love, to be entirely free from that quality of selfishness
which is frequently the chief constituent of the passion, and sometimes its
only one! The reddleman's disinterestedness was so well deserving of
respect that it overshot respect by being barely comprehended; and she
almost thought it absurd.

'Then we are both of one mind at last,' she said.

'Yes,' replied Venn gloomily. 'But if you would tell me, miss, why you
take such an interest in her, I should be easier. It is so sudden and strange.'

Eustacia appeared at a loss. 'I cannot tell you that, reddleman,' she said
coldly.

Venn said no more. He pocketed the letter, and, bowing to Eustacia,
went away.

Rainbarrow had again become blended with night when Wildeve
ascended the long acclivity at its base. On his reaching the top a shape
grew up from the earth immediately behind him. It was that of Eustacia's
emissary. He slapped Wildeve on the shoulder. The feverish young
innkeeper and ex-engineer started like Satan at the touch of Ithuriel's
spear.

'The meeting is always at eight o'clock, at this place,' said Venn, 'and
here we are – we three.'

'We three?' said Wildeve, looking quickly around.

'Yes; you, and I, and she. This is she.' He held up the letter and parcel.

Wildeve took them wonderingly. 'I don't quite see what this means,'
he said. 'How do you come here? There must be some mistake.'

'It will be cleared from your mind when you have read the letter.

Lanterns for one.' The reddleman struck a light, kindled an inch of tallow-candle which he had brought, and sheltered it with his cap.

'Who are you?' said Wildeve, discerning by the candlelight an obscure rubicundity of person in his companion. 'You are the reddleman I saw on the hill this morning – why, you are the man who –'

'Please read the letter.'

'If you had come from the other one I shouldn't have been surprised,' murmured Wildeve as he opened the letter and read. His face grew serious.

To Mr Wildeve.

After some thought I have decided once and for all that we must hold no further communication. The more I consider the matter the more I am convinced that there must be an end to our acquaintance. Had you been uniformly faithful to me throughout these two years you might now have some ground for accusing me of heartlessness; but if you calmly consider what I bore during the period of your desertion, and how I passively put up with your courtship of another without once interfering, you will, I think, own that I have a right to consult my own feelings when you come back to me again. That these are not what they were towards you may, perhaps, be a fault in me, but it is one which you can scarcely reproach me for when you remember how you left me for Thomasin.

The little articles you gave me in the early part of our friendship are returned by the bearer of this letter. They should rightly have been sent back when I first heard of your engagement to her.

EUSTACIA

By the time that Wildeve reached her name the blankness with which he had read the first half of the letter intensified to mortification. 'I am made a great fool of, one way and another,' he said pettishly. 'Do you know what is in this letter?'

The reddleman hummed a tune.

'Can't you answer me?' asked Wildeve warmly.

'Ru-um-tum-tum,' sang the reddleman.

Wildeve stood looking on the ground beside Venn's feet, till he allowed his eyes to travel upwards over Diggory's form, as illuminated by the candle, to his head and face. 'Ha-ha! Well, I suppose I deserve it, considering how I have played with them both,' he said at last, as much to himself as to Venn. 'But of all the odd things that ever I knew, the oddest is that you should so run counter to your own interests as to bring this to me.'

'My interests?'

'Certainly. 'Twas your interest not to do anything which would send me courting Thomasin again, now she has accepted you – or something like it. Mrs Yeobright says you are to marry her. 'Tisn't true, then?'

'Good Lord! I heard of this before, but didn't believe it. When did she say so?'

Wildeve began humming as the reddleman had done.

'I don't believe it now,' cried Venn.

'Ru-um-tum-tum,' sang Wildeve.

'O Lord – how we can imitate!' said Venn contemptuously. 'I'll have this out. I'll go straight to her.'

Diggory withdrew with an emphatic step, Wildeve's eye passing over his form in withering derision, as if he were no more than a heath-cropper. When the reddleman's figure could no longer be seen, Wildeve himself descended and plunged into the rayless hollow of the vale.

To lose the two women – he who had been the well-beloved of both – was too ironical an issue to be endured. He could only decently save himself by Thomasin; and once he became her husband, Eustacia's repentance, he thought, would set in for a long and bitter term. It was no wonder that Wildeve, ignorant of the new man at the back of the scene, should have supposed Eustacia to be playing a part. To believe that the letter was not the result of some momentary pique, to infer that she really gave him up to Thomasin, would have required previous knowledge of her transfiguration by that man's influence. Who was to know that she had grown generous in the greediness of a new passion, that in coveting one cousin she was dealing liberally with another, that in her eagerness to appropriate she gave way?

Full of this resolve to marry in haste, and wring the heart of the proud girl, Wildeve went his way.

Meanwhile Diggory Venn had returned to his van, where he stood looking thoughtfully into the stove. A new vista was opened up to him. But, however promising Mrs Yeobright's views of him might be as a candidate for her niece's hand, one condition was indispensable to the favour of Thomasin herself, and that was a renunciation of his present wild mode of life. In this he saw little difficulty.

He could not afford to wait till the next day before seeing Thomasin and detailing his plan. He speedily plunged himself into toilet operations, pulled a suit of cloth clothes from a box, and in about twenty minutes stood before the van-lantern as a reddleman in nothing but his face, the vermilion shades of which were not to be removed in a day. Closing the door and fastening it with a padlock Venn set off towards Blooms-End.

He had reached the white palings and laid his hand upon the gate when the door of the house opened, and quickly closed again. A female form had glided in. At the same time a man, who had seemingly been standing with the woman in the porch, came forward from the house till he was face to face with Venn. It was Wildeve again.

'Man alive, you've been quick at it,' said Diggory sarcastically.

'And you slow, as you will find,' said Wildeve. 'And,' lowering his voice, 'you may as well go back again now. I've claimed her, and got her. Good night, reddleman!' Thereupon Wildeve walked away.

Venn's heart sank within him, though it had not risen unduly high. He stood leaning over the palings in an indecisive mood for nearly a quarter of an hour. Then he went up the garden-path, knocked, and asked for Mrs Yeobright.

Instead of requesting him to enter she came to the porch. A discourse was carried on between them in low measured tones for the space of ten minutes or more. At the end of the time Mrs Yeobright went in, and Venn sadly retracted his steps into the heath. When he had again regained his van he lit the lantern, and with an apathetic face at once began to pull off his best clothes, till in the course of a few minutes he reappeared as the confined and irretrievable reddleman that he had seemed before.

* VIII *

Firmness Is Discovered in a Gentle Heart

ON that evening the interior of Blooms-End, though cosy and comfortable, had been rather silent. Clym Yeobright was not at home. Since the Christmas party he had gone on a few days' visit to a friend about ten miles off.

The shadowy form seen by Venn to part from Wildeve in the porch, and quickly withdraw into the house, was Thomasin's. On entering she threw down a cloak which had been carelessly wrapped round her, and came forward to the light, where Mrs Yeobright sat at her work-table, drawn up within the settle, so that part of it projected into the chimney-corner.

'I don't like your going out after dark alone, Tamsin,' said her aunt quietly, without looking up from her work.

'I have only been just outside the door.'

'Well?' inquired Mrs Yeobright, struck by a change in the tone of Thomasin's voice, and observing her. Thomasin's cheek was flushed to a pitch far beyond that which it had reached before her troubles, and her eyes glittered.

'It was *he* who knocked,' she said.

'I thought as much.'

'He wishes the marriage to be at once.'

'Indeed! What – is he anxious?' Mrs Yeobright directed a searching look upon her niece. 'Why did not Mr Wildeve come in?'

'He did not wish to. You are not friends with him, he says. He would like the wedding to be the day after tomorrow, quite privately; at the church of his parish – not at ours.'

'Oh! And what did you say?'

'I agreed to it,' Thomasin answered firmly. 'I am a practical woman now. I don't believe in hearts at all. I would marry him under any circumstances since – since Clym's letter.'

A letter was lying on Mrs Yeobright's work-basket, and at Thomasin's words her aunt reopened it, and silently read for the tenth time that day:

What is the meaning of this silly story that people are circulating about Thomasin and Mr Wildeve? I should call such a scandal humiliating if there was the least chance of its being true. How could such a gross falsehood have arisen? It is said that one should go abroad to hear news of home, and I appear to have done it. Of course I contradict the tale everywhere; but it is very vexing, and I wonder how it could have originated. It is too ridiculous that such a girl as Thomasin could so mortify us as to get jilted on the wedding-day. What has she done?

'Yes,' Mrs Yeobright said sadly, putting down the letter. 'If you think you can marry him, do so. And since Mr Wildeve wishes it to be unceremonious, let it be that too. I can do nothing. It is all in your own hands now. My power over your welfare came to an end when you left this house to go with him to Anglebury.' She continued, half in bitterness, 'I may almost ask, why do you consult me in the matter at all? If you had gone and married him without saying a word to me, I could hardly have been angry – simply because, poor girl, you can't do a better thing.'

'Don't say that and dishearten me.'

'You are right: I will not.'

'I do not plead for him, aunt. Human nature is weak, and I am not a blind woman to insist that he is perfect. I did think so, but I don't now. But I know my course, and you know that I know it. I hope for the best.'

'And so do I, and we will both continue to,' said Mrs Yeobright, rising and kissing her. 'Then the wedding, if it comes off, will be on the morning of the very day Clym comes home?'

'Yes. I decided that it ought to be over before he came. After that you can look him in the face, and so can I. Our concealments will matter nothing.'

Mrs Yeobright moved her head in thoughtful assent, and presently said, 'Do you wish me to give you away? I am willing to undertake that, you know, if you wish, as I was last time. After once forbidding the banns I think I can do no less.'

'I don't think I will ask you to come,' said Thomasin reluctantly, but with decision. 'It would be unpleasant, I am almost sure. Better let there be only strangers present, and none of my relations at all. I would rather have it so. I do not wish to do anything which may touch your credit, and I feel that I should be uncomfortable if you were there, after what has passed. I am only your niece, and there is no necessity why you should concern yourself more about me.'

'Well, he has beaten us,' her aunt said. 'It really seems as if he had been playing with you in this way in revenge for my humbling him as I did by standing up against him at first.'

'O no, aunt,' murmured Thomasin.

They said no more on the subject then. Diggory Venn's knock came soon after; and Mrs Yeobright, on returning from her interview with him in the porch, carelessly observed, 'Another lover has come to ask for you.'

'No?'

'Yes; that queer young man Venn.'

'Asks to pay his addresses to me?'

'Yes; and I told him he was too late.'

Thomasin looked silently into the candle-flame. 'Poor Diggory!' she said, and then aroused herself to other things.

The next day was passed in mere mechanical deeds of preparation, both the women being anxious to immerse themselves in these to escape the emotional aspect of the situation. Some wearing apparel and other articles were collected anew for Thomasin, and remarks on domestic details were frequently made, so as to obscure any inner misgivings about her future as Wildeve's wife.

The appointed morning came. The arrangement with Wildeve was that he should meet at the church to guard against any unpleasant curiosity which might have affected them had they been seen walking off together in the usual country way.

Aunt and niece stood together in the bedroom where the bride was dressing. The sun, where it could catch it, made a mirror of Thomasin's hair, which she always wore braided. It was braided according to a calendric system: the more important the day the more numerous the strands in the braid. On ordinary working-days she braided it in threes; on ordinary Sundays in fours; at May-polings, gipsyings, and the like, she braided it in fives. Years ago she had said that when she married she would braid it in sevens. She had braided it in sevens today.

'I have been thinking that I will wear my blue silk after all,' she said. 'It *is* my wedding day, even though there may be something sad about the time. I mean,' she added, anxious to correct any wrong impression, 'not sad in itself, but in its having had great disappointment and trouble before it.'

Mrs Yeobright breathed in a way which might have been called a sigh. 'I almost wish Clym had been at home,' she said. 'Of course you chose the time because of his absence.'

'Partly. I have felt that I acted unfairly to him in not telling him all; but, as it was done not to grieve him, I thought I would carry out the plan to its end, and tell the whole story when the sky was clear.'

'You are a practical little woman,' said Mrs Yeobright, smiling. 'I wish you and he – no, I don't wish anything. There, it is nine o'clock,' she interrupted, hearing a whizz and a dinging downstairs.

'I told Damon I would leave at nine,' said Thomasin, hastening out of the room.

Her aunt followed. When Thomasin was going up the little walk from the door to the wicket-gate, Mrs Yeobright looked reluctantly at her, and said, 'It is a shame to let you go alone.'

'It is necessary,' said Thomasin.

'At any rate,' added her aunt with forced cheerfulness, 'I shall call upon you this afternoon, and bring the cake with me. If Clym has returned by that time he will perhaps come too. I wish to show Mr Wildeve that I bear him no ill-will. Let the past be forgotten. Well, God bless you! There, I don't believe in old superstitions, but I'll do it.' She threw a slipper at the retreating figure of the girl, who turned, smiled, and went on again.

A few steps further, and she looked back. 'Did you call me, aunt?' she tremulously inquired. 'Good-bye!'

Moved by an uncontrollable feeling as she looked upon Mrs Yeobright's worn, wet face, she ran back, when her aunt came forward, and they met again. 'O – Tamsie,' said the elder, weeping, 'I don't like to let you go.'

'I – I – am –' Thomasin began, giving way likewise. But, quelling her grief, she said, 'Good-bye!' again and went on.

Then Mrs Yeobright saw a little figure wending its way between the scratching furze-bushes, and diminishing far up the valley – a pale-blue spot in a vast field of neutral brown, solitary and undefended except by the power of her own hope.

But the worst feature in the case was one which did not appear in the landscape; it was the man.

The hour chosen for the ceremony by Thomasin and Wildeve had been so timed as to enable her to escape the awkwardness of meeting her cousin Clym, who was returning the same morning. To own to the partial truth of what he had heard would be distressing as long as the humiliating position resulting from the event was unimproved. It was only after a second and successful journey to the altar that she could lift up her head and prove the failure of the first attempt a pure accident.

She had not been gone from Blooms-End more than half an hour when Yeobright came by the meads from the other direction and entered the house.

'I had an early breakfast,' he said to his mother after greeting her. 'Now I could eat a little more.'

They sat down to the repeated meal, and he went on in a low, anxious voice, apparently imagining that Thomasin had not yet come downstairs. 'What's this I have heard about Thomasin and Mr Wildeve?'

'It is true in many points,' said Mrs Yeobright quietly; 'but it is all right now, I hope.' She looked at the clock.

'True?'

'Thomasin is gone to him today.'

Clym pushed away his breakfast. 'Then there is a scandal of some sort, and that's what's the matter with Thomasin. Was it this that made her ill?'

'Yes. Not a scandal: a misfortune. I will tell you all about it, Clym. You must not be angry, but you must listen, and you'll find that what we have done has been done for the best.'

She then told him the circumstances. All that he had known of the affair before he returned from Paris was that there had existed an attachment between Thomasin and Wildeve, which his mother had at first discountenanced, but had since, owing to the arguments of Thomasin, looked upon in a little more favourable light. When she, therefore, proceeded to explain all he was greatly surprised and troubled.

'And she determined that the wedding should be over before you came back,' said Mrs Yeobright, 'that there might be no chance of her meeting you, and having a very painful time of it. That's why she has gone to him; they have arranged to be married this morning.'

'But I can't understand it,' said Yeobright, rising. ' 'Tis so unlike her. I can see why you did not write to me after her unfortunate return home. But why didn't you let me know when the wedding was going to be – the first time?'

'Well, I felt vexed with her just then. She seemed to me to be obstinate; and when I found that you were nothing in her mind I vowed that she should be nothing in yours. I felt that she was only my niece after all; I told her she might marry, but that I should take no interest in it, and should not bother you about it either.'

'It wouldn't have been bothering me. Mother, you did wrong.'

'I thought it might disturb you in your business, and that you might throw up your situation, or injure your prospects in some way because of it, so I said nothing. Of course, if they had married at that time in a proper manner, I should have told you at once.'

'Tamsin actually being married while we are sitting here!'

'Yes. Unless some accident happens again, as it did the first time. It may, considering he's the same man.'

'Yes, and I believe it will. Was it right to let her go? Suppose Wildeve is really a bad fellow?'

'Then he won't come, and she'll come home again.'

'You should have looked more into it.'

'It is useless to say that,' his mother answered with an impatient look of sorrow. 'You don't know how bad it has been here with us all these weeks, Clym. You don't know what a mortification anything of that sort is to a woman. You don't know the sleepless nights we've had in this house, and the almost bitter words that have passed between us since that Fifth of November. I hope never to pass seven such weeks again. Tamsin has not gone outside the door, and I have been ashamed to look anybody in the face; and now you blame me for letting her do the only thing that can be done to set that trouble straight.'

'No,' he said slowly. 'Upon the whole I don't blame you. But just consider how sudden it seems to me. Here was I, knowing nothing; and then I am told all at once that Tamsie is gone to be married. Well, I suppose there was nothing better to do. Do you know, mother,' he continued after a moment or two, looking suddenly interested in his own past history, 'I once thought of Tamsin as a sweetheart? Yes, I did. How odd boys are! And when I came home and saw her this time she seemed so much more affectionate than usual, that I was quite reminded of those days, particularly on the night of the party, when she was unwell. We had the party just the same – was not that rather cruel to her?'

'It made no difference. I had arranged to give one, and it was not worth while to make more gloom than necessary. To begin by shutting ourselves up and telling you of Tamsin's misfortunes would have been a poor sort of welcome.'

Clym remained thinking. 'I almost wish you had not had that party,' he said; 'and for other reasons. But I will tell you in a day or two. We must think of Tamsin now.'

They lapsed into silence. 'I'll tell you what,' said Yeobright again, in a tone which showed some slumbering feeling still. 'I don't think it kind to Tamsin to let her be married like this, and neither of us there to keep up her spirits or care a bit about her. She hasn't disgraced herself, or done anything to deserve that. It is bad enough that the wedding should be so hurried and unceremonious, without our keeping away from it in addition. Upon my soul, 'tis almost a shame. I'll go.'

'It is over by this time,' said his mother with a sigh; 'unless they were late, or he –'

'Then I shall be soon enough to see them come out. I don't quite like your keeping me in ignorance, mother, after all. Really, I half hope he has failed to meet her!'

'And ruined her character?'

'Nonsense: that wouldn't ruin Thomasin.'

He took up his hat and hastily left the house. Mrs Yeobright looked rather unhappy, and sat still, deep in thought. But she was not long left alone. A few minutes later Clym came back again, and in his company came Diggory Venn.

'I find there isn't time for me to get there,' said Clym.

'Is she married?' Mrs Yeobright inquired, turning to the reddleman a face in which a strange strife of wishes, for and against, was apparent.

Venn bowed. 'She is, ma'am.'

'How strange it sounds,' murmured Clym.

'And he didn't disappoint her this time?' said Mrs Yeobright.

'He did not. And there is now no slight on her name. I was hastening ath'art to tell you at once, as I saw you were not there.'

'How came you to be there? How did you know it?' she asked.

'I have been in that neighbourhood for some time, and I saw them go in,' said the reddleman. 'Wildeve came up to the door, punctual as the clock. I didn't expect it of him.' He did not add, as he might have added, that how he came to be in that neighbourhood was not by accident; that, since Wildeve's resumption of his right to Thomasin, Venn, with the thoroughness which was part of his character, had determined to see the end of the episode.

'Who was there?' said Mrs Yeobright.

'Nobody hardly. I stood right out of the way, and she did not see me.' The reddleman spoke huskily, and looked into the garden.

'Who gave her away?'

'Miss Vye.'

'How very remarkable! Miss Vye! It is to be considered an honour, I suppose?'

'Who's Miss Vye?' said Clym.

'Captain Vye's granddaughter, of Mistover Knap.'

'A proud girl from Budmouth,' said Mrs Yeobright. 'One not much to my liking. People say she's a witch, but of course that's absurd.'

The reddleman kept to himself his acquaintance with that fair personage, and also that Eustacia was there because he went to fetch her, in accordance with a promise he had given as soon as he learnt that the marriage was to take place. He merely said, in continuation of the story –

'I was sitting on the churchyard-wall when they came up, one from one way, the other from the other; and Miss Vye was walking thereabouts, looking at the head-stones. As soon as they had gone in I went to the door, feeling I should like to see it, as I knew her so well. I pulled off my boots because they were so noisy, and went up into the gallery. I saw then that the parson and clerk were already there.'

'How came Miss Vye to have anything to do with it, if she was only on a walk that way?'

'Because there was nobody else. She had gone into the church just before me, not into the gallery. The parson looked round before beginning, and as she was the only one near he beckoned to her, and she went up to the rails. After that, when it came to signing the book she pushed up her veil and signed; and Tamsin seemed to thank her for her kindness.' The reddleman told the tale thoughtfully, for there lingered upon his vision the changing colour of Wildeve, when Eustacia lifted the thick veil which had concealed her from recognition and looked calmly into his face. 'And then,' said Diggory sadly, 'I came away, for her history as Tamsin Yeobright was over.'

'I offered to go,' said Mrs Yeobright regretfully. 'But she said it was not necessary.'

'Well, it is no matter,' said the reddleman. 'The thing is done at last as it was meant to be at first, and God send her happiness. Now I'll wish you good morning.'

He placed his cap on his head and went out.

From that instant of leaving Mrs Yeobright's door, the reddleman was seen no more in or about Egdon Heath for a space of many months. He vanished entirely. The nook among the brambles where his van had been standing was as vacant as ever the next morning, and scarcely a sign remained to show that he had been there, excepting a few straws, and a little redness on the turf, which was washed away by the next storm of rain.

The report that Diggory had brought of the wedding, correct as far as it went, was deficient in one significant particular, which had escaped him through his being at some distance back in the church. When Thomasin was tremblingly engaged in signing her name Wildeve had flung towards Eustacia a glance that said plainly, 'I have punished you now.' She had replied in a low tone – and he little thought how truly – 'You mistake; it gives me sincerest pleasure to see her your wife today.'

BOOK THIRD

THE FASCINATION

I

'My Mind to Me a Kingdom Is'

In Clym Yeobright's face could be dimly seen the typical countenance of the future. Should there be a classic period to art hereafter, its Pheidias may produce such faces. The view of life as a thing to be put up with, replacing that zest for existence which was so intense in early civilizations, must ultimately enter so thoroughly into the constitution of the advanced races that its facial expression will become accepted as a new artistic departure. People already feel that a man who lives without disturbing a curve of feature, or setting a mark of mental concern anywhere upon himself, is too far removed from modern perceptiveness to be a modern type. Physically beautiful men – the glory of the race when it was young – are almost an anachronism now; and we may wonder whether, at some time or other, physically beautiful women may not be an anachronism likewise.

The truth seems to be that a long line of disillusive centuries has permanently displaced the Hellenic idea of life, or whatever it may be called. What the Greeks only suspected we know well; what their Aeschylus imagined our nursery children feel. That old-fashioned revelling in the general situation grows less and less possible as we uncover the defects of natural laws, and see the quandary that man is in by their operation.

The lineaments which will get embodied in ideals based upon this new recognition will probably be akin to those of Yeobright. The observer's eye was arrested, not by his face as a picture, but by his face as a page; not by what it was, but by what it recorded. His features were attractive in the light of symbols, as sounds intrinsically common become attractive in language, and as shapes intrinsically simple become interesting in writing.

He had been a lad of whom something was expected. Beyond this all had been chaos. That he would be successful in an original way, or that he would go to the dogs in an original way, seemed equally probable. The only absolute certainty about him was that he would not stand still in the circumstances amid which he was born.

Hence, when his name was casually mentioned by neighbouring yeomen, the listener said, 'Ah, Clym Yeobright: what is he doing now?' When the instinctive question about a person is, What is he doing? it is felt that he will not be found to be, like most of us, doing nothing in particular. There is an indefinite sense that he must be invading some region of singularity, good or bad. The devout hope is that he is doing well. The secret faith is that he is making a mess of it. Half a dozen comfortable marketmen, who were habitual callers at the Quiet Woman as they passed by in their carts, were partial to the topic. In fact, though they were not Egdon men, they could hardly avoid it while they sucked their long clay tubes and regarded the heath through the window. Clym had been so inwoven with the heath in his boyhood that hardly anybody could look upon it without thinking of him. So the subject recurred: if he were making a fortune and a name, so much the better for him; if he were making a tragical figure in the world, so much the better for a narrative.

The fact was that Yeobright's fame had spread to an awkward extent before he left home. 'It is bad when your fame outruns your means,' said the Spanish Jesuit Gracian. At the age of six he had asked a Scripture riddle: 'Who was the first man known to wear breeches?' and applause had resounded from the very verge of the heath. At seven he painted the Battle of Waterloo with tiger-lily pollen and black-currant juice, in the absence of water-colours. By the time he reached twelve he had in this manner been heard of as artist and scholar for at least two miles round. An individual whose fame spreads three or four thousand yards in the time taken by the fame of others similarly situated to travel six or eight hundred, must of necessity have something in him. Possibly Clym's fame, like Homer's, owed something to the accidents of his situation; nevertheless famous he was.

He grew up and was helped out in life. That waggery of fate which started Clive as a writing clerk, Gay as a linen-draper, Keats as a surgeon, and a thousand others in a thousand other odd ways, banished the wild and ascetic heath lad to a trade whose sole concern was with the especial symbols of self-indulgence and vainglory.

The details of this choice of a business for him it is not necessary to give. At the death of his father a neighbouring gentleman had kindly undertaken to give the boy a start; and this assumed the form of sending him to Budmouth. Yeobright did not wish to go there, but it was the only feasible opening. Thence he went to London; and thence, shortly after, to Paris, where he had remained till now.

Something being expected of him, he had not been at home many days before a great curiosity as to why he stayed on so long began to arise in the heath. The natural term of a holiday had passed, yet he still remained. On the Sunday morning following the week of Thomasin's marriage a discussion on this subject was in progress at a hair-cutting before Fairway's house. Here the local barbering was always done at this hour on this day; to be followed by the great Sunday wash of the inhabitants at noon, which in its turn was followed by the great Sunday dressing an hour later. On Egdon Heath Sunday proper did not begin till dinner-time, and even then it was a somewhat battered specimen of the day.

These Sunday-morning hair-cuttings were performed by Fairway; the victim sitting on a chopping-block in front of the house, without a coat, and the neighbours gossiping around, idly observing the locks of hair as they rose upon the wind after the snip, and flew away out of sight to the four quarters of the heavens. Summer and winter the scene was the same, unless the wind were more than usually blusterous, when the stool was shifted a few feet round the corner. To complain of cold in sitting out of doors, hatless and coatless, while Fairway told true stories between the cuts of the scissors, would have been to pronounce yourself no man at once. To flinch, exclaim, or move a muscle of the face at the small stabs under the ear received from those instruments, or at scarifications of the neck by the comb, would have been thought a gross breach of good manners, considering that Fairway did it all for nothing. A bleeding about the poll on Sunday afternoons was amply accounted for by the explanation, 'I have had my hair cut, you know.'

The conversation on Yeobright had been started by a distant view of the young man rambling leisurely across the heath before them.

'A man who is doing well elsewhere wouldn't bide here two or three weeks for nothing,' said Fairway. 'He's got some project in 's head – depend upon that.'

'Well, 'a can't keep a diment shop here,' said Sam.

'I don't see why he should have had them two heavy boxes home if he had not been going to bide; and what there is for him to do here the Lord in heaven knows.'

Before many more surmises could be indulged in Yeobright had come near; and seeing the hair-cutting group he turned aside to join them. Marching up, and looking critically at their faces for a moment, he said, without introduction, 'Now, folks, let me guess what you have been talking about.'

'Ay, sure, if you will,' said Sam.

'About me.'

'Now, it is a thing I shouldn't have dreamed of doing, otherwise,' said Fairway in a tone of integrity; 'but since you have named it, Master Yeobright, I'll own that we was talking about 'ee. We were wondering what could keep you home here molly-horning about when you have made such a world-wide name for yourself in the nick-nack trade – now, that's the truth o't.'

'I'll tell you,' said Yeobright, with unexpected earnestness. 'I am not sorry to have the opportunity. I've come home because, all things considered, I can be a trifle less useless here than anywhere else. But I have only lately found this out. When I first got away from home I thought this place was not worth troubling about. I thought our life here was contemptible. To oil your boots instead of blacking them, to dust your coat with a switch instead of a brush: was there ever anything more ridiculous? I said.'

'So 'tis; so 'tis!'

'No, no – you are wrong; it isn't.'

'Beg your pardon, we thought that was your maning?'

'Well, as my views changed my course became very depressing. I found that I was trying to be like people who had hardly anything in common with myself. I was endeavouring to put off one sort of life for another sort of life, which was not better than the life I had known before. It was simply different.'

'True; a sight different,' said Fairway.

'Yes, Paris must be a taking place,' said Humphrey. 'Grand shop-winders, trumpets, and drums; and here be we out of doors in all winds and weathers –'

'But you mistake me,' pleaded Clym. 'All this was very depressing. But not so depressing as something I next perceived – that my business was the idlest, vainest, most effeminate business that ever a man could be put to. That decided me: I would give it up and try to follow some rational occupation among the people I knew best, and to whom I could be of most use. I have come home; and this is how I mean to carry out my plan. I shall keep a school as near to Egdon as possible, so as to be able to walk over here and have a night-school in my mother's house. But I must study a little at first, to get properly qualified. Now, neighbours, I must go.'

And Clym resumed his walk across the heath.

'He'll never carry it out in the world,' said Fairway. 'In a few weeks he'll learn to see things otherwise.'

' 'Tis good-hearted of the young man,' said another. 'But, for my part, I think he had better mind his business.'

* II *

The New Course Causes Disappointment

YEOBRIGHT loved his kind. He had a conviction that the want of most men was knowledge of a sort which brings wisdom rather than affluence. He wished to raise the class at the expense of individuals rather than individuals at the expense of the class. What was more, he was ready at once to be the first unit sacrificed.

In passing from the bucolic to the intellectual life the intermediate stages are usually two at least, frequently many more; and one of these stages is almost sure to be worldly advance. We can hardly imagine bucolic placidity quickening to intellectual aims without imagining social aims as the transitional phase. Yeobright's local peculiarity was that in striving at high thinking he still cleaved to plain living – nay, wild and meagre living in many respects, and brotherliness with clowns.

He was a John the Baptist who took ennoblement rather than repentance for his text. Mentally he was in a provincial future, that is, he was in many points abreast with the central town thinkers of his date. Much of this development he may have owed to his studious life in Paris, where he had become acquainted with ethical systems popular at the time.

In consequence of this relatively advanced position, Yeobright might have been called unfortunate. The rural world was not ripe for him. A man should be only partially before his time: to be completely to the vanward in aspirations is fatal to fame. Had Philip's warlike son been intellectually so far ahead as to have attempted civilization without bloodshed, he would have been twice the godlike hero that he seemed, but nobody would have heard of an Alexander.

In the interests of renown the forwardness should lie chiefly in the capacity to handle things. Successful propagandists have succeeded because the doctrine they bring into form is that which their listeners have for some time felt without being able to shape. A man who advocates aesthetic effort and deprecates social effort is only likely to be understood by a class to which social effort has become a stale matter. To argue upon the possibility of culture before luxury to the bucolic world may be to argue truly, but it is an attempt to disturb a sequence to which humanity has been long accustomed. Yeobright preaching to the Egdon eremites that they might rise to a serene comprehensiveness without going through the process of enriching themselves, was not unlike arguing to ancient Chaldeans that in ascending from earth to the pure empyrean it was not necessary to pass first into the intervening heaven of ether.

Was Yeobright's mind well-proportioned? No. A well-proportioned mind is one which shows no particular bias; one of which we may safely say that it will never cause its owner to be confined as a madman, tortured as a heretic, or crucified as a blasphemer. Also, on the other hand, that it will never cause him to be applauded as a prophet, revered as a priest, or exalted as a king. Its usual blessings are happiness and mediocrity. It produces the poetry of Rogers, the paintings of West, the statecraft of North, the spiritual guidance of Tomline; enabling its possessors to find their way to wealth, to wind up well, to step with dignity off the stage, to die comfortably in their beds, and to get the decent monument which, in many cases, they deserve. It never would have allowed Yeobright to do such a ridiculous thing as throw up his business to benefit his fellow-creatures.

He walked along towards home without attending to paths. If any one knew the heath well it was Clym. He was permeated with its scenes, with its substance, and with its odours. He might be said to be its product. His eyes had first opened thereon; with its appearance all the first images of his memory were mingled; his estimate of life had been coloured by it; his toys had been the flint knives and arrow-heads which he found there, wondering why stones should 'grow' to such odd shapes; his flowers, the purple bells and yellow furze; his animal kingdom, the snakes and croppers; his society, its human haunters. Take all the varying hates felt by Eustacia Vye towards the heath, and translate them into loves, and you have the heart of Clym. He gazed upon the wide prospect as he walked, and was glad.

To many persons this Egdon was a place which had slipped out of its century generations ago, to intrude as an uncouth object into this. It was an obsolete thing, and few cared to study it. How could this be otherwise in the days of square fields, plashed hedges, and meadows watered on a plan so rectangular that on a fine day they look like silver gridirons? The farmer, in his ride, who could smile at artificial grasses, look with solicitude at the coming corn, and sigh with sadness at the fly-eaten turnips, bestowed upon the distant upland of heath nothing better than a frown. But as for Yeobright, when he looked from the heights on his way he could not help indulging in a barbarous satisfaction at observing that, in some of the attempts at reclamation from the waste, tillage, after holding on for a year or two, had receded again in despair, the ferns and furze-tufts stubbornly reasserting themselves.

He descended into the valley, and soon reached his home at Blooms-End. His mother was snipping dead leaves from the window-plants. She looked up at him as if she did not understand the meaning of his long stay with her; her face had worn that look for several days. He could perceive that the curiosity which had been shown by their hair-cutting group amounted in his mother to concern. But she had asked no question with her lips, even when the arrival of his trunks suggested that he was not going to leave her soon. Her silence besought an explanation of him more loudly than words.

'I am not going back to Paris again, mother,' he said. 'At least, in my old capacity. I have given up the business.'

Mrs Yeobright turned in pained surprise. 'I thought something was amiss, because of the boxes. I wonder you did not tell me sooner.'

'I ought to have done it. But I have been in doubt whether you would be pleased with my plan. I was not quite clear on a few points myself. I am going to take an entirely new course.'

'I am astonished, Clym. How can you want to do better than you've been doing?'

'Very easily. But I shall not do better in the way you mean; I suppose it will be called doing worse. But I hate that business of mine, and I want to do some worthy thing before I die. As a schoolmaster I think to do it – a schoolmaster to the poor and ignorant, to teach them what nobody else will.'

'After all the trouble that has been taken to give you a start, and when there is nothing to do but to keep straight on towards affluence, you say you will be a poor man's schoolmaster. Your fancies will be your ruin, Clym.'

Mrs Yeobright spoke calmly, but the force of feeling behind the words was but too apparent to one who knew her as well as her son did. He did not answer. There was in his face that hopelessness of being understood which comes when the objector is constitutionally beyond the reach of a logic that, even under favouring conditions, is almost too coarse a vehicle for the subtlety of the argument.

No more was said on the subject till the end of dinner. His mother then began, as if there had been no interval since the morning. 'It disturbs me, Clym, to find that you have come home with such thoughts as those. I hadn't the least idea that you meant to go backward in the world by your own free choice. Of course, I have always supposed you were going to push straight on, as other men do – all who deserve the name – when they have been put in a good way of doing well.'

'I cannot help it,' said Clym, in a troubled tone. 'Mother, I hate the flashy business. Talk about men who deserve the name, can any man deserving the name waste his time in that effeminate way, when he sees half the world going to ruin for want of somebody to buckle to and teach them how to breast the misery they are born to? I get up every morning and see the whole creation groaning and travailing in pain, as St Paul says, and yet there am I, trafficking in glittering splendours with wealthy women and titled libertines, and pandering to the meanest vanities – I, who have health and strength enough for anything. I have been troubled in my mind about it all the year, and the end is that I cannot do it any more.'

'Why can't you do it as well as others?'

'I don't know, except that there are many things other people care for which I don't; and that's partly why I think I ought to do this. For one thing, my body does not require much of me. I cannot enjoy delicacies; good things are wasted upon me. Well, I ought to turn that defect to advantage, and by being able to do without what other people require I can spend what such things cost upon anybody else.'

Now, Yeobright, having inherited some of these very instincts from the woman before him, could not fail to awaken a reciprocity in her through her feelings, if not by arguments, disguise it as she might for his good. She spoke with less assurance. 'And yet you might have been a wealthy man if you had only persevered. Manager to that large diamond establishment – what better can a man wish for? What a post of trust and respect! I suppose you will be like your father; like him, you are getting weary of doing well.'

'No,' said her son; 'I am not weary of that, though I am weary of what you mean by it. Mother, what is doing well?'

Mrs Yeobright was far too thoughtful a woman to be content with ready definitions, and, like the 'What is wisdom?' of Plato's Socrates, and the 'What is truth?' of Pontius Pilate, Yeobright's burning question received no answer.

The silence was broken by the clash of the garden gate, a tap at the door, and its opening. Christian Cantle appeared in the room in his Sunday clothes.

It was the custom on Egdon to begin the preface to a story before absolutely entering the house, so as to be well in for the body of the narrative by the time visitor and visited stood face to face. Christian had been saying to them while the door was leaving its latch, 'To think that I, who go from home but once in a while, and hardly then, should have been there this morning!'

' 'Tis news you have brought us, then, Christian?' said Mrs Yeobright.

'Ay, sure, about a witch, and ye must overlook my time o' day; for, says I, "I must go and tell 'em, though they won't have half done dinner." I assure ye it made me shake like a driven leaf. Do ye think any harm will come o't?'

'Well – what?'

'This morning at church we was all standing up, and the pa'son said, "Let us pray." "Well," thinks I, "one may as well kneel as stand"; so down I went; and, more than that, all the rest were as willing to oblige the man as I. We hadn't been hard at it for more than a minute when a most terrible screech sounded through church, as if somebody had just gied up their heart's blood. All the folks jumped up, and then we found that Susan Nunsuch had pricked Miss Vye with a long stocking-needle, as she had threatened to do as soon as ever she could get the young lady to church, where she don't come very often. She've waited for this chance for weeks, so as to draw her blood and put an end to the bewitching of Susan's children that has been carried on so long. Sue followed her into church, sat next to her, and as soon as she could find a chance in went the stocking-needle into my lady's arm.'

'Good heaven, how horrid!' said Mrs Yeobright.

'Sue pricked her that deep that the maid fainted away; and as I was afeard there might be some tumult among us, I got behind the bass-viol and didn't see no more. But they carried her out into the air, 'tis said; but when they looked round for Sue she was gone. What a scream that girl gied, poor thing! There were the pa'son in his surplice holding up his hand and saying, "Sit down, my good people, sit down!" But the deuce a bit would they sit down. O, and what d'ye think I found out, Mrs Yeobright? The pa'son wears a suit of clothes under his surplice! – I could see his black sleeve when he held up his arm.'

' 'Tis a cruel thing,' said Yeobright.

'Yes,' said his mother.

'The nation ought to look into it,' said Christian. 'Here's Humphrey coming, I think.'

In came Humphrey. 'Well, have ye heard the news? But I see you have. 'Tis a very strange thing that whenever one of Egdon folk goes to church some rum job or other is sure to be doing. The last time one of us was there was when neighbour Fairway went in the fall; and that was the day you forbad the banns, Mrs Yeobright.'

'Has the cruelly treated girl been able to walk home?' said Clym.

'They say she got better, and went home very well. And now I've told it I must be moving homeward myself.'

THE RETURN OF THE NATIVE

'And I,' said Humphrey. 'Truly now we shall see if there's anything in what folks say about her.'

When they were gone into the heath again Yeobright said quietly to his mother, 'Do you think I have turned teacher too soon?'

'It is right that there should be schoolmasters, and missionaries, and all such men,' she replied. 'But it is right, too, that I should try to lift you out of this life into something richer, and that you should not come back again, and be as if I had not tried at all.'

Later in the day Sam, the turf-cutter, entered. 'I've come a-borrowing, Mrs Yeobright. I suppose you have heard what's been happening to the beauty on the hill?'

'Yes, Sam: half a dozen have been telling us.'

'Beauty?' said Clym.

'Yes, tolerably well-favoured,' Sam replied. 'Lord! all the country owns that 'tis one of the strangest things in the world that such a woman should have come to live up there.'

'Dark or fair?'

'Now, though I've seen her twenty times, that's a thing I cannot call to mind.'

'Darker than Tamsin,' murmured Mrs Yeobright.

'A woman who seems to care for nothing at all, as you may say.'

'She is melancholy, then?' inquired Clym.

'She mopes about by herself, and don't mix in with the people.'

'Is she a young lady inclined for adventures?'

'Not to my knowledge.'

'Doesn't join in with the lads in their games, to get some sort of excitement in this lonely place?'

'No.'

'Mumming, for instance?'

'No. Her notions are different. I should rather say her thoughts were far away from here, with lords and ladies she'll never know, and mansions she'll never see again.'

Observing that Clym appeared singularly interested Mrs Yeobright said rather uneasily to Sam, 'You see more in her than most of us do. Miss Vye is to my mind too idle to be charming. I have never heard that she is of any use to herself or to other people. Good girls don't get treated as witches even on Egdon.'

'Nonsense – that proves nothing either way,' said Yeobright.

'Well, of course I don't understand such niceties,' said Sam, withdrawing from a possibly unpleasant argument; 'and what she is we must wait for time to tell us. The business that I have really called about is this, to borrow the longest and strongest rope you have. The captain's bucket has dropped into the well, and they are in want of water; and as all the chaps are at home today we think we can get it out for him. We have three cart-ropes already, but they won't reach to the bottom.'

Mrs Yeobright told him that he might have whatever ropes he could find in the outhouse, and Sam went out to search. When he passed by the door Clym joined him, and accompanied him to the gate.

'Is this young witch-lady going to stay long at Mistover?' he asked.

'I should say so.'

'What a cruel shame to ill-use her! She must have suffered greatly – more in mind than in body.'

' 'Twas a graceless trick – such a handsome girl, too. You ought to see her, Mr Yeobright, being a young man come from far, and with a little more to show for your years than most of us.'

'Do you think she would like to teach children?' said Clym.

Sam shook his head. 'Quite a different sort of body from that, I reckon.'

'O, it was merely something which occurred to me. It would of course be necessary to see her and talk it over – not an easy thing, by the way, for my family and hers are not very friendly.'

'I'll tell you how you mid see her, Mr Yeobright,' said Sam. 'We are going to grapple for the bucket at six o'clock tonight at her house, and you could lend a hand. There's five or six coming, but the well is deep, and another might be useful, if you don't mind appearing in that shape. She's sure to be walking round.'

'I'll think of it,' said Yeobright; and they parted.

He thought of it a good deal; but nothing more was said about Eustacia inside the house at that time. Whether this romantic martyr to superstition and the melancholy mummer he had conversed with under the full moon were one and the same person remained as yet a problem.

* III *

The First Act in a Timeworn Drama

THE afternoon was fine, and Yeobright walked on the heath for an hour with his mother. When they reached the lofty ridge which divided the valley of Blooms-End from the adjoining valley they stood still and looked round. The Quiet Woman Inn was visible on the low margin of the heath in one direction, and afar on the other hand rose Mistover Knap.

'You mean to call on Thomasin?' he inquired.

'Yes. But you need not come this time,' said his mother.

'In that case I'll branch off here, mother. I am going to Mistover.'

Mrs Yeobright turned to him inquiringly.

'I am going to help them get the bucket out of the captain's well,' he continued. 'As it is so very deep I may be useful. And I should like to see this Miss Vye – not so much for her good looks as for another reason.'

'Must you go?' his mother asked.

'I thought to.'

And they parted. 'There is no help for it,' murmured Clym's mother gloomily as he withdrew. 'They are sure to see each other. I wish Sam would carry his news to other houses than mine.'

Clym's retreating figure got smaller and smaller as it rose and fell over the hillocks on his way. 'He is tender-hearted,' said Mrs Yeobright to herself while she watched him; 'otherwise it would matter little. How he's going on!'

He was, indeed, walking with a will over the furze, as straight as a line, as if his life depended upon it. His mother drew a long breath, and, abandoning the visit to Thomasin, turned back. The evening films began to make nebulous pictures of the valleys, but the high lands still were raked by the declining rays of the winter sun, which glanced on Clym as he walked forward, eyed by every rabbit and fieldfare around, a long shadow advancing in front of him.

On drawing near to the furze-covered bank and ditch which fortified the captain's dwelling he could hear voices within, signifying that operations had been already begun. At the side-entrance gate he stopped and looked over.

Half a dozen able-bodied men were standing in a line from the well-mouth, holding a rope which passed over the well-roller into the depths below. Fairway, with a piece of smaller rope round his body, made fast to one of the standards, to guard against accidents, was leaning over the opening, his right hand clasping the vertical rope that descended into the well.

'Now, silence, folks,' said Fairway.

The talking ceased, and Fairway gave a circular motion to the rope, as if he were stirring batter. At the end of a minute a dull splashing reverberated from the bottom of the well; the helical twist he had imparted to the rope had reached the grapnel below.

'Haul!' said Fairway; and the men who held the rope began to gather it over the wheel.

'I think we've got sommat,' said one of the haulers-in.

'Then pull steady,' said Fairway.

They gathered up more and more, till a regular dripping into the well could be heard below. It grew smarter with the increasing height of the bucket, and presently a hundred and fifty feet of rope had been pulled in.

Fairway then lit a lantern, tied it to another cord, and began lowering it into the well beside the first. Clym came forward and looked down. Strange humid leaves, which knew nothing of the seasons of the year, and quaint-natured mosses were revealed on the wellside as the lantern descended; till its rays fell upon a confused mass of rope and bucket dangling in the dank, dark air.

'We've only got en by the edge of the hoop – steady, for God's sake!' said Fairway.

They pulled with the greatest gentleness, till the wet bucket appeared about two yards below them, like a dead friend come to earth again. Three or four hands were stretched out, then jerk went the rope, whizz went the wheel, the two foremost haulers fell backward, the beating of a falling body was heard, receding down the sides of the well, and a thunderous uproar arose at the bottom. The bucket was gone again.

'Damn the bucket!' said Fairway.

'Lower again,' said Sam.

'I'm as stiff as a ram's horn stooping so long,' said Fairway, standing up and stretching himself till his joints creaked.

'Rest a few minutes, Timothy,' said Yeobright. 'I'll take your place.'

The grapnel was again lowered. Its smart impact upon the distant water reached their ears like a kiss, whereupon Yeobright knelt down, and leaning over the well began dragging the grapnel round and round as Fairway had done.

'Tie a rope round him – it is dangerous!' cried a soft and anxious voice somewhere above them.

Everybody turned. The speaker was a woman, gazing down upon the group from an upper window, whose panes blazed in the ruddy glare from the west. Her lips were parted and she appeared for the moment to forget where she was.

The rope was accordingly tied round his waist, and the work proceeded. At the next haul the weight was not heavy, and it was discovered that they had only secured a coil of the rope detached from the bucket. The tangled mass was thrown into the background. Humphrey took Yeobright's place, and the grapnel was lowered again.

Yeobright retired to the heap of recovered rope in a meditative mood. Of the identity between the lady's voice and that of the melancholy mummer he had not a moment's doubt. 'How thoughtful of her!' he said to himself.

Eustacia, who had reddened when she perceived the effect of her exclamation upon the group below, was no longer to be seen at the window, though Yeobright scanned it wistfully. While he stood there the men at the well succeeded in getting up the bucket without a mishap. One of them then went to inquire for the captain, to learn what orders he wished to give for mending the well-tackle. The captain proved to be away from home; and Eustacia appeared at the door and came out. She had lapsed into an easy and dignified calm, far removed from the intensity of life in her words of solicitude for Clym's safety.

'Will it be possible to draw water here tonight?' she inquired.

'No, miss; the bottom of the bucket is clean knocked out. And as we can do no more now we'll leave off, and come again tomorrow morning.'

'No water,' she murmured, turning away.

'I can send you up some from Blooms-End,' said Clym, coming forward and raising his hat as the men retired.

Yeobright and Eustacia looked at each other for one instant, as if each had in mind those few moments during which a certain moonlight scene was common to both. With the glance the calm fixity of her features sublimed itself to an expression of refinement and warmth: it was like garish noon rising to the dignity of sunset in a couple of seconds.

'Thank you; it will hardly be necessary,' she replied.

'But if you have no water?'

'Well, it is what I call no water,' she said, blushing, and lifting her long-lashed eyelids as if to lift them were a work requiring consideration. 'But my grandfather calls it water enough. I'll show you what I mean.'

She moved away a few yards, and Clym followed. When she reached the corner of the enclosure, where the steps were formed for mounting the boundary bank, she sprang up with a lightness which seemed strange after her listless movement towards the well. It incidentally showed that her apparent languor did not arise from lack of force.

Clym ascended behind her, and noticed a circular burnt patch at the top of the bank. 'Ashes?' he said.

'Yes,' said Eustacia. 'We had a little bonfire here last Fifth of November, and those are the marks of it.'

On that spot had stood the fire she had kindled to attract Wildeve.

'That's the only kind of water we have,' she continued, tossing a stone into the pool, which lay on the outside of the bank like the white of an eye without its pupil. The stone fell with a flounce, but no Wildeve appeared on the other side, as on a previous occasion there. 'My grandfather says he lived for more than twenty years at sea on water twice as bad as that,' she went on, 'and considers it quite good enough for us here on an emergency.'

'Well, as a matter of fact there are no impurities in the water of these pools at this time of the year. It has only just rained into them.'

She shook her head. 'I am managing to exist in a wilderness, but I cannot drink from a pond,' she said.

Clym looked towards the well, which was now deserted, the men having gone home. 'It is a long way to send for springwater,' he said, after a silence. 'But since you don't like this in the pond, I'll try to get you some myself.' He went back to the well. 'Yes, I think I could do it by tying on this pail.'

'But, since I would not trouble the men to get it, I cannot in conscience let you.'

'I don't mind the trouble at all.'

He made fast the pail to the long coil of rope, put it over the wheel, and allowed it to descend by letting the rope slip through his hands. Before it had gone far, however, he checked it.

'I must make fast the end first, or we may lose the whole,' he said to Eustacia, who had drawn near. 'Could you hold this a moment, while I do it – or shall I call your servant?'

'I can hold it,' said Eustacia; and he placed the rope in her hands, going then to search for the end.

'I suppose I may let it slip down?' she inquired.

'I would advise you not to let it go far,' said Clym. 'It will get much heavier, you will find.'

However, Eustacia had begun to pay out. While he was tying she cried, 'I cannot stop it!'

Clym ran to her side, and found he could only check the rope by twisting the loose part round the upright post, when it stopped with a jerk. 'Has it hurt you?'

'Yes,' she replied.

'Very much?'

'No; I think not.' She opened her hands. One of them was bleeding; the rope had dragged off the skin. Eustacia wrapped it in her handkerchief.

'You should have let go,' said Yeobright. 'Why didn't you?'

'You said I was to hold on . . . This is the second time I have been wounded today.'

'Ah, yes; I have heard of it. I blush for my native Egdon. Was it a serious injury you received in church, Miss Vye?'

There was such an abundance of sympathy in Clym's tone that Eustacia slowly drew up her sleeve and disclosed her round white arm. A bright red spot appeared on its smooth surface, like a ruby on Parian marble.

'There it is,' she said, putting her finger against the spot.

'It was dastardly of the woman,' said Clym. 'Will not Captain Vye get her punished?'

'He is gone from home on that very business. I did not know that I had such a magic reputation.'

'And you fainted?' said Clym, looking at the scarlet little puncture as if he would like to kiss it and make it well.

'Yes, it frightened me. I had not been to church for a long time. And now I shall not go again for ever so long – perhaps never. I cannot face their eyes after this. Don't you think it dreadfully humiliating? I wished I was dead for hours after, but I don't mind now.'

'I have come to clean away these cobwebs,' said Yeobright. 'Would you like to help me – by high class teaching? We might benefit them much.'

'I don't quite feel anxious to. I have not much love for my fellow-creatures. Sometimes I quite hate them.'

'Still I think that if you were to hear my scheme you might take an interest in it. There is no use in hating people – if you hate anything, you should hate what produced them.'

'Do you mean Nature? I hate her already. But I shall be glad to hear your scheme at any time.'

The situation had now worked itself out, and the next natural thing was for them to part. Clym knew this well enough, and Eustacia made a move of conclusion; yet he looked at her as if he had one word more to say. Perhaps if he had not lived in Paris it would never have been uttered.

'We have met before,' he said, regarding her with rather more interest than was necessary.

'I do not own it,' said Eustacia, with a repressed, still look.

'But I may think what I like.'

'Yes.'

'You are lonely here.'

'I cannot endure the heath, except in its purple season. The heath is a cruel taskmaster to me.'

'Can you say so?' he asked. 'To my mind it is most exhilarating, and strengthening, and soothing. I would rather live on these hills than anywhere else in the world.'

'It is well enough for artists; but I never would learn to draw.'

'And there is a very curious Druidical stone just out there.' He threw a pebble in the direction signified. 'Do you often go to see it?'

'I was not even aware that there existed any such curious Druidical stone. I am aware that there are Boulevards in Paris.'

Yeobright looked thoughtfully on the ground. 'That means much,' he said.

'It does indeed,' said Eustacia.

'I remember when I had the same longing for town bustle. Five years of a great city would be a perfect cure for that.'

'Heaven send me such a cure! Now, Mr Yeobright, I will go indoors and plaster my wounded hand.'

They separated, and Eustacia vanished in the increasing shade. She seemed full of many things. Her past was a blank, her life had begun. The effect upon Clym of this meeting he did not fully discover till some time after. During his walk home his most intelligible sensation was that his scheme had somehow become glorified. A beautiful woman had been intertwined with it.

On reaching the house he went up to the room which was to be made his study, and occupied himself during the evening in unpacking his books from the boxes and arranging them on shelves. From another box he drew a lamp and a can of oil. He trimmed the lamp, arranged his table, and said, 'Now, I am ready to begin.'

He rose early the next morning, read two hours before breakfast by the light of his lamp – read all the morning, all the afternoon. Just when the sun was going down his eyes felt weary, and he leant back in his chair.

His room overlooked the front of the premises and the valley of the heath beyond. The lowest beams of the winter sun threw the shadow of the house over the palings, across the grass margin of the heath, and far up the vale, where the chimney outlines and those of the surrounding treetops stretched forth in long dark prongs. Having been seated at work all day, he decided to take a turn upon the hills before it got dark; and, going out forthwith, he struck across the heath towards Mistover.

It was an hour and a half later when he again appeared at the garden gate. The shutters of the house were closed, and Christian Cantle, who had been wheeling manure about the garden all day, had gone home. On entering he found that his mother, after waiting a long time for him, had finished her meal.

'Where have you been, Clym?' she immediately said. 'Why didn't you tell me that you were going away at this time?'

'I have been on the heath.'

'You'll meet Eustacia Vye if you go up there.'

Clym paused a minute. 'Yes, I met her this evening,' he said, as though it were spoken under the sheer necessity of preserving honesty.

'I wondered if you had.'

'It was no appointment.'

'No; such meetings never are.'

'But you are not angry, mother?'

'I can hardly say that I am not. Angry? No. But when I consider the usual nature of the drag which causes men of promise to disappoint the world I feel uneasy.'

'You deserve credit for the feeling, mother. But I can assure you that you need not be disturbed by it on my account.'

'When I think of you and your new crotchets,' said Mrs Yeobright, with some emphasis, 'I naturally don't feel so comfortable as I did a twelvemonth ago. It is incredible to me that a man accustomed to the attractive women of Paris and elsewhere should be so easily worked upon by a girl in a heath. You could just as well have walked another way.'

'I had been studying all day.'

'Well, yes,' she added more hopefully, 'I have been thinking that you might get on as a schoolmaster, and rise that way, since you really are determined to hate the course you were pursuing.'

Yeobright was unwilling to disturb this idea, though his scheme was far enough removed from one wherein the education of youth should be made a mere channel of social ascent. He had no desires of that sort. He had reached the stage in a young man's life when the grimness of the general human situation first becomes clear; and the realization of this causes ambition to halt awhile. In France it is not uncustomary to commit suicide at this stage; in England we do much better, or much worse, as the case may be.

The love between the young man and his mother was strangely invisible now. Of love it may be said, the less earthly the less demonstrative. In its absolutely indestructible form it reaches a profundity in which all exhibition of itself is painful. It was so with these. Had conversations between them been overheard, people would have said, 'How cold they are to each other!'

His theory and his wishes about devoting his future to teaching had made an impression on Mrs Yeobright. Indeed, how could it be otherwise when he was a part of her – when their discourses were as if carried on between the right and the left hands of the same body? He had despaired of reaching her by argument; and it was almost as a discovery to him that he could reach her by a magnetism which was as superior to words as words are to yells.

Strangely enough he began to feel now that it would not be so hard to persuade her who was his best friend that comparative poverty was essentially the higher course for him, as to reconcile to his feelings the act of persuading her. From every provident point of view his mother was so undoubtedly right, that he was not without a sickness of heart in finding he could shake her.

She had a singular insight into life, considering that she had never mixed with it. There are instances of persons who, without clear ideas of the things they criticize, have yet had clear ideas of the relations of those things. Blacklock, a poet blind from his birth, could describe visual objects with accuracy; Professor Sanderson, who was also blind, gave excellent lectures on colour, and taught others the theory of ideas which they had and he had not. In the social sphere these gifted ones are mostly women; they can watch a world which they never saw, and estimate forces of which they have only heard. We call it intuition.

What was the great world to Mrs Yeobright? A multitude whose tendencies could be perceived, though not its essences. Communities were seen by her as from a distance; she saw them as we see the throngs which cover the canvases of Sallaert, Van Alsloot, and others of that school – vast masses of beings, jostling, zigzagging, and processioning in definite directions, but whose features are indistinguishable by the very comprehensiveness of the view.

One could see that, as far as it had gone, her life was very complete on its reflective side. The philosophy of her nature, and its limitation by circumstances, was almost written in her movements. They had a majestic foundation, though they were far from being majestic; and they had a groundwork of assurance, but they were not assured. As her once elastic walk had become deadened by time, so had her natural pride of life been hindered in its blooming by her necessities.

The next slight touch in the shaping of Clym's destiny occurred a few days after. A barrow was opened on the heath, and Yeobright attended the operation, remaining away from his study during several hours. In the afternoon Christian returned from a journey in the same direction, and Mrs Yeobright questioned him.

'They have dug a hole, and they have dug things like flower-pots upside down, Mis'ess Yeobright; and inside these be real charned bones. They have carried 'em off to men's houses; but I shouldn't like to sleep where they will bide. Dead folks have been known to come and claim their own. Mr Yeobright had got one pot of the bones, and was going to bring 'em home – a real skellington bones – but 'twas ordered otherwise. You'll be relieved to hear that he gave away his, pot and all, on second thoughts; and a blessed thing for ye, Mis'ess Yeobright, considering the wind o' nights.'

'Gave it away?'

'Yes. To Miss Vye. She has a cannibal taste for such churchyard furniture seemingly.'

'Miss Vye was there too?'

'Ay, 'a b'lieve she was.'

When Clym came home, which was shortly after, his mother said, in a curious tone, 'The urn you had meant for me you gave away.'

Yeobright made no reply; the current of her feeling was too pronounced to admit it.

The early weeks of the year passed on. Yeobright certainly studied at home, but he also walked much abroad, and the direction of his walk was always towards some point of a line between Mistover and Rainbarrow.

The month of March arrived, and the heath showed its first faint signs of awakening from winter trance. The awakening was almost feline in its stealthiness. The pool outside the bank by Eustacia's dwelling, which seemed as dead and desolate as ever to an observer who moved and made noises in his observation, would gradually disclose a state of great animation when silently watched awhile. A timid animal world had come to life for the season. Little tadpoles and efts began to bubble up through the water, and to race along beneath it; toads made noises like very young ducks, and advanced to the margin in twos and threes; overhead, bumble-bees flew hither and thither in the thickening light, their drone coming and going like the sound of a gong.

On an evening such as this Yeobright descended into the Blooms-End valley from beside that very pool, where he had been standing with another person quite silently and quite long enough to hear all this puny stir of resurrection in nature; yet he had not heard it. His walk was rapid as he came down, and he went with a springy tread. Before entering upon his mother's premises he stopped and breathed. The light which shone forth on him from the window revealed that his face was flushed and his eye bright. What it did not show was something which lingered upon his lips like a seal set there. The abiding presence of this impress was so real that he hardly dared to enter the house, for it seemed as if his mother might say, 'What red spot is that glowing upon your mouth so vividly?'

But he entered soon after. The tea was ready, and he sat down opposite his mother. She did not speak many words; and as for him, something had been just done and some words had been just said on the hill which prevented him from beginning a desultory chat. His mother's taciturnity was not without ominousness, but he appeared not to care. He knew why she said so little, but he could not remove the cause of her bearing towards him. These half-silent sittings were far from uncommon with them now. At last Yeobright made a beginning of what was intended to strike at the whole root of the matter.

'Five days have we sat like this at meals with scarcely a word. What's the use of it, mother?'

'None,' said she, in a heart-swollen tone. 'But there is only too good a reason.'

'Not when you know all. I have been waiting to speak about this, and I am glad the subject is begun. The reason, of course, is Eustacia Vye.

Well, I confess I have seen her lately, and have seen her a good many times.'

'Yes, yes; and I know what that amounts to. It troubles me, Clym. You are wasting your life here; and it is solely on account of her. If it had not been for that woman you would never have entertained this teaching scheme at all.'

Clym looked hard at his mother. 'You know that is not it,' he said.

'Well, I know you had decided to attempt it before you saw her; but that would have ended in intentions. It was very well to talk of, but ridiculous to put in practice. I fully expected that in the course of a month or two you would have seen the folly of such self-sacrifice, and would have been by this time back again to Paris in some business or other. I can understand objections to the diamond trade – I really was thinking that it might be inadequate to the life of a man like you even though it might have made you a millionaire. But now I see how mistaken you are about this girl I doubt if you could be correct about other things.'

'How am I mistaken in her?'

'She is lazy and dissatisfied. But that is not all of it. Supposing her to be as good a woman as any you can find, which she certainly is not, why do you wish to connect yourself with anybody at present?'

'Well, there are practical reasons,' Clym began, and then almost broke off under an overpowering sense of the weight of argument which could be brought against his statement. 'If I take a school an educated woman would be invaluable as a help to me.'

'What! you really mean to marry her?'

'It would be premature to state that plainly. But consider what obvious advantages there would be in doing it. She –'

'Don't suppose she has any money. She hasn't a farthing.'

'She is excellently educated, and would make a good matron in a boarding-school. I candidly own that I have modified my views a little, in deference to you; and it should satisfy you. I no longer adhere to my intention of giving with my own mouth rudimentary education to the lowest class. I can do better. I can establish a good private school for farmers' sons, and without stopping the school I can manage to pass examinations. By this means, and by the assistance of a wife like her –'

'O, Clym!'

'I shall ultimately, I hope, be at the head of one of the best schools in the county.'

Yeobright had enunciated the word 'her' with a fervour which, in conversation with a mother, was absurdly indiscreet. Hardly a maternal heart within the four seas could, in such circumstances, have helped being irritated at that ill-timed betrayal of feeling for a new woman.

'You are blinded, Clym,' she said warmly. 'It was a bad day for you when you first set eyes on her. And your scheme is merely a castle in the air built on purpose to justify this folly which has seized you, and to salve your conscience on the irrational situation you are in.'

'Mother, that's not true,' he firmly answered.

'Can you maintain that I sit and tell untruths, when all I wish to do is to save you from sorrow? For shame, Clym! But it is all through that woman – a hussy!'

Clym reddened like fire and rose. He placed his hand upon his mother's shoulder and said, in a tone which hung strangely between entreaty and command. 'I won't hear it. I may be led to answer you in a way which we shall both regret.'

His mother parted her lips to begin some other vehement truth, but on looking at him she saw that in his face which led her to leave the words unsaid. Yeobright walked once or twice across the room, and then suddenly went out of the house. It was eleven o'clock when he came in, though he had not been further than the precincts of the garden. His mother was gone to bed. A light was left burning on the table, and supper was spread. Without stopping for any food he secured the doors and went upstairs.

* IV *

An Hour of Bliss and Many Hours of Sadness

THE next day was gloomy enough at Blooms-End. Yeobright remained in his study, sitting over the open books; but the work of those hours was miserably scant. Determined that there should be nothing in his conduct towards his mother resembling sullenness, he had occasionally spoken to her on passing matters, and would take no notice of the brevity of her replies. With the same resolve to keep up a show of conversation he said, about seven o'clock in the evening, 'There's an eclipse of the moon tonight. I am going out to see it.' And, putting on his overcoat, he left her.

The low moon was not as yet visible from the front of the house, and Yeobright climbed out of the valley until he stood in the full flood of her light. But even now he walked on, and his steps were in the direction of Rainbarrow.

In half an hour he stood at the top. The sky was clear from verge to verge, and the moon flung her rays over the whole heath, but without sensibly lighting it, except where paths and water-courses had laid bare the white flints and glistening quartz sand, which made streaks upon the general shade. After standing awhile he stooped and felt the heather. It was dry, and he flung himself down upon the barrow, his face towards the moon, which depicted a small image of herself in each of his eyes.

He had often come up here without stating his purpose to his mother; but this was the first time that he had been ostensibly frank as to his purpose while really concealing it. It was a moral situation which, three months earlier, he could hardly have credited of himself. In returning to labour in this sequestered spot he had anticipated an escape from the chafing of social necessities; yet behold they were here also. More than ever he longed to be in some world where personal ambition was not the only recognized form of progress – such, perhaps, as might have been the case at some time or other in the silvery globe then shining upon him. His eye travelled over the length and breadth of that distant country – over the Bay of Rainbows, the sombre Sea of Crises, the Ocean of Storms, the Lake of Dreams, the vast Walled Plains, and the wondrous Ring Mountains – till he almost felt himself to be voyaging bodily through its wild scenes, standing on its hollow hills, traversing its deserts, descending its vales and old sea bottoms, or mounting to the edges of its craters.

While he watched the far-removed landscape a tawny stain grew into being on the lower verge: the eclipse had begun. This marked a preconcerted moment: for the remote celestial phenomenon had been pressed into sublunary service as a lover's signal. Yeobright's mind flew back to earth at the sight; he arose, shook himself, and listened. Minute after minute passed by, perhaps ten minutes passed, and the shadow on the moon perceptibly widened. He heard a rustling on his left hand, a cloaked figure with an upturned face appeared at the base of the Barrow, and Clym descended. In a moment the figure was in his arms, and his lips upon hers.

'My Eustacia!'

'Clym, dearest!'

Such a situation had less than three months brought forth.

They remained long without a single utterance, for no language could reach the level of their condition: words were as the rusty implements of a by-gone barbarous epoch, and only to be occasionally tolerated.

'I began to wonder why you did not come,' said Yeobright, when she had withdrawn a little from his embrace.

'You said ten minutes after the first mark of shade on the edge of the moon; and that's what it is now.'

'Well, let us only think that here we are.'

Then, holding each other's hand, they were again silent, and the shadow on the moon's disc grew a little larger.

'Has it seemed long since you last saw me?' she asked.

'It has seemed sad.'

'And not long? That's because you occupy yourself, and so blind yourself to my absence. To me, who can do nothing, it has been like living under stagnant water.'

'I would rather bear tediousness, dear, than have time made short by such means as have shortened mine.'

'In what way is that? You have been thinking you wished you did not love me.'

'How can a man wish that, and yet love on? No, Eustacia.'

'Men can, women cannot.'

'Well, whatever I may have thought, one thing is certain – I do love you – past all compass and description. I love you to oppressiveness – I, who have never before felt more than a pleasant passing fancy for any woman I have ever seen. Let me look right into your moonlit face, and dwell on every line and curve in it! Only a few hair-breadths make the difference between this face and faces I have seen many times before I knew you; yet what a difference – the difference between everything and nothing at all. One touch on that mouth again! there, and there, and there. Your eyes seem heavy, Eustacia!'

'No, it is my general way of looking. I think it arises from my feeling sometimes an agonizing pity for myself that I ever was born.'

'You don't feel it now?'

'No. Yet I know that we shall not love like this always. Nothing can ensure the continuance of love. It will evaporate like a spirit, and so I feel full of fears.'

'You need not.'

'Ah, you don't know. You have seen more than I, and have been into cities and among people that I have only heard of, and have lived more years than I; but yet I am older at this than you. I loved another man once, and now I love you.'

'In God's mercy don't talk so, Eustacia!'

'But I do not think I shall be the one who wearies first. It will, I fear, end in this way: your mother will find out that you meet me, and she will influence you against me!'

'That can never be. She knows of these meetings already.'

'And she speaks against me?'

'I will not say.'

'There, go away! Obey her. I shall ruin you. It is foolish of you to meet me like this. Kiss me, and go away for ever. For ever – do you hear – for ever!'

'Not I.'

'It is your only chance. Many a man's love has been a curse to him.'

'You are desperate, full of fancies, and wilful; and you misunderstand. I have an additional reason for seeing you tonight besides love of you. For though, unlike you, I feel our affection may be eternal, I feel with you in this, that our present mode of existence cannot last.'

'Oh! 'tis your mother. Yes, that's it! I knew it.'

'Never mind what it is. Believe this, I cannot let myself lose you. I must have you always with me. This very evening I do not like to let you go. There is only one cure for this anxiety, dearest – you must be my wife.'

She started: then endeavoured to say calmly, 'Cynics say that cures the anxiety by curing the love.'

'But you must answer me. Shall I claim you some day – I don't mean at once?'

'I must think,' Eustacia murmured. 'At present speak of Paris to me. Is there any place like it on earth?'

'It is very beautiful. But will you be mine?'

'I will be nobody else's in the world – does that satisfy you?'

'Yes, for the present.'

'Now tell me of the Tuileries, and the Louvre,' she continued evasively.

'I hate talking of Paris! Well, I remember one sunny room in the Louvre which would make a fitting place for you to live in – the Galerie d'Apollon. Its windows are mainly east; and in the early morning, when the sun is bright, the whole apartment is in a perfect blaze of splendour. The rays bristle and dart from the encrustations of gilding to the magnificent inlaid coffers, from the coffers to the gold and silver plate, from the plate to the jewels and precious stones, from these to the enamels, till there is a perfect network of light which quite dazzles the eye. But now, about our marriage –'

'And Versailles – the King's Gallery is some such gorgeous room, is it not?'

'Yes. But what's the use of talking of gorgeous rooms? By the way, the little Trianon would suit us beautifully to live in, and you might walk in the gardens in the moonlight and think you were in some English shrubbery; it is laid out in English fashion.'

'I should hate to think that!'

'Then you could keep to the lawn in front of the Grand Palace. All about there you would doubtless feel in a world of historical romance.'

He went on, since it was all new to her, and described Fontainebleau, St Cloud, the Bois, and many other familiar haunts of the Parisians; till she said –

'When used you to go to these places?'

'On Sundays.'

'Ah, yes. I dislike English Sundays. How I should chime in with their manners over there! Dear Clym, you'll go back again?'

Clym shook his head, and looked at the eclipse.

'If you'll go back again I'll – be something,' she said tenderly, putting her head near his breast. 'If you'll agree I'll give my promise, without making you wait a minute longer.'

'How extraordinary that you and my mother should be of one mind about this!' said Yeobright. 'I have vowed not to go back, Eustacia. It is not the place I dislike; it is the occupation.'

'But you can go in some other capacity.'

'No. Besides, it would interfere with my scheme. Don't press that, Eustacia. Will you marry me?'

'I cannot tell.'

'Now – never mind Paris; it is no better than other spots. Promise, sweet!'

'You will never adhere to your education plan, I am quite sure; and then it will be all right for me; and so I promise to be yours for ever and ever.'

Clym brought her face towards his by a gentle pressure of the hand, and kissed her.

'Ah! but you don't know what you have got in me,' she said. 'Sometimes I think there is not that in Eustacia Vye which will make a good homespun wife. Well, let it go – see how our time is slipping, slipping, slipping!' She pointed towards the half eclipsed moon.

'You are too mournful.'

'No. Only I dread to think of anything beyond the present. What is, we know. We are together now, and it is unknown how long we shall be so: the unknown always fills my mind with terrible possibilities, even when I may reasonably expect it to be cheerful . . . Clym, the eclipsed moonlight shines upon your face with a strange foreign colour, and shows its shape as if it were cut out in gold. That means that you should be doing better things than this.'

'You are ambitious, Eustacia – no, not exactly ambitious, luxurious. I ought to be of the same vein, to make you happy, I suppose. And yet, far from that, I could live and die in a hermitage here, with proper work to do.'

There was that in his tone which implied distrust of his position as a solicitous lover, a doubt if he were acting fairly towards one whose tastes touched his own only at rare and infrequent points. She saw his meaning, and whispered, in a low, full accent of eager assurance, 'Don't mistake me, Clym: though I should like Paris, I love you for yourself alone. To be your wife and live in Paris would be heaven to me; but I would rather live with you in a hermitage here than not be yours at all. It is gain to me either way, and very great gain. There's my too candid confession.'

'Spoken like a woman. And now I must soon leave you. I'll walk with you towards your house.'

'But must you go home yet?' she asked. 'Yes, the sand has nearly slipped away, I see, and the eclipse is creeping more and more. Don't go yet! Stop till the hour has run itself out; then I will not press you any more. You will go home and sleep well; I keep sighing in my sleep! Do you ever dream of me?'

'I cannot recollect a clear dream of you.'

'I see your face in every scene of my dreams, and hear your voice in every sound. I wish I did not. It is too much what I feel. They say such love never lasts. But it must! And yet once, I remember, I saw an officer of the Hussars ride down the street at Budmouth, and though he was a total stranger and never spoke to me, I loved him till I thought I should really die of love – but I didn't die, and at last I left off caring for him. How terrible it would be if a time should come when I could not love you, my Clym!'

'Please don't say such reckless things. When we see such a time at hand we will say, "I have outlived my faith and purpose," and die. There, the hour has expired: now let us walk on.'

Hand in hand they went along the path towards Mistover. When they were near the house he said, 'It is too late for me to see your grandfather tonight. Do you think he will object to it?'

'I will speak to him. I am so accustomed to be my own mistress that it did not occur to me that we should have to ask him.'

Then they lingeringly separated, and Clym descended towards Blooms-End.

And as he walked further and further from the charmed atmosphere of his Olympian girl his face grew sad with a new sort of sadness. A perception of the dilemma in which his love had placed him came back in full force. In spite of Eustacia's apparent willingness to wait through the period of an unpromising engagement, till he should be established in his new pursuit, he could not but perceive at moments that she loved him rather as a visitant from a gay world to which she rightly belonged than as a man with a purpose opposed to that recent past of his which so interested her. Often at their meetings a word or a sigh escaped her. It meant that, though she made no conditions as to his return to the French capital, this was what she secretly longed for in the event of marriage; and it robbed him of many an otherwise pleasant hour. Along with that came the widening breach between himself and his mother. Whenever any little occurrence had brought into more prominence than usual the disappointment that he was causing her it had sent him on lone and moody walks; or he was kept awake a great part of the night by the turmoil of spirit which such a recognition created. If Mrs Yeobright could only have been led to see what a sound and worthy purpose this purpose of his was and how little it was being affected by his devotion to Eustacia, how differently would she regard him!

Thus as his sight grew accustomed to the first blinding halo kindled about him by love and beauty, Yeobright began to perceive what a strait he was in. Sometimes he wished that he had never known Eustacia, immediately to retract the wish as brutal. Three antagonistic growths had to be kept alive: his mother's trust in him, his plan for becoming a teacher, and Eustacia's happiness. His fervid nature could not afford to relinquish one of these, though two of the three were as many as he could hope to preserve. Though his love was as chaste as that of Petrarch for his Laura, it had made fetters of what previously was only a difficulty. A position which was not too simple when he stood wholehearted had become indescribably complicated by the addition of Eustacia. Just when his mother was beginning to tolerate one scheme he had introduced another still bitterer than the first, and the combination was more than she could bear.

V

Sharp Words Are Spoken, and a Crisis Ensues

WHEN Yeobright was not with Eustacia he was sitting slavishly over his books; when he was not reading he was meeting her. These meetings were carried on with the greatest secrecy.

One afternoon his mother came home from a morning visit to Thomasin. He could see from a disturbance in the lines of her face that something had happened.

'I have been told an incomprehensible thing,' she said mournfully. 'The captain has let out at the Woman that you and Eustacia Vye are engaged to be married.'

'We are,' said Yeobright. 'But it may not be yet for a very long time.'

'I should hardly think it *would* be yet for a very long time! You will take her to Paris, I suppose?' She spoke with weary hopelessness.

'I am not going back to Paris.'

'What will you do with a wife, then?'

'Keep a school in Budmouth, as I have told you.'

'That's incredible! The place is overrun with schoolmasters. You have no special qualifications. What possible chance is there for such as you?'

'There is no chance of getting rich. But with my system of education, which is as new as it is true, I shall do a great deal of good to my fellow-creatures.'

'Dreams, dreams! If there had been any system left to be invented they would have found it out at the universities long before this time.'

'Never, mother. They cannot find it out, because their teachers don't come in contact with the class which demands such a system – that is, those who have had no preliminary training. My plan is one for instilling high knowledge into empty minds without first cramming them with what has to be uncrammed again before true study begins.'

'I might have believed you if you had kept yourself free from entanglements; but this woman – if she had been a good girl it would have been bad enough; but being –'

'She is a good girl.'

'So you think. A Corfu bandmaster's daughter! What has her life been? Her surname even is not her true one.'

'She is Captain Vye's granddaughter, and her father merely took her mother's name. And she is a lady by instinct.'

'They call him "captain", but anybody is captain.'

'He was in the Royal Navy!'

'No doubt he has been to sea in some tub or other. Why doesn't he look after her? No lady would rove about the heath at all hours of the day and night as she does. But that's not all of it. There was something queer between her and Thomasin's husband at one time – I am as sure of it as that I stand here.'

'Eustacia has told me. He did pay her a little attention a year ago; but there's no harm in that. I like her all the better.'

'Clym,' said his mother with firmness, 'I have no proofs against her, unfortunately. But if she makes you a good wife, there has never been a bad one.'

'Believe me, you are almost exasperating,' said Yeobright vehemently. 'And this very day I had intended to arrange a meeting between you. But you give me no peace; you try to thwart my wishes in everything.'

'I hate the thought of any son of mine marrying badly! I wish I had never lived to see this; it is too much for me – it is more than I dreamt!' She turned to the window. Her breath was coming quickly, and her lips were pale, parted, and trembling.

'Mother,' said Clym, 'whatever you do, you will always be dear to me – that you know. But one thing I have a right to say, which is, that at my age I am old enough to know what is best for me.'

Mrs Yeobright remained for some time silent and shaken, as if she could say no more. Then she replied, 'Best? Is it best for you to injure your prospects for such a voluptuous, idle woman as that? Don't you see that by the very fact of your choosing her you prove that you do not know what is best for you? You give up your whole thought – you set your whole soul – to please a woman.'

'I do. And that woman is you.'

'How can you treat me so flippantly!' said his mother, turning again to him with a tearful look. 'You are unnatural, Clym, and I did not expect it.'

'Very likely,' said he cheerlessly. 'You did not know the measure you were going to mete me, and therefore did not know the measure that would be returned to you again.'

'You answer me; you think only of her. You stick to her in all things.'

'That proves her to be worthy. I have never yet supported what is bad. And I do not care only for her. I care for you and for myself, and for anything that is good. When a woman once dislikes another she is merciless!'

'O Clym! please don't go setting down as my fault what is your obstinate wrong-headedness. If you wished to connect yourself with an unworthy person why did you come home here to do it? Why didn't you do it in Paris? – it is more the fashion there. You have come only to distress me, a lonely woman, and shorten my days! I wish that you would bestow your presence where you bestow your love!'

Clym said huskily, 'You are my mother. I will say no more – beyond this, that I beg your pardon for having thought this my home. I will no longer inflict myself upon you; I'll go.' And he went out with tears in his eyes.

It was a sunny afternoon at the beginning of summer, and the moist hollows of the heath had passed from their brown to their green stage.

Yeobright walked to the edge of the basin which extended down from Mistover and Rainbarrow. By this time he was calm, and he looked over the landscape. In the minor valleys, between the hillocks which diversified the contour of the vale, the fresh young ferns were luxuriantly growing up, ultimately to reach a height of five or six feet. He descended a little way, flung himself down in a spot where a path emerged from one of the small hollows, and waited. Hither it was that he had promised Eustacia to bring his mother this afternoon, that they might meet and be friends. His attempt had utterly failed.

He was in a nest of vivid green. The ferny vegetation round him, though so abundant, was quite uniform: it was a grove of machine-made foliage, a world of green triangles with saw-edges and not a single flower. The air was warm with a vaporous warmth, and the stillness was unbroken. Lizards, grasshoppers, and ants were the only living things to be beheld. The scene seemed to belong to the ancient world of the carboniferous period, when the forms of plants were few, and of the fern kind; when there was neither bud nor blossom, nothing but a monotonous extent of leafage, amid which no bird sang.

When he had reclined for some considerable time, gloomily pondering, he discerned above the ferns a drawn bonnet of white silk approaching from the left, and Yeobright knew directly that it covered the head of her he loved. His heart awoke from its apathy to a warm excitement, and, jumping to his feet, he said aloud, 'I knew she was sure to come.'

She vanished in a hollow for a few moments, and then her whole form unfolded itself from the brake.

'Only you here?' she exclaimed, with a disappointed air, whose hollowness was proved by her rising redness and her half-guilty low laugh. 'Where is Mrs Yeobright?'

'She has not come,' he replied in a subdued tone.

'I wish I had known that you would be here alone,' she said seriously, 'and that we were going to have such an idle, pleasant time as this. Pleasure not known beforehand is half wasted; to anticipate it is to double it. I have not thought once today of having you all to myself this afternoon, and the actual moment of a thing is so soon gone.'

'It is indeed.'

'Poor Clym!' she continued, looking tenderly into his face. 'You are sad. Something has happened at your home. Never mind what is – let us only look at what seems.'

'But, darling, what shall we do?' said he.

'Still go on as we do now – just live on from meeting to meeting, never minding about another day. You, I know, are always thinking of that – I can see you are. But you must not – will you, dear Clym?'

'You are just like all women. They are ever content to build their lives on any incidental position that offers itself; whilst men would fain make a globe to suit them. Listen to this, Eustacia. There is a subject I have determined to put off no longer. Your sentiment on the wisdom of *Carpe diem* does not impress me today. Our present mode of life must shortly be brought to an end.'

'It is your mother!'

'It is. I love you none the less in telling you; it is only right you should know.'

'I have feared my bliss,' she said, with the merest motion of her lips. 'It has been too intense and consuming.'

'There is hope yet. There are forty years of work in me yet, and why should you despair? I am only at an awkward turning. I wish people wouldn't be so ready to think that there is no progress without uniformity.'

'Ah – your mind runs off to the philosophical side of it. Well, these sad and hopeless obstacles are welcome in one sense, for they enable us to look with indifference upon the cruel satires that Fate loves to indulge in. I have heard of people, who, upon coming suddenly into happiness, have died from anxiety lest they should not live to enjoy it. I felt myself in that whimsical state of uneasiness lately; but I shall be spared it now. Let us walk on.'

Clym took the hand which was already bared for him – it was a favourite way with them to walk bare hand in bare hand – and led her through the ferns. They formed a very comely picture of love at full flush, as they walked along the valley that late afternoon, the sun sloping down on their right, and throwing their thin spectral shadows, tall as poplar trees, far out across the furze and fern. Eustacia went with her head thrown back fancifully, a certain glad and voluptuous air of triumph pervading her eyes at having won by her own unaided self a man who was her perfect complement in attainments, appearance, and age. On the young man's part, the paleness of face which he had brought with him from Paris, and the incipient marks of time and thought, were less perceptible than when he returned, the healthful and energetic sturdiness which was his by nature having partially recovered its original proportions. They wandered onward till they reached the nether margin of the heath, where it became marshy, and merged in moorland.

'I must part from you here, Clym,' said Eustacia.

They stood still and prepared to bid each other farewell. Everything before them was on a perfect level. The sun, resting on the horizon line, streamed across the ground from between copper-coloured and lilac clouds, stretched out in flats beneath a sky of pale soft green. All dark objects on the earth that lay towards the sun were overspread by a purple haze, against which groups of wailing gnats shone out, rising upwards and dancing about like sparks of fire.

'O! this leaving you is too hard to bear!' exclaimed Eustacia in a sudden whisper of anguish. 'Your mother will influence you too much; I shall not be judged fairly, it will get afloat that I am not a good girl, and the witch story will be added to make me blacker!'

'They cannot. Nobody dares to speak disrespectfully of you or of me.'

'O how I wish I was sure of never losing you – that you could not be able to desert me anyhow!'

Clym stood silent a moment. His feelings were high, the moment was passionate, and he cut the knot.

'You shall be sure of me, darling,' he said, folding her in his arms. 'We will be married at once.'

'O Clym!'

'Do you agree to it?'

'If – if we can.'

'We certainly can, both being of full age. And I have not followed my occupation all these years without having accumulated money; and if you will agree to live in a tiny cottage somewhere on the heath, until I take a house in Budmouth for the school, we can do it at a very little expense.'

'How long shall we have to live in the tiny cottage, Clym?'

'About six months. At the end of that time I shall have finished my reading – yes, we will do it, and this heartaching will be over. We shall, of course, live in absolute seclusion, and our married life will only begin to outward view when we take the house in Budmouth, where I have already addressed a letter on the matter. Would your grandfather allow you?'

'I think he would – on the understanding that it should not last longer than six months.'

'I will guarantee that, if no misfortune happens.'

'If no misfortune happens,' she repeated slowly.

'Which is not likely. Dearest, fix the exact day.'

And then they consulted on the question, and the day was chosen. It was to be a fortnight from that time.

This was the end of their talk, and Eustacia left him. Clym watched her as she retired towards the sun. The luminous rays wrapped her up with her increasing distance, and the rustle of her dress over the sprouting sedge and grass died away. As he watched, the dead flat of the scenery overpowered him, though he was fully alive to the beauty of that untarnished early summer green which was worn for the nonce by the poorest blade. There was something in its oppressive horizontality which too much reminded him of the arena of life; it gave him a sense of bare equality with, and no superiority to, a single living thing under the sun.

Eustacia was now no longer the goddess but the woman to him, a being to fight for, support, help, be maligned for. Now that he had reached a cooler moment he would have preferred a less hasty marriage; but the card was laid, and he determined to abide by the game. Whether Eustacia was to add one other to the list of those who love too hotly to love long and well, the forthcoming event was certainly a ready way of proving.

* VI *

Yeobright Goes, and the Breach Is Complete

ALL that evening smart sounds denoting an active packing up came from Yeobright's room to the ears of his mother downstairs.

Next morning he departed from the house and again proceeded across the heath. A long day's march was before him, his object being to secure a dwelling to which he might take Eustacia when she became his wife. Such a house, small, secluded, and with its windows boarded up, he had casually observed a month earlier, about two miles beyond the village of East Egdon, and six miles distant altogether; and thither he directed his steps today.

The weather was far different from that of the evening before. The yellow and vapoury sunset which had wrapped up Eustacia from his parting gaze had presaged change. It was one of those not infrequent days of an English June which are as wet and boisterous as November. The cold clouds hastened on in a body, as if painted on a moving slide. Vapours from other continents arrived upon the wind, which curled and parted round him as he walked on.

At length Clym reached the margin of a fir and beech plantation that had been enclosed from heath land in the year of his birth. Here the trees, laden heavily with their new and humid leaves, were now suffering more damage than during the highest winds of winter, when the boughs are specially disencumbered to do battle with the storm. The wet young beeches were undergoing amputations, bruises, cripplings, and harsh lacerations, from which the wasting sap would bleed for many a day to come, and which would leave scars visible till the day of their burning. Each stem was wrenched at the root, where it moved like a bone in its socket, and at every onset of the gale convulsive sounds came from the branches, as if pain were felt. In a neighbouring brake a finch was trying to sing; but the wind blew under his feathers till they stood on end, twisted round his little tail, and made him give up his song.

Yet a few yards to Yeobright's left, on the open heath, how ineffectively gnashed the storm! Those gusts which tore the trees merely waved the furze and heather in a light caress. Egdon was made for such times as these.

Yeobright reached the empty house about mid-day. It was almost as lonely as that of Eustacia's grandfather, but the fact that it stood near a heath was disguised by a belt of firs which almost enclosed the premises. He journeyed on about a mile further to the village in which the owner lived, and, returning with him to the house, arrangements were completed, and the man undertook that one room at least should be ready for occupation the next day. Clym's intention was to live there alone until Eustacia should join him on their wedding-day.

Then he turned to pursue his way homeward through the drizzle that had so greatly transformed the scene. The ferns, among which he had lain in comfort yesterday, were dripping moisture from every frond, wetting his legs through as he brushed past; and the fur of the rabbits leaping before him was clotted into dark locks by the same watery surrounding.

He reached home damp and weary enough after his ten-mile walk. It had hardly been a propitious beginning, but he had chosen his course, and would show no swerving. The evening and the following morning were spent in concluding arrangements for his departure. To stay at home a minute longer than necessary after having once come to his determination would be, he felt, only to give new pain to his mother by some word, look, or deed.

He had hired a conveyance and sent off his goods by two o'clock that day. The next step was to get some furniture, which, after serving for temporary use in the cottage, would be available for the house at Budmouth when increased by goods of a better description. A mart extensive enough for the purpose existed at Anglebury, some miles beyond the spot chosen for his residence, and there he resolved to pass the coming night.

It now only remained to wish his mother good-bye. She was sitting by the window as usual when he came downstairs.

'Mother, I am going to leave you,' he said, holding out his hand.

'I thought you were, by your packing,' replied Mrs Yeobright in a voice from which every particle of emotion was painfully excluded.

'And you will part friends with me?'

'Certainly, Clym.'

'I am going to be married on the twenty-fifth.'

'I thought you were going to be married.'

'And then – and then you must come and see us. You will understand me better after that, and our situation will not be so wretched as it is now.'

'I do not think it likely I shall come to see you.'

'Then it will not be my fault or Eustacia's, mother. Good-bye!'

He kissed her cheek, and departed in great misery, which was several hours in lessening itself to a controllable level. The position had been such that nothing more could be said without, in the first place, breaking down a barrier; and that was not to be done.

No sooner had Yeobright gone from his mother's house than her face changed its rigid aspect for one of blank despair. After a while she wept, and her tears brought some relief. During the rest of the day she did nothing but walk up and down the garden path in a state bordering on stupefaction. Night came, and with it but little rest. The next day, with an instinct to do something which should reduce prostration to mournfulness, she went to her son's room, and with her own hands arranged it in order, for an imaginary time when he should return again. She gave some attention to her flowers, but it was perfunctorily bestowed, for they no longer charmed her.

It was a great relief when, early in the afternoon, Thomasin paid her an unexpected visit. This was not the first meeting between the relatives since Thomasin's marriage; and past blunders having been in a rough way rectified, they could always greet each other with pleasure and ease.

The oblique band of sunlight which followed her through the door became the young wife well. It illuminated her as her presence illuminated the heath. In her movements, in her gaze, she reminded the beholder of a feathered creature who lived around her home. All similes and allegories concerning her began and ended with birds. There was as much variety in her motions as in their flight. When she was musing she was a kestrel, which hangs in the air by an invisible motion of its wings. When she was in a high wind her light body was blown against trees and banks like a heron's. When she was frightened she darted noiselessly like a kingfisher. When she was serene she skimmed like a swallow, and that is how she was moving now.

'You are looking very blithe, upon my word, Tamsie,' said Mrs Yeobright, with a sad smile. 'How is Damon?'

'He is very well.'

'Is he kind to you, Thomasin?' And Mrs Yeobright observed her narrowly.

'Pretty fairly.'

'Is that honestly said?'

'Yes, aunt. I would tell you if he were unkind.' She added, blushing, and with hesitation, 'He – I don't know if I ought to complain to you about this, but I am not quite sure what to do. I want some money, you know, aunt – some to buy little things for myself – and he doesn't give me any. I don't like to ask him; and yet, perhaps, he doesn't give it me because, he doesn't know. Ought I to mention it to him, aunt?'

'Of course you ought. Have you never said a word on the matter?'

'You see, I had some of my own,' said Thomasin evasively; 'and I have not wanted any of his until lately. I did just say something about it last week; but he seems – not to remember.'

'He must be made to remember. You are aware that I have a little box full of spade-guineas, which your uncle put into my hands to divide between yourself and Clym whenever I chose. Perhaps the time has come when it should be done. They can be turned into sovereigns at any moment.'

'I think I should like to have my share – that is, if you don't mind.'

'You shall, if necessary. But it is only proper that you should first tell your husband distinctly that you are without any, and see what he will do.'

'Very well, I will . . . Aunt, I have heard about Clym. I know you are in trouble about him, and that's why I have come.'

Mrs Yeobright turned away, and her features worked in her attempt to conceal her feelings. Then she ceased to make any attempt, and said, weeping, 'O Thomasin, do you think he hates me? How can he bear to grieve me so, when I have lived only for him through all these years?'

'Hate you – no,' said Thomasin soothingly. 'It is only that he loves her too well. Look at it quietly – do. It is not so very bad of him. Do you know, I thought it not the worst match he could have made. Miss Vye's family is a good one on her mother's side; and her father was a romantic wanderer – a sort of Greek Ulysses.'

'It is no use, Thomasin; it is no use. Your intention is good; but I will not trouble you to argue. I have gone through the whole that can be said on either side times, and many times. Clym and I have not parted in anger; we have parted in a worse way. It is not a passionate quarrel that would have broken my heart; it is the steady opposition and persistence in going wrong that he has shown. O Thomasin, he was so good as a little boy – so tender and kind!'

'He was, I know.'

'I did not think one whom I called mine would grow up to treat me like this. He spoke to me as if I opposed him to injure him. As though I could wish him ill!'

'There are worse women in the world than Eustacia Vye.'

'There are too many better; that's the agony of it. It was she, Thomasin, and she only, who led your husband to act as he did: I would swear it!'

'No,' said Thomasin eagerly. 'It was before he knew me that he thought of her, and it was nothing but a mere flirtation.'

'Very well; we will let it be so. There is little use in unravelling that now. Sons must be blind if they will. Why is it that a woman can see from a distance what a man cannot see close? Clym must do as he will – he is nothing more to me. And this is maternity – to give one's best years and best love to ensure the fate of being despised!'

'You are too unyielding. Think how many mothers there are whose sons have brought them to public shame by real crimes before you feel so deeply a case like this.'

'Thomasin, don't lecture me – I can't have it. It is the excess above what we expect that makes the force of the blow, and that may not be greater in their case than in mine: they may have foreseen the worst . . . I am wrongly made, Thomasin,' she added, with a mournful smile. 'Some widows can guard against the wounds their children give them by turning their hearts to another husband and beginning life again. But I always was a poor, weak, one-idea'd creature – I had not the compass of heart nor the enterprise for that. Just as forlorn and stupefied as I was when my husband's spirit flew away I have sat ever since – never attempting to mend matters at all. I was comparatively a young woman then, and I might have had another family by this time, and have been comforted by them for the failure of this one son.'

'It is more noble in you that you did not.'

'The more noble, the less wise.'

'Forget it, and be soothed, dear aunt. And I shall not leave you alone for long. I shall come and see you every day.'

And for one week Thomasin literally fulfilled her word. She endeavoured to make light of the wedding; and brought news of the preparations, and that she was invited to be present. The next week she was rather unwell, and did not appear. Nothing had as yet been done about the guineas, for Thomasin feared to address her husband again on the subject, and Mrs Yeobright had insisted upon this.

One day just before this time Wildeve was standing at the door of the Quiet Woman. In addition to the upward path through the heath to Rainbarrow and Mistover, there was a road which branched from the highway a short distance below the inn, and ascended to Mistover by a circuitous and easy incline. This was the only route on that side for vehicles to the captain's retreat. A light cart from the nearest town descended the road, and the lad who was driving pulled up in front of the inn for something to drink.

'You come from Mistover?' said Wildeve.

'Yes. They are taking in good things up there. Going to be a wedding.' And the driver buried his face in his mug.

Wildeve had not received an inkling of the fact before, and a sudden expression of pain overspread his face. He turned for a moment into the passage to hide it. Then he came back again.

'Do you mean Miss Vye?' he said. 'How is it – that she can be married so soon?'

'By the will of God and a ready young man, I suppose.'

'You don't mean Mr Yeobright?'

'Yes. He has been creeping about with her all the spring.'

'I suppose – she was immensely taken with him?'

'She is crazy about him, so their general servant of all work tells me. And that lad Charley that looks after the horse is all in a daze about it. The stun-poll has got fondlike of her.'

'Is she lively – is she glad? Going to be married so soon – well!'

'It isn't so very soon.'

'No; not so very soon.'

Wildeve went indoors to the empty room, a curious heartache within him. He rested his elbow upon the mantelpiece and his face upon his hand. When Thomasin entered the room he did not tell her of what he had heard. The old longing for Eustacia had reappeared in his soul: and it was mainly because he had discovered that it was another man's intention to possess her.

To be yearning for the difficult, to be weary of that offered; to care for the remote, to dislike the near; it was Wildeve's nature always. This is the true mark of the man of sentiment. Though Wildeve's fevered feeling had not been elaborated to real poetical compass, it was of the standard sort. He might have been called the Rousseau of Egdon.

* VII *

The Morning and the Evening of a Day

THE wedding morning came. Nobody would have imagined from appearances that Blooms-End had any interest in Mistover that day. A solemn stillness prevailed around the house of Clym's mother, and there was no more animation indoors. Mrs Yeobright, who had declined to attend the ceremony, sat by the breakfast-table in the old room which communicated immediately with the porch, her eyes listlessly directed towards the open door. It was the room in which, six months earlier, the merry Christmas party had met, to which Eustacia came secretly and as a stranger. The only living thing that entered now was a sparrow; and seeing no movements to cause alarm, he hopped boldly round the room, endeavoured to go out by the window, and fluttered among the pot-flowers. This roused the lonely sitter, who got up, released the bird, and went to the door. She was expecting Thomasin, who had written she would wish to have the money, and that she would if possible call this day.

Yet Thomasin occupied Mrs Yeobright's thoughts but slightly as she looked up the valley of the heath, alive with butterflies, and with grasshoppers whose husky noises on every side formed a whispered chorus. A domestic drama, for which the preparations were now being made a mile or two off, was but little less vividly present to her eyes than if enacted before her. She tried to dismiss the vision, and walked about the garden-plot; but her eyes ever and anon sought out the direction of the parish church to which Mistover belonged, and her excited fancy clove the hills which divided the building from her eyes. The morning wore away. Eleven o'clock struck: could it be that the wedding was then in progress? It must be so. She went on imagining the scene at the church, which he had by this time approached with his bride. She pictured the little group of children by the gate as the pony-carriage drove up, in which, as Thomasin had learnt, they were going to perform the short journey. Then she saw them enter and proceed to the chancel and kneel; and the service seemed to go on.

She covered her face with her hands. 'O, it is a mistake!' she groaned. 'And he will rue it some day, and think of me!'

While she remained thus, overcome by her forebodings, the old clock indoors whizzed forth twelve strokes. Soon after, faint sounds floated to her ear from afar over the hills. The breeze came from that quarter, and it had brought with it the notes of distant bells, gaily starting off in a peal: one, two, three, four, five. The ringers at East Egdon were announcing the nuptials of Eustacia and her son.

'Then it is over,' she murmured. 'Well, well! and life too will be over soon. And why should I go on scalding my face like this? Cry about one thing in life, cry about all; one thread runs through the whole piece. And yet we say, "a time to laugh!" '

Towards evening Wildeve came. Since Thomasin's marriage Mrs Yeobright had shown towards him that grim friendliness which at last arises in all such cases of undesired affinity. The vision of what ought to have been is thrown aside in sheer weariness, and browbeaten human endeavour listlessly makes the best of the fact that is. Wildeve, to do him justice, had behaved very courteously to his wife's aunt; and it was with no surprise that she saw him enter now.

'Thomasin has not been able to come, as she promised to do,' he replied to her inquiry, which had been anxious, for she knew that her niece was badly in want of money. 'The captain came down last night and personally pressed her to join them today. So, not to be unpleasant, she determined to go. They fetched her in the pony-chaise, and are going to bring her back.'

'Then it is done,' said Mrs Yeobright. 'Have they gone to their new home?'

'I don't know. I have had no news from Mistover since Thomasin left to go.'

'You did not go with her?' said she, as if there might be good reasons why.

'I could not,' said Wildeve, reddening slightly. 'We could not both leave the house; it was rather a busy morning, on account of Anglebury Great Market. I believe you have something to give to Thomasin? If you like, I will take it.'

Mrs Yeobright hesitated, and wondered if Wildeve knew what the something was. 'Did she tell you of this?' she inquired.

'Not particularly. She casually dropped a remark about having arranged to fetch some article or other.'

'It is hardly necessary to send it. She can have it whenever she chooses to come.'

'That won't be yet. In the present state of her health she must not go on walking so much as she has done.' He added, with a faint twang of sarcasm, 'What wonderful thing is it that I cannot be trusted to take?'

'Nothing worth troubling you with.'

'One would think you doubted my honesty,' he said, with a laugh, though his colour rose in a quick resentfulness frequent with him.

'You need think no such thing,' said she drily. 'It is simply that I, in common with the rest of the world, feel that there are certain things which had better be done by certain people than by others.'

'As you like, as you like,' said Wildeve laconically. 'It is not worth arguing about. Well, I think I must turn homeward again, as the inn must not be left in charge of the lad and the maid only.'

He went his way, his farewell being scarcely so courteous as his greeting. But Mrs Yeobright knew him thoroughly by this time, and took little notice of his manner, good or bad.

When Wildeve was gone Mrs Yeobright stood and considered what would be the best course to adopt with regard to the guineas, which she had not liked to entrust to Wildeve. It was hardly credible that Thomasin had told him to ask for them, when the necessity for them had arisen from the difficulty of obtaining money at his hands. At the same time Thomasin really wanted them, and might be unable to come to Blooms-End for another week at least. To take or send the money to her at the inn would be impolitic, since Wildeve would pretty surely be present, or would discover the transaction; and if, as her aunt suspected, he treated her less kindly than she deserved to be treated, he might then get the whole sum out of her gentle hands. But on this particular evening Thomasin was at Mistover, and anything might be conveyed to her there without the knowledge of her husband. Upon the whole the opportunity was worth taking advantage of.

Her son, too, was there, and was now married. There could be no more proper moment to render him his share of the money than the present. And the chance that would be afforded her, by sending him this gift, of showing how far she was from bearing him ill-will, cheered the sad mother's heart.

She went upstairs and took from a locked drawer a little box, out of which she poured a hoard of brown unworn guineas that had lain there many a year. There were a hundred in all, and she divided them into two heaps, fifty each. Tying up these in small canvas bags, she went down to the garden and called to Christian Cantle, who was loitering about in hope of a supper which was not really owed him. Mrs Yeobright gave him the money-bags, charged him to go to Mistover, and on no account to deliver them into any one's hands save her son's and Thomasin's. On further thought she deemed it advisable to tell Christian precisely what the two bags contained, that he might be fully impressed with their importance. Christian pocketed the money-bags, promised the greatest carefulness, and set out on his way.

'You need not hurry,' said Mrs Yeobright. 'It will be better not to get there till after dusk, and then nobody will notice you. Come back here to supper, if it is not too late.'

It was nearly nine o'clock when he began to ascend the vale towards Mistover; but the long days of summer being at their climax, the first obscurity of evening had only just begun to tan the landscape. At this point of his journey Christian heard voices, and found that they proceeded from a company of men and women who were traversing a hollow ahead of him, the tops only of their heads being visible.

He paused and thought of the money he carried. It was almost too early even for Christian seriously to fear robbery; nevertheless he took a precaution which ever since his boyhood he had adopted whenever he carried more than two or three shillings upon his person – a precaution somewhat like that of the owner of the Pitt Diamond when filled with similar misgivings. He took off his boots, untied the guineas, and emptied the contents of one little bag into the right boot, and of the other into the left, spreading them as flatly as possible over the bottom of each, which was really a spacious coffer by no means limited to the size of the foot. Pulling them on again and lacing them to the very top, he proceeded on his way, more easy in his head than under his soles.

His path converged towards that of the noisy company, and on coming nearer he found to his relief that they were several Egdon people whom he knew very well, while with them walked Fairway, of Blooms-End.

'What! Christian going too?' said Fairway as soon as he recognized the new-comer. 'You've got no young woman nor wife to your name to gie a gown-piece to, I'm sure.'

'What d'ye mean?' said Christian.

'Why, the raffle. The one we go to every year. Going to the raffle as well as ourselves?'

'Never knew a word o't. Is it like cudgel-playing or other sportful forms of bloodshed? I don't want to go, thank you, Mister Fairway, and no offence.'

'Christian don't know the fun o't, and 'twould be a fine sight for him,' said a buxom woman. 'There's no danger at all, Christian. Every man puts in a shilling apiece, and one wins a gown-piece for his wife or sweetheart if he's got one.'

'Well, as that's not my fortune there's no meaning in it to me. But I should like to see the fun, if there's nothing of the black art in it, and if a man may look on without cost or getting into any dangerous wrangle?'

'There will be no uproar at all,' said Timothy. 'Sure, Christian, if you'd like to come we'll see there's no harm done.'

'And no ba'dy gaieties, I suppose? You see, neighbours, if so, it would be setting father a bad example, as he is so light moral'd. But a gown-piece for a shilling, and no black art — 'tis worth looking in to see, and it wouldn't hinder me half an hour. Yes, I'll come, if you'll step a little way towards Mistover with me afterwards, supposing night should have closed in, and nobody else is going that way?'

One or two promised; and Christian, diverging from his direct path, turned round to the right with his companions towards the Quiet Woman.

When they entered the large common room of the inn they found assembled there about ten men from among the neighbouring population, and the group was increased by the new contingent to double that number. Most of them were sitting round the room in seats divided by wooden elbows like those of crude cathedral stalls, which were carved with the initials of many an illustrious drunkard of former times who had passed his days and his nights between them, and now lay as an alcoholic cinder in the nearest churchyard. Among the cups on the long table before the sitters lay an open parcel of light drapery — the gown piece, as it was called — which was to be raffled for. Wildeve was standing with his back to the fireplace, smoking a cigar; and the promoter of the raffle, a packman from a distant town, was expatiating upon the value of the fabric as material for a summer dress.

'Now, gentlemen,' he continued, as the new-comers drew up to the table, 'there's five have entered, and we want four more to make up the number. I think, by the faces of those gentlemen who have just come in, that they are shrewd enough to take advantage of this rare opportunity of beautifying their ladies at a very trifling expense.'

Fairway, Sam, and another placed their shillings on the table, and the man turned to Christian.

'No, sir,' said Christian, drawing back, with a quick gaze of misgiving. 'I am only a poor chap come to look on, an it please ye, sir. I don't so much as know how you do it. If so be I was sure of getting it I would put down the shilling; but I couldn't otherwise.'

'I think you might almost be sure,' said the pedlar. 'In fact, now I look into your face, even if I can't say you are sure to win, I can say that I never saw anything look more like winning in my life.'

'You'll anyhow have the same chances as the rest of us,' said Sam.

'And the extra luck of being the last comer,' said another.

'And I was born wi' a caul, and perhaps can be no more ruined than drowned?' Christian added, beginning to give way.

Ultimately Christian laid down his shilling, the raffle began, and the dice went round. When it came to Christian's turn he took the box with a trembling hand, shook it fearfully, and threw a pair-royal. Three of the others had thrown common low pairs, and all the rest mere points.

'The gentleman looked like winning, as I said,' observed the chapman blandly. 'Take it, sir; the article is yours.'

'Haw-haw-haw!' said Fairway. 'I'm damned if this isn't the quarest start that ever I knowed!'

'Mine?' asked Christian, with a vacant stare from his target eyes. 'I – I haven't got neither maid, wife, nor widder belonging to me at all, and I'm afeared it will make me laughed at to ha'e it, Master Traveller. What with being curious to join in I never thought of that? What shall I do wi' a woman's clothes in my bedroom, and not lose my decency!'

'Keep 'em, to be sure,' said Fairway, 'if it is only for luck. Perhaps 'twill tempt some woman that thy poor carcase had no power over when standing empty-handed.'

'Keep it, certainly,' said Wildeve, who had idly watched the scene from a distance.

The table was then cleared of the articles, and the men began to drink.

'Well, to be sure!' said Christian, half to himself. 'To think I should have been born so lucky at this, and not have found it out until now! What curious creatures these dice be – powerful rulers of us all, and yet at my command! I am sure I never need be afeared of anything after this.' He handled the dice fondly one by one. 'Why, sir,' he said in a confidential whisper to Wildeve, who was near his left hand, 'if I could only use this power that's in me of multiplying money I might do some good to a near relation of yours, seeing what I've got about me of hers – eh?' He tapped one of his money-laden boots upon the floor.

'What do you mean?' said Wildeve.

'That's a secret. Well, I must be going now.' He looked anxiously towards Fairway.

'Where are you going?' Wildeve asked.

'To Mistover Knap. I have to see Mrs Thomasin there – that's all.'

'I am going there, too, to fetch Mrs Wildeve. We can walk together.'

Wildeve became lost in thought, and a look of inward illumination came into his eyes. It was money for his wife that Mrs Yeobright could not trust him with. 'Yet she could trust this fellow,' he said to himself. 'Why doesn't that which belongs to the wife belong to the husband too?'

He called to the pot-boy to bring him his hat, and said, 'Now, Christian, I am ready.'

'Mr Wildeve,' said Christian timidly, as he turned to leave the room, 'would you mind lending me them wonderful little things that carry my luck inside 'em, that I might practise a bit by myself, you know?' He looked wistfully at the dice and box lying on the mantelpiece.

'Certainly,' said Wildeve carelessly. 'They were only cut out by some lad with his knife, and are worth nothing.' And Christian went back and privately pocketed them.

Wildeve opened the door and looked out. The night was warm and cloudy. 'By Gad! 'tis dark,' he continued. 'But I suppose we shall find our way.'

'If we should lose the path it might be awkward,' said Christian. 'A lantern is the only shield that will make it safe for us.'

'Let's have a lantern by all means.' The stable-lantern was fetched and lighted. Christian took up his gown-piece, and the two set out to ascend the hill.

Within the room the men fell into chat till their attention was for a moment drawn to the chimney-corner. This was large, and, in addition to its proper recess, contained within its jambs, like many on Egdon, a receding seat, so that a person might sit there absolutely unobserved, provided there was no fire to light him up, as was the case now and throughout the summer. From the niche a single object protruded into the light from the candles on the table. It was a clay pipe, and its colour was reddish. The men had been attracted to this object by a voice behind the pipe asking for a light.

'Upon my life it fairly startled me when the man spoke!' said Fairway, handling a candle. 'Oh – 'tis the reddleman! You've kept a quiet tongue, young man.'

'Yes, I had nothing to say,' observed Venn. In a few minutes he arose and wished the company good night.

Meanwhile Wildeve and Christian had plunged into the heath.

It was a stagnant, warm, and misty night, full of all the heavy perfumes of new vegetation not yet dried by hot sun, and among these particularly the scent of the fern. The lantern, dangling from Christian's hand, brushed the feathery fronds in passing by, disturbing moths and other winged insects, which flew out and alighted upon its horny panes.

'So you have money to carry to Mrs Wildeve?' said Christian's companion, after a silence. 'Don't you think it very odd that it shouldn't be given to me?'

'As a man and wife be one flesh, 'twould have been all the same, I
should think,' said Christian. 'But my strict documents was, to give the
money into Mrs Wildeve's hand: and 'tis well to do things right.'

'No doubt,' said Wildeve. Any person who had known the circumstances might have perceived that Wildeve was mortified by the discovery
that the matter in transit was money, and not, as he had supposed when
at Blooms-End, some fancy nick-nack which only interested the two
women themselves. Mrs Yeobright's refusal implied that his honour was
not considered to be of sufficiently good quality to make him a safe bearer
of his wife's property.

'How very warm it is tonight, Christian!' he said, panting, when they
were nearly under Rainbarrow. 'Let us sit down for a few minutes, for
Heaven's sake.'

Wildeve flung himself down on the soft ferns; and Christian, placing
the lantern and parcel on the ground, perched himself in a cramped
position hard by, his knees almost touching his chin. He presently thrust
one hand into his coat-pocket and began shaking it about.

'What are you rattling in here?' said Wildeve.

'Only the dice, sir,' said Christian, quickly withdrawing his hand.
'What magical machines these little things be, Mr Wildeve! 'Tis a game
I should never get tired of. Would you mind my taking 'em out and
looking at 'em for a minute, to see how they are made? I didn't like
to look close before the other men, for fear they should think it bad
manners in me.' Christian took them out and examined them in the
hollow of his hand by the lantern light. 'That these little things should
carry such luck, and such charm, and such a spell, and such power in
'em, passes all I ever heard or zeed,' he went on, with a fascinated
gaze at the dice, which, as is frequently the case in country places,
were made of wood, the points being burnt upon each face with the
end of a wire.

'They are a great deal in a small compass, you think?'

'Yes. Do ye suppose they really be the devil's playthings, Mr Wildeve?
If so, 'tis no good sign that I be such a lucky man.'

'You ought to win some money, now that you've got them. Any
woman would marry you then. Now is your time, Christian, and I would
recommend you not to let it slip. Some men are born to luck, some are
not. I belong to the latter class.'

'Did you ever know anybody who was born to it besides myself?'

'O yes. I once heard of an Italian, who sat down at a gaming-table with
only a louis (that's a foreign sovereign) in his pocket. He played on for
twenty-four hours, and won ten thousand pounds, stripping the bank he
had played against. Then there was another man who had lost a thousand
pounds, and went to the broker's next day to sell stock, that he might pay
the debt. The man to whom he owed the money went with him in a
hackney-coach; and to pass the time they tossed who should pay the fare.
The ruined man won, and the other was tempted to continue the game,
and they played all the way. When the coachman stopped he was told to

drive home again: the whole thousand pounds had been won back by the man who was going to sell.'

'Ha – ha – splendid!' exclaimed Christian. 'Go on – go on!'

'Then there was a man of London, who was only a waiter at White's club-house. He began playing first half-crown stakes, and then higher and higher, till he became very rich, got an appointment in India, and rose to be Governor of Madras. His daughter married a member of parliament, and the Bishop of Carlisle stood godfather to one of the children.'

'Wonderful! wonderful!'

'And once there was a young man in America who gambled till he had lost his last dollar. He staked his watch and chain; and lost as before: staked his umbrella; lost again; staked his hat; lost again: staked his coat and stood in his shirt-sleeve; lost again. Began taking off his breeches, and then a looker-on gave him a trifle for his pluck. With this he won. Won back his coat, won back his hat, won back his umbrella, his watch, his money, and went out of the door a rich man.'

'O, 'tis too good – it takes away my breath! Mr Wildeve, I think I will try another shilling with you, as I am one of that sort; no danger can come o't, and you can afford to lose.'

'Very well,' said Wildeve, rising. Searching about with the lantern, he found a large flat stone, which he placed between himself and Christian, and sat down again. The lantern was opened to give more light, and its rays directed upon the stone. Christian put down a shilling, Wildeve another, and each threw. Christian won. They played for two. Christian won again.

'Let us try four,' said Wildeve. They played for four. This time the stakes were won by Wildeve.

'Ah, those little accidents will, of course, sometimes happen to the luckiest man,' he observed.

'And now I have no more money!' exclaimed Christian excitedly. 'And yet, if I could go on, I should get it back again, and more. I wish this was mine.' He struck his boot upon the ground, so that the guineas chinked within.

'What! you have not put Mrs Wildeve's money there?'

'Yes. 'Tis for safety. Is it any harm to raffle with a married lady's money when, if I win, I shall only keep my winnings, and give her her own all the same; and if t'other man wins, her money will go to the lawful owner?'

'None at all.'

Wildeve had been brooding ever since they started on the mean estimation in which he was held by his wife's friends; and it cut his heart severely. As the minutes passed he had gradually drifted into a revengeful intention without knowing the precise moment of forming it. This was to teach Mrs Yeobright a lesson, as he considered it to be; in other words, to show her if he could, that her niece's husband was the proper guardian of her niece's money.

'Well, here goes!' said Christian, beginning to unlace one boot. 'I shall dream of it nights and nights, I suppose; but I shall always swear my flesh don't crawl when I think o't!'

He thrust his hand into the boot and withdrew one of poor Thomasin's precious guineas, piping hot. Wildeve had already placed a sovereign on the stone. The game was then resumed. Wildeve won first, and Christian ventured another, winning himself this time. The game fluctuated, but the average was in Wildeve's favour. Both men became so absorbed in the game they took no heed of anything but the pigmy objects immediately beneath their eyes; the flat stone, the open lantern, the dice, and the few illuminated fern-leaves which lay under the light, were the whole world to them.

At length Christian lost rapidly; and presently, to his horror, the whole fifty guineas belonging to Thomasin had been handed over to his adversary.

'I don't care – I don't care!' he moaned, and desperately set about untying his left boot to get at the other fifty. 'The devil will toss me into the flames on his three-pronged fork for this night's work, I know! But perhaps I shall win yet, and then I'll get a wife to sit up with me o' nights, and I won't be afeard, I won't! Here's another for'ee, my man!' He slapped another guinea down upon the stone, and the dice-box was rattled again.

Time passed on. Wildeve began to be as excited as Christian himself. When commencing the game his intention had been nothing further than a bitter practical joke on Mrs Yeobright. To win the money, fairly or otherwise, and to hand it contemptuously to Thomasin in her aunt's presence, had been the dim outline of his purpose. But men are drawn from their intentions even in the course of carrying them out, and it was extremely doubtful, by the time the twentieth guinea had been reached, whether Wildeve was conscious of any other intention than that of winning for his own personal benefit. Moreover, he was now no longer gambling for his wife's money, but for Yeobright's; though of this fact Christian, in his apprehensiveness, did not inform him till afterwards.

It was nearly eleven o'clock, when, with almost a shriek, Christian placed Yeobright's last gleaming guinea upon the stone. In thirty seconds it had gone the way of its companions.

Christian turned and flung himself on the ferns in a convulsion of remorse. 'O, what shall I do with my wretched self?' he groaned. 'What shall I do? Will any good Heaven hae mercy upon my wicked soul?'

'Do? Live on just the same.'

'I won't live on just the same! I'll die! I say you are a – a –'

'A man sharper than my neighbour.'

'Yes, a man sharper than my neighbour; a regular sharper!'

'Poor chips-in-porridge, you are very unmannerly.'

'I don't know about that! And I say you be unmannerly. You've got money that isn't your own. Half the guineas are poor Mr Clym's.'

'How's that?'

'Because I had to gie fifty of 'em to him. Mrs Yeobright said so.'

'Oh? . . . Well, 'twould have been more graceful of her to have given them to his wife Eustacia. But they are in my hands now.'

Christian pulled on his boots, and with heavy breathings, which could be heard to some distance, dragged his limbs together, arose, and tottered away out of sight. Wildeve set about shutting the lantern to return to the house, for he deemed it too late to go to Mistover to meet his wife, who was to be driven home in the captain's four-wheel. While he was closing the little horn door a figure rose from behind a neighbouring bush and came forward into the lantern light. It was the reddleman approaching.

* VIII *

A New Force Disturbs the Current

WILDEVE stared. Venn looked coolly towards Wildeve, and, without a word being spoken, he deliberately sat himself down where Christian had been seated, thrust his hand into his pocket, drew out a sovereign, and laid it on the stone.

'You have been watching us from behind that bush?' said Wildeve.

The reddleman nodded. 'Down with your stake,' he said. 'Or haven't you pluck enough to go on?'

Now, gambling is a species of amusement which is much more easily begun with full pockets than left off with the same; and though Wildeve in a cooler temper might have prudently declined this invitation, the excitement of his recent success carried him completely away. He placed one of the guineas on the slab beside the reddleman's sovereign. 'Mine is a guinea,' he said.

'A guinea that's not your own,' said Venn sarcastically.

'It is my own,' answered Wildeve haughtily. 'It's my wife's, and what is hers is mine.'

'Very well; let's make a beginning.' He shook the box, and threw eight, ten, and nine; the three casts amounted to twenty-seven.

This encouraged Wildeve. He took the box; and his three casts amounted to forty-five.

Down went another of the reddleman's sovereigns against his first one which Wildeve laid. This time Wildeve threw fifty-one points, but no pair. The reddleman looked grim, threw a raffle of aces, and pocketed the stakes.

'Here you are again,' said Wildeve contemptuously. 'Double the stakes.'

He laid two of Thomasin's guineas, and the reddleman his two pounds. Venn won again. New stakes were laid on the stone, and the gamblers proceeded as before.

Wildeve was a nervous and excitable man; and the game was beginning to tell upon his temper. He writhed, fumed, shifted his seat; and the beating of his heart was almost audible. Venn sat with lips impassively closed and eyes reduced to a pair of unimportant twinkles; he scarcely appeared to breathe. He might have been an Arab, or an automaton; he would have been like a red-sandstone statue but for the motion of his arm with the dice-box.

The game fluctuated, now in favour of one, now in favour of the other, without any great advantage on the side of either. Nearly twenty minutes were passed thus. The light of the candle had by this time attracted heathflies, moths, and other winged creatures of night, which floated round the lantern, flew into the flame, or beat about the faces of the two players.

But neither of the men paid much attention to these things, their eyes being concentrated upon the little flat stone, which to them was an arena vast and important as a battle-field. By this time a change had come over the game; the reddleman won continually. At length sixty guineas – Thomasin's fifty, and ten of Clym's – had passed into his hands. Wildeve was reckless, frantic, exasperated.

' "Won back his coat," ' said Venn slily.

Another throw, and the money went the same way.

' "Won back his hat," ' continued Venn.

'Oh, oh!' said Wildeve.

' "Won back his watch, won back his money, and went out of the door a rich man," ' added Venn sentence by sentence, as stake after stake passed over to him.

'Five more!' shouted Wildeve, dashing down the money. 'And three casts be hanged – one shall decide.'

The red automaton opposite lapsed into silence, nodded, and followed his example. Wildeve rattled the box, and threw a pair of sixes and five points. He clapped his hands; 'I have done it this time – hurrah!'

'There are two playing, and only one has thrown,' said the reddleman, quietly bringing down the box. The eyes of each were then so intently converged upon the stone that one could fancy their beams were visible, like rays in a fog.

Venn lifted the box, and behold a triplet of sixes was disclosed.

Wildeve was full of fury. While the reddleman was grasping the stakes Wildeve seized the dice and hurled them, box and all, into the darkness, uttering a fearful imprecation. Then he arose and began stamping up and down like a madman.

'It is all over, then?' said Venn.

'No, no!' cried Wildeve. 'I mean to have another chance yet. I must!'

'But, my good man what have you done with the dice?'

'I threw them away – it was a momentary irritation. What a fool I am! Here – come and help me to look for them – we must find them again.'

Wildeve snatched up the lantern and began anxiously prowling among the furze and fern.

'You are not likely to find them there,' said Venn, following. 'What did you do such a crazy thing as that for? Here's the box. The dice can't be far off.'

Wildeve turned the light eagerly upon the spot where Venn had found the box, and mauled the herbage right and left. In the course of a few minutes one of the dice was found. They searched on for some time, but no other was to be seen.

'Never mind,' said Wildeve; 'let's play with one.'

'Agreed,' said Venn.

Down they sat again, and recommenced with single guinea stakes; and the play went on smartly. But Fortune had unmistakably fallen in love with the reddleman tonight. He won steadily, till he was the owner of fourteen more of the gold pieces. Seventy-nine of the hundred guineas were his, Wildeve possessing only twenty-one. The aspect of the two opponents was now singular. Apart from motions, a complete diorama of the fluctuations of the game went on in their eyes. A diminutive candle-flame was mirrored in each pupil, and it would have been possible to distinguish therein between the moods of hope and the moods of abandonment, even as regards the reddleman, though his facial muscles betrayed nothing at all. Wildeve played on with the recklessness of despair.

'What's that?' he suddenly exclaimed, hearing a rustle; and they both looked up.

They were surrounded by dusky forms between four and five feet high, standing a few paces beyond the rays of the lantern. A moment's inspection revealed that the encircling figures were heath-croppers, their heads being all towards the players, at whom they gazed intently.

'Hoosh!' said Wildeve; and the whole forty or fifty animals at once turned and galloped away. Play was again resumed.

Ten minutes passed away. Then a large death's head moth advanced from the obscure outer air, wheeled twice round the lantern, flew straight at the candle, and extinguished it by the force of the blow. Wildeve had just thrown, but had not lifted the box to see what he had cast; and now it was impossible.

'What the infernal!' he shrieked. 'Now, what shall we do? Perhaps I have thrown six – have you any matches?'

'None,' said Venn.

'Christian had some – I wonder where he is. Christian!'

But there was no reply to Wildeve's shout, save a mournful whining from the herons which were nesting lower down the vale. Both men looked blankly round without rising. As their eyes grew accustomed to the darkness they perceived faint greenish points of light among the grass and fern. These lights dotted the hillside like stars of a low magnitude.

'Ah – glowworms,' said Wildeve. 'Wait a minute. We can continue the game.'

Venn sat still, and his companion went hither and thither till he had gathered thirteen glowworms – as many as he could find in a space of four or five minutes – upon a foxglove leaf which he pulled for the purpose. The reddleman vented a low humourous laugh when he saw his adversary return with these. 'Determined to go on, then?' he said drily.

'I always am!' said Wildeve angrily. And shaking the glowworms from the leaf he ranged them with a trembling hand in a circle on the stone, leaving a space in the middle for the descent of the dice-box, over which thirteen tiny lamps threw a pale phosphoric shine. The game was again renewed. It happened to be that season of the year at which glowworms put forth their greatest brilliancy, and the light they yielded was more than ample for the purpose, since it is possible on such nights to read the handwriting of a letter by the light of two or three.

The incongruity between the men's deeds and their environment was great. Amid the soft juicy vegatation of the hollow in which they sat, the motionless and the uninhabited solitude, intruded the chink of guineas, the rattle of dice, the exclamations of the reckless players.

Wildeve had lifted the box as soon as the lights were obtained, and the solitary die proclaimed that the game was still against him.

'I won't play any more: you've been tampering with the dice,' he shouted.

'How – when they were your own?' said the reddleman.

'We'll change the game: the lowest point shall win the stake – it may cut off my ill luck. Do you refuse?'

'No – go on,' said Venn.

'O, there they are again – damn them!' cried Wildeve, looking up. The heath-croppers had returned noiselessly, and were looking on with erect heads just as before, their timid eyes fixed upon the scene, as if they were wondering what mankind and candle-light could have to do in these haunts at this untoward hour.

'What a plague those creatures are – staring at me so!' he said, and flung a stone, which scattered them; when the game was continued as before.

Wildeve had now ten guineas left; and each laid five. Wildeve threw three points; Venn two, and raked in the coins. The other seized the die, and clenched his teeth upon it in sheer rage, as if he would bite it in pieces. 'Never give in – here are my last five!' he cried, throwing them down. 'Hang the glowworms – they are going out. Why don't you burn, you little fools? Stir them up with a thorn.'

He probed the glowworms with a bit of stick, and rolled them over, till the bright side of their tails was upwards.

'There's light enough. Throw on,' said Venn.

Wildeve brought down the box within the shining circle and looked eagerly. He had thrown ace. 'Well done! – I said it would turn, and it has turned.' Venn said nothing; but his hand shook slightly.

He threw ace also.

'O!' said Wildeve. 'Curse me!'

The die smacked the stone a second time. It was ace again. Venn looked gloomy, threw: the die was seen to be lying in two pieces, the cleft sides uppermost.

'I've thrown nothing at all,' he said.

'Serves me right – I split the die with my teeth. Here – take your money. Blank is less than one.'

'I don't wish it.'

'Take it, I say – you've won it!' And Wildeve threw the stakes against the reddleman's chest. Venn gathered them up, arose, and withdrew from the hollow, Wildeve sitting stupefied.

When he had come to himself he also arose, and, with the extinguished lantern in his hand, went towards the high-road. On reaching it he stood still. The silence of night pervaded the whole heath except in one direction; and that was towards Mistover. There he could hear the noise of light wheels, and presently saw two carriage-lamps descending the hill. Wildeve screened himself under a bush and waited.

The vehicle came on and passed before him. It was a hired carriage, and behind the coachman were two persons whom he knew well. There sat Eustacia and Yeobright, the arm of the latter being round her waist. They turned the sharp corner at the bottom towards the temporary home which Clym had hired and furnished, about five miles to the eastward.

Wildeve forgot the loss of the money at the sight of his lost love, whose preciousness in his eyes was increasing in geometrical progression with each new incident that reminded him of their hopeless division. Brimming with the subtilized misery that he was capable of feeling, he followed the opposite way towards the inn.

About the same moment that Wildeve stepped into the highway Venn also had reached it at a point a hundred yards further on; and he, hearing the same wheels, likewise waited till the carriage should come up. When he saw who sat therein he seemed to be disappointed. Reflecting a minute or two, during which interval the carriage rolled on, he crossed the road, and took a short cut through the furze and heath to a point where the turnpike-road bent round in ascending a hill. He was now again in front of the carriage, which presently came up at a walking pace. Venn stepped forward and showed himself.

Eustacia started when the lamp shone upon him, and Clym's arm was involuntarily withdrawn from her waist. He said, 'What, Diggory? You are having a lonely walk.'

'Yes – I beg your pardon for stopping you,' said Venn. 'But I am waiting about for Mrs Wildeve: I have something to give her from Mrs Yeobright. Can you tell me if she's gone home from the party yet?'

'No. But she will be leaving soon. You may possibly meet her at the corner.'

Venn made a farewell obeisance, and walked back to his former position, where the by-road from Mistover joined the highway. Here he remained fixed for nearly half an hour; and then another pair of lights came down the hill. It was the old-fashioned wheeled nondescript belonging to the captain, and Thomasin sat in it alone, driven by Charley.

The reddleman came up as they slowly turned the corner. 'I beg pardon for stopping you, Mrs Wildeve,' he said. 'But I have something to give you privately from Mrs Yeobright.' He handed a small parcel; it consisted of the hundred guineas he had just won, roughly twisted up in a piece of paper.

Thomasin recovered from her surprise, and took the packet. 'That's all, ma'am – I wish you good-night,' he said, and vanished from her view.

Thus Venn, in his anxiety to rectify matters, had placed in Thomasin's hands not only the fifty guineas which rightly belonged to her, but also the fifty intended for her cousin Clym. His mistake had been based upon Wildeve's words at the opening of the game, when he indignantly denied that the guineas was not his own. It had not been comprehended by the reddleman that at half-way through the performance the game was continued with the money of another person; and it was an error which afterwards helped to cause more misfortune than treble the loss in money value could have done.

The night was now somewhat advanced; and Venn plunged deeper into the heath, till he came to a ravine where his van was standing – a spot not more than two hundred yards from the site of the gambling bout. He entered this movable home of his, lit his lantern, and, before closing his door for the night, stood reflecting on the circumstances of the preceding hours. While he stood the dawn grew visible in the north-east quarter of the heavens, which, the clouds having cleared off, was bright with a soft sheen at this midsummer time, though it was only between one and two o'clock. Venn, thoroughly weary, then shut his door and flung himself down to sleep.

BOOK FOURTH

THE CLOSED DOOR

I

The Rencounter by the Pool

THE July sun shone over Egdon and fired its crimson heather to scarlet. It was the one season of the year, and the one weather of the season, in which the heath was gorgeous. This flowering period represented the second or noontide division in the cycle of those superficial changes which alone were possible here; it followed the green or young-fern period, representing the morn, and preceded the brown period, when the heath-bells and ferns would wear the russet tinges of evening; to be in turn displaced by the dark hue of the winter period, representing night.

Clym and Eustacia, in their little house at Alderworth, beyond East Egdon, were living on with a monotony which was delightful to them. The heath and changes of weather were quite blotted out from their eyes for the present. They were enclosed in a sort of luminous mist, which hid from them surroundings of any inharmonious colour, and gave to all things the character of light. When it rained they were charmed, because they could remain indoors together all day with such a show of reason; when it was fine they were charmed, because they could sit together on the hills. They were like those double stars which revolve round and round each other, and from a distance appear to be one. The absolute solitude in which they lived intensified their reciprocal thoughts; yet some might have said that it had the disadvantage of consuming their mutual affections at a fearfully prodigal rate. Yeobright did not fear for his own part; but recollection of Eustacia's old speech about the evanescence of love, now apparently forgotten by her, sometimes caused him to ask himself a question; and he recoiled at the thought that the quality of finiteness was not foreign to Eden.

When three or four weeks had been passed thus, Yeobright resumed his reading in earnest. To make up for lost time he studied indefatigably, for he wished to enter his new profession with the least possible delay.

Now, Eustacia's dream had always been that, once married to Clym, she would have the power of inducing him to return to Paris. He had carefully withheld all promise to do so; but would he be proof against her coaxing and argument? She had calculated to such a degree on the probability of success that she had represented Paris, and not Budmouth, to her grandfather as in all likelihood their future home. Her hopes were bound up in this dream. In the quiet days since their marriage, when Yeobright had been poring over her lips, her eyes, and the lines of her face, she had mused and mused on the subject, even while in the act of returning his gaze; and now the sight of the books, indicating a future which was antagonistic to her dream, struck her with a positively painful jar. She was hoping for the time when, as the mistress of some pretty establishment, however small, near a Parisian Boulevard, she would be passing her days on the skirts at least of the gay world, and catching stray wafts from those town pleasures she was so well fitted to enjoy. Yet Yeobright was as firm in the contrary intention as if the tendency of marriage were rather to develop the fantasies of young philanthropy than to sweep them away.

Her anxiety reached a high pitch; but there was something in Clym's undeviating manner which made her hesitate before sounding him on the subject. At this point in their experience, however, an incident helped her. It occurred one evening about six weeks after their union, and arose entirely out of the unconscious misapplication by Venn of the fifty guineas intended for Yeobright.

A day or two after the receipt of the money Thomasin had sent a note to her aunt to thank her. She had been surprised at the largeness of the amount; but as no sum had ever been mentioned she set that down to her late uncle's generosity. She had been strictly charged by her aunt to say nothing to her husband of this gift; and Wildeve, as was natural enough, had not brought himself to mention to his wife a single particular of the midnight scene in the heath. Christian's terror, in like manner, had tied his tongue on the share he took in that proceeding; and hoping that by some means or other the money had gone to its proper destination, he simply asserted as much, without giving details.

Therefore, when a week or two had passed away, Mrs Yeobright began to wonder why she never heard from her son of the receipt of the present; and to add gloom to her perplexity came the possibility that resentment might be the cause of his silence. She could hardly believe as much, but why did he not write? She questioned Christian, and the confusion in his answer would at once have led her to believe that something was wrong, had not one-half of his story been corroborated by Thomasin's note.

Mrs Yeobright was in this state of uncertainty when she was informed one morning that her son's wife was visiting her grandfather at Mistover. She determined to walk up the hill, see Eustacia, and ascertain from her daughter-in-law's lips whether the family guineas, which were to Mrs Yeobright what family jewels are to wealthier dowagers, had miscarried or not.

When Christian learnt where she was going his concern reached its height. At the moment of her departure he could prevaricate no longer, and, confessing to the gambling, told her the truth as far as he knew it – that the guineas had been won by Wildeve.

'What, is he going to keep them?' Mrs Yeobright cried.

'I hope and trust not!' moaned Christian. 'He's a good man, and perhaps will do right things. He said you ought to have gied Mr Clym's share to Eustacia, and that's perhaps what he'll do himself.'

To Mrs Yeobright, as soon as she could calmly reflect, there was much likelihood in this, for she could hardly believe that Wildeve would really appropriate money belonging to her son. The intermediate course of giving it to Eustacia was the sort of thing to please Wildeve's fancy. But it filled the mother with anger none the less. That Wildeve should have got command of the guineas after all, and should rearrange the disposal of them, placing Clym's share in Clym's wife's hands, because she had been his own sweetheart, and might be so still, was as irritating a pain as any that Mrs Yeobright had ever borne.

She instantly dismissed the wretched Christian from her employ for his conduct in the affair; but, feeling quite helpless and unable to do without him, told him afterwards that he might stay a little longer if he chose. Then she hastened off to Eustacia, moved by a much less promising emotion towards her daughter-in-law than she had felt half an hour earlier, when planning her journey. At that time it was to inquire in a friendly spirit if there had been any accidental loss; now it was to ask plainly if Wildeve had privately given her money which had been intended as a sacred gift to Clym.

She started at two o'clock, and her meeting with Eustacia was hastened by the appearance of the young lady beside the pool and bank which bordered her grandfather's premises, where she stood surveying the scene, and perhaps thinking of the romantic enactments it had witnessed in past days. When Mrs Yeobright approached, Eustacia surveyed her with the calm stare of a stranger.

The mother-in-law was the first to speak. 'I was coming to see you,' she said.

'Indeed!' said Eustacia with surprise, for Mrs Yeobright, much to the girl's mortification, had refused to be present at the wedding. 'I did not at all expect you.'

'I was coming on business only,' said the visitor, more coldly than at first. 'Will you excuse my asking this – Have you received a gift from Thomasin's husband?'

'A gift?'

'I mean money!'

'What – I myself?'

'Well, I meant yourself, privately – though I was not going to put it in that way.'

'Money from Mr Wildeve? No – never! Madam, what do you mean by that?' Eustacia fired up all too quickly, for her own consciousness of the old attachment between herself and Wildeve led her to jump to the conclusion that Mrs Yeobright also knew of it, and might have come to accuse her of receiving dishonourable presents from him now.

'I simply ask the question,' said Mrs Yeobright. 'I have been –'

'You ought to have better opinions of me – I feared you were against me from the first!' exclaimed Eustacia.

'No. I was simply for Clym,' replied Mrs Yeobright, with too much emphasis in her earnestness. 'It is the instinct of every one to look after their own.'

'How can you imply that he required guarding against me?' cried Eustacia, passionate tears in her eyes. 'I have not injured him by marrying him! What sin have I done that you should think so ill of me? You had no right to speak against me to him when I have never wronged you.'

'I only did what was fair under the circumstances,' said Mrs Yeobright more softly. 'I would rather not have gone into this question at present, but you compel me. I am not ashamed to tell you the honest truth. I was firmly convinced that he ought not to marry you – therefore I tried to dissuade him by all the means in my power. But it is done now, and I have no idea of complaining any more. I am ready to welcome you.'

'Ah, yes, it is very well to see things in that business point of view,' murmured Eustacia with a smothered fire of feeling. 'But why should you think there is anything between me and Mr Wildeve? I have a spirit as well as you. I am indignant; and so would any woman be. It was a condescension in me to be Clym's wife, and not a manoeuvre, let me remind you; and therefore I will not be treated as a schemer whom it becomes necessary to bear with because she has crept into the family.'

'Oh!' said Mrs Yeobright, vainly endeavouring to control her anger. 'I have never heard anything to show that my son's lineage is not as good as the Vyes' – perhaps better. It is amusing to hear you talk of condescension.'

'It was condescension, nevertheless,' said Eustacia vehemently. 'And if I had known then what I know now, that I should be living in this wild heath a month after my marriage, I – I should have thought twice before agreeing.'

'It would be better not to say that; it might not sound truthful. I am not aware that any deception was used on his part – I know there was not – whatever might have been the case on the other side.'

'This is too exasperating!' answered the younger woman huskily, her face crimsoning, and her eyes darting light. 'How can you dare to speak to me like that? I insist upon repeating to you that had I known that my life would from my marriage up to this time have been as it is, I should have said No. I don't complain. I have never uttered a sound of such a thing to him; but it is true. I hope therefore that in the future you will be silent on my eagerness. If you injure me now you injure yourself.'

'Injure you? Do you think I am an evil-disposed person?'

'You injured me before my marriage, and you have now suspected me of secretly favouring another man for money!'

'I could not help what I thought. But I have never spoken of you outside my house.'

'You spoke of me within it, to Clym, and you could not do worse.'

'I did my duty.'

'And I'll do mine.'

'A part of which will possibly be to set him against his mother. It is always so. But why should I not bear it as others have borne it before me!'

'I understand you,' said Eustacia, breathless with emotion. 'You think me capable of every bad thing. Who can be worse than a wife who encourages a lover, and poisons her husband's mind against his relative? Yet that is now the character given to me. Will you not come and drag him out of my hands?'

Mrs Yeobright gave back heat for heat.

'Don't rage at me, madam! It ill becomes your beauty, and I am not worth the injury you may do it on my account, I assure you. I am only a poor old woman who has lost a son.'

'If you had treated me honourably you would have had him still,' Eustacia said, while scalding tears trickled from her eyes. 'You have brought yourself to folly; you have caused a division which can never be healed!'

'I have done nothing. This audacity from a young woman is more than I can bear.'

'It was asked for; you have suspected me, and you have made me speak of my husband in a way I would not have done. You will let him know that I have spoken thus, and it will cause misery between us. Will you go away from me? You are no friend!'

'I will go when I have spoken a word. If any one says I have come here to question you without good grounds for it, that person speaks untruly. If any one says that I attempted to stop your marriage by any but honest means, that person, too, does not speak the truth. I have fallen on an evil time; God has been unjust to me in letting you insult me! Probably my son's happiness does not lie on this side of the grave, for he is a foolish man who neglects the advice of his parent. You, Eustacia, stand on the edge of a precipice without knowing it. Only show my son one-half the temper you have shown me today – and you may before long – and you will find that though he is as gentle as a child with you now, he can be as hard as steel!'

The excited mother then withdrew, and Eustacia, panting, stood looking into the pool.

* II *

He Is Set Upon by Adversities; but He Sings a Song

THE result of that unpropitious interview was that Eustacia, instead of passing the afternoon with her grandfather, hastily returned home to Clym, where she arrived three hours earlier than she had been expected.

She came indoors with her face flushed, and her eyes still showing traces of her recent excitement. Yeobright looked up astonished; he had never seen her in any way approaching to that state before. She passed him by, and would have gone upstairs unnoticed, but Clym was so concerned that he immediately followed her.

'What is the matter, Eustacia?' he said. She was standing on the hearthrug in the bedroom, looking upon the floor, her hands clasped in front of her, her bonnet yet unremoved. For a moment she did not answer; and then she replied in a low voice –

'I have seen your mother; and I will never see her again!'

A weight fell like a stone upon Clym. That same morning, when Eustacia had arranged to go and see her grandfather, Clym had expressed a wish that she would drive down to Blooms-End and inquire for her mother-in-law, or adopt any other means she might think fit to bring about a reconciliation. She had set out gaily; and he had hoped for much.

'Why is this?' he asked.

'I cannot tell – I cannot remember. I met your mother. And I will never meet her again.'

'Why?'

'What do I know about Mr Wildeve now? I won't have wicked opinions passed on me by anybody. O! it was too humiliating to be asked if I had received any money from him, or encouraged him, or something of the sort – I don't exactly know what!'

'How could she have asked you that?'

'She did.'

'Then there must have been some meaning in it. What did my mother say besides?'

'I don't know what she said, except in so far as this, that we both said words which can never be forgiven!'

'O, there must be some misapprehension. Whose fault was it that her meaning was not made clear?'

'I would rather not say. It may have been the fault of the circumstances, which were awkward at the very least. O Clym – I cannot help expressing it – this is an unpleasant position that you have placed me in. But you must improve it – yes, say you will – for I hate it all now! Yes, take me to Paris, and go on with your old occupation, Clym! I don't mind how humbly we live there at first, if it can only be Paris, and not Egdon Heath.'

'But I have quite given up the idea,' said Yeobright, with surprise. 'Surely I never led you to expect such a thing?'

'I own it. Yet there are thoughts which cannot be kept out of mind, and that one was mine. Must I not have a voice in the matter, now I am your wife and the sharer of your doom?'

'Well, there are things which are placed beyond the pale of discussion; and I thought this was specially so, and by mutual agreement.'

'Clym, I am unhappy at what I hear,' she said in a low voice; and her eyes drooped, and she turned away.

This indication of an unexpected mine of hope in Eustacia's bosom disconcerted her husband. It was the first time that he had confronted the fact of the indirectness of a woman's movement towards her desire. But his intention was unshaken, though he loved Eustacia well. All the effect that her remark had upon him was a resolve to chain himself more closely than ever to his books, so as to be the sooner enabled to appeal to substantial results from another course in arguing against her whim.

Next day the mystery of the guineas was explained. Thomasin paid them a hurried visit, and Clym's share was delivered up to him by her own hands. Eustacia was not present at the time.

'Then this is what my mother meant,' exclaimed Clym. 'Thomasin, do you know that they have had a bitter quarrel?'

There was a little more reticence now than formerly in Thomasin's manner towards her cousin. It is the effect of marriage to engender in several directions some of the reserve it annihilates in one. 'Your mother told me,' she said quietly. 'She came back to my house after seeing Eustacia.'

'The worst thing I dreaded has come to pass. Was mother much disturbed when she came to you, Thomasin?'

'Yes.'

'Very much indeed?'

'Yes.'

Clym leant his elbow upon the post of the garden gate, and covered his eyes with his hand.

'Don't trouble about it, Clym. They may get to be friends.'

He shook his head. 'Not two people with inflammable natures like theirs. Well, what must be will be.'

'One thing is cheerful in it – the guineas are not lost.'

'I would rather have lost them twice over than have had this happen.'

Amid these jarring events Yeobright felt one thing to be indispensable – that he should speedily make some show of progress in his scholastic plan. With this view he read far into the small hours during many nights.

One morning, after a severer strain than usual, he awoke with a strange sensation in his eyes. The sun was shining directly upon the window-blind, and at his first glance thitherward a sharp pain obliged him to close his eyelids quickly. At every new attempt to look about him the same morbid sensibility to light was manifested, and excoriating tears ran down his cheeks. He was obliged to tie a bandage over his brow while dressing; and during the day it could not be abandoned. Eustacia was thoroughly alarmed. On finding that the case was no better the next morning they decided to send to Anglebury for a surgeon.

Towards evening he arrived, and pronounced the disease to be acute inflammation induced by Clym's night studies, continued in spite of a cold previously caught, which had weakened his eyes for the time.

Fretting with impatience at this interruption to a task he was so anxious to hasten, Clym was transformed into an invalid. He was shut up in a room from which all light was excluded, and his condition would have been one of absolute misery had not Eustacia read to him by the glimmer of a shaded lamp. He hoped that the worst would soon be over; but at the surgeon's third visit he learnt to his dismay that although he might venture out of doors with shaded eyes in the course of a month, all thought of pursuing his work, or of reading print of any description, would have to be given up for a long time to come.

One week and another week wore on, and nothing seemed to lighten the gloom of the young couple. Dreadful imaginings occurred to Eustacia, but she carefully refrained from uttering them to her husband. Suppose he should become blind, or, at all events, never recover sufficient strength of sight to engage in an occupation which would be congenial to her feelings, and conduce to her removal from this lonely dwelling among the hills? That dream of beautiful Paris was not likely to cohere into substance in the presence of this misfortune. As day after day passed by, and he got no better, her mind ran more and more in this mournful groove, and she would go away from him into the garden and weep despairing tears.

Yeobright thought he would send for his mother; and then he thought he would not. Knowledge of his state could only make her the more unhappy; and the seclusion of their life was such that she would hardly be likely to learn the news except through a special messenger. Endeavouring to take the trouble as philosophically as possible, he waited on till the third week had arrived, when he went into the open air for the first time since the attack. The surgeon visited him again at this stage, and Clym urged him to express a distinct opinion. The young man learnt with added surprise that the date at which he might expect to resume his labours was as uncertain as ever, his eyes being in that peculiar state which, though affording him sight enough for walking about, would not admit of their being strained upon any definite object without incurring the risk of reproducing ophthalmia in its acute form.

Clym was very grave at the intelligence, but not despairing. A quiet firmness, and even cheerfulness, took possession of him. He was not to be blind; that was enough. To be doomed to behold the world through smoked glass for an indefinite period was bad enough, and fatal to any kind of advance; but Yeobright was an absolute stoic in the face of mishaps which only affected his social standing; and, apart from Eustacia, the humblest walk of life would satisfy him if it could be made to work in with some form of his culture scheme. To keep a cottage night-school was one such form; and his affliction did not master his spirit as it might otherwise have done.

He walked through the warm sun westward into those tracts of Egdon with which he was best acquainted, being those lying nearer to his old home. He saw before him in one of the valleys the gleaming of whetted iron, and advancing, dimly perceived that the shine came from the tool of a man who was cutting furze. The worker recognized Clym, and Yeobright learnt from the voice that the speaker was Humphrey.

Humphrey expressed his sorrow at Clym's condition; and added, 'Now, if yours was low-class work like mine, you could go on with it just the same.'

'Yes; I could,' said Yeobright musingly. 'How much do you get for cutting these faggots?'

'Half-a-crown a hundred, and in these long days I can live very well on the wages.'

During the whole of Yeobright's walk home to Alderworth he was lost in reflections which were not of an unpleasant kind. On his coming up to the house Eustacia spoke to him from the open window, and he went across to her.

'Darling,' he said, 'I am much happier. And if my mother were reconciled to me and to you I should, I think, be happy quite.'

'I fear that will never be,' she said, looking afar with her beautiful stormy eyes. 'How *can* you say "I am happier," and nothing changed?'

'It arises from my having at last discovered something I can do, and get a living at, in this time of misfortune.'

'Yes?'

'I am going to be a furze and turf-cutter.'

'No, Clym!' she said, the slight hopefulness previously apparent in her face going off again, and leaving her worse than before.

'Surely I shall. Is it not very unwise in us to go on spending the little money we've got when I can keep down expenditure by an honest occupation? The outdoor exercise will do me good, and who knows but that in a few months I shall be able to go on with my reading again?'

'But my grandfather offers to assist us, if we require assistance.'

'We don't require it. If I go furze-cutting we shall be fairly well off.'

'In comparison with slaves, and the Israelites in Egypt, and such people!' A bitter tear rolled down Eustacia's face, which he did not see. There had been *nonchalance* in his tone, showing her that he felt no absolute grief at a consummation which to her was a positive horror.

The very next day Yeobright went to Humphrey's cottage, and borrowed of him leggings, gloves, a whet-stone, and a hook, to use till he should be able to purchase some for himself. Then he sallied forth with his new fellow-labourer and old acquaintance, and selecting a spot where the furze grew thickest he struck the first blow in his adopted calling. His sight, like the wings in 'Rasselas', though useless to him for his grand purpose, sufficed for this strait, and he found that when a little practice should have hardened his palms against blistering he would be able to work with ease.

Day after day he rose with the sun, buckled on his leggings, and went off to the rendezvous with Humphrey. His custom was to work from four o'clock in the morning till noon; then, when the heat of the day was at its highest, to go home and sleep for an hour or two; afterwards coming out again and working till dusk at nine.

This man from Paris was now so disguised by his leather accoutrements, and by the goggles he was obliged to wear over his eyes, that his closest friend might have passed by without recognizing him. He was a brown spot in the midst of an expanse of olive-green gorse, and nothing more. Though frequently depressed in spirit when not actually at work, owing to thoughts of Eustacia's position and his mother's estrangement, when in the full swing of labour he was cheerfully disposed and calm.

His daily life was of a curious microscopic sort, his whole world being limited to the circuit of a few feet from his person. His familiars were creeping and winged things, and they seemed to enroll him in their band. Bees hummed around his ears with an intimate air, and tugged at the heath and furze-flowers at his side in such numbers as to weigh them down to the sod. The strange amber-coloured butterflies which Egdon produced, and which were never seen elsewhere, quivered in the breath of his lips, alighted upon his bowed back, and sported with the glittering point of his hook as he flourished it up and down. Tribes of emerald-green grasshoppers leaped over his feet, falling awkwardly on their backs, heads, or hips, like unskilful acrobats, as chance might rule; or engaged themselves in noisy flirtations under the fern-fronds with silent ones of homely hue. Huge flies, ignorant of larders and wire-netting, and quite in a savage state, buzzed about him without knowing that he was a man. In and out of the fern-dells snakes glided in their most brilliant blue and yellow guise, it being the season immediately following the shedding of their old skins, when their colours are brightest. Litters of young rabbits came out from their forms to sun themselves upon hillocks, the hot beams blazing though the delicate tissue of each thin-fleshed ear, and firing it to a blood-red transparency in which the veins could be seen. None of them feared him.

The monotony of his occupation soothed him, and was in itself a pleasure. A forced limitation of effort offered a justification of homely courses to an unambitious man, whose conscience would hardly have allowed him to remain in such obscurity while his powers were unimpeded. Hence Yeobright sometimes sang to himself, and when obliged to accompany Humphrey in search of brambles for faggot-bonds he would amuse his companion with sketches of Parisian life and character, and so while away the time.

On one of these warm afternoons Eustacia walked out alone in the direction of Yeobright's place of work. He was busily chopping away at the furze, a long row of faggots which stretched downward from his position representing the labour of the day. He did not observe her approach, and she stood close to him, and heard his undercurrent of song. It shocked her. To see him there, a poor afflicted man, earning money by the sweat of his brow, had at first moved her to tears; but to hear him sing and not at all rebel against an occupation which, however satisfactory to himself, was degrading to her, as an educated lady-wife, wounded her through. Unconscious of her presence, he still went on singing:

> 'Le point du jour
> À nos bosquets rend toute leur parure;

Flore est plus belle à son retour;
L'oiseau reprend doux chant d'amour;
Tout célèbre dans la nature
    Le point du jour.

'Le point du jour
Cause parfois, cause douleur extrême;
Que l'espace des nuits est court
Pour le berger brûlant d'amour,
Forcé de quitter ce qu'il aime
Au point du jour!'

It was bitterly plain to Eustacia that he did not care much about social failure; and the proud fair woman bowed her head and wept in sick despair at thought of the blasting effect upon her own life of that mood and condition in him. Then she came forward.

'I would starve rather than do it!' she exclaimed vehemently. 'And you can sing! I will go and live with my grandfather again!'

'Eustacia! I did not see you, though I noticed something moving,' he said gently. He came forward, pulled off his huge leather glove, and took her hand. 'Why do you speak in such a strange way? It is only a little old song which struck my fancy when I was in Paris, and now just applies to my life with you. Has your love for me all died, then, because my appearance is no longer that of a fine gentleman?'

'Dearest, you must not question me unpleasantly, or it may make me not love you.'

'Do you believe it possible that I would run the risk of doing that?'

'Well, you follow out your own ideas, and won't give in to mine when I wish you to leave off this shameful labour. Is there anything you dislike in me that you act so contrarily to my wishes? I am your wife, and why will you not listen? Yes, I am your wife indeed!'

'I know what that tone means.'

'What tone?'

'The tone in which you said, "Your wife indeed." It meant, "Your wife, worse luck." '

'It is hard in you to probe me with that remark. A woman may have reason, though she is not without heart, and if I felt "worse luck", it was no ignoble feeling – it was only too natural. There, you see that at any rate I do not attempt untruths. Do you remember how, before we were married, I warned you that I had not good wifely qualities?'

'You mock me to say that now. On that point at least the only noble course would be to hold your tongue, for you are still queen of me, Eustacia, though I may no longer be king of you.'

'You are my husband. Does not that content you?'

'Not unless you are my wife without regret.'

'I cannot answer you. I remember saying that I should be a serious matter on your hand.'

'Yes, I saw that.'

'Then you were too quick to see! No true lover would have seen any such thing; you are too severe upon me, Clym – I don't like your speaking so at all.'

'Well, I married you in spite of it, and don't regret doing so. How cold you seem this afternoon! and yet I used to think there never was a warmer heart than yours.'

'Yes, I fear we are cooling – I see it as well as you,' she sighed mournfully. 'And how madly we loved two months ago! You were never tired of contemplating me, nor I of contemplating you. Who could have thought then that by this time my eyes would not seem so very bright to yours, nor your lips so very sweet to mine? Two months – is it possible? Yes, 'tis too true!'

'You sigh, dear, as if you were sorry for it; and that's a hopeful sign.'

'No. I don't sigh for that. There are other things for me to sigh for, or any other woman in my place.'

'That your chances in life are ruined by marrying in haste an unfortunate man?'

'Why will you force me, Clym, to say bitter things? I deserve pity as much as you. As much? — I think I deserve it more. For you can sing! It would be a strange hour which should catch me singing under such a cloud as this! Believe me, sweet, I could weep to a degree that would astonish and confound such an elastic mind as yours. Even had you felt careless about your own affliction, you might have refrained from singing out of sheer pity for mine. God! if I were a man in such a position I would curse rather than sing.'

Yeobright placed his hand upon her arm. 'Now, don't you suppose, my inexperienced girl, that I cannot rebel, in high Promethean fashion, against the gods and fate as well as you. I have felt more steam and smoke of that sort than you have ever heard of. But the more I see of life the more do I perceive that there is nothing particularly great in its greatest walks, and therefore nothing particularly small in mine of furze-cutting. If I feel that the greatest blessings vouchsafed to us are not very valuable, how can I feel it to be any great hardship when they are taken away? So I sing to pass the time. Have you indeed lost all tenderness for me, that you begrudge me a few cheerful moments?'

'I have still some tenderness left for you.'

'Your words have no longer their old flavour. And so love dies with good fortune!'

'I cannot listen to this, Clym – it will end bitterly,' she said in a broken voice. 'I will go home.'

III

She Goes Out to Battle against Depression

A FEW days later, before the month of August had expired, Eustacia and Yeobright sat together at their early dinner. Eustacia's manner had become of late almost apathetic. There was a forlorn look about her beautiful eyes which, whether she deserved it or not, would have excited pity in the breast of any one who had known her during the full flush of her love for Clym. The feelings of husband and wife varied, in some measure, inversely with their positions. Clym, the afflicted man, was cheerful; and he even tried to comfort her, who had never felt a moment of physical suffering in her whole life.

'Come, brighten up, dearest; we shall be all right again. Some day perhaps I shall see as well as ever. And I solemnly promise that I'll leave off cutting furze as soon as I have the power to do anything better. You cannot seriously wish me to stay idling at home all day?'

'But it is so dreadful – a furze-cutter! and you a man who have lived about the world, and speak French, and German, and who are fit for what is so much better than this.'

'I suppose when you first saw me and heard about me I was wrapped in a sort of golden halo to your eyes – a man who knew glorious things, and had mixed in brilliant scenes – in short, an adorable, delightful, distracting hero?'

'Yes,' she said, sobbing.

'And now I am a poor fellow in brown leather.'

'Don't taunt me. But enough of this. I will not be depressed any more. I am going from home this afternoon, unless you greatly object. There is to be a village picnic – a gipsying, they call it – at East Egdon, and I shall go.'

'To dance?'

'Why not? You can sing.'

'Well, well, as you will. Must I come to fetch you?'

'If you return soon enough from your work. But do not inconvenience yourself about it. I know the way home, and the heath has no terror for me.'

'And can you cling to gaiety so eagerly as to walk all the way to a village festival in search of it?'

'Now, you don't like my going alone! Clym, you are not jealous?'

'No. But I would come with you if it could give you any pleasure; though, as things stand, perhaps you have too much of me already. Still, I somehow wish that you did not want to go. Yes, perhaps I am jealous; and who could be jealous with more reason than I, a half-blind man, over such a woman as you?'

'Don't think like it. Let me go, and don't take all my spirits away!'

'I would rather lose all my own, my sweet wife. Go and do whatever you like. Who can forbid your indulgence in any whim? You have all my heart yet, I believe; and because you bear with me, who am in truth a drag upon you, I owe you thanks. Yes, go alone and shine. As for me, I will stick to my doom. At that kind of meeting people would shun me. My hook and gloves are like the St Lazarus rattle of the leper, warning the world to get out of the way of a sight that would sadden them.' He kissed her, put on his leggings, and went out.

When he was gone she rested her head upon her hands and said to herself, 'Two wasted lives – his and mine. And I am come to this! Will it drive me out of my mind?'

She cast about for any possible course which offered the least improvement on the existing state of things, and could find none. She imagined how all those Budmouth ones who should learn what had become of her would say, 'Look at the girl for whom nobody was good enough!' To Eustacia the situation seemed such a mockery of her hopes that death appeared the only door of relief if the satire of Heaven should go much further.

Suddenly she aroused herself and exclaimed, 'But I'll shake it off. Yes, I *will* shake it off! No one shall know my suffering. I'll be bitterly merry, and ironically gay, and I'll laugh in derision! And I'll begin by going to this dance on the green.'

She ascended to her bedroom and dressed herself with scrupulous care. To an onlooker her beauty would have made her feelings almost seem reasonable. The gloomy corner into which accident as much as indiscretion had brought this woman might have led even a moderate partisan to feel that she had cogent reasons for asking the Supreme Power by what right a being of such exquisite finish had been placed in circumstances calculated to make of her charms a curse rather than a blessing.

It was five in the afternoon when she came out from the house ready for her walk. There was material enough in the picture for twenty new conquests. The rebellious sadness that was rather too apparent when she sat indoors without a bonnet was cloaked and softened by her outdoor attire, which always had a sort of nebulousness about it, devoid of harsh edges anywhere; so that her face looked from its environment as from a cloud, with no noticeable lines of demarcation between flesh and clothes. The heat of the day had scarcely declined as yet and she went along the sunny hills at a leisurely pace, there being ample time for her idle expedition. Tall ferns buried her in their leafage whenever her path lay through them, which now formed miniature forests, though not one stem of them would remain to bud the next year.

The site chosen for the village festivity was one of the lawn-like oases which were occasionally, yet not often, met with on the plateaux of the heath district. The brakes of furze and fern terminated abruptly round the margin, and the grass was unbroken. A green cattle-track skirted the spot, without, however, emerging from the screen of fern, and this path Eustacia followed, in order to reconnoitre the group before joining it.

The lusty notes of the East Egdon band had directed her unerringly, and she now beheld the musicians themselves, sitting in a blue waggon with red wheels scrubbed as bright as new, and arched with sticks, to which boughs and flowers were tied. In front of this was the grand central dance of fifteen or twenty couples, flanked by minor dances of inferior individuals whose gyrations were not always in strict keeping with the tune.

The young men wore blue and white rosettes, and with a flush on their faces footed it to the girls, who, with the excitement and the exercise, blushed deeper than the pink of their numerous ribbons. Fair ones with long curls, fair ones with short curls, fair ones with love-locks, fair ones with braids, flew round and round; and a beholder might well have wondered how such a prepossessing set of young women of like size, age, and disposition, could have been collected together where there were only one or two villages to choose from. In the background was one happy man dancing by himself, with closed eyes, totally oblivious of all the rest. A fire was burning under a pollard thorn a few paces off, over which three kettles hung in a row. Hard by was a table where elderly dames prepared tea, but Eustacia looked among them in vain for the cattle-dealer's wife who had suggested that she should come, and had promised to obtain a courteous welcome for her.

This unexpected absence of the only local resident whom Eustacia knew considerably damaged her scheme for an afternoon of reckless gaiety. Joining in became a matter of difficulty, notwithstanding that, were she to advance, cheerful dames would come forward with cups of tea and make much of her as a stranger of superior grace and knowledge to themselves. Having watched the company through the figures of two dances, she decided to walk a little further, to a cottage where she might get some refreshment, and then return homeward in the shady time of evening.

This she did; and by the time that she retraced her steps towards the scene of the gipsying, which it was necessary to repass on her way to Alderworth, the sun was going down. The air was now so still that she could hear the band afar off, and it seemed to be playing with more spirit, if that were possible, than when she had come away. On reaching the hill the sun had quite disappeared; but this made little difference either to Eustacia or to the revellers, for a round yellow moon was rising before her, though its rays had not yet outmastered those from the west. The dance was going on just the same, but strangers had arrived and formed a ring around the figure, so that Eustacia could stand among these without a chance of being recognized.

A whole village-full of sensuous emotion, scattered abroad all the year long, surged here in a focus for an hour. The forty hearts of those waving couples were beating as they had not done since, twelve months before, they had come together in similar jollity. For the time Paganism was revived in their hearts, the pride of life was all in all, and they adored none other than themselves.

How many of those impassioned but temporary embraces were destined to become perpetual was possibly the wonder of some of those who indulged in them, as well as of Eustacia who looked on. She began to envy those pirouetters, to hunger for the hope and happiness which the fascination of the dance seemed to engender within them. Desperately fond of dancing herself, one of Eustacia's expectations of Paris had been the opportunity it might afford her of indulgence in this favourite pastime. Unhappily, that expectation was now extinct within her for ever.

Whilst she abstractedly watched them spinning and fluctuating in the increasing moonlight she suddenly heard her name whispered by a voice over her shoulder. Turning in surprise, she beheld at her elbow one whose presence instantly caused her to flush to the temples.

It was Wildeve. Till this moment he had not met her eye since the morning of his marriage, when she had been loitering in the church, and had startled him by lifting her veil and coming forward to sign the register as witness. Yet why the sight of him should have instigated that sudden rush of blood she could not tell.

Before she could speak he whispered, 'Do you like dancing as much as ever?'

'I think I do,' she replied in a low voice.

'Will you dance with me?'

'It would be a great change for me; but will it not seem strange?'

'What strangeness can there be in relations dancing together?'

'Ah – yes, relations. Perhaps none.'

'Still, if you don't like to be seen, pull down your veil; though there is not much risk of being known by this light. Lots of strangers are here.'

She did as he suggested; and the act was a tacit acknowledgement that she accepted his offer.

Wildeve gave her his arm and took her down on the outside of the ring to the bottom of the dance, which they entered. In two minutes more they were involved in the figure and began working their way upwards to the top. Till they had advanced halfway thither Eustacia wished more than once that she had not yielded to his request; from the middle to the top she felt that, since she had come out to seek pleasure, she was only doing a natural thing to obtain it. Fairly launched into the ceaseless glides and whirls which their new position as top couple opened up to them, Eustacia's pulses began to move too quickly for longer rumination of any kind.

Through the length of five-and-twenty couples they threaded their giddy way, and a new vitality entered her form. The pale ray of evening lent a fascination to the experience. There is a certain degree and tone of light which tends to disturb the equilibrium of the senses, and to promote dangerously the tenderer moods; added to movement, it drives the emotions to rankness, the reason becoming sleepy and unperceiving in inverse proportion; and this light fell now upon these two from the disc of the moon. All the dancing girls felt the symptoms, but Eustacia most of all. The grass under their feet became trodden away, and the hard beaten surface of the sod, when viewed aslant towards the moonlight, shone like a polished table. The air became quite still; the flag above the waggon which held the musicians clung to the pole, and the players appeared only in outline against the sky; except when the circular mouths of the trombone, ophicleide, and French horn gleamed out like huge eyes from the shade of their figures. The pretty dresses of the maids lost their subtler day colours and showed more or less of a misty white. Eustacia floated round and round on Wildeve's arm, her face rapt and statuesque; her soul had passed away from and forgotten her features, which were left empty and quiescent, as they always are when feeling goes beyond their register.

How near she was to Wildeve! it was terrible to think of. She could feel his breathing, and he, of course, could feel hers. How badly she had treated him! yet, here they were treading one measure. The enchantment of the dance surprised her. A clear line of difference divided like a tangible fence her experience within this maze of motion from her experience without it. Her beginning to dance had been like a change of atmosphere; outside, she had been steeped in arctic frigidity by comparison with the tropical sensations here. She had entered the dance from the troubled hours of her late life as one might enter a brilliant chamber after a night walk in a wood. Wildeve by himself would have been merely an agitation; Wildeve added to the dance, and the moonlight, and the secrecy, began to be a delight. Whether his personality supplied the greater part of this sweetly compounded feeling, or whether the dance and the scene weighed the more therein, was a nice point upon which Eustacia herself was entirely in a cloud.

People began to say 'Who are they?' but no invidious inquiries were made. Had Eustacia mingled with the other girls in their ordinary daily walks the case would have been different; here she was not inconvenienced by excessive inspection, for all were wrought to their brightest grace by the occasion. Like the planet Mercury surrounded by the lustre of sunset, her permanent brilliancy passed without much notice in the temporary glory of the situation.

As for Wildeve, his feelings are easy to guess. Obstacles were a ripening sun to his love, and he was at this moment in a delirium of exquisite misery. To clasp as his for five minutes what was another man's through all the rest of the year was a kind of thing he of all men could appreciate. He had long since begun to sigh again for Eustacia; indeed, it may be asserted that signing the marriage register with Thomasin was the natural signal to his heart to return to its first quarters, and that the extra complication of Eustacia's marriage was the one addition required to make that return compulsory.

Thus, for different reasons, what was to the rest an exhilarating movement was to these two a riding upon the whirlwind. The dance had come like an irresistible attack upon whatever sense of social order there was in their minds, to drive them back into old paths which were now doubly irregular. Through three dances in succession they spun their way; and then, fatigued with the incessant motion, Eustacia turned to quit the circle in which she had already remained too long. Wildeve led her to a grassy mound a few yards distant, where she sat down, her partner standing beside her. From the time that he addressed her at the beginning of the dance till now they had not exchanged a word.

'The dance and the walking have tired you?' he said tenderly.

'No; not greatly.'

'It is strange that we should have met here of all places, after missing each other so long.'

'We have missed because we tried to miss, I suppose.'

'Yes. But you began that proceeding – by breaking a promise.'

'It is scarcely worth while to talk of that now. We have formed other ties since then – you no less than I.'

'I am sorry to hear that your husband is ill.'

'He is not ill – only incapacitated.'

'Yes: that is what I mean. I sincerely sympathize with you in your trouble. Fate has treated you cruelly.'

She was silent awhile. 'Have you heard that he has chosen to work as a furze-cutter?' she said in a low, mournful voice.

'It has been mentioned to me,' answered Wildeve hesitatingly. 'But I hardly believed it.'

'It is true. What do you think of me as a furze-cutter's wife?'

'I think the same as ever of you, Eustacia. Nothing of that sort can degrade you: you ennoble the occupation of your husband.'

'I wish I could feel it.'

'Is there any chance of Mr Yeobright getting better?'

'He thinks so. I doubt it.'

'I was quite surprised to hear that he had taken a cottage. I thought, in common with other people, that he would have taken you off to a home in Paris immediately after you had married him. "What a gay, bright future she has before her!" I thought. He will, I suppose, return there with you, if his sight gets strong again?'

Observing that she did not reply he regarded her more closely. She was almost weeping. Images of a future never to be enjoyed, the revived sense of her bitter disappointment, the picture of the neighbours' suspended ridicule which was raised by Wildeve's words, had been too much for proud Eustacia's equanimity.

Wildeve could hardly control his own too forward feelings when he saw her silent perturbation. But he affected not to notice this, and she soon recovered her calmness.

'You did not intend to walk home by yourself?' he asked.

'O yes,' said Eustacia. 'What could hurt me on this heath, who have nothing?'

'By diverging a little I can make my way home the same as yours. I shall be glad to keep you company as far as Throope Corner.' Seeing that

Eustacia sat on in hesitation he added, 'Perhaps you think it unwise to be seen in the same road with me after the events of last summer?'

'Indeed I think no such thing,' she said haughtily. 'I shall accept whose company I choose, for all that may be said by the miserable inhabitants of Egdon.'

'Then let us walk on – if you are ready. Our nearest way is towards that holly-bush with the dark shadow that you see down there.'

Eustacia arose, and walked beside him in the direction signified, brushing her way over the damping heath and fern, and followed by the strains of the merrymakers, who still kept up the dance. The moon had now waxed bright and silvery, but the heath was proof against such illumination, and there was to be observed the striking scene of a dark, rayless tract of country under an atmosphere charged from its zenith to its extremities with whitest light. To an eye above them their two faces would have appeared amid the expanse like two pearls on a table of ebony.

On this account the irregularities of the path were not visible, and Wildeve occasionally stumbled; whilst Eustacia found it necessary to perform some graceful feats of balancing whenever a small tuft of heather or root of furze protruded itself through the grass of the narrow track and entangled her feet. At these junctures in her progress a hand was invariably stretched forward to steady her, holding her firmly until smooth ground was again reached, when the hand was again withdrawn to a respectful distance.

They performed the journey for the most part in silence, and drew near to Throope Corner, a few hundred yards from which a short path branched away to Eustacia's house. By degrees they discerned coming towards them a pair of human figures, apparently of the male sex.

When they came a little nearer Eustacia broke the silence by saying, 'One of those men is my husband. He promised to come to meet me.'

'And the other is my greatest enemy,' said Wildeve.

'It looks like Diggory Venn.'

'That is the man.'

'It is an awkward meeting,' said she; 'but such is my fortune. He knows too much about me, unless he could know more, and so prove to himself that what he now knows counts for nothing. Well, let it be: you must deliver me up to them.'

'You will think twice before you direct me to do that. Here is a man who has not forgotten an item in our meetings at Rainbarrow: he is in company with your husband. Which of them, seeing us together here, will believe that our meeting and dancing at the gipsy-party was by chance?'

'Very well,' she whispered gloomily. 'Leave me before they come up.'

Wildeve bade her a tender farewell, and plunged across the fern and furze, Eustacia slowly walking on. In two or three minutes she met her husband and his companion.

'My journey ends here for tonight, reddleman,' said Yeobright as soon as he perceived her. 'I turn back with this lady. Good night.'

'Good night, Mr Yeobright,' said Venn. 'I hope to see you better soon.'

The moonlight shone directly upon Venn's face as he spoke, and revealed all its lines to Eustacia. He was looking suspiciously at her. That Venn's keen eye had discerned what Yeobright's feeble vision had not – a man in the act of withdrawing from Eustacia's side – was within the limits of the probable.

If Eustacia had been able to follow the reddleman she would soon have found striking confirmation of her thought. No sooner had Clym given her his arm and led her off the scene than the reddleman turned back from the beaten track towards East Egdon, whither he had been strolling merely to accompany Clym in his walk, Diggory's van being again in the neighbourhood. Stretching out his long legs he crossed the pathless portion of the heath somewhat in the direction which Wildeve had taken. Only a man accustomed to nocturnal rambles could at this hour have descended those shaggy slopes with Venn's velocity without falling headlong into a pit, or snapping off his leg by jamming his foot into some rabbit-burrow. But Venn went on without much inconvenience to himself, and the course of his scamper was towards the Quiet Woman Inn. This place he reached in about half an hour, and he was well aware that no person who had been near Throope Corner when he started could have got down there before him.

The lonely inn was not yet closed, though scarcely an individual was there, the business done being chiefly with travellers who passed the inn on long journeys, and these had now gone on their way. Venn went to the public room, called for a mug of ale, and inquired of the maid in an indifferent tone if Mr Wildeve was at home.

Thomasin sat in an inner room and heard Venn's voice. When customers were present she seldom showed herself, owing to her inherent dislike for the business; but perceiving that no one else was there tonight she came out.

'He is not at home yet, Diggory,' she said pleasantly. 'But I expected him sooner. He has been to East Egdon to buy a horse.'

'Did he wear a light wideawake?'

'Yes.'

'Then I saw him at Throope Corner, leading one home,' said Venn drily. 'A beauty, with a white face and a mane as black as night. He will soon be here, no doubt.' Rising and looking for a moment at the pure, sweet face of Thomasin, over which a shadow of sadness had passed since the time when he had last seen her, he ventured to add, 'Mr Wildeve seems to be often away at this time.'

'Oh yes,' cried Thomasin in what was intended to be a tone of gaiety. 'Husbands will play the truant, you know. I wish you could tell me of some secret plan that would help me to keep him home at my will in the evenings.'

'I will consider if I know of one,' replied Venn in that same light tone which meant no lightness. And then he bowed in a manner of his own invention and moved to go. Thomasin offered him her hand; and without a sigh, though with food for many, the reddleman went out.

When Wildeve returned, a quarter of an hour later, Thomasin said simply, and in the abashed manner usual with her now, 'Where is the horse, Damon?'

'O, I have not bought it, after all. The man asks too much.'

'But somebody saw you at Throope Corner leading it home – a beauty, with a white face and a mane as black as night.'

'Ah!' said Wildeve, fixing his eyes upon her; 'who told you that?'

'Venn the reddleman.'

The expression of Wildeve's face became curiously condensed. 'That is a mistake – it must have been someone else,' he said slowly and testily, for he perceived that Venn's countermoves had begun again.

* IV *

Rough Coercion Is Employed

THOSE words of Thomasin, which seemed so little, but meant so much, remained in the ears of Diggory Venn: 'Help me to keep him home in the evenings.'

On this occasion Venn had arrived on Egdon Heath only to cross to the other side: he had no further connection with the interests of the Yeobright family, and he had a business of his own to attend to. Yet he suddenly began to feel himself drifting into the old track of manoeuvring on Thomasin's account.

He sat in his van and considered. From Thomasin's words and manner he had plainly gathered that Wildeve neglected her. For whom could he neglect her if not for Eustacia? Yet it was scarcely credible that things had come to such a head as to indicate that Eustacia systematically encouraged him. Venn resolved to reconnoitre somewhat carefully the lonely road which led along the vale from Wildeve's dwelling to Clym's house at Alderworth.

At this time, as has been seen, Wildeve was quite innocent of any predetermined act of intrigue, and except at the dance on the green he had not once met Eustacia since her marriage. But that the spirit of intrigue was in him had been shown by a recent romantic habit of his: a habit of going out after dark and strolling towards Alderworth, there looking at the moon and stars, looking at Eustacia's house, and walking back at leisure.

Accordingly, when watching on the night after the festival, the reddleman saw him ascend by the little path, lean over the front gate of Clym's garden, sigh, and turn to go back again. It was plain that Wildeve's intrigue was rather ideal than real. Venn retreated before him down the hill to a place where the path was merely a deep groove between the heather; here he mysteriously bent over the ground for a few minutes, and retired. When Wildeve came on to that spot his ankle was caught by something, and he fell headlong.

As soon as he had recovered the power of respiration he sat up and listened. There was not a sound in the gloom beyond the spiritless stir of the summer wind. Feeling about for the obstacle which had flung him down, he discovered that two tufts of heath had been tied together across the path, forming a loop, which to a traveller was certain overthrow. Wildeve pulled off the string that bound them, and went on with tolerable quickness. On reaching home he found the cord to be of a reddish colour. It was just what he had expected.

Although his weaknesses were not specially those akin to physical fear, this species of *coup-de-Jarnac* from one he knew too well troubled the mind of Wildeve. But his movements were unaltered thereby. A night or two later he again went along the vale to Alderworth, taking the precaution of keeping out of any path. The sense that he was watched, that craft was employed to circumvent his errant tastes, added piquancy to a journey so entirely sentimental, so long as the danger was of no fearful sort. He imagined that Venn and Mrs Yeobright were in league, and felt that there was a certain legitimacy in combating such a coalition.

The heath tonight appeared to be totally deserted: and Wildeve, after looking over Eustacia's garden gate for some little time, with a cigar in his mouth, was tempted by the fascination that emotional smuggling had for his nature to advance towards the window, which was not quite closed, the blind being only partly drawn down. He could see into the room, and Eustacia was sitting there alone. Wildeve contemplated her for a minute, and then retreating into the heath beat the ferns lightly, whereupon moths flew out alarmed. Securing one, he returned to the window, and holding the moth to the chink, opened his hand. The moth made towards the candle upon Eustacia's table, hovered round it two or three times, and flew into the flame.

Eustacia started up. This had been a well-known signal in old times when Wildeve had used to come secretly wooing to Mistover. She at once knew that Wildeve was outside, but before she could consider what to do her husband came in from upstairs. Eustacia's face burnt crimson at the animation that it too frequently lacked.

'You have a very high colour, dearest,' said Yeobright, when he came close enough to see it. 'Your appearance would be no worse if it were always so.'

'I am warm,' said Eustacia. 'I think I will go into the air for a few minutes.'

'Shall I go with you?'

'O no. I am only going to the gate.'

She arose, but before she had time to get out of the room a loud rapping began upon the front door.

'I'll go – I'll go,' said Eustacia in an unusually quick tone for her; and she glanced eagerly towards the window whence the moth had flown; but nothing appeared there.

'You had better not at this time of the evening,' he said. Clym stepped before her into the passage, and Eustacia waited, her somnolent manner covering her inner heat and agitation.

She listened, and Clym opened the door. No words were uttered outside, and presently he closed it and came back, saying, 'Nobody was there. I wonder what that could have meant?'

He was left to wonder during the rest of the evening, for no explanation offered itself, and Eustacia said nothing, the additional fact that she knew of only adding more mystery to the performance.

Meanwhile a little drama had been acted outside which saved Eustacia from all possibility of compromising herself that evening at least. While Wildeve had been preparing his moth-signal another had come behind him up to the gate. This man, who carried a gun in his hand, looked on for a moment at the other's operation by the window, walked up to the house, knocked at the door, and then vanished round the corner and over the hedge.

'Damn him!' said Wildeve. 'He has been watching me again.'

As his signal had been rendered futile by this uproarious rapping Wildeve withdrew, passed out at the gate, and walked quickly down the path without thinking of anything except getting away unnoticed. Half-way down the hill the path ran near a knot of stunted hollies, which in the general darkness of the scene stood as the pupil in a black eye. When Wildeve reached this point a report startled his ear, and a few spent gunshots fell among the leaves around him.

There was no doubt that he himself was the cause of that gun's discharge; and he rushed into the clump of hollies, beating the bushes furiously with his stick; but nobody was there. This attack was a more serious matter than the last, and it was some time before Wildeve recovered his equanimity. A new and most unpleasant system of menace had begun, and the intent appeared to be to do him grievous bodily harm. Wildeve had looked upon Venn's first attempt as a species of horse-play, which the reddleman had indulged in for want of knowing better; but now the boundary-line was passed which divides the annoying from the perilous.

Had Wildeve known how thoroughly in earnest Venn had become he might have been still more alarmed. The reddleman had been almost exasperated by the sight of Wildeve outside Clym's house, and he was prepared to go to any lengths short of absolutely shooting him, to terrify the young innkeeper out of his recalcitrant impulses. The doubtful legitimacy of such rough coercion did not disturb the mind of Venn. It troubles few such minds in such cases, and sometimes this is not to be regretted. From the impeachment of Strafford to Farmer Lynch's short way with the scamps of Virginia there have been many triumphs of justice which are mockeries of law.

About half a mile below Clym's secluded dwelling lay a hamlet where lived one of the two constables who preserved the peace in the parish of Alderworth, and Wildeve went straight to the constable's cottage. Almost the first thing that he saw on opening the door was the constable's truncheon hanging to a nail, as if to assure him that here were the means to his purpose. On inquiry, however, of the constable's wife he learnt that the constable was not at home. Wildeve said he would wait.

The minutes ticked on, and the constable did not arrive. Wildeve cooled down from his state of high indignation to a restless dissatisfaction with himself, the scene, the constable's wife, and the whole set of circumstances. He arose and left the house. Altogether, the experience of that evening had had a cooling, not to say a chilling, effect on misdirected tenderness, and Wildeve was in no mood to ramble again to Alderworth after nightfall in hope of a stray glance from Eustacia.

Thus far the reddleman had been tolerably successful in his rude contrivances for keeping down Wildeve's inclination to rove in the evening. He had nipped in the bud the possible meeting between Eustacia and her old lover this very night. But he had not anticipated that the tendency of his action would be to divert Wildeve's movement rather than to stop it. The gambling with the guineas had not conduced to make him a welcome guest to Clym; but to call upon his wife's relative was natural, and he was determined to see Eustacia. It was necessary to choose some less untoward hour than ten o'clock at night. 'Since it is unsafe to go in the evening,' he said, 'I'll go by day.'

Meanwhile Venn had left the heath and gone to call upon Mrs Yeobright, with whom he had been on friendly terms since she had learnt what a providential countermove he had made towards the restitution of the family guineas. She wondered at the lateness of his call, but had no objection to see him.

He gave her a full account of Clym's affliction, and of the state in which he was living; then, referring to Thomasin, touched gently upon the apparent sadness of her days. 'Now, ma'am, depend upon it,' he said, 'you couldn't do a better thing for either of 'em than to make yourself at home in their houses, even if there should be a little rebuff at first.'

'Both she and my son disobeyed me in marrying; therefore I have no interest in their households. Their troubles are of their own making.' Mrs Yeobright tried to speak severely; but the account of her son's state had moved her more than she cared to show.

'Your visits would make Wildeve walk straighter than he is inclined to do, and might prevent unhappiness down the heath.'

'What do you mean?'

'I saw something tonight out there which I didn't like at all. I wish your son's house and Mr Wildeve's were a hundred miles apart instead of four or five.'

'Then there *was* an understanding between him and Clym's wife when he made a fool of Thomasin!'

'We'll hope there's no understanding now.'

'And our hope will probably be very vain. O Clym! O Thomasin!'

'There's no harm done yet. In fact, I've persuaded Wildeve to mind his own business.'

'How?'

'O, not by talking – by a plan of mine called the silent system.'

'I hope you'll succeed.'

'I shall if you help me by calling and making friends with your son. You'll have a chance then of using your eyes.'

'Well, since it has come to this,' said Mrs Yeobright sadly, 'I will own to you, reddleman, that I thought of going. I should be much happier if we were reconciled. The marriage is unalterable, my life may be cut short, and I should wish to die in peace. He is my only son; and since sons are made of such stuff I am not sorry I have no other. As for Thomasin, I never expected much from her; and she has not disappointed me. But I forgave her long ago; and I forgive him now. I'll go.'

At this very time of the reddleman's conversation with Mrs Yeobright at Blooms-End another conversation on the same subject was languidly proceeding at Alderworth.

All the day Clym had borne himself as if his mind were too full of its own matter to allow him to care about outward things, and his words now showed what had occupied his thoughts. It was just after the mysterious knocking that he began the theme. 'Since I have been away today, Eustacia, I have considered that something must be done to heal up this ghastly breach between my dear mother and myself. It troubles me.'

'What do you propose to do?' said Eustacia abstractedly, for she could not clear away from her the excitement caused by Wildeve's recent manoeuvre for an interview.

'You seem to take a very mild interest in what I propose, little or much,' said Clym, with tolerable warmth.

'You mistake me,' she answered, reviving at his reproach. 'I am only thinking.'

'What of?'

'Partly of that moth whose skeleton is getting burnt up in the wick of the candle,' she said slowly. 'But you know I always take an interest in what you say.'

'Very well, dear. Then I think I must go and call upon her.' . . . He went on with tender feeling: 'It is a thing I am not at all too proud to do, and only a fear that I might irritate her has kept me away so long. But I must do something. It is wrong in me to allow this sort of thing to go on.'

'What have you to blame yourself about?'

'She is getting old, and her life is lonely, and I am her only son.'

'She has Thomasin.'

'Thomasin is not her daughter; and if she were that would not excuse me. But this is beside the point. I have made up my mind to go to her, and all I wish to ask you is whether you will do your best to help me – that is, forget the past; and if she shows her willingness to be reconciled, meet her half-way by welcoming her to our house, or by accepting a welcome to hers?'

At first Eustacia closed her lips as if she would rather do anything on the whole globe than what he suggested. But the lines of her mouth softened with thought, though not so far as they might have softened; and she said, 'I will put nothing in your way; but after what has passed it is asking too much that I go and make advances.'

'You never distinctly told me what did pass between you.'

'I could not do it then, nor can I now. Sometimes more bitterness is sown in five minutes than can be got rid of in a whole life; and that may be the case here.' She paused a few moments, and added, 'If you had never returned to your native place, Clym, what a blessing it would have been for you! . . . It has altered the destinies of –'

'Three people.'

'Five,' Eustacia thought; but she kept that in.

* V *

The Journey across the Heath

THURSDAY, the thirty-first of August, was one of a series of days during which snug houses were stifling, and when cool draughts were treats; when cracks appeared in clayey gardens, and were called 'earthquakes' by apprehensive children; when loose spokes were discovered in the wheels of carts and carriages; and when stinging insects haunted the air, the earth, and every drop of water that was to be found.

In Mrs Yeobright's garden large-leaved plants of a tender kind flagged by ten o'clock in the morning: rhubarb bent downward at eleven; and even stiff cabbages were limp by noon.

It was about eleven o'clock on this day that Mrs Yeobright started across the heath towards her son's house, to do her best in getting reconciled with him and Eustacia, in conformity with her words to the reddleman. She had hoped to be well advanced in her walk before the heat of the day was at its highest, but after setting out she found that this was not to be done. The sun had branded the whole heath with his mark, even the purple heath-flowers having put on a brownness under the dry blazes of the few preceding days. Every valley was filled with air like that of a kiln, and the clean quartz sand of the winter water-courses, which formed summer paths, had undergone a species of incineration since the drought had set in.

In cool, fresh weather Mrs Yeobright would have found no inconvenience in walking to Alderworth, but the present torrid attack made the journey a heavy undertaking for a woman past middle age; and at the end of the third mile she wished that she had hired Fairway to drive her a portion at least of the distance. But from the point at which she had arrived it was as easy to reach Clym's house as to get home again. So she went on, the air around her pulsating silently, and oppressing the earth with lassitude. She looked at the sky overhead, and saw that the sapphirine hue of the zenith in spring and early summer had been replaced by a metallic violet.

Occasionally she came to a spot where independent worlds of ephemerons were passing their time in mad carousal, some in the air, some on the hot ground and vegetation, some in the tepid and stringy water of a nearly dried pool. All the shallower ponds had decreased to a vaporous mud amid which the maggoty shapes of innumerable obscure creatures could be indistinctly seen, heaving and wallowing with enjoyment. Being a woman not disinclined to philosophize she sometimes sat down under her umbrella to rest and to watch their happiness, for a certain hopefulness as to the result of her visit gave ease to her mind, and between important thoughts left it free to dwell on any infinitesimal matter which caught her eyes.

Mrs Yeobright had never before been to her son's house, and its exact position was unknown to her. She tried one ascending path and another, and found that they led her astray. Retracing her steps she perceived at a distance a man at work. She went towards him and inquired the way.

The labourer pointed out the direction, and added, 'Do you see that furze-cutter, ma'am, going up that footpath yond?'

Mrs Yeobright strained her eyes, and at last said that she did perceive him.

'Well, if you follow him you can make no mistake. He's going to the same place, ma'am.'

She followed the figure indicated. He appeared of a russet hue, not more distinguishable from the scene around him than the green caterpillar from the leaf it feeds on. His progress when actually walking was more rapid than Mrs Yeobright's; but she was enabled to keep at an equable distance from him by his habit of stopping whenever he came to a brake of brambles, where he paused awhile. On coming in her turn to each of these spots she found half a dozen long limp brambles which he had cut from the bush during his halt and laid out straight beside the path. They were evidently intended for furze-faggot bonds which he meant to collect on his return.

The silent being who thus occupied himself seemed to be of no more account in life than an insect. He appeared as a mere parasite of the heath, fretting its surface in his daily labour as a moth frets a garment, entirely engrossed with its products, having no knowledge of anything in the world but fern, furze, heath, lichens, and moss.

The furze-cutter was so absorbed in the business of his journey that he never turned his head; and his leather-legged and gauntleted form at length became to her as nothing more than a moving handpost to show her the way. Suddenly she was attracted to his individuality by observing peculiarities in his walk. It was a gait she had seen somewhere before; and the gait revealed the man to her, as the gait of Ahimaaz in the distant plain made him known to the watchman of the king. 'His walk is exactly as my husband's used to be,' she said; and then the thought burst upon her that the furze-cutter was her son.

She was scarcely able to familiarize herself with this strange reality. She had been told that Clym was in the habit of cutting furze, but she had supposed that he occupied himself with the labour only at odd times, by way of useful pastime; yet she now beheld him as a furze-cutter and nothing more – wearing the regulation dress of the craft, and thinking the regulation thoughts, to judge by his motions. Planning a dozen hasty schemes for at once preserving him and Eustacia from this mode of life she throbbingly followed the way, and saw him enter his own door.

At one side of Clym's house was a knoll, and on the top of the knoll a clump of fir trees so highly thrust up into the sky that their foliage from a distance appeared as a black spot in the air above the crown of the hill. On reaching this place Mrs Yeobright felt distressingly agitated, weary, and unwell. She ascended, and sat down under their shade to recover herself, and to consider how best to break the ground with Eustacia, so as not to irritate a woman underneath whose apparent indolence lurked passions even stronger and more active than her own.

The trees beneath which she sat were singularly battered, rude, and wild, and for a few minutes Mrs Yeobright dismissed thoughts of her own storm-broken and exhausted state to contemplate theirs. Not a bough in the nine trees which composed the group but was splintered, looped, and distorted by the fierce weather that there held them at its mercy whenever it prevailed. Some were blasted and split as if by lightning, black stains as from fire marking their sides, while the ground at their feet was strewn with dead fir-needles and heaps of cones blown down in the gales of past years. The place was called the Devil's Bellows, and it was only necessary to come there on a March or November night to discover the forcible reasons for that name. On the present heated afternoon, when no perceptible wind was blowing, the trees kept up a perpetual moan which one could hardly believe to be caused by the air.

Here she sat for twenty minutes or more ere she could summon resolution to go down to the door, her courage being lowered to zero by her physical lassitude. To any other person than a mother it might have seemed a little humiliating that she, the elder of the two women, should be the first to make advances. But Mrs Yeobright had well considered all that, and she only thought how best to make her visit appear to Eustacia not abject but wise.

From her elevated position the exhausted woman could perceive the roof of the house below, and the garden and the whole enclosure of the little domicile. And now, at the moment of rising, she saw a second man approaching the gate. His manner was peculiar, hesitating, and not that of a person come on business or by invitation. He surveyed the house with interest, and then walked round and scanned the outer boundary of the garden, as one might have done had it been the birthplace of Shakespeare, the prison of Mary Stuart, or the Château of Hougomont. After passing round and again reaching the gate he went in. Mrs Yeobright was vexed at this, having reckoned on finding her son and his wife by themselves; but a moment's thought showed her that the presence of an acquaintance would take off the awkwardness of her first appearance in the house, by confining the talk to general matters until she had begun to feel comfortable with them. She came down the hill to the gate, and looked into the hot garden.

There lay the cat asleep on the bare gravel of the path, as if beds, rugs, and carpets were unendurable. The leaves of the hollyhocks hung like half-closed umbrellas, the sap almost simmered in the stems, and foliage with a smooth surface glared like metallic mirrors. A small apple tree, of the sort called Ratheripe, grew just inside the gate, the only one which throve in the garden, by reason of the lightness of the soil; and among the fallen apples on the ground beneath were wasps rolling drunk with the juice, or creeping about the little caves in each fruit which they had eaten out before stupefied by its sweetness. By the door lay Clym's furze-hook and the last handful of faggot-bonds she had seen him gather; they had plainly been thrown down there as he entered the house.

* VI *

A Conjuncture, and Its Result upon the Pedestrian

WILDEVE, as has been stated, was determined to visit Eustacia boldly, by day, and on the easy terms of a relation, since the reddleman had spied out and spoilt his walks to her by night. The spell that she had thrown over him in the moonlight dance made it impossible for a man having no strong puritanic force within him to keep away altogether. He merely calculated on meeting her and her husband in an ordinary manner, chatting a little while, and leaving again. Every outward sign was to be conventional; but the one great fact would be there to satisfy him: he would see her. He did not even desire Clym's absence, since it was just possible that Eustacia might resent any situation which could compromise her dignity as a wife, whatever the state of her heart towards him. Women were often so.

He went accordingly; and it happened that the time of his arrival coincided with that of Mrs Yeobright's pause on the hill near the house. When he had looked round the premises in the manner she had noticed he went and knocked at the door. There was a few minutes' interval, and then the key turned in the lock, the door opened, and Eustacia herself confronted him.

Nobody could have imagined from her bearing now that here stood the woman who had joined with him in the impassioned dance of the week before, unless indeed he could have penetrated below the surface and gauged the real depth of that still stream.

'I hope you reached home safely?' said Wildeve.

'O yes,' she carelessly returned.

'And were you not tired the next day? I feared you might be.'

'I was rather. You need not speak low – nobody will overhear us. My small servant is gone on an errand to the village.'

'Then Clym is not at home?'

'Yes, he is.'

'O! I thought that perhaps you had locked the door because you were alone and were afraid of tramps.'

'No – here is my husband.'

They had been standing in the entry. Closing the front door and turning the key, as before, she threw open the door of the adjoining room and asked him to walk in. Wildeve entered, the room appearing to be empty; but as soon as he had advanced a few steps he started. On the hearth rug lay Clym asleep. Beside him were the leggings, thick boots, leather gloves, and sleeve-waistcoat in which he worked.

'You may go in; you will not disturb him,' she said, following behind. 'My reason for fastening the door is that he may not be intruded upon by any chance comer while lying here, if I should be in the garden or upstairs.'

'Why is he sleeping there?' said Wildeve in low tones.

'He is very weary. He went out at half-past four this morning, and has been working ever since. He cuts furze because it is the only thing he can do that does not put any strain upon his poor eyes.' The contrast between the sleeper's appearance and Wildeve's at this moment was painfully apparent to Eustacia, Wildeve being elegantly dressed in a new summer suit and light hat; and she continued: 'Ah! you don't know how differently he appeared when I first met him, though it is such a little while ago. His hands were as white and soft as mine; and look at them now, how rough and brown they are! His complexion is by nature fair, and that rusty look he has now, all of a colour with his leather clothes, is caused by the burning of the sun.'

'Why does he go out at all?' Wildeve whispered.

'Because he hates to be idle; though what he earns doesn't add much to our exchequer. However, he says that when people are living upon their capital they must keep down current expenses by turning a penny where they can.'

'The fates have not been kind to you, Eustacia Yeobright.'

'I have nothing to thank them for.'

'Nor has he – except for their one great gift to him.'

'What's that?'

Wildeve looked her in the eyes.

Eustacia blushed for the first time that day. 'Well, I am a questionable gift,' she said quietly. 'I thought you meant the gift of content – which he has, and I have not.'

'I can understand content in such a case – though how the outward situation can attract him puzzles me.'

'That's because you don't know him. He's an enthusiast about ideas, and careless about outward things. He often reminds me of the Apostle Paul.'

'I am glad to hear that he's so grand in character as that.'

'Yes; but the worst of it is that though Paul was excellent as a man in the Bible he would hardly have done in real life.'

Their voices had instinctively dropped lower, though at first they had taken no particular care to avoid awakening Clym. 'Well, if that means that your marriage is a misfortune to you, you know who is to blame,' said Wildeve.

'The marriage is no misfortune in itself,' she retorted with some little petulance. 'It is simply the accident which has happened since that has been the cause of my ruin. I have certainly got thistles for figs in a worldly sense, but how could I tell what time would bring forth.'

'Sometimes, Eustacia, I think it is a judgement upon you. You rightly belonged to me, you know; and I had no idea of losing you.'

'No, it was not my fault! Two could not belong to you; and remember that, before I was aware, you turned aside to another woman. It was cruel levity in you to do that. I never dreamt of playing such a game on my side till you began it on yours.'

'I meant nothing by it,' replied Wildeve. 'It was a mere interlude. Men are given to the trick of having a passing fancy for somebody else in the midst of a permanent love, which reasserts itself afterwards just as before. On account of your rebellious manner to me I was tempted to go further than I should have done; and when you still would keep playing the same tantalizing part I went further still, and married her.' Turning and looking again at the unconscious form of Clym he murmured, 'I am afraid that you don't value your prize, Clym . . . He ought to be happier than I in one thing at least. He may know what it is to come down in the world, and to be afflicted with a great personal calamity; but he probably doesn't know what it is to lose the woman he loved.'

'He is not ungrateful for winning her,' whispered Eustacia, 'and in that respect he is a good man. Many women would go far for such a husband. But do I desire unreasonably much in wanting what is called life – music, poetry, passion, war, and all the beating and pulsing that is going on in the great arteries of the world? That was the shape of my youthful dream; but I did not get it. Yet I thought I saw the way to it in my Clym.'

'And you only married him on that account?'

'There you mistake me. I married him because I loved him, but I won't say that I didn't love him partly because I thought I saw a promise of that life in him.'

'You have dropped into your old mournful key.'

'But I am not going to be depressed,' she cried perversely. 'I began a new system by going to that dance, and I mean to stick to it. Clym can sing merrily; why should not I?'

Wildeve looked thoughtfully at her. 'It is easier to say you will sing than to do it; though if I could I would encourage you in your attempt. But as life means nothing to me, without one thing which is now impossible, you will forgive me for not being able to encourage you.'

'Damon, what is the matter with you, that you speak like that?' she asked, raising her deep shady eyes to his.

'That's a thing I shall never tell plainly; and perhaps if I try to tell you in riddles you will not care to guess them.'

Eustacia remained silent for a minute, and she said, 'We are in a strange relationship today. You mince matters to an uncommon nicety. You mean, Damon, that you still love me. Well, that gives me sorrow, for I am not made so entirely happy by my marriage that I am willing to spurn you for the information, as I ought to do. But we have said too much about this. Do you mean to wait until my husband is awake?'

'I thought to speak to him; but it is unnecessary, Eustacia, if I offend you by not forgetting you, you are right to mention it; but do not talk of spurning.'

She did not reply, and they stood looking musingly at Clym as he slept on in that profound sleep which is the result of physical labour carried on in circumstances that wake no nervous fear.

'God, how I envy him that sweet sleep!' said Wildeve. 'I have not slept like that since I was a boy – years and years ago.'

While they thus watched him a click at the gate was audible, and a knock came to the door. Eustacia went to a window and looked out.

Her countenance changed. First she became crimson, and then the red subsided till it even partially left her lips.

'Shall I go away?' said Wildeve, standing up.

'I hardly know.'

'Who is it?'

'Mrs Yeobright. O, what she said to me that day! I cannot understand this visit – what does she mean? And she suspects that past time of ours.'

'I am in your hands. If you think she had better not see me here I'll go into the next room.'

'Well, yes: go.'

Wildeve at once withdrew; but before he had been half a minute in the adjoining apartment Eustacia came after him.

'No,' she said, 'we won't have any of this. If she comes in she must see you – and think if she likes there's something wrong! But how can I open the door to her, when she dislikes me – wishes to see not me, but her son? I won't open the door!'

Mrs Yeobright knocked again more loudly.

'Her knocking will, in all likelihood, awaken him,' continued Eustacia; 'and then he will let her in himself. Ah – listen.'

They could hear Clym moving in the other room, as if disturbed by the knocking, and he uttered the word 'Mother'.

'Yes – he is awake – he will go to the door,' she said, with a breath of relief. 'Come this way. I have a bad name with her, and you must not be seen. Thus I am obliged to act by stealth, not because I do ill, but because others are pleased to say so.'

By this time she had taken him to the back door, which was open, disclosing a path leading down the garden. 'Now, one word, Damon,' she remarked as he stepped forth. 'This is your first visit here; let it be your last. We have been hot lovers in our time, but it won't do now. Good-bye.'

'Good-bye,' said Wildeve. 'I have had all I came for, and I am satisfied.'

'What was it?'

'A sight of you. Upon my eternal honour I came for no more.'

Wildeve kissed his hand to the beautiful girl he addressed, and passed into the garden, where she watched him down the path, over the stile at the end, and into the ferns outside, which brushed his hips as he went along till he became lost in their thickets. When he had quite gone she slowly turned, and directed her attention to the interior of the house.

But it was possible that her presence might not be desired by Clym and his mother at this moment of their first meeting, or that it would be superfluous. At all events, she was in no hurry to meet Mrs Yeobright. She resolved to wait till Clym came to look for her, and glided back into the garden. Here she idly occupied herself for a few minutes, till finding no notice was taken of her she retraced her steps through the house to the front, where she listened for voices in the parlour. But hearing none she opened the door and went in. To her astonishment Clym lay precisely where Wildeve and herself had left him, his sleep apparently unbroken. He had been disturbed and made to dream and murmur by the knocking, but he had not awakened. Eustacia hastened to the door, and in spite of her reluctance to open it to a woman who had spoken of her so bitterly, she unfastened it and looked out. Nobody was to be seen. There, by the scraper, lay Clym's hook and the handful of faggot-bonds he had brought home; in front of her were the empty path, the garden gate standing slightly ajar; and, beyond, the great valley of purple heath thrilling silently in the sun. Mrs Yeobright was gone.

Clym's mother was at this time following a path which lay hidden from Eustacia by a shoulder of the hill. Her walk thither from the garden gate had been hasty and determined, as of a woman who was now no less anxious to escape from the scene than she had previously been to enter it. Her eyes were fixed on the ground; within her two sights were graven – that of Clym's hook and brambles at the door, and that of a woman's face at a window. Her lips trembled, becoming unnaturally thin as she murmured, ' 'Tis too much — Clym, how can he bear to do it! He is at home; and yet he lets her shut the door against me!'

In her anxiety to get out of the direct view of the house she had diverged from the straightest path homeward, and while looking about to regain it she came upon a little boy gathering whortleberries in a hollow. The boy was Johnny Nunsuch, who had been Eustacia's stoker at the bonfire, and, with the tendency of a minute body to gravitate towards a greater, he began hovering round Mrs Yeobright as soon as she appeared, and trotted on beside her without perceptible consciousness of his act.

Mrs Yeobright spoke to him as one in a mesmeric sleep. ' 'Tis a long way home, my child, and we shall not get there till evening.'

'I shall,' said her small companion. 'I am going to play marnels afore supper, and we go to supper at six o'clock, because father comes home. Does your father come home at six too?'

'No: he never comes; nor my son either, nor anybody.'

'What have made you so down? Have you seen a ooser?'

'I have seen what's worse – a woman's face looking at me through a window-pane.'

'Is that a bad sight?'

'Yes. It is always a bad sight to see a woman looking out at a weary wayfarer and not letting her in.'

'Once when I went to Throope Great Pond to catch effets I seed myself looking up at myself, and I was frightened and jumped back like anything.'

. . . 'If they had only shown signs of meeting my advances half-way how well it might have been done! But there is no chance. Shut out! She must have set him against me. Can there be beautiful bodies without hearts inside? I think so. I would not have done it against a neighbour's cat on such a fiery day as this!'

'What is it you say?'

'Never again – never! Not even if they send for me!'

'You must be a very curious woman to talk like that.'

'O no, not at all,' she said, returning to the boy's prattle. 'Most people who grow up and have children talk as I do. When you grow up your mother will talk as I do too.'

'I hope she won't; because 'tis very bad to talk nonsense.'

'Yes, child; it is nonsense, I suppose. Are you not nearly spent with the heat?'

'Yes. But not so much as you be.'

'How do you know?'

'Your face is white and wet, and your head is hanging-down-like.'

'Ah, I am exhausted from inside.'

'Why do you, every time you take a step, go like this?' The child in speaking gave to his motion the jerk and limp of an invalid.

'Because I have a burden which is more than I can bear.'

The little boy remained silently pondering, and they tottered on side by side until more than a quarter of an hour had elapsed, when Mrs Yeobright, whose weakness plainly increased, said to him, 'I must sit down here to rest.'

When she had seated herself he looked long in her face and said, 'How funny you draw your breath – like a lamb when you drive him till he's nearly done for. Do you always draw your breath like that?'

'Not always.' Her voice was now so low as to be scarcely above a whisper.

'You will go to sleep there, I suppose, won't you? You have shut your eyes already.'

'No. I shall not sleep much till – another day, and then I hope to have a long, long one – very long. Now can you tell me if Rimsmoor Pond is dry this summer?'

'Rimsmoor Pond is, but Oker's Pool isn't, because he is deep, and is never dry – 'tis just over there.'

'Is the water clear?'

'Yes, middling – except where the heath-croppers walk into it.'

'Then, take this, and go as fast as you can, and dip me up the clearest you can find. I am very faint.'

She drew from the small willow reticule that she carried in her hand an old-fashioned china teacup without a handle; it was one of half a dozen of the same sort lying in the reticule, which she had preserved ever since her childhood, and had brought with her today as a small present for Clym and Eustacia.

The boy started on his errand, and soon came back with the water, such as it was. Mrs Yeobright attempted to drink, but it was so warm as to give her nausea, and she threw it away. Afterwards she still remained sitting, with her eyes closed.

The boy waited, played near her, caught several of the little brown butterflies which abounded, and then said as he waited again, 'I like going on better than biding still. Will you soon start again?'

'I don't know.'

'I wish I might go on by myself,' he resumed, fearing, apparently, that he was to be pressed into some unpleasant service. 'Do you want me any more, please?'

Mrs Yeobright made no reply.

'What shall I tell mother?' the boy continued.

'Tell her you have seen a broken-hearted woman cast off by her son.'

Before quite leaving her he threw upon her face a wistful glance, as if he had misgivings on the generosity of forsaking her thus. He gazed into her face in a vague, wondering manner, like that of one examining some strange old manuscript the key to whose characters is undiscoverable. He was not so young as to be absolutely without a sense that sympathy was demanded, he was not old enough to be free from the terror felt in childhood at beholding misery in adult quarters hitherto deemed impregnable; and whether she were in a position to cause trouble or to suffer from it, whether she and her affliction were something to pity or something to fear, it was beyond him to decide. He lowered his eyes and went on without another word. Before he had gone half a mile he had forgotten all about her, except that she was a woman who had sat down to rest.

Mrs Yeobright's exertions, physical and emotional, had well-nigh prostrated her; but she continued to creep along in short stages with long breaks between. The sun had now got far to the west of south and stood directly in her face, like some merciless incendiary, brand in hand, waiting to consume her. With the departure of the boy all visible animation disappeared from the landscape, though the intermittent husky notes of the male grasshoppers from every tuft of furze were enough to show that amid the prostration of the larger animal species an unseen insect world was busy in all the fulness of life.

In two hours she reached a slope about three-fourths the whole distance from Alderworth to her own home, where a little patch of shepherd's-thyme intruded upon the path; and she sat down upon the perfumed mat it formed there. In front of her a colony of ants had established a thoroughfare across the way, where they toiled a never-ending and heavy-laden throng. To look down upon them was like observing a city street from the top of a tower. She remembered that this bustle of ants had been in progress for years at the same spot – doubtless those of the old times were the ancestors of these which walked there now. She leant back to obtain more thorough rest, and the soft eastern portion of the sky was as great a relief to her eyes as the thyme was to her head. While she looked a heron arose on that side of the sky and flew on with his face towards the sun. He had come dripping wet from some pool in the valleys, and as he flew the edges and lining of his wings, his thighs, and his breast were so caught by the bright sunbeams that he appeared as if formed of burnished silver. Up in the zenith where he was seemed a free and happy place, away from all contact with the earthly ball to which she was pinioned; and she wished that she could arise uncrushed from its surface and fly as he flew then.

But, being a mother, it was inevitable that she should soon cease to ruminate upon her own condition. Had the track of her next thought been marked by a streak in the air, like the path of a meteor, it would have shown a direction contrary to the heron's, and have descended to the eastward upon the roof of Clym's house.

VII

The Tragic Meeting of Two Old Friends

HE in the meantime had aroused himself from sleep, sat up, and looked around. Eustacia was sitting in a chair hard by him, and though she held a book in her hand she had not looked into it for some time.

'Well, indeed!' said Clym, brushing his eyes with his hands. 'How soundly I have slept! I have had such a tremendous dream, too: one I shall never forget.'

'I thought you had been dreaming,' said she.

'Yes. It was about my mother. I dreamt that I took you to her house to make up differences, and when we got there we couldn't get in, though she kept on crying to us for help. However, dreams are dreams. What o'clock is it, Eustacia?'

'Half-past two.'

'So late, is it? I didn't mean to stay so long. By the time I have had something to eat it will be after three.'

'Ann is not come back from the village, and I thought I would let you sleep on till she returned.'

Clym went to the window and looked out. Presently he said, musingly, 'Week after week passes, and yet mother does not come. I thought I should have heard something from her long before this.'

Misgiving, regret, fear, resolution, ran their swift course of expression in Eustacia's dark eyes. She was face to face with a monstrous difficulty, and she resolved to get free of it by postponement.

'I must certainly go to Blooms-End soon,' he continued, 'and I think I had better go alone.' He picked up his leggings and gloves, threw them down again, and added, 'As dinner will be so late today I will not go back to the heath, but work in the garden till the evening, and then, when it will be cooler, I will walk to Blooms-End. I am quite sure that if I make a little advance mother will be willing to forget all. It will be rather late before I can get home, as I shall not be able to do the distance either way in less than an hour and a half. But you will not mind for one evening, dear? What are you thinking of to make you look so abstracted?'

'I cannot tell you,' she said heavily. 'I wish we didn't live here, Clym. The world seems all wrong in this place.'

'Well – if we make it so. I wonder if Thomasin has been to Blooms-End lately. I hope so. But probably not, as she is, I believe, expecting to be confined in a month or so. I wish I had thought of that before. Poor mother must indeed be very lonely.'

'I don't like you going tonight.'

'Why not tonight?'

'Something may be said which will terribly injure me.'

'My mother is not vindictive,' said Clym, his colour faintly rising.

'But I wish you would not go,' Eustacia repeated in a low tone. 'If you agree not to go tonight I promise to go by myself to her house tomorrow, and make it up with her, and wait till you fetch me.'

'Why do you want to do that at this particular time, when at every previous time that I have proposed it you have refused?'

'I cannot explain further than that I should like to see her alone before you go,' she answered, with an impatient move of her head, and looking at him with an anxiety more frequently seen upon those of a sanguine temperament than upon such as herself.

'Well, it is very odd that just when I had decided to go myself you should want to do what I proposed long ago. If I wait for you to go tomorrow another day will be lost; and I know I shall be unable to rest another night without having been. I want to get this settled, and will. You must visit her afterwards: it will be all the same.'

'I could even go with you now?'

'You could scarcely walk there and back without a longer rest than I shall take. No, not tonight, Eustacia.'

'Let it be as you say, then,' she replied in the quiet way of one who, though willing to ward off evil consequences by a mild effort, would let events fall out as they might sooner than wrestle hard to direct them.

Clym then went into the garden; and a thoughtful languor stole over Eustacia for the remainder of the afternoon, which her husband attributed to the heat of the weather.

In the evening he set out on the journey. Although the heat of summer was yet intense the days had considerably shortened, and before he had advanced a mile on his way all the heath purples, browns, and greens had merged in a uniform dress without airiness or gradation, and broken only by touches of white where the little heaps of clean quartz sand showed the entrance to a rabbit-burrow, or where the white flints of a footpath lay like a thread over the slopes. In almost every one of the isolated and stunted thorns which grew here and there a night-hawk revealed his presence by whirring like the clack of a mill as long as he could hold his breath, then stopping, flapping his wings, wheeling round the bush, alighting, and after a silent interval of listening beginning to whirr again. At each brushing of Clym's feet white miller-moths flew into the air just high enough to catch upon their dusty wings the mellowed light from the west, which now shone across the depressions and levels of the ground without falling thereon to light them up.

Yeobright walked on amid this quiet scene with a hope that all would soon be well. Three miles on he came to a spot where a soft perfume was wafted across his path, and he stood still for a moment to inhale the familiar scent. It was the place at which, four hours earlier, his mother had sat down exhausted on the knoll covered with shepherd's-thyme. While he stood a sound between a breathing and a moan suddenly reached his ears.

He looked to where the sound came from; but nothing appeared there save the verge of the hillock stretching against the sky in an unbroken line. He moved a few steps in that direction, and now he perceived a recumbent figure almost close at his feet.

Among the different possibilities as to the person's individuality there did not for a moment occur to Yeobright that it might be one of his own family. Sometimes furze-cutters had been known to sleep out of doors at these times, to save a long journey homeward and back again; but Clym remembered the moan and looked closer, and saw that the form was feminine; and a distress came over him like cold air from a cave. But he was not absolutely certain that the woman was his mother till he stooped and beheld her face, pallid, and with closed eyes.

His breath went, as it were, out of his body and the cry of anguish which would have escaped him died upon his lips. During the momentary interval that elapsed before he became conscious that something must be done all sense of time and place left him, and it seemed as if he and his mother were as when he was a child with her many years ago on this heath at hours similar to the present. Then he awoke to activity; and bending yet lower he found that she still breathed, and that her breath though feeble was regular, except when disturbed by an occasional gasp.

'O, what is it! Mother, are you very ill – you are not dying?' he cried, pressing his lips to her face. 'I am your Clym. How did you come here? What does it all mean?'

At that moment the chasm in their lives which his love for Eustacia had caused was not remembered by Yeobright, and to him that present joined continuously with that friendly past that had been their experience before the division.

She moved her lips, appeared to know him, but could not speak; and then Clym strove to consider how best to move her, as it would be necessary to get her away from the spot before the dews were intense. He was able-bodied, and his mother was thin. He clasped his arms round her, lifted her a little, and said, 'Does that hurt you?'

She shook her head, and he lifted her up; then, at a slow pace, went onward with his load. The air was now completely cool; but whenever he passed over a sandy patch of ground uncarpeted with vegetation there was reflected from its surface into his face the heat which it had imbibed during the day. At the beginning of his undertaking he had thought but little of the distance which yet would have to be traversed before Blooms-End could be reached; but though he had slept that afternoon he soon began to feel the weight of his burden. Thus he proceeded, like Aeneas with his father; the bats circling round his head, nightjars flapping their wings within a yard of his face, and not a human being within call.

While he was yet nearly a mile from the house his mother exhibited signs of restlessness under the constraint of being borne along, as if his arms were irksome to her. He lowered her upon his knees and looked around. The point they had now reached, though far from any road, was not more than a mile from the Blooms-End cottages occupied by Fairway, Sam, Humphrey, and the Cantles. Moreover, fifty yards off stood a hut, built of clods and covered with thin turves, but now entirely disused. The simple outline of the lonely shed was visible, and thither he determined to direct his steps. As soon as he arrived he laid her down carefully by the entrance, and then ran and cut with his pocket-knife an armful of the dryest fern. Spreading this within the shed, which was entirely open on one side, he placed his mother thereon: then he ran with all his might towards the dwelling of Fairway.

Nearly a quarter of an hour had passed, disturbed only by the broken breathing of the sufferer, when moving figures began to animate the line between heath and sky. In a few moments Clym arrived with Fairway, Humphrey, and Susan Nunsuch; Olly Dowden, who had chanced to be at Fairway's, Christian and Grandfer Cantle following helter-skelter behind. They had brought a lantern and matches, water, a pillow, and a few other articles which had occurred to their minds in the hurry of the moment. Sam had been despatched back again for brandy, and a boy brought Fairway's pony, upon which he rode off to the nearest medical man, with directions to call at Wildeve's on his way, and inform Thomasin that her aunt was unwell.

Sam and the brandy soon arrived, and it was administered by the light of the lantern; after which she became sufficiently conscious to signify by signs that something was wrong with her foot. Olly Dowden at length understood her meaning, and examined the foot indicated. It was swollen and red. Even as they watched the red began to assume a more livid colour, in the midst of which appeared a scarlet speck, smaller than a pea, and it was found to consist of a drop of blood, which rose above the smooth flesh of her ankle in a hemisphere.

'I know what it is,' cried Sam. 'She has been stung by an adder!'

'Yes,' said Clym instantly. 'I remember when I was a child seeing just such a bite. O, my poor mother!'

'It was my father who was bit,' said Sam. 'And there's only one way to cure it. You must rub the place with the fat of other adders, and the only way to get that is by frying them. That's what they did for him.'

' 'Tis an old remedy,' said Clym distrustfully, 'and I have doubts about it. But we can do nothing else till the doctor comes.'

' 'Tis a sure cure,' said Olly Dowden, with emphasis. 'I've used it when I used to go out nursing.'

'Then we must pray for daylight, to catch them,' said Clym gloomily.

'I will see what I can do,' said Sam.

He took a green hazel which he had used as a walking-stick, split it at the end, inserted a small pebble, and with the lantern in his hand went out into the heath. Clym had by this time lit a small fire, and despatched Susan Nunsuch for a frying-pan. Before she had returned Sam came in with three adders, one briskly coiling and uncoiling in the cleft of the stick, and the other two hanging dead across it.

'I have only been able to get one alive and fresh as he ought to be,' said Sam. 'These limp ones are two I killed today at work; but as they don't die till the sun goes down they can't be very stale meat.'

The live adder regarded the assembled group with a sinister look in its small black eye, and the beautiful brown and jet pattern on its back seemed to intensify with indignation. Mrs Yeobright saw the creature, and the creature saw her: she quivered throughout, and averted her eyes.

'Look at that,' murmured Christian Cantle. 'Neighbours, how do we know but that something of the old serpent in God's garden, that gied the apple to the young woman with no clothes, lives on in adders and snakes still? Look at his eye – for all the world like a villainous sort of black currant. 'Tis to be hoped he can't ill-wish us! There's folks in heath who've been overlooked already. I will never kill another adder as long as I live.'

'Well, 'tis right to be afeard of things, if folks can't help it,' said Grandfer Cantle. ' 'Twould have saved me many a brave danger in my time.'

'I fancy I heard something outside the shed,' said Christian. 'I wish troubles would come in the daytime, for then a man could show his courage, and hardly beg for mercy of the most broomstick old woman he should see, if he was a brave man, and able to run out of her sight!'

'Even such an ignorant fellow as I should know better than do that,' said Sam.

'Well, there's calamities where we least expect it, whether or no. Neighbours, if Mrs Yeobright were to die, d'ye think we should be took up and tried for the manslaughter of a woman?'

'No, they couldn't bring it in as that,' said Sam, 'unless they could prove we had been poachers at some time of our lives. But she'll fetch round.'

'Now, if I had been stung by ten adders I should hardly have lost a day's work for't,' said Grandfer Cantle. 'Such is my spirit when I am on my mettle. But perhaps 'tis natural in a man trained for war. Yes, I've gone through a good deal; but nothing ever came amiss to me after I joined the Locals in four.' He shook his head and smiled at a mental picture of himself in uniform. 'I was always first in the most galliantest scrapes in my younger days!'

'I suppose that was because they always used to put the biggest fool afore,' said Fairway from the fire, beside which he knelt, blowing it with his breath.

'D'ye think so, Timothy?' said Grandfer Cantle, coming forward to Fairway's side with sudden depression in his face. 'Then a man may feel for years that he is good solid company, and be wrong about himself after all?'

'Never mind that question, Grandfer. Stir your stumps and get some more sticks. 'Tis very nonsense of an old man to prattle so when life and death's in mangling.'

'Yes, yes,' said Grandfer Cantle, with melancholy conviction. 'Well, this is a bad night altogether for them that have done well in their time; and if I were ever such a dab at the hautboy or tenor-viol, I shouldn't have the heart to play tunes upon 'em now.'

Susan now arrived with the frying-pan, when the live adder was killed and the heads of the three taken off. The remainders, being cut into lengths and split open, were tossed into the pan, which began hissing and crackling over the fire. Soon a rill of clear oil trickled from the carcases, whereupon Clym dipped the corner of his handkerchief into the liquid and anointed the wound.

* VIII *

Eustacia Hears of Good Fortune, and Beholds Evil

IN the meantime Eustacia, left alone in her cottage at Alderworth, had become considerably depressed by the posture of affairs. The consequences which might result from Clym's discovery that his mother had been turned from his door that day were likely to be disagreeable, and this was a quality in events which she hated as much as the dreadful.

To be left to pass the evening by herself was irksome to her at any time, and this evening it was more irksome than usual by reason of the excitements of the past hours. The two visits had stirred her into restlessness. She was not wrought to any great pitch of uneasiness by the probability of appearing in an ill light in the discussion between Clym and his mother, but she was wrought to vexation; and her slumbering activities were quickened to the extent of wishing that she had opened the door. She had certainly believed that Clym was awake, and the excuse would be an honest one as far as it went; but nothing could save her from censure in refusing to answer at the first knock. Yet, instead of blaming herself for the issue she laid the fault upon the shoulders of some indistinct, colossal Prince of the World, who had framed her situation and ruled her lot.

At this time of the year it was pleasanter to walk by night than by day, and when Clym had been absent about an hour she suddenly resolved to go out in the direction of Blooms-End, on the chance of meeting him on his return. When she reached the garden gate she heard wheels approaching, and looking round beheld her grandfather coming up in his car.

'I can't stay a minute, thank ye,' he answered to her greeting. 'I am to East Egdon; but I came round here just to tell you the news. Perhaps you have heard – about Mr Wildeve's fortune?'

'No,' said Eustacia blankly.

'Well, he has come into a fortune of eleven thousand pounds – uncle died in Canada, just after hearing that all his family, whom he was sending home, had gone to the bottom in the *Cassiopeia*; so Wildeve has come into everything, without in the least expecting it.'

Eustacia stood motionless awhile. 'How long has he known of this?' she asked.

'Well, it was known to him this morning early, for I knew it at ten o'clock, when Charley came back. Now, he is what I call a lucky man. What a fool you were, Eustacia!'

'In what way?' she said, lifting her eyes in apparent calmness.

'Why, in not sticking to him when you had him.'

'Had him, indeed!'

'I did not know there had ever been anything between you till lately; and, faith, I should have been hot and strong against it if I had known; but since it seems that there was some sniffing between ye, why the deuce didn't you stick to him?'

Eustacia made no reply, but she looked as if she could say as much upon that subject as he if she chose.

'And how is your poor purblind husband?' continued the old man. 'Not a bad fellow either, as far as he goes.'

'He is quite well.'

'It is a good thing for his cousin what-d'ye-call-her? By George, you ought to have been in that galley, my girl! Now I must drive on. Do you want any assistance? What's mine is yours, you know.'

'Thank you, grandfather, we are not in want at present,' she said coldly. 'Clym cuts furze, but he does it mostly as a useful pastime, because he can do nothing else.'

'He is paid for his pastime, isn't he? Three shillings a hundred, I heard.'

'Clym has money,' she said, colouring; 'but he likes to earn a little.'

'Very well; good night.' And the captain drove on.

When her grandfather was gone Eustacia went on her way mechanically; but her thoughts were no longer concerning her mother-in-law and Clym. Wildeve, notwithstanding his complaints against his fate, had been seized upon by destiny and placed in the sunshine once more. Eleven thousand pounds! From every Egdon point of view he was a rich man. In Eustacia's eyes, too, it was an ample sum – one sufficient to supply those wants of hers which had been stigmatized by Clym in his more austere moods as vain and luxurious. Though she was no lover of money she loved what money could bring; and the new accessories she imagined around him clothed Wildeve with a great deal of interest. She recollected now how quietly well-dressed he had been that morning: he had probably put on his newest suit, regardless of damage by briars and thorns. And then she thought of his manner towards herself.

'O I see it, I see it,' she said. 'How much he wishes he had me now, that he might give me all I desire!'

In recalling the details of his glances and words – at the time scarcely regarded – it became plain to her how greatly they had been dictated by his knowledge of this new event. 'Had he been a man to bear a jilt ill-will he would have told me of his good fortune in crowing tones;

instead of doing that he mentioned not a word, in deference to my misfortunes, and merely implied that he loved me still, as one superior to him.'

Wildeve's silence that day on what had happened to him was just the kind of behaviour calculated to make an impression on such a woman. Those delicate touches of good taste were, in fact, one of the strong points in his demeanour towards the other sex. The peculiarity of Wildeve was that, while at one time passionate, upbraiding, and resentful towards a woman, at another he would treat her with such unparalleled grace as to make previous neglect appear as no discourtesy, injury as no insult, interference as a delicate attention, and the ruin of her honour as excess of chivalry. This man, whose admiration today Eustacia had disregarded, whose good wishes she had scarcely taken the trouble to accept, whom she had shown out of the house by the back door, was the possessor of eleven thousand pounds – a man of fair professional education, and one who had served his articles with a civil engineer.

So intent was Eustacia upon Wildeve's fortunes that she forgot how much closer to her own course were those of Clym; and instead of walking on to meet him at once she sat down upon a stone. She was disturbed in her reverie by a voice behind, and turning her head beheld the old lover and fortunate inheritor of wealth immediately beside her.

She remained sitting, though the fluctuation in her look might have told any man who knew her so well as Wildeve that she was thinking of him.

'How did you come here?' she said in her clear low tone. 'I thought you were at home.'

'I went on to the village after leaving your garden; and now I have come back again: that's all. Which way are you walking, may I ask?'

She waved her hand in the direction of Blooms-End. 'I am going to meet my husband. I think I may possibly have got into trouble whilst you were with me today.'

'How could that be?'

'By not letting in Mrs Yeobright.'

'I hope that visit of mine did you no harm.'

'None. It was not your fault,' she said quietly.

By this time she had risen; and they involuntarily sauntered on together, without speaking, for two or three minutes; when Eustacia broke silence by saying, 'I assume I must congratulate you.'

'On what? O yes; on my eleven thousand pounds, you mean. Well, since I didn't get something else, I must be content with getting that.'

'You seem very indifferent about it. Why didn't you tell me today when you came?' she said in the tone of a neglected person. 'I heard of it quite by accident.'

'I did mean to tell you,' said Wildeve. 'But I – well, I will speak frankly – I did not like to mention it when I saw, Eustacia, that your star was not high. The sight of a man lying wearied out with hard work, as your husband lay, made me feel that to brag of my own fortune to you would be greatly out of place. Yet, as you stood there beside him, I could not help feeling too that in many respects he was a richer man than I.'

At this Eustacia said, with slumbering mischievousness, 'What, would you exchange with him – your fortune for me?'

'I certainly would,' said Wildeve.

'As we are imagining what is impossible and absurd, suppose we change the subject?'

'Very well; and I will tell you of my plans for the future, if you care to hear them. I shall permanently invest nine thousand pounds, keep one thousand as ready money, and with the remaining thousand travel for a year or so.'

'Travel? What a bright idea! Where will you go to?'

'From here to Paris, where I shall pass the winter and spring. Then I shall go to Italy, Greece, Egypt, and Palestine, before the hot weather comes on. In the summer I shall go to America; and then, by a plan not yet settled, I shall go to Australia and round to India. By that time I shall have begun to have had enough of it. Then I shall probably come back to Paris again, and there I shall stay as long as I can afford to.'

'Back to Paris again,' she murmured in a voice that was nearly a sigh. She had never once told Wildeve of the Parisian desires which Clym's description had sown in her; yet here was he involuntarily in a position to gratify them. 'You think a good deal of Paris?' she added.

'Yes. In my opinion it is the central beauty-spot of the world.'

'And in mine! And Thomasin will go with you?'

'Yes, if she cares to. She may prefer to stay at home.'

'So you will be going about, and I shall be staying here!'

'I suppose you will. But we know whose fault that is.'

'I am not blaming you,' she said quickly.

'Oh, I thought you were. If ever you *should* be inclined to blame me, think of a certain evening by Rainbarrow, when you promised to meet me and did not. You sent me a letter; and my heart ached to read that as I hope yours never will. That was one point of divergence. I then did something in haste . . . But she is a good women, and I will say no more.'

'I know that the blame was on my side that time,' said Eustacia. 'But it had not always been so. However, it is my misfortune to be too sudden in feeling. O Damon, don't reproach me any more – I can't bear that.'

They went on silently for a distance of two or three miles, when Eustacia said suddenly, 'Haven't you come out of your way, Mr Wildeve?'

'My way is anywhere tonight. I will go with you as far as the hill on which we can see Blooms-End, as it is getting late for you to be alone.'

'Don't trouble. I am not obliged to be out at all. I think I would rather you did not accompany me further. This sort of thing would have an odd look if known.'

'Very well, I will leave you.' He took her hand unexpectedly, and kissed it – for the first time since her marriage. 'What light is that on the hill?' he added, as it were to hide the caress.

She looked, and saw a flickering firelight proceeding from the open side of a hovel a little way before them. The hovel, which she had hitherto always found empty, seemed to be inhabited now.

'Since you have come so far,' said Eustacia, 'will you see me safely past that hut? I thought I should have met Clym somewhere about here, but as he doesn't appear I will hasten on and get to Blooms-End before he leaves.'

They advanced to the turf-shed, and when they got near it the firelight and the lantern inside showed distinctly enough the form of a woman reclining on a bed of fern, a group of heath men and women standing around her. Eustacia did not recognize Mrs Yeobright in the reclining figure, nor Clym as one of the standers-by till she came close. Then she quickly pressed her hand upon Wildeve's arm and signified to him to come back from the open side of the shed into the shadow.

'It is my husband and his mother,' she whispered in an agitated voice. 'What can it mean? Will you step forward and tell me?'

Wildeve left her side and went to the back wall of the hut. Presently Eustacia perceived that he was beckoning to her, and she advanced and joined him.

'It is a serious case,' said Wildeve.

From their position they could hear what was proceeding inside.

'I cannot think where she could have been going,' said Clym to some one. 'She had evidently walked a long way, but even when she was able to speak just now she would not tell me where. What do you really think of her?'

'There is a great deal to fear,' was gravely answered, in a voice which Eustacia recognized as that of the only surgeon in the district. 'She had suffered somewhat from the bite of the adder; but it is exhaustion which has overpowered her. My impression is that her walk must have been exceptionally long.'

'I used to tell her not to overwalk herself this weather,' said Clym, with distress. 'Do you think we did well in using the adder's fat?'

'Well, it is a very ancient remedy – the old remedy of the viper-catchers, I believe,' replied the doctor. 'It is mentioned as an infallible ointment by Hoffman, Mead, and I think the Abbé Fontana. Undoubtedly it was as good a thing as you could do; though I question if some other oils would not have been equally efficacious.'

'Come here, come here!' was then rapidly said in anxious female tones; and Clym and the doctor could be heard rushing forward from the back part of the shed to where Mrs Yeobright lay.

'O, what is it?' whispered Eustacia.

' 'Twas Thomasin who spoke,' said Wildeve. 'Then they have fetched her. I wonder if I had better go in – yet it might do harm.'

For a long time there was utter silence among the group within; and it was broken at last by Clym saying, in an agonized voice, 'O doctor, what does it mean?'

The doctor did not reply at once; ultimately he said, 'She is sinking fast. Her heart was previously affected, and physical exhaustion has dealt the finishing blow.'

Then there was a weeping of women, then waiting, then hushed exclamations, then a strange gasping sound, then a painful stillness.

'It is all over,' said the doctor.

Further back in the hut the cotters whispered, 'Mrs Yeobright is dead.'

Almost at the same moment the two watchers observed the form of a small old-fashioned child entering at the open side of the shed. Susan Nunsuch, whose boy it was, went forward to the opening and silently beckoned to him to go back.

'I've got something to tell 'ee, mother,' he cried in a shrill tone. 'That woman asleep there walked along with me today; and she said I was to say that I had seed her, and she was a broken-hearted woman and cast off by her son, and then I came on home.'

A confused sob as from a man was heard within, upon which Eustacia gasped faintly, 'That's Clym – I must go to him – yet dare I do it? No: come away!'

When they had withdrawn from the neighbourhood of the shed she said huskily, 'I am to blame for this. There is evil in store for me.'

'Was she not admitted to your house after all?' Wildeve inquired.

'No; and that's where it all lies! O, what shall I do! I shall not intrude upon them: I shall go straight home. Damon, good-bye! I cannot speak to you any more now.'

They parted company; and when Eustacia had reached the next hill she looked back. A melancholy procession was wending its way by the light of the lantern from the hut towards Blooms-End. Wildeve was nowhere to be seen.

BOOK FIFTH

THE DISCOVERY

* I *

'Wherefore Is Light Given to Him That Is in Misery'

ONE evening, about three weeks after the funeral of Mrs Yeobright, when the silver face of the moon sent a bundle of beams directly upon the floor of Clym's house at Alderworth, a woman came forth from within. She reclined over the garden gate as if to refresh herself awhile. The pale lunar touches which make beauties of hags lent divinity to this face, already beautiful.

She had not long been there when a man came up the road and with some hesitation said to her, 'How is he tonight, ma'am, if you please?'

'He is better, though still very unwell, Humphrey,' replied Eustacia.

'Is he light-headed, ma'am?'

'No. He is quite sensible now.'

'Do he rave about his mother just the same, poor fellow?' continued Humphrey.

'Just as much, though not quite so wildly,' she said in a low voice.

'It was very unfortunate, ma'am, that the boy Johnny should ever ha' told him his mother's dying words, about her being broken-hearted and cast off by her son. 'Twas enough to upset any man alive.'

Eustacia made no reply beyond that of a slight catch in her breath, as of one who fain would speak but could not; and Humphrey, declining her invitation to come in, went away.

Eustacia turned, entered the house, and ascended to the front bedroom, where a shaded light was burning. In the bed lay Clym, pale, haggard, wide awake, tossing to one side and to the other, his eyes lit by a hot light, as if the fire in their pupils were burning up their substance.

'Is it you, Eustacia?' he said as she sat down.

'Yes, Clym. I have been down to the gate. The moon is shining beautifully, and there is not a leaf stirring.'

'Shining, is it? What's the moon to a man like me? Let it shine – let anything be, so that I never see another day! . . . Eustacia, I don't know where to look: my thoughts go through me like swords. O, if any man wants to make himself immortal by painting a picture of wretchedness, let him come here!'

'Why do you say so?'

'I cannot help feeling that I did my best to kill her.'

'No, Clym.'

'Yes, it was so; it is useless to excuse me! My conduct to her was too hideous – I made no advances; and she could not bring herself to forgive me. Now she is dead! If I had only shown myself willing to make it up with her sooner, and we had been friends, and then she had died, it wouldn't be so hard to bear. But I never went near her house, so she never came near mine, and didn't know how welcome she would have been – that's what troubles me. She did not know I was going to her house that very night, for she was too insensible to understand me. If she had only come to see me! I longed that she would. But it was not to be.'

There escaped from Eustacia one of those shivering sighs which used to shake her like a pestilent blast. She had not yet told.

But Yeobright was too deeply absorbed in the ramblings incidental to his remorseful state to notice her. During his illness he had been continually talking thus. Despair had been added to his original grief by the unfortunate disclosure of the boy who had received the last words of Mrs Yeobright – words too bitterly uttered in an hour of misapprehension. Then his distress had overwhelmed him, and he longed for death as a field labourer longs for the shade. It was the pitiful sight of a man standing in the very focus of sorrow. He continually bewailed his tardy journey to his mother's house, because it was an error which could never be rectified, and insisted that he must have been horribly perverted by some fiend not to have thought before that it was his duty to go to her, since she did not come to him. He would ask Eustacia to agree with him in his self-condemnation; and when she, seared inwardly by a secret she dared not tell, declared that she could not give an opinion, he would say, 'That's because you didn't know my mother's nature. She was always ready to forgive if asked to do so; but I seemed to her to be as an obstinate child, and that made her unyielding. Yet not unyielding: she was proud and reserved, no more . . . Yes, I can understand why she held out against me so long. She was waiting for me. I dare say she said a hundred times in her sorrow, "What a return he makes for all the sacrifices I have made for him!" I never went to her! When I set out to visit her it was too late. To think of that is nearly intolerable!'

Sometimes his condition had been one of utter remorse, unsoftened by a single tear of pure sorrow: and then he writhed as he lay, fevered far more by thought than by physical ills. 'If I could only get one assurance that she did not die in a belief that I was resentful,' he said one day when in this mood, 'it would be better to think of than a hope of heaven. But that I cannot do.'

'You give yourself up too much to this wearying despair,' said Eustacia. 'Other men's mothers have died.'

'That doesn't make the loss of mine less. Yet it is less the loss than the circumstances of the loss. I sinned against her, and on that account there is no light for me.'

'She sinned against you, I think.'

'No: she did not. I committed the guilt; and may the whole burden be upon my head!'

'I think you might consider twice before you say that,' Eustacia replied.

'Single men have, no doubt, a right to curse themselves as much as they please; but men with wives involve two in the doom they pray down.'

'I am in too sorry a state to understand what you are refining on,' said the wretched man. 'Day and night shout at me, "You have helped to kill her." But in loathing myself I may, I own, be unjust to you, my poor wife. Forgive me for it, Eustacia, for I scarcely know what I do.'

Eustacia was always anxious to avoid the sight of her husband in such a state as this, which had become as dreadful to her as the trial scene was to Judas Iscariot. It brought before her eyes the spectre of a worn-out woman knocking at a door which she would not open; and she shrank from contemplating it. Yet it was better for Yeobright himself when he spoke openly of his sharp regret, for in silence he endured infinitely more, and would sometimes remain so long in a tense, brooding mood, consuming himself by the gnawing of his thought, that it was imperatively necessary to make him talk aloud, that his grief might in some degree expend itself in the effort.

Eustacia had not been long indoors after her look at the moonlight when a soft footstep came up to the house, and Thomasin was announced by the woman downstairs.

'Ah, Thomasin! Thank you for coming tonight,' said Clym when she entered the room. 'Here am I, you see. Such a wretched spectacle am I, that I shrink from being seen by a single friend, and almost from you.'

'You must not shrink from me, dear Clym,' said Thomasin earnestly, in that sweet voice of hers which came to a sufferer like fresh air into a Black Hole. 'Nothing in you can ever shock me or drive me away. I have been here before, but you don't remember it.'

'Yes, I do; I am not delirious, Thomasin, nor have I been so at all. Don't you believe that if they say so. I am only in great misery at what I have done: and that, with the weakness, makes me seem mad. But it has not upset my reason. Do you think I should remember all about my mother's death if I were out of my mind? No such good luck. Two months and a half, Thomasin, the last of her life, did my poor mother live alone, distracted and mourning because of me; yet she was unvisited by me, though I was living only six miles off. Two months and a half – seventy-five days did the sun rise and set upon her in that deserted state which a dog didn't deserve! Poor people who had nothing in common with her would have cared for her, and visited her had they known her sickness and loneliness; but I, who should have been all to her, stayed away like a cur. If there is any justice in God let Him kill me now. He has nearly blinded me, but that is not enough. If He would only strike me with more pain I would believe in Him for ever!'

'Hush, hush! O, pray, Clym, don't, don't say it!' implored Thomasin, affrighted into sobs and tears; while Eustacia, at the other side of the room, though her pale face remained calm, writhed in her chair. Clym went on without heeding his cousin.

'But I am not worth receiving further proof even of Heaven's repro-bation. Do you think, Thomasin, that she knew me – that she did not die in that horrid mistaken notion about my not forgiving her, which I can't tell you how she acquired? If you could only assure me of that! Do you think so, Eustacia? Do speak to me.'

'I think I can assure you that she knew better at last,' said Thomasin. The pallid Eustacia said nothing.

'Why didn't she come to my house? I would have taken her in and showed her how I loved her in spite of all. But she never came; and I didn't go to her, and she died on the heath like an animal kicked out, nobody to help her till it was too late. If you could have seen her, Thomasin, as I saw her – a poor dying woman, lying in the dark upon the bare ground, moaning, nobody near, believing she was utterly deserted by all the world, it would have moved you to anguish, it would have moved a brute. And this poor woman my mother! No wonder she said to the child, "You have seen a broken-hearted woman." What a state she must have been brought to, to say that! and who can have done it but I? It is too dreadful to think of, and I wish I could be punished more heavily than I am. How long was I what they called out of my senses?'

'A week, I think.'

'And then I became calm.'

'Yes, for four days.'

'And now I have left off being calm.'

'But try to be quiet: please do, and you will soon be strong. If you could remove that impression from your mind –'

'Yes, yes,' he said impatiently. 'But I don't want to get strong. What's the use of my getting well? It would be better for me if I die, and it would certainly be better for Eustacia. Is Eustacia there?'

'Yes.'

'It would be better for you, Eustacia, if I were to die?'

'Don't press such a question, dear Clym.'

'Well, it really is but a shadowy supposition; for unfortunately I am going to live. I feel myself getting better. Thomasin, how long are you going to stay at the inn, now that all this money has come to your husband?'

'Another month or two, probably; until my illness is over. We cannot get off till then. I think it will be a month or more.'

'Yes, yes. Of course. Ah, Cousin Tamsie, you will get over your trouble – one little month will take you through it, and bring something to console you; but I shall never get over mine, and no consolation will come!'

'Clym, you are unjust to yourself. Depend upon it, aunt thought kindly of you. I know that, if she had lived, you would have been reconciled with her.'

'But she didn't come to see me, though I asked her, before I married, if she would come. Had she come, or had I gone there, she would never have died saying, "I am a broken-hearted woman, cast off by my son." My door has always been open to her – a welcome here has always awaited her. But that she never came to see.'

'You had better not talk any more now, Clym,' said Eustacia faintly from the other part of the room, for the scene was growing intolerable to her.

'Let me talk to you instead for the little time I shall be here,' Thomasin said soothingly. 'Consider what a one-sided way you have of looking at the matter, Clym. When she said that to the little boy you had not found her and taken her into your arms: and it might have been uttered in a moment of bitterness. It was rather like aunt to say things in haste. She sometimes used to speak so to me. Though she did not come, I am convinced that she thought of coming to see you. Do you suppose a man's mother could live two or three months without one forgiving thought? She forgave me; and why should she not have forgiven you?'

'You laboured to win her round; I did nothing. I, who was going to teach people the higher secrets of happiness, did not know how to keep out of that gross misery which the most untaught are wise enough to avoid.'

'How did you get here tonight, Thomasin?' said Eustacia.

'Damon set me down at the end of the lane. He has driven into East Egdon on business, and he will come and pick me up by-and-by.'

Accordingly they soon after heard the noise of wheels. Wildeve had come, and was waiting outside with his horse and gig.

'Send out and tell him I will be down in two minutes,' said Thomasin.

'I will run down myself,' said Eustacia.

She went down. Wildeve had alighted, and was standing before the horse's head when Eustacia opened the door. He did not turn for a moment, thinking the comer Thomasin. Then he looked, started ever so little, and said one word: 'Well?'

'I have not yet told him,' she replied in a whisper.

'Then don't do so till he is well – it will be fatal. You are ill yourself.'

'I am wretched . . . O Damon,' she said, bursting into tears, 'I – I can't tell you how unhappy I am! I can hardly bear this. I can tell nobody of my trouble – nobody knows of it but you.'

'Poor girl!' said Wildeve, visibly affected at her distress, and at last led on so far as to take her hand. 'It is hard, when you have done nothing to deserve it, that you should have got involved in such a web as this. You were not made for these sad scenes. I am to blame most. If I could only have saved you from it all!'

'But, Damon, please pray tell me what I must do? To sit by him hour after hour, and hear him reproach himself as being the cause of her death, and to know that I am the sinner, if any human being is at all, drives me into cold despair. I don't know what to do. Should I tell him or should I not tell him? I always am asking myself that. O, I want to tell him; and yet I am afraid. If he finds it out he must surely kill me, for nothing else will be in proportion to his feelings now. "Beware the fury of a patient man" sounds day by day in my ears as I watch him.'

'Well, wait till he is better, and trust to chance. And when you tell, you must only tell part – for his own sake.'

'Which part should I keep back?'

Wildeve paused. 'That I was in the house at the time,' he said in a low tone.

'Yes; it must be concealed, seeing what has been whispered. How much easier are hasty actions than speeches that will excuse them!'

'If he were only to die –' Wildeve murmured.

'Do not think of it! I would not buy hope of immunity by so cowardly a desire even if I hated him. Now I am going up to him again. Thomasin bade me tell you she would be down in a few minutes. Good-bye.'

She returned, and Thomasin soon appeared. When she was seated in the gig with her husband, and the horse was turning to go off, Wildeve lifted his eyes to the bedroom windows. Looking from one of them he could discern a pale, tragic face watching him drive away. It was Eustacia's.

* II *

A Lurid Light Breaks In upon a Darkened Understanding

CLYM's grief became mitigated by wearing itself out. His strength returned, and a month after the visit of Thomasin he might have been seen walking about the garden. Endurance and despair, equanimity and gloom, the tints of health and the pallor of death, mingled weirdly in his face. He was now unnaturally silent upon all of the past that related to his mother; and though Eustacia knew that he was thinking of it none the less, she was only too glad to escape the topic ever to bring it up anew. When his mind had been weaker his heart had led him to speak out; but reason having now somewhat recovered itself he sank into taciturnity.

One evening when he was thus standing in the garden, abstractedly spudding up a weed with his stick, a bony figure turned the corner of the house and came up to him.

'Christian, isn't it?' said Clym. 'I am glad you have found me out. I shall soon want you to go to Blooms-End and assist me in putting the house in order. I suppose it is all locked up as I left it?'

'Yes, Mister Clym.'

'Have you dug up the potatoes and other roots?'

'Yes, without a drop o' rain, thank God. But I was coming to tell 'ee of something else which is quite different from what we have lately had in the family. I am sent by the rich gentleman at the Woman, that we used to call the landlord, to tell 'ee that Mrs Wildeve is doing well of a girl, which was born punctually at one o'clock at noon, or a few minutes more or less; and 'tis said that expecting of this increase is what have kept 'em there since they came into their money.'

'And she is getting on well, you say?'

'Yes, sir. Only Mr Wildeve is twanky because 'tisn't a boy – that's what they say in the kitchen, but I was not supposed to notice that.'

'Christian, now listen to me.'

'Yes, sure, Mr Yeobright.'

'Did you see my mother the day before she died?'

'No, I did not.'

Yeobright's face expressed disappointment.

'But I zeed her the morning of the same day she died.'

Clym's look lighted up. 'That's nearer still to my meaning,' he said.

'Yes, I know 'twas the same day; for she said, "I be going to see him, Christian; so I shall not want any vegetables brought in for dinner." '

'See whom?'

'See you. She was going to your house, you understand.'

Yeobright regarded Christian with intense surprise. 'Why did you never mention this?' he said. 'Are you sure it was my house she was coming to?'

'O yes. I didn't mention it because I've never zeed you lately. And as she didn't get there it was all nought, and nothing to tell.'

'And I have been wondering why she should have walked in the heath on that hot day! Well, did she say what she was coming for? It is a thing, Christian, I am very anxious to know.'

'Yes, Mister Clym. She didn't say it to me, though I think she did to one here and there.'

'Do you know one person to whom she spoke of it?'

'There is one man, please, sir, but I hope you won't mention my name to him, as I have seen him in strange places, particular in dreams. One night last summer he glared at me like Famine and Sword, and it made me feel so low that I didn't comb out my few hairs for two days. He was standing, as it might be, Mister Yeobright, in the middle of the path to Mistover, and your mother came up, looking as pale—'

'Yes, when was that?'

'Last summer, in my dream.'

'Pooh! Who's the man?'

'Diggory, the reddleman. He called upon her and sat with her the evening before she set out to see you. I hadn't gone home from work when he came up to the gate.'

'I must see Venn – I wish I had known it before,' said Clym anxiously. 'I wonder why he has not come to tell me?'

'He went out of Egdon Heath the next day, so would not be likely to know you wanted him.'

'Christian,' said Clym, 'you must go and find Venn. I am otherwise engaged, or I would go myself. Find him at once, and tell him I want to speak to him.'

'I am a good hand at hunting up folk by day,' said Christian, looking dubiously round at the declining light; 'but as to night-time, never is such a bad hand as I, Mister Yeobright.'

'Search the heath when you will, so that you bring him soon. Bring him tomorrow, if you can.'

Christian then departed. The morrow came, but no Venn. In the evening Christian arrived, looking very weary. He hd been searching all day, and had heard nothing of the reddleman.

'Inquire as much as you can tomorrow without neglecting your work,' said Yeobright. 'Don't come again till you have found him.'

The next day Yeobright set out for the old house at Blooms-End, which, with the garden, was now his own. His severe illness had hindered all preparations for his removal thither; but it had become necessary that he should go and overlook its contents, as administrator to his mother's little property; for which purpose he decided to pass the next night on the premises.

He journeyed onward, not quickly or decisively, but in the slow walk of one who has been awakened from a stupefying sleep. It was early afternoon when he reached the valley. The expression of the place, the tone of the hour, were precisely those of many such occasions in days gone by; and these antecedent similarities fostered the illusion that she, who was there no longer, would come out to welcome him. The garden gate was locked and the shutters were closed, just as he himself had left them on the evening after the funeral. He unlocked the gate, and found that a spider had already constructed a large web, tying the door to the lintel, on the supposition that it was never to be opened again. When he had entered the house and flung back the shutters he set about his task of overhauling the cupboards and closets, burning papers, and considering how best to arrange the place for Eustacia's reception, until such time as he might be in a position to carry out his long-delayed scheme, should that time ever arrive.

As he surveyed the rooms he felt strongly disinclined for the alterations which would have to be made in the time-honoured furnishing of his parents and grandparents, to suit Eustacia's modern ideas. The gaunt oak-cased clock, with the picture of the Ascension on the door-panel and the Miraculous Draught of Fishes on the base; his grandmother's corner cupboard with the glass door, through which the spotted china was visible; the dumb-waiter; the wooden tea-trays; the hanging fountain with the brass tap – whither would these venerable articles have to be banished?

He noticed that the flowers in the window had died for want of water, and he placed them out upon the ledge, that they might be taken away. While thus engaged he heard footsteps on the gravel without, and somebody knocked at the door.

Yeobright opened it, and Venn was standing before him.

'Good morning,' said the reddleman. 'Is Mrs Yeobright at home?'

Yeobright looked upon the ground. 'Then you have not seen Christian or any of the Egdon folks?' he said.

'No. I have only just returned after a long stay away. I called here the day before I left.'

'And you have heard nothing?'

'Nothing.'

'My mother is – dead.'

'Dead!' said Venn mechanically.

'Her home now is where I shouldn't mind having mine.'

Venn regarded him, and then said, 'If I didn't see your face I could never believe your words. Have you been ill?'

'I had an illness.'

'Well, the change! When I parted from her a month ago everything seemed to say that she was going to begin a new life.'

'And what seemed came true.'

'You say right, no doubt. Trouble has taught you a deeper vein of talk than mine. All I meant was regarding her life here. She has died too soon.'

'Perhaps through my living too long. I have had a bitter experience on that score this past month, Diggory. But come in; I have been wanting to see you.'

He conducted the reddleman into the large room where the dancing had taken place the previous Christmas; and they sat down in the settle together. 'There's the cold fireplace, you see,' said Clym. 'When that half-burnt log and those cinders were alight she was alive! Little has been changed here yet. I can do nothing. My life creeps like a snail.'

'How came she to die?' said Venn.

Yeobright gave him some particulars of her illness and death, and continued: 'After this no kind of pain will ever seem more than an indisposition to me. – I began saying that I wanted to ask you something, but I stray from subjects like a drunken man. I am anxious to know what my mother said to you when she last saw you. You talked with her a long time, I think?'

'I talked with her more than half an hour.'

'About me?'

'Yes. And it must have been on account of what we said that she was on the heath. Without question she was coming to see you.'

'But why should she come to see me if she felt so bitter against me? There's the mystery.'

'Yet I know she quite forgave 'ee.'

'But, Diggory – would a woman, who had quite forgiven her son, say, when she felt herself ill on the way to his house, that she was broken-hearted because of his ill-usage? Never!'

'What I know is that she didn't blame you at all. She blamed herself for what had happened, only herself. I had it from her own lips.'

'You had it from her lips that I had *not* ill-treated her; and at the same time another had it from her lips that I *had* ill-treated her? My mother was no impulsive woman who changed her opinion every hour without reason. How can it be, Venn, that she should have told such different stories in close succession?'

'I cannot say. It is certainly odd, when she had forgiven you, and had forgiven your wife, and was going to see ye on purpose to make friends.'

'If there was one thing wanting to bewilder me it was this incomprehensible thing! . . . Diggory, if we, who remain alive, were only allowed to hold conversation with the dead – just once, a bare minute, even through a screen of iron bars, as with persons in prison – what we might learn! How many who now ride smiling would hide their heads! And this mystery – I should then be at the bottom of it at once. But the grave has for ever shut her in; and how shall it be found out now?'

No reply was returned by his companion, since none could be given; and when Venn left, a few minutes later, Clym had passed from the dullness of sorrow to the fluctuation of carking incertitude.

He continued in the same state all the afternoon. A bed was made up for him in the same house by a neighbour, that he might not have to return again the next day; and when he retired to rest in the deserted place it was only to remain awake hour after hour thinking the same thoughts. How to discover a solution to this riddle of death seemed a query of more importance than highest problems of the living. There was housed in his memory a vivid picture of the face of a little boy as he entered the hovel where Clym's mother lay. The round eyes, eager gaze, the piping voice which enunciated the words, had operated like stilettos on his brain.

A visit to the boy suggested itself as a means of gleaning new particulars; though it might be quite unproductive. To probe a child's mind after the lapse of six weeks, not for facts which the child had seen and understood, but to get at those which were in their nature beyond him, did not promise much; yet when every obvious channel is blocked we grope towards the small and obscure. There was nothing else left to do; after that he would allow the enigma to drop into the abyss of undiscoverable things.

It was about daybreak when he had reached this decision, and he at once arose. He locked up the house and went out into the green patch which merged in heather further on. In front of the white garden-palings the path branched into three like a broad-arrow. The road to the right led to the Quiet Woman and its neighbourhood; the middle track led to Mistover Knap; the left-hand track led over the hill to another part of Mistover, where the child lived. On inclining into the latter path Yeobright felt a creeping chilliness, familiar enough to most people, and probably caused by the unsunned morning air. In after days he thought of it as a thing of singular significance.

When Yeobright reached the cottage of Susan Nunsuch, the mother of the boy he sought, he found that the inmates were not yet astir. But in upland hamlets the transition from a-bed to abroad is surprisingly swift and easy. There no dense partition of yawns and toilets divides humanity by night from humanity by day. Yeobright tapped at the upper window-sill, which he could reach with his walking-stick; and in three or four minutes the woman came down.

It was not till this moment that Clym recollected her to be the person who had behaved so barbarously to Eustacia. It partly explained the insuavity with which the woman greeted him. Moreover, the boy had been ailing again; and Susan now, as ever since the night when he had been pressed into Eustacia's service at the bonfire, attributed his indispositions to Eustacia's influence as a witch. It was one of those sentiments which lurk like moles underneath the visible surface of manners, and may have been kept alive by Eustacia's entreaty to the captain, at the time that he had intended to prosecute Susan for the pricking in church, to let the matter drop; which he accordingly had done.

Yeobright overcame his repugnance, for Susan had at least borne his mother no ill-will. He asked kindly for the boy; but her manner did not improve.

'I wish to see him,' continued Yeobright, with some hesitation; 'to ask him if he remembers anything more of his walk with my mother than what he has previously told.'

She regarded him in a peculiar and criticizing manner. To anybody but a half-blind man it would have said, 'You want another of the knocks which have already laid you so low.'

She called the boy downstairs, asked Clym to sit down on a stool, and continued, 'Now, Johnny, tell Mr Yeobright anything you can call to mind.'

'You have not forgotten how you walked with the poor lady on that hot day?' said Clym.

'No,' said the boy.

'And what she said to you?'

The boy repeated the exact words he had used on entering the hut. Yeobright rested his elbow on the table and shaded his face with his hand; and the mother looked as if she wondered how a man could want more of what had stung him so deeply.

'She was going to Alderworth when you first met her?'

'No; she was coming away.'

'That can't be.'

'Yes; she walked along with me. I was coming away too.'

'Then where did you first see her?'

'At your house.'

'Attend, and speak the truth!' said Clym sternly.

'Yes, sir; at your house was where I seed her first.'

Clum started up, and Susan smiled in an expectant way which did not embellish her face; it seemed to mean, 'Something sinister is coming!'

'What did she do at my house?'

'She went and sat under the trees at the Devil's Bellows.'

'Good God! this is all news to me!'

'You never told me this before?' said Susan.

'No, mother; because I didn't like to tell 'ee I had been so far. I was picking black-hearts, and went further than I meant.'

'What did she do then?' said Yeobright.

'Looked at a man who came up and went into your house.'

'That was myself – a furze-cutter, with brambles in his hand.'

'No; 'twas not you. 'Twas a gentleman. You had gone in afore.'

'Who was he?'

'I don't know.'

'Now tell me what happened next.'

'The poor lady went and knocked at your door, and the lady with black hair looked out of the side window at her.'

The boy's mother turned to Clym and said, 'This is something you didn't expect?'

Yeobright took no more notice of her than if he had been of stone. 'Go on, go on,' he said hoarsely to the boy.

'And when she saw the young lady look out of the window the old lady knocked again; and when nobody came she took up the furze-hook and looked at it, and put it down again, and then she looked at the faggot-bonds; and then she went away, and walked across to me, and blowed her breath very hard, like this. We walked on together, she and I, and I talked to her and she talked to me a bit, but not much, because she couldn't blow her breath.'

'O!' murmured Clym, in a low tone, and bowed his head. 'Let's have more,' he said.

'She couldn't talk much, and she couldn't walk; and her face was, O so queer!'

'How was her face?'

'Like yours is now.'

The woman looked at Yeobright, and beheld him colourless, in a cold sweat. 'Isn't there meaning in it?' she said stealthily. 'What do you think of her now?'

'Silence!' said Clym fiercely. And, turning to the boy, 'And then you left her to die?'

'No,' said the woman, quickly and angrily. 'He did not leave her to die! She sent him away. Whoever says he forsook her says what's not true.'

'Trouble no more about that,' answered Clym, with a quivering mouth. 'What he did is a trifle in comparison with what he saw. Door kept shut, did you say? Kept shut, she looking out of windows? Good heart of God! – what does it mean?'

The child shrank away from the gaze of his questioner.

'He said so,' answered the mother, 'and Johnny's a God-fearing boy and tells no lies.'

' "Cast off by my son!" No, by my best life, dear mother, it is not so! But by your son's, your son's – May all murderesses get the torment they deserve!'

With these words Yeobright went forth from the little dwelling. The pupils of his eyes, fixed steadfastly on blankness, were vaguely lit with an icy shine; his mouth had passed into the phase more or less imaginatively rendered in studies of Oedipus. The strangest deeds were possible to his mood. But they were not possible to his situation. Instead of there being before him the pale face of Eustacia, and masculine shape unknown, there was only the imperturbable countenance of the heath, which, having defied the cataclysmal onsets of the centuries, reduced to insignificance by its seamed and antique features the wildest turmoil of a single man.

* III *

Eustacia Dresses Herself on a Black Morning

A CONSCIOUSNESS of a vast impassivity in all which lay around him took possession even of Yeobright in his wild walk towards Alderworth. He had once before felt in his own person this overpowering of the fervid by the inanimate; but then it had tended to enervate a passion far sweeter than that which at present pervaded him. It was once when he stood parting from Eustacia in the moist still levels beyond the hills.

But dismissing all this he went onward home, and came to the front of his house. The blinds of Eustacia's bedroom were still closely drawn, for she was no early riser. All the life visible was in the shape of a solitary thrush cracking a small snail upon the door-stone for his breakfast, and his tapping seemed a loud noise in the general silence which prevailed; but on going to the door Clym found it unfastened, the young girl who attended upon Eustacia being astir in the back part of the premises. Yeobright entered and went straight to his wife's room.

The noise of his arrival must have aroused her, for when he opened the door she was standing before the looking-glass in her night-dress, the ends of her hair gathered into one hand, with which she was coiling the whole mass round her head, previous to beginning toilette operations. She was not a woman given to speaking first at a meeting, and she allowed Clym to walk across in silence, without turning her head. He came behind her, and she saw his face in the glass. It was ashy, haggard, and terrible. Instead of starting towards him in sorrowful surprise, as even Eustacia, undemonstrative wife as she was, would have done in days before she burdened herself with a secret, she remained motionless, looking at him in the glass. And while she looked the carmine flush with which warmth and sound sleep had suffused her cheeks and neck, dissolved from view, and the death-like pallor in his face flew across into hers. He was close enough to see this, and the sight instigated his tongue.

'You know what is the matter,' he said huskily. 'I see it in your face.'

Her hand relinquished the rope of hair and dropped to her side, and the pile of tresses, no longer supported, fell from the crown of her head about her shoulders and over the white nightgown. She made no reply.

'Speak to me,' said Yeobright peremptorily.

The blanching process did not cease in her, and her lips now became as white as her face. She turned to him and said, 'Yes, Clym, I'll speak to you. Why do you return so early? Can I do anything for you?'

'Yes, you can listen to me. It seems that my wife is not very well?'

'Why?'

'Your face, my dear; your face. Or perhaps it is the pale morning light which takes your colour away? Now I am going to reveal a secret to you. Ha-ha!'

'O, that is ghastly!'

'What?'

'Your laugh.'

'There's reason for ghastliness. Eustacia, you have held my happiness in the hollow of your hand, and like a devil you have dashed it down!'

She started back from the dressing-table, retreated a few steps from him, and looked him in the face. 'Ah! you think to frighten me,' she said, with a slight laugh. 'Is it worth while? I am undefended, and alone.'

'How extraordinary!'

'What do you mean?'

'As there is ample time I will tell you, though you know well enough. I mean that it is extraordinary that you should be alone in my absence. Tell me, now, where is he who was with you on the afternoon of the thirty-first of August? Under the bed? Up the chimney?'

A shudder overcame her and shook the light fabric of her night-dress throughout. 'I do not remember dates so exactly,' she said. 'I cannot recollect that anybody was with me besides yourself.'

'The day I mean,' said Yeobright, his voice growing louder and harsher, 'was the day you shut the door against my mother and killed her. O, it is too much – too bad!' He leant over the footpiece of the bedstead for a few moments, with his back towards her; then rising again: 'Tell me, tell me! tell me – do you hear?' he cried, rushing up to her and seizing her by the loose folds of her sleeve.

The superstratum of timidity which often overlies those who are daring and defiant at heart had been passed through, and the mettlesome substance of the woman was reached. The red blood inundated her face, previously so pale.

'What are you going to do?' she said in a low voice, regarding him with a proud smile. 'You will not alarm me by holding on so; but it would be a pity to tear my sleeve.'

Instead of letting go he drew her closer to him. 'Tell me the particulars of – my mother's death,' he said in a hard, panting whisper; 'or – I'll – I'll –'

'Clym,' she answered slowly, 'do you think you dare do anything to me that I dare not bear? But before you strike me listen. You will get nothing from me by a blow, even though it should kill me, as it probably will. But perhaps you do not wish me to speak – killing may be all you mean?'

'Kill you! Do you expect it?'

'I do.'

'Why?'

'No less degree of rage against me will match your previous grief for her.'

'Phew – I shall not kill you,' he said contemptuously, as if under a sudden change of purpose. 'I did think of it; but – I shall not. That would be making a martyr of you, and sending you to where she is; and I would keep you away from her till the universe come to an end, if I could.'

'I almost wish you would kill me,' said she with gloomy bitterness. 'It is with no strong desire, I assure you, that I play the part I have lately played on earth. You are no blessing, my husband.'

'You shut the door – you looked out of the window upon her – you had a man in the house with you – you sent her away to die. The inhumanity – the treachery – I will not touch you – stand away from me – and confess every word!'

'Never! I'll hold my tongue like the very death that I don't mind meeting, even though I can clear myself of half you believe by speaking. Yes. I will! Who of any dignity would take the trouble to clear cobwebs from a wild man's mind after such language as this? No; let him go on, and think his narrow thoughts, and run his head into the mire. I have other cares.'

' 'Tis too much – but I must spare you.'

'Poor charity.'

'By my wretched soul you sting me, Eustacia! I can keep it up, and hotly too. Now, then, madam, tell me his name!'

'Never, I am resolved.'

'How often does he write to you? Where does he put his letters – when does he meet you? Ah, his letters! Do you tell me his name?'

'I do not.'

'Then I'll find it myself.' His eye had fallen upon a small desk that stood near, on which she was accustomed to write her letters. He went to it. It was locked.

'Unlock this!'

'You have no right to say it. That's mine.'

Without another word he seized the desk and dashed it to the floor. The hinge burst open, and a number of letters tumbled out.

'Stay!' said Eustacia, stepping before him with more excitement than she had hitherto shown.

'Come, come! stand away! I must see them.'

She looked at the letters as they lay, checked her feeling, and moved indifferently aside; when he gathered them up, and examined them.

By no stretch of meaning could any but a harmless construction be placed upon a single one of the letters themselves. The solitary exception was an empty envelope directed to her, and the handwriting was Wildeve's. Yeobright held it up. Eustacia was doggedly silent.

'Can you read, madam? Look at this envelope. Doubtless we shall find more soon, and what was inside them. I shall no doubt be gratified by learning in good time what a well-finished and full-blown adept in a certain trade my lady is.'

'Do you say it to me – do you?' she gasped.

He searched further, but found nothing more. 'What was in the letter?' he said.

'Ask the writer. Am I your hound that you should talk to me in this way?'

'Do you brave me? do you stand me out, mistress? Answer. Don't look at me with those eyes as if you would bewitch me again! Sooner than that I die. You refuse to answer?'

'I wouldn't tell you after this, if I were as innocent as the sweetest babe in heaven!'

'Which you are not.'

'Certainly I am not absolutely,' she replied. 'I have not done what you suppose; but if to have done no harm at all is the only innocence recognized, I am beyond forgiveness. But I require no help from your conscience.'

'You can resist, and resist again! Instead of hating you I could, I think, mourn for and pity you, if you were contrite, and would confess all. Forgive you I never can. I don't speak of your lover – I will give you the benefit of the doubt in that matter, for it only affects me personally. But the other: had you half-killed *me*, had it been that you wilfully took the sight away from these feeble eyes of mine, I could have forgiven you. But *that's* too much for nature!'

'Say no more. I will do without your pity. But I would have saved you from uttering what you will regret.'

'I am going away now. I shall leave you.'

'You need not go, as I am going myself. You will keep just as far away from me by staying here.'

'Call her to mind – think of her – what goodness there was in her: it showed in every line of her face! Most women, even when but slightly annoyed, show a flicker of evil in some curl of the mouth or some corner of the cheek; but as for her, never in her angriest moments was there anything malicious in her look. She was angered quickly, but she forgave just as readily, and underneath her pride there was the meekness of a child. What came of it? – what cared you? You hated her just as she was learning to love you. O! couldn't you see what was best for you, but must bring a curse upon me, and agony and death upon her, by doing that cruel deed! What was the fellow's name who was keeping you company and causing you to add cruelty to her to your wrong to me? Was it Wildeve? Was it poor Thomasin's husband? Heaven, what wickedness! Lost your voice, have you? It is natural after detection of that most noble trick . . . Eustacia, didn't any tender thought of your own mother lead you to think of being gentle to mine at such a time of weariness? Did not one grain of pity enter your heart as she turned away? Think what a vast opportunity was then lost of beginning a forgiving and honest course. Why did not you kick him out, and let her in, and say, I'll be an honest wife and a noble woman from this hour? Had I told you to go and quench eternally our last flickering chance of happiness here you could have done no worse. Well, she's asleep now; and have you a hundred gallants, neither they nor you can insult her any more.'

'You exaggerate fearfully,' she said in a faint, weary voice; 'but I cannot enter into my defence – it is not worth doing. You are nothing to me in future, and the past side of the story may as well remain untold. I have lost all through you, but I have not complained. Your blunders and misfortunes may have been a sorrow to you, but they have been a wrong to me. All persons of refinement have been scared away from me since I sank into the mire of marriage. Is this your cherishing – to put me into a hut like this, and keep me like the wife of a hind? You deceived me – not by words, but by appearances, which are less seen through than words. But the place will serve as well as any other – as somewhere to pass from – into my grave.' Her words were smothered in her throat, and her head drooped down.

'I don't know what you mean by that. Am I the cause of your sin?' (Eustacia made a trembling motion towards him.) 'What, you can begin to shed tears and offer me your hand? Good God! can you? No, not I. I'll not commit the fault of taking that.' (The hand she had offered dropped nervelessly, but the tears continued flowing.) 'Well, yes, I'll take it, if only for the sake of my own foolish kisses that were wasted there before I knew what I cherished. How bewitched I was! How could there be any good in a woman that everybody spoke ill of?'

'O, O, O!' she cried, breaking down at last; and, shaking with sobs which choked her, she sank upon her knees. 'O, will you have done! O, you are too relentless – there's a limit to the cruelty of savages! I have held out long – but you crush me down. I beg for mercy – I cannot bear this any longer – it is inhuman to go further with this! If I had – killed your – mother with my own hand – I should not deserve such a scourging to the bone as this. O, O! God have mercy upon a miserable woman! . . . You have beaten me in this game – I beg you to stay your hand in pity! . . . I confess that I – wilfully did not undo the door the first time she knocked – but – I – should have unfastened it the second – if I had not thought you had gone to do it yourself. When I found you had not I opened it, but she was gone. That's the extent of my crime – towards *her*. Best natures commit bad faults sometimes, don't they? – I think they do. Now I will leave you – for ever and ever!'

'Tell all, and I *will* pity you. Was the man in the house with you Wildeve?'

'I cannot tell,' she said desperately through her sobbing. 'Don't insist further – I cannot tell. I am going from this house. We cannot both stay here.'

'You need not go: I will go. You can stay here.'

'No, I will dress, and then I will go.'

'Where?'

'Where I came from, or *else*where.'

She hastily dressed herself, Yeobright moodily walking up and down the room the whole of the time. At last all her things were on. Her little hands quivered so violently as she held them to her chin to fasten her bonnet that she could not tie the strings, and after a few moments she relinquished the attempt. Seeing this he moved forward and said, 'Let me tie them.'

She assented in silence, and lifted her chin. For once at least in her life she was totally oblivious of the charm of her attitude. But he was not, and he turned his eyes aside, that he might not be tempted to softness.

The strings were tied; she turned from him. 'Do you still prefer going away yourself to my leaving you?' he inquired again.

'I do.'

'Very well – let it be. And when you will confess to the man I may pity you.'

She flung her shawl about her and went downstairs, leaving him standing in the room.

Eustacia had not long been gone when there came a knock at the door of the bedroom; and Yeobright said, 'Well?'

It was the servant; and she replied, 'Somebody from Mrs Wildeve's have called to tell 'ee that the mis'ess and the baby are getting on wonderful well, and the baby's name is to be Eustacia Clementine.' And the girl retired.

'What a mockery!' said Clym. 'This unhappy marriage of mine to be perpetuated in that child's name!'

* IV *

The Ministrations of a Half-Forgotten One

EUSTACIA's journey was at first as vague in direction as that of thistledown
on the wind. She did not know what to do. She wished it had been night
instead of morning, that she might at least have borne her misery without
the possibility of being seen. Tracing mile after mile along between the
dying ferns and the wet white spiders' webs, she at length turned her
steps towards her grandfather's house. She found the front door closed
and locked. Mechanically she went round to the end where the stable
was, and on looking in at the stable-door she saw Charley standing
within.

'Captain Vye is not at home?' she said.

'No, ma'am,' said the lad in a flutter of feeling; 'he's gone to
Weatherbury, and won't be home till night. And the servant is gone
home for a holiday. So the house is locked up.'

Eustacia's face was not visible to Charley as she stood at the doorway,
her back being to the sky, and the stable but indifferently lighted; but the
wildness of her manner arrested his attention. She turned and walked
away across the enclosure to the gate, and was hidden by the bank.

When she had disappeared Charley, with misgiving in his eyes, slowly
came from the stable-door, and going to another point in the bank he
looked over. Eustacia was leaning against it on the outside, her face
covered with her hands, and her head pressing the dewy heather which
bearded the bank's outer side. She appeared to be utterly indifferent to the
circumstance that her bonnet, hair, and garments were becoming wet and
disarranged by the moisture of her cold, harsh pillow. Clearly something
was wrong.

Charley had always regarded Eustacia as Eustacia had regarded Clym
when she first beheld him – as a romantic and sweet vision, scarcely
incarnate. He had been so shut off from her by the dignity of her look and
the pride of her speech, except at that one blissful interval when he was
allowed to hold her hand, that he had hardly deemed her a woman,
wingless and earthly, subject to household conditions and domestic jars.
The inner details of her life he had only conjectured. She had been a
lovely wonder, predestined to an orbit in which the whole of his own was
but a point; and this sight of her leaning like a helpless, despairing
creature against a wild wet bank, filled him with an amazed horror. He
could no longer remain where he was. Leaping over, he came up, touched
her with his finger, and said tenderly, 'You are poorly, ma'am. What can
I do?'

Eustacia started up, and said, 'Ah, Charley – you have followed me.
You did not think when I left home in the summer that I should come
back like this!'

'I did not, dear ma'am. Can I help you now?'

'I am afraid not. I wish I could get into the house. I feel giddy – that's all.'

'Lean on my arm, ma'am, till we get to the porch; and I will try to open the door.'

He supported her to the porch, and there depositing her on a seat hastened to the back, climbed to a window by the help of a ladder, and descending inside opened the door. Next he assisted her into the room, where there was an old-fashioned horsehair settee as large as a donkey-waggon. She lay down here, and Charley covered her with a cloak he found in the hall.

'Shall I get you something to eat and drink?' he said.

'If you please, Charley. But I suppose there is no fire?'

'I can light it, ma'am.'

He vanished, and she heard a splitting of wood and a blowing of bellows; and presently he returned, saying, 'I have lighted a fire in the kitchen, and now I'll light one here.'

He lit the fire, Eustacia dreamily observing him from her couch. When it was blazing up he said, 'Shall I wheel you round in front of it, ma'am, as the morning is chilly?'

'Yes, if you like.'

'Shall I go and bring the victuals now?'

'Yes, do,' she murmured languidly.

When he had gone, and the dull sounds occasionally reached her ears of his movements in the kitchen, she forgot where she was, and had for a moment to consider by an effort what the sounds meant. After an interval which seemed short to her whose thoughts were elsewhere, he came in with a tray on which steamed tea and toast, though it was nearly lunchtime.

'Place it on the table,' she said. 'I shall be ready soon.'

He did so, and retired to the door: when, however, he perceived that she did not move he came back a few steps.

'Let me hold it to you, if you don't wish to get up,' said Charley. He brought the tray to the front of the couch, where he knelt down, adding, 'I will hold it for you.'

Eustacia sat up and poured out a cup of tea. 'You are very kind to me, Charley,' she murmured as she sipped.

'Well, I ought to be,' said he diffidently, taking great trouble not to rest his eyes upon her, though this was their only natural position, Eustacia being immediately before him. 'You have been kind to me.'

'How have I?' said Eustacia.

'You let me hold your hand when you were a maiden at home.'

'Ah, so I did. Why did I do that? My mind is lost – it had to do with the mumming, had it not?'

'Yes, you wanted to go in my place.'

'I remember. I do indeed remember – too well!'

She again became utterly downcast; and Charley, seeing that she was not going to eat or drink any more, took away the tray.

Afterwards he occasionally came in to see if the fire was burning, to ask her if she wanted anything, to tell her that the wind had shifted from south to west, to ask her if she would like him to gather her some blackberries; to all which inquiries she replied in the negative or with indifference.

She remained on the settee some time longer, when she aroused herself and went upstairs. The room in which she had formerly slept still remained much as she had left it, and the recollection this forced upon her of her own greatly changed and infinitely worsened situation again set on her face the undetermined and formless misery which it had worn on her first arrival. She peeped into her grandfather's room, through which the fresh autumn air was blowing from the open window. Her eye was arrested by what was a familiar sight enough, though it broke upon her now with a new significance.

It was a brace of pistols, hanging near the head of her grandfather's bed, which he always kept there loaded, as a precaution against possible burglars, the house being very lonely. Eustacia regarded them long, as if they were the page of a book in which she read a new and strange matter. Quickly, like one afraid of herself, she returned downstairs and stood in deep thought.

'If I could only do it!' she said. 'It would be doing much good to myself and all connected with me, and no harm to a single one.'

The idea seemed to gather force within her, and she remained in a fixed attitude nearly ten minutes, when a certain finality was expressed in her gaze, and no longer the blankness of indecision.

She turned and went up the second time – softly and stealthily now – and entered her grandfather's room, her eyes at once seeking the head of the bed. The pistols were gone.

The instant quashing of her purpose by their absence affected her brain as a sudden vacuum affects the body: she nearly fainted. Who had done this? There was only one person on the premises besides herself. Eustacia involuntarily turned to the open window which overlooked the garden as far as the bank that bounded it. On the summit of the latter stood Charley, sufficiently elevated by its height to see into the room. His gaze was directed eagerly and solicitously upon her.

She went down downstairs to the door and beckoned to him.

'You have taken them away?'

'Yes, ma'am.'

'Why did you do it?'

'I saw you looking at them too long.'

'What has that to do with it?'

'You have been heart-broken all the morning, as if you did not want to live.'

'Well?'

'And I could not bear to leave them in your way. There was meaning in your look at them.'

'Where are they now?'

'Locked up.'

'Where?'

'In the stable.'

'Give them to me.'

'No, ma'am.'

'You refuse?'

'I do. I care too much for you to give 'em up.'

She turned aside, her face for the first time softening from the stony immobility of the earlier day, and the corners of her mouth resuming something of that delicacy of cut which was always lost in her moments of despair. At last she confronted him again.

'Why should I not die if I wish?' she said tremulously. 'I have made a bad bargain with life, and I am weary of it – weary. And now you have hindered my escape. O, why did you, Charley! What makes death painful except the thought of others' grief? – and that is absent in my case, for not a sigh would follow me!'

'Ah, it is trouble that has done this! I wish in my very soul that he who brought it about might die and rot, even if 'tis transportation to say it!'

'Charley, no more of that. What do you mean to do about this you have seen?'

'Keep it close as night, if you promise not to think of it again.'

'You need not fear. The moment has passed. I promise.' She then went away, entered the house, and lay down.

Later in the afternoon her grandfather returned. He was about to question her categorically; but on looking at her he withheld his words.

'Yes, it is too bad to talk of,' she slowly returned in answer to his glance. 'Can my old room be got ready for me tonight, grandfather? I shall want to occupy it again.'

He did not ask what it all meant, or why she had left her husband, but ordered the room to be prepared.

V

An Old Move Inadvertently Repeated

CHARLEY'S attentions to his former mistress were unbounded. The only solace to his own trouble lay in his attempts to relieve hers. Hour after hour he considered her wants: he thought of her presence there with a sort of gratitude, and, while uttering imprecations on the cause of her unhappiness, in some measure blessed the result. Perhaps she would always remain there, he thought, and then he would be as happy as he had been before. His dread was lest she should think fit to return to Alderworth, and in that dread his eyes, with all the inquisitiveness of affection, frequently sought her face when she was not observing him, as he would have watched the head of a stockdove to learn if it contemplated flight. Having once really succoured her, and possibly preserved her from the rashest of acts, he mentally assumed in addition a guardian's responsibility for her welfare.

For this reason he busily endeavoured to provide her with pleasant distractions, bringing home curious objects which he found in the heath, such as white trumpet-shaped mosses, red-headed lichens, stone arrow-heads used by the old tribes on Egdon, and faceted crystals from the hollows of flints. These he deposited on the premises in such positions that she should see them as if by accident.

A week passed, Eustacia never going out of the house. Then she walked into the enclosed plot and looked through her grandfather's spy-glass, as she had been in the habit of doing before her marriage. One day she saw, at a place where the high-road crossed the distant valley, a heavily laden waggon passing along. It was piled with household furniture. She looked again and again, and recognized it to be her own. In the evening her grandfather came indoors with a rumour that Yeobright had removed that day from Alderworth to the old house at Blooms-End.

On another occasion when reconnoitring thus she beheld two female figures walking in the vale. The day was fine and clear; and the persons not being more than half a mile off she could see their every detail with the telescope. The woman walking in front carried a white bundle in her arms, from one end of which hung a long appendage of drapery; and when the walkers turned, so that the sun fell more directly upon them, Eustacia could see that the object was a baby. She called Charley, and asked him if he knew who they were, though she well guessed.

'Mrs Wildeve and the nurse-girl,' said Charley.

'The nurse is carrying the baby?' said Eustacia.

'No, 'tis Mrs Wildeve carrying that,' he answered, 'and the nurse walks behind carrying nothing.'

The lad was in good spirits that day, for the fifth of November had again come round, and he was planning yet another scheme to divert her from her too absorbing thoughts. For two successive years his mistress had seemed to take pleasure in lighting a bonfire on the bank overlooking the valley; but this year she had apparently quite forgotten the day and the customary deed. He was careful not to remind her, and went on with his secret preparations for a cheerful surprise, the more zealously that he had been absent last time and unable to assist. At every vacant minute he hastened to gather furze-stumps, thorn-tree roots, and other solid materials from the adjacent slopes, hiding them from cursory view.

The evening came, and Eustacia was still seemingly unconscious of the anniversary. She had gone indoors after her survey through the glass, and had not been visible since. As soon as it was quite dark Charley began to build the bonfire, choosing precisely that spot on the bank which Eustacia had chosen at previous times.

When all the surrounding bonfires had burst into existence Charley kindled his, and arranged its fuel so that it should not require tending for some time. He then went back to the house, and lingered round the door and windows till she should by some means or other learn of his achievement and come out to witness it. But the shutters were closed, the door remained shut, and no heed whatever seemed to be taken of his performance. Not liking to call her he went back and replenished the fire, continuing to do this for more than half an hour. It was not till his stock of fuel had greatly diminished that he went to the back door and sent in to beg that Mrs Yeobright would open the window-shutters and see the sight outside.

Eustacia, who had been sitting listlessly in the parlour, started up at the intelligence and flung open the shutters. Facing her on the bank blazed the fire, which at once sent a ruddy glare into the room where she was, and overpowered the candles.

'Well done, Charley!' said Captain Vye from the chimney-corner. 'But I hope it is not my wood that he's burning . . . Ah, it was this time last year that I met with that man Venn, bringing home Thomasin Yeobright – to be sure it was! Well, who would have thought that girl's troubles would have ended so well? What a snipe you were in that matter, Eustacia! Has your husband written to you yet?'

'No,' said Eustacia, looking vaguely through the window at the fire, which just then so much engaged her mind that she did not resent her grandfather's blunt opinion. She could see Charley's form on the bank, shovelling and stirring the fire; and there flashed upon her imagination some other form which that fire might call up.

She left the room, put on her garden-bonnet and cloak, and went out. Reaching the bank she looked over with a wild curiosity and misgiving, when Charley said to her, with a pleased sense of himself, 'I made it o' purpose for you, ma'am.'

'Thank you,' she said hastily. 'But I wish you to put it out now.'

'It will soon burn down,' said Charley, rather disappointed. 'Is it not a pity to knock it out?'

'I don't know,' she musingly answered.

They stood in silence, broken only by the crackling of the flames, till Charley, perceiving that she did not want to talk to him, moved reluctantly away.

Eustacia remained within the bank looking at the fire, intending to go indoors, yet lingering still. Had she not by her situation been inclined to hold in indifference all things honoured of the gods and of men she would probably have come away. But her state was so hopeless that she could play with it. To have lost is less disturbing than to wonder if we may possibly have won: and Eustacia could now, like other people at such a stage, take a standing-point outside herself, observe herself as a disinterested spectator, and think what a sport for Heaven this woman Eustacia was.

While she stood she heard a sound. It was the splash of a stone in the pond.

Had Eustacia received the stone full in the bosom her heart could not have given a more decided thump. She had thought of the possibility of such a signal in answer to that which had been unwittingly given by Charley; but she had not expected it yet. How prompt Wildeve was! Yet how could he think her capable of deliberately wishing to renew their assignations now? An impulse to leave the spot, a desire to stay, struggled within her; and the desire held its own. More than that it did not do, for she refrained even from ascending the bank and looking over. She remained motionless, not disturbing a muscle of her face or raising her eyes; for were she to turn up her face the fire on the bank would shine upon it, and Wildeve might be looking down.

There was a second splash into the pond.

Why did he stay so long without advancing and looking over? Curiosity had its way: she ascended one or two of the earth-steps in the bank and glanced out.

Wildeve was before her. He had come forward after throwing the last pebble, and the fire now shone into each of their faces from the bank stretching breast-high between them.

'I did not light it!' cried Eustacia quickly. 'It was lit without my knowledge. Don't, don't come over to me!'

'Why have you been living here all these days without telling me? You have left your home. I fear I am something to blame for this?'

'I did not let in his mother; that's how it is!'

'You do not deserve what you have got, Eustacia; you are in great misery; I see it in your eyes, your mouth, and all over you. My poor, poor girl!' He stepped over the bank. 'You are beyond everything unhappy!'

'No, no; not exactly –'

'It has been pushed too far – it is killing you: I do think it!'

Her usually quiet breathing had grown quicker with his words. 'I – I –' she began, and then burst into quivering sobs, shaken to the very heart by the unexpected voice of pity – a sentiment whose existence in relation to herself she had almost forgotten.

This outbreak of weeping took Eustacia herself so much by surprise that she could not leave off, and she turned aside from him in some shame, though turning hid nothing from him. She sobbed on desperately; then the outpour lessened, and she became quieter. Wildeve had resisted the impulse to clasp her, and stood without speaking.

'Are you not ashamed of me, who used never to be a crying animal?' she asked in a weak whisper as she wiped her eyes. 'Why didn't you go away? I wish you had not seen quite all that; it reveals too much by half.'

'You might have wished it, because it makes me as sad as you,' he said with emotion and deference. 'As for revealing – the word is impossible between us two.'

'I did not send for you – don't forget it, Damon; I am in pain, but I did not send for you! As a wife, at least, I've been straight.'

'Never mind – I came. O, Eustacia, forgive me for the harm I have done you in these two past years! I see more and more that I have been your ruin.'

'Not you. This place I live in.'

'Ah, your generosity may naturally make you say that. But I am the culprit. I should either have done more or nothing at all.'

'In what way?'

'I ought never to have hunted you out; or, having done it, I ought to have persisted in retaining you. But of course I have no right to talk of that now. I will only ask this: can I do anything for you? Is there anything on the face of the earth that a man can do to make you happier than you are at present? If there is, I will do it. You may command me, Eustacia, to the limit of my influence; and don't forget that I am richer now. Surely something can be done to save you from this! Such a rare plant in such a wild place it grieves me to see. Do you want anything bought? Do you want to go anywhere? Do you want to escape the place altogether? Only say it, and I'll do anything to put an end to those tears, which but for me would never have been at all.'

'We are each married to another person,' she said faintly; 'and assistance from you would have an evil sound – after – after –'

'Well, there's no preventing slanderers from having their fill at any time; but you need not be afraid. Whatever I may feel I promise you on my word of honour never to speak to you about – or act upon – until you say I may. I know my duty to Thomasin quite as well as I know my duty to you as a woman unfairly treated. What shall I assist you in?'

'In getting away from here.'

'Where do you wish to go to?'

'I have a place in my mind. If you could help me as far as Budmouth I can do all the rest. Steamers sail from there across the Channel, and so I can get to Paris, where I want to be. Yes,' she pleaded earnestly, 'help me to get to Budmouth harbour without my grandfather's or my husband's knowledge, and I can do all the rest.'

'Will it be safe to leave you there alone?'

'Yes, yes. I know Budmouth well.'

'Shall I go with you? I am rich now.'

She was silent.

'Say yes, sweet!'

She was silent still.

'Well, let me know when you wish to go. We shall be at our present house till December; after that we remove to Casterbridge. Command me in anything till that time.'

'I will think of this,' she said hurriedly. 'Whether I can honestly make use of you as a friend, or must close with you as a lover – that is what I must ask myself. If I wish to go and decide to accept your company I will signal to you some evening at eight o'clock punctually, and this will mean that you are to be ready with a horse and trap at twelve o'clock the same night to drive me to Budmouth harbour in time for the morning boat.'

'I will look out every night at eight, and no signal shall escape me.'

'Now please go away. If I decide on this escape I can only meet you once more unless – I cannot go without you. Go – I cannot bear it longer. Go – go!'

Wildeve slowly went up the steps and descended into the darkness on the other side; and as he walked he glanced back, till the bank blotted out her form from his further view.

* VI *

Thomasin Argues with her Cousin, and He Writes a Letter

YEOBRIGHT was at this time at Blooms-End hoping that Eustacia would return to him. The removal of furniture had been accomplished only that day, though Clym had lived in the old house for more than a week. He had spent the time in working about the premises, sweeping leaves from the garden-paths, cutting dead stalks from the flower-beds, and nailing up creepers which had been displaced by the autumn winds. He took no particular pleasure in these deeds, but they formed a screen between himself and despair. Moreover, it had become a religion with him to preserve in good condition all that had lapsed from his mother's hands to his own.

During these operations he was constantly on the watch for Eustacia. That there should be no mistake about her knowing where to find him he had ordered a notice-board to be affixed to the garden gate at Alderworth, signifying in white letters whither he had removed. When a leaf floated to the earth he turned his head, thinking it might be her footfall. A bird searching for worms in the mould of the flower-beds sounded like her hand on the latch of the gate; and at dusk, when soft, strange ventrilo-quisms came from holes in the ground, hollow stalks, curled dead leaves, and other crannies whereon breezes, worms, and insects can work their will, he fancied that they were Eustacia, standing without and breathing wishes of reconciliation.

Up to this hour he had persevered in his resolve not to invite her back. At the same time the severity with which he had treated her lulled the sharpness of his regret for his mother, and awoke some of his old solicitude for his mother's supplanter. Harsh feelings produce harsh usage, and this by reaction quenches the sentiments that gave it birth. The more he reflected the more he softened. But to look upon his wife as innocence in distress was impossible, though he could ask himself whether he had given her quite time enough – if he had not come a little too suddenly upon her on that sombre morning.

Now that the first flush of his anger had paled he was disinclined to ascribe to her more than an indiscreet friendship with Wildeve, for there had not appeared in her manner the signs of dishonour. And this once admitted, an absolutely dark interpretation of her act towards his mother was no longer forced upon him.

On the evening of the fifth November his thoughts of Eustacia were intense. Echoes from those past times when they had exchanged tender words all day long came like the diffused murmur of a seashore left miles behind. 'Surely,' he said, 'she might have brought herself to communicate with me before now, and confess honestly what Wildeve was to her.'

Instead of remaining at home that night he determined to go and see Thomasin and her husband. If he found opportunity he would allude to the cause of the separation between Eustacia and himself, keeping silence, however, on the fact that there was a third person in his house when his mother was turned away. If it proved that Wildeve was innocently there he would doubtlessly openly mention it. If he were there with unjust intentions Wildeve, being a man of quick feeling, might possibly say something to reveal the extent to which Eustacia was compromised.

But on reaching his cousin's house he found that only Thomasin was at home, Wildeve being at that time on his way towards the bonfire innocently lit by Charley at Mistover. Thomasin then, as always, was glad to see Clym, and took him to inspect the sleeping baby, carefully screening the candlelight from the infant's eyes with her hand.

'Tamsin, have you heard that Eustacia is not with me now?' he said when they had sat down again.

'No,' said Thomasin, alarmed.

'And not that I have left Alderworth?'

'No. I never hear tidings from Alderworth unless you bring them. What is the matter?'

Clym in a disturbed voice related to her his visit to Susan Nunsuch's boy, the revelation he had made, and what had resulted from his charging Eustacia with having wilfully and heartlessly done the deed. He suppressed all mention of Wildeve's presence with her.

'All this, and I not knowing it!' murmured Thomasin in an awestruck tone. 'Terrible! What could have made her – O, Eustacia! And when you found it out you went in hot haste to her? Were you too cruel? – or is she really so wicked as she seems?'

'Can a man be too cruel to his mother's enemy?'

'I can fancy so.'

'Very well, then – I'll admit that he can. But now what is to be done?'

'Make it up again – if a quarrel so deadly can ever be made up. I almost wish you had not told me. But do try to be reconciled. There are ways, after all, if you both wish to.'

'I don't know that we do both wish to make it up,' said Clym. 'If she had wished it, would she not have sent to me by this time?'

'You seem to wish to, and yet you have not sent to her.'

'True; but I have been tossed to and fro in doubt if I ought, after such strong provocation. To see me now, Thomasin, gives you no idea of what I have been; of what depths I have descended to in these few last days. O, it was a bitter shame to shut out my mother like that! Can I ever forget it, or even agree to see her again?'

'She might not have known that anything serious would come of it, and perhaps she did not mean to keep aunt out altogether.'

'She says herself that she did not. But the fact remains that keep her out she did.'

'Believe her sorry, and send for her.'

'How if she will not come?'

'It will prove her guilty, by showing that it is her habit to nourish enmity. But I do not think that for a moment.'

'I will do this. I will wait for a day or two longer – not longer than two days certainly; and if she does not send to me in that time I will indeed send to her. I thought to have seen Wildeve here tonight. Is he from home?'

Thomasin blushed a little. 'No,' she said. 'He is merely gone out for a walk.'

'Why didn't he take you with him? The evening is fine. You want fresh air as well as he.'

'Oh, I don't care for going anywhere; besides, there is baby.'

'Yes, yes. Well, I have been thinking whether I should not consult your husband about this as well as you,' said Clym steadily.

'I fancy I would not,' she quickly answered. 'It can do no good.'

Her cousin looked her in the face. No doubt Thomasin was ignorant that her husband had any share in the events of that tragic afternoon; but her countenance seemed to signify that she concealed some suspicion or thought of the reputed tender relations between Wildeve and Eustacia in days gone by.

Clym, however, could make nothing of it, and he rose to depart, more in doubt than when he came.

'You will write to her in a day or two?' said the young woman earnestly. 'I do so hope the wretched separation may come to end.'

'I will,' said Clym; 'I don't rejoice in my present state at all.'

And he left her and climbed over the hill to Blooms-End. Before going to bed he sat down and wrote the following letter:

MY DEAR EUSTACIA, – I must obey my heart without consulting my reason too closely. Will you come back to me? Do so, and the past shall never be mentioned. I was too severe; but O, Eustacia, the provocation! You don't know, you never will know, what those words of anger cost me which you drew down upon yourself. All that an honest man can promise you I promise now, which is that from me you shall never suffer anything on this score again. After all the vows we have made, Eustacia, I think we had better pass the remainder of our lives in trying to keep them. Come to me, then, even if you reproach me. I have thought of your sufferings that morning on which I parted from you; I know they were genuine, and they are as much as you ought to bear. Our love must still continue. Such hearts as ours would never have been given us but to be concerned with each other. I could not ask you back at first, Eustacia, for I was unable to persuade myself that he who was with you was not there as a lover. But if you will come and explain distracting appearances I do not question that you can show your honesty to me. Why have you not come before? Do you think I will not listen to you? Surely not, when you remember the kisses and vows we exchanged under the summer moon. Return then, and you shall be warmly welcomed. I can no longer think of you to your prejudice – I am but too much absorbed in justifying you. – Your husband as ever,

CLYM

'There,' he said, as he laid it in his desk, 'that's a good thing done. If she does not come before tomorrow night I will send it to her.'

Meanwhile, at the house he had just left Thomasin sat sighing uneasily. Fidelity to her husband had that evening induced her to conceal all suspicion that Wildeve's interest in Eustacia had not ended with his marriage. But she knew nothing positive; and though Clym was her well-beloved cousin there was one nearer to her still.

When a little later, Wildeve returned from his walk to Mistover, Thomasin said, 'Damon, where have you been? I was getting quite frightened, and thought you had fallen into the river. I dislike being in the house by myself.'

'Frightened?' he said, touching her cheek as if she were some domestic animal. 'Why, I thought nothing could frighten you. It is that you are getting proud, I am sure, and don't like living here since we have risen above our business. Well, it is a tedious matter, this getting a new house; but I couldn't have set about it sooner, unless our ten thousand pounds had been a hundred thousand, when we could have afforded to despise caution.'

'No – I don't mind waiting – I would rather stay here twelve months longer than run any risk with baby. But I don't like your vanishing so in the evenings. There's something on your mind – I know there is, Damon.

You go about so gloomily, and look at the heath as if it were somebody's gaol instead of a nice wild place to walk in.'

He looked towards her with pitying surprise. 'What, do you like Egdon Heath?' he said.

'I like what I was born near to; I admire its grim old face.'

'Pooh, my dear. You don't know what you like.'

'I am sure I do. There's only one thing unpleasant about Egdon.'

'What's that?'

'You never take me with you when you walk there. Why do you wander so much in it yourself if you so dislike it?'

The inquiry, though a simple one, was plainly disconcerting, and he sat down before replying. 'I don't think you often see me there. Give an instance.'

'I will,' she answered triumphantly. 'When you went out this evening I thought that as baby was asleep I would see where you were going to so mysteriously without telling me. So I ran out and followed behind you. You stopped at the place where the road forks, looked round at the bonfires, and then said, "Damn it, I'll go!" And you went quickly up the left-hand road. Then I stood and watched you.'

Wildeve frowned, afterwards saying, with a forced smile, 'Well, what wonderful discovery did you make?'

'There – now you are angry, and we won't talk of this any more.' She went across to him, sat on a footstool, and looked up in his face.

'Nonsense!' he said; 'that's how you always back out. We will go on with it now we have begun. What did you next see? I particularly want to know.'

'Don't be like that, Damon!' she murmured. 'I didn't see anything. You vanished out of sight, and then I looked round at the bonfires and came in.'

'Perhaps this is not the only time you have dogged my steps. Are you trying to find out something bad about me?'

'Not at all! I have never done such a thing before, and I shouldn't have done it now if words had not sometimes been dropped about you.'

'What *do* you mean?' he impatiently asked.

'They say – they say you used to go to Alderworth in the evenings, and it puts into my mind what I have heard about –'

Wildeve turned angrily and stood up in front of her. 'Now,' he said, flourishing his hand in the air, 'just out with it, madam! I demand to know what remarks you have heard.'

'Well, I heard that you used to be very fond of Eustacia – nothing more than that, though dropped in a bit-by-bit way. You ought not to be angry!'

He observed that her eyes were brimming with tears. 'Well,' he said, 'there is nothing new in that, and of course I don't mean to be rough towards you, so you need not cry. Now, don't let us speak of the subject any more.'

And no more was said, Thomasin being glad enough of a reason for not mentioning Clym's visit to her that evening, and his story.

* VII *

The Night of the Sixth of November

HAVING resolved on flight Eustacia at times seemed anxious that something should happen to thwart her own intention. The only event that could really change her position was the appearance of Clym. The glory which had encircled him as her lover was departed now; yet some good simple quality of his would occasionally return to her memory and stir a momentary throb of hope that he would again present himself before her. But calmly considered it was not likely that such a severance as now existed would ever close up: she would have to live on as a painful object, isolated, and out of place. She had used to think of the heath alone as an uncongenial spot to be in; she felt it now of the whole world.

Towards evening on the sixth her determination to go away again revived. About four o'clock she packed up anew the few small articles she had brought in her flight from Alderworth, and also some belonging to her which had been left here: the whole formed a bundle not too large to be carried in her hand for a distance of a mile or two. The scene without grew darker; mud-coloured clouds bellied downwards from the sky like vast hammocks slung across it, and with the increase of night a stormy wind arose; but as yet there was no rain.

Eustacia could not rest indoors, having nothing more to do, and she wandered to and fro on the hill, not far from the house she was soon to leave. In these desultory ramblings she passed the cottage of Susan Nunsuch, a little lower down than her grandfather's. The door was ajar, and a riband of bright firelight fell over the ground without. As Eustacia crossed the firebeams she appeared for an instant as distinct as a figure in a phantasmagoria – a creature of light surrounded by an area of darkness: the moment passed, and she was absorbed in night again.

A woman who was sitting inside the cottage had seen and recognized her in that momentary irradiation. This was Susan herself, occupied in preparing a posset for her little boy, who, often ailing, was now seriously unwell. Susan dropped the spoon, shook her fist at the vanished figure, and then proceeded with her work in a musing, absent way.

At eight o'clock, the hour at which Eustacia had promised to signal to

Wildeve if ever she signalled at all, she looked around the premises to learn if the coast was clear, went to the furze-rick, and pulled thence a long-stemmed bough of that fuel. This she carried to the corner of the bank, and, glancing behind to see if the shutters were all closed, she struck a light, and kindled the furze. When it was thoroughly ablaze Eustacia took it by the stem and waved it in the air above her head till it had burned itself out.

She was gratified, if gratification were possible to such a mood, by seeing a similar light in the vicinity of Wildeve's residence a minute or two later. Having agreed to keep watch at this hour every night, in case she should require assistance, this promptness proved how strictly he had held to his word. Four hours after the present time, that is, at midnight, he was to be ready to drive her to Budmouth, as prearranged.

Eustacia returned to the house. Supper having been got over she retired early, and sat in her bedroom waiting for the time to go by. The night being dark and threatening Captain Vye had not strolled out to gossip in any cottage or to call at the inn, as was sometimes his custom on these long autumn nights; and he sat sipping grog alone downstairs. About ten o'clock there was a knock at the door. When the servant opened it the rays of the candle fell upon the form of Fairway.

'I was a-forced to go to Lower Mistover tonight,' he said; 'and Mr Yeobright asked me to leave this here on my way; but, faith, I put it in the lining of my hat, and thought no more about it till I got back and was hasping my gate before going to bed. So I have run back with it at once.'

He handed a letter and went his way. The girl brought it to the captain, who found that it was directed to Eustacia. He turned it over and over, and fancied that the writing was her husband's, though he could not be sure. However, he decided to let her have it at once if possible, and took it up stairs for that purpose; but on reaching the door of her room and looking in at the keyhole he found there was no light within, the fact being that Eustacia, without undressing, had flung herself upon the bed, to rest and gather a little strength for her coming journey. Her grandfather concluded from what he saw that he ought not to disturb her; and descending again to the parlour he placed the letter on the mantelpiece to give it to her in the morning.

At eleven o'clock he went to bed himself, smoked for some time in his bedroom, put out his light at half-past eleven, and then, as was his invariable custom, pulled up the blind before getting into bed, that he might see which way the wind blew on opening his eyes in the morning, his bedroom window commanding a view of the flagstaff and vane. Just as he had lain down he was surprised to observe the white pole of the staff flash into existence like a streak of phosphorus drawn downwards across the shade of night without. Only one explanation met this – a light had been suddenly thrown upon the pole from the direction of the house. As everybody had retired to rest the old man felt it necessary to get out of bed, open the window softly, and look to the right and left. Eustacia's bedroom was lighted up, and it was the shine from her window which had lighted the pole. Wondering what had aroused her he remained undecided at the window, and was thinking of fetching the letter to slip it under her door, when he heard a slight brushing of garments on the partition dividing his room from the passage.

The captain concluded that Eustacia, feeling wakeful, had gone for a book, and would have dismissed the matter as unimportant if he had not also heard her distinctly weeping as she passed.

'She is thinking of that husband of hers,' he said to himself. 'Ah, the silly goose! she had no business to marry him. I wonder if that letter is really his?'

He arose, threw his boat-cloak round him, opened the door, and said, 'Eustacia!' There was no answer. 'Eustacia!' he repeated louder, 'there is a letter on the mantelpiece for you.'

But no response was made to this statement save an imaginary one from the wind, which seemed to gnaw at the corners of the house, and the stroke of a few drops of rain upon the windows.

He went on to the landing, and stood waiting nearly five minutes. Still she did not return. He went back for a light, and prepared to follow her; but first he looked into her bedroom. There, on the outside of the quilt, was the impression of her form, showing that the bed had not been opened; and, what was more significant, she had not taken her candlestick downstairs. He was now thoroughly alarmed; and hastily putting on his clothes he descended to the front door, which he himself had bolted and locked. It was now unfastened. There was no longer any doubt that Eustacia had left the house at this midnight hour; and whither could she have gone? To follow her was almost impossible. Had the dwelling stood in an ordinary road, two persons setting out, one in each direction, might have made sure of overtaking her; but it was a hopeless task to seek for anybody on a heath in the dark, the practicable directions for flight across it from any point being as numerous as the meridians radiating from the pole. Perplexed what to do he looked into the parlour, and was vexed to find that the letter still lay there untouched.

At half-past eleven, finding that the house was silent, Eustacia had lighted her candle, put on some warm outer wrappings, taken her bag in her hand, and, extinguishing the light again, descended the staircase. When she got into the outer air she found that it had begun to rain, and as she stood pausing at the door it increased, threatening to come on heavily. But having committed herself to this line of action there was no retreating for bad weather. Even the receipt of Clym's letter would not have stopped her now. The gloom of the night was funereal; all nature seemed clothed in crape. The spiky points of the fir trees behind the house rose into the sky like the turrets and pinnacles of an abbey. Nothing below the horizon was visible save a light which was still burning in the cottage of Susan Nunsuch.

Eustacia opened her umbrella and went out from the enclosure by the steps over the bank, after which she was beyond all danger of being perceived. Skirting the pool she followed the path towards Rainbarrow, occasionally stumbling over twisted furze-roots, tufts of rushes, or oozing lumps of fleshy fungi, which at this season lay scattered about the heath like the rotten liver and lungs of some colossal animal. The moon and stars were closed up by cloud and rain to the degree of extinction. It was a night which led the traveller's thoughts instinctively to dwell on nocturnal scenes of disaster in the chronicles of the world, on all that is terrible and dark in history and legend – the last plague of Egypt, the destruction of Sennacherib's host, the agony in Gethsemane.

Eustacia at length reached Rainbarrow, and stood still there to think. Never was harmony more perfect than that between the chaos of her mind and the chaos of the world without. A sudden recollection had flashed on her this moment: she had not money enough for undertaking a long journey. Amid the fluctuating sentiments of the day her unpractical mind had not dwelt on the necessity of being well-provided, and now that she thoroughly realized the conditions she sighed bitterly and ceased to stand erect, gradually crouching down under the umbrella as if she were drawn into the Barrow by a hand from beneath. Could it be that she was to remain a captive still? Money: she had never felt its value before. Even to efface herself from the country means were required. To ask Wildeve for pecuniary aid without allowing him to accompany her was impossible to a woman with a shadow of pride left in her: to fly as his mistress – and she knew that he loved her – was of the nature of humiliation.

Any one who had stood by now would have pitied her, not so much on account of her exposure to weather, and isolation from all of humanity except the mouldered remains inside the tumulus; but for that other form of misery which was denoted by the slightly rocking movement that her feelings imparted to her person. Extreme unhappiness weighed visibly upon her. Between the drippings of the rain from her umbrella to her mantle, from her mantle to the heather, from the heather to the earth, very similar sounds could be heard coming from her lips; and the tearfulness of the outer scene was repeated upon her face. The wings of her soul were broken by the cruel obstructiveness of all about her; and even had she seen herself in a promising way of getting to Budmouth, entering a steamer, and sailing to some opposite port, she would have been but little more buoyant, so fearfully malignant were other things. She uttered words aloud. When a woman in such a situation, neither old, deaf, crazed, nor whimsical, takes upon herself to sob and soliloquize aloud there is something grievous the matter.

'Can I go, can I go?' she moaned. 'He's not *great* enough for me to give myself to – he does not suffice for my desire! . . . If he had been a Saul or a Búonaparte – ah! But to break my marriage vow for him – it is too poor a luxury! . . . And I have no money to go alone! And if I could, what comfort to me? I must drag on next year, as I have dragged on this year, and the year after that as before. How I have tried and tried to be a splendid woman, and how destiny has been against me! . . . I do not

deserve my lot!' she cried in a frenzy of bitter revolt. 'O, the cruelty of
putting me into this ill-conceived world! I was capable of much; but I
have been injured and blighted and crushed by things beyond my control!
O, how hard it is of Heaven to devise such tortures for me, who have
done no harm to Heaven at all!'

The distant light which Eustacia had cursorily observed in leaving the
house came, as she had divined, from the cottage-window of Susan
Nunsuch. What Eustacia did not divine was the occupation of the woman
within at that moment. Susan's sight of her passing figure earlier in the
evening, not five minutes after the sick boy's exclamation, 'Mother, I do
feel so bad!' persuaded the matron that an evil influence was certainly
exercised by Eustacia's propinquity.

On this account Susan did not go to bed as soon as the evening's work
was over, as she would have done at ordinary times. To counteract the
malign spell which she imagined poor Eustacia to be working, the boy's
mother busied herself with a ghastly invention of superstition, calculated
to bring powerlessness, atrophy, and annihilation on any human being
against whom it was directed. It was a practice well known on Egdon at
that date, and one that is not quite extinct at the present day.

She passed with her candle into an inner room, where, among other
utensils, were two large brown pans, containing together perhaps a
hundredweight of liquid honey, the produce of the bees during the
foregoing summer. On a shelf over the pans was a smooth and solid
yellow mass of a hemispherical form, consisting of beeswax from the
same take of honey. Susan took down the lump, and, cutting off several
thin slices, heaped them in an iron ladle, with which she returned to the
living-room, and placed the vessel in the hot ashes of the fireplace. As
soon as the wax had softened to the plasticity of dough she kneaded the
pieces together. And now her face became more intent. She began
moulding the wax; and it was evident from her manner of manipulation
that she was endeavouring to give it some preconceived form. The form
was human.

By warming and kneading, cutting and twisting, dismembering and
re-joining the incipient image she had in about a quarter of an hour
produced a shape which tolerably well resembled a woman, and was
about six inches high. She laid it on the table to get cold and hard.
Meanwhile she took the candle and went upstairs to where the little boy
was lying.

'Did you notice, my dear, what Mrs Eustacia wore this afternoon
besides the dark dress?'

'A red ribbon round her neck.'

'Anything else?'

'No – except sandal-shoes.'

'A red ribbon and sandal-shoes,' she said to herself.

Mrs Nunsuch went and searched till she found a fragment of the
narrowest red ribbon, which she took downstairs and tied round the neck

of the image. Then fetching ink and a quill from the rickety bureau by the window, she blackened the feet of the image to the extent presumably covered by shoes; and on the instep of each foot marked cross-lines in the shape taken by the sandal-strings of those days. Finally she tied a bit of black thread round the upper part of the head, in faint resemblance to a snood worn for confining the hair.

Susan held the object at arm's length and contemplated it with a satisfaction in which there was no smile. To anybody acquainted with the inhabitants of Egdon Heath the image would have suggested Eustacia Yeobright.

From her work-basket in the window-seat the woman took a paper of pins, of the old long and yellow sort whose heads were disposed to come off at their first usage. These she began to thrust into the image in all directions, with apparently excruciating energy. Probably as many as fifty were thus inserted, some into the head of the wax model, some into the shoulders, some into the trunk, some upwards through the soles of the feet, till the figure was completely permeated with pins.

She turned to the fire. It had been of turf; and though the high heap of ashes which turf fires produce was somewhat dark and dead on the outside, upon raking it abroad with the shovel the inside of the mass showed a glow of red heat. She took a few pieces of fresh turf from the chimney-corner and built them together over the glow, upon which the fire brightened. Seizing with the tongs the image that she had made of Eustacia, she held it in the heat, and watched it as it began to waste slowly away. And while she stood thus engaged there came from between her lips a murmur of words.

It was a strange jargon – the Lord's Prayer repeated backwards – the incantation usual in proceedings for obtaining unhallowed assistance against an enemy. Susan uttered the lugubrious discourse three times slowly, and when it was completed the image had considerably diminished. As the wax dropped into the fire a long flame arose from the spot, and curling its tongue round the figure ate still further into its substance. A pin occasionally dropped with the wax, and the embers heated it red as it lay.

* VIII *

Rain, Darkness, and Anxious Wanderers

WHILE the effigy of Eustacia was melting to nothing, and the fair woman herself was standing on Rainbarrow, her soul in an abyss of desolation seldom plumbed by one so young, Yeobright sat lonely at Blooms-End. He had fulfilled his word to Thomasin by sending off Fairway with the letter to his wife, and now waited with increased impatience for some sound or signal of her return. Were Eustacia still at Mistover the very least he expected was that she would send him back a reply tonight by the same hand; though, to leave all to her inclination, he had cautioned Fairway not to ask for an answer. If one were handed to him he was to bring it immediately; if not, he was to go straight home without troubling to come round to Blooms-End again that night.

But secretly Clym had a more pleasing hope. Eustacia might possibly decline to use her pen – it was rather her way to work silently – and surprise him by appearing at his door. How fully her mind was made up to do otherwise he did not know.

To Clym's regret it began to rain and blow hard as the evening advanced. The wind rasped and scraped at the corners of the house, and filliped the eavesdroppings like peas against the panes. He walked restlessly about the untenanted rooms, stopping strange noises in windows and doors by jamming splinters of wood into the casements and crevices, and pressing together the lead-work of the quarries where it had become loosened from the glass. It was one of those nights when cracks in the walls of old churches widen, when ancient stains on the ceilings of decayed manor-houses are renewed and enlarged from the size of a man's hand to an area of many feet. The little gate in the palings before his dwelling continually opened and clicked together again, but when he looked out eagerly nobody was there; it was as if invisible shapes of the dead were passing in on their way to visit him.

Between ten and eleven o'clock, finding that neither Fairway nor anybody else came to him, he retired to rest, and despite his anxieties soon fell asleep. His sleep, however, was not very sound, by reason of the expectancy he had given way to, and he was easily awakened by a knocking which began at the door about an hour after. Clym arose and looked out of the window. Rain was still falling heavily, the whole expanse of heath before him emitting a subdued hiss under the downpour. It was too dark to see anything at all.

'Who's there?' he cried.

Light footsteps shifted their position in the porch, and he could just distinguish in a plaintive female voice the words, 'O Clym, come down and let me in!'

He flushed hot with agitation. 'Surely it is Eustacia!' he murmured. If so, she had indeed come to him unawares.

He hastily got a light, dressed himself, and went down. On his flinging open the door the rays of the candle fell upon a woman closely wrapped up, who at once came forward.

'Thomasin!' he exclaimed in an indescribable tone of disappointment. 'It is Thomasin, and on such a night as this! O, where is Eustacia?'

Thomasin it was, wet, frightened, and panting.

'Eustacia? I don't know, Clym; but I can think,' she said with much perturbation. 'Let me come in and rest – I will explain this. There is a great trouble brewing – my husband and Eustacia!'

'What, what?'

'I think my husband is going to leave me or do something dreadful – I don't know what – Clym, will you go and see? I have nobody to help me but you! Eustacia has not yet come home?'

'No.'

She went on breathlessly: 'Then they are going to run off together! He came indoors tonight about eight o'clock and said in an off-hand way, "Tamsie, I have just found that I must go a journey." "When?" I said. "Tonight," he said. "Where?" I asked him. "I cannot tell you at present," he said; "I shall be back again tomorrow." He then went and busied himself in looking up his things, and took no notice of me at all. I expected to see him start, but he did not, and then it came to be ten o'clock, when he said, "You had better go to bed." I didn't know what to do, and I went to bed. I believe he thought I fell asleep, for half an hour after that he came up and unlocked the oak chest we keep money in when we have much in the house and took out a roll of something which I believe was bank-notes, though I was not aware that he had 'em there. These he must have got from the bank when he went there the other day. What does he want bank-notes for, if he is only going off for a day? When he had gone down I thought of Eustacia, and how he had met her the night before – I know he did meet her, Clym, for I followed him part of the way; but I did not like to tell you when you called, and so make you think ill of him, as I did not think it was so serious. Then I could not stay in bed: I got up and dressed myself, and when I heard him out in the stable I thought I would come and tell you. So I came downstairs without any noise and slipped out.'

'Then he was not absolutely gone when you left?'

'No. Will you, dear Cousin Clym, go and try to persuade him not to go? He takes no notice of what I say, and puts me off with the story of his going on a journey, and will be home tomorrow, and all that; but I don't believe it. I think you could influence him.'

'I'll go,' said Clym. 'O, Eustacia!'

Thomasin carried in her arms a large bundle; and having by this time seated herself she began to unroll it, when a baby appeared as the kernel to the husks – dry, warm, and unconscious of travel or rough weather. Thomasin briefly kissed the baby, and then found time to begin crying as she said, 'I brought baby, for I was afraid what might happen to her. I suppose it will be her death, but I couldn't leave her with Rachel!'

Clym hastily put together the logs on the hearth, raked abroad the embers, which were scarcely yet extinct, and blew up a flame with the bellows.

'Dry yourself,' he said. 'I'll go and get some more wood.'

'No, no – don't stay for that. I'll make up the fire. Will you go at once – please will you?'

Yeobright ran upstairs to finish dressing himself. While he was gone another rapping came to the door. This time there was no delusion that it might be Eustacia's: the footsteps just preceding it had been heavy and slow. Yeobright, thinking it might possibly be Fairway with a note in answer, descended again and opened the door.

'Captain Vye?' he said to a dripping figure.

'Is my granddaughter here?' said the captain.

'No.'

'Then where is she?'

'I don't know.'

'But you ought to know – you are her husband.'

'Only in name apparently,' said Clym with rising excitement. 'I believe she means to elope tonight with Wildeve. I am just going to look to it.'

'Well, she has left my house; she left about half an hour ago. Who's sitting there?'

'My cousin Thomasin.'

The captain bowed in a preoccupied way to her. 'I only hope it is no worse than an elopement,' he said.

'Worse? What's worse than the worst a wife can do?'

'Well, I have been told a strange tale. Before starting in search of her I called up Charley, my stable-lad. I missed my pistols the other day.'

'Pistols?'

'He said at the time that he took them down to clean. He has now owned that he took them because he saw Eustacia looking curiously at them; and she afterwards owned to him that she was thinking of taking her life, but bound him to secrecy, and promised never to think of such a thing again. I hardly suppose she will ever have bravado enough to use one of them; but it shows what has been lurking in her mind; and people who think of that sort of thing once think of it again.'

'Where are the pistols?'

'Safely locked up. O no, she won't touch them again. But there are more ways of letting out life than through a bullet-hole. What did you quarrel about so bitterly with her to drive her to this? You must have treated her badly indeed. Well, I was always against the marriage, and I was right.'

'Are you going with me?' said Yeobright, paying no attention to the captain's latter remark. 'If so I can tell you what we quarrelled about as we walk along.'

'Where to?'

'To Wildeve's – that was her destination, depend upon it.'

Thomasin here broke in, still weeping: 'He said he was only going on a sudden short journey; but if so why did he want so much money? O, Clym, what do you think will happen? I am afraid that you, my poor baby, will soon have no father left to you!'

'I am off now,' said Yeobright, stepping into the porch.

'I would fain go with 'ee,' said the old man doubtfully. 'But I begin to be afraid that my legs will hardly carry me there such a night as this. I am not so young as I was. If they are interrupted in their flight she will be sure to come back to me, and I ought to be at the house to receive her. But be it as 'twill I can't walk to the Quiet Woman, and that's an end on't. I'll go straight home.'

'It will perhaps be best,' said Clym. 'Thomasin, dry yourself, and be as comfortable as you can.'

With this he closed the door upon her, and left the house in company with Captain Vye, who parted from him outside the gate, taking the middle path, which led to Mistover. Clym crossed by the right-hand track towards the inn.

Thomasin, being left alone, took off some of her wet garments, carried the baby upstairs to Clym's bed, and then came down to the sitting-room again, where she made a larger fire, and began drying herself. The fire soon flared up the chimney, giving the room an appearance of comfort that was doubled by contrast with the drumming of the storm without, which snapped at the window-panes and breathed into the chimney strange low utterances that seemed to be the prologue to some tragedy.

But the least part of Thomasin was in the house, for her heart being at ease about the little girl upstairs she was mentally following Clym on his journey. Having indulged in this imaginary peregrination for some considerable interval, she became impressed with a sense of the intolerable slowness of time. But she sat on. The moment then came when she could scarcely sit longer; and it was like a satire on her patience to remember that Clym could hardly have reached the inn as yet. At last she went to the baby's bedside. The child was sleeping soundly; but her imagination of possibly disastrous events at her home, the predominance within her of the unseen over the seen, agitated her beyond endurance. She could not refrain from going down and opening the door. The rain still continued, the candlelight falling upon the nearest drops and making glistening darts of them as they descended across the throng of invisible ones behind. To plunge into that medium was to plunge into water slightly diluted with air. But the difficulty of returning to her house at this moment made her all the more desirous of doing so: anything was better than suspense. 'I have come here well enough,' she said, 'and why shouldn't I go back again? It is a mistake for me to be away.'

She hastily fetched the infant, wrapped it up, cloaked herself as before, and shovelling the ashes over the fire, to prevent accidents, went into the open air. Pausing first to put the door-key in its old place behind the shutter, she resolutely turned her face to the confronting pile of firmamental darkness beyond the palings, and stepped into its midst. But Thomasin's imagination being so actively engaged elsewhere, the night and the weather had for her no terror beyond that of their actual discomfort and difficulty.

She was soon ascending Blooms-End valley and traversing the undulations on the side of the hill. The noise of the wind over the heath was shrill, and as if it whistled for joy at finding a night so congenial as this. Sometimes the path led her to hollows between thickets of tall and dripping bracken, dead, though not yet prostrate, which enclosed her like a pool. When they were more than usually tall she lifted the baby to the top of her head, that it might be out of the reach of their drenching fronds. On higher ground, where the wind was brisk and sustained, the rain flew in a level flight without sensible descent, so that it was beyond all power to imagine the remoteness of the point at which it left the bosoms of the clouds. Here self-defence was impossible, and individual drops stuck into her like the arrows into Saint Sebastian. She was enabled to avoid puddles by the nebulous paleness which signified their presence, though beside anything less dark than the heath they themselves would have appeared as blackness.

Yet in spite of all this Thomasin was not sorry that she had started. To her there were not, as to Eustacia, demons in the air, and malice in every bush and bough. The drops which lashed her face were not scorpions, but prosy rain; Egdon in the mass was no monster whatever, but impersonal open ground. Her fears of the place were rational, her dislikes of its worst moods reasonable. At this time it was in her view a windy, wet place, in which a person might experience much discomfort, lose the path without care, and possibly catch cold.

If the path is well known the difficulty at such times of keeping therein is not altogether great, from its familiar feel to the feet; but once lost it is irrecoverable. Owing to her baby, who somewhat impeded Thomasin's view forward and distracted her mind, she did at last lose the track. This mishap occurred when she was descending an open slope about two-thirds home. Instead of attempting, by wandering hither and thither, the hopeless task of finding such a mere thread, she went straight on, trusting for guidance to her general knowledge of the contours, which was scarcely surpassed by Clym's or by that of the heath-croppers themselves.

At length Thomasin reached a hollow and began to discern through the rain a faint blotted radiance, which presently assumed the oblong form of an open door. She knew that no house stood hereabouts, and was soon aware of the nature of the door by its height above the ground.

'Why, it is Diggory Venn's van, surely!' she said.

A certain secluded spot near Rainbarrow was, she knew, often Venn's chosen centre when staying in this neighbourhood; and she guessed at once that she had stumbled upon this mysterious retreat. The question arose in her mind whether or not she should ask him to guide her into the path. In her anxiety to reach home she decided that she would appeal to him, notwithstanding the strangeness of appearing before his eyes at this place and season. But when, in pursuance of this resolve, Thomasin reached the van and looked in she found it to be untenanted; though there was no doubt that it was the reddleman's. The fire was burning in the stove, the lantern hung from the nail. Round the doorway the floor was merely sprinkled with rain, and not saturated, which told her that the door had not long been opened.

While she stood uncertainly looking in Thomasin heard a footstep advancing from the darkness behind her; and turning, beheld the well-known form in corduroy, lurid from head to foot, the lantern beams falling upon him through an intervening gauze of raindrops.

'I thought you went down the slope,' he said, without noticing her face. 'How do you come back here again?'

'Diggory?' said Thomasin faintly.

'Who are you?' said Venn, still unperceiving. 'And why were you crying so just now?'

'O, Diggory! don't you know me?' said she. 'But of course you don't, wrapped up like this. What do you mean? I have not been crying here, and I have not been here before?'

Venn then came nearer till he could see the illuminated side of her form.

'Mrs Wildeve!' he exclaimed, starting. 'What a time for us to meet! And the baby too! What dreadful thing can have brought you out on such a night as this?'

She could not immediately answer; and without asking her permission he hopped into his van, took her by the arm, and drew her up after him.

'What is it?' he continued when they stood within.

'I have lost my way coming from Blooms-End, and I am in a great hurry to get home. Please show me as quickly as you can! It is so silly of me not to know Egdon better, and I cannot think how I came to lose the path. Show me quickly, Diggory, please.'

'Yes, of course. I will go with 'ee. But you came to me before this, Mrs Wildeve?'

'I only came this minute.'

'That's strange. I was lying down here asleep about five minutes ago, with the door shut to keep out the weather, when the brushing of a woman's clothes over the heath-bushes just outside woke me up (for I don't sleep heavy), and at the same time I heard a sobbing or crying from the same woman. I opened my door and held out my lantern, and just as far as the light would reach I saw a woman: she turned her head when the light sheened on her, and then hurried on downhill. I hung up the lantern, and was curious enough to pull on my things and dog her a few steps, but I could see nothing of her any more. That was where I had been when you came up; and when I saw you I thought you were the same one.'

'Perhaps it was one of the heath-folk going home?'

'No, it couldn't be. 'Tis too late. The noise of her gown over the he'th was of a whistling sort that nothing but silk will make.'

'It wasn't I, then. My dress is not silk, you see . . . Are we anywhere in a line between Mistover and the inn?'

'Well, yes; not far out.'

'Ah, I wonder if it was she! Diggory, I must go at once!'

She jumped down from the van before he was aware, when Venn unhooked the lantern and leaped down after her. 'I'll take the baby, ma'am,' he said. 'You must be tired out by the weight.'

Thomasin hesitated a moment, and then delivered the baby into Venn's hands. 'Don't squeeze her, Diggory,' she said, 'or hurt her little arm; and keep the cloak close over her like this, so that the rain may not drop in her face.'

'I will,' said Venn earnestly. 'As if I could hurt anything belonging to you!'

'I only meant accidentally,' said Thomasin.

'The baby is dry enough, but you are pretty wet,' said the reddleman when, in closing the door of his cart to padlock it, he noticed on the floor a ring of water-drops where her cloak had hung from her.

Thomasin followed him as he wound right and left to avoid the larger bushes, stopping occasionally and covering the lantern, while he looked over his shoulder to gain some idea of the position of Rainbarrow above them, which it was necessary to keep directly behind their backs to preserve a proper course.

'You are sure the rain does not fall upon baby?'

'Quite sure. May I ask how old he is, ma'am?'

'He!' said Thomasin reproachfully. 'Anybody can see better than that in a moment. She is nearly two months old. How far is it now to the inn?'

'A little over a quarter of a mile.'

'Will you walk a little faster?'

'I was afraid you could not keep up.'

'I am very anxious to get there. Ah, there is a light from the window!'

' 'Tis not from the window. That's a gig-lamp, to the best of my belief.

'O!' said Thomasin in despair. 'I wish I had been there sooner – give me the baby, Diggory – you can go back now.'

'I must go all the way,' said Venn. 'There is a quag between us and that light, and you will walk into it up to your neck unless I take you round.'

'But the light is at the inn, and there is no quag in front of that.'

'No, the light is below the inn some two or three hundred yards.'

'Never mind,' said Thomasin hurriedly. 'Go towards the light, and not towards the inn.'

'Yes,' answered Venn, swerving round in obedience; and, after a pause, 'I wish you would tell me what this great trouble is. I think you have proved that I can be trusted.'

'There are some things that cannot be – cannot be told to –' And then her heart rose into her throat, and she could say no more.

IX

Sights and Sounds Draw the Wanderers Together

HAVING seen Eustacia's signal from the hill at eight o'clock, Wildeve immediately prepared to assist her in her flight, and, as he hoped, accompany her. He was somewhat perturbed, and his manner of informing Thomasin that he was going on a journey was in itself sufficient to rouse her suspicions. When she had gone to bed he collected the few articles he would require, and went upstairs to the money-chest, whence he took a tolerably bountiful sum in notes, which had been advanced to him on the property he was so soon to have in possession, to defray expenses incidental to the removal.

He then went to the stable and coach-house to assure himself that the horse, gig, and harness were in a fit condition for a long drive. Nearly half an hour was spent thus, and on returning to the house Wildeve had no thought of Thomasin being anywhere but in bed. He had told the stable-lad not to stay up, leading the boy to understand that his departure would be at three or four in the morning; for this, though an exceptional hour, was less strange than midnight, the time actually agreed on, the packet from Budmouth sailing between one and two.

At last all was quiet, and he had nothing to do but to wait. By no effort could he shake off the oppression of spirits which he had experienced ever since his last meeting with Eustacia, but he hoped there was that in his situation which money could cure. He had persuaded himself that to act not ungenerously towards his gentle wife by settling on her the half of his property, and with chivalrous devotion towards another and greater woman by sharing her fate, was possible. And though he meant to adhere to Eustacia's instructions to the letter, to deposit her where she wished and to leave her, should that be her will, the spell that she had cast over him intensified, and his heart was beating fast in the anticipated futility of such commands in the face of a mutual wish that they should throw in their lot together.

He would not allow himself to dwell long upon these conjectures, maxims, and hopes, and at twenty minutes to twelve he again went softly to the stable, harnessed the horse, and lit the lamps, whence, taking the horse by the head, he led him with the covered car out of the yard to a spot by the roadside some quarter of a mile below the inn.

Here Wildeve waited, slightly sheltered from the driving rain by a high bank that had been cast up at this place. Along the surface of the road where lit by the lamps the loosened gravel and small stones scudded and clicked together before the wind, which, leaving them in heaps, plunged into the heath and boomed across the bushes into darkness. Only one sound rose above this din of weather, and that was the roaring of a ten-hatch weir to the southward, from a river in the meads which formed the boundary of the heath in this direction.

He lingered on in perfect stillness till he began to fancy that the midnight hour must have struck. A very strong doubt had arisen in his mind if Eustacia would venture down the hill in such weather; yet knowing her nature he felt that she might. 'Poor thing! 'tis like her ill-luck,' he murmured.

At length he turned to the lamp and looked at his watch. To his surprise it was nearly a quarter past midnight. He now wished that he had driven up the circuitous road to Mistover, a plan not adopted because of the enormous length of the route in proportion to that of the pedestrian's path down the open hillside, and the consequent increase of labour for the horse.

At this moment a footstep approached; but the light of the lamp being in a different direction the comer was not visible. The step paused, then came on again.

'Eustacia?' said Wildeve.

The person came forward, and the light fell upon the form of Clym, glistening with wet, whom Wildeve immediately recognized; but Wildeve, who stood behind the lamp, was not at once recognized by Yeobright.

He stopped as if in doubt whether this waiting vehicle could have anything to do with the flight of his wife or not. The sight of Yeobright at once banished Wildeve's sober feelings, who saw him again as the deadly rival from whom Eustacia was to be kept at all hazards. Hence Wildeve did not speak, in the hope that Clym would pass by without particular inquiry.

While they both hung thus in hesitation a dull sound became audible above the storm and wind. Its origin was unmistakable – it was the fall of a body into the stream in the adjoining mead, apparently at a point near the weir.

Both started. 'Good God! can it be she?' said Clym.

'Why should it be she?' said Wildeve, in his alarm forgetting that he had hitherto screened himself.

'Ah! – that's you, you traitor, is it?' cried Yeobright. 'Why should it be she? Because last week she would have put an end to her life if she had been able. She ought to have been watched! Take one of the lamps and come with me.'

Yeobright seized the one on his side and hastened on; Wildeve did not wait to unfasten the other, but followed at once along the meadow-track to the weir, a little in the rear of Clym.

Shadwater Weir had at its foot a large circular pool, fifty feet in diameter, into which the water flowed through ten huge hatches, raised and lowered by a winch and cogs in the ordinary manner. The sides of the pool were of masonry, to prevent the water from washing away the bank; but the force of the stream in winter was sometimes such as to undermine the retaining wall and precipitate it into the hole. Clym reached the hatches, the framework of which was shaken to its foundations by the velocity of the current. Nothing but the froth of the waves could be discerned in the pool below. He got upon the plank bridge over the race, and holding to the rail, that the wind might not blow him off, crossed to the other side of the river. There he leant over the wall and lowered the lamp, only to behold the vortex formed at the curl of the returning current.

Wildeve meanwhile had arrived on the former side, and the light from Yeobright's lamp shed a flecked and agitated radiance across the weir-pool, revealing to the ex-engineer the tumbling courses of the currents from the hatches above. Across this gashed and puckered mirror a dark body was slowly borne by one of the backward currents.

'O, my darling!' exclaimed Wildeve in an agonized voice; and, without showing sufficient presence of mind even to throw off his great-coat, he leaped into the boiling caldron.

Yeobright could now also discern the floating body, though but indistinctly; and imagining from Wildeve's plunge that there was life to be saved he was about to leap after. Bethinking himself of a wiser plan he placed the lamp against a post to make it stand upright, and running round to the lower part of the pool, where there was no wall, he sprang in and boldly waded upwards towards the deeper portion. Here he was taken off his legs, and in swimming was carried round into the centre of the basin, where he perceived Wildeve struggling.

While these hasty actions were in progress here, Venn and Thomasin had been toiling through the lower corner of the heath in the direction of the light. They had not been near enough to the river to hear the plunge, but they saw the removal of the carriage-lamp, and watched its motion into the mead. As soon as they reached the car and horse Venn guessed that something new was amiss, and hastened to follow in the course of the moving light. Venn walked faster than Thomasin, and came to the weir alone.

The lamp placed against the post by Clym still shone across the water, and the reddleman observed something floating motionless. Being encumbered with the infant he ran back to meet Thomasin.

'Take the baby, please, Mrs Wildeve,' he said hastily. 'Run home with her, call the stable-lad, and make him send down to me any men who may be living near. Somebody has fallen into the weir.'

Thomasin took the child and ran. When she came to the covered car the horse, though fresh from the stable, was standing perfectly still, as if conscious of misfortune. She saw for the first time whose it was. She nearly fainted, and would have been unable to proceed another step but that the necessity of preserving the little girl from harm nerved her to an amazing self-control. In this agony of suspense she entered the house, put the baby in a place of safety, woke the lad and the female domestic, and ran out to give the alarm at the nearest cottage.

Diggory, having returned to the brink of the pool, observed that the small upper hatches of floats were withdrawn. He found one of these lying upon the grass, and taking it under one arm, and with his lantern in his hand, entered at the bottom of the pool as Clym had done. As soon as he began to be in deep water he flung himself across the hatch; thus supported he was able to keep afloat as long as he chose, holding the lantern aloft with his disengaged hand. Propelled by his feet he steered round and round the pool, ascending each time by one of the back streams and descending in the middle of the current.

At first he could see nothing. Then amidst the glistening of the whirlpools and the white clots of foam he distinguished a woman's bonnet floating alone. His search was now under the left wall, when something came to the surface almost close beside him. It was not, as he had expected, a woman, but a man. The reddleman put the ring of the lantern between his teeth, seized the floating man by the collar, and, holding on to the hatch with the remaining arm, struck out into the strongest race, by which the unconscious man, the hatch, and himself were carried down the stream. As soon as Venn found his feet dragging over the pebbles of the shallower part below he secured his footing and waded towards the brink. There, where the water stood at about the height of his waist, he flung away the hatch, and attempted to drag forth the man. This was a matter of great difficulty, and he found as the reason that the legs of the unfortunate stranger were tightly embraced by the arms of another man, who had hitherto been entirely beneath the surface.

At this moment his heart bounded to hear footsteps running towards him, and two men, roused by Thomasin, appeared at the brink above. They ran to where Venn was, and helped him in lifting out the apparently drowned persons, separating them, and laying them out upon the grass. Venn turned the light upon their faces. The one who had been uppermost was Yeobright; he who had been completely submerged was Wildeve.

'Now we must search the hole again,' said Venn. 'A woman is in there somewhere. Get a pole.'

One of the men went to the foot-bridge and tore off the handrail. The reddleman and the two others then entered the water together from below as before, and with their united force probed the pool forwards to where it sloped down to its central depth. Venn was not mistaken in supposing that any person who had sunk for the last time would be washed down to this point, for when they had examined to about half-way across something impeded their thrust.

'Pull it forward,' said Venn, and they raked it in with the pole till it was close to their feet.

Venn vanished under the stream, and came up with an armful of wet drapery enclosing a woman's cold form, which was all that remained of the desperate Eustacia.

When they reached the bank there stood Thomasin, in a stress of grief, bending over the two unconscious ones who already lay there. The horse and car were brought to the nearest point in the road, and it was the work of a few minutes only to place the three in the vehicle. Venn led on the horse, supporting Thomasin upon his arm, and the two men followed, till they reached the inn.

The woman who had been shaken out of her sleep by Thomasin had hastily dressed herself and lighted a fire, the other servant being left to snore on in peace at the back of the house. The insensible forms of Eustacia, Clym and Wildeve were then brought in and laid on the carpet, with their feet to the fire, when such restorative processes as could be thought of were adopted at once, the stableman being in the meantime sent for a doctor. But there seemed to be not a whiff of life left in either of the bodies. Then Thomasin, whose stupor of grief had been thrust off awhile by frantic action, applied a bottle of hartshorn to Clym's nostrils, having tried it in vain upon the other two. He sighed.

'Clym's alive!' she exclaimed.

He soon breathed distinctly, and again and again did she attempt to revive her husband by the same means; but Wildeve gave no sigh. There was too much reason to think that he and Eustacia both were for ever beyond the reach of stimulating perfumes. Their exertions did not relax till the doctor arrived, when, one by one, the senseless three were taken upstairs and put into warm beds.

Venn soon felt himself relieved from further attendance, and went to the door, scarcely able yet to realize the strange catastrophe that had befallen the family in which he took so great an interest. Thomasin surely would be broken down by the sudden and overwhelming nature of this event. No firm and sensible Mrs Yeobright lived now to support the gentle girl through the ordeal; and, whatever an unimpassioned spectator might think of her loss of such a husband as Wildeve, there could be no doubt that for the moment she was distracted and horrified by the blow. As for himself, not being privileged to go to her and comfort her, he saw no reason for waiting longer in a house where he remained only as a stranger.

He returned across the heath to his van. The fire was not yet out, and everything remained as he had left it. Venn now bethought himself of his clothes, which were saturated with water to the weight of lead. He changed them, spread them before the fire, and lay down to sleep. But it was more than he could do to rest here while excited by a vivid imagination of the turmoil they were in at the house he had quitted, and, blaming himself for coming away, he dressed in another suit, locked up the door, and again hastened across to the inn. Rain was still falling heavily when he entered the kitchen. A bright fire was shining from the hearth, and two women were bustling about, one of whom was Olly Dowden.

'Well, how is it going on now?' said Venn in a whisper.

'Mr Yeobright is better; but Mrs Yeobright and Mr Wildeve are dead and cold. The doctor says they were quite gone before they were out of the water.'

'Ah! I thought as much when I hauled 'em up. And Mrs Wildeve?'

'She is as well as can be expected. The doctor had her put between blankets, for she was almost as wet as they that had been in the river, poor young thing. You don't seem very dry, reddleman.'

'O, 'tis not much. I have changed my things. This is only a little dampness I've got coming through the rain again.'

'Stand by the fire. Mis'ess says you be to have whatever you want, and she was sorry when she was told that you'd gone away.'

Venn drew near to the fireplace, and looked into the flames in an absent mood. The steam came from his leggings and ascended the chimney with the smoke, while he thought of those who were upstairs. Two were corpses, one had barely escaped the jaws of death, another was sick and a widow. The last occasion on which he had lingered by that fireplace was when the raffle was in progress; when Wildeve was alive and well; Thomasin active and smiling in the next room; Yeobright and Eustacia just made husband and wife, and Mrs Yeobright living at Blooms-End. It had seemed at that time that the then position of affairs was good for at least twenty years to come. Yet, of all the circle, he himself was the only one whose situation had not materially changed.

While he ruminated a footstep descended the stairs. It was the nurse, who brought in her hand a rolled mass of wet paper. The woman was so engrossed with her occupation that she hardly saw Venn. She took from a cupboard some pieces of twine, which she strained across the fireplace, tying the end of each piece to the firedog, previously pulled forward for the purpose, and, unrolling the wet papers, she began pinning them one by one to the strings in a manner of clothes on a line.

'What be they?' said Venn.

'Poor master's bank-notes,' she answered. 'They were found in his pocket when they undressed him.'

'Then he was not coming back again for some time?' said Venn.

'That we shall never know,' said she.

Venn was loth to depart, for all on earth that interested him lay under this roof. As nobody in the house had any more sleep that night, except the two who slept for ever, there was no reason why he should not remain. So he retired into the niche of the fireplace where he had used to sit, and there he continued, watching the steam from the double row of bank-notes as they waved backwards and forwards in the draught of the chimney till their flaccidity was changed to dry crispness throughout. Then the woman came and unpinned them, and, folding them together, carried the handful upstairs. Presently the doctor appeared from above with the look of a man who could do no more, and, pulling on his gloves, went out of the house, the trotting of his horse soon dying away upon the road.

At four o'clock there was a gentle knock at the door. It was from Charley, who had been sent by Captain Vye to inquire if anything had been heard of Eustacia. The girl who admitted him looked in his face as if she did not know what answer to return, and showed him in to where Venn was seated, saying to the reddleman, 'Will you tell him, please?'

Venn told. Charley's only utterance was a feeble, indistinct sound. He stood quite still; then he burst out spasmodically, 'I shall see her once more?'

'I dare say you may see her,' said Diggory gravely. 'But hadn't you better run and tell Captain Vye?'

'Yes, yes. Only I do hope I shall see her just once again.'

'You shall,' said a low voice behind; and starting round they beheld by the dim light a thin, pallid, almost spectral form, wrapped in a blanket, and looking like Lazarus coming from the tomb.

It was Yeobright. Neither Venn nor Charley spoke, and Clym continued: 'You shall see her. There will be time enough to tell the captain when it gets daylight. You would like to see her too – would you not, Diggory? She looks very beautiful now.'

Venn assented by rising to his feet, and with Charley he followed Clym to the foot of the staircase, where he took off his boots; Charley did the same. They followed Yeobright upstairs to the landing, where there was a candle burning, which Yeobright took in his hand, and with it led the way into an adjoining room. Here he went to the bedside and folded back the sheet.

They stood silently looking upon Eustacia, who, as she lay there still in death, eclipsed all her living phases. Pallor did not include all the quality of her complexion, which seemed more than whiteness; it was almost light. The expression of her finely carved mouth was pleasant, as if a sense of dignity had just compelled her to leave off speaking. Eternal rigidity had seized upon it in a momentary transition between fervour and resignation. Her black hair was looser now than either of them had ever seen it before, and surrounded her brow like a forest. The stateliness of look which had been almost too marked for a dweller in a country domicile had at last found an artistically happy background.

Nobody spoke, till at length Clym covered her and turned aside. 'Now come here,' he said.

They went to a recess in the same room, and there, on a smaller bed, lay another figure – Wildeve. Less repose was visible in his face than in Eustacia's, but the same luminous youthfulness overspread it, and the least sympathetic observer would have felt at sight of him now that he was born for a higher destiny than this. The only sign upon him of his recent struggle for life was in his finger-tips, which were worn and scarified in his dying endeavours to obtain a hold on the face of the weir-wall.

Yeobright's manner had been so quiet, he had uttered so few syllables since his reappearance, that Venn imagined him resigned. It was only when they had left the room and stood upon the landing that the true state of his mind was apparent. Here he said, with a wild smile, inclining his head towards the chamber in which Eustacia lay, 'She is the second woman I have killed this year. I was a great cause of my mother's death; and I am the chief cause of hers.'

'How?' said Venn.

'I spoke cruel words to her, and she left my house. I did not invite her back till it was too late. It is I who ought to have drowned myself. It would have been a charity to the living had the river overwhelmed me and borne her up. But I cannot die. Those who ought to have lived lie dead; and here am I alive!'

'But you can't charge yourself with crimes in that way,' said Venn. 'You may as well say that the parents be the cause of a murder by the child, for without the parents the child would never have been begot.'

'Yes, Venn, that is very true; but you don't know all the circumstances. If it had pleased God to put an end to me it would have been a good thing for all. But I am getting used to the horror of my existence. They say that a time comes when men laugh at misery through long acquaintance with it. Surely that time will soon come to me!'

'Your aim has always been good,' said Venn. 'Why should you say such desperate things?'

'No, they are not desperate. They are only hopeless; and my great regret is that for what I have done no man or law can punish me!'

BOOK SIXTH

AFTERCOURSES

I

The Inevitable Movement Onward

THE story of the deaths of Eustacia and Wildeve was told throughout Egdon, and far beyond, for many weeks and months. All the known incidents of their love were enlarged, distorted, touched up, and modified, till the original reality bore but a slight resemblance to the counterfeit presentation by surrounding tongues. Yet, upon the whole, neither the man nor the woman lost dignity by sudden death. Misfortune had struck them gracefully, cutting off their erratic histories with a catastrophic dash, instead of, as with many, attenuating each life to an uninteresting meagreness, through long years of wrinkles, neglect, and decay.

On those most nearly concerned the effect was somewhat different. Strangers who had heard of many such cases now merely heard of one more; but immediately where a blow falls no previous imaginings amount to appreciable preparation for it. The very suddenness of her bereavement dulled, to some extent, Thomasin's feelings; yet, irrationally enough, a consciousness that the husband she had lost ought to have been a better man did not lessen her mourning at all. On the contrary, this fact seemed at first to set off the dead husband in his young wife's eyes, and to be the necessary cloud to the rainbow.

But the horrors of the unknown had passed. Vague misgivings about her future as a deserted wife were at an end. The worst had once been matter of trembling conjecture; it was now matter of reason only, a limited badness. Her chief interest, the little Eustacia, still remained. There was humility in her grief, no defiance in her attitude; and when this is the case a shaken spirit is apt to be stilled.

Could Thomasin's mournfulness now and Eustacia's serenity during life have been reduced to common measure, they would have touched the same mark nearly. But Thomasin's former brightness made shadow of that which in a sombre atmosphere was light itself.

The spring came and calmed her; the summer came and soothed her; the autumn arrived, and she began to be comforted, for her little girl was strong and happy, growing in size and knowledge every day. Outward events flattered Thomasin not a little. Wildeve had died intestate, and she and the child were his only relatives. When administration had been granted, all the debts paid, and the residue of her husband's uncle's property had come into her hands, it was found that the sum waiting to be invested for her own and the child's benefit was little less than ten thousand pounds.

Where should she live? The obvious place was Blooms-End. The old rooms, it is true, were not much higher than the between-decks of a frigate, necessitating a sinking in the floor under the new clock-case she brought from the inn, and the removal of the handsome brass knobs on its head, before there was height for it to stand; but, such as the rooms were, there were plenty of them, and the place was endeared to her by every early recollection. Clym very gladly admitted her as a tenant, confining his own existence to two rooms at the top of the back staircase, where he lived on quietly, shut off from Thomasin and the three servants she had thought fit to indulge in now that she was a mistress of money, going his own ways, and thinking his own thoughts.

His sorrows had made some change in his outward appearance; and yet the alteration was chiefly within. It might have been said that he had a wrinkled mind. He had no enemies, and he could get nobody to reproach him, which was why he so bitterly reproached himself.

He did sometimes think he had been ill-used by fortune, so far as to say that to be born is a palpable dilemma, and that instead of men aiming to advance in life with glory they should calculate how to retreat out of it without shame. But that he and his had been sarcastically and pitilessly handled in having such irons thrust into their souls he did not maintain long. It is usually so, except with the sternest of men. Human beings, in their generous endeavour to construct a hypothesis that shall not degrade a First Cause, have always hesitated to conceive a dominant power of lower moral quality than their own; and, even while they sit down and weep by the waters of Babylon, invent excuses for the oppression which prompts their tears.

Thus, though words of solace were vainly uttered in his presence, he found relief in a direction of his own choosing when left to himself. For a man of his habits the house and the hundred and twenty pounds a year which he had inherited from his mother were enough to supply all worldly needs. Resources do not depend upon gross amounts, but upon the proportion of spendings to takings.

He frequently walked the heath alone, when the past seized upon him with its shadowy hand, and held him there to listen to its tale. His imagination would then people the spot with its ancient inhabitants: forgotten Celtic tribes trod their tracks about him, and he could almost live among them, look in their faces, and see them standing beside the barrows which swelled around, untouched and perfect as at the time of their erection. Those of the dyed barbarians who had chosen the cultivable tracts were, in comparison with those who had left their marks here, as writers on paper besides writers on parchment. Their records had perished long ago by the plough, while the works of these remained. Yet they all had lived and died unconscious of the different fates awaiting their relics. It reminded him that unforseen factors operate in the evolution of immortality.

Winter again came round, with its winds, frosts, tame robins, and sparkling starlight. The year previous Thomasin had hardly been conscious of the season's advance; this year she laid her heart open to external influences of every kind. The life of this sweet cousin, her baby, and her servants, came to Clym's senses only in the form of sounds through a wood partition as he sat over books of exceptionally large type; but his ear became at last so accustomed to these slight noises from the other part of the house that he almost could witness the scenes they signified. A faint beat of half-seconds conjured up Thomasin rocking the cradle, a wavering hum meant that she was singing the baby to sleep, a crunching of sand as between millstones raised the picture of Humphrey's, Fairway's, or Sam's heavy feet crossing the stone floor of the kitchen; a light boyish step, and a gay tune in a high key, betokened a visit from Grandfer Cantle; a sudden break-off in the Grandfer's utterances implied the application to his lips of a mug of small beer; a bustling and slamming of doors meant starting to go to market; for Thomasin, in spite of her added scope for gentility, led a ludicrously narrow life, to the end that she might save every possible pound for her little daughter.

One summer day Clym was in the garden, immediately outside the parlour-window, which was as usual open. He was looking at the pot-flowers on the sill; they had been revived and restored by Thomasin to the state in which his mother had left them. He heard a slight scream from Thomasin, who was sitting inside the room.

'O, how you frightened me!' she said to some one who had entered. 'I thought you were the ghost of yourself.'

Clym was curious enough to advance a little further and look in at the window. To his astonishment there stood within the room Diggory Venn, no longer a reddleman, but exhibiting the strangely altered hues of an ordinary Christian countenance, white shirt-front, light flowered waistcoat, blue-spotted neckerchief, and bottle-green coat. Nothing in this appearance was at all singular but the fact of its great difference from what he had formerly been. Red, and all approach to red, was carefully excluded from every article of clothes upon him; for what is there that persons just out of harness dread so much as reminders of the trade which has enriched them?

Yeobright went round to the door and entered.

'I was so alarmed!' said Thomasin, smiling from one to the other. 'I couldn't believe that he had got white of his own accord! It seemed supernatural.'

'I gave up dealing in reddle last Christmas,' said Venn. 'It was a profitable trade, and I found that by that time I had made enough to take the dairy of fifty cows that my father had in his lifetime. I always thought of getting to that place again if I changed at all; and now I am there.'

'How did you manage to become white, Diggory?' Thomasin asked.

'I turned so by degrees, ma'am.'

'You look much better than ever you did before.'

Venn appeared confused; and Thomasin, seeing how inadvertently she had spoken to a man who might possibly have tender feelings for her still, blushed a little. Clym saw nothing of this, and added good-humouredly –

'What shall we have to frighten Thomasin's baby with, now you have become a human being again?'

'Sit down, Diggory,' said Thomasin, 'and stay to tea.'

Venn moved as if he would retire to the kitchen, when Thomasin said with pleasant pertness as she went on with some sewing, 'Of course you must sit down here. And where does your fifty-cow dairy lie, Mr Venn?'

'At Stickleford – about two miles to the right of Alderworth, ma'am, where the meads begin. I have thought that if Mr Yeobright would like to pay me a visit sometimes he shouldn't stay away for want of asking. I'll not bide to tea this afternoon, thank'ee, for I've got something on hand that must be settled. 'Tis Maypole-day tomorrow, and the Shadwater folk have clubbed with a few of your neighbours here to have a pole just outside your palings in the heath, as it is a nice green place.' Venn waved his elbow towards the patch in front of the house. 'I have been talking to Fairway about it,' he continued, 'and I said to him that before we put up the pole it would be as well to ask Mrs Wildeve.'

'I can say nothing against it,' she answered. 'Our property does not reach an inch further than the white palings.'

'But you might not like to see a lot of folk going crazy round a stick, under your very nose?'

'I shall have no objection at all.'

Venn soon after went away, and in the evening Yeobright strolled as far as Fairway's cottage. It was a lovely May sunset, and the birch trees which grew on this margin of the vast Egdon wilderness had put on their new leaves, delicate as butterflies' wings, and diaphanous as amber. Beside Fairway's dwelling was an open space recessed from the road, and here were now collected all the young people from within a radius of a couple of miles. The pole lay with one end supported on a trestle, and women were engaged in wreathing it from the top downwards with wildflowers. The instincts of merry England lingered on here with exceptional vitality, and the symbolic customs which tradition has attached to each season of the year were yet a reality on Egdon. Indeed, the impulses of all such outlandish hamlets are pagan still: in these spots homage to nature, self-adoration, frantic gaieties, fragments of Teutonic rites to divinities whose names are forgotten, seem in some way or other to have survived medieval doctrine.

Yeobright did not interrupt the preparations, and went home again. The next morning, when Thomasin withdrew the curtains of her bedroom window, there stood the Maypole in the middle of the green, its top cutting into the sky. It had sprung up in the night, or rather early morning, like Jack's bean-stalk. She opened the casement to get a better view of the garlands and posies that adorned it. The sweet perfume of the flowers had already spread into the surrounding air, which, being free from every taint, conducted to her lips a full measure of the fragrance received from the spire of blossom in its midst. At the top of the pole were crossed hoops decked with small flowers; beneath these came a milk-white zone of Maybloom; then a zone of bluebells, then of cowslips, then of lilacs, then of ragged-robins, daffodils, and so on, till the lowest stage was reached. Thomasin noticed all these, and was delighted that the May-revel was to be so near.

When afternoon came people began to gather on the green, and Yeobright was interested enough to look out upon them from the open window of his room. Soon after this Thomasin walked out from the door immediately below and turned her eyes up to her cousin's face. She was dressed more gaily than Yeobright had ever seen her dress since the time of Wildeve's death, eighteen months before; since the day of her marriage even she had not exhibited herself to such advantage.

'How pretty you look today, Thomasin!' he said. 'Is it because of the Maypole?'

'Not altogether.' And then she blushed and dropped her eyes, which he did not specially observe, though her manner seemed to him to be rather peculiar, considering that she was only addressing himself. Could it be possible that she had put on her summer clothes to please him?

He recalled her conduct towards him throughout the last few weeks, when they had often been working together in the garden, just as they had formerly done when they were boy and girl under his mother's eye. What if her interest in him were not so entirely that of a relative as it had formerly been? To Yeobright any possibility of this sort was a serious matter; and he almost felt troubled at the thought of it. Every pulse of loverlike feeling which had not been stilled during Eustacia's lifetime had gone into the grave with her. His passion for her had occurred too far on in his manhood to leave fuel enough on hand for another fire of that sort, as may happen with more boyish loves. Even supposing him capable of loving again, that love would be a plant of slow and laboured growth, and in the end only small and sickly, like an autumn-hatched bird.

He was so distressed by this new complexity that when the enthusiastic brass band arrived and struck up, which it did about five o'clock, with apparently wind enough among its members to blow down his house, he withdrew from his rooms by the back door, went down the garden, through the gate in the hedge, and away out of sight. He could not bear to remain in the presence of enjoyment today, though he had tried hard.

Nothing was seen of him for four hours. When he came back by the same path it was dusk, and the dews were coating every green thing. The boisterous music had ceased; but, entering the premises as he did from behind, he could not see if the May party had all gone till he had passed through Thomasin's division of the house to the front door. Thomasin was standing within the porch alone.

She looked at him reproachfully. 'You went away just when it began, Clym,' she said.

'Yes. I felt I could not join in. You went out with them, of course?'

'No, I did not.'

'You appeared to be dressed on purpose.'

'Yes, but I could not go out alone; so many people were there. One is there now.'

Yeobright strained his eyes across the dark-green patch beyond the paling, and near the black form of the Maypole he discerned a shadowy figure, sauntering idly up and down. 'Who is it?' he said.

'Mr Venn,' said Thomasin.

'You might have asked him to come in, I think, Tamsie. He has been very kind to you first and last.'

'I will now,' she said; and, acting on the impulse, went through the wicket to where Venn stood under the Maypole.

'It is Mr Venn, I think?' she inquired.

Venn started as if he had not seen her – artful man that he was – and said, 'Yes.'

'Will you come in?'

'I am afraid that I –'

'I have seen you dancing this evening, and you had the very best of the girls for your partners. Is it that you won't come in because you wish to stand here, and think over the past hours of enjoyment?'

'Well, that's partly it,' said Mr Venn, with ostentatious sentiment. 'But the main reason why I am biding here like this is that I want to wait till the moon rises.'

'To see how pretty the Maypole looks in the moonlight?'

'No. To look for a glove that was dropped by one of the maidens.'

Thomasin was speechless with surprise. That a man who had to walk some four or five miles to his home should wait here for such a reason pointed to only one conclusion: the man must be amazingly interested in that glove's owner.

'Were you dancing with her, Diggory?' she asked, in a voice which revealed that he had made himself considerably more interesting to her by this disclosure.

'No,' he sighed.

'And you will not come in, then?'

'Not tonight, thank you, ma'am.'

'Shall I lend you a lantern to look for the young person's glove, Mr Venn?'

'O no; it is not necessary, Mrs Wildeve, thank you. The moon will rise in a few minutes.'

Thomasin went back to the porch. 'Is he coming in?' said Clym, who had been waiting where she had left him.

'He would rather not tonight,' she said, and then passed by into the house; whereupon Clym too retired to his own rooms.

When Clym was gone Thomasin crept upstairs in the dark, and, just listening by the cot, to assure herself that the child was asleep, she went to the window, gently lifted the corner of the white curtain, and looked out. Venn was still there. She watched the growth of the faint radiance appearing in the sky by the eastern hill, till presently the edge of the moon burst upwards and flooded the valley with light. Diggory's form was now distinct on the green; he was moving about in a bowed attitude, evidently scanning the grass for the precious missing article, walking in zigzags right and left till he should have passed over every foot of the ground.

'How very ridiculous!' Thomasin murmured to herself, in a tone which was intended to be satirical. 'To think that a man should be so silly as to go mooning about like that for a girl's glove! A respectable dairyman, too, and a man of money as he is now. What a pity!'

At last Venn appeared to find it; whereupon he stood up and raised it to his lips. Then placing it in his breast-pocket – the nearest receptacle to a man's heart permitted by modern raiment – he ascended the valley in a mathematically direct line towards his distant home in the meadows.

* II *

Thomasin Walks in a Green Place by the Roman Road

CLYM saw little of Thomasin for several days after this; and when they met she was more silent than usual. At length he asked her what she was thinking of so intently.

'I am thoroughly perplexed,' she said candidly. 'I cannot for my life think who it is that Diggory Venn is so much in love with. None of the girls at the Maypole were good enough for him, and yet she must have been there.'

Clym tried to imagine Venn's choice for a moment; but ceasing to be interested in the question he went on again with his gardening.

No clearing up of the mystery was granted her for some time. But one afternoon Thomasin was upstairs getting ready for a walk, when she had occasion to come to the landing and call 'Rachel.' Rachel was a girl about thirteen, who carried the baby out for airings; and she came upstairs at the call.

'Have you seen one of my last new gloves about the house, Rachel?' inquired Thomasin. 'It is the fellow to this one.'

Rachel did not reply.

'Why don't you answer?' said her mistress.

'I think it is lost, ma'am.'

'Lost? Who lost it? I have never worn them but once.'

Rachel appeared as one dreadfully troubled, and at last began to cry.

'Please, ma'am, on the day of the Maypole I had none to wear, and I seed yours on the table, and I thought I would borrow 'em. I did not mean to hurt 'em at all, but one of them got lost. Somebody gave me some money to buy another pair for you, but I have not been able to go anywhere to get 'em.'

'Who's somebody?'

'Mr Venn.'

'Did he know it was my glove?'

'Yes. I told him.'

Thomasin was so surprised by the explanation that she quite forgot to lecture the girl, who glided silently away. Thomasin did not move further than to turn her eyes upon the grass-plat where the Maypole had stood. She remained thinking, then said to herself that she would not go out that afternoon, but would work hard at the baby's unfinished lovely plaid frock, cut on the cross in the newest fashion. How she managed to work hard, and yet do no more than she had done at the end of two hours, would have been a mystery to any one not aware that the recent incident was of a kind likely to divert her industry from a manual to a mental channel.

Next day she went her ways as usual, and continued her custom of walking in the heath with no other companion than little Eustacia, now of the age when it is a matter of doubt with such characters whether they are intended to walk through the world on their hands or on their feet; so that they get into painful complications by trying both. It was very pleasant to Thomasin, when she had carried the child to some lonely place, to give her a little private practice on the green turf and shepherd's-thyme, which formed a soft mat to fall headlong upon when equilibrium was lost.

Once, when engaged in this system of training, and stooping to remove bits of stick, fern-stalks, and other such fragments from the child's path, that the journey might not be brought to an untimely end by some insuperable barrier a quarter of an inch high, she was alarmed by discovering that a man on horseback was almost close beside her, the soft natural carpet having muffled the horse's tread. The rider, who was Venn, waved his hat in the air and bowed gallantly.

'Diggory, give me my glove,' said Thomasin, whose manner it was under any circumstances to plunge into the midst of a subject which engrossed her.

Venn immediately dismounted, put his hand in his breast-pocket, and handed the glove.

'Thank you. It was very good of you to take care of it.'

'It is very good of you to say so.'

'O no. I was quite glad to find you had it. Everybody gets so indifferent that I was surprised to know you thought of me.'

'If you had remembered what I was once you wouldn't have been surprised.'

'Ah, no,' she said quickly. 'But men of your character are mostly so independent.'

'What is my character?' he asked.

'I don't exactly know,' said Thomasin simply, 'except it is to cover up your feelings under a practical manner, and only to show them when you are alone.'

'Ah, how do you know that?' said Venn strategically.

'Because,' said she, stopping to put the little girl, who had managed to get herself upside down, right end up again, 'because I do.'

'You mustn't judge by folks in general,' said Venn. 'Still I don't know much what feelings are now-a-days. I have got so mixed up with business of one sort and t'other that my soft sentiments are gone off in vapour like. Yes, I am given up body and soul to the making of money. Money is all my dream.'

'O Diggory, how wicked!' said Thomasin reproachfully, and looking at him in exact balance between taking his words seriously and judging them as said to tease her.

'Yes, 'tis rather a rum course,' said Venn, in the bland tone of one comfortably resigned to sins he could no longer overcome.

'You, who used to be so nice!'

'Well, that's an argument I rather like, because what a man has once been he may be again.' Thomasin blushed. 'Except that it is rather harder now,' Venn continued.

'Why?' she asked.

'Because you be richer than you were at that time.'

'O no – not much. I have made it nearly all over to the baby, as it was my duty to do, except just enough to live on.'

'I am rather glad of that,' said Venn softly, and regarding her from the corner of his eye, 'for it makes it easier for us to be friendly.'

Thomasin blushed again, and, when a few more words had been said of a not unpleasing kind, Venn mounted his horse and rode on.

This conversation had passed in a hollow of the heath near the old Roman road, a place much frequented by Thomasin. And it might have been observed that she did not in future walk that way less often from having met Venn there now. Whether or not Venn abstained from riding thither because he had met Thomasin in the same place might easily have been guessed from her proceedings about two months later in the same year.

* III *

The Serious Discourse of Clym with His Cousin

THROUGHOUT this period Yeobright had more or less pondered on his duty to his cousin Thomasin. He could not help feeling that it would be a pitiful waste of sweet material if the tender-natured thing should be doomed from this early stage of her life onwards to dribble away her winsome qualities on lonely gorse and fern. But he felt this as an economist merely, and not as a lover. His passion for Eustacia had been a sort of conserve of his whole life, and he had nothing more of that supreme quality left to bestow. So far the obvious thing was not to entertain any idea of marriage with Thomasin, even to oblige her.

But this was not all. Years ago there had been in his mother's mind a great fancy about Thomasin and himself. It had not positively amounted to a desire, but it had always been a favourite dream. That they should be man and wife in good time, if the happiness of neither were endangered thereby, was the fancy in question. So that what course save one was there now left for any son who reverenced his mother's memory as Yeobright did? It is an unfortunate fact that any particular whim of parents, which might have been dispersed by half an hour's conversation during their lives, becomes sublimated by their deaths into a fiat the most absolute, with such results to conscientious children as those parents, had they lived, would have been the first to decry.

Had only Yeobright's own future been involved he would have proposed to Thomasin with a ready heart. He had nothing to lose by carrying out a dead mother's hope. But he dreaded to contemplate Thomasin wedded to the mere corpse of a lover that he now felt himself to be. He had but three activities alive in him. One was his almost daily walk to the little graveyard wherein his mother lay; another, his just as frequent visits by night to the more distant enclosure, which numbered his Eustacia among its dead; the third was self-preparation for a vocation which alone seemed likely to satisfy his cravings – that of an itinerant preacher of the eleventh commandment. It was difficult to believe that Thomasin would be cheered by a husband with such tendencies as these.

Yet he resolved to ask her, and let her decide for herself. It was even with a pleasant sense of doing his duty that he went downstairs to her one evening for this purpose, when the sun was printing on the valley the same long shadow of the house-top that he had seen lying there times out of number while his mother lived.

Thomasin was not in her room, and he found her in the front garden. 'I have long been wanting, Thomasin,' he began, 'to say something about a matter that concerns both our futures.'

'And you are going to say it now?' she remarked quickly, colouring as she met his gaze. 'Do stop a minute, Clym, and let me speak first, for, oddly enough, I have been wanting to say something to you.'

'By all means say on, Tamsie.'

'I suppose nobody can overhear us?' she went on, casting her eyes around and lowering her voice. 'Well, first you will promise me this – that you won't be angry and call me anything harsh if you disagree with what I propose?'

Yeobright promised, and she continued: 'What I want is your advice, for you are my relation – I mean, a sort of guardian to me – aren't you, Clym?'

'Well, yes, I suppose I am; a sort of guardian. In fact, I am, of course,' he said, altogether perplexed as to her drift.

'I am thinking of marrying,' she then observed blandly. 'But I shall not marry unless you assure me that you approve of such a step. Why don't you speak?'

'I was taken rather by surprise. But, nevertheless, I am very glad to hear such news. I shall approve, of course, dear Tamsie. Who can it be? I am quite at a loss to guess. No, I am not – 'tis the old doctor! – not that I mean to call him old, for he is not very old after all. Ah – I noticed when he attended you last time!'

'No, no,' she said hastily. ' 'Tis Mr Venn.'

Clym's face suddenly became grave.

'There, now, you don't like him, and I wish I hadn't mentioned him!' she exclaimed almost petulantly. 'And I shouldn't have done it, either, only he keeps on bothering me so till I don't know what to do!'

Clym looked at the heath. 'I like Venn well enough,' he answered at last. 'He is a very honest and at the same time astute man. He is clever too, as is proved by his having got you to favour him. But really, Thomasin, he is not quite –'

'Gentleman enough for me? That is just what I feel. I am sorry now that I asked you, and I won't think any more of him. At the same time I must marry him if I marry anybody – that I *will* say!'

'I don't see that,' said Clym, carefully concealing every clue to his own interrupted intention, which she plainly had not guessed. 'You might marry a professional man, or somebody of that sort, by going into the town to live and forming acquaintances there.'

'I am not fit for town life – so very rural and silly as I always have been. Do not you yourself notice my countrified ways?'

'Well, when I came home from Paris I did, a little; but I don't now.'

'That's because you have got countrified too. O, I couldn't live in a street for the world! Egdon is a ridiculous old place; but I have got used to it, and I couldn't be happy anywhere else at all.'

'Neither could I,' said Clym.

'Then how could you say that I should marry some town man? I am sure, say what you will, that I must marry Diggory, if I marry at all. He has been kinder to me than anybody else, and has helped me in many ways that I don't know of!' Thomasin almost pouted now.

'Yes, he has,' said Clym in a neutral tone. 'Well, I wish with all my heart that I could say, marry him. But I cannot forget what my mother thought on that matter, and it goes rather against me not to respect her opinion. There is too much reason why we should do the little we can to respect it now.'

'Very well, then,' sighed Thomasin. 'I will say no more.'

'But you are not bound to obey my wishes. I merely say what I think.'

'O no – I don't want to be rebellious in that way,' she said sadly. 'I had no business to think of him – I ought to have thought of my family. What dreadfully bad impulses there are in me!' Her lip trembled, and she turned away to hide a tear.

Clym, though vexed at what seemed her unaccountable taste, was in a measure relieved to find that at any rate the marriage question in relation to himself was shelved. Through several succeeding days he saw her at different times from the window of his room moping disconsolately about the garden. He was half angry with her for choosing Venn; then he was grieved at having put himself in the way of Venn's happiness, who was, after all, as honest and persevering a young fellow as any on Egdon, since he had turned over a new leaf. In short, Clym did not know what to do.

When next they met she said abruptly, 'He is much more respectable now than he was then!'

'Who? O yes – Diggory Venn.'

'Aunt only objected because he was a reddleman.'

'Well, Thomasin, perhaps I don't know all the particulars of my mother's wish. So you had better use your own discretion.'

'You will always feel that I slighted your mother's memory.'

'No, I will not. I shall think you are convinced that, had she seen Diggory in his present position, she would have considered him a fitting husband for you. Now, that's my real feeling. Don't consult me any more, but do as you like, Thomasin. I shall be content.'

It is to be supposed that Thomasin was convinced; for a few days after this, when Clym strayed into a part of the heath that he had not lately visited, Humphrey, who was at work there, said to him, 'I am glad to see that Mrs Wildeve and Venn have made it up again, seemingly.'

'Have they?' said Clym abstractedly.

'Yes; and he do contrive to stumble upon her whenever she walks out on fine days with the chiel. But, Mr Yeobright, I can't help feeling that your cousin ought to have married you. 'Tis a pity to make two chimley-corners where there need be only one. You could get her away from him now, 'tis my belief, if you were only to set about it.'

'How can I have the conscience to marry after having driven two women to their deaths? Don't think such a thing, Humphrey. After my experience I should consider it too much of a burlesque to go to church and take a wife. In the words of Job, "I have made a covenant with mine eyes; why then should I think upon a maid?" '

'No, Mr Clym, don't fancy that about driving two women to their deaths. You shouldn't say it.'

'Well, we'll leave that out,' said Yeobright. 'But anyhow God has set a mark upon me which wouldn't look well in a love-making scene. I have two ideas in my head, and no others. I am going to keep a night-school; and I am going to turn preacher. What have you got to say to that, Humphrey?'

'I'll come and hear 'ee with all my heart.'

'Thanks. 'Tis all I wish.'

As Clym descended into the valley Thomasin came down by the other path, and met him at the gate. 'What do you think I have to tell you, Clym?' she said, looking archly over her shoulder at him.

'I can guess,' he replied.

She scrutinized his face. 'Yes, you guess right. It is going to be after all. He thinks I may as well make up my mind, and I have got to think so too. It is to be on the twenty-fifth of next month, if you don't object.'

'Do what you think right, dear. I am only too glad that you see your way clear to happiness again. My sex owes you every amends for the treatment you received in days gone by.' ★

★ IV ★

Cheerfulness Again Asserts Itself at Blooms-End, and Clym Finds His Vocation

ANYBODY who had passed through Blooms-End about eleven o'clock on the morning fixed for the wedding would have found that, while Yeobright's house was comparatively quiet, sounds denoting great activity came from the dwelling of his nearest neighbour, Timothy Fairway. It was chiefly a noise of feet, briskly crunching hither and thither over the sanded floor within. One man only was visible outside, and he seemed to be later at an appointment than he had intended to be, for he hastened up to the door, lifted the latch, and walked in without ceremony.

★ The writer may state here that the original conception of the story did not design a marriage between Thomasin and Venn. He was to have retained his isolated and weird character to the last, and to have disappeared mysteriously from the heath, nobody knowing whither – Thomasin remaining a widow. But certain circumstances of serial publication led to a change of intent.

Readers can therefore choose between endings, and those with an austere artistic code can assume the more consistent conclusion to be the true one.

The scene within was not quite the customary one. Standing about the room was the little knot of men who formed the chief part of the Egdon coterie, there being present Fairway himself, Grandfer Cantle, Humphrey, Christian, and one or two turf-cutters. It was a warm day, and the men were as a matter of course in their shirtsleeves, except Christian, who had always a nervous fear of parting with a scrap of his clothing when in anybody's house but his own. Across the stout oak table in the middle of the room was thrown a mass of striped linen, which Grandfer Cantle held down on one side, and Humphrey on the other, while Fairway rubbed its surface with a yellow lump, his face being damp and creased with the effort of the labour.

'Waxing a bed-tick, souls?' said the new-comer.

'Yes, Sam,' said Grandfer Cantle, as a man too busy to waste words. 'Shall I stretch this corner a shade tighter, Timothy?'

Fairway replied, and the waxing went on with unabated vigour. ' 'Tis going to be a good bed, by the look o't,' continued Sam, after an interval of silence. 'Who may it be for?'

' 'Tis a present for the new folks that's going to set up house-keeping,' said Christian, who stood helpless and overcome by the majesty of the proceedings.

'Ah, to be sure; and a valuable one, 'a b'lieve.'

'Beds be dear to fokes that don't keep geese, bain't they, Mister Fairway?' said Christian, as to an omniscient being.

'Yes,' said the furze-dealer, standing up, giving his forehead a thorough mopping, and handing the beeswax to Humphrey, who succeeded at the rubbing forthwith. 'Not that this couple be in want of one, but 'twas well to show 'em a bit of friendliness at this great racketing vagary of their lives. I set up both my own daughters in one when they was married, and there have been feathers enough for another in the house the last twelve months. Now then, neighbours, I think we have laid on enough wax. Grandfer Cantle, you turn the tick the right way outwards, and then I'll begin to shake the feathers.'

When the bed was in proper trim Fairway and Christian brought forward vast paper bags, stuffed to the full, but light as balloons, and began to turn the contents of each into the receptacle just prepared. As bag after bag was emptied, airy tufts of down and feathers floated about the room in increasing quantity till, through a mishap of Christian's, who shook the contents of one bag outside the tick, the atmosphere of the room became dense with gigantic flakes, which descended upon the workers like a windless snowstorm.

'I never saw such a clumsy chap as you, Christian,' said Grandfer Cantle severely. 'You might have been the son of a man that's never been outside Blooms-End in his life for all the wit you have. Really all the soldiering and smartness in the world in the father seems to count for nothing in forming the nater of the son. As far as that chiel Christian is concerned I might as well have stayed at home and seed nothing, like all the rest of ye here. Though, as far as myself is concerned, a dashing spirit has counted for sommat, to be sure!'

'Don't ye let me down so, father; I feel no bigger than a ninepin after it. I've made but a bruckle hit, I'm afeard.'

'Come, come. Never pitch yerself in such a low key as that, Christian; you should try more,' said Fairway.

'Yes, you should try more,' echoed the Grandfer with insistence, as if he had been the first to make the suggestion. 'In common conscience every man ought either to marry or go for a soldier. 'Tis a scandal to the nation to do neither one nor t'other. I did both, thank God! Neither to raise men nor to lay 'em low – that shows a poor do-nothing spirit indeed.'

'I never had the nerve to stand fire,' faltered Christian. 'But as to marrying, I own I've asked here and there, though without much fruit from it. Yes, there's some house or other that might have had a man for a master – such as he is – that's now ruled by a woman alone. Still it might have been awkward if I had found her; for, d'ye see, neighbours, there'd have been nobody left at home to keep down father's spirits to the decent pitch that becomes a old man.'

'And you've your work cut out to do that, my son,' said Grandfer Cantle smartly. 'I wish that the dread of infirmities was not so strong in me! – I'd start the very first thing tomorrow to see the world over again! But seventy-one, though nothing at home, is a high figure for a rover . . . Ay, seventy-one last Candlemas-day. Gad, I'd sooner have it in guineas than in years!' And the old man sighed.

'Don't you be mournful, Grandfer,' said Fairway. 'Empty some more feathers into the bed-tick, and keep up yer heart. Though rather lean in the stalks you be a green-leaved old man still. There's time enough left to ye yet to fill whole chronicles.'

'Begad, I'll go to 'em, Timothy – to the married pair!' said Grandfer Cantle in an encouraged voice, and starting round briskly. 'I'll go to 'em tonight and sing a wedding song, hey? 'Tis like me to do so, you know; and they'd see it as such. My "Down in Cupid's Gardens" was well liked in four; still, I've got others as good, and even better. What do you say to my

> 'She cal'-led to' her love'
> From the lat'-tice a-bove,
> "O, come in' from the fog'-gy fog'-gy dew'." '

'Twould please 'em well at such a time! Really, now I come to think of it, I haven't turned my tongue in my head to the shape of a real good song since Old Midsummer night, when we had the "Barley Mow" at the Woman; and 'tis a pity to neglect your strong point where there's few that have the compass for such things!'

'So 'tis, so 'tis,' said Fairway. 'Now gie the bed a shake down. We've put in seventy pound of best feathers, and I think that's as many as the tick will fairly hold. A bit and a drap wouldn't be amiss now, I reckon.

Christian, maul down the victuals from corner-cupboard if canst reach, man, and I'll draw a drap o' sommat to wet it with.'

They sat down to a lunch in the midst of their work, feathers around, above, and below them; the original owners of which occasionally came to the open door and cackled begrudgingly at sight of such a quantity of their old clothes.

'Upon my soul I shall be chokt,' said Fairway when, having extracted a feather from his mouth, he found several others floating on the mug as it was handed round.

'I've swallered several; and one had a tolerable quill,' said Sam placidly from the corner.

'Hullo – what's that – wheels I hear coming?' Grandfer Cantle exclaimed, jumping up and hastening to the door. 'Why, 'tis they back again: I didn't expect 'em yet this half-hour. To be sure, how quick marrying can be done when you are in the mind for't!'

'O yes, it can soon be *done*,' said Fairway, as if something should be added to make the statement complete.

He arose and followed the Grandfer, and the rest also went to the door. In a moment an open fly was driven past, in which sat Venn and Mrs Venn, Yeobright, and a grand relative of Venn's who had come from Budmouth for the occasion. The fly had been hired at the nearest town, regardless of distance and cost, there being nothing on Egdon Heath, in Venn's opinion, dignified enough for such an event when such a woman as Thomasin was the bride; and the church was too remote for a walking bridal-party.

As the fly passed the group which had run out from the homestead they shouted 'Hurrah!' and waved their hands; feathers and down floating from their hair, their sleeves, and the folds of their garments at every motion, and Grandfer Cantle's seals dancing merrily in the sunlight as he twirled himself about. The driver of the fly turned a supercilious gaze upon them; he even treated the wedded pair themselves with something like condescension; for in what other state than heathen could people, rich or poor, exist who were doomed to abide in such a world's end as Egdon? Thomasin showed no such superiority to the group at the door, fluttering her hand as quickly as a bird's wing towards them, and asking Diggory, with tears in her eyes, if they ought not to alight and speak to these kind neighbours. Venn, however, suggested that, as they were all coming to the house in the evening, this was hardly necessary.

After this excitement the saluting party returned to their occupation, and the stuffing and sewing was soon afterwards finished, when Fairway harnessed a horse, wrapped up the cumbrous present, and drove off with it in the cart to Venn's house at Stickleford.

Yeobright, having filled the office at the wedding-service which naturally fell to his hands, and afterwards returned to the house with the husband and wife, was indisposed to take part in the feasting and dancing that wound up the evening. Thomasin was disappointed.

'I wish I could be there without dashing your spirits,' he said. 'But I might be too much like the skull at the banquet.'

'No, no.'

'Well, dear, apart from that, if you would excuse me, I should be glad. I know it seems unkind; but, dear Thomasin, I fear I should not be happy in the company – there, that's the truth of it. I shall always be coming to see you at your new home, you know, so that my absence now will not matter.'

'Then I give in. Do whatever will be most comfortable to yourself.'

Clym retired to his lodging at the housetop much relieved and occupied himself during the afternoon in noting down the heads of a sermon, with which he intended to initiate all that really seemed practicable of the scheme that had originally brought him hither, and that he had so long kept in view under various modifications, and through evil and good report. He had tested and weighed his convictions again and again, and saw no reason to alter them, though he had considerably lessened his plan. His eyesight, by long humouring in his native air, had grown stronger, but not sufficiently strong to warrant his attempting his extensive educational project. Yet he did not repine: there was still more than enough of an unambitious sort to tax all his energies and occupy all his hours.

Evening drew on, and sounds of life and movement in the lower part of the domicile became more pronounced, the gate in the palings clicking incessantly. The party was to be an early one, and all the guests were assembled long before it was dark. Yeobright went down the back staircase and into the heath by another path than that in front, intending to walk in the open air till the party was over, when he would return to wish Thomasin and her husband good-bye as they departed. His steps were insensibly bent towards Mistover by the path that he had followed on that terrible morning when he learnt the strange news from Susan's boy.

He did not turn aside to the cottage, but pushed on to an eminence, whence he could see over the whole quarter that had once been Eustacia's home. While he stood observing the darkening scene somebody came up. Clym, seeing him but dimly, would have let him pass by silently, had not the pedestrian, who was Charley, recognized the young man and spoken to him.

'Charley, I have not seen you for a length of time,' said Yeobright. 'Do you often walk this way?'

'No,' the lad replied. 'I don't often come outside the bank.'

'You were not at the Maypole.'

'No,' said Charley, in the same listless tone. 'I don't care for that sort of thing now.'

'You rather liked Miss Eustacia, didn't you?' Yeobright gently asked. Eustacia had frequently told him of Charley's romantic attachment.

'Yes, very much. Ah, I wish –'

'Yes?'

'I wish, Mr Yeobright, you could give me something to keep that once belonged to her – if you don't mind.'

'I shall be very happy to. It will give me very great pleasure, Charley. Let me think what I have of hers that you would like. But come with me to the house, and I'll see.

They walked towards Blooms-End together. When they reached the front it was dark, and the shutters were closed, so that nothing of the interior could be seen.

'Come round this way,' said Clym. 'My entrance is at the back for the present.'

The two went round and ascended the crooked stair in darkness till Clym's sitting-room on the upper floor was reached, where he lit a candle, Charley entering gently behind. Yeobright searched his desk, and taking out a sheet of tissue-paper unfolded from it two or three undulating locks of raven hair, which fell over the paper like black streams. From these he selected one, wrapped it up, and gave it to the lad, whose eyes had filled with tears. He kissed the packet, put it in his pocket, and said in a voice of emotion, 'O, Mr Clym, how good you are to me!'

'I will go a little way with you,' said Clym. And amid the noise of merriment from below they descended. Their path to the front led them close to a little side-window, whence the rays of candles streamed across the shrubs. The window, being screened from general observation by the bushes, had been left unblinded, so that a person in this private nook could see all that was going on within the room which contained the wedding-guests, except in so far as vision was hindered by the green antiquity of the panes.

'Charley, what are they doing?' said Clym. 'My sight is weaker again tonight, and the glass of the window is not good.'

Charley wiped his own eyes, which were rather blurred with moisture, and stepped closer to the casement. 'Mr Venn is asking Christian Cantle to sing,' he replied; 'and Christian is moving about in his chair as if he were much frightened at the question, and his father has struck up a stave instead of him.'

'Yes, I can hear the old man's voice,' said Clym. 'So there's to be no dancing, I suppose. And is Thomasin in the room? I see something moving in front of the candles that resembles her shape, I think.'

'Yes. She do seem happy. She is red in the face, and laughing at something Fairway has said to her. O my!'

'What noise was that?' said Clym.

'Mr Venn is so tall that he has knocked his head against the beam in gieing a skip as he passed under. Mrs Venn has run up quite frightened and now she's put her hand to his head to feel if there's a lump. And now they be all laughing again as if nothing had happened.'

'Do any of them seem to care about my not being there?' Clym asked.

'No, not a bit in the world. Now they are all holding up their glasses and drinking somebody's health.'

'I wonder if it is mine?'

'No, 'tis Mr and Mrs Venn's, because he is making a hearty sort of speech. There – now Mrs Venn has got up, and is going away to put on her things, I think.'

'Well, they haven't concerned themselves about me, and it is quite right they should not. It is all as it should be, and Thomasin at least is happy. We will not stay any longer now, as they will soon be coming out to go home.'

He accompanied the lad into the heath on his way home, and, returning alone to the house a quarter of an hour later, found Venn and Thomasin ready to start, all the guests having departed in his absence. The wedded pair took their seats in the four-wheeled dogcart which Venn's head milker and handy man had driven from Stickleford to fetch them in; little Eustacia and the nurse were packed securely upon the open flap behind; and the milker, on an ancient overstepping pony, whose shoes clashed like cymbals at every tread, rode in the rear, in the manner of a body-servant of the last century.

'Now we leave you in absolute possession of your own house again,' said Thomasin as she bent down to wish her cousin good-night. 'It will be rather lonely for you, Clym, after the hubbub we have been making.'

'O, that's no inconvenience,' said Clym, smiling rather sadly. And then the party drove off and vanished in the night-shades, and Yeobright entered the house. The ticking of the clock was the only sound that greeted him, for not a soul remained; Christian, who acted as cook, valet, and gardener to Clym, sleeping at his father's house. Yeobright sat down in one of the vacant chairs, and remained in thought a long time. His mother's old chair was opposite; it had been sat in that evening by those who had scarcely remembered that it ever was hers. But to Clym she was almost a presence there, now as always. Whatever she was in other people's memories, in his she was the sublime saint whose radiance even his tenderness for Eustacia could not obscure. But his heart was heavy; that mother had *not* crowned him in the day of his espousals and in the day of the gladness of his heart. And events had borne out the accuracy of her judgement, and proved the devotedness of her care. He should have heeded her for Eustacia's sake even more than for his own. 'It was all my fault,' he whispered. 'O, my mother, my mother! would to God that I could live my life again, and endure for you what you endured for me!'

On the Sunday after this wedding an unusual sight was to be seen on Rainbarrow. From a distance there simply appeared to be a motionless figure standing on the top of the tumulus, just as Eustacia had stood on that lonely summit some two years and a half before. But now it was fine warm weather, with only a summer breeze blowing, and early afternoon instead of dull twilight. Those who ascended to the immediate neigh-bourhood of the Barrow perceived that the erect form in the centre, piercing the sky, was not really alone. Round him upon the slopes of the Barrow a number of heathmen and women were reclining or sitting at their ease. They listened to the words of the man in their midst, who was preaching, while they abstractedly pulled heather, stripped ferns, or tossed pebbles down the slope. This was the first of a series of moral lectures or Sermons on the Mount, which were to be delivered from the same place every Sunday afternoon as long as the fine weather lasted.

The commanding elevation of Rainbarrow had been chosen for two reasons: first, that it occupied a central position among the remote cottages around; secondly, that the preacher thereon could be seen from all adjacent points as soon as he arrived at his post, the view of him being thus a convenient signal to those stragglers who wished to draw near. The speaker was bareheaded, and the breeze at each waft gently lifted and lowered his hair, somewhat too thin for a man of his years, these still numbering less than thirty-three. He wore a shade over his eyes, and his face was pensive and lined; but, though these bodily features were marked with decay there was no defect in the tones of his voice, which were rich, musical, and stirring. He stated that his discourses to people were to be sometimes secular, and sometimes religious, but never dogmatic; and that his texts would be taken from all kinds of books. This afternoon the words were as follows:

' "And the king rose up to meet her, and bowed himself unto her, and sat down on his throne, and caused a seat to be set for the king's mother; and she sat on his right hand. Then she said, I desire one small petition of thee; I pray thee say me not nay. And the king said unto her, Ask on, my mother: for I will not say thee nay." '

Yeobright had, in fact, found his vocation in the career of an itinerant open-air preacher and lecturer on morally unimpeachable subjects; and from this day he laboured incessantly in that office, speaking not only in simple language on Rainbarrow and in the hamlets round, but in a more cultivated strain elsewhere – from the steps and porticoes of town-halls, from market-crosses, from conduits, on esplanades and on wharves, from the parapets of bridges, in barns and outhouses, and all other such places in the neighbouring Wessex towns and villages. He left alone creeds and systems of philosophy, finding enough and more than enough to occupy his tongue in the opinions and actions common to all good men. Some believed him, and some believed not; some said that his words were commonplace, others complained of his want of theological doctrine; while others again remarked that it was well enough for a man to take to preaching who could not see to do anything else. But everywhere he was kindly received, for the story of his life had become generally known.

THE LIFE AND DEATH OF

THE MAYOR
OF
CASTERBRIDGE

A STORY OF A MAN OF
CHARACTER

AUTHOR'S PREFACE

READERS of the following story who have not yet arrived at middle age are asked to bear in mind that, in the days recalled by the tale, the home Corn Trade, on which so much of the action turns, had an importance that can hardly be realized by those accustomed to the sixpenny loaf of the present date, and to the present indifference of the public to harvest weather.

The incidents narrated arise mainly out of three events, which chanced to range themselves in the order and at or about the intervals of time here given, in the real history of the town called Casterbridge and the neighbouring country. They were the sale of a wife by her husband, the uncertain harvests which immediately preceded the repeal of the Corn Laws, and the visit of a Royal personage to the aforesaid part of England.

The present edition of the volume, like the previous one, contains nearly a chapter which did not at first appear in any English copy, though it was printed in the serial issue of the tale, and in the American edition. The restoration was made at the instance of some good judges across the Atlantic, who strongly represented that the home edition suffered from the omission. Some shorter passages and names, omitted or altered for reasons which no longer exist, in the original printing of both English and American editions, have also been replaced or inserted.

The story is more particularly a study of one man's deeds and character than, perhaps, any other of those included in my Exhibition of Wessex life. Objections have been raised to the Scotch language of Mr Farfrae, the second character; and one of his fellow-countrymen went so far as to declare that men beyond the Tweed did not and never could say 'warrld', 'cannet', 'advairrtisment' and so on. As this gentleman's pronunciation in correcting me seemed to my Southron ear an exact repetition of what my spelling implied, I was not struck with the truth of his remark, and somehow we did not get any forwarder in the matter. It must be remembered that the Scotchman of the tale is represented not as he would appear to other Scotchmen, but as he would appear to people of outer regions. Moreover, no attempt is made herein to reproduce his entire pronunciation phonetically, any more than that of the Wessex speakers. I should add, however, that this new edition of the book has had the accidental advantage of a critical overlooking by a professor of the tongue in question – one of undoubted authority: – in fact he is a gentleman who adopted it for urgent personal reasons in the first year of his existence.

Furthermore, a charming non-Scottish lady, of strict veracity and admitted penetration, the wife of a well-known Caledonian, came to the writer shortly after the story was first published, and inquired if Farfrae were not drawn from her husband, for he seemed to her to be the living portrait of that (doubtless) happy man. It happened that I had never thought of her husband in constructing Farfrae. I trust therefore that Farfrae may be allowed to pass, if not as a Scotchman to Scotchmen, as a Scotchman to Southerners.

The novel was first published complete, in two volumes, in May 1886.

February 1895–May 1912   T.H.

ONE evening of late summer, before the nineteenth century had reached one-third of its span, a young man and woman, the latter carrying a child, were approaching the large village of Weydon-Priors, in Upper Wessex, on foot. They were plainly but not ill clad, though the thick hoar of dust which had accumulated on their shoes and garments from an obviously long journey lent a disadvantageous shabbiness to their appearance just now.

The man was of fine figure, swarthy, and stern in aspect; and he showed in profile a facial angle so slightly inclined as to be almost perpendicular. He wore a short jacket of brown corduroy, newer than the remainder of his suit, which was a fustian waistcoat with white horn buttons, breeches of the same, tanned leggings, and a straw hat overlaid with black glazed canvas. At his back he carried by a looped strap a rush basket, from which protruded at one end the crutch of a hayknife, a wimble for hay-bonds being also visible in the aperture. His measured, springless walk was the walk of the skilled countryman as distinct from the desultory shamble of the general labourer; while in the turn and plant of each foot there was, further, a dogged and cynical indifference personal to himself, showing its presence even in the regularly interchanging fustian folds, now in the left leg, now in the right, as he paced along.

What was really peculiar, however, in this couple's progress, and would have attracted the attention of any casual observer otherwise disposed to overlook them, was the perfect silence they preserved. They walked side by side in such a way as to suggest afar off the low, easy, confidential chat of people full of reciprocity; but on closer view it could be discerned that the man was reading, or pretending to read, a ballad sheet which he kept before his eyes with some difficulty by the hand that was passed through the basket strap. Whether this apparent cause were the real cause, or whether it were an assumed one to escape an intercourse that would have been irksome to him, nobody but himself could have said precisely; but his taciturnity was unbroken, and the woman enjoyed no society whatever from his presence. Virtually she walked the highway alone, save for the child she bore. Sometimes the man's bent elbow almost touched her shoulder, for she kept as close to his side as was possible without actual contact; but she seemed to have no idea of taking his arm, nor he of offering it; and far from exhibiting surprise at his ignoring silence she appeared to receive it as a natural thing. If any word at all were uttered by the little group, it was an occasional whisper of the woman to the child – a tiny girl in short clothes and blue boots of knitted yarn – and the murmured babble of the child in reply.

The chief – almost the only – attraction of the young woman's face was its mobility. When she looked down sideways to the girl she became pretty, and even handsome, particularly that in the action her features caught slantwise the rays of the strongly coloured sun, which made transparencies of her eyelids and nostrils and set fire on her lips. When she plodded on in the shade of the hedge, silently thinking, she had the hard, half-apathetic expression of one who deems anything possible at the hands of Time and Chance except, perhaps, fair play. The first phase was the work of Nature, the second probably of civilization.

That the man and woman were husband and wife, and the parents of the girl in arms, there could be little doubt. No other than such relationship would have accounted for the atmosphere of stale familiarity which the trio carried along with them like a nimbus as they moved down the road.

The wife mostly kept her eyes fixed ahead, though with little interest – the scene for that matter being one that might have been matched at almost any spot in any country in England at this time of the year; a road neither straight nor crooked, neither level nor hilly, bordered by hedges, trees, and other vegetation, which had entered the blackened-green stage of colour that doomed leaves pass through on their way to dingy, and yellow, and red. The grassy margin of the bank, and the nearest hedgerow boughs, were powdered by the dust that had been stirred over them by hasty vehicles, the same dust as it lay on the road deadening their footfalls like a carpet; and this, with the aforesaid total absence of conversation, allowed every extraneous sound to be heard.

For a long time there was none, beyond the voice of a weak bird singing a trite old evening song that might doubtless have been heard on the hill at the same hour, and with the selfsame trills, quavers, and breves, at any sunset of that season for centuries untold. But as they approached the village sundry distant shouts and rattles reached their ears from some elevated spot in that direction, as yet screened from view by foliage. When the outlying houses of Weydon-Priors could just be descried, the family group was met by a turnip-hoer with his hoe on his shoulder, and his dinner-bag suspended from it. The reader promptly glanced up.

'Any trade doing here?' he asked phlegmatically, designating the village in his van by a wave of the broadsheet. And thinking the labourer did not understand him, he added, 'Anything in the hay-trussing line?'

The turnip-hoer had already begun shaking his head. 'Why, save the man, what wisdom's in him that 'a should come to Weydon for a job of that sort this time o' year?'

'Then is there any house to let – a little small new cottage just a-builded, or such like?' asked the other.

The pessimist still maintained a negative. 'Pulling down is more the nater of Weydon. There were five houses cleared away last year, and three this; and the volk nowhere to go – no, not so much as a thatched hurdler; that's the way o' Weydon-Priors.'

The hay-trusser, which he obviously was, nodded with some supercil-iousness. Looking towards the village, he continued, 'There is something going on here, however, is there not?'

'Ay. 'Tis Fair Day. Though what you hear now is little more than the clatter and scurry of getting away the money o' children and fools, for the real business is done earlier than this. I've been working within sound o't all day, but I didn't go up – not I. 'Twas no business of mine.'

The trusser and his family proceeded on their way, and soon entered the Fair-field, which showed standing-places and pens where many hundreds of horses and sheep had been exhibited and sold in the forenoon, but were now in great part taken away. At present, as their informant had observed, but little real business remained on hand, the chief being the sale by auction of a few inferior animals, that could not otherwise be disposed of, and had been absolutely refused by the better class of traders, who came and went early. Yet the crowd was denser now than during the morning hours, the frivolous contingent of visitors, including journey-men out for a holiday, a stray soldier or two home on furlough, village shopkeepers, and the like, having latterly flocked in; persons whose activities found a congenial field among the peep-shows, toy-stands, waxworks, inspired monsters, disinterested medical men who travelled for the public good, thimble-riggers, nick-nack vendors, and readers of Fate.

Neither of our pedestrians had much heart for these things, and they looked around for a refreshment tent among the many which dotted the down. Two, which stood nearest to them in the ochreous haze of expiring sunlight, seemed almost equally inviting. One was formed of new, milk-hued canvas, and bore red flags on its summit; it announced 'Good Homebrewed Beer, Ale and Cyder'. The other was less new; a little iron stove-pipe came out of it at the back, and in front appeared the placard, 'Good Furmity Sold Hear'. The man mentally weighed the two inscrip-tions, and inclined to the former tent.

'No – no – the other one,' said the woman. 'I always like furmity; and so does Elizabeth-Jane; and so will you. It is nourishing after a long hard day.'

'I've never tasted it,' said the man. However, he gave way to her representations, and they entered the furmity booth forthwith.

A rather numerous company appeared within, seated at the long narrow tables that ran down the tent on each side. At the upper end stood a stove, containing a charcoal fire, over which hung a three-legged crock, sufficiently polished round the rim to show that it was made of bell-metal. A haggish creature of about fifty presided, in a white apron, which, as it threw an air of respectability over her as far as it extended, was made so wide as to reach nearly round her waist. She slowly stirred the contents of the pot. The dull scrape of her large spoon was audible throughout the tent as she thus kept from burning the mixture of corn in the grain, flour, milk, raisins, currants, and what not, that composed the antiquated slop in which she dealt. Vessels holding the separate ingredients stood on a white-clothed table of boards and trestles close by.

The young man and woman ordered a basin each of the mixture, steaming hot, and sat down to consume it at leisure. This was very well so far, for furmity, as the woman had said, was nourishing, and as proper a food as could be obtained within the four seas; though, to those not accustomed to it, the grains of wheat swollen as large as lemon-pips, which floated on its surface, might have a deterrent effect at first.

But there was more in that tent than met the cursory glance; and the man, with the instinct of a perverse character, scented it quickly. After a mincing attack on his bowl, he watched the hag's proceedings from the corner of his eye, and saw the game she played. He winked to her, and passed up his basin in reply to her nod; when she took a bottle from under the table, slily measured out a quantity of its contents, and tipped the same into the man's furmity. The liquor poured in was rum. The man as slily sent back money in payment.

He found the concoction, thus strongly laced, much more to his satisfaction than it had been in its natural state. His wife had observed the proceeding with much uneasiness; but he persuaded her to have hers laced also, and she agreed to a milder allowance after some misgiving.

The man finished his basin, and called for another, the rum being signalled for in yet stronger proportion. The effect of it was soon apparent in his manner, and his wife but too sadly perceived that in strenuously steering off the rocks of the licensed liquor-tent she had only got into maelstrom depths here amongst the smugglers.

The child began to prattle impatiently, and the wife more than once said to her husband, 'Michael, how about our lodging? You know we may have trouble in getting it if we don't go soon.'

But he turned a deaf ear to those bird-like chirpings. He talked loud to the company. The child's black eyes, after slow, round, ruminating gazes at the candles when they were lighted, fell together; then they opened, then they shut again, and she slept.

At the end of the first basin the man had risen to serenity; at the second he was jovial; at the third, argumentative; at the fourth, the qualities signified by the shape of his face, the occasional clench of his mouth, and the fiery spark of his dark eye, began to tell in his conduct; he was overbearing – even brilliantly quarrelsome.

The conversation took a high turn, as it often does on such occasions. The ruin of good men by bad wives, and, more particularly, the frustration of many a promising youth's high aims and hopes and the extinction of his energies by an early imprudent marriage, was the theme.

'I did for myself that way thoroughly,' said the trusser, with a contemplative bitterness that was well-nigh resentful. 'I married at eighteen, like the fool that I was; and this is the consequence o't.' He pointed at himself and family with a wave of the hand intended to bring out the penuriousness of the exhibition.

The young woman his wife, who seemed accustomed to such remarks, acted as if she did not hear them, and continued her intermittent private words on tender trifles to the sleeping and waking child, who was just big enough to be placed for a moment on the bench beside her when she wished to ease her arms. The man continued –

'I haven't more than fifteen shillings in the world, and yet I am a good experienced hand in my line. I'd challenge England to beat me in the fodder business; and if I were a free man again I'd be worth a thousand pound before I'd done o't. But a fellow never knows these little things till all chance of acting upon 'em is past.'

The auctioneer selling the old horses in the field outside could be heard saying, 'Now this is the last lot – now who'll take the last lot for a song? Shall I say forty shillings? 'Tis a very promising brood-mare, a trifle over five years old, and nothing the matter with the hoss at all, except that she's a little holler in the back and had her left eye knocked out by the kick of another, her own sister, coming along the road.'

'For my part I don't see why men who have got wives and don't want 'em shouldn't get rid of 'em as these gipsy fellows do their old horses,' said the man in the tent. 'Why shouldn't they put 'em up and sell 'em by auction to men who are in need of such articles? Hey? Why, begad, I'd sell mine this minute if anybody would buy her!'

'There's them that would do that,' some of the guests replied, looking at the woman, who was by no means ill-favoured.

'True,' said a smoking gentleman, whose coat had the fine polish about the collar, elbows, seams, and shoulder-blades that long-continued friction with grimy surfaces will produce, and which is usually more desired on furniture than on clothes. From his appearance he had possibly been in former time groom or coachman to some neighbouring county family. 'I've had my breedings in as good circles, I may say, as any man,' he added, 'and I know true cultivation, or nobody do; and I can declare she's got it – in the bone, mind ye, I say – as much as any female in the fair – though it may want a little bringing out.' Then, crossing his legs, he resumed his pipe with a nicely-adjusted gaze at a point in the air.

The fuddled young husband stared for a few seconds at this unexpected praise of his wife, half in doubt of the wisdom of his own attitude towards the possessor of such qualities. But he speedily lapsed into his former conviction, and said harshly –

'Well, then, now is your chance; I am open to an offer for this gem o' creation.'

She turned to her husband and murmured, 'Michael, you have talked this nonsense in public places before. A joke is a joke, but you may make it once too often, mind!'

'I know I've said it before; I meant it. All I want is a buyer.'

At the moment a swallow, one among the last of the season, which had by chance found its way through an opening into the upper part of the tent, flew to and fro in quick curves above their heads, causing all eyes to follow it absently. In watching the bird till it made its escape the assembled company neglected to respond to the workman's offer, and the subject dropped.

But a quarter of an hour later the man, who had gone on lacing his furmity more and more heavily, though he was either so strong-minded or such an intrepid toper that he still appeared fairly sober, recurred to the old strain, as in a musical fantasy the instrument fetches up the original theme. 'Here – I am waiting to know about this offer of mine. The woman is no good to me. Who'll have her?'

The company had by this time decidedly degenerated, and the renewed inquiry was received with a laugh of appreciation. The woman whispered; she was imploring and anxious: 'Come, come, it is getting dark, and this nonsense won't do. If you don't come along, I shall go without you. Come!'

She waited and waited; yet he did not move. In ten minutes the man broke in upon the desultory conversation of the furmity drinkers with, 'I asked this question, and nobody answered to 't. Will any Jack Rag or Tom Straw among ye buy my goods?'

The woman's manner changed, and her face assumed the grim shape and colour of which mention has been made.

'Mike, Mike,' said she; 'this is getting serious. O! – too serious!'

'Will anybody buy her?' said the man.

'I wish somebody would,' said she firmly. 'Her present owner is not at all to her liking!'

'Nor you to mine,' said he. 'So we are agreed about that. Gentlemen, you hear? It's an agreement to part. She shall take the girl if she wants to, and go her ways. I'll take my tools, and go my ways. 'Tis simple as Scripture history. Now then, stand up, Susan, and show yourself.'

'Don't, my chiel,' whispered a buxom staylace dealer in voluminous petticoats, who sat near the woman; 'yer good man don't know what he's saying.'

The woman, however, did stand up. 'Now, who's auctioneer?' cried the hay-trusser.

'I be,' promptly answered a short man, with a nose resembling a copper knob, a damp voice, and eyes like buttonholes. 'Who'll make an offer for this lady?'

The woman looked on the ground, as if she maintained her position by a supreme effort of will.

'Five shillings,' said someone, at which there was a laugh.

'No insults,' said the husband. 'Who'll say a guinea?'

Nobody answered; and the female dealer in staylaces interposed.

'Behave yerself moral, good man, for Heaven's love! Ah, what a cruelty is the poor soul married to! Bed and board is dear at some figures, 'pon my 'vation 'tis!'

'Set it higher, auctioneer,' said the trusser.

'Two guineas!' said the auctioneer; and no one replied.

'If they don't take her for that, in ten seconds they'll have to give more,' said the husband. 'Very well. Now, auctioneer, add another.'

'Three guineas – going for three guineas!' said the rheumy man.

'No bid?' said the husband. 'Good Lord, why she's cost me fifty times the money, if a penny. Go on.'

'Four guineas!' cried the auctioneer.

'I'll tell ye what – I won't sell her for less than five,' said the husband, bringing down his fist so that the basins danced. 'I'll sell her for five guineas to any man that will pay me the money, and treat her well; and he shall have her for ever, and never hear aught o' me. But she shan't go for less. Now then – five guineas – and she's yours. Susan, you agree?'

She bowed her head with absolute indifference.

'Five guineas,' said the auctioneer, 'or she'll be withdrawn. Do anybody give it? The last time. Yes or no?'

'Yes,' said a loud voice from the doorway.

All eyes were turned. Standing in the triangular opening which formed the door of the tent was a sailor, who, unobserved by the rest, had arrived there within the last two or three minutes. A dead silence followed his affirmation.

'You say you do?' asked the husband, staring at him.

'I say so,' replied the sailor.

'Saying is one thing, and paying is another. Where's the money?'

The sailor hesitated a moment, looked anew at the woman, came in, unfolded five crisp pieces of paper, and threw them down upon the table-cloth. They were Bank-of-England notes for five pounds. Upon the face of this he chinked down the shillings severally – one, two, three, four, five.

The sight of real money in full amount, in answer to a challenge for the same till then deemed slightly hypothetical, had a great effect upon the spectators. Their eyes became riveted upon the faces of the chief actors, and then upon the notes as they lay, weighted by the shillings, on the table.

Up to this moment it could not positively have been asserted that the man, in spite of his tantalizing declaration, was really in earnest. The spectators had indeed taken the proceedings throughout as a piece of mirthful irony carried to extremes; and had assumed that, being out of work, he was, as a consequence, out of temper with the world, and society, and his nearest kin. But with the demand and response of real cash the jovial frivolity of the scene departed. A lurid colour seemed to fill the tent, and change the aspect of all therein. The mirth-wrinkles left the listeners' faces, and they waited with parting lips.

'Now,' said the woman, breaking the silence, so that her low dry voice sounded quite loud, 'before you go further, Michael, listen to me. If you touch that money, I and this girl go with the man. Mind, it is a joke no longer.'

'A joke? Of course it is not a joke!' shouted her husband, his resentment rising at her suggestion. 'I take the money: the sailor takes you. That's plain enough. It has been done elsewhere – and why not here?'

' 'Tis quite on the understanding that the young woman is willing,' said the sailor blandly. 'I wouldn't hurt her feelings for the world.'

'Faith, nor I,' said her husband. 'But she is willing, provided she can have the child. She said so only the other day when I talked o't!'

'That you swear?' said the sailor to her.

'I do,' said she, after glancing at her husband's face and seeing no repentance there.

'Very well, she shall have the child, and the bargain's complete,' said the trusser. He took the sailor's notes and deliberately folded them, and put them with the shillings in a high remote pocket, with an air of finality.

The sailor looked at the woman and smiled. 'Come along!' he said kindly. 'The little one too – the more the merrier!' She paused for an instant, with a close glance at him. Then dropping her eyes again, and saying nothing, she took up the child and followed him as he made towards the door. On reaching it, she turned, and pulling off her wedding-ring, flung it across the booth in the hay-trusser's face.

'Mike,' she said, 'I've lived with thee a couple of years, and had nothing but temper! Now I'm no more to 'ee; I'll try my luck elsewhere. 'Twill be better for me and Elizabeth-Jane, both. So good-bye!'

Seizing the sailor's arm with her right hand, and mounting the little girl on her left, she went out of the tent sobbing bitterly.

A stolid look of concern filled the husband's face, as if, after all, he had not quite anticipated this ending; and some of the guests laughed.

'Is she gone?' he said.

'Faith, ay; she's gone clane enough,' said some rustics near the door.

He rose and walked to the entrance with the careful tread of one conscious of his alcoholic load. Some others followed, and they stood looking into the twilight. The difference between the peacefulness of interior nature and the wilful hostilities of mankind was very apparent at this place. In contrast with the harshness of the act just ended within the tent was the sight of several horses crossing their necks and rubbing each other lovingly as they waited in patience to be harnessed for the homeward journey. Outside the fair, in the valleys and woods, all was quiet. The sun had recently set, and the west heaven was hung with rosy cloud, which seemed permanent, yet slowly changed. To watch it was like looking at some grand feat of stagery from a darkened auditorium. In presence of this scene after the other there was a natural instinct to abjure man as the blot on an otherwise kindly universe; till it was remembered that all terrestrial conditions were intermittent, and that mankind might some night be innocently sleeping when these quiet objects were raging loud.

'Where do the sailor live?' asked a spectator, when they had vainly gazed around.

'God knows that,' replied the man who had seen high life. 'He's without doubt a stranger here.'

'He came in about five minutes ago,' said the furmity woman, joining the rest with her hands on her hips. 'And then 'a stepped back, and then 'a looked in again. I'm not a penny the better for him.'

'Serves the husband well be-right,' said the staylace vendor. 'A comely respectable body like her – what can a man want more? I glory in the woman's sperrit. I'd ha' done it myself – 'od sent if I wouldn't, if a husband had behaved so to me! I'd go, and 'a might call, and call, till his keacorn was raw; but I'd never come back no, not till the great trumpet, would I!'

'Well, the woman will be better off,' said another of a more deliberate turn. 'For seafaring natures be very good shelter for shorn lambs, and the man do seem to have plenty of money, which is what she'd not been used to lately, by all showings.'

'Mark me – I'll not go after her!' said the trusser, returning doggedly to his seat. 'Let her go! If she's up to such vagaries she must suffer for 'em. She'd no business to take the maid – 'tis my maid; and if it were the doing again she shouldn't have her!'

Perhaps from some little sense of having countenanced an indefensible proceeding, perhaps because it was late, the customers thinned away from the tent shortly after this episode. The man stretched his elbows forward on the table, leant his face upon his arms, and soon began to snore. The furmity seller decided to close for the night, and after seeing the rum-bottles, milk, corn, raisins, etc., that remained on hand, loaded into the cart, came to where the man reclined. She shook him, but could not wake him. As the tent was not to be struck that night, the fair continuing for two or three days, she decided to let the sleeper, who was obviously no tramp, stay where he was, and his basket with him. Extinguishing the last candle, and lowering the flap of the tent, she left it, and drove away.

* II *

THE morning sun was streaming through the crevices of the canvas when the man awoke. A warm glow pervaded the whole atmosphere of the marquee, and a single big blue fly buzzed musically round and round it. Besides the buzz of the fly there was not a sound. He looked about – at the benches – at the table supported by trestles – at his basket of tools – at the stove where the furmity had been boiled – at the empty basins – at some shed grains of wheat – at the corks which dotted the grassy floor. Among the odds and ends he discerned a little shining object, and picked it up. It was his wife's ring.

A confused picture of the events of the previous evening seemed to come back to him, and he thrust his hand into his breast-pocket. A rustling revealed the sailor's bank-notes thrust carelessly in.

This second verification of his dim memories was enough; he knew now they were not dreams. He remained seated, looking on the ground for some time. 'I must get out of this as soon as I can,' he said deliberately at last, with the air of one who could not catch his thoughts without pronouncing them. 'She's gone – to be sure she is – gone with that sailor who bought her, and little Elizabeth-Jane. We walked here, and I had the furmity, and rum in it – and sold her. Yes, that's what's happened, and here am I. Now, what am I to do – am I sober enough to walk, I wonder?' He stood up, found that he was in fairly good condition for progress, unencumbered. Next he shouldered his tool basket, and found he could carry it. Then lifting the tent door he emerged into the open air.

Here the man looked around with gloomy curiosity. The freshness of the September morning inspired and braced him as he stood. He and his family had been weary when they arrived the night before, and they had observed but little of the place; so that he now beheld it as a new thing. It exhibited itself as the top of an open down, bounded on one extreme by a plantation, and approached by a winding road. At the bottom stood the village which lent its name to the upland and the annual fair that was held thereon. The spot stretched downward into valleys, and onward to other uplands, dotted with barrows, and trenched with the remains of pre-historic forts. The whole scene lay under the rays of a newly risen sun, which had not as yet dried a single blade of the heavily dewed grass, whereon the shadows of the yellow and red vans were projected far away, those thrown by the felloe of each wheel being elongated in shape to the orbit of a comet. All the gipsies and showmen who had remained on the ground lay snug within their carts and tents, or wrapped in horse-cloths under them, and were silent and still as death, with the exception of an occasional snore that revealed their presence. But the Seven Sleepers had a dog; and dogs of the mysterious breeds that vagrants own, that are as much like cats as dogs and as much like foxes as cats, also lay about here. A little one started up under one of the carts, barked as a matter of principle, and quickly lay down again. He was the only positive spectator of the hay-trusser's exit from the Weydon Fair-field.

This seemed to accord with his desire. He went on in silent thought, unheeding the yellowhammers which flitted about the hedges with straws in their bills, the crowns of the mushrooms, and the tinkling of local sheep-bells, whose wearers had had the good fortune not to be included in the fair. When he reached a lane, a good mile from the scene of the previous evening, the man pitched his basket and leant upon a gate. A difficult problem or two occupied his mind.

'Did I tell my name to anybody last night, or didn't I tell my name?' he said to himself; and at last concluded that he did not. His general demeanour was enough to show how he was surprised and nettled that his wife had taken him so literally – as much could be seen in his face, and in the way he nibbled a straw which he pulled from the hedge. He knew that she must have been somewhat excited to do this; moreover, she must have believed that there was some sort of binding force in the transaction. On this latter point he felt almost certain, knowing her freedom from levity of character, and the extreme simplicity of her intellect. There may, too, have been enough recklessness and resentment beneath her ordinary placidity to make her stifle any momentary doubts. On a previous occasion when he had declared during a fuddle that he would dispose of her as he had done, she had replied that she would not hear him say that many times more before it happened, in the resigned tones of a fatalist . . . 'Yet she knows I am not in my senses when I do that!' he exclaimed. 'Well, I must walk about till I find her . . . Seize her, why didn't she know better than bring me into this disgrace!' he roared out. 'She wasn't queer if I was. 'Tis like Susan to show some idiotic simplicity. Meek – that meekness has done me more harm than the bitterest temper!'

When he was calmer he turned to his original conviction that he must somehow find her and his little Elizabeth-Jane, and put up with the shame as best he could. It was of his own making, and he ought to bear it. But first he resolved to register an oath, a greater oath than he had ever sworn before: and to do it properly he required a fit place and imagery; for there was something fetichistic in this man's beliefs.

He shouldered his basket and moved on, casting his eyes inquisitively round upon the landscape as he walked, and at the distance of three or four miles perceived the roofs of a village and the tower of a church. He instantly made towards the latter object. The village was quite still, it being that motionless hour of rustic daily life which fills the interval between the departure of the field-labourers to their work, and the rising of their wives and daughters to prepare the breakfast for their return. Hence he reached the church without observation, and the door being only latched he entered. The haytrusser deposited his basket by the font, went up the nave till he reached the altar-rails, and opening the gate entered the sacrarium, where he seemed to feel a sense of the strangeness for a moment; then he knelt upon the foot-pace. Dropping his head upon the clamped book which lay on the Communion-table, he said aloud –

'I, Michael Henchard, on this morning of the sixteenth of September, do take an oath before God here in this solemn place that I will avoid all strong liquors for the space of twenty-one years to come, being a year for every year that I have lived. And this I swear upon the book before me; and may I be strook dumb, blind, and helpless, if I break this my oath!'

When he had said it and kissed the big book, the hay-trusser arose, and seemed relieved at having made a start in a new direction. While standing in the porch a moment he saw a thick jet of wood smoke suddenly start up from the red chimney of a cottage near, and knew that the occupant had just lit her fire. He went round to the door, and the housewife agreed to prepare him some breakfast for a trifling payment, which was done. Then he started on the search for his wife and child.

The perplexing nature of the undertaking became apparent soon enough. Though he examined and inquired, and walked hither and thither day after day, no such characters as those he described had anywhere been seen since the evening of the fair. To add to the difficulty he could gain no sound of the sailor's name. As money was short with him he decided, after some hesitation, to spend the sailor's money in the prosecution of this search; but it was equally in vain. The truth was that a certain shyness of revealing his conduct prevented Michael Henchard from following up the investigation with the loud hue-and-cry such a pursuit demanded to render it effectual; and it was probably for this reason that he obtained no clue, though everything was done by him that did not involve an explanation of the circumstances under which he had lost her.

Weeks counted up to months, and still he searched on, maintaining himself by small jobs of work in the intervals. By this time he had arrived at a seaport, and there he derived intelligence that persons answering somewhat to his description had emigrated a little time before. Then he said he would search no longer, and that he would go and settle in the district which he had had for some time in his mind. Next day he started, journeying south-westward, and did not pause, except for nights' lodgings, till he reached the town of Casterbridge, in a far distant part of Wessex.

* III *

THE highroad into the village of Weydon-Priors was again carpeted with dust. The trees had put on as of yore their aspect of dingy green, and where the Henchard family of three had once walked along, two persons not unconnected with that family walked now.

The scene in its broad aspect had so much of its previous character, even to the voices and rattle from the neighbouring village down, that it might for that matter have been the afternoon following the previously recorded episode. Change was only to be observed in details; but here it was obvious that a long procession of years had passed by. One of the two who walked the road was she who had figured as the young wife of Henchard on the previous occasion; now her face had lost much of its rotundity; her skin had undergone a textural change; and though her hair had not lost colour it was considerably thinner than heretofore. She was dressed in the mourning clothes of a widow. Her companion, also in black, appeared as a well-formed young woman about eighteen, completely possessed of that ephemeral precious essence youth, which is itself beauty, irrespective of complexion or contour.

A glance was sufficient to inform the eye that this was Susan Henchard's grown-up daughter. While life's middle summer had set its hardening mark on the mother's face, her former spring-like specialities were transferred so dexterously by Time to the second figure, her child, that the absence of certain facts within her mother's knowledge from the girl's mind would have seemed for the moment, to one reflecting on those facts, to be a curious imperfection in Nature's powers of continuity.

They walked with joined hands, and it could be perceived that this was the act of simple affection. The daughter carried in her outer hand a withy basket of old-fashioned make; the mother a blue bundle, which contrasted oddly with her black stuff gown.

Reaching the outskirts of the village they pursued the same track as formerly, and ascended to the fair. Here, too, it was evident that the years had told. Certain mechanical improvements might have been noticed in the roundabouts and high-fliers, machines for testing rustic strength and weight, and in the erections devoted to shooting for nuts. But the real business of the fair had considerably dwindled. The new periodical great markets of neighbouring towns were beginning to interfere seriously with the trade carried on here for centuries. The pens for sheep, the tie-ropes for horses, were about half as long as they had been. The stalls of tailors, hosiers, coopers, linen-drapers, and other such trades had almost disappeared, and the vehicles were far less numerous. The mother and daughter threaded the crowd for some little distance, and then stood still.

'Why did we hinder our time by coming in here? I thought you wished to get onward?' said the maiden.

'Yes, my dear Elizabeth-Jane,' explained the other. 'But I had a fancy for looking up here.'

'Why?'

'It was here I first met with Newson – on such a day as this.'

'First met with father here? Yes, you have told me so before. And now he's drowned and gone from us!' As she spoke the girl drew a card from her pocket and looked at it with a sigh. It was edged with black, and inscribed within a design resembling a mural tablet were the words, 'In affectionate memory of Richard Newson, mariner, who was unfortunately lost at sea, in the month of November 184–, aged forty-one years.'

'And it was here,' continued her mother, with more hesitation, 'that I last saw the relation we are going to look for – Mr Michael Henchard.'

'What is his exact kin to us, mother? I have never clearly had it told me.'

'He is, or was – for he may be dead – a connection by marriage,' said her mother deliberately.

'That's exactly what you have said a score of times before!' replied the young woman, looking about her inattentively. 'He's not a near relation, I suppose?'

'Not by any means.'

'He was a hay-trusser, wasn't he, when you last heard of him?'

'He was.'

'I suppose he never knew me?' the girl innocently continued.

Mrs Henchard paused for a moment, and answered uneasily, 'Of course not, Elizabeth-Jane. But come this way.' She moved on to another part of the field.

'It is not much use inquiring here for anybody, I should think,' the daughter observed, as she gazed round about. 'People at fairs change like the leaves of trees; and I daresay you are the only one here today who was here all those years ago.'

'I am not so sure of that,' said Mrs Newson, as she now called herself, keenly eyeing something under a green bank a little way off. 'See there.'

The daughter looked in the direction signified. The object pointed out was a tripod of sticks stuck into the earth, from which hung a three-legged crock, kept hot by a smouldering wood fire beneath. Over the pot stooped an old woman, haggard, wrinkled, and almost in rags. She stirred the contents of the pot with a large spoon, and occasionally croaked in a broken voice, 'Good furmity sold here!'

It was indeed the former mistress of the furmity tent – once thriving, cleanly, white-aproned, and chinking with money – now tentless, dirty, owning no tables or benches, and having scarce any customers except two small whity-brown boys, who came up and asked for 'A ha'p'orth, please – good measure,' which she served in a couple of chipped yellow basins of commonest clay.

'She was here at that time,' resumed Mrs Newson, making a step as if to draw nearer.

'Don't speak to her – it isn't respectable!' urged the other.

'I will just say a word – you, Elizabeth-Jane, can stay here.'

The girl was not loth, and turned to some stalls of coloured prints while her mother went forward. The old woman begged for the latter's custom as soon as she saw her, and responded to Mrs Henchard-Newson's request for a pennyworth with more alacrity than she had shown in selling sixpennyworth in her younger days. When the *soi-disant* widow had taken the basin of thin poor slop that stood for the rich concoction of the former time, the hag opened a little basket behind the fire, and looking up slily, whispered, 'Just a thought o' rum in it? – smuggled, you know – say two penn'orth – 'twill make it slip down like cordial!'

Her customer smiled bitterly at this survival of the old trick, and shook her head with a meaning the old woman was far from translating. She pretended to eat a little of the furmity with the leaden spoon offered, and as she did so said blandly to the hag, 'You've seen better days?'

'Ah, ma'am – well ye may say it!' responded the old woman, opening the sluices of her heart forthwith. 'I've stood in this fairground, maid, wife, and widow, these nine-and-thirty year, and in that time have known what it was to do business with the richest stomachs in the land! Ma'am you'd hardly believe that I was once the owner of a great pavilion-tent that was the attraction of the fair. Nobody could come, nobody could go, without having a dish of Mrs Goodenough's furmity. I knew the clergy's taste, and dandy gent's taste; I knew the town's taste, the country's taste. I even knowed the taste of the coarse shameless females. But Lord's my life – the world's no memory; straightforward dealings don't bring profit – 'tis the sly and the underhand that get on in these times!'

Mrs Newson glanced round – her daughter was still bending over the distant stalls. 'Can you call to mind,' she said cautiously to the old woman, 'the sale of a wife by her husband in your tent eighteen years ago today?'

The hag reflected, and half shook her head. 'If it had been a big thing I should have minded it in a moment,' she said. 'I can mind every serious fight o' married parties, every murder, every manslaughter, even every pocket-picking – leastwise large ones – that 't has been my lot to witness. But a selling? Was it done quiet-like?'

'Well, yes. I think so.'

The furmity woman half shook her head again. 'And yet,' she said, 'I do. At any rate, I can mind a man doing something o' the sort – a man in a cord jacket, with a basket of tools; but, Lord bless ye, we don't gi'e it head-room, we don't, such as that. The only reason why I can mind the man is that he came back here to the next year's fair, and told me quite private-like that if a woman ever asked for him I was to say he had gone to – where? – Casterbridge – yes – to Casterbridge, said he. But, Lord's my life, I shouldn't ha' thought of it again!'

Mrs Newson would have rewarded the old woman as far as her small means afforded had she not discreetly borne in mind that it was by that unscrupulous person's liquor her husband had been degraded. She briefly thanked her informant, and rejoined Elizabeth, who greeted her with, 'Mother, do let's go on – it was hardly respectable for you to buy refreshment there. I see none but the lowest do.'

'I have learned what I wanted, however,' said her mother quietly. 'The last time our relative visited this fair he said he was living at Casterbridge. It is a long, long way from here, and it was many years ago that he said it; but there I think we'll go.'

With this they descended out of the fair, and went onward to the village, where they obtained a night's lodging.

IV

HENCHARD'S wife acted for the best, but she had involved herself in difficulties. A hundred times she had been upon the point of telling her daughter Elizabeth-Jane the true story of her life, the tragical crisis of which had been the transaction at Weydon Fair, when she was not much older than the girl now beside her. But she had refrained. An innocent maiden had thus grown up in the belief that the relations between the genial sailor and her mother were the ordinary ones that they had always appeared to be. The risk of endangering a child's strong affection by disturbing ideas which had grown with her growth was to Mrs Henchard too fearful a thing to contemplate. It had seemed, indeed, folly to think of making Elizabeth-Jane wise.

But Susan Henchard's fear of losing her dearly loved daughter's heart by a revelation had little to do with any sense of wrong-doing on her own part. Her simplicity – the original ground of Henchard's contempt for her – had allowed her to live on in the conviction that Newson had acquired a morally real and justifiable right to her by his purchase – though the exact bearings and legal limits of that right were vague. It may seem strange to sophisticated minds that a sane young matron could believe in the seriousness of such a transfer; and were there not numerous other instances of the same belief the thing might scarcely be credited. But she was by no means the first or last peasant woman who had religiously adhered to her purchaser, as too many rural records show.

The history of Susan Henchard's adventures in the interim can be told in two or three sentences. Absolutely helpless she had been taken off to Canada, where they had lived several years without any great worldly success, though she worked as hard as any woman could to keep their cottage cheerful and well-provided. When Elizabeth-Jane was about twelve years old the three returned to England, and settled at Falmouth, where Newson made a living for a few years as boatman and general handy shoreman.

He then engaged in the Newfoundland trade, and it was during this period that Susan had an awakening. A friend to whom she confided her history ridiculed her grave acceptance of her position; and all was over with her peace of mind. When Newson came home at the end of one winter he saw that the delusion he had so carefully sustained had vanished for ever.

There was then a time of sadness, in which she told him her doubts if she could live with him longer. Newson left home again on the Newfoundland trade when the season came round. The vague news of his loss at sea a little later on solved a problem which had become torture to her meek conscience. She saw him no more.

Of Henchard they heard nothing. To the liege subjects of Labour, the England of those days was a continent, and a mile a geographical degree.

Elizabeth-Jane developed early into womanliness. One day, a month or so after receiving intelligence of Newson's death off the Bank of Newfoundland, when the girl was about eighteen, she was sitting on a willow chair in the cottage they still occupied, working twine nets for the fishermen. Her mother was in a back corner of the same room, engaged in the same labour; and dropping the heavy wood needle she was filling she surveyed her daughter thoughtfully. The sun shone in at the door upon the young woman's head and hair, which was worn loose, so that the rays streamed into its depths as into a hazel copse. Her face, though somewhat wan and incomplete, possessed the raw materials of beauty in a promising degree. There was an under-handsomeness in it, struggling to reveal itself through the provisional curves of immaturity, and the casual disfigurements that resulted from the straitened circumstances of their lives. She was handsome in the bone, hardly as yet handsome in the flesh. She possibly might never be fully handsome, unless the carking accidents of her daily existence could be evaded before the mobile parts of her countenance had settled to their final mould.

The sight of the girl made her mother sad – not vaguely, but by logical inference. They both were still in that strait-waistcoat of poverty from which she had tried so many times to be delivered for the girl's sake. The woman had long perceived how zealously and constantly the young mind of her companion was struggling for enlargement; and yet now, in her eighteenth year, it still remained but little unfolded. The desire – sober and repressed – of Elizabeth-Jane's heart was indeed to see, to hear, and to understand. How could she become a woman of wider knowledge, higher repute – 'better', as she termed it – this was her constant inquiry of her mother. She sought further into things than other girls in her position ever did, and her mother groaned as she felt she could not aid in the search.

The sailor, drowned or no, was probably now lost to them; and Susan's staunch, religious adherence to him as her husband in principle, till her views had been disturbed by enlightenment, was demanded no more. She asked herself whether the present moment, now that she was a free woman again, were not as opportune a one as she would find in a world where everything had been so inopportune, for making a desperate effort to advance Elizabeth. To pocket her pride and search for the first husband seemed, wisely or not, the best initiatory step. He had possibly drunk himself into his tomb. But he might, on the other hand, have had too much sense to do so; for in her time with him he had been given to bouts only, and was not a habitual drunkard.

At any rate, the propriety of returning to him, if he lived, was unquestionable. The awkwardness of searching for him lay in enlightening Elizabeth, a proceeding which her mother could not endure to contemplate. She finally resolved to undertake the search without confiding to the girl her former relations with Henchard, leaving it to him if they found him to take what steps he might choose to that end. This will account for their conversation at the fair and the half-informed state in which Elizabeth was led onward.

In this attitude they proceeded on their journey, trusting solely to the dim light afforded of Henchard's whereabouts by the furmity woman. The strictest economy was indispensable. Sometimes they might have been seen on foot, sometimes on farmers' waggons, sometimes in carriers' vans; and thus they drew near Casterbridge. Elizabeth-Jane discovered to her alarm that her mother's health was not what it once had been, and there was ever and anon in her talk that renunciatory tone which showed that, but for the girl, she would not be very sorry to quit a life she was growing thoroughly weary of.

It was on a Friday evening, near the middle of September, and just before dusk, that they reached the summit of a hill within a mile of the place they sought. There were high-banked hedges to the coach-road here, and they mounted upon the green turf within, and sat down. The spot commanded a full view of the town and its environs.

'What an old-fashioned place it seems to be!' said Elizabeth-Jane, while her silent mother mused on other things than topography. 'It is huddled all together; and it is shut in by a square wall of trees, like a plot of garden ground by a box-edging.'

Its squareness was, indeed, the characteristic which most struck the eye in this antiquated borough, the borough of Casterbridge – at that time, recent as it was, untouched by the faintest sprinkle of modernism. It was compact as a box of dominoes. It had no suburbs – in the ordinary sense. Country and town met at a mathematical line.

To birds of the more soaring kind Casterbridge must have appeared on this fine evening as a mosaic-work of subdued reds, browns, greys, and crystals, held together by a rectangular frame of deep green. To the level eye of humanity it stood as an indistinct mass behind a dense stockade of limes and chestnuts, set in the midst of miles of rotund down and concave field. The mass became gradually dissected by the vision into towers, gables, chimneys, and casements, the highest glazings shining bleared and bloodshot with the coppery fire they caught from the belt of sunlit cloud in the west.

From the centre of each side of this tree-bound square ran avenues east, west, and south into the wide expanse of cornland and coomb to the distance of a mile or so. It was by one of these avenues that the pedestrians were about to enter. Before they had risen to proceed two men passed outside the hedge, engaged in argumentative conversation.

'Why, surely,' said Elizabeth, as they receded, 'those men mentioned the name of Henchard in their talk – the name of our relative?'

'I thought so too,' said Mrs Newson.

'That seems a hint to us that he is still here.'

'Yes.'

'Shall I run after them, and ask them about him –'

'No, no, no! Not for the world just yet. He may be in the workhouse, or in the stocks, for all we know.'

'Dear me – why should you think that, mother?'

''Twas just something to say – that's all! But we must make private inquiries.'

Having sufficiently rested they proceeded on their way at even-fall. The dense trees of the avenue rendered the road dark as a tunnel, though the open land on each side was still under a faint daylight; in other words, they passed down a midnight between two gloamings. The features of the town had a keen interest for Elizabeth's mother, now that the human side came to the fore. As soon as they had wandered about they could see that the stockade of gnarled trees which framed in Casterbridge was itself an avenue, standing on a low green bank or escarpment, with a ditch yet visible without. Within the avenue and bank was a wall more or less discontinuous, and within the wall were packed the abodes of the burghers.

Though the two women did not know it these external features were but the ancient defences of the town, planted as a promenade.

The lamplights now glimmered through the engirdling trees, conveying a sense of great snugness and comfort inside, and rendering at the same time the unlighted country without strangely solitary and vacant in aspect, considering its nearness to life. The difference between burgh and champaign was increased, too, by sounds which now reached them above others – the notes of a brass band. The travellers returned into the High Street, where there were timber houses with overhanging storeys, whose small-paned lattices were screened by dimity curtains on a drawing-string, and under whose barge-boards old cobwebs waved in the breeze. There were houses of brick-nogging, which derived their chief support from those adjoining. There were slate roofs patched with tiles, and tile roofs patched with slate, with occasionally a roof of thatch.★

The agricultural and pastoral character of the people upon whom the town depended for its existence was shown by the class of objects displayed in the shop windows. Scythes, reap-hooks, sheep-shears, bill-hooks, spades, mattocks, and hoes at the ironmonger's; bee-hives, butter-firkins, churns, milking stools and pails, hay-rakes, field-flagons, and seed-lips at the cooper's; cart-ropes and plough-harness at the saddler's; carts, wheel-barrows, and mill-gear at the wheelwright's and machinist's; horse-embrocations at the chemist's; at the glover's and leather-cutter's, hedging-gloves, thatchers' knee-caps, ploughmen's leggings, villagers' pattens and clogs.

They came to a grizzled church, whose massive square tower rose unbroken into the darkening sky, the lower parts being illuminated by the nearest lamps sufficiently to show how completely the mortar from the joints of the stonework had been nibbled out by time and weather, which had planted in the crevices thus made little tufts of stone-crop and grass almost as far up as the very battlements. From this tower the clock struck eight, and thereupon a bell began to toll with a peremptory clang. The curfew was still rung in Casterbridge, and it was utilized by the

★ Most of these old houses have now been pulled down (1912).

inhabitants as a signal for shutting their shops. No sooner did the deep notes of the bell throb between the house-fronts than a clatter of shutters arose from the whole length of the High Street. In a few minutes business at Casterbridge was ended for the day.

Other clocks struck eight from time to time – one gloomily from the gaol, another from the gable of an almshouse, with a preparative creak of machinery, more audible than the note of the bell; a row of tall, varnished case-clocks from the interior of a clock-maker's shop joined in one after another just as the shutters were enclosing them, like a row of actors delivering their final speeches before the fall of the curtain; then chimes were heard stammering out the Sicilian Mariners' Hymn;* so that chronologists of the advanced school were appreciably on their way to the next hour before the whole business of the old one was satisfactorily wound up.

In an open space before the church walked a woman with her gown-sleeves rolled up so high that the edge of her underlinen was visible, and her skirt tucked up through her pocket hole. She carried a loaf under her arm from which she was pulling pieces of bread, and handing them to some other women who walked with her; which pieces they nibbled critically. The sight reminded Mrs Henchard-Newson and her daughter that they had an appetite; and they inquired of the woman for the nearest baker's.

'Ye may as well look for manna-food as good bread in Casterbridge just now,' she said, after directing them. 'They can blare their trumpets and thump their drums, and have their roaring dinners' – waving her hand towards a point further along the street, where the brass band could be seen standing in front of an illuminated building – 'but we must needs be put-to for want of a wholesome crust. There's less good bread than good beer in Casterbridge now.'

'And less good beer than swipes,' said a man with his hands in his pockets.

'How does it happen there's no good bread?' asked Mrs Henchard.

'Oh, 'tis the corn-factor – he's the man that our millers and bakers all deal wi', and he has sold 'em growed wheat, which they didn't know was growed, so they *say*, till the dough ran all over the ovens like quicksilver; so that the loaves be as flat as toads, and like suet pudden inside. I've been a wife, and I've been a mother, and I never see such unprincipled bread in Casterbridge as this before. – But you must be a real stranger here not to know what's made all the poor volks' insides plim like blowed bladders this week?'

'I am,' said Elizabeth's mother shyly.

Not wishing to be observed further till she knew more of her future in this place, she withdrew with her daughter from the speaker's side. Getting a couple of biscuits at the shop indicated as a temporary substitute for a meal, they next bent their steps instinctively to where the music was playing.

* These chimes, like those of other country churches, have been silenced for many years.

V

A FEW score yards brought them to the spot where the town band was now shaking the window-panes with the strains of 'The Roast Beef of Old England'.

The building before whose doors they had pitched their music-stands was the chief hotel in Casterbridge – namely, the King's Arms. A spacious bow-window projected into the street over the main portico, and from the open sashes came the babble of voices, the jingle of glasses, and the drawing of cords. The blinds, moreover, being left unclosed, the whole interior of this room could be surveyed from the top of a flight of stone steps to the road-waggon office opposite, for which reason a knot of idlers had gathered there.

'We might, perhaps, after all, make a few inquiries about – our relation Mr Henchard,' whispered Mrs Newson who, since her entry into Casterbridge had seemed strangely weak and agitated, 'And this, I think, would be a good place for trying it – just to ask, you know, how he stands in the town – if he is here, as I think he must be. You, Elizabeth-Jane, had better be the one to do it. I'm too worn out to do anything – pull down your fall first.'

She sat down upon the lowest step, and Elizabeth-Jane obeyed her directions and stood among the idlers.

'What's going on tonight?' asked the girl, after singling out an old man and standing by him long enough to acquire a neighbourly right to converse.

'Well, ye must be a stranger sure,' said the old man, without taking his eyes from the window. 'Why, 'tis a great public dinner of the gentle-people and such like leading volk – wi' the Mayor in the chair. As we plainer fellows bain't invited, they leave the winder-shutters open that we may get jist a sense o't out here. If you mount the steps you can see 'em. That's Mr Henchard, the Mayor, at the end of the table, a-facing ye; and that's the Council men right and left . . . Ah, lots of them when they begun life were no more than I be now!'

'Henchard!' said Elizabeth-Jane, surprised, but by no means suspecting the whole force of the revelation. She ascended to the top of the steps.

Her mother, though her head was bowed, had already caught from the inn-window tones that strangely riveted her attention before the old man's words, 'Mr Henchard, the Mayor', reached her ears. She arose, and stepped up to her daughter's side as soon as she could do so without showing exceptional eagerness.

The interior of the hotel dining-room was spread out before her, with its tables, and glass, and plate, and inmates. Facing the window, in the chair of dignity, sat a man about forty years of age; of heavy frame, large features, and commanding voice; his general build being rather coarse than compact. He had a rich complexion, which verged on swarthiness, a flashing black eye, and dark, bushy brows and hair. When he indulged in an occasional loud laugh at some remark among the guests, his large mouth parted so far back as to show to the rays of the chandelier a full score or more of the two-and-thirty sound white teeth that he obviously still could boast of.

That laugh was not encouraging to strangers; and hence it may have been well that it was rarely heard. Many theories might have been built upon it. It fell in well with conjectures of a temperament which would have no pity for weakness, but would be ready to yield ungrudging admiration to greatness, and strength. Its producer's personal goodness, if he had any, would be of a very fitful cast – an occasional almost oppressive generosity rather than a mild and constant kindness.

Susan Henchard's husband – in law, at least – sat before them, matured in shape, stiffened in line, exaggerated in traits; disciplined, thought-marked – in a word, older. Elizabeth, encumbered with no recollections as her mother was, regarded him with nothing more than the keen curiosity and interest which the discovery of such unexpected social standing in the long-sought relative naturally begot. He was dressed in an old-fashioned evening suit, an expanse of frilled shirt showing on his broad breast; jewelled studs, and a heavy gold chain. Three glasses stood at his right hand; but, to his wife's surprise, the two for wine were empty, while the third, a tumbler, was half full of water.

When last she had seen him he was sitting in a corduroy jacket, fustian waistcoat and breeches, and tanned leather leggings, with a basin of hot furmity before him. Time, the magician, had wrought much here. Watching him, and thus thinking of past days, she became so moved that she shrank back against the jamb of the waggon-office doorway to which the steps gave access, the shadow from it conveniently hiding her features. She forgot her daughter till a touch from Elizabeth-Jane aroused her. 'Have you seen him, mother?' whispered the girl.

'Yes, yes,' answered her companion hastily. 'I have seen him, and it is enough for me! Now I only want to go – pass away – die.'

'Why – O what?' She drew closer, and whispered in her mother's ear, 'Does he seem to you not likely to befriend us? I thought he looked a generous man. What a gentleman he is, isn't he? and how his diamond studs shine! How strange that you should have said he might be in the stocks, or in the workhouse, or dead! Did ever anything go more by contraries! Why do you feel so afraid of him? I am not at all; I'll call upon him – he can but say he don't own such remote kin.'

'I don't know at all – I can't tell what to set about. I feel so down.'

'Don't be that, mother, now we have got here and all! Rest there where you be a little while – I will look on and find out more about him.'

'I don't think I can ever meet Mr Henchard. He is not how I thought he would be – he overpowers me! I don't wish to see him any more.'

'But wait a little time and consider.'

Elizabeth-Jane had never been so much interested in anything in her life as in their present position, partly from the natural elation she felt at discovering herself akin to a coach; and she gazed again at the scene. The younger guests were talking and eating with animation; their elders were searching for titbits, and sniffing and grunting over their plates like sows nuzzling for acorns. Three drinks seemed to be sacred to the company – port, sherry, and rum; outside which old-established trinity few or no palates ranged.

A row of ancient rummers with ground figures on their sides, and each primed with a spoon, was now placed down the table, and these were promptly filled with grog at such high temperatures as to raise serious considerations for the articles exposed to its vapours. But Elizabeth-Jane noticed that, though this filling went on with great promptness up and down the table, nobody filled the Mayor's glass, who still drank large quantities of water from the tumbler behind the clump of crystal vessels intended for wine and spirits.

'They don't fill Mr Henchard's wine-glasses,' she ventured to say to her elbow acquaintance, the old man.

'Ah, no; don't ye know him to be the celebrated abstaining worthy of that name? He scorns all tempting liquors; never touches nothing. O yes, he've strong qualities that way. I have heard tell that he swore a gospel oath in by-gone times, and has bode by it ever since. So they don't press him, knowing it would be unbecoming in the face of that; for yer gospel oaths is a serious thing.'

Another elderly man, hearing this discourse, now joined in by inquiring, 'How much longer have he got to suffer from it, Solomon Longways?'

'Another two year, they say. I don't know the why and the wherefore of his fixing such a time, for 'a never has told anybody. But 'tis exactly two calendar years longer, they say. A powerful mind to hold out so long!'

'True . . . But there's great strength in hope. Knowing that in four-and-twenty months' time ye'll be out of your bondage, and able to make up for all you've suffered, by partaking without stint – why, it keeps a man up, no doubt.'

'No doubt, Christopher Coney, no doubt. And 'a must need such reflections – a lonely widow man,' says Longways.

'When did he lose his wife?' asked Elizabeth.

'I never knowed her. 'Twas afore he came to Casterbridge,' Solomon Longways replied with terminative emphasis, as if the fact of his ignorance of Mrs Henchard were sufficient to deprive her history of all interest. 'But I know that 'a's a banded teetotaller, and that if any of his men be ever so little overtook by a drop he's down upon 'em as stern as the Lord upon the jovial Jews.'

'Has he many men, then?' said Elizabeth-Jane.

'Many! Why, my good maid, he's the powerfullest member of the Town Council, and quite a principal man in the country round besides. Never a big dealing in wheat, barley, oats, hay, roots, and such-like but Henchard's got a hand in it. Ay, and he'll go into other things too; and that's where he makes his mistake. He worked his way up from nothing when 'a came here; and now he's a pillar of the town. Not but what he's been shaken a little to-year about this bad corn he has supplied in his contracts. I've seen the sun rise over Durnover Moor these nine-and-sixty year, and though Mr Henchard has never cussed me unfairly ever since I've worked for'n, seeing I be but a little small man, I must say that I have never before tasted such rough bread as has been made from Henchard's wheat lately. 'Tis that growed out that ye could a'most call it malt, and there's a list at bottom o' the loaf as thick as the sole of one's shoe.'

The band now struck up another melody, and by the time it was ended the dinner was over, and speeches began to be made. The evening being calm, and the windows still open, these orations could be distinctly heard. Henchard's voice arose above the rest; he was telling a story of his hay-dealing experiences, in which he had outwitted a sharper who had been bent upon outwitting him.

'Ha-ha-ha!' responded his audience at the upshot of the story; and hilarity was general till a new voice arose with, 'This is all very well; but how about the bad bread?'

It came from the lower end of the table, where there sat a group of minor tradesmen who, although part of the company, appeared to be a little below the social level of the others; and who seemed to nourish a certain independence of opinion and carry on discussions not quite in harmony with those at the head; just as the west end of a church is sometimes persistently found to sing out of time and tune with the leading spirits in the chancel.

This interruption about the bad bread afforded infinite satisfaction to the loungers outside, several of whom were in the mood which finds its pleasure in others' discomfiture; and hence they echoed pretty freely, 'Hey! How about the bad bread, Mr Mayor?' Moreover, feeling none of the restraints of those who shared the feast, they could afford to add, 'You rather ought to tell the story o' that, sir!'

The interruption was sufficient to compel the Mayor to notice it.

'Well, I admit that the wheat turned out badly,' he said. 'But I was taken in in buying it as much as the bakers who bought it 'o me.'

'And the poor folk who had to eat it whether or no,' said the inharmonious man outside the window.

Henchard's face darkened. There was temper under the thin bland surface – the temper which, artificially intensified, had banished a wife nearly a score of years before.

'You must make allowances for the accidents of a large business,' he said. 'You must bear in mind that the weather just at the harvest of that corn was worse than we have known it for years. However, I have mended my arrangements on account o't. Since I have found my business too large to be well looked after by myself alone, I have advertised for a thorough good man as manager of the corn department. When I've got him you will find these mistakes will no longer occur – matters will be better looked into.'

'But what are you going to do to repay us for the past?' inquired the man who had before spoken, and who seemed to be a baker or miller. 'Will you replace the grown flour we've still got by sound grain?'

Henchard's face had become still more stern at these interruptions, and he drank from his tumbler of water as if to calm himself or gain time. Instead of vouchsafing a direct reply, he stiffly observed –

'If anybody will tell me how to turn grown wheat into wholesome wheat I'll take it back with pleasure. But it can't be done.'

Henchard was not to be drawn again. Having said this, he sat down.

* VI *

NOW the group outside the window had within the last few minutes been reinforced by new arrivals, some of them respectable shopkeepers and their assistants, who had come out for a whiff of air after putting up the shutters for the night; some of them of a lower class. Distinct from either there appeared a stranger – a young man of remarkably pleasant aspect – who carried in his hand a carpet-bag of the smart floral pattern prevalent in such articles at that time.

He was ruddy and of a fair countenance, bright-eyed, and slight in build. He might possibly have passed by without stopping at all, or at most for half a minute to glance in at the scene, had not his advent coincided with the discussion on corn and bread; in which event this history had never been enacted. But the subject seemed to arrest him, and he whispered some inquiries of the other bystanders, and remained listening.

When he heard Henchard's closing words, 'It can't be done', he smiled impulsively, drew out his pocket-book, and wrote down a few words by the aid of the light in the window. He tore out the leaf, folded and directed it, and seemed about to throw it in through the open sash upon the dining-table; but, on second thoughts, edged himself through the loiterers, till he reached the door of the hotel, where one of the waiters who had been serving inside was now idly leaning against the door-post.

'Give this to the Mayor at once,' he said, handing in his hasty note.

Elizabeth-Jane had seen his movements and heard the words, which attracted her both by their subject and by their accent – a strange one for those parts. It was quaint and northerly.

The waiter took the note, while the young stranger continued –

'And can ye tell me of a respectable hotel that's a little more moderate than this?'

The waiter glanced indifferently up and down the street.

'They say the Three Mariners, just below here, is a very good place,' he languidly answered; 'but I have never stayed there myself.'

The Scotchman, as he seemed to be, thanked him, and strolled on in the direction of the Three Mariners aforesaid, apparently more concerned about the question of an inn than about the fate of his note, now that the momentary impulse of writing it was over. While he was disappearing slowly down the street the waiter left the door, and Elizabeth-Jane saw with some interest the note brought into the dining-room and handed to the Mayor.

Henchard looked at it carelessly, unfolded it with one hand, and glanced it through. Thereupon it was curious to note an unexpected effect. The nettled, clouded aspect which had held possession of his face since the subject of his corn-dealings had been broached, changed itself into one of arrested attention. He read the note slowly, and fell into thought, not moody, but fitfully intense, as that of a man who has been captured by an idea.

By this time toasts and speeches had given place to songs, the wheat subject being quite forgotten. Men were putting their heads together in twos and threes, telling good stories, with pantomimic laughter which reached convulsive grimace. Some were beginning to look as if they did not know how they had come there, what they had come for, or how they were going to get home again; and provisionally sat on with a dazed smile. Square-built men showed a tendency to become hunchbacks; men with a dignified presence lost it in a curious obliquity of figure, in which their features grew disarranged and one-sided; whilst the heads of a few who had dined with extreme thoroughness were somehow sinking into their shoulders, the corners of their mouth and eyes being bent upwards by the subsidence. Only Henchard did not conform to these flexuous changes; he remained stately and vertical, silently thinking.

The clock struck nine. Elizabeth-Jane turned to her companion. 'The evening is drawing on, mother,' she said. 'What do you propose to do?'

She was surprised to find how irresolute her mother had become. 'We must get a place to lie down in,' she murmured. 'I have seen – Mr Henchard; and that's all I wanted to do.'

'That's enough for tonight, at any rate,' Elizabeth-Jane replied soothingly. 'We can think tomorrow what is best to do about him. The question now is – is it not? – how shall we find a lodging?'

As her mother did not reply Elizabeth-Jane's mind reverted to the words of the waiter, that the Three Mariners was an inn of moderate charges. A recommendation good for one person was probably good for another. 'Let's go where the young man has gone to,' she said. 'He is respectable. What do you say?'

Her mother assented, and down the street they went.

In the meantime the Mayor's thoughtfulness, engendered by the note as stated, continued to hold him in abstraction; till, whispering to his neighbour to take his place, he found opportunity to leave the chair. This was just after the departure of his wife and Elizabeth.

Outside the door of the assembly-room he saw the waiter, and beckoning to him asked who brought the note which had been handed in a quarter of an hour before.

'A young man, sir – a sort of traveller. He was a Scotchman seemingly.'

'Did he say how he had got it?'

'He wrote it himself, sir, as he stood outside the window.'

'Oh – wrote it himself . . . Is the young man in the hotel?'

'No, sir. He went to the Three Mariners, I believe.'

The Mayor walked up and down the vestibule of the hotel with his hands under his coat tails, as if he were merely seeking a cooler atmosphere than that of the room he had quitted. But there could be no doubt that he was in reality still possessed to the full by the new idea, whatever that might be. At length he went back to the door of the dining-room, paused, and found that the songs, toasts, and conversation were proceeding quite satisfactorily without his presence. The Corporation, private residents, and major and minor tradesmen had, in fact, gone in for comforting beverages to such an extent that they had quite forgotten, not only the Mayor, but all those vast political, religious, and social differences which they felt necessary to maintain in the daytime, and which separated them like iron grills. Seeing this the Mayor took his hat, and when the waiter had helped him on with a thin holland overcoat, went out and stood under the portico.

Very few persons were now in the street; and his eyes, by a sort of attraction, turned and dwelt upon a spot about a hundred yards further down. It was the house to which the writer of the note had gone – the Three Mariners – whose two prominent Elizabethan gables, bow-window, and passage-light could be seen from where he stood. Having kept his eyes on it for a while he strolled in that direction.

This ancient house of accommodation for man and beast, now, unfortunately, pulled down, was built of mellow sandstone, with mullioned windows of the same material, markedly out of perpendicular from the settlement of foundations. The bay window projecting into the street, whose interior was so popular among the frequenters of the inn, was closed with shutters, in each of which appeared a heart-shaped aperture, somewhat more attenuated in the right and left ventricles than is seen in Nature. Inside these illuminated holes, at a distance of about three inches, were ranged at this hour, as every passer knew, the ruddy polls of Billy Wills the glazier, Smart the shoe-maker, Buzzford the general dealer, and others of a secondary set of worthies, of a grade somewhat below that of the diners at the King's Arms, each with his yard of clay.

A four-centred Tudor arch was over the entrance, and over the arch the signboard, now visible in the rays of an opposite lamp. Hereon the Mariners, who had been represented by the artist as persons of two dimensions only – in other words, flat as a shadow – were standing in a row in paralysed attitudes. Being on the sunny side of the street the three comrades had suffered largely from warping, splitting, fading, and shrinkage, so that they were but a half-invisible film upon the reality of the grain, and knots, and nails, which composed the signboard. As a matter of fact, this state of things was not so much owing to Stannidge the landlord's neglect, as from the lack of a painter in Casterbridge who would undertake to reproduce the features of men so traditional.

A long, narrow, dimly-lit passage gave access to the inn, within which passage the horses going to their stalls at the back, and the coming and departing human guests, rubbed shoulders indiscriminately, the latter running no slight risk of having their toes trodden upon by the animals. The good stabling and the good ale of the Mariners, though somewhat difficult to reach on account of there being but this narrow way to both, were nevertheless perseveringly sought out by the sagacious old heads who knew what was what in Casterbridge.

Henchard stood without the inn for a few instants; then lowering the dignity of his presence as much as possible by buttoning the brown holland coat over his shirt-front, and in other ways toning himself down to his ordinary everyday appearance, he entered the inn door.

* VII *

ELIZABETH-JANE and her mother had arrived some twenty minutes earlier. Outside the house they had stood and considered whether even this homely place, though recommended as moderate, might not be too serious in its prices for their light pockets. Finally, however, they had found courage to enter, and duly met Stannidge the landlord; a silent man, who drew and carried frothing measures to this room and to that, shoulder to shoulder with his waiting-maids – a stately slowness, however, entering into his ministrations by contrast with theirs, as became one whose service was somewhat optional. It would have been altogether optional but for the orders of the landlady, a person who sat in the bar, corporeally motionless, but with a flitting eye and quick ear, with which she observed and heard through the open door and hatchway the pressing needs of customers whom her husband overlooked though close at hand. Elizabeth and her mother were passively accepted as sojourners, and shown to a small bedroom under one of the gables, where they sat down.

The principle of the inn seemed to be to compensate for the antique awkwardness, crookedness, and obscurity of the passages, floors, and windows, by quantities of clean linen spread about everywhere, and this had a dazzling effect upon the travellers.

''Tis too good for us – we can't meet it!' said the elder woman, looking round the apartment with misgivings as soon as they were left alone.

'I fear it is, too,' said Elizabeth. 'But we must be respectable.'

'We must pay our way even before we must be respectable,' replied her mother. 'Mr Henchard is too high for us to make ourselves known to him, I much fear; so we've only our own pockets to depend on.'

'I know what I'll do,' said Elizabeth-Jane after an interval of waiting, during which their needs seemed quite forgotten under the press of business below. And leaving the room, she descended the stairs and penetrated to the bar.

If there was one good thing more than another which characterized this single-hearted girl it was a willingness to sacrifice her personal comfort and dignity to the common weal.

'As you seem busy here tonight, and mother's not well off, might I take out part of our accommodation by helping?' she asked of the landlady.

The latter, who remained as fixed in the arm-chair as if she had been melted into it when in a liquid state, and could not now be unstuck, looked the girl up and down inquiringly, with her hands on the chair-arms. Such arrangements as the one Elizabeth proposed were not uncommon in country villages; but, though Casterbridge was old-fashioned, the custom was well-nigh obsolete here. The mistress of the house, however, was an easy woman to strangers, and she made no objection. Thereupon Elizabeth, being instructed by nods and motions from the taciturn landlord as to where she could find the different things, trotted up and down stairs with materials for her own and her parent's meal.

While she was doing this the wood partition in the centre of the house thrilled to its centre with the tugging of a bell-pull upstairs. A bell below tinkled a note that was feebler in sound than the twanging of wires and cranks that had produced it.

''Tis the Scotch gentleman,' said the landlady omnisciently; and turning her eyes to Elizabeth, 'Now then, can you go and see if his supper is on the tray? If it is you can take it up to him. The front room over this.'

Elizabeth-Jane, though hungry, willingly postponed serving herself awhile, and applied to the cook in the kitchen, whence she brought forth the tray of supper viands, and proceeded with it upstairs to the apartment indicated. The accommodation of the Three Mariners was far from spacious, despite the fair area of ground it covered. The room demanded by intrusive beams and rafters, partitions, passages, staircases, disused ovens, settles, and four-posters, left comparatively small quarters for human beings. Moreover, this being at a time before home-brewing was abandoned by the smaller victuallers, and a house in which the twelve-bushel strength was still religiously adhered to by the landlord in his ale, the quality of the liquor was the chief attraction of the premises, so that everything had to make way for utensils and operations in connection therewith. Thus Elizabeth found that the Scotchman was located in a room quite close to the small one that had been allotted to herself and her mother.

When she entered nobody was present but the young man himself – the same whom she had seen lingering without the windows of the King's Arms Hotel. He was now idly reading a copy of the local paper, and was hardly conscious of her entry, so that she looked at him quite coolly, and saw how his forehead shone where the light caught it, and how nicely his hair was cut, and the sort of velvet-pile or down that was on the skin at the back of his neck, and how his cheek was so truly curved as to be part of a globe, and how clearly drawn were the lids and lashes which hid his bent eyes.

She set down the tray, spread his supper, and went away without a word. On her arrival below the landlady, who was as kind as she was fat and lazy, saw that Elizabeth-Jane was rather tired, though in her earnestness to be useful she was waiving her own needs altogether. Mrs Stannidge thereupon said with a considerate peremptoriness that she and her mother had better take their own suppers if they meant to have any.

Elizabeth fetched their simple provisions, as she had fetched the Scotchman's, and went up to the little chamber where she had left her mother, noiselessly pushing open the door with the edge of the tray. To her surprise her mother, instead of being reclined on the bed where she had left her, was in an erect position, with lips parted. At Elizabeth's entry she lifted her finger.

The meaning of this was soon apparent. The room allotted to the two women had at one time served as a dressing-room to the Scotchman's chamber, as was evidenced by signs of a door of communication between them – now screwed up and pasted over with the wall paper. But, as is frequently the case with hotels of far higher pretensions than the Three Mariners, every word spoken in either of these rooms was distinctly audible in the other. Such sounds came through now.

Thus silently conjured Elizabeth deposited the tray, and her mother whispered as she drew near, ''Tis he.'

'Who?' said the girl.

'The Mayor.'

The tremors in Susan Henchard's tone might have led any person but one so perfectly unsuspicious of the truth as the girl was to surmise some closer connection than the admitted simple kinship as a means of accounting for them.

Two men were indeed talking in the adjoining chamber, the young Scotchman and Henchard, who, having entered the inn while Elizabeth-Jane was in the kitchen waiting for the supper, had been deferentially conducted upstairs by host Stannidge himself. The girl noiselessly laid out their little meal, and beckoned to her mother to join her, which Mrs

Henchard mechanically did, her attention being fixed on the conversation through the door.

'I merely strolled in on my way home to ask you a question about something that has excited my curiosity,' said the Mayor, with careless geniality. 'But I see you have not finished supper.'

'Ay, but I will be done in a little! Ye needn't go, sir. Take a seat. I've almost done, and it makes no difference at all.'

Henchard seemed to take the seat offered, and in a moment he resumed: 'Well, first I should ask, did you write this?' A rustling of paper followed.

'Yes, I did,' said the Scotchman.

'Then,' said Henchard, 'I am under the impression that we have met by accident while waiting for the morning to keep an appointment with each other? My name is Henchard; ha'n't you replied to an advertisement for a corn-factor's manager that I put into the paper – ha'n't you come here to see me about it?'

'No,' said the Scotchman, with some surprise.

'Surely you are the man,' went on Henchard insistingly, 'who arranged to come and see me? Joshua, Joshua, Jipp – Jopp – what was his name?'

'You're wrong!' said the young man. 'My name is Donald Farfrae. It is true I am in the corren trade – but I have replied to no advairrtisement, and arranged to see no one. I am on my way to Bristol – from there to the other side of the warrld, to try my fortune in the great wheat-growing districts of the West! I have some inventions useful to the trade, and there is no scope for developing them here.'

'To America – well, well,' said Henchard, in a tone of disappointment, so strong as to make itself felt like a damp atmosphere. 'And yet I could have sworn you were the man!'

The Scotchman murmured another negative, and there was a silence, till Henchard resumed: 'Then I am truly and sincerely obliged to you for the few words you wrote on that paper.'

'It was nothing, sir.'

'Well, it has a great importance for me just now. This row about my grown wheat, which I declare to Heaven I didn't know to be bad till the people came complaining, has put me to my wits' end. I've some hundreds of quarters of it on hand; and if your renovating process will make it wholesome, why, you can see what a quag 'twould get me out of. I saw in a moment there might be truth in it. But I should like to have it proved; and of course you don't care to tell the steps of the process sufficiently for me to do that, without my paying ye well for't first.'

The young man reflected a moment or two. 'I don't know that I have any objection,' he said. 'I'm going to another country, and curing bad corn is not the line I'll take up there. Yes, I'll tell ye the whole of it – you'll make more out of it heere than I will in a foreign country. Just look heere a minute, sir. I can show ye by a sample in my carpet-bag.'

The click of a lock followed, and there was a sifting and rustling; then a discussion about so many ounces to the bushel, and drying, and refrigerating, and so on.

'These few grains will be sufficient to show ye with,' came in the young fellow's voice; and after a pause, during which some operation seemed to be intently watched by them both, he exclaimed. 'There, now, do you taste that.'

'It's complete! – quite restored, or – well – nearly.'

'Quite enough restored to make good seconds out of it,' said the Scotchman. 'To fetch it back entirely is impossible; Nature won't stand so much as that, but heere you go a great way towards it. Well, sir, that's the process; I don't value it, for it can be but of little use in countries where the weather is more settled than in ours; and I'll be only too glad if it's of service to you.'

'But hearken to me,' pleaded Henchard. 'My business, you know, is in corn and in hay; but I was brought up as a hay-trusser simply, and hay is what I understand best, though I now do more in corn than in the other. If you'll accept the place, you shall manage the corn branch entirely, and receive a commission in addition to salary.'

'You're liberal – very liberal; but no, no – I cannet!' the young man still replied, with some distress in his accents.

'So be it!' said Henchard conclusively. 'Now – to change the subject – one good turn deserves another; don't stay to finish that miserable supper. Come to my house; I can find something better for 'ee than cold ham and ale.'

Donald Farfrae was grateful – said he feared he must decline – that he wished to leave early next day.

'Very well,' said Henchard quickly, 'please yourself. But I tell you, young man, if this holds good for the bulk, as it has done for the sample, you have saved my credit, stranger though you be. What shall I pay you for this knowledge?'

'Nothing at all, nothing at all. It may not prove necessary to ye to use if often, and I don't value it at all. I thought I might just as well let ye know, as you were in a difficulty, and they were harrd upon ye.'

Henchard paused. 'I shan't soon forget this,' he said. 'And from a stranger! . . . I couldn't believe you were not the man I had engaged! Says I to myself "He knows who I am, and recommends himself by this stroke." And yet it turns out, after all, that you are not the man who answered my advertisement, but a stranger!'

'Ay, ay; that's so,' said the young man.

Henchard again suspended his words, and then his voice came thoughtfully: 'Your forehead, Farfrae, is something like my poor brother's – now dead and gone; and the nose, too, isn't unlike his. You must be, what – five foot nine, I reckon? I am six foot one and a half out of my shoes. But what of that? In my business, 'tis true that strength and bustle build up a firm. But judgement and knowledge are what keep it established. Unluckily, I am bad at science, Farfrae; bad at figures – a rule o' thumb sort of man. You are just the reverse – I can see that. I have been looking for such as you these two year, and yet you are not for me. Well, before I go, let me ask this: Though you are not the young man I thought you were, what's the difference? Can't ye stay just the same? Have you really made up your mind about this American notion? I won't mince matters. I feel you would be invaluable to me – that needn't be said – and if you bide and be my manager, I will make it worth your while.'

'My plans are fixed,' said the young man, in negative tones. 'I have formed a scheme, and so we need na say any more about it. But will you not drink with me, sir? I find this Casterbridge ale warreming to the stomach.'

'No, no; I fain would, but I can't,' said Henchard gravely, the scraping of his chair informing the listeners that he was rising to leave. 'When I was a young man I went in for that sort of thing too strong – far too strong – and was well-nigh ruined by it! I did a deed on account of it which I shall be ashamed of to my dying day. It made such an impression on me that I swore, there and then, that I'd drink nothing stronger than tea for as many years as I was old that day. I have kept my oath; and though, Farfrae, I am sometimes that dry in the dog days that I could drink a quarter-barrel to the pitching, I think o' my oath, and touch no strong drink at all.'

'I'll no' press ye, sir – I'll no' press ye. I respect your vow.'

'Well, I shall get a manager somewhere, no doubt,' said Henchard, with strong feeling in his tones. 'But it will be long before I see one that would suit me so well!'

The young man appeared much moved by Henchard's warm convictions of his value. He was silent till they reached the door. 'I wish I could stay – sincerely I would like to,' he replied. 'But no – it cannet be! it cannet! I want to see the warrld.'

* VIII *

THUS they parted; and Elizabeth-Jane and her mother remained each in her thoughts over their meal, the mother's face being strangely bright since Henchard's avowal of shame for a past action. The quivering of the partition to its core presently denoted that Donald Farfrae had again rung his bell, no doubt to have his supper removed; for humming a tune, and walking up and down, he seemed to be attracted by the lively burst of conversation and melody from the general company below. He sauntered out upon the landing, and descended the staircase.

When Elizabeth-Jane had carried down his supper tray, and also that used by her mother and herself, she found the bustle of serving to be at its height below, as it always was at this hour. The young woman shrank from having anything to do with the ground-floor serving, and crept silently about observing the scene – so new to her, fresh from the seclusion of a seaside cottage. In the general sitting-room, which was large, she remarked the two or three dozen strong-backed chairs that stood round against the wall, each fitted with its genial occupant; the sanded floor; the black settle which, projecting end-wise from the wall within the door, permitted Elizabeth to be a spectator of all that went on without herself being particularly seen.

The young Scotchman had just joined the guests. These, in addition to the respectable master-tradesmen occupying the seats of privilege in the bow-window and its neighbourhood, included an inferior set at the unlighted end, whose seats were mere benches against the wall, and who drank from cups instead of from glasses. Among the latter she noticed some of those personages who had stood outside the windows of the King's Arms.

Behind their backs was a small window, with a wheel ventilator in one of the panes, which would suddenly start off spinning with a jingling sound, as suddenly stop, and as suddenly start again.

While thus furtively making her survey the opening words of a song greeted her ears from the front of the settle, in a melody and accent of peculiar charm. There had been some singing before she came down; and now the Scotchman had made himself so soon at home that, at the request of some of the master-tradesmen, he, too, was favouring the room with a ditty.

Elizabeth-Jane was fond of music; she could not help pausing to listen; and the longer she listened the more she was enraptured. She had never heard any singing like this; and it was evident that the majority of the audience had not heard such frequently, for they were attentive to a much greater degree than usual. They neither whispered, nor drank, nor dipped their pipe-stems in their ale to moisten them, nor pushed the mug to their neighbours. The singer himself grew emotional, till she could imagine a tear in his eye as the words went on:

> 'It's hame, and it's hame, hame fain would I be,
> O hame, hame, hame to my ain countree!
> There's an eye that ever weeps, and a fair face will be fain,
> As I pass through Annan Water with my bonnie bands again;
> When the flower is in the bud, and the leaf upon the tree,
> The lark shall sing me hame to my ain countree!'

There was a burst of applause, and a deep silence which was even more eloquent than the applause. It was of such a kind that the snapping of a pipe-stem too long for him by old Solomon Longways, who was one of those gathered at the shady end of the room, seemed a harsh and irreverent act. Then the ventilator in the window-pane spasmodically started off for a new spin, and the pathos of Donald's song was temporarily effaced.

''Twas not amiss – not at all amiss!' muttered Christopher Coney, who was also present. And removing his pipe a finger's breadth from his lips, he said aloud, 'Draw on the next verse, young gentleman, please.'

'Yes. Let's have it again, stranger,' said the glazier, a stout, bucket-headed man, with a white apron rolled up round his waist. 'Folks don't lift up their hearts like that in this part of the world.' And turning aside, he said in undertones, 'Who is the young man? – Scotch, d'ye say?'

'Yes, straight from the mountains of Scotland, I believe,' replied Coney.

Young Farfrae repeated the last verse. It was plain that nothing so pathetic had been heard at the Three Mariners for a considerable time. The difference of accent, the excitability of the singer, the intense local feeling, and the seriousness with which he worked himself up to a climax, surprised this sect of worthies, who were only too prone to shut up their emotions with caustic words.

'Danged if our country down here is worth singing about like that!' continued the glazier, as the Scotchman again melodized with a dying fall, 'My ain countree!' 'When you take away from among us the fools and the rogues, and the lammigers, and the wanton hussies, and the slatterns, and such like, there's cust few left to ornament a song with in Casterbridge, or the country round.'

'True,' said Buzzford, the dealer, looking at the grain of the table. 'Casterbridge is a old, hoary place o' wickedness, by all account. 'Tis recorded in history that we rebelled against the King one or two hundred years ago, in the time of the Romans, and that lots of us was hanged on Gallows Hill, and quartered, and our different jints sent about the country like butcher's meat; and for my part I can well believe it.'

'What did ye come away from yer own country for, young maister, if ye be so wownded about it?' inquired Christopher Coney, from the background, with the tone of a man who preferred the original subject. 'Faith, it wasn't worth your while on our account, for, as Maister Billy Wills says, we be bruckle folk here – the best o' us hardly honest sometimes, what with hard winters, and so many mouths to fill, and God-a'mighty sending his little taties so terrible small to fill 'em with. We don't think about flowers and fair faces, not we – except in the shape o' cauliflowers and pigs' chaps.'

'But no!' said Donald Farfrae, gazing round into their faces with earnest concern; 'the best of ye hardly honest – not that surely? None of ye has been stealing what didn't belong to him?'

'Lord! no, no!' said Solomon Longways, smiling grimly. 'That's only his random way o' speaking. 'A was always such a man of under-thoughts.' (And reprovingly towards Christopher): 'Don't ye be so over-familiar with a gentleman that ye know nothing of – and that's travelled a'most from the North Pole.'

Christopher Coney was silenced, and as he could get no public sympathy, he mumbled his feelings to himself: 'Be dazed, if I loved my country half as well as the young feller do, I've live by claning my neighbour's pigsties afore I'd go away! For my part I've no more love for my country than I have for Botany Bay!'

'Come,' said Longways; 'let the young man draw onwards with his ballet, or we shall be here all night.'

'That's all of it,' said the singer apologetically.

'Soul of my body, then we'll have another!' said the general dealer.

'Can you turn a strain to the ladies, sir?' inquired a fat woman with a figured purple apron, the waist-string of which was overhung so far by her sides as to be invisible.

'Let him breathe – let him breathe, Mother Cuxsom. He hain't got his second wind yet,' said the master glazier.

'O yes, but I have!' exclaimed the young man; and he at once rendered 'O Nannie' with faultless modulations, and another or two of the like sentiment, winding up at their earnest request with 'Auld Lang Syne'.

By this time he had completely taken possession of the hearts of the Three Mariners' inmates, including even old Coney. Notwithstanding an occasional odd gravity which awoke their sense of the ludicrous for the moment, they began to view him through a golden haze which the tone of his mind seemed to raise around him. Casterbridge had sentiment – Casterbridge had romance; but this stranger's sentiment was of differing quality. Or rather, perhaps, the difference was mainly superficial; he was to them like the poet of a new school who takes his contemporaries by storm; who is not really new, but is the first to articulate what all his listeners have felt, thought but dimly till then.

The silent landlord came and leant over the settle while the young man sang; and even Mrs Stannidge managed to unstick herself from the framework of her chair in the bar and get as far as the door-post, which movement she accomplished by rolling herself round, as a cask is trundled on the chine by a drayman without losing much of its perpendicular.

'And are you going to bide in Casterbridge, sir?' she asked.

'Ah – no!' said the Scotchman, with melancholy fatality in his voice, 'I'm only passing thirrough! I am on my way to Bristol, and on frae there to foreign parts.'

'We be truly sorry to hear it,' said Solomon Longways. 'We can ill afford to lose tuneful wynd-pipes like yours when they fall among us. And verily, to mak' acquaintance with a man a-come from so far, from the land o' perpetual snow, as we may say, where wolves and wild boars and other dangerous animalcules be as common as blackbirds hereabouts – why, 'tis a thing we can't do every day; and there's good sound information for bide-at-homes like we when such a man opens his mouth.'

'Nay, but ye mistake my country,' said the young man, looking round upon them with tragic fixity, till his eye lighted up and his cheek kindled with a sudden enthusiasm to right their errors. 'There are not perpetual snow and wolves at all in it! – except snow in winter, and – well – a little in summer just sometimes, and a "gaberlunzie" or two stalking about here and there, if ye may call them dangerous. Eh, but you should take a summer jarreny to Edinboro', and Arthur's Seat, and all round there, and then go on to the lochs, and all the Highland scenery – in May and June – and you would never say 'tis the land of wolves and perpetual snow!'

'Of course not – it stands to reason,' said Buzzford. ''Tis barren ignorance that leads to such words. He's a simple home-spun man, that never was fit for good company – think nothing of him, sir.'

'And do ye carry your flock bed, and your quilt, and your crock, and your bit chiney? or do ye go in bare bones, as I may say?' inquired Christopher Coney.

'I've sent on my luggage – though it isn't much; for the voyage is long.' Donald's eyes dropped into a remote gaze as he added: 'But I said to myself, "Never a one of the prizes of life will I come by unless I undertake it!" and I decided to go.'

A general sense of regret, in which Elizabeth-Jane shared not least, made itself apparent in the company. As she looked at Farfrae from the back of the settle she decided that his statements showed him to be no less thoughtful than his fascinating melodies revealed him to be cordial and impassioned. She admired the serious light in which he looked at serious things. He had seen no jest in ambiguities and roguery, as the Casterbridge toss-pots had done; and rightly not – there was none. She disliked those wretched humours of Christopher Coney and his tribe; and he did not appreciate them. He seemed to feel exactly as she felt about life and its surroundings – that they were a tragical rather than a comical thing; that though one could be gay on occasion, moments of gaiety were interludes, and no part of the actual drama. It was extraordinary how similar their views were.

Though it was still early the young Scotchman expressed his wish to retire, whereupon the landlady whispered to Elizabeth to run upstairs and turn down his bed. She took a candlestick and proceeded on her mission, which was the act of a few moments only. When, candle in hand, she reached the top of the stairs on her way down again, Mr Farfrae was at the foot coming up. She could not very well retreat; they met and passed in the turn of the staircase.

She must have appeared interesting in some way – notwithstanding her plain dress – or rather, possibly, in consequence of it, for she was a girl characterized by earnestness and soberness of mien, with which simple drapery accorded well. Her face flushed, too, at the slight awkwardness of the meeting, and she passed him with her eyes bent on the candle-flame that she carried just below her nose. Thus it happened that when confronting her he smiled; and then, with the manner of a temporarily light-hearted man, who has started himself on a flight of song whose momentum he cannot readily check, he softly tuned an old ditty that she seemed to suggest –

> 'As I came in by my bower door,
>   As day was waxin' wearie,
> Oh wha came tripping down the stair
>   But bonnie Peg my dearie.'

Elizabeth-Jane, rather disconcerted, hastened on; and the Scotchman's voice died away, humming more of the same within the closed door of his room.

Here the scene and sentiment ended for the present. When, soon after, the girl rejoined her mother, the latter was still in thought – on quite another matter than a young man's song.

'We've made a mistake,' she whispered (that the Scotchman might not overhear). 'On no account ought ye to have helped serve here tonight. Not because of ourselves, but for the sake of *him*. If he should befriend us, and take us up, and then find out what you did when staying here, 'twould grieve and wound his natural pride as Mayor of the town.'

Elizabeth, who would perhaps have been more alarmed at this than her mother had she known the real relationship, was not much disturbed about it as things stood. Her 'he' was another man than her poor mother's. 'For myself,' she said, 'I didn't at all mind waiting a little upon him. He's so respectable, and educated – far above the rest of 'em in the inn. They thought him very simple not to know their grim broad way of talking about themselves here. But of course he didn't know – he was too refined in his mind to know such things!' Thus she earnestly pleaded.

Meanwhile, the 'he' of her mother was not so far away as even they thought. After leaving the Three Mariners he had sauntered up and down the empty High Street, passing and repassing the inn in his promenade. When the Scotchman sang his voice had reached Henchard's ears through the heart-shaped holes in the window-shutters, and had led him to pause outside them a long while.

'To be sure, to be sure, how that fellow does draw me!' he had said to himself. 'I suppose 'tis because I'm so lonely. I'd have given him a third share in the business to have stayed!'

* IX *

WHEN Elizabeth-Jane opened the hinged casement next morning the mellow air brought in the feel of imminent autumn almost as distinctly as if she had been in the remotest hamlet. Casterbridge was the complement of the rural life around; not its urban opposite. Bees and butterflies in the cornfields at the top of the town, who desired to get to the meads at the bottom, took no circuitous course, but flew straight down High Street without any apparent consciousness that they were traversing strange latitudes. And in autumn airy spheres of thistledown floated into the same street, lodged upon the shop fronts, blew into drains, and innumerable tawny and yellow leaves skimmed along the pavement, and stole through people's doorways into their passages with a hesitating scratch on the floor, like the skirts of timid visitors.

Hearing voices, one of which was close at hand, she withdrew her head and glanced from behind the window-curtains. Mr Henchard – now habited no longer as a great personage, but as a thriving man of business – was pausing on his way up the middle of the street, and the Scotchman was looking from the window adjoining her own. Henchard, it appeared, had gone a little way past the inn before he had noticed his acquaintance of the previous evening. He came back a few steps, Donald Farfrae opening the window further.

'And you are off soon, I suppose?' said Henchard upwards.

'Yes – almost this moment, sir,' said the other. 'Maybe I'll walk on till the coach makes up on me.'

'Which way?'

'The way ye are going.'

'Then shall we walk together to the top o' town?'

'If ye'll wait a minute,' said the Scotchman.

In a few minutes the latter emerged, bag in hand. Henchard looked at the bag as at an enemy. It showed there was no mistake about the young man's departure. 'Ah, my lad,' he said, 'you should have been a wise man, and have stayed with me.'

'Yes, yes – it might have been wiser,' said Donald looking microscopically at the houses that were furthest off. 'It is only telling ye the truth when I say my plans are vague.'

They had by this time passed on from the precincts of the inn and Elizabeth-Jane heard no more. She saw that they continued in conversation, Henchard turning to the other occasionally, and emphasizing some remark with a gesture. Thus they passed the King's Arms Hotel, the Market House, St Peter's churchyard wall, ascending to the upper end of the long street till they were small as two grains of corn; when they bent suddenly to the right into the Bristol Road, and were out of view.

'He was a good man – and he's gone,' she said to herself. 'I was nothing to him, and there was no reason why he should have wished me goodbye.'

The simple thought, with its latent sense of slight, had moulded itself out of the following little fact: when the Scotchman came out at the door he had by accident glanced up at her; and then he had looked away again without nodding, or smiling, or saying a word.

'You are still thinking, mother,' she said, when she turned inwards.

'Yes; I am thinking of Mr Henchard's sudden liking for that young man. He was always so. Now, surely, if he takes so warmly to people who are not related to him at all, may he not take as warmly to his own kin?'

While they debated this question a procession of five large waggons went past, laden with hay up to the bedroom windows. They came in from the country, and the steaming horses had probably been travelling a great part of the night. To the shaft of each hung a little board, on which was painted in white letters, 'Henchard, cornfactor and hay-merchant'. The spectacle renewed his wife's conviction that, for her daughter's sake, she should strain a point to rejoin him.

The discussion was continued during breakfast, and the end of it was that Mrs Henchard decided, for good or for ill, to send Elizabeth-Jane with a message to Henchard, to the effect that his relative Susan, a sailor's widow, was in the town; leaving it to him to say whether or not he would recognize her. What had brought her to this determination were chiefly two things. He had been described as a lonely widower; and he had expressed shame for a past transaction of his life. There was promise in both.

'If he says no,' she enjoined, as Elizabeth-Jane stood, bonnet on, ready to depart; 'if he thinks it does not become the good position he has reached to in the town, to own – to let us call on him as – his distant kinsfolk, say, "Then, sir, we would rather not intrude; we will leave Casterbridge as quietly as we have come, and go back to our own country." . . . I almost feel that I would rather he did say so, as I have not seen him for so many years, and we are so – little allied to him!'

'And if he say yes?' inquired the more sanguine one.

'In that case,' answered Mrs Henchard cautiously, 'ask him to write me a note, saying when and how he will see us – or *me*.'

Elizabeth-Jane went a few steps towards the landing. 'And tell him,' continued her mother, 'that I full know I have no claim upon him – that I am glad to find he is thriving; that I hope his life may be long and happy – there, go.' Thus with a half-hearted willingness, a smothered reluctance, did the poor forgiving woman start her unconscious daughter on this errand.

It was about ten o'clock, and market-day, when Elizabeth paced up the High Street, in no great hurry; for to herself her position was only that of a poor relation deputed to hunt up a rich one. The front doors of the private houses were mostly left open at this warm autumn time, no thought of umbrella stealers disturbing the minds of the placid burgesses. Hence, through the long, straight, entrance passages thus unclosed could be seen, as through tunnels, the mossy gardens at the back, glowing with nasturtiums, fuchsias, scarlet geraniums, 'bloody warriors', snapdragons, and dahlias, this floral blaze being backed by crusted grey stone-work remaining from a yet remoter Casterbridge than the venerable one visible in the street. The old-fashioned fronts of these houses, which had older than old-fashioned backs, rose sheer from the pavement, into which the bow-windows protruded like bastions, necessitating a pleasing *chassez-déchassez* movement to the time-pressed pedestrian at every few yards. He was bound also to evolve other Terpsichorean figures in respect of door-steps, scrapers, cellar-hatches, church buttresses, and the overhang-ing angles of walls which, originally unobtrusive, had become bow-legged and knock-kneed.

In addition to these fixed obstacles which spoke so cheerfully of individual unrestraint as to boundaries, movables occupied the path and roadway to a perplexing extent. First the vans of the carriers in and out of Casterbridge, who hailed from Mellstock, Weatherbury, The Hintocks, Sherton-abbas, Kingsbere, Overcombe, and many other towns and villages round. Their owners were numerous enough to be regarded as a tribe, and had almost distinctiveness enough to be regarded as a race. Their vans had just arrived, and were drawn up on each side of the street in close file, so as to form at places a wall between the pavement and the roadway. Moreover every shop pitched out half of its contents upon trestles and boxes on the kerb, extending the display each week a little further and further into the roadway, despite the expostulations of the two feeble old constables, until there remained but a tortuous defile for carriages down the centre of the street, which afforded fine opportunities for skill with the reins. Over the pavement on the sunny side of the way hung shopblinds so constructed as to give the passenger's hat a smart buffet off his head, as from the unseen hands of Cranstoun's Goblin Page, celebrated in romantic lore.

Horses for sale were tied in rows, their forelegs on the pavement, their hind legs in the street, in which position they occasionally nipped little boys by the shoulder who were passing to school. And any inviting recess in front of a house that had been modestly kept back from the general line was utilized by pig-dealers as a pen for their stock.*

The yeomen, farmers, dairymen, and townsfolk, who came to transact business in these ancient streets, spoke in other ways than by articulation. Not to hear the words of your interlocutor in metropolitan centres is to know nothing of his meaning. Here the face, the arms, the hat, the stick, the body throughout spoke equally with the tongue. To express satisfaction the Casterbridge marketman added to his utterance a broadening of the cheeks, a crevicing of the eyes, a throwing back of the shoulders, which was intelligible from the other end of the street. If he wondered, though all Henchard's carts and waggons were rattling past him, you knew it from perceiving the inside of his crimson mouth, and a target-like circling of his eyes. Deliberation caused sundry attacks on the moss of adjoining walls with the end of his stick, a change of his hat from the horizontal to the less so; a sense of tediousness announced itself in a lowering of the person by spreading the knees to a lozenge-shaped aperture and contorting the arms. Chicanery, subterfuge, had hardly a place in the streets of this honest borough to all appearance; and it was said that the lawyers in the Court House hard by occasionally threw in strong arguments for the other side out of pure generosity (though apparently by mischance) when advancing their own.

Thus Casterbridge was in most respects but the pole, focus, or nerve-knot of the surrounding country life; differing from the many

* The reader will scarcely need to be reminded that time and progress have obliterated from the town that suggested these descriptions many or most of the old-fashioned features here enumerated.

manufacturing towns which are as foreign bodies set down, like boulders on a plain, in a green world with which they have nothing in common. Casterbridge lived by agriculture at one remove further from the fountain-head than the adjoining villages – no more. The townsfolk understood every fluctuation in the rustic's condition, for it affected their receipts as much as the labourer's; they entered into the troubles and joys which moved the aristocratic families ten miles round – for the same reason. And even at the dinner-parties of the professional families the subjects of discussion were corn, cattle-disease, sowing and reaping, fencing and planting; while politics were viewed by them less from their own standpoint of burgesses with rights and privileges than from the stand-point of their county neighbours.

All the venerable contrivances and confusions which delighted the eye by their quaintness, and in a measure reasonableness, in this rare old market-town, were metropolitan novelties to the unpractised eyes of Elizabeth-Jane, fresh from netting fish seines in a seaside cottage. Very little inquiry was necessary to guide her footsteps. Henchard's house was one of the best, faced with dull red-and-grey old brick. The front door was open, and, as in other houses, she could see through the passage to the end of the garden – nearly a quarter of a mile off.

Mr Henchard was not in the house, but in the store-yard. She was conducted into the mossy garden, and through a door in the wall, which was studded with rusty nails speaking of generations of fruit-trees that had been trained there. The door opened upon the yard, and here she was left to find him as she could. It was a place flanked by hay-barns, into which tons of fodder, all in trusses, were being packed from the waggons she had seen pass the inn that morning. On other sides of the yard were wooden granaries on stone staddles, to which access was given by Flemish ladders, and a store-house several floors high. Wherever the doors of these places were open, a closely packed throng of bursting wheat-sacks could be seen standing inside, with the air of awaiting a famine that would not come.

She wandered about this place, uncomfortably conscious of the impend-ing interview, till she was quite weary of searching; she ventured to inquire of a boy in what quarter Mr Henchard could be found. He directed her to an office which she had not seen before, and knocking at the door she was answered by a cry of 'Come in'.

Elizabeth turned the handle; and there stood before her, bending over some sample-bags on a table, not the corn-merchant, but the young Scotchman Mr Farfrae – in the act of pouring some grains of wheat from one hand to the other. His hat hung on a peg behind him, and the roses of his carpet-bag glowed from the corner of the room.

Having toned her feelings and arranged words on her lips for Mr Henchard, and for him alone, she was for the moment confounded.

'Yes, what is it?' said the Scotchman, like a man who permanently ruled there.

She said she wanted to see Mr Henchard.

'Ah, yes; will you wait a minute? He's engaged just now,' said the young man, apparently not recognizing her as the girl at the inn. He handed her a chair, bade her sit down, and turned to his sample-bags again. While Elizabeth-Jane sits waiting in great amaze at the young man's presence we may briefly explain how he came there.

When the two new acquaintances had passed out of sight that morning towards the Bath and Bristol road they went on silently, except for a few commonplaces, till they had gone down an avenue on the town walls called the Chalk Walk, leading to an angle where the North and West escarpments met. From this high corner of the square earthworks a vast extent of country could be seen. A footpath ran steeply down the green slope, conducting from the shady promenade on the walls to a road at the bottom of the scarp. It was by this path the Scotchman had to descend.

'Well, here's success to 'ee,' said Henchard, holding out his right hand and leaning with his left upon the wicket which protected the descent. In the act there was the inelegance of one whose feelings are nipped and wishes defeated. 'I shall often think of this time, and of how you came at the very moment to throw a light upon my difficulty.'

Still holding the young man's hand he paused, and then added deliberately: 'Now I am not the man to let a cause be lost for want of a word. And before ye are gone for ever I'll speak. Once more, will ye stay? There it is, flat and plain. You can see that it isn't all selfishness that makes me press 'ee; for my business is not quite so scientific as to require an intellect entirely out of the common. Others would do for the place without doubt. Some selfishness perhaps there is, but there is more; it isn't for me to repeat what. Come bide with me – and name your own terms. I'll agree to 'em willingly and 'ithout a word of gainsaying; for, hang it, Farfrae, I like thee well!'

The young man's hand remained steady in Henchard's for a moment or two. He looked over the fertile country that stretched beneath them, then backward along the shaded walk reaching to the top of the town. His face flushed.

'I never expected this – I did not!' he said. 'It's Providence! Should any one go against it? No; I'll not go to America; I'll stay and be your man!'

His hand, which had lain lifeless in Henchard's, returned the latter's grasp.

'Done,' said Henchard.

'Done,' said Donald Farfrae.

The face of Mr Henchard beamed forth a satisfaction that was almost fierce in its strength. 'Now you are my friend!' he exclaimed. 'Come back to my house; let's clinch it at once by clear terms, so as to be comfortable in our minds.' Farfrae caught up his bag and retraced the North-West Avenue in Henchard's company as he had come. Henchard was all confidence now.

'I am the most distant fellow in the world when I don't care for a man,' he said. 'But when a man takes my fancy he takes it strong. Now I am sure you can eat another breakfast? You couldn't have eaten much so

early, even if they had anything at that place to gi'e thee, which they
hadn't; so come to my house and we will have a solid, staunch tuck-in,
and settle terms in black-and-white if you like; though my word's my
bond. I can always make a good meal in the morning. I've got a splendid
cold pigeon-pie going just now. You can have some home-brewed if you
want to, you know.'

'It is too airly in the morning for that,' said Farfrae with a smile.

'Well, of course, I didn't know. I don't drink it because of my oath; but
I am obliged to brew for my work-people.'

Thus talking they returned, and entered Henchard's premises by the
back way or traffic entrance. Here the matter was settled over the
breakfast, at which Henchard heaped the young Scotchman's plate to a
prodigal fulness. He would not rest satisfied till Farfrae had written for
his luggage from Bristol, and despatched the letter to the post-office.
When it was done this man of strong impulses declared that his new
friend should take up his abode in his house – at least till some suitable
lodgings could be found.

He then took Farfrae round and showed him the places, and the stores
of grain, and other stock; and finally entered the offices where the younger
of them has already been discovered by Elizabeth.

* X *

WHILE she still sat under the Scotchman's eyes a man came up to the
door, reaching it as Henchard opened the door of the inner office to admit
Elizabeth. The new-comer stepped forward like the quicker cripple at
Bethesda, and entered in her stead. She could hear his words to Henchard:
'Joshua Jopp, sir – by appointment – the new manager.'

'The new manager! – he's in his office,' said Henchard bluntly.

'In his office!' said the man, with a stultified air.

'I mentioned Thursday,' said Henchard; 'and as you did not keep your
appointment, I have engaged another manager. At first I thought he must
be you. Do you think I can wait when business is in question?'

'You said Thursday or Saturday, sir,' said the new-comer, pulling out
a letter.

'Well, you are too late,' said the corn-factor. 'I can say no more.'

'You as good as engaged me,' murmured the man.

'Subject to an interview,' said Henchard. 'I am sorry for you – very
sorry indeed. But it can't be helped.'

There was no more to be said, and the man came out, encountering Elizabeth-Jane in his passage. She could see that his mouth twitched with anger, and that bitter disappointment was written in his face everywhere.

Elizabeth-Jane now entered, and stood before the master of the premises. His dark pupils – which always seemed to have a red spark of light in them, though this could hardly be a physical fact – turned indifferently round under his dark brows until they rested on her figure. 'Now then, what is it, my young woman?' he said blandly.

'Can I speak to you – not on business, sir?' said she.

'Yes – I suppose.' He looked at her more thoughtfully.

'I am sent to tell you, sir,' she innocently went on, 'that a distant relative of yours by marriage, Susan Newson, a sailor's widow, is in the town; and to ask whether you would wish to see her.'

The rich *rouge-et-noir* of his countenance underwent a slight change. 'Oh – Susan is – still alive?' he asked with difficulty.

'Yes, sir.'

'Are you her daughter?'

'Yes, sir – her only daughter.'

'What – do you call yourself – your Christian name?'

'Elizabeth-Jane, sir.'

'Newson?'

'Elizabeth-Jane Newson.'

This at once suggested to Henchard that the transaction of his early married life at Weydon Fair was unrecorded in the family history. It was more than he could have expected. His wife had behaved kindly to him in return for his unkindness, and had never proclaimed her wrong to her child or to the world.

'I am – a good deal interested in your news,' he said. 'And as this is not a matter of business, but pleasure, suppose we go indoors.'

It was with a gentle delicacy of manner, surprising to Elizabeth, that he showed her out of the office and through the outer room, where Donald Farfrae was overhauling bins and samples with the inquiring inspection of a beginner in charge. Henchard preceded her through the door in the wall to the suddenly changed scene of the garden and flowers, and onward into the house. The dining-room to which he introduced her still exhibited the remnants of the lavish breakfast laid for Farfrae. It was furnished to profusion with heavy mahogany furniture of the deepest red-Spanish hues. Pembroke tables, with leaves hanging so low that they well-nigh touched the floor, stood against the walls on legs and feet shaped like those of an elephant, and on one lay three huge folio volumes – a Family Bible, a 'Josephus', and a 'Whole Duty of Man'. In the chimney corner was a fire-grate with a fluted semicircular back, having urns and festoons cast in relief thereon; and the chairs were of the kind which, since that day, has cast lustre upon the names of Chippendale and Sheraton, though, in point of fact, their patterns may have been such as those illustrious carpenters never saw or heard of.

'Sit down – Elizabeth-Jane – sit down,' he said, with a shake in his voice as he uttered her name; and sitting down himself he allowed his hands to hang between his knees, while he looked upon the carpet. 'Your mother, then, is quite well?'

'She is rather worn out, sir, with travelling.'

'A sailor's widow – when did he die?'

'Father was lost last spring.'

Henchard winced at the word 'father', thus applied. 'Do you and she come from abroad – America or Australia?' he asked.

'No. We have been in England some years. I was twelve when we came here from Canada.'

'Ah; exactly.' By such conversation he discovered the circumstances which had enveloped his wife and her child in such total obscurity that he had long ago believed them to be in their graves. These things being clear, he returned to the present. 'And where is your mother staying?'

'At the Three Mariners.'

'And you are her daughter Elizabeth-Jane?' repeated Henchard. He arose, came close to her, and glanced in her face. 'I think,' he said, suddenly turning away with a wet eye, 'you shall take a note from me to your mother. I should like to see her . . . She is not left very well off by her late husband?' His eye fell on Elizabeth's clothes, which, though a respectable suit of black, and her very best, were decidedly old-fashioned even to Casterbridge eyes.

'Not very well,' she said, glad that he had divined this without her being obliged to express it.

He sat down at the table and wrote a few lines; next taking from his pocket-book a five-pound note, which he put in the envelope with the letter, adding to it, as by an after-thought, five shillings. Sealing the whole up carefully, he directed it to 'Mrs Newson, Three Mariners Inn', and handed the packet to Elizabeth.

'Deliver it to her personally, please,' said Henchard. 'Well, I am glad to see you here, Elizabeth-Jane – very glad. We must have a long talk together – but not just now.'

He took her hand at parting, and held it so warmly that she, who had known so little friendship, was much affected, and tears rose to her aerial-grey eyes. The instant that she was gone Henchard's state showed itself more distinctly; having shut the door he sat in his dining-room stiffly erect, gazing at the opposite wall as if he read his history there.

'Begad!' he suddenly exclaimed, jumping up. 'I didn't think of that. Perhaps these are impostors – and Susan and the child dead after all!'

However, a something in Elizabeth-Jane soon assured him that, as regarded her, at least, there could be little doubt. And a few hours would settle the question of her mother's identity; for he had arranged in his note to see her that evening.

'It never rains but it pours!' said Henchard. His keenly excited interest in his new friend the Scotchman was now eclipsed by this event; and Donald Farfrae saw so little of him during the rest of the day that he wondered at the suddenness of his employer's moods.

In the meantime Elizabeth had reached the inn. Her mother, instead of taking the note with the curiosity of a poor woman expecting assistance, was much moved at sight of it. She did not read it at once, asking Elizabeth to describe her reception, and the very words Mr Henchard used. Elizabeth's back was turned when her mother opened the letter. It ran thus: –

Meet me at eight o'clock this evening, if you can, at the Ring on the Budmouth road. The place is easy to find. I can say no more now. The news upsets me almost. The girl seems to be in ignorance. Keep her so till I have seen you.

M.H.

He said nothing about the enclosure of five guineas. The amount was significant; it may tacitly have said to her that he bought her back again. She waited restlessly for the close of the day, telling Elizabeth-Jane that she was invited to see Mr Henchard; that she would go alone. But she said nothing to show that the place of meeting was not at his house, nor did she hand the note to Elizabeth.

* XI *

THE Ring at Casterbridge was merely the local name of one of the finest Roman Amphitheatres, if not the very finest, remaining in Britain.

Casterbridge announced old Rome in every street, alley, and precinct. It looked Roman, bespoke the art of Rome, concealed dead men of Rome. It was impossible to dig more than a foot or two deep about the town fields and gardens without coming upon some tall soldier or other of the Empire, who had lain there in his silent unobtrusive rest for a space of fifteen hundred years. He was mostly found lying on his side, in an oval scoop in the chalk, like a chicken in its shell; his knees drawn up to his chest; sometimes with the remains of his spear against his arm; a fibula or brooch of bronze on his breast or forehead; an urn at his knees, a jar at his throat, a bottle at his mouth; and mystified conjecture pouring down upon him from the eyes of Casterbridge street boys and men, who had turned a moment to gaze at the familiar spectacle as they passed by.

Imaginative inhabitants, who would have felt an unpleasantness at the discovery of a comparatively modern skeleton in their gardens, were quite unmoved by these hoary shapes. They had lived so long ago, their time was so unlike the present, their hopes and motives were so widely removed from ours, that between them and the living there seemed to stretch a gulf too wide for even a spirit to pass.

The Amphitheatre was a huge circular enclosure, with a notch at opposite extremities of its diameter north and south. From it sloping internal form it might have been called the spittoon of Jötuns. It was to Casterbridge what the ruined Coliseum is to modern Rome, and was nearly of the same magnitude. The dusk of evening was the proper hour at which a true impression of this suggestive place could be received. Standing in the middle of the arena at that time there by degrees became apparent its real vastness, which a cursory view from the summit at noon-day was apt to obscure. Melancholy, impressive, lonely, yet accessible from every part of the town, the historic circle was the frequent spot for appointments of a furtive kind. Intrigues were arranged there; tentative meetings were there experimented after divisions and feuds. But one kind of appointment – in itself the most common of any – seldom had place in the Amphitheatre: that of happy lovers.

Why, seeing that it was pre-eminently an airy, accessible, and seques-tered spot for interviews, the cheerfullest form of those occurrences never took kindly to the soil of the ruin, would be a curious inquiry. Perhaps it was because its associations had about them something sinister. Its history proved that. Apart from the sanguinary nature of the games originally played therein, such incidents attached to its past as these: that for scores of years the town-gallows had stood at one corner; that in 1705 a woman who had murdered her husband was half-strangled and then burnt there in the presence of ten thousand spectators. Tradition reports that at a certain stage of the burning her heart burst and leapt out of her body, to the terror of them all, and that not one of those ten thousand people ever cared particularly for hot roast after that. In addition to these old tragedies, pugilistic encounters almost to the death had come off down to recent dates in that secluded arena, entirely invisible to the outside world save by climbing to the top of the enclosure, which few townspeople in the daily round of their lives ever took the trouble to do. So that, though close to the turnpike-road, crimes might be perpetrated there unseen at mid-day.

Some boys had latterly tried to impart gaiety to the ruin by using the central arena as a cricket-ground. But the game usually languished for the aforesaid reason – the dismal privacy which the earthen circle enforced, shutting out every appreciative passer's vision, every commendatory remark from outsiders – everything, except the sky; and to play at games in such circumstances was like acting to an empty house. Possibly, too, the boys were timid, for some old people said that at certain moments in the summer time, in broad daylight, persons sitting with a book or dozing in the arena had, on lifting their eyes, beheld the slopes lined with a gazing legion of Hadrian's soldiery as if watching the gladiatorial combat; and had heard the roar of their excited voices; that the scene would remain but a moment, like a lightning flash, and then disappear.

It was related that there still remained under the south entrance excavated cells for the reception of the wild animals and athletes who took part in the games. The arena was still smooth and circular, as if used for its original purpose not so very long ago. The sloping pathways by which spectators had ascended to their seats were pathways yet. But the whole was grown over with grass, which now, at the end of summer, was bearded with withered bents that formed waves under the brush of the wind, returning to the attentive ear Aeolian modulations, and detaining for moments the flying globes of thistledown.

Henchard had chosen this spot as being the safest from observation which he could think of for meeting his long-lost wife, and at the same time as one easily to be found by a stranger after nightfall. As Mayor of the town, with a reputation to keep up, he could not invite her to come to his house till some definite course had been decided on.

Just before eight he approached the deserted earthwork, and entered by the south path which descended over the *débris* of the former dens. In a few moments he could discern a female figure creeping in by the great north gap, or public gateway. They met in the middle of the arena. Neither spoke just at first – there was no necessity for speech – and the poor woman leant against Henchard, who supported her in his arms.

'I don't drink,' he said in a low, halting, apologetic voice. 'You hear, Susan? – I don't drink now – I haven't since that night.' Those were his first words.

He felt her bow her head in acknowledgement that she understood. After a minute or two he again began:

'If I had know you were living, Susan! But there was every reason to suppose you and the child were dead and gone. I took every possible step to find you – travelled – advertised. My opinion at last was that you had started for some colony with that man, and had been drowned on your voyage out. Why did you keep silent like this?'

'O Michael! because of him – what other reason could there be? I thought I owed him faithfulness to the end of one of our lives – foolishly I believed there was something solemn and binding in the bargain; I thought that even in honour I dared not desert him when he had paid so much for me in good faith. I meet you now only as a widow – I consider myself that, and that I have no claim upon you. Had he not died I should never have come – never! Of that you may be sure.'

'Ts-s-s! How could you be so simple?'

'I don't know. Yet it would have been very wicked – if I had not thought like that!' said Susan, almost crying.

'Yes – yes – so it would. It is only that which makes me feel 'ee an innocent woman. But – to lead me into this!'

'What, Michael?' she asked, alarmed.

'Why, this difficulty about our living together again, and Elizabeth-Jane. She cannot be told all – she would so despise us both that – I could not bear it!'

'That was why she was brought up in ignorance of you. I could not bear it either.'

'Well – we must talk of a plan for keeping her in her present belief, and getting matters straight in spite of it. You have heard I am in a large way of business here – that I am Mayor of the town, and churchwarden, and I don't know what all?'

'Yes,' she murmured.

'These things, as well as the dread of the girl discovering our disgrace, make it necessary to act with extreme caution. So that I don't see how you two can return openly to my house as the wife and daughter I once treated badly, and banished from me; and there's the rub o't.'

'We'll go away at once. I only came to see –'

'No, no, Susan; you are not to go – you mistake me!' he said, with kindly severity. 'I have thought of this plan: that you and Elizabeth take a cottage in the town as the widow Mrs Newson and her daughter; that I meet you, court you, and marry you, Elizabeth-Jane coming to my house as my step-daughter. The thing is so natural and easy it is half done in thinking o't. This would leave my shady, headstrong, disgraceful life as a young man absolutely unopened; the secret would be yours and mine only; and I should have the pleasure of seeing my own only child under my roof, as well as my wife.'

'I am quite in your hands, Michael,' she said meekly. I came here for the sake of Elizabeth; for myself, if you tell me to leave again tomorrow morning, and never come near you more, I am content to go.'

'Now, now; we don't want to hear that,' said Henchard gently. 'Of course you won't leave again. Think over the plan I have proposed for a few hours; and if you can't hit upon a better one we'll adopt it. I have to be away for a day or two on business, unfortunately; but during that time you can get lodgings – the only ones fit for you are those over the china-shop in High Street – and you can also look for a cottage.'

'If the lodgings are in High Street they are dear, I suppose?'

'Never mind – you *must* start genteel if our plan is to be carried out. Look to me for money. Have you enough till I come back?'

'Quite,' said she.

'And are you comfortable at the inn?'

'O yes.'

'And the girl is quite safe from learning the shame of her case and ours? – that's what makes me most anxious of all.'

'You would be surprised to find how unlikely she is to dream of the truth. How could she ever suppose such a thing?'

'True!'

'I like the idea of repeating our marriage,' said Mrs Henchard, after a pause. 'It seems the only right course, after all this. Now I think I must go back to Elizabeth-Jane, and tell her that our kinsman, Mr Henchard, kindly wishes us to stay in the town.'

'Very well – arrange that yourself. I'll go some way with you.'

'No, no. Don't run any risk!' said his wife anxiously. 'I can find my way back – it is not late. Please let me go alone.'

'Right,' said Henchard. 'But just one word. Do you forgive me, Susan?'

She murmured something; but seemed to find it difficult to frame her answer.

'Never mind – all in good time,' said he. 'Judge me by my future works – good-bye!'

He retreated, and stood at the upper side of the Amphitheatre while his wife passed out through the lower way, and descended under the trees to the town. Then Henchard himself went homeward, going so fast that by the time he reached his door he was almost upon the heels of the unconscious woman from whom he had just parted. He watched her up the street, and turned into his house.

* XII *

ON entering his own door after watching his wife out of sight, the Mayor walked on through the tunnel-shaped passage into the garden, and thence by the back door towards the stores and granaries. A light shone from the office-window, and there being no blind to screen the interior Henchard could see Donald Farfrae still seated where he had left him, initiating himself into the managerial work of the house by overhauling the books. Henchard entered, merely observing, 'Don't let me interrupt you, if ye will stay so late.'

He stood behind Farfrae's chair, watching his dexterity in clearing up the numerical fogs which had been allowed to grow so thick in Henchard's books as almost to baffle even the Scotchman's perspicacity. The corn-factor's mien was half admiring, and yet it was not without a dash of pity for the tastes of any one who could care to give his mind to such finnikin details. Henchard himself was mentally and physically unfit for grubbing subtleties from soiled paper; he had in a modern sense received the education of Achilles, and found penmanship a tantalizing art.

'You shall do no more tonight,' he said at length, spreading his great hand over the paper. 'There is time enough tomorrow. Come indoors with me and have some supper. Now you shall! I am determined on't.' He shut the account-books with friendly force.

Donald had wished to get to his lodgings; but he already saw that his friend and employer was a man who knew no moderation in his requests and impulses, and he yielded gracefully. He liked Henchard's warmth, even if it inconvenienced him; the great difference in their characters adding to the liking.

They locked up the office, and the young man followed his companion through the private little door which, admitting directly into Henchard's garden, permitted a passage from the utilitarian to the beautiful at one step. The garden was silent, dewy, and full of perfume. It extended a long way back from the house, first as lawn and flower-beds, then as fruit-garden, where the long-tied espaliers, as old as the old house itself, had grown so stout, and cramped, and gnarled that they had pulled their stakes out of the ground and stood distorted and writhing in vegetable agony, like leafy Laocoöns. The flowers which smelt so sweetly were not discernible; and they passed through them into the house.

The hospitalities of the morning were repeated, and when they were over Henchard said, 'Pull your chair round to the fireplace, my dear fellow, and let's make a blaze – there's nothing I hate like a black grate, even in September.' He applied a light to the laid-in fuel, and a cheerful radiance spread around.

'It is odd,' said Henchard, 'that two men should meet as we have done on a purely business ground, and that at the end of the first day I should wish to speak to 'ee on a family matter. But, damn it all, I am a lonely man, Farfrae: I have nobody else to speak to; and why shouldn't I tell it to 'ee?'

'I'll be glad to hear it, if I can be of any service,' said Donald, allowing his eyes to travel over the intricate wood-carvings of the chimney-piece, representing garlanded lyres, shields, and quivers, on either side of a draped ox-skull, and flanked by heads of Apollo and Diana in low relief.

'I've not been always what I am now,' continued Henchard, his firm deep voice being ever so little shaken. He was plainly under that strange influence which sometimes prompts men to confide to the new-found friend what they will not tell to the old. 'I began life as a working hay-trusser, and when I was eighteen I married on the strength o' my calling. Would you think me a married man?'

'I heard in the town that you were a widower.'

'Ah, yes – you would naturally have heard that. Well, I lost my wife nineteen years ago or so – by my own fault . . . This is how it came about. One summer evening I was travelling for employment, and she was walking at my side, carrying the baby, our only child. We came to a booth in a country fair. I was a drinking man at that time.'

Henchard paused a moment, threw himself back so that his elbow rested on the table, his forehead being shaded by his hand, which, however, did not hide the marks of introspective inflexibility on his features as he narrated in fullest details the incidents of the transaction with the sailor. The tinge of indifference which had at first been visible in the Scotchman now disappeared.

Henchard went on to describe his attempts to find his wife; the oath he swore; the solitary life he led during the years which followed. 'I have kept my oath for nineteen years,' he went on; 'I have risen to what you see me now.'

'Ay!'

'Well – no wife could I hear of in all that time; and being by nature something of a woman-hater, I have found it no hardship to keep mostly at a distance from the sex. No wife could I hear of, I say, till this very day. And now – she has come back.'

'Come back, has she!'

'This morning – this very morning. And what's to be done?'

'Can ye no' take her and live with her, and make some amends?'

'That's what I've planned and proposed. But, Farfrae,' said Henchard gloomily, 'by doing right with Susan I wrong another innocent woman.'

'Ye don't say that?'

'In the nature of things, Farfrae, it is almost impossible that a man of my sorts should have the good fortune to tide through twenty years o' life without making more blunders than one. It has been my custom for many years to run across to Jersey in the way of business, particularly in the potato and root season. I do a large trade wi' them in that line. Well, one autumn when stopping there I fell quite ill, and in my illness I sank into one of those gloomy fits I sometimes suffer from, on account o' the loneliness of my domestic life, when the world seems to have the blackness of hell, and, like Job, I could curse the day that gave me birth.'

'Ah, no, I never feel like it,' said Farfrae.

'Then pray to God that you never may, young man. While in this state I was taken pity on by a woman – a young lady I should call her, for she was of good family, well bred, and well educated – the daughter of some harum-scarum military officer who had got into difficulties, and had his pay sequestrated. He was dead now, and her mother too, and she was as lonely as I. This young creature was staying at the boarding-house where I happened to have my lodging; and when I was pulled down she took upon herself to nurse me. Heaven knows why, for I wasn't worth it. But being together in the same house, and her feelings warm, we got naturally intimate. I won't go into particulars of what our relations were. It is enough to say that we honestly meant to marry. There arose a scandal, which did me no harm, but was of course ruin to her. Though, Farfrae, between you and me, as man and man, I solemnly declare that philandering with womankind has neither been my vice nor my virtue. She was terribly careless of appearances, and I was perhaps more, because o' my dreary state; and it was through this that the scandal arose. At last I was well and came away. When I was gone she suffered much on my account, and didn't forget to tell me so in letters one after another; till, latterly, I felt I owed her something, and thought that, as I had not heard of Susan for so long, I would make this other one the only return I could make, and ask her if she would run the risk of Susan being alive (very slight as I believed) and marry me, such as I was. She jumped for joy, and we should no doubt soon have been married – but, behold, Susan appears!'

Donald showed his deep concern at a complication so far beyond the degree of his simple experiences.

'Now see what injury a man may cause around him! Even after that wrong-doing at the fair when I was young, if I had never been so selfish as to let this giddy girl devote herself to me over at Jersey, to the injury of her name, all might now be well. Yet, as it stands, I must bitterly disappoint one of these women; and it is the second. My first duty is to Susan – there's no doubt about that.'

'They are both in a very melancholy position, and that's true!' murmured Donald.

'They are! For myself I don't care – 'twill all end one way. But these two.' Henchard paused in reverie. 'I feel I should like to treat the second, no less than the first, as kindly as a man can in such a case.'

'Ah, well, it cannet be helped!' said the other, with philosophic woefulness. 'You mun write to the young lady, and in your letter you must put it plain and honest that it turns out she cannet be your wife, the first having come back; that ye cannet see her more; and that – ye wish her weel.'

'That won't do. 'Od seize it, I must do a little more than that! I must – though she did always brag about her rich uncle or rich aunt, and her expectations from 'em – I must send a useful sum of money to her, I suppose – just as a little recompense, poor girl . . . Now, will you help me in this, and draw up an explanation to her of all I've told ye, breaking it as gently as you can? I'm so bad at letters.'

'And I will.'

'Now, I haven't told you quite all yet. My wife Susan has my daughter with her – the baby that was in her arms at the fair; and this girl knows nothing of me beyond that I am some sort of relation by marriage. She has grown up in the belief that the sailor to whom I made over her mother, and who is now dead, was her father, and her mother's husband. What her mother has always felt, she and I together feel now – that we can't proclaim our disgrace to the girl by letting her know the truth. Now what would you do? – I want your advice.'

'I think I'd run the risk, and tell her the truth. She'll forgive ye both.'

'Never!' said Henchard. 'I am not going to let her know the truth. Her mother and I be going to marry again; and it will not only help us to keep our child's respect, but it will be more proper. Susan looks upon herself as the sailor's widow, and won't think o' living with me as formerly without another religious ceremony – and she's right.'

Farfrae thereupon said no more. The letter to the young Jersey woman was carefully framed by him, and the interview ended, Henchard saying, as the Scotchman left, 'I feel it a great relief, Farfrae, to tell some friend o' this! You see now that the Mayor of Casterbridge is not so thriving in his mind as it seems he might be from the state of his pocket.'

'I do. And I'm sorry for ye!' said Farfrae.

When he had gone Henchard copied the letter, and, enclosing a cheque, took it to the post-office, from which he walked back thoughtfully.

'Can it be that it will go off so easily!' he said. 'Poor thing – God knows! Now then, to make amends to Susan!'

XIII

THE cottage which Michael Henchard hired for his wife Susan under her name of Newson – in pursuance of their plan – was in the upper or western part of the town, near the Roman wall, and the avenue which overshadowed it. The evening sun seemed to shine more yellowly there than anywhere else this autumn – stretching its rays, as the hours grew later, under the lowest sycamore boughs, and steeping the ground-floor of the dwelling, with its green shutters, in the substratum of radiance which the foliage screened from the upper parts. Beneath these sycamores on the town walls could be seen from the sitting-room the tumuli and earth forts of the distant uplands; making it altogether a pleasant spot, with the usual touch of melancholy that a past-marked prospect lends.

As soon as the mother and daughter were comfortably installed, with a white-aproned servant and all complete, Henchard paid them a visit, and remained to tea. During the entertainment Elizabeth was carefully hoodwinked by the very general tone of the conversation that prevailed – a proceeding which seemed to afford some humour to Henchard, though his wife was not particularly happy in it. The visit was repeated again and again with business-like determination by the Mayor, who seemed to have schooled himself into a course of strict mechanical rightness towards this woman of prior claim, at any expense to the later one and to his own sentiments.

One afternoon the daughter was not indoors when Henchard came, and he said drily, 'This is a very good opportunity for me to ask you to name the happy day, Susan.'

The poor woman smiled faintly; she did not enjoy pleasantries on a situation into which she had entered solely for the sake of her girl's reputation. She like them so little, indeed, that there was room for wonder why she had countenanced deception at all, and had not bravely let the girl know her history. But the flesh is weak; and the true explanation came in due course.

'O Michael!' she said, 'I am afraid all this is taking up your time and giving trouble – when I did not expect any such thing!' And she looked at him and at his dress as a man of affluence, and at the furniture he had provided for the room – ornate and lavish to her eyes.

'Not at all,' said Henchard, in rough benignity. 'This is only a cottage – it costs me next to nothing. And as to taking up my time' – here his red and black visage kindled with satisfaction – 'I've a splendid fellow to superintend my business now – a man whose like I've never been able to lay hands on before. I shall soon be able to leave everything to him, and have more time to call my own than I've had for these last twenty years.'

Henchard's visits here grew so frequent and so regular that it soon became whispered, and then openly discussed, in Casterbridge that the masterful, coercive Mayor of the town was captured and enervated by the genteel widow Mrs Newson. His well-known haughty indifference to the society of womankind, his silent avoidance of converse with the sex, contributed a piquancy to what would otherwise have been an unromantic matter enough. That such a poor fragile woman should be his choice was inexplicable, except on the ground that the engagement was a family affair in which sentimental passion had no place; for it was known that they were related in some way. Mrs Henchard was so pale that the boys called her 'The Ghost'. Sometimes Henchard overheard this epithet when they passed together along the Walks – as the avenues on the walls were named – at which his face would darken with an expression of destructiveness towards the speakers ominous to see; but he said nothing.

He pressed on the preparations for his union, or rather reunion, with this pale creature in a dogged, unflinching spirit which did credit to his conscientiousness. Nobody would have conceived from his outward demeanour that there was no amatory fire or pulse of romance acting as stimulant to the bustle going on in his gaunt, great house; nothing but three large resolves – one, to make amends to his neglected Susan; another, to provide a comfortable home for Elizabeth-Jane under his paternal eye; and a third, to castigate himself with the thorns which these restitutory acts brought in their train; among them the lowering of his dignity in public opinion by marrying so comparatively humble a woman.

Susan Henchard entered a carriage for the first time in her life when she stepped into the plain brougham which drew up at the door on the wedding-day to take her and Elizabeth-Jane to church. It was a windless morning of warm November rain, which floated down like meal, and lay in a powdery form on the nap of hats and coats. Few people had gathered round the church door though they were well packed within. The Scotchman, who assisted as groomsman, was of course, the only one present, beyond the chief actors, who knew the true situation of the contracting parties. He, however, was too inexperienced, too thoughtful, too judicial, too strongly conscious of the serious side of the business, to enter into the scene in its dramatic aspect. That required the special genius of Christopher Coney, Solomon Longways, Buzzford, and their fellows. But they knew nothing of the secret; though, as the time for coming out of church drew on, they gathered on the pavement adjoining, and expounded the subject according to their lights.

' 'Tis five-and-forty years since I had my settlement in this here town,' said Coney; 'but daze me if ever I see a man wait so long before to take so little! There's a chance even for thee after this, Nance Mockridge.' The remark was addressed to a woman who stood behind his shoulder – the same who had exhibited Henchard's bad bread in public when Elizabeth and her mother entered Casterbridge.

'Be cust if I'd marry any such as he, or thee either,' replied that lady. 'As for thee, Christopher, we know what ye be, and the less said the better. And as for he – well, there – (lowering her voice) 'tis said 'a was a poor parish 'prentice – I wouldn't say it for all the world – but 'a was a poor parish 'prentice, that began life wi' no more belonging to 'en than a carrion crow.'

'And now he's worth ever so much a minute,' murmured Longways. 'When a man is said to be worth so much a minute, he's a man to be considered!'

Turning, he saw a circular disc reticulated with creases, and recognized the smiling countenance of the fat woman who had asked for another song at the Three Mariners. 'Well, Mother Cuxsom,' he said, 'how's this? Here's Mrs Newson, a mere skellinton, has got another husband to keep her, while a woman of your tonnage have not.'

'I have not. Nor another to beat me . . . Ah, yes, Cuxsom's gone, and so shall leather breeches!'

'Yes; with the blessing of God leather breeches shall go.'

' 'Tisn't worth my old while to think of another husband,' continued Mrs Cuxsom. 'And yet I'll lay my life I'm as respectable born as she.'

'True; your mother was a very good woman – I can mind her. She were rewarded by the Agricultural Society for having begot the greatest number of healthy children without parish assistance, and other virtuous marvels.'

' 'Twas that that kept us so low upon the ground – that great hungry family.'

'Ay. Where the pigs be many the wash runs thin.'

'And dostn't mind how mother would sing, Christopher?' continued Mrs Cuxsom, kindling at the retrospection; 'and how we went with her to the party at Mellstock, do ye mind? – at old Dame Ledlow's, farmer Shiner's aunt, do ye mind? – she we used to call Toad-skin, because her face were so yaller and freckled, do ye mind?'

'I do, hee-hee, I do!' said Christopher Coney.

'And well do I – for I was getting up husband-high at that time – one-half girl, and t'other half woman, as one may say. And canst mind' – she prodded Solomon's shoulder with her finger-tip, while her eyes twinkled between the crevices of their lids – 'canst mind the sherry-wine, and the zilver-snuffers, and Joan Dummett was took bad when we were coming home, and Jack Griggs was forced to carry her through the mud; and how 'a let her fall in Diaryman Sweetapple's cow-barton, and we had to clane her gown wi' grass – never such a mess as 'a were in?'

'Ay – that I do – hee-hee, such doggery as there was in them ancient days, to be sure! Ah, the miles I used to walk then; and now I can hardly step over a furrow!'

Their reminiscences were cut short by the appearance of the reunited pair – Henchard looking round upon the idlers with that ambiguous gaze of his, which at one moment seemed to mean satisfaction, and at another fiery disdain.

'Well – there's a difference between 'em, though he do call himself a teetotaller,' said Nance Mockridge. 'She'll wish her cake dough afore she's done of him. There's a bluebeardy look about 'en; and 'twill out in time.'

'Stuff – he's well enough! Some folk want their luck buttered. If I had a choice as wide as the ocean sea I wouldn't wish for a better man. A poor twanking woman like her – 'tis a godsend for her, and hardly a pair of jumps or night-rail to her name.'

The plain little brougham drove off in the mist, and the idlers dispersed. 'Well, we hardly know how to look at things in these times!' said Solomon. 'There was a man dropped down dead yesterday, not so very many miles from here; and what wi' that, and this moist weather, 'tis scarce worth one's while to begin any work o' consequence today. I'm in such a low key with drinking nothing but small table ninepenny this last week or two that I shall call and warm up at the Mar'ners as I pass along.'

'I don't know but that I may as well go with 'ee, Solomon,' said Christopher: 'I'm as clammy as a cockle-snail.'

* XIV *

A MARTINMAS summer of Mrs Henchard's life set in with her entry into her husband's large house and respectable social orbit; and it was as bright as such summers well can be. Lest she should pine for deeper affection than he could give he made a point of showing some semblance of it in external action. Among other things he had the iron railings, that had smiled sadly in dull rust for the last eighty years, painted a bright green, and the heavy-barred, small-paned Georgian sash windows enlivened with three coats of white. He was as kind to her as a man, mayor, and churchwarden could possibly be. The house was large, the rooms lofty, and the landings wide; and the two unassuming women scarcely made a perceptible addition to its contents.

To Elizabeth-Jane the time was a most triumphant one. The freedom she experienced, the indulgence with which she was treated, went beyond her expectations. The reposeful, easy, affluent life to which her mother's marriage had introduced her was, in truth, the beginning of a great change in Elizabeth. She found she could have nice personal possessions and ornaments for the asking, and, as the medieval saying puts it 'Take, have, and keep, are pleasant words.' With peace of mind came development, and with development beauty. Knowledge – the result of great natural insight – she did not lack; learning, accomplishments – those, alas, she had not; but as the winter and spring passed by her thin face and figure filled out in rounder and softer curves; the lines and contractions upon her young brow went away; the muddiness of skin which she had looked upon as her lot by nature departed with a change to abundance of good things, and a bloom came upon her cheek. Perhaps, too, her grey, thoughtful eyes revealed an arch gaiety sometimes; but this was infrequent; the sort of wisdom which looked from their pupils did not readily keep company with these lighter moods. Like all people who have known rough times, light-heartedness seemed to her too irrational and inconsequent to be indulged in except as a reckless dram now and then; for she had been too early habituated to anxious reasoning to drop the habit suddenly. She felt none of those ups and downs of spirit which beset so many people without cause; never – to paraphrase a recent poet – never a gloom in Elizabeth-Jane's soul but she well knew how it came there; and her present cheerfulness was fairly proportionate to her solid guarantees for the same.

It might have been supposed that, given a girl rapidly becoming good-looking, comfortably circumstanced, and for the first time in her life commanding ready money, she would go and make a fool of herself by dress. But no. The reasonableness of almost everything that Elizabeth did was nowhere more conspicuous that in this question of clothes. To keep in the rear of opportunity in matters of indulgence is as valuable a habit as to keep abreast of opportunity in matters of enterprise. This unsophisticated girl did it by an innate perceptiveness that was almost genius. Thus she refrained from bursting out like a water-flower that spring, and clothing herself in puffings and knick-knacks, as most of the Casterbridge girls would have done in her circumstances. Her triumph was tempered by circumspection; she had still that fieldmouse fear of the coulter of destiny despite fair promise, which is common among the thoughtful who have suffered early from poverty and oppression.

'I won't be too gay on any account,' she would say to herself. 'It would be tempting Providence to hurl mother and me down, and afflict us again as He used to do.

We now see her in a black silk bonnet, velvet mantle or silk spencer, dark dress, and carrying a sunshade. In this latter article she drew the line at ringe, and had it plain edged, with a little ivory ring for keeping it closed. It was odd about the necessity for that sunshade. She discovered that with the clarification of her complexion and the birth of pink cheeks her skin had grown more sensitive to the sun's rays. She protected those cheeks forthwith, deeming spotlessness part of womanliness.

Henchard had become very fond of her, and she went out with him more frequently than with her mother now. Her appearance one day was so attractive that he looked at her critically.

'I happened to have the ribbon by me, so I made it up,' she faltered, thinking him perhaps dissatisfied with some rather bright trimming she had donned for the first time.

'Ay – of course – to be sure,' he replied in his leonine way. 'Do as you like – or rather as your mother advises ye. 'Od send – I've nothing to say to't!'

Indoors she appeared with her hair divided by a parting that arched like a white rainbow from ear to ear. All in front of this line was covered with a thick encampment of curls; all behind was dressed smoothly, and drawn to a knob.

The three members of the family were sitting at breakfast one day, and Henchard was looking silently, as he often did, at this head of hair, which in colour was brown – rather light than dark. 'I thought Elizabeth-Jane's hair – didn't you tell me that Elizabeth-Jane's hair promised to be black when she was a baby?' he said to his wife.

She looked startled, jerked her foot warningly, and murmured, 'Did I?'

As soon as Elizabeth was gone to her own room Henchard resumed. 'Begad, I nearly forgot myself just now! What I meant was that the girl's hair certainly looked as if it would be darker, when she was a baby.'

'It did; but they alter so,' replied Susan.

'Their hair gets darker, I know – but I wasn't aware it lightened ever?'

'O yes.' And the same uneasy expression came out on her face, to which the future held the key. It passed as Henchard went on:

'Well, so much the better. Now, Susan, I want to have her called Miss Henchard – not Miss Newson. Lots o' people do it already in carelessness – it is her legal name – so it may as well be made her usual name – I don't like t'other name at all for my own flesh and blood. I'll advertise it in the Casterbridge paper – that's the way they do it. She won't object.'

'No. O no. But –'

'Well, then, I shall do it,' said he, peremptorily. 'Surely, if she's willing, you must wish it as much as I?'

'O yes – if she agrees let us do it by all means,' she replied.

Then Mrs Henchard acted somewhat inconsistently; it might have been called falsely, but that her manner was emotional and full of the earnestness of one who wishes to do right at great hazard. She went to Elizabeth-Jane, whom she found sewing in her own sitting-room upstairs, and told her what had been proposed about her surname. 'Can you agree – is it not a slight upon Newson – now he's dead and gone?'

Elizabeth reflected. 'I'll think of it, mother,' she answered.

When, later in the day, she saw Henchard, she adverted to the matter at once, in a way which showed that the line of feeling started by her mother had been persevered in. 'Do you wish this change so very much, sir?' she asked.

'Wish it? Why, my blessed fathers, what an ado you women make about a trifle! I proposed it – that's all. Now, 'Lizabeth-Jane, just please yourself. Curse me if I care what you do. Now, you understand, don't 'ee go agreeing to it to please me.'

Here the subject dropped, and nothing more was said, and nothing was done, and Elizabeth still passed as Miss Newson, and not by her legal name.

Meanwhile the great corn and hay traffic conducted by Henchard throve under the management of Donald Farfrae as it had never thriven before. It had formerly moved in jolts; now it went on oiled castors. The old crude *vivâ voce* system of Henchard, in which everything depended upon his memory, and bargains were made by the tongue alone, was swept away. Letters and ledgers took the place of 'I'll do't', and 'you shall hae't'; and, as in all such cases of advance, the rugged picturesqueness of the old method disappeared with its inconveniences.

The position of Elizabeth-Jane's room – rather high in the house, so that it commanded a view of the hay-stores and granaries across the garden – afforded her opportunity for accurate observation of what went on there. She saw that Donald and Mr Henchard were inseparables. When walking together Henchard would lay his arm familiarly on his manager's shoulder, as if Farfrae were a young brother, bearing so heavily that his slight figure bent under the weight. Occasionally she would hear a perfect cannonade of laughter from Henchard, arising from something Donald had said, the latter looking quite innocent and not laughing at all. In Henchard's somewhat lonely life he evidently found the young man as desirable for comradeship as he was useful for consultations. Donald's brightness of intellect maintained in the corn-factor the admiration it had won at the first hour of their meeting. The poor opinion, and but ill-concealed, that he entertained of the slim Farfrae's physical girth, strength, and dash was more than counterbalanced by the immense respect he had for his brains.

Her quiet eye discerned that Henchard's tigerish affection for the younger man, his constant liking to have Farfrae near him, now and then resulted in a tendency to domineer, which, however, was checked in a moment when Donald exhibited marks of real offence. One day, looking down on their figures from on high, she heard the latter remark, as they stood in the doorway between the garden and yard, that their habit of walking and driving about together rather neutralized Farfrae's value as a second pair of eyes, which should be used in places where the principal was not. ' 'Od damn it,' cried Henchard, 'what's all the world! I like a fellow to talk to. Now come along and hae some supper, and don't take too much thought about things, or ye'll drive me crazy.'

When she walked with her mother, on the other hand, she often beheld the Scotchman looking at them with a curious interest. The fact that he had met her at the Three Mariners was insufficient to account for it, since on the occasion on which she had entered his room he had never raised his eyes. Besides, it was at her mother more particularly than at herself that he looked, to Elizabeth-Jane's half-conscious, simple-minded, perhaps pardonable, disappointment. Thus she could not account for this interest by her own attractiveness, and she decided that it might be apparent only – a way of turning his eyes that Mr Farfrae had.

She did not divine the ample explanation of his manner, without personal vanity, that was afforded by the fact of Donald being the depositary of Henchard's confidence in respect of his past treatment of the pale, chastened mother who walked by her side. Her conjectures on that past never went further than faint ones based on things casually heard and seen – mere guesses that Henchard and her mother might have been lovers in their younger days, who had quarrelled and parted.

Casterbridge, as has been hinted, was a place deposited in the block upon a corn-field. There was no suburb in the modern sense, or transitional intermixture of town and down. It stood, with regard to the wide fertile land adjoining, clean-cut and distinct, like a chessboard on a green table-cloth. The farmer's boy could sit under his barley-mow and pitch a stone into the office-window of the town-clerk; reapers at work among the sheaves nodded to acquaintances standing on the pavement-corner; the red-robed judge, when he condemned a sheep-stealer, pronounced sentence to the tune of Baa, that floated in at the window from the remainder of the flock browsing hard by; and at executions the waiting crowd stood in a meadow immediately before the drop, out of which the cows had been temporarily driven to give the spectators room.

The corn grown on the uplands side of the borough was garnered by farmers who lived in an eastern purlieu called Durnover. Here wheat-ricks overhung the old Roman street, and thrust their eaves against the church tower; green-thatched barns, with doorways as high as the gates of Solomon's temple, opened directly upon the main thoroughfare. Barns indeed were so numerous as to alternate with every half-dozen houses along the way. Here lived burgesses who daily walked the fallow; shepherds in an intra-mural squeeze. A street of farmers' homesteads – a street ruled by a mayor and corporation, yet echoing with the thump of the flail, the flutter of the winnowing-fan, and the purr of the milk into the pails – a street which had nothing urban in it whatever – this was the Durnover end of Casterbridge.

Henchard, as was natural, dealt largely with this nursery or bed of small farmers close at hand – and his waggons were often down that way. One day, when arrangements were in progress for getting home corn from one of the aforesaid farms, Elizabeth-Jane received a note by hand, asking her to oblige the writer by coming at once to a granary on Durnover Hill. As this was the granary whose contents Henchard was removing, she thought the request had something to do with his business, and proceeded thither as soon as she had put on her bonnet. The granary was just within the farm-yard, and stood on stone staddles, high enough for persons to walk under. The gates were open, but nobody was within. However, she entered and waited. Presently she saw a figure approaching the gate – that of Donald Farfrae. He looked up at the church clock, and came in. By some unaccountable shyness, some wish not to meet him there alone, she quickly ascended the step-ladder leading to the granary door, and entered it before he had seen her. Farfrae advanced, imagining himself in solitude; and a few drops of rain beginning to fall he moved and stood under the shelter where she had just been standing. Here he leant against one of the staddles, and gave himself up to patience. He, too, was plainly expecting some one; could it be herself? If so, why? In a few minutes he looked at his watch, and then pulled out a note, a duplicate of the one she had herself received.

The situation began to be very awkward, and the longer she waited the more awkward it became. To emerge from a door just above his head and descend the ladder, and show she had been hiding there, would look so very foolish that she still waited on. A winnowing machine stood close beside her, and to relieve her suspense she gently moved the handle; whereupon a cloud of wheat husks flew out into her face, and covered her clothes and bonnet, and stuck into the fur of her victorine. He must have heard the slight movement for he looked up, and then ascended the steps.

'Ah – it's Miss Newson,' he said as soon as he could see into the granary. 'I didn't know you were there. I have kept the appointment, and am at your service.'

'O Mr Farfrae,' she faltered; 'so have I. But I didn't know it was you who wished to see me, otherwise I –'

'I wished to see you? Oh no – at least, that is, I am afraid there may be a mistake.'

'Didn't you ask me to come here? Didn't you write this?' Elizabeth held out her note.

'No. Indeed, at no hand would I have thought of it! And for you – didn't you ask me? This is not your writing?' And he held up his.

'By no means.'

'And is that really so! Then it's somebody wanting to see us both. Perhaps we would do well to wait a little longer.'

Acting on this consideration they lingered, Elizabeth-Jane's face being arranged to an expression of preternatural composure, and the young Scot, at every footstep in the street without looking from under the granary to see if the passer were about to enter and declare himself their summoner. They watched individual drops of rain creeping down the thatch of the opposite rick – straw after straw – till they reached the bottom; but nobody came, and the granary roof began to drip.

'The person is not likely to be coming,' said Farfrae. 'It's a trick perhaps, and if so, it's a great pity to waste our time like this, and so much to be done.'

' 'Tis a great liberty,' said Elizabeth.

'It's true, Miss Newson. We'll hear news of this some day, depend on't, and who it was that did it. I wouldn't stand for it hindering myself; but you, Miss Newson –'

'I don't mind – much,' she replied.

'Neither do I.'

They lapsed again into silence. 'You are anxious to get back to Scotland, I suppose, Mr Farfrae?' she inquired.

'O no, Miss Newson. Why would I be?'

'I only supposed you might be from the song you sang at the Three Mariners – about Scotland and home, I mean – which you seemed to feel so deep down in your heart; so that we all felt for you.'

'Ay – and I did sing there – I did – But, Miss Newson' – and Donald's voice musically undulated between two semitones, as it always did when he became earnest – 'it's well you feel a song for a few minutes, and your eyes they get quite tearful; but you finish it, and for all you felt you don't mind it or think of it again for a long while. O no, I don't want to go back! Yet I'll sing the song to you wi' pleasure whenever you like. I could sing it now, and not mind at all?'

'Thank you, indeed. But I fear I must go – rain or no.'

'Ay! Then, Miss Newson, ye had better say nothing about this hoax, and take no heed of it. And if the person should say anything to you, be civil to him or her, as if you did not mind it – so you'll take the clever person's laugh away.' In speaking his eyes became fixed upon her dress, still sown with wheat husks. 'There's husks and dust on you. Perhaps you don't know it?' he said, in tones of extreme delicacy. 'And it's very bad to let rain come upon clothes when there's chaff on them. It washes in and spoils them. Let me help you – blowing is the best.'

As Elizabeth neither assented nor dissented Donald Farfrae began blowing her back hair, and her side hair, and her neck, and the crown of her bonnet, and the fur of her victorine, Elizabeth saying, 'O, thank you,' at every puff. At last she was fairly clean, though Farfrae, having got over his first concern at the situation, seemed in no manner of hurry to be gone.

'Ah – now I'll go and get ye an umbrella,' he said.

She declined the offer, stepped out and was gone. Farfrae walked slowly after, looking thoughtfully at her diminishing figure, and whistling in undertones, 'As I came down through Cannobie'.

* XV *

At first Miss Newson's budding beauty was not regarded with much interest by anybody in Casterbridge. Donald Farfrae's gaze, it is true, was now attracted by the Mayor's so-called step-daughter, but he was only one. The truth is that she was but a poor illustrative instance of the prophet Baruch's sly definition: 'The virgin that loveth to go gay'.

When she walked abroad she seemed to be occupied with an inner chamber of ideas, and to have slight need for visible objects. She formed curious resolves on checking gay fancies in the matter of clothes, because it was inconsistent with her past life to blossom gaudily the moment she had become possessed of money. But nothing is more insidious than the evolution of wishes from mere fancies, and of wants from mere wishes. Henchard gave Elizabeth-Jane a box of delicately-tinted gloves one spring day. She wanted to wear them to show her appreciation of his kindness, but she had no bonnet that would harmonize. As an artistic indulgence she thought she would have such a bonnet. When she had a bonnet that would go with the gloves she had no dress that would go with the bonnet. It was now absolutely necessary to finish; she ordered the requisite article, and found that she had no sunshade to go with the dress. In for a penny in for a pound; she bought the sunshade, and the whole structure was at last complete.

Everybody was attracted, and some said that her bygone simplicity was the art that conceals art, the 'delicate imposition' of Rochefoucauld; she had produced an effect, a contrast, and it had been done on purpose. As a matter of fact this was not true, but it had its result; for as soon as Casterbridge thought her artful it thought her worth notice. 'It is the first time in my life that I have been so much admired,' she said to herself; 'though perhaps it is by those whose admiration is not worth having.'

But Donald Farfrae admired her, too; and altogether the time was an exciting one; sex had never before asserted itself in her so strongly, for in former days she had perhaps been too impersonally human to be distinctively feminine. After an unprecedented success one day she came indoors, went upstairs, and leant upon her bed face downwards, quite forgetting the possible creasing and damage. 'Good Heaven,' she whispered, 'can it be? Here am I setting up as the town beauty!'

When she had thought it over, her usual fear of exaggerating appearances engendered a deep sadness. 'There is something wrong in all this,' she mused. 'If they only knew what an unfinished girl I am — that I can't talk Italian, or use globes, or show any of the accomplishments they learn at boarding-schools, how they would despise me! Better sell all this finery and buy myself grammar-books and dictionaries and a history of all the philosophies!'

She looked from the window and saw Henchard and Farfrae in the hay-yard talking, with that impetuous cordiality on the Mayor's part, and genial modesty on the younger man's, that was now so generally observable in their intercourse. Friendship between man and man; what a rugged strength there was in it, as evinced by these two. And yet the seed that was to lift the foundation of this friendship was at that moment taking root in a chink of its structure.

It was about six o'clock; the men were dropping off homeward one by one. The last to leave was a round shouldered, blinking young man of nineteen or twenty, whose mouth fell ajar on the slightest provocation, seemingly because there was no chin to support it. Henchard called aloud to him as he went out of the gate. 'Here — Abel Whittle!'

Whittle turned, and ran back a few steps. 'Yes, sir,' he said, in breathless deprecation, as if he knew what was coming next.

'Once more — be in time tomorrow morning. You see what's to be done, and you hear what I say, and you know I'm not going to be trifled with any longer.'

'Yes, sir.' Then Abel Whittle left, and Henchard and Farfrae; and Elizabeth saw no more of them.

Now there was good reason for this command on Henchard's part. Poor Abel, as he was called, had an inveterate habit of over-sleeping himself and coming late to his work. His anxious will was to be among the earliest; but if his comrades omitted to pull the string that he always tied round his great toe and left hanging out of the window for that purpose, his will was as wind. He did not arrive in time.

As he was often second hand at the hay-weighing, or at the crane which lifted the sacks, or was one of those who had to accompany the waggons into the country to fetch away stacks that had been purchased, this affliction of Abel's was productive of much inconvenience. For two mornings in the present week he had kept the others waiting nearly an hour; hence Henchard's threat. It now remained to be seen what would happen tomorrow.

Six o'clock struck, and there was no Whittle. At half-past six Henchard entered the yard; the waggon was horsed that Abel was to accompany; and the other man had been waiting twenty minutes. Then Henchard swore, and Whittle coming up breathless at that instant, the corn-factor turned on him, and declared with an oath that this was the last time; that if he were behind once more, by God, he would come and drag him out o' bed.

'There is sommit wrong in my make, your worshipful!' said Abel, 'especially in the inside, whereas my poor dumb brain gets as dead as a clot afore I've said my few scrags of prayers. Yes – it came on as a stripling, just afore I'd got man's wages, whereas I never enjoy my bed at all, for no sooner do I lie down than I be asleep, and afore I be awake I be up. I've fretted my gizzard green about it, maister, but what can I do? Now last night, afore I went to bed, I only had a scantling o' cheese and –'

'I don't want to hear it!' roared Henchard. 'Tomorrow the waggons must start at four, and if you're not here, stand clear. I'll mortify thy flesh for thee!'

'But let me clear up my points, your worshipful –'

Henchard turned away.

'He asked me and he questioned me, and then 'a wouldn't hear my points!' said Abel, to the yard in general. 'Now, I shall twitch like a moment-hand all night tonight for fear o' him!'

The journey to be taken by the waggons next day was a long one into Blackmoor Vale, and at four o'clock lanterns were moving about the yard. But Abel was missing. Before either of the other men could run to Abel's and warn him, Henchard appeared in the garden doorway. 'Where's Abel Whittle? Not come after all I've said? Now I'll carry out my word, by my blessed fathers – nothing else will do him any good! I'm going up that way.'

Henchard went off, entered Abel's house, a little cottage in Back Street, the door of which was never locked because the inmates had nothing to lose. Reaching Whittle's bedside the corn factor shouted a bass note so vigorously that Abel started up instantly, and beholding Henchard standing over him, was galvanized into spasmodic movements which had not much relation to getting on his clothes.

'Out of bed, sir, and off to the granary, or you leave my employ today! 'Tis to teach ye a lesson. March on; never mind your breeches!'

The unhappy Whittle threw on his sleeve waistcoat, and managed to get into his boots at the bottom of the stairs, while Henchard thrust his hat over his head. Whittle then trotted on down Back Street, Henchard walking sternly behind.

Just at this time Farfrae, who had been to Henchard's house to look for him, came out of the back gate, and saw something white fluttering in the morning gloom, which he soon perceived to be the part of Abel's shirt that showed below his waistcoat.

'For maircy's sake, what object's this?' said Farfrae, following Abel into the yard, Henchard being some way in the rear by this time.

'Ye see, Mr Farfrae,' gibbered Abel with a resigned smile of terror, 'he said he'd mortify my flesh if so be I didn't get up sooner, and now he's a-doing on't! Ye see it can't be helped, Mr Farfrae; things do happen queer sometimes! Yes – I'll go to Blackmoor Vale half naked as I be, since he do command; but I shall kill myself afterwards; I can't outlive the disgrace; for the women-folk will be looking out of their winders at my mortification all the way along, and laughing me to scorn as a man 'ithout breeches! You know how I feel such things, Maister Farfrae, and how forlorn thoughts get hold upon me. Yes – I shall do myself harm – I feel it coming on!'

'Get back home, and slip on your breeches, and come to wark like a man! If ye go not, you'll ha'e your death standing there!'

'I'm afeard I mustn't! Mr Henchard said –'

'I don't care what Mr Henchard said, nor anybody else! 'Tis simple foolishness to do this. Go and dress yourself instantly, Whittle.'

'Hullo, hullo!' said Henchard, coming up behind. 'Who's sending him back?'

All the men looked towards Farfrae.

'I am,' said Donald. 'I say this joke has been carried far enough.'

'And I say it hasn't! Get up in the waggon, Whittle.'

'Not if I am manager,' said Farfrae. 'He either goes home, or I march out of this yard for good.'

Henchard looked at him with a face stern and red. But he paused for a moment, and their eyes met. Donald went up to him, for he saw in Henchard's look that he began to regret this.

'Come,' said Donald quietly, 'a man o' your position should ken better, sir! It is tyrannical and no worthy of you.'

' 'Tis not tyrannical!' murmured Henchard, like a sullen boy. 'It is to make him remember!' He presently added, in a tone of one bitterly hurt: 'Why did you speak to me before them like that, Farfrae? You might have stopped till we were alone. Ah – I know why! I've told ye the secret o' my life – fool that I was to do't – and you take advantage of me!'

'I had forgot it,' said Farfrae simply.

Henchard looked on the ground, said nothing more, and turned away. During the day Farfrae learnt from the men that Henchard had kept

Abel's old mother in coals and snuff all the previous winter, which made him less antagonistic to the corn-factor. But Henchard continued moody and silent, and when one of the men inquired of him if some oats should be hoisted to an upper floor or not, he said shortly, 'Ask Mr Farfrae. He's master here!'

Morally he was; there could be no doubt of it. Henchard, who had hitherto been the most admired man in his circle, was the most admired no longer. One day the daughters of a deceased farmer in Durnover wanted an opinion on the value of their haystack, and sent a messenger to ask Mr Farfrae to oblige them with one. The messenger, who was a child, met in the yard not Farfrae, but Henchard.

'Very well,' he said. 'I'll come.'

'But please will Mr Farfrae come? said the child.

'I am going that way . . . Why Mr Farfrae?' said Henchard, with the fixed look of thought. 'Why do people always want Mr Farfrae?'

'I suppose because they like him so – that's what they say.'

'Oh – I see – that's what they say – hey? They like him because he's cleverer than Mr Henchard, and because he knows more; and in short, Mr Henchard can't hold a candle to him – hey?'

'Yes – that's just it, sir – some of it.'

'Oh, there's more? Of course there's more! What besides? Come, here's sixpence for a fairing.'

' "And he's better-tempered, and Henchard's a fool to him," they say. And when some of the women were a-walking home they said, "He's a diment – he's a chap o' wax – he's the best – he's the horse for my money," says they. And they said, "He's the most understanding man o' them two by long chalks. I wish he was the master instead of Henchard," they said.'

'They'll talk any nonsense,' Henchard replied with covered gloom. 'Well, you can go now. And *I* am coming to value the hay, d'ye hear? – I.' The boy departed, and Henchard murmured, 'Wish he were master here, do they?'

He went towards Durnover. On his way he overtook Farfrae. They walked on together, Henchard looking mostly on the ground.

'You're no yoursel' the day?' Donald inquired.

'Yes, I am very well,' said Henchard.

'But ye are a bit down – surely ye are down? Why, there's nothing to be angry about! 'Tis splendid stuff that we've got from Blackmoor Vale. By the by, the people in Durnover want their hay valued.'

'Yes. I am going there.'

'I'll go with ye.'

As Henchard did not reply Donald practised a piece of music *sotto voce*, till, getting near the bereaved people's door, he stopped himself –

'Ah, as their father is dead I won't go on with such as that. How could I forget?'

'Do you care so very much about hurting folks' feelings?' observed Henchard with a half sneer. 'You do, I know – especially mine!'

'I am sorry if I have hurt yours, sir,' replied Donald, standing still, with a second expression of the same sentiment in the regretfulness of his face. 'Why should you say it – think it?'

The cloud lifted from Henchard's brow, and as Donald finished the corn-merchant turned to him, regarding his breast rather than his face.

'I have been hearing things that vexed me,' he said. ' 'Twas that made me short in manner – made me overlook what you really are. Now, I don't want to go in here about this hay – Farfrae, you can do it better than I. They sent for 'ee, too. I have to attend a meeting of the Town Council at eleven, and 'tis drawing on for't.'

They parted thus in renewed friendship, Donald forbearing to ask Henchard for meanings that were not very plain to him. On Henchard's part there was now again repose; and yet, whenever he thought of Farfrae, it was with a dim dread; and he often regretted that he had told the young man his whole heart, and confided to him the secrets of his life.

* XVI *

ON this account Henchard's manner towards Farfrae insensibly became more reserved. He was courteous – too courteous – and Farfrae was quite surprised at the good breeding which now for the first time showed itself among the qualities of a man he had hitherto thought undisciplined, if warm and sincere. The corn-factor seldom or never again put his arm upon the young man's shoulder so as to nearly weigh him down with the pressure of mechanized friendship. He left off coming to Donald's lodgings and shouting into the passage, 'Hoy, Farfrae, boy, come and have some dinner with us! Don't sit here in solitary confinement!' But in the daily routine of their business there was little change.

Thus their lives rolled on till a day of public rejoicing was suggested to the country at large in celebration of a national event that had recently taken place.

For some time Casterbridge, by nature slow, made no response. Then one day Donald Farfrae broached the subject to Henchard by asking if he would have any objection to lend some rick-cloths to himself and a few others, who contemplated getting up an entertainment of some sort on the day named, and required a shelter for the same, to which they might charge admission at the rate of so much a head.

'Have as many cloths as you like,' Henchard replied.

When his manager had gone about the business Henchard was fired with emulation. It certainly had been very remiss of him, as Mayor, he thought, to call no meeting ere this, to discuss what should be done on this holiday. But Farfrae had been so cursed quick in his movements as to give old-fashioned people in authority no chance of the initiative. However, it was not too late; and on second thoughts he determined to take upon his own shoulders the responsibility of organizing some amusements, if the other Councilmen would leave the matter in his hands. To this they quite readily agreed, the majority being fine old crusted characters who had a decided taste for living without worry.

So Henchard set about his preparations for a really brilliant thing – such as should be worthy of the venerable town. As for Farfrae's little affair, Henchard nearly forgot it; except once now and then when, on it coming into his mind, he said to himself, 'Charge admission at so much a head – just like a Scotchman! – who is going to pay anything a head?' The diversions which the Mayor intended to provide were to be entirely free.

He had grown so dependent upon Donald that he could scarcely resist calling him in to consult. But by sheer self-coercion he refrained. No, he thought, Farfrae would be suggesting such improvements in his damned luminous way that in spite of himself he, Henchard, would sink to the position of second fiddle, and only scrape harmonies to his manager's talents.

Everybody applauded the Mayor's proposed entertainment, especially when it became known that he meant to pay for it all himself.

Close to the town was an elevated green spot surrounded by an ancient square earthwork – earthworks square, and not square, were as common as blackberries hereabout – a spot whereon the Casterbridge people usually held any kind of merry-making, meeting, or sheep-fair that required more space than the streets would afford. On one side it sloped to the river Froom, and from any point a view was obtained of the country round for many miles. This pleasant upland was to be the scene of Henchard's exploit.

He advertised about the town, in long posters of a pink colour, that games of all sorts would take place here; and set to work a little battalion of men under his own eye. They erected greasy-poles for climbing, with smoked hams and local cheese at the top. They placed hurdles in rows for jumping over; across the river they laid a slippery pole, with a live pig of the neighbourhood tied at the other end, to become the property of the man who could walk over and get it. There were also provided wheelbarrows for racing, donkeys for the same, a stage for boxing, wrestling, and drawing blood generally; sacks for jumping in. Moreover, not forgetting his principles, Henchard provided a mammoth tea, of which everybody who lived in the borough was invited to partake without payment. The tables were laid parallel with the inner slope of the rampart, and awnings were stretched overhead.

Passing to and fro the Mayor beheld the unattractive exterior of Farfrae's erection in the West Walk, rick-cloths of different sizes and colours being hung up to the arching trees without any regard to appearance. He was easy in his mind now, for his own preparations far transcended these.

The morning came. The sky, which had been remarkably clear down to within a day or two, was overcast, and the weather threatening, the wind having an unmistakable hint of water in it. Henchard wished he had not been quite so sure about the continuance of a fair season. But it was too late to modify or postpone, and the proceedings went on. At twelve o'clock the rain began to fall, small and steady, commencing and increasing so insensibly that it was difficult to state exactly when dry weather ended or wet established itself. In an hour the slight moisture resolved itself into a monotonous smiting of earth by heaven, in torrents to which no end could be prognosticated.

A number of people had heroically gathered in the field, but by three o'clock Henchard discerned that his project was doomed to end in failure. The hams at the top of the poles dripped watered smoke in the form of a brown liquor, the pig shivered in the wind, the grain of the deal tables showed through the sticking tableclothes, for the awning allowed the rain to drift under at its will, and to enclose the sides at this hour seemed a useless undertaking. The landscape over the river disappeared; the wind played on the tent-cords in Aeolian improvisations; and at length rose to such a pitch that the whole erection slanted to the ground, those who had taken shelter within it having to crawl out on their hands and knees.

But towards six the storm abated, and a drier breeze shook the moisture from the grass bents. It seemed possible to carry out the programme after all. The awning was set up again; the band was called out from its shelter, and ordered to begin, and where the tables had stood a place was cleared for dancing.

'But where are the folk?' said Henchard, after the lapse of half-an-hour, during which time only two men and a woman had stood up to dance. 'The shops are all shut. Why don't they come?'

'They are at Farfrae's affair in the West Walk,' answered a Councilman who stood in the field with the Mayor.

'A few, I suppose. But where are the body o' 'em?'

'All out of doors are there.'

'Then the more fools they!'

Henchard walked away moodily. One or two young fellows gallantly came to climb the poles, to save the hams from being wasted; but as there were no spectators, and the whole scene presented the most melancholy appearance, Henchard gave orders that the proceedings were to be suspended, and the entertainment closed, the food to be distributed among the poor people of the town. In a short time nothing was left in the field but a few hurdles, the tents, and the poles.

Henchard returned to his house, had tea with his wife and daughter, and then walked out. It was now dusk. He soon saw that the tendency of all promenaders was towards a particular spot in the Walks, and eventually proceeded thither himself. The notes of a stringed band came from the enclosure that Farfrae had erected – the pavilion as he called it – and when the Mayor reached it he perceived that a gigantic tent had been ingeniously constructed without poles or ropes. The densest point of the avenue of sycamores had been selected, where the boughs made a closely interlaced vault overhead; to these boughs the canvas had been hung, and a barrel roof was the result. The end towards the wind was enclosed, the other end was open. Henchard went round and saw the interior.

In form it was like the nave of a cathedral with one gable removed, but the scene within was anything but devotional. A reel or fling of some sort was in progress; and the usually sedate Farfrae was in the midst of the other dancers in the costume of a wild Highlander, flinging himself about and spinning to the tune. For a moment Henchard could not help laughing. Then he perceived the immense admiration for the Scotchman that revealed itself in the women's faces; and when his exhibition was over, and a new dance proposed, and Donald had disappeared for a time to return in his natural garments, he had an unlimited choice of partners, every girl being in a coming-on disposition towards one who so thoroughly understood the poetry of motion as he.

All the town crowded to the Walk, such a delightful idea of a ballroom never having occurred to the inhabitants before. Among the rest of the onlookers were Elizabeth and her mother – the former thoughtful yet much interested, her eyes beaming with a longing lingering light, as if Nature had been advised by Correggio in their creation. The dancing progressed with unabated spirit, and Henchard walked and waited till his wife should be disposed to go home. He did not care to keep in the light, and when he went into the dark it was worse, for there he heard remarks of a kind which were becoming too frequent:

'Mr Henchard's rejoicings couldn't say good morning to this,' said one. 'A man must be a headstrong stunpoll to think folk would go up to that bleak place today.'

The other answered that people said it was not only in such things as those that the Mayor was wanting. 'Where would his business be if it were not for this young fellow? 'Twas verily Fortune sent him to Henchard. His accounts were like a bramblewood when Mr Farfrae came. He used to reckon his sacks by chalk strokes all in a row like garden-palings, measure his ricks by stretching with his arms, weigh his trusses by a lift, judge his hay by a chaw, and settle the price with a curse. But now this accomplished young man does it all by ciphering and mensuration. Then the wheat – that sometimes used to taste so strong o' mice when made into bread that people could fairly tell the breed – Farfrae has a plan for purifying, so that nobody would dream the smallest four-legged beast had walked over it once. O yes, everybody is full of him, and the care Mr Henchard has to keep him, to be sure!' concluded this gentleman.

'But he won't do it for long, good-now,' said the other.

'No!' said Henchard to himself behind the tree. 'Of if he do, he'll be honeycombed clean out of all the character and standing that he's built up in these eighteen year!'

He went back to the dancing pavilion. Farfrae was footing a quaint little dance with Elizabeth-Jane – an old country thing, the only one she knew, and though he considerately toned down his movements to suit her demurer gait, the pattern of the shining little nails in the soles of his boots became familiar to the eyes of every bystander. The tune had enticed her into it; being a tune of a busy, vaulting, leaping sort – some low notes on the silver string of each fiddle, then a skipping on the small, like running up and down ladders – 'Miss M'Leod of Ayr' was its name, so Mr Farfrae had said, and that it was very popular in his own country.

It was soon over, and the girl looked at Henchard for approval; but he did not give it. He seemed not to see her. 'Look here, Farfrae,' he said, like one whose mind was elsewhere, 'I'll go to Port-Bredy Great Market tomorrow myself. You can stay and put things in your clothes-box, and recover strength to your knees after your vagaries.' He planted on Donald an antagonistic glare that had begun as a smile.

Some other townsmen came up, and Donald drew aside. 'What's this, Henchard,' said Alderman Tubber, applying his thumb to the corn-factor like a cheese-taster. 'An opposition randy to yours, eh? Jack's as good as his master, eh? Cut ye out quite, hasn't he?'

'You see, Mr Henchard,' said the lawyer, another good-natured friend, 'where you made the mistake was in going so far afield. You should have taken a leaf out of his book, and have had your sports in a sheltered place like this. But you didn't think of it, you see; and he did, and that's where he's beat you.'

'He'll be top-sawyer soon of you two, and carry all afore him,' added jocular Mr Tubber.

'No,' said Henchard gloomily. 'He won't be that, because he's shortly going to leave me.' He looked towards Donald, who had again come near. 'Mr Farfrae's time as my manager is drawing to a close – isn't it, Farfrae?'

The young man, who could now read the lines and folds of Henchard's strongly-traced face as if they were clear verbal inscriptions, quietly assented; and when people deplored the fact, and asked why it was, he simply replied that Mr Henchard no longer required his help.

Henchard went home, apparently satisfied. But in the morning, when his jealous temper had passed away, his heart sank within him at what he had said and done. He was the more disturbed when he found that this time Farfrae was determined to take him at his word.

XVII

ELIZABETH-JANE had perceived from Henchard's manner that in assenting to dance she had made a mistake of some kind. In her simplicity she did not know what it was till a hint from a nodding acquaintance enlightened her. As the Mayor's step-daughter, she learnt, she had not been quite in her place in treading a measure amid such a mixed throng as filled the dancing pavilion.

Thereupon her ears, cheeks, and chin glowed like live coals at the dawning of the idea that her tastes were not good enough for her position, and would bring her into disgrace.

This made her very miserable, and she looked about for her mother; but Mrs Henchard, who had less idea of conventionality than Elizabeth herself, had gone away, leaving her daughter to return at her own pleasure. The latter moved into the dark dense old avenues, or rather vaults of living woodwork, which ran along the town boundary, and stood reflecting.

A man followed in a few minutes, and her face being towards the shine from the tent he recognized her. It was Farfrae – just come from the dialogue with Henchard which had signified his dismissal.

'And it's you, Miss Newson? – and I've been looking for ye everywhere!' he said, overcoming a sadness imparted by the estrangement with the corn-merchant. 'May I walk on with you as far as your street-corner?'

She thought there might be something wrong in this, but did not utter any objection. So together they went on, first down the West Walk, and then into the Bowling Walk, till Farfrae said, 'It's like that I'm going to leave you soon.'

She faltered 'Why?'

'Oh – as a mere matter of business – nothing more. But we'll not concern ourselves about it – it is for the best. I hoped to have another dance with you.'

She said she could not dance – in any proper way.

'Nay, but you do! It's the feeling for it rather than the learning of steps that makes pleasant dancers . . . I fear I offend your father by getting up this! And now, perhaps, I'll have to go to another part o' the warrld altogether!'

This seemed such a melancholy prospect that Elizabeth-Jane breathed a sigh – letting it off in fragments that he might not hear her. But darkness makes people truthful, and the Scotchman went on impulsively – perhaps he had heard her after all:

'I wish I was richer, Miss Newson; and your stepfather had not been offended; I would ask you something in a short time – yes, I would ask you tonight. But that's not for me!'

What he would have asked her he did not say, and instead of

encouraging him she remained incompetently silent. Thus afraid one of another they continued their promenade along the walls till they got near the bottom of the Bowling Walk; twenty steps further and the trees would end, and the street-corner and lamps appear. In consciousness of this they stopped.

'I never found out who it was that sent us to Durnover granary on a fool's errand that day,' said Donald, in his undulating tones. 'Did ye ever know yourself, Miss Newson?'

'Never,' said she.

'I wonder why they did it!'

'For fun, perhaps.'

'Perhaps it was not for fun. It might have been that they thought they would like us to stay waiting there, talking to one another? Ay, well! I hope you Casterbridge folk will not forget me if I go.'

'That I'm sure we won't!' she said earnestly. 'I – wish you wouldn't go at all.'

They had got into the lamplight. 'Now, I'll think over that,' said Donald Farfrae. 'And I'll not come up to your door; but part from you here; lest it make your father more angry still.'

They parted, Farfrae returning into the dark Bowling Walk, and Elizabeth-Jane going up the street. Without any consciousness of what she was doing she started running with all her might till she reached her father's door. 'O dear me – what am I at?' she thought, as she pulled up breathless.

Indoors she fell to conjecturing the meaning of Farfrae's enigmatic words about not daring to ask her what he fain would. Elizabeth, that silent observing woman, had long noted how he was rising in favour among the townspeople; and knowing Henchard's nature now she had feared that Farfrae's days as manager were numbered; so that the announcement gave her little surprise. Would Mr Farfrae stay in Casterbridge despite his words and her father's dismissal? His occult breathings to her might be solvable by his course in that respect.

The next day was windy – so windy that walking in the garden she picked up a portion of the draft of a letter on business in Donald Farfrae's writing, which had flown over the wall from the office. The useless scrap she took indoors, and began to copy the calligraphy, which she much admired. The letter began 'Dear Sir', and presently writing on a loose slip 'Elizabeth-Jane', she laid the latter over 'Sir', making the phrase 'Dear Elizabeth-Jane'. When she saw the effect a quick red ran up her face and warmed her through, though nobody was there to see what she had done. She quickly tore up the slip, and threw it away. After this she grew cool and laughed at herself, walked about the room, and laughed again; not joyfully, but distressfully rather.

It was quickly known in Casterbridge that Farfrae and Henchard had decided to dispense with each other. Elizabeth-Jane's anxiety to know if Farfrae were going away from the town reached a pitch that disturbed her, for she could no longer conceal from herself the cause. At length the news reached her that he was not going to leave the place. A man following the same trade as Henchard, but on a very small scale, had sold his business to Farfrae, who was forthwith about to start as corn and hay merchant on his own account.

Her heart fluttered when she heard of this step of Donald's, proving that he meant to remain; and yet, would a man who cared one little bit for her have endangered his suit by setting up a business in opposition to Mr Henchard's? Surely not; and it must have been a passing impulse only which had led him to address her so softly.

To solve the problem whether her appearance on the evening of the dance were such as to inspire a fleeting love at first sight, she dressed herself up exactly as she had dressed then – the muslin, the spencer, the sandals, the parasol – and looked in the mirror. The picture glassed back was, in her opinion, precisely of such a kind as to inspire that fleeting regard, and no more – 'just enough to make him silly, and not enough to keep him so,' she said luminously; and Elizabeth thought, in a much lower key, that by this time he had discovered how plain and homely was the informing spirit of that pretty outside.

Hence, when she felt her heart going out to him, she would say to herself with a mock pleasantry that carried an ache with it, 'No, no, Elizabeth-Jane – such dreams are not for you!' She tried to prevent herself from seeing him, and thinking of him; succeeding fairly well in the former attempt, in the latter not so completely.

Henchard, who had been hurt at finding that Farfrae did not mean to put up with his temper any longer, was incensed beyond measure when he learnt what the young man had done as an alternative. It was in the town-hall, after a council meeting, that he first became aware of Farfrae's *coup* for establishing himself independently in the town; and his voice might have been heard as far as the town-pump expressing his feelings to his fellow councilmen. Those tones showed that, though under a long reign of self-control he had become Mayor and churchwarden and what not, there was still the same unruly volcanic stuff beneath the rind of Michael Henchard as when he had sold his wife at Weydon Fair.

'Well, he's a friend of mine, and I'm a friend of his – or if we are not, what are we? 'Od send, if I've not been his friend, who has, I should like to know? Didn't he come here without a sound shoe to his voot? Didn't I keep him here – help him to a living? Didn't I help him to money, or whatever he wanted? I stuck out for no terms – I said "Name your own price." I'd have shared my last crust with that young fellow at one time, I liked him so well. And now he's defied me! But damn him, I'll have a tussle with him now – at fair buying and selling, mind – at fair buying and selling! And if I can't overbid such a stripling as he, then I'm not wo'th a varden! We'll show that we know our business as well as one here and there!'

His friends of the Corporation did not specially respond. Henchard was less popular now than he had been when, nearly two years before, they had voted him to the chief magistracy on account of his amazing energy. While they had collectively profited by this quality of the corn-factor's they had been made to wince individually on more than one occasion. So he went out of the hall and down the street alone.

Reaching home he seemed to recollect something with a sour satisfaction. He called Elizabeth-Jane. Seeing how he looked when she entered she appeared alarmed.

'Nothing to find fault with,' he said, observing her concern. 'Only I want to caution you, my dear. That man, Farfrae – it is about him. I've seen him talking to you two or three times – he danced with 'ee at the rejoicings, and came home with 'ee. Now, now, no blame to you. But just hearken: Have you made him any foolish promise? Gone the least bit beyond sniff and snaff at all?'

'No. I have promised him nothing.'

'Good. All's well that ends well. I particularly wish you not to see him again.'

'Very well, sir.'

'You promise?'

She hesitated for a moment, and then said –

'Yes, if you much wish it.'

'I do. He's an enemy to our house!'

When she had gone he sat down, and wrote in a heavy hand to Farfrae thus:–

SIR, – I make request that henceforth you and my step-daughter be as strangers to each other. She on her part has promised to welcome no more addresses from you; and I trust, therefore, you will not attempt to force them upon her.

M. HENCHARD

One would almost have supposed Henchard to have had policy to see that no better *modus vivendi* could be arrived at with Farfrae than by encouraging him to become his son-in-law. But such a scheme for buying over a rival had nothing to recommend it to the Mayor's headstrong faculties. With all domestic *finesse* of that kind he was hopelessly at variance. Loving a man or hating him, his diplomacy was as wrongheaded as a buffalo's; and his wife had not ventured to suggest the course which she, for many reasons, would have welcomed gladly.

Meanwhile Donald Farfrae had opened the gates of commerce on his own account at a spot on Durnover Hill – as far as possible from Henchard's stores, and with every intention of keeping clear of his former friend and employer's customers. There was, it seemed to the younger man, room for both of them and to spare. The town was small, but the corn and hay-trade was proportionately large, and with his native sagacity he saw opportunity for a share of it.

So determined was he to do nothing which should seem like trade-antagonism to the Mayor that he refused his first customer – a large farmer of good repute – because Henchard and this man had dealt together within the preceding three months.

'He was once my friend,' said Farfrae, 'and it's not for me to take business from him. I am sorry to disappoint you, but I cannot hurt the trade of a man who's been so kind to me.'

In spite of this praiseworthy course the Scotchman's trade increased. Whether it were that his northern energy was an over-mastering force among the easy-going Wessex worthies, or whether it was sheer luck, the fact remained that whatever he touched he prospered in. Like Jacob in Padan-Aram, he would no sooner humbly limit himself to the ringstraked-and-spotted exceptions of trade than the ringstraked-and-spotted would multiply and prevail.

But most probably luck had little to do with it. Character is Fate, said Novalis, and Farfrae's character was just the reverse of Henchard's, who might be described as Faust has been described – as a vehement gloomy being who had quitted the ways of vulgar men, without light to guide him on a better way.

Farfrae duly received the request to discontinue attentions to Elizabeth-Jane. His acts of that kind had been so slight that the request was almost superfluous. Yet he had felt a considerable interest in her, and after some cogitation he decided that it would be as well to enact no Romeo part just then – for the young girl's sake no less than his own. Thus the incipient attachment was stifled down.

A time came when, avoid collision with his former friend as he might, Farfrae was compelled, in sheer self-defence, to close with Henchard in mortal commercial combat. He could no longer parry the fierce attacks of the latter by simple avoidance. As soon as their war of prices began everybody was interested, and some few guessed the end. It was, in some degree, Northern insight matched against Southron doggedness – the dirk against the cudgel – and Henchard's weapon was one which, if it did not deal ruin at the first or second stroke, left him afterwards well-nigh at his antagonist's mercy.

Almost every Saturday they encountered each other amid the crowd of farmers which thronged about the market-place in the weekly course of their business. Donald was always ready, and even anxious, to say a few friendly words; but the Mayor invariably gazed stormfully past him, like one who had endured and lost on his account, and could in no sense forgive the wrong; nor did Farfrae's snubbed manner of perplexity at all appease him. The large farmers, corn-merchants, millers, auctioneers, and others had each an official stall in the cornmarket room, with their names painted thereon; and when to the familiar series of 'Henchard', 'Everdene', 'Shiner', 'Darton', and so on, was added one inscribed 'Farfrae', in staring new letters, Henchard was stung into bitterness; like Bellerophon, he wandered away from the crowd, cankered in soul.

From that day Donald Farfrae's name was seldom mentioned in Henchard's house. If at breakfast or dinner Elizabeth-Jane's mother inadvertently alluded to her favourite's movements, the girl would implore her by a look to be silent; and her husband would say, 'What – are you, too, my enemy?'

XVIII

THERE came a shock which had been foreseen for some time by Elizabeth, as the box passenger foresees the approaching jerk from some channel across the highway.

Her mother was ill – too unwell to leave her room. Henchard, who treated her kindly, except in moments of irritation, sent at once for the richest, busiest doctor, whom he supposed to be the best. Bedtime came, and they burnt a light all night. In a day or two she rallied.

Elizabeth, who had been staying up, did not appear at breakfast on the second morning, and Henchard sat down alone. He was startled to see a letter for him from Jersey in a writing he knew too well, and had expected least to behold again. He took it up in his hands and looked at it as at a picture, a vision, a vista of past enactments; and then he read it as an unimportant finale to conjecture.

The writer said that she at length perceived how impossible it would be for any further communications to proceed between them now that his re-marriage had taken place. That such re-union had been the only straightforward course open to him she was bound to admit.

'On calm reflection, therefore,' she went on, 'I quite forgive you for landing me in such a dilemma, remembering that you concealed nothing before our ill-advised acquaintance; and that you really did set before me in your grim way the fact of there being a certain risk in intimacy with you, slight as it seemed to be after fifteen or sixteen years of silence on your wife's part. I thus look upon the whole as a misfortune of mine, and not a fault of yours.

'So that, Michael, I must ask you to overlook those letters with which I pestered you day after day in the heat of my feelings. They were written whilst I thought your conduct to me cruel; but now I know more particulars of the position you were in I see how inconsiderate my reproaches were.

'Now you will, I am sure, perceive that the one condition which will make any future happiness possible for me is that the past connection between our lives be kept secret outside this isle. Speak of it I know you will not; and I can trust you not to write of it. One safeguard more remains to be mentioned – that no writings of mine, or trifling articles belonging to me, should be left in your possession through neglect or forgetfulness. To this end may I request you to return to me any such you may have, particularly the letters written in the first abandonment of feeling.

'For the handsome sum you forwarded to me as a plaster to the wound I heartily thank you.

'I am now on my way to Bristol, to see my only relative. She is rich, and I hope will do something for me. I shall return through Casterbridge and Budmouth, where I shall take the packet-boat. Can you meet me with the letters and other trifles? I shall be in the coach which changes horses at the Antelope Hotel at half past five Wednesday evening; I shall be wearing a Paisley shawl with a red centre, and thus may easily be found. I should prefer this plan of receiving them to having them sent. – I remain still, yours ever,

LUCETTA'

Henchard breathed heavily. 'Poor thing – better you had not known me! Upon my heart and soul, if ever I should be left in a position to carry out that marriage with thee, I *ought* to do it – I ought to do it, indeed!'

The contingency that he had in his mind was, of course, the death of Mrs Henchard.

As requested, he sealed up Lucetta's letters, and put the parcel aside till the day she had appointed; this play of returning them by hand being apparently a little *ruse* of the young lady for exchanging a word or two with him on past times. He would have preferred not to see her; but deeming that there could be no great harm in acquiescing thus far, he went at dusk and stood opposite the coach-office.

The evening was chilly, and the coach was late. Henchard crossed over to it while the horses were being changed; but there was no Lucetta inside or out. Concluding that something had happened to modify her arrangements he gave the matter up and went home, not without a sense of relief.

Meanwhile Mrs Henchard was weakening visibly. She could not go out of doors any more. One day, after much thinking which seemed to distress her, she said she wanted to write something. A desk was put upon her bed with pen and paper, and at her request she was left alone. She remained writing for a short time, folded her paper carefully, called Elizabeth-Jane to bring a taper and wax, and then, still refusing assistance, sealed up the sheet, directed it, and locked it in her desk. She had directed it in these words:–

'*Mr Michael Henchard. Not to be opened till Elizabeth-Jane's wedding-day.*'

The latter sat up with her mother to the utmost of her strength night after night. To learn to take the universe seriously there is no quicker way than to watch – to be a 'waker', as the country-people call it. Between the hours at which the last toss-pot went by and the first sparrow shook himself, the silence in Casterbridge – barring the rare sound of the watchman – was broken in Elizabeth's ear only by the time-piece in the bedroom ticking frantically against the clock on the stairs; ticking harder and harder till it seemed to clang like a gong; and all this while the subtle-souled girl asking herself why she was born, why sitting in a room, and blinking at the candle; why things around her had taken the shape they wore in preference to every other possible shape. Why they stared at her so helplessly, as if waiting for the touch of some wand that should release them from terrestrial constraint; what that chaos called consciousness, which spun in her at this moment like a top, tended to, and began in. Her eyes fell together; she was awake, yet she was asleep.

A word from her mother roused her. Without preface, and as the continuation of a scene already progressing in her mind, Mrs Henchard said: 'You remember the note sent to you and Mr Farfrae – asking you to meet some one in Durnover Barton – and that you thought it was a trick to make fools of you?'

'Yes.'

'It was not to make fools of you – it was done to bring you together. 'Twas I did it.'

'Why?' said Elizabeth, with a start.

'I – wanted you to marry Mr Farfrae.'

'O mother!' Elizabeth-Jane bent down her head so much that she looked quite into her own lap. But as her mother did not go on, she said, 'What reason?'

'Well, I had a reason. 'Twill out one day. I wish it could have been in my time! But there – nothing is as you wish it! Henchard hates him.'

'Perhaps they'll be friends again,' murmured the girl.

'I don't know – I don't know.' After this her mother was silent, and dozed; and she spoke on the subject no more.

Some little time later on Farfrae was passing Henchard's house on a Sunday morning, when he observed that the blinds were all down. He rang the bell so softly that it only sounded a single full note and a small one; and then he was informed that Mrs Henchard was dead – just dead – that very hour.

At the town-pump there were gathered when he passed a few old inhabitants, who came there for water whenever they had, as at present, spare time to fetch it, because it was purer from that original fount than from their own wells. Mrs Cuxsom, who had been standing there for an indefinite time with her pitcher, was describing the incidents of Mrs Henchard's death, as she had learnt them from the nurse.

'And she was as white as marble-stone,' said Mrs Cuxsom. 'And likewise such a thoughtful woman, too – ah, poor soul – that a' minded every little thing that wanted tending. "Yes," says she, "when I'm gone, and my last breath's blowed, look in the top drawer o' the chest in the back room by the window, and you'll find all my coffin clothes; a piece of flannel – that's to put under me, and the little piece is to put under my head; and my new stockings for my feet – they are folded alongside, and all my other things. And there's four ounce pennies, the heaviest I could find, a-tied up in bits of linen, for weights – two for my right eye and two for my left," she said. "And when you've used 'em, and my eyes don't open no more, bury the pennies, good souls, and don't ye go spending 'em, for I shouldn't like it. And open the windows as soon as I am carried out, and make it as cheerful as you can for Elizabeth-Jane." '

'Ah, poor heart!'

'Well, and Martha did it, and buried the ounce pennies in the garden. But if ye'll believe words, that man, Christopher Coney, went and dug 'em up, and spent 'em at the Three Mariners. "Faith," he said, "why should death rob life o' fourpence? Death's not of such good report that we should respect 'en to that extent," says he.'

' 'Twas a cannibal deed!' deprecated her listeners.

'Gad, then, I won't quite ha'e it,' said Solomon Longways. 'I say it today, and 'tis a Sunday morning, and I wouldn't speak wrongfully for a zilver zixpence at such a time. I don't see noo harm in it. To respect the dead is sound doxology; and I wouldn't sell skellintons – leastwise respectable skellintons – to be varnished for 'natomies, except I were out o' work. But money is scarce, and throats get dry. Why *should* death rob life o'fourpence? I say there was no treason in it.'

'Well, poor soul; she's helpless to hinder that or anything now,' answered Mother Cuxsom. 'And all her shining keys will be took from her, and her cupboards opened; and little things a' didn't wish seen, anybody will see; and her wishes and ways will all be as nothing!'

* XIX *

HENCHARD and Elizabeth sat conversing by the fire. It was three weeks after Mrs Henchard's funeral; the candles were not lighted, and a restless, acrobatic flame, poised on a coal, called from the shady walls the smiles of all shapes that could respond – the old pier-glass, with gilt columns and huge entablature, the picture-frames, sundry knobs and handles, and the brass rosette at the bottom of each riband bell-pull on either side of the chimney-piece.

'Elizabeth, do you think much of old times?' said Henchard.

'Yes, sir; often,' said she.

'Who do you put in your pictures of 'em?'

'Mother and father – nobody else hardly.'

Henchard always looked like one bent on resisting pain when Elizabeth-Jane spoke of Richard Newson as 'father'. 'Ah! I am out of all that, am I not?' he said . . . 'Was Newson a kind father?'

'Yes, sir; very.'

Henchard's face settled into an expression of stolid loneliness which gradually modulated into something softer. 'Suppose I had been your real father?' he said. 'Would you have cared for me as much as you cared for Richard Newson?'

'I can't think it,' she said quickly. 'I can think of no other as my father, except my father.'

Henchard's wife was dissevered from him by death; his friend and helper Farfrae by estrangement; Elizabeth-Jane by ignorance. It seemed him that only one of them could possibly be recalled, and that was the girl. His mind began vibrating between the wish to reveal himself to her and the policy of leaving well alone, till he could no longer sit still. He walked up and down, and then he came and stood behind her chair, looking down upon the top of her head. He could no longer restrain his impulse. 'What did your mother tell you about me – my history?' he asked.

'That you were related by marriage.'

'She should have told more – before you knew me! Then my task would not have been such a hard one . . . Elizabeth, it is I who am your father, and not Richard Newson. Shame alone prevented your wretched parents from owning this to you while both of 'em were alive.'

The back of Elizabeth's head remained still, and her shoulders did not denote even the movements of breathing. Henchard went on: 'I'd rather have your scorn, your fear, anything than your ignorance; 'tis that I hate. Your mother and I were man and wife when we were young. What you saw was our second marriage. Your mother was too honest. We had thought each other dead – and – Newson became her husband.'

This was the nearest approach Henchard could make to the full truth. As far as he personally was concerned he would have screened nothing; but he showed a respect for the young girl's sex and years worthy of a better man.

When he had gone on to give details which a whole series of slight unregarded incidents in her past life strangely corroborated; when, in short, she believed his story to be true, she became greatly agitated, and turning round to the table flung her face upon it weeping.

'Don't cry – don't cry!' said Henchard, with vehement pathos, 'I can't bear it, I won't bear it. I am your father; why should you cry? Am I so dreadful, so hateful to 'ee? Don't take against me, Elizabeth-Jane!' he cried, grasping her wet hand. 'Don't take against me – though I was a drinking man once and used your mother roughly – I'll be kinder to you than *he* was! I'll do anything, if you will only look upon me as your father!'

She tried to stand up and confront him trustfully; but she could not; she was troubled at his presence, like the brethren at the avowal of Joseph.

'I don't want you to come to me all of a sudden,' said Henchard in jerks, and moving like a great tree in a wind. 'No, Elizabeth, I don't. I'll go away and not see you till tomorrow, or when you like; and then I'll show 'ee papers to prove my words. There, I am gone, and won't disturb you any more . . . 'Twas I that chose your name, my daughter; your mother wanted it Susan. There, don't forget 'twas I gave you your name!' He went out at the door and shut her softly in, and she heard him go away into the garden. But he had not done. Before she had moved, or in any way recovered from the effect of his disclosure, he reappeared.

'One word more, Elizabeth,' he said. 'You'll take my surname now – hey? Your mother was against it; but it will be much more pleasant to me. 'Tis legally yours, you know. But nobody need know that. You shall take it as if by choice. I'll talk to my lawyer – I don't know the law of it exactly; but will you do this – let me put a few lines into the newspaper that such is to be your name?'

'If it is my name I must have it, mustn't I?' she asked.

'Well, well; usage is everything in these matters.'

'I wonder why mother didn't wish it?'

'Oh, some whim of the poor soul's. Now get a bit of paper and draw up a paragraph as I shall tell you. But let's have a light.'

'I can see by the firelight,' she answered. 'Yes – I'd rather.'

'Very well.'

She got a piece of paper, and bending over the fender wrote at his dictation words which he had evidently got by heart from some advertisement or other – words to the effect that she, the writer, hitherto known as Elizabeth-Jane Newson, was going to call herself Elizabeth-Jane Henchard forthwith. It was done, and fastened up and directed to the office of the *Casterbridge Chronicle*.

'Now,' said Henchard, with the blaze of satisfaction that he always emitted when he had carried his point – though tenderness softened it this time – 'I'll go upstairs and hunt for some documents that will prove it all to you. But I won't trouble you with them till tomorrow. Good-night, my Elizabeth-Jane!'

He was gone before the bewildered girl could realize what it all meant, or adjust her filial sense to the new centre of gravity. She was thankful that he had left her to herself for the evening, and sat down over the fire. Here she remained in silence, and wept – not for her mother now, but for the genial sailor Richard Newson, to whom she seemed doing a wrong.

Henchard in the meantime had gone upstairs. Papers of a domestic nature he kept in a drawer in his bedroom, and this he unlocked. Before turning them over he leant back and indulged in reposeful thought. Elizabeth was his at last and she was a girl of such good sense and kind heart that she would be sure to like him. He was the kind of man whom some human object for pouring out his heat upon – were it emotive or were it choleric – was almost a necessity. The craving of his heart for the re-establishment of this tenderest human tie had been great during his wife's lifetime, and now he had submitted to its mastery without reluctance and without fear. He bent over the drawer again, and proceeded in his search.

Among the other papers had been placed the contents of his wife's little desk, the keys of which had been handed to him at her request. Here was the letter addressed to him with the restriction. *'Not to be opened till Elizabeth-Jane's wedding-day.'*

Mrs Henchard, though more patient than her husband, had been no practical hand at anything. In sealing up the sheet, which was folded and tucked in without an envelope, in the old-fashioned way, she had overlaid the junction with a large mass of wax without the requisite under-touch of the same. The seal had cracked, and the letter was open. Henchard had no reason to suppose the restriction one of serious weight, and his feeling for his late wife had not been of the nature of deep respect. 'Some trifling fancy or other of poor Susan's, I suppose,' he said; and without curiosity he allowed his eyes to scan the letter:–

MY DEAR MICHAEL, – For the good of all of us I have kept one thing a secret from you till now. I hope you will understand why; I think you will; though perhaps you may not forgive me. But, dear Michael, I have done it for the best. I shall be in my grave when you read this, and Elizabeth-Jane will have a home. Don't curse me, Mike – think of how I was situated. I can hardly write it, but here it is. Elizabeth-Jane is not your Elizabeth-Jane – the child who was in my arms when you sold me. No; she died three months after that, and this living one is my other husband's. I christened her by the same name we had given to the first, and she filled up the ache I felt at the other's loss. Michael, I am dying, and I might have held my tongue; but I could not. Tell her husband of this or not, as you may judge; and forgive, if you can, a woman you once deeply wronged, as she forgives you.

SUSAN HENCHARD

Her husband regarded the paper as if it were a windowpane through which he saw for miles. His lips twitched, and he seemed to compress his frame, as if to bear better. His usual habit was not to consider whether destiny were hard upon him or not – the shape of his ideas in cases of affliction being simply a moody 'I am to suffer, I perceive.' 'This much scourging, then, is it for me?' But now through his passionate head there stormed this thought – that the blasting disclosure was what he had deserved.

His wife's extreme reluctance to have the girl's name altered from Newson to Henchard was now accounted for fully. It furnished another illustration of that honesty in dishonesty which had characterized her in other things.

He remained unnerved and purposeless for near a couple of hours; till he suddenly said, 'Ah – I wonder if it is true!'

He jumped up in an impulse, kicked off his slippers, and went with a candle to the door of Elizabeth-Jane's room, where he put his ear to the keyhole and listened. She was breathing profoundly. Henchard softly turned the handle, entered, and shading the light, approached the bedside. Gradually bringing the light from behind a screening curtain he held it in such manner that it fell slantwise on her face without shining on her eyes. He steadfastly regarded her features.

They were fair; his were dark. But this was an unimportant preliminary. In sleep there come to the surface buried genealogical facts, ancestral curves, dead men's traits, which the mobility of daytime animation screens and overwhelms. In the present statuesque repose of the young girl's countenance Richard Newson's was unmistakably reflected. He could not endure the sight of her, and hastened away.

Misery taught him nothing more than defiant endurance of it. His wife was dead, and the first impulse for revenge died with the thought that she was beyond him. He looked out at the night as at a fiend. Henchard, like all his kind, was superstitious, and he could not help thinking that the concatenation of events this evening had produced was the scheme of some sinister intelligence bent on punishing him. Yet they had developed naturally. If he had not revealed his past history to Elizabeth he would not have searched the drawer for papers, and so on. The mockery was, that he should have no sooner taught a girl to claim the shelter of his paternity than he discovered her to have no kinship with him.

This ironical sequence of things angered him like an impish trick from a fellow-creature. Like Prester John's, his table had been spread, and infernal harpies had snatched up the food. He went out of the house, and moved sullenly onward down the pavement till he came to the bridge at the bottom of the High Street. Here he turned in upon a bypath on the river bank, skirting the north-east limits of the town.

These precincts embodied the mournful phases of Casterbridge life, as the south avenues embodied its cheerful moods. The whole way along here was sunless, even in summer time; in spring, white frosts lingered here when other places were steaming with warmth; while in winter it was the seed-field of all aches, rheumatisms, and torturing cramps of the year. The Casterbridge doctors must have pined away for want of sufficient nourishment but for the configuration of the landscape on the north-eastern side.

The river – slow, noiseless, and dark – the Schwarzwasser of Caster-bridge – ran beneath a low cliff, the two together forming a defence which had rendered walls and artificial earthworks on this side unnecessary. Here were ruins of a Franciscan priory, and a mill attached to the same, the water of which roared down a back-hatch like the voice of desolation. Above the cliff, and behind the river, rose a pile of buildings, and in the front of the pile a square mass cut into the sky. It was like a pedestal lacking its statue. This missing feature, without which the design remained incomplete, was, in truth, the corpse of a man; for the square mass formed the base of the gallows, the extensive buildings at the back being the county gaol. In the meadow where Henchard now walked the mob were wont to gather whenever an execution took place, and there to the tune of the roaring weir they stood and watched the spectacle.

The exaggeration which darkness imparted to the glooms of this region impressed Henchard more than he had expected. The lugubrious harmony of the spot with his domestic situation was too perfect for him, impatient of effects, scenes and adumbrations. It reduced his heartburning to melancholy, and he exclaimed, 'Why the deuce did I come here!' He went on past the cottage in which the old local hangman had lived and died, in times before that calling was monopolized over all England by a single gentleman; and climbed up by a steep back lane into the town.

For the sufferings of that night, engendered by his bitter disappoint-ment, he might well have been pitied. He was like one who had half fainted, and could neither recover nor complete the swoon. In words he could blame his wife, but not in his heart; and had he obeyed the wise directions outside her letter this pain would have been spared him for long – possibly for ever, Elizabeth-Jane seeming to show no ambition to quit her safe and secluded maiden courses for the speculative path of matrimony.

The morning came after this night of unrest, and with it the necessity for a plan. He was far too self-willed to recede from a position, especially as it would involve humiliation. His daughter he had asserted her to be, and his daughter she should always think herself, no matter what hypocrisy it involved.

But he was ill-prepared for the first step in this new situation. The moment he came into the breakfast-room Elizabeth advanced with open confidence to him and took him by the arm.

'I have thought and thought all night of it,' she said frankly. 'And I see that everything must be as you say. And I am going to look upon you as the father that you are, and not to call you Mr Henchard any more. It is so plain to me now. Indeed, father, it is. For, of course, you would not have done half the things you have done for me, and let me have my own way so entirely, and bought me presents, if I had only been your stepdaughter! He – Mr Newson – whom my poor mother married by such a strange mistake' (Henchard was glad that he had disguised matters here), 'was very kind – O so kind!' (she spoke with tears in her eyes); 'but that is not the same thing as being one's real father after all. Now, father, breakfast is ready!' said she cheerfully.

Henchard bent and kissed her cheek. The moment and the act he had prefigured for weeks with a thrill of pleasure; yet it was no less than a miserable insipidity to him now that it had come. His reinstatement of her mother had been chiefly for the girl's sake, and the fruition of the whole scheme was such dust and ashes as this.

* **XX** *

OF all the enigmas which ever confronted a girl there can have been seldom one like that which followed Henchard's announcement of himself to Elizabeth as her father. He had done it in an ardour and an agitation which had half carried the point of affection with her; yet, behold, from the next morning onwards his manner was constrained as she had never seen it before.

The coldness soon broke out into open chiding. One grievous failing of Elizabeth's was her occasional pretty and picturesque use of dialect words – those terrible marks of the beast to the truly genteel.

It was dinner-time – they never met except at meals – and she happened to say when he was rising from table, wishing to show him something, 'If you'll bide where you be a minute, father, I'll get it.'

' "Bide where you be," ' he echoed sharply. 'Good God, are you only fit to carry wash to a pig-trough, that ye use such words as those?'

She reddened with shame and sadness.

'I meant "Stay where you are", father,' she said, in a low, humble voice. 'I ought to have been more careful.'

He made no reply, and went out of the room.

The sharp reprimand was not lost upon her, and in time it came to pass that for 'fay' she said 'succeed'; that she no longer spoke of 'dumbledores' but of 'humble bees'; no longer said of young men and women that they 'walked together', but that they were 'engaged'; that she grew to talk of 'greggles' as 'wild hyacinths'; that when she had not slept she did not quaintly tell the servants next morning that she had been 'hagrid', but that she had 'suffered from indigestion'.

These improvements, however, are somewhat in advance of the story. Henchard, being uncultivated himself, was the bitterest critic the fair girl could possibly have had of her own lapses – really slight now, for she read omnivorously. A gratuitous ordeal was in store for her in the matter of her handwriting. She was passing the dining-room door one evening, and had occasion to go in for something. It was not till she had opened the door that she knew the Mayor was there in the company of a man with whom he transacted business.

'Here, Elizabeth-Jane,' he said, looking round at her, 'just write down what I tell you – a few words of an agreement for me and this gentleman to sign. I am a poor tool with a pen.'

'Be jowned, and so be I,' said the gentleman.

She brought forward blotting-book, paper, and ink, and sat down.

'Now then – "An agreement entered into this sixteenth day of October" – write that first.'

She started the pen in an elephantine march across the sheet. It was a splendid round, bold hand of her own conception, a style that would have stamped a woman as Minerva's own in more recent days. But other ideas reigned then. Henchard's creed was that proper young girls wrote ladies'-hand – nay, he believed that bristling characters were as innate and inseparable a part of refined womanhood as sex itself. Hence when, instead of scribbling, like the Princess Ida. –

> In such a hand as when a field of corn
> Bows all its ears before the roaring East,

Elizabeth-Jane produced a line of chain-shot and sand-bags, he reddened in angry shame for her, and, peremptorily saying, 'Never mind – I'll finish it,' dismissed her there and then.

Her considerate disposition became a pitfall to her now. She was, it must be admitted, sometimes provokingly and unnecessarily willing to saddle herself with manual labours. She would go to the kitchen instead of ringing, 'Not to make Phoebe come up twice.' She went down to her knees, shovel in hand, when the cat overturned the coal-scuttle; moreover, she would persistently thank the parlour-maid for everything, till one day, as soon as the girl was gone from the room, Henchard broke out with, 'Good God, why dostn't leave off thanking that girl as if she were

a goddess-born! Don't I pay her a dozen pound a year to do things for
'ee?' Elizabeth shrank so visibly at the exclamation that he became sorry
a few minutes after, and said that he did not mean to be rough.

These domestic exhibitions were the small protruding needle-rocks
which suggested rather than revealed what was underneath. But his
passion had less terror for her than his coldness. The increasing frequency
of the latter mood told her the sad news that he disliked her with a
growing dislike. The more interesting that her appearance and manners
became under the softening influences which she could now command,
and in her wisdom did command, the more she seemed to estrange him.
Sometimes she caught him looking at her with a louring invidiousness
that she could hardly bear. Not knowing his secret it was a cruel mockery
that she should for the first time excite his animosity when she had taken
his surname.

But the most terrible ordeal was to come. Elizabeth had latterly been
accustomed of an afternoon to present a cup of cider or ale and bread-
and-cheese to Nance Mockridge, who worked in the yard wimbling hay-
bonds. Nance accepted this offering thankfully at first; afterwards as a
matter or course. On a day when Henchard was on the premises he saw
his step-daughter enter the hay-barn on this errand; and, as there was no
clear spot on which to deposit the provisions, she at once set to work
arranging two trusses of hay as a table, Mockridge meanwhile standing
with her hands on her hips, easefully looking at the preparations on her
behalf.

'Elizabeth, come here!' said Henchard; and she obeyed.

'Why do you lower yourself so confoundedly?' he said with suppressed
passion. 'Haven't I told you o't fifty times? Hey? Making yourself a
drudge for a common workwoman of such a character as hers! Why, ye'll
disgrace me to the dust!'

Now these words were uttered loud enough to reach Nance inside the
barn door, who fired up immediately at the slur upon her personal
character. Coming to the door she cried, regardless of consequences,
'Come to that, Mr Michael Henchard, I can let 'ee know she've waited on
worse!'

'Then she must have had more charity than sense,' said Henchard.

'O no, she hadn't. 'Twere not for charity but for hire; and at a public-
house in this town!'

'It is not true!' cried Henchard indignantly.

'Just ask her,' said Nance, folding her naked arms in such a manner
that she could comfortably scratch her elbows.

Henchard glanced at Elizabeth-Jane, whose complexion, now pink and
white from confinement, lost nearly all of the former colour. 'What does
this mean?' he said to her. 'Anything or nothing?'

'It is true,' said Elizabeth-Jane. 'But it was only –'

'Did you do it, or didn't you? Where was it?'

'At the Three Mariners; one evening for a little while, when we were
staying there.'

Nance glanced triumphantly at Henchard, and sailed into the barn; for assuming that she was to be discharged on the instant she had resolved to make the most of her victory. Henchard, however, said nothing about discharging her. Unduly sensitive on such points by reason of his own past, he had the look of one completely ground down to the last indignity. Elizabeth followed him to the house like a culprit; but when she got inside she could not see him. Nor did she see him again that day.

Convinced of the scathing damage to his local repute and position that must have been caused by such a fact, though it had never before reached his own ears, Henchard showed a positive distaste for the presence of this girl not his own, whenever he encountered her. He mostly dined with the farmers at the market-room of one of the two chief hotels, leaving her in utter solitude. Could he have seen how she made use of those silent hours he might have found reason to reverse his judgement on her quality. She read and took notes incessantly, mastering facts with painful laborious-ness, but never flinching from her self-imposed task. She began the study of Latin, incited by the Roman characteristics of the town she lived in. 'If I am not well-informed it shall be by no fault of my own,' she would say to herself through the tears that would occasionally glide down her peachy cheeks when she was fairly baffled by the portentous obscurity of many of these educational works.

Thus she lived on, a dumb, deep-feeling, great-eyed creature, construed by not a single contiguous being; quenching with patient fortitude her incipient interest in Farfrae, because it seemed to be one-sided, unmaid-enly, and unwise. True, that for reasons best known to herself, she had, since Farfrae's dismissal, shifted her quarters from the back room affording a view of the yard (which she had occupied with such zest) to a front chamber overlooking the street; but as for the young man, whenever he passed the house he seldom or never turned his head.

Winter had almost come, and unsettled weather made her still more dependent upon indoor resources. But there were certain early winter days in Casterbridge – days of firmamental exhaustion which followed angry south-westerly tempests – when, if the sun shone, the air was like velvet. She seized on these days for her periodical visits to the spot where her mother lay buried – the still-used burial-ground of the old Roman-British city, whose curious feature was this, its continuity as a place of sepulture. Mrs Henchard's dust mingled with the dust of women who lay ornamented with glass hairpins and amber necklaces, and men who held in their mouths coins of Hadrian, Posthumus, and the Constantines.

Half-past ten in the morning was about her hour for seeking this spot – a time when the town avenues were deserted as the avenues of Karnac. Business had long since passed down them into its daily cells, and Leisure had not arrived there. So Elizabeth-Jane walked and read, or looked over the edge of the book to think, and thus reached the churchyard.

There, approaching her mother's grave, she saw a solitary dark figure in the middle of the gravel-walk. This figure, too, was reading; but not from a book: the words which engrossed it being the inscription on Mrs

Henchard's tombstone. The personage was in mourning like herself, was about her age and size, and might have been her wraith or double, but for the fact that it was a lady much more beautifully dressed than she. Indeed, comparatively indifferent as Elizabeth-Jane was to dress, unless for some temporary whim or purpose, her eyes were arrested by the artistic perfection of the lady's appearance. Her gait, too, had a flexuousness about it, which seemed to avoid angularity of movement less from choice than from predisposition. It was a revelation to Elizabeth that human beings could reach this stage of external development – she had never suspected it. She felt all the freshness and grace to be stolen from herself on the instant by the neighbourhood of such a stranger. And this was in face of the fact that Elizabeth could have been writ handsome, while the young lady was simply pretty.

Had she been envious she might have hated the woman; but she did not do that – she allowed herself the pleasure of feeling fascinated. She wondered where the lady had come from. The stumpy and practical walk of honest homeliness which mostly prevailed there, the two styles of dress thereabout, the simple and the mistaken, equally avouched that this figure was no Casterbridge woman's, even if a book in her hand resembling a guide-book had not also suggested it.

The stranger presently moved from the tombstone of Mrs Henchard, and vanished behind the corner of the wall. Elizabeth went to the tomb herself; beside it were two footprints distinct in the soil, signifying that the lady had stood there a long time. She returned homeward, musing on what she had seen, as she might have mused on a rainbow or the Northern Lights, a rare butterfly or a cameo.

Interesting as things had been out of doors, at home it turned out to be one of her bad days. Henchard, whose two years' mayoralty was ending, had been made aware that he was not to be chosen to fill a vacancy in the list of aldermen; and that Farfrae was likely to become one of the Council. This caused the unfortunate discovery that she had played the waiting-maid in the town of which he was Mayor to rankle in his mind yet more poisonously. He had learnt by personal inquiry at the time that it was to Donald Farfrae – that treacherous upstart – that she had thus humiliated herself. And though Mrs Stannidge seemed to attach no great importance to the incident – the cheerful souls at the Three Mariners having exhausted its aspects long ago – such was Henchard's haughty spirit that the simple thrifty deed was regarded as little less than a social catastrophe by him.

Ever since the evening of his wife's arrival with her daughter there had been something in the air which had changed his luck. That dinner at the King's Arms with his friends had been Henchard's Austerlitz: he had had his successes since, but his courses had not been upward. He was not to be numbered among the aldermen – that Peerage of burghers – as he had expected to be, and the consciousness of this soured him today.

'Well, where have you been?' he said to her with off-hand laconism.

'I've been strolling in the Walks and churchyard, father, till I feel quite leery.' She clapped her hand to her mouth, but too late.

This was just enough to incense Henchard after the other crosses of the day. 'I *won't* have you talk like that!' he thundered. ' "Leery", indeed. One would think you worked upon a farm! One day I learn that you lend a hand in public-houses. Then I hear that you talk like a clodhopper. I'm burned, if it goes on, this house can't hold us two.'

The only way of getting a single pleasant thought to go to sleep upon after this was by recalling the lady she had seen that day, and hoping she might see her again.

Meanwhile Henchard was sitting up, thinking over his jealous folly in forbidding Farfrae to pay his addresses to this girl who did not belong to him, when if he had allowed them to go on he might not have been encumbered with her. At last he said to himself with satisfaction as he jumped up and went to the writing-table: 'Ah! he'll think it means peace, and a marriage portion – not that I don't want my house to be troubled with her, and no portion at all!' He wrote as follows: –

Sir, – On consideration, I don't wish to interfere with your courtship of Elizabeth-Jane, if you care for her. I therefore withdraw my objection; excepting in this – that the business be not carried on in my house. – Yours,

M. Henchard

Mr Farfrae

The morrow, being fairly fine, found Elizabeth-Jane again in the churchyard; but while looking for the lady she was startled by the apparition of Farfrae, who passed outside the gate. He glanced up for a moment from a pocket-book in which he appeared to be making figures as he went; whether or not he saw her he took no notice, and disappeared.

Unduly depressed by a sense of her own superfluity she thought he probably scorned her; and quite broken in spirit sat down on a bench. She fell into painful thought on her position, which ended with her saying quite loud, 'O, I wish I was dead with dear mother!'

Behind the bench was a little promenade under the wall where people sometimes walked instead of on the gravel. The bench seemed to be touched by something; she looked round, and a face was bending over her, veiled, but still distinct, the face of the young woman she had seen yesterday.

Elizabeth-Jane looked confounded for a moment, knowing she had been overheard, though there was pleasure in her confusion. 'Yes, I heard you,' said the lady, in a vivacious voice, answering her look. 'What can have happened?'

'I don't – I can't tell you,' said Elizabeth, putting her hand to her face to hide a quick flush that had come.

There was no movement or word for a few seconds; then the girl felt that the young lady was sitting down beside her.

'I guess how it is with you,' said the latter. 'That was your mother.' She waved her hand towards the tombstone. Elizabeth looked up at her as if inquiring to herself whether there should be confidence. The lady's manner was so desirous, so anxious, that the girl decided there should be confidence. 'It was my mother,' she said, 'my old friend.'

'But your father, Mr Henchard. He is living?'

'Yes, he is living,' said Elizabeth-Jane.

'Is he not kind to you?'

'I've no wish to complain of him.'

'There has been a disagreement?'

'A little.'

'Perhaps you were to blame,' suggested the stranger.

'I was – in many ways,' sighed the meek Elizabeth. 'I swept up the coals when the servant ought to have done it; and I said I was leery; – and he was angry with me.'

The lady seemed to warm towards her for that reply. 'Do you know the impression your words give me?' she said ingenuously. 'That he is a hot-tempered man – a little proud – perhaps ambitious; but not a bad man.' Her anxiety not to condemn Henchard while siding with Elizabeth was curious.

'O no; certainly not *bad*,' agreed the honest girl. 'And he has not even been unkind to me till lately – since mother died. But it has been very much to bear while it has lasted. All is owing to my defects, I daresay; and my defects are owing to my history.'

'What is your history?'

Elizabeth-Jane looked wistfully at her questioner. She found that her questioner was looking at her; turned her eyes down; and then seemed compelled to look back again. 'My history is not gay or attractive,' she said. 'And yet I can tell it, if you really want to know.'

The lady assured her that she did want to know; whereupon Elizabeth-Jane told the tale of her life as she understood it, which was in general the true one, except that the sale at the fair had no part therein.

Contrary to the girl's expectation her new friend was not shocked. This cheered her; and it was not till she thought of returning to that home in which she had been treated so roughly of late that her spirits fell.

'I don't know how to return,' she murmured. 'I think of going away. But what can I do? Where can I go?'

'Perhaps it will be better soon,' said her friend gently. 'So I would not go far. Now what do you think of this: I shall soon want somebody to live in my house, partly as house-keeper, partly as companion; would you mind coming to me? But perhaps –'

'O yes,' cried Elizabeth, with tears in her eyes. 'I would indeed – I would do anything to be independent; for then perhaps my father might get to love me. But, ah!'

'What?'

'I am no accomplished person. And a companion to *you* must be that.'

'O, not necessarily.'

'Not? But I can't help using rural words sometimes, when I don't mean to.'

'Never mind, I shall like to know them.'

'And – O, I know I shan't do!' – she cried with a distressful laugh. 'I accidently learned to write round hand instead of ladies'-hand. And, of course, you want someone who can write that?'

'Well, no.'

'What, not necessary to write ladies'-hand?' cried the joyous Elizabeth. 'Not at all.'

'But where do you live?'

'In Casterbridge, or rather I shall be living here after twelve o'clock today.'

Elizabeth expressed her astonishment.

'I have been staying at Budmouth for a few days while my house was getting ready. The house I am going into is that one they call High-Place Hall – the old stone one looking down the lane to the Market. Two or three rooms are fit for occupation, though not all: I sleep there tonight for the first time. Now will you think over my proposal, and meet me here the first fine day next week, and say if you are still in the same mind?'

Elizabeth, her eyes shining at this prospect of a change from an unbearable position, joyfully assented; and the two parted at the gate of the churchyard.

* XXI *

As a maxim glibly repeated from childhood remains practically unmarked till some mature experience enforces it, so did this High-Place Hall now for the first time really show itself to Elizabeth-Jane, though her ears had heard its name on a hundred occasions.

Her mind dwelt upon nothing else but the stranger, and the house and her own chance of living there, all the rest of the day. In the afternoon she had occasion to pay a few bills in the town and do a little shopping, when she learnt that what was a new discovery to herself had become a common topic about the streets. High-Place Hall was undergoing repair; a lady was coming there to live shortly; all the shop-people knew it, and had already discounted the chance of her being a customer.

Elizabeth-Jane could, however, add a capping touch to information so new to her in the bulk. The lady, she said, had arrived that day.

When the lamps were lighted, and it was yet not so dark as to render chimneys, attics, and roofs invisible, Elizabeth, almost with a lover's feeling, thought she would like to look at the outside of High-Place Hall. She went up the street in that direction.

The Hall, with its grey *façade* and parapet, was the only residence of its sort so near the centre of the town. It had, in the first place, the characteristics of a country mansion – birds' nests in its chimneys, damp nooks where fungi grew, and irregularities of surface direct from Nature's trowel. At night the forms of passengers were patterned by the lamps in black shadows upon the pale walls.

This evening motes of straw lay around, and other signs of the premises having been in that lawless condition which accompanies the entry of a new tenant. The house was entirely of stone, and formed an example of dignity without great size. It was not altogether aristocratic, still less consequential, yet the old-fashioned stranger instinctively said, 'Blood built it, and Wealth enjoys it,' however vague his opinions of those accessories might be.

Yet as regards the enjoying it the stranger would have been wrong, for until this very evening, when the new lady had arrived, the house had been empty for a year or two, while before that interval its occupancy had been irregular. The reason of its unpopularity was soon made manifest. Some of its rooms overlooked the market-place; and such a prospect from such a house was not considered desirable or seemly by its would-be occupiers.

Elizabeth's eyes sought the upper rooms, and saw lights there. The lady had obviously arrived. The impression that this woman of comparatively practised manner had made upon the studious girl's mind was so deep that she enjoyed standing under an opposite archway merely to think that the charming lady was inside the confronting walls, and to wonder what she was doing. Her admiration for the architecture of that front was entirely on account of the inmate it screened. Though for that matter the architecture deserved admiration, or at least study, on its own account. It was Palladian, and like most architecture erected since the Gothic age was a compilation rather than a design. But its reasonableness made it impressive. It was not rich, but rich enough. A timely consciousness of the ultimate vanity of human architecture, no less than of other human things, had prevented artistic superfluity.

Men had till quite recently been going in and out with parcels and packing-cases, rendering the door and hall within like a public thoroughfare. Elizabeth trotted through the open door in the dusk, but becoming alarmed at her own temerity she went quickly out again by another which stood open in the lofty wall of the back court. To her surprise she found herself in one of the little-used alleys of the town. Looking round at the door which had given her egress, by the light of the solitary lamp fixed in the alley, she saw that it was arched and old – older even than the house itself. The door was studded, and the keystone of the arch was a mask. Originally the mask had exhibited a comic leer, as could still be discerned; but generations of Casterbridge boys had thrown stones at the mask, aiming at its open mouth; and the blows thereon had chipped off the lips and jaws as if they had been eaten away by disease. The appearance was so ghastly by the weakly lamp-glimmer that she could not bear to look at it – the first unpleasant feature of her visit.

The position of the queer old door and the odd presence of the leering mask suggested one thing above all others as appertaining to the mansion's past history – intrigue. By the alley it had been possible to come unseen from all sorts of quarters in the town – the old play-house, the old bull-stake, the old cock-pit, the pool wherein nameless infants had been used to disappear. High-Place Hall could boast of its conveniences undoubtedly.

She turned to come away in the nearest direction homeward, which was down the alley, but hearing footsteps approaching in that quarter, and having no great wish to be found in such a place at such a time she quickly retreated. There being no other way out she stood behind a brick pier till the intruder should have gone his ways.

Had she watched she would have been surprised. She would have seen that the pedestrian on coming up made straight for the arched doorway: that as he paused with his hand upon the latch the lamplight fell upon the face of Henchard.

But Elizabeth-Jane clung so closely to her nook that she discerned nothing of this. Henchard passed in, as ignorant of her presence as she was ignorant of his identity, and disappeared in the darkness. Elizabeth came out a second time into the alley, and made the best of her way home.

Henchard's chiding, by begetting in her a nervous fear of doing anything definable as unlady-like, had operated thus curiously in keeping them unknown to each other at a critical moment. Much might have resulted from recognition – at the least a query on either side in one and the self-same form: What could he or she possibly be doing there?

Henchard, whatever his business at the lady's house, reached his own home only a few minutes later than Elizabeth-Jane. Her plan was to broach the question of leaving his roof this evening; the events of the day had urged her to the course. But its execution depended upon his mood, and she anxiously awaited his manner towards her. She found that it had changed. He showed no further tendency to be angry; he showed something worse. Absolute indifference had taken the place of irritability; and his coldness was such that it encouraged her to departure, even more than hot temper could have done.

'Father, have you any objection to my going away?' she asked.

'Going away! No – none whatever. Where are you going?'

She thought it undesirable and unnecessary to say anything at present about her destination to one who took so little interest in her. He would know that soon enough. 'I have heard of an opportunity of getting more cultivated and finished, and being less idle,' she answered, with hesitation. 'A chance of a place in a household where I can have advantages of study, and seeing refined life.'

'Then make the best of it, in Heaven's name – if you can't get cultivated where you are.'

'You don't object?'

'Object – I? Ho – no! Not at all.' After a pause he said, 'But you won't have enough money for this lively scheme without help, you know? If you like I should be willing to make you an allowance, so that you be not bound to live upon the starvation wages refined folk are likely to pay 'ee.'

She thanked him for this offer.

'It had better be done properly,' he added after a pause. 'A small annuity is what I should like you to have – so as to be independent of me – and so that I may be independent of you. Would that please ye?'

'Certainly.'

'Then I'll see about it this very day.' He seemed relieved to get her off his hands by this arrangement, and as far as they were concerned the matter was settled. She now simply waited to see the lady again.

The day and the hour came; but a drizzling rain fell. Elizabeth-Jane, having now changed her orbit from one of gay independence to laborious self-help, thought the weather good enough for such declined glory as hers, if her friend would only face it – a matter of doubt. She went to the boot-room where her pattens had hung ever since her apotheosis, took them down, had their mildewed leathers blacked, and put them on as she had done in old times. Thus mounted, and with cloak and umbrella, she went off to the place of appointment – intending, if the lady were not there, to call at the house.

One side of the churchyard – the side towards the weather – was sheltered by an ancient thatched mud wall whose eaves overhung as much as one or two feet. At the back of the wall was a corn-yard with its granary and barns – the place wherein she had met Farfrae many months earlier. Under the projection of the thatch she saw a figure. The young lady had come.

Her presence so exceptionally substantiated the girl's utmost hopes that she almost feared good fortune. Fancies find room in the strongest minds. Here, in a churchyard old as civilization, in the worst of weathers, was a strange woman of curious fascinations never seen elsewhere: there might be some devilry about her presence. However, Elizabeth went on to the church tower, on whose summit the rope of a flag-staff rattled in the wind; and thus she came to the wall.

The lady had such a cheerful aspect in the drizzle that Elizabeth forgot her fancy. 'Well,' said the lady, a little of the whiteness of her teeth appearing with the word through the black fleece that protected her face, 'have you decided?'

'Yes, quite,' said the other eagerly.

'Your father is willing?'

'Yes.'

'Then come along.'

'When?'

'Now – as soon as you like. I had a good mind to send to you to come to my house, thinking you might not venture up here in the wind. But as I like getting out of doors, I thought I would come and see first.'

'It was my own thought.'

'That shows we shall agree. Then can you come today? My house is so hollow and dismal that I want some living thing there.'

'I think I might be able to,' said the girl, reflecting.

Voices were borne over to them at that instant on the wind and raindrops from the other side of the wall. There came such words as 'sacks', 'quarters', 'threshing', 'tailing', 'next Saturday's market', each sentence being disorganized by the gusts like a face in a cracked mirror. Both the women listened.

'Who are those?' said the lady.

'One is my father. He rents that yard and barn.'

The lady seemed to forget the immediate business in listening to the technicalities of the corn trade. At last she said suddenly, 'Did you tell him where you were going to?'

'No.'

'O – how was that?'

'I thought it safer to get away first – as he is so uncertain in his temper.'

'Perhaps you are right . . . Besides, I have never told you my name. It is Miss Templeman . . . Are they gone – on the other side?'

'No. They are only gone up into the granary.'

'Well, it is getting damp here. I shall expect you today – this evening, say, at six.'

'Which way shall I come, ma'am?'

'The front way – round by the gate. There is no other that I have noticed.'

Elizabeth-Jane had been thinking of the door in the alley.

'Perhaps, as you have not mentioned your destination, you may as well keep silent upon it till you are clear off. Who knows but that he may alter his mind?'

Elizabeth-Jane shook her head. 'On consideration I don't fear it,' she said sadly. 'He has grown quite cold to me.'

'Very well. Six o'clock then.'

When they had emerged upon the open road and parted, they found enough to do in holding their bowed umbrellas to the wind. Nevertheless the lady looked in at the corn-yard gates as she passed them, and paused on one foot for a moment. But nothing was visible there save the ricks, and the humpbacked barn cushioned with moss, and the granary rising against the church-tower behind, where the smacking of the rope against the flag-staff still went on.

Now Henchard had not the slightest suspicion that Elizabeth-Jane's movement was to be so prompt. Hence when, just before six, he reached home and saw a fly at the door from the King's Arms, and his stepdaughter, with all her little bags and boxes, getting into it, he was taken by surprise.

'But you said I might go, father?' she explained through the carriage window.

'Said! – yes. But I thought you meant next month, or next year. 'Od, seize it – you take time by the forelock! This, then, is how you be going to treat me for all my trouble about ye?'

'O father! how can you speak like that? It is unjust of you!' she said with spirit.

'Well, well, have your own way,' he replied. He entered the house, and, seeing that all her things had not yet been brought down, went up to her room to look on. He had never been there since she had occupied it. Evidences of her care, of her endeavours for improvement, were visible all around, in the form of books, sketches, maps, and little arrangements for tasteful effects. Henchard had known nothing of these efforts. He gazed at them, turned suddenly about, and came down to the door.

'Look here,' he said, in an altered voice – he never called her by name now – 'don't 'ee go away from me. It may be I've spoke roughly to you – but I've been grieved beyond everything by you – there's something that caused it.'

'By me?' she said, with deep concern. 'What have I done?'

'I can't tell you now. But if you'll stop, and go on living as my daughter, I'll tell you all in time.'

But the proposal had come ten minutes too late. She was in the fly – was already, in imagination, at the house of the lady whose manner had such charms for her. 'Father,' she said, as considerately as she could, 'I think it best for us that I go on now. I need not stay long; I shall not be far away; and if you want me badly I can soon come back again.'

He nodded ever so slightly, as a receipt of her decision and no more. 'You are not going far, you say. What will be your address, in case I wish to write to you? Or am I not to know?'

'Oh yes – certainly. It is only in the town – High-Place Hall.'

'Where?' said Henchard, his face stilling.

She repeated the words. He neither moved nor spoke, and waving her hand to him in utmost friendliness she signified to the flyman to drive up the street.

* XXII *

WE go back for a moment to the preceding night, to account for Henchard's attitude.

At the hour when Elizabeth-Jane was contemplating her stealthy reconnoitring excursion to the abode of the lady of her fancy, he had been not a little amazed at receiving a letter by hand in Lucetta's well-known characters. The self-repression, the resignation of her previous communication had vanished from her mood; she wrote with some of the natural lightness which had marked her in their early acquaintance.

HIGH-PLACE HALL

MY DEAR MR HENCHARD, – Don't be surprised. It is for your good and mine, as I hope, that I have come to live at Casterbridge – for how long I cannot tell. That depends upon another; and he is a man, and a merchant, and a Mayor, and one who has the first right to my affections.

Seriously, *mon ami*, I am not so light-hearted as I may seem to be from this. I have come here in consequence of hearing of the death of your wife – whom you used to think of as dead so many years before! Poor woman, she seems to have been a sufferer, though uncomplaining, and though weak in intellect not an imbecile. I am glad you acted fairly by her. As soon as I knew she was no more, it was brought home to me very forcibly by my conscience that I ought to endeavour to disperse the shade which my *étourderie* flung over my name, by asking you to carry out your promise to me. I hope you are of the same mind, and that you will take steps to this end. As, however, I did not know how you were situated, or what had happened since our separation, I decided to come and establish myself here before communicating with you.

You probably feel as I do about this. I shall be able to see you in a day or two. Till then, farewell. – Yours,

LUCETTA

P.S. – I was unable to keep my appointment to meet you for a moment or two in passing through Casterbridge the other day. My plans were altered by my family event, which it will surprise you to hear of.

Henchard had already heard that High-Place Hall was being prepared for a tenant. He said with a puzzled air to the first person he encountered, 'Who is coming to live at the Hall?'

'A lady of the name of Templeman, I believe, sir,' said his informant.

Henchard thought it over. 'Lucetta is related to her, I suppose,' he said to himself. 'Yes, I must put her in a proper position, undoubtedly.'

It was by no means with the oppression that would once have accompanied the thought that he regarded the moral necessity now; it was, indeed, with interest, if not warmth. His bitter disappointment at finding Elizabeth-Jane to be none of his, and himself a childless man, had left an emotional void in Henchard that he unconsciously craved to fill. In this frame of mind, though without strong feeling, he had strolled up the alley and into High-Place Hall by the postern at which Elizabeth had so nearly encountered him. He had gone on thence into the court, and inquired of a man whom he saw unpacking china from a crate if Miss Le Sueur was living there. Miss Le Sueur had been the name under which he had known Lucetta – or 'Lucette', as she had called herself at that time.

The man replied in the negative; that Miss Templeman only had come. Henchard went away, concluding that Lucetta had not as yet settled in.

He was in this interested stage of the inquiry when he witnessed

Elizabeth-Jane's departure the next day. On hearing her announce the address there suddenly took possession of him the strange thought that Lucetta and Miss Templeman were one and the same person, for he could recall that in her season of intimacy with him the name of the rich relative whom he had deemed somewhat a mythical personage had been given as Templeman. Though he was not a fortune-hunter, the possibility that Lucetta had been sublimed into a lady of means by some munificent testament on the part of this relative lent a charm to her image which it might not otherwise have acquired. He was getting on towards the dead level of middle age, when material things increasingly possess the mind.

But Henchard was not left long in suspense. Lucetta was rather addicted to scribbling, as had been shown by the torrent of letters after the *fiasco* in their marriage arrangements, and hardly had Elizabeth gone away when another note came to the Mayor's house from High-Place Hall.

'I am in residence,' she said, 'and comfortable, though getting here has been a wearisome undertaking. You probably know what I am going to tell you, or do you not? My good Aunt Templeman, the banker's widow, whose very existence you used to doubt, much more her affluence, has lately died, and bequeathed some of her property to me. I will not enter into details except to say that I have taken her name – as a means of escape from mine, and its wrongs.

'I am now my own mistress, and have chosen to reside in Casterbridge – to be tenant of High-Place Hall, that at least you may be put to no trouble if you wish to see me. My first intention was to keep you in ignorance of the changes in my life till you should meet me in the street; but I have thought better of this.

'You probably are aware of my arrangement with your daughter, and have doubtless laughed at the – what shall I call it? – practical joke (in all affection) of my getting her to live with me. But my first meeting with her was purely an accident. Do you see, Michael, partly why I have done it? – why, to give you an excuse for coming here as if to visit *her*, and thus to form my acquaintance naturally. She is a dear, good girl, and she thinks you have treated her with undue severity. You may have done so in your haste, but not deliberately, I am sure. As the result has been to bring her to me I am not disposed to upbraid you. – In haste, yours always,

LUCETTA'

The excitement which these announcements produced in Henchard's gloomy soul was to him most pleasurable. He sat over his dining-table long and dreamily, and by an almost mechanical transfer the sentiments which had run to waste since his estrangement from Elizabeth-Jane and Donald Farfrae gathered around Lucetta before they had grown dry. She was plainly in a very coming-on disposition for marriage. But what else could a poor woman be who had given her time and heart to him so thoughtlessly, at that former time, as to lose her credit by it? Probably conscience no less than affection had brought her here. On the whole he did not blame her.

'The artful little woman!' he said, smiling (with reference to Lucetta's adroit and pleasant manoeuvre with Elizabeth-Jane).

To feel that he would like to see Lucetta was with Henchard to start for her house. He put on his hat and went. It was between eight and nine o'clock when he reached her door. The answer brought him was that Miss Templeman was engaged for that evening; but that she would be happy to see him the next day.

'That's rather like giving herself airs!' he thought. 'And considering what we –' But after all, she plainly had not expected him, and he took the refusal quietly. Nevertheless he resolved not to go next day. 'These cursed woman – there's not an inch of straight grain in 'em!' he said.

Let us follow the track of Mr Henchard's thought as if it were a clue line, and view the interior of High-Place Hall on this particular evening.

On Elizabeth-Jane's arrival she had been phlegmatically asked by an elderly woman to go upstairs and take off her things. She had replied with great earnestness that she would not think of giving that trouble, and on the instant divested herself of her bonnet and cloak in the passage. She was then conducted to the first door on the landing, and left to find her way further alone.

The room disclosed was prettily furnished as a boudoir or small drawing-room, and on a sofa with two cylindrical pillows reclined a dark-haired, large-eyed, pretty woman, of unmistakably French extraction on one side or the other. She was probably some years older than Elizabeth, and had a sparkling light in her eye. In front of the sofa was a small table, with a pack of cards scattered upon it faces upward.

The attitude had been so full of abandonment that she bounded up like a spring on hearing the door open.

Perceiving that it was Elizabeth she lapsed into ease, and came across to her with a reckless skip that innate grace only prevented from being boisterous.

'Why, you are late,' she said, taking hold of Elizabeth-Jane's hands.

'There were so many little things to put up.'

'And you seem dead-alive and tired. Let me try to enliven you by some wonderful tricks I have learnt, to kill the time. Sit there and don't move.' She gathered up the pack of cards, pulled the table in front of her, and began to deal them rapidly, telling Elizabeth to choose some.

'Well, have you chosen?' she asked, flinging down the last card.

'No,' stammered Elizabeth, arousing herself from a reverie. 'I quite forgot, I was thinking of – you, and me – and how strange it is that I am here.'

Miss Templeman looked at Elizabeth-Jane with interest, and laid down the cards. 'Ah! never mind,' she said. 'I'll lie here while you sit by me; and we'll talk.'

Elizabeth drew up silently to the head of the sofa, but with obvious pleasure. It could be seen that though in years she was younger than her entertainer in manner and general vision she seemed more of the sage. Miss Templeman deposited herself on the sofa in her former flexuous position, and throwing her arm above her brow – somewhat in the pose of a well-known conception of Titian's – talked up at Elizabeth-Jane invertedly across her forehead and arm.

'I must tell you something,' she said. 'I wonder if you have suspected it. I have only been mistress of a large house and a fortune a little while.'

'Oh – only a little while?' murmured Elizabeth-Jane, her countenance slightly falling.

'As a girl I lived about in garrison towns and elsewhere with my father, till I was quite flighty and unsettled. He was an officer in the army. I should not have mentioned this had I not thought it best you should know the truth.'

'Yes, yes.' She looked thoughtfully round the room – at the little square piano with brass inlayings, at the window-curtains, at the lamp, at the fair and dark kings and queens on the card-table, and finally at the inverted face of Lucetta Templeman whose large lustrous eyes had such an odd effect upside down.

Elizabeth's mind ran on acquirements to an almost morbid degree. 'You speak French and Italian fluently, no doubt,' she said. 'I have not been able to get beyond a wretched bit of Latin yet.'

'Well, for that matter, in my native isle speaking French does not go for much. It is rather the other way.'

'Where is your native isle?'

It was with rather more reluctance that Miss Templeman said, 'Jersey. There they speak French on one side of the street and English on the other, and a mixed tongue in the middle of the road. But it is a long time since I was there. Bath is where my people really belong to, though my ancestors in Jersey were as good as anybody in England. They were the Le Sueurs, an old family who have done great things in their time. I went back and lived there after my father's death. But I don't value such past matters, and am quite an English person in my feelings and tastes.'

Lucetta's tongue had for a moment outrun her discretion. She had arrived at Casterbridge as a Bath lady, and there were obvious reasons why Jersey should drop out of her life. But Elizabeth had tempted her to make free, and a deliberately formed resolve had been broken.

It could not, however, have been broken in safer company. Lucetta's words went no further, and after this day she was so much upon her guard that there appeared no chance of her identification with the young Jersey woman who had been Henchard's dear comrade at a critical time. Not the least amusing of her safeguards was her resolute avoidance of a French word if one by accident came to her tongue more readily than its English equivalent. She shirked it with the suddenness of the weak Apostle at the accusation, 'Thy speech betrayeth thee!'

Expectancy sat visibly upon Lucetta the next morning. She dressed herself for Mr Henchard, and restlessly awaited his call before mid-day; as he did not come she waited on through the afternoon. But she did not tell Elizabeth that the person expected was the girl's stepfather.

They sat in adjoining windows of the same room in Lucetta's great stone mansion, netting, and looking out upon the market, which formed an animated scene. Elizabeth could see the crown of her stepfather's hat among the rest beneath, and was not aware that Lucetta watched the same object with yet intenser interest. He moved about amid the throng, at this point lively as an ant-hill; elsewhere more reposeful, and broken up by stalls of fruit and vegetables. The farmers as a rule preferred the open *carrefour* for their transactions, despite its inconvenient jostlings and the danger from crossing vehicles, to the gloomy sheltered market-room provided for them. Here they surged on this one day of the week, forming a little world of leggings, switches, and sample-bags; men of extensive stomachs, sloping like mountain sides; men whose heads in walking swayed as the trees in November gales; who in conversing varied their attitudes much, lowering themselves by spreading their knees, and thrusting their hands into the pockets of remote inner jackets. Their faces radiated tropical warmth; for though when at home their countenances varied with the seasons, their market-faces all the year round were glowing little fires.

All over-clothes here were worn as if they were an inconvenience, a hampering necessity. Some men were well-dressed; but the majority were careless in that respect, appearing in suits which were historical records of their wearer's deeds, sun-scorchings, and daily struggles for many years past. Yet many carried ruffled cheque-books in their pockets which regulated at the bank hard by a balance of never less than four figures. In fact, what these gibbous human shapes specially represented was ready money – money insistently ready – not ready next year like a nobleman's – often not merely ready at the bank like a professional man's, but ready in their large plump hands.

It happened that today there rose in the midst of them all two or three tall apple-trees standing as if they grew on the spot; till it was perceived that they were held by men from the cider districts who came here to sell them, bringing the clay of their county on their boots. Elizabeth-Jane, who had often observed them, said, 'I wonder if the same trees come every week?'

'What trees?' said Lucetta, absorbed in watching for Henchard.

Elizabeth replied vaguely, for an incident checked her. Behind one of the trees stood Farfrae, briskly discussing a sample-bag with a farmer. Henchard had come up, accidentally encountering the young man, whose face seemed to inquire, 'Do we speak to each other?'

She saw her stepfather throw a shine into his eye which answered 'No!' Elizabeth-Jane sighed.

'Are you particularly interested in anybody out there?' said Lucetta.

'O no,' said her companion, a quick red shooting over her face.

Luckily Farfrae's figure was immediately covered by the apple-tree.

Lucetta looked hard at her. 'Quite sure?' she said.

'O yes,' said Elizabeth-Jane.

Again Lucetta looked out. 'They are all farmers, I suppose?' she said.

'No. There's Mr Bulge – he's a wine merchant; there's Benjamin Brownlet – a horse dealer; and Kitson, the pig breeder; and Yopper, the auctioneer; besides maltsters, and millers – and so on.' Farfrae stood out quite distinctly now; but she did not mention him.

The Saturday afternoon slipped on thus desultorily. The market changed from the sample-showing hour to the idle hour before starting homewards, when tales were told. Henchard had not called on Lucetta though he had stood so near. He must have been too busy, she thought. He would come on Sunday or Monday.

The days came but not the visitor, though Lucetta repeated her dressing with scrupulous care. She was disheartened. It may at once be declared that Lucetta no longer bore towards Henchard all that warm allegiance which had characterized her in their first acquaintance; the then unfortunate issue of things had chilled pure love considerably. But there remained a conscientious wish to bring about her union with him, now that there was nothing to hinder it – to right her position – which in itself was a happiness to sigh for. With strong social reasons on her side why their marriage should take place there had ceased to be any worldly reason on his why it should be postponed, since she had succeeded to fortune.

Tuesday was the great Candlemas fair. At breakfast she said to Elizabeth-Jane quite coolly: 'I imagine your father may call to see you today. I suppose he stands close by in the market-place with the rest of the corn-dealers?'

She shook her head. 'He won't come.'

'Why?'

'He has taken against me,' she said in a husky voice.

'You have quarrelled more deeply than I know of.'

Elizabeth, wishing to shield the man she believed to be her father from any charge of unnatural dislike, said 'Yes.'

'Then where you are is, of all places, the one he will avoid?'

Elizabeth nodded sadly.

Lucetta looked blank, twitched up her lovely eyebrows and lips, and burst into hysterical sobs. Here was disaster – her ingenious scheme completely stultified.

'O, my dear Miss Templeman – what's the matter?' cried her companion.

'I like your company much!' said Lucetta, as soon as she could speak.

'Yes, yes – and so do I yours!' Elizabeth chimed in soothingly.

'But – but –' She could not finish the sentence, which was, naturally, that if Henchard had such a rooted dislike for the girl as now seemed to be the case, Elizabeth-Jane would have to be got rid of – a disagreeable necessity.

A provisional resource suggested itself. 'Miss Henchard – will you go on an errand for me as soon as breakfast is over? – Ah, that's very good of you. Will you go and order –' Here she enumerated several commissions at sundry shops, which would occupy Elizabeth's time for the next hour or two, at least.

'And have you ever seen the Museum?'

Elizabeth-Jane had not.

'Then you should do so at once. You can finish the morning by going

there. It is an old house in a back street – I forget where – but you'll find
out – and there are crowds of interesting things – skeletons, teeth, old
pots and pans, ancient boots and shoes, birds' eggs – all charmingly
instructive. You'll be sure to stay till you get quite hungry.'

Elizabeth hastily put on her things and departed. 'I wonder why she
wants to get rid of me today!' she said sorrowfully as she went. That her
absence, rather than her services or instruction, was in request, had been
readily apparent to Elizabeth-Jane, simple as she seemed, and difficult as
it was to attribute a motive for the desire.

She had not been gone ten minutes when one of Lucetta's servants was
sent to Henchard's with a note. The contents were briefly:

DEAR MICHAEL, – You will be standing in view of my house today for two or
three hours in the course of your business, so do please call and see me. I am sadly
disappointed that you have not come before, for can I help anxiety about my own
equivocal relation to you? – especially now my aunt's fortune has brought me
more prominently before society? Your daughter's presence here may be the cause
of your neglect; and I have therefore sent her away for the morning. Say you come
on business – I shall be quite alone.

LUCETTA

When the messenger returned her mistress gave directions that if a
gentleman called he was to be admitted at once, and sat down to await
results.

Sentimentally she did not much care to see him – his delays had wearied
her; but it was necessary; and with a sigh she arranged herself picturesquely
in the chair; first this way, then that; next so that the light fell over her
head. Next she flung herself on the couch in the cyma-recta curve which
so became her, and with her arm over her brow looked towards the door.
This, she decided, was the best position after all; and thus she remained
till a man's step was heard on the stairs. Whereupon Lucetta, forgetting
her curve (for Nature was too strong for Art as yet), jumped up and ran
and hid herself behind one of the window-curtains in a freak of timidity.
In spite of the waning of passion the situation was an agitating one – she
had not seen Henchard since his (supposed) temporary parting from her
in Jersey.

She could hear the servant showing the visitor into the room, shutting
the door upon him, and leaving as if to go and look for her mistress.
Lucetta flung back the curtain with a nervous greeting. The man before
her was not Henchard.

XXIII

A CONJECTURE that her visitor might be some other person had, indeed, flashed through Lucetta's mind when she was on the point of bursting out; but it was just too late to recede.

He was years younger than the Mayor of Casterbridge; fair, fresh, and slenderly handsome. He wore genteel cloth leggings with white buttons, polished boots with infinite lace holes, light cord breeches under a black velveteen coat and waistcoat; and he had a silver-topped switch in his hand. Lucetta blushed, and said with a curious mixture of pout and laugh on her face – 'O, I've made a mistake!'

The visitor, on the contrary, did not laugh half a wrinkle.

'But I'm very sorry!' he said, in deprecating tones. 'I came and I inquired for Miss Henchard, and they showed me up heere, and in no case would I have caught ye so unmannerly if I had known!'

'I was the unmannerly one,' said she.

'But is it that I have come to the wrong house, madam?' said Mr Farfrae, blinking a little in his bewilderment and nervously tapping his legging with his switch.

'O no, sir, – sit down. You must come and sit down now you are here,' replied Lucetta kindly, to relieve his embarrassment. 'Miss Henchard will be here directly.'

Now this was not strictly true; but that something about the young man – that hyperborean crispness, stringency, and charm, as of a well-braced musical instrument, which had awakened the interest of Henchard, and of Elizabeth-Jane, and of the Three Mariners' jovial crew, at sight, made his unexpected presence here attractive to Lucetta. He hesitated, looked at the chair, thought there was no danger in it (though there was), and sat down.

Farfrae's sudden entry was simply the result of Henchard's permission to him to see Elizabeth if he were minded to woo her. At first he had taken no notice of Henchard's brusque letter; but an exceptionally fortunate business transaction put him on good terms with everybody, and revealed to him that he could undeniably marry if he chose. Then who so pleasing, thrifty, and satisfactory in every way as Elizabeth-Jane? Apart from her personal recommendations a reconciliation with his former friend Henchard would, in the natural course of things, flow from such a union. He therefore forgave the Mayor his curtness; and this morning on his way to the fair he had called at her house, where he learnt that she was staying at Miss Templeman's. A little stimulated at not finding her ready and waiting – so fanciful are men! – he hastened on to High-Place Hall to encounter not Elizabeth but its mistress herself.

'The fair today seems a large one,' she said when, by a natural deviation, their eyes sought the busy scene without. 'Your numerous fairs and markets keep me interested. How many things I think of while I watch from here!'

He seemed in doubt how to answer, and the babble without reached them as they sat – voices as of wavelets on a lopping sea, one ever and anon rising above the rest. 'Do you look out often?' he asked.

'Yes – very often.'

'Do you look for any one you know?'

Why should she have answered as she did?

'I look as at a picture merely. But,' she went on, turning pleasantly to him, 'I may do so now – I may look for you. You are always there, are you not? Ah – I don't mean it seriously! But it is amusing to look for somebody one knows in a crowd, even if one does not want him. It takes off the terrible oppressiveness of being surrounded by a throng, and having no point of junction with it through a single individual.'

'Ah! Maybe you'll be very lonely, ma'am?'

'Nobody knows how lonely.'

'But you are rich, they say?'

'If so, I don't know how to enjoy my riches. I came to Casterbridge thinking I should like to live here. But I wonder if I shall.'

'Where did ye come from, ma'am?'

'The neighbourhood of Bath.'

'And I from near Edinboro',' he murmured. 'It's better to stay at home, and that's true; but a man must live where his money is made. It is a great pity, but it's always so! Yet I've done very well this year. O yes,' he went on with ingenuous enthusiasm. 'You see that man with the drab kerseymere coat? I bought largely of him in the autumn when wheat was down, and then afterwards when it rose a little I sold off all I had! It brought only a small profit to me; while the farmers kept theirs, expecting higher figures – yes, though the rats were gnawing the ricks hollow. Just when I sold the markets went lower, and I brought up the corn of those who had been holding back at less price than my first purchases. And then,' cried Farfrae impetuously, his face alight, 'I sold it a few weeks after, when it happened to go up again! And so, by contenting mysel' with small profits frequently repeated, I soon made five hundred pounds – yes!' – (bringing down his hand upon the table, and quite forgetting where he was) – 'while the others by keeping theirs in hand made nothing at all!'

Lucetta regarded him with a critical interest. He was quite a new type of person to her. At last his eye fell upon the lady's and their glances met.

'Ay, now, I'm wearying you!' he exclaimed.

She said, 'No, indeed,' colouring a shade.

'What then?'

'Quite otherwise. You are most interesting.'

It was now Farfrae who showed the modest pink.

'I mean all you Scotchmen,' she added in hasty correction. 'So free from Southern extremes. We common people are all one way or the other

– warm or cold, passionate or frigid. You have both temperatures going on in you at the same time.'

'But how do you mean that? Ye were best to explain clearly, ma'am.'

'You are animated – then you are thinking of getting on. You are sad the next moment – then you are thinking of Scotland and friends.'

'Yes. I think of home sometimes!' he said simply.

'So do I – as far as I can. But it was an old house where I was born, and they pulled it down for improvements, so I seem hardly to have any home to think of now.'

Lucetta did not add, as she might have done, that the house was in St Helier, and not in Bath.

'But the mountains, and the mists and the rocks, they are there! And don't they seem like home?'

She shook her head.

'They do to me – they do to me,' he murmured. And his mind could be seen flying away northwards. Whether its origin were national or personal, it was quite true what Lucetta had said, that the curious double strands in Farfrae's thread of life – the commercial and the romantic – were very distinct at times. Like the colours in a variegated cord those contrasts could be seen intertwisted, yet not mingling.

'You are wishing you were back again,' said she.

'Ah, no, ma'am,' said Farfrae, suddenly recalling himself.

The fair without the windows was now raging thick and loud. It was the chief hiring fair of the year, and differed quite from the market of a few days earlier. In substance it was a whitey-brown crowd flecked with white – this being the body of labourers waiting for places. The long bonnets of the women, like waggon-tilts, their cotton gowns and checked shawls, mixed with the carter's smock-frocks; for they, too, entered into the hiring. Among the rest, at the corner of the pavement, stood an old shepherd, who attracted the eyes of Lucetta and Farfrae by his stillness. He was evidently a chastened man. The battle of life had been a sharp one with him, for, to begin with, he was a man of small frame. He was now so bowed by hard work and years that, approaching from behind, a person could hardly see his head. He had planted the stem of his crook in the gutter and was resting upon the bow, which was polished to silver brightness by the long friction of his hands. He had quite forgotten where he was, and what he had come for, his eyes being bent on the ground. A little way off negotiations were proceeding which had reference to him; but he did not hear them, and there seemed to be passing through his mind pleasant visions of the hiring successes of his prime, when his skill laid open to him any farm for the asking.

The negotiations were between a farmer from a distant county and the old man's son. In these there was a difficulty. The farmer would not take the crust without the crumb of the bargain, in other words, the old man without the younger; and the son had a sweetheart on his present farm, who stood by, waiting the issue with pale lips.

'I'm sorry to leave ye, Nelly,' said the young man with emotion. 'But, you see, I can't starve father, and he's out o'work at Lady-day. 'Tis only thirty-five mile.'

The girl's lips quivered. 'Thirty-five mile!' she murmured. 'Ah! 'tis enough! I shall never see 'ee again!' It was, indeed, a hopeless length of traction for Dan Cupid's magnet; for young men were young men at Casterbridge as elsewhere.

'O! no, no – I never shall,' she insisted, when he pressed her hand; and she turned her face to Lucetta's wall to hide her weeping. The farmer said he would give the young man half-an-hour for his answer, and went away, leaving the group sorrowing.

Lucetta's eyes, full of tears, met Farfrae's. His, too, to her surprise, were moist at the scene.

'It is very hard,' she said with strong feelings. 'Lovers ought not to be parted like that! O, if I had my wish, I'd let people live and love at their pleasure!'

'Maybe I can manage that they'll not be parted,' said Farfrae. 'I want a young carter; and perhaps I'll take the old man too – yes; he'll not be very expensive, and doubtless he will answer my pairrpose somehow.'

'O, you are so good!' she cried, delighted. 'Go and tell them, and let me know if you have succeeded!'

Farfrae went out, and she saw him speak to the group. The eyes of all brightened; the bargain was soon struck. Farfrae returned to her immediately it was concluded.

'It is kind-hearted of you, indeed,' said Lucetta. 'For my part, I have resolved that all my servants shall have lovers if they want them! Do make the same resolve.'

Farfrae looked more serious, waving his head a half turn. 'I must be a little stricter than that,' he said.

'Why?'

'You are a – a thriving woman; and I am a struggling hay-and-corn merchant.'

'I am a very ambitious woman.'

'Ah, well, I cannet explain. I don't know how to talk to ladies, ambitious or no; and that's true,' said Donald with grave regret. 'I try to be civil to a' folk – no more!'

'I see you are as you say,' replied she, sensibly getting the upper hand in these exchanges of sentiment. Under this revelation of insight Farfrae again looked out of the window into the thick of the fair.

Two farmers met and shook hands, and being quite near the window their remarks could be heard as others' had been.

'Have you seen young Mr Farfrae this morning?' asked one. 'He promised to meet me here at the stroke of twelve; but I've gone athwart and about the fair half-a-dozen times, and never a sign of him: though he's mostly a man to his word.'

'I quite forgot the engagement,' murmured Farfrae.

'Now you must go,' said she; 'must you not?'

'Yes,' he replied. But he still remained.

'You had better go,' she urged. 'You will lose a customer.'

'Now, Miss Templeman, you will make me angry,' exclaimed Farfrae.

'Then suppose you don't go; but stay a little longer?'

He looked anxiously at the farmer who was seeking him, and who just then ominously walked across to where Henchard was standing, and he looked into the room and at her. 'I like staying; but I fear I must go!' he said. 'Business ought not to be neglected, ought it?'

'Not for a single minute.'

'It's true. I'll come another time – if I may, ma'am?'

'Certainly,' she said. 'What has happened to us today is very curious.'

'Something to think over when we are alone, it's like to be?'

'Oh, I don't know that. It is commonplace after all.'

'No, I'll not say that. O no!'

'Well, whatever it has been, it is now over; and the market calls you to be gone.'

'Yes, yes. Market – business! I wish there were no business in the warrld.'

Lucetta almost laughed – she would quite have laughed – but that there was a little emotion going in her at the time. 'How you change!' she said. 'You should not change like this.'

'I have never wished such things before,' said the Scotchman, with a simple, shamed, apologetic look for his weakness. 'It is only since coming heere and seeing you!'

'If that's the case, you had better not look at me any longer. Dear me, I feel I have demoralized you!'

'But look or look not, I will see you in my thoughts. Well, I'll go – thank you for the pleasure of this visit.'

'Thank you for staying.'

'Maybe I'll get into my market-mind when I've been out a few minutes,' he murmured. 'But I don't know – I don't know!'

As he went she said eagerly, 'You may hear them speak of me in Casterbridge as time goes on. If they tell you I'm a coquette, which some may, because of the incidents of my life, don't believe it, for I am not.'

'I swear I will not!' he said fervidly.

Thus the two. She had enkindled the young man's enthusiasm till he was quite brimming with sentiment; while he, from merely affording her a new form of idleness, had gone on to wake her serious solicitude. Why was this? They could not have told.

Lucetta as a young girl would hardly have looked at a tradesman. But her ups and downs, capped by her indiscretions with Henchard, had made her uncritical as to station. In her poverty she had met with repulse from the society to which she had belonged, and she had no great zest for renewing an attempt upon it now. Her heart longed for some ark into which it could fly and be at rest. Rough or smooth she did not care so long as it was warm.

Farfrae was shown out, it having entirely escaped him that he had called to see Elizabeth. Lucetta at the window watched him threading the maze of farmers and farmers' men. She could see by his gait that he was conscious of her eyes, and her heart went out to him for his modesty – pleaded with her sense of his unfitness that he might be allowed to come again. He entered the market-house, and she could see him no more.

Three minutes later, when she had left the window, knocks, not of multitude but of strength, sounded through the house, and the waiting-maid tripped up.

'The Mayor,' she said.

Lucetta had reclined herself, and was looking dreamily through her fingers. She did not answer at once, and the maid repeated the information with the addition, 'And he's afraid he hasn't much time to spare, he says.'

'Oh! Then tell him that as I have a headache I won't detain him today.'

The message was taken down, and she heard the door close.

Lucetta had come to Casterbridge to quicken Henchard's feelings with regard to her. She had quickened them, and now she was indifferent to the achievement.

Her morning view of Elizabeth-Jane as a disturbing element changed, and she no longer felt strongly the necessity of getting rid of the girl for her stepfather's sake. When the young woman came in, sweetly unconscious of the turn in the tide, Lucetta went up to her, and said quite sincerely –

'I'm so glad you've come. You'll live with me a long time, won't you?'

Elizabeth as a watch-dog to keep her father off – what a new idea. Yet it was not unpleasing. Henchard had neglected her all these days, after compromising her indescribably in the past. The least he could have done when he found himself free, and herself affluent, would have been to respond heartily and promptly to her invitation.

Her emotions rose, fell, undulated, filled her with wild surmise at their suddenness; and so passed Lucetta's experiences of that day.

* XXIV *

POOR Elizabeth-Jane, little thinking what her malignant star had done to blast the budding attentions she had won from Donald Farfrae, was glad to hear Lucetta's words about remaining.

For in addition to Lucetta's house being a home, that raking view of the market-place which it afforded had as much attraction for her as for Lucetta. The *carrefour* was like the regulation Open Place in spectacular dramas, where the incidents that occur always happen to bear on the lives of the adjoining residents. Farmers, merchants, dairymen, quacks, hawkers, appeared there from week to week, and disappeared as the afternoon wasted away. It was the node of all orbits.

From Saturday to Saturday was as from day to day with the two young women now. In an emotional sense they did not live at all during the intervals. Whenever they might go wandering on other days, on market-day they were sure to be at home. Both stole sly glances out of the window at Farfrae's shoulders and poll. His face they seldom saw, for, either through shyness, or not to disturb his mercantile mood, he avoided looking towards their quarters.

Thus things went on, till a certain market-morning brought a new sensation. Elizabeth and Lucetta were sitting at breakfast when a parcel containing two dresses arrived for the latter from London. She called Elizabeth from her breakfast, and entering her friend's bedroom Elizabeth saw the gowns spread out on the bed, one of a deep cherry colour, the other lighter – a glove lying at the end of each sleeve, a bonnet at the top of each neck, and parasols across the gloves, Lucetta standing beside the suggested human figure in an attitude of contemplation.

'I wouldn't think so hard about it,' said Elizabeth, marking the intensity with which Lucetta was alternating the question whether this or that would suit best.

'But settling upon new clothes is so trying,' said Lucetta. 'You are that person' (pointing to one of the arrangements), 'or you are *that* totally different person' (pointing to the other), 'for the whole of the coming spring: and one of the two, you don't know which, may turn out to be very objectionable.'

It was finally decided by Miss Templeman that she would be the cherry-coloured person at all hazards. The dress was pronounced to be a fit, and Lucetta walked with it into the front room, Elizabeth following her.

The morning was exceptionally bright for the time of year. The sun fell so flat on the houses and pavement opposite Lucetta's residence that they poured their brightness into her rooms. Suddenly, after a rumbling of wheels, there were added to this steady light a fantastic series of circling irradiations upon the ceiling, and the companions turned to the window. Immediately opposite a vehicle of strange description had come to a standstill, as if it had been placed there for exhibition.

It was the new-fashioned agricultural implement called a horse-drill, till then unknown, in its modern shape, in this part of the country, where the venerable seed-lip was still used for sowing as in the days of the Heptarchy. Its arrival created about as much sensation in the corn-market as a flying machine would create at Charing Cross. The farmers crowded round it, women drew near it, children crept under and into it. The machine was painted in bright hues of green, yellow, and red, and it resembled as a whole a compound of hornet, grass-hopper, and shrimp, magnified enormously. Or it might have been likened to an upright musical instrument with the front gone. That was how it struck Lucetta. 'Why, it is a sort of agricultural piano,' she said.

'It has something to do with corn,' said Elizabeth.

'I wonder who thought of introducing it here?'

Donald Farfrae was in the minds of both as the innovator, for though not a farmer he was closely leagued with farming operations. And as if in response to their thought he came up at that moment, looked at the machine, walked round it, and handled it as if he knew something about its make. The two watchers had inwardly started at his coming, and Elizabeth left the window, went to the back of the room, and stood as if absorbed in the panelling of the wall. She hardly knew that she had done this till Lucetta, animated by the conjunction of her new attire with the sight of Farfrae, spoke out: 'Let us go and look at the instrument, whatever it is.'

Elizabeth-Jane's bonnet and shawl were pitchforked on in a moment, and they went out. Among all the agriculturists gathering round the only appropriate possessor of the new machine seemed to be Lucetta, because she alone rivalled it in colour.

They examined it curiously; observing the rows of trumpet-shaped tubes one within the other, the little scoops, like revolving salt-spoons, which tossed the seed into the upper ends of the tubes that conducted it to the ground; till somebody said, 'Good morning, Elizabeth-Jane.' She looked up, and there was her stepfather.

His greeting had been somewhat dry and thunderous, and Elizabeth-Jane, embarrassed out of her equanimity, stammered at random, 'This is the lady I live with, father – Miss Templeman.'

Henchard put his hand to his hat, which he brought down with a great wave till it met his body at the knees. Miss Templeman bowed. 'I am happy to become acquainted with you, Mr Henchard,' she said. 'This is a curious machine.'

'Yes,' Henchard replied; and he proceeded to explain it, and still more forcibly to ridicule it.

'Who brought it here?' said Lucetta.

'Oh, don't ask me, ma'am!' said Henchard. 'The thing – why 'tis impossible it should act. 'Twas brought here by one of our machinists on the recommendation of a jumped-up jackanapes of a fellow who thinks –' His eye caught Elizabeth-Jane's imploring face, and he stopped, probably thinking that the suit might be progressing.

He turned to go away. Then something seemed to occur which his stepdaughter fancied must really be a hallucination of hers. A murmur apparently came from Henchard's lips in which she detected the words, 'You refused to see me!' reproachfully addressed to Lucetta. She could not believe that they had been uttered by her stepfather; unless, indeed, they might have been spoken to one of the yellow-gaitered farmers near them. Yet Lucetta seemed silent; and then all thought of the incident was dissipated by the humming of a song which sounded as though from the interior of the machine. Henchard had by this time vanished into the market-house, and both the women glanced towards the corn-drill. They could see behind it the bent back of a man who was pushing his head into the internal works to master their simple secrets. The hummed song went on –

> ''Tw—s on a s—m—r aftern—n,
> A wee be—re the s—n w—nt d—n,
> When Kitty wi' a braw n—w g—wn
> C—me ow're the h—lls to Gowrie.'

Elizabeth-Jane had apprehended the singer in a moment, and looked guilty of she did not know what. Lucetta next recognized him, and more mistress of herself said archly, 'The "Lass of Gowrie" from the inside of a seed-drill – what a phenomenon!'

Satisfied at last with his investigation the young man stood upright, and met their eyes across the summit.

'We are looking at the wonderful new drill,' Miss Templeman said. 'But practically it is a stupid thing – is it not?' she added, on the strength of Henchard's information.

'Stupid? O no!' said Farfrae gravely. 'It will revolutionize sowing heereabout! No more sowers flinging their seed about broadcast, so that some falls by the wayside and some among thorns, and all that. Each grain will go straight to its intended place, and nowhere else whatever!'

'Then the romance of the sower is gone for good,' observed Elizabeth-Jane, who felt herself at one with Farfrae in Bible-reading at least. ' "He that observeth the wind shall not sow," so the Preacher said; but his words will not be to the point any more. How things change!'

'Ay; ay . . . It must be so!' Donald admitted, his gaze fixing itself on a blank point far away. 'But the machines are already very common in the East and North of England,' he added apologetically.

Lucetta seemed to be outside this train of sentiment, her acquaintance with the Scriptures being somewhat limited. 'Is the machine yours?' she asked of Farfrae.

'O no, madam,' said he, becoming embarrassed and deferential at the sound of her voice, though with Elizabeth-Jane he was quite at his ease. 'No, no – I merely recommended that it should be got.'

In the silence which followed Farfrae appeared only conscious of her; to have passed from perception of Elizabeth into a brighter sphere of existence than she appertained to. Lucetta, discerning that he was much mixed that day, partly in his mercantile mood and partly in his romantic one, said gaily to him –

'Well, don't forsake the machine for us,' and went indoors with her companion.

The latter felt that she had been in the way, though why was unaccountable to her. Lucetta explained the matter somewhat by saying when they were again in the sitting-room –

'I had occasion to speak to Mr Farfrae the other day, and so I knew him this morning.'

Lucetta was very kind towards Elizabeth that day. Together they saw the market thicken, and in course of time thin away with the slow decline of the sun towards the upper end of the town, its rays taking the street endways and enfilading the long thoroughfare from top to bottom. The gigs and vans disappeared one by one till there was not a vehicle in the street. The time of the riding world was over; the pedestrian world held sway. Field labourers and their wives and children trooped in from the villages for their weekly shopping, and instead of a rattle of wheels and a tramp of horses ruling the sounds as earlier, there was nothing but the shuffle of many feet. All the implements were gone; all the farmers; all the moneyed class. The character of the town's trading had changed from bulk to multiplicity, and pence were handled now as pounds had been handled earlier in the day.

Lucetta and Elizabeth looked out upon this, for though it was night and the street lamps were lighted, they had kept their shutters unclosed. In the faint blink of the fire they spoke more freely.

'Your father was distant with you,' said Lucetta.

'Yes.' And having forgotten the momentary mystery of Henchard's seeming speech to Lucetta she continued, 'It is because he does not think I am respectable. I have tried to be so more that you can imagine, but in vain! My mother's separation from my father was unfortunate for me. You don't know what it is to have shadows like that upon your life.'

Lucetta seemed to wince. 'I do not – of that kind precisely,' she said, 'but you may feel a – sense of disgrace – shame – in other ways.'

'Have you ever had any such feeling?' said the younger innocently.

'O no,' said Lucetta quickly. 'I was thinking of – what happens sometimes when women get themselves in strange positions in the eyes of the world from no fault of their own.'

'It must make them very unhappy afterwards.'

'It makes them anxious; for might not other women despise them?'

'Not altogether despise them. Yet not quite like or respect them.'

Lucetta winced again. Her past was by no means secure from investigation, even in Casterbridge. For one thing Henchard had never returned to her the cloud of letters she had written and sent him in her first excitement. Possibly they were destroyed; but she could have wished that they had never been written.

The rencounter with Farfrae and his bearing towards Lucetta had made the reflective Elizabeth more observant of her brilliant and amiable companion. A few days afterwards, when her eyes met Lucetta's as the latter was going out, she somehow knew that Miss Templeman was nourishing a hope of seeing the attractive Scotchman. The fact was printed large all over Lucetta's cheeks and eyes to any one who could read her as Elizabeth-Jane was beginning to do. Lucetta passed on and closed the street door.

A seer's spirit took possession of Elizabeth, impelling her to sit down by the fire and divine events so surely from data already her own that they could be held as witnessed. She followed Lucetta thus mentally – saw her encounter Donald somewhere as if by chance – saw him wear his special look when meeting women, with an added intensity because this one was

Lucetta. She depicted his impassioned manner; beheld the indecision of both between their lothness to separate and their desire not to be observed; depicted their shaking of hands; how they probably parted with frigidity in their general contour and movements, only in the smaller features showing the spark of passion, thus invisible to all but themselves. This discerning silent witch had not done thinking of these things when Lucetta came noiselessly behind her and made her start.

It was all true as she had pictured – she could have sworn it. Lucetta had a heightened luminousness in her eye over and above the advanced colour of her cheeks.

'You've seen Mr Farfrae,' said Elizabeth demurely.

'Yes,' said Lucetta. 'How did you know?'

She knelt down on the hearth and took her friend's hands excitedly in her own. But after all she did not say when or how she had seen him or what he had said.

That night she became restless; in the morning she was feverish; and at breakfast-time she told her companion that she had something on her mind – something which concerned a person in whom she was interested much. Elizabeth was earnest to listen and sympathize.

'This person – a lady – once admired a man much – very much,' she said tentatively.

'Ah,' said Elizabeth-Jane.

'They were intimate – rather. He did not think so deeply of her as she did of him. But in an impulsive moment, purely out of reparation, he proposed to make her his wife. She agreed. But there was an unexpected hitch in the proceedings; though she had been so far compromised with him that she felt she could never belong to another man, as a pure matter of conscience, even if she should wish to. After that they were much apart, heard nothing of each other for a long time, and she felt her life closed up for her.'

'Ah – poor girl!'

'She suffered much on account of him; though I should add that he could not altogether be blamed for what had happened. At last the obstacle which separated them was providentially removed; and he came to marry her.'

'How delightful!'

'But in the interval she – my poor friend – had seen a man she liked better than him. Now comes the point: Could she in honour dismiss the first?'

'A new man she liked better – that's bad!'

'Yes,' said Lucetta, looking pained at a boy who was swinging the town pump-handle. 'It is bad! Though you must remember that she was forced into an equivocal position with the first man by an accident – that he was not so well educated or refined as the second, and that she had discovered some qualities in the first that rendered him less desirable as a husband than she had at first thought him to be.'

'I cannot answer,' said Elizabeth-Jane thoughtfully. 'It is so difficult. It wants a Pope to settle that!'

'You prefer not to, perhaps?' Lucetta showed in her appealing tone how much she leant on Elizabeth's judgement.

'Yes, Miss Templeman,' admitted Elizabeth. 'I would rather not say.'

Nevertheless, Lucetta seemed relieved by the simple fact of having opened out the situation a little, and was slowly convalescent of her headache. 'Bring me a looking-glass. How do I appear to people?' she said languidly.

'Well – a little worn,' answered Elizabeth, eyeing her as a critic eyes a doubtful painting; fetching the glass she enabled Lucetta to survey herself in it, which Lucetta anxiously did.

'I wonder if I wear well, as times go!' she observed after a while.

'Yes – fairly.'

'Where am I worst?'

'Under your eyes – I notice a little brownness there.'

'Yes. That is my worst place, I know. How many years more do you think I shall last before I get hopelessly plain?'

There was something curious in the way in which Elizabeth, though the younger, had come to play the part of experienced sage in these discussions. 'It may be five years,' she said judicially. 'Or with a quiet life, as many as ten. With no love you might calculate on ten.'

Lucetta seemed to reflect on this as on an unalterable, impartial verdict. She told Elizabeth-Jane no more of the past attachment she had roughly abumbrated as the experiences of a third person; and Elizabeth, who in spite of her philosophy was very tender-hearted, sighed that night in bed at the thought that her pretty, rich Lucetta did not treat her to the full confidence of names and dates in her confessions. For by the 'she' of Lucetta's story Elizabeth had not been beguiled.

* XXV *

THE next phase of the supersession of Henchard in Lucetta's heart was an experiment in calling on her performed by Farfrae with some apparent trepidation. Conventionally speaking he conversed with both Miss Templeman and her companion; but in fact it was rather that Elizabeth sat invisible in the room. Donald appeared not to see her at all, and answered her wise little remarks with curtly indifferent monosyllables, his looks and faculties hanging on the woman who could boast of a more Protean variety in her phases, moods, opinions, and also principles, than could Elizabeth. Lucetta had persisted in dragging her into the circle; but she had remained like an awkward third point which that circle would not touch.

Susan Henchard's daughter bore up against the frosty ache of the treatment, as she had borne up under worst things, and contrived as soon as possible to get out of the inharmonious room without being missed. The Scotchman seemed hardly the same Farfrae who had danced with her and walked with her in a delicate poise between love and friendship – that period in the history of a love when alone it can be said to be unalloyed with pain.

She stoically looked from her bedroom window, and contemplated her fate as if it were written on the top of the church-tower hard by. 'Yes,' she said at last, bringing down her palm upon the sill with a pat: '*He* is the second man of that story she told me!'

All this time Henchard's smouldering sentiments towards Lucetta had been fanned into higher and higher inflammation by the circumstances of the case. He was discovering that the young woman for whom he once felt a pitying warmth which had been almost chilled out of him by reflection, was, when now qualified with a slight inaccessibility and a more matured beauty, the very being to make him satisfied with life. Day after day proved to him, by her silence, that it was no use to think of bringing her round by holding aloof; so he gave in, and called upon her again, Elizabeth-Jane being absent.

He crossed the room to her with a heavy tread of some awkwardness, his strong, warm gaze upon her – like the sun beside the moon in comparison with Farfrae's modest look – and with something of a hail-fellow bearing, as, indeed, was not unnatural. But she seemed so transubstantiated by her change of position, and held out her hand to him in such cool friendship, that he became deferential, and sat down with a perceptible loss of power. He understood but little of fashion in dress, yet enough to feel himself inadequate in appearance beside her whom he had hitherto been dreaming of as almost his property. She said something very polite about his being good enough to call. This caused him to recover balance. He looked her oddly in the face, losing his awe.

'Why, of course I have called, Lucetta,' he said. 'What does that nonsense mean? You know I couldn't have helped myself if I had wished – that is, if I had any kindness at all. I've called to say that I am ready, as soon as custom will permit, to give you my name in return for your devotion, and what you lost by it in thinking too little of yourself and too much of me; to say that you can fix the day or month, with my full consent, whenever in your opinion it would be seemly: you know more of these things than I.'

'It is full early yet,' she said evasively.

'Yes, yes; I suppose it is. But you know, Lucetta, I felt directly my poor ill-used Susan died, and when I could not bear the idea of marrying again, that after what had happened between us it was my duty not to let any unnecessary delay occur before putting things to rights. Still, I wouldn't call in a hurry, because – well, you can guess how this money you've come into made me feel.' His voice slowly fell; he was conscious that in this room his accents and manner wore a roughness not observable in the street. He looked about the room at the novel hangings and ingenious furniture with which she had surrounded herself.

'Upon my life I didn't know such furniture as this could be bought in Casterbridge,' he said.

'Nor can it be,' said she. 'Nor will it till fifty years more of civilization have passed over the town. It took a waggon and four horses to get it here.'

'H'm. It looks as if you were living on capital.'

'O no, I am not.'

'So much the better. But the fact is, your setting up like this makes my bearing towards you rather awkward.'

'Why?'

An answer was not really needed, and he did not furnish one. 'Well,' he went on, 'there's nobody in the world I would have wished to see enter into this wealth before you, Lucetta, and nobody, I am sure, who will become it more.' He turned to her with congratulatory admiration so fervid that she shrank somewhat, notwithstanding that she knew him so well.

'I am greatly obliged to you for all that,' said she, rather with an air of speaking ritual. The stint of reciprocal feeling was perceived, and Henchard showed chagrin at once – nobody was more quick to show that than he.

'You may be obliged or not for't. Though the things I say may not have the polish of what you've lately learnt to expect for the first time in your life, they are real, my lady Lucetta.'

'That's rather a rude way of speaking to me,' pouted Lucetta, with stormy eyes.

'Not at all!' replied Henchard hotly. 'But there, there, I don't wish to quarrel with 'ee. I come with an honest proposal for silencing your Jersey enemies, and you ought to be thankful.'

'How can you speak so!' she answered, firing quickly. 'Knowing that my only crime was the indulging in a foolish girl's passion for you with too little regard for correctness, and that I was what *I* call innocent all the time they called me guilty, you ought not to be so cutting! I suffered enough at that worrying time, when you wrote to tell me of your wife's return and my consequent dismissal, and if I am a little independent now, surely the privilege is due me!'

'Yes, it is,' he said. 'But it is not by what is, in this life, but by what appears, that you are judged; and I therefore think you ought to accept me – for your own good name's sake. What is known in your native Jersey may get known here.'

'How you keep on about Jersey! I am English!'

'Yes, yes. Well, what do you say to my proposal?'

For the first time in their acquaintance Lucetta had the move; and yet she was backward. 'For the present let things be,' she said with some embarrassment. 'Treat me as an acquaintance; and I'll treat you as one. Time will –' she stopped; and he said nothing to fill the gap for awhile, there being no pressure of half acquaintance to drive them into speech if they were not minded for it.

'That's the way the wind blows, is it?' he said at last grimly, nodding an affirmative to his own thoughts.

A yellow flood of reflected sunlight filled the room for a few instants. It was produced by the passing of a load of newly trussed hay from the country, in a waggon marked with Farfrae's name. Beside it rode Farfrae himself on horseback. Lucetta's face became – as a woman's face becomes when the man she loves rises upon her gaze like an apparition.

A turn of the eye by Henchard, a glance from the window, and the secret of her inaccessibility would have been revealed. But Henchard in estimating her tone was looking down so plumb-straight that he did not note the warm consciousness upon Lucetta's face.

'I shouldn't have thought it – I shouldn't have thought it of women!' he said emphatically by-and-by, rising and shaking himself into activity; while Lucetta was so anxious to divert him from any suspicion of the truth that she asked him to be in no hurry. Bringing him some apples she insisted upon paring one for him.

He would not take it. 'No, no; such is not for me,' he said drily, and moved to the door. At going out he turned his eye upon her.

'You came to live in Casterbridge entirely on my account,' he said. 'Yet now you are here you won't have anything to say to my offer!'

He had hardly gone down the staircase when she dropped upon the sofa and jumped up again in a fit of desperation. 'I *will* love him!' she cried passionately; 'as for *him* – he's hot-tempered and stern, and it would be madness to bind myself to him knowing that. I won't be a slave to the past – I'll love where I choose!'

Yet having decided to break away from Henchard one might have supposed her capable of aiming higher than Farfrae. But Lucetta reasoned nothing: she feared hard words from the people with whom she had been earlier associated; she had no relatives left; and with native lightness of heart took kindly to what fate offered.

Elizabeth-Jane, surveying the position of Lucetta between her two lovers from the crystalline sphere of a straightforward mind, did not fail to perceive that her father, as she called him, and Donald Farfrae became more desperately enamoured of her friend every day. On Farfrae's side it was the unforced passion of youth. On Henchard's the artificially stimulated coveting of maturer age.

The pain she experienced from the almost absolute obliviousness to her existence that was shown by the pair of them became at times half dissipated by her sense of its humourousness. When Lucetta had pricked her finger they were as deeply concerned as if she were dying; when she herself had been seriously sick or in danger they uttered a conventional word of sympathy at the news, and forgot all about it immediately. But, as regarded Henchard, this perception of hers also caused her some filial grief; she could not help asking what she had done to be neglected so, after the professions of solicitude he had made. As regarded Farfrae, she thought, after honest reflection, that it was quite natural. What was she beside Lucetta? – as one of the 'meaner beauties of the night', when the moon had risen in the skies.

She had learnt the lesson of renunciation, and was as familiar with the wreck of each day's wishes as with the diurnal setting of the sun. If her earthly career had taught her few book philosophies it had at least well practised her in this. Yet her experience had consisted less in a series of pure disappointments than in a series of substitutions. Continually it had happened that what she had desired had not been granted her, and that what had been granted her she had not desired. So she viewed with an approach to equanimity the now cancelled days when Donald had been her undeclared lover, and wondered what unwished-for thing Heaven might send her in place of him.

* XXVI *

IT chanced that on a fine spring morning Henchard and Farfrae met in the chestnut-walk which ran along the south wall of the town. Each had just come out from his early breakfast, and there was not another soul near. Henchard was reading a letter from Lucetta, sent in answer to a note from him, in which she made some excuse for not immediately granting him a second interview that he had desired.

Donald had no wish to enter into conversation with his former friend on their present constrained terms; neither would he pass him in scowling silence. He nodded, and Henchard did the same. They had receded from each other several paces when a voice cried 'Farfrae!' It was Henchard's, who stood regarding him.

'Do you remember,' said Henchard, as if it were the presence of the thought and not of the man which made him speak, 'do you remember my story of that second woman – who suffered for her thoughtless intimacy with me?'

'I do,' said Farfrae.

'Do you remember my telling 'ee how it all began and how it ended?'

'Yes.'

'Well, I have offered to marry her now that I can; but she won't marry me. Now what would you think of her – I put it to you?'

'Well, ye owe her nothing more now,' said Farfrae heartily.

'It is true,' said Henchard, and went on.

That he had looked up from a letter to ask his question completely shut out from Farfrae's mind all vision of Lucetta as the culprit. Indeed, her present position was so different from that of the young woman of Henchard's story as of itself to be sufficient to blind him absolutely to her identity. As for Henchard, he was reassured by Farfrae's words and manner against a suspicion which had crossed his mind. They were not those of a conscious rival.

Yet that there was rivalry by some one he was firmly persuaded. He could feel it in the air around Lucetta, see it in the turn of her pen. There was an antagonistic force in exercise, so that when he had tried to hang near her he seemed standing in a refluent current. That it was not innate caprice he was more and more certain. Her windows gleamed as if they did not want him; her curtains seemed to hang slily, as if they screened an ousting presence. To discover whose presence that was – whether really Farfrae's after all, or another's – he exerted himself to the utmost to see her again; and at length succeeded.

At the interview, when she offered him tea, he made it a point to launch a cautious inquiry if she knew Mr Farfrae.

O yes, she knew him, she declared; she could not help knowing almost everybody in Casterbridge, living in such a gazebo over the centre and arena of the town.

'Pleasant young fellow,' said Henchard.

'Yes,' said Lucetta.

'We both know him,' said kind Elizabeth-Jane, to relieve her companion's divined embarrassment.

There was a knock at the door; literally, three full knocks and a little one at the end.

'That kind of knock means half-and-half – somebody between gentle and simple,' said the corn-merchant to himself. 'I shouldn't wonder therefore if it is he.' In a few seconds surely enough Donald walked in.

Lucetta was full of little fidgets and flutters, which increased Henchard's suspicions without affording any special proof of their correctness. He was well-nigh ferocious at the sense of the queer situation in which he stood towards this woman. One who had reproached him for deserting her when calumniated, who had urged claims upon his consideration on that account, who had lived waiting for him, who at the first decent moment had come to ask him to rectify, by making her his, the false position into which she had placed herself for his sake; such she had been. And now he sat at her tea-table eager to gain her attention, and in his amatory rage feeling the other man present to be a villain, just as any young fool of a lover might feel.

They sat stiffly side by side at the darkening table, like some Tuscan painting of the two disciples supping at Emmaus. Lucetta, forming the third and haloed figure, was opposite them; Elizabeth-Jane, being out of the game, and out of the group, could observe all from afar, like the evangelist who had to write it down: that there were long spaces of taciturnity, when all exterior circumstance was subdued to the touch of spoons and china, the click of a heel on a pavement under the window, the passing of a wheel-barrow or cart, the whistling of the carter, the gush of water into householders' buckets at the town-pump opposite; the exchange of greetings among their neighbours, and the rattle of the yokes by which they carried off their evening supply.

'More bread-and-butter?' said Lucetta to Henchard and Farfrae equally, holding out between them a plateful of long slices. Henchard took a slice by one end and Donald by the other; each feeling certain he was the man meant; neither let go, and the slice came in two.

'Oh – I am so sorry!' cried Lucetta, with a nervous titter. Farfrae tried to laugh; but he was too much in love to see the incident in any but a tragic light.

'How ridiculous of all three of them!' said Elizabeth to herself.

Henchard left the house with a ton of conjecture, though without a grain of proof, that the counter-attraction was Farfrae; and therefore he would not make up his mind. Yet to Elizabeth-Jane it was plain as the town-pump that Donald and Lucetta were incipient lovers. More than once, in spite of her care, Lucetta had been unable to restrain her glance from flitting across into Farfrae's eyes like a bird to its nest. But Henchard was constructed upon too large a scale to discern such minutiae as these by any evening light, which to him were as the notes of an insect that lie above the compass of the human ear.

But he was disturbed. And the sense of occult rivalry in suitorship was so much superadded to the palpable rivalry of their business lives. To the coarse materiality of that rivalry it added an inflaming soul.

The thus vitalized antagonism took the form of action by Henchard sending for Jopp, the manager originally displaced by Farfrae's arrival. Henchard had frequently met this man about the streets, observed that his clothing spoke of neediness, heard that he lived in Mixen Lane – a back slum of the town, the *pis aller* of Casterbridge domiciliation – itself almost a proof that a man had reached a stage when he would not stick at trifles.

Jopp came after dark, by the gates of the store-yard, and felt his way through the hay and straw to the office where Henchard sat in solitude awaiting him.

'I am again out of a foreman,' said the corn-factor. 'Are you in a place?'

'Not so much as a beggar's, sir.'

'How much do you ask?'

Jopp named his price, which was very moderate.

'When can you come?'

'At this hour and moment, sir,' said Jopp, who, standing hands-pocketed at the street corner till the sun had faded the shoulders of his coat to scarecrow green, had regularly watched Henchard in the market-place, measured him, and learnt him, by virtue of the power which the still man has in his stillness of knowing the busy one better than he knows himself. Jopp, too, had had a convenient experience; he was the only one in Casterbridge besides Henchard and the close-lipped Elizabeth who knew that Lucetta came truly from Jersey, and but proximately from Bath. 'I know Jersey, too, sir,' he said. 'Was living there when you used to do business that way. O yes – have often seen ye there.'

'Indeed! Very good. Then the thing is settled. The testimonials you showed me when you first tried for't are sufficient.'

That characters deteriorate in time of need possibly did not occur to Henchard. Jopp said, 'Thank you,' and stood more firmly, in the consciousness that at last he officially belonged to that spot.

'Now,' said Henchard, digging his strong eyes into Jopp's face, 'one thing is necessary to me, as the biggest corn-and-hay-dealer in these parts. The Scotchman, who's taking the town trade so bold into his hands, must be cut out. D'ye hear? We two can't live side by side – that's clear and certain.'

'I've seen it all,' said Jopp.

'By fair competition I mean, of course,' Henchard continued. 'But as hard, keen, and unflinching as fair – rather more so. By such a desperate bid against him for the farmers' custom as will grind him into the ground – starve him out. I've capital, mind ye, and I can do it.'

'I'm all that way of thinking,' said the new foreman. Jopp's dislike of Farfrae as the man who had once usurped his place, while it made him a willing tool, made him, at the same time, commercially as unsafe a colleague as Henchard could have chosen.

'I sometimes think,' he added, 'that he must have some glass that he sees next year in. He has such a knack of making everything bring him fortune.'

'He's deep beyond all honest men's discerning; but we must make him shallower. We'll under-sell him, and over-buy him, and so snuff him out.'

They then entered into specific details of the process by which this would be accomplished, and parted at a late hour.

Elizabeth-Jane heard by accident that Jopp had been engaged by her stepfather. She was so fully convinced that he was not the right man for the place that, at the risk of making Henchard angry, she expressed her apprehension to him when they met. But it was done to no purpose. Henchard shut up her argument with a sharp rebuff.

The season's weather seemed to favour their scheme. The time was in the years immediately before foreign competition had revolutionized the trade in grain; when still as from the earliest ages, the wheat quotations from month to month depended entirely upon the home harvest. A bad harvest, or the prospect of one, would double the price of corn in a few weeks; and the promise of a good yield would lower it as rapidly. Prices were like the roads of the period, steep in gradient, reflecting in their phases the local conditions, without engineering, levellings, or averages.

The farmer's income was ruled by the wheat-crop within his own horizon, and the wheat-crop by the weather. Thus, in person, he became a sort of flesh-barometer, with feelers always directed to the sky and wind around him. The local atmosphere was everything to him; the atmospheres of other countries a matter of indifference. The people, too, who were not farmers, the rural multitude, saw in the god of the weather a more important personage than they do now. Indeed, the feeling of the peasantry in this matter was so intense as to be almost unrealizable in these equable days. Their impulse was well-nigh to prostrate themselves in lamentation before untimely rains and tempests, which came as the Alastor of those households whose crime it was to be poor.

After midsummer they watched the weather-cocks as men waiting in antechambers watch the lackey. Sun elated them; quiet rain sobered them; weeks of watery tempest stupefied them. That aspect of the sky which they now regarded as disagreeable they then beheld as maleficent.

It was June, and the weather was very unfavourable. Casterbridge, being as it were the bell-board on which all the adjacent hamlets and villages sounded their notes, was decidedly dull. Instead of new articles in the shop-windows those that had been rejected in the foregoing summer were brought out again; superseded reap-hooks, badly-shaped rakes, shop-worn leggings, and time-stiffened water-tights reappeared, furbished up as near to new as possible.

Henchard, backed by Jopp, read a disastrous garnering, and resolved to base his strategy against Farfrae upon that reading. But before acting he wished – what so many have wished – that he could know for certain what was at present only strong probability. He was superstitious – as such headstrong natures often are – and he nourished in his mind an idea bearing on the matter; an idea he shrank from disclosing even to Jopp.

In a lonely hamlet a few miles from the town – so lonely that what are called lonely villages were teeming by comparison – there lived a man of curious repute as a forecaster or weather-prophet. The way to his house was crooked and miry – even difficult in the present unpropitious season. One evening when it was raining so heavily that ivy and laurel resounded like distant musketry, and an out-door man could be excused for shrouding himself to his ears and eyes, such a shrouded figure on foot might have been perceived travelling in the direction of the hazel-copse which dripped over the prophet's cot. The turnpike-road became a lane, the lane a cart-track, the cart-track a bridle-path, the bridle-path a foot-way, the foot-way overgrown. The solitary walker slipped here and there, and stumbled over the natural springes formed by the brambles, till at length he reached the house, which, with its garden, was surrounded with a high, dense hedge. The cottage, comparatively a large one, had been built of mud by the occupier's own hands, and thatched also by himself. Here he had always lived, and here it was assumed he would die.

He existed on unseen supplies; for it was an anomalous thing that while there was hardly a soul in the neighbourhood but affected to laugh at this man's assertions, uttering the formula, 'There's nothing in 'em', with full assurance on the surface of their faces, very few of them were unbelievers in their secret hearts. Whenever they consulted him they did it 'for a fancy'. When they paid him they said, 'Just a trifle for Christmas', or 'Candlemas', as the case might be.

He would have preferred more honesty in his clients, and less sham ridicule; but fundamental belief consoled him for superficial irony. As stated, he was enabled to live; people supported him with their backs turned. He was sometimes astonished that men could profess so little and believe so much at his house, when at church they professed so much and believed so little.

Behind his back he was called 'Wide-oh', on account of his reputation; to his face 'Mr' Fall.

The hedge of his garden formed an arch over the entrance, and a door was inserted as in a wall. Outside the door the tall traveller stopped, bandaged his face with a handkerchief as if he were suffering from toothache, and went up the path. The window shutters were not closed, and he could see the prophet within, preparing his supper.

In answer to the knock Fall came to the door, candle in hand. The visitor stepped back a little from the light, and said, 'Can I speak to 'ee?' in significant tones. The other's invitation to come in was responded to by the country formula, 'This will do, thank 'ee', after which the householder has no alternative but to come out. He placed the candle on the corner of the dresser, took his hat from a nail, and joined the stranger in the porch, shutting the door behind him.

'I've long heard that you can – do things of a sort?' began the other, repressing his individuality as much as he could.

'Maybe so, Mr Henchard,' said the weather-caster.

'Ah – why do you call me that?' asked the visitor with a start.

'Because it's your name. Feeling you'd come I've waited for 'ee; and thinking you might be leery from your walk I laid two supper plates – look ye here.' He threw open the door and disclosed the supper-table, at which appeared a second chair, knife and fork, plate and mugs, as he had declared.

Henchard felt like Saul at his reception by Samuel; he remained in silence for a few moments, then throwing off the disguise of frigidity which he had hitherto preserved, he said, 'Then I have not come in vain . . . Now, for instance, can ye charm away warts?'

'Without trouble.'

'Cure the evil?'

'That I've done – with consideration – if they will wear the toad-bag by night as well as by day.'

'Forecast the weather?'

'With labour and time.'

'Then take this,' said Henchard. ' 'Tis a crown-piece. Now, what is the harvest fortnight to be? When can I know?'

'I've worked it out already, and you can know at once.' (The fact was that five farmers had already been there on the same errand from different parts of the country.) 'By the sun, moon, and stars, by the clouds, the winds, the trees, and grass, the candleflame and swallows, the smell of the herbs; likewise by the cats' eyes, the ravens, the leeches, the spiders, and the dungmixen, the last fortnight in August will be – rain and tempest.'

'You are not certain, of course?'

'As one can be in a world where all's unsure. 'Twill be more like living in Revelations this autumn than in England. Shall I sketch it out for 'ee in a scheme?'

'O no, no,' said Henchard. 'I don't altogether believe in forecasts, come to second thoughts on such. But I –'

'You don't – you don't – 'tis quite understood,' said Wide-oh, without a sound of scorn. 'You have given me a crown because you've one too many. But won't you join me at supper, now 'tis waiting and all?'

Henchard would gladly have joined; for the savour of the stew had floated from the cottage into the porch with such appetizing distinctness that the meat, the onions, the pepper, and the herbs could be severally recognized by his nose. But as sitting down to hob-and-nob there would have seemed to mark him too implicitly as the weather-caster's apostle, he declined, and went his way.

The next Saturday Henchard bought grain to such an enormous extent that there was quite a talk about his purchases among his neighbours the lawyer, the wine merchant, and the doctor; also on the next, and on all available days. When his granaries were full to choking, all the weather-cocks of Casterbridge creaked and set their faces in another direction, as if tired of the south-west. The weather changed; the sunlight, which had been like tin for weeks, assumed the hues of topaz. The temperament of the welkin passed from the phlegmatic to the sanguine; an excellent harvest was almost a certainty; and as a consequence prices rushed down.

All these transformations, lovely to the outsider, to the wrong-headed corn-dealer were terrible. He was reminded of what he had well known before, that a man might gamble upon the square green areas of fields as readily as upon those of a card-room.

Henchard had backed bad weather, and apparently lost. He had mistaken the turn of the flood for the turn of the ebb. His dealings had been so extensive that settlement could not long be postponed, and to settle he was obliged to sell off corn that he had bought only a few weeks before at figures higher by many shillings a quarter. Much of the corn he had never seen; it had not even been moved from the ricks in which it lay stacked miles away. Thus he lost heavily.

In the blaze of an early August day he met Farfrae in the market-place. Farfrae knew of his dealings (though he did not guess their intended bearing on himself) and commiserated with him; for since their exchange of words in the South Walk they had been on stiffly speaking terms. Henchard for the moment appeared to resent the sympathy; but he suddenly took a careless turn.

'Ho, no no! – nothing serious, man!' he cried with fierce gaiety. 'These things always happen, don't they? I know it has been said that figures have touched me tight lately; but is that anything rare? The case is not so bad as folk make out perhaps. And dammy, a man must be a fool to mind the common hazards of trade!'

But he had to enter the Casterbridge Bank that day for reasons which had never before sent him there – and to sit a long time in the partners' room with a constrained bearing. It was rumoured soon after that much real property as well as vast stores of produce, which had stood in Henchard's name in the town neighbourhood, was actually the possession of his bankers.

Coming down the steps of the bank he encountered Jopp. The gloomy transactions just completed within had added fever to the original sting of Farfrae's sympathy that morning, which Henchard fancied might be satire disguised, so that Jopp met with anything but a bland reception. The latter was in the act of taking off his hat to wipe his forehead, and saying, 'A fine hot day,' to an acquaintance.

'You can wipe and wipe, and say, "A fine hot day," can ye!' cried Henchard in a savage undertone, imprisoning Jopp between himself and the bank wall. 'If it hadn't been for your blasted advice it might have been a fine day enough! Why did you let me go on, hey? – when a word of doubt from you or anybody would have made me think twice! For you can never be sure of weather till 'tis past.'

'My advice, sir, was to do what you thought best.'

'A useful fellow! And the sooner you help somebody else in that way the better!' Henchard continued his address to Jopp in similar terms till it ended in Jopp's dismissal there and then, Henchard turning upon his heel and leaving him.

'You shall be sorry for this, sir; sorry as a man can be!' said Jopp, standing pale, and looking after the corn-merchant as he disappeared in the crowd of market-men hard by.

*   * XXVII *

IT was the eve of the harvest. Prices being low Farfrae was buying. As was usual, after reckoning too surely on famine weather the local farmers had flown to the other extreme, and (in Farfrae's opinion) were selling off too recklessly – calculating with just a trifle too much certainty upon an abundant yield. So he went on buying old corn at its comparatively ridiculous price: for the produce of the previous year, though not large, had been of excellent quality.

When Henchard had squared his affairs in a disastrous way and got rid of his burdensome purchases at a monstrous loss, the harvest began. There were three days of excellent weather, and then – 'What if that curst conjuror should be right after all!' said Henchard.

The fact was, that no sooner had the sickles begun to play than the atmosphere suddenly felt as if cress would grow in it without other nourishment. It rubbed people's cheeks like damp flannel when they walked abroad. There was a gusty, high, warm wind; isolated raindrops starred the window-panes at remote distances: the sunlight would flap out like a quickly opened fan, throw the pattern of the window upon the floor of the room in a milky, colourless shine, and withdraw as suddenly as it had appeared.

From that day and hour it was clear that there was not to be so successful an ingathering after all. If Henchard had only waited long enough he might at least have avoided loss though he had not made a profit. But the momentum of his character knew no patience. At this turn of the scales he remained silent. The movements of his mind seemed to tend to the thought that some power was working against him.

'I wonder,' he asked himself with eerie misgiving; 'I wonder if it can be that somebody has been roasting a waxen image of me, or stirring an unholy brew to confound me! I don't believe in such power; and yet – what if they should ha' been doing it!' Even he could not admit that the perpetrator, if any, might be Farfrae. These isolated hours of superstition came to Henchard in time of moody depression, when all his practical largeness of view had oozed out of him.

Meanwhile Donald Farfrae prospered. He had purchased in so depressed a market that the present moderate stiffness of prices was sufficient to pile for him a large heap of gold where a little one had been.

'Why, he'll soon be Mayor!' said Henchard. It was indeed hard that the speaker should, of all others, have to follow the triumphal chariot of this man to the Capitol.

The rivalry of the masters was taken up by the men.

September-night shades had fallen upon Casterbridge; the clocks had struck half-past eight, and the moon had risen. The streets of the town were curiously silent for such a comparatively early hour. A sound of jangling horse-bells and heavy wheels passed up the street. These were followed by angry voices outside Lucetta's house, which led her and Elizabeth-Jane to run to the windows, and pull up the blinds.

The neighbouring Market House and Town Hall abutted against its next neighbour the Church except in the lower storey, where an arched thoroughfare gave admittance to a large square called Bull Stake. A stone post rose in the midst, to which the oxen had formerly been tied for baiting with dogs to make them tender before they were killed in the adjoining shambles. In a corner stood the stocks.

The thoroughfare leading to this spot was now blocked by two four-horse waggons and horses, one laden with hay-trusses, the leaders having already passed each other, and become entangled head to tail. The passage of the vehicles might have been practicable if empty; but built up with hay to the bedroom windows as one was, it was impossible.

'You must have done it a' purpose!' said Farfrae's waggoner. 'You can hear my horses' bells half-a-mile such a night as this!'

'If ye'd been minding your business instead of zwailing along in such a gawk-hammer way, you would have zeed me!' retorted the wroth representative of Henchard.

However, according to the strict rule of the road it appeared that Henchard's man was most in the wrong; he therefore attempted to back into the High Street. In doing this the near hind-wheel rose against the churchyard wall, and the whole mountainous load went over, two of the four wheels rising in the air, and the legs of the thill horse.

Instead of considering how to gather up the load the two men closed in a fight with their fists. Before the first round was quite over Henchard came upon the spot, somebody having run for him.

Henchard sent the two men staggering in contrary directions by collaring one with each hand, turned to the horse that was down, and extricated him after some trouble. He then inquired into the circumstances; and seeing the state of his waggon and its load began hotly rating Farfrae's man.

Lucetta and Elizabeth-Jane had by this time run down to the street corner, whence they watched the bright heap of new hay lying in the moon's rays, and passed and re-passed by the forms of Henchard and the waggoners. The women had witnessed what nobody else had seen – the origin of the mishap; and Lucetta spoke.

'I saw it all, Mr Henchard,' she cried; 'and your man was most in the wrong!'

Henchard paused in his harangue and turned. 'Oh, I didn't notice you, Miss Templeman,' said he. 'My man in the wrong? Ah, to be sure; to be sure! But I beg your pardon notwithstanding. The other's is the empty waggon, and he must have been most to blame for coming on.'

'No; I saw it, too,' said Elizabeth-Jane. 'And I can assure you he couldn't help it.'

'You can't trust *their* senses!' murmured Henchard's man.

'Why not?' asked Henchard sharply.

'Why, you see, sir, all the women side with Farfrae – being a damn young dand – or the sort that he is – one that creeps into a maid's heart like the giddying worm into a sheep's brain – making crooked seem straight to their eyes!'

'But do you know who that lady is you talk about in such a fashion? Do you know that I pay my attentions to her, and have for some time? Just be careful!'

'Not I. I know nothing, sir, outside eight shillings a week.'

'And that Mr Farfrae is well aware of it? He's sharp in trade, but he wouldn't do anything so underhand as what you hint at.'

Whether because Lucetta heard this low dialogue, or not, her white figure disappeared from her doorway inward, and the door was shut before Henchard could reach it to converse with her further. This disappointed him, for he had been sufficiently disturbed by what the man had said to wish to speak to her more closely. While pausing the old constable came up.

'Just see that nobody drives against that hay and waggon tonight, Stubberd,' said the corn-merchant. 'It must bide till the morning, for all hands are in the fields still. And if any coach or road-waggon wants to come along, tell 'em they must go round by the back street, and be hanged to 'em . . . Any case tomorrow up in Hall?'

'Yes, sir. One in number, sir.'

'Oh, what's that?'

'An old flagrant female, sir, swearing and committing a nuisance in a horrible profane manner against the church wall, sir, as if 'twere no more that a pot-house! That's all, sir.'

'Oh. The Mayor's out o' town, isn't he?'

'He is, sir.'

'Very well, then I'll be there. Don't forget to keep an eye on that hay. Good night t' 'ee.'

During those moments Henchard had determined to follow up Lucetta notwithstanding her elusiveness, and he knocked for admission.

The answer he received was an expression of Miss Templeman's sorrow at being unable to see him again that evening because she had an engagement to go out.

Henchard walked away from the door to the opposite side of the street, and stood by his hay in a lonely reverie, the constable having strolled elsewhere, and the horses being removed. Though the moon was not bright as yet there were no lamps lighted, and he entered the shadow of one of the projecting jambs which formed the thoroughfare to Bull Stake; here he watched Lucetta's door.

Candle-lights were flitting in and out of her bedroom, and it was obvious that she was dressing for the appointment, whatever the nature of that might be at such an hour. The lights disappeared, the clock struck nine, and almost at the moment Farfrae came round the opposite corner and knocked. That she had been waiting just inside for him was certain, for she instantly opened the door herself. They went together by the way of a back lane westward, avoiding the front street; guessing where they were going he determined to follow.

The harvest had been so delayed by the capricious weather that whenever a fine day occurred all sinews were strained to save what could be saved of the damaged drops. On account of the rapid shortening of the days the harvesters worked by moonlight. Hence tonight the wheat-fields abutting on the two sides of the square formed by Casterbridge town were animated by the gathering hands. Their shouts and laughter had reached Henchard at the Market House, while he stood there waiting, and he had little doubt from the turn which Farfrae and Lucetta had taken that they were bound for the spot.

Nearly the whole town had gone into the fields. The Casterbridge populace still retained the primitive habit of helping one another in time of need; and thus, though the corn belonged to the farming section of the little community – that inhabiting the Durnover quarter – the remainder was no less interested in the labour of getting it home.

Reaching the top of the lane Henchard crossed the shaded avenue on the walls, slid down the green rampart, and stood amongst the stubble. The 'stitches' or shocks rose like tents about the yellow expanse, those in the distance becoming lost in the moonlight hazes.

He had entered at a point removed from the scene of immediate operations; but two others had entered at that place and he could see them winding among the shocks. They were paying no regard to the direction of their walk, whose vague serpentining soon began to bear down towards Henchard. A meeting promised to be awkward, and he therefore stepped into the hollow of the nearest shock, and sat down.

'You have my leave,' Lucetta was saying gaily. 'Speak what you like.'

'Well, then,' replied Farfrae, with the unmistakable inflection of the lover pure, which Henchard had never heard in full resonance on his lips before, 'you are sure to be much sought after for your position, wealth, talents, and beauty. But will ye resist the temptation to be one of those ladies with lots of admirers – ay – and be content to have only a homely one?'

'And he the speaker?' said she, laughing. 'Very well, sir, what next?'

'Ah! I'm afraid that what I feel will make me forget my manners!'

'Then I hope you'll never have any, if you lack them only for that cause.' After some broken words which Henchard lost she added, 'Are you sure you won't be jealous?'

Farfrae seemed to assure her that he would not, by taking her hand.

'You are convinced, Donald, that I love nobody else,' she presently said. 'But I should wish to have my own way in some things.'

'In everything! What special thing did you mean?'

'If I wished not to live always in Casterbridge, for instance upon finding that I should not be happy here?'

Henchard did not hear the reply; he might have done so and much more, but he did not care to play the eavesdropper. They went on towards the scene of activity, where the sheaves were being handed, a dozen a minute, upon the carts and waggons which carried them away.

Lucetta insisted on parting from Farfrae when they drew near the workpeople. He had some business with them and, though he entreated her to wait a few minutes, she was inexorable, and tripped off homeward alone.

Henchard thereupon left the field and followed her. His state of mind was such that on reaching Lucetta's door he did not knock but opened it, and walked straight up to her sitting-room, expecting to find her there. But the room was empty, and he perceived that in his haste he had somehow passed her on the way hither. He had not to wait many minutes, however, for he soon heard her dress rustling in the hall, followed by a soft closing of the door. In a moment she appeared.

The light was so low that she did not notice Henchard at first. As soon as she saw him she uttered a little cry, almost of terror.

'How can you frighten me so?' she exclaimed, with a flushed face. 'It is past ten o'clock, and you have no right to surprise me here at such a time.'

'I don't know that I've not the right. At any rate I have the excuse. Is it so necessary that I should stop to think of manners and customs?'

'It is too late for propriety, and might injure me.'

'I called an hour ago, and you would not see me, and I thought you were in when I called now. It is you, Lucetta, who are doing wrong. It is not proper in 'ee to throw me over like this. I have a little matter to remind you of, which you seem to forget.'

She sank into a chair, and turned pale.

'I don't want to hear it – I don't want to hear it!' she said through her hands, as he, standing close to the edge of her gown, began to allude to the Jersey days.

'But you ought to hear it,' said he.

'It came to nothing; and through you. Then why not leave me the freedom that I gained with such sorrow! Had I found that you proposed to marry me for pure love I might have felt bound now. But I soon learnt that you had planned it out of mere charity – almost as an unpleasant duty – because I had nursed you, and compromised myself, and you thought you must repay me. After that I did not care for you so deeply as before.'

'Why did you come here to find me, then?'

'I thought I ought to marry you for conscience' sake, since you were free, even though I – did not like you so well.'

'And why then don't you think so now?'

She was silent. It was only too obvious that conscience had ruled well enough till new love had intervened and usurped that rule. In feeling this she herself forgot for the moment her partially justifying argument – that having discovered Henchard's infirmities of temper, she had some excuse for not risking her happiness in his hands after once escaping them. The only thing she could say was, 'I was a poor girl then; and now my circumstances have altered, so I am hardly the same person.'

'That's true. And it makes the case awkward for me. But I don't want to touch your money. I am quite willing that every penny of your property shall remain to your personal use. Besides, that argument has nothing in it. The man you are thinking of is no better than I.'

'If you were as good as he you would leave me!' she cried passionately.

This unluckily aroused Henchard. 'You cannot in honour refuse me,' he said. 'And unless you give me your promise this very night to be my wife, before a witness, I'll reveal our intimacy – in common fairness to other men!'

A look of resignation settled upon her. Henchard saw its bitterness; and had Lucetta's heart been given to any other man in the world than Farfrae he would probably have had pity upon her at that moment. But the supplanter was the upstart (as Henchard called him) who had mounted into prominence upon his shoulders, and he could bring himself to show no mercy.

Without another word she rang the bell, and directed that Elizabeth-Jane should be fetched from her room. The latter appeared, surprised in the midst of her lucubrations. As soon as she saw Henchard she went across to him dutifully.

'Elizabeth-Jane,' he said, taking her hand, 'I want you to hear this.' And turning to Lucetta: 'Will you, or will you not, marry me?'

'If you – wish it, I must agree!'

'You say yes?'

'I do.'

No sooner had she given the promise than she fell back in a fainting state.

'What dreadful thing drives her to say this, father, when it is such a pain to her?' asked Elizabeth, kneeling down by Lucetta. 'Don't compel her to do anything against her will! I have lived with her, and know that she cannot bear much.'

'Don't be a no'thern simpleton!' said Henchard drily. 'This promise will leave him free for you, if you want him, won't it?'

At this Lucetta seemed to wake from her swoon with a start.

'Him? Who are you talking about?' she said wildly.

'Nobody, as far as I am concerned,' said Elizabeth firmly.

'Oh – well. Then it is my mistake,' said Henchard. 'But the business is between me and Miss Templeman. She agrees to be my wife.'

'But don't dwell on it just now,' entreated Elizabeth, holding Lucetta's hand.

'I don't wish to, if she promises,' said Henchard.

'I have, I have,' groaned Lucetta, her limbs hanging like flails, from very misery and faintness. 'Michael, please don't argue it any more!'

'I will not,' he said. And taking up his hat he went away.

Elizabeth-Jane continued to kneel by Lucetta. 'What is this?' she said. 'You called my father "Michael" as if you knew him well? And how is it he has this power over you, that you promise to marry him against your will? Ah – you have many many secrets from me!'

'Perhaps you have some from me,' Lucetta murmured with closed eyes, little thinking, however, so unsuspicious was she, that the secret of Elizabeth's heart concerned the young man who had caused this damage to her own.

'I would not – do anything against you at all!' stammered Elizabeth, keeping in all signs of emotion till she was ready to burst. 'I cannot understand how my father can command you so; I don't sympathize with him in it at all. I'll go to him and ask him to release you.'

'No, no,' said Lucetta. 'Let it all be.'

XXVIII

THE next morning Henchard went to the Town Hall below Lucetta's house, to attend Petty Sessions, being still a magistrate for the year by virtue of his late position as Mayor. In passing he looked up at her windows, but nothing of her was to be seen.

Henchard as a Justice of the Peace may at first seem to be an even greater incongruity than Shallow and Silence themselves. But his rough and ready perceptions, his sledge-hammer directness, had often served him better than nice legal knowledge in despatching such simple business as fell to his hands in this Court. Today Dr Chalkfield, the Mayor for the year, being absent, the corn-merchant took the big chair, his eyes still abstractedly stretching out of the window to the ashlar front of High-Place Hall.

There was one case only, and the offender stood before him. She was an old woman of mottled countenance, attired in a shawl of that nameless tertiary hue which comes, but cannot be made – a hue neither tawny, russet, hazel, nor ash; a sticky black bonnet that seemed to have been worn in the country of the Psalmist where the clouds drop fatness: and an apron that had been white in times so comparatively recent as still to contrast visibly with the rest of her clothes. The steeped aspect of the woman as a whole showed her to be no native of the country-side or even of a country-town.

She looked cursorily at Henchard and the second magistrate, and Henchard looked at her, with a momentary pause, as if she had reminded him indistinctly of somebody or something which passed from his mind as quickly as it had come. 'Well, and what has she been doing?' he said, looking down at the charge-sheet.

'She is charged, sir, with the offence of disorderly female and nuisance,' whispered Stubberd.

'Where did she do that?' said the other magistrate.

'By the church, sir, of all the horrible places in the world! – I caught her in the act, your worship.'

'Stand back then,' said Henchard, 'and let's hear what you've got to say.'

Stubberd was sworn, the magistrate's clerk dipped his pen, Henchard being no note-taker himself, and the constable began –

'Hearing a' illegal noise I went down the street at twenty-five minutes past eleven p.m. on the night of the fifth instinct, Hannah Dominy. When I had –'

'Don't go on so fast, Stubberd,' said the clerk.

The constable waited, with his eyes on the clerk's pen; till the latter stopped scratching, and said, 'yes.' Stubberd continued: 'When I had proceeded to the spot I saw defendant at another spot, namely, the gutter.' He paused, watching the point of the clerk's pen again.

'Gutter, yes, Stubberd.'

'Spot measuring twelve feet nine inches or thereabouts, from where I –' Still careful not to outrun the clerk's penmanship Stubberd pulled up again; for having got his evidence by heart it was immaterial to him whereabouts he broke off.

'I object to that,' spoke up the old woman, ' "spot measuring twelve feet nine or thereabouts from where I," is not sound testimony!'

The magistrates consulted, and the second one said that the bench was of opinion that twelve feet nine inches from a man on his oath was admissible.

Stubberd, with a suppressed gaze of victorious rectitude at the old woman, continued: 'Was standing myself. She was wambling about quite dangerous to the thoroughfare, and when I approached to draw near she committed the nuisance, and insulted me.'

' "Insulted me." . . . Yes, what did she say?'

'She said, "Put away that dee lantern," she says.'

'Yes.'

'Says she, "Dost hear, old turmit-head? Put away that dee lantern. I have floored fellows a dee sight finer-looking than a dee fool like thee, you son of a bee, dee me if I haint," she says.'

'I object to that conversation!' interposed the old woman. 'I was not capable enough to hear what I said, and what is said out of my own hearing is not evidence.'

There was another stoppage for consultation, a book was referred to, and finally Stubberd was allowed to go on again. The truth was that the old woman had appeared in court so many more times than the magistrates themselves, that they were obliged to keep a sharp look-out upon their procedure. However, when Stubberd had rambled on a little further Henchard broke out impatiently, 'Come – we don't want to hear any more of them cust dees and bees! Say the words out like a man, and don't be so modest, Stubberd; or else leave it alone!' Turning to the woman, 'Now then, have you any questions to ask him, or anything to say?'

'Yes,' she replied with a twinkle in her eye; and the clerk dipped his pen.

'Twenty years ago or thereabout I was selling of furmity in a tent at Weydon Fair –'

' "Twenty years ago" – well, that's beginning at the beginning; suppose you go back to the Creation!' said the clerk, not without satire.

But Henchard stared, and quite forgot what was evidence and what was not.

'A man and a woman with a little child came into my tent,' the woman continued. 'They sat down and had a basin apiece. Ah, Lord's my life! I was of a more respectable station in the world then than I am now, being a land smuggler in a large way of business; and I used to season my furmity with rum for them who asked fo't. I did it for the man; and then he had more and more; till at last he quarrelled with his wife, and offered to sell her to the highest bidder. A sailor came in and bid five guineas, and paid the money, and led her away. And the man who sold his wife in that fashion is the man sitting there in the great big chair.' The speaker concluded by nodding her head at Henchard and folding her arms.

Everybody looked at Henchard. His face seemed strange, and in tint as if it had been powdered over with ashes. 'We don't want to hear your life and adventures,' said the second magistrate sharply, filling the pause which followed. 'You've been asked if you've anything to say bearing on the case.'

'That bears on the case. It proves that he's no better than I, and has no right to sit there in judgement upon me.'

''Tis a concocted story,' said the clerk. 'So hold your tongue!'

'No – 'tis true.' The words came from Henchard. ''Tis as true as the light,' he said slowly. 'And upon my soul it does prove that I'm no better than she! And to keep out of any temptation to treat her hard for revenge, I'll leave her to you.'

The sensation in the court was indescribably great. Henchard left the chair, and came out, passing through a group of people on the steps and outside that was much larger than usual; for it seemed that the old furmity dealer had mysteriously hinted to the denizens of the lane in which she had been lodging since her arrival, that she knew a queer thing or two about their great local man Mr Henchard, if she chose to tell it. This had brought them hither.

'Why are there so many idlers round the Town Hall today?' said Lucetta to her servant when the case was over. She had risen late, and had just looked out of the window.

'Oh, please, ma'am, 'tis this larry about Mr Henchard. A woman has proved that before he became a gentleman he sold his wife for five guineas in a booth at a fair.'

In all the accounts which Henchard had given her of the separation from his wife Susan for so many years, of his belief in her death, and so on, he had never clearly explained the actual and immediate cause of that separation. The story she now heard for the first time.

A gradual misery overspread Lucetta's face as she dwelt upon the promise wrung from her the night before. At bottom, then, Henchard was this. How terrible a contingency for a woman who should commit herself to his care.

During the day she went out to the Ring and to other places, not coming in till nearly dusk. As soon as she saw Elizabeth-Jane after her return indoors she told her that she had resolved to go away from home to the seaside for a few days – to Port-Bredy; Casterbridge was so gloomy.

Elizabeth, seeing that she looked wan and disturbed, encouraged her in the idea, thinking a change would afford her relief. She could not help suspecting that the gloom which seemed to have come over Casterbridge in Lucetta's eyes might be partially owing to the fact that Farfrae was away from home.

Elizabeth saw her friend depart for Port-Bredy, and took charge of

High-Place Hall till her return. After two or three days of solitude and incessant rain Henchard called at the house. He seemed disappointed to hear of Lucetta's absence, and though he nodded with outward indifference he went away handling his beard with a nettled mien.

The next day he called again. 'Is she come now?' he asked.

'Yes. She returned this morning,' replied his stepdaughter. 'But she is not indoors. She has gone for a walk along the turnpike-road to Port-Bredy. She will be home by dusk.'

After a few words, which only served to reveal his restless impatience, he left the house again.

* XXIX *

At this hour Lucetta was bounding along the road to Port-Bredy just as Elizabeth had announced. That she had chosen for her afternoon walk the road along which she had returned to Casterbridge three hours earlier in a carriage was curious – if anything should be called curious in concatenations of phenomena wherein each is known to have its accounting cause. It was the day of the chief market – Saturday – and Farfrae for once had been missed from his corn-stand in the dealers' room. Nevertheless, it was known that he would be home that night – 'for Sunday', as Casterbridge expressed it.

Lucetta, in continuing her walk, had at length reached the end of the ranked trees which bordered the highway in this and other directions out of the town. This end marked a mile; and here he stopped.

The spot was a vale between two gentle acclivities, and the road, still adhering to its Roman foundation, stretched onward straight as a surveyor's line till lost to sight on the most distant ridge. There was neither hedge nor tree in the prospect now, the road clinging to the stubbly expanse of corn-land like a stripe to an undulating garment. Near her was a barn – the single building of any kind within her horizon.

She strained her eyes up the lessening road, but nothing appeared thereon – not so much as a speck. She sighed one word – 'Donald!' and turned her face to the town for retreat.

Here the case was different. A single figure was approaching her – Elizabeth-Jane's.

Lucetta, in spite of her loneliness, seemed a little vexed. Elizabeth's face, as soon as she recognized her friend, shaped itself into affectionate lines while yet beyond speaking distance. 'I suddenly thought I would come and meet you,' she said, smiling.

Lucetta's reply was taken from her lips by an unexpected diversion. A by-road on her right hand descended from the fields into the highway at the point where she stood, and down the track a bull was rambling uncertainly towards her and Elizabeth, who, facing the other way, did not observe him.

In the latter quarter of each year cattle were at once the mainstay and the terror of families about Casterbridge and its neighbourhood, where breeding was carried on with Abrahamic success. The head of stock driven into and out of the town at this season to be sold by the local auctioneer was very large; and all these horned beasts, in travelling to and fro, sent women and children to shelter as nothing else could do. In the main the animals would have walked along quietly enough; but the Casterbridge tradition was that to drive stock it was indispensable that hideous cries, coupled with Yahoo antics and gestures, should be used, large sticks flourished, stray dogs called in, and in general everything done that was likely to infuriate the viciously disposed and terrify the mild. Nothing was commoner than for a householder on going out of his parlour to find his hall or passage full of little children, nurse-maids, aged women, or a ladies' school, who apologized for their presence by saying, 'A bull passing down street from the sale.'

Lucetta and Elizabeth regarded the animal in doubt, he meanwhile drawing vaguely towards them. It was a large specimen of the breed, in colour rich dun, though disfigured at present by splotches of mud about his seamy sides. His horns were thick and tipped with brass; his two nostrils like the Thames Tunnel as seen in the perspective toys of yore. Between them, through the gristle of his nose, was a stout copper ring, welded on, and irremovable as Gurth's collar of brass. To the ring was attached an ash staff about a yard long, which the bull with the motions of his head flung about like a flail.

It was not till they observed this dangling stick that the young women were really alarmed; for it revealed to them that the bull was an old one, too savage to be driven, which had in some way escaped, the staff being the means by which the drover controlled him and kept his horns at arms' length.

They looked round for some shelter or hiding-place, and thought of the barn hard by. As long as they had kept their eyes on the bull he had shown some deference in his manner of approach; but no sooner did they turn their backs to seek the barn than he tossed his head and decided to thoroughly terrify them. This caused the two helpless girls to run wildly, whereupon the bull advanced in a deliberate charge.

The barn stood behind a green slimy pond, and it was closed save as to one of the usual pair of doors facing them, which had been propped open by a hurdle-stake, and for this opening they made. The interior had been cleared by a recent bout of threshing except at one end, where there was a stack of dry clover. Elizabeth-Jane took in the situation. 'We must climb up there,' she said.

But before they had even approached it they heard the bull scampering through the pond without, and in a second he dashed into the barn, knocking down the hurdle-stake in passing; the heavy door slammed behind him; and all three were imprisoned in the barn together. The mistaken creature saw them, and stalked towards the end of the barn into which they had fled. The girls doubled so adroitly that their pursuer was against the wall when the fugitives were already half way to the other end. By the time that his length would allow him to turn and follow them thither they had crossed over; thus the pursuit went on, the hot air from his nostrils blowing over them like a sirocco, and not a moment being attainable by Elizabeth or Lucetta in which to open the door. What might have happened had their situation continued cannot be said; but in a few moments a rattling of the door distracted their adversary's attention, and a man appeared. He ran forward towards the leading-staff, seized it, and wrenched the animal's head as if he would snap it off. The wrench was in reality so violent that the thick neck seemed to have lost its stiffness and to become half-paralysed, whilst the nose dropped blood. The premeditated human contrivance of the nose-ring was too cunning for impulsive brute force, and the creature flinched.

The man was seen in the partial gloom to be large-framed and unhesitating. He led the bull to the door, and the light revealed Henchard. He made the bull fast without, and re-entered to the succour of Lucetta; for he had not perceived Elizabeth, who had climbed onto the clover-heap. Lucetta was hysterical, and Henchard took her in his arms and carried her to the door.

'You – have saved me!' she cried, as soon as she could speak.

'I have returned your kindness,' he responded tenderly. 'You once saved me.'

'How – comes it to be you – you?' she asked, not heeding his reply.

'I came out here to look for you. I have been wanting to tell you something these two or three days; but you have been away, and I could not. Perhaps you cannot talk now?'

'Oh – no! Where is Elizabeth?'

'Here am I!' cried the missing one cheerfully; and without waiting for the ladder to be placed she slid down the face of the clover-stack to the floor.

Henchard supporting Lucetta on one side, and Elizabeth-Jane on the other, they went slowly along the rising road. They had reached the top and were descending again when Lucetta, now much recovered, recollected that she had dropped her muff in the barn.

'I'll run back,' said Elizabeth-Jane. 'I don't mind it at all, as I am not tired as you are.' She thereupon hastened down again to the barn, the others pursuing their way.

Elizabeth soon found the muff, such an article being by no means small at that time. Coming out she paused to look for a moment at the bull, now rather to be pitied with his bleeding nose, having perhaps rather intended a practical joke than a murder. Henchard had secured him by jamming the staff into the hinge of the barn-door, and wedging it there with a stake. At length she turned to hasten onward after her contemplation, when she saw a green-and-black gig approaching from the contrary direction, the vehicle being driven by Farfrae.

His presence here seemed to explain Lucetta's walk that way. Donald saw her, drew up, and was hastily made acquainted with what had occurred. At Elizabeth-Jane mentioning how greatly Lucetta had been jeopardized, he exhibited an agitation different in kind no less than in intensity from any she had seen in him before. He became so absorbed in the circumstances that he scarcely had sufficient knowledge of what he was doing to think of helping her up beside him.

'She has gone on with Mr Henchard, you say?' he inquired at last.

'Yes. He is taking her home. They are almost there by this time.'

'And you are sure she can get home?'

Elizabeth-Jane was quite sure.

'Your stepfather saved her?'

'Entirely.'

Farfrae checked his horse's pace; she guessed why. He was thinking that it would be best not to intrude on the other two just now. Henchard had saved Lucetta, and to provoke a possible exhibition of her deeper affection for himself was as ungenerous as it was unwise.

The immediate subject of their talk being exhausted she felt more embarrassed at sitting thus beside her past lover; but soon the two figures of the others were visible at the entrance to the town. The face of the woman was frequently turned back, but Farfrae did not whip on the horse. When these reached the town walls Henchard and his companion had disappeared down the street. Farfrae set down Elizabeth-Jane on her expressing a particular wish to alight there, and drove round to the stables at the back of his lodgings.

On this account he entered the house through his garden, and going up to his apartments found them in a particularly disturbed state, his boxes being hauled out upon the landing, and his bookcase standing in three pieces. These phenomena, however, seemed to cause him not the least surprise. 'When will everything be sent up?' he said to the mistress of the house, who was superintending.

'I am afraid not before eight, sir,' said she. 'You see we wasn't aware till this morning that you were going to move, or we could have been forwarder.'

'A – well, never mind, never mind!' said Farfrae cheerily. 'Eight o'clock will do well enough if it be not later. Now, don't ye be standing here talking, or it will be twelve, I doubt.' Thus speaking he went out by the front door and up the street.

During this interval Henchard and Lucetta had had experiences of a different kind. After Elizabeth's departure for the muff the corn-merchant opened himself frankly, holding her hand within his arm, though she would fain have withdrawn it. 'Dear Lucetta, I have been very, very anxious to see you these two or three days,' he said; 'ever since I saw you last! I have thought over the way I got your promise that night. You said to me, "If I were a man I should not insist." That cut me deep. I felt that there was some truth in it. I don't want to make you wretched; and to marry me just now would do that as nothing else could – it is but too plain. Therefore I agree to an indefinite engagement – to put off all thought of marriage for a year or two.'

'But – but – can I do nothing of a different kind?' said Lucetta. 'I am full of gratitude to you – you have saved my life. And your care of me is like coals of fire on my head! I am a monied person now. Surely I can do something in return for your goodness – something practical?'

Henchard remained in thought. He had evidently not expected this. 'There is one thing you might do, Lucetta,' he said. 'But not exactly of that kind.'

'Then of what kind is it?' she asked with renewed misgiving.

'I must tell you a secret to ask it. – You may have heard that I have been unlucky this year? I did what I have never done before – speculated rashly; and I lost. That's just put me in a strait.'

'And you would wish me to advance some money?'

'No, no!' said Henchard, almost in anger. 'I'm not the man to sponge on a woman, even though she may be so nearly my own as you. No, Lucetta; what you can do is this; and it would save me. My great creditor is Grower, and it is at his hands I shall suffer if at anybody's; while a fortnight's forbearance on his part would be enough to allow me to pull through. This may be got out of him in one way – that you would let it be known to him that you are my intended – that we are to be quietly married in the next fortnight. – Now stop, you haven't heard all! Let him have this story, without, of course, any prejudice to the fact that the actual engagement between us is to be a long one. Nobody else need know: you could go with me to Mr Grower and just let me speak to 'ee before him as if we were on such terms. We'll ask him to keep it secret. He will willingly wait then. At the fortnight's end I shall be able to face him; and I can coolly tell him all is postponed between us for a year or two. Not a soul in the town need know how you've helped me. Since you wish to be of use, there's your way.'

It being now what the people called the 'pinking in' of the day, that is the quarter-hour just before dusk, he did not at first observe the result of his own words upon her.

'If it were anything else,' she began, and the dryness of her lips was represented in her voice.

'But it is such a little thing!' he said, with a deep reproach. 'Less than you have offered – just the beginning of what you have so lately promised! I could have told him as much myself, but he would not have believed me.'

'It is not because I won't – it is because I absolutely can't,' she said, with rising distress.

'You are provoking!' he burst out. 'It is enough to make me force you to carry out at once what you have promised.'

'I cannot!' she insisted desperately.

'Why? When I have only within these few minutes released you from your promise to do the thing off-hand.'

'Because – he was a witness!'

'Witness? Of what?'

'If I must tell you –. Don't, don't upbraid me!'

'Well! Let's hear what you mean?'

'Witness of my marriage – Mr Grower was!'

'Marriage?'

'Yes. With Mr Farfrae. O Michael! I am already his wife. We were married this week at Port-Bredy. There were reasons against our doing it here. Mr Grower was a witness because he happened to be at Port-Bredy at the time.'

Henchard stood as if idiotized. She was so alarmed at his silence that she murmured something about lending him sufficient money to tide over the perilous fortnight.

'Married him?' said Henchard at length. 'My good – what, married him whilst – bound to marry me?'

'It was like this,' she explained, with tears in her eyes and quavers in her voice; 'don't – don't be cruel! I loved him so much, and I thought you might tell him of the past – and that grieved me! And then, when I had promised you, I learnt of the rumour that you had – sold your first wife at a fair like a horse or cow! How could I keep my promise after hearing that? I could not risk myself in your hands; it would have been letting myself down to take your name after such a scandal. But I knew I should lose Donald if I did not secure him at once – for you would carry out your threat of telling him of our former acquaintance, as long as there was a chance of keeping me for yourself by doing so. But you will not do so now, will you, Michael? for it is too late to separate us.'

The notes of St Peter's bells in full peal had been wafted to them while she spoke; and now the genial thumping of the town band, renowned for its unstinted use of the drum-stick, throbbed down the street.

'Then this racket they are making is on account of it, I suppose?' said he.

'Yes – I think he has told them, or else Mr Grower has . . . May I leave you now? My – he was detained at Port-Bredy today, and sent me on a few hours before him.'

'Then it is *his wife's* life I have saved this afternoon.'

'Yes – and he will be for ever grateful to you.'

'I am much obliged to him . . . O you false woman!' burst from Henchard. 'You promised me!'

'Yes, yes! But it was under compulsion, and I did not know all your past –'

'And now I've a mind to punish you as you deserve! One word to this bran-new husband of how you courted me, and your precious happiness is blown to atoms!'

'Michael – pity me, and be generous!'

'You don't deserve pity! You did; but you don't now.'

'I'll help you to pay off your debt.'

'A pensioner of Farfrae's wife – not I! Don't stay with me longer – I shall say something worse. Go home!'

She disappeared under the trees of the south walk as the band came round the corner, awaking the echoes of every stock and stone in celebration of her happiness. Lucetta took no heed, but ran up the back street and reached her own home unperceived.

* XXX *

FARFRAE'S words to his landlady had referred to the removal of his boxes and other effects from his late lodgings to Lucetta's house. The work was not heavy, but it had been much hindered on account of the frequent pauses necessitated by exclamations of surprise at the event, of which the good woman had been briefly informed by letter a few hours earlier.

At the last moment of leaving Port-Bredy, Farfrae, like John Gilpin, had been detained by important customers, whom, even in the exceptional circumstances, he was not the man to neglect. Moreover, there was a convenience in Lucetta arriving first at her house. Nobody there as yet knew what had happened; and she was best in a position to break the news to the inmates, and give directions for her husband's accommodation. He had, therefore, sent on his two-days' bride in a hired brougham, whilst he went across the country to a certain group of wheat and barley ricks a few miles off, telling her the hour at which he might be expected the same evening. This accounted for her trotting out to meet him after their separation of four hours.

By a strenuous effort, after leaving Henchard she calmed herself in readiness to receive Donald at High-Place Hall when he came on from his lodgings. One supreme fact empowered her to this, the sense that, come what would, she had secured him. Half-an-hour after her arrival he walked in, and she met him with a relieved gladness, which a month's perilous absence could not have intensified.

'There is one thing I have not done; and yet it is important,' she said earnestly, when she had finished talking about the adventure with the bull. 'That is, broken the news of our marriage to my dear Elizabeth-Jane.'

'Ah, and you have not?' he said thoughtfully. 'I gave her a lift from the barn homewards; but I did not tell her either; for I thought she might have heard of it in the town, and was keeping back her congratulations from shyness, and all that.'

'She can hardly have heard of it. But I'll find out; I'll go to her now. And, Donald, you don't mind her living on with me just the same as before? She is so quiet and unassuming.'

'O no, indeed I don't,' Farfrae answered with, perhaps, a faint awkwardness. 'But I wonder if she would care to?'

'O yes!' said Lucetta eagerly. 'I am sure she would like to. Besides, poor thing, she has no other home.'

Farfrae looked at her and saw that she did not suspect the secret of her more reserved friend. He liked her all the better for the blindness. 'Arrange as you like with her by all means,' he said. 'It is I who have come to your house, not you to mine.'

'I'll run and speak to her,' said Lucetta.

When she got upstairs to Elizabeth-Jane's room the latter had taken off her out-door things, and was resting over a book. Lucetta found in a moment that she had not yet learnt the news.

'I did not come down to you, Miss Templeman,' she said simply. 'I was coming to ask if you had quite recovered from your fright, but I found you had a visitor. What are the bells ringing for, I wonder? And the band, too, is playing. Somebody must be married; or else they are practising for Christmas.'

Lucetta uttered a vague 'Yes', and seating herself by the other young woman looked musingly at her. 'What a lonely creature you are,' she presently said; 'never knowing what's going on, or what people are talking about everywhere with keen interest. You should get out, and gossip about as other women do, and then you wouldn't be obliged to ask me a question of that kind. Well, now, I have something to tell you.'

Elizabeth-Jane said she was so glad, and made herself receptive.

'I must go rather a long way back,' said Lucetta, the difficulty of explaining herself satisfactorily to the pondering one beside her growing more apparent at each syllable. 'You remember that trying case of conscience I told you of some time ago – about the first lover and the second lover?' She let out in jerky phrases a leading word or two of the story she had told.

'O yes – I remember; the story of *your friend*,' said Elizabeth drily, regarding the irises of Lucetta's eyes as though to catch their exact shade. 'The two lovers – the old and the new: how she wanted to marry the second, but felt she ought to marry the first; so that she neglected the better course to follow the evil, like the poet Ovid I've just been construing: "Video meliora proboque, deteriora sequor." '

'Oh no; she didn't follow evil exactly!' said Lucetta hastily.

'But you said that she – or as I may say *you*' – answered Elizabeth, dropping the mask, 'were in honour and conscience bound to marry the first?'

Lucetta's blush at being seen through came and went again before she replied anxiously, 'You will never breathe this, will you, Elizabeth-Jane?'

'Certainly not, if you say not.'

'Then I will tell you that the case is more complicated – worse, in fact – than it seemed in my story. I and the first man were thrown together in a strange way, and felt that we ought to be united, as the world had talked of us. He was a widower, as he supposed. He had not heard of his first wife for many years. But the wife returned, and we parted. She is now dead; and the husband comes paying me addresses again, saying, "Now we'll complete our purpose." But, Elizabeth-Jane, all this amounts to a new courtship of me by him; I was absolved from all vows by the return of the other woman.'

'Have you not lately renewed your promise?' said the younger with quiet surmise. She had divined Man Number One.

'That was wrung from me by a threat.'

'Yes, it was. But I think when any one gets coupled up with a man in the past so unfortunately as you have done, she ought to become his wife if she can, even if she were not the sinning party.'

Lucetta's countenance lost its sparkle. 'He turned out to be a man I should be afraid to marry,' she pleaded. 'Really afraid! And it was not till after my renewed promise that I knew it.'

'Then there is only one course left to honesty. You must remain a single woman.'

'But think again! Do consider –'

'I am certain,' interrupted her companion hardily. 'I have guessed very well who the man is. My father; and I say it is him or nobody for you.'

Any suspicion of impropriety was to Elizabeth-Jane like a red rag to a bull. Her craving for correctness of procedure was, indeed, almost vicious. Owing to her early troubles with regard to her mother a semblance of irregularity had terrors for her which those whose names are safeguarded from suspicion know nothing of. 'You ought to marry Mr Henchard or nobody – certainly not another man!' she went on with a quivering lip in whose movement two passions shared.

'I don't admit that!' said Lucetta passionately.

'Admit it or not, it is true!'

Lucetta covered her eyes with her right hand, as if she could plead no more, holding out her left to Elizabeth-Jane.

'Why, you *have* married him!' cried the latter, jumping up with pleasure after a glance at Lucetta's fingers. 'When did you do it? Why did you not tell me, instead of teasing me like this? How very honourable of you! He did treat my mother badly once, it seems, in a moment of intoxication. And it is true that he is stern sometimes. But you will rule him entirely, I am sure, with your beauty and wealth and accomplishments. You are the woman he will adore, and we shall all three be happy together now!'

'O, my Elizabeth-Jane!' cried Lucetta distressfully. ''Tis somebody else that I have married! I was so desperate – so afraid of being forced to anything else – so afraid of revelations that would quench his love for me, that I resolved to do it off-hand, come what might, and purchase a week of happiness at any cost!'

'You – have – married Mr Farfrae!' cried Elizabeth-Jane, in Nathan tones.

Lucetta bowed. She had recovered herself.

'The bells are ringing on that account,' she said. 'My husband is downstairs. He will live here till a more suitable house is ready for us; and I have told him that I want you to stay with me just as before.'

'Let me think of it alone,' the girl quickly replied, corking up the turmoil of her feeling with grand control.

'You shall. I am sure we shall be happy together.'

Lucetta departed to join Donald below, a vague uneasiness floating over her joy at seeing him quite at home there. Not on account of her friend Elizabeth did she feel it: for of the bearings of Elizabeth-Jane's emotions she had not the least suspicion; but on Henchard's alone.

Now the instant decision of Susan Henchard's daughter was to dwell in that house no more. Apart from her estimate of the propriety of Lucetta's conduct, Farfrae had been so nearly her avowed lover that she felt she could not abide there.

It was still early in the evening when she hastily put on her things and went out. In a few minutes, knowing the ground, she had found a suitable lodging, and arranged to enter it that night. Returning and entering noiselessly she took off her pretty dress and arrayed herself in a plain one, packing up the other to keep as her best; for she would have to be very economical now. She wrote a note to leave for Lucetta, who was closely shut up in the drawing-room with Farfrae; and then Elizabeth-Jane called a man with a wheelbarrow; and seeing her boxes put into it she trotted off down the street to her rooms. They were in the street in which Henchard lived, and almost opposite his door.

Here she sat down and considered the means of subsistence. The little annual sum settled on her by her stepfather would keep body and soul together. A wonderful skill in netting of all sorts – acquired in childhood by making seines in Newson's home – might serve her in good stead; and her studies, which were pursued unremittingly, might serve her in still better.

By this time the marriage that had taken place was known throughout Casterbridge; had been discussed noisily on kerb-stones, confidentially behind counters, and jovially at the Three Mariners. Whether Farfrae would sell his business and set up for a gentleman on his wife's money, or whether he would show independence enough to stick to his trade in spite of his brilliant alliance, was a great point of interest.

XXXI

THE retort of the furmity-woman before the magistrates had spread; and in four-and-twenty hours there was not a person in Casterbridge who remained unacquainted with the story of Henchard's mad freak at Weydon-Priors Fair, long years before. The amends he had made in after life were lost sight of in the dramatic glare of the original act. Had the incident been well known of old and always, it might by this time have grown to be lightly regarded as the rather tall wild oat, but well-nigh the single one, of a young man with whom the steady and mature (if somewhat head-strong) burgher of today had scarcely a point in common. But the act having lain as dead and buried ever since, the interspace of years was unperceived; and the black spot of his youth wore the aspect of a recent crime.

Small as the police-court incident had been in itself, it formed the edge or turn in the incline of Henchard's fortunes. On that day – almost at that minute – he passed the ridge of prosperity and honour, and began to descend rapidly on the other side. It was strange how soon he sank in esteem. Socially he had received a startling fillip downwards; and, having already lost commercial buoyancy from rash transactions, the velocity of his descent in both aspects became accelerated every hour.

He now gazed more at the pavements and less at the house-fronts when he walked about; more at the feet and leggings of men, and less into the pupils of their eyes with the blazing regard which formerly had made them blink.

New events combined to undo him. It had been a bad year for others besides himself, and the heavy failure of a debtor whom he had trusted generously completed the overthrow of his tottering credit. And now, in his desperation, he failed to preserve that strict correspondence between bulk and sample which is the soul of commerce in grain. For this, one of his men was mainly to blame; that worthy, in his great unwisdom, having picked over the sample of an enormous quantity of second-rate corn which Henchard had in hand, and removed the pinched, blasted, and smutted grains in great numbers. The produce if honestly offered would have created no scandal; but the blunder of misrepresentation, coming at such a moment, dragged Henchard's name into the ditch.

The details of his failure were of the ordinary kind. One day Elizabeth-Jane was passing the King's Arms, when she saw people bustling in and out more than usual when there was no market. A bystander informed her, with some surprise at her ignorance, that it was a meeting of the Commissioners under Mr Henchard's bankruptcy. She felt quite tearful, and when she heard that he was present in the hotel she wished to go in and see him, but was advised not to intrude that day.

The room in which debtor and creditors had assembled was a front one, and Henchard, looking out of the window, had caught sight of

Elizabeth-Jane through the wire blind. His examination had closed, and the creditors were leaving. The appearance of Elizabeth threw him into a reverie; till turning his face from the window, and towering above all the rest, he called their attention for a moment more. His countenance had somewhat changed from its flush of prosperity; the black hair and whiskers were the same as ever, but a film of ash was over the rest.

'Gentlemen,' he said, 'over and above the assets that we've been talking about, and that appear on the balance-sheet, there be these. It all belongs to ye, as much as everything else I've got, and I don't wish to keep it from you, not I.' Saying this, he took his gold watch from his pocket and laid it on the table; then his purse – the yellow canvas money-bag, such as was carried by all farmers and dealers – untying it, and shaking the money out upon the table beside the watch. The latter he drew back quickly for an instant, to remove the hair-guard made and given him by Lucetta. 'There, now you have all I've got in the world,' he said. 'And I wish for your sakes 'twas more.'

The creditors, farmers almost to a man, looked at the watch, and at the money, and into the street; when Farmer James Everdene of Weatherbury spoke.

'No, no, Henchard,' he said warmly. 'We don't want that. 'Tis honourable in ye; but keep it. What do you say, neighbours – do ye agree?'

'Ay, sure: we don't wish it at all,' said Grower, another creditor.

'Let him keep it, of course,' murmured another in the background – a silent, reserved young man named Boldwood; and the rest responded unanimously.

'Well,' said the senior Commissioner, addressing Henchard, 'though the case is a desperate one, I am bound to admit that I have never met a debtor who behaved more fairly. I've proved the balance-sheet to be as honestly made out as it could possibly be; we have had no trouble; there have been no evasions and no concealments. The rashness of dealing which led to this unhappy situation is obvious enough; but as far as I can see every attempt has been made to avoid wronging anybody.'

Henchard was more affected by this than he cared to let them perceive, and he turned aside to the window again. A general murmur of agreement followed the Commissioner's words; and the meeting dispersed. When they were gone Henchard regarded the watch they had returned to him. ''Tisn't mine by rights,' he said to himself. 'Why the devil didn't they take it? – I don't want what don't belong to me!' Moved by a recollection he took the watch to the maker's just opposite, sold it there and then for what the tradesman offered, and went with the proceeds to one among the smaller of his creditors, a cottager of Durnover in straitened circumstances, to whom he handed the money.

When everything was ticketed that Henchard had owned, and the auctions were in progress, there was quite a sympathetic reaction in the town, which till then for some time past had done nothing but condemn him. Now that Henchard's whole career was pictured distinctly to his neighbours, and they could see how admirably he had used his one talent of energy to create a position of affluence out of absolutely nothing – which was really all he could show when he came to the town as a journeyman hay-trusser, with his wimble and knife in his basket – they wondered and regretted his fall.

Try as she might, Elizabeth could never meet with him. She believed in him still, though nobody else did; and she wanted to be allowed to forgive him for his roughness to her, and to help him in his trouble.

She wrote to him; he did not reply. She then went to his house – the great house she had lived in so happily for a time – with its front of dun brick, vitrified here and there, and its heavy sash-bars – but Henchard was to be found there no more. The ex-Mayor had left the house of his prosperity, and gone into Jopp's cottage by the Priory Mill – the sad purlieu to which he had wandered on the night of his discovery that she was not his daughter. Thither she went.

Elizabeth thought it odd that he had fixed on this spot to retire to, but assumed that necessity had no choice. Trees which seemed old enough to have been planted by the friars still stood around, and the back hatch of the original mill yet formed a cascade which had raised its terrific roar for centuries. The cottage itself was built of old stones from the long dismantled Priory, scraps of tracery, moulded window-jambs, and arch-labels, being mixed in with the rubble of the walls.

In this cottage he occupied a couple of rooms, Jopp, whom Henchard had employed, abused, cajoled, and dismissed by turns, being the householder. But even here her stepfather could not be seen.

'Not by his daughter?' pleaded Elizabeth.

'By nobody – at present: that's his order,' she was informed.

Afterwards she was passing by the corn-stores and hay-barns which had been the headquarters of his business. She knew that he ruled there no longer; but it was with amazement that she regarded the familiar gateway. A smear of decisive lead-coloured paint had been laid on to obliterate Henchard's name, though its letters dimly loomed through like ships in a fog. Over these, in fresh white, spread the name of Farfrae.

Abel Whittle was edging his skeleton in at the wicket, and she said, 'Mr Farfrae is master here?'

'Yaas, Miss Henchet,' he said, 'Mr Farfrae have bought the concern and all of we work-folk with it; and 'tis better for us than 'twas – though I shouldn't say that to you as a daughter-law. We work harder, but we bain't made afeard now. It was fear made my few poor hairs so thin! No busting out, no slamming of doors, no meddling with yer eternal soul and all that; and though 'tis a shilling a week less I'm the richer man; for what's all the world if yer mind is always in a larry, Miss Henchet?'

The intelligence was in a general sense true; and Henchard's stores, which had remained in a paralysed condition during the settlement of his bankruptcy, were stirred into activity again when the new tenant had possession. Thenceforward the full sacks, looped with the shining chain, went scurrying up and down under the cathead, hairy arms were thrust out from the different door-ways, and the grain was hauled in; trusses of hay were tossed anew in and out of the barns, and the wimbles creaked; while the scales and steel-yards began to be busy where guess-work had formerly been the rule.

* XXXII *

Two bridges stood near the lower part of Casterbridge town. The first, of weather-stained brick, was immediately at the end of High Street, where a diverging branch from that thoroughfare ran round to the low-lying Durnover Lanes; so that the precincts of the bridge formed the merging point of respectability and indigence. The second bridge, of stone, was further out on the highway – in fact, fairly in the meadows, though still within the town boundary.

These bridges had speaking countenances. Every projection in each was worn down to obtuseness partly by weather, more by friction from generations of loungers, whose toes and heels had from year to year made restless movements against these parapets, as they had stood there meditating on the aspect of affairs. In the case of the more friable bricks and stones even the flat faces were worn into hollows by the same mixed mechanism. The masonry of the top was clamped with iron at each joint; since it had been no uncommon thing for desperate men to wrench the coping off and throw it down the river, in reckless defiance of the magistrates.

For to this pair of bridges gravitated all the failures of the town; those who had failed in business, in love, in sobriety, in crime. Why the unhappy hereabout usually chose the bridges for their meditations in preference to a railing, a gate, or a stile, was not so clear.

There was a marked difference of quality between the personages who haunted the near bridge of brick and the personages who haunted the far one of stone. Those of lowest character preferred the former, adjoining the town; they did not mind the glare of the public eye. They had been of comparatively no account during their successes; and, though they might feel dispirited, they had no particular sense of shame in their ruin. Their hands were mostly kept in their pockets; they wore a leather strap round their hips or knees, and boots that required a great deal of lacing, but seemed never to get any. Instead of sighing at their adversities they spat, and instead of saying the iron had entered into their souls they said they were down on their luck. Jopp in his times of distress had often stood here; so had Mother Cuxsom, Christopher Coney, and poor Abel Whittle.

The *misérables* who would pause on the remoter bridge were of a politer stamp. They included bankrupts, hypochondriacs, persons who were what is called 'out of a situation' from fault or lucklessness, the inefficient of the professional class – shabby-genteel men, who did not know how to get rid of the weary time between breakfast and dinner, and the yet more weary time between dinner and dark. The eyes of this species were mostly directed over the parapet upon the running water below. A man seen there looking thus fixedly into the river was pretty sure to be one whom the world did not treat kindly for some reason or other. While one in straits on the townward bridge did not mind who saw him so, and kept his back to the parapet to survey the passers-by, one in straits on this never faced the road, never turned his head at coming footsteps, but, sensitive to his own condition, watched the current whenever a stranger approached, as if some strange fish interested him, though every finned thing had been poached out of the river years before.

There and thus they would muse; if their grief were the grief of oppression they would wish themselves kings; if their grief were poverty, wish themselves millionaires; if sin, they would wish they were saints or angels; if despised love, that they were some much-courted Adonis of county fame. Some had been known to stand and think so long with this fixed gaze downward that eventually they had allowed their poor carcases to follow that gaze; and they were discovered the next morning out of reach of their troubles, either here or in the deep pool called Blackwater, a little higher up the river.

To this bridge came Henchard, as other unfortunates had come before him, his way thither being by the riverside path on the chilly edge of the town. Here he was standing one windy afternoon when Durnover church clock struck five. While the gusts were bringing the notes to his ears across the damp intervening flat a man passed behind him and greeted Henchard by name. Henchard turned slightly and saw that the comer was Jopp, his old foreman, now employed elsewhere, to whom, though he hated him, he had gone for lodgings because Jopp was the one man in Casterbridge whose observation and opinion the fallen corn-merchant despised to the point of indifference.

Henchard returned him a scarcely perceptible nod, and Jopp stopped.

'He and she are gone into their new house today,' said Jopp.

'Oh,' said Henchard absently. 'Which house is that?'

'Your old one.'

'Gone into my house?' And starting up Henchard added, '*My* house of all others in the town!'

'Well, as somebody was sure to live there, and you couldn't, it can do 'ee no harm that he's the man.'

It was quite true: he felt that it was doing him no harm. Farfrae, who had already taken the yards and stores, had acquired possession of the house for the obvious convenience of its contiguity. And yet this act of his taking up residence within those roomy chambers while he, their former tenant, lived in a cottage, galled Henchard indescribably.

Jopp continued: 'And you heard of that fellow who bought all the best furniture at your sale? He was bidding for no other than Farfrae all the while! It has never been moved out of the house, as he'd already got the lease.'

'My furniture too! Surely he'll buy my body and soul like-wise!'

'There's no saying he won't, if you be willing to sell.' And having planted these wounds in the heart of his once imperious master Jopp went on his way; while Henchard stared and stared into the racing river till the bridge seemed moving backward with him.

The low land grew blacker, and the sky a deeper grey. When the landscape looked like a picture blotted in with ink, another traveller approached the great stone bridge. He was driving a gig, his direction being also townwards. On the round of the middle of the arch the gig stopped. 'Mr Henchard?' came from it in the voice of Farfrae. Henchard turned his face.

Finding that he had guessed rightly Farfrae told the man who accompanied him to drive home; while he alighted and went up to his former friend.

'I have heard that you think of emigrating, Mr Henchard,' he said. 'Is it true? I have a real reason for asking.'

Henchard withheld his answer for several instants, and then said, 'Yes; it is true. I am going where you were going to a few years ago, when I prevented you and got you to bide here. 'Tis turn and turn about, isn't it! Do ye mind how we stood like this in the Chalk Walk when I persuaded 'ee to stay? You then stood without a chattel to your name, and I was the master of the house in Corn Street. But now I stand without a stick or a rag, and the master of that house is you.'

'Yes, yes; that's so! It's the way o' the warrld,' said Farfrae.

'Ha, ha, true!' cried Henchard, throwing himself into a mood of jocularity. 'Up and down! I'm used to it. What's the odds after all!'

'Now listen to me, if it's no taking up your time,' said Farfrae, 'just as I listened to you. Don't go. Stay at home.'

'But I can do nothing else, man!' said Henchard scornfully. 'The little money I have will just keep body and soul together for a few weeks, and no more. I have not felt inclined to go back to journeywork yet; but I can't stay doing nothing, and my best chance is elsewhere.'

'No; but what I propose is this – if ye will listen. Come and live in your old house. We can spare some rooms very well – I am sure my wife would not mind it at all – until there's an opening for ye.'

Henchard started. Probably the picture drawn by the unsuspecting Donald of himself under the same roof with Lucetta was too striking to be received with equanimity. 'No, no,' he said gruffly; 'we should quarrel.'

'You should hae a part to yourself,' said Farfrae; 'and nobody to interfere wi' you. It will be a deal healthier than down there by the river where you live now.'

Still Henchard refused. 'You don't know what you ask,' he said. 'However, I can do no less than thank 'ee.'

They walked into the town together side by side, as they had done when Henchard persuaded the young Scotchman to remain. 'Will you come in and have some supper?' said Farfrae when they reached the middle of the town, where their paths diverged right and left.

'No, no.'

'Bye-the-bye, I had nearly forgot. I bought a good deal of your furniture.'

'So I have heard.'

'Well, it was no that I wanted it so very much for myself; but I wish ye to pick out all that you care to have – such things as may be endeared to ye by associations, or particularly suited to your use. And take them to your own house – it will not be depriving me; we can do with less very well, and I will have plenty of opportunities of getting more.'

'What – give it to me for nothing?' said Henchard. 'But you paid the creditors for it!'

'Ah, yes; but maybe it's worth more to you than it is to me.'

Henchard was a little moved. 'I – sometimes think I've wronged 'ee!' he said, in tones which showed the disquietude that the night shades hid in his face. He shook Farfrae abruptly by the hand, and hastened away as if unwilling to betray himself further. Farfrae saw him turn through the thoroughfare into Bull Stake and vanish down towards the Priory Mill.

Meanwhile Elizabeth-Jane, in an upper room no larger than the Prophet's chamber, and with the silk attire of her palmy days packed away in a box, was netting with great industry between the hours which she devoted to studying such books as she could get hold of.

Her lodgings being nearly opposite her stepfather's former residence, now Farfrae's, she could see Donald and Lucetta speeding in and out of their door with all the bounding enthusiasm of their situation. She avoided looking that way as much as possible, but it was hardly in human nature to keep the eyes averted when the door slammed.

While living on thus quietly she heard the news that Henchard had caught cold and was confined to his room – possibly a result of standing about the meads in damp weather. She went off to his house at once. This time she was determined not to be denied admittance, and made her way upstairs. He was sitting up in the bed with a greatcoat round him, and at first resented her intrusion. 'Go away – go away,' he said. 'I don't like to see 'ee!'

'But, father –'

'I don't like to see 'ee,' he repeated.

However, the ice was broken, and she remained. She made the room more comfortable, gave directions to the people below, and by the time she went away had reconciled her stepfather to her visiting him.

The effect, either of her ministrations or of her mere presence, was a rapid recovery. He soon was well enough to go out; and now things seemed to wear a new colour in his eyes. He no longer thought of emigration, and thought more of Elizabeth. The having nothing to do made him more dreary than any other circumstance; and one day, with better views of Farfrae than he had held for some time, and a sense that honest work was not a thing to be ashamed of, he stoically went down to Farfrae's yard and asked to be taken on as a journeyman hay-trusser. He was engaged at once. This hiring of Henchard was done through a foreman, Farfrae feeling that it was undesirable to come personally in contact with the ex-corn-factor more than was absolutely necessary. While anxious to help him he was well aware by this time of his uncertain temper, and thought reserved relations best. For the same reason his orders to Henchard to proceed to this and that country farm trussing in the usual way were always given through a third person.

For a time these arrangements worked well, it being the custom to truss in the respective stack-yards, before bringing it away, the hay bought at the different farms about the neighbourhood; so that Henchard was often absent at such places the whole week long. When this was all done, and Henchard had become in a measure broken in, he came to work daily on the home premises like the rest. And thus the once flourishing merchant and Mayor and what not stood as a day-labourer in the barns and granaries he formerly had owned.

'I have worked as a journeyman before now, ha'n't I?' he would say in his defiant way; 'and why shouldn't I do it again?' But he looked a far different journeyman from the one he had been in his earlier days. Then he had worn clean, suitable clothes, light and cheerful in hue; leggings yellow as marigolds, corduroys immaculate as new flax, and a neckerchief like a flower-garden. Now he wore the remains of an old blue cloth suit of his gentlemanly times, a rusty silk hat, and a once black satin stock, soiled and shabby. Clad thus he went to and fro, still comparatively an active man – for he was not much over forty – and saw with the other men in the yard Donald Farfrae going in and out of the green door that led to the garden, and the big house, and Lucetta.

At the beginning of the winter it was rumoured about Casterbridge that Mr Farfrae, already in the Town Council, was to be proposed for Mayor in a year or two.

'Yes; she was wise, she was wise in her generation!' said Henchard to himself when he heard of this one day on his way to Farfrae's hay-barn. He thought it over as he wimbled his bonds, and the piece of news acted as a reviviscent breath to that old view of his – of Donald Farfrae as his triumphant rival who rode rough-shod over him.

'A fellow of his age going to be mayor, indeed!' he murmured with a corner-drawn smile on his mouth. 'But 'tis her money that floats en upward. Ha-ha – how cust odd it is! Here be I, his former master, working for him as man, and he the man standing as master, with my house and my furniture and my what-you-may-call wife all his own.'

He repeated these things a hundred times a day. During the whole period of his acquaintance with Lucetta he had never wished to claim her as his own so desperately as he now regretted her loss. It was no mercenary hankering after her fortune that moved him; though that fortune had been the means of making her so much the more desired by giving her the air of independence and sauciness which attracts men of his composition. It had given her servants, house, and fine clothing – a setting that invested Lucetta with a startling novelty in the eyes of him who had known her in her narrow days.

He accordingly lapsed into moodiness, and at every allusion to the possibility of Farfrae's near election to the municipal chair his former hatred of the Scotchman returned. Concurrently with this he underwent a moral change. It resulted in his significantly saying every now and then, in tones of recklessness, 'Only a fortnight more!' – 'Only a dozen days!' and so forth, lessening his figures day by day.

'Why d'ye say only a dozen days?' asked Solomon Longways as he worked beside Henchard in the granary weighing oats.

'Because in twelve days I shall be released from my oath.'

'What oath?'

'The oath to drink no spirituous liquid. In twelve days it will be twenty-one years since I swore it, and then I mean to enjoy myself, please God!'

Elizabeth-Jane sat at her window one Sunday, and while there she heard in the street below a conversation which introduced Henchard's name. She was wondering what was the matter, when a third person who was passing by asked the question in her mind.

'Michael Henchard have busted out drinking after taking nothing for twenty-one years!'

Elizabeth-Jane jumped up, put on her things, and went out.

* XXXIII *

AT this date there prevailed in Casterbridge a convivial custom – scarcely recognized as such, yet none the less established. On the afternoon of every Sunday a large contingent of the Casterbridge journeymen – steady church-goers and sedate characters – having attended service, filed from the church doors across the way to the Three Mariners inn. The rear was usually brought up by the choir, with their bass-viols, fiddles, and flutes under their arms.

The great point, the point of honour, on these sacred occasions was for each man to strictly limit himself to half-a-pint of liquor. This scrupulosity was so well understood by the landlord that the whole company was served in cups of that measure. They were all exactly alike – straight-sided, with two leafless lime-trees done in eel-brown on the sides – one towards the drinker's lips, the other confronting his comrade. To wonder how many of these cups the landlord possessed altogether was a favourite exercise of children in the marvellous. Forty at least might have been seen at these times in the large room, forming a ring round the margin of the great sixteen-legged oak table, like the monolithic circle at Stonehenge in its pristine days. Outside and above the forty cups came a circle of forty smoke-jets from forty clay pipes; outside the pipes the countenances of the forty church-goers, supported at the back by a circle of forty chairs.

The conversation was not the conversation of weekdays, but a thing altogether finer in point and higher in tone. They invariably discussed the sermon, dissecting it, weighing it, as above or below the average – the general tendency being to regard it as a scientific feat or performance which had no relation to their own lives, except as between critics and the thing criticized. The bass-viol player and the clerk usually spoke with more authority than the rest on account of their official connection with the preacher.

Now the Three Mariners was the inn chosen by Henchard as the place for closing his long term of dramless years. He had so timed his entry as to be well established in the large room by the time the forty church-goers entered to their customary cups. The flush upon his face proclaimed at once that the vow of twenty-one years had lapsed, and the era of recklessness begun anew. He was seated on a small table, drawn up to the side of the massive oak reserved for the churchmen, a few of whom nodded to him as they took their places and said, 'How be ye, Mr Henchard? Quite a stranger here.'

Henchard did not take the trouble to reply for a few moments, and his eyes rested on his stretched-out legs and boots. 'Yes,' he said at length; 'that's true. I've been down in spirit for weeks; some of ye know the cause. I am better now; but not quite serene. I want you fellows of the choir to strike up a tune; and what with that and this brew of Stannidge's, I am in hopes of getting altogether out of my minor key.'

'With all my heart,' said the first fiddle. 'We've let back our strings, that's true; but we can soon pull 'em up again. Sound A, neighbours, and give the man a stave.'

'I don't care a curse what the words be,' said Henchard. 'Hymns, ballets, or rantipole rubbish; the Rogue's March or the cherubim's warble – 'tis all the same to me if 'tis good harmony, and well put out.'

'Well – heh, heh – it may be we can do that, and not a man among us that have sat in the gallery less than twenty year,' said the leader of the band. 'As 'tis Sunday, neighbours, suppose we raise the Fourth Psa'm, to Samuel Wakely's tune, as improved by me?'

'Hang Samuel Wakely's tune, as improved by thee!' said Henchard. 'Chuck across one of your psalters – old Wiltshire is the only tune worth singing – the psalm-tune that would make my blood ebb and flow like the sea when I was a steady chap. I'll find some words to fit en.' He took one of the psalters and began turning over the leaves.

Chancing to look out of the window at that moment he saw a flock of people passing by, and perceived them to be the congregation of the upper church, now just dismissed, their sermon having been a longer one than that the lower parish was favoured with. Among the rest of the leading inhabitants walked Mr Councillor Farfrae with Lucetta upon his arm, the observed and imitated of all the smaller tradesmen's woman-kind. Henchard's mouth changed a little, and he continued to turn over the leaves.

'Now then,' he said, 'Psalm the Hundred-and-Ninth, to the tune of Wiltshire: verses ten to fifteen. I gi'e ye the words:

'His seed shall orphans be, his wife
    A widow plunged in grief;
His vagrant children beg their bread
    Where none can give relief.

'His ill-got riches shall be made
    To usurers a prey;
The fruit of all his toil shall be
    By strangers borne away.

'None shall be found that to his wants
    Their mercy will extend,
Or to his helpless orphan seed
    The least assistance lend.

'A swift destruction soon shall seize
    On his unhappy race;
And the next age his hated name
    Shall utterly deface.'

'I know the Psa'am – I know the Psa'am!' said the leader hastily; 'but I would as lief not sing it. 'Twasn't made for singing. We chose it once when the gipsy stole the pa'son's mare, thinking to please him, but pa'son was quite upset. Whatever Servant David were thinking about when he made a Psalm that nobody can sing without disgracing himself, I can't fathom! Now then, the Fourth Psalm, to Samuel Wakely's tune, as improved by me.'

''Od seize your sauce – I tell ye to sing the Hundred-and-Ninth to Wiltshire, and sing it you shall!' roared Henchard. 'Not a single one of all the droning crew of ye goes out of this room till that Psalm is sung!' He slipped off the table, seized the poker, and going to the door placed his back against it. 'Now then, go ahead, if you don't wish to have your cust pates broke!'

'Don't 'ee, don't 'ee take on so! – As 'tis the Sabbath-day, and 'tis Servant David's words and not ours, perhaps we don't mind for once, hey?' said one of the terrified choir, looking round upon the rest. So the instruments were turned and the comminatory verses sung.

'Thank ye, thank ye,' said Henchard in a softened voice, his eyes growing downcast, and his manner that of a man much moved by the strains. 'Don't you blame David,' he went on in low tones, shaking his head without raising his eyes. 'He knew what he was about when he wrote that! . . . If I could afford it, be hanged if I wouldn't keep a church choir at my own expense to play and sing to me at these low, dark times of my life. But the bitter thing is, that when I was rich I didn't need what I could have, and now I be poor I can't have what I need!'

While they paused, Lucetta and Farfrae passed again, this time homeward, it being their custom to take, like others, a short walk out on the highway and back, between church and tea-time. 'There's the man we've been singing about,' said Henchard.

The players and singers turned their heads and saw his meaning. 'Heaven forbid!' said the bass-player.

''Tis the man,' repeated Henchard doggedly.

'Then if I'd known,' said the performer on the clarionet solemnly, 'that 'twas meant for a living man, nothing should have drawn out of my wynd-pipe the breath for that Psalm, so help me!'

'Nor from mine,' said the first singer. 'But, thought I, as it was made so long ago perhaps there isn't much in it, so I'll oblige a neighbour; for there's nothing to be said against the tune.'

'Ah, my boys, you've sung it,' said Henchard triumphantly. 'As for him, it was partly by his songs that he got over me, and heaved me out . . . I could double him up like that – and yet I don't.' He laid the poker across his knee, bent it as if it were a twig, flung it down, and came away from the door.

It was at this time that Elizabeth-Jane, having heard where her stepfather was, entered the room with a pale and agonized countenance. The choir and the rest of the company moved off, in accordance with their half-pint regulation. Elizabeth-Jane went up to Henchard, and entreated him to accompany her home.

By this hour the volcanic fires of his nature had burnt down, and having drunk no great quantity as yet he was inclined to acquiesce. She took his arm, and together they went on. Henchard walked blankly, like a blind man, repeating to himself the last words of the singers –

'And the next age his hated name
Shall utterly deface.'

At length he said to her, 'I am a man to my word. I have kept my oath for twenty-one years; and now I can drink with a good conscience . . . If I don't do for him – well, I am a fearful practical joker when I choose! He has taken away everything from me, and by heavens, if I meet him I won't answer for my deeds!'

These half-uttered words alarmed Elizabeth – all the more by reason of the still determination of Henchard's mien.

'What will you do?' she asked cautiously, while trembling with disquietude, and guessing Henchard's allusion only too well.

Henchard did not answer, and they went on till they had reached his cottage. 'May I come in?' she said.

'No, no; not today,' said Henchard; and she went away; feeling that to caution Farfrae was almost her duty, as it was certainly her strong desire.

As on the Sunday, so on the week-days, Farfrae and Lucetta might have been seen flitting about the town like two butterflies – or rather like a bee and a butterfly in league for life. She seemed to take no pleasure in going anywhere except in her husband's company; and hence when business would not permit him to waste an afternoon she remained indoors waiting for the time to pass till his return, her face being visible to Elizabeth-Jane from her window aloft. The latter, however, did not say to herself that Farfrae should be thankful for such devotion, but, full of her reading, she cited Rosalind's exclamation: 'Mistress, know yourself; down on your knees and thank Heaven fasting for a good man's love.'

She kept her eye upon Henchard also. One day he answered her inquiry for his health by saying that he could not endure Abel Whittle's pitying eyes upon him while they worked together in the yard. 'He is such a fool,' said Henchard, 'that he can never get out of his mind the time when I was master there.'

'I'll come and wimble for you instead of him, if you will allow me,' said she. Her motive on going to the yard was to get an opportunity of observing the general position of affairs on Farfrae's premises now that her stepfather was a workman there. Henchard's threats had alarmed her so much that she wished to see his behaviour when the two were face to face.

For two or three days after her arrival Donald did not make any appearance. Then one afternoon the green door opened, and through came, first Farfrae, and at his heels Lucetta. Donald brought his wife forward without hesitation, it being obvious that he had no suspicion whatever of any antecedents in common between her and the now journeyman hay-trusser.

Henchard did not turn his eyes towards either of the pair, keeping them fixed on the bond he twisted, as if that alone absorbed him. A feeling of delicacy, which ever prompted Farfrae to avoid anything that might seem like triumphing over a fallen rival, led him to keep away from the hay-barn where Henchard and his daughter were working, and to go on to the corn department. Meanwhile Lucetta, never having been informed that Henchard had entered her husband's service, rambled straight on to the barn, where she came suddenly upon Henchard, and gave vent to a little 'Oh!' which the happy and busy Donald was too far off to hear. Henchard, with withering humility of demeanour, touched the brim of his hat to her as Whittle and the rest had done, to which she breathed a dead-alive 'Good afternoon'.

'I beg your pardon, ma'am?' said Henchard, as if he had not heard.

'I said good afternoon,' she faltered.

'O yes, good afternoon, ma'am,' he replied, touching his hat again. 'I am glad to see you, ma'am.' Lucetta looked embarrassed, and Henchard continued: 'For we humble workmen here feel it a great honour that a lady should look in and take an interest in us.'

She glanced at him entreatingly; the sarcasm was too bitter, too unendurable.

'Can you tell me the time, ma'am?' he asked.

'Yes,' she said hastily; 'half-past four.'

'Thank 'ee. An hour and a half longer before we are released from work. Ah, ma'am, we of the lower classes know nothing of the gay leisure that such as you enjoy!'

As soon as she could do so Lucetta left him, nodded and smiled to Elizabeth-Jane, and joined her husband at the other end of the enclosure, where she could be seen leading him away by the outer gates, so as to avoid passing Henchard again. That she had been taken by surprise was obvious. The result of this casual rencounter was that the next morning a note was put into Henchard's hand by the postman.

'Will you,' said Lucetta, with as much bitterness as she could put into a small communication, 'will you kindly undertake not to speak to me in the biting undertones you used today, if I walk through the yard at any time? I bear you no ill-will, and I am only too glad that you should have employment of my dear husband; but in common fairness treat me as his wife, and do not try to make me wretched by covert sneers. I have committed no crime, and done you no injury.'

'Poor fool!' said Henchard with fond savagery, holding out the note. 'To know no better than commit herself in writing like this! Why, if I were to show that to her dear husband – pooh!' He threw the letter into the fire.

Lucetta took care not to come again among the hay and corn. She would rather have died than run the risk of encountering Henchard at such close quarters a second time. The gulf between them was growing wider every day. Farfrae was always considerate to his fallen acquaintance; but it was impossible that he should not, by degrees, cease to regard the ex-corn-merchant as more than one of his other workmen. Henchard saw this, and concealed his feelings under a cover of stolidity, fortifying his heart by drinking more freely at the Three Mariners every evening.

Often did Elizabeth-Jane, in her endeavours to prevent his taking other liquor, carry tea to him in a little basket at five o'clock. Arriving one day on this errand she found her stepfather was measuring up clover-seed and rape-seed in the corn-stores on the top floor, and she ascended to him. Each floor had a door opening into the air under a cat-head, from which a chain dangled for hoisting the sacks.

When Elizabeth's head rose through the trap she perceived that the upper door was open, and that her stepfather and Farfrae stood just within it in conversation, Farfrae being nearest the dizzy edge, and Henchard a little way behind. Not to interrupt them she remained on the steps without raising her head any higher. While waiting thus she saw – or fancied she saw, for she had a terror of feeling certain – her stepfather slowly raise his hand to a level behind Farfrae's shoulders, a curious expression taking possession of his face. The young man was quite unconscious of the action, which was so indirect that, if Farfrae had observed it, he might almost have regarded it as an idle outstretching of the arm. But it would have been possible, by a comparatively light touch, to push Farfrae off his balance, and send him head over heels into the air.

Elizabeth felt quite sick at heart on thinking of what this *might* have meant. As soon as they turned she mechanically took the tea to Henchard, left it, and went away. Reflecting, she endeavoured to assure herself that the movement was an idle eccentricity, and no more. Yet, on the other hand, his subordinate position in an establishment where he once had been master might be acting on him like an irritant poison; and she finally resolved to caution Donald.

* XXXIV *

NEXT morning, accordingly, she rose at five o'clock and went into the street. It was not yet light; a dense fog prevailed, and the town was as silent as it was dark, except that from the rectangular avenues which framed in the borough there came a chorus of tiny rappings, caused by the fall of water-drops condensed on the boughs; now it was wafted from the West Walk, now from the South Walk; and then from both quarters simultaneously. She moved on to the bottom of Corn Street, and, knowing his time well, waited only a few minutes before she heard the familiar bang of his door, and then his quick walk towards her. She met him at the point where the last tree of the engirding avenue flanked the last house in the street.

He could hardly discern her till, glancing inquiringly, he said, 'What – Miss Henchard – and are ye up so airly?'

She asked him to pardon her for waylaying him at such an unseemly time. 'But I am anxious to mention something,' she said. 'And I wished not to alarm Mrs Farfrae by calling.'

'Yes?' said he, with the cheeriness of a superior. 'And what may it be? It's very kind of ye, I'm sure.'

She now felt the difficulty of conveying to his mind the exact aspect of possibilities in her own. But she somehow began, and introduced Henchard's name, 'I sometimes fear,' she said with an effort, 'that he may be betrayed into some attempt to – insult you, sir.'

'But we are the best of friends?'

'Or to play some practical joke upon you, sir. Remember that he has been hardly used.'

'But we are quite friendly?'

'Or to do something – that would injure you – hurt you – wound you.' Every word cost her twice its length of pain. And she could see that Farfrae was still incredulous. Henchard, a poor man in his employ, was not to Farfrae's view the Henchard who had ruled him. Yet he was not only the same man, but that man with his sinister qualities, formerly latent, quickened into life by his buffetings.

Farfrae, happy, and thinking no evil, persisted in making light of her fears. Thus they parted, and she went homeward, journeymen now being in the street, waggoners going to the harness-makers for articles left to be repaired, farm-horses going to the shoeing-smiths, and the sons of labour showing themselves generally on the move. Elizabeth entered her lodging unhappily, thinking she had done no good, and only made herself appear foolish by her weak note of warning.

But Donald Farfrae was one of those men upon whom an incident is never absolutely lost. He revised impressions from a subsequent point of view, and the impulsive judgement of the moment was not always his permanent one. The vision of Elizabeth's earnest face in the rimy dawn came back to him several times during the day. Knowing the solidity of her character he did not treat her hints altogether as idle sounds.

But he did not desist from a kindly scheme on Henchard's account that engaged him just then; and when he met Lawyer Joyce, the town-clerk, later in the day, he spoke of it as if nothing had occurred to damp it.

'About that little seedsman's shop,' he said; 'the shop overlooking the churchyard, which is to let. It is not for myself I want it, but for our unlucky fellow-townsman Henchard. It would be a new beginning for him, if a small one; and I have told the Council that I would head a private subscription among them to set him up in it – that I would be fifty pounds, if they would make up the other fifty among them.'

'Yes, yes; so I've heard; and there's nothing to say against it for that matter,' the town-clerk replied, in his plain, frank way. 'But, Farfrae, others see what you don't. Henchard hates 'ee – ay, hates 'ee; and 'tis right that you should know it. To my knowledge he was at the Three Mariners last night, saying in public that about you which a man ought not to say about another.'

'Is that so – ah, is that so?' said Farfrae, looking down. 'Why should he do it?' added the young man bitterly; 'what harm have I done him that he should try to wrong me?'

'God only knows,' said Joyce, lifting his eyebrows. 'It shows much long-suffering in you to put up with him, and keep him in your employ.'

'But I cannet discharge a man who was once a good friend to me? How can I forget that when I came here 'twas he enabled me to make a footing for mysel'? No, no. As long as I've a day's wark to offer he shall do it if he chooses. 'Tis not I who will deny him such a little as that. But I'll drop the idea of establishing him in a shop till I can think more about it.'

It grieved Farfrae much to give up this scheme. But a damp having been thrown over it by these and other voices in the air, he went and countermanded his orders. The then occupier of the shop was in it when Farfrae spoke to him, and feeling it necessary to give some explanation of his withdrawal from the negotiation Donald mentioned Henchard's name, and stated that the intentions of the Council had been changed.

The occupier was much disappointed, and straightaway informed Henchard, as soon as he saw him, that a scheme of the Council for setting him up in a shop had been knocked on the head by Farfrae. And thus out of error enmity grew.

When Farfrae got indoors that evening the tea-kettle was singing on the high hob of the semi-egg-shaped grate. Lucetta, light as a sylph, ran forward and seized his hands, whereupon Farfrae duly kissed her.

'Oh!' she cried playfully, turning to the window. 'See – the blinds are not drawn down, and the people can look in – what a scandal!'

When the candles were lighted, the curtains drawn, and the twain sat at tea, she noticed that he looked serious. Without directly inquiring why she let her eyes linger solicitously on his face.

'Who has called?' he absently asked. 'Any folk for me?'

'No,' said Lucetta. 'What's the matter, Donald?'

'Well – nothing worth talking of,' he responded sadly.

'Then, never mind it. You will get through it. Scotchmen are always lucky.'

'No – not always!' he said, shaking his head gloomily as he contemplated a crumb on the table. 'I know many who have not been so! There was Sandy Macfarlane, who started to America to try his fortune, and he was drowned; and Archibald Leith, he was murdered! And poor Willie Dunbleeze and Maitland Macfreeze – they fell into bad courses, and went the way of all such!'

'Why – you old goosey – I was only speaking in a general sense, of course! You are always so literal. Now when we have finished tea, sing me that funny song about high-heeled shoon and siller tags, and the one-and-forty wooers.'

'No, no. I couldna sing tonight! It's Henchard – he hates me; so that I may not be his friend if I would. I would understand why there should be a wee bit envy; but I cannet see a reason for the whole intensity of what he feels. Now, can you, Lucetta? It is more like old-fashioned rivalry in love than just a bit of rivalry in trade.'

Lucetta had grown somewhat wan. 'No,' she replied.

'I give him employment – I cannet refuse it. But neither can I blind myself to the fact that with a man of passions such as his, there is no safeguard for conduct!'

'What have you heard – O Donald, dearest?' said Lucetta in alarm. The words on her lips were 'anything about me?' – but she did not utter them. She could not, however, suppress her agitation, and her eyes filled with tears.

'No, no – it is not so serious as ye fancy,' declared Farfrae soothingly; though he did not know its seriousness so well as she.

'I wish you would do what we have talked of,' mournfully remarked Lucetta. 'Give up business, and go away from here. We have plenty of money, and why should we stay?'

Farfrae seemed seriously disposed to discuss this move, and they talked thereon till a visitor was announced. Their neighbour Alderman Vatt came in.

'You've heard, I suppose, of poor Doctor Chalkfield's death? Yes – died this afternoon at five,' said Mr Vatt. Chalkfield was the Councilman who had succeeded to the Mayoralty in the preceding November.

Farfrae was sorry at the intelligence, and Mr Vatt continued: 'Well, we know he's been going some days, and as his family is well provided for we must take it all as it is. Now I have called to ask 'ee this – quite privately. If I should nominate 'ee to succeed him, and there should be no particular opposition, will 'ee accept the chair?'

'But there are folk whose turn is before mine; and I'm over young, and may be thought pushing!' said Farfrae after a pause.

'Not at all. I don't speak for myself only, several have named it. You won't refuse?'

'We thought of going away,' interposed Lucetta, looking at Farfrae anxiously.

'It was only a fancy,' Farfrae murmured. 'I wouldna refuse if it is the wish of a respectable majority in the Council.'

'Very well, then, look upon yourself as elected. We have had older men long enough.'

When he was gone Farfrae said musingly, 'See now how it's ourselves that are ruled by the Powers above us! We plan this, but we do that. If they want to make me Mayor I will stay, and Henchard must rave as he will.'

From this evening onward Lucetta was very uneasy. If she had not been imprudence incarnate she would not have acted as she did when she met Henchard by accident a day or two later. It was in the bustle of the market, when no one could readily notice their discourse.

'Michael,' said she, 'I must again ask you what I asked you months ago – to return me any letters or papers of mine that you may have – unless you have destroyed them? You must see how desirable it is that the times at Jersey should be blotted out, for the good of all parties.'

'Why, bless the woman! – I packed up every scrap of your handwriting to give you in the coach – but you never appeared.'

She explained how the death of her aunt had prevented her taking the journey on that day. 'And what became of the parcel then?' she asked.

He could not say – he would consider. When she was gone he recollected that he had left a heap of useless papers in his former dining-room safe – built up in the wall of his old house – now occupied by Farfrae. The letters might have been amongst them.

A grotesque grin shaped itself on Henchard's face. Had that safe been opened?

On the very evening which followed this there was a great ringing of bells in Casterbridge, and the combined brass, wood, catgut, and leather bands played round the town with more prodigality of percussion-notes than ever. Farfrae was Mayor – the two-hundredth odd of a series forming an elective dynasty dating back to the days of Charles I – and the fair Lucetta was the courted of the town . . . But, ah! that worm i' the bud – Henchard; what he could tell!

He, in the meantime, festering with indignation at some erroneous intelligence of Farfrae's opposition to the scheme for installing him in the little seed-shop, was greeted with the news of the municipal election (which, by reason of Farfrae's comparative youth and his Scottish nativity – a thing unprecedented in the case – had an interest far beyond the ordinary). The bell-ringing and the band-playing, loud as Tamerlane's trumpet, goaded the downfallen Henchard indescribably: the ousting now seemed to him to be complete.

The next morning he went to the corn-yard as usual, and about eleven o'clock Donald entered through the green door, with no trace of the worshipful about him. The yet more emphatic change of places between him and Henchard which this election had established renewed a slight embarrassment in the manner of the modest younger man; but Henchard showed the front of one who had overlooked all this; and Farfrae met his amenities half-way at once.

'I was going to ask you,' said Henchard, 'about a packet that I may possibly have left in my old safe in the dining-room.' He added particulars.

'If so, it is there now,' said Farfrae. 'I have never opened the safe at all as yet; for I keep ma papers at the bank, to sleep easy o' nights.'

'It was not of much consequence – to me,' said Henchard. 'But I'll call for it this evening, if you don't mind?'

It was quite late when he fulfilled his promise. He had primed himself with grog, as he did very frequently now, and a curl of sardonic humour hung on his lip as he approached the house, as though he were contemplating some terrible form of amusement. Whatever it was, the incident of his entry did not diminish its force, this being his first visit to the house since he had lived there as owner. The ring of the bell spoke to him like the voice of a familiar drudge who had been bribed to forsake him; the movements of the doors were revivals of dead days.

Farfrae invited him into the dining-room, where he at once unlocked the iron safe built into the wall, *his*, Henchard's safe, made by an ingenious locksmith under his direction. Farfrae drew thence the parcel, and other papers, with apologies for not having returned them.

'Never mind,' said Henchard drily. 'The fact is they are letters mostly . . . Yes,' he went on, sitting down and unfolding Lucetta's passionate bundle, 'here they be. That ever I should see 'em again! I hope Mrs Farfrae is well after her exertions yesterday?'

'She has felt a bit weary; and has gone to bed airly on that account.'

Henchard returned to the letters, sorting them over with interest, Farfrae being seated at the other end of the dining-table. 'You don't forget, of course,' he resumed, 'that curious chapter in the history of my past which I told you of, and that you gave me some assistance in? These letters are, in fact, related to that unhappy business. Though, thank God, it is all over now.'

'What became of the poor woman?' asked Farfrae.

'Luckily she married, and married well,' said Henchard. 'So that these reproaches she poured out on me do not now cause me any twinges, as they might otherwise have done . . . Just listen to what an angry woman will say!'

Farfrae, willing to humour Henchard, though quite uninterested, and bursting with yawns, gave well mannered attention.

' "For me," ' Henchard read, ' "there is practically no future. A creature too unconventionally devoted to you – who feels it impossible that she can be wife of any other man; and who is yet no more to you than the first woman you meet in the street – such am I. I quite acquit you of any intention to wrong me, yet you are the door through which wrong has come to me. That in the event of your present wife's death you will place me in her position is a consolation so far as it goes – but how far does it go? Thus I sit here, forsaken by my few acquaintance, and forsaken by you!" '

'That's how she went on to me,' said Henchard, 'acres of words like that, when what had happened was what I could not cure.'

'Yes,' said Farfrae absently, 'it is the way wi' women.' But the fact was that he knew very little of the sex; yet detecting a sort of resemblance in style between the effusions of the woman he worshipped and those of the supposed stranger, he concluded that Aphrodite ever spoke thus, whosoever the personality she assumed.

Henchard unfolded another letter, and read it through likewise, stopping at the subscription as before. 'Her name I don't give,' he said blandly. 'As I didn't marry her, and another man did, I can scarcely do that in fairness to her.'

'Tr-rue, tr-rue,' said Farfrae. 'But why didn't you marry her when your wife Susan died?' Farfrae asked this and the other questions in the comfortably indifferent tone of one whom the matter very remotely concerned.

'Ah – well you may ask that!' said Henchard, the new-moon-shaped grin adumbrating itself again upon his mouth. 'In spite of all her protestations, when I came forward to do so, as in generosity bound, she was not the woman for me.'

'She had already married another – maybe?'

Henchard seemed to think it would be sailing too near the wind to descend further into particulars, and he answered 'Yes.'

'The young lady must have had a heart that bore transplanting very readily!'

'She had, she had,' said Henchard emphatically.

He opened a third and fourth letter, and read. This time he approached the conclusion as if the signature were indeed coming with the rest. But again he stopped short. The truth was that, as may be divined, he had quite intended to effect a grand catastrophe at the end of this drama by reading out the name; he had come to the house with no other thought. But sitting there in cold blood he could not do it. Such a wrecking of hearts appalled even him. His quality was such that he could have annihilated them both in the heat of action; but to accomplish the deed by oral poison was beyond the nerve of his enmity.

* XXXV *

As Donald stated, Lucetta had retired early to her room because of fatigue. She had, however, not gone to rest, but sat in the bedside chair reading and thinking over the events of the day. At the ringing of the door-bell by Henchard she wondered who it should be that would call at that comparatively late hour. The dining-room was almost under her bedroom; she could hear that somebody was admitted there, and presently the indistinct murmur of a person reading became audible.

The usual time for Donald's arrival upstairs came and passed, yet still the reading and conversation went on. This was very singular. She could think of nothing but that some extraordinary crime had been committed, and that the visitor, whoever he might be, was reading an account of it from a special edition of the *Casterbridge Chronicle*. At last she left the room, and descended the stairs. The dining-room door was ajar, and in the silence of the resting household the voice and words were recognizable before she reached the lower flight. She stood transfixed. Her own words greeted her in Henchard's voice, like spirits from the grave.

Lucetta leant upon the banister with her cheek against the smooth hand-rail, as if she would make a friend of it in her misery. Rigid in this position, more and more words fell successively upon her ear. But what amazed her most was the tone of her husband. He spoke merely in the accents of a man who made a present of his time.

'One word,' he was saying, as the crackling of paper denoted that Henchard was unfolding yet another sheet. 'Is it quite fair to this young woman's memory to read at such length to a stranger what was intended for your eye alone?'

'Well, yes,' said Henchard. 'By not giving her name make it an example of all womankind, and not a scandal to one.'

'If I were you I would destroy them,' said Farfrae, giving more thought to the letters than he had hitherto done. 'As another man's wife it would injure the woman if it were known.'

'No, I shall not destroy them,' murmured Henchard, putting the letters away. Then he arose, and Lucetta heard no more.

She went back to her bedroom in a semi-paralysed state. For very fear she could not undress, but sat on the edge of the bed, waiting. Would Henchard let out the secret in his parting words? Her suspense was terrible. Had she confessed all to Donald in their early acquaintance he might possibly have got over it, and married her just the same – unlikely as it had once seemed; but for her or any one else to tell him now would be fatal.

The door slammed; she could hear her husband bolting it. After looking round in his customary way he came leisurely up the stairs. The spark in her eyes well-nigh went out when he appeared round the bedroom door. Her gaze hung doubtful for a moment, then to her joyous amazement she saw that he looked at her with the rallying smile of one who had just been relieved of a scene that was irksome. She could hold out no longer, and sobbed hysterically.

When he had restored her Farfrae naturally enough spoke of Henchard. 'Of all men he was the least desirable as a visitor,' he said; 'but it is my belief that he's just a bit crazed. He has been reading to me a long lot of letters relating to his past life; and I could do no less than indulge him by listening.'

This was sufficient. Henchard, then, had not told. Henchard's last words to Farfrae, in short, as he stood on the doorstep, had been these: 'Well – I'm obliged to 'ee for listening. I may tell more about her some day.'

Finding this, she was much perplexed as to Henchard's motives in opening the matter at all; for in such cases we attribute to an enemy a power of consistent action which we never find in ourselves or in our friends; and forget that abortive efforts from want of heart are as possible to revenge as to generosity.

Next morning Lucetta remained in bed, meditating how to parry this incipient attack. The bold stroke of telling Donald the truth, dimly conceived, was yet too bold; she she dreaded lest in doing so he, like the rest of the world, should believe that the episode was rather her fault than her misfortune. She decided to employ persuasion – not with Donald, but with the enemy himself. It seemed the only practicable weapon left her as a woman. Having laid her plan she rose, and wrote to him who kept her on these tenterhooks:

'I overheard your interview with my husband last night, and saw the drift of your revenge. The very thought of it crushes me! Have pity on a distressed woman! If you could see me you would relent. You do not know how anxiety has told upon me lately. I will be at the Ring at the time you leave work – just before the sun goes down. Please come that way. I cannot rest till I have seen you face to face, and heard from your mouth that you will carry this horse-play no further.'

To herself she said, on closing up this appeal: 'If ever tears and pleadings have served the weak to fight the strong, let them do so now!'

With this view she made a toilette which differed from all she had ever attempted before. To heighten her natural attractions had hitherto been the unvarying endeavour of adult life, and one in which she was no novice. But now she neglected this, and even proceeded to impair the natural presentation. Beyond a natural reason for her slightly drawn look, she had not slept all the previous night, and this had produced upon her pretty though slightly worn features the aspect of a countenance ageing prematurely from extreme sorrow. She selected – as much from want of spirit as design – her poorest, plainest, and longest discarded attire.

To avoid the contingency of being recognized she veiled herself, and slipped out of the house quickly. The sun was resting on the hill like a drop of blood on an eyelid by the time she had got up the road opposite the amphitheatre, which she speedily entered. The interior was shadowy, and emphatic of the absence of every living thing.

She was not disppointed in the fearful hope with which she awaited him. Henchard came over the top, descended, and Lucetta waited breathlessly. But having reached the arena she saw a change in his bearing: he stood still at a little distance from her; she could not think why.

Nor could any one else have known. The truth was that in appointing this spot, and this hour, for the rendezvous, Lucetta had unwittingly backed up her entreaty by the strongest argument she could have used outside words, with this man of moods, glooms, and superstitions. Her figure in the midst of the huge enclosure, the unusual plainness of her dress, her attitude of hope and appeal, so strongly revived in his soul the memory of another ill-used woman who had stood there and thus in bygone days, and had now passed away into her rest, that he was unmanned, and his heart smote him for having attempted reprisals on one of a sex so weak. When he approached her, and before she had spoken a word, her point was half gained.

His manner as he had come down had been one of cynical carelessness; but he now put away his grim half-smile, and said in a kindly subdued tone, 'Good night t'ye. Of course I'm glad to come if you want me.'

'O, thank you,' she said apprehensively.

'I am sorry to see 'ee looking so ill,' he stammered with unconcealed compunction.

She shook her head. 'How can you be sorry,' she asked, 'when you deliberately cause it?'

'What!' said Henchard uneasily. 'Is it anything I have done that has pulled you down like that?'

'It is all your doing,' said she. 'I have no other grief. My happiness would be secure enough but for your threats. O Michael! don't wreck me like this! You might think that you have done enough! When I came here

I was a young woman; now I am rapidly becoming an old one. Neither my husband nor any other man will regard me with interest long.'

Henchard was disarmed. His old feeling of supercilious pity for womankind in general was intensified by this suppliant appearing here as the double of the first. Moreover, that thoughtless want of foresight which had led to all her trouble remained with poor Lucetta still; she had come to meet him here in this compromising way without perceiving the risk. Such a woman was very small deer to hunt; he felt ashamed, lost all zest and desire to humiliate Lucetta there and then, and no longer envied Farfrae his bargain. He had married money, but nothing more. Henchard was anxious to wash his hands of the game.

'Well, what do you want me to do?' he said gently. 'I am sure I shall be very willing. My reading of those letters was only a sort of practical joke, and I revealed nothing.'

'To give me back the letters and any papers you may have that breathe of matrimony or worse.'

'So be it. Every scrap shall be yours . . . But, between you and me, Lucetta, he is sure to find out something of the matter, sooner or later.'

'Ah!' she said with eager tremulousness; 'but not till I have proved myself a faithful and deserving wife to him, and then he may forgive me everything!'

Henchard silently looked at her: he almost envied Farfrae such love as that, even now. 'H'm – I hope so,' he said. 'But you shall have the letters without fail. And your secret shall be kept. I swear it.'

'How good you are! – how shall I get them?'

He reflected, and said he would send them the next morning. 'Now don't doubt me,' he added. 'I can keep my word.'

* XXXVI *

RETURNING from her appointment Lucetta saw a man waiting by the lamp nearest to her own door. When she stopped to go in he came and spoke to her. It was Jopp.

He begged her pardon for addressing her. But he had heard that Mr Farfrae had been applied to by a neighbouring corn-merchant to recommend a working partner; if so, he wished to offer himself. He could give good security, and had stated as much to Mr Farfrae in a letter; but he would feel much obliged if Lucetta would say a word in his favour to her husband.

'It is a thing I know nothing about,' said Lucetta coldly.

'But you can testify to my trustworthiness better than anybody, ma'am,' said Jopp. 'I was in Jersey several years, and knew you there by sight.'

'Indeed,' she replied. 'But I knew nothing of you.'

'I think, ma'am, that a word or two from you would secure for me what I covet very much,' he persisted.

She steadily refused to have anything to do with the affair, and cutting him short, because of her anxiety to get indoors before her husband should miss her, left him on the pavement.

He watched her till she had vanished, and then went home. When he got there he sat down in the fireless chimney corner looking at the iron dogs, and the wood laid across them for heating the morning kettle. A movement upstairs disturbed him, and Henchard came down from his bedroom, where he seemed to have been rummaging boxes.

'I wish,' said Henchard, 'you would do me a service, Jopp, now – tonight, I mean, if you can. Leave this at Mrs Farfrae's for her. I should take it myself, of course, but I don't wish to be seen there.'

He handed a package in brown paper, sealed. Henchard had been as good as his word. Immediately on coming indoors he had searched over his few belongings; and every scrap of Lucetta's writing that he possessed was here. Jopp indifferently expressed his willingness.

'Well, how have ye got on today?' his lodger asked. 'Any prospect of an opening?'

'I am afraid not,' said Jopp, who had not told the other of his application to Farfrae.

'There never will be in Casterbridge,' declared Henchard decisively. 'You must roam further afield.' He said good night to Jopp, and returned to his own part of the house.

Jopp sat on till his eyes were attracted by the shadow of the candle-snuff on the wall, and looking at the original he found that he had formed itself into a head like a red-hot cauliflower. Henchard's packet next met his gaze. He knew there had been something of the nature of wooing between Henchard and the now Mrs Farfrae; and his vague ideas on the subject narrowed themselves down to these: Henchard had a parcel belonging to Mrs Farfrae, and he had reasons for not returning that parcel to her in person. What could be inside it? So he went on and on till, animated by resentment at Lucetta's haughtiness, as he thought it, and curiosity to learn if there were any weak sides to this transaction with Henchard, he examined the package. The pen and all its relations being awkward tools in Henchard's hands he had affixed the seals without an impression, it never occurring to him that the efficacy of such a fastening depended on this. Jopp was far less a tyro; he lifted one of the seals with his penknife peeped in at the end thus opened, saw that the bundle consisted of letters; and, having satisfied himself thus far, sealed up the end again by simply softening the wax with the candle, and went off with the parcel as requested.

His path was by the river-side at the foot of the town. Coming into the light at the bridge which stood at the end of High Street he beheld lounging thereon Mother Cuxsom and Nance Mockridge.

'We be just going down Mixen Lane way, to look into Peter's Finger afore creeping to bed,' said Mrs Cuxsom. 'There's a fiddle and tambourine going on there. Lord, what's all the world – do ye come along too, Jopp – 'twon't hinder ye five minutes.'

Jopp had mostly kept himself out of this company, but present circumstances made him somewhat more reckless than usual, and without many words he decided to go to his destination that way.

Though the upper part of Durnover was mainly composed of a curious congeries of barns and farmsteads, there was a less picturesque side to the parish. This was Mixen Lane, now in great part pulled down.

Mixen Lane was the Adullam of all the surrounding villages. It was the hiding-place of those who were in distress, and in debt, and trouble of every kind. Farm-labourers and other peasants, who combined a little poaching with their farming, and a little brawling and bibbing with their poaching, found themselves sooner or later in Mixen Lane. Rural mechanics too idle to mechanize, rural servants too rebellious to serve, drifted or were forced into Mixen Lane.

The lane and its surrounding thicket of thatched cottages stretched out like a spit into the moist and misty lowland. Much that was sad, much that was low, some things that were baneful, could be seen in Mixen Lane. Vice ran freely in and out certain of the doors of the neighbourhood; recklessness dwelt under the roof with the crooked chimney; shame in some bow-windows; theft (in times of privation) in the thatched and mud-walled houses by the sallows. Even slaughter had not been altogether unknown here. In a block of cottages up an alley there might have been erected an altar to disease in years gone by. Such was Mixen Lane in the times when Henchard and Farfrae were Mayors.

Yet this mildewed leaf in the sturdy and flourishing Casterbridge plant lay close to the open country; not a hundred yards from a row of noble elms, and commanding a view across the moor of airy uplands and corn-fields, and mansions of the great. A brook divided the moor from the tenements, and to outward view there was no way across it – no way to the houses but round about by the road. But under every householder's stairs there was kept a mysterious plank nine inches wide; which was a secret bridge.

If you, as one of those refugee householders, came in from business after dark – and this was the business time here – you stealthily crossed the moor, approached the border of the aforesaid brook, and whistled opposite the house to which you belonged. A shape thereupon made its appearance on the other side bearing the bridge on end against the sky; it was lowered; you crossed, and a hand helped you to land yourself, together with the pheasants and hares gathered from neighbouring manors. You sold them slily the next morning, and the day after you stood before the magistrates with the eye of all your sympathizing neighbours concentrated on your back. You disappeared for a time; then you were again found quietly living in Mixen Lane.

Walking along the lane at dusk the stranger was struck by two or three peculiar features therein. One was an intermittent rumbling from the back premises of the inn half-way up; this meant a skittle alley. Another was the extensive prevalence of whistling in the various domiciles – a piped note of some kind coming from nearly every open door. Another was the frequency of white aprons over dingy gowns among the women around the doorways. A white apron is a suspicious vesture in situations where spotlessness is difficult; moreover, the industry and cleanliness which the white apron expressed were belied by the postures and gaits of the women who wore it – their knuckles being mostly on their hips (an attitude which lent them the aspect of two-handled mugs), and their shoulders against door-posts; while there was a curious alacrity in the turn of each honest woman's head upon her neck and in the twirl of her honest eyes, at any noise resembling a masculine footfall along the lane.

Yet amid so much that was bad needy respectability also found a home. Under some of the roofs abode pure and virtuous souls whose presence there was due to the iron hand of necessity, and to that alone. Families from decayed villages – families of that once bulky, but now nearly extinct, section of village society called 'liviers', or lifeholders – copyholders and others, whose roof-trees had fallen for some reason or other, compelling them to quit the rural spot that had been their home for generations – came here, unless they chose to lie under a hedge by the wayside.

The inn called Peter's Finger was the church of Mixen Lane.

It was centrally situated, as such places should be, and bore about the same social relation to the Three Mariners as the latter bore to the King's Arms. At first sight the inn was so repectable as to be puzzling. The front door was kept shut, and the step was so clean that evidently but few persons entered over its sanded surface. But at the corner of the public-house was an alley, a mere slit, dividing it from the next building. Half-way up the alley was a narrow door shiny and paintless from the rub of infinite hands and shoulders. This was the actual entrance to the inn.

A pedestrian would be seen abstractedly passing along Mixen Lane; and then, in a moment, he would vanish, causing the gazer to blink like Ashton at the disappearance of Ravenswood. That abstracted pedestrian had edged into the slit by the adroit fillip of his person sideways; from the slit he edged into the tavern by a similar exercise of skill.

The company at the Three Mariners were persons of quality in comparison with the company which gathered here; though it must be admitted that the lowest fringe of the Mariners' party touched the crest of Peter's at points. Waifs and strays of all sorts loitered about here. The landlady was a virtuous woman who years ago had been unjustly sent to gaol as an accessory to something or other after the fact. She underwent her twelvemonth, and had worn a martyr's countenance ever since, except at times of meeting the constable who apprehended her, when she winked her eye.

To this house Jopp and his acquaintants had arrived. The settles on which they sat down were thin and tall, their tops being guyed by pieces of twine to hooks in the ceiling; for when the guests grew boisterous the settles would rock and overturn without some such security. The thunder of bowls echoed from the backyard; swingels hung behind the blower of the chimney; and ex-poachers and ex-gamekeepers, whom squires had persecuted without a cause, sat elbowing each other – men who in past times had met in fights under the moon, till lapse of sentences on the one part, and loss of favour and expulsion from service on the other, brought them here together to a common level, where they sat calmly discussing old times.

'Dos't mind how you could jerk a trout ashore with a bramble, and not ruffle the stream, Charl?' a deposed keeper was saying. ' 'Twas at that I caught 'ee once, if you can mind?'

'That can I. But the worst larry for me was that pheasant business at Yalbury Wood. Your wife swore false that time, Joe – O, by Gad, she did – there's no denying it.'

'How was that?' asked Jopp.

'Why – Joe closed wi' me, and we rolled down together, close to his garden hedge. Hearing the noise, out ran his wife with the oven pyle, and it being dark under the trees she couldn't see which was uppermost. "Where beest thee, Joe, under or top?" she screeched. "O – under, by Gad!" says he. She then began to rap down upon my skull, back, and ribs with the pyle till we'd roll over again. "Where beest now, dear Joe, under or top?" she'd scream again. By George, 'twas through her I was took! And then when we got up in hall she sware that the cock pheasant was one of her rearing, when 'twas not your bird at all, Joe; 'twas Squire Brown's bird – that's whose 'twas – one that we'd picked off as we passed his wood, an hour afore. It did hurt my feelings to be so wronged! . . . Ah well – 'tis over now.'

'I might have had 'ee days afore that,' said the keeper. 'I was within a few years of 'ee dozens of times, with a sight more of birds than that poor one.'

'Yes – 'tis not our greatest doings that the world gets wind of,' said the furmity-woman, who, lately settled in this purlieu, sat among the rest. Having travelled a great deal in her time she spoke with cosmopolitan largeness of idea. It was she who presently asked Jopp what was the parcel he kept so snugly under his arm.

'Ah, therein lies a grand secret,' said Jopp. 'It is the passion of love. To think that a woman should love one man so well, and hate another so unmercifully.'

'Who's the object of your meditation, sir.'

'One that stand high in this town. I'd like to shame her! Upon my life, 'twould be as good as a play to read her love-letters, the proud piece of silk and wax-work! For 'tis her love-letters that I've got here.'

'Love-letters? then let's hear 'em, good soul,' said Mother Cuxsom. 'Lord, do ye mind, Richard, what fools we used to be when we were younger? Getting a schoolboy to write ours for us; and giving him a penny, do ye mind, not to tell other folks what he'd put inside, do ye mind?'

By this time Jopp had pushed his finger under the seals, and unfastened the letters, tumbling them over and picking up one here and there at random, which he read aloud. These passages soon began to uncover the secret which Lucetta had so earnestly hoped to keep buried, though the epistles, being allusive only, did not make it altogether plain.

'Mrs Farfrae wrote that!' said Nance Mockridge. ' 'Tis a humbling thing for us, as respectable women, that one of the same sex could do it. And now she's vowed herself to another man!'

'So much the better for her,' said the aged furmity-woman. 'Ah, I saved her from a real bad marriage, and she's never been the one to thank me.'

'I say, what a good foundation for a skimmity-ride,' said Nance.

'True,' said Mrs Cuxsom, reflecting. ' 'Tis as good a ground for a skimmity-ride as ever I knowed; and it ought not to be wasted. The last one seen in Casterbridge must have been ten years ago, if a day.'

At this moment there was a shrill whistle, and the landlady said to the man who had been called Charl, ' 'Tis Jim coming in. Would ye go and let down the bridge for me?'

Without replying Charl and his comrade Joe rose, and receiving a lantern from her went out at the back door and down the garden-path, which ended abruptly at the edge of the stream already mentioned. Beyond the stream was the open moor, from which a clammy breeze smote upon their faces as they advanced. Taking up the board that had lain in readiness one of them lowered it across the water, and the instant its further end touched the ground footsteps entered upon it, and there appeared from the shade a stalwart man with straps round his knees, a double-barrelled gun under his arm and some birds slung up behind him. They asked him if he had had much luck.

'Not much,' he said indifferently. 'All safe inside?'

Receiving a reply in the affirmative he went on inwards, the other withdrawing the bridge and beginning to retreat in his rear. Before, however, they had entered the house a cry of 'Ahoy' from the moor led them to pause.

The cry was repeated. They pushed the lantern into an outhouse, and went back to the brink of the stream.

'Ahoy – is this the way to Casterbridge?' said some one from the other side.

'Not in particular,' said Charl. 'There's a river afore 'ee.'

'I don't care – here's for through it!' said the man in the moor. 'I've had travelling enough for today.'

'Stop a minute, then,' said Charl, finding that the man was no enemy. 'Joe, bring the plank and lantern; here's somebody that's lost his way. You should have kept along the turnpike road, friend, and not have strook across here.'

'I should – as I see now. But I saw a light here, and says I to myself, that's an outlying house, depend on't.'

The plank was now lowered; and the stranger's form shaped itself from the darkness. He was a middle-aged man, with hair and whiskers prematurely grey, and a broad and genial face. He had crossed on the plank without hesitation, and seemed to see nothing odd in the transit. He thanked them, and walked between them up the garden. 'What place is this?' he asked, when they reached the door.

'A public-house.'

'Ah. Perhaps it will suit me to put up at. Now then, come in and wet your whistle at my expense for the lift over you have given me.'

They followed him into the inn, where the increased light exhibited him as one who would stand higher in an estimate by the eye than in one by the ear. He was dressed with a certain clumsy richness – his coat being furred, and his head covered by a cap of seal-skin, which, though the nights were chilly, must have been warm for the daytime, spring being somewhat advanced. In his hand he carried a small mahogany case, strapped, and clamped with brass.

Apparently surprised at the kind of company which confronted him through the kitchen door, he at once abandoned his idea of putting up at the house; but taking the situation lightly, he called for glasses of the best, paid for them as he stood in the passage, and turned to proceed on his way by the front door. This was barred, and while the landlady was unfastening it the conversation about the skimmington was continued in the sitting-room, and reached his ears.

'What do they mean by a "skimmity-ride"?' he asked.

'O, sir!' said the landlady, swinging her long earrings with deprecating modesty; ' 'tis a' old foolish thing they do in these parts when a man's wife is – well, not too particularly his own. But as a respectable householder I don't encourage it.'

'Still, are they going to do it shortly? It is a good sight to see, I suppose?'

'Well, sir!' she simpered. And then, bursting into naturalness, and glancing from the corner of her eye, ' 'Tis the funniest thing under the sun! And it costs money.'

'Ah! I remember hearing of some such thing. Now I shall be in Casterbridge for two or three weeks to come, and should not mind seeing the performance. Wait a moment.' He turned back, entered the sitting-room, and said, 'Here, good folks; I should like to see the old custom you are talking of, and I don't mind being something towards it – take that.' He threw a sovereign on the table and returned to the landlady at the door, of whom, having inquired the way into the town, he took his leave.

'There were more where that one came from,' said Charl, when the sovereign had been taken up and handed to the landlady for safe keeping. 'By George! we ought to have got a few more while we had him here.'

'No, no,' answered the landlady. 'This is a respectable house, thank God! And I'll have nothing done but what's honourable.'

'Well,' said Jopp; 'now we'll consider the business begun, and will soon get it in train.'

'We will!' said Nance. 'A good laugh warms my heart more than a cordial, and that's the truth on't.'

Jopp gathered up the letters, and it being now somewhat late he did not attempt to call at Farfrae's with them that night. He reached home, sealed them up as before, and delivered the parcel at its address next morning. Within an hour its contents were reduced to ashes by Lucetta, who, poor soul! was inclined to fall down on her knees in thankfulness that at last no evidence remained of the unlucky episode with Henchard in her past. For though hers had been rather the laxity of inadvertence than of intention, that episode, if known, was not the less likely to operate fatally between herself and her husband.

* XXXVII *

SUCH was the state of things when the current affairs of Casterbridge were interrupted by an event of such magnitude that its influence reached to the lowest social stratum there, stirring the depths of its society simultaneously with the preparations for the skimmington. It was one of those excitements which, when they move a country town, leave a permanent mark upon its chronicles, as a warm summer permanently marks the ring in the tree-trunk corresponding to its date.

A Royal Personage was about to pass through the borough on his course further west, to inaugurate an immense engineering work out that way. He had consented to halt half-an-hour or so in the town, and to receive an address from the corporation of Casterbridge, which, as a representative centre of husbandry, wished thus to express its sense of the great services he had rendered to agricultural science and economics, by his zealous promotion of designs for placing the art of farming on a more scientific footing.

Royalty had not been seen in Casterbridge since the days of the third King George, and then only by candlelight for a few minutes, when that monarch, on a night-journey, had stopped to change horses at the King's Arms. The inhabitants therefore decided to make a thorough *fête carillonnée* of the unwonted occasion. Half-an-hour's pause was not long, it is true; but much might be done in it by a judicious grouping of incidents, above all, if the weather were fine.

The address was prepared on parchment by an artist who was handy at ornamental lettering, and was laid on with the best gold-leaf and colours that the sign-painter had in his shop. The Council met on the Tuesday before the appointed day, to arrange the details of the procedure. While they were sitting, the door of the Council Chamber standing open, they heard a heavy footstep coming up the stairs. It advanced along the passage, and Henchard entered the room, in clothes of frayed and threadbare shabbiness, the very clothes which he had used to wear in the primal days when he had sat among them.

'I have a feeling,' he said, advancing to the table and laying his hand upon the green cloth, 'that I should like to join ye in this reception of our illustrious visitor. I suppose I could walk with the rest?'

Embarrassed glances were exchanged by the Council, and Grower nearly ate the end of his quillpen off, so gnawed he it during the silence. Farfrae the young Mayor, who by virtue of his office sat in the large chair, intuitively caught the sense of the meeting, and as spokesman was obliged to utter it, glad as he would have been that the duty should have fallen to another tongue.

'I hardly see that it would be proper, Mr Henchard,' said he. 'The Council are the Council, and as ye are no longer one of the body, there would be an irregularity in the proceeding. If ye were included, why not others?'

'I have a particular reason for wishing to assist at the ceremony.'

Farfrae looked round. 'I think I have expressed the feeling of the Council,' he said.

'Yes, yes,' from Dr Bath, Lawyer Long, Alderman Tubber, and several more.

'Then I am not to be allowed to have anything to do with it officially?'

'I am afraid so; it is out of the question indeed. But of course you can see the doings full well, such as they are to be, like the rest of the spectators.'

Henchard did not reply to that very obvious suggestion, and turning on his heel, went away.

It had been only a passing fancy of his, but opposition crystallized it into a determination. 'I'll welcome his Royal Highness, or nobody shall!' he went about saying. 'I am not going to be sat upon by Farfrae, or any of the rest of the paltry crew! You shall see.'

The eventful morning was bright, a full-faced sun confronting early window-gazers eastward, and all perceived (for they were practised in weather-lore) that there was permanence in the glow. Visitors soon began to flock in from county houses, villages, remote copses, and lonely uplands, the latter in oiled boots and tilt bonnets, to see the reception, or if not to see it, at any rate to be near it. There was hardly a workman in the town who did not put a clean shirt on. Solomon Longways, Christopher Coney, Buzzford, and the rest of that fraternity, showed their sense of the occasion by advancing their customary eleven o'clock pint to half-past ten; from which they found a difficulty in getting back to the proper hour for several days.

Henchard had determined to do no work that day. He primed himself in the morning with a glass of rum, and walking down the street met Elizabeth-Jane, whom he had not seen for a week. 'It was lucky,' he said to her, 'my twenty-one years expired before this came on, or I should never have had the nerve to carry it out.'

'Carry out what?' said she, alarmed.

'This welcome I am going to give our Royal visitor.'

She was perplexed. 'Shall we go and see it together?' she said.

'See it! I have other fish to fry. You see it. It will be worth seeing!'

She could do nothing to elucidate this, and decked herself out with a heavy heart. As the appointed time drew near she got sight again of her stepfather. She thought he was going to the Three Mariners; but no, he elbowed his way through the gay throng to the shop of Woolfrey, the draper. She waited in the crowd without.

In a few minutes he emerged, wearing, to her surprise, a brilliant rosette, which more suprising still, in his hand he carried a flag of somewhat homely construction, formed by tacking one of the small Union Jacks, which abounded in the town today, to the end of a deal wand – probably the roller from a piece of calico. Henchard rolled up his flag on the doorstep, put it under his arm, and went down the street.

Suddenly the taller members of the crowd turned their heads, and the shorter stood on tiptoe. It was said that the Royal *cortège* approached. The railway had stretched out an arm towards Casterbridge at this time, but had not reached it by several miles as yet; so that the intervening distance, as well as the remainder of the journey, was to be traversed by road in the old fashion. People thus waited – the county families in their carriages, the masses on foot – and watched the far-stretching London highway to the ringing of bells and chatter of tongues.

From the background Elizabeth-Jane watched the scene. Some seats had been arranged from which ladies could witness the spectacle, and the front seat was occupied by Lucetta, the Mayor's wife, just at present. In the road under her eyes stood Henchard. She appeared so bright and pretty that, as it seemed, he was experiencing the momentary weakness of wishing for her notice. But he was far from attractive to a woman's eye, ruled as that is so largely by the superficies of things. He was not only a journeyman, unable to appear as he formerly had appeared, but he disdained to appear as well as he might. Everybody else, from the Mayor to the washer-woman, shone in new vesture according to means; but Henchard had doggedly retained the fretted and weather-beaten garments of bygone years.

Hence, alas, this occurred: Lucetta's eyes slid over him to this side and to that without anchoring on his features – as gaily dressed women's eyes will too often do on such occasions. Her manner signified quite plainly that she meant to know him in public no more.

But she was never tired of watching Donald, as he stood in animated converse with his friends a few yards off, wearing round his young neck the official gold chain with great square links, like that round the Royal unicorn. Every trifling emotion that her husband showed as he talked had its reflex on her face and lips, which moved in little duplicates to his. She was living his part rather then her own, and cared for no one's situation but Farfrae's that day.

At length a man stationed at the furthest turn of the high road, namely, on the second bridge of which mention has been made, gave a signal; and the Corporation in their robes proceeded from the front of the Town Hall to the archway erected at the entrance to the town. The carriages containing the Royal visitor and his suite arrived at the spot in a cloud of dust, a procession was formed, and the whole came on to the Town Hall at a walking pace.

This spot was the centre of interest. There were a few clear yards in front of the Royal carriage, sanded; and into this space a man stepped before any one could prevent him. It was Henchard. He had unrolled his private flag, and removing his hat he staggered to the side of the slowing vehicle, waving the Union Jack to and fro with his left hand, while he blandly held out his right to the Illustrious Personage.

All the ladies said with bated breath, 'Oh, look there!' and Lucetta was ready to faint. Elizabeth-Jane peeped through the shoulders of those in front, saw what it was, and was terrified; and then her interest in the spectacle as a strange phenomenon got the better of her fear.

Farfrae, with Mayoral authority, immediately rose to the occasion. He seized Henchard by the shoulder, dragged him back, and told him roughly to be off. Henchard's eyes met his, and Farfrae observed the fierce light in them despite his excitement and irritation. For a moment Henchard stood his ground rigidly; then by an unaccountable impulse gave way and retired. Farfrae glanced to the ladies' gallery, and saw that his Calphurnia's cheek was pale.

'Why – it is your husband's old patron!' said Mrs Blowbody, a lady of the neighbourhood who sat beside Lucetta.

'Patron!' said Donald's wife with quick indignation.

'Do you say the man is an acquaintance of Mr Farfrae's?' observed Mrs Bath, the physician's wife, a new-comer to the town through her recent marriage with the doctor.

'He works for my husband,' said Lucetta.

'Oh – is that all? They have been saying to me that it was through him your husband first got a footing in Casterbridge. What stories people will tell!'

'They will indeed. It was not so at all. Donald's genius would have enabled him to get a footing anywhere, without anybody's help! He would have just the same if there had been no Henchard in the world!'

It was partly Lucetta's ignorance of the circumstances of Donald's arrival which led her to speak thus; partly the sensation that everybody seemed bent on snubbing her at this triumphant time. The incident had occupied but a few moments, but it was necessarily witnessed by the Royal Personage, who, however, with practised tact, affected not to have noticed anything unusual. He alighted, the Mayor advanced, the address was read; the Illustrious Personage replied, then said a few words to Farfrae, and shook hands with Lucetta as the Mayor's wife. The ceremony occupied but a few minutes, and the carriages rattled heavily as Pharaoh's chariots down Corn Street and out upon the Budmouth Road, in continuation of the journey coastward.

In the crowd stood Coney, Buzzford, and Longways. 'Some difference between him now and when he zung at the Dree Mariners,' said the first. ' 'Tis wonderful how he could get a lady of her quality to go snacks wi' en in such quick time.'

'True. Yet how folk do worship fine clothes! Now there's a better-looking woman than she that nobody notices at all, because she's akin to that hontish fellow Henchard.'

'I could worship ye, Buzz, for saying that,' remarked Nance Mockridge. 'I do like to see the trimming pulled off such Christmas candles. I am quite unequal to the part of villain myself, or I'd gi'e all my small silver to see that lady toppered. . . . and perhaps I shall soon,' she added significantly.

'That's not a noble passiont for a 'oman to keep up,' said Longways.

Nance did not reply, but every one knew what she meant. The ideas diffused by the reading of Lucetta's letters at Peter's Finger had condensed into a scandal, which was spreading like a miasmatic fog through Mixen Lane, and thence up the back streets of Casterbridge.

This mixed assemblage of idlers known to each other presently fell apart into two bands by a process of natural selection, the frequenters of Peter's Finger going off Mixen Lanewards, where most of them lived, while Coney, Buzzford, Longways, and that connection remained in the street.

'You know what's brewing down there, I suppose?' said Buzzford mysteriously to the others.

Coney looked at him. 'Not the skimmity-ride?'

Buzzford nodded.

'I have my doubts if it will be carried out,' said Longways. 'If they are getting it up they are keeping it mighty close.'

'I heard they were thinking of it a fortnight ago, at all events.'

'If I were sure o't I'd lay information,' said Longways emphatically. ' 'Tis too rough a joke, and apt to wake riots in towns. We know that the Scotchman is a right enough man, and that this lady has been a right enough 'oman since she came here, and if there was anything wrong about her afore, that's their business, not ours.'

Coney reflected. Farfrae was still liked in the community; but it must be owned that, as the Mayor and man of money, engrossed with affairs and ambitions, he had lost in the eyes of the poorer inhabitants something of that wondrous charm which he had had for them as a light-hearted penniless young man who sang ditties as readily as the birds in the trees. Hence the anxiety to keep him from annoyance showed not quite the ardour that would have animated it in former days.

'Suppose we make inquiration into it, Christopher,' continued Longways; 'and if we find there's really anything in it, drop a letter to them most concerned, and advise 'em to keep out of the way?'

This course was decided on, and the group separated, Buzzford saying to Coney, 'Come, my ancient friend; let's move on. There's nothing more to see here.'

These well-intentioned ones would have been surprised had they known how ripe the great jocular plot really was. 'Yes, tonight,' Jopp had said to the Peter's party at the corner of Mixen Lane. 'As a wind-up to the Royal visit the hit will be all the more pat by reason of their great elevation today.'

To him, at least, it was not a joke, but a retaliation.

* XXXVIII *

THE proceedings had been brief – too brief – to Lucetta, whom an intoxicating *Weltlust* had fairly mastered; but they had brought her a great triumph nevertheless. The shake of the Royal hand still lingered in her fingers; and the chit-chat she had overheard, that her husband might possibly receive the honour of knighthood, though idle to a degree, seemed not the wildest vision; stranger things had occurred to men so good and captivating as her Scotchman was.

After the collision with the Mayor, Henchard had withdrawn behind the ladies' stand; and there he stood, regarding with a stare of abstraction the spot on the lapel of his coat where Farfrae's hand had seized it. He put his own hand there, as if he could hardly realize such an outrage from one whom it had once been his wont to treat with ardent generosity. While pausing in this half-stupefied state the conversation of Lucetta with the other ladies reached his ears; and he distinctly heard her deny him – deny that he had assisted Donald, that he was anything more than a common journeyman.

He moved on homeward, and met Jopp in the archway to the Bull Stake. 'So you've had a snub,' said Jopp.

'And what if I have?' answered Henchard sternly.

'Why, I've had one too, so we are both under the same cold shade.' He briefly related his attempt to win Lucetta's intercession.

Henchard merely heard this story, without taking it deeply in. His own relation to Farfrae and Lucetta overshadowed all kindred ones. He went on saying brokenly to himself, 'She has supplicated to me in her time; and now her tongue won't own me nor her eyes see me! . . . And he – how angry he looked. He drove me back as if I were a bull breaking fence . . . I look like a lamb, for I saw it could not be settled there. He can rub brine on a green wound! . . . But he shall pay for it, and she shall be sorry. It must come to a tussle – face to face; and then we'll see how a coxcomb can front a man!'

Without further reflection the fallen merchant, bent on some wild purpose, ate a hasty dinner and went forth to find Farfrae. After being injured by him as a rival, and snubbed by him as a journeyman, the crowning degradation had been reserved for this day – that he should be shaken at the collar by him as a vagabond in the face of the whole town.

The crowds had dispersed. But for the green arches which still stood as they were erected Casterbridge life had resumed its ordinary shape. Henchard went down Corn Street till he came to Farfrae's house, where he knocked, and left a message that he would be glad to see his employer at the granaries as soon as he conveniently could come there. Having done this he proceeded round to the back and entered the yard.

Nobody was present, for, as he had been aware, the labourers and carters were enjoying a half-holiday on account of the events of the morning – though the carters would have to return for a short time later on, to feed and litter down the horses. He had reached the granary steps and was about to ascend, when he said to himself aloud, 'I'm stronger than he.'

Henchard returned to a shed, where he selected a short piece of rope from several pieces that were lying about; hitching one end of this to a nail, he took the other in his right hand and turned himself bodily round, while keeping his arm against his side; by this contrivance he pinioned the arm effectively. He now went up the ladders to the top floor of the corn-stores.

It was empty except of a few sacks, and at the further end was the door often mentioned, opening under the cathead and chain that hoisted the sacks. He fixed the door open and looked over the sill. There was a depth of thirty or forty feet to the ground; here was the spot on which he had been standing with Farfrae when Elizabeth-Jane had seen him lift his arm, with many misgivings as to what the movement portended.

He retired a few steps into the loft and waited. From this elevated perch his eye could sweep the roofs round about, the upper parts of the luxurious chestnut trees, now delicate in leaves of a week's age, and the dropping boughs of the limes; Farfrae's garden and the green door leading therefrom. In course of time – he could not say how long – that green door opened and Farfrae came through. He was dressed as if for a journey. The low light of the nearing evening caught his head and face when he emerged from the shadow of the wall, warming them to a complexion of flame-colour. Henchard watched him with his mouth firmly set, the squareness of his jaw and the verticality of his profile being unduly marked.

Farfrae came on with one hand in his pocket, and humming a tune in a way which told that the words were most in his mind. They were those of the song he had sung when he arrived years before at the Three Mariners, a poor young man, adventuring for life and fortune, and scarcely knowing whitherward:–

> 'And here's a hand, my trusty fiere,
>   And gie's a hand o' thine.'

Nothing moved Henchard like an old melody. He sank back. 'No; I can't do it!' he gasped. 'Why does the infernal fool begin that now!'

At length Farfrae was silent, and Henchard looked out of the loft door. 'Will ye come up here?' he said.

'Ay, man,' said Farfrae. 'I couldn't see ye. What's wrang?'

A minute later Henchard heard his feet on the lowest ladder. He heard him land on the first floor, ascend and land on the second, begin the ascent to the third. And then his head rose through the trap behind.

'What are you doing up here at this time?' he asked, coming forward. 'Why didn't ye take your holiday like the rest of the men?' He spoke in a tone which had just severity enough in it to show that he remembered the untoward event of the forenoon, and his conviction that Henchard had been drinking.

Henchard said nothing; but going back he closed the stair hatchway, and stamped upon it so that it went tight into its frame; he next turned to the wondering man, who by this time observed that one of Henchard's arms was bound to his side.

'Now,' said Henchard quietly, 'we stand face to face – man and man. Your money and your fine wife no longer lift 'ee above me as they did but now, and my poverty does not press me down.'

'What does it all mean?' asked Farfrae simply.

'Wait a bit, my lad. You should ha' thought twice before you affronted to extremes a man who had nothing to lose. I've stood your rivalry, which ruined me, and your snubbing, which humbled me; but your hustling, that disgraced me, I won't stand!'

Farfrae warmed a little at this. 'Ye'd no business there,' he said.

'As much as any one among ye! What, you forward stripling, tell a man of my age he'd no business there!' The anger-vein swelled in his forehead as he spoke.

'You insulted Royalty, Henchard; and 'twas my duty, as the chief magistrate, to stop you.'

'Royalty be damned,' said Henchard. 'I am as loyal as you, come to that!'

'I am not here to argue. Wait till you cool doon, wait till you cool; and you will see things the same way as I do.'

'You may be the one to cool first,' said Henchard grimly. 'Now this is the case. Here be we, in this four-square loft, to finish out that little wrestle you began this morning. There's the door, forty foot above ground. One of us two puts the other out by that door – the master stays inside. If he likes he may go down afterwards and give the alarm that the other has fallen out by accident – or he may tell the truth – that's his business. As the strongest man I've tied one arm to take no advantage of 'ee. D'ye understand? Then here's at 'ee!'

There was no time for Farfrae to do aught but one thing, to close with Henchard, for the latter had come on at once. It was a wrestling match, the object of each being to give his antagonist a back fall; and on Henchard's part, unquestionably, that it should be through the door.

At the outset Henchard's hold by his only free hand, the right, was on the left side of Farfrae's collar, which he firmly grappled, the latter holding Henchard by his collar with the contrary hand. With his right he endeavoured to get hold of his antagonist's left arm, which, however, he could not do, so adroitly did Henchard keep it in the rear as he gazed upon the lowered eyes of his fair and slim antagonist.

Henchard planted the first toe forward, Farfrae crossing him with his; and thus far the struggle had very much the appearance of the ordinary wrestling of those parts. Several minutes were passed by them in this attitude, the pair rocking and writhing like trees in a gale, both preserving an absolute silence. By this time their breathing could be heard. Then Farfrae tried to get hold of the other side of Henchard's collar, which was resisted by the larger man exerting all his force in a wrenching movement, and this part of the struggle ended by his forcing Farfrae down on his knees by sheer pressure of one of his muscular arms. Hampered as he was, however, he could not keep him there, and Farfrae finding his feet again the struggle proceeded as before.

By a whirl Henchard brought Donald dangerously near the precipice; seeing his position the Scotchman for the first time locked himself to his adversary, and all the efforts of that infuriated Prince of Darkness – as he might have been called from his appearance just now – were inadequate to lift or loosen Farfrae for a time. By an extraordinary effort he succeeded at last, though not until they had got far back again from the fatal door. In doing so Henchard contrived to turn Farfrae a complete somersault. Had Henchard's other arm been free it would have been all over with Farfrae then. But again he regained his feet, wrenching Henchard's arm considerably, and causing him sharp pain, as could be seen from the twitching of his face. He instantly delivered the younger man an annihilating turn by the left fore-hip, as it used to be expressed, and following up his advantage thrust him towards the door, never loosening his hold till Farfrae's fair head was hanging over the window-sill, and his arm dangling down outside the wall.

'Now,' said Henchard between his gasps, 'this is the end of what you began this morning. Your life is in my hands.'

'Then take it, take it!' said Farfrae. 'Ye've wished to long enough!'

Henchard looked down upon him in silence, and their eyes met. 'O Farfae! – that's not true!' he said bitterly. 'God is my witness that no man ever loved another as I did thee at one time . . . And now – though I came here to kill 'ee, I cannot hurt thee! Go and give me in charge – do what you will – I care nothing for what comes of me!'

He withdrew to the back part of the loft, loosened his arm, and flung himself into a corner upon some sacks, in the abandonment of remorse. Farfrae regarded him in silence; then went to the hatch and descended through it. Henchard would fain have recalled him; but his tongue failed in its task, and the young man's steps died on his ear.

Henchard took his full measure of shame and self-reproach. The scenes of his first acquaintance with Farfrae rushed back upon him – that time when the curious mixture of romance and thrift in the young man's composition so commanded his heart that Farfrae could play upon him as on an instrument. So thoroughly subdued was he that he remained on the sacks in a crouching attitude, unusual for a man, and for such a man. Its womanliness sat tragically on the figure of so stern a piece of virility. He heard a conversation below, the opening of the coach-house door, and the putting in of a horse, but took no notice.

Here he stayed till the thin shades thickened to opaque obscurity, and the loft-door became an oblong of gray light – the only visible shape around. At length he arose, shook the dust from his clothes wearily, felt his way to the hatch, and gropingly descended the steps till he stood in the yard.

'He thought highly of me once,' he murmured. 'Now he'll hate me and despise me for ever!'

He became possessed by an overpowering wish to see Farfrae again that night, and by some desperate pleading to attempt the well-nigh impossible task of winning pardon for his late mad attack. But as he walked towards Farfrae's door he recalled the unheeded doings in the yard while he had lain above in a sort of stupor. Farfrae he remembered had gone to the stable and put the horse into the gig; while doing so Whittle had brought him a letter; Farfrae had then said that he would not go towards Budmouth as he had intended – that he was unexpectedly summoned to Weatherbury, but meant to call at Mellstock on his way thither, that place lying but one or two miles out of his course.

He must have come prepared for a journey when he first arrived in the yard, unsuspecting enmity; and he must have drive off (though in a changed direction) without saying a word to any one on what had occurred between themselves.

It would therefore be useless to call at Farfrae's house till very late.

There was no help for it but to wait till his return, though waiting was almost torture to his restless and self-accusing soul. He walked about the streets and outskirts of the town, lingering here and there till he reached the stone bridge of which mention has been made, an accustomed halting-place with him now. Here he spent a long time, the purl of waters through the weirs meeting his ear, and the Casterbridge lights glimmering at no great distance off.

While leaning thus upon the parapet his listless attention was awakened by sounds of an unaccustomed kind from the town quarter. They were a confusion of rhythmical noises, to which the streets added yet more confusion by encumbering them with echoes. His first incurious thought that the clangour arose from the town band, engaged in an attempt to round off a memorable day by a burst of evening harmony, was contradicted by certain peculiarities of reverberation. But inexplicability did not rouse him to more than a cursory heed; his sense of degradation was too strong for the admission of foreign ideas; and he leant against the parapet as before.

* XXXIX *

When Farfrae descended out of the loft breathless from his encounter with Henchard, he paused at the bottom to recover himself. He arrived at the yard with the intention of putting the horse into the gig himself (all the men having a holiday), and driving to a village on the Budmouth Road. Despite the fearful struggle he decided still to persevere in his journey, so as to recover himself before going indoors and meeting the eyes of Lucetta. He wished to consider his course in a case so serious.

When he was just on the point of driving off Whittle arrived with a note badly addressed, and bearing the word 'immediate' upon the outside. On opening it he was surprised to see that it was unsigned. It contained a brief request that he would go to Weatherbury that evening about some business which he was conducting there. Farfrae knew nothing that could make it pressing; but as he was bent upon going out he yielded to the anonymous request, particularly as he had a call to make at Mellstock which could be included in the same tour. Thereupon he told Whittle of his change of direction, in words which Henchard had overheard; and set out on his way. Farfrae had not directed his man to take the message indoors, and Whittle had not been supposed to do so on his own responsibility.

Now the anonymous letter was a well-intentioned but clumsy contrivance of Longways and other of Farfrae's men to get him out of the way for the evening, in order that the satirical mummery should fall flat, if it were attempted. By giving open information they would have brought down upon their heads the vengeance of those among their comrades who enjoyed these boisterous old games; and therefore the plan of sending a letter recommended itself by its indirectness.

For poor Lucetta they took no protective measure, believing with the majority there was some truth in the scandal, which she would have to bear as she best might.

It was about eight o'clock, and Lucetta was sitting in the drawing-room alone. Night had set in for more than half an hour, but she had not had the candles lighted, for when Farfrae was away she preferred waiting for him by the firelight, and, if it were not too cold, keeping one of the window-sashes a little way open that the sound of his wheels might reach her ears early. She was leaning back in her chair, in a more hopeful mood than she had enjoyed since her marriage. The day had been such a success; and the temporary uneasiness which Henchard's show of effrontery had wrought in her disappeared with the quiet disappearance of Henchard himself under her husband's reproof. The floating evidence of her absurd passion for him, and its consequences, had been destroyed, and she really seemed to have no cause for fear.

The reverie in which these and other subjects mingled was disturbed by a hubbub in the distance, that increased moment by moment. It did not greatly surprise her, the afternoon having been given up to recreation by a majority of the populace since the passage of the Royal equipages. But her attention was at once riveted to the matter by the voice of a maid-servant next door, who spoke from an upper window across the street to some other maid even more elevated than she.

'Which way be they going now?' inquired the first with interest.

'I can't be sure for a moment,' said the second, 'because of the malter's chimbley. O yes – I can see 'em. Well, I declare, I declare!'

'What, what?' from the first, more enthusiastically.

'They are coming up Corn Street after all! They sit back to back!'

'What – two of 'em – are there two figures?'

'Yes. Two images on a donkey, back to back, their elbows tied to one another's! She's facing the head, and he's facing the tail.'

'Is it meant for anybody particular?'

'Well – it mid be. The man has got on a blue coat and kerseymere leggings; he has black whiskers, and a reddish face. 'Tis a stuffed figure, with a falseface.'

The din was increasing now – then it lessened a little.

'There – I shan't see, after all!' cried the disappointed first maid.

'They have gone into a back street – that's all,' said the one who occupied the enviable position in the attic. 'There – now I have got 'em all endways nicely!'

'What's the woman like? Just say, and I can tell in a moment if 'tis meant for one I've in mind.'

'My – why – 'tis dressed just as *she* was dressed when she sat in the front seat at the time the play-actors came to the Town Hall!'

Lucetta started to her feet; and almost at the instant the door of the room was quickly and softly opened. Elizabeth-Jane advanced into the firelight.

'I have come to see you,' she said breathlessly. 'I did not stop to knock – forgive me! I see you have not shut your shutters, and the window is open.'

Without waiting for Lucetta's reply she crossed quickly to the window and pulled out one of the shutters. Lucetta glided to her side. 'Let it be – hush!' she said peremptorily, in a dry voice, while she seized Elizabeth-Jane by the hand, and held up her finger. Their intercourse had been so low and hurried that not a word had been lost of the conversation without; which had thus proceeded:

'Her neck is uncovered, and her hair in bands, and her back-comb in place; she's got on a puce silk, and white stockings and coloured shoes.'

Again Elizabeth-Jane attempted to close the window, but Lucetta held her by main force.

' 'Tis me!' she said, with a face pale as death. 'A procession – a scandal – an effigy of me, and him!'

The look of Elizabeth betrayed that the latter knew it already.

'Let us shut it out,' coaxed Elizabeth-Jane, noting that the rigid wildness of Lucetta's features was growing yet more rigid and wild with the nearing of the noise and laughter. 'Let us shut it out!'

'It is no use!' she shrieked out. 'He will see it, won't he? Donald will see it! He is just coming home – and it will break his heart – he will never love me any more – and O, it will kill me – kill me!'

Elizabeth-Jane was frantic now. 'O, can't something be done to stop it?' she cried. 'Is there nobody to do it – not one?'

She relinquished Lucetta's hands, and ran to the door. Lucetta herself, saying recklessly 'I will see it!' turned to the window, threw up the sash, and went out upon the balcony. Elizabeth immediately followed her, and put her arm round her to pull her in. Lucetta's eyes were straight upon the spectacle of the uncanny revel, now advancing rapidly. The numerous lights around the two effigies threw them up into lurid distinctness; it was impossible to mistake the pair for other than the intended victims. 'Come in, come in,' implored Elizabeth; 'and let me shut the window!'

'She's me – she's me – even to the parasol – my green parasol!' cried Lucetta with a wild laugh as she stepped in. She stood motionless for one second – then fell heavily to the floor.

Almost at the instant of her fall the rude music of the skimmington ceased. The roars of sarcastic laughter went off in ripples, and the trampling died out like the rustle of a spent wind. Elizabeth was only indirectly conscious of this; she had rung the bell, and was bending over Lucetta, who remained convulsed on the carpet in the paroxysms of an epileptic seizure. She rang again and again, in vain; the probability being that the servants had all run out of the house to see more of the Daemonic Sabbath than they could see within.

At last Farfrae's man, who had been agape on the door-step, came up; then the cook. The shutters, hastily pushed to by Elizabeth, were quite closed, a light was obtained, Lucetta carried to her room, and the man sent off for a doctor. While Elizabeth was undressing her she recovered consciousness; but as soon as she remembered what had passed the fit returned.

The doctor arrived with unhoped-for promptitude; he had been standing at his door, like others, wondering what the uproar meant. As soon as he saw the unhappy sufferer he said, in answer to Elizabeth's mute appeal, 'This is serious.'

'It is a fit,' Elizabeth said.

'Yes. But a fit in the present state of her health means mischief. You must send at once for Mr Farfrae. Where is he?'

'He has driven into the country, sir,' said the parlour-maid; 'to some place on the Budmouth Road. He's likely to be back soon.'

'Never mind; he must be sent for, in case he should not hurry.' The doctor returned to the bedside again. The man was despatched, and they soon heard him clattering out of the yard at the back.

Meanwhile Mr Benjamin Grower, that prominent burgess of whom mention has been already made, hearing the din of cleavers, tongs, tambourines, kits, crouds, humstrums, serpents, rams'-horns and other historical kinds of music as he sat indoors in the High Street, had put on his hat and gone out to learn the cause. He came to the corner above Farfrae's, and soon guessed the nature of the proceedings; for being a native of the town he had witnessed such rough jests before. His first move was to search hither and thither for the constables; there were two in the town, shrivelled men whom he ultimately found in hiding up an alley yet more shrivelled than usual, having some not ungrounded fears that they might be roughly handled if seen.

'What can we two poor lammigers do against such a multitude!' expostulated Stubberd, in answer to Mr Grower's chiding. ' 'Tis tempting 'em to commit *felo de se* upon us, and that would be the death of the perpetrator; and we wouldn't be the cause of a fellow-creature's death on no account, not we!'

'Get some help, then! Here, I'll come with you. We'll see what a few words of authority can do. Quick now; have you got your staves?'

'We didn't want the folk to notice us as law officers, being so short-handed, sir; so we pushed our Gover'ment staves up this water-pipe.'

'Out with 'em, and come along, for Heaven's sake! Ah, here's Mr Blowbody; that's lucky.' (Blowbody was the third of the three borough magistrates.)

'Well, what's the row?' said Blowbody. 'Got their names – hey?'

'No. Now,' said Grower to one of the constables, 'you go with Mr Blowbody round by the Old Walk and come up the street; and I'll go with Stubberd straight forward. By this plan we shall have 'em between us. Get their names only; no attack or interruption.'

Thus they started. But as Stubberd with Mr Grower advanced into Corn Street, whence the sounds had proceeded, they were surprised that no procession could be seen. They passed Farfrae's, and looked to the end

of the street. The lamp flames waved, the Walk trees soughed, a few
loungers stood about with their hands in their pockets. Everything was
as usual.

'Have you seen a motley crowd making a disturbance?' Grower said
magisterially to one of these in a fustian jacket, who smoked a short pipe
and wore straps round his knees.

'Beg yer pardon, sir?' blandly said the person addressed, who was no
other than Charl, of Peter's Finger. Mr Grower repeated the words.

Charl shook his head to the zero of childlike ignorance. 'No; we haven't
seen anything; have we, Joe? And you was here afore I.'

Joseph was quite as blank as the other in his reply.

'H'm – that's odd,' said Mr Grower. 'Ah – here's a respectable man
coming that I know by sight. Have you,' he inquired, addressing the
nearing shape of Jopp, 'have you seen any gang of fellows making a devil
of a noise – skimmington riding, or something of the sort?'

'Oh no – nothing, sir,' Jopp replied, as if receiving the most singular
news. 'But I've not been far tonight, so perhaps –'

'Oh, 'twas here – just here,' said the magistrate.

'Now I've noticed, come to think o't, that the wind in the Walk trees
makes a peculiar poetical-like murmur tonight, sir; more than common;
so perhaps 'twas that?' Jopp suggested, as he rearranged his hand in his
greatcoat pocket (where it ingeniously supported a pair of kitchen tongs
and a cow's horn, thrust up under his waistcoat).

'No, no, no, – d'ye think I'm a fool? Constable, come this way. They
must have gone into the back street.'

Neither in back street nor in front street, however, could the disturbers
be perceived; and Blowbody and the second constable, who came up at
this time, brought similar intelligence. Effigies, donkey, lanterns, band,
all had disappeared like the crew of *Comus*.

'Now,' said Mr Grower, 'there's only one thing more we can do. Get
ye half-a-dozen helpers, and go in a body to Mixen Lane, and into Peter's
Finger. I'm much mistaken if you don't find a clue to the perpetrators
there.'

The rusty-jointed executors of the law mustered assistance as soon as
they could, and the whole party marched off to the lane of notoriety. It
was no rapid matter to get there at night, not a lamp or glimmer of any
sort offering itself to light the way, except an occasional pale radiance
through some window-curtain, or through the chink of some door which
could not be closed because of the smoky chimney within. At last they
entered the inn boldly, by the till then bolted front-door, after a
prolonged knocking of loudness commensurate with the importance of
their standing.

In the settles of the large room, guyed to the ceiling by cords as usual
for stability, an ordinary group sat drinking and smoking with statuesque
quiet of demeanour. The landlady looked mildly at the invaders, saying
in honest accents, 'Good evening, gentlemen; there's plenty of room. I
hope there's nothing amiss?'

They looked round the room. 'Surely,' said Stubberd to one of the men, 'I saw you by now in Corn Street – Mr Grower spoke to 'ee?'

The man, who was Charl, shook his head absently. 'I've been here this last hour, hain't I, Nance?' he said to the woman who meditatively sipped her ale near him.

'Faith, that you have. I came in for my quiet supper-time half-pint, and you was here then, as all the rest.'

The other constable was facing the clock-case, where he saw reflected in the glass a quick motion by the landlady. Turning sharply, he caught her closing the oven-door.

'Something curious about that oven, ma'am!' he observed advancing, opening it, and drawing out a tambourine.

'Ah,' she said apologetically, 'that's what we keep here to use when there's a little quiet dancing. You see damp weather spoils it, so I put it there to keep it dry.'

The constable nodded knowingly; but what he knew was nothing. Nohow could anything be elicited from this mute and inoffensive assembly. In a few minutes the investigators went out, and joining those of their auxiliaries who had been left at the door they pursued their way elsewhither.

* XL *

LONG before this time Henchard, weary of his ruminations on the bridge, had repaired towards the town. When he stood at the bottom of the street a procession burst upon his view, in the act of turning out of an alley just above him. The lanterns, horns, and multitude startled him; he saw the mounted images, and knew what it all meant.

They crossed the way, entered another street, and disappeared. He turned back a few steps and was lost in grave reflection, finally wending his way homeward by the obscure river-side path. Unable to rest there he went to his step-daughter's lodging, and was told that Elizabeth-Jane had gone to Mrs Farfrae's. Like one acting in obedience to a charm, and with a nameless apprehension, he followed in the same direction in the hope of meeting her, the roysterers having vanished. Disappointed in this he gave the gentlest of pulls to the door-bell, and then learnt particulars of what had occurred, together with the doctor's imperative orders that Farfrae should be brought home, and how they had set out to meet him on the Budmouth Road.

'But he has gone to Mellstock and Weatherbury!' exclaimed Henchard, now unspeakably grieved. 'Not Budmouth way at all.'

But, alas! for Henchard; he had lost his good name. They would not believe him, taking his words but as the frothy utterances of recklessness. Though Lucetta's life seemed at that moment to depend upon her husband's return (she being in great mental agony lest he should never know the unexaggerated truth of her past relations with Henchard), no messenger was despatched towards Weatherbury. Henchard, in a state of bitter anxiety and contrition, determined to seek Farfrae himself.

To this end he hastened down the town, ran along the eastern road over Durnover moor, up the hill beyond, and thus onward in the moderate darkness of this spring night till he had reached a second and almost a third hill about three miles distant. In Yalbury Bottom, or Plain, at the foot of the hill, he listened. At first nothing, beyond his own heart-throbs, was to be heard but the slow wind making its moan among the masses of spruce and larch of Yalbury Wood which clothed the heights on either hand; but presently there came the sound of light wheels whetting their felloes against the newly stoned patches of road, accompanied by the distant glimmer of lights.

He knew it was Farfae's gig descending the hill from an indescribable personality in its noise, the vehicle having been his own till bought by the Scotchman at the sale of his effects. Henchard thereupon retraced his steps along Yalbury Plain, the gig coming up with him as its driver slackened speed between two plantations.

It was a point in the highway near which the road to Mellstock branched off from the homeward direction. By diverging to that village, as he had intended to do, Farfrae might probably delay his return by a couple of hours. It soon appeared that his intention was to do so still, the light swerving towards Cuckoo Lane, the by-road aforesaid. Farfrae's off giglamp flashed in Henchard's face. At the same time, Farfrae discerned his late antagonist.

'Farfrae – Mr Farfrae!' cried the breathless Henchard, holding up his hand.

Farfrae allowed the horse to turn several steps into the branch lane before he pulled up. He then drew rein, and said 'Yes?' over his shoulder, as one would towards a pronounced enemy.

'Come back to Casterbridge at once!' Henchard said. 'There's something wrong at your house – requiring your return. I've run all the way here on purpose to tell ye.'

Farfrae was silent, and at his silence Henchard's soul sank within him. Why had he not, before this, thought of what was only too obvious? He who, four hours earlier, had enticed Farfrae into a deadly wrestle stood now in the darkness of late night-time on a lonely road, inviting him to come a particular way, where an assailant might have confederates, instead of going his purposed way, where there might be a better opportunity of guarding himself from attack. Henchard could almost feel this view of things in course of passage through Farfrae's mind.

'I have to go to Mellstock,' said Farfrae coldly, as he loosened his rein to move on.

'But,' implored Henchard, 'the matter is more serious then your business at Mellstock. It is – your wife! She is ill. I can tell you particulars as we go along.'

The very agitation and abruptness of Henchard increased Farfrae's suspicion that this was a *ruse* to decoy him on to the next wood, where might be effectually compassed what, from policy or want of nerve, Henchard had failed to do earlier in the day. He started the horse.

'I know what you think,' deprecated Henchard running after, almost bowed down with despair as he perceived the image of unscrupulous villainy that he assumed in his former friend's eyes. 'But I am not what you think!' he cried hoarsely. 'Believe me, Farfrae; I have come entirely on your own and your wife's account. She is in danger. I know no more; and they want you to come. Your man has gone the other way in a mistake. O Farfrae! don't mistrust me – I am a wretched man; but my heart is true to you still!'

Farfrae, however, did distrust him utterly. He knew his wife was with child, but he had left her not long ago in perfect health; and Henchard's treachery was more credible than his story. He had in his time heard bitter ironies from Henchard's lips, and there might be ironies now. He quickened the horse's pace, and had soon risen in the high country lying between there and Mellstock, Henchard's spasmodic run after him lending yet more substance to his thought of evil purposes.

The gig and its driver lessened against the sky in Henchard's eyes; his exertions for Farfrae's good had been in vain. Over this repentant sinner, at least, there was to be no joy in heaven. He cursed himself like a less scrupulous Job, as a vehement man will do when he loses self-respect, the last mental prop under poverty. To this he had come after a time of emotional darkness of which the adjoining woodland shade afforded inadequate illustration. Presently he began to walk back again along the way by which he had arrived. Farfrae should at all events have no reason for delay upon the road by seeing him there when he took his journey homeward later on.

Arriving at Casterbridge Henchard went again to Farfrae's house to make inquiries. As soon as the door opened anxious faces confronted his from the staircase, hall, and landing; and they all said in grievous disappointment, 'O – it is not he!' The manservant, finding his mistake, had long since returned, and all hopes had been centred upon Henchard.

'But haven't you found him?' said the doctor.

'Yes . . . I cannot tell 'ee!' Henchard replied as he sank down on a chair within the entrance. He can't be home for two hours.'

'H'm,' said the surgeon, returning upstairs.

'How is she?' asked Henchard of Elizabeth, who formed one of the group.

'In great danger, father. Her anxiety to see her husband makes her fearfully restless. Poor woman – I fear they have killed her!'

Henchard regarded the sympathetic speaker for a few instants as if she struck him in a new light; then, without further remark, went out of the door and onward to his lonely cottage. So much for man's rivalry, he thought. Death was to have the oyster, and Farfrae and himself the shells. But about Elizabeth-Jane; in the midst of his gloom she seemed to him as a pin-point of light. He had liked the look of her face as she answered him from the stairs. There had been affection in it, and above all things what he desired now was affection from anything that was good and pure. She was not his own; yet, for the first time, he had a faint dream that he might get to like her as his own, – if she would only continue to love him.

Jopp was just going to bed when Henchard got home. As the latter entered the door Jopp said, 'This is rather bad about Mrs Farfrae's illness.'

'Yes,' said Henchard shortly, though little dreaming of Jopp's complicity in the night's harlequinade, and raising his eyes just sufficiently to observe that Jopp's face was lined with anxiety.

'Somebody has called for you,' continued Jopp, when Henchard was shutting himself into his own apartment. 'A kind of traveller, or sea-captain of some sort.'

'Oh? – who could he be?'

'He seemed a well-be-doing man – had grey hair and a broadish face; but he gave no name, and no message.'

'Nor do I gi'e him any attention.' And, saying this, Henchard closed his door.

The divergence to Mellstock delayed Farfrae's return very nearly the two hours of Henchard's estimate. Among the other urgent reasons for his presence had been the need of his authority to send to Budmouth for a second physician; and when at length Farfrae did come back he was in a state bordering on distraction at his misconception of Henchard's motives.

A messenger was despatched to Budmouth, late as it had grown; the night wore on, and the other doctor came in the small hours. Lucetta had been much soothed by Donald's arrival; he seldom or never left her side; and when, immediately after his entry, she had tried to lisp out to him the secret which so oppressed her, he checked her feeble words, lest talking should be dangerous, assuring her there was plenty of time to tell him everything.

Up to this time he knew nothing of the skimmington-ride. The dangerous illness and miscarriage of Mrs Farfrae was soon rumoured through the town, and an apprehensive guess having been given as to its cause by the leaders in the exploit, compunction and fear threw a dead silence over all particulars of their orgie; while those immediately around Lucetta would not venture to add to her husband's distress by alluding to the subject.

What, and how much, Farfrae's wife ultimately explained to him of her past entanglement with Henchard, when they were alone in the solitude of that sad night, cannot be told. That she informed him of the bare facts of her peculiar intimacy with the corn-merchant became plain from Farfrae's own statements. But in respect of her subsequent conduct – her motive in coming to Casterbridge to unite herself with Henchard – her assumed justification in abandoning him when she discovered reasons for fearing him (though in truth her inconsequent passion for another man at first sight had most to do with that abandonment) – her method of reconciling to her conscience a marriage with the second when she was in a measure committed to the first: to what extent she spoke of these things remained Farfrae's secret alone.

Besides the watchman who called the hours and weather in Casterbridge that night there walked a figure up and down Corn Street hardly less frequently. It was Henchard's, whose retiring to rest had proved itself a futility as soon as attempted; and he gave it up to go hither and thither, and make inquiries about the patient every now and then. He called as much on Farfrae's account as on Lucetta's, and on Elizabeth-Jane's even more than on either's. Shorn one by one of all other interests, his life seemed centring on the personality of the stepdaughter whose presence but recently he could not endure. To see her on each occasion of his inquiry at Lucetta's was a comfort to him.

The last of his calls was made about four o'clock in the morning, in the steely light of dawn. Lucifer was fading into day across Durnover Moor, the sparrows were just alighting into the street, and the hens begun to cackle from the outhouses. When within a few yards of Farfrae's he saw the door gently opened, and a servant raise her hand to the knocker, to untie the piece of cloth which had muffled it. He went across, the sparrows in his way scarcely flying up from the road-litter, so little did they believe in human aggression at so early a time.

'Why do you take off that?' said Henchard.

She turned in some surprise at his presence, and did not answer for an instant or two. Recognizing him, she said, 'Because they may knock as loud as they will; she will never hear it any more.'

* XLI *

HENCHARD went home. The morning having now fully broke he lit his fire, and sat abstractedly beside it. He had not sat there long when a gentle footstep approached the house and entered the passage, a finger tapping lightly at the door. Henchard's face brightened, for he knew the motions to be Elizabeth's. She came into his room, looking wan and sad.

'Have you heard?' she asked. 'Mrs Farfrae! She is – dead! Yes, indeed – about an hour ago!'

'I know it,' said Henchard. 'I have but lately come in from there. It is so very good of 'ee, Elizabeth, to come and tell me. You must be so tired out, too, with sitting up. Now do you bide here with me this morning. You can go and rest in the other room; and I will call 'ee when breakfast is ready.'

To please him, and herself – for this recent kindliness was winning a surprised gratitude from the lonely girl – she did as he bade her, and lay down on a sort of couch which Henchard had rigged up out of a settle in the adjoining room. She could hear him moving about in his preparations; but her mind ran most strongly on Lucetta, whose death in such fullness of life and amid such cheerful hopes of maternity was appallingly unexpected. Presently she fell asleep.

Meanwhile her stepfather in the outer room had set the breakfast in readiness; but finding that she dozed he would not call her; he waited on, looking into the fire and keeping the kettle boiling with housewifely care, as if it were an honour to have her in his house. In truth, a great change had come over him with regard to her, and he was developing the dream of a future lit by her filial presence, as though that way alone could happiness lie.

He was disturbed by another knock at the door, and rose to open it, rather deprecating a call from anybody just then. A stoutly built man stood on the doorstep, with an alien, unfamiliar air about his figure and bearing – an air which might have been called colonial by people of cosmopolitan experience. It was the man who had asked the way at Peter's Finger. Henchard nodded, and looked inquiry.

'Good morning, good morning,' said the stranger with profuse heartiness. 'Is it Mr Henchard I am talking to?'

'My name is Henchard.'

'Then I've caught 'ee at home – that's right. Morning's the time for business, says I. Can I have a few words with you?'

'By all means,' Henchard answered, showing the way in.

'You may remember me?' said his visitor, seating himself.

Henchard observed him indifferently, and shook his head.

'Well – perhaps you may not. My name is Newson.'

Henchard's face and eyes seemed to die. The other did not notice it. 'I know the name well,' Henchard said at last, looking on the floor.

'I make no doubt of that. Well, the fact is, I've been looking for 'ee this fortnight past. I landed at Havenpool and went through Casterbridge on my way to Falmouth, and when I got there, they told me you had some years before been living at Casterbridge. Back came I again, and by long and by late I got here by coach, ten minutes ago. "He lives down by the mill," says they. So here I am. Now – that transaction between us some twenty years agone – 'tis that I've called about. 'Twas a curious business.

I was younger then than I am now, and perhaps the less said about it, in one sense, the better.'

'Curious business! 'Twas worse than curious. I cannot even allow that I'm the man you met then. I was not in my senses, and a man's senses are himself.'

'We were young and thoughtless,' said Newson. 'However, I've come to mend matters rather than open arguments. Poor Susan – hers was a strange experience.'

'It was.'

'She was a warm-hearted, home-spun woman. She was not what they call shrewd or sharp at all – better she had been.'

'She was not.'

'As you in all likelihood know, she was simple-minded enough to think that the sale was in a way binding. She was as guiltless o' wrong-doing in that particular as a saint in the clouds.'

'I know it, I know it. I found it out directly,' said Henchard, still with averted eyes. 'There lay the sting o't to me. If she had seen it as what it was she would never have left me. Never! But how should she be expected to know? What advantages had she? None. She could write her own name, and no more.'

'Well, it was not in my heart to undeceive her when the deed was done,' said the sailor of former days. 'I thought, and there was not much vanity in thinking it, that she would be happier with me. She was fairly happy, and I never would have undeceived her till the day of her death. Your child died; she had another, and all went well. But a time came – mind me, a time always does come. A time came – it was some while after she and I and the child returned from America – when somebody she had confided her history to, told her my claim to her was a mockery, and made a jest of her belief in my right. After that she was never happy with me. She pined and pined, and socked and sighed. She said she must leave me, and then came the question of our child. Then a man advised me how to act, and I did it, for I thought it was best. I left her at Falmouth, and went off to sea. When I got to the other side of the Atlantic there was a storm, and it was supposed that a lot of us including myself, had been washed overboard. I got ashore at Newfoundland, and then I asked myself what I should do. "Since I'm here, here I'll bide," I thought to myself; "'twill be most kindness to her, now she's taken against me, to let her believe me lost; for," I thought, "while she supposes us both alive she'll be miserable; but if she thinks me dead she'll go back to him, and the child will have a home." I've never returned to this country till a month ago, and I found that, as I had supposed, she went to you, and my daughter with her. They told me in Falmouth that Susan was dead. But my Elizabeth-Jane – where is she?'

'Dead likewise,' said Henchard doggedly. 'Surely you learnt that too?'

The sailor started up, and took an enervated pace or two down the room. 'Dead!' he said, in a low voice. 'Then what's the use of my money to me?'

Henchard, without answering, shook his head as if that were rather a question for Newson himself than for him.

'Where is she buried?' the traveller inquired.

'Beside her mother,' said Henchard, in the same stolid tones.

'When did she die?'

'A year ago and more,' replied the other without hesitation.

The sailor continued standing. Henchard never looked up from the floor. At last Newson said: 'My journey hither has been for nothing! I may as well go as I came! It has served me right. I'll trouble you no longer.'

Henchard heard the retreating footsteps of Newson upon the sanded floor, the mechanical lifting of the latch, the slow opening and closing of the door that was natural to a baulked or dejected man; but he did not turn his head. Newson's shadow passed the window. He was gone.

Then Henchard, scarcely believing the evidence of his senses, rose from his seat amazed at what he had done. It had been the impulse of a moment. The regard he had lately acquired for Elizabeth, the new-sprung hope of his loneliness that she would be to him a daughter of whom he could feel as proud as of the actual daughter she still believed herself to be, had been stimulated by the unexpected coming of Newson to a greedy exclusiveness in relation to her; so that the sudden prospect of her loss had caused him to speak mad lies like a child, in pure mockery of consequences. He had expected questions to close in round him, and unmask his fabrication in five minutes; yet such questioning had not come. But surely they would come; Newson's departure could be but momentary; he would learn all by inquiries in the town; and return to curse him, and carry his last treasure away!

He hastily put on his hat, and went out in the direction that Newson had taken. Newson's back was soon visible up the road, crossing Bull-stake. Henchard followed; and saw his visitor stop at the King's Arms, where the morning coach which had brought him waited half-an-hour for another coach which crossed there. The coach Newson had come by was about to move again. Newson mounted; his luggage was put in, and in a few minutes the vehicle disappeared with him.

He had not so much as turned his head. It was an act of simple faith in Henchard's words – faith so simple as to be almost sublime. The young sailor who had taken Susan Henchard on the spur of the moment and on the faith of a glance at her face, more than twenty years before, was still living and acting under the form of the grizzled traveller who had taken Henchard's words on trust so absolute as to shame him as he stood.

Was Elizabeth-Jane to remain his by virtue of this hardy invention of a moment? 'Perhaps not for long,' said he. Newson might converse with his fellow-travellers, some of whom might be Casterbridge people; and the trick would be discovered.

This probability threw Henchard into a defensive attitude, and instead of considering how best to right the wrong, and acquaint Elizabeth's father with the truth at once, he bethought himself of ways to keep the

position he had accidentally won. Towards the young woman herself his
affection grew more jealously strong with each new hazard to which his
claim to her was exposed.

He watched the distant highway expecting to see Newson return on
foot, enlightened and indignant, to claim his child. But no figure
appeared. Possibly he had spoken to nobody on the coach, but buried his
grief in his own heart.

His grief! – what was it, after all, to that which he, Henchard, would
feel at the loss of her? Newson's affection, cooled by years, could not
equal his who had been constantly in her presence. And thus his jealous
soul speciously argued to excuse the separation of father and child.

He returned to the house half expecting that she would have vanished.
No; there she was – just coming out from the inner room, the marks of
sleep upon her eyelids, and exhibiting a generally refreshed air.

'O father!' she said, smiling. 'I had no sooner lain down that I napped,
though I did not mean to. I wonder I did not dream about poor Mrs
Farfrae, after thinking of her so; but I did not. How strange it is that we
do not often dream of latest events, absorbing as they may be.'

'I am glad you have been able to sleep,' he said, taking her hand with
anxious proprietorship – an act which gave her a pleasant surprise.

They sat down to breakfast, and Elizabeth-Jane's thoughts reverted to
Lucetta. Their sadness added charm to a countenance whose beauty had
ever lain in its meditative soberness.

'Father,' she said, as soon as she recalled herself to the outspread meal,
'it is so kind of you to get this nice breakfast with your own hands, and
I idly asleep the while.'

'I do it every day,' he replied. 'You have left me; everybody has left me;
how should I live but by my own hands.'

'You are very lonely, are you not?'

'Ay, child – to a degree that you know nothing of! It is my own fault.
You are the only one who has been near me for weeks. And you will
come no more.'

'Why do you say that? Indeed I will, if you would like to see me.'

Henchard signified dubiousness. Though he had so lately hoped that
Elizabeth-Jane might again live in his house as daughter, he would not
ask her to do so now. Newson might return at any moment, and what
Elizabeth would think of him for his deception it were best to bear apart
from her.

When they had breakfasted his stepdaughter still lingered, till the
moment arrived at which Henchard was accustomed to go to his daily
work. Then she arose, and with assurances of coming again soon went up
the hill in the morning sunlight.

'At this moment her heart is as warm towards me as mine is towards
her; she would live with me here in this humble cottage for the asking!
Yet before the evening probably he will have come; and then she will
scorn me!'

This reflection, constantly repeated by Henchard to himself, accompanied him everywhere through the day. His mood was no longer that of the rebellious, ironical, reckless misadventurer; but the leaden gloom of one who has lost all that can make life interesting, or even tolerable. There would remain nobody for him to be proud of, nobody to fortify him; for Elizabeth-Jane would soon be but as a stranger, and worse. Susan, Farfrae, Lucetta, Elizabeth – all had gone from him, one after one, either by his fault or by his misfortune.

In place of them he had no interest, hobby, or desire. If he could have summoned music to his aid his existence might even now have been borne; for with Henchard music was of regal power. The merest trumpet or organ tone was enough to move him, and high harmonies transubstantiated him. But hard fate had ordained that he should be unable to call up this Divine spirit in his need.

The whole land ahead of him was as darkness itself; there was nothing to come, nothing to wait for. Yet in the natural course of life he might possibly have to linger on earth another thirty or forty years – scoffed at; at best pitied.

The thought of it was unendurable.

To the east of Casterbridge lay moors and meadows through which much water flowed. The wanderer in this direction who should stand still for a few moments on a quiet night, might hear singular symphonies from these waters, as from a lampless orchestra, all playing in their sundry tones from near and far parts of the moor. At a hole in a rotten weir they executed a recitative; where a tributary brook fell over a stone breastwork they trilled cheerily; under an arch they performed a metallic cymballing; and at Durnover Hole they hissed. The spot at which their instrumentation rose loudest was a place called Ten Hatches, whence during high springs there proceeded a very fugue of sounds.

The river here was deep and strong at all times, and the hatches on this account were raised and lowered by cogs and a winch. A path led from the second bridge over the highway (so often mentioned) to these Hatches, crossing the stream at their head by a narrow plank-bridge. But after night-fall human beings were seldom found going that way, the path leading only to a deep reach of the stream called Blackwater, and the passage being dangerous.

Henchard, however, leaving the town by the east road, proceeded to the second, or stone bridge, and thence struck into this path of solitude, following its course beside the stream till the dark shapes of the Ten Hatches cut the sheen thrown upon the river by the weak lustre that still lingered in the west. In a second or two he stood beside the weir-hole where the water was at its deepest. He looked backwards and forwards, and no creature appeared in view. He then took off his coat and hat, and stood on the brink of the stream with his hands clasped in front of him.

While his eyes were bent on the water beneath there slowly became visible a something floating in the circular pool formed by the wash of centuries; the pool he was intending to make his deathbed. At first it was indistinct by reason of the shadow from the bank; but it emerged thence and took shape, which was that of a human body, lying stiff and stark upon the surface of the stream.

In the circular current imparted by the central flow the form was brought forward, till it passed under his eyes; and then he perceived with a sense of horror that it was *himself*. Not a man somewhat resembling him, but one in all respects his counterpart, his actual double, was floating as if dead in Ten Hatches Hole.

The sense of the supernatural was strong in this unhappy man, and he turned away as one might have done in the actual presence of an appalling miracle. He covered his eyes and bowed his head. Without looking again into the stream he took his coat and hat, and went slowly away.

Presently he found himself by the door of his own dwelling. To his surprise Elizabeth-Jane was standing there. She came forward, spoke, called him 'father' just as before. Newson, then, had not even yet returned.

'I thought you seemed very sad this morning,' she said, 'so I have come again to see you. Not that I am anything but sad myself. But everybody and everything seem against you so; and I know you must be suffering.'

How this woman divined things! Yet she had not divined their whole extremity.

He said to her, 'Are miracles still worked, do ye think, Elizabeth? I am not a read man. I don't know so much as I could wish. I have tried to peruse and learn all my life; but the more I try to know the more ignorant I seem.'

'I don't quite think there are any miracles nowadays,' she said.

'No interference in the case of desperate intentions, for instance? Well, perhaps not, in a direct way. Perhaps not. But will you come and walk with me, and I will show 'ee what I mean?'

She agreed willingly, and he took her over the highway, and by the lonely path to Ten Hatches. He walked restlessly, as if some haunting shade, unseen of her, hovered round him and troubled his glance. She would gladly have talked of Lucetta, but feared to disturb him. When they got near the weir he stood still, and asked her to go forward and look into the pool, and tell him what she saw.

She went, and soon returned to him. 'Nothing,' she said.

'Go again,' said Henchard, 'and look narrowly.'

She proceeded to the river brink a second time. On her return, after some delay, she told him that she saw something floating round and round there; but what it was she could not discern. It seemed to be a bundle of old clothes.

'Are they like mine?' asked Henchard.

'Well – they are. Dear me – I wonder if – Father, let us go away!'

'Go and look once more; and then we will get home.'

She went back, and he could see her stoop till her head was close to the margin of the pool. She started up, and hastened back to his side.

'Well,' said Henchard; 'what do you say now?'

'Let us go home.'

'But tell me – do – what is it floating there?'

'The effigy,' she answered hastily. 'They must have thrown it into the river higher up amongst the willows at Blackwater, to get rid of it in their alarm at discovery by the magistrates; and it must have floated down here.'

'Ah – to be sure – the image o' me! But where is the other? Why that one only? . . . That performance of theirs killed her, but kept me alive!'

Elizabeth-Jane thought and thought of these words 'kept me alive', as they slowly retraced their way to the town, and at length guessed their meaning. 'Father! – I will not leave you alone like this!' she cried. 'May I live with you, and tend upon you as I used to do? I do not mind your being poor. I would have agreed to come this morning, but you did not ask me.'

'May you come to me?' he cried bitterly. 'Elizabeth, don't mock me! If you only would come!'

'I will,' said she.

'How will you forgive all my roughness in former days? You cannot!'

'I have forgotten it. Talk of that no more.'

Thus she assured him, and arranged their plans for reunion; and at length each went home. Then Henchard shaved for the first time during many days, and put on clean linen, and combed his hair; and was a man resuscitated thenceforward.

The next morning the fact turned out to be as Elizabeth-Jane had stated; the effigy was discovered by a cowherd, and that of Lucetta a little higher up in the same stream. But as little as possible was said of the matter, and the figures were privately destroyed.

Despite this natural solution of the mystery Henchard no less regarded it as an intervention that the figure should have been floating there. Elizabeth-Jane heard him say, 'Who is such a reprobate as I! And yet it seems that even I be in Somebody's hand!'

* XLII *

BUT the emotional conviction that he was in Somebody's hand began to die out of Henchard's breast as time slowly removed into distance the event which had given that feeling birth. The apparition of Newson haunted him. He would surely return.

Yet Newson did not arrive. Lucetta had been borne along the churchyard path; Casterbridge had for the last time turned its regard upon her, before proceeding to its work as if she had never lived. But Elizabeth remained undisturbed in the belief of her relationship to Henchard, and now shared his home. Perhaps, after all, Newson was gone for ever.

In due time the bereaved Farfrae had learnt the, at least, proximate cause of Lucetta's illness and death; and his first impulse was naturally enough to wreak vengeance in the name of the law upon the perpetrators of the mischief. He resolved to wait till the funeral was over ere he moved in the matter. The time having come he reflected. Disastrous as the result had been, it was obviously in no way foreseen or intended by the thoughtless crew who arranged the motley procession. The tempting prospect of putting to the blush people who stand at the head of affairs – that supreme and piquant enjoyment of those who writhe under the heel of the same – had alone animated them, so far as he could see; for he knew nothing of Jopp's incitements. Other considerations were also involved. Lucetta had confessed everything to him before her death, and it was not altogether desirable to make much ado about her history, alike for her sake, for Henchard's, and for his own. To regard the event as an untoward accident seemed, to Farfrae, truest consideration for the dead one's memory, as well as best philosophy.

Henchard and himself mutually forbore to meet. For Elizabeth's sake the former had fettered his pride sufficiently to accept the small seed and root business which some of the Town Council, headed by Farfrae, had purchased to afford him a new opening. Had he been only personally concerned Henchard, without doubt, would have declined assistance even remotely brought about by the man whom he had so fiercely assailed. But the sympathy of the girl seemed necessary to his very existence; and on her account pride itself wore the garments of humility.

Here they settled themselves; and on each day of their lives Henchard anticipated her every wish with a watchfulness in which paternal regard was heightened by a burning jealous dread of rivalry. Yet that Newson would ever now return to Casterbridge to claim her as a daughter there was little reason to suppose. He was a wanderer and a stranger, almost an alien; he had not seen his daughter for several years; his affection for her could not in the nature of things be keen; other interests would probably soon obscure his recollections of her, and prevent any such renewal of inquiry into the past as would lead to a discovery that she was still a creature of the present. To satisfy his conscience somewhat Henchard repeated to himself that the lie which had retained for him the coveted treasure had not been deliberately told to that end, but had come from him as the last defiant word of a despair which took no thought of consequences. Furthermore he pleaded within himself that no Newson could love her as he loved her, or would tend her to his life's extremity as he was prepared to do cheerfully.

Thus they lived on in the shop overlooking the churchyard, and nothing occurred to mark their days during the remainder of the year. Going out but seldom, and never on a market-day they saw Donald

Farfrae only at rarest intervals, and then mostly as a transitory object in the distance of the street. Yet he was pursuing his ordinary avocations, smiling mechanically to fellow-tradesmen, and arguing with bargainers – as bereaved men do after a while.

Time, 'in his own grey style', taught Farfrae how to estimate his experience of Lucetta – all that it was, and all that it was not. There are men whose hearts insist upon a dogged fidelity to some image or cause thrown by chance into their keeping, long after their judgement has pronounced it no rarity – even the reverse, indeed; and without them the band of the worthy is incomplete. But Farfrae was not of those. It was inevitable that the insight, briskness, and rapidity of his nature should take him out of the dead blank which his loss threw about him. He could not but perceive that by the death of Lucetta he had exchanged a looming misery for a simple sorrow. After that revelation of her history, which must have come sooner or later in any circumstances, it was hard to believe that life with her would have been productive of further happiness.

But as a memory, notwithstanding such conditions, Lucetta's image still lived on with him, her weaknesses provoking only the gentlest criticism, and her suffering's attenuating wrath at her concealments to a momentary spark now and then.

By the end of a year Henchard's little retail seed and grain shop, not much larger than a cupboard, had developed its trade considerably, and the stepfather and daughter enjoyed much serenity in the pleasant, sunny corner in which it stood. The quiet bearing of one who brimmed with an inner activity characterized Elizabeth-Jane at this period. She took long walks into the country two or three times a week, mostly in the direction of Budmouth. Sometimes it occurred to him that when she sat with him in the evening after these invigorating walks she was civil rather than affectionate; and he was troubled; one more bitter regret being added to those he had already experienced at having, by his severe censorship, frozen up her precious affection when originally offered.

She had her own way in everything now. In going and coming, in buying and selling, her word was law.

'You have got a new muff, Elizabeth,' he said to her one day quite humbly.

'Yes; I bought it,' she said.

He looked at it again as it lay on an adjoining table. The fur was of a glossy brown, and, though he was no judge of such articles, he thought it seemed an unusually good one for her to possess.

'Rather costly, I suppose, my dear, was it not?' he hazarded.

'It was rather above my figure,' she said quietly. 'But it is not showy.'

'O no,' said the netted lion, anxious not to pique her in the least.

Some little time after, when the year had advanced into another spring, he paused opposite her empty bedroom in passing it. He thought of the time when she had cleared out of his then large and handsome house in Corn Street, in consequence of his dislike and harshness, and he had looked into her chamber in just the same way. The present room was much humbler, but what struck him about it was the abundance of books lying everywhere. Their number and quality made the meagre furniture that supported them seem absurdly disproportionate. Some, indeed many, must have been recently purchased; and though he encouraged her to buy in reason, he had no notion that she indulged her innate passion so extensively in proportion to the narrowness of their income. For the first time he felt a little hurt by what he thought her extravagance, and resolved to say a word to her about it. But, before he had found the courage to speak, an event happened which set his thoughts flying in quite another direction.

The busy time of the seed trade was over; and the quiet weeks that preceded the hay-season had come – setting their special stamp upon Casterbridge by thronging the market with wood rakes, new waggons in yellow, green, and red, formidably scythes, and pitch-forks of prong sufficient to skewer up a small family. Henchard, contrary to his wont, went out one Saturday afternoon towards the market place, from a curious feeling that he would like to pass a few minutes on the spot of his former triumphs. Farfrae, to whom he was still a comparative stranger, stood a few steps below the Corn Exchange door – a usual position with him at this hour – and he appeared lost in thought about something he was looking at a little way off.

Henchard's eyes followed Farfrae's, and he saw that the object of his gaze was no sample-showing farmer, but his own stepdaughter, who had just come out of a shop over the way. She, on her part, was quite unconscious of his attention, and in this was less fortunate than those young women whose very plumes, like those of Juno's bird, are set with Argus eyes whenever possible admirers are within ken.

Henchard went away, thinking that perhaps there was nothing significant after all in Farfrae's look at Elizabeth-Jane at that juncture. Yet he could not forget that the Scotchman had once shown a tender interest in her, of a fleeting kind. Thereupon promptly came to the surface that idiosyncrasy of Henchard's which had ruled his courses from the beginning and had mainly made him what he was. Instead of thinking that a union between his cherished stepdaughter and the energetic thriving Donald was a thing to be desired for her good and his own, he hated the very possibility.

Time had been when such instinctive opposition would have taken shape in action. But he was not now the Henchard of former days. He schooled himself to accept her will, in this as in other matters, as absolute and unquestionable. He dreaded lest an antagonistic word should lose for him such regard as he had regained from her by his devotion, feeling that to retain this under separation was better than to incur her dislike by keeping her near.

But the mere thought of such separation fevered his spirit much, and in the evening he said, with the stillness of suspense: 'Have you seen Mr Farfrae today, Elizabeth?'

Elizabeth-Jane started at the question; and it was with some confusion that she replied 'No.'

'Oh – that's right – that's right . . . It was only that I saw him in the street when we both were there.' He was wondering if her embarrassment justified him in a new suspicion – that the long walks which she had latterly been taking, that the new books which had so surprised him, had anything to do with the young man. She did not enlighten him, and lest silence should allow her to shape thoughts unfavourable to their present friendly relations, he diverted the discourse into another channel.

Henchard was, by original make, the last man to act stealthily, for good or for evil. But the *solicitus timor* of his love – the dependence upon Elizabeth's regard into which he had declined (or, in another sense, to which he had advanced) – denaturalized him. He would often weigh and consider for hours together the meaning of such and such a deed or phrase of hers, when a blunt settling question would formerly have been his first instinct. And now, uneasy at the thought of a passion for Farfrae which should entirely displace her mild filial sympathy with himself, he observed her going and coming more narrowly.

There was nothing secret in Elizabeth-Jane's movements beyond what habitual reserve induced; and it may at once be owned on her account that she was guilty of occasional conversations with Donald when they chanced to meet. Whatever the origin of her walks on the Budmouth Road, her return from those walks was often coincident with Farfrae's emergence from Corn Street for a twenty minutes' blow on that rather windy highway – just to winnow the seeds and chaff out of him before sitting down to tea, as he said. Henchard became aware of this by going to the Ring, and, screened by its enclosure, keeping his eye upon the road till he saw them meet. His face assumed an expression of extreme anguish.

'Of her, too, he means to rob me!' he whispered. 'But he has the right. I do not wish to interfere.'

The meeting, in truth, was of a very innocent kind, and matters were by no means so far advanced between the young people as Henchard's jealous grief inferred. Could he have heard such conversation as passed he would have been enlightened thus much:

He. – 'You like walking this way, Miss Henchard – and is it not so?' (uttered in his undulatory accents, and with an appraising, pondering gaze at her).

She. – 'O yes. I have chosen this road latterly. I have no great reason for it.'

He. – 'But that may make a reason for others.'

She (reddening). – 'I don't know that. My reason, however, such as it is, is that I wish to get a glimpse of the sea every day.'

He. – 'Is it a secret why?'

She (reluctantly). – 'Yes.'

He (with the pathos of one of his native ballads). – 'Ah, I doubt there will be any good in secrets! A secret cast a deep shadow over my life. And well you know what it was.'

Elizabeth admitted that she did, but she refrained from confessing why the sea attracted her. She could not herself account for it fully, not knowing the secret possibly to be that, in addition to early marine associations, her blood was a sailor's.

'Thank you for those new books, Mr Farfrae,' she added shyly. 'I wonder if I ought to accept so many!'

'Ay! why not? It gives me more pleasure to get them for you, than you to have them!'

'It cannot!'

They proceeded along the road together till they reached the town, and their paths diverged.

Henchard vowed that he would leave them to their own devices, put nothing in the way of their courses, whatever they might mean. If he were doomed to be bereft of her, so it must be. In the situation which their marriage would create he could see no *locus standi* for himself at all. Farfrae would never recognize him more than superciliously; his poverty ensured that, no less than his past conduct. And so Elizabeth would grow to be a stranger to him, and the end of his life would be friendless solitude.

With such a possibility impending he could not help watchfulness. Indeed, within certain lines, he had the right to keep an eye upon her as his charge. The meetings seemed to become matters of course with them on special days of the week.

At last full proof was given him. He was standing behind a wall close to the place at which Farfrae encountered her. He heard the young man address her as 'Dearest Elizabeth-Jane', and then kiss her, the girl looking quickly round to assure herself that nobody was near.

When they were gone their way Henchard came out from the wall, and mournfully followed them to Casterbridge. The chief looming trouble in this engagement had not decreased. Both Farfrae and Elizabeth-Jane, unlike the rest of the people, must suppose Elizabeth to be his actual daughter, from his own assertion while he himself had the same belief; and though Farfrae must have so far forgiven him as to have no objection to own him as a father-in-law, intimate they could never be. Thus would the girl, who was his only friend, be withdrawn from him by degrees through her husband's influence, and learn to despise him.

Had she lost her heart to any other man in the world than the one he had rivalled, cursed, wrestled with for life in days before his spirit was broken, Henchard would have said, 'I am content.' But content with the prospect as now depicted was hard to acquire.

There is an outer chamber of the brain in which thoughts unowned, unsolicited, and of noxious kind, are sometimes allowed to wander for a moment prior to being sent off whence they came. One of these thoughts sailed into Henchard's ken now.

Suppose he were to communicate to Farfrae the fact that his betrothed was not the child of Michael Henchard at all – legally, nobody's child; how would that correct and leading townsman receive the information?

He might possibly forsake Elizabeth-Jane, and then she would be her stepsire's own again.

Henchard shuddered, and exclaimed, 'God forbid such a thing! Why should I still be subject to these visitations of the devil, when I try so hard to keep him away?'

* XLIII *

WHAT Henchard saw thus early was, naturally enough, seen at a little later date by other people. That Mr Farfrae 'walked with that bankrupt Henchard's stepdaughter, of all women', became a common topic in the town, the simple perambulating term being used hereabout to signify a wooing; and the nineteen superior young ladies of Casterbridge, who had each looked upon herself as the only woman capable of making the merchant Councilman happy, indignantly left off going to the church Farfrae attended, left off conscious mannerisms, left off putting him in their prayers at night amongst their blood relations; in short, reverted to their natural courses.

Perhaps the only inhabitants of the town to whom this looming choice of the Scotchman's gave unmixed satisfaction were the members of the philosophic party, which included Longways, Christopher Coney, Billy Wills, Mr Buzzford, and the like. The Three Mariners having been, years before, the house in which they had witnessed the young man and woman's first and humble appearance on the Casterbridge stage, they took a kindly interest in their career, not unconnected, perhaps, with visions of festive treatment at their hands hereafter. Mrs Stannidge, having rolled into the large parlour one evening and said that it was a wonder such a man as Mr Farfrae, 'a pillow of the town', who might have chosen one of the daughters of the professional men or private residents, should stoop so low, Coney ventured to disagree with her.

'No, ma'am, no wonder at all. 'Tis she that's a stooping to he – that's my opinion. A widow man – whose first wife was no credit to him – what is it for a young perusing woman that's her own mistress and well liked? But as a neat patching up of things I see much good in it. When a man have put up a tomb of best marble-stone to the other one, as he've done, and weeped his fill, and thought it all over, and said to hisself, "T'other took me in; I knowed this one first; she's a sensible piece for a partner, and there's no faithful woman in high life now", – well, he may do worse than not to take her, if she's tender-inclined.'

Thus they talked at the Mariners. But we must guard against a too liberal use of the conventional declaration that a great sensation was caused by the prospective event, that all the gossips' tongues were set wagging thereby, and so on, even though such a declaration might lend some *éclat* to the career of our poor only heroine. When all has been said about busy rumourers, a superficial and temporary thing is the interest of anybody in affairs which do not directly touch them. It would be a truer representation to say that Casterbridge (ever excepting the nineteen young ladies) looked up for a moment at the news, and withdrawing its attention, went on labouring and victualling, bringing up its children, and burying its dead, without caring a little for Farfrae's domestic plans.

Not a hint of the matter was thrown out to her stepfather by Elizabeth herself or by Farfrae either. Reasoning of the cause of their reticence he concluded that, estimating him by his past, the throbbing pair were afraid to broach the subject, and looked upon him as an irksome obstacle whom they would be heartily glad to get out of the way. Embittered as he was against society, this moody view of himself took deeper and deeper hold of Henchard, till the daily necessity of facing mankind, and of them particularly Elizabeth-Jane, became well-nigh more than he could endure. His health declined; he became morbidly sensitive. He wished he could escape those who did not want him, and hide his head for ever.

But what if he were mistaken in his views, and there were no necessity that his own absolute separation from her should be involved in the incident of her marriage?

He proceeded to draw a picture of the alternative – himself living like a fangless lion about the back rooms of a house in which his stepdaughter was mistress; an inoffensive old man, tenderly smiled on by Elizabeth, and good-naturedly tolerated by her husband. It was terrible to his pride to think of descending so low; and yet, for the girl's sake he might put up with anything; even from Farfrae; even snubbings and masterful tongue-scourgings. The privilege of being in the house she occupied would almost outweigh the personal humiliation.

Whether this were a dim possibility or the reverse, the courtship – which it evidently now was – had an absorbing interest for him.

Elizabeth, as has been said, often took her walks on the Budmouth Road, and Farfrae as often made it convenient to create an accidental meeting with her there. Two miles out, a quarter of a mile from the highway, was the prehistoric fort called Mai Dun, of huge dimensions and many ramparts, within or upon whose enclosures a human being, as seen from the road, was but an insignificant speck. Hitherward Henchard often resorted, glass in hand, and scanned the hedgeless *Via* – for it was the original track laid out by the legions of the Empire – to a distance of two or three miles, his object being to read the progress of affairs between Farfrae and his charmer.

One day Henchard was at this spot when a masculine figure came along the road from Budmouth, and lingered. Applying his telescope to his eye Henchard expected that Farfrae's features would be disclosed as usual. But the lenses revealed that today the man was not Elizabeth-Jane's lover.

It was one clothed as a merchant captain; and as he turned in his scrutiny of the road he revealed his face. Henchard lived a lifetime the moment he saw it. The face was Newson's.

Henchard dropped the glass, and for some seconds made no other movement. Newson waited, and Henchard waited – if that could be called a waiting which was a transfixture. But Elizabeth-Jane did not come. Something or other had caused her to neglect her customary walk that day. Perhaps Farfrae and she had chosen another road for variety's sake. But what did that amount to? She might be here tomorrow, and in any case Newson, if bent on a private meeting and a revelation of the truth to her, would soon make his opportunity.

Then he would tell her not only of his paternity, but of the ruse by which he had been once sent away. Elizabeth's strict nature would cause her for the first time to despise her stepfather, would root out his image as that of an arch-deceiver, and Newson would reign in her heart in his stead.

But Newson did not see anything of her that morning. Having stood still awhile he at last retraced his steps, and Henchard felt like a condemned man who has a few hours' respite. When he reached his own house he found her there.

'O father!' she said innocently, 'I have had a letter – a strange one – not signed. Somebody has asked me to meet him, either on the Budmouth Road at noon today, or in the evening at Mr Farfrae's. He says he came to see me some time ago, but a trick was played him, so that he did not see me. I don't understand it; but between you and me I think Donald is at the bottom of the mystery, and that it is a relation of his who wants to pass an opinion on his choice. But I did not like to go till I had seen you. Shall I go?'

Henchard replied heavily, 'Yes; go.'

The question of his remaining in Casterbridge was for ever disposed of by this closing in of Newson on the scene. Henchard was not the man to stand the certainty of condemnation on a matter so near his heart. And being an old hand at bearing anguish in silence, and haughty withal, he resolved to make as light as he could of his intention, while immediately taking his measures.

He surprised the young woman whom he had looked upon as his all in this world by saying to her, as if he did not care about her more: 'I am going to leave Casterbridge, Elizabeth-Jane.'

'Leave Casterbridge!' she cried, 'and leave – me?'

'Yes, this little shop can be managed by you alone as well as by us both; I don't care about shops and streets and folk – I would rather get into the country by myself, out of sight, and follow my own ways, and leave you to yours.'

She looked down and her tears fell silently. It seemed to her that this resolve of his had come on account of her attachment and its probable result. She showed her devotion to Farfrae, however, by mastering her emotion and speaking out.

'I am sorry you have decided on this,' she said with difficult firmness. 'For I thought it probable – possible – that I might marry Mr Farfrae some little time hence, and I did not know that you disapproved of the step!'

'I approve of anything you desire to do, Izzy,' said Henchard huskily. 'If I did not approve it would be no matter! I wish to go away. My presence might make things awkward in the future; and, in short, it is best that I go.'

Nothing that her affection could urge would induce him to reconsider his determination; for she could not urge what she did not know – that when she should learn he was not related to her other than as a step-parent she would refrain from despising him, and that when she knew what he had done to keep her in ignorance she would refrain from hating him. It was his conviction that she would not so refrain; and there existed as yet neither word nor event which could argue it away.

'Then,' she said at last, 'you will not be able to come to my wedding; and that is not as it ought to be.'

'I don't want to see it – I don't want to see it!' he exclaimed; adding more softly, 'but think of me sometimes in your future life – you'll do that, Izzy? – think of me when you are living as the wife of the richest, the foremost man in the town, and don't let my sins, *when you know them all*, cause 'ee to quite forget that though I loved 'ee late I loved 'ee well.'

'It is because of Donald!' she sobbed.

'I don't forbid you to marry him,' said Henchard. 'Promise not to quite forget me when –' He meant when Newson should come.

She promised mechanically, in her agitation; and the same evening at dusk Henchard left the town, to whose development he had been one of the chief stimulants for many years. During the day he had bought a new tool-basket, cleaned up his old hay-knife and wimble, set himself up in fresh leggings, knee-naps and corduroys, and in other ways gone back to the working clothes of his young manhood, discarding for ever the shabby-genteel suit of cloth and rusty silk hat that since his decline had characterized him in the Casterbridge street as a man who had seen better days.

He went secretly and alone, not a soul of the many who had known him being aware of his departure. Elizabeth-Jane accompanied him as far as the second bridge on the highway – for the hour of her appointment with the unguessed visitor at Farfrae's had not yet arrived – and parted from him with unfeigned wonder and sorrow, keeping him back a minute or two before finally letting him go. She watched his form diminish across the moor, the yellow rush-basket at his back moving up and down with each tread, and the creases behind his knees coming and going alternately till she could no longer see them. Though she did not know it Henchard formed at this moment much the same picture as he had presented when entering Casterbridge for the first time nearly a quarter of a century before; except, to be sure, that the serious addition to his years had considerably lessened the spring of his stride, that his state of hopelessness had weakened him, and imparted to his shoulders, as weighted by the basket, a perceptible bend.

He went on till he came to the first milestone, which stood in the bank, half way up a steep hill. He rested his basket on the top of the stone, placed his elbows on it, and gave way to a convulsive twitch, which was worse than a sob, because it was so hard and so dry.

'If I had only got her with me – if I only had!' he said. 'Hard work would be nothing to me then! But that was not to be. I – Cain – go alone as I deserve – an outcast and a vagabond. But my punishment is *not* greater than I can bear!'

He sternly subdued his anguish, shouldered his basket, and went on.

Elizabeth, in the meantime, had breathed him a sigh, recovered her equanimity, and turned her face to Casterbridge. Before she had reached the first house she was met in her walk by Donald Farfrae. This was evidently not their first meeting that day; they joined hands without ceremony, and Farfrae anxiously asked, 'And is he gone – and did you tell him? – I mean of the other matter – not of ours.'

'He is gone; and I told him all I knew of your friend. Donald, who is he?'

'Well, well, dearie; you will know soon about that. And Mr Henchard will hear of it if he does not go far.'

'He will go far – he's bent upon getting out of sight and sound!'

She walked beside her lover, and when they reached the Crossways, or Bow, turned with him into Corn Street instead of going straight on to her own door. At Farfrae's house they stopped and went in.

Farfrae flung open the door of the ground-floor sitting-room, saying, 'There he is waiting for you,' and Elizabeth entered. In the arm-chair sat the broad-faced genial man who had called on Henchard on a memorable morning between one and two years before this time, and whom the latter had seen mount the coach and depart within half-an-hour of his arrival. It was Richard Newson. The meeting with the light-hearted father from whom she had been separated half-a-dozen years, as if by death, need hardly be detailed. It was an affecting one, apart from the question of paternity. Henchard's departure was in a moment explained. When the true facts came to be handled the difficulty of restoring her to her old belief in Newson was not so great as might have seemed likely, for Henchard's conduct itself was a proof that those facts were true. Moreover, she had grown up under Newson's paternal care; and even had Henchard been her father in nature, this father in early domiciliation might almost have carried the point against him, when the incidents of her parting with Henchard had a little worn off.

Newson's pride in what she had grown up to be was more than he could express. He kissed her again and again.

'I've saved you the trouble to come and meet me – ha-ha!' said Newson. 'The fact is that Mr Farfrae here, he said, "Come up and stop with me for a day or two, Captain Newson, and I'll bring her round." "Faith," says I, "so I will"; and here I am.'

'Well, Henchard is gone,' said Farfrae, shutting the door. 'He has done it all voluntarily, and, as I gather from Elizabeth, he has been very nice with her. I was got rather uneasy; but all is as it should be, and we will have no more deefficulties at all.'

'Now, that's very much as I thought,' said Newson, looking into the face of each by turns. 'I said to myself, ay, a hundred times, when I tried to get a peep at her unknown to herself – "Depend upon it, 'tis best that I should live on quiet for a few days like this till something turns up for the better." I now know you are all right, and what can I wish for more?'

'Well, Captain Newson, I will be glad to see ye here every day now, since it can do no harm,' said Farfrae. 'And what I've been thinking is that the wedding may as well be kept under my own roof, the house being large, and you being in lodgings by yourself – so that a great deal of trouble and expense would be saved ye? – and 'tis a convenience when a couple's married not to hae far to go to get home!'

'With all my heart,' said Captain Newson; 'since, as ye say, it can do no harm, now poor Henchard's gone; though I wouldn't have done it otherwise, or put myself in his way at all; for I've already in my lifetime been an intruder into his family quite as far as politeness can be expected to put up with. But what do the young woman say herself about it? Elizabeth, my child, come and hearken to what we be talking about, and not bide staring out o' the window as if ye didn't hear.'

'Donald and you must settle it,' murmured Elizabeth, still keeping up a scrutinizing gaze at some small object in the street.

'Well, then,' continued Newson, turning anew to Farfrae with a face expressing thorough entry into the subject, 'that's how we'll have it. And, Mr Farfrae, as you provide so much, and houseroom, and all that, I'll do my part in the drinkables, and see to the rum and schiedam – maybe a dozen jars will be sufficient? – as many of the folk will be ladies, and perhaps they won't drink hard enough to make a high average in the reckoning? But you know best. I've provided for men and shipmates times enough, but I'm as ignorant as a child how many glasses of grog a woman, that's not a drinking woman, is expected to consume at these ceremonies?'

'Oh, none – we'll no want much of that – O no!' said Farfrae, shaking his head with appalled gravity. 'Do you leave all to me.'

When they had gone a little further in these particulars Newson, leaning back in his chair and smiling reflectively at the ceiling, said, 'I've never told ye, or have I, Mr Farfrae, how Henchard put me off the scent that time?'

He expressed ignorance of what the Captain alluded to.

'Ah, I thought I hadn't. I resolved that I would not, I remember, not to hurt the man's name. But now he's gone I can tell ye. Why, I came to Casterbridge nine or ten months before that day last week that I found ye out. I had been here twice before then. The first time I passed through the town on my way westward, not knowing Elizabeth lived here. Then hearing at some place – I forget where – that a man of the name of Henchard had been mayor here, I came back, and called at his house one morning. The old rascal! – he said Elizabeth-Jane had died years ago.'

Elizabeth now gave earnest heed to his story.

'Now, it never crossed my mind that the man was selling me a packet,' continued Newson. 'And, if you'll believe me, I was that upset, that I went back to the coach that had brought me, and took passage onward without lying in the town half-an-hour. Ha-ha! – 'twas a good joke, and well carried out, and I give the man credit for't!'

Elizabeth-Jane was amazed at the intelligence. 'A joke? – O no!' she cried. 'Then he kept you from me, father, all those months, when you might have been here?'

The father admitted that such was the case.

'He ought not to have done it!' said Farfrae.

Elizabeth sighed. 'I said I would never forget him. But O! I think I ought to forget him now!'

Newson, like a good many rovers and sojourners among strange men and strange moralities, failed to perceive the enormity of Henchard's crime, notwithstanding that he himself had been the chief sufferer therefrom. Indeed, the attack upon the absent culprit waxing serious, he began to take Henchard's part.

'Well, 'twas not ten words that he said, after all,' Newson pleaded. 'And how could he know that I should be such a simpleton as to believe him? 'Twas as much my fault as his, poor fellow!'

'No,' said Elizabeth-Jane firmly, in her revulsion of feeling. 'He knew your disposition – you always were so trusting, father; I've heard my mother say so hundreds of times – and he did it to wrong you. After weaning me from you these five years by saying he was my father, he should not have done this.'

Thus they conversed; and there was nobody to set before Elizabeth any extenuation of the absent one's deceit. Even had he been present Henchard might scarce have pleaded it, so little did he value himself or his good name.

'Well, well – never mind – it is all over and past,' said Newson good-naturedly. 'Now, about this wedding again.'

XLIV

MEANWHILE, the man of their talk had pursued his solitary way eastward till weariness overtook him, and he looked about for a place of rest. His heart was so exacerbated at parting from the girl that he could not face an inn, or even a household of the most humble kind; and entering a field he lay down under a wheatrick, feeling no want of food. The very heaviness of his soul caused him to sleep profoundly.

The bright autumn sun shining into his eyes across the stubble awoke him the next morning early. He opened his basket and ate for his breakfast what he had packed for his supper; and in doing so overhauled the remainder of his kit. Although everything he brought necessitated carriage at his own back, he had secreted among his tools a few of Elizabeth-Jane's cast-off belongings, in the shape of gloves, shoes, a scrap of her handwriting, and the like; and in his pocket he carried a curl of her hair. Having looked at these things he closed them up again, and went onward.

During five consecutive days Henchard's rush basket rode along upon his shoulder between the highway hedges, the new yellow of the rushes catching the eye of an occasional field-labourer as he glanced through the quickset, together with the wayfarer's hat and head, and down-turned face, over which the twig shadows moved in endless procession. It now became apparent that the direction of his journey was Weydon-Priors, which he reached on the afternoon of the sixth day.

The renowned hill whereon the annual fair had been held for so many generations was now bare of human beings, and almost of aught besides. A few sheep grazed thereabout, but these ran off when Henchard halted upon the summit. He deposited his basket upon the turf, and looked about with sad curiosity; till he discovered the road by which his wife and himself had entered on the upland so memorable to both, five-and-twenty years before.

'Yes, we came up that way,' he said, after ascertaining his bearings. 'She was carrying the baby, and I was reading a ballet-sheet. Then we crossed about here – she so sad and weary, and I speaking to her hardly at all, because of my cursed pride and mortification at being poor. Then we saw the tent – that must have stood more this way.' He walked to another spot; it was not really where the tent had stood, but it seemed so to him. 'Here we went in, and here we sat down. I faced this way. Then I drank, and committed my crime. It must have been just on that very pixy-ring that she was standing when she said her last words to me before going off with him; I can hear their sound now, and the sound of her sobs: "O Mike! I've lived with thee all this while, and had nothing but temper. Now I'm no more to 'ee – I'll try my luck elsewhere." '

He experienced not only the bitterness of a man who finds, in looking back upon an ambitious course, that what he has sacrificed in sentiment was worth as much as what he has gained in substance; but the superadded bitterness of seeing his very recantation nullified. He had been sorry for all this long ago; but his attempts to replace ambition by love had been as fully foiled as his ambition itself. His wronged wife had foiled them by a fraud so grandly simple as to be almost a virtue. It was an odd sequence that out of all this tampering with social law came that flower of Nature, Elizabeth. Part of his wish to wash his hands of life arose from his perception of its contrarious inconsistencies – of Nature's jaunty readiness to support unorthodox social principles.

He intended to go on from this place – visited as an act of penance – into another part of the country altogether. But he could not help thinking of Elizabeth, and the quarter of the horizon in which she lived. Out of this it happened that the centrifugal tendency imparted by weariness of the world was counteracted by the centripetal influence of his love for his stepdaughter. As a consequence, instead of following a straight course yet further away from Casterbridge, Henchard gradually, almost unconsciously, deflected from that right line of his first intention; till by degrees, his wandering, like that of the Canadian woodsman, became part of a circle of which Casterbridge formed the centre. In ascending any particular hill he ascertained the bearings as nearly as he could by means of the sun, moon, or stars, and settled in his mind the exact direction in which Casterbridge and Elizabeth-Jane lay. Sneering at himself for his weakness he yet every hour – nay, every few minutes – conjectured her actions for the time being – her sitting down and rising up, her goings and comings, till thought of Newson's and Farfrae's counter-influence would pass like a cold blast over a pool, and efface her image. And then he would say of himself, 'O you fool! All this about a daughter who is no daughter of thine!'

At length he obtained employment at his own occupation of hay-trusser, work of that sort being in demand at this autumn time. The scene of his hiring was a pastoral farm near the old western highway, whose course was the channel of all such communications as passed between the busy centres of novelty and the remote Wessex boroughs. He had chosen the neighbourhood of this artery from a sense that, situated here, though at a distance of fifty miles, he was virtually nearer to her whose welfare was so dear than he would be at a roadless spot only half as remote.

And thus Henchard found himself again on the precise standing which he had occupied a quarter of a century before. Externally there was nothing to hinder his making another start on the upward slope, and by his new lights achieving higher things than his soul in its half-formed state had been able to accomplish. But the ingenious machinery contrived by the Gods for reducing human possibilities of amelioration to a minimum – which arranges that wisdom to do shall come *pari passu* with the departure of zest for doing – stood in the way of all that. He had no wish to make an arena a second time of a world that had become a mere painted scene to him.

Very often, as his hay-knife crunched down among the sweet-smelling grassy stems, he would survey mankind and say to himself: 'Here and everywhere be folk dying before their time like frosted leaves, though wanted by their families, the country, and the world; while I, an outcast, an encumberer of the ground, wanted by nobody, and despised by all, live on against my will!'

He often kept an eager ear upon the conversation of those who passed along the road – not from a general curiosity by any means – but in the hope that among these travellers between Casterbridge and London some would, sooner or later, speak of the former place. The distance, however, was too great to lend much probability to his desire; and the highest result of his attention to wayside words was that he did indeed hear the name 'Casterbridge' uttered one day by the driver of a road-waggon. Henchard ran to the gate of the field he worked in, and hailed the speaker, who was a stranger.

'Yes – I've come from there, maister,' he said, in answer to Henchard's inquiry. 'I trade up and down, ye know; though, what with this travelling without horses that's getting so common, my work will soon be done.'

'Anything moving in the old place, mid I ask?'

'All the same as usual.'

'I've heard that Mr Farfrae, the late mayor, is thinking of getting married. Now is that true or not?'

'I couldn't say for the life o' me. O no, I should think not.'

'But yes, John – you forget,' said a woman inside the waggon-tilt. 'What were them packages we carr'd there at the beginning o' the week? Surely they said a wedding was coming off soon – on Martin's Day?'

The man declared he remembered nothing about it; and the waggon went on jangling over the hill.

Henchard was convinced that the woman's memory served her well. The date was an extremely probable one, there being no reason for delay on either side. He might, for that matter, write and inquire of Elizabeth; but his instinct for sequestration had made the course difficult. Yet before he left her she had said that for him to be absent from her wedding was not as she wished it to be.

The remembrance would continually revive in him now that it was not Elizabeth and Farfrae who had driven him away from them, but his own haughty sense that his presence was no longer desired. He had assumed the return of Newson without absolute proof that the Captain meant to return; still less that Elizabeth-Jane would welcome him; and with no proof whatever that if he did return he would stay. What if he had been mistaken in his views; if there had been no necessity that his own absolute separation from her he loved should be involved in these untoward incidents? To make one more attempt to be near her: to go back; to see her, to plead his cause before her, to ask forgiveness for his fraud, to endeavour strenuously to hold his own in her love; it was worth the risk of repulse, ay, of life itself.

But how to initiate this reversal of all his former resolves without causing husband and wife to despise him for his inconsistency was a question which made him tremble and brood.

He cut and cut his trusses two days more, and then he concluded his hesitancies by a sudden reckless determination to go to the wedding festivity. Neither writing nor message would be expected of him. She had regretted his decision to be absent – his unanticipated presence would fill the little unsatisfied corner that would probably have place in her just heart without him.

To intrude as little of his personality as possible upon a gay event with which that personality could show nothing in keeping, he decided not to make his appearance till evening – when stiffness would have worn off, and a gentle wish to let bygones be bygones would exercise its sway in all hearts.

He started on foot, two mornings before St Martin's-tide, allowing himself about sixteen miles to perform for each of the three days' journey, reckoning the wedding-day as one. There were only two towns, Melchester and Shottsford, of any importance along his course, and at the latter he stopped on the second night, not only to rest, but to prepare himself for the next evening.

Possessing no clothes but the working suit he stood in – now stained and distorted by their two months of hard usage, he entered a shop to make some purchases which should put him, externally at any rate, a little in harmony with the prevailing tone of the morrow. A rough yet respectable coat and hat, a new shirt and neck-cloth, were the chief of these; and having satisfied himself that in appearance at least he would not offend her, he proceeded to the more interesting particular of buying her some present.

What should that present be? He walked up and down the street regarding dubiously the display in the shop windows, from a gloomy sense that what he might most like to give her would be beyond his miserable pocket. At length a caged goldfinch met his eye. The cage was a plain and small one, the shop humble, and on inquiry he concluded he could afford the modest sum asked. A sheet of newspaper was tied round the little creature's wire prison, and with the wrapped up cage in his hand Henchard sought a lodging for the night.

Next day he set out upon the last stage, and was soon within the district which had been his dealing ground in bygone years. Part of the distance he travelled by carrier, seating himself in the darkest corner at the back of that trader's van; and as the other passengers, mainly women going short journeys, mounted and alighted in front of Henchard, they talked over much local news, not the least portion of this being the wedding then in course of celebration at the town they were nearing. It appeared from their accounts that the town band had been hired for the evening party, and, lest the convivial instincts of that body should get the better of their skill, the further step had been taken of engaging the string band from Budmouth, so that there would be a reserve of harmony to fall back upon in case of need.

He heard, however, but few particulars beyond those known to him already, the incident of the deepest interest on the journey being the soft pealing of the Casterbridge bells, which reached the travellers' ears while the van paused on the top of Yalbury Hill to have the drag lowered. The time was just after twelve o'clock.

Those notes were a signal that all had gone well; that there had been no slip 'twixt cup and lip in this case; that Elizabeth-Jane and Donald Farfrae were man and wife.

Henchard did not care to ride any further with his chattering companions after hearing this sound. Indeed, it quite unmanned him; and in pursuance of his plan of not showing himself in Casterbridge street till evening, lest he should mortify Farfrae and his bride, he alighted here, with his bundle and bird-cage, and was soon left as a lonely figure on the broad white highway.

It was the hill near which he had waited to meet Farfrae, almost two years earlier, to tell him of the serious illness of his wife Lucetta. The place was unchanged; the same larches sighed the same notes; but Farfrae had another wife – and, as Henchard knew, a better one. He only hoped that Elizabeth-Jane had obtained a better home than had been hers at the former time.

He passed the remainder of the afternoon in a curious high-strung condition, unable to do much but think of the approaching meeting with her, and sadly satirize himself for his emotions thereon, as a Samson shorn. Such an innovation on Casterbridge customs as a flitting of bridegroom and bride from the town immediately after the ceremony, was not likely, but if it should have taken place he would wait till their return. To assure himself on this point he asked a market-man when near the borough if the newly-married couple had gone away, and was promptly informed that they had not; they were at that hour, according to all accounts, entertaining a houseful of guests at their home in Corn Street.

Henchard dusted his boots, washed his hands at the riverside, and proceeded up the town under the feeble lamps. He need have made no inquiries beforehand, for on drawing near Farfrae's residence it was plain to the least observant that festivity prevailed within, and that Donald himself shared it, his voice being distinctly audible in the street, giving strong expression to a song of his dear native country that he loved so well as never to have revisited it. Idlers were standing on the pavement in front; and wishing to escape the notice of these Henchard passed quickly on to the door.

It was wide open; the hall was lighted extravagantly, and people were going up and down the stairs. His courage failed him; to enter footsore, laden, and poorly dressed in to the midst of such resplendency was to bring needless humiliation upon her he loved, if not to court repulse from her husband. Accordingly he went round into the street at the back that he knew so well, entered the garden, and came quietly into the house through the kitchen, temporarily depositing the bird and cage under a bush outside, to lessen the awkwardness of his arrival.

Solitude and sadness had so emolliated Henchard that he now feared circumstances he would formerly have scorned, and he began to wish that he had not taken upon himself to arrive at such a juncture. However, his progress was made unexpectedly easy by his discovering alone in the kitchen an elderly woman who seemed to be acting as provisional house-keeper during the convulsions from which Farfrae's establishment was just then suffering. She was one of those people whom nothing surprises, and though to her, a total stranger, his request must have seemed odd, she willingly volunteered to go up and inform the master and mistress of the house that 'a humble old friend' had come.

On second thoughts she said that he had better not wait in the kitchen, but come up into the little back-parlour, which was empty. He thereupon followed her thither, and she left him. Just as she had got across the landing to the door of the best parlour a dance was struck up, and she returned to say that she would wait till that was over before announcing him – Mr and Mrs Farfrae having both joined in the figure.

The door of the front room had been taken off its hinges to give more space, and that of the room Henchard sat in being ajar, he could see fractional parts of the dancers whenever their gyrations brought them near the doorway, chiefly in the shape of the skirts of dresses and stream-ing curls of hair; together with about three-fifths of the band in profile, including the restless shadow of a fiddler's elbow, and the tip of the bass-viol bow.

The gaiety jarred upon Henchard's spirits; and he could not quite understand why Farfrae, a much-sobered man, and a widower, who had had his trials, should have cared for it all, notwithstanding the fact that he was quite a young man still, and quickly kindled to enthusiasm by dance and song. That the quiet Elizabeth, who had long ago appraised life at a moderate value, and who knew in spite of her maidenhood that marriage was as a rule no dancing matter, should have had zest for this revelry surprised him still more. However, young people could not be quite old people, he concluded, and custom was omnipotent.

With the progress of the dance the performers spread out somewhat, and then for the first time he caught a glimpse of the once despised daughter who had mastered him, and made his heart ache. She was in a dress of white silk or satin, he was not near enough to say which – snowy white, without a tinge of milk or cream; and the expression of her face was one of nervous pleasure rather than of gaiety. Presently Farfrae came round, his exuberant Scotch movement making him conspicuous in a moment. The pair were not dancing together, but Henchard could discern that whenever the changes of the figure made them the partners of a moment their emotions breathed a much subtler essence than at other times.

By degrees Henchard became aware that the measure was trod by some one who out-Farfraed Farfrae in saltatory intenseness. This was strange, and it was stranger to find that eclipsing personage was Elizabeth-Jane's partner. The first time that Henchard saw him he was sweeping grandly round, his head quivering and low down, his legs in the form of an X and his back towards the door. The next time he came round in the other direction, his white waistcoat preceding his face, and his toes preceding his white waistcoat. That happy face – Henchard's complete discomfiture lay in it. It was Newson's, who had indeed come and supplanted him.

Henchard pushed to the door, and for some seconds made no other movement. He rose to his feet, and stood like a dark ruin, obscured by 'the shade from his own soul upthrown'.

But he was no longer the man to stand these reverses unmoved. His agitation was great, and he would fain have been gone, but before he could leave the dance had ended, the housekeeper had informed Elizabeth-Jane of the stranger who awaited her, and she entered the room immediately.

'Oh – it is – Mr Henchard!' she said, starting back.

'What; Elizabeth?' he cried, as he seized her hand. 'What do you say? – Mr Henchard? Don't, don't scourge me like that! Call me worthless old Henchard – anything – but don't 'ee be so cold as this! O my maid – I see you have another – a real father in my place. Then you know all; but don't give all your thought to him! Do ye save a little room for me!'

She flushed up, and gently drew her hand away. 'I could have loved you always – I would have gladly,' said she. 'But how can I when I know you have deceived me so – so bitterly deceived me! You persuaded me that my father was not my father – allowed me to live on in ignorance of the truth for years; and then when he, my warm-hearted real father, came to find me, cruelly sent him away with a wicked invention of my death, which nearly broke his heart. O how can I love as I once did a man who has served us like this!'

Henchard's lips half parted to begin an explanation. But he shut them up like a vice, and uttered not a sound. How should he, there and then, set before her with any effect the palliatives of his great faults – that he had himself been deceived in her identity at first, till informed by her mother's letter that his own child had died; that, in the second accusation, his lie had been the last desperate throw of a gamester who loved her affection better than his own honour? Among the many hindrances to such a pleading not the least was this, that he did not sufficiently value himself to lessen his sufferings by strenuous appeal or elaborate argument.

Waiving, therefore, his privilege of self-defence, he regarded only her discomposure. 'Don't ye distress yourself on my account,' he said, with proud superiority. 'I would not wish it – at such a time, too, as this. I have done wrong in coming to 'ee – I see my error. But it is only for once, so forgive it. I'll never trouble 'ee again, Elizabeth-Jane – no, not to my dying day! Good night. Good-bye!'

Then, before she could collect her thoughts, Henchard went out from her rooms, and departed from the house by the back way as he had come; and she saw him no more.

XLV

IT was about a month after the day which closed as in the last chapter. Elizabeth-Jane had grown accustomed to the novelty of her situation, and the only difference between Donald's movements now and formerly was that he hastened indoors rather more quickly after business hours than he had been in the habit of doing for some time.

Newson had stayed in Casterbridge three days after the wedding party (whose gaiety, as might have been surmised, was of his making rather than of the married couple's), and was stared at and honoured as became the returned Crusoe of the hour. But whether or not because Casterbridge was difficult to excite by dramatic returns and disappearances, through having been for centuries an assize town, in which sensational exits from the world, antipodean absences, and such like, were half-yearly occurrences, the inhabitants did not altogether lose their equanimity on his account. On the fourth morning he was discovered disconsolately climbing a hill, in his craving to get a glimpse of the sea from somewhere or other. The contiguity of salt water proved to be such a necessity of his existence that he preferred Budmouth as a place of residence, notwithstanding the society of his daughter in the other town. Thither he went, and settled in lodgings in a green-shuttered cottage which had a bow-window, jutting out sufficiently to afford glimpses of a vertical strip of blue sea to any one opening the sash, and leaning forward far enough to look through a narrow lane of tall intervening houses.

Elizabeth-Jane was standing in the middle of her upstairs parlour, critically surveying some re-arrangement of articles with her head to one side, when the housemaid came in with the announcement, 'Oh, please ma'am, we know now how that bird-cage came there.'

In exploring her new domain during the first week of residence, gazing with critical satisfaction on this cheerful room and that, penetrating cautiously into dark cellars, sallying forth with gingerly tread to the garden, now leaf-strewn by autumn winds, and thus, like a wise field-marshal, estimating the capabilities of the site whereon she was about to open her house-keeping campaign – Mrs Donald Farfrae had discovered in a screened corner a new bird-cage, shrouded in newspaper, and at the bottom of the cage a little ball of feathers – and dead body of a goldfinch. Nobody could tell her how the bird and cage had come there; though that the poor little songster had been starved to death was evident. The sadness of the incident had made an impression on her. She had not been able to forget it for days, despite Farfrae's tender banter; and now when the matter had been nearly forgotten it was again revived.

'Oh, please ma'am, we know how that bird-cage came there. That farmer's man who called on the evening of the wedding – he was seen wi' it in his hand as he came up the street; and 'tis thoughted that he put it down while he came in with his message, and then went away forgetting where he had left it.'

This was enough to set Elizabeth thinking, and in thinking she seized hold of the idea, at one feminine bound, that the caged bird had been brought by Henchard for her as a wedding gift and token of repentance. He had not expressed to her any regrets or excuses for what he had done in the past; but it was a part of his nature to extenuate nothing, and live on as one of his own worst accusers. She went out, looked at the cage, buried the starved little singer, and from that hour her heart softened towards the self-alienated man.

When her husband came in she told him her solution of the bird-cage mystery; and begged Donald to help her in finding out, as soon as possible, whither Henchard had banished himself, that she might make her peace with him; try to do something to render his life less that of an outcast, and more tolerable to him. Although Farfrae had never so passionately liked Henchard as Henchard had liked him, he had, on the other hand, never so passionately hated him in the same direction as his former friend had done; and he was therefore not the least indisposed to assist Elizabeth-Jane in her laudable plan.

But it was by no means easy to set about discovering Henchard. He had apparently sunk into the earth on leaving Mr and Mrs Farfrae's door. Elizabeth-Jane remembered what he had once attempted; and trembled.

But though she did not know it Henchard had become a changed man since then – as far, that is, as change of emotional basis can justify such a radical phrase; and she needed not to fear. In a few days Farfrae's inquiries elicited that Henchard had been seen by one who knew him walking steadily along the Melchester highway eastward, at twelve o'clock at night – in other words, retracing his steps on the road by which he had come.

This was enough; and the next morning Farfrae might have been discovered driving his gig out of Casterbridge in that direction, Elizabeth-Jane sitting beside him, wrapped in a thick flat fur – the victorine of the period – her complexion somewhat richer than formerly, and an incipient matronly dignity, which the serene Minerva-eyes of one 'whose gestures beamed with mind' made becoming, settling on her face. Having herself arrived at a promising haven from at least the grosser troubles of her life, her object was to place Henchard in some similar quietude before he should sink into the lower stage of existence which was only too possible to him now.

After driving along the highway for a few miles they made further inquiries, and learnt of a road-mender, who had been working thereabouts for weeks, that he had observed such a man at the time mentioned; he had left the Melchester coach-road at Weatherbury by a forking highway which skirted the north of Egdon Heath. Into this road they directed the horse's head, and soon were bowling across that ancient country whose surface never had been stirred to a finger's depth, save by the scratchings of rabbits, since brushed by the feet of the earliest tribes. The tumuli these had left behind, dun and shagged with heather, jutted roundly into the sky from the uplands, as though they were the full breasts of Diana Multimammia supinely extended there.

They searched Egdon, but found no Henchard. Farfrae drove onward, and by the afternoon reached the neighbourhood of some extension of the heath to the north of Anglebury, a prominent feature of which, in the form of a blasted clump of firs on the summit of a hill, they soon passed under. That the road they were following had, up to this point, been Henchard's track on foot they were pretty certain; but the ramifications which now began to reveal themselves in the route made further progress in the right direction a matter of pure guess-work, and Donald strongly advised his wife to give up the search in person, and trust to other means for obtaining news of her stepfather. They were now a score of miles at least from home, but, by resting the horse for a couple of hours at a village they had just traversed, it would be possible to get back to Casterbridge that same day; while to go much further afield would reduce them to the necessity of camping out for the night; 'and that will make a hole in a sovereign,' said Farfrae. She pondered the position, and agreed with him.

He accordingly drew rein, but before reversing their direction paused a moment and looked vaguely round upon the wide country which the elevated position disclosed. While they looked a solitary human form came from under the clump of trees, and crossed ahead of them. The person was some labourer; his gait was shambling, his regard fixed in front of him as absolutely as if he wore blinkers; and in his hand he carried a few sticks. Having crossed the road he descended into a ravine, where a cottage revealed itself, which he entered.

'If it were not so far away from Casterbridge I should say that must be poor Whittle. 'Tis just like him,' observed Elizabeth-Jane.

'And it may be Whittle, for he's never been to the yard these three weeks, going away without saying any word at all; and I owing him for two days' work, without knowing who to pay it to.'

The possibility led them to alight, and at least make an inquiry at the cottage. Farfrae hitched the reins to the gate-post, and they approached what was of humble dwellings surely the humblest. The walls, built of kneaded clay originally faced with a trowel, had been worn by years of rain-washings to a lumpy crumbling surface, channelled and sunken from its plane, its gray rents held together here and there by a leafy strap of ivy which could scarcely find substance enough for the purpose. The rafters were sunken, and the thatch of the roof in ragged holes. Leaves from the fence had been blown into the corners of the doorway, and lay there undisturbed. The door was ajar; Farfrae knocked; and he who stood before them was Whittle, as they had conjectured.

His face showed marks of deep sadness, his eyes lighting on them with an unfocused gaze; and he still held in his hand the few sticks he had been out to gather. As soon as he recognized them he started.

'What, Abel Whittle; is it that ye are heere?' said Farfrae.

'Ay, yes, sir! You see he was kind-like to mother when she wer here below, though 'a was rough to me.'

'Who are you talking of?'

'O sir – Mr Henchet! Didn't ye know it? He's just gone – about half-an-hour ago, by the sun; for I've got no watch to my name.'

'Not – dead?' faltered Elizabeth-Jane.

'Yes, ma'am, he's gone! He was kind-like to mother when she wer here below, sending her the best ship-coal, and hardly any ashes from it at all; and taties, and such-like that were very needful to her. I seed en go down street on the night of your worshipful's wedding to the lady at yer side, and I thought he looked low and faltering. And I followed en over Grey's Bridge, and he turned and zeed me, and said, "You go back!" But I followed, and he turned again, and said, "Do you hear, sir? Go back!" But I zeed that he was low, and I followed on still. Then 'a said, "Whittle, what do ye follow me for when I've told ye to go back all these times?" And I said, "Because, sir, I see things be bad with 'ee, and yer wer kind-like to mother if ye were rough to me, and I would fain be kind-like to you." Then he walked on, and I followed; and he never complained at me no more. We walked on like that all night; and in the blue o' the morning, when 'twas hardly day, I looked ahead o' me, and I zeed that he wambled, and could hardly drag along. By that time we had got past here, but I had seen that this house was empty as I went by and I got him to come back; and I took down the boards from the windows, and helped him inside. "What, Whittle," he said, "and can ye really be such a poor fond fool as to care for such a wretch as I!" Then I went on further, and some neighbourly woodmen lent me a bed, and a chair, and a few other traps, and we brought 'em here, and made him as comfortable as we could. But he didn't gain strength, for you see, ma'am, he couldn't eat – no, no appetite at all – and he got weaker; and today he died. One of the neighbours have gone to get a man to measure him.'

'Dear me – is that so!' said Farfrae.

As for Elizabeth, she said nothing.

'Upon the head of his bed he pinned a piece of paper, with some writing upon it,' continued Abel Whittle. 'But not being a man o' letters, I can't read writing; so I don't know what it is. I can get it and show ye.'

They stood in silence while he ran into the cottage; returning in a moment with a crumpled scrap of paper. On it there was pencilled as follows:

Michael Henchard's Will

That Elizabeth-Jane Farfrae be not told of my death, or made to grieve on account of me.

> & that I be not bury'd in consecrated ground.
> & that no sexton be asked to toll the bell.
> & that nobody is wished to see my dead body.
> & that no murners walk behind me at my funeral.

& that no flours be planted on my grave.
& that no man remember me.
To this I put my name.

MICHAEL HENCHARD

'What are we to do?' said Donald, when he had handed the paper to her.

She could not answer distinctly. 'O Donald!' she said at last through her tears, 'what bitterness lies there! O I would not have minded so much if it had not been for my unkindness at that last parting! . . . But there's no altering – so it must be.'

What Henchard had written in the anguish of his dying was respected as far as practicable by Elizabeth-Jane, though less from a sense of the sacredness of last words, as such, than from her independent knowledge that the man who wrote them meant what he said. She knew the directions to be a piece of the same stuff that his whole life was made of, and hence were not to be tampered with to give herself a mournful pleasure, or her husband credit for large-heartedness.

All was over at last, even her regrets for having misunderstood him on his last visit, for not having searched him out sooner, though these were deep and sharp for a good while. From this time forward Elizabeth-Jane found herself in a latitude of calm weather, kindly and grateful in itself, and doubly so after the Capharnaum in which some of her preceding years had been spent. As the lively and sparkling emotions of her early married life cohered into an equable serenity, the finer movements of her nature found scope in discovering to the narrow-lived ones around her the secret (as she had once learnt it) of making limited opportunities endurable; which she deemed to consist in the cunning enlargement, by a species of microscopic treatment, of those minute forms of satisfaction that offer themselves to everybody not in positive pain; which, thus handled, have much of the same inspiriting effect upon life as wider interests cursorily embraced.

Her teaching had a reflex action upon herself, insomuch that she thought she could perceive no great personal difference between being respected in the nether parts of Casterbridge and glorified at the uppermost end of the social world. Her position was, indeed, to a marked degree one that, in common phrase, afforded much to be thankful for. That she was not demonstratively thankful was no fault of hers. Her experience had been of a kind to teach her, rightly or wrongly, that the doubtful honour of a brief transit through a sorry world hardly called for effusiveness, even when the path was suddenly irradiated at some half-way point by daybeams rich as hers. But her strong sense that neither she nor any human being deserved less than was given, did not blind her to the fact that there were others receiving less who had deserved much more. And in being forced to class herself among the fortunate she did not cease to wonder at the persistence of the unforeseen, when the one to whom such unbroken tranquillity had been accorded in the adult stage was she whose youth had seemed to teach that happiness was but the occasional episode in a general drama of pain.